The FLOWER Mosaic

Frances Siân Doyle

Edited by Bernard Gavin

authorHOUSE®

AuthorHouse™ UK
1663 Liberty Drive
Bloomington, IN 47403 USA
www.authorhouse.co.uk
Phone: 0800.197.4150

Published by AuthorHouse 09/28/2018

ISBN: 978-1-5462-9649-2 (sc)
ISBN: 978-1-5462-9650-8 (e)

Print information available on the last page.

For

Doon

No better tribute could I give

List of Characters

France; College de Clermont
Father Manare; *college Principal*
Father Barzini, *Hebrew and Greek scholar*
Father Eduard, *herbalist*
Father de Sacy
Father Bernardo d'Aguila
Friar Patrick O'Healy, *an Irish Franciscan visitor*
Brother Daniel de Collier
Brother Foucauld
Brother Benedict
Tom Sanders
Jan Coecke
Hernando Nunez
Goronwy Glyn-Parry
Emlyn Tomas
(*students*: Tom Sanders, Jan Coecke, Hernando Nunez, Goronwy Glyn-Parry, Emlyn Tomas)
Fra Pietro Sebastiano da Firenze, *a Florentine visitor*
Eugine and Isabelle Benoit, *cloth and wool merchants* (Dieppe)

Rouen
Carmelia Grimani, *Don Carlos; daughter*
Pellegrina, *her maid*
Adriana Martinelli, *her godmother*
Josquin, *a mercenary*
Wendelin Tieffenbrucker,* *German carpenter and lute maker*
Eva, *his wife*
Angelo Corberio, *mercenary captain*
Giles de Saint Remy, *mercenary overseer*
Alessandro and Celio, *mercenaries*

Constantinople Istanbul
Ismael of Damascus, *merchant*
Koçi, *his servant*
Symeon, *physician*
Abu Abdullah of Ulcinj, *merchant*
Sultan Selim,* *ruler of the Ottoman Empire*

Wales
Ambrose Chillingworth, *English traveller and wool merchant*
Christopher, *his son*
Aled and Jack Jones, *his servants*
Matthew Wheatland, *his manager*
Dafydd Allen, *master of le Mychelle,*
Gruffydd Hiraethog, *wool farmer*
Twm, *his servant*
Anne, *his daughter*
Squire Hugh Morgan of Plas Newydd, *son*
Elisabeth, *Hugh's wife*
Owain Morgan, *Hugh's son*
Ellen Morgan, *his step daughter*
Harriet Crew, *Owain's future wife*
Robert Jenkinson, *friend to Owain*
Stephen Howell, friend to Owain
Connie O'Neill, *Irish servant to Ellen*
John Talbot, *Catholic priest*
John Moore, *wool manager*
Rhys and Tom Tilbury, *young Jesuit novices*
Thomas Mostyn, *Catholic sympathiser*
Robert Persons,* *leader of Catholic rebels*
Mafanwy Fawr, *a local healer*

Geraint and Gerald Glyn-Parry
Branwen, *their mother*
Rhys Llwyd
Madog Mathaw, Sinon Ddu, *hired men*
Idris Hughes, *a sheriff's man*

Venice

Bartolomeo Varini, *manager of the Lanarca Salt Company*
Jacopo and Maria, *servants to Bartolomeo*
Andrea, *thier son*
Zia Carlina, *a neighbour and friend*
Alessandro Balsamo *(deceased)*
Fiorenza Caterina Balsamo, *his widow*
Maria, *her maid*
Enrico de Martoni, *notary*
Tomasso di Vincentini, *merchant adventurer*
Scipione Barozzi, *manager of the Eastern Spice Company*
Marco, *his servant*
Don Carlos Grimani, *Venetian nobleman*
Juliana, his wife
Cristoforo and Roberto, *(deceased) Grimani's sons*
Lorenzo Grimani, his *grandson*
Paolo Grimani, his *grandson*
Uglino, *pageboy*
Giuseppe, *servant*
Zorzo Vecelli, *manager*
Paolo Mannutio Aldus, *book printer*
Aldo il Giovane, *his son*
Giorgio and Jerome Pesaro, *merchants*
Cesare Zatta, *captain of Grimani's war galley* Theo Tieffenbrucker,* *Wendelin's brother* Mariebella, *Theo's wife*
Umbaldo, *an apprentice*
Sebastiano Erizzo, *Venetian Senator*

Geneva

Abraham Oertel
Theodoric Molino *agent*
Pompeo Diodati, *a merchant banker*
Karenina, his wife

Milan

Girolamo Favorino of Pavia,* *astrologer* Thomas Becheart, *courier*
Madonna Teresa Portormo
Rosalina and Bettina, *her nieces*
Marino, Robusti Ottavio and Sandrino Agazzari, *actors and musicians*

At Sea

Gaspare Maria del Monte, *Genoese seaman*
Cesare Faliero, *galley captain*
Quirini, *boatswain*
Matteo Sarzana, the captain of the Maria

Others

Queen Elisabeth of England*
Philip II, King of Spain*
Charles IX King of France*
Catherine d' Medici,* *his mother*
Duke of Alva,* *Netherlands overlord*
Mary Stuart,* *abdicated Queen of Scotland.* William Cecil,* *Secretary of State to the Queen of England*
Don Gueru de Spes,* *Spanish ambassador*
William Salesbury*, Welsh scholar
Sir Thomas Gresham,* *English merchant*
William Allen,* *English exile a Jesuit*
Sebastiano Venier,* *governor of Candia*
Don Diego de Luzon
Miguel de Cervantes Saavedra*
* (actual characters in history)

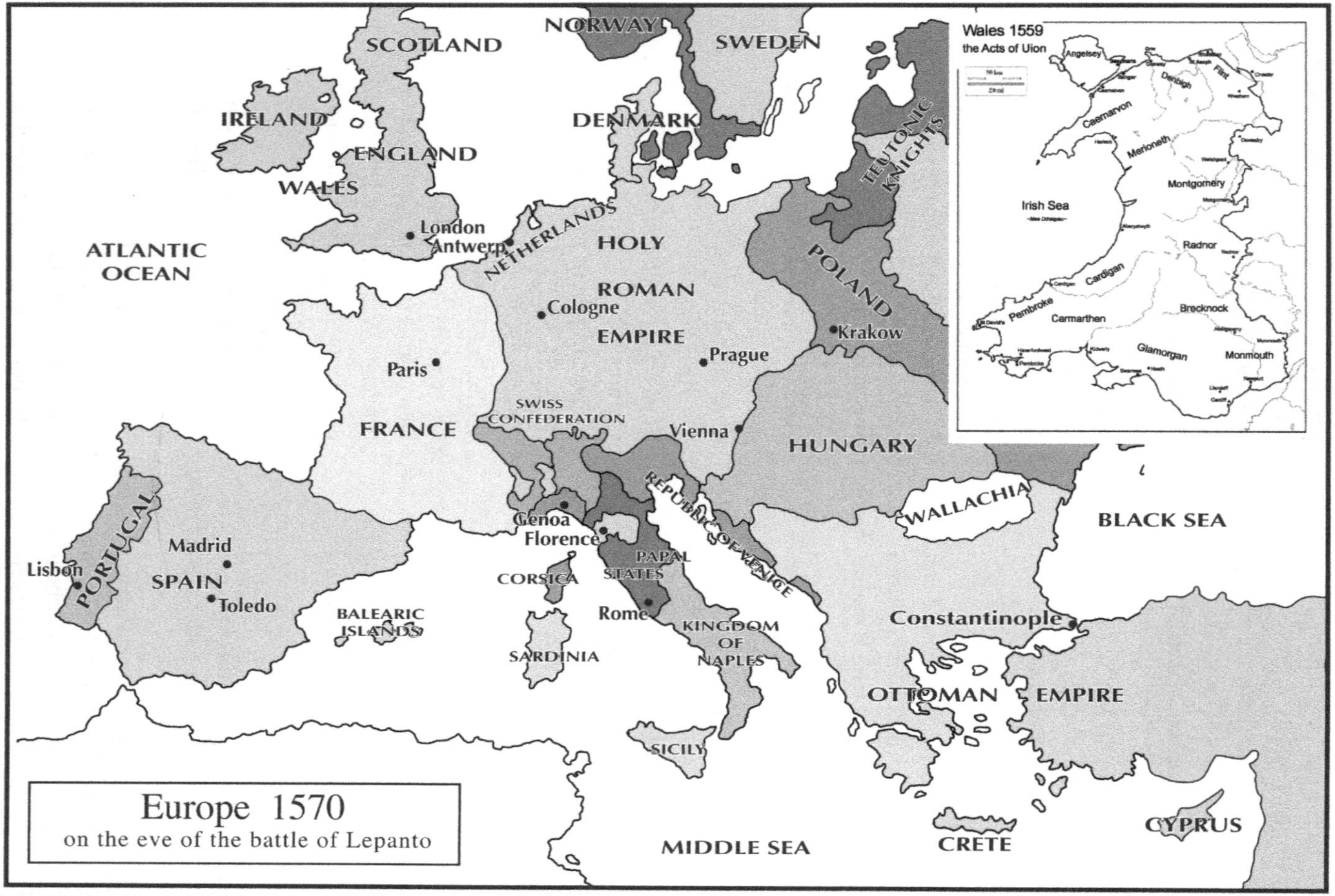

Europe 1570
on the eve of the battle of Lepanto

The mountain snow: the stag doth fly,
the wind above the rocks doth sigh,
love cannot in concealment lie.

The mountain snow: the grove is dark,
the raven black, the hound doth bark,
God keep you from all evil work.

The mountain snow: the crust is sound,
the wind doth twist the reeds around.
Where ignorance is, no grace is found.

PROLOGUE

Istanbul 1568

The ring of camel and goat bells wavered over the hill long before the travellers came into view. On the hill-crest, a single rider pulled in his Persian mare. A musical bracelet chimed on his slender wrist as he pulled the rein. He was Koçi, the slave of Ismael the Syrian who rode below in a sea of dust.

The caravan spread over the grasslands like the scintillating swarf from an alchemist's cauldron, led by a shifting blanket of three-hundred sheep and dozens of Bactrian camels. Servants' voices rose in excitement, clicking their tongues and urging their beasts towards the caravanserai. The camels could smell the fodder and warmth and their great heads, with knob-bed ears and beguiling lashes, thrust forward eagerly. Colourful tassels swung from ear and nose; tassels threaded with gold, vermilion, cerise and madder and twisted with shimmering tinsels. Against the furred flanks, faded bundles were tided securely; the dull coverings concealed a wealth of fringed silks, supple leathers and exquisite jasper carpets; riches of untold price and exotic origin.

The traders were clad in dull quilted wool and worn leathers. Their heads capped in colourful felt edged with long fur, or enfolded in a fantasy of knotted turban. Lit by the citrine of setting sun, man and beast paced the grasslands; indistinguishable in the swirling dust.

Koçi hooked his red booted foot over the saddle, crossing elegant hands over his bent knee. He watched the procession as he had across thousands of leagues of steppe and mountainous track. He could see his master, Ismael the Syrian conversing with his travelling companion, Abu Abdullah of Ulcinj. With a fleeting glance at the caravanserai half a mile away, Koçi thumped his mare with a single heel and rode leisurely down towards the two merchants.

'With the blessing of Allah, who has guided us in His wisdom thus far, we will reach Uskudar before the sun of tomorrow sinks into Marmara,' said Abu Abdullah. 'You and I my friend will drink sherbet and savour peaches and lamb of unsurpassed tenderness. And the catamites! Pleasure gained at a journey's end is unparalleled.'

'Greater is the pleasure of reaping its riches.' Ismael replied. Under his fur rimmed hat he smiled, his eyes cast in darkness by the wide shaggy brim. Nine feet of camel shuffled past him; twin tufted humps just visible under four-hundred pounds of canvas-wrapped silk.

'But what changes have come now that the Law Giver is gone? God forever grant him peace in Paradise,' Abu Abdullah lamented. A tear dewed his eye, shivered down his dark seamed cheek and rolled into his black beard. The last time Abu had come to Stamboul, Sultan Suleyman had ruled the Ottoman Empire; a ruler whom Abu had held in deep regard. Now, Suleyman's son, Selim was the Ottoman sultan and in his four years of rule the Empire had gained little.

Ismael glanced knowingly at the friend who had accompanied him from Samarkand. All around them servants, slaves, soldiers and merchants urged the burdened beasts forward. The young men like Koçi, raced their handsome horses, thundering across the dried grass towards comfort and food. Watching them, Ismael said, 'We ride like princes, Abu. But shall we allow these children to excel us in horsemanship?'

Teeth flashing like a sickle in his enormous black beard, Abu Abdullah of Ulcinj needed no further invitation. He drove his shadowy stallion forward with a cry on his lips and lifted his turbaned head to the red sky, his wide frame rocking with laughter.

Released from his characteristic seriousness, Ismael touched spur to the flanks of his horse. Both merchants bent low over the arched necks, orange and grey manes slapping their faces, as they swept towards the Caravanserai.

They arrived as the last daylight faded from the sky. Notes from a pipe rose and dipped, beseechingly. A goat-skin drum began to beat. A group of Arab boys with liquid eyes swayed girlish hips and moved their long, brown hands tapping on tambourine. Koçi watched them under long lashes. They were beautiful the Arabians.

Cooking fires sent spirals of blue, charcoal-scented smoke into the darkening sky. Traders and buyers, servants, slaves and herdsmen, water carriers, soldiers, beggars and lively children, wandered about lazily or squatted around the coffee seller or played a game with fist hollows and camel droppings. Story tellers sat under the leafy roofs of cedar and wild olive, twisting rope while they gathered an audience with their mellow voices.

Ismael and Koçi sat relaxed in an alcove carved into the wall of the caravanserai. This was the final stop on the Asian side of the Bosphorus, where the travellers planned to stay for three days. At the Caravanserai many sales were agreed upon before the goods flowed on to the Stamboul markets. Ismael intended to contact buyers, conclude sales and arrange for others. He had ordered plates of food for the visiting merchants and carpets and bolsters were spread for their comfort. Koçi lit candles made from Russian bee's wax, which glowed with soft inviting light and kept the biting insects away.

A breeze flapped the awning under which they sat; swallows swooped in the evening sky, taking pleasure from their skill on the wing. From among the slaves and camels, Daud the camel-boy sauntered towards them his hands dangling from a stick across his shoulders. He dropped down beside Koçi and dipped a chunk of flat bread into a shared soup bowl, circles of goat fat floated on the cooling surface. He said, 'the she-camels are milked Lord.' This was the final task that had been repeated on each night of the journey.

Ismael leaned back against the wall and closed his eyes listening to the sounds of the caravanserai and the whining barter of the traders. He was freshly dressed in sheepskins and leather with a new fur-trimmed cap. His embroidered boots had tassels hanging from the back entwined with seed pearls. He had seen a few traders and had set a price for the camels. He would not be moved from it, nor would he be fooled by tales of hungry children and greedy wives.

Koçi yawned. After seven years, there were none now who would know little Koçi at the Serai Palace where he had come as a child gathered in the *Devshirme*. Travelling to the furthest reaches of China and back again, had changed Koçi—as it had his lord Ismael. Koçi was nearly twenty, his skin was soft and his eyes were beautiful and he moved with the grace of the Arab boys who danced to the tapping drum. He began to grow restless as the traders continued to haggle over the price of the camels. He got to his feet lithely and strolled through the camp making his bracelet bells chime as he walked. He wandered through the camel lines, nodding here and there to a servant or slave whom he had befriended on the journey. He and Ismael had come now to a new beginning; the carefree life of the nomad left behind them. A journey's end had its sorrow as well as its joy.

A pleasant voice spoke behind him. 'You are the slave of Ismael of Bursa?'

When he turned Koçi saw a distinguished looking man dressed in the plain gown and white turban of the Ulema—the school of sacred law and theology from the Topkapi Palace.

'May I guide you?' Koçi asked. He guessed that by now, that the camel buyers would have left satisfied or not. The stranger nodded and followed him to where Ismael was sitting.

When they had exchanged courteous greeting and asked after family, heath and business, the visitor broached the subject of the meeting. 'You are favoured,' he said addressing the Syrian. 'The Imperial Council has invited you to attend the Divan. Hearing of your reputable fame the Mufti of Stamboul, has requested your learned knowledge of travel be revealed to him'

Ismael showed no change of expression, if he was afraid of what this might entail, he kept his emotion hidden. 'I am honoured by the Sheikh-ul-Islam' he replied, 'I will make it my duty to attend.'

After the man had left them, Koçi was startled to hear his master's soft laughter. 'Lord what amuses thee?' he said in soft Arabic.

'I have sold the camels,' said Ismael, ignoring the question. He had shared hashish with the camel dealers from Uskudar, his eyes danced in the dim light; his risible eyes that brought lovers to his arms without complaint but would not turn with the same invitation to Koçi.

'Daud will not be very happy.' Koçi replied.

'I've sold him too. Tomorrow we shall pay a visit to the Gypsies of Balatmahalle. They are excellent horse breeders.'

'Are we to move so soon?' asked Koçi.

'After I have told the Sheikh-ul-Islam all he wishes to know about the Portuguese.'

'He does not wish then to ask you of your experience lord?'

Ismael gathered up his blankets to rest. 'There are a hundred travellers such as me,' he replied, 'but very few who have knowledge of the Portuguese and the sea route they use to the east. The mufti wishes to expand on his knowledge in this matter, among other things.'

'What will you do? I am afraid for you…'

'I shall not be delayed long.' Ismael replied reassuringly, 'Do not worry, I owe nothing to the Portuguese and have nothing to fear from the sultan.' He paused and looked up to the starlit sky, a sky he had not seen for a long time. 'Should a man fear to tread on the path of his destiny?' he said softly

'Wine long nurtured is sweet lord.' Koçi replied with a beautiful smile.

'Is it Koçi? I find it otherwise.'

'How can you lord when it is a cup you have yet to taste?'

BOOK ONE

The Jesuit

Chapter 1 Paris, April 1568

One cold mid-April dawn in 1568, a miracle occurred at College de Clermont in Paris. On his way to chapel, Brother Daniel de Collier was chewing on a new baked loaf *before mass,* when he was stopped abruptly by a trail of luminous footprints glistening on the path before him. He blinked, blessed himself and approached the open chapel door holding his breath.

In the dawn, the chapel interior was gloomy. Brother Daniel could just make out the dim shape of the statue of the Blessed Virgin, aglow with dawn light from a window to the right of the altar. It was here that the steps began, seeming to step delicately off the plinth; they were a startling, glowing white. Brother Daniel turned about and retraced the trail treading carefully.

Dawn tinged the sky in apricot and turquoise. Outside the church, the prints led along a cobbled path to the cloister and continued under a stone archway. Brother Daniel was astounded; he had been chosen to witness a miracle. The Blessed Virgin had most certainly walked in the night. What else could have left steps as pure as new fallen snow? He scurried along, his dark habit rustling around his ankles and his sandals soaking up the dew. The pure footprints ran twice around the nodding jonquils and entered the convent through a side archway. Brother Daniel wove faithfully onwards, through the dark cloister to the teaching monk's cells. The footsteps suddenly disappeared under the door to the cell of Father Barzini; a renowned reader of Greek and Hebrew, who had brought his learning from Florence to bestow upon the young Jesuit students of College de Clermont.

'How favoured in the eyes of God is Father Barzini,' whispered Brother Daniel reverently. He bent closely to the ground and noticed that another trail of milky prints left the door and disappeared into the shadows. A booming voice spoke beside him and made him jump in terror.

'Is it ill you are there Brother Danny, to be kneeling as if it's judgement day?'

Recovering himself, Brother Daniel looked up. It was the meddlesome Irish friar, Patrick O'Healy, who was visiting Paris on his way back from Rome; Franciscan monks where not over welcome at the Jesuit school.

'I am not ill thank you.' Brother Daniel replied indignantly. 'I have found a miraculous wonder. Look at the footprints of the Blessed Virgin, from the chapel right up to the door of Father Barzini of Florence.'

'There's a wonder to be sure,' Friar Patrick O'Healy replied seriously, his mouth set in a line and his fluffy orange eyebrows lowered in concentration. 'Sure there t' footprints of t' Holy Mother herself, though a bit large I have t' say. And would you know it? …they come right back out again.'

'We must follow them.' Brother Daniel insisted.

They followed. Outside the buttery, they fell into step with the Brothers Benedict and Foucauld and told them of the miracle. All along the way Brother Daniel de Clarion proclaimed the miracle to the brothers. Friar Patrick O'Healy encouraged them with his rolling Gaelic Irish that no one understood.

'So great is the power of God,' said Brother Benedict, drawn in enthusiastically, 'that the blessed Virgin has trodden straight up the herb garden wall on the corner by Father Eluard's fig tree.'

'I would have thought,' added Brother Foucauld thoughtfully, 'that the Blessed Virgin would float rather than walk.'

By the time the group reached the chapel door, there were seven brothers of the Society of Jesus, five novices and Friar O'Healy who placed his large freckled hands on the doors and pushed them open. They all entered like a flock of nervous starlings. The church was still dark with the shadows of night. Only a threaded glimmer of sun touched the window and filtered through the intricacy of lead and stained glass above the altar. The Blessed Virgin had walked right back to her niche in the wall. She stood as she always had stood; her benign lips as pink as the dawn, her compassionate eyes the pellucid blue of a summer sky and her feet, white as dove wings, planted reassuringly upon the serpent. In unison, the brothers dropped to their knees emitting a dry whisper of cloth, a rattle of rosaries and a sigh of prodigious bewilderment.

The miracle worker was a young student, presently hidden in the confessional and hardly daring to breathe. He knew that if he was found there, the miracle he had created would be reduced to the level of an irreligious prank and he would be punished. He had to escape the church. He straightened and crept out of the confining space as silent as a spirit. The front entrance was out of the question; they would see him as he rounded the baptismal font. He slid along the side wall and reached the sacristy door concealed behind a curtain. He put his hand on the handle and froze.

The main doors flew open emitting a shaft of sunlight bobbing with tonsured heads. Father Manare, the Principal of the College de Clermont entered, his was expression stern.

The student pulled on the door, it was locked. Crouching, he scuttled back and hid behind a lectern, while a throng of Jesuits pattered purposefully down the central aisle.

'There, there!' cried Brother Daniel de Clarion; as soon as he caught sight of his superior, 'footprints that are the purest white of heaven,' he breathed reverently.

Father Manare bent and dipped a finger to a footprint as if it were some delicate dish. He sniffed and wrinkled his nose. 'The purest white of gypsum' he said rising to his full height. 'Brother Daniel have you roused the whole community for the sake of a practical joke?'

Brother Daniel turned as pink as a dog-rose. 'I...' he spluttered. 'You could not possibly think that I...?'

'Precisely' snapped Father Manare. He swept his hooded gaze over the gathering of teachers, novices and students. 'Therefore: who?'

The student kept to the shadows, his clothes were speckled with whitewash. Unable to see what was happening, he closed his eyes and stopped breathing. The lectern wobbled. A book resting on the top, slithered, rocked on a corner and fell. It slapped the flag stones and sixty eyes turned in curiosity.

'What was that?' Father Manare demanded glaring at an owl-faced novice. 'You, yes you. Go and see what is there!'

The hidden student froze and braced himself. Around the lectern, a known face appeared, wide-eyed with surprise. The crouching student breathed out in relief. He winked and put a finger to his lips. It was to no avail.

The novice, Goronwy Glyn-Parry, shouted when he recognized his friend. 'Emlyn Tomas! What are you doing here?'

Emlyn Tomas, creator of miracles, cringed and shook his head. At home in Wales Goronwy Glyn-Parry's voice could be heard from Bryn Gop to Moel Hiraethog, in the confines of the modest church, it was exceptional.

'Oh,' whispered his betrayer in dismay.

'Thank you Goronwy,' said Emlyn pleasantly. 'No doubt Father Barzini will not appreciate a nightly visitation from the Blessed Virgin, I will be beaten and not be able to sit down for a week'. He stood up, dusted his jerkin and held his head up, resigned to whatever befell.

This was the third time they had caught him making mischief this year, it was only April. What he had done, although amusing, was sacrilegious and could not be condoned. He hoped he would be dismissed from the order of Jesuits: If not, he would have to dream up more devilish means of escaping.

The brothers of the Society of Jesus descended on him like carrion birds. A stick hooked around his neck and yanked him backwards. He tumbled over.

'Emile Thomas!' thundered Father Barzini, (he refused to say Emlyn, considering it a pagan name). He was a large man with a ring of white hair circling his gleaming scalp. Above his trembling jowls, his eyes were fierce and black. 'Get from this house of God you wretched sinner!'

The stick came down with every word. Emlyn protected his head with his hands and began to run along the wall. Blows continued to rain down on back and shoulders. There was no escaping the wrath of Father Barzini.

'Irreverent miscreant dog...Obscene, lascivious worm ...'

Goronwy winced and turned to Daniel de Clarion, 'this time they will beat him until his bones show,' he whispered.

Daniel de Clarion nodded sagely.

'...impure, wicked serpent!'

Many hours later Father de Sacy went to search for Emlyn Tomas, whom he had taught for the past four years. He knew where to find him when he was in trouble, not on his knees in the church as the other brothers believed, but in the library. That morning, Father de Sacy had returned from a trip to Rouen. He had brought an old acquaintance of Emlyn's back with him. But, the meeting would have to wait. Father de Sacy wished that he had come sooner; he would have tried to prevent the unsparing beating the Welsh student had received. It was becoming increasingly difficult to save the youngster from the messes he got himself into, and Father de Sacy had to step carefully when confronting the superior of the Jesuit school, Father Manare. The principal had asked de Sacy to talk with Emlyn, to see if he could discover the answers to Emlyn's disruptive behaviour

Emlyn was standing at the far end of a long, baize-covered table. He was reading. Father de Sacy closed the door and stood with his hands clasped in front, entwined with his ivory rosary. Emlyn looked up and offered an innocent, disarming smile. His large, dove-grey eyes were as clear as a child's. His face was as pale as paper, framed with untidy, dark hair that fell in a tangle of curls and ringlets.

Father de Sacy paced the floor; his eyes cast downward in thought. He paused at one of the windows that ran the length of the room, allowing maximum light for the sake of reading. The library was the Society's pride and joy. Outside, in the afternoon sunlight, Paris heaved with activity. He could not see the city behind the high cloister wall, but he could hear it; the bang of hammer, the buzz of saw and the calling voices tinged with merriment. It was near to the feast of Easter and the town was in preparation for the processions and the royal visits.

He transferred his hands to his back, rattling the beads. Without turning, he said 'On my arrival here, I heard that two miracles occurred last night. One of which you are well aware. The other, which you did not take into account while producing the first, is that the Holy Virgin's delicate feet, grew four sizes larger as she stepped from her plinth. It was a childish prank Emlyn.'

'Father it was well meant, I only...'

'How old are you Emlyn?' Father de Sacy turned away from the light.

'Seventeen'

'So, we are agreed that you are no longer a child? Why do you antagonize us so? It is not as if we are humourless in this house. The Society of Jesus realizes the value of a lightened heart; they encourage music, mime, sport and song and even the antics of the tumbler, the juggler, the fool. There are many paths to men's joy. But, in the right place Emlyn, in the right place. The antics you constantly involve yourself in are the acts of a child, not of a young man contemplating the priesthood.'

Emlyn's head was bent; his hands were white, clasping the book. He looked pale and highly strung, he had hardly moved since Father de Sacy had entered the room. He offered no answer. Ask him to talk of Cicero and Seneca, Virgil and Ovid or any of the ancient writers, then he would speak openly and intelligently and in any of the five languages he had mastered; his great capacity for knowledge was the reason the Jesuits wanted to keep him under their influence and make him a full member of their society. However, Emlyn's incessant need to create mayhem and chaos drove many in the community to abandon their devotion to the youth; a sound beating was the resolution to most misdemeanour's. After four years at the Parisian Jesuit School, sound beatings had little effect on Emlyn.

Father de Sacy fingered his rosary. 'Before vespers, you are summoned before your superiors to answer for your behaviour today,' he stated glumly. 'You will have much explaining to do. They may well consider your dismissal from the order.'

Emlyn looked up, his eyes momentary alight.

De Sacy walked around the table and stood beside him, looking at him intently. 'There are important matters to consider, now that your future here has been jeopardized,' he said stiffly. 'It was your uncle's wish that when you reached the age of eighteen, you would become a priest.'

Emlyn kept his eyes lowered. 'When I came here over four years ago, my uncle was a Catholic,' he explained. 'But now, he has adopted the safer way of the Reformers. This was done so that he could remain a squire and hold on to his estates in Wales, which would be difficult if he were still Catholic. What his plans for me were four years ago, no longer hold any significance.'

'That could not have been easy for him,' de Sacy replied uneasily. 'The heretic English queen demands much from her subjects. If you needed to return to your uncle, would you be made welcome as a priest?'

Emlyn offered a smile edged with bitterness. 'He would not be pleased to see his Catholic nephew arrive on his door step, he would probably turn me about and send me back here. To put it lightly, priests are not encouraged at present by Queen Elizabeth.'

Fully aware of the situation in England, De Sacy nodded gravely. He said, 'you know how keen our superior is to have you join our order.' Although dismissal would be threatened, the order would do much to keep a hold on this young novice.

Emlyn lifted his eyes and regarded the priest openly. 'If by these recent actions I am to be dismissed, I shall go to Gruffydd Hiraethog, my grandfather.' Emlyn paused, his eyes dreamy. 'He always wanted me to stay in Wales, to become a bard,' he added.

'What…a simple rhymester?' Father de Sacy was greatly surprised.

'Yes, a poet, a harper or some other occupation that would keep the old customs of Wales alive. Hiraethog has never been daunted by the English or the Reformers. He is a bard himself, a staunch Catholic, and much respected. The Queen has recently allowed the festival of bards and musicians to continue. It has been banned for many years. Hiraethog has written to me and asked me to come, if I am able.'

'Why did you not mention this before now?'

Emlyn dragged his hand through his untidy hair and mumbled, 'I have been refused permission by our principal to leave the school so am unlikely to attend the Bardic festival.'

Father de Sacy nodded slowly. Was this the reason behind this mornings prank? Did Emlyn want to be dismissed? But, with all his gifts, Emlyn would make a fine Jesuit, no matter what the teachers and brothers had to say concerning his conduct; the principal Manare would find some argument to still their complaints and change their minds. He had plans for Emlyn Thomas. 'Emlyn, all this foolishness about the gypsum footprints, appears to be in response to this request from your grandfather and the principals decision. Do you seek dismissal so avidly?'

Ignoring the questions, Emlyn said softly. 'Hiraethog's is the hand that first set my fingers to the harp. He awoke in me the love of song and music.'

'Has it been so unpleasant for you here?' Father de Sacy asked, as understanding flowed through his mind.

'I have learned much Father, and am indebted to those who have taught me.' Emlyn replied. 'I think you know me well enough to know what I want the most.'

Father de Sacy considered what he knew of Emlyn's history. His mother had married an Italian merchant and left Wales to live in Venice. It was known, that in the five years of marriage, she gave birth to two sons. Soon after the second son was born, the merchant died tragically at sea, leaving a young widow. She had mysteriously disappeared, and Emlyn had been born long after the merchant's death which had led to much speculation and rumour concerning Emlyn's illegitimate status. If the collage principal wanted to make a Jesuit out of this promising young man, the accusation of illegitimacy must be irradiated. Father de Sacy had been given the responsibility to discover the truth concerning Emlyn's birth, it was a difficult task.

From whatever his beginnings, Emlyn had arrived in Wales at the age of six, accompanied by a Franciscan priest. He had lived for five years in his uncle's household, before being sent to France. His childhood in Wales had been a life of little comfort or affection and his uncle had sent him to be trained by the Jesuits.

Father de Sacy knew of the deep need Emlyn held to know the truth of his origins. He suspected that Emlyn would not become Jesuit or bard or anything else, until he found answers to the mysteries that plagued him. Investigations so far had failed to provide a satisfying explanation. After much letter writing, de Sacy had eventually found the Franciscan who had taken Emlyn to his uncle in Wales. The man's response to Father de Sacy's inquiries had been enthusiastic, but tight lipped. The Franciscan had recently arrived in France and written to de Sacy requesting a visit. Emlyn had been made aware of the inquiries

De Sacy cleared his throat and grimaced. 'Do you know the reason for my visit to Rouen?'

Emlyn looked at him in puzzlement and then his expression cleared. 'Did you find the Franciscan?' he asked cautiously.

'Yes. I have found your Franciscan,' de Sacy said. 'He came to France by sea. He is an elderly man and I believe the journey tired him. However, I brought him back with me.'

Emlyn frowned; slow to take in the information. 'Here?'

De Sacy smiled. 'He is in the garden with your friend Goronwy. I think it would be better for you to see him before you are summoned by our principal; what you discover about your origins may have some significance on the decisions made.'

Emlyn nodded, looking thoughtful.

'You know that Father Manare would like to know if you are…' de Sacy paused awkwardly.

'Legitimate?' Emlyn finished for him. Something mischievous lit his expression.

De Sacy cleared his throat. He had promised himself that he would not keep Emlyn in the dark. 'I suspect that our principal may require a promise from you. He may well demand that you begin preparation to be ordained.'

Emlyn nodded, serious now. 'He and I have spoken thus before.'

'Then see this Franciscan first and hear what he has to say. I'm afraid that Goronwy will have besmirched your reputation with tales of miracles by now, so you do not go to this meeting as anonymous as you might wish.'

Emlyn's head lifted and his disarming smile returned.

Chapter 2 Paris

Father De Sacy accompanied Emlyn to the garden where the Franciscan, Fra Sebastiano waited. They could hear Goronwy's voice before they rounded the high wall. He was, as De Sacy had guessed, relating the story of the miracle. That was the trouble with Goronwy; he always charged into a situation with bells ringing and trumpets blaring. He never took time to think before he spoke or acted.

Emlyn and Goronwy had been friends for many years. Recently, Emlyn had noticed a change in him. It was as if he was constrained; as if, for once in his life, he was unable to speak of what concerned him. This worried Emlyn. He was also concerned that Goronwy would be witness to whatever the Franciscan had to tell. Emlyn never spoke about his past, nor voiced the need that drove him to discover the truth. If he had done so, the whole of Paris would be aware of his predicament. But his worries were needless; Father de Sacy, denying satisfaction to his own curiosity, drew Goronwy away from the gathering and made up some excuse as they left the enclosure.

The Franciscan friar was old and rounded. He was dressed in a worn habit and scuffed sandals. He did not rise from the bench, but rested his hands on his stick and subjected Emlyn to an examination. Emlyn remained standing, after his severe beating from Father Barzini to sit would not bring comfort. Time stood still. Bird song filled the well tended garden and the scent of spring flowers wafted on the light breeze. White doves played and cooed in the midst of green shoots and white cherry blossom encircling a shrine to the Blessed Virgin. Emlyn could hear a choir practising in the church near by, the singing clear and beautiful. A viol creaked into song joined by a hesitant rebec and the cajoling voice of a patient teacher.

Fra Sebastiano adjusted his weight and bent his head. He said, 'I am pleasantly surprised by this music. The French are equal now, if not better, than those of Florence whom I last heard sing the light hearted scherzo and the contrapuntal canzonet. Your friend has told me that you are a valued addition to the musicians here. It is good to praise God with the utmost of our talent.'

Emlyn did not reply. He looked at the friar and liked what he saw, but nothing stirred in his memory. Fra Sebastiano was white haired and his brown skin was seamed like a walnut. His eyes were umber brown twinkling as merrily as a child's. 'You are nothing like the boy who arrived from Cetua all that time ago, now you are grown to a man,' he said. 'There is no need for you to remain standing, sit down; this is a story long in the telling.'

Emlyn took a step back and lowered himself with extreme care to a bench opposite.

Fra Sebastiano bowed his head to hide his smile. 'Do they call you Emile now?'

'Only if they are French, the brothers here, prefer Emile. In Wales I am still called Emlyn it is the name of King Arthur's magician, bestowed upon me by my grandfather.'

'Then they do not call you by your baptismal name, Thomas? I thought it was your father's name.'

'There is no man I name father.' Emlyn replied, with no show of emotion. 'I am probably my uncle's bastard or his sister's bastard. Some say I am a by-blow of my grandfather's, from when he was in France fighting.'

'Yet, they took you in at this school, illegitimate though you say you are?'

Emlyn looked down at his hands. 'The generous donation to the college from my uncle caused them to overlook my birth status.'

'You do not remember me then? I am Fra Pietro Sebastiano da Firenze, the priest who brought you to your uncle's house, all those years ago. You may have remembered your life before then, I could not be sure, it is for this reason that I came now to see you.' He paused and listened to the silence between them. 'I knew, from your family, that your mother had married an Italian merchant and that she disappeared soon after his death, no one knows what became of her. I cannot promise you any answers. If you wish, I will go from here and what there is, will remain unsaid.'

This was a puzzling statement and it worked as the Franciscan intended; it aroused Emlyn's curiosity further. He looked expectantly to the friar. 'Are you saying that I will be so distressed by what I hear, that I would be better off not knowing?'

'That is for you to decide. I do not know where your loyalty lies.' Fra Sebastiano paused thoughtfully. 'If you are going to join the Society of Jesus, it may be better to remain ignorant. Your teachers here will not use bad clay to mould their future priests. Don't mistake me, you are not as such yourself, but the question of your illegitimate birth may be turned against you.'

Emlyn sighed, he felt both excited and dismayed. 'The brothers here would like me to join their community, but I cannot commit myself without knowing who my father was. Can you tell me the name of my father?'

Fra Sebastiano reached into the fold of his habit and brought out a small, tooled leather box. It fitted neatly into his palm. He ran a finger over the faded lettering, flecked now with gold, were once it had flowed. 'This, is all there is from your father, at least that is what I have presumed.' He said. 'What it means is as much a puzzle to me as it will be to you. I have held it for you for many years. The reason why I did so will be self explanatory when you open it.' He reached forward and placed the box in Emlyn's hands.

Emlyn held the box and saw that his hand trembled. He looked closely, the lettering was Arabic. '*La ilahah illa Allah*' He had little knowledge of the script but had seen this particular swirling image often enough to know the meaning. He said softly, 'There is no God but Allah'.

Fra Sebastiano nodded slowly and remained silent, watching the youth in front of him for a few minutes. The doves continued to coo and the choir to sing softly in harmony. 'Have you ever heard of the place named Cetua?' he asked.

Emlyn placed the box beside him and looked up, his dark eyes momentarily puzzled. Then his expression cleared and he said, 'It is in North Africa, across the sea from Seville. I believe the Portuguese have a fort there, I may be mistaken.'

Fra Sebastiano smiled, pleased with the answer. He settled more comfortably and began his tale. 'I was brought up in the environs' of Santa Croce in Florence, but my work has taken me all over Europe and the Levant. On one bright day, over eleven years ago I was in Lisbon at the house of our order. I was summoned by our superior, Father Nunez and told that a Portuguese ship had come to harbour and the captain needed to speak urgently with me. The ship was the *Madre de Deus,* newly arrived from Cetua. I had assumed that the summons would be a problem of translation or a similar matter that called on the experience I had acquired in my travels. It was known too, that I intended to journey to England at the behest of the Holy Father. England was then under the rule of Mary Tudor and with a Catholic queen on the throne the Franciscans, among many, hoped to rebuild their ruined houses and schools.

'The captain of the *Madre de Deus* was a brightly dressed gentleman Gaspar Fernandes. He grasped my hands in his and planted wet kisses on each cheek. *'I can see that you are a good man Fra Sebastiano'* he had cried, clapping his hands, *'truly a man blessed by God. It is through the goodness of my heart that I undertook this task. It hurts me sorely to be forced to pass it to another, but what choice do I have?'*

'Fernandes informed me that he had brought a passenger from Cetua, a passenger who needed escorting to his family in England. While he had been in Cetua a veiled lady accompanied by a child had approached the ship's padre. She bade him in the name of God, to take the child aboard and to insure that he would reach his family in England. The boy was the son of her mistress, she explained. It was her greatest wish that he be baptised and brought up for the church. The woman had begged with such earnest and pressed gems into the padre's hands. Moved to pity, he agreed, he asked the woman to accompany him herself. She cried anew, although she would reveal nothing concerning her mistress, she explained that she could not abandon her mistress to stand alone among the unbelievers.'

It took Emlyn a moment to realize the friar had stopped speaking, but he didn't speak himself. He picked up the old box and held it on his knee without attempting to open it. He had known something of this story, but had believed that he had come from Lisbon in Portugal and not Cetua in North Africa. He suppressed a shudder, shocked by the implications of what he heard.

'When I first saw this young child,' continued the Franciscan, his voice gentle as the scented breeze, 'his face under an elaborate headdress was pale; the eyes huge and grey, smeared with tears. The defiance of his stance belonged to princes. He greeted me with '*Salaam Aleikum*. Father Nunez thought the child was a Moor and insisted that he must be baptised immediately. As I was leaving for England in four days taking the child with me, I agreed that this would be wise. I had a chance before that, to question the foundling put into my care. I had often dealt with children; the homeless urchins that ran wild along the banks of the Arno in Florence, so I was patient and took the boy to the bath house. His hair, when revealed, was the silvery-warm yellow of ripe straw. His cheeks were rounded and pink as was the rest of him; pampered and well fed with skin as soft as rose petals. I guessed that he was used to the service of slaves and probably reared in a wealthy house, maybe the son of a pasha or someone of wealth and influence. But, when he turned for his back to be washed, I saw on his right shoulder, a brand. I could not decipher the mark but knew that it was one of ownership, from whatever house the boy had come from, he had been a slave and so too, must have been his mother.'

'Wait!' Emlyn stood suddenly and walked away, unable to take in what he was hearing. He stopped by the shrine, his breath restricted and his mind reeling. 'Go on,' he said, without turning.

Fra Sebastiano remained seated; he cleared his throat and after a moment continued. 'I told the child of the journey we would take to England but he did not understand me. Form the little Arabic I had learned, I gathered that his name was Saiah or Toma. But he also spoke in a tongue that I had not heard before, but I gathered that it was Irish perhaps or Scottish, which I had heard at the court of France, an unusual language for a boy coming from the deserts of Africa. As time was short, we baptised him Thomas, after St. Thomas Aquinas, and hoped that he would outlive the early influences of his short life to become a good Christian. That account Emlyn, is how you came to Lisbon and into my care.'

Emlyn felt a wave of anguish and heat wash over him. He knew there was more to learn, but he could not hear of it yet. What it all meant was too difficult to consider yet. He returned to the bench and sat, feeling exhausted and battered.

Fra Sebastiano leaned forward and griped his shoulder. 'Do not despair,' he said. 'I see now that our efforts have been rewarded, for you are now grown to manhood and contemplate the priesthood. If you are to overcome your difficulties here, your mother's wish will be granted.'

Emlyn shook the hand away and dropped his head into his hands. The singing had come to an end and even the birds seemed silenced by what had been revealed. *If you wish, I will go from here and what there is, will remain unsaid.*

'Take your time Emlyn and look in the box,' Fra Sebastiano said. 'When you are ready you will find me at the Franciscan house here in Paris and we can talk more on this.'

Emlyn rose slowly, holding the box in two hands. He said, 'When Pandora opened her box, she brought misery into the world. Will I bring the same upon myself by opening this?'

The Franciscan smiled. 'Who knows? If I were in your position, I would not be able to leave it closed. Come now help an old man and give me your arm.'

Emlyn helped him to rise and held his arm as they made their way out of the garden. Before they parted company, Fra Sebastiano exclaimed and came to a sudden stop. 'There is another matter of which you must be made aware before I leave you. Do not be concerned, it is of a pleasant nature.' Fra Sebastiano laughed. 'And it may well help with some answers. The merchant your mother married in Italy was a Venetian was he not, by the name of Cristoforo Grimani?'

Emlyn nodded reluctantly, not wanting to hear any more.

'I carried a letter from Florence to a child at a convent in Rouen. This girl has the same name.' Fra Sebastiano announced. 'It is a charming convent the girls were out gathering flowers to adorn the road for the procession after Easter. So I was not able to speak with her directly. However, the Mother Superior was kind enough to see me. She informed me that the girl has been with them since the age of seven. Her name is Carmelia Grimani and her family is from Venice. I believe her to be a relation of yours, probably a cousin or niece. I have told Father de Sacy who may be able to assist you in finding out more and perhaps arranging a visit.'

'I don't understand.' Emlyn replied. His thoughts were confused and the distress caused by what he had heard left him unable to grasp any clear meaning. He needed to be alone.

Fra Sebastiano resumed walking. 'Now,' he sighed. 'I have heard that you harbour a brother Franciscan here, I am expected to bring him back with me.'

Emlyn shook his head to clear it. 'That will be the Irishman friar Patrick O'Healy.'

'Then I shall collect him and be on my way. You and I will speak again when you have had a chance to absorb all I have said. You know where to find me?'

'Thank you, Fra Sebastiano. I will call on you when I am able.' Emlyn was not so sure that he wanted to learn more. He knew with certainty, that what he now knew concerning his early origins could not be revealed to Father Manare. Emlyn's mind reeled at the possibilities. After she had left Venice had his mother been enslaved? What if his early beginnings had been those of a Muslim? Father Manare would be quite horrified if it was all true. Emlyn gazed at the box. It was a sort of Pandora's Box and he hadn't even peered inside.

When Emlyn returned to the common sleeping room, he was relieved to see that it was empty. He held the box in one hand and traced his finger over the Islamic inscription on the lid. He took a deep breath preparing to lift it when there was a sound of scraping outside and voices calling. Cursing, Emlyn hurried to the wall where his secret hiding place was, a neglected hole in the stone where he hid a few treasured possessions. He put the box inside and pushed the bed forward to conceal it.

The door opened emitting a streak of slanting sunlight. 'Emlyn?' said someone from the door. 'Are you in there?' The voice was rich, mellow and deep. It was Goronwy Glyn-Parry, who had innocently betrayed him in the church. He was speaking Welsh. 'Thank God!' he laughed. 'Emlyn I'm sorry. I did not think. I thought, well, you know I'm not...' he stumbled to a halt.

Emlyn moved into the light of the only window in the long room. The beating he had received for his prank from Father Barzini had been relentless, he had tried to ignore the pain all morning, but he could no longer turn his mind from it. Outside, he could see the stable where mules stamped restlessly and warm sunlight gleamed on the yellow straw. The sound of counterpoint came from the church across the yard, the choir was now practising a *Salve Regina* for High Mass. Emlyn and Goronwy should have been with them.

Goronwy said, 'We missed you at the Easter play. It was quite good too. Brother de Mare thinks it will do wonders in converting the heathen. The moral play, he says, explains itself. The Jesuits are going to use them to convert the savages. Mime and mimicry will take the place of words. Emlyn you look a bit strange'. Goronwy walked up to him. 'Who was the man from Florence was he any relation to Barzini? What did the want?'

Emlyn shook his head. Goronwy's rattling was too much to comprehend now, when so many other thoughts intruded. He actually felt quite sick.

Goronwy said, 'I had the job of looking after your sheep this morning, they were determined to eat Father Eluard's herb garden and his rooty plants from the New World. Are you all right?' Goronwy splashed water into a beaker and sat on the seat near the window. He held up the water as if a peace offering.

Emlyn stretched out on a bench he could not sit but he could lie on his stomach. He accepted the cup and placed it carefully beside him. He dropped his head onto folded arms. The sheep which Goronwy referred to were Murano sheep, which Emlyn had acquired for his grandfather in order to breed them with the Welsh stock to improve the wool. Goronwy was going to take them to Wales.

Goronwy said, 'Take your shirt off. I've brought hot water with Father Eluard's herb potion in it, it's mixed with butter. Father Barzini has the Book of Job for you to translate and Father Bernardo d'Aguila says that if you cannot play your lute on Easter Sunday because of what has happened, he shall use Father Barzini's guts for lute strings. Jack Turnbull says that ever since you fiddled with his...Emlyn?'

Emlyn was not asleep, although he wished he was Goronwy was boring him to sleep. Peeling the shirt off was painful.

Goronwy was unfeeling enough to laugh. 'You look as if you've sat on hot harp strings.' He squeezed out a cloth above a basin, and gently began to wash the nasty wounds.

Emlyn let Goronwy get on with it. He and Emlyn had been children when they had come here, empty vessels into which the Jesuits could pour their learning. Emlyn had never regretted learning and knew that he had been fortunate to gain such an education. The Jesuits had taught him other things; they had taught him how to fear the devil; shown him how small he was beneath the awesome power of a vengeful God. They had not taught courage or how to wield a sword, but he had learned how to hate.

Goronwy would be returning home to Wales within a few days, going home with a purpose. Goronwy and his faithful followers were going to convert the Protestants and show them the error of their ways. He had always been full of plans and schemes to reach this end. Emlyn thought that it would be good to return home to Wales with Goronwy, but would it be possible? When he could trust himself to speak, he said 'Goronwy, they may not let me stay here after this matter today. I am to meet with Father Manare later for my future to be decided.'

'They will make a fuss Emlyn, but they will let you stay.' Goronwy replied cheerfully. 'You have been punished enough. The best thing you can do is forget the whole thing. Put it behind you and stay out of trouble until I come back. Don't worry, all will be forgotten and forgiven ...'

The words Emlyn had heard so often, drifted in and out of hearing.

'We are doing the right thing! Remember, we are the Crusaders for the Cause! What an army we are going to lead into Wales to clear out the heretics. We will do it Emlyn, you and I and a thousand Jesuits I can see that a little beating may put you off for a while. You will get your enthusiasm back once you have stopped hurting. Anyway it's your own fault. You always will go tom-fooling about the…'

Dreamily, Emlyn remembered a drift of thought, 'Goronwy? I think I have a cousin or a niece.'

'Bastards don't have cousins,' said Goronwy cheerfully.

'Nor do bastards become Jesuits' Emlyn replied smugly.

Chapter 3 Istanbul 1568

In the slave market of Galata, Koçi sat in the full sun, flicking a frayed stick in the dust at his feet. From here he could see the blue-gold sea surrounding the minarets of Constantinople, all aglow with sunlight. It held no mystery for Koçi; he preferred to remain on this side of the Golden Horn away from the Topkapi Palace which brought fearful memories. Since they had arrived in the city his master, Ismael the Syrian, came and went to the Turkish Palace whenever he pleased. Ismael liked to keep company with the learned men of the Ulema where they heard from him about the Portuguese and whatever else he elected to tell them, in exchange for favour He was there now with the old men bent over manuscripts and maps and ancient writings. While thus, his poor slave Koçi waited in the dusty heat for the slave dealer, Abu Abdullah of Ulcinj to arrive.

Soon after they had arrived in Uskudar, Ismael had bought house slaves from Abu. These were sent to a house which Ismael had bought without even seeing it; he said that he knew of it. Koçi had seen the house two days before. They had ridden out and had stopped on the top of a rise to view the buildings from a distance. Koçi had been disappointed. They looked down on a mound of gnarled branches crawling with leaves and flowers, with tall palms in shaggy abundance above. Ismael had eased his weight in the saddle. The new mare stamped, shaking the heavy tassels on her rein, ringing the bells of her harness.

Koçi had said, 'You have bought the nest of a giant bird, Lord.'

Ismael laughed. 'No Koçi I have bought Paradise.' He thudded his mare's flanks and thundered down the slope.

Koçi had galloped after him, filled with joyful abandon, knowing that he could not catch up. Ismael had been right about the gypsies of Balatmahalle; they did sell wonderful horses.

A high wall surrounded a house that seemed as ancient as the city itself, inured to time, awash with the flavour of Byzantine. The trees in the courtyard were gnarled and overgrown, the vines so old that they had brought down the trellising, captured it in twined embraces until it had rotted away. The walls were a mixture of mosaic, plaster and stone, fused by time. Where once a fountain had stood, there was a wide, clear pond, messy with weeds and broken stones. There was a great deal of work to be done before the house was habitable. Ismael had viewed all with pleasure. Standing inside the gate, he had laughed and held out his arms as if to embrace what he beheld.

There were salamanders in the pond, these, Ismael had taken an exceptional interest in. He had crouched at the edge and dipped his hand into the clear water. Disinterested, Koçi had sat beside him and watched. The merchant remained still and patient until a salamander came close. With a sudden movement, he snatched and brought the creature out, caged within his ringed fingers. The fingers unfurled slowly like an opening lily and the tiny salamander lay curled in his hand. It was pink-brown, glistening with moisture. The feathered head lifted, preparing to flee. Ismael sat motionless until the tiny dragon grew courageous and padded to the tip of his fingers. He lowered his hand and the salamander plopped into the water, leaving circles of light and shadow to mark its passing. When Ismael had looked up, his expression was playful.

Koçi's feet had spun on the gravel as he rose and left him

Now as he waited for the slave dealer, Koçi grimaced at the memory. He knew that rare expression of his master's when he had held the salamander; it was not as innocent as it appeared.

Abu Abdullah of Ulcinj arrived with a gift for his beloved friend Ismael, the gift of a black slave. Abu patted the new slave affectionately. 'He reads, he writes, he plays with numbers and is learned in medicine, invaluable!' he laughed. 'Unfortunately he is Christian, but he does not look like one.'

It was looks that interested Koçi more; he would not welcome competition for the attentions of Ismael. If the black slave had a brain and a wealth of experience, the attention of Ismael would be diverted enough; it would not do for him to be slender and graceful as well.

He was not slender and graceful; this was the first point that Koçi noticed when Abu Abdullah came out into the sunlight with the slave walking at his side. The man was sulking and his ears were outside the folds of his turban. His features were gravely handsome and his eyes thoughtful. He was of average height with narrow shoulders, the rest of him was covered by a long white robe; on his feet were flat slippers embroidered with gold thread and coral beads. Koçi was pleased, for the man was at least the age of Ismael, if not older. Abu took the slave's arm and pushed him onwards affectionately.

Koçi didn't stand up; to do so would invite the embrace of Abu, who was large and greasy with patchouli oil. Koçi had shared his bed once or twice on the journey from Samarkand. The Arab was a gentle and affectionate man. Koçi knew what lay behind this gift; Ismael was going to Damascus and Abu Abdullah hoped that with this new slave he could persuade the master to present him with Koçi, in return.

'Where is my *Muhibbi*,' wailed Abu, wringing his plump hands. 'Where is my beloved friend?'

'He has not returned sidi.' Koçi answered nonchalantly. 'He has found favour with the Sultan and walks where most men fear to tread.'

'In Sha Allah,' Abu thumped the black slave between the shoulders. 'This is Symeon,' he announced. 'His old master prepares for Paradise, even his physicians' skill can not prevent the inevitable.'

'In Sha Allah,' intoned Koçi and Symeon simultaneously.

Abu frowned at them and continued, 'I promised the good medical man that I would find an excellent master for his favoured slave. My friend Ismael is the perfect choice. Symeon will be a great help to him in his business. And, I give him from the goodness of my heart, completely free of charge.'

Addressing Symeon in Turkish, which Abu refused to adopt, Koçi said 'My master has already bought his household slaves from this man. Abu Abdullah can afford to be generous with the gift of you.'

Symeon smiled. His teeth were even and unbroken; his eyes aglitter with humour 'Abu Abdullah is not known for his generosity,' he said. 'Maybe he will expect payment in some form or other.' They left the slave dealer and Koçi took Symeon to the old house they were staying at, to await his new master.

The Syrian did not return that night or the following day. Koçi took two horses and returned to the harbour to watch the public barges, fearing that his master was detained at the palace against his will. But Ismael came across that evening in a fishing boat, looking tired but pleased. Ismael walked casually from the water edge. He was dressed like a Turk, in a new furred robe, blazing with gems and his dazzling white turban was pinned with a gold clasp and an ostrich feather dyed purple. He looked as magnificent as a pasha. Koçi watched and felt his heartbeat quicken. He ran to greet his beloved master and spoke of what was most on his mind. 'Lord, Abu Abdullah has sent you the gift of a slave. He is...'

'The African, Symeon?' Ismael said. He smiled and winked. 'I have sold him to a Venetian trader, along with my remaining goods.'

Koçi stepped back in surprise. 'Master you have not beheld him. How can you know that is he of no worth to you?'

'Do you like him, Koçi?' said Ismael. 'Then I am sorry, but it is done. He is a Christian so it is better that he serves a Christian'.

'What will you say to sidi Abu?'

'I will thank Abu for the generosity of his gift. Then I will go to Damascus.'

Koçi cast him a sidelong glance, fluttering his lashes like a camel, presenting the smile that captivated everyone else, that never worked on his master.

Ismael shook his head, a faint smile lifting the corners of his neat beard. 'I want no servant with me when I go, I am tired of servants. Wait in the house I have bought, that is so favoured by Allah. Grow vines upon the trellises.'

Koçi dropped the pretence, his sorrow deep. He led his master to the horses.

When Ismael mounted he did not turn toward the hills above Galata, but moved instead under a crumbling arch which led to the covered market.

Koçi said, 'You do not come home, Lord?'

Ismael rubbed his eyes with a tired gesture. 'Soon,' he replied. 'Take the man, Symeon to the harbour, to the Venetian Ballie. He is to board the *Cornucopia,* a caravel due to sail for Venice in the morning.'

Chapter 4 Paris

The last war between England and France had ended with the Treaty of Troyes in 1564. England had bitterly lost Calais; her last long held foothold in France. Queen Elizabeth ruled the only Protestant kingdom in Europe. A protestant queen ruling a protestant country forced families who were devoted to Catholicism to seek an education for their offspring abroad. College de Clermont in Paris offered a solution; a new approach to Catholic education; instruction in grammar, humanities, rhetoric, theology, scripture, geography and languages, including those of the orient. Pre-Christian Philosopher's were not shunned nor were the ideas of the changing world around them. The Jesuits believed that languages were the key to the door of ignorance; to learn Hebrew and Arabic was to open the gates of Jerusalem; the mastery of Persian and Turkish would bring down the Minarets of Constantinople and return it to Christendom; excellence in the Germanic tongues and the English dialects would drive the heretic back to the righteous path.

The power and influence of Rome had lessened in significance in Northern Europe and the Jesuits were the answer to all who denied the leadership of the Pope in Rome. They were his ears, his eyes and his hands; theirs were the feet that trod lands old and new to take the word of God to the heathen or to re-educate the wayward. They had already infiltrated every court of Europe- except the court of Elizabeth, Queen of England. They had come so far in such a short time, that this was seen as just a temporary state of affairs. The re-conversion of England was a burning ambition in their motto, '*Ad majorem Dei gloriam*' -To the Greater Glory of God.

Students had arrived in droves from England to escape the religious reform, some to France to study at Louvain or Paris, while others fled to the Netherlands. They had leadership, every English exile accepted in one of the schools was considered a future priest and a soldier of God prepared to spread the true faith. At College de Clermont, Father Manare drummed the message into the hearts of his flock with thunderous conviction. He looked upon them with special affection, those brave spirits who have fled their homes in the wake of terrible persecution. 'We could not in truth call ourselves Christian, if we did not open our doors and hearts to this homeless, leaderless flock and make them strong again to continue the work of God.'

This was a message Emlyn had heard often enough. The first time, he had been an undersized boy of thirteen years, arriving at the college with Goronwy. It seemed right to recall that incident, now that his meeting with Father Manare and the members of the Society was over. He awaited their decision, knowing that his future was no longer as sure as it had been. Most of them wanted him to leave the college. Father Barzini had suggested that as soon as possible could not be soon enough. Yet, Father de Sacy had spoken eloquently on the advantages that Emlyn could offer the society if he were able to remain. Emlyn had felt for a moment that the words would sway the decision, but then the argument had intensified.

'His behaviour is disrespectful. He tied the skirts of a lady of ill repute to Monsignor the Cardinal of Lorraine's hose strings!'

'He spilled madder into the Abbot's milk, driving the God fearing man to his knees!'

'He tied bells and clappers to the students on retreat!'

'He fights with the university students at wherever opportunity arises; he has run imp-wild in the streets causing no end of mischief!'

'Did he not, but last month, let loose a plague of frogs in the herbarium?'

'He is remarkable with languages,' Father de Sacy had repeated throughout. 'He needs to mature, as all boys do.'

'I agree, if you knocked the fool out of him, he would make a good man of God,' Father Manare had said in weak defence. 'God chooses his army with care and I do not deny that I see in this young Welshman the making of such a one.'

'Nonsense' Father Barzini had spluttered disrespectfully. None objected, they all knew what generous donors the family Barzini was to the order. To strengthen his argument Barzini had then brought forth the one accusation that none of them could argue against. 'We shun certain men from joining our society; those who are wed or in servitude, or are mentally deficient. We also bar those of bad habits Father Superior, those lacking intelligence and those of questionable birth who suffer from inconsistency and worldliness. Are we to welcome one as base born as he in to our flock? Do we to turn to the misbegotten?'

'It is only rumoured that the boy may be illegitimate,' Father Manare had answered in quiet response. 'We are not certain.'

The room where Emlyn awaited his reckoning was cold and seemed to grow colder with the waiting there was no fire at the hearth. His eyes searched the well-stocked book shelves and picked out at least six titles that should have been burnt, if the order of the Pope was to be obeyed. Emlyn's curiosity over these forbidden volumes increased while he waited. He sighed and let his eyes roam away from the books; over the vellum and neatly stacked papers, the ornate ink holder and pens and quills. There were maps on the walls, dotted with red wax to indicate where the Jesuit colleges were in Europe, and the missions in further, mysterious places, said to be inhabited by idol worshippers. There was no red wax upon the tiny kingdom of England.

Noise from outside intruded: the clang of a blacksmith's hammer and the complaining snort from the horse he was shoeing; the tramps of feet and slap of sandals on paving as boys moved from class to refectory; a work bell calling the artisans' day to a close; the high voice of a boy calling out his wares; a cockerel crowing to the dipping of the sun. All were the sounds he had lived with for four years, the sounds of belonging and being tied to the rhythms of one place.

Emlyn felt cold and sick, he closed his eyes and thought reluctantly of his mother. The inner presence came soaring to his mind, a voice, coloured by visions and dreams; rich in hue and scent and emotion; utterly concealed within. Emlyn shook it away. He had said nothing to the Jesuits about his meeting with Fra Sebastiano and what he had learned about himself. 'Cetua?' he whispered softly. It was a great distance away, on the very tip of North Africa, before the great continent sloped away to greet the cold Atlantic. The scrap of surrounding land was Portugal's tiny foothold on a vast and terrifying land mass. Cetua was a port where troops were kept to foray out occasionally to harass the Moors. Even after nearly a hundred years of occupation, Portugal had been ineffectual and the great caravans had moved their markets to other sites along the North African coast.

The door opened and Father Manare entered. The hair beneath his round cap was damp and curled with perspiration and his eyes carried an expression of tired patience. He lowered himself into his velvet covered chair with a sigh. The chair was a gift from the Cardinal de Bourbon and had become Father Manare's favoured place from which to control the running of his college. He arranged his habit about him and sat forward in a businesslike manner.

'Emile, you are problem and promise rolled into one being,' he announced tiredly. 'Many would like to see the back of you, but I know it would be wrong to dismiss you without considerable thought.' He paused, fixing Emlyn with a piercing glare. 'It is not easy to belong to this Society of Jesus, Emile. Only a strong heart can survive here. We Jesuits have seen our windows stoned and the filth thrown into our house. We have too often stood under siege. But we will persevere, through patience and prayer and respect. You were sent to us for the purpose of joining our order and you are aware of my hope that every student who enters the portals of College de Clermont will go out again as a Jesuit. Such a life could still be possible for you.'

Emlyn looked up. 'Perhaps God has another purpose in mind for me, Father. I would make an unhappy priest.' He knew the words had been ill chosen as soon as he voiced them.

'Your own spiritual strength is equalled by few.' Father Manare continued softly, looking disappointed. 'But, I would be the last, as God is my witness, to deny your evident unsuitability; wild spirits would be hard tried, shackled to the obedience required here. Yet, anchored to a strong source, that energy could be channelled and redirected, put to the use of God, rather than destruction. You are young and inexperienced, but the Lord would not have blessed you with the gift of tongues and music unless He had good reason. Do you believe that you have both the courage and strength to take up the gauntlet Emile?'

'I do not know about courage and strength,' Emlyn replied humbly. 'But Father you know yourself, that whether I am expelled from here or not, there are other matters that influence such a decision. As Farther Barzini clearly pointed out.'

'Do not think I have not considered this problem Emile, I have thought long on it. Your legitimacy can not be proven, but nor can it be disproved. Some answers must be found and I think the only person capable of discovering the truth is you.' Father Manare produced a letter from within his gown and placed it purposefully on the table. He took a deep breath before he spoke. 'It is my decision that you return home to your family for a few months. It will allow these recent events to settle down.'

Emlyn gasped in surprise.

'I know, I refused your request earlier, to attend some ceremony or other,' Father Manare explained. 'Matters have changed since then, and this letter is from your uncle, he requests my permission personally. It seems the ceremony...the...'

'The Eisteddfod,' said Emlyn, unable to help himself. 'It is an ancient celebration of music and poetry and a gathering of the bards. Surely the letter was not from my uncle, Father, but from my grandfather, to whom the Eisteddfod is of great importance.'

'I see,' continued Father Manare. 'Well, whatever, but while you are there, I want you to do all you can to discover your parentage. I will write to your uncle and inquire into the matter; he may be able to provide proof. Was there not some suggestion that your father was an Italian seaman?'

Emlyn felt his skin burn with indignation. 'My mother was married to an Italian merchant; he died at sea two years before I was born. I believe that I have told you this before Father.'

'I see, I see. Still, there may have been some mistake in the calculations. I will urge your uncle to put matters right and when you return to us in the autumn, we will see if we have a Jesuit in you or not. By then you will be in your eighteenth year and able to take holy orders. I will voice my decision to our brothers.' The principal rose and crossed the room. At the door he turned and said, 'Stay here a while, and think carefully on this Emile. May God give you comfort.'

Emlyn allowed himself to relax only when the door had closed firmly behind the principal. It seemed that Father Manare was quite willing to overlook illegitimacy. He was a kind and patient man, Emlyn knew that his uncle would not be persuaded to take part in whatever deception the Jesuit required of him. If proof of a legitimate birth was what Father Manare needed, he would never get it in Wales. Emlyn was free to go to Wales with Goronwy. He was free to follow whatever path he chose.

He thought of the unopened leather-bound box hidden in the wall. Would it provide clues to resolve the mystery surrounding his mother? He would have to contrive some way of seeing the child Fra Sebastiano had told him about in Rouen, perhaps she might supply some answers. Emlyn's mind was numb, the day seemed so long that he felt as if he had missed a night and could think of nothing but sleep.

He should have cautioned himself against such optimism. Father Barzini, subject of the miraculous visitation, had not forgotten him. He opened the door with enough violence to make Emlyn leap to his feet. Dark, fierce eyes bored into him as the Florentine ordered him to go straight to the church to spend the night on his knees. Resigned, Emlyn walked across the courtyard to the church. The daylight was softening towards dusk. He noticed a splash of gypsum here and there on the tiles of the cloister. He smiled. Had the miraculous footprints only been this morning?

***

A young novice stared dreamily out of a window in her Rouen convent; a soft breeze lifted her veil. In the sky, the yellow sun slipped into swathes of moody-grey cloud, colours dancing on the surface of the Seine. The reflective river wound towards the sea, a thick, mirrored worm prickly with dark ships. Towering hills rose into the dusky sky like bastions defending the old merchant town.

Inside the convent walls, old apple trees swelled with new growth, early blossom, already burst, shed petals to embroider the grass, all rich and thick with silver twilight moisture. Pale hands reached out to pull the shutters closed, the room was plunged to darkness. The novice paused by the door, she turned to be sure the room was in order before she left.

She dipped her fingers to the door-font of holy water. A blessing, she thought with rancour, a pattern repeated, an ending to each and every day for the last seven years! Was she to endure a further seven? Her family had forgotten her existence. Her romantic dreams were shattered as she contemplated a life of being forgotten.

Carmelia Grimani was small for her age, her face was pale and her eyes a deep earth-brown. Her hair was very long and as dark as night, she had plaited it into two strands, as thick as her wrist.

She crossed the courtyard and stopped near the fish pond; a pool still dark and cold from winter. She could see the old, gnarled willow by the convent wall, green fresh leaves waved in the night wind; not yet thick enough to cover the hole in the wall. This was a small opening through which the young girl had wiggled to freedom on occasions. As an escapee, she always dressed as a boy, it was the only way she could escape the convent walls and walk anonymous into the bustle of life in the river port. She loved the harbour and the tall ships, they promised longed for romantic adventure.

At first, she had ventured out on her own on rare occasions. But, her maid Pellegrina had recently discovered her escapades and insisted on becoming part of them. Pellegrina was not as pious as she appeared and her knowledge of men, which she had recently revealed to her young mistress, was astonishing. At times, when the sun shone and the babble of mingled languages rang through the air, Carmelia thought of Italy. She longed to travel back over the Alps she had crossed as a child. She could not remember her parents well. There was a miniature of her mother in her room. But, if she passed her elderly father on the street, she was afraid that she would not know him and was certain that he would not see her as his child. She was not dressed to escape tonight and it was too early. She turned away and hurried back as she saw a nun running towards her.

'Carmel!' the nun was running, her veil flapping. 'Come quickly child,' she called. 'Your godmother is here.' This was said in awe. The nun touched her forehead and made the sign of the cross as if to avert evil.

'Sister Helen,' said Carmelia falling into step beside her. 'Are you afraid?'

'I can't say I am comforted by having that Mademoiselle Adriana Martinelli, here among us. Do you know child that she cured the Cardinal of Poitou of his complaint by casting a spell on the good man's pillow? And he had travelled far and wide to find a cure for his complaint.'

'What was his complaint?' Carmelia asked curiously.

'What matters more,' said Sister Helen emphatically, 'is that he was so grateful, and him being a man of God, that he showered her with gold!'

'You exaggerate Sister!'

'Only a little my dear,' said Sister Helen with her nose in the air.

'I am sure that the good Lord had a hand in it somewhere,' said Carmelia reassuringly.

Carmelia knew that they disapproved of her godmother here. Rumour abounded concerning the life of Adriana Martinelli: she invited poets and artists to her house; she encouraged musicians and players, both noble and plebeian; she dabbled in alchemy; single and married men came and went as they pleased. She welcomed men and women from all backgrounds under her accommodating roof, Huguenot and Catholic alike! Adriana was widowed, which seemed to make matters worse. Carmelia herself was afraid of her godmother and believed everything the nuns told her. The bold smile she offered Sister Helen was merely a mask in the face of her own fear.

Down the corridor, their skirts rustled against baskets heaped with bright flower petals, the scent was overwhelming. They had been gathered in preparation for the Easter procession in three days. Carmelia and Sister Helen paused before a heavy wooden door, studded with brass. It remained firmly closed after they had knocked.

Sister Helen grasped her rosary and whispered a Hail Mary.; she got through four, before the door creaked open.

The abbess of the convent stood on the threshold with her hands clasped together at her waist. She was a comfortably stout woman, with a matronly look about her. It was a mistake to take this mild appearance on face value; the abbess had a will of iron and ruled her convent with the astuteness of a banker. Her eyes were cold and her mouth was set in its usual straight line, drawn down by age. She could smile and often did, she was capable of warmth and affection when need arose, but her usual demeanour was one of stern authority. 'You may leave us,' she said to Sister Helen. The sister scuttled off as fast as her short legs would take her. Carmelia entered the room and saw her godmother standing by the fire.

Madame Adriana Martinelli was thin, superior and ageless. A woman of striking beauty with a presence that demanded instant respect. She was dressed in black brocade, an austere outfit with very little to lighten it. Two ropes of grey pearls hung from neck to waist. Her hair was always hidden. Today she wore a puffed velvet cap, brimmed with dark embroidery and seed pearls.

Carmelia dropped in a curtsey. She had seen her godmother on few occasions during her stay in the convent, and had occasionally gone to Chartres, where her godmother kept her scandalous country house.

'Dear, dear me,' said Madame Adriana Martinelli. She looked Carmelia up and down and shook her head in despair.

Carmelia remained silent. She had forgotten that her skirts were rumpled and heavy with moisture from the walk through the unkempt garden.

'Whatever are we to do with you child?' Adriana snapped. 'It is unfortunate that you are not blessed with great beauty, but I suppose you will have to do. A little care here and there could do wonders.'

'You might think to add a prayer or two, Mademoiselle Martinelli,' added the abbess. 'Carmel is far from becoming a responsible adult. She is a quiet girl and obedient, but she does dream so. It is so difficult to keep her attention.'

Carmelia felt herself shrink under their scrutiny.

'And just as difficult to keep her tidy, it would appear,' said Adriana Martinelli. Her voice was not cynical. Peeking nervously at her, Carmelia saw for a fleeting moment that her godmother was smiling affectionately. The smile soon disappeared and the mask of haughty indifference returned.

'Come closer child,' ordered the abbess. 'Don't stand there like a bedraggled orphan.'

Carmelia crept a few steps closer, her head lowered. Her godmother walked forward and took her arm, drawing her towards the light of the wall lamps. 'I am in Rouen for a short visit, and with some news,' Adriana explained. 'The abbess tells me that you have had a visitor?'

'Have I?' Carmelia was sure she would have remembered. Life was so dull at times a visitor would have been more than welcome.

'A Franciscan,' Adriana added. 'Fra Pietro Sebastiano da Firenze, not a name one would treat with ignorance. I understand that you were not present when he called?'

'No Madonna,' whispered Carmelia. She had never heard of Fra Pietro Sebastiano da Firenze. 'I did not know. Was it of some importance?'

'Who can say as you were not here to greet him?' Adriana said with a trace of annoyance.

The abbess cleared her throat, she said. 'That infamous friar did call. He is known to your father Carmelia, Carlos Grimani. He delivered some letters from your family, which I shall give to you presently.'

Carmelia almost squealed with joy. 'If he was a Franciscan from Florence,' she burst out, 'he probably carried word of my... about Lorenzo. He is actually my nephew, though he is older than I. Lorenzo has been a novice with the Franciscans in Florence for two years. He writes to me often.' She was sorry that she had missed her visitor with news from Lorenzo, his letters were always amusing. Although she had not seen him for over four years, he kept a close affection between them through his letters, Carmelia wrote back with the same enthusiasm.

'I am sure you two have much to discuss,' announced the abbess, sweeping towards the door. Carmelia was left alone with her godmother.

Adriana spoke as soon as the door closed. 'And I, have received word from your father.'

Carmelia looked up and met her eyes. They were unfathomable.

Adriana continued, 'He wishes you to consider marriage.'

Carmelia was astonished. Although she dreamed about her future, the prospect of real marriage had never entered her mind. 'So soon?' she gasped, 'and to whom?'

'Why are you surprised child?' Adriana asked. 'You are now fourteen, by the time the arrangements are made you will be fifteen. I myself was wed twice by then. I have wed twice more since. They were elderly men, God keep them.'

Carmelia shuddered. 'Will he be old?'

'Whoever the fortunate groom is, I do not know. Your father omitted the information; I doubt that even he has decided. But you can be sure Carmelia that he will be rich. I can't see your father settle for anyone who is not at least as wealthy as himself. It may even be possible that the chosen husband is young and handsome; stranger things have happened.' Adriana Martinelli held out her arms and the earlier smile returned to soften her face.

Carmelia stepped forward and returned her godmother's embrace.

Releasing her, Madame Adriana said, 'Do not fret Carmelia. Do you think that your godmother would allow her little girl to wed an ancient monster?'

Carmelia felt the tension between them dissipate. 'No,' she replied forcing a smile. 'Do you think your influence could stretch to a perfect, handsome prince?'

'Maybe even a sea prince?'

The simple words made Carmelia suddenly cold. She felt as if a cloud had passed over the sun. 'Any prince,' she laughed nervously as she felt her panic rise. She turned away as tears flowed over her lashes and ran down her cheeks.

Her godmother took her hand and coaxed her towards a chair where she sat, pulling Carmelia down to sit at her feet. Her voice revealed a tenderness that Carmelia had rarely heard before. Madame Adriana Martinelli was not a woman used to showing her emotions. 'My very dear Little Dove,' she said softly. 'You are like a daughter to me, I have held you in my arms as my own child when you were first brought into this world and you have been dear to me ever since. It is now a time of change. Do not forget what you have learned in this peaceful convent. Though you may have often wished to fly from here, you will find in times to come, that this is the safest place you will ever be. You will look upon it with great affection and fond memory.'

Carmelia did not much care for what she knew of the world outside these protective walls, yet it beckoned her or she would have never escaped the confines of the convent through the secret break in the wall. 'I thought I might remain here all my life,' she answered.

Adriana patted her hand and tucked a stray tendril of dark hair back into place. 'That would be shame indeed. You are destined for greater things. If God gives you a good husband and grants you sons and daughters, then you will be blessed undeniably. What gives greater pleasure to a woman than the child she bears? Before then, you will be brought to the world and I shall prepare you for it. You will come and stay with me after Easter, while we await your father's instructions. There is so much you must learn.'

Carmelia felt a little calmer. 'Mademoiselle, I shall look forward to that.'

'And you will enjoy it,' said Adriana enthusiastically. 'I will instruct you how to dress with a good sense of decency and never adorn yourself with too much finery- that is a mark of vanity most unattractive in a young girl. Finery is for old women who have nothing of their beauty left to show. The lessons of modesty and decorum you have received here, will serve you well for the rest of your life. Your chosen husband must receive your respect and duty so your reputation is of paramount importance. Never do anything that will bring disgrace upon you.' Adriana bent forward and took Carmelia's face in the frame of her hands. 'Dear Carmelia, I am sure you will live in love and peace. You must honour your father and bring no shame to his great name. May God prosper you, Little Dove and grant to you the happiness you deserve.'

***

Emlyn rose from his knees and sat on the bench. He was not sure which position offered more discomfort, but it was easier to sleep sitting than kneeling. Brother Daniel de Collier had joined him in prayer and had instantly fallen asleep. Emlyn was seated near to the Blessed Virgin; the serene statue seemed to smile in the dim candle light. Emlyn closed his eyes. But sleep would not come; his mind was filled with thoughts of all that had occurred that day. At least Goronwy would be overjoyed that Emlyn was to join him on his journey home.

Goronwy had returned to Wales often over the years, and kept in touch with his large family. Emlyn had stayed in Paris the whole time, he never heard from his uncle, Hugh of Plas Newydd, and only heard from his grandfather now and then. The old man had taken the trouble to keep Emlyn informed of family news and the odd bits of gossip. Emlyn was looking forward to seeing him and knew that old Gruffydd would be delighted that Emlyn was probably not going to be a Jesuit. Gruffydd owned extensive pasture land that he had developed and made profitable over the years. He had named Emlyn as his heir, much to the annoyance of Emlyn's uncle, who saw the land as his, by right of inheritance under the recent laws imposed by England. Unlike his grandfather, who refused to acknowledge such laws, Emlyn could see that his uncle was right and that the promise of inheritance from Gruffydd was nothing more than an illusion. When Emlyn returned home, the old quarrels would be renewed and Gruffydd would adhere to the old customs of Wales as he always did, causing more harm than good. Emlyn was not interested in the old quarrels; what he wanted from Gruffydd now, was the story of his mother, a subject which Gruffydd had avoided.

Emlyn had buried memories of his mother. When he did force himself to remember, she seemed to be always surrounded with light, like a saint. Shimmering gauze draped her dark hair and gems glinted at her brow and neck. There was sadness in her eyes and sadness in her smile. She spoke softly and always in Welsh, telling her son the legends and the heroic tales, as if she had always known that his life would not be with hers. He had no memory of his father, but was aware of a wisp of imagery, as if something nagged at the edges of his awareness. Emlyn forced the thoughts away; such memories always brought a sense of confusion and a sadness that he could never understand. Did the box that Fra Sebastiano had brought him contain the answers he sought?

Brother Daniel de Collier continued in undisturbed slumber; the fringe of his tonsure rising and falling with soft snores. Emlyn sat for over an hour, watching the candles diminish. It was a place of deep peace and worked like a balm on his raw emotions. He was roused from his revere by a sharp hiss from the church doorway. He looked around quickly and saw Goronwy signalling in silence. Emlyn got up quietly and went to join him.

Goronwy grasped his sleeve and pulled him out of sight of Brother Daniel, should the good brother awaken. 'Well?' Goronwy demanded in a fierce whisper.

Emlyn said, 'if you haven't brought me any supper. I'm going to eat the candles.'

Goronwy pushed a small loaf and a piece of cheese into his hand. Emlyn took it gratefully. He refused to speak until he had eaten every crumb. When he was done, he said, 'I'm coming back home with you.'

Goronwy didn't look overjoyed. He looked horrified. 'You can't,' he yelped.

'What? Why not? I thought you would be pleased.'

Goronwy turned red and looked at his feet. Eventually he said 'I'm sorry, you are right, I am pleased. I don't know what came over me. But there are…' he stumbled to a halt. 'There is something I didn't tell you about. There was no need, as you were not coming back with me and it seemed wise to keep quiet.'

Emlyn sighed, 'You may as well tell me.' Goronwy had been keeping some strange company lately and could have well been dragged into some plot. 'Would it have anything to do with those English visitors we had from Louvain? You spoke to one of them earnestly and met him again during the days following. Was it William Allen?'

Goronwy shrugged, the tightness leaving his broad shoulders. He nodded his head in affirmation. 'William Allen is going to Rome later this year. He has every hope that the Holy Father will grant him permission and blessing to start a Jesuit school of his own. Allen intends to found it especially for the Catholics flying from the tyranny of England.' Goronwy swallowed nervously. 'I know what you are thinking,' he said. 'I don't want to hear it.'

'You should tell me the rest,' Emlyn replied.

'All right,' Goronwy agreed, 'but you are only going to argue with me'

'I won't.'

'I am taking the means for making a printing press back to Wales. Me, and a few others, are going to print pamphlets and distribute them to the Catholics wherever they are. You have always told me about the power of the written word, well now we can see that power working for ourselves. We can reach the ear of every Catholic, man, woman and child in Wales who are still faithful to the old ways. We can communicate with thousands.'

'Goronwy, what are you thinking of?' gasped Emlyn. 'I can't believe what I am hearing. You may not wish for argument but, have you considered the consequences if you are discovered?'

'This has all been arranged. We are all organized into teams and work together to one end. I am to pick up the letter blocks in Rouen from Wendelin Tieffenbrucker, you know, the German lute maker. No one will suspect anything. You said you would not argue!'

'You will be discovered as soon as you arrive in England,' said Emlyn. 'You will be thrown into the Tower and hung at Tyburn. Worse still, they do not favour hanging much these days, at least not unto death. *A heuo ddrain na cherdded yn droednoeth!*'

'Leave it Emlyn,' said Goronwy darkly. 'I am not going to arrive in England.'

Emlyn swung away in anger. 'Where else is there to spread your rebellious scribbling?'

Goronwy smiled sourly. 'You're not thinking Emlyn.'

'Wales?' gasped Emlyn in disbelief. 'Well, there you are you may as well get hung drawn and quartered in Wrexham or Beaumaris. At least the watching crowd will call you traitor in Welsh!'

'Emlyn you're being foolish. The risk is small and the reward is great. I knew you wouldn't understand. I knew you would treat this as if it were some joke.' Goronwy turned away, his face darkened with anger. He turned with his hand on the door and said, 'When have you ever done anything worthy in the eyes of God?'

Before Emlyn could voice his disbelief, Goronwy was gone. Emlyn returned to his hard bench. He did very little praying that night. The day had begun with what he thought was a light-hearted prank, and had progressed into inexplicable incredulity.

Chapter 5 Paris

Early the next morning, Emlyn just managed to catch the end of the line of novices filing into the refectory. Many of them silently congratulated him on his latest prank. When he sat down, an English student Tom Sanders thumped him on the back just to give him an excuse to wince and tell them all about the severity of his beating. Emlyn glowed contently. When Father de Sacy left the room on some unaccountable errand, the students all clustered around him. 'Do you know what happened while you were away?' Tom Sanders said enthusiastically.

'I wasn't away,' said Emlyn. 'I was fasting and praying. What?'

They all laughed and made him wait. 'Footprints,' said Tom, 'two of them, planted squarely outside the latrines; just two, a left one and a right one.'

'No one knows who left them there,' said Jan Coecke, a student from Brussels. 'Only that it could not have been you, you were to busy fasting and praying.'

Emlyn laughed. There was hope for the College yet, he had a successor.

'Father Barzini thinks that you are planning something with the Franciscans,' said Jan. 'They were not impressed with your recent visitor. Friar Patrick O'Healy is bad enough on Jesuit ground, but the famous Fra Pietro Sebastiano da Firenze appearing at the gates, had them all whispering in corners.'

'Is Fra Sebastiano famous?' Emlyn asked, but before he could inquire further, Father de Sacy reappeared, clapping his hands sharply for order.

It was not until the late afternoon that Emlyn was given permission to leave college and visit the Franciscan community. Emlyn did not tell Goronwy where he was going. He knew he would have to offer an explanation about the friar soon. Emlyn hurried to his room to collect the box Fra Sebastiano had given him. Burning with curiosity he opened the lid carefully, not knowing what to expect. He gasped in astonishment and stood for some minutes shock-still, staring into the box. Then he shut it and left the room; his thoughts in turmoil.

He wove through Paris, keeping an eye out for university students, who were never friendly, and arrived at the door of the Franciscan house just as it was opening.

'Saints alive it's yourself,' said Friar Patrick O'Healy, nearly knocking him over. 'Emlyn Tomas of the White Virgin, tis a fine, merry dance you've led them good brothers of the Holy Father. Throwing you out are they?'

Emlyn grinned. Friar Patrick O'Healy was the only one who had fully appreciated the miracle of the Virgin.

'You look half starved,' said the Irishman. 'Or is this to show the good friars here, that a Welshman can out fast an Irishman?'

'Well there you are see,' Emlyn replied. 'I could starve better than you any day and pray better. Look at the belly on you! It'll never enter the Pearly Gates. You should change orders. The Jesuits do a lovely bowl of gruel once a fortnight and keep you in fine fettle chasing heretics; you get a bowl of beans too if you catch one, though you'd be hard pressed to find a leek'.

Friar Patrick O'Healy grasped a handful of Emlyn's jerkin and pulled him in through the door. 'Leeks is it?' he said 'and where'd you be finding a leek in this fair city, where they eat nothing if doesn't have a wobble to it?'

He managed to get away eventually. Unlike the Jesuits, the Franciscans liked Friar O'Healy. When he had arrived the day before with Fra Sebastiano, they were all speeded up a step or two; they smiled and laughed and followed his booming voice, rejuvenated by his active, chattering presence.

The room into which Emlyn was shown was warm, smelling of herbs and vinegar. It was comfortable with sunlight streaming through the glazed window and a cheerful tapestry softening the wall. There was a brazier lit and a lectern piled with books. Fra Sebastiano was in bed, propped up on feather stuffed pillows while he wrote, busily splashing ink on the coverlet. He looked up when Emlyn entered. Without offering a greeting, he said, 'Did you open it?'

'Yes.' Emlyn answered. 'Did you?'

'Of course, God forgive me my curiosity. You have come to discover its secrets. Sit by here, you look cold. Have you eaten?'

'Yes. A few days ago,' Emlyn smiled. The Franciscans did keep a good kitchen; it was one of the arguable points of difference between the two houses.

Fra Sebastiano called a novice by ringing a hand bell. 'Bring some food, Jacque,' he said, when the boy appeared. 'I think we are going to need enough for three, or perhaps you had better make it four.'

When the boy had gone, Emlyn brought out the box and opened it. He spilled the contents over the bed. A myriad of gems lay glittering on the humble cloth. They were of equal size; diamonds, emeralds, sapphires, rubies, rock crystals, blood stones and pearls. The facets were alive with light. Some were clasped in gold fittings, as if broken from a necklace, but each fitting was different; claws and beaks, eyes and curled feathers, petals and leaves and flowers.

'Are they real?' Emlyn asked in an awed whisper.

Fra Sebastiano nodded his untidy head and pursed his lips in thought. 'They are real and they are worth a great deal. Like the box, I would say that they were made in Moorish Spain.' He picked up a single blue rock crystal and held it to the light. 'The ancients tell us, that this is made from ice, frozen so hard that were it to be placed in a furnace, it will never melt.' He selected another and hummed before he spoke. 'The bloodstone, see the tiny drops of red captured within? Many think that this is the blood of Christ. And the sapphire is said in ancient legend, to be a captured drop of amrita, the drink of the gods that brings immortality. Unfortunately they do not provide the answers you seek rather; they give you another puzzle to solve. Could they have some connection with your father? Perhaps he was a man of some wealth.'

Emlyn said, 'If they are of great value, why would ...' he paused, in inexplicable difficulty.

'Your mother entrust them to a small child?' Fra Sebastiano finished helpfully. 'I do not know Emlyn. That is for you to recall, if it is within your power to do so.'

At a loud knock on the door, Emlyn swept the gems back into the box, not knowing why he felt so cautious. Food arrived, piled high on a tray. Although Emlyn could not see the head behind the tray, he recognized the freckled feet.

Friar Patrick O'Healy placed the tray on a table near the fire and began to unload it. His head shone. 'Is it four mouths we have to feed in here now? He said.

'Emlyn is seventeen,' said Fra Sebastiano, in way of explanation.

Friar O'Healy unloaded the platters of sausages, sliced onions, goat cheese, loaves with the steam coming off them in mouth-watering wafts, pickled dates, dried herrings, a jug of deep red wine, a pot of sauce and an egg; all came out on to the table until it was overburdened. Emlyn swallowed noisily.

Friar O'Healy pulled up a chair and began to devour. 'Is it not hungry you are? And me walking the Seine and back again for want of a leek?' he said.

Emlyn needed no further encouragement; he set to and stuffed himself. The egg was for Fra Sebastiano. They put up with the Irishman because he was there for the duration of the meal. After it, while Emlyn scraped the plates and licked the rim of the empty sauce pot, Friar O'Healy stretched his powerful legs out and settled for a sleep or a listen, depending.

While he remained, Emlyn and Fra Sebastiano were unwilling to continue their earlier discussion. Emlyn wiped his hands on his jerkin and drained the small cup of wine that Fra Sebastiano had allowed him; then he set himself to amuse. He winked at the Florentine and turned to the big Irishman. 'Friar O'Healy,' he said. 'Have you heard the tale of Twm Sion Catti of Tregaron and the porridge pot with the hole?'

'I have not,' said the Irishman. 'God's truth, if there's a tale to be told I'm all for listening.'

And so he did. Afterwards, he sent his booming laugh right through the convent and Emlyn was rewarded by the sound of sandals and French voices that came to take the Irishman away. The room seemed deathly silent after he had gone. Emlyn sighed. Fra Sebastiano was watching him with a thoughtful expression. Emlyn began to tidy up the plates and cups. He said 'Why did Friar O'Healy go to Rome?'

'He has not told me,' answered Fra Sebastiano. 'I suspect that he was kept waiting at the Vatican and came away without seeing the Holy Father. Don't be fooled by that warm friendly attitude. Friar O'Healy is determined in his purpose and unafraid to upset a few important heads while about it.'

'It will be to do with Ireland,' said Emlyn thoughtfully. 'They want freedom from English rule, as we do in Wales. But with no power, no army and no leaders, there is little point in hoping for such, in Wales anyway. Besides, the desolation of the monasteries and churches swept through Wales with hardly a ripple.'

Fra Sebastiano smiled. 'Your Wales is better off accepting the inevitable. There is great wisdom in thought before action. Perhaps a country that does not rise to arms when the call comes has a greater purpose in mind.'

Emlyn sat on the stool by the brazier. He said, 'The Jesuits encourage us to gather huge support, to storm through England and return it to the church in Rome. They believe in the fight against the reformation and will eagerly rise to arms when called.'

Fra Sebastiano growled. 'Ah, yes. The Jesuits,' he said dispassionately. 'England is indeed a beleaguered isle, beset by enemies. But, you know my son your queen is greatly admired and even feared. The seeds of doubt sown by the likes of Luther and Calvin have come from years of doubt and question. We live in a time of change, and would be better advised to learn to live with it rather than battle against it.'

'You are Catholic and you say that?'

'I am old and I say that.' Fra Sebastiano settled himself more comfortably on the pillows. 'I took you to England all those years ago at the time when Queen Mary had come to the throne and the schism between England and Rome was healed. When the queen was wed to King Philip of Spain, England was answerable to the Holy Father once more. The purpose for my own visit was to see what could be done for the restoration of the monasteries, our own house included. You and I Emlyn were part of the Spanish king's entourage.

'At the time, I had no idea what I was to do with you. Your mother had provided a letter, which you had brought from Cetua, but it was written in a Celtic language that I had never come across. It seemed best to get it translated at the first opportunity. It was my intention to take you to your family, once we discovered who they were. You and I had a room at Court, next to the Spanish Ambassador. I have rarely been housed better, before or since. You won the hearts of the Queen's ladies by playing the spinet. While I went about my clerical and religious duties, which kept me busy for several days, you were taken by those charming companions to visit the menagerie. They informed me that they had a unicorn there, but I never got to see it.

'After making a few inquiries, I learned that your mother's letter was written in Welsh and I was taken to the house of the renowned mathematician, astrologer and cartographer, Doctor John Dee, who was familiar with the language. The room I was shown to was an apothecary's. There were phials and skulls, glass pots and clay pots, books, scrolls, maps, pickled objects, desiccated frogs and dried bits and pieces hanging off the ceiling. Doctor Dee told me he knew the family the letter was intended for. Apparently, your grandfather, Gruffydd Hiraethog, had been a gun founder for old King Henry. He had been granted land by the King after the French wars and had retired to Wales. So this necromancer, Doctor John Dee, translated your mother's letter to me. Her instructions were really quite simple; she wanted her son to be brought up as a good Catholic and to become a priest. She could not have known the troubles that would come to England then, or that in order to follow her wishes, your uncle would have to send you here to France. So you see Emlyn, we went there, you and I on that long and pleasant journey to your home and I handed you to your grandfather. Since then, I have known about you. Do you remember the scholarly man who lives with your grandfather?'

'Yes,' Emlyn replied, 'he is old John Talbot.'

'Well, he and I have corresponded on occasion. I had thought you were destined for the priesthood until I received a letter form father De Sacy asking me to find out what I could about your history. Since then, and as I had to come to Paris anyway, I felt it my duty to find you if I could, and return the box to you.'

Emlyn looked up. He said, 'grandfather never told me about Cetua, nor did my uncle ever mention it.'

'That must be so,' said Fra Sebastiano with a sigh. 'God forgive me my son, I never told them either. I kept the box, because I felt that you would never see it again unless I did so. What business it was of mine, only the good Lord can answer. I knew nothing of your family, so I said nothing of Cetua and told them you had been brought to me in Lisbon. Now only you can further unravel the mystery.'

Emlyn said, 'What I do recall is little and my mothers name was never uttered.' He brought out the box again and ran his fingers over the faded tracery. The meaning of the box and its contents were still a puzzle.

Fra Sebastiano reached out and patted him affectionately on the arm. 'It is your mother's gift. Whoever she was, she has given you wealth Emlyn, enough to make your own choices.'

Startled, Emlyn said, 'This is that sort of wealth?'

'The gems are of good quality they will fetch a good price if you sell them.'

Emlyn opened the lid and poured the jewels out on to the bed. He pushed them around with his finger delighting in the way they captured the light and spun light about the walls. He examined a tiny dragon-shaped clasp one of the eyes was missing. He could not consider the value; these glittering stones held a different meaning for him.

Fra Sebastiano watched him. 'You must take great care that no one knows about these. Such jewels can bring the worse out in men, and beware that they do not bring the worse out in you.'

Emlyn picked up a single ruby. It was so dark, that the colour could only be detected in full light. A blood-red fire shone from the depth like a single baleful eye. It hung from a clasp shaped like a claw, as if held in captivity. 'I will find out what I can of their origin,' he replied. 'Perhaps they will unravel the mystery of my mother's fate. Though where and how to begin is beyond me.'

'With God,' said Fra Sebastiano. 'Pray Emlyn, and wait for God's guidance. When I return to Italy, I shall do what I can to discover what happened to your mother. In Venice, the name Grimani is much respected, we even have one in our monastery in Florence, a Lorenzo, I believe. If you are connected to this family, it will not be difficult to find out.'

Emlyn said, 'Fra Sebastiano, I could go to Venice myself.'

Fra Sebastiano laughed softly. 'You could indeed. You stand at a cross-road, my child. Only God knows what will come of all this.'

'I saved you some blood-pudding,' said Goronwy, as Emlyn sat beside him later in the refectory. 'It's to remind you of home.'

Emlyn accepted the meat, grateful that Goronwy seemed willing to forget their earlier disagreement.

Goronwy smiled. 'I wonder what it is like now at home. I got a letter from my brother Gareth, saying they have another baby, a girl. I am looking forward to seeing them all.'

Emlyn reached for bread. 'You are an uncle three times over now. Soon there will be enough Glyn-Parry's to provide a choir at Chester cathedral.'

'What happened with Fra Pietro Sebastiano da Firenze?' said Goronwy sharply.

Emlyn caught the note of resentment. He had told Goronwy nothing about Fra Sebastiano. He said, 'I went to see him and we talked and ate lots of food. Have you ever thought of becoming a Franciscan Goronwy? They serve much better food there.'

'You're trying to change the subject,' Goronwy said. 'What did you talk about? I mean why would the man come all the way from Italy just to see you?'

'He didn't. He is in Paris for a different reason. Goronwy, he's the friar who first brought me to Wales. He was just curious to see how I had turned out. That's all there is to it. He did tell me the story. I was handed to him and he brought me to England, when he accompanied the party of King Philip of Spain.'

Goronwy looked at him suspiciously; when he next spoke he used Welsh. 'I know you well enough to see that you are holding something back. I suppose pressing you, will only make you more reluctant, but you can't blame me for trying. You don't seem to see how important it is to know whether you can be a priest or not.'

Emlyn shook his head; he was so tired that he wished to sleep for a week. 'You're imagining things.' His skin prickled. It was always difficult to lie to Goronwy. Goronwy was so determined that they would both have a great part to play in returning Catholicism to England; it was becoming harder to talk with him about anything else.

They left College de Clermont the following day. They were late in starting as Emlyn found it necessary to bid farewell to all who had taught or befriended him since he had been there. Goronwy was annoyed; it wasn't as if they were not coming back. He was further irritated by the six sheep that Emlyn insisted on bringing. The arrival of the sheep at the college six months previously, had caused quite a stir, but they were tolerated by father Abelard who was of a soft nature and treated all God's creatures with care. They had come from Spain with Hernando Nunez, a fellow student whose family had made their wealth through wool. 'We have the best sheep in the world,' Hernando had boasted. To prove the fact he had brought six ewes back with him when he had returned from a visit to his family. Hernando Nunez was extravagant. Emlyn had not expected the gift of sheep but had been forced to accept them. In Wales the best wool for export was produced. The Spanish sheep too, had fine, long wool. There were advantages to be gained in breeding the two. Emlyn's Grandfather, Gruffydd Hiraethog already had a reputation as a fine wool producer, his wool was in much demand, especially at the cloth market of Blackfriars in London.

To pass the time and make the walk less tiring, Goronwy told Emlyn all about his plans once he got the printing press set up in Wales. Emlyn listened without interruption for twenty miles. To convince him, Goronwy explained about the Welsh Catholics from the noble families who had first thought of the ambitious project. It was they who provided the money to pay the carpenter for the woodblocks. Goronwy had the responsibility to see it all delivered to Wales. He carried a heavy purse to pay the craftsman in Rouen. 'There are many staunch Catholics at home who depend on the success of all this,' he emphasized at the end of his enthusiastic monologue.

'What exactly are you taking to Wales?' Emlyn asked.

'The means to print,' said Goronwy. 'What do you think I've been trying to tell you for the past four hours?'

'About what you intend to do once you, and whatever it is, are safely in Wales. You are risking so much. Why not use a cider press? It would be easier.'

'I know that!' Goronwy groaned lifting his eyes heavenward. 'But, no one in Wales could produce the wooden letter blocks. That's what we are going to collect in Rouen from Wendelin Tieffenbrucker.'

Emlyn smiled and shook his head, he knew Tieffenbrucker. He was a German craftsman who had gained fame for his superior musical instruments. Emlyn said 'Well, I hope you didn't tell him what they are for. Wendelin would rather die than spread the word of Catholicism. He's a Calvinist.'

'Are you tup?' Goronwy laughed. 'Of course I haven't. Anyway, he is less likely to ask questions if you come there with me. You can admire his lutes while I load up the boxes and the herrings.'

'Herrings?'

'That's how they will be hidden, in boxes of dried herrings.' Goronwy explained. He stopped walking. 'Come on Emlyn, you have to join me in this.'

Emlyn whistled to the sheep and they fell into step with him as if following a mother. When he turned to Goronwy, his expression had become serious. 'I am not convinced that you are wise in this wild scheme Goronwy. Besides, I value my life more.'

'Don't be a fool Emlyn. Have you forgotten all that we planned together? This must have something to do with that Franciscan who came looking for you and who told you something that you cannot tell a friend who has stayed by you since the beginning.' Goronwy resumed walking, his expression sullen.

'I have told you already Goronwy. He was the monk who brought me to my uncle when I was a child. You know the story, you were there.'

'I accept that,' said Goronwy. 'It was years ago. So how did he know you were in Paris then?'

Emlyn cleared his throat and took a deep breath. 'He knew where to find me because he is a man of letters and he wrote to John Talbot on occasion. I didn't know anything about it, nor, I suspect did Gruffydd.'

John Talbot was a priest who had lost everything when the churches and monasteries had been brought to ruin in old King Henry's day. Since then, he had lived with Gruffydd Hiraethog and had kept the spirit of the old faith alive by saying mass on a Sunday at various secret houses, or on the mountainside, where discovery was near impossible. He wrote letters copiously and kept up with news of the struggles in Europe. Goronwy had always felt a deep respect for him and believed what Emlyn said of him; it was just like John Talbot to keep in touch with the Italian friar. But Emlyn was keeping *something* back.

They came to a small hamlet, a huddle of buildings crouched near the river Seine with a tall church spire announcing its presence. As the light was fading, they begged shelter for themselves and the sheep in a barn at the side of the road. Leaving Emlyn there, Goronwy walked into the village to bring back food and beer.

Left to alone Emlyn sank into the dry straw with a groan of pleasure. He pulled his boots off and rubbed his blistered feet. The night turned cold and Emlyn pulled his worn cloak about his shoulders. He had no desire to be pulled into Goronwy's scheming, he may have made promises once, but that had been years ago. In the last few days, everything had changed and he was on his way to Wales, he doubted if he would return. In the last four years he had learned everything his mind could encompass; it remained to be seen whether he could better his situation because of it.

He ran his fingers along the edge of his padded jerkin, feeling the tiny bumps under the cloth where he had sewn the gems securely. He worried that they would mysteriously disappear. He had never owned anything that caused so much concern. Emlyn kept his secret. If he told Goronwy about them; Goronwy would turn them to coin and put that to use in his noble cause.

Goronwy returned with a jug of beer, bread, a hard cheese, dried fish and half a candle. Emlyn was impressed. They ate in silence while Emlyn thought how he was going to explain his own plans to Goronwy. He licked the grease off his fingers and wiped them dry on the cloth of his hose. He lay back in the crackle of straw and laced his fingers behind his head. 'Do you remember the name of the Italian my mother married?'

Goronwy took a long swallow of beer before he answered. 'Giovanni? Ghisi? Guicciardini?'

'Grimani' Emlyn finished. 'Fra Pietro Sebastiano told me about the girl in a convent in Rouen with the same name. She might be my cousin.'

'Is that what all this evasion has been about?' Goronwy laughed. 'They will never let you near a convent, or me. Look at us Emlyn, we're like vagabonds and as unwashed, and we're hardly gentlemen.'

Emlyn grinned. 'I've thought about that. It is all a matter of timing. Do you think we can reach Rouen before Saturday?'

Goronwy's mood mellowed. 'What did you have in mind?'

Chapter 6 Venice/Istanbul

Venice, the most dazzling, beautiful city of all, rose out of the sea like the aqueous city of Neptune, beseeching, tempting, scandalous and irresistible. This was not a clean city; rubbish, street filth and the contents of thousands of chamber pots, went straight into the maze of canals. The tide removed most of it, flowing through the remote inlets, collecting the garbage and surging out with it past the Lagoon to the sea; what it left, clung to the steps and crumbling walls of water-logged houses.

A Venetian merchant was never just a merchant; some were also pirates and plunderers, warriors and princes of the sea. Theirs was a way echoed through a thousand years of success, following in the tradition of their Phoenician ancestors. For centuries the elegant galleys had dominated the trade routes over the Mediterranean, through the Straights of Gibraltar to the ports of northern Europe. The key to the Venetians' present success lay in their strong connections with the Ottoman Turks. A relationship which was regarded sourly by Christian Europe, but nor sourly enough to sever the source of the rare, luxury goods it craved from the golden city of Constantinople.

Bartolomeo Varini hastened his steps as he crossed the bridge over Rio di S. Polo. He was leaving the environs of the church of Santa Maria Gloriosa dei Frari, where he had attended the funeral of his employer, Alessandro Balsamo. Bartolomeo had left as soon as he was able; he did not want anyone to follow him. He had seen the Venetian mercantile families there, glowering under their lowered brows and fur trimmed hats. They had attended out of respect for the deceased, Alessandro Balsamo. To have not turned up for the funeral would have shown the powerful families to be niggardly. Some may have attended out of honest sympathy, but these were few. Alessandro Balsamo had owed most of them money or favour Now that he was dead; they were ready to swoop down on Bartolomeo Varini like crows after battle.

Bartolomeo was the manager of the Lanarca Salt Company. It was owned by two men, one who was now interned in the Franciscan church which Bartolomeo had fled from, the other, a certain Tomasso di Vincentini, whom Bartolomeo knew little about. Tomasso di Vincentini never came to Venice. With the death of Alessandro Balsamo, and with the absence of his wife, who was in Cyprus, Bartolomeo was left with the unpleasant responsibility of paying off the debts the company had incurred. As there was not enough to pay them all; some would be disappointed. Bartolomeo could see little hope for the future; he considered the possibility of ending his days in a debtor's cell.

It began to rain. He had left his hat behind. Nothing would induce him to return for it, even the exposure of his balding head. Bartolomeo miserably paid the ferry-man to take him across the Canal Grande. Most of Venice, including the San Marco piazza, was flooded from the Acqua Alta, the high spring tide. Another inch and it would have spilled into the Basilica. As it was, it was quite convenient for everyone, if you had the money to pay the Gondola you hardly had to walk at all. If not, Venice was impossible to cross without getting wet up to the knees. Bartolomeo prepared for a soaking.

Nothing had turned out as he had hoped. He had dreamed of making a comfortable living for himself in the growing company. He had thought of marrying a respectable woman who would not be daunted by his over large features, and children would have completed his vision. But the years had passed and his hopes had dwindled. Varini was of medium stature with long arms and legs that stuck out, giving the impression of a featherless bird. His knees were permanently bent from an illness he had suffered in childhood. Apart from preventing him from running very fast, this peculiarity did not inhibit him; he never had cause to run fast anywhere. His face was round and he smiled often without showing his teeth. As his mouth was long, the smile, gathered up his dimples, creased his cheeks, and seemed to go all the way to his ears; considering his predicament, could not find a smile at present.

It took him over an hour to reach the Street of Spices, where the warehouse and business premises stood. The canals were quiet; for the start of the trading season, this was not very promising. Venice had lost her monopoly on spice since Vasco de Garma had rounded the Horn of Africa, and secured a route for Portugal to the Eastern markets. Looking at the emptiness about him, Bartolomeo wondered if they had secured the salt market too. In rained just long enough for Bartolomeo to reach his door and enter dripping. The clouds drew back and the setting sun shone on the Lagoon turning it to silver.

There was one gleam to be realized from Alessandro Balsamo's untimely death; now Bartolomeo could open the cupboard above the doorway. He now had sole possession of the key that he had never possessed before. Alessandro Balsamo had always been very secretive about this cupboard. In it, Bartolomeo knew, was kept the correspondence from the company's other owner, Tomasso di Vincentini who never came to Venice. Bartolomeo gathered that he lived in Venetian owned Cyprus, which was where the company's salt came from. There was one point however which caused Bartolomeo to doubt the truth of this. In Lanarca, on the southern coast of Cyprus, the company gathered salt from a series of lakes that dried up in July revealing the crust of salt. In control of this task, was the company's Cyprus manager, Enrico de Martoni. Enrico wrote often to Bartolomeo, never once had he mentioned Tomasso di Vincentini. If the man lived on Cyprus at all, he showed little interest in the Lanarca Salt Company. Why Alessandro Balsamo had treated it all to with the utmost secrecy was an enigma. This partner had frequently sent substantial sums of money to the Venetian side of the business. Alessandro Balsamo had put it to little beneficial use; he had been an incessant gambler.

Perhaps that explains the secrecy, thought Bartolomeo as he pulled a stool under the secret cupboard. It was possible that Alessandro had been afraid that this Vincentini would turn up and demand an explanation. The stool wobbled under his weight. Bartolomeo reached up, inserted the key and swung the door open. It didn't contain any money. There was a box with a scarp of silk tied around it, a bundle of similarly tied letters and a pyramid of time-worn scrolls. Bartolomeo Varini pulled them all out and stacked them on the table under the window. He scrambled about until he found a half-filled bottle of wine and a cup; this was going to be a lengthy task. The daylight was rapidly fading. He placed a new candle in the holder and put flame to the wick.

Only the guttering breath of the dying candle drew Bartolomeo's attention away from his reading. The flame hissed in a pool of wax leaving the room in darkness. Varini sat back, seeing nothing, his mind a whirl of thoughts. So enraptured was he, that the hours of night had passed without his knowledge. He could make out the grey shapes of objects in the room as the early light of dawn penetrated.

Bartolomeo stretched, stood and turned to the window. He gazed out at the shadowy shapes of palaces, churches and huddled houses rising out of the mist. As the light strengthened, a smile transformed his features. While engrossed in the letters he had often come across a line such as 'Tell Bartolomeo to see Romero about the alterations to the caravel' or

'Bartolomeo will know where to get alum should you need it to trade with the Foscari.' As far as he was aware, Bartolomeo had never met Tomasso di Vincentini. So why would the man make such suggestions to Alessandro Balsamo? The letters were all signed simply with just the name 'Tomasso.' They were lengthy and told much of the places they were written from; Alexandria, Trebizond, Stamboul, Chios, Sophia, Tunis and, an odd one here and there from Lanarca in Cyprus. They were all concerned with trade advantages, none of which Alessandro Balsamo had ever taken advantage of. To Bartolomeo, whose ear was trained to the buying and selling on the Rialto, the suggestions which Tomasso di Vincentini had made had a ring of genius about them. If only this man had been in Venice, reflected Bartolomeo, I would have realized my dreams and probably his too.

The correspondence covered a period of five years; each distinctly marked with the date when written. The puzzle that now confronted Bartolomeo was that the last letter written by the industrious merchant was over seven years old. If there were any others, they were not in Alessandro Balsamo's secret hoard. Bartolomeo began to wonder if there still was a Tomasso di Vincentini.

Fiorenza Caterina Balsamo stood on the deck of the *Cornucopia* with her maid, Maria, watching the loading of ships and the unloading of ships and all the busy bustle of the Golden Horn. She had left Cyprus with her notary Enrico de Martoni two weeks previously. He periodically returned to Venice on behalf of the company and had offered to escort her. After her husband Alessandro's death, which she had heard about six weeks previously, Fiorenza discovered that she was now a partner in the Lanarca Salt Company. She would have to make some decisions concerning its future. She had cried when it was expected of her, but to none had she admitted her overwhelming relief. She had disliked her husband, Alessandro. Even though he had died leaving her with his debts and his crumbling business, she was still glad to be free of him.

She and the notary, Enrico had waited on board the caravel for three hours; assailed by the noise and the insufferable heat, with no sign that the ship was ready to sail. The *Cornucopia* was ill fitted and dirty and the crew looked as if they had been dragged out of some unmentionable gutter. If they did not sail soon, she conjectured they may as well not sail at all; the best part of the day had already gone. They were waiting for the arrival of another passenger.

There were many merchants like Tomasso di Vincentini, who hired ships or passage on them and tried their fortunes on the sea and its exotic ports of call. This was how Venice had founded and ruled her empire. Some beggared themselves and returned to the mercy of their families or returned not at all; inexperience leading to often violent death. But others, because the reward of the Middle Sea was abundant, had made their fortunes and founded their own empires.

It was not so common now; the character portrayed in Tomasso di Vincentini was one of a dying profession. Softened and overfed with indulgence, many Venetians had turned away from the sea and its difficult treasure. They had turned their interest inward, planted land with profitable crops and built their magnificent palaces, from which to enjoy their bounty. There was no diminishing of wealth in the Mediterranean, but now the competition was greater.

Fiorenza startled when the gangplank rattled beneath her, horses were being brought on board. Horses were common enough; but these were costly, desert-bred mares with dainty legs, rolling eyes and long flying hair. The horses were followed by bundles and boxes, barrels and sea trunks, two racing hounds and a dozen cages with parrots and monkeys. Some of the bundles were betrayed by scent. Fiorenza recognized spice and the essences of perfume; sandalwood, rose and musk vied with cinnamon and clove. Fiorenza wrinkled her nose and sneezed finding the mixture overwhelming. Her curiosity was ignited.

A man approached the caravel, accompanied by a black servant. He was dressed in dark Venetian cloth and carried a bundle of scrolls under his arm. This, thought Fiorenza, can only be Tomasso di Vincentini; perhaps the ship would leave before nightfall after all.

'He is a man of taste who shows a preference for quality as well as quantity,' said Enrico, the notary, coming up beside her.

'I don't think he is Cypriot' said Fiorenza.

The notary frowned. 'No, he is originally from Padua. I believe he has a house in Cyprus. Perhaps it is a matter on which you can converse.'

'Perhaps,' agreed Fiorenza. 'I know nothing about him. Like you dear Enrico, Alessandro was uncharacteristically secretive about his partner in business.' Curiosity induced her to lean over the wooden rail. All she saw was Tomasso di Vincentini's shoulders and hat, which was board-brimmed and feathered, after the current taste in Spanish apparel. Then he looked up and she met the blaze of his eyes. Fiorenza felt her heart miss a beat. She caught her breath, surprised. Was it fear this man caused her to feel or something else? He did not spare her more than a brief, disinterested glance, then his face was hidden again by the brim of his hat and his voice rose in strident Greek. Fiorenza smiled at his anger. Did he not know how disorganized matters were dealt with in Stamboul?

Before evening, the *Cornucopia* nosed out to sea, pulled by harbour boats until she was free to unfurl her sails in open water. Fiorenza stayed aboveboard to watch the diminishing city. Then she turned to the wind and thought of Venice without Alessandro. She would miss her daughter, left in Cyprus, but she longed for Venice with a physical hunger.

The captain was Marco Erizzo, a Ragustan, with a fierce look about him, which Fiorenza hoped would keep the motley crew in order. The richly clad merchant stood at the rail of the caravel; looking with a deep, unsettling expression on the shrinking minarets. Constantinople, with its smells of rotting fish and garlic sauce, dropped from the horizon and the *Cornucopia* bravely set her bow to the Aegean Sea. Her dirty, patched sails filled with wind; her faded, splintered boards creaked in rhythm to her sea dance.

At first, Fiorenza kept to her cabin, immersed in thought. There was no one now to whom she must account to for her actions; this realization was a pleasant surprise. She felt a flood of pure joy run through her as it had not done since childhood. How seldom it was that a woman could say that the world was her oyster? The one shadow in her joy was that the Signori of Venice might use their influence to marry her off to some enterprising merchant. Many widows lost their freedom through such interference.

The days grew hotter and the nights brought little relief. Finding the confines of her cabin stifling, Fiorenza took her lute and went upon the deck. Maria, her maid followed and grumbled inaudibly. Laughter greeted Fiorenza first, from a group of sailors who sat shirtless on the deck. They ate from a plate of olives placed on the boards. Tomasso di Vincentini sat with them, he was telling a story. Fiorenza edged closer and soon gathered that the words were distasteful to a lady's ears; seeing her, the crew quieted and the soft voice stumbled to a halt.

Flushing, Maria said, 'My lady we should keep to our cabin. To do otherwise is to tempt the devil to wickedness.'

Tomasso di Vincentini rose, pulling together his shirt strings unselfconsciously, at their ends, hung gold acorns that flashed in the sun like his earring. He was tall and bearded, a striking man, whose face was lined with a wealth of experience. His eyes were un-Venetian grey.

'Please do not end your entertainment for my sake,' said Fiorenza.

He smiled, his teeth showing white and even against his greying beard. He examined her with undisguised curiosity. He bowed and said, 'I could not hope to compete in face of such tempting promise, Madonna.'

Her cheeks burned. She felt confused and angry with herself. Although they had been introduced briefly, he had made no mention of the fact that they were now partners in business.

'Do you play well?' he asked indicating the lute.

Recovering her composure, she said 'Yes. I have had time.'

One of the crew, barely into manhood, leaped up and rolled a barrel forward, righting it for her to sit upon. He was Greek and his eyes shone, framed with silken lashes. She accepted gratefully and settled with her lute. They would enjoy the bawdy, sailors' songs; she knew enough of those, including the various wordings. She chose instead to play a saraband. The sailors stood up and danced in stately parody of courtiers; their steps slow and exaggerated, their manner comical and light-hearted. Fiorenza sang. After the first few verses, Tomasso di Vincentini sang with her, faltering on the words or making them up as he went along. They began a conversation in song, the words polite but suggestive. The crew laughed, adding an occasional line. The Greek boy, sweet thing, looked confused. So, thank the Saints, did Maria. Shortly after, Fiorenza surrendered her seat and her lute to the Greek boy, who played love songs. She stood and marvelled at the beauty of the Aegean as the *Cornucopia* bobbed her way through the Cycladese, the tiny islands of classical fable. The sky was a wash of orange and deep vermilion and on the horizon lay the island of Naxos nestled behind Venetian walls.

Behind her, the voice of Tomasso di Vincentini spoke softly into the gathering dark. 'The nymphs of mythical Nysa cared for Dionysus in his youth. In time, to Naxos came the honey-fed Dionysus, wreathed in joy and crowned in ivy. There his eyes fell upon Ariadne weeping for Theseus, her lost love. The young god, being a youth of virtue and love, consoled her, wooed her and, eventually wed her. The vine of Naxos, Madonna, still flows with the sweet nectar of that marriage feast. But gone are the Maenads and the Satyrs, the Sileni and the half-horsed Centaurs.'

'For my part,' said Fiorenza, 'I am glad. I should not know what to say to one if I had the misfortune to come across it. Do we go, like Dionysus to Naxos?'

Vincentini came and stood beside her, looking out over the sea. 'There is no need,' he replied. 'The ship has provision enough. If the Madonna wishes to break her voyage, we could pause there for a day. I have cargo to collect offshore.'

'That would cause some delay. Do you not want to beat the trading galleys to Venice?'

'I will, come what may,' he answered. 'You will excuse me Madonna; there are matters which require my attention?' He bowed and left her before she could reply.

Fiorenza bit her lip. She was angry for letting him know she had made inquiries into his affairs. It was his own fault, he assumed, as so many did that she knew nothing. But she had learned what she could of the business with the valuable, if begrudged help of the notary, Enrico. She was not ignorant of the ways of merchandising.

Fiorenza sat quietly sewing on deck with Maria blushing beside her. Maria was typically Venetian, round faced and inclined towards stoutness, the crew teased her. The evening was golden and the tasks of the day were done. Fiorenza watched the idle sailors come to sit with Tomasso di Vincentini, asking for a tale or a song. They treated him with a friendly respect and he found time for them. Fiorenza listened to him. He was a good story teller, his voice rising and falling, carrying his audience transfixed, on journeys of incredible places and deeds of fantastical daring. His hands were delicate; the slender wrists and ringed fingers accompanying his words with a language of their own.

Now while he spoke, his hands were not taking part, they worked with pestle and mortar, crushing peppercorns, filling the air with spicy scent; his words halted frequently by a sneeze. His dogs lay curled at his feet, sniffling from the effects of blown pepper. The ship had been lying off Naxos since the previous evening, but made no attempt to seek shelter at the harbour. Fiorenza could see the twelve towers of the Chora rising above the olive groves and lemon trees. She listened to the soft voice and closed her eyes.

'...Now come the Turks to pick the islands, like beads off the string of the Venetian necklace. Naxos lies in a Corsair's paradise. Every inlet, cave or bay of these islands, offers a lair to pirates and their own tiny kingdom, should they so desire. The jaws of the Venetian Lion are weak.'

Fiorenza opened her eyes, ready to object to this view concerning the power of Venice, but she did not speak. Bare feet thudded on the boards. Voices yelled in Greek. There was a boat approaching.

Without stopping his pepper grinding, Tomasso looked up. The approaching boat offered no threat; it was small and weighed down with cargo. When it drew alongside, Tomasso leapt aboard with the ease of one born to the sea. He shouted greetings and instructions. His Greek so fast Fiorenza was unable to follow. The cargo, as she had guessed, was wine, barrels and barrels which took over an hour to haul aboard and store in the hold. With the boat, came a Franciscan bound for Venice, Fra Vitale di Baganza, Fiorenza was grateful to see him. No ship should sail without a man of God aboard. Tomasso di Vincentini seemed a little put out by the man's arrival.

Enrico, her notary watched all with a mistrustful glare. 'Is Naxos Venetian still?' he said doubtfully. 'I would not be surprised to find our friend dealing with the Turks, the crew of that boat look like Turkish pirates. And what of that sly servant he keeps? As dark as a Blackamoor.'

'Don't be silly Enrico,' scolded Fiorenza. 'You will insist upon seeking a shadow in every corner. Black slaves are really quite fashionable, my sister Giovanna has two. Do try and get on with the man, after all, we are partners in business, at least until we reach Venice.'

'If we reach Venice,' Enrico replied. He frowned, his mouth set in a line of mistrust. Although nearly a hundred years had passed since the Turks had taken the island of Negroponte from Venice, the memory lingered bitterly in the hearts of most Venetians; for every man had been butchered and every woman and child enslaved. Although they traded with the Ottoman Turks, most Venetians harboured a well nurtured hatred.

With the island of Naxos, well astern, a storm darkened the sky ahead. Still bathed in garish sunlight, the *Cornucopia* reared on sliver crested-waves and plunged into turquoise depths with a shower of silver sea foam. The wind filled her three triangular sails and drove her towards the next port of call, Candia -the birth place of Zeus.

Tomasso di Vincentini was uneasy. He worried about returning to Venice after so long an absence. He remained in his cabin writing letters. The motion of the ship and the constant confinement unnerved him. The inkwell slid rattling from side to side, its black contents slopping over the rim, spoiling his work. He pushed the stopper in and placed it on a narrow shelf where it could do less mischief, then methodically cleaned his quills.

He had never considered the death of Alessandro Balsamo in his careful planning. Instead of the smiling, round merchant banker, he now had a widow to deal with. His feelings on the matter were mixed. Alessandro, beyond all expectations, had kept their business interests in absolute secrecy, like a true Venetian. His widow knew nothing of the long laid plans, nor had the sour Enrico been told more than was necessary. It could not remain so for much longer.

Tomasso yawned and stretched. He roused his new servant, Symeon, who was curled asleep in the corner with the hounds. Tomasso had acquired him only a day before leaving Constantinople. He said, 'Ask Madonna Fiorenza Balsamo if she is free to join me.'

'That is good Master,' Symeon replied. 'You need the care of a woman to smooth away your fears, which I believe are great. I rejoice that you wish for her.'

'Symeon you are an oaf! I don't know what prompted me to buy you. If you were a good Christian you would know that such a suggestion is unfitting and insulting to the lady.'

'I am a good Christian Master.'

Tomasso smiled. 'We have matters to discuss, and bring the notary.'

Symeon bowed himself out of the door.

Soon Tomasso had his guests seated in the small cabin as comfortably as the rolling sea allowed. Fiorenza was dressed in black with her hair concealed beneath a veil. She seemed composed and had lightened the effect with the addition of a string of pearls and a showing of white, embroidered sleeves. Tomasso poured ruby wine, half filling the glasses because of the motion of the sea.

'It tastes remarkably like Malmsey,' said Fiorenza sipping the sanguine liquid. 'Don't you agree?'

'Remarkably,' said Enrico.

After thanking them for coming, Tomasso said, 'I have called you both here to discuss the Lanarca Salt Company in which we share an interest. Madonna, you will of course want to end our partnership, but if I could…'

'I do not,' said Fiorenza with a finality that made both men look at her with surprise. 'I realize that I may not be the partner you would have chosen, but there is no reason why I cannot continue where Alessandro left off. God rest his soul.'

Enrico looked at her in disbelief. 'Madonna, what about your brother-in-law, who has stated that he would be more than willing to relieve you of this burden, and to see that you are comfortable until you wed again. Sell the business to him, with Messer Vincentini's agreement of course. All will be admirably taken care of without you worrying about anything.'

Tomasso watched them with interest.

'Precisely Enrico,' said Fiorenza. 'However, as we are making matters clear, it is deceptive to allow Messer Vincentini here, to believe that we are a thriving, successful company and that we are free of debt. Indeed Messer, we are in danger of losing our salt trade and all else will follow.'

Tomasso was amazed that he had learned so much in so short a time. 'I am sorry,' he said, 'I did not know. Has Lake Lanarca lost its salt? I see no other way in which the salt trade could falter.'

'It contains as much salt as ever,' said Enrico mournfully. 'But we have suffered. Two years past, we lost two of our salt ships, laden with cargo. As you can guess, the loss was substantial and, as yet, we have been unable to recover sufficiently. But Emilo Gabrieli, the lady's brother by marriage, has generously offered to buy the business once we have recovered our loss.'

'Rot Enrico!' said Fiorenza 'My brother-in-law's offer could not be considered generous. As you well know we have been forced to refuse it.'

'But Madonna,' pleaded Enrico, looking as if he wished to be anywhere but here, 'now the situation is much changed. The death of your husband leaves us with no alternative. You are unlearned of the ways of trade and a woman…'

Fiorenza folded her arms stubbornly. 'Does Emilo's promise to you Enrico for further, beneficial employment, flavour your council?'

'That makes no difference, Madonna,' said Enrico offended. 'As you know, your interests and continued welfare are my prime concern.'

Tomasso listened and watched trying to judge their relationship and their capability. The widow certainly showed an unexpected determination, her knowledge was not limited to self interest. Women, he had discovered, when they were not couched in the restrictions of custom, made equal merchants to men, often better.

Enrico turned to him, appealing to his age and experience. 'Messer Vincentini,' he began, 'as you have been a near silent partner for some time, you may not be aware of all that has befallen the company,'

Tomasso said, 'I have corresponded with Alessandro always and through him with the Venetian manager, Bartolomeo Varini. I have continuously sent goods to Constantinople. I believed the profits made to be considerable by the time they reached the Italian markets and beyond. To what use where they put?'

Enrico twisted his fingers together nervously. 'To buy ships,' he replied. 'Three ships, to replace the ageing vessels we had, and the upkeep of the business in Cyprus, the hiring of men and mules and the paying of taxes, which are crippling in the Sublime Porte. It is some years since we heard from you; we thought that some misfortune had befallen you. I am delighted of course that this was not the case. After the loss of the two ships, to theft or storm, we have been unable to regain our markets. We run a third of what we used to, trust has faltered.'

'You do not know how these ships met with misfortune?'

'We could not discover what had occurred. It was not possible Messer, to fall back upon our bankers, they insisted upon evidence, before they would even consider insurance. This in turn, marred our reputation and lost us custom. Messer Balsamo was exceptionally distraught. It has been a struggle ever since. Poor Alessandro to have died thus,' said Enrico with tears lighting his eyes and his voice genuinely tinged with frustration and regret, whether for himself or his employer, was unclear. He continued, 'Messer, you have brought much cargo aboard this ship. May I inquire as to its nature?'

Tomasso smiled. Before he replied, he refilled their glasses while they sat in ill concealed curiosity. Then he looked at them each in turn. Enrico, he judged could be trusted so long as he suffered no personal loss and his loyalty to Alessandro Balsamo's widow seemed genuine. Fiorenza had courage and a taste for adventure which Tomasso admired. It was not all he admired about the woman; he tried not to think about that.

'Signora, I will put to you a proposal,' he explained. 'I am willing to renew our partnership. But if this is not to your liking, you may set up a business of your own, or retire, or remarry as you wish. I will see that expenses you incur will be met, and that a house and servants will be provided for you, in Venice or elsewhere. It is a promised I made to your husband when I heard of his marriage to you. Do you have children?'

'A daughter, Florinda,' said Fiorenza. 'She has remained in Cyprus, where my family has long made their lives and their fortune.

'Not salt surely?' Tomasso laughed.

Fiorenza smiled. 'Your offer is generous and beyond my expectations. But you mentioned a renewal of the partnership? I would be interested to hear what you intend to do before I make a decision.'

Tomasso looked at them both. He said, 'I bought this ship in Constantinople, there is…'

Enrico spluttered. 'You have been cheated Messer!' he exclaimed 'If I had know you required a vessel to purchase, I would have been only too willing to assist you in its choosing. The *Cornucopia* is…'

'Is Venetian, Enrico,' Tomasso interrupted, 'and is as sound as you could wish. She is of the new style and can sail all through the year. Her appearance is meant to deceive; we do not want to attract pirates. The *Cornucopia* carries enough cargo to heal all hurts. Most of it is my own. But what remains could see the company, not only repay its debt but also regain its markets and expand upon them.'

Enrico stood up smiling. 'Is this true? You are sent by God Messer,' he exclaimed clasping his hands together.

Tomasso raised an eyebrow. 'I may be sent by God Enrico, but it is not my intention to be your saviour in the Lanarca salt trade. What I suggest, is that we sell the salt business, we have no further need of it. A new company will be formed which will trade not in salt but in its close relative spice. I have established a supplier in Constantinople, who will obtain goods for me at half the price paid in Cairo.'

'That is impossible Messer,' said Enrico 'The spice market there is in severe decline since the Portuguese discovered a route to the Indies. They now avoid the Muslims and their taxes, and have cornered the market. We cannot escape Muslim taxes.'

'I have devised a way to do so, through a Syrian merchant,' said Tomasso, irritated by the notary. 'I shall command sixty-five per cent of this company and all decisions will be finalized by me.'

'It will be a surprise to Venice,' said Enrico. 'Questions will be asked.'

'There will always be those who pry and question.' Tomasso agreed. 'But, the Signori of Venice will rejoice to have their streets perfumed with Eastern spice once more, they will not ask too close how this came about.' Tomasso paused and rose from the table. 'Enrico, secrecy is the backbone of a good company, so long as none learn of our source, none can intrude upon it.'

'It all sounds daunting,' said Fiorenza. 'It sounds exciting, but I'm not sure...'

Tomasso said, 'I will also put the matter to the Venetian Manager, Bartolomeo Varini. But if we are to all agree, I will not have my judgement questioned. Put your trust in me and you will have no reason for regret.'

Fiorenza stood up. 'I am decided,' she said. 'There is no need for deliberation. It will be expected of me to mourn for a respectable time but, I am as secretive as a stone. Messer Vincentini and I cannot wait to begin.'

Tomasso took her hand to steady her as she swayed with the motion of the ship. 'Madonna, I am delighted,' he said gracefully kissing her hand. He turned to the notary 'Enrico?'

'I, of course, see no choice in the matter,' Enrico replied, smiling with admiration. 'We would be fools indeed not to take advantage of your proposal. Your trust will never be misplaced. You have my loyalty. I am admittedly, ever loyal to the pursuit of riches.'

Tomasso unsteadily filled their glasses to the brim. He held his own up. Caught in a shaft of sunlight, it sent a myriad of dancing light about the cabin. 'Alla salute!' He touched his glass to theirs, 'To a new venture!'

They dutifully drained their exceptional wine, oblivious to the fact that they had been skilfully deceived.

Chapter 7 Rouen

Emlyn, Goronwy and the flock of Murano sheep reached Rouen on the evening of Friday. The town windows and balconies were hung with garlands and pennants in preparation for the Easter festival. Goronwy found room at an inn off the Place du March, where he had stayed on similar journeys.

While they were eating, they were joined by a fellow guest, a Dutch soldier, fair haired, blue-eyed and handsome, who introduced himself merely as Josquin. When they had finished their meal, Emlyn asked him if he knew of the convent which Fra Sebastiano had told him about. 'I just want to know how to get there,' he explained.

The soldier smiled. 'I can tell you nothing. Nuns hold my interest not at all. Brides of Christ, what use could they be to a man of my romantic tastes?' He paused and sipped his beer thoughtfully. 'Women covered from feet to throat or not at all, are all the same. A little praise, a little complement and they swoon at my feet. What is it you wish to discover?'

Emlyn believed him. As well as his good looks, Josquin was neat and surprisingly well spoken. Emlyn said, 'There is a girl there who is a distant cousin. I thought it only correct to give her greeting while I am here.'

'Is she pretty?'

'I don't know.' Emlyn snapped, irritated. 'She is just a child.'

Josquin laughed. 'I will tell you where it is. In return, I want something.'

'What do you require?'

Josquin's expression darkened. 'Tell me about the Irishman, O'Healy.'

Emlyn and Goronwy stared at him in astonishment. 'I've never heard of him,' said Emlyn.

'Tell you what?' Goronwy asked at the same time.

Josquin eyed them both expectantly.

'We hardly know him,' Emlyn amended. 'He's just a brown friar going home to Ireland. What is your interest in him?'

Josquin shook his head. 'You and your companion are leaving France; does he intend to accompany you? I need to know because he carries a letter for me.'

'No,' answered Emlyn, suddenly suspicious. How did this man know so much? 'We don't know anything about him, not even that he was travelling the same road.'

Josquin sat in thought for a moment. 'Of course you suspect me of wishing the man harm. I have no intention of harming him. I have an urgent matter to discuss with him, but it is unlikely that I will be able to find him before I return to the Netherlands.'

'The Netherlands?' said Goronwy. 'Are you going to fight with the Duke of Alva?' He ignored Emlyn, kicking at his leg under the table. 'The Duke has been appointed by the King of Spain to eradicate heresy. He brought a band of mercenaries over the Alps, most of them from the Spanish owned Italian states, but some from France and the Netherlands. I assumed that you were connected to them. We all fight to free this land and others from Protestant influence.'

'Well you assumed wrong,' Josquin replied.

Even in the semi-darkness, Emlyn could see the anger in his eyes. 'You are not Catholic?'

Josquin stood suddenly. 'I assume now that you will tell me nothing concerning the Irish friar?'

'I'm sorry,' said Emlyn.

Josquin regarded Emlyn with hostility. 'You can see the convent from the end of this road. The novices will be decorating the road with petals tomorrow for the Easter procession,' he explained. 'I bid you good night.'

As soon as the soldier had left, Goronwy said, 'what was all that about?'

'I don't know. But, if we should meet Friar Patrick O'Healy, a word of warning in his ear might not go amiss.'

'He is not with the Duke of Alva is he, this Josquin?' asked Goronwy.

'No' Emlyn snapped. 'Believe it or not Goronwy, Alva is no friend to England either. This war in the Netherlands will bring England's trade to a standstill. I do not know why you support it'

'Why care?' Goronwy said casually. 'Bring England to her knees through trade embargoes and the Queen will be forced to return to the rule of Rome. The Duke of Alva works in our favour Emlyn. He invites the English Catholics to fight with him.'

Emlyn fought to control his anger. He firmly believed that the more the pressure put on England, the harder England would resist. Not only would England be affected by the disruption in trade, but also Wales and the wool trade of his grandfather, Gruffydd Hiraethog. 'Would you join Alva and his *'council of blood*? It is an organization that can only bring bloodshed.'

'You have no idea.' Goronwy answered, his face suffused with anger.

Before they retired, Goronwy mentioned that he wished to collect an inordinate amount of dried fish to take on the voyage. Dried fish and printing presses in Wales? Emlyn went to bed worried.

The following morning he and Goronwy visited the work shop of Wendelin Tieffenbrucker, a German carpenter. The carpenters' apprentices made letters for printing presses out of rose wood; but the man himself was most famous for making the most beautiful lutes in France. Because of his own interests in lutes, Emlyn knew the German well and held him in high esteem.

Before they reached the workshop, Goronwy said 'What are we going to do about Friar O'Healy? You know that he is bound for Ireland and therefore quite lightly to be sailing on *Le Mychelle*, the boat we will take ourselves.'

'Are you concerned for his safety or that he will discover what you are up to?' Emlyn replied.

'I think that the less who know the better,' Goronwy replied, 'and I would not trust O'Healy to keep his big mouth shut if I told him anything either.'

'You need not worry,' said Emlyn reassuringly. 'O'Healy has just come from Rome, he went to see the pontiff about the future of Ireland, but was not granted an audience.'

Goronwy offered nothing further.

Inside the workshop, Wendelin Tieffenbrucker was bent over a wide table. Sunlight streamed from the window beside him, lighting a shaft of floating sawdust and providing Tieffenbrucker with an iridescent halo. He was a large, softly rounded man with a thatch of hair the colour of corn stalks. He had a handsome, bushy moustache the same hue as his hair and above it, candid eyes as blue and clear as summer sky. His nose was round and large and his smile, when given, was generous. On the benches beside him, his three apprentices worked in silence, heads turned to their work. The room smelled of wood resin and shellac. Tieffenbrucker looked up as his visitors entered and smiled. 'Emlyn, what a surprise to see you, have you come to charm my lutes to sing?'

Emlyn had first met the German a year ago, on a visit with his music teacher Father Alonso d'Aguila. He found Tieffenbrucker's lutes irresistible; his fingers itched to play them whenever he saw them. He visited the workshop whenever he came to Rouen. One of his greatest hopes was to eventually own a Tieffenbrucker lute. He thought about the jewels he had sewn into his jerkin and wondered what they were worth. Was there enough to buy a lute? But now was not the time for self indulgence, Goronwy would probably explode if Emlyn deviated from the task at hand. He tore his eyes away from the musical instruments, promising himself to return if possible to procure a fine lute, one with intricately carved ivory set in the centre rose.

Tieffenbrucker made the wood blocks for printing for the Jesuits, whom he did not like. But business was business and left no room for personal opinions. Rouen was a large printing centre, if somewhat disrupted by what was allowed to be printed and what was forbidden. The German did feel deep sympathy for the young student Emlyn who's flair at plucking a lute, was better than anything he had heard before. It seemed such a waste to lock such talent up in a monastery, when the boy could find a beneficial future at the court in Mantua or Ferrara or Prague or Vienna. Tieffenbrucker had broached the subject often, but the boy was not free to make his own decisions. Today, Tieffenbrucker had business with Emlyn's formidable-looking companion, who did not invite speculative discussion.

After they had seen the printing blocks and Goronwy had paid for them, Emlyn ran off to the nearest hiring stable and hired a horse and cart to carry them to Le Havre. Goronwy had been provided with enough silver by the Catholic, Welsh noblemen, who had instigated the scheme, to buy the merchandise necessary for making a printing press and to ensure that it arrived in Wales safely.

Following Goronwy's instructions, Emlyn called at the fish sellers on his way back and bought enough dried fish to feed a band of mercenaries. He thought it was ridiculous to be taking fish to Wales which had an exceptional fishing economy. He wondered if the thought would occur to Goronwy or, worse still, to the searchers at the harbour in Conway when they arrived there. But it was early in the year and the fishing fleet that left North Wales for Newfoundland, would not yet have returned with their rich catch. Dried herring would probably be quite acceptable.

By late morning, he and Goronwy had packed the wood printing blocks under the herrings so that they were well hidden. The boxes looked normal and only close investigation or betrayal could lead to their discovery. Goronwy cheered up considerably. They collected the sheep from the yard at the inn, loaded them onto the cart and set off in the warm sun to search for nuns with baskets of flower petals.

Before they reached the bridge, they saw instead, the large figure of Friar Patrick O'Healy. They pulled their hoods over their heads, but to no effect, the Irishman still recognized them.

Carmelia had spent the best part of the day creating a flower-petal mosaic of the Sacred Heart. By this time tomorrow, she mused sadly, the Cardinal of Lorraine will have trodden on it and the priests and acolytes behind him will have scattered the rest to the winds. But, now it looked perfect. The central heart had been the most difficult; red being rare in April. Carmelia had overcome the problem by using young unopened leaves, still pink and bronze in their winter casings. All that remained to be done was a small line of white, but Carmelia had run out of petals. She was far up the road and it was quite a walk to where the others worked at similar patterns. She made her way towards them, glancing frequently backwards to be sure that no harm befell her artistic creation. She beseeched the Lord to keep the day bright and calm and windless; she could not foresee any other trouble. Across the river form where the procession would begin, the flower festooned road led to the Priory of Bonne-Nouvelle.

Carmelia walked by the other petal designs examining them with an eye for perfection. There was a cross of Jerusalem; a *fleur de lis*, bright with irises; the cross of St. John and a Lamb of God, nearly as perfect as her own creation.

Seeing her approach, Sister Helen straightened and massaged her aching back with the heel of her hand, groaning theatrically.

Carmelia smiled. 'Sister Helen, I need more white petals. Are these spare?'

'Most certainly not,' Sister Helen replied. 'Have you seen the Cross of St. John?'

'It's yellow,' laughed Carmelia. 'Do you think the Knights of St. John will mind?' She crouched near the flower basket and ran her fingers through the soft petals. 'You have more than enough here Sister... Please? I only need a handful or two. I'll bring the rest back.'

'You impossible girl,' Sister Helen laughed. 'Those eyes will charm the birds from the sky. Take what you need then. And hurry up child or we'll be leaving you behind.'

Carmelia stood and kissed her, then swept up the basket. Her plaits swung, her grey skirts brushed the ground and petals spilled like snow drops behind her as she hurried back up the road. She knelt down and began to place the petals in a white band across the Sacred Heart. She was meticulous, ensuring that each petal fell in the same direction as not to distract from the perfection of the whole. The warm air was perfumed with nectar. The cathedral bells rang over the walled town announcing the hour.

Friar O'Healy was not overweight; he was large, from his bulbous sandaled toes to the top of his freckled, red-encircled tonsure. He joined the two Welshmen eagerly. They had a horse and cart which was an advantage he couldn't ignore. The cart was pulled by a tired brown mare with soft eyes and a grey nose. Having pulled carts for most of her life, no amount of cursing or kicking or pulling would induce her to quicken her pace. The pace slowed further when the large friar pulled himself up on to the bench. He said 'Well there you are, and ready to offer a humble and tired friar a ride. I am as ever ready to call down the grace of God on a generous soul.'

Emlyn lowered his already blistered feet to the ground, preferring to walk. He took the mare's rein and led her towards the bridge, his high spirits draining away like spilled wine.

Friar O'Healy began to sing. His idea of music differed startlingly from everyone else. When Friar O'Healy strung notes together, they were so discordant that they put the cries of a slaughtered piglet to shame. When the friar lifted his head and emitted a particularly strange collection of sounds, it was too much for Goronwy, it had to be stopped. Goronwy said 'We bumped into a mercenary last night who was looking for you.'

Friar O'Healy's lamentation reduced to a buzzing hum.

'I don't think he had your welfare in mind.' Goronwy added. 'He said you had a letter for him.'

The humming ceased altogether. The friar looked up and his ginger eyebrows rose in question. Goronwy explained the conversation they had with Josquin and Friar O'Healy shook his head and pursed his lips in thought. 'Faith, there's a powerful lot of fussing about the comings and going of me all of a sudden. A letter you say?'

He seemed undisturbed but Goronwy kept him talking to prevent him from bursting into song.

Emlyn ignored them; he had worries of his own. He had discovered where the sisters of St. Claire were decorating the road for the Cardinal of Lorraine, but he and Goronwy had spent most of the day collecting horse and cart and wood blocks and herrings; it was unlikely that the nuns and their charges were still there.

To add to his worries, the mare was having difficulty negotiating the bridge. It was busy from both directions; there was a group of noble women showing their fluttering satins and furs, trailed after by liveried servants with banners held high, two women with large bundles and smiles on their round faces, a man with a ladder followed by a boy carrying paint, a flock of choir boys, three monks, two old men struggling under the weight of a tray full of honey pots, four soldiers, a dray piled high with beer barrels, a two-wheeled cart stacked with chickens in wicker baskets and the mercenary Josquin, who was standing at the end of the bridge.

Goronwy guided the horse and cart to one side as the beer cart rumbled by. Because he was above Emlyn, he could see to the other side of the bridge. There was a splash of brilliant yellow and green and pink, stretched out across the lane where such colour shouldn't be. He had seen this sort of decoration before on the feast of Corpus Christi; flower petal mosaics lining the route of holy processions; beautiful, images created from petals painstakingly fashioned over many hours by countless loving hands. 'Emlyn,' he shouted 'look over there!'

When the bee cart had passed, Emlyn saw the nuns. They were in the distance and rapidly making their way in the direction of Bonne-Nouvelle. Emlyn cursed; if he did not manage to see Carmelia Grimani now, the chance would be lost to him. He tightened his grip on the mare's chin strap and pulled her into the throng of people and animals, ignoring Goronwy's shouts and curses. They had reached the end of the bridge when Emlyn saw Josquin put a blow pipe to his lips. The mare suddenly rolled her eyes and tossed her head. The cart nudged the men with the honey pots and they lost their grip on the tray.

Emlyn pulled the mare back and stammered an apology. By then, the situation was out of his hands. The mare suddenly pulled away with a terrified whinny and the rein tore out of Emlyn's hand. Out of control, the horse charged straight into a two-wheeled chicken cart and the chicken baskets fell onto the road. Goronwy's cart thundered onwards and Friar O'Healy performed a head-over-heels, bounced and rolled off the cart, his eyes filled with an expression of extreme surprise and his feet trapped in wicker baskets. The cart sped on bumping and leaping over the chickens. The baskets burst with a shower of straw and feathers, spilling in a ruinous mess across the road. Emlyn ran after the cart.

The cart rumbled towards the nuns and they fled, flapping like doomed moths to the roadside, their flower petal mosaics abandoned. The sudden movement caused the mare to rear and turn. The sheep spilled out the back. Goronwy hung on, shouting and pulling the reins, white faced with fury. A wheel came loose and the mare came to an abrupt stop. The cart collapsed and the horse slid on her haunches into a carpet of delicately laid blossom depicting the Sacred Heart.

Emlyn tripped over and sat in a tangle of baskets and chickens. The poultry owner ran about in circles, frantically trying to trap the hens as they ran helter-skelter for freedom. Emlyn was helpless with astonishment. He stood up. He saw a stout nun with a face like thunder approaching. She was joined by the red faced Irish friar, a furious chicken owner, Goronwy and a whole choir of clacking nuns. Emlyn began to walk backwards, his hands held out in pacifying gestures.

Friar Patrick O'Healy had the longest stride and anger lent him strength. He reached out and grasped a handful of Emlyn's collar and shook him like a rattle, letting fly an expressive, unsparing tirade of abuse that caused the Mother Superior to turn purple.

Emlyn struggled and choked and hit out at the friar's ample midriff. It was like hitting a stone. Nevertheless, Friar O'Healy dropped him. The nuns arrived and Emlyn wished the ground would open and swallow him up. Everyone was shouting and screaming at once. Eyes bulged under furious brows and wimples, tongues cursed, berated and nagged non-stop and arms flew every which way.

'What about my chickens?'

'Mother Mary!'

'Unbearable wretch, what have you done?'

'Jesus, Mary and Joseph!'

A basket flew through the air and hit Emlyn above his ear splattering him with daffodils.

Help came from an unexpected direction. The mercenary, Josquin appeared and held out his arms to encircle an armful of distressed damsels. His touch was gentle and reassuring and his voice so beguiling under the high-pitched tattle, that the nuns quieted considerably and melted into silence.

'Sisters, sisters,' Josquin soothed in his Dutch-French, 'let us not carry on as if we lack compassion and forgiveness in our hearts. The good Lord teaches us to harbour no ill feeling towards our neighbour.' He turned to face the Abbess.

She looked him up and down with a scrutinizing eye, judging his value, estimating how much she could add to the restoration of the church roof. Josquin raised an inquisitive eyebrow and caught on immediately. He withdrew his dagger from his belt, an action that caused the ladies to squeal, and then cut the jewelled buttons from his doublet. Without a word he handed the generous donation to the Abbess. After that, matters had a wonderful way of solving themselves.

There were chickens, sheep and herrings scattered across the road, but the letter blocks remained neatly boxed and had suffered no harm. Josquin wisely disappeared. Under the Abbess's disapproving gaze, Friar O'Healy, Goronwy and Emlyn were instructed to repair the flower mosaics. A few novices came to direct their clumsy attempts. Emlyn spoke to them quickly and they pointed to a novice who worked alone to restore her own work which had been scattered in the mayhem.

Carmelia reworked her petal mosaic in furious silence. Head bent, hands busy, she failed to see the youth, as he bent to the same task. They bumped heads. Carmelia leaped back with a startled cry.

'Mademoiselle!' He cried he put his hand on her arm to steady her.

'Oaf!' she retorted pulling away. 'What ever possessed you to cause such mischief? You have destroyed it!' Carmelia exercised some of her more colourful French, until she saw him turn white and back away from her.

'I do apologize mademoiselle; it was not my fault, though few here will believe me.' He took the basket from her saying 'Here let me. Do these white ones go by here?' His smile was captivating.

'You will never restore it to what it was.' Carmelia replied sulkily. She calmed down. The clumsy youth was a little older than she was. His hair was in ringlets like the love locks of the university students in Paris; it was as dark as her own and was speckled with petals.

He said, 'say that you forgive Mademoiselle? I could not bear to think that I had been the cause of your sorrow. Are you a novice here in Rouen?'

Carmelia felt the colour rise to her cheeks, she dropped her eyes. 'I am not a novice,' she said quietly. 'I am staying with the nuns for my schooling.'

'Carmelia,' he said softly.

'How do you know my name?'

'I asked your friends,' he replied. 'You may find it hard to believe, but I hoped that I could find you here and speak with you before all this happened. It didn't turn out quite as I wished.'

'You are right,' she replied. 'I do find that hard to believe.'

'My name is Emlyn Tomas,' he said. 'And I intended to speak with you because I believe that we may be distantly related.'

'I have never heard of you,' said Carmelia 'What you say is exceptionally unlikely, my family is from Venice.'

He pushed the hair out of his eyes. 'I have made matters much worse for myself than they could possibly have been. I should have approached this with more reason. I thought to take advantage of the opportunity. I didn't think I would be allowed to see you once you returned to your convent. Would that be permissible?'

'After what you have done here, most certainly not,' Carmelia laughed, looking him up and down.

He crouched to put down the basket and looked up at her. His eyes were the colour of the sky. 'How can I see you then?'

Carmelia looked away, suddenly feeling uncomfortable. 'You don't know what you are saying,' she whispered fiercely. 'Such a visit is unheard of. We are forbidden visitors…even priests.'

Still crouched, he reached out and grasped the hem of her Carmelia's skirt. 'That would be Fra Sebastiano da Firenze. He came to see me too. Carmelia do you know a Cristoforo Grimani? Please answer me!'

Carmelia snatched her skirt away from his grasp, stepped away from him and gathered up the basket. Her heart was thudding with fright. 'Yes, but he's dead,' she snapped back at him. 'He died years ago at sea before I was born.'

From across the road the abbess shouted, 'Carmel!'

Emlyn stood up and firmly gripped her arm. 'Was he married to a woman named Anne? I am sorry if I frighten you. It is of the utmost importance.'

Carmelia tried to pull away but he tightened his grip and his eyes entreated her to answer. 'I think so,' she said quickly. 'It was along time ago. My family does not speak of it. That is all I know so please release me or I shall scream.'

He let go as if she was on fire. 'I implore you tell me, who your father is?'

'Please leave me!'

He took a step back, his expression disappointed. 'I am sorry. Thank you, Carmelia.'

She retreated running to the abbess. When she looked back he stood in the road looking at her.

Carmelia stayed close to the Abbess until the flower mosaics had been restored. The Abbess approached the chicken farmer and managed to get hold of a pair of fine hens; she could be very persuasive when the need arose.

The farmer shrugged. He knew the Abbess from passed acquaintance. 'When I have lost so many,' he said, 'why not two more? Take them reverend mother, please enjoy them, they are yours to eat or to lay eggs.'

'Thank you Domenique,' she replied. 'I shall remember you in my prayers.'

The sisters wove down the road with swaying skirts, but the Abbess, swung around to face the travellers and fixed the Irish friar with a piercing glare. 'Brother Patrick!' she said, having already been introduced. The tone of the voice was such that the big man assumed the stance of a guilty schoolboy. Satisfied, she continued 'I believe you owe the Almighty an act of confession. If I were your confessor, I would ensure that you remain on your knees a long while in repenting for your active misuse of the Lord's name!' She turned again and tapped Carmelia sharply so that her head faced the right direction and marched her troop away.

Carmelia looked back and saw that the strange young man had returned to the cart and was being shouted at by everyone else. Even though he had frightened her, she wished that she had been able to talk with him longer but she did not know why. She could not wait to tell her maid Pellegrina. Pellegrina was always talking about boys. 'Emlyn Tomas,' she said to herself. 'What sort of name is that for anybody? Well, he is most certainly not from Venice!'

Friar O'Healy began to laugh. Now that it was all over, he could appreciate the humour of the situation. He walked up to Emlyn and grasped his arm. 'As ye have sown,' he said shaking his head, 'so shall ye reap. You can mend the cart.'

It was a difficult task. The wheel had both come loose and one side of the cart was almost reduced to planking. O'Healy sat by the side of the road offering advice while Emlyn crouched down and began to assemble the bits. Goronwy appeared at his side. He did not offer to help. He said 'Why Emlyn? In God's name why?'

Ignoring the question Emlyn said, 'Did you see that girl I was talking to? Do you know what her name was? Carmelia…'

'No!' Goronwy shouted. 'No, I am not going to sit here and listen to you prattle on about some girl until I have an honest answer to my question. For once in your life Emlyn Tomas give me a straight answer!'

'A straight answer,' Emlyn mumbled around a mouth full of nails. He removed one and held it to a piece of wood, banging it into place with a stone. 'There isn't one' he finished.

'I won't accept that.'

'I don't know, nor why you assume that all this was caused by me. No harm has come of it. Your precious letters are safe.'

'You call this no harm!' Goronwy demanded thumping the cart in anger.

'It's repairable,' said Emlyn.

'Repair it on your own then!' Goronwy snapped. He stormed off.

It began to rain. Left to himself, Emlyn thought about Carmelia. Not so much about the girl herself, for she was but a child, but about the name Grimani. Cristoforo Grimani was the Italian merchant his mother had run off with. It was the only information about his wayward mother that he had been able to extract from his grandfather who believed in letting well alone. What you do not know, he had said, you will never suffer from. And the girl had said something very similar... *my family does not speak of it.*

He hit his finger with the stone and spat the nails out with a curse. He had learned nothing new. Why not forget it, as everyone advised? Why go chasing after something that had happened years ago and could have no influence on the future? Gruffydd Hiraethog had provided a future for him, should he decline holy orders. That future was a promise of freedom and land and the opportunity to make a living as a wool grower. He had thought about it more and more since his grandfather's last letter. Besides, Gruffydd wanted to train him in the old bardic traditions. Bards need no titles he had said. A bard is greatly respected in Wales and, if he is worthy, his reputation alone is enough to grant him all he reaches for. A bastard therefore, thought Emlyn, could be a bard. A bard could own land and stand equal with other men. How much simpler it would be to settle down to such a life and put behind him the haunting dreams of his past.

Emlyn resumed his work patiently and slowly soaked to the skin. When he had reassembled the cart, Goronwy came to help him, lifting the cart with ease as Emlyn fitted the wheel. They secured the boxes and gathered the wet sheep.

When all was at last sorted out, Friar O'Healy discovered that he had lost his pouch. He searched frantically for it, muttering in Gaelic and mopping the rain from his pink head with his sleeve. Goronwy offered to search the cart, keeping the friar away from the herring and the wood blocks. Friar O'Healy cradled his head in his large hands. He looked more angry than upset.

Feeling pity, Emlyn said 'Have you lost something of great value then?'

Friar O'Healy dropped his hands and shook his head. 'There's no wish in me for naught but me own sweet soil,' he moaned. 'I carried a letter for one Don Diego; a Spanish gentleman fighting the heathens with the Duke of Alva. An' there was I giving my word that I'd see the letter safe to his very hands.' He suddenly sat up, his eyes wide. 'Faith, it was that black hearted thief!'

'Who?'

Friar O'Healy hawked and spat. 'Thief and murdering robber, that's what he is. An' you saw how helpful the man was just now? He took me pouch, God rot him!'

'Do you mean the mercenary Josquin?' Emlyn asked, not surprised. He had seen the blow pipe and knew why the mare had bolted, but had not known the reason for it until now.

Friar O'Healy looked at Emlyn carefully as if judging his trustworthiness. 'The letter sure contained information concerning the wages to pay Alva's troops in the Netherlands. This Josquin's no fool, he plans ahead. Now he knows by what route the coin is coming.'

'You mean Josquin intends to rob this...Diego'

'You have it in a nut shell to be sure,' said the friar. He put a finger to his lips in caution. 'Tell not a soul now or I might well find an ear interested in the business of printing. I have a mind to stay in this fair place now.'

'You're not coming with us?' Emlyn asked failing to keep the relief form his voice.

Friar O'Healy thumped him on the back, gave a wink and sauntered off, waving a hand and calling to Goronwy as he went.

Emlyn and Goronwy climbed on to the cart and continued their journey towards the harbour.

Chapter 8 Venice/Crete

Weeks after the funeral of the Venetian merchant, Alessandro Balsamo, Bartolomeo Varini's fears became a reality. He had watched the ships come in and none had carried the Cyprus manager, Enrico, or Alessandro's widow, Fiorenza. Bartolomeo had dealt with matters himself. With apologies and reluctance, he had sent off most of the company's employees. He had given them good references and found most of them positions in other trading houses. Only two apprentices remained and the steward Jacopo and his family, who had been with Bartolomeo from the start. Now the accounting tables were empty and the building already looked dejected and worn.

Bartolomeo had searched Alessandro's room and found a single letter from Tomasso di Vincentini. It was recent and stated that the merchant intended to return to Venice. Alessandro had received it just two days before his death. Its presence explained a great deal to Bartolomeo. In true Roman style, Alessandro had taken his own life rather than the face the circumstances. The fact that he had committed suicide had been kept from public knowledge. Its disclosure could only bring further harm to his already tarnished reputation.

'Rest in peace now Alessandro,' Bartolomeo muttered to himself. 'None can call you to answer from the grave.' He was walking to the Rialto, to keep an early appointment. The sky above was blue and profound, the sun already merciless. Dressed in black, Bartolomeo wilted under its unforgiving glare. He arrived at the prearranged meeting place and waited alone with only the grumbles of his stomach for company.

The man who had requested to see him was a young merchant banker, Paolo Grimani. The request was on behalf of his grandfather, the greatly respected Don Carlos Grimani. Bartolomeo had some idea what the meeting would be about. Fortunately, Alessandro Balsamo had owed the Grimani nothing; for some unaccountable reason, he had never had anything to do with the Grimani family. Although Bartolomeo had often urged his employer to accept the financial help offered by Don Carlos,

Alessandro had always dismissed the idea and refused to speak further on it. Now Alessandro is gone, surmised the lawyer, and I would be more that willing to listen to the great patron. I will wait though, to see if the mysterious Tomasso di Vincentini makes an appearance, before I make a decision. But how long can the wolves be held at the door before they break through and demand their due?

Paolo Grimani was a striking youth of twenty-two. His hair was naturally fair, the envy of nearly every woman in Venice. Bartolomeo had once worked for his father, Cristoforo, before he had joined the Lanarca salt business. Cristoforo Grimani had died tragically at sea and his wife had disappeared assumed dead. The tragic deaths had left two sons orphaned, Lorenzo and Paolo. The two boys had been brought up by their grandfather Don Carlos Grimani. They had become as sons to him and were the heirs to his great fortune. The older youth, Lorenzo, much against his family's wishes, had devoted his life to the church.

Paolo Grimani arrived in a gondola which was fringed and canopied; baring the insignia of the house. With him were two servants, one black and one white. They were dressed in lime-green hose and matching tunics, edged with silver braid. Bartolomeo winced when he saw them.

Paolo leapt from the boat to the Rialto steps and greeted the lawyer jovially. 'Come aboard Messer Varini,' he said. 'It is cooler on the water and we have wine to refresh you.'

Bartolomeo thanked him graciously and complied to his wishes. He made polite inquiries after Paolo's family. He had heard that the Patron had not been quite himself recently.

'He tries to cheat time,' said Paolo in explanation, 'but nothing will stay the scythe of ageing and inevitable death.'

'God forbid!' Bartolomeo exclaimed. He was surprised at Paolo's choice of words. Paolo did not look the least bit perturbed; contrary, he looked quite pleased with the prospect.

The two Venetian gentlemen lounged in comfort while the boat sped over the Lagoon with the ease of a swan. Paolo spoke of the death of Alessandro with respect. 'As you are aware,' he added, 'my grandfather has interest in the Lanarca Salt Company. He is aware of the tremendous debts your employer accumulated before his sad demise.'

'Not so tremendous,' said Bartolomeo defensively.

'In spite of all this,' continued Paolo, 'and with all due respect, my Grandfather is interested in buying the Lanarca Salt Company. As you must be aware, Don Carlos has his own salt shipping business. It makes sense to have the Cyprus salt managed by one company.

'No doubt your words are true,' Bartolomeo replied uneasily. 'However, I do not have the authority to negotiate a sale.'

'But there are none here who can but you Messer Varini. The unfortunate widow has yet to come to Venice and soon you will have visitors who will require a settlement of the moneys owed. How do you propose to meet these?'

Bartolomeo flushed with anger. He took time to calm himself before he answered. Was Paolo so impolitely direct because of his youth and inexperience? Or was he guided to act thus by his grandfather? This was not the first time Don Carlos had showed an interest in the Lanarca Salt Company. Looking at the youth disdainfully Bartolomeo said, 'As I have pointed out, it is not my place to decide which course to take. I am assured that Madonna Fiorenza Balsamo is on her way. She will be here in less than a week. There is also Alessandro's partner, to consider. It is also his intention to come to Venice.'

'Partner?' Paolo said in surprise. 'This is news indeed. But think, Messer Varini, how much they would appreciate a solving of their problems; to arrive and find that all has been arranged for them. The widow most surely, would be grateful. This partner, you mentioned his name?'

'No I did not,' said the lawyer firmly. 'It escapes me at present. He has been partner up until now, in name only.' Bartolomeo mopped his brow. 'You will excuse me? I am sickened by the heat.' He assumed a miserable expression.

'Of course!' Paolo exclaimed with concern.' I should never forgive myself were you to be taken ill on any account of mine.' He signalled for the gondola to turn toward the shore. 'When may I suggest making an offer for the company?'

Bartolomeo moaned painfully and clutched his stomach.

Paolo touched his shoulder, his face a mask of concern, he said, 'I shall send a servant for a physician.'

'That will not be necessary,' groaned Bartolomeo. 'If you could see me to my door I would be more than grateful.'

'Certainly,' agreed Paolo. He redirected the gondolier, his expression peeved.

To put him at his ease, Bartolomeo said, 'Perhaps if your esteemed grandfather could make his offer in writing, I could consider it when I am recovered?'

'There is no need,' said Paolo brightly. 'I have it here already. You will forgive my presumption?'

Bartolomeo groaned and moaned and writhed about. Any more of this, he thought, and I really shall be ill!

But Paolo said nothing more on the subject until they reached the trading house. Bartolomeo was assisted inside by the two servants. 'I will leave this with your steward!' Paolo called after him.

Bartolomeo grunted in reply and waved his false gratitude before the servants left. His steward Jacopo ran up to him looking worried. Sinking into a chair Bartolomeo smiled at him. 'Do not be concerned Jacopo,' he said waving him away. 'It was all but farce, to escape a sticky situation.'

A sea storm built up, two hundred miles off the African coast. Terrifying in its majesty and lit by eerie, sun-infused mists, the towering rock of Crete shuddered out of the sea. Torrential rain drenched the craggy slopes, clouds swathed the mountain and yawning ravines. Winds howled through the halls were the Minotaur had once blew his steamy breath and pounded the earth with his cloven hooves. Crete the Isle of Bulls had cherished and nurtured its Pagan gods. The storm growled and foamed against the coast of Iraklion.

Venice had renamed Crete, Candia and they had built a ducal palace and a basilica of San Marco, with its winged lion and lofty flag poles, in imitation of Venice. There was also a campanile, an arsenal and elegant loggias. At present the balconies were empty, the potted flowers flattened by rain. Around the Piazza, the houses of the military command were shut against the deafening downpour. The bell tower of St. Titus was silent. The soaked lion flag coiled around its pole like a spent serpent. Serpentine too, were the harbour and city walls, the gun turrets manned with grumbling city guards. The rain poured straight from the heavens washing away the soil; flooding the streets and courtyards.

Struggling past the storm dark fortress of La Rocca al Mare, the *Cornucopia* acknowledged the muffled cannon that announced her routine arrival. Her dirty sails and creaking boards nosed her into the safety of the mole. Near the quay, greyed with rain, stood rows of warehouses where the hidden cargoes were stored before shipment to the Republic of Venice. There were also sheds for ship building. Wooden, insect legs supported half built galleys, caravels and fishing boats.

A small boat came out to the *Cornucopia*, carrying the searchers and officials, who must know where every ship was bound for and from what port it came. They were reluctant in the task, the weather was so unpleasant. 'Would the esteemed gentleman, the lady and their retinue, return with them to the warmth and comfort of the loggia?'

Expecting this, Fiorenza had dressed for the occasion and selected the best of her jewels. She still wore black, but it was alight with beads and circlets of African gold. At her throat shone an astonishing stone, as green as envy, it was a gift from her new partner in business. Her hair was still covered but the veil less heavy. She contrived a wistful look of sorrow. Enrico had replaced his usual worn doublet with a newer one, to little affect. He fussed and hovered about Fiorenza like a stork without a nest.

Tomasso di Vincentini had a ring on every finger, each worth the contents of a warehouse. He wore his wide hat without its feathers; the brim was pinned back with a gold framed diamond the size of a cowrie shell; from his ear hung his familiar earring. With him stood his servant Symeon and Fra Vitale di Baganza who looked cold in his friar's cowl and inadequate sandals. These two had become friends on the voyage. The friar expressed a wish to visit the cathedral of St. Titus and Symeon was going with him, he missed the feeling of solid ground underfoot.

Sebastiano Venier was governor of Candia. He was a sharp-eyed, thunderous old warrior, who took pleasure in crushing the Turk whenever opportunity offered. He sat in his dining room, alone at a long table, eating vanilla custard. Rain washed the windows reducing visibility to a fog. He had heard the boom of cannon, but paid it no heed. He already had the details of the incoming ship, a shabby caravel, some merchant of little importance who would not demand his attention. He was annoyed, therefore, when a servant came up to him to inform him that he had guests.

'Who?' he demanded gruffly.

'A lady excellence,' the servant replied nervously. 'Madonna Fiorenza Caterina Balsamo and a merchant Tomasso di Vincentini.'

'Ah,' breathed the veteran. 'See to their comfort, Pio. I will join them presently.' Venier had custard to finish, the delicious dish he would not put aside for any man, or woman. He knew of the lady vaguely, he had entertained her husband at this very table; a jovial man he remembered who liked to make a wager and usually lost. It would be discourteous to ignore the lady's presence.

He did more than make them welcome, he provided a feast on silver platters and attended by matching servants. As governor of Candia, Venier's duties were irksome, but he would not allow good manners to fall. After introductions and a showing of sorrow at the widow's loss, Venier asked them about the Turks, his sole interest. 'Have you seen a war fleet in

Constantinople? I fear the Ottomans will try to take Candia. I will be here waiting for them. They will need more than the protection of Allah to succeed. Not only do we have God and San Marco on our side my friends, but also me, Sebastiano Venier, whom no Turk can pass without exposing his top knot to paradise.'

'Sultan Selim's eye, Excellency,' said Tomasso di Vincentini 'is not turned to Candia, sweet though her wines are. The Sultan looks elsewhere.'

'Where will he turn to do battle?' Venier questioned roughly.

'There is fear that he may turn to Spain where the Moors are driven almost to the very sea by their Spanish overlords.'

'About time too!' Venier exclaimed. 'Why Emperor Charles has allowed them to remain on Christian soil, practising their unholy rituals is beyond me.'

'I believe the emperor's son, Philip is now king of Spain Excellency,' corrected the merchant. 'He will, no doubt, persecute all who bow to Mecca.'

'You sound as if you do not agree sir! You cannot sympathize with the heathen?'

'I am sure,' interrupted Fiorenza, 'that Messer Vincentini meant nothing of the sort. More blancmange Excellency?'

Tomasso di Vincentini fumbled awkwardly with his fork. Venier understood; he himself had taken a good while to learn to use the fandangle. 'Have you not come across the fork Messer? They are popular in Venice,' he explained.

'Introduced by your friends the Muslim, I believe,' said Fiorenza sweetly.

'Surely not!' exclaimed Venier. 'They were Venetian before they were anything else.'

Fiorenza bowed her head, 'I am sure you are correct Excellency, forgive me.'

Venier's eyed the merchant. He felt a nagging stir of recognition. The name was not familiar, but there was something about the smile and the calculating grey eyes that tugged at his memory. The man had no manners talking as he did of war and Turks in the company of a lady. Madonna Fiorenza was as she should be, lighting the dour afternoon with chatter about fashions, music, food and the current dances and performances in Venice. Her knowledge on such trivia was substantial. Poised with a purple fig on the end of her fork, she said, 'What was the reference of sweet wine in relation to the Sultan? I was led to believe, the Islamic law forbids the fruit of the vine.'

Tomasso looked up at her with an expression of annoyance. 'That is so Madonna,' he replied, 'but the present Sultan compares wine unto the beauty of a woman and finds it superior. The Sultan can make his own laws as he is Defender of the Faithful, chosen by Allah as the Holy Father is chosen by God, therefore his word is sacred. He has changed the shariah to suit his tastes. Needless to say, it has met with opposition.'

The governor laughed. 'Perhaps they will turn on each other and give us no further concern.' Then on a more serious note he added, 'Messer Vincentini, you are well versed in the ways of the Turk.'

'I was taught by a wise soldier,' the merchant replied, 'to know my enemy. It was a lesson I learned before I could lift a sword.'

It was also a lesson Venier had taught to all the youths sent to him to learn sword-play, when he was younger. Had he taught this man? He said, 'You are from the Brenta you say? I know the area well and have known good friends there.'

Vincentini smiled pleasantly. He signalled to a servant to bring his cloak. He said, 'Forgive me Excellency. If there was time, we could perhaps talk and find mutual acquaintances. It is to my sorrow that this is denied us. I am sure it would benefit us both.'

To Venier's mind came the memory of a boy attacking him from behind a farm gate, the stabbing 'to death' with a wooden sword, laughing at his own cunning. Venier raised a hand in a commanding gesture that even Tomasso could not ignore. 'Tell me,' he said softly. 'Do you know Capaccio?'

With a raised eyebrow the merchant said, 'The painter?'

'No, I was thinking of another branch of that illustrious family.'

'I am sorry to disappoint you,' Vincentini replied lightly. He took the weight of his damp cloak on his shoulders. He bowed. 'It has been an evening of pleasure which I shall remember with gratitude.'

'Of course,' said Venier rising, banishing memories from his mind. 'I too have enjoyed such knowledgeable company and pray that it can be repeated at greater leisure. An escort will walk you to the waterfront.' He turned to the lady, who was making no preparation for leaving. 'Madonna, I offer further hospitality should you wish to spend a night away from the discomfort of sea. There are rooms prepared.'

'Thank you Excellency. I am delighted to accept.' Fiorenza replied.

Tomasso bowed to her. 'I will call for you at dawn. Do you think you could be ready?'

Venier laughed. 'A lady is never ready. They are ruled by a time that cannot be ordered.'

In spite of the governor's predictions, Fiorenza was ready by dawn. She had been ready for an hour and had shared breakfast with the governor on the balcony; a meal of flat bread, fried fish, pomegranates and slices of sweet orange. Tomasso di Vincentini arrived in a manner totally unexpected, he brought the horses from the caravel, saddled and bridled, tossing their heads in eagerness to run. They looked perfectly beautiful.

He drew up in the courtyard and looked up to where Fiorenza stood on the balcony. Without dismounting, he called, 'I thought you would like a ride, before we sail again. You can ride I assume?'

'You assumed correctly Ser Vincentini,' she replied. She wished she was not dressed in her best. 'You have three horses?'

'Do you require an attendant? Maria?'

She said, 'No, Maria dislikes riding. Do we ride far?'

'There is little time. I mean to be away before the day is much older.'

Fiorenza walked down and stood by the horses, stroking silken mane, waiting for assistance. The merchant belatedly, leapt down and lifted her into the saddle. Fiorenza shivered at his touch. She wondered why he had such an affect on her. Over the last few days, she had thought of a proposal to make to him. She wished it only to be of benefit the company, but was honest enough to admit that Vincentini's manner and mystery affected her in a way altogether different.

They rode out past the church and saw Fra Vitale di Baganza, standing waist-deep in children. He waved happily to them. The rain had gone. The countryside looked clean and glistening, puddles lay everywhere. Before they had gone far, Fiorenza's dress was splashed with mud. As soon as they had left the gates of Iraklion, Tomasso spurred the horses into a gallop, they needed no urging.

Fiorenza felt the release and freedom. She had learned to ride as a child and the spirited mares were to her liking. Hooves thundering, they flew over rutted tracks, crushing tufts of sweet thyme. Gentle wind unfurled tails and manes and undid the tie in Tomasso's hair. Behind him, Fiorenza took time to watch him. He seemed so free of trouble. He turned laughing to her as they approached a low gate. Fiorenza urged her mare forward and took the jump without falter. A little ahead, she drew her horse in to walk and the merchant pulled in to match her pace.

Fiorenza said, 'Messer Vincentini, I could not help but notice your dislike for the governor. Was it dislike?'

'No, more an irritation. I find the military mind seldom sees beyond it's own profession. I meant no discourtesy. Were you offended?'

'No, I was amused. At breakfast he has asked me questions concerning your family, he thinks he knows you.'

'Were you able to enlighten the inquisitive governor, Madonna?'

'I wish you would not call me Madonna all the time. You may call me Fiorenza, we are together in business.'

'Agreed, Fiorenza,' he replied, squinting with the sun in his eyes.

As he did not offer, she said, 'May I call you Tomasso?'

'By all means.'

'And, something of yourself...That is if you don't mind?' Why did he make things so difficult? She looked at his long fingered hands bereft of rings they entwined the rein.

Surprisingly, he answered her. 'My father grew saffron. We had a farm encompassed by a bend on the river Brenta. I grew up there and then I went my own way, now all my family are dead.' His eyes lifted. 'That is my history, Fiorenza.'

'I'm sorry your family passed away,' she said, caught by his bitterness. 'You must have been a disappointment to them.'

'The less we touch on the matter, the better we'll agree.' He spurred his horse forward in anger and left her standing.

She pulled in her horse in fiercely as it fought to bounce away. She felt the sting of tears, she had been foolish. In the calmness of her cabin, she had considered the possibility of marriage to Tomasso di Vincentini in order to strengthen their partnership. She was prepared for a negative answer. But, if he gave himself time to consider, what could his objections be? She considered the brief account he had offered of his family. He had risen from a humble beginning, how had he come to such riches? It seemed as if his own interests occupied him more than any concerns about a new business, he was preoccupied. Fiorenza wondered how he would survive under the inquisitive rivalry of other Venetian merchants. It meant much in Venice to be part of the city, to have relations and friends with influence that one could relay on.

The mare stamped. Insects buzzed in the dry grass and fluttered over mounds of scented marjoram. Above the waves, sea birds cried and dived after fish; the storm had boiled the sea and brought easy pickings. The landscape was patched with tawny brown, heliotrope mountains rose above, scared with deep morning shadows. The merchant waited for her on the crest of a hill between cedar trees that stood like sentinels overlooking the sea. Fiorenza rode toward him without haste.

Tomasso rode down to her. He said, 'We have idled long enough. It is time to return.'

Now that the chance was offered, a rare occasion when they were both away from others, Fiorenza fumbled for words. In the end, finding no better way, she said, 'Have you considered marriage, Messer Vincentini? I have a proposition…'

'No,' the reply came without a pause.

'I was referring to an arrangement with myself. That is…the new company might benefit...' Fiorenza stopped, overwhelmed with embarrassment.

His horse spun as he drew the rein. He looked at her in incredulous astonishment. His brows drew together and his eyes blazed.

Fiorenza looked away, feeling the enormity of her mistake. She felt the colour rise to her cheeks. She urged her horse forward and was some way ahead, when she summoned up the courage to stop and look back.

He sat with head bowed. His mare stamped and flicked at flies with her tail. Tomasso had taken off his hat and the sun lit his hair, showing more grey than black. The noise of sea-birds intruded. Time froze between them.

Fiorenza turned away and dug her heels in to her horse's flank. The mare tossed her head and at the bite of a whip, stretched out into a ground-eating gallop. She flew past carob trees and crumbling walls and vine-hung trellises. She was near the walls of Iraklion when the thunder of hooves came up behind her. The mares were equally matched, but as much as she urged, she felt the gap between them close. She bent down, whispering in the silky ears. Ahead, a donkey, invisible burdened with straw, brayed and kicked as it was pulled to the side by the owner the Cretan voiced well used curses directed at the Venetian overlords. Goats and goat-boy scattered from the road.

Drawing level, Tomasso reached out and grasped a rein, hauling them both to an untidy stop. Fiorenza lifted her whip and struck him to force him to release her. He held on, fighting for control of his horse and hers. The animals reared in panic and plunged from the road. Fiorenza brought her whip down repeatedly on the hand that prevented her escape.

The mares galloped towards a high stone wall and a pair of towering windmills, arms whirring and creaking in the wind. With snorts and neighs of protest, the horses slowed and came to an unwilling, nervous stop at the base of the wall.

Vincentini was laughing. He dismounted, breathless, still retaining a hold on Fiorenza's rein. He sat down abruptly, fighting to control his mirth.

Fiorenza just sat and watched him. Her own anger boiled, strengthened now by disbelief.

Tomasso rose unsteadily and without asking, caught her around the waist and swung her down from the saddle. She stood close beside him, looking up into his laughing eyes.

'Do not be angry, Fiorenza.'

'I am not angry!' she screamed back at him.

'Please, let us sit. There is much you do not know of me. If you did, you would never have put to me such a tempting proposal.'

'I thought only to benefit the company,' she snapped. 'Do you know what becomes of a successful widow in Venice? Ironically, I was safe enough being a share holder of the sorry salt business. If this spice trade prospers, the Senate will feel obliged to trap me with some convenient family allegiance which may not be to my liking.'

Tomasso led her under the shadow of the wall and smoothed the grass for her to sit. She remained standing. He produced a leather bottle that she refused when offered. He said, 'Your idea is one of good sense and I do not turn it down lightly. However, there are matters to which I must attend before I could consider marriage. I am not free to do so.'

Fiorenza sighed and felt her anger drain away, but not the discomfort. She had known him for weeks only, it was folly. She said, 'I too am sorry. It was presumptuous of me.'

He smiled at her and pulled her down to sit beside him. 'If you wish Fiora,' he said, 'I offer you my protection as guardian. Any future plans the Senate may have on your welfare, shall have to be dealt with through me. I shall make your wishes clear and can protect you from an undesirable match. You may remain free of ties for as long as you wish. Indeed I am surprised that you wish to wed at all, for a woman, your position could not be freer. Have you thought of becoming a courtesan?'

She thought him serious, but his eyes shone with humour. He had shortened her name, unknowingly to what it was when she was a child. She wanted to know more about him. She had connections, and no man's past could remain hidden for long in the bustle of Venice. She summoned up a smile. Her attraction toward him and his mystery was enhanced, but she felt an underlying fear; he was not all he seemed.

The wharf chain lifted and strong wind filled the sails of the *Cornucopia* thrusting her into open water. Provisioned and watered, she pointed her bow to the Ionian Sea and the long, hazardous stretch between Italy and the coast of Dalmatia. Fat and low in the water, she ran for Venice, freshly filled with olive oil, fresh vegetables and corn, bound for the granaries of the Republic of Venice.

The crew of the caravel answered immediately on the rare occasions Tomasso overrode the authority of the Ragustan captain. Tomasso knew the nature of the sea, he made this evident in his every action, so they would gain confidence in him and leap to his commands should the need arise.

Exercising his hounds in the narrow confines of the deck, he often saw Fiorenza watching him. He felt his eyes lazily stray in her direction and remain there until she looked away. She was not the least bit abashed, she often smiled at him but she did not invite conversation, beyond what was necessary. He often wondered what the colour of her hair was. In spite of his refusal, he knew the fruit was offered still, if he wished to taste it. His eyes acknowledged her offer but his hand never reached out. He could hear her lute at times and her sweet voice rise from within. There might be time, thought Tomasso, to taste of that fruit when all is done and if I live to taste it.

Chapter 9 Wales May

Conway castle stood on a headland overlooking the wide river estuary and the fishing village of Aberconwy. It was built with seven great towers and five smaller ones. The walls stretched out from the main building surrounding the whole town with twenty-seven further towers. These were twined at the three major gates. When the castle had been built by Edward I, the danger had been from the Welsh on whose land it was built.

The town of Conway had become a backwater which men passed through on their way to Ireland or somewhere else. No traveller ever stayed very long. Sir Henry Conway and his lady rarely visited the castle; they were there now; their personal standard fluttered in the breeze above the castle. Conway was crowded. It was time of the Spring Fair, the one occasion in the year that made the old walled town worth visiting.

Ambrose Chillingworth was a wool merchant and a member of the Muscovy Merchant Company. This is how he represented himself to most men he did business with, but his interests were wider and his knowledge more extensive. He was an English gentleman with an undying loyalty to England and the proud, indecisive Queen Elizabeth. Merchants like Ambrose bought and sold plots, gossip and small talk. They were often bankers and as such exerted a powerful influence on the monarchs of Europe, who so often needed to beg and to borrow.

That morning, as Ambrose Chillingworth left the Dancing Bear inn, he was itching from head to foot. He vowed never to stay under the cobweb draped ceiling again. He was used to more comfortable accommodation. It was a cloudy day in late May. Wet, soggy blossom piled in corners and chilly winds strong enough to whip the cloak off your back, howled around the castle walls. Ambrose shivered as he shut the door firmly and finally behind him. Wales was never blessed with pleasant weather, so he had been told by a colleague at court.

Ambrose was sixty-two, a solid robust man who had led an active life in pursuit of his occupation, the export trade in cloth. This had been chiefly centred in Antwerp, with the English Merchant Adventurers. Not long before this, Calais had been the gateway to the markets of Europe.

After two hundred years of English occupation Calais had been taken back by France in the last year of Queen Mary Tudor's reign.

In the years that followed, English traders searched for markets beyond Europe. The Muscovy Merchant Company had been founded to explore these new markets in the east, they had met with mixed success. Ambrose Chillingworth had travelled twice to Russia and was well aware of the enormous difficulties of travel and the expense incurred. A group of West Country merchants had nosed into the lucrative African slave trade. But this was a perilous and risky business. Ambrose, always on the look out for profit, had sent his son Christopher with the last Barbary ships under Jack Hawkins, ships that carried slaves for the Spanish markets in the Indies.

Ambrose had arrived in Conwy the night before with three servants. His own man, a small, dour Englishman named Matthew and two hired servants, Aled and Jack Jones. Ambrose had hired them in Chester, on the recommendation of their previous master, a certain Richard Clough, whom Ambrose had met at Antwerp. Ambrose had come to Wales to buy wool, it was of the best quality available in Europe. He hoped to take it direct to the markets of Italy. If he succeeded in this, the venture could bring greater profits than trading through the Italian wool buyers in Antwerp.

At the dock gate, Ambrose found his Welsh servants waiting for him. Aled and Jack were grinning. They were brothers, but did not look alike, Jack was a strong simple minded man with a thick thatch of blond hair. His size and obvious strength were valuable assets went travelling along the forested roads between the Welsh towns were thieves prayed on travellers. Aled at twenty was the younger. He was tall and bony with a neat bowl-cut of mud brown hair. Under dark brows, his eyes were the same brown, intense and serious. His previous employer Richard Clough had taught Aled to write and read a further advantage was that Aled knew everyone who was worth knowing in North Wales and was vaguely related to most of them. Ambrose hoped these boys would lead him to the sheep farmers who were not already bound by trade agreement to deliver their wool to the London market at Blackfriars.

The two servants were grinning. They greeted the merchant with a shy cheerfulness. They were young lads and it didn't take much to guess how they had spent the night. It did nothing to lighten Ambrose's humour. It was going to rain. The sky was grey; the sea was grey and flat as slate. There was nothing good about the morning at all.

Aled had informed him of a local sheep farmer, by the name of Gruffydd Hiraethog who was in Conway to meet his grandson, arriving from France on the *le Mychelle* due in that day. There would also be samples at the fair of the superior wool produced by the Welshman which Ambrose could inspect. 'You'll not find better this side of the Pyrenees' Aled had assured him.

The *le Mychelle* nosed up the river estuary to the harbour. After a wet spring and countless weeks of gloom, a crack appeared in the clouds and rare sunlight flooded through. Ambrose looked over the wharf to the *le Mychelle*. Her fresh painted colours winked brightly in the new sunlight. Aled had found him a barrel to sit on so h he had a good view and kept him from being jostled by the crowd.

Ambrose asked Aled, 'if the wool farmer is here, on the wharf, Will you know him if you see him?'

'There's no mistaking Gruffydd Hiraethog,' Aled replied. 'He is known well in these parts for his skill as a bard, I have never met him but I know his grandson Emlyn Tomas, he's been in France studying with the Jesuits.'

'Not very wise these days,' said Ambrose.

'True enough,' Aled replied. 'It may interest you know that he is bringing sheep with him.'

Ambrose laughed dryly. 'What fool would bring sheep into Wales? It's already got more sheep than Welshmen.'

The fool that would was nestled among the *le Mychelle's* cargo. It was a very mixed lading. There were boxes and bundles, butts of wine and barrels of honey and sugar and black soap, a hogshead of vinegar, three fardels of canvas, two bundles of teasel staffs and a massive mill stone. The sheep Emlyn had brought with him had been put into slated crates since leaving Le Havre. They had bleated pitifully over every wave. It had annoyed everybody aboard. The wind had been meagre, the seamen were ill tempered and eager to get in the inns that lined the wharf. After four years of learning to be good members of the Society of Jesus, Emlyn Tomas and his friend Goronwy Glyn Parry had worked their passage home like common seamen.

The master of *le Mychelle*, Dafydd Allen, had often taken students as passengers. They usually turned green a mile out to sea and remained green until their feet returned to *Terra Firma*. Students rarely had the means to pay their way and these two had been no exception. They knew nothing about handling a ship, but were willing enough to do as he asked and only one had turned green and remained incapable for a few days. The tall one was quiet and as strong as an ox. The other, the younger one was a cheerful lad, the jokes and insults rained on him continually by the seamen had produced no effect whatever. Dafydd Allen suspected that the lad might be a bit daft, but if daftness brought such good nature, where was the harm in it?

The voyage had not been a good one nor had it been terrible. The upset was more to do with a string of mishaps than anything else. The seaman's porridge had mysteriously turned blue between the cook's galley and the wooden platters it was dished up on. one of the crew, Ieran had caught his foot an a tangle of rope and hung off the yard-arm for an hour yelling until someone got him down. Once when they had pulled a good catch from the sea, all the fish had slipped out of the wooden pail, slithered across the tilting deck and leaped back into the water. The crew had mumbled about bad luck, but Dafydd Allen put it down to misfortune. When misfortune rode with the *le Mychelle*, it was best to double your prayers and get the voyage over and done with, as quickly as possible.

As *le Mychelle* neared Conway, the Captain felt his shoulders un-knot and gave order for the cargo to be got ready for unloading. As none could leave the ship until this was done, willing hands completed the task before the *le Mychelle* bumped against the harbour wall. There were cheers and waves from the waiting crowd and a creaky set of blocks and tackle was brought into service to help unload heavier packages. The crew was always quick and efficient at this as it was the end of the voyage. Spirits were high and the two students were getting a double dose of ribald humour. In his cabin, Dafydd Allen knelt for a private prayer of thanksgiving. Then he combed his generous moustache, put on his best doublet and a new French hat and emerged into the sunlight to meet the custom officials.

The seamen began muttering and scowling at the crowd for some reason. There appeared to be a problem. The town bailiff was on the quay-side with a group of armed men. He was trying to make his way to the ship and looked to be in a foul temper. Noise and confusion grew as boxes of dried herring were handed over the side and butts of wine and vinegar were eased down the sloping planks. The rope and tackle was fixed to the millstone and the crowd was pushing and jostling and the noise was becoming deafening.

The voice of the Bailiff roared out above the clamour, ordering his men to move forward. They began clearing the way, with the flat of their swords and the handles of their pikes. Gradually the crowd was forced into some sort of order, as they were driven back from the ship's side. A strange sense of quiet fell upon the scene. The neglected millstone turned sluggishly on the tackle; the blocks creaked as they held the weight of it high in the air. The whole quay-side was a jumble of spilled cargo, except where the boxes of dried fish were stacked safely beside a couple of sea trunks and a few small barrels.

The brothers Aled and Jack emerged from the crowd to stand beside Ambrose Chillingworth. The merchant looked at them, seeking some sort of explanation.

Jack shrugged. He said 'The Bailiff wants to search the *le Mychelle*.'

'Whatever for?' Ambrose inquired.

'Weapons and other forbidden things I expect.' Aled replied.

Weapons and contraband usually meant rebellion and rebellion these days meant Catholics. After ten years of relative peace, Queen Elizabeth's England was beginning to stir with unrest. Ambrose had heard of it all as he travelled about the country. He was a tolerant man and was not prepared to involve himself in an way. The quay stank of rotting fish; he wrinkled his nose and closed his eyes. Things were seldom as straight forward as you wished them to be.

On the deck of the *le Mychelle*, Emlyn began to busy himself with the sheep crates.

'Dewi Sant! What are you doing?' Goronwy said in disbelief. He had his thick arms locked around a barrel of soap, ready to carry it to the gang plank. He looked worried.

Emlyn raised an eyebrow innocently. 'letting the sheep out,' he said.

Goronwy looked at him with a pained expression 'You can't do that, not here, all hell will break loose. Look at their rolling eyes.'

Emlyn was sitting on the wooden crate unfastening the rope ties. Wet noses and woolly ears poked between the slats. He said, 'Can't you see Goronwy? There are twelve helmets approaching, with soldier's heads under them and twelve pikes and a bailiff. If they search the ship's cargo, as I am sure they will, they will discover the wood blocks. They only have to overturn the fish boxes to find what we are bringing into Wales. Then will come the questions and the forced answers and then we will be put to stew in some rotting, rat infested cell, to await the bailiff's pleasure. Then we'll have our ears chopped off.'

Watching the soldiers walking up the boarding plank, Goronwy began to panic. 'I see little point in releasing the sheep,' he said nervously. 'What will that achieve?'

'Confusion,' Emlyn replied simply.

Goronwy remembered the chickens in Rouen and the miracle of the Virgin's footprints and the countless other occasions when Emlyn had created confusion. This thought Goronwy is not the time or place for pranks. He said 'If you think for one moment, that I am going to allow you to ruin everything after such planning and expense...'

'I am not going to ruin anything,' Emlyn said 'Ieran is.'

'Ieran?' Goronwy asked. 'How?'

Emlyn turned to look at a hogshead of Gascony wine, which he had slept near to all the way from France. He had already loosed the bung. He took a leather helmet from one of the boxes and moved towards the barrel. Slowly and deliberately, he eased the bung and let a ruby trickle of wine to fill the helmet. As he guessed, his action did not go unnoticed.

Math of Merioneth had sailed with the *le Mychelle* since he had been a small boy of twelve. He was a very large man with an overgrown beard and an abusive manner, a seaman and not one who would miss the chance of good draft of wine. Going ashore was going to be delayed now with the searching. Math nudged his friend Ieran, the same unfortunate man who was found mysteriously dangling in the rigging a few days earlier. Both seamen approached Emlyn Tomas and the barrel.

With his helmet of wine balanced beside him, Emlyn watched them approach. He was still fiddling with a rope on the sheep pen.

Goronwy looked cross and suspicious and worried all at the same time. He was all those things. He didn't trust Emlyn when he had that mild, inoffensive look about him. It usually meant the reverse.

Turning to him with sudden serious urgency, Emlyn said 'Go on, unload the rest of the herring boxes or the chance will be wasted!'

Goronwy nodded nervously and moved away.

Math spat on the planking. 'Now then Ieran,' he said. 'Why is it 'e's bringing them sheep to Wales?'

'Well 'e's from Rhuddlan see so what can you expect?' Ieran replied. 'Though it could be that they're related, them sheep an' 'im is long lost cousins by the look of them.'

Math smiled showing his four remaining black teeth. 'An' as them sheep doesn't drink wine...?' He reached for the helmet.

Just as his hand reached the spot, Emlyn nimbly whisked the wine away and looked directly into the eyes of Math. His own eyes appeared to be out of focus. He mumbled thickly 'Are we there then? Is this Conway?'

'E's bin at that wine all morning! Come now lad, give it 'ere!' Ieran demanded, pushing his way forward.

Emlyn dropped the tangle of rope keeping one end in his hand. He swung it back and forth and stood up. He was a head shorter than the seaman. With his free hand, he lifted the helmet to his lips and took a long, audible swallow. He licked his lips and backed a step. With a wicked grin he said, 'Care for another swing in the rigging Ieran?'

Ieran looked at the rope and a series of expressions moved across his face ending in a furious scowl. His eyes bulged and his face reddened with anger. 'The Devil, You did that?' he spluttered. It made no difference to Ieran that the *le Mychelle* was docked and half unloaded or that there were soldiers thumping up and down and poking into everything. He went for Emlyn with his big horny hands outstretched ready to strangle.

Emlyn dropped the helmet. He bounced away behind the sheep crate, still holding the rope.

Ieran followed with a string of curses.

Emlyn tugged the rope briskly.

The loop tightened around Ieran's legs. He fell into the sheep crate, splintering the wooden slats. The sheep, burst away in all directions. The bung on the hogshead had not been replaced, wine spilled over the fardels of canvas and soaked into a bale of fancy brocade. Upset by a bleating ewe, teasel staffs clattered among the balls of woad and jars of madder. A hogshead of vinegar burst in the process and ruined a sack of English hops and a packet of precious Papal alum in the process. The barrel of black soap overturned and upset the box of helmets.

On the quay, Goronwy was busy unloading herrings.

With a look of mischief Emlyn took off toward the forecastle.

Everyone aboard left what they were doing to watch what was happening. When Ieran had untangled himself, he and Math charged after Emlyn.

Emlyn cavorted among the items of cargo. A butt of honey flew at Math and burst when it hit him on the shoulder. The floor swam with red wine and red madder and blue woad balls and powdered alum, sticky with honey. Coral beads and pearl buttons burst out of a coffer and bounced on to the planks disappearing between the cracks. Soon most of the crew of the *le Mychelle* had joined in the chase. The Bailiff and his men gave up inspecting the ship's cargo and joined the pursuit around the deck.

On shore, Ambrose opened his eyes. Seamen and soldiers were shouting and running in all directions. A cart suddenly appeared through the east harbour gate pulled by what looked like a runaway horse. Everyone scattered to get out of the way, until it came to an abrupt halt next to were the mill stone hung by the neatly stacked boxes of dried herring on the quay-side.

Ambrose put his dignity to one side and stood up on the barrel. From his perch he could see a thin youth with patched, darned hose and red boots like those worn by the troubadours. He was clambering up the mast rigging. Stuffed in the front of his jerkin was an assortment of items that he hurled at his pursuers. Cheeses flew through the air unravelling linen. Two helmets were followed by a shower of raisins. A lady's glove packed with black soap hit the Master, Dafydd Allen and knocked off his fine new hat. A headless fish hit Ieran across the mouth cutting off his curses.

The youth was perched high on a yard-arm, his missiles running out. Ambrose could see six men climbing after him. As they neared the top, Emlyn slithered to the end of the spar. A few of the spectators below cheered him on. The rest showed upturned, angry faces and some had drawn swords.

'Emlyn Tomas is home again,' laughed Aled. 'They have nearly caught him!'

And so they had. Math and Ieran were moving along the spar like two beetles, closing in on their prey. Emlyn edged to the end, calling out insults in French. He swung his feet down, hanging on to the yard-arm with his hands. They could all see what he intended to do; he was going to leap over on to the block and tackle from which the millstone hung. It was risky jump with a long drop to the ground below. Guessing the next move, Math reached out with a snarl.

Emlyn was no longer there. A gasp rose from the onlookers as he flew through the air. To the surprise of a few and the disappointment of many, Emlyn reached his goal. The block and tackle creaked and the mill stone swayed dangerously. The cart was now loaded with herring. The horse stamped and then trotted towards the gate, thee men leapt on as the cart it moved away.

Ambrose realized that he was the only one who had taken any notice of the cart, all other eyes were fixed on the youth. He was holding onto the crane hook, with his feet guiding the stone into a slow spin. The crowd shrieked and fell back away from the *le Mychelle,* afraid that the stone would fall and crush them. The young man looked down on the result of his work that morning and the smile left his face. He had blue and red streaks running down his torn tunic, it had lost a sleeve and most of the lace.

Red faced with fury; Dafydd Allen shook his fist. 'Come down,' he shouted. 'Or I'll have them hang you were you stand! Then I'll skin you and use your guts for halyards!'

Pointing an accusing finger at Ieran, Emlyn said, 'It was an accident. That man tried to throttle me. I ran in fear for my life.'

Turning to the people of Conway, Dafydd Allen offered them a broad wink. 'He fears for his life,' he said mockingly. 'I cannot think why.'

They all laughed. It had been entertaining. Aloft on the rigging, Ieran and Math had fashioned hanging knots out of Emlyn's discarded piece of rope. They swung them threateningly. The Bailiff ordered the crane-men to lower the mill stone and with it, the trouble maker Emlyn Tomas. A small group of young men clapped their hands and shouted to Emlyn in Welsh. Everyone who had goods aboard the *le Mychelle* were shouting angrily.

Clearly, above it all was the voice of the lady of Conway herself. It was her brocade and her cheeses that were ruined. It was her beads and baubles that were lost under the planking. 'That buffoon should be thoroughly beaten, quartered alive and thrown to the dogs.' she pronounced.

The Bailiff added, 'By the time I have finished with him ma'am, there will be nothing left for the dogs!'

Emlyn's feet had hardly left the mill stone when the balief's men leapt on him and bore him to the ground. He offered them no resistance. He smiled at them and received a savage kick for his efforts. He had led them on a wild chase and caused delay and upheaval on a day that should have been a happy occasion.

Ambrose climbed off his barrel. The mood of the crowd was turning ugly. They were screaming abuse and pelting the young man with stones and rubbish. It could turn into a lynching. The merchant decided to make himself scarce. He could always complete his business when matters had cooled down. It was no concern of his. Aled and Jack had disappeared into the crowd. This made Ambrose angry; they had run off without his leave. With his brows knit, he stormed off towards the dock gate. 'I knew today would be luckless!' he muttered to himself.

A cart had overturned in the narrow street; it had lost a wheel. Ambrose recognized it as the one that had taken away the fish boxes during all the confusion. A few men stood around offering suggestions to the cart owner. The merchant's suspicions had been aroused when he had seen the cart hastily leave the dock. Not wanting to be involved in whatever they were up to, Ambrose ducked through a dark doorway to cut through a store house to the street on the other side. There was no other side.

The room he had entered was dim with a ragged cloth hung over the small window, cutting out the light. Heavy beams ran across the ceiling.

Fishing nets and lobster pots hung from the walls. It smelled of dried herrings. On the floor was the source of the smell. The fish boxes were open, the fish scattered revealing the hidden contents of the boxes. About them stood three rough looking men, others lurked in the shadows. An older man sat astride a box and stared at Ambrose in astonishment.

His hair was as white as thistle-down, as was his long beard that was brushed and glistening. His round eyes, blue as mountain harebells, peered from under white, bushy brows.

Ambrose took a few steps into the room and stood stock still. There was no mistaking the contents of the boxes. Any educated man could see what they were, sets of carved wooden letters which were used for printing together with bundles of paper and printed pamphlets. These were all being packed into empty flour sacks in a great hurry. Weapons and other forbidden things, thought Ambrose. I have walked into a nest of scheming Catholics! These men had not anticipated the break down of the cart otherwise they would have been well away by now. Ambrose had seen the block letters that were not meant to be seen; he now understood that the destructive acrobatics of the youth on the boat had been to draw attention away from the unloading of this illicit cargo. Noise from the crowd outside was muffled by the thick walls. Inside, the men eyed Ambrose with hostility. One of them took a step forward and spoke harshly to the others in Welsh. Ambrose backed a few steps and came to an awkward stop against something large and unyielding. He turned around slowly. It was his servant Jack, as solid as a tree. Jack gave him a huge smile and grunted. Aled Jones appeared from the shadow by the wall. He looked shamefaced. 'Master Chillingworth,' he said with a nervous grin. 'What are you doing here?'

'Look Aled,' said Ambrose. He held up his hands to show them that he was unarmed. 'I've seen nothing. I'll be on my way and I won't whisper a word.'

'Chillingworth,' echoed the older man leaping up from his box. 'Aled what do you mean by leading this man here?'

'I was going to tell you,' said Aled defensively, turning to face him. 'He employed us in Chester. He wants to buy wool. I did not bring him here he came here on his own.'

'Chillingworth,' the old man repeated. 'Do you know who he is?'

Aled shrugged his shoulders. The others hastily threw sacks over the remaining wood blocks and moved closer, standing around in a loose circle.

Ambrose dropped his arms to his sides and swallowed nervously.

'He is one of the Queen's men, a financial agent,' continued the elderly man. 'He is a spy in the pay of Sir Thomas Gresham!'

'Nonsense,' said Ambrose calmly. He had never seen this man before, but the things he said were a little too close to the truth. 'I admit I have served her Royal Majesty in the capacity of financial adviser once or twice. I admit also that Sir Thomas Gresham is known to me, as he is to any English merchant in Antwerp. I am no spy.'

'Are you Catholic?'

'No.' Ambrose admitted, feeling that he would be better served by truth.

'Cut his throat,' said one of the men gruffly. He was a thin man with a balding head and large ears. He walked forward and stood menacingly in front of the merchant. He drew a wide, short blade from his belt. It shone dully, as did the cruel smile on the man's narrow face.

'No!' Aled shouted. He placed himself between the armed man and the merchant. 'Are we murderers? He is a wool buyer and I am sure he has no interest in what we do here.'

Ambrose was surprised and relieved at this defence. 'Thank you Aled,' he said, placing a hand on the boy's shoulder. 'The lad is right you have nothing to fear from me.'

'Oh but I am afraid we have,' said the older man. 'You cannot be allowed to go free after what you have seen. It is unfortunate for you that we were delayed by the mishap with the cart otherwise we could have been away from here. You will have to come with us until I decide what to do about you.' He turned away and swept his eyes over the room. 'Morris, put up your knife! Robert get this stuff packed away and be quick about it, you too Rhys. We must be away from here as soon as we can.'

While they busied themselves with their preparations, Ambrose thought he might be able to creep away unnoticed. He inched towards the door. It burst open and another younger man entered, one that Ambrose had seen leaving the ship.

'men are coming this way,' he shouted, his voice high in panic.

'Ah, Goronwy,' exclaimed the white haired man. 'A fine guard you make! Learn to think before you speak. Next time you burst in like that I will let Morris cut your throat. He is itching to test his blade on this Englishman here. Now, who is coming?'

Goronwy stared at the merchant incomprehensibly then he looked away. 'Emlyn has started a riot. If we don't do something, they will hang him from the nearest branch.'

The door shook as a fist pounded on it from the outside. It burst open the bailiff stood in the entrance. Behind him stood his men. Beyond them, the crowd arrived and stumbled to a halt with Emlyn Tomas held fast among them. They were armed with sticks and stones and anything that had come to hand.

Inside, the Catholics all stopped what they were doing and stared up, wild eyed with fear. Even the old man was speechless. The bailiff looked from one to the other. When he saw the merchant, his eyes travelled up and down the length of him; taking in the rich fur lined cloth, the fine leather boots and the haughty glare.

Ambrose stood in front of him and blocked his view of the room. He straightened to his full height and put his wide girth to good use. His black gown and his velvet hat, placed just so, gave him the look of an irate bishop. He kept his voice light and pleasant. 'What has occurred here bailiff? Can I be of any assistance?'

The bailiff tried to look over his shoulder and failed as Ambrose shifted his position.

'Come, come,' said Ambrose taking his arm in a friendly but firm grip. 'What is all the commotion about?' He guided the bailiff out of the door.

'Is this your cursed cart out here?' the bailiff asked when they were outside.

'A small mishap,' Ambrose explained. 'I am sure these good people of Conway will assist in removing it.' Then Ambrose Chillingworth took over the situation with the authority of a school master; his voice, deep and commanding, carried over the heads of the crowd. 'Ah, Emlyn my boy there you are! I did not get here in time to meet the *le Mychelle*, but here you are, God be praised. What's this? Are you being held?'

'Do you know this youth?' demanded the bailiff pushing his way in front.

'Why yes my good man,' Ambrose replied, patting the bailiff affectionately on the shoulder. 'And whatever he has done, I am sure can be put to rights over a cup of ale. Do you know a good clean tavern here? I am new to your town, I find it quite charming.'

'You are not going to put all this to rights over an ale jug,' the bailiff replied angrily. The crowd murmured in agreement.

Ambrose smiled at them all. He walked over to the ones who held the prisoner and compelled them with friendly nods and gestures to release the boy. Ambrose took Emlyn's arm and turned back to face the bailiff. 'I am willing to meet any expense that goes without saying. You will find me more than generous in this, especially for the inconvenience to yourself in your public office.'

The bailiff's anger melted. He smiled and nodded his head. But a few among the crowd raised their voices in objection. They shuffled their feet but remained standing together in a threatening mass.

'Let us be done with this,' said Ambrose soothingly. 'Today is for good cheer and feasting. A free cask of ale in the tavern for the men here, ladies go off and put on your fine dresses. I'm sure there must be stalls to be raised and produce to be sorted. Whatever will happen to the festival? I'll keep this one out of harms way. You can be assured that the punishment he suffers at my hands will be far better than any thrashing you can give him here.'

They laughed in agreement. They saw the sense in his words and began to drift away to make their preparations for the fair. The bailiff took over, ushering the people along. He stood back and waited patiently for the merchant, his date with an ale cup and a nice fat purse. The freed prisoner sank to the ground with a groan. He had his head down cradled in his arms, his hair and clothing were wet and his breath ragged.

Ambrose bent and helped Emlyn to his feet. He said 'I hope the reward is worth the sacrifice?'

The bowed head lifted and revealed wide eyes of a blue-grey. Emlyn Tomas looked full into the light and their brightness was startling and disquieting, like deep, blue pools lit with sunlight. 'I don't know why you helped' he said, 'but it is fortunate for me that you did. I think I was in for a right stoning there. I don't know how I can thank you enough.'

'I do,' said Ambrose severely. 'You can return to the *le Mychelle* and clear up all the mess you made. I want a full accounting of all that is broken, marred, ruined or lost.'

He walked off with the bailiff, chattering as he went. Behind him the old man and the smugglers stood stupefied with relief.

'Ah!' Ambrose exclaimed when they came to the bailiff's favourite inn. 'The Dancing Bear, how delightful.'

Chapter 10 Wales

Matthew Wheatland, Ambrose Chillingworth's English servant, had a face which reflected his dour nature; deep lines from his thin nose drew down the corners of his mouth and continued down his long, pointed chin. His brows were set at a melancholy angle and his forehead was creased with lines of worry. The overall effect was one of mournful dejection like a sad dog left out in the cold. He had spent the morning searching out for better accommodation for his master. He had found nothing within the town walls and was returning to the harbour when he spotted one of the Welsh servants, sitting on a bench outside the Dancing Bear. It was Aled Jones.

'He's inside,' the boy said as Matthew drew level.

'What! After he told to me he'd never enter its odorous doors again?' Matthew answered.

'He is with the bailiff,' Aled continued. 'He would probably be glad of an excuse to end the meeting.'

'The bailiff?' Matthew was perplexed. 'What's happened? And why can't you find an excuse for him to leave?'

Aled looked at his feet and mumbled some answer.

'What?' said Matthew impatiently, bending towards him. He got on surprisingly well with Aled, considering the lad was Welsh.

Aled lifted his head and sighed deeply. 'It's better that you hear it all from him, and it's better if you go and interrupt the meeting; I'm out of favour.'

Matthew straightened, sniffed, wriggled his nose and pushed through the door of the Dancing Bear. He spotted the merchant and the bailiff immediately. They were seated near the hearth; the rest of the room was empty. The town's people had made their way uphill towards the castle meadow, where most of the festivities would be held.

Matthew could see what course to take from the expression on Ambrose's face. He walked straight up to them. He assumed a worried expression. 'Are you the bailiff? You're needed up at the castle. I have searched all over for you. A bull has run riot in the field, threatening to bring down the very walls of the castle. You can hear the hullabaloo from here, if you've a keen ear. All hell has broken loose and your name is on the lips of every trader with his stall upturned!'

The bailiff leapt to his feet. He stuffed the remains of a pie in his mouth with one hand and brushed away the crumbs from his tunic with the other. He swept up a purse of money from the table and pushed it into his belt. 'I'd better hurry,' he mumbled around a mouthful. 'Do you know I had forgotten all about the fair! Will you be staying?'

'No,' said Ambrose rising to his feet. 'I won't stay, but I will leave word here where I can be found should it be absolutely necessary. I'll go now and settle with the ship's master. Then, God willing, we can then let the matter rest.'

The bailiff disappeared with apologies and stammered excuses. He was paid well enough not to even think about the incident again.

Ambrose sat down, slowly poured a cup a watery ale and pushed it towards his servant. 'A well constructed lie Matthew,' he commented. 'Soon you will be as wily as any merchant.'

Matthew sat down opposite and drank his ale while Ambrose related whole sorry tale of the morning's events.

'...and, if that is not bad enough,' concluded Ambrose, 'I have a feeling that the older man is the one whom I hoped to purchase wool from. He must be, otherwise, why would Aled and his lump of a brother have been there?'

'Aled is outside, looking sorry for himself,' said Matthew thoughtfully.

'Then send him in and let's get to the bottom of this before I have emptied my purse and am reduced to beggary.'

A few minutes later, Aled stood before him with a shamefaced expression.

'So!' Ambrose scolded. 'You belong to a group of scheming Catholics intent on stirring up rebellion with the aid of a printing press?'

'Yes, but if only...'

'And this Griffith, whatever-his-name-is, who also happens to produce the best wool in Wales, is the leader of this little army of monks?'

'No, not the leader just,' Aled paused. 'Master Chillingworth, if only you had not entered that building.'

'I never consider 'ifs,' said Ambrose. 'The matter which concerns me above all others is the fact that you Aled Jones, are in my employ. And I tell you straight, no servant of mine goes off and involves himself in some harebrained scheme that may put his master in danger. While you work for me, you obey me alone. Is that understood?'

'I would not have gone off like that if Goronwy had not asked it of me; it was because of all the confusion,' Aled replied, his hands held in front of him.

'What could have been does not concern me. This has cost me dear enough already. What has been done about the upset cargo?'

'It was not as bad as it appeared,' answered Aled. His voice lost its whining tone and sounded more optimistic. 'The rest of our people are doing all they can to set it to rights but the ship's master is very angry and demands that the costs be met. They'll all be down there still, including Gruffydd Hiraethog. If you still want to buy wool, I'm sure he would be more than willing after all you have done. We are not a gang of thieves and cut throats, master Ambrose. No harm would have come to you, they were only trying to frighten you so that you wouldn't run off and call the bailiff and his men, that's all.'

'What would be the point in me doing that?' Ambrose scoffed incredulously. 'I assume that very soon after I left, there would be nothing in that warehouse but herrings. Beside, you overestimate yourselves, I have neither the time nor the interest to become involved. Right now, I am sure the inn keeper would like to close, we're leaving.'

'To the harbour?' Aled asked. He was smiling.

Ambrose rose and pulled a purse from the folds of his gown. He gave a few coins to Matthew to pay the inn keeper and then he turned to Aled. He pulled the draw strings of the purse and handed it to the Welsh man. 'Aled this is yours, for you and your brother.'

'What for?' Aled accepted the purse as he spoke.

'You are dismissed from my service. I would be hard pressed to find another as expensive as yourself.'

Protestations and apologies had no effect on Ambrose. He swept out of the Dancing Bear leaving them both standing and staring after him.

Emlyn was on his hands and knees teasing coral beads from between the planking on the *le Michelle*. From where he knelt he could see Gruffydd Hiraethog and Dafydd Allen in earnest discussion. They had been talking for nearly an hour, when they were joined by and a fashionably dressed young man. Emlyn recognised him though four years had passed since he had seen him last. The young nobleman was Sir Henry Conwy. He had taken over Bodrhyuddan Hall when his father had died in a hunting accident the year before. The lands were on the outskirts of Rhuddlan and adjoined the estate of Emlyn's uncle. The Bodrhyuddan family were staunch Catholics. Goronwy had explained that it was they who had financed the printing press and the considerable cost of the block letters. Emlyn could well understand the young man's anxiety after the morning's events. Emlyn kept his head down and got on with the task. He smiled. He had come back to Wales.

Sometime later, Ambrose Chillingworth joined the group on the quay side. Emlyn sat up and watched the merchant approach. He wore a neat beard that was a uniform grey like his hair. He was well built with a tenancy towards stoutness. In his black attire he looked more like a physician than a merchant, but the cloth was expensive, a knee length doublet with dark red piping on the breast, black hose, fine leather boots that reached his knees, and a swirling cloak trimmed with marten. He was frowning; the dark brows meeting over serious brown eyes and the thin lips compressed in a stern, unforgiving line.

From where he worked, Emlyn could not hear what was being said. But it must have been all settled amicably for Dafydd Allen smiled and the English merchant lost his frown. Gruffydd Hiraethog, having discovered the merchant's desire for wool, took Ambrose Chillingworth by the arm and marched him up the hill towards the castle. Emlyn watched them go. Whatever the earlier meeting had been about, it was over. Sir Henry left with Dafydd Allen, leaving only Goronwy, the two servants and some other helpers to continue with the task of clearing up the mess. Emlyn left the ship and joined Goronwy. For a while they both looked at each other silently. Emlyn wasn't quite sure how his friend had taken all this.

Then, gradually Goronwy's expression relaxed into a broad grin. He slapped Emlyn on the back heartily and laughed. 'We did it Emlyn. In spite of everything, we did it!'

Emlyn breathed a sigh of relief. It was a further hour before the work was completed and they were free to seek their own entertainment.

The Conwy Spring fair was a grand occasion. From all over the borough, people brought their farm animals and produce to sell at the market; cattle and sheep, fattened on spring pastures had crowded the roads and bridges all morning. Now they were penned in enclosures where they could best be admired by the farmers, butchers and hide merchants. The drovers bought them for English markets and took them as far as Brentwood and Maidenstone. Others were taken to the Bush and Bartholomew fairs where they were resold and fattened to grace the dinner tables of London. Sacks of wheat, barley and oats were brought on stout wagons pulled by oxen. The farmer's wives brought flax and hemp for spinning and woven Welsh cloth. Others brought beans and peas, grown in their garden plots. Pies, pickles and cakes were stacked under bright awnings. There were capons boiled with lard, salted ducks, smoked geese, grisly chickens, mottled pig puddings, sausages, herrings and goat cheese. Smells both pleasant and unpleasant, assailed the passers by.

The town crier periodically rang his bell and bellowed out the order of the market and the fair. There were five prisoners for the public whipping post, two thieves, two women who had not attended church on the Sabbath and a miserable creature calling himself a physician who had poisoned half the town with his 'elixir'.

Sellers stood at corners with cakes, honey, soap and buttons. Acrobats spun in the air from towering human ladders, five men high, Jugglers sent coloured balls and batons spinning in rotation.

In the castle grounds, games had been organised; strong-man contests, wrestling bouts, oiled poles; with the prize of a piglet for the one who stayed on the longest, merry-go-rounds, May poles and ball games. And, to round off the afternoon's entertainment, an archery contest. For this there were many contestants, the prize for the best archer was a Spanish mare with an ornate saddle, donated by Sir Henry Conway, who, at present was having his ear bent by his wife bemoaning the lost of her beads and buttons.

Everywhere there was noise and music. Vast quantities of food and ales were consumed. Fools capered, children ran uncontrolled and pick-pockets wandered through the rich pickings. Escorted ladies quarrelled over bits of lace and ribbons and old hags haggled over the price of jam.

Late into this merry medley came Emlyn, Goronwy, Aled and Jack. Emlyn had a mask with a long nose and a red and yellow hat with bells dangling from the corners. After a ferocious argument with Jack, Aled was forced into buying the same for his brother.

'Two of a kind,' said Goronwy with a sardonic grin.

Emlyn made straight for the tottering human ladder. There were fourteen men standing in a towering triangle while the last climbed steadily to the top. He had just achieved his objective and had lifted his hands to the applause of the crowd, when Emlyn approached them from behind and began to clamber up. The watchers howled with joy; some recognised the trouble-maker from the events at the harbour that morning. Unable to act, the acrobats cursed the intruder as he trod on shoulders and heads. When he reached the top man, Emlyn climbed on to his back and then up on to his shoulders. The human pyramid swayed back and forth for balance shouting in anxiety and anger. Then they were all silent, striving for control. Emlyn placed his hands on the top man's head. The tumblers knew what he was going to do; for their own safety rather than his, they stood rock steady. With a jerk, Emlyn lifted his feet and swung them gracefully up above his head in a handstand. The audience held their breath. Emlyn grabbed his jingling hat before he lost it.

The man beneath him knew how to dislodge the intruder from his perch. Emlyn's hand dropped, grasping a handful of hair. In an untidy sprawl of legs and arms he toppled form one layer to the next, stepping on heads and ears, drawing gasps from the audience as he made a pretence of falling with each unsteady step. When he reached the ground, they crowded about him clapping and cheering, giving him the praise that was due to the glowering acrobats. The crowd began to drift away; after seeing a fifteen-man pyramid, a fourteen-man one offered little in comparison.

The young men wove in and out of the stalls, crunching crusty pies, and buns stuffed with raisins all washed down with cups of cider. Aled had money to spend. He teased the baker's plump daughter and got chased off by the girl's even plumper mother; she was armed with a meat cleaver. Emlyn watched all the girls until Goronwy reminded him of his vocation.

Aled said, 'Emlyn thinks of girls seventy five per cent of the day with steam coming out of his ears, the other twenty five per cent is spent in thinking about why he is thinking about girls.'

They all laughed even Goronwy.

They walked the rolling barrel, tried to lift a cow, joined the ring of dancers around the May Pole until they were driven off for tangling it up, and then watched Jack win the day on the greased pole. He came away stinking of rancid fat and grinning from ear to ear; under his arm a piglet squealed and struggled to escape. By then they had arrived at the stocks where the criminals were shackled for their crimes. They were sitting in a pile of rotting garbage and being pelted with old mangle worsels.

Emlyn did not join in this entertainment. He was well aware that he could have been sitting there himself, had the English merchant not intervened. It would have been too humiliating. He had heard that his uncle was here at the fair and with him his son Owain, his second wife Elizabeth and her daughter Ellen. Emlyn felt that he should seek them out and pay his respects but he was afraid that his uncle may already have heard from Father Manare and the meeting could turn out to be unpleasant. Emlyn pulled on his mask and his hat with the bells; feeling a bit more confident behind the disguise. He walked down to the sheep pens in search of his grandfather Gruffydd Hiraethog.

Gruffydd Hiraethog had two children who had survived the rigours of childhood. The youngest, his son, was now an influential man of thirty six, squire Hugh of Plas Newydd. Five years previously, Hugh had married a wealthy widow twelve years his elder. He had lost his first wife after the birth of his son Owain. With the widow, had come Ellen, a step daughter younger than Owain. The marriage had benefited Hugh greatly, for he now ran the farming lands on the outskirts of Rhuddlan that had been left to Helen when her first husband died. Hugh had not settled there to enjoy his wealth in comfort; he had worked hard to better it. He had become a leading figure in the community and had taken on his responsibilities with diligence and a strong will that soon earned him a fearful respect among his fellow landowners. Hugh had become a Protestant to marry Helen Boutflower. This had started a bitter rift between himself and his father, Gruffydd. They had hardly spoken to each other for over four years.

Gruffydd's other child was his daughter Anne, Emlyn's mother. She had left Wales as a young girl of sixteen, run off to marry an Italian sea captain whom she had met in Bristol while visiting there with her father. Gruffydd had not seen her again. Headstrong and determined, she had gone against his will. At first she had written often, telling him of her two sons and of the colourful life she led in Venice. After her husband had been killed during a sea battle, Anne had written to her father, informing him that she intended to return to Wales with her two children. It was the last time he had heard from her. He had received word, over two years later, from a man who had worked for her husband and herself after his death. Bartolomeo Varini had informed Gruffydd that she too had died at sea on a journey to Cyprus. Gruffydd had arranged masses to be said for her and in time, had placed her sadly in his memories of the past.

Five years later, the arrival of an Italian friar and a small boy in a hay cart had changed matter's considerably. That boy was Emlyn, whom, the friar had said, claimed to be Anne's son. The child then, could speak little Welsh and no English and the truth of his origin was in doubt. There had been nothing more form Anne. The child was obviously not one of the sons born to her Italian husband. Gruffydd had written letters, sent messages and made inquiries of Carlos Grimani, Anne's father in law. He had replied with surprise and disbelief and even gone so far as to suggest that the boy could well be a bastard planted on Gruffydd by some woman he had lain with during his travel s in France. Gruffydd's son, Hugh had agreed. He had never treated his new nephew with anything but scorn. Against all advice, Gruffydd had accepted the boy, insisting that anyone who had known Anne could see that he was the image of his mother.

There was also the little package which Emlyn had brought with him. It had contained a book of psalms illustrated with miniatures and decorated with red and gold beads. This book alone was enough to convince Gruffydd; he had given it to his daughter for her seventh birthday and on the front leaf, in faded ink were the few lines he had written for her in Latin. *Dominus custodiat introitum tuum et exitum tuum ex hoc nunc et usque in sæculum, a* prayer to protect her and keep her safe.

Now, as Emlyn walked towards him, Gruffydd saw him remove a mask and thought that he looked more like his mother than ever. The fine bones, the dark curling hair and the eyes the colour of dove's wings were all the same as Anne's.

Gruffydd's dogs bounded out to meet him. 'Are you coming to the archery butts?' Emlyn called.

'Are you competing?' Gruffydd replied, 'Owain is.'

'It hadn't occurred to me,' answered Emlyn thoughtfully, 'until now. Do I want a Spanish mare?'

Gruffydd laughed at this presumption. 'You wouldn't have a chance Emlyn bach, Owain has carried off the prize these last three years running, while you have done nothing more strenuous that turn book pages.'

'I kept my bow,' Emlyn replied defensively. 'Goronwy and I practised three times a week on a field by the Seine. Look!' he held out his arm proudly tensing his muscle. He knew that it was more due to the acrobatics that the Jesuits encouraged for the plays, rather than the archery, which they had not practised as often as he had said.

Gruffydd obliged him and was surprised. In spite of the thinness, the arms were as hard and unyielding as a tree branch. 'You must compete then,' he said. He never missed an opportunity to push Emlyn forward, to prove that this grandson was just as good as the other.

'I'd rather not,' said Emlyn. 'I have not held a bow for a month nor do I want to draw attention to myself. I have not seen my uncle yet.'

'So? What has any of that got to do with anything?'

'I might loose.'

Gruffydd grasped his arm and led him towards the sheep pen where Ambrose Chillingworth stood with his servant Matthew.

'Trefor!' Gruffydd called as they approached. His farm manager answered the summons and came running across a stretch of grass. He was a solid, dark Welshman. His black hair was short cropped, his eyes dark and serious and his nose askew, broken during a fight three years before. Since the age of fifteen he had worked for Gruffydd and could be relied upon to run the holding during his master's frequent absences. In his hand he carried a long bow.

'There,' said Gruffydd. 'Take that Emlyn, and practice. Trefor go and enter Emlyn's name in the archery competition.'

'No Tad-cu.' Emlyn protested 'I...'

'No? Come boy it is only a game and you can't hide from them forever. I have arranged for you to accompany me on the harp this evening. I have written a special *Englyn.*'

'What!' Emlyn cried. 'Tad-cu I wish you had asked me first. I am no longer the child that must me ordered and organised. Have I no will of my own?'

Gruffydd laughed and patted his grandson on the back. 'Not a shred,' he replied. He sat on the bench beside Ambrose Chillingworth and had Trefor put up a hay bale with a target on it.

Scarcely able to contain his anger, Emlyn practised shooting for an hour. He hit just twice. The bow was inferior and his mind churned with anxiety, fear and lack of confidence. When his companions found him, they only laughed when they discovered what he was going to do.

Emlyn's cheeks reddened with shame. In a last attempt to avoid his fate, he said, 'Goronwy is better then I am Tad-cu, why not have him shoot in my place?'

'That's not true!' Goronwy replied, ignoring Emlyn's hostile glare. 'Beside, I would not put myself up against that lot of nobles and gentlemen and neither should you.'

'Nor I,' said Aled Jones who stood beside him. 'I'm sure the winner is chosen before they begin.'

'What do you mean boy?' Gruffydd asked suspiciously.

'You don't think they are going to give that fine horse as a prise to just anyone do you master Gruffydd?' Aled answered. 'They will find some reason for disqualifying the true winner and the contest will be fixed so that Owain wins. That's the way it was last year.'

'That is a serious accusation, Aled Jones.'

'Sorry master Gruffydd. Forget I ever spoke. I'm sure I was mistaken anyway.'

'Quite so!' Ambrose Chillingworth agreed.

Resigned to his fate, Emlyn heard the blast of trumpets summoning the competitors. He turned to Aled and said 'Can you send someone to fetch my own bow? It's at the inn of The Hat on the harbour.'

'Jack will go,' said Aled.

Jack nodded his fair head and widened his perpetual grin. Emlyn explained to him in detail exactly where to find the bow and Jack ran off in a shuffling gait leaving his piglet behind with the penned sheep.

Slowly Emlyn began to walk towards the castle. The others babbled on excitedly beside him.

Flags fluttered from the towers and banners stirred in the light breeze from the sea. Within the grounds stood a group of foppishly dressed young men who were waiting to take part in the archery contest; among them stood Emlyn's cousin Owain. They hated each other with a bitter rivalry that had existed between them since childhood. Following his father's example, he had treated his bastard cousin with scorn and contempt. He always took pleasure in insulting Emlyn or involving him in some scheme or wrong doing for which Emlyn invariably took the blame.

But Emlyn was not defenceless. At first he had fought Owain with fists, feet, teeth and nails until his uncle had shown him by harsh punishment, the futility of his actions. Emlyn had turned to his lessons with a determination to better his cousin. It was one field in which Owain had never been able to get the better of him. They had been a Catholic family then and Emlyn's willingness to learn had led to his uncle's decision, to send the boy to France to be educated for a life in the church. Squire Hugh had considered it an excellent solution and had even made a generous donation to the Society of Jesus to insure that the unwanted boy did not return. Unknown to Emlyn, Squire Hugh would be quite willing to swear to the boys' legitimacy, should Father Manare inquire into the matter.

Owain was in Conwy to meet the parents of his betrothed, Harriet Crew. Her family had come to the festival. Owain was going to have to pretend an interest. He had met the girl at the age of seven. Now she was sixteen and said to be plain. He was not interested. Her family was descended from the Norman barons de Montalt who owned land in Mold and Ysceifiog. They had a son, off somewhere in Europe. It was to be a match that would benefit both families. But what Owain wanted more than anything else, were the rich grazing lands in the rounded hills that rose above the vale of Conwy; owned at present by his grandfather Gruffydd Hiraethog.

Owain was twenty and had grown up as handsome as they had all hoped he would. He had the corn-flower blue eyes and the flaxen hair of his mother. Emlyn, he reflected, used to be a dirty sort of brown colour. He might have had a wash or two since he had left at the age of thirteen but he had never been much to look at against the classical looks of his cousin.

Owain now had two friends of his own age with him; sons of landowners like himself. The tallest was Robert Jenkinson, round shouldered, with a trim waist and a long thin face. He was dressed like a courtier, 'foppish' his father called him; as if to further prove this point, Robert wore an extraordinary hat. It sat on his mouse brown hair resembling an empty sack with tassels and fringes and feathers dangling from it.

The other man was of a sober nature. Stephen Howell of Tywysog, the youngest son of four who had no hope of inheriting his father's estate. He considered himself a scholar and a poet and was forever boring his friends with his tedious, badly constructed verse. He was small and dark, a typical Welshman. This fact annoyed him considerably. It was popular among young nobles to adopt the English tongue and customs, now that Wales was firmly established as part of Queen Elizabeth's England. Of the three young men, Stephen Howell was the only one who could speak Welsh with any fluency. The people of Conwy stopped their work, momentarily to stare at Owain and his friends with rude hostility; they despised them for being noblemen's sons turned English.

Owain stood gracefully, one hand at his hip above the skirt of his slashed doublet. It was as yellow as buttercups. His hose, were white and showed off his muscular legs to perfection; at least Mari Gwladys Pugh, above the apothecary had said so; Owain, had spent a comfortable night there. From his other hand, his expensive hat dangled, trailing swan feathers in the grime.

'Owain, is that your grandfather the bard?' Stephen Howell asked, watching a group enter the clearing.

Owain spun around in alarm. He was afraid of Gruffydd Hiraethog. This stern religious man never stopped berating him for his lack of Welsh and never spoke to him in any other tongue. Owain went out of his way to avoid a meeting whenever he could. This time, in the company of his friends, he stood his ground and waited for them to approach.

Gruffydd noticed him. He offered a minimal nod in his direction but continued on his way with no intention of pausing. Owain released a breath of relief and examined the old man's companions. He recognised one with surprise; Goronwy the forester's son who had gone to Paris with Emlyn.

'Good God!' Robert Jenkinson exclaimed. 'Is that your Emlyn, the one with the fool's hat?'

Owain looked closer. It was indeed Emlyn. He was holding a bow. Owain burst into laughter.

'I thought he was going to be a priest,' said Stephen.

'The papists must have let him out.' Owain replied. 'I wonder if father knows.'

'I saw him this morning at the harbour,' said Robert. 'Remember I told you all about it and you weren't listening? Well he was the one that started it all.'

Owain's mouth set in a sneer. 'That's a relief,' he said. 'Emlyn may have grown an inch or two but he hasn't changed any other way. He's not going to compete for the mare is he?'

'Don't worry Owain,' said Robert reassuringly. 'He probably hasn't held a bow since he left.'

There were many competitors. A length of grass had been cleared of stall holders and dogs and children and refuse. At the far end three targets were mounted. Each archer fired three arrows into the target. Out of this the best were selected to compete in the final game. Stephen Howell had made a hopeless shot and had not been selected for the following try, archery was not among his talents.

Owain, Stephen and Robert walked over to where the prize stood. They passed Emlyn where he stood waiting his turn with a grim expression; beside him stood Goronwy. Owain stopped. He folded his arms across his fine doublet and looked at Emlyn with disdain before moving away. Emlyn said nothing.

Owain and his friends walked over to see the Spanish horse. She was a graceful creature the colour of sand; tossing her arched neck. Her silken flanks shone from brushing and the silver in her harness winked in the bright sunlight.

'She is the most beautiful horse I have ever seen,' said Owain.

'She's a fine looking beast,' agreed Robert. 'Her legs are so slender and graceful though, they might snap like dry branches if she ran on rough ground.'

'I do not intend to run her on rough ground.' Owain replied.

Awaiting his turn, Emlyn stood before the butts and held a finger to the wind. He felt better now with his own bow in his hand, but he still felt uneasy to compete against his cousin.

'They will probably lengthen the distance as they go along,' Goronwy said squinting his eyes at the distance. 'Anyway, you can't possibly win nor should you try.'

'Why not?' Emlyn replied indignantly. 'I have as much chance as Owain.'

'But what if you do win?'

'Then I will have a good horse and saddle and will make Owain furious.'

'That's what you want isn't it? Emlyn you are not thinking. If you take the prize_'

'God willing.'

'If you take the prize, then Owain will be more than furious. Have you forgotten how he is? He will hound you and badger you and give you no peace until he has won it from you. He will make your life a misery and that means mine too. We will not be left in peace to print the pamphlets. If he discovers what we are up to, then nothing would please him more than to see us weighed down with chains and led off to the hangman's noose.'

'I hadn't thought of that,' said Emlyn thoughtfully. 'Still he will never discover our whereabouts and this will be a wonderful chance to better him.'

'Look, it's your turn,' said Goronwy biting his nail with worry. 'Remember what I said and shoot badly.'

Emlyn took his place and measured the distance. He stood poised for a moment and then loosed his arrows rapidly one after the other. They thudded into the centre. Three golds! A gasp rose from the onlookers. Emlyn turned to Goronwy and smiled.

Goronwy did not smile back. 'As always Emlyn Tomas, you are acting like a fool. The last thing we need at present is to draw further attention to ourselves, and you have done nothing but that ever since we arrived!'

Emlyn looked at him in surprise. Since they had left France, Goronwy had become very serious. It was difficult to get a laugh out of him any more.

'I did not want this Goronwy,' he said throwing his bow to the ground. 'Nor was I particularly taken with risking my life so that we could off-load everything from the ship without anyone noticing. As you see, I have a good chance of winning that horse and_'

'And, you will not give it up to safeguard all that we have worked for?'

'I didn't say that!'

'But that's what you mean to do! Look they are all gathering for the final shoot, to watch the great Emlyn Tomas better his cousin and march off with the prize.' Goronwy's words were tinged with disdain. 'Emlyn do not cause us any trouble here. If you insist on winning this, your involvement in our cause is finished!'

Emlyn laughed in disbelief.

Goronwy turned his back and marched off to join Gruffydd Hiraethog and the English merchant who had taken seats on the benches provided for the spectators.

Emlyn watched him go, seriously concerned by his friend's words.

A fanfare of trumpets commanded the attention of all. Flags waved, pennants streamed, bets were placed and the people of Conwy settled down to hear the Justice of Chester and North Wales give his annual speech. It promised to be as dull, colourless and as rambling as it always was; it also promised to be in English, which meant it would have to be endured twice with the translation of the interpreter.

The speech began: Fans fluttered in the hands of twittering ladies; the elderly, who had seen it all before, yawned and nodded off and bored children fidgeted and fretted. The twelve competitors waited impatiently and the hot sun baked them all the way through the droning soliloquy.

Here was gathered the pride of North Wales. The landowners, some who could claim proud descent from the Welsh princes and the rest who boasted an impressive pedigree from wherever they could find one adaptable enough to fit their needs. The least drop of royal blood gave a man excuse to hold up his head and call himself noble and with this nobility, came the mansions and the land. These were more often pre-church lands, which sustained a squire's family, servants and a style of life that was luxurious and impressive. Among those gathered were the Mostyns of Flint, the Herberts, the Gruffydds of Penrhyn, the Bulkeleys of Holywell, the Wynns of Gwydir and the Morgans of Rhuddlan. With these were the wealthy clergymen, the lesser squires, successful yeomen, the merchants and affluent burgesses, who could outshine any landlord in their expensive, boastful attire. They all sat under the sun, ignoring the Justice of Chester and North Wales, exchanging news and views, setting up deals and even discussing advantageous marriages.

Gruffydd Hiraethog sat with the English merchant. Ambrose had bought all his wool and had arranged to travel up the vale to buy more which Gruffydd had held back to sell at Blackfriars later that year. After their first encounter in the warehouse, they got on remarkably well and sat chatting amiably on many topics of shared interest. After seeing Emlyn shoot for the selection, they had both placed their money on him with hopes of doubling it. This had been a costly day for the English merchant.

At last the speech came to a blessed end. The stout Justice of the Peace sat down amidst polite applause, and then stood up again, halting the trumpeter before he blew, so his cheeks deflated like an empty water skin. 'There is just the matter of the Knappan,' said the Justice of the Peace. 'Merioneth have challenged Flint. The Knappan will be held in October as is traditional and any who wish to attend are welcome.'

A cheer rose from the town's people and the visitors that drown all else. When it had subsided, the raucous trumpet blew, awakening all who had managed to stay asleep through the speech. The final contest was about to begin.

The archers were divided into four groups of three. They all watched the first set, a drover, a glover and a woodsman's son. The shooting fell short of expectations. In the next set, Owain took his place with an air of confidence, beside him stood Robert Jenkinson. They were both cheered on from the side by Stephen Howell and a group of the squire's men.

Emlyn walked up and down nervously. He couldn't see Goronwy anywhere. The argument had left Emlyn feeling more determined to win than ever. He had greeted his cousin and had thought for a moment that Owain was going to answer him, but after his moment of hesitation Owain had shown his sneering smile and walked off without a word. Emlyn stood still and watched his cousin shoot.

Owain had removed his buttercup-yellow doublet and now stood striped to shirt and hose. The white cloth and the fair hair presented a picture of perfection. Nervously, Jenkinson fired first, one arrow flying off over the castle wall, ruining his chances. Owain's bow sang with the first released arrow. It flew straight and true and hit the target in the centre. Taking careful aim, he shot the next barb. It thudded just below the first, still in the centre ring. The third arrow flew and nestled beside them. A cheer went up from the watchers and under it, the curses of those who had bet against him. Owain bowed elegantly and turned to face his cousin. He gave Emlyn a superior glare and bowed his head like a perfect gentleman.

Emlyn tightened the strap of protective leather on his wrist and stepped forward into his position. He shot as he had the first time, letting the arrows fly in quick succession; all three thumped quivering into the middle of the target. More cheers rose from the crowd. Emlyn walked back to let the next group fire. He looked smugly across at Owain. Owain glared back with challenge.

When the final four where selected, the targets were drawn back further. The remaining contestants drew straws to decide in which order to fire. Emlyn groaned; he was last and before him Owain. The drover shot first, two arrows in the centre and one off to the right side. A butcher's son took his turn and lost one arrow in the grass beside the target. A sympathetic groan came from the town's people who had hoped their man would win the day. He turned, smiled at them and then bowed to the gentry who were sitting on the benches.

Owain's eyes burned with animosity; his angelic face was ruined by the ugly sneer he directed towards Emlyn.

Emlyn said, 'What are you going to do, glare me to death or fire your darts? We are all waiting.'

Owain spat at his feet. 'The horse is mine,' he growled.

'First, you will have to win it,' Emlyn replied.

Owain drew bow and released his first arrow. A freak breeze blew it off its path and nudged it just off centre. Owain cursed. The next two flew true, hissing through the air and landing where they were intended. The onlookers mumbled and clapped thinly. Owain stormed off the field and threw his bow to the ground in temper.

Emlyn contained his elation. He moved to his place and stood still with a whispered prayer on his breath. The crowd were silent. He let his first arrow fly. It whistled as it flew and spat straw as it whacked the mark. Careful this time, Emlyn notched his next dart and with measured slowness, aimed it and let it fly. It followed the same path as the first. A rustle of movement ran through the spectators and then they were silent waiting as if they held their breath.

Emlyn held the arrow, already taut, and raised his eyes to the target. A man had moved away from the crowd and stood dangerously close to the butt. Emlyn felt his muscle jump and quiver. It was Goronwy. He stood with arms folded, legs apart as if tempting his friend to shoot him. Even with the distance between them, Emlyn could see the scowl on his face, the dark brows nearly meeting in the middle and the fierce eyes burning beneath them. His words ran through Emlyn's mind. *'If you insist on winning this, your involvement in our cause is finished!'*

Emlyn stood, frozen in indecision. The declining sun beat on the back of his neck as all waited for him to shoot. The only sound was the cawing of the ravens nestling on top of a disused castle tower. To better Owain was the thought foremost in his mind, but with Goronwy's appearance a nagging doubt had set in. His arm began to ache with the strain; the point of the arrow wavered. He felt sweat running from his brow down his cheek. An anguished groan escaped him. Gritting his teeth, he lifted his bow and shot up towards the tower, just as a raven rose into the air. The arrow took the bird clean through the breast. With a startled croak it plummeted to the ground, fluttered and lay dead. To all that watched, it was a perfect shot, a display of a master bowman, although the youth had now lost the game.

Followed by Stephen Howell and Robert Jenkinson, Owain stormed across the space between himself and his cousin. Reaching Emlyn, he shoved him backwards. Emlyn staggered a few steps and stared at him.

Red faced with fury Owain glared back. 'Are you trying to make a fool of me!' He reached out his hands.

Stephen and Robert caught his arms and held him. 'Not here Owain! Keep it for the Knappan,' Stephen warned. He was afraid that a brawl would begin in front of the Mayor of Conwy and all the gathered nobles.

'What have I done?' Emlyn protested. 'You have won the mare haven't you? That's what you wanted.'

Too late, he realised the enormity of his mistake. His own pride had blinded him to the outcome. Owain had won, but the competition had not been fair. To all the eyes that watched, Emlyn had given the game to his cousin, a gallant chivalrous gesture. To Owain it did not appear as such. And nor, thought Emlyn with regret, would it appear as such to Goronwy.

Chapter 11 Venice

There was only one candle lit in the warehouse. It's dim light flickered on salt cones and lit the table where Bartolomeo Varini poured over his ledgers. It was a fruitless effort, debts ate into his reserves. All it promised was a short future. Since the owner was dead and his wife absent, he himself, as manager of the company had nothing to look forward to but a cell in a debtor's prison.

Torrential rain hammered on the tiled roof and dribbled in through the door, collecting in a corner where salt dissolved unseen. The room was damp and dark and cold. Varini shivered, his quill shivered with him, scattering blots over the column of numbers. He groaned aloud and sniffed. Had he really ever dreamt he would run the Lanarca Salt company from a creamy palace on the Rialto? It was, without doubt, Alessandro's fault. But Alessandro is beyond from all the worry now, mused Bartolomeo. probably strumming a harp and looking down from his cloud at his poor, miserable notary, scribbling away in a mean pool of light, with holes in his shoes and no wine to warm his blood.

The warehouse was windowless and as dark as a coffin, there had been little need for illumination. Outside the high double doors there was a courtyard leading to the canal, where tables were set up in times of trading. Salt and grain had been the only commodities in which Bartolomeo Varini had dealt. It had been a monotonous business but had gone well enough in the beginning.

Bartolomeo had often sailed to Cyprus with the Beirut trading fleet. Cyprus had been cleverly enticed into the Venetian empire through marriage of the Venetian, Carlotta Corner to the ruling Lugusta King, Zacco. The king had unfortunately died soon after; the circumstances of his death leaving a pall of suspicion. He had left an infant to succeed him. Venice had felt it her duty to provide Cyprus and its queen with an armed garrison and war galleys to protect her harbours. The child was defenceless, so defenceless that he did not survive his first year of life, leaving a wholly

Venetian queen to rule. She was given little choice but to hand her island kingdom to her overlords the Venetian Senate.

Venice had reaped the riches for seventy years. As the island lay off the coast of North Africa, on the trade route to Beirut, it paid the Senate well. From Cyprus came cotton and sugar, Massey wine, salt and grain and copper, amianthus and umber. Her fortified cities were fat and rich

It was very late by the time Jacopo, the house servant arrived to take his master home. Bartolomeo Varini didn't hear him come. He failed to catch the creak of the door or notice the flare of light from Jacopo's lamp. Jacopo stood for a while and watched him with affection, 'Messer?'

Varini jumped with fright. He dropped his pen, upset his ink and lost his eye glasses. 'Must you go creeping around the place like a lost soul!'

Jacopo's round face shone with the smile that made his cheeks glow like apples. His eyes glittered. He looked as if he was just about to produce a surprise. 'There is a man to see you,' he said, 'just arrived.'

Varini felt his heart miss a beat. Had they come for him then? Would he see the next sunrise whilst tied to the pillory, jeered at, covered in peelings and refuse? He sniffed and straightened, replacing his eye glasses. 'Who is it?'

'I do not know. He is mysterious.'

A strange choice of word for Jacopo, thought Bartolomeo. 'Did he tell you no name or are your manners such that you did not ask one?'

'No name,' said Jacopo. 'Wealthy though; a merchant, a nobleman flashing with jewels and as dark as a Morrisco.'

Not the Arsenotti then. 'Have you left him to flash his jewels in the rain?'

'He is in the shop, I left him with a lamp.'

'That was thoughtful of you Jacopo.'

'That is why I have this poor lamp which gave you a fright.'

Varini stacked his papers and placed them in a worn satchel. He licked his fingers and snuffed out the candle. What urgent matter would bring a man out seeking him on a night like this? Nothing but ill, no doubt.

Leaving Jacopo to lock the warehouse, Bartolomeo walked around to the shop, sloshed up the steps and opened the door. Rain dribbled down his neck; he had forgotten his hat. It was near dark within, but he could see the figure seated behind the counter, reading by the light of Jacopo's lamp, just a little better than the other. There were jewels, flashing off doublet, fingers and an ear. Bartolomeo stood taking in the richness of dress, the bent head, the silvering beard. 'My apologies Messer,' he said. 'You have waited long? How my I assist you?'

Unsurprised, the visitor closed the book gently and rose to his feet. He said nothing, merely stood in his splendid fur trimmed cloak. Even in the poor light, Bartolomeo could see that he was smiling. There was something vaguely familiar about him. Hopefully, Bartolomeo said, 'Is it a transaction?'

'Do you not know me? 'Tolomeo you old rogue,' said the visitor. 'You are thinner, balder and your nose has grown and your eyes have acquired glass coverings. I take it that you did not receive word from this wretched galley slave. That explains the lack of fireworks, flags and festoons?'

Now, there was no doubt in Bartolomeo's mind. The years tumbled away. Impossible though it seemed, he knew then, that this was the merchant Tomasso di Vincentini, Alessandro's partner in the Lanarca Salt Company. When Bartolomeo had last seen him he was known as Tomasso Cappaccio, the changed name had deceived him until now. It had been close to twenty years since Tomasso had left Venice chained to a galley oar. 'Tomasso is it really you?'

'Yes it's me. Am I welcome?'

Bartolomeo choked, he was overjoyed. 'Welcome! By the Virgin of the Rushes, of course you are welcome! I would not have known you! Dear Lord it has been so long. I never thought to see you ever again. Forgive me I thought the galleys had killed you.'

'Well, I am not dead,' said the merchant, walking up to him. 'Did you receive any of my letters?'

e Bartolomeo embraced him planting a kiss on each sun browned cheek. No he hadn't but he'd read them all since. This was not the time to broach the problem. He said, 'Yes, yes, most of them. You look magnificent! You have met with success?'

'Success? Yes more than you could wish for. I have met a few other things though along the way. This can't wait 'Tolomeo. Come to my ship, we have a cargo to unload.'

'You have a ship? That is splendid!' Bartolomeo exclaimed. 'I cannot believe this is you Tomasso! Of course I will come. Now in the dark? What have you brought?'

Tomasso took him by the elbow and guided him to the door. 'Well,' he said pulling it open, 'it is not salt. Wait and see. Jacopo didn't recognise me either.'

'Jacopo wouldn't recognise his own wife in full sunlight. Do you know he has eleven children now?' Smiling, Bartolomeo stepped out into the rain.

In the great Venetian harbour of Bacino di San Marco, hundreds of ships either lay at anchor or slipped night and day about their business; their masts to the sky like a forest of topless trees. From gondolas to galleasses, the traffic on the Lagoon was never still: it filtered through the blood stream of the city, the warren of canals, and out to the empire of islands and sheltered coasts on sea routes to the Orient. The Arsenal was were the of the long, war galleys were built

Bartolomeo was not impressed with the caravel that Tomasso led him to and said so, when they bumped alongside the, dirty salt stained prow.

'She is not meant to impress,' said Tomasso. 'Once you crack the case of that dull nut, I think 'impressed' will be inappropriate. Her name, *Cornucopia* is well suited.'

The crew had already started with the unloading. The boxes, bundles, barrels and crates were taken by barge to the warehouse and stacked beside the damp salt. Bartolomeo watched it all with mounting excitement. Into the last boat, two triple-locked sea trunks were lowered, the last of the cargo to empty from the *Cornucopia.* Tomasso di Vincentini presented the crew with butts of wine. Bartolomeo noticed the brand that was burnt onto the barrels and was surprised, it represented a wolf's head and was the symbol of the trading house of Don Carlos Grimani. Bartolomeo said nothing, perhaps things had changed since he had last seen Tomasso; Grimani had condemned Tomasso to be chained to a galley oar of a Greek ship bound for the Levant. Galley slaves did not live long, even the strongest rarely survived for more than four years. But Tomasso was here to prove different. Somehow he had become Tomasso di Vincentini and had founded the salt company with Alessandro who had been his friend from childhood. There were many questions that Bartolomeo wanted to ask, but he voiced none of them, there would be time enough. And because he had enough troubles at present, he concentrated more on the matter at hand.

When all was completed, he said, 'You have been to the Customs house? There is nothing unlawful in this?'

Tomasso winked at him, but offered no explanation.

The crew were paid off and free to enjoy the pleasures of Venice, the last boats moved off in a jagged line, lamps on their bows illuminating the water. In the rain and the dark they seemed unreal. To Bartolomeo the whole evening seemed unreal. Tomasso remained mischievously secretive. But the notary had not traded on the Street of Spices for nothing; he could smell the exotic aroma. A thrill of excitement ran though him and he knew that Lanarca Salt company had solved its problems. He would not waste his remaining years in a cold cell with only criminals and rats to see him to his grave.

When they were alone in the salt warehouse, except for Tomasso's four large guards, Tomasso lit candles and lamps until the whole room glowed like daylight. He took an ornate dagger, its hilt studded with pearls, and cut the ropes of an oil-cloth bundle. Layers of protective hessian peeled back, before his hands fell on a splash of yellow.

It was silk.

Silk cloth its self was not uncommon, it was even manufactured from raw silk in Venice or available from Constantinople, beautifully finished in the old Byzantine factories. But this was different. This was the most sought after, treasured fabric of all time. Since it had first been brought from the East to Europe, there was none more intoxicating in its beauty and none more hungered after. Nobles and wealthy merchants, princes and kings, all were undeterred by the outrageous cost. This silk from the Orient showed both the taste and the wealth of the wearer.

Once the fabric was unfolded, it captured the light like gold. Bartolomeo could only stare open mouthed and round eyed, a shuddering sigh escaped him. Saffron yellow embroidered with sea waves, clouds and golden dragons, moons, stars, mountains and rivers. Glittering silver and gold threads swam among impossible colours enhanced with beads and tiny pearls. It was the most magnificent cloth Bartolomeo had ever laid his eyes on, and he suspected it numbered among the most priceless cloths ever to cross the Venetian Lagoon.

'Do you have much of this?' he asked breathlessly; eyes aglow with wonder.

Tomasso smiled smugly. 'One bale of blue, a red another of green and a black,' he replied, 'and there are twelve bales of unadorned silk, all of superior quality.'

'I have never seen anything like it, as if it were sewn by heaven or woven by enchantment. If you get the price you ask, if such a thing can be put upon it, you will...'

'...be as rich as Croesus? No, Bartolomeo. Though in time I should see good reward, and this is not all.'

'There is more?'

'Enamel trinkets, gold thread, ivory, porcelain, rugs, carpets, caged birds and lacquered boxes all luxury baubles and beads to feed the vanity of dignitaries.'

'You have brought all that to Venice? Tomasso who else knows?'

'Of this? None save you 'Tolomeo.'

'You have not declared it to the officials?'

'Most of the cargo is spice, the wealth of Venice. They were content to tax this at the normal rate. They are not fools 'Tolomeo and will turn a blind eye were they are well paid. The cloth was declared as raw silk. I've bought horses and caged birds for ladies' gardens and monkeys too. I heard they were popular again. The widow Fiorenza has arranged for their storage,' said Tomasso. Then, because the notary offered no answer, 'Was I wrong? Are monkeys not favoured?'

'They are, they are,' said Bartolomeo thoroughly bemused, soon they will take over from the cats, Venice abounds with them. Personally I can not abide the screeching creatures. It seems you have all but slaves Tomasso...Do you have slaves?"

'I considered it, but they are a troublesome commodity, they take too much space and need to be fed,' the merchant replied and then added, 'What there is will bring wealth enough. Fiorenza and Enrico, the Cypriot factor, travelled from Constantinople with me. The taxes were paid out of the Lanarca account.'

Bartolomeo sat down, dizzy with the implications of what he beheld. 'There is nothing of Lanarca Salt to pay with, but I trust this will soon change. Alessandro's widow, does she know?'

'Only of the spice, and that is enough to fill her coffer's, there is more too.'

'Spare me Tomasso!'

'I mean more spice, yet to be shipped from Constantinople, I thought it unwise to flood the market. I have a reliable agent there.'

'But there is no market to flood, Venice has lost her foothold on the spice trade. Our Flanders galleys carry less and less to the Low countries and the ports of England. The Portuguese rule the sea route to the Indies and have made it their market. The Turks have imposed higher taxes on spice arriving via Arabia and the Red Sea and Egypt to be stored in the scented markets of Cairo. They have made it a hard commodity to profit by. There is spice to be had, for those who can afford it. If what you say is true, it will delight the Serenissima.'

'Assuredly.'

'Do you know what you are about?'

When Tomasso covered the cloth, it was as if the sun went behind a rain cloud, so intense had been its colour. Looking at the manager with a triumphant smile, Tomasso took a lamp from the table and taking his arm, walked with him to where the sacks and barrels were newly stacked against the far wall.

'This,' he said holding the light up high, 'is black pepper from the Indies and cinnamon and cloves from there too. This is ginger and there turmeric, from the ports of Calicut. These are nutmegs from the Moluccas. I did have two sacks of cardamom, but was offered too good a price to refuse in Medina, the Arabs have a great fondness for cardamom. The ginger I would like to sell to an English agent, if one can be found, they pay a good price for it there. All this means we are rich and we can sit among the noble families of Venice...should we wish to.'

'You cannot hope to keep this hidden,' said Bartolomeo.

The smile dropped and Tomasso looked at him seriously. 'None have seen it but you. For the time being we need to keep it secret. After a few days when we have make the necessary contacts matters will change.'

'Why have you shown me?'

'Because I need your help on the Rialto. And I want you to benefit from it.'

Bartolomeo suppressed a shiver, not knowing whether it was one of excitement or of fear. Tomasso looked exotic and foreign in the golden light, like a prince out of legend. Bartolomeo said, 'You are dressed like a prince and shining with success of your venture.'

'That was for you 'Tolomeo,' Tomasso replied smiling. He sat down with a wary sigh. 'Beside, it is my nature to be flamboyant.'

'Flamboyance is for youth, the taste in Venice is sober.'

'Don't worry 'Tolomeo I know many guises. Tomorrow I must visit the Senate, although I would wish for a day or two of peace and may even get it before trading starts.'

'I think you will; for buyers must be informed and be given time to gather. There will be a high demand and you will not be able to satisfy all. This is bound to upset some.'

'I care not,' answered Tomasso. 'We will sell the Lanarca Salt company.'

'Why?' Bartolomeo asked in disbelief. 'You will have heard from Enrico and the widow that Alessandro made unwise investments, it is true, but it can now be rectified. We have had forceful offers for the company, including the buildings at Lanarca and all the workings. But there will be no need now to sell. Cypriot Salt is reliable if well managed and financed.'

'Not for much longer,' said Tomasso. Then he added, 'I thought the widow's brother wished to buy the company? What forceful offers? Are these from elsewhere?'

'From a certain business that has great holdings in Cyprus and wishes to expand until it owns the whole island and runs it as a personal kingdom. You will know of course to who I am referring?'

Tomasso looked up with a raised eyebrow.

Bartolomeo Varini nodded slowly. He remembered that gesture, the eyebrow was scarred now, a thin line dividing the dark arch, but it was the same.

An expression of delight lit Tomasso's face making him look ten years younger. 'Don Carlos Grimani?'

Bartolomeo did not share his pleasure. 'He runs part of the salt lake business,' he explained. 'From that point of view it makes sense, it is in his interest to run it all, the whole consignment of salt for Venice held in one hand. It has been five weeks since he first showed an interest; the pressure has increased ever since.'

Tomasso found two wooden cups and a bottle with cobwebs on it. He opened it, sniffed the contents and drew back with a start. 'How long have you had this 'Tolomeo? It smells like bilge water!' He filled the cups. 'To Grimani,' he said. He raised the cup to his lips without drinking. 'Things could not have turned out better. I take it, you have not accepted his offers?'

'No indeed, though he was not unreasonable, a better offer than Fiorenza's brother-in-law, who is not really interested but feels bound to assist the widow. Grimani's last offer was just this morning. I will admit that I was considering it seriously. I have the figure and the letter here, do you want to see them?'

'No. Whatever it is, we will take it. Sell Grimani all the salt he desires.'

Bartolomeo sat down and drained his wine with a splutter of disgust. 'Are you going to tell me Why?'

'We have no need of it 'Tolomeo. We will start a new company. With the contacts I have made, trade with the East will be possible for a number of years.'

'You are the same Tomasso, although to look at...well I would have passed you on the street and not known you. The Senate and the merchants are running around in circles while the empire crumbles to the Turk, and you come sailing in with a wealth of scented gold, and contacts along that arduous route for more. If you have no need of the salt, why give the benefit to Grimani? And after all that has happened in the past.'

Tomasso put his cup down. He looked up at the manager, the flash of his ring in the lamp light was mirrored in his steady gaze. He said, 'Because Cyprus, the Isle of Aphrodite will soon be invaded by the Turks.'

Bartolomeo offered a smile of disbelief. 'The Turks? There has been an odd rumour here too. When have we not been at odds with the Ottomans? Suleyman is dead, now they have all gone off to dig ditches in the Crimea and net Russian slaves for their harems. The loss of Cyprus would cripple many a mercantile empire, but none can bring themselves to face the prospect. Many believe it would not suit the Sultan to offend Venice and so lose her favour and her door to Europe.'

'The Senate are blind!' Tomasso replied in exasperation. 'Did the Turks consider the offence to Venice when they took Euboea and the islands of the Cyclades? When the Council of Ten wept at the loss of Methoni, did their tears bring it back? I fear Venice underestimates the power of Islam.'

'It may be so, but it is not going to happen for many a year. There is much salt to be shaken from Lanarca, before it flavours the meat on Mohammedans platters. Why favour Grimani with the sale when others, like the widow's brother, what's-his-name, could benefit?'

'I have good reasons 'Tolomeo, you can be sure there is nothing kind about them. Did you think my heart had softened? That I come ready to forgive?'

'Well...no, but...' Bartolomeo stuttered. He would never think that, the hatred that had burned in Tomasso so long ago, was with him still. Nor was he the young man who had been dragged off to the galleys for duelling in the street with Roberto, Don Carols' son. Bartolomeo said, 'So you plan to sell to Grimani and see him fail?'

'How could I have planned that?' Tomasso replied. 'I had no idea he was interested. However I am delighted that he is...Will it be possible to eat? It has been a long day.'

Bartolomeo leapt to his feet. 'Of course! Forgive me. I sent Jacopo back hours ago, food will be ready. We will leave all until tomorrow. I won't be the same man as awoke this day as awakes tomorrow.'

When the lights were snuffed Bartolomeo turned to check the guards. Then he splashed out into the dark. He had found his hat but the rain had stopped. The night was clear. A sickle moon sat in the velvet sky like a wide yellow grin. A thousand stars lit the heavens. Water lapped steps and gurgled under bridges. Venice lay silent in the early hours of the morning.

On their way to the canal Tomasso stopped and turned, 'I have not used my true name, Capaccio for many years 'Tolomeo. Could you explain my presence as some visiting cousin or something?'

Bartolomeo looked at him with a puzzled expression. 'What cousin?'

'It is a new identity I wish to adopt,' Tomasso explained. 'As you say, there are bound to be questions when we launch ourselves into the market. I have to be someone and I can't be who I am, as I am supposed to be long dead.'

'I see,' said Bartolomeo thoughtfully. 'I do come from a large family that includes some adventurous types such as yourself. In fact, I have a second cousin who resides at Kerkyra, on the Dalmatian coast, he's a horse breeder. He would be the best one to adopt, for the time being. I will send word to let him know, should any inquiries be made. But what of the widow and Enrico?'

'To them I am Tomasso di Vincentini and have been all this time. Why would they speak against me when they would suffer nothing but loss?'

'Well if they are so sworn, then a cousin you shall be. His name is Andrea Spinola but you could easily change it, as he has not been here for years.'

'I assume that Alessandro kept the secret of my identity better that I ever imagined? Would the name Vincentini suffice?'

Bartolomeo grinned and swept off his hat, bowing courteously. He said 'Welcome to Venice dear cousin!'

To Bartolomeo's surprise, Tomasso sang a boat song as they continued on their way. As his voice was not of the excellence boasted by the Gondoliers, shutters banged open and objects rained down with curses from irate sleepers. Tomasso ducked laughing and splashing through puddles.

He is maddened by moonlight, thought Bartolomeo. Narrowly missing the contents of a chamber pot, he said, 'How did you get through the land of Turks with all this?'

In the middle of a bridge Tomasso paused in his cavorting. 'On a camel,' he replied.

***

As dawn broke over the palace of Don Carlos Grimani, a young servant stood outside his master's bedchamber. Beside him stood Giuseppe, the old steward. He was mild eyed, white haired and had the patience of Job. On the floor was a neat stack of clean towels and an ornate jug of steaming water. It had been refilled three times, for the water had cooled from waiting.

'Listen to me Uglino,' said Giuseppe in a whisper. 'You are new here, whatever you see behind this door must never be revealed to a living soul. Do you understand me?'

'Yes,' replied Uglino in the same hushed voice.

'If you ever feel tempted,' continued Giuseppe, 'you will be found floating face down in the Lagoon, as many before you have ended their days in Venice.'

Awed and unable to answer, Uglino nodded his head and swallowed with a loud gulp. What happened on the other side of the door? Was the great man a necromancer? Did he practice back arts in the hours of darkness? The thought of what he would see on the other side of the door made him frightened, yet curious.

Uglino had been a page boy for just one day. He felt uncomfortable yet very proud of his new livery of green and blue. Though not normally a vain boy, he couldn't resist the urge to strut about with a feeling of self importance. Earlier, when the head steward, Giuseppe had asked if he knew where Alessandro Balsamo the salt merchant used to live, he'd answered with a feeling of pride and confidence. Of course he knew the house; it was very near to where he lived before coming to the Grimani palace. Uglino's family were poor and he had suffered all his life from the taunts and jeers of the other children in the neighbourhood; particularly from one older boy, Andrea who was the son of a servant in the same salt merchant's house.

When Giuseppe had then asked him if he could take a letter there, Uglino had been overjoyed. How he would enjoy the look on Andrea's face when the bully saw him dressed in the fine livery of the patron of Venice himself! But Uglino had been disappointed; on the five occasions when he had called to deliver the letters, his hated rival and enemy had been nowhere in sight, Uglino had only seen the notary, Bartolomeo Varini. He would have to wait to savour his revenge.

Now Uglino had been summoned to the presence of Don Carlos himself. Judging from the look of old Giuseppe and the threatening words he was using, he was about to witness something of great secrecy and importance.

But Gieseppe's words had nothing to do with mystery or necromancy, they had been to caution the boy against the dangers of a loose tongue. His master, Don Carlos was a man of rich and varied appetite, some of his habits could even be described as offensive, crude and beneath the dignity of the position he held in Venetian society. The less that was known about the private life of Don Carlos Grimani, the better for all concerned.

On the other side of the door the great man was awake. He rolled over and let out a low, long moan. He was of considerable weight and the large bed creaked and groaned. His toes curled in protest as he placed them on the cold tiled floor. He had a crushing headache. During the night, his nightshirt had rolled up and escaped over his head, leaving him only in his skin, revealing to the room his layers and layers of quivering fat.

He rose unsteadily, broke wind and waddled over to the privy. The floor was littered with half consumed food, spilled wine and broken Murano glass. His foot nudged the pee-pot, slopping its rancid contents over the carpet. He spat at it and thumped the window open. It was still dark outside. He added his contribution to the overburdened canal with a sigh of content and shook himself dry splashing the window. His head continued to pound as he squeezed his eyes shut and rubbed the back of his neck to ease the pain.

A sleepy, seductive voice called from the bed. 'Caaarloss.'

The great man peered through the grey light in its direction. He could make out a mound of milky white flesh tangled in sheeting. She looked strange and unreal. He couldn't remember anything about her. She sat up, beautiful with a river of glossy black curls tumbling over a smooth shoulder. 'Carlos?' She held the bedclothes open in invitation.

The magnificent ignored her and pulled on a robe of Damascus silk. It was red and grubby and stained from the night's revelry. The action made his headache increase. He walked to the table in the centre of the room and pulled a leg off a cold, half-eaten chicken. He bit into the meat and his round cheeks shone with grease.

'Come to bed my Minotaur,' she called.

'Go! Get out!' Don Carlos snapped. He approached, spitting out chicken bones as he walked.

She moved like a Goddess; her skin young and smooth. From years of practice, her smile was generous. It never reached her eyes and she never failed to keep the tinge of pretence out of her husky laughter. Rosa di Turchino, she called herself, the Turkish Rose. Named not after her mixed blood, whatever that was, but from the colour she always wore, a rare dusky-pink cloth dyed for her in Florence. It was a quality that few whores could afford.

Carlos threw the stripped bone at her; she had done nothing to ease his worry. He had received news that his ships from Cyprus had been attacked by pirates and lost to him. A years vintage! A year's supply of Malmsey wine. The loss would not bring him to his knees, but it would take a long time to recover it.

Rosa di Turchino knelt and coiled her serpentine arms around his neck, stroking the oily skirt of curls that circled his baldness. He pushed her away. Her eyes flashed. She sulked and collected her pink clothes, every movement was slow and provoking. She gave him a sidelong, pouting glance and stroked a rose feather over her moon-white breasts. She fluttered her lashes, but whatever spell she had held over him was broken with daylight and reality. Seeing his lip curl with disgust, she draped her silks and feathers over her shoulder and walked to the door. Before she reached it, she turned and sent him a kiss and a look full of promise, should he care to send for her again. She let loose a tingle of laughter and swung the doors open just as she was, half naked. For a moment, she stood in a mist of pink silk before the mantle settled over her shoulders and swaying hips.

Don Carlos sat on the bed and sank down into himself, filled with self pity.

Outside the door, Uglino was waiting with his newly filled jug of steaming water. He was thinking about all the horrible things he was about to see, about which he must never mention a word. Thinking with half anticipation and half fear of things which threatened his very life. Then the terrible doors swung open and Uglino shut his eyes and then opened them again. His mouth dropped open. There stood Rosa di Turchino, hardly clothed at all. It that fraction of a second, before she swirled the silk about her, the gaps in Uglino's education about women were deliciously filled. Rosa walked alluringly away, the two servants beneath her notice.

Giuseppe slapped the boy across the ear and Uglino came back down to earth. He was a bit disappointed. In spite of the beauty of Rosa di Turchino, Uglino had expected something of a dire nature to emerge from the room. He knew all about Don Carlos, most people did and his sisters had often chattered over the family meal about the padrone, they followed the same profession as Rosa, but in a less well thought of area of Venice, where the foreign ships came in.

Down the corridor behind them came the purposeful steps of Paolo Grimani, Don Carlos' grandson. He spoke as he drew level, 'Is the master up Giuseppe?'

'Just about to rise Master Paolo,' replied Giuseppe with a humble bow.

Uglino did likewise. He admired Paolo Grimani more than any man in Venice. He was tall and as handsome as a prince and always dressed in the current fashions and colours that the noblemen wore. This morning, Paolo was wearing stripped hose and a blue doublet. The cloth was edged with gold brocade and artfully puckered and pleated with invisible stitches. The gold chain he wore had links as thick as baby's fingers. His hair was golden yellow with wheaten streaks through it like the mane of a lion.

Don Carlos bellowed for his servants and they crept in. Uglino was afraid of the old man, but there were no other terrors lurking behind the door. He could not keep the tremor out of this hands as he poured water into a deep bowl. It was porcelain, encircled with golden cherubs. When Don Carlos stepped into it, Uglino was afraid it would break, so huge was he compared to its delicacy.

Paolo Grimani dropped into a chair draping his long legs over the chair arms. He began to clean his nails with a small peeling knife. 'Good morning Padrone,' he said. 'I hope I find you well?'

'How can I be well? I am stricken,' snarled the elderly man.

'Not stricken enough to by-pass a nights entertainment I see,' said Paolo. 'We have suffered a set back, we can recover, it is only one season's produce. And we are insured against such a loss.'

'Insured yes, but questions are being asked.'

'Such as?'

'Such as, why did the thieves not take the ships? I still have the three ships, bereft of their crew and cargo. They will travel back with the Alexandrian fleet, if enough men can be found to crew them. And maybe we will discover some answers. Until then, who is going to believe that this is not some scheme? Why did I ever let myself be talked into letting my ships sail with no protection?"

Paolo said, 'I can't remember anyone talking you into it. You managed that decision quite well on your own.'

Carlos shivered as Uglino washed him with fine soap and a sea sponge. Trembling like a leaf, Uglino dropped the soap. It plopped into the bowl and slid between the great man's feet. 'Pick it up oaf!' Carlos snapped, slapping Uglino across the ear. Now! Before I catch my death.'

Paolo let out a contented chuckle. Don Carlos turned to him with a look that he feared. 'I was laughing at your servant,' said Paolo quickly. 'He has two swollen ears already and if he harms a hair on your august self, I shall cut off his member and feed it to him personally.'

It was too much for Uglino. He backed away chewing his lower lip. Giuseppe continued to wash his master as if nothing was amiss. Carlos Grimani examined Uglino with a critical eye. You, what's your name?'

'Ug...Ug...Uglino, Patron.'

'Ah yes, the messenger boy whom I sent to the salt dealer's house. I want you to go there again.' Carlos turned to his grandson. 'Paolo, that the fool Bartolomeo Varini wishes a meeting to discuss the sale of the company. As you were unsuccessful with your last attempt, you can arrange this one?'

'I was not unsuccessful,' Paolo protested. 'I did not press him over much I admit, but Bartolomeo Varini was taken ill and I could only see him to his home.'

'He was wiggling out of it,' scoffed Carlos, snatching a towel from his servant. 'You are young in this business Paolo and I do not expect you to see through men's guile and pretence yet. You will learn in time.'

The morning ceremony continued in silence. Through the window drifted voices from the Grand Canal, distant and sleepy, and the cooing of doves as they struggled for a hold on the narrow window ledge. Layers of rich cloth went over Carlos Grimani followed by embroidered satin hose, silk shirt and a long doublet of heavy velvet. It was blood red, sewn with seed pearls and criss-crossed with gold braided cord. To this were added his jewels and chains of gold. He looked hugely magnificent, transformed by cloth and riches into the great patron of seamen and merchants who ranked high among the wealthiest and noblest men in Venice.

'So Paolo,' he said swinging around to his grandson and towering above him. "Did you speak to your brother?"

'Grandfather I did and to great length, but Lorenzo would not heed my advice. Why should he? He is the older and has never thought anything that I had to say was worth listening to.'

Grimani frowned. 'I had hoped that you, more that any one else would be able to talk him out of becoming a priest. I need him here. He would not have been fooled by Bartolomeo Varini.'

Paolo's dark brows lowered over his lion-like eyes. 'I have obeyed your every wish,' he protested. 'Yet you have hammered me with his misplaced ability for years. You snap your fingers and I always jump to obey.'

'And continue to do so,' said Don Carlos stroking the fur collar Giuseppe had laid over his wide shoulders. 'Before I hand you the reins of power, you have much to learn. You are my grandson, I understand your injury. My wife tells me that you are the best. She has been a mother to you, her handsome Paolo. I know she believes so, but to me, you have yet to prove yourself.'

'You sent me away to study, to learn from the classics. What could they have known of the markets today? Is learning retorie a skill required for buying salt? I am not to be locked up in stuffy rooms with stuffy books and stuffy people! There is nothing to be achieved from learning, but stuffing to impress.'

'Then remain home and be unlearned. It is time you were wed to a good wealthy girl. The details of your careless social life reach me often, so that is a manly task you should be well capable of. Do you father bastards Paolo? I myself have fifteen.'

'Is that the latest count?' Paolo queried cynically. He himself liked to live well too; to drink with his friends, to rise to every challenge they set him, whether in sport, play or loves' spicy challenges. He knew that his grandfather's words were untrue; as far as Paolo was aware there were no bastards claiming him as father. Paolo caressed his stripped thigh, smoothing out an odd wrinkle in the cloth. He said, 'I probably can produce three bastards to your every one.'

'You mean you do not know?' Don Carlos threaded his fingers with rings. 'If they lived they would have come and told you by now, they always do. Of course they can never prove anything, but base born children have their uses.'

'Would it not be better,' said Paolo, 'to wait until your daughter Carmelia comes home from France before I consider marriage? After all, it was your intention to send for her.'

Don Carlos looked at him carefully. 'I did have a husband in mind for her, Alfonso de Vio. Unfortunately I have recently heard that the man is dying. He may be dead already, so I am forced into finding another. She will marry a wealthy man Paolo. I care not who, so long as he has wealth enough to increase our gain. Advantageous marriages is what daughters are for.'

'Then why do you not send for her? If you bring her away from that convent you have shut her up in since childhood. She would be the most wanted maiden in Venice.'

'I have,' said Don Carlos. 'She will return to us before the winter. It is true that the future of this great family lies with you and my daughter. I had hoped that your brother Lorenzo, who is gifted as your father was, would have taken over from me and so allowed me to retire in comfort. But now Lorenzo has decided to join the church. He is lost to me. All that trouble so many years ago and all for naught.'

When Paolo had left the room, the patron sat on the wide window seat. The room was nearly in order. Paolo was not a bad boy, a bit wild but it became a youth to be wild, so long as he did not upset anybody. Paolo's friends were of equal footing. They hung around the Stamperia in Campo di San Agostino, the printing house of Paolo Mannutio and his son Aldo il Giovane. It had been a famous gathering place for learned men when old Theobaldo Mannutio was alive. Now the young men were not so learned, but it was still considered a respectable place to meet and talk of books. Carlos did not think that Paolo talked of books.

Carlos Grimani stared over the canal. It was busy now, the boats slithering through the water were piled high with market produce. The sun had risen, steaming away the moisture. His oldest son Cristoforo, had died at sea over twenty seven years ago. Don Carlos had hoped that of the two sons he had left, Lorenzo would have been the one to follow him in business. Lorenzo had grown to look so much like his father that Don Carlos was constantly reminded of Cristoforo and the hatred that had existed between them.

Carlos bitterly regretted his actions of the past. He had disowned his son Cristoforo. They had always disagreed. But Cristoforo's choice of wife had brought about the final confrontation. She had brought no gain into the Grimani empire when it had been climbing to fame and fortune. And, more disgraceful still, she had been a foreigner! Cristoforo had died at sea without attempting to mend the break between them. Carlos had no choice but to befriend the widow and gather her two sons, Lorenzo and Paolo, into his fold. The window had been difficult about the arrangement. He had sent her away. But she had cursed him at their parting, in her foul, guttural tongue. *As God be my witness, I curse thee! No child will ever grow form your loins. I curse your bloodline, may it shrivel and die with you Carlos Grimani. You will live to rue this day!*

Soon after that, Roberto, Grimani's youngest son had been killed in a street fight. Both his sons were killed in the prime of their life and left only the two babes. Grimani's hopes for the future had lain with the two grandsons. Lorenzo had chosen a life of chastity and if Paolo's seed failed to bear fruit, an end would come to his own bloodline which could trace its ancestors back to Venice's early beginnings. A Grimani had been one of the first over the walls of Constantinople when it fell to Venice during the fourth crusade. The treasure plundered then still maintained the wealth of Grimani and Ca de Blanco. A later Grimani had captured a Genoese galley worth quarter of a million ducats off the coast of Salonica, just eighty years before. Philosophers, Cardinals, physicians, architects, artists, writers and even a Doge had borne the fabled name of Grimani.

Carlos could not allow it to end. He had taken his grandsons from their disgraced mother, had showered them with encouragement and praise. Carlos himself had defied the woman's curse. He had wed again, after his first wife's death. He had wed a young, beautiful girl half his age, Juliana. Although they had no son and she was sick from continuous miscarriages, they did have a daughter. It was through Paolo, Carmelia and whomever Carlos chose for her husband, that the Grimani blood would prosper for generations to come.

Carlos knew better than most, how to rule and how to fit each man with the task he was suited to. He was afraid that Paolo would never head this mercantile empire with anything but fumbling failure. He turned to his new servant. 'Uglino?'

'Y...yes patron?' Uglino stammered in reply.

'Ah, you are a pretty boy. What would you like most at the moment?' Carlos' voice was as gentle as a loving father.

'Padrone?'

'Come boy, tell me something you would like to have.'

Uglino was stunned. He thought quickly, knowing that the opportunity would not be available for long. He was aware that he had to give a sensible answer and not one of greed that could halt the flow of favour before he had gained anything. 'I would like a dog Padrone,' he answered.

'Ah ha, A dog?'

'Yes. A big fierce one.'

'Ah,' sighed Carlos softly. 'Here is a boy who asks so little, Giuseppe, I find that refreshing. You shall have a dog Uglino, you shall have two. But you must earn your reward.'

'Anything Padrone,' Uglino replied with a wide grin. He would always be afraid of the great man, but he felt that a step had been climbed. If he earned his master's confidence and trust, he, little Uglino, could do quite well for himself. He would rise above his enemies.

Don Carlos called for pen and paper. Uglino leapt to find them but Giuseppe, from long experience, was already holding them out. He was smiling at Uglino and gave him a concealed wink. Another letter was written to Bartolomeo Varini, inviting him and the bereaved Fiorenza Caterina Balsamo, should she so desire, to attend a meeting.

Chapter 12 Venice

In the modest house on the Canale delle Torreselle, Tomasso di Vincentini was seated on a window ledge in the kitchen when Bartolomeo stumbled down the three steps into the warmth of the room. There was an empty bottle overturned on the table and another stood beside it drained of its contents. Tomasso di Vincentini, the master of the house, was drunk.

Bartolomeo said, 'You look as if you have not slept at all.'

Tomasso shook his head, pushing back a tangle of hair.

The day before, he had visited the Senate and the collegio and he had waited for hours before seeing them. They had been reluctant to listen to his warning concerning the growing threat from the Ottoman Sultan and his interest in taking Cyprus. He had listened to their arguments but not responded to them. Before he left, he urged them to heed his warning, to be prepared. Tomasso shrugged, that was their loss not his, he had done what he could.

He was wrapped in a fringed bedgown, he had been drinking solidly through the night. Only here, at the end of his journey and surrounded with memories, did he let his defences drop to indulge in the wine so long untouched. On the dawn of his vengeance, he allowed himself this luxury.

To Bartolomeo now, he looked nothing like the sea prince who had arrived in the cloak of darkness. Tomasso looked red eyed and dishevelled, but the dangerous power of the man still lurked beneath his show of indifference; like something hidden under a blanket that none dared disturb.

'Are the servants still abed?' Bartolomeo asked as he entered the room and pushed the doors closed behind him.

'I have told them to make themselves scarce,' said Tomasso, 'there are too many children.'

Bartolomeo moved to a bench at the table, empty of its usual string of chattering children, and sat down. He looked up at the bearded face with its unsteady gaze. 'I am afraid of what you are about to begin,' he said.

'You need not be,' Tomasso replied with a wave of his hand. 'I intend to take a little amusement, as I deserve, at someone else's expense. I have more than paid for it. Now I propose to have it. If you disapprove, I ask only your confidence until it is over or exposed.'

'This is to be nothing quick is it? You have sharpened your talons and will now close in on Grimani, not for the kill, but for the torment. The merchants will be drawing lots for your murder.'

'And you, 'Tolomeo?'

'I am a man of Venice and always will be. Disrupt trade and you harm the city.'

'How very patriotic of you,' said Tomasso leaving his perch on the window ledge. 'Venice acts as always, in it's own interests. Don't worry, I wish the Signori no harm.' He began to pace the room, pausing when he reached the table to refill his cup from the last dregs of the bottle. The wine had given him a crushing headache. 'In this sweet city which you hold so dear to your heart,' he continued, 'resides but one that I would injure, one that I would strip of his wealth, his reputation and all that he holds dear, then I shall close in and reveal to him the reasons behind his suffering before I finish him off in the most painful way possible.'

Bartolomeo shivered. He said, 'On the Rialto yesterday, I heard that three Venetian ships on their journey from Cyprus, were boarded and robbed by corsairs. The cargo is missing and the crew. What has become of them I wonder? Do they lie at the bottom of the sea? Do they carry the chains of slavery? But what has set tongues wagging, is the ships. What enterprising corsair would return three sea-worthy vessels to Venice? They were brought back empty with the Beirut fleet. The loss will serve a crippling blow to the owner; they had been carrying barrels of Malmsey.'

On the other side of the room, Tomasso pushed open the window casements and stood between them watching the new day and breathing the salt laden air. 'How very unfortunate,' he said.

Bartolomeo did not mention the barrels of Malmsey he had seen on the night of Tomasso's arrival that had been branded with the Grimani symbol. Perhaps it was just coincidence, he preferred to think so, but his mind told him otherwise.

Tomasso suddenly turned away from the window as if bored or impatient. 'It can not be helped that you will know some of the moves I intend to make,' he said, 'but I have no intention of drawing you or any other, into it's conspiracy. 'Tolomeo, I am not a fit companion at present, I shall leave before my tongue runs away.'

Bartolomeo stood and walked up to him, to stand face to face. 'Before you do,' he said, 'there are a few things of which you should be made aware. Many years have passed since you were judged so wrongly by the Senate and Don Carlos Grimani. If you have not forgotten, Venice has.'

Tomasso sat on the window ledge. Again he dragged ringless fingers through his hair. Loosened from the ties, it fell untidy beneath his shoulders and across his forehead. He looked burdened and tired beyond tolerance.

Bartolomeo said, 'You are committed to your path. You wish to bring down, disgrace and eventually kill a dangerous and powerful man. To achieve that, you will need help and influence and you will need protective friends. You asked it of me when you arrived, what has made you change your mind?'

Tomasso dropped his hands, they were marked with the filth and dust of the warehouse, where he had spent most of the night moving things with his silent guards. He considered the notary a moment before he replied. 'For the sake of the spice 'Tolomeo, I would have your help, but not for the other. Trust is not a commodity I trade in freely; I have learned to be secretive. In your case it is unfortunate that I laid it upon you. Whatever I set out to do I will achieve. By the time I am through, there will be more than fingers burned. I will be well blessed indeed, if I escape it unscathed.'

'And if,' said Bartolomeo cautiously, 'you inadvertently drag innocents in your wake, will that not burn your conscience? What of her sons? Or have you left your soul on some caravan route along with the camel dung?'

Tomasso swore. He swept his cup from the ledge and smashed it. He fixed Bartolomeo with a stare of numbing hostility. 'I will fulfil the obligations I have set myself, without your righteous flapping! My soul, which has been the subject of some inquiry, remains with me and is unquestionably my own. I shall slip in to this world of commerce and change my coat with the ease of the salamander. There will doubtless be losses and I would not have you among their number.'

'The game is yours,' said Bartolomeo. 'However, I am as caught up in it as a sardine in a fishing net; I could not know what I do and not be caught so; that places me, like it or not, under the wings of your vengeance. All I can hope is, that they are as protective as the wings of a hen and that the only fingers burnt, apart from your antagonists, will be your own.'

The tension left Tomasso, he laughed openly; the only show so far of the wine he had consumed. 'It is you 'Tolomeo, for the love of God, who insists on providing the wings. Do you think that I need protection?' He dissolved into mirth.

Bartolomeo felt the colour burn his cheeks and the indignant anger behind it. 'Venice is tied up as tight as silk,' he replied angrily. 'If you think it an easy task to move in with your spice and your glitter, to nudge aside well established relationships and to break in to a network that spans from the Black Sea to the shores of England with the ease of swatting a fly, then I wish you well of it. I should leave you to blunder your way to failure.'

Tomasso recovered his composure. ''Tolomeo Varini, you are talking me sober. Venice is not what she once was. Where one empire falls another steps in to take its place, it is the nature of empires to totter and crumble. Merchants here are not ignorant of this decline. If they still have the sense that brought them to wealth and power, they will realise the advantages in what I came to offer. Gold, 'Tolomeo, speaks louder than allegiance, than relationships in trade or otherwise. They will overstep loyalties for profit, as they do the world over.' Tomasso paused, drained of emotion. 'Forgive me 'Tolomeo, I am a fool and befuddled with wine.'

'Then you welcome my support?'

'If you insist upon it.'

'You realise that there will be hostility, and not only from Grimani. There has already been a tattle of rumour concerning the Cyprus ships, not concerning you, but if it was by your hand that it came about...'

'I knew of it,' said Tomasso gravely.

'Knew of it?'

Tomasso stood unsteadily. 'The ships were captained by a man who would not turn away Turkish gold. He has died for his duplicity, therefore, can cast no light on whoever filled his purse. As the oarsmen on the ships were Muslim, they are freed from slavery and will see this as the mercy of Allah.'

'How do you know that much?'

'I inquired in the right places. But unless I had sprouted wings, and not those of a hen, there was not the time or the opportunity to act. Do not question me 'Tolomeo.'

'So you have influence enough it seems, with the heathen. You merely bought the stolen Malmsey from pirates and washed your hands of the deed?'

Tomasso's patience was running out. 'It may appear that the attack on the ships was directed solely at Carlos Grimani. It may also be possible that it was organised and paid for by Tomasso di Vincentini. The wine, you have seen was bought in Naxos. You may assume what you will.'

'Naxos?' said Bartolomeo surprised. 'I assume you derived pleasure from its purchase?'

Tomasso's eyes crinkled at the corners but they remained unlit, as cold as fish scales. He said, 'I did. If you are offended by that, back away now as I have advised you, for it is nothing to the pleasure yet to come.'

Risking his anger, Bartolomeo offered one last warning. 'Grimani will kill you. But I will stand by to pick up the pieces.'

'Nonsense!' Tomasso exclaimed. 'Did you not know that he already has? He killed me and every thing I loved years ago. I was already dead when he sold me to the galleys. Being dead there is nothing he can do to cause me discomfort. There may well be pieces to pick up at the end of this, but they will not be mine.'

Bartolomeo walked away towards the door. The confrontation had left him shaken and aware of his limitations. Tomasso would not have his motives questioned. He had allowed Bartolomeo to do so only because of the loyalty he had shown to Tomasso since he had returned. But Bartolomeo felt he had to try at least to sway this bitter man from his grim purpose. 'What of her sons?' Bartolomeo had asked, but Tomasso had ignored that question; perhaps it was one he was not yet ready to face.

The same day, Don Carlos Grimani's new page boy Uglino, paid another visit to the salt dealer's house. Uglino travelled over the sun-lit canal by gondola. He felt important as he sat under the fringed canopy been rowed by a liveried servant. In Uglino's hand there was a tubular box carrying Don Grimani's letter to the salt company's manager, Bartolomeo Varini. When they had crossed the Grand Canal, the gondola slid through darkness into a narrow canal shadowed by high houses. It was chill and damp and the walls were streaked with algae and black mould. They approached as if through a dark tunnel, but when Uglino saw the bridge over the Canale delle Torreselle, it was splashed in yellow sunlight. On it, with dirty feet dangled over the edge, was Andrea, Uglino childhood enemy. Andrea was eating bright fruit and his cheeks bulged with a huge mouthful.

Uglino brushed imaginary dirt off his fine clothes, straightened his green hat with its feather arranged over his shoulder, tucked the leather box under his arm and stood up in full view. His chest swelled with pride. Andrea saw him, Uglino was sure of that, but Andrea's expression did not change. He just sat there and swinging his legs and looking aggressive. Not even a raised eyebrow interrupted the chewing.

Uglino stared at him with all the hostility he could muster. He wasn't put off by Andrea's pretended lack of interest. How could anyone not see the new Uglino, all dressed up with his hair twisted into handsome ringlets? How could Andrea not notice what good fortune had come to the boy he had bullied and teased?

Andrea did notice. Nothing happened in Venice that Andrea did not know about as soon as it occurred. He had scampered through the streets and paddled through the blue-green canals since he had been a small child. He was a street urchin of the best type. A pickpocket, a thief at the market stalls who had never been caught. He knew where to get the best oranges, the tenderest crabs and lobsters, the juiciest cucumbers, the softest bread and the succulent pies that were left to cool on window sills. He was the son of the steward Jacopo's, who had worked for Varini for many years.

Beside him there was a neat pile of fish heads that he had collected for soup. Andrea picked one up and threw it. Then, with rapid accuracy, he threw the rest.

The first one hit Uglino on the side of the head, dislodged his hat and smearing him with rotting flesh. The following grisly missals hit thighs, arms and chest and the final one hit him square between his astonished eyes. Uglino's hat fell into the water and the gondolier collapsed into whoops of breathless laughter. Andrea sauntered off with the arrogance of a Castilian.

Uglino spluttered and cursed and stood, knees together arms akimbo as the narrow boat sped under the bridge unattended. It went under at an awkward angle. Blinded by fish scales, Uglino failed to duck. The bridge hit him on the forehead and sent him sprawling backwards into the fine canopy. The material, hitherto held taunt by withys, ripped and collapsed. The oil lamps on either side, snapped, became tangled in bullion tassels and spilled their contents. The Gondolier's revered picture of Our Lady of the Fishes, flew into the air, plopped into the canal, floated momentarily and spiralled to the bottom. The Gondolier let out a wail of dismay. The boat thudded to a halt, spilling Uglino half out on to the steps of the salt dealer's house.

He got the audience he craved. All stopped what they were doing and watched with growing pleasure. They howled with laughter; they pointed fingers and slapped their thighs. Uglino was red as a crab, smeared with fish and lamp oil and tied up in a tangle of the brocade canopy. He dragged himself up the steps and turned his back on them all. He stood shuddering with rage and shame.

The door to the house was open and in it stood Andrea's father Jacopo. He was desperately trying to control himself as tears streamed from his eyes and he clamped a hand over his mouth. Across the bridge, the hilarious cackle of an old crone undid him. He spluttered, gasped and clutched his sides, convulsed with silent howls. He did manage to grasp Uglino's arm and drag him through the door. When it closed, Jacopo slid to the floor in a shuddering ball of uncontrollable mirth.

Uglino was filthy, tattered and stank worse than a fish wife. He stood in a puddle of dirty canal water with a googly, dull fish eye dangling from his ear. He held out the leather box to the quivering heap beneath him.

Jacopo was beyond control. Seeing Uglino's unique earring, set him off again.

'A letter for the manager Varini,' said Uglino, controlling the seething anger and shame with a note of scorn in his voice.

In spite of the ridiculous looking speaker, the words sobered Jacopo enough to gain command of himself. He led Uglino through to the kitchen, not trusting himself to speak.

On the table, still chewing, sat the instigator of Uglino's downfall. With a snarl of fury, Uglino flew at Andrea, quite prepared to kill him with his bare hands.

Andrea leaped off the table and out of the back window upsetting a flower pot. Before it dropped, he grasped it and threw it at Uglino.

Uglino ducked this time. The pot crashed into the wall behind him with a shower of terracotta and petals. By the time he had recovered, Andrea had disappeared. Only his voice remained chanting ridicule that echoed around the walls of the room until it faded in the distance. Uglino sank to the floor and wept.

Jacopo helped him undress and threw the ruined clothes into a wooden bucket that he placed outside the door. He gave Uglino soap and warm water to wash himself. The smell lingered.

'Don't worry Uglino,' Jacopo said to comfort him. 'You will be able to see the funny side of it all when you are dry and fully recovered from your ordeal.'

'I am going to kill him,' said Uglino bitterly. 'I'm going to kill him, but before I do, I'm going to make him suffer and suffer until he begs for mercy.'

Jacopo patted him reluctantly on the head. 'You won't feel so bad about it after a day or two.' he said 'Were you delivering a letter?'

'I will not forget it!' Uglino vowed. 'Never! Never! Never!'

'Come on lad. Don't take on so. I will make sure Andrea gets a beating for it. I will do it myself,' said Jacopo, but he wondered what Uglino had done to deserve such treatment. Andrea was wild but rarely malicious. He gave the sorry looking boy a cup of warmed wine. Uglino's eyes were fiercely burning with hatred. Jacopo had no doubt that the boy would carry his hatred to the grave.

Until Uglino's memorable arrival, the house had been quiet. The new master had made it quite clear that Jacopo's large family were to make themselves scarce. Tomasso had returned from his second visit to the Senate where he had spent the best part of the morning. Jacopo and his wife Maria had dealt with the morning's activities. Maria had taken the children to her sister's house that was full of more children and sticky cakes.

Tomasso had taken the room upstairs, one that had been empty and bare of furnishings for many years. Now it was richly furnished with oriental carpets and luxurious cloth, with chests of heavy black wood, carved chairs upholstered with brocade and a bed so large it would sleep seven in comfort. The master of the house was rarely seen and the servants soon learned how much he valued his privacy.

Bartolomeo's little room was at the front of the house. He was not asleep; he had been watching the comical events below. It had happened while he was dressing and had cheered him up enormously. He allowed things to settle before he emerged. He headed for the kitchen and stopped in the doorway. 'What an awful smell Jacopo. What are you cooking? Entrails?'

Jacopo gave a demonstration of his excellent facial expressions so that, by the time Bartolomeo had fully entered the room, he knew not to make any further reference to the hilarious incident. He greeted Uglino cordially and accepted the damp letter carrier, turning away to hide his smile.

'It is from Don Carlos Grimani,' said Uglino, resuming his role of page boy with a scrap of salvaged pride. 'I am forbidden to return without an answer Messer Varini.'

'Of course,' Bartolomeo replied, 'and an answer you shall have.' He could not subject the boy to further disappointment, the poor child had suffered enough.

Tomasso was alone in the library when Bartolomeo brought him the letter. He was wearing a simple black doublet, tasteful, expensive and exceptionally Venetian. He stood by the wide window gazing out on to the roof tops of Venice.

Bartolomeo said, 'It is from Grimani. I fear it's contents. It is probably an offer far beneath our expectation, now that I have informed him we will sell.' He broke the seal and unrolled the letter. After a moment reading, he said, 'He wishes us to meet him and his secretary. Now the stage is set. He knows well how to manipulate others into a compromising position. It would be wise to step with care. The page boy tells me that he is forbidden to return without an answer.'

'Write a letter to inform Don Carlos you will be willing to attend a meeting to discuss the sale. Tomorrow we open for business, so you will see him in four days. By then the spice will be sold.' Tomasso paused, then turning once more to the window he said, 'I wonder would Grimani know me? Has he changed much?'

'None will know you for the man you were and I think you will find him much changed, he has certainly eaten well over the years. It is said that his health is failing. He is still as much in control as he has ever been, and greatly respected. I don't know if he could forget the man who killed his son Roberto, though. Remember the one you...'

'Struck in self defence? God curse the day!'

'Yes, well, he died soon after you had been taken and sold to the galleys.' Bartolomeo turned to leave. He had reached the door before Tomasso spoke.

'What happened to Anna's sons? Have they grown up to be fat, healthy Grimani?'

Bartolomeo turned around with his hand on the door frame. He felt that the question was for his benefit. This was the first time Tomasso had mentioned the name of the woman he had loved then. Tomasso did not care about the fate of her two boys who had inadvertently caused so much pain and suffering. Bartolomeo said, 'The younger boy, Paolo is unruly and very popular with the youths of Venice. He cannot wait to see old Grimani in the grave, or at the very least, retired. All Venice knows of the relationship between them. Paolo was sent to me with the first offer for the company. The older one, Lorenzo, is to become a priest.'

Tomasso laughed. It was not a pleasant sound and Bartolomeo felt a shiver run down his spine.

Fiorenza Caterina Balsamo was staying at the house of Emilo Gabrieli, her sister's husband. The house was on the quiet Rio di Santa Caterina. The loggias were long and cool and pooled with shadows. Wherever possibility offered, plants crawled up the pink walls, tumbled over balconies, sprouted in profusion from urns, casks, pots, boxes and amphorae. Chosen for fragrance and beauty the overgrown plants had earned the tall house the title of Ca' de Paradiasia. Among the drooping, flower-laden boughs, hung bird cages intricately fashioned from Lagoon reeds, the birds sang and twittered all day long. At night there were still the bells to listen to, hung from silken threads on the branches were the wind set them chiming. The gardens were the ingenious invention of Fiorenza's sister Giovanna, who as a young wife, had become bored, waiting for her husband to return between trading journeys. This miraculous garden had been her love and passion ever since. Even during the summer months of sickness and heat, when many Venetians left the city, Giovanna would not leave her garden.

The house and the warm welcome offered by her older sister worked like a balm on Fiorenza. She recovered from the long sea voyage and from the rejection of Tomasso di Vincentini. Gabrieli's house was a bustle of constant activity, crawling with servants and children; sons, daughters, nieces, nephews, numerable grandchildren and cousins. They all seemed to share the looks of the Zappe, Fiorenza and Giovanna's Cypriot family. All had the same melting long-lashed eyes set in cherubic faces and a tendency towards stoutness. Fiorenza could not tell one from the other nor could she keep up with whom they all belonged to. Giovanna was wonderful with children.

There were quiet places to be found amidst all this; places children were forbidden unless invited. The Ca' de Paradiasia attracted some very interesting people. On some days the artists came and the poets and writers, always with ladies among them and they brought musicians too. These were favoured by Giovanna who wrote verse herself in the style of Petrach. On other days, there were scholars of Latin and Greek, historians and physicians. All men of learning were made welcome by Emilo Gabrieli. Giovanna had often complained, during the years of the early marriage about Emilo and his love of books.

Emilo had been relieved when Fiorenza told him of the arrangements that had been made for the Lanarca Salt Company, he had been reluctant to involve himself in the salt business, and had only done so because of Giovanna's urging. He was glad that the responsibility was no longer his and offered a warm welcome to Fiorenza.

So there were interesting people to meet at the house, and Fiorenza found the ladies of Venice to be most informative. Word came now and again from Tomasso di Vincentini or about Tomasso di Vincentini. She discovered that soon she was very likely to be rich. From time to time, Giovanna and her husband mentioned the possibility of remarrying.

A week after her arrival, Fiorenza was sitting in the back courtyard with a group of chattering ladies. They were discussing Giovanna's peacock, which was white and missing half of it's tail feathers. Fiorenza looked at the bird sorrowfully.

'That was little Olivi's doing,' Giovanna explained. 'He is my youngest nephew. He took the feathers and sold them to Eugena Cavallini for her hat. Sold them mind! He is a true Gabrieli.'

'That boy should be thrashed,' said the youngest member of the gathering. She was Giovanna's daughter Emilia. Beside her, sat an elegant woman who had been introduced to Fiorenza simply as Bianca, a much respected courtesan and a valued ally in the art of gossip. She had dropped by to discuss the merits of using lemon juice in the preservation of peaches, so she had said on arrival. Fiorenza had embroidered a whole iris on to cloth she was working on and had heard no mention of peaches. She did learn some interesting and often hilarious facts concerning the nobility of Venice; these privileged few were obviously material for common gossip. The fifth member of the party was Emilia's companion the lovely Madalana de Claudio Mazzocchi.

Fiorenza threaded her needle with a strand of blue. The sun was very hot. Fiorenza half listened to the town gossip. '...Carrying for five months before she knew she was with child!' Bianca screeched.

'Poor, unfortunate girl,' said Giovanna shaking her head over her own sewing. It was a christening robe, her thirteenth that she was embroidering with white lilies.

'She is as fat as a sow,' said the lovely Madalana. 'She must have paid a man to lie with her.'

'And who is the fortunate father?' Giovanna asked, without lifting her head. The sun was bright on her lace cap and on the brown curls that escaped around the edges. Light bounced off the gold on her finger as she worked the neat, rhythmic stitches.

'You'll never guess...' said Bianca.

A Negro servant entered the garden, depriving them of this tasty morsel of gossip. 'There is a visitor for Madonna Fiorenza Caterina Balsamo,' he rolled off his tongue with elegance.

They all looked from him to Fiorenza.

'There is a gentleman caller Madonna. He is Tomasso di Vincentini,' the servant said. Giovanna's daughter Emilia and her friend Madalana, stood up and rushed to the balcony like a pair of butterflies. From there they would see anyone who came calling at the house.

'Well Balthazar?' Giovanna said to the servant.

'Madonna,' said Balthazar in a quiet tone, 'he has a monkey with him and a black servant. He says it is for the Madonna's children.'

'The monkey or the servant?' said Bianca with a smirk.

Balthazar turned to Fiorenza. 'He says that he will wait, Madonna, until you are ready.'

'And who is this mysterious Tomasso di Vincentini?' Bianca asked. 'We have all been so curious.'

Fiorenza looked up and found the slanted eyes appraising her. She said, 'You do not know Bianca? I would have thought his secrets would be uncovered by now, after all, he has been here nearly a week.'

'Not from lack of trying,' said Bianca sharply. 'What is the name Vincentini? I would guess that it is not a family name of any account, yet it is on many lips.'

Giovanna stood and placed her sewing on the stool. She grasped Fiorenza's sleeve. 'Forgive me sister,' she said urging her forward. 'We simply must have a look, mustn't we Bianca?' They all trooped up to the balcony where the two girls already stood giggling and blushing.

Fiorenza felt her cheeks burn. She tucked a stray strand of hair under her veil. 'He was my husband's business partner,' she explained. 'The call is probably for the purpose of business.'

'Oh really?' Bianca retorted. 'Don't tell me that you have not heard all the talk?'

'What talk?'

'All Venice watches this Tomasso di Vincentini,' Bianca said. 'He is surrounded with exotic romance. He is wealthy and unwed! Don't, I pray, tell me that you have been on the same ship as he for weeks and not noticed. But then, of course, you are so recently widowed,' she added with a touch of malice.

Fiorenza smothered her anger. Nothing was ever secret in Venice, on the other hand, nor was the truth ever as it seemed. With Giovanna and Bianca in attendance, it was wiser to play along. Fiorenza peered discreetly over the balcony.

There was no sign of Tomasso di Vincentini or a black servant or a monkey.

'If you are looking for me, I am here,' said the cynical voice she recognised. He had entered the house below and crossed to the courtyard without them noticing.

He was standing on the sunlit tiles beneath them with his hands held, palm up as if in supplication. Curling from his wide hat was a white peacock feather. From a delicate hand there dangled a woven, gilded cage with a wide eyed marmoset inside.

'My servant tells me you have a brought a monkey for the children Messer Vincentini,' said Giovanna. She rescued them all from further embarrassment and descended the steps.

'Your servant speaks true Madonna,' he said. He kissed Giovanna's hand and then kissed Emilia's hand and Bianca's and Madalana's and lastly, Fiorenza's. For her, he added a wink. He bedazzled them all with his un-Venetian eyes and his jewels. He was good at dealing with women and managed to get free of them in a short time, without answering Bianca's questions. He had brought Symeon, the servant who had made the voyage from Stamboul with him. Symeon remained in the gondola and greeted Fiorenza cheerfully when she descended the steps from the house. Tomasso bowed and offered her his hand as she climbed into the boat. He explained that he had found a house in a quieter part of Venice that he wanted her to consider for her own use. They would call there before going to the house on Canal delle Torresselle to discuss company business. Fiorenza felt a sudden inexplicable fear. She sent for her maid Maria, for the sake of propriety.

Hours later, in the warm glow of evening, the owners and employees of Lanarca Salt, met at the house on Canale delle Torreselle. Gardens were rare in Venice, where there was little room to plant them. For those who could not live without them, there was always a flat roof. This one was lined with potted geraniums and still boasted the exotic trees that the long dead Cristoforo had brought from his travels. Under Jacopo's knowing care the tall palms thrived and even provided dates. Above the fringed leaves the sky was a wash of brilliant tangerine, mirrored in the Lagoon, it bathed everywhere in golden light. The air was filled with the scent of flowers and the citrus tang of the young lemons on the potted trees.

This was where the company finalised the arrangements for the sale of the salt business and the discussed the start of the new Eastern Spice Company. Tomasso had arranged the meeting with a touch of perfection and provided the best meal, so Fiorenza said, to be had in all of Venice. Bartolomeo agreed and even Enrico, the Cypriot manager, who was sniffing with a cold, growled in agreement. They were to start business the following morning and had already, by word and promise, sold most of their existing stock.

Fiorenza was dressed in emerald green, a rich satin that shimmered in the warm light. Her hair was concealed beneath a blue hat twisted with green silk; from this hung a fat tassel, trembling beside her ear. Tomasso found himself watching her. Her round face turned to him and she held his gaze for a moment before turning away with a dimpled smile. At her throat, on a chain of gold, lay the emerald Tomasso had given her. He had done that for spiteful reasons and was sorry. Before he got to know her better, he had tried to tie her to him by encouraging her through greed or gratitude. Fiorenza had shown a taste for neither; her interest in him was of a nature that Tomasso had no time for and no interest in.

Still, he dragged his eyes away from her with reluctance. 'The *Cornucopia*,' he said leaning back in his chair, 'will take a week to be refitted and loaded before she returns to Constantinople. By then, we should have ample moneys to fund her.'

'By this time tomorrow we will certainly have enough,' said Bartolomeo enthusiastically. He folded his arms and smiled smugly. 'The Loredan have first choice and the rest is assured a sale. I found an English merchant for the ginger. You were right Tomasso, he offered me a price I could not refuse. For the rest I have had to turn down generous offers. If only we had more spice, we need never look back.'

'We will have,' said Tomasso, 'but not until the summer, when the ship returns. At present it is necessary to employ a manager for the Turkish side of business whom I can send with the caravel.'

Fiorenza sat forward and placed her hands on the table, fixing him with her direct stare. 'You will not be returning yourself?' she asked.

'That will not be possible,' Tomasso replied. 'There are pressing matters to which I must attend before I am free to travel.' He turned to his manager. "Tolomeo, I need you here in Venice. Fiorenza waits here for her daughter's arrival from Cyprus, and in any case, I would not send so attractive a woman to deal with the Turk, they may wish to keep her.' He smiled at her and she blushed charmingly. He switched his gaze to the notary, 'And Enrico?'

'I am not going back.' Enrico answered with an expression of horror. His nose was red and shining from constant rubbing. He sniffed. 'I have only just got here. Anyway...'

'...You are neither suited to the task nor capable,' finished the master unkindly. 'Therefore we will have to employ another. As I am not knowledgeable in this matter, I wondered if any of you might think of someone suitable?'

They sat in silent thought and watched the sun turn the day into molten gold as it sank towards the far Apennines. 'I know of one,' said Fiorenza her eyes alight, 'if he could be persuaded, Scipione Barozzi.'

'Ah yes!' Bartolomeo cried, 'Scipione. He is a scholar who works in the Ducal Palace and he would be willing.'

'A scholar?' Tomasso repeated doubtfully.

'Perhaps that was an understatement,' Bartolomeo replied. 'He is a man of exceptional worth and knows more about the Turks than most, from what I have heard.'

'Also,' said Fiorenza, her hand extended for emphasis, 'he knows most of the merchants on the Rialto and all there is to know about them. I don't think he has been to Stamboul, indeed, I don't think he has ever left Venice, but given the chance, he would be a man to be valued and trusted. In his present position he is undervalued to the point of insult.'

Tomasso looked at them thoughtfully. He had to rely on their judgement here, but he could make a few discrete inquiries of his own. It was necessary that this appointment to be their choice and not his. Bartolomeo's opinion mattered a great deal and if he agreed with Fiora about this Scipione Barozzi, than Tomasso was willing to give the man a try. He hoped that he was as capable as they made him sound, for, with no experience, the man would have to be good indeed. Enrico looked miserable. Tomasso said, 'Do you know this man Enrico?'

'I am surprised that you consider my opinion at all.' Enrico replied sulkily.

Tomasso said, 'You are a man of letters Enrico and you do not require the use of an abacus to keep your accounts. These skills are as valuable to me as the talents of the others. I am sorry if I offended you.'

Enrico looked astonished and then brightened under this praise, he even managed a half smile. 'Scipione Barozzi,' he said pursing his lips and releasing them with a smacking sound. He sat in thought for moment and then added, 'From a family of no account. Trained in Sienna. He has been in the employ of the Senate for many years and is more than capable in his position as a minor lawyer. He is perhaps hampered from advancing himself for lack of funds and influence. He is an unusual choice, but I do not think we will be disappointed.'

Tomasso stretched and released a yawn. 'Can you approach him in this, 'Tolomeo?'

'I will make arrangement for you to meet him,' Bartolomeo answered. He had learnt how to judge the master's moods, and so realised that they had all been dismissed. He stood and gathered his papers, feeling pleased at the way matters were turning out concerning the business.

Tomasso was left alone on the roof with the potted trees whispering around him. It was a place of memories. He rested his head on his arms and stared over the low wall overlooking the canal. The presence of Fiora had forced upon him memories which he usually kept himself from thinking about. Here, in this garden, he had sat with Anna and watched her sons play. In this house he had fought with Roberto Grimani, until Anna had broken a vase over the man's head and brought that conflict to an end. Here he had priced her jewels for her, and sold them so that she could leave Venice and return to England with her children, far from the clutches of Carlos Grimani. Here he had fallen in love with her and brought all her plans of escape to ruin. Under this same sky in the warmth of a summer night, he had asked her to be his wife.

Anna had loved this place and the people around her. And it was much the same still.

The shutters of a window opposite creaked back and Maria Foscini, a fisherman's wife, emerged with her arms loaded with bedding. She shook the quilts out over the balcony, snapping them in the air. She did the same thing every evening, singing as she worked. Her voice was sweet and in keeping with the gentle light and the lethargic time of day. Beneath her, her husband was tying up his boat and haggling with an old crone, over the price of an octopus.

Down the narrow walk-way came old Babbett, as bowed as Atlas under her burden of troubles. On her arm was her familiar basket filled with fish heads and scraps from the market. She called out as she walked, in her high pitched summons. 'Here my beauties, come to Babbett my little treasures. Fish, fish, fish! Kitty, kitty kitty!' Out they came. black, brown, white and grey, speckled, striped, mottled, an ear torn on an old ginger tom, a tail missing on another. And the young adolescents, tails in the air, bounding and frolicking but keeping a respectable distance from their elders. Out came the fish heads and bits and pieces, flopping on the pathway behind the feline guardian. They trotted after her, a bite for every one. Their mews increased and mingled with Maria Foscini's sweet voice above. Cats poured out of every crack and door and crumbling archway, off roof tops and window sills, pattering over arched bridges and over the bobbing gondolas that were moored for the night. They knew the sound of Babbett's frequent call; she cared for them like no other.

Tomasso closed his eyes on this part of Venice that he had known at a different time. In spite of her foreign origins, his beloved Anna had felt close to these people. She had felt herself a neighbour almost as close as family. Tomasso had shut his mind against such memories because of the deep pain they caused him. Time had not lessened the pain and he felt weakened by Anna's spirit which seemed to be a part of this place now as it had been then. He wondered if these people remembered. They did not remember him; they treated him with respect as the master of the house and the children looked upon him with awe. He preferred to keep it that way.

Down in the kitchen, Jacopo sat with his head on folded arms. He was mooning out of the window, watching a young woman. Jacopo's wife Maria, the mother of his numerous children, would probably beat him to death if she saw him. Jacopo had discovered, on making a few discreet inquiries, that the young woman was named Rosa and that she was a prostitute who had come to stay with Zia Carlina, the old woman across the canal. Jacopo didn't care what she was, he kept repeating her name over and over. She was his beautiful Gypsy and she was obviously aware of the effect she had on men such as he. Her long-lashed eyes cast sidelong glances as she stepped out of the door across the canal, laden with the privy pot and a bag of peelings. Jacopo shivered all over, satisfied just to drink in her slender form and the fall of her silky hair, as black as midnight. Her bright skirts, yellow be-ribboned with blue, were hitched up showing narrow brown feet and slim ankles. Around one, a glint of silver showed. Jacopo couldn't take his eyes off it. He sighed and let out a long, bear-like moan. There was not a woman alive to compare with her. What a delight to behold, a full, high breasted, round hipped, delicious woman. One to bury his head in and suffocate in kisses.

She shook the bag of peelings out into the canal. The receding tide caught them and carried them sluggishly out to sea. She bent to pick up the pot, every movement admirable. Then she screamed and dropped it. Her hands flew up and her eyes were wide with horror. Her screams went on and on.

In the library Fiorenza was dressed in her warm cloak, ready to make her return journey. She stood still, shocked by the intensity of the chilling sound that ran though her from head to foot. She gathered up her dark skirts and ran for the stairs. Tomasso ran from the roof and followed her and behind came Bartolomeo Varini.

Windows opened, heads emerged, voices called out in question. Feet ran to the source of the terrible cries.

Jacopo was the first to arrive. Fiorenza came quickly after him and stopped at his side abruptly. They all stood, struck momentarily to silence at what they saw.

Festooned with browning petals, left over from a wedding earlier in the day, the boy Andrea lay in the canal. His face was turned to the sky, his eyes glaring sightless. The undercurrents played with his lifeless limbs deceptively. Sickened moans and cries of sorrow came from the onlookers. Hands fluttered in blessing and clutched companions in shared compassion.

'Holy Virgin protect us!' Maria Foscini gasped.

'Get him out!' Fiorenza cried. She could not believe what she saw.

Jacopo grasped an oar and gently pulled his son's body towards them. It sank, overturned and bobbed up. The garland of petals dispersed. The men leaned over and pulled Andrea out. Water poured away from his sodden clothing and emptied from his blind eyes.

'He has drowned!' Zia Carlina exclaimed.

'No,' said Jacopo. Tears rolled freely down his cheeks as he embraced his son.

The fisherman pushed forward and said, 'Andrea could swim like an eel. I have seen him myself, diving for oysters.'

'Is there some mark to show how he...?'

They turned the sad body over. There was no wound, nothing to show how the street urchin had come to his death. Only the staring eyes.

Bartolomeo said, 'You don't think it could have been the boy, Uglino?'

Jacopo shook his head and held the body closer, buying his head in the damp hair.

'Come away 'Tolomeo,' said Tomasso quietly. 'Tell me more about the incident this morning with Grimani's page boy.'

Chapter 13 Wales

As Emlyn had anticipated, Goronwy had been furious about the way he lost the archery contest. He advised Emlyn to disappear for a few weeks until Owain's anger had calmed down. The day after the spring festival, Emlyn travelled up the mountains with Gruffydd Hiraethog accompanied by the English merchant, Chillingworth and his manager. Aled and Jack, in spite of protestations, had been dismissed with no recommendation from their previous employer.

After the fair, Ambrose Chillingworth had found better accommodation at a town house where Gruffydd stayed. It was the house of a Jewish merchant that boasted nine chimneys 'And never a thread of smoke from any of them' Gruffydd had commented on entering, which was untrue for they were provided with every comfort and were provided with a festive breakfast by their genial host before they started on their journey next morning.

Ambrose was secretly pleased that matters had turned out as they had. Gruffydd Hiraethog and his active grandson felt that they stood in debt to him for the way he had handled the incident at the harbour. They were well aware that matters could have turned out very differently, and that they could well have ended up with the boy awaiting trial for treason.

Ambrose knew the advantages of maintaining debtors; many people owed him favours. But it was not this that decided him to include Gruffydd Hiraethog in his mercantile scheming. He had found in Gruffydd Hiraethog a kindred spirit. Gruffydd knew a great deal concerning the wool trade and could provide the merchant with a yearly supply of good quality wool for which there was so much demand in the markets of Europe and beyond. Ambrose considered inviting the Welshman to accompany him to Italy, thus doubling the cloth and the profit.

Higher and higher they climbed from the Conwy valley with the austere beauty of the mountains unfolding before them. The track they followed was cut into the rock by thousands of cloven feet, by generation after generation of sheep following the same route. In parts the path crumbled from the steep slope. The short grass was mottled with wild thyme and mossy hummocks with curled, new ferns. Protruding white rocks held tiny pools of rain water from the downpour of the night before. Gruffydd's lands where suitable only for grazing but it was good grazing and the flocks were vast, spreading down the hillsides like clouds. Here and there was evidence of other work, mills, barns and the scent of a tannery prevailing the air.

As they reached the top of the hill, the wind hit with breathtaking strength. It smelled of sea and summer. Ambrose breathed it deeply and Emlyn was filled with the madness of the wind. He ran shouting to the sheep with a dog bounding at his side. Overhead gulls fluttered like torn rags.

At the top of Moelfre Isaf, they turned downward into a narrow vale where a river wound through rich, damp hillsides. It was evening and the air was soft and blurred with smoky mist lingering in the hollows. The track had become a stony road and on either side thick woodland grew with a tangle of undergrowth. The musty shadows twittered with birdsong and the voice of a stream muttered through deep green pools and chattered over moss-cushioned rocks. Branches arched overhead creating a tunnel of dancing sunlight.

Before them lay a clearing bathed in warm evening sunlight and Gruffydd Hiraethog's house, nestled against a craggy backdrop. Barns and outbuildings squared off an area of ground, sparse of grass and packed hard by years of hooves, feet and cart-wheels. It was a bustle of activity. Men ran out to take charge of the sheep, dogs barked, servants hurried to take the mules and horses and women squealed in the bake-house. The master had returned.

After they had eaten, and Emlyn had run off to renew acquaintances, Gruffydd took his English guest to the Solar and poured him Gascony wine. The Solar was long and narrow and ran the full length of the house on the upper story. A log fire burned in the hearth sending flickering shadows about the room. It was comfortably furnished and held an enviable amount of books. Tired from the long ride, Ambrose sank into a padded chair and watched the last shreds of daylight disappear from the sky in a wash of vermilion.

Stretching comfortably, he said, 'A man could easily spend his waning years in such a place as this.'

'Then stay for a while,' said Gruffydd, 'or must you hurry your wool to the London markets?'

'I cannot afford to stay,' Ambrose replied, 'and nor do I intend to visit Blackfriars to sell the wool.'

'Then you are going to Antwerp?'

'I will pass through Antwerp, if it is still open to us which I very much doubt.' Ambrose replied with a sigh. 'Now many merchants deal at the German port of Emden, or through the ports of Hamburg and La Rochelle. Some even send their cloth to Italy by sea. There is the difficulty of a blockade on English goods. The Duke of Alva intends to cripple English trade in the Netherlands it is not very healthy to trade there at present.'

'Well by sea offers little better,' said Gruffydd thoughtfully. 'The Channel is swarming with pirates; you would have little chance of getting your cloth through that way.'

Ambrose smiled. 'There are pirates and there are pirates. Most of them are English and leave English ships alone, preying only on the Spanish and French. Italy still holds strength at sea; there are few pirates who would be brave enough to take on a Venetian or Ragustan fleet.'

'You intend your wool for the Italian market? Surely Blackfriars is where the Italians buy their wool?'

'True, and they make great profits by the time they sell it to the Levant. I would that these profits were mine.'

Gruffydd scratched his head and looked at the merchant with a critical eye. 'That road is closed too,' he said. 'Aside from the obvious difficulties, the Hanse merchants dominate the trade in Northern Europe and the Italians dominate the rest and that is without considering the influence of Spain. You would be better to return to Russia, at least there you are guaranteed the profits you're after.'

Unperturbed Ambrose said, 'You have no idea my friend what a journey to Russia entails. Apart from the loss of ships to the sea of ice, there are wild, man-eating tribes to contend with, the dishonesty of the various traders and a frozen, barbarous landscape that I would compare to hell, did I not know that hell was molten fire. You are right. There are vast profits to be made if a man could survive all this, the corruption at the court of Ivan the Terrible and the hazardous journey all the way back. It is not courage that I lack here, in my desire never to sit a frozen sled drawn by the thought of profit. Common sense tells me that my chances of surviving such an ordeal a third time is testing God's patience. Beside, it is not for the betterment of the Muscovy Company that I wish to trade, but for my own advantage. I am sixty-two and any profits that I make from now on shall be for my own comfort and for that of my son.'

Gruffydd smiled.'So you hope to avoid the ravages of the Spanish Netherlands and the hostilities of France to reach Italy with the wool?'

'Right to the heart of Venice,' said Ambrose smugly. 'By next Spring we should have a clearer idea of the situation in Antwerp. Trade usually manages to raise its head above adversary.'

With a deep frown Gruffydd replied, 'It can do Europe little good blockading our cloth trade as we supply most of their cloth. The blockade will bring powerful voices raised up in objection, Genoa, Lucca and Venice to name but a few.'

'More powerful than Spain?' Ambrose answered. 'It is Spain who rules the roost now in her determination to preserve the faith you yourself hold to. And Spain spreads her influence across Europe, from the English Channel to Sicily.'

'Hence the blockade?'

'Hence the blockade. What a tangled web England weaves, now that she is the head of the Reformed church. Let us hope she does not tie herself into a knot too intricate to be undone. Never mix trade with politics Gruffydd; they only harm each other.'

Gruffydd stood up and stared out of the dark window. After a while he turned and said 'If you cannot go by sea for fear of pirates, and Antwerp is closed to you, and the markets of Hamburg and La Rochelle remain on shaky ground because of their Huguenot connections, what choice is left?'

Ambrose said, 'I take it over the Alps on a train of mules. I can hire mercenaries and all the help needed for a safe journey. I have buyers. I'll carry it right up to the Lagoon and there will be nothing lost but expenses. We could double the wool by next spring.'

'We?'

'Why not? From here to Italy all in our hands and under our control.'

Gruffydd thoughtfully refilled the two glasses. Some time passed before he replied 'It is a brave idea and I would be a fool not to consider it. But you said to me a short while ago, that a man could easily spend his waning years in such a place as this. I put eight years on your sixty-two, I am an old man and I will not stray from here again. I could not for I have this land on which many depend and I have taken on the responsibility of preserving the bardic traditions here; that, I will achieve to some extent, before I leave this life.'

'That is well,' Ambrose replied. 'Indeed I had not thought you would agree. But you need not travel with me, merely offer me your financial support and send a representative and your own wool packs.'

Gruffydd's harebell eyes peered from above the rim of his glass. He said 'It is my hope that Emlyn will take this land and it's produce when I am gone. He has no parent but I. My son Hugh is well established and comfortable enough to last him two lifetimes. Owain, with his coming marriage, will have more than he can manage. It is a great pity that they cannot be content to have it so. In case of disquiet and feud, I have moneys put away for Emlyn's future. I could invest this in your enterprise, were I sure of your success.'

'None can be sure of what the future holds,' Ambrose replied, running a ringed hand through his grey hair. 'I would be a fool if I undertook this journey without care and information. Care can be bought and information can be bought. With enough financial protection the chances of failure are minimal.'

Gruffydd looked at him thoughtfully. 'Europe is under the sway of the Catholic church,' he replied. 'What of the dangers of travelling as a Protestant?'

'These difficulties can be overcome,' said Ambrose uncomfortably.

'How? By changing your faith?'

Ambrose placed his glass carefully on the floor and looked at his host. He was too set in his ways to change. He believed in the Reformation and all it stood for, but this was not a safe subject to discuss with a man prepared to risk his life in bringing a printing press to Wales. 'I will go anyway my friend,' he said softly, 'as was my intention before I came here. I merely offered you the chance of participating for mutual financial gain. The question of how we believe in God is neither here nor there. You would be surprised at the power of merchants. They provide the blood stream of the commercial world, without which, monarchies and the banks they depend on would whither and fall.'

'Do you count yourself among these?'

Ambrose smiled warily; it was all the answer he was prepared to give.

'I will consider your proposal,' said Gruffydd acknowledging the caution in the words. 'And we will leave the question of God to those better suited to answer it.'

The following morning Gruffydd stood on the wooden balcony that overlooked the hall. Below he could see Emlyn, teasing the hounds and talking with the servants. They were going out to hunt with Gruffydd's falcons, up on the steep hillsides where the perfection of the bird's flight could be admired in full.

Emlyn had played the harp, at the feast held after the fair in Conwy, while Gruffydd had told of the glory of battle lost and won in Wales' war torn history. Gruffydd had little chance to see the boy alone since. Emlyn had played remarkably well, if somewhat softly. It was Gruffydd's wish that his grandson compete in the great gathering of bards and harpers that was to be held in Caerwys later in the year. So keen was I, he thought, to have the boy named Harper, that I wrote to the School in Paris requesting that they give Emlyn leave to take part in the Eisteddfod. He has said nothing of their reaction.

After many years of secrecy, the Eisteddfod was to be held openly by request of the Queen. Too many vagrants had taken to the roads claiming to be bards and harpers and begging hospitality in return for their skill. More often that not, these were poor representatives of the ancient craft and had brought scorn to the name of Bard. The Queen had ordered that twenty esteemed gentlemen of North Wales be selected to judge and sort out the true artists from the beggars. Being a bard of some renown himself, Gruffydd Hiraethog was one of the twenty judges chosen to separate the thrush from the sparrow.

Gruffydd had hoped that Emlyn would learn the ways, if not as a bard then as a harper. As a child Emlyn had shown his love for making music. Delighted with this, Gruffydd had taught the boy all he knew. Emlyn was now a superior harper to the master who had taught him. Gruffydd's heart had filled with pride when Emlyn had played at the Conwy feast. His extraordinary skill was noted by those that mattered, for there were some in that hall who would sit in judgement at the Eisteddfod. Perhaps, thought Gruffydd wistfully, acclaim at the Eisteddfod will change his mind about the priesthood, if that was what Emlyn wanted. A Catholic priest could not inherit this land.

It was not until late afternoon that Gruffydd had the chance to talk with his grandson. Ambrose Chillingworth sat in a chair by the window of the solar, reading. He had bought all the wool Gruffydd had in stock and planned to return to his home in Southampton before the end of the week. They had not broached the subject of the trek over the Alps, planned for the following spring. Throughout the day Gruffydd had thought long about the offer of partnership but he could not bring himself to a decision. Several times he had asked himself why he had been invited to partake in this endeavour. Ambrose Chillingworth was invested with by an aura of calm and confidence. Enough to tempt a unicorn from the other world, thought Gruffydd. He could not think of any better suited to the task than this English merchant. Was Ambrose asking for the favour done in Conwy to now be returned?

Emlyn had been out all day, riding over Gruffydd's lands and flying the hawks until the birds had tired and were disinterested.

'You should have seen Hywel fly!' Emlyn said, entering the solar like a blast of wind. 'You would never think that he was old and grey.'

'Like me?' Gruffydd said, laughing. 'Though I cannot claim to fly to catch my daily bread.'

Emlyn was smiling. He was splattered with mud and dressed in the same patched outfit he had worn on arriving in Wales, worse now from that ordeal. His hair was loose and tossed into untidy ringlets by the wind. He looked wind blown and full of energy. His nose was reddened by the sun.

'Sit down,' commanded Gruffydd. 'You make me feel jumpy. I wish to talk with you.' They spoke in Welsh as Gruffydd never spoke English unless he had to.

Emlyn sat by the hearth and pulled off his muddy boots. 'You should have come with us,' he said.

'Hawking is for young men.' Gruffydd replied, 'I am not going to get younger and this is what I want to talk about.'Gruffydd hesitated, rubbing a hand over his whiskers. He cleared his throat. 'Emlyn, you will be eighteen soon. You will be an age to take holy orders. There is a matter on which we must speak before you decide.'

'No,' said Emlyn. The smile left his face suddenly, as if he had been struck. 'Tad-cu there is something I have not told you. I was meaning to as soon as the chance arrived. It's just that, well...'

'What?'

'There are a few things. First I upset Owain the other day by shooting that bird.'

'I'm not surprised. You robbed him of a clean win and worse, you lost me money. I thought your enmity with your cousin was forgotten. It is not wise to bring it all up again.'

'I did not intend to start it afresh, it was just the way things turned out. Goronwy said I was not to go near the printing because of it. He is afraid that Owain will seek me out and discover what we are doing.'

Gruffydd looked at him with surprise. 'Goronwy said that?'

Emlyn nodded sullenly. 'We quarrelled but he can't do much without me.'

'Well now,' said Gruffydd. He leaned back in his chair, smiling at Emlyn's presumption. The boy was too sure of himself. 'I am pleased to hear that Goronwy has discovered the benefits of common sense even if you haven't. He is right in not wanting to draw attention to himself. There are other matters on which you could turn your attention, some work I would like you to do for me. Before you return to France, I want you to accompany me on a few meetings I am asked to attend.'

With his head down, digging at the cracks in the hearth stone with a blunt fingernail Emlyn muttered, 'There is something else, concerning Collage de Clermont' He stopped and seemed at a loss for words.

Gruffydd sat patiently waiting for him to finish. He glanced across the room and Ambrose winked at him. Gruffydd remembered that he had mentioned a son, although he did not understand the conversation, the merchant would know something of the trials and troubles of youth. Gruffydd wondered if four years of strict schooling had put Emlyn off the idea of becoming a Jesuit or that four years of Emlyn Tomas had put the Jesuits off having him. He was grown now and the experience was bound to have had it's effect. When no explanation followed, he said, 'Is there some problem with the Jesuits?'

'A bastard cannot be ordained,' said Emlyn. 'Father Manare has written to uncle to discover the history of my ill begotten birth.'

'Ill begotten!' Gruffydd replied raising his voice. 'Ill begotten? Emlyn no one is ill begotten. You have a father the same as any man. Under Welsh law the fact that you have no knowledge of who he was, is neither here nor there. How often must I tell you this to put your mind at rest?'

Emlyn stood up abruptly. 'You can repeat it until doom's day Tad-cu; still I would not be satisfied and nor would anybody else! Welsh law no longer applies. Anyway I do not even have your family name to boast of.'

'You want to be a Morgan? Do you ever hear me called such?'

'No but that is different. You are named bard, a name given to you in honour of your art. All know who you are, unfortunately all know who I am not. Why in Christ's name did I get called Tomas?'

'Your mother must have had her reasons. Is it so adverse that much mystery surrounds your birth? You are more fortunate than most fatherless bastards Emlyn. Why not look on this good fortune and look towards your future instead of being embittered about what might have been.'

Emlyn swung around to face him. 'I am not given the chance to look anywhere but at what I am. Did you think a school of novices would allow me to forget it?'

Gruffydd stood and placed his hands on Emlyn shoulders, surprised that the boy was half a head taller than him. Emlyn looked at him steadily with the eyes of his mother, the same smoky blue-grey, the same dark arched brows, the same stubborn determination. 'Where does your anger stem from?' Gruffydd asked softy. 'Is it, in all honesty, because you cannot become a priest?'

'No.' Emlyn replied shrugging his shoulders. 'If I was accepted into the Society of Jesus, I would never know who I was and I would never find peace from that. I don't wholly reject that way of life, I don't feel free to commit myself to it.'

Gruffydd smiled tenderly. This is what he had longed to hear. Emlyn had taken the first step away from the destiny planned for him, so meticulously by his uncle.

He said 'You are Emlyn Tomas and you are my grandson and my heir. You could be many things, your life is yet to begin.'

Emlyn pulled away and sat back down on his hearth stone. 'You do not even know if I am your daughter's son for certain.'

Gruffydd shook his head, stroking his long beard on the breast of his doublet. 'There is no doubt in my mind that you are Anne's son; you look even more like her now than ever and you have her temperament, up and down, up and down just like Welsh weather. Why do you doubt my word?'

'Because the last you knew of her was the news that she had drown and that was before I was born.' Emlyn dragged his fingers through his unkempt hair. Looking up he said, 'Sit down Tad-cu. I will tell you what I have learned since.'

Gruffydd resumed his seat and listened to the story that Emlyn had heard from Fra Sebastiano. He knew that the friar had brought Emlyn from Portugal; he was surprised to learn what had happened before. When Emlyn had finished, Gruffydd thought long on what had been revealed. Eventually he said, 'I knew that Anne could not have drown at sea. The Italian family she wed into may have believed that was true, they wrote and told me so, but it is obvious that matters did not occur as they thought. It was not the sea that claimed her, rather it was some pirate, some Corsair that sold her into slavery. This happens often enough Emlyn even on our own coast line, as it did in Barmouth some fifteen years ago. So the man who fathered you could be...'

Emlyn leapt to his feet, anger and injury burning in his eyes. 'What I am,' he said grinding the words between clenched teeth, 'is a heathen corsair's bastard!'

Before Gruffydd could reply, Emlyn crossed the room, pulled the double doors open aggressively and stormed out, banging them behind him with such fury that they boomed closed and shuddered on the hinges.

Behind him, Gruffydd smiled and, if he had been younger he would have clicked his heels in the air. It did not matter to him what Emlyn was or had been. What did matter to the old bard, was that Emlyn Tomas was not going to be a priest; could not be a priest. Emlyn was now free to seriously consider his future and to inherit these Welsh pastures that Gruffydd had built up and developed with that thought in mind. It would be an advantage however, if he could clear away the name of Bastard, before he inherited his grandfather's lands. Gruffydd felt a warm glow kindle inside him with the realisation that Anne might still live; no matter that it was in some foreign, far off place; where church bells and Christian prayers were never heard, where an other god was worshipped. Emlyn's reaction to this news was obviously disquieting. Until he accepted it or discovered the truth, he would not find peace within himself. Gruffydd's frown made his head ache.

'Trouble?' Ambrose said from across the room.

Gruffydd had forgotten him. 'No, no trouble at all,' he replied. 'And yes.'

'And yes, what?' Ambrose inquired with a puzzled frown.

'On one condition.'

Ambrose rose from the chair, still looking beguiled.

Gruffydd crossed the room to a stout table where wine and glasses stood. He spoke while he poured. 'Yes I will help finance you on your journey to Italy, though my guess is that you are well off enough to do it all yourself. Before we seal our agreement, I ask for one condition.'

'Being what?'

'That you take my grandson, Emlyn with you.'

'A fledgling Jesuit! Are you serious?' Ambrose spluttered in disbelief. 'We have managed thus far to keep our religious differences to ourselves. If this is some scheme of your?'

'No at all,' said Gruffydd, his eyes twinkling like a bubbling brook. 'He is not going to become a priest. Emlyn is free to follow a different path.'

'No,' said Ambrose adamantly.

Blinded with tears of frustration and shame, Emlyn spilled down the stairs without noticing them. He collided with something soft at the bottom. There was a squeal and a flurry of cloth. Unable to keep his balance, Emlyn tripped over the damp contents of a laundry basket that wrapped around his ankles. The curses that came out of him would have earned him a sound beating if he had been within the hearing of Father Barzini. As it was, they earned him shocked disapproval from the face that stared at him from the rim of the now empty wash basket.

'Why Master Emlyn!' She stared at him with an expression of horror. The basket fell from her hands.

Sprawled on the floor, Emlyn clawed at the cloth that covered his face and heard it rip before he gained his sight again. His mouth dropped open.

Blodeuedd Hewitt was pursued by every male, in various fashion, from the age of six to seventy. She was aware of the impression she made and had learnt to make good use of it. Although she was spoken for and soon to wed, to discover that even the priestly master Emlyn was not immune to her charm, was the crowning of her artistry. As any modest, well-bred maiden would, with down cast eyes, she raised a delicate hand to her mouth to partially hide a smile, gathered a handful of skirt with the other and fled to the kitchen, being sure to flash her admirer a smile that was both shy and inviting.

Emlyn's mouth snapped shut when she disappeared. He stood up slowly with Gruffydd's torn nightshirt hanging around his neck like a garland. Forgetting his shame of moments earlier, he gathered up the laundry into a trailing bundle and stumbled, tripping over it as he made his way across the yard to the kitchen.

The room was a large square with a long table running down the centre. From the beamed ceiling, herbs and dried flowers hung in bunches and from the walls hung meat hooks, spoons, pot and pans and all the paraphernalia for preparing the master's meals. Arched windows let in a flood of warm sunshine. There were two women and a young girl, whom Emlyn did not recognise, making bread at the table, up to their elbows in flour. A fire burnt and spluttered from the fat of three roasting birds strung together on a spit above the flames. A thin yellow dog watched it attentively, drool hanging from his mouth.

Beside it, an old man dozed with the kitchen cat on his knee. John Talbot was the priest who had been made homeless after King Henry's dissolution of religious houses. He had lived with Gruffydd ever since. It was through the efforts of this sleeping old man and the letters from Father de Sacy, that Fra Sebastiano had been made aware of Emlyn's upbringing.

Blodeuedd Hewitt was standing in the shaft of sunlight, untying the strings of her bonnet. Released, her warm brown hair fell as straight as blown grass to her waist. By then Emlyn had worked out who she was, the plump, twelve year old daughter of Trefor Hewitt, Gruffydd's farm manager who had lent Emlyn his bow at the Conwy fair; except Blodeuedd wasn't twelve any more nor was she plump. She was alluring and shapely with eyes the colour of the wet moss that clings to river stones.

Although Emlyn thought about girls a great deal, when he was faced with one, he never knew quite what to do or say. He was fine with children like the little novice Carmelia Grimani, but this girl left him speechless. He stood by the door feeling awkward with his arms loaded with washing. A sensation of prickles ran through him like a shower of icicles. He felt his knees weaken as she came toward him, her hips swinging, her lips tilted at the corners and her cloud-white arms held out to relieve him of his burden.

She said, 'Did you not bring the basket?'

'eh?' Emlyn grunted in bemused response.

'The basket for the washing,' she explained.

'I forgot it.' Emlyn stammered.

'Well now there's daft you are. How am I going to carry it out to dry?'

'Don't you talk like that Blodeuedd Hewitt!' One of the older woman at the table warned.

'I'll carry it for you,' said Emlyn ignoring her. 'I was going out anyway.'

Blodeuedd pushed passed him to get through the door, leaning close as if she had missed her step. She heard him gasp and felt him shiver.

He followed her like a devoted lap dog, trailing washing across the yard, through the gate to the herb garden, past the neat rows of greenery, over the grass on the other side and up to the hedgerow where the cloth would be draped to dry.

Blodeuedd dutifully blushed and giggled and artfully dodged between the hedges as he reached a tentative hand out, the cloth falling into a mound at his feet.

'You're very pretty Blodeuedd,' he said. He took a corner of sheeting and pinned it on a hawthorn.

'There's a poet you are Emlyn Tomas,' she replied scornfully, peering from a frame of elder flowers. 'Can't you come up with a better line than that to charm a girl?'

Emlyn looked at his feet. 'I would if I had time to think one up,' he said. 'I'll write you a poem if you like.'

She squealed delightfully. 'No one has written me a poem not ever.' she said.

'I'll write you one this very day.' Emlyn said, 'in praise of your pure beauty and your green eyes and your lips as soft as rose petals.'

Blodeuedd came from behind the elder bush to stand close to him.

The air was filled with the scents of early summer, birds twittered in the woods near by, blossom dispensed bees and butterflies and the sun sank towards the distant sea washing the sky with a flush of gold. Blodeuedd's hair floated like a gossamer web caught on the gentle breeze and her soft skin blushed with the glow of sunset.

Emlyn held his breath and stared lovingly at her, drowning in her mossy eyes, leaning forward, a hair's breath away from her soft lips. Of their own volition, his hands reached out and clasped her waist; his lips crossed the tiny gulf that divided them from hers. Emlyn kissed her.

Ambrose stood by the window with his hands clasped behind his back. The long cuffs, edged with lace fell over his fingers. At his neck a collar trimmed with the same lace, lay neatly across his shoulders. He released his hands and leaned forward, closer to the window. It overlooked the herb garden and the two young people embraced amidst the laundry-strewn bushes. Ambrose pulled at his ear lobe and smiled in amusement. Our young troubadour has recovered, he thought, form whatever it was that upset him but a moment ago.

Gruffydd approached carrying a dish of fruit. He peered over the merchants shoulder. 'Blodeuedd Hewitt!' he exclaimed.

'I beg your pardon?' said Ambrose, the words had sounded like a curse to him.

'He'll get no more than a chaste kiss from that one if he's wise,' Gruffydd explained. 'She's to wed Jasper Overbury, the tanner from Llanrwst before the month is out. He's a big lad and if he catches him...'

'Well I can't blame him for trying,' said Ambrose. 'She's a pretty lass. I'd have done the same at seventeen. I am pleased to see that the Jesuits have not knocked that natural instinct out of the boy.'

'Then you will take him with you in the spring?' Gruffydd asked hopefully.

So loud was the roar that came from outside that they both heard it quite clearly. Soon after, a big man thrust through the barn doors and stormed out with his fists clenched. Ambrose released a snort of laughter. 'That, I take it is your large tanner.'

Gruffydd nodded his white head, making tutting sounds and grinning.

By the hedgerow, Emlyn broke away from the girl. She squealed and flapped her hands, giggling. Reaching them, Jasper, the tanner made a grab for Emlyn. He swerved away, running behind the hawthorn. The tanner followed in swift pursuit. Emlyn ran back towards the house, looking worried. The large young tanner grasped a log form the ground and hurled it through the air.

It caught Emlyn behind the knees and sent him sprawling into the mud. By the time he regained his feet, the irate suitor of Blodeuedd Hewitt had caught up. He caught hold of a handful of Emlyn's clothing and lifted him from the ground. Emlyn struggled, but it was useless. The tanner took a firmer hold on him and hurled him away.

Emlyn landed face first in the manure pile outside the barn.

Ambrose laughed heartily. 'You want me to take that with me? Can you see such a boy take on the responsibilities that will be required on such a venture?'

'I want you to take him because he is like this.' Gruffydd answered. 'I will employ another to accompany him and to take on the responsibilities.'

Ambrose did not turn away from the scene below. Emlyn was sitting up, steaming with manure that covered him from head to foot. A few of the farm hands were preventing Jasper Overbury from further vengeance. They held him firmly and voices rose in argument. 'I'll take him,' said Ambrose. He was highly amused. 'You're right. A boy like that needs direction, my own was the same.'

Gruffydd lifted the dish of early wild strawberries and held them temptingly under the merchants nose. Their eyes met and held for a moment. Gruffydd said, 'Where is he now, your son?'

'Christopher is half way to the New World, God willing,' said Ambrose. He helped himself to a miniature rosy fruit at the top of the pile. 'He is with the slaver Jack Hawkins, carrying a live cargo to the Spanish there. On his last trip Hawkins made a good profit selling Africans, he hopes to repeat it.'

'It's a questionable trade,' said Gruffydd chewing pensively.

'How so?' Ambrose asked, turning to face him.'They are not Christian souls.'

'No, but they could be. A profitable trade I agree, but a dirty one. I hear that the poor souls will throw themselves and their children overboard, so terrified are they to leave their own land. I believe that they are God's creatures like you and me. For that reason, I cannot condone the practice of slavers.'

Ambrose meticulously folded back his cuffs before he took two strawberries from the bowl. 'It is an ancient, lucrative trade,' he answered. 'They may suffer hardship, but their souls are redeemed by their owners, they all become good Christians in the end. The benefit far out weighs the suffering.'

'Still I would not have thought you a man to deal in human flesh,' said Gruffydd scathingly.

'Nor am I and my son Christopher is no slaver, he has no stomach for it. He travels with the fleet for the purpose of other trade. There are many new dyes and spices and plants with health giving properties, for which there is a growing demand in Europe. Why should Spain be the only one to benefit? As you know the lands to the East are barred to us by the infidel. If England is to find a route to the East, it will not be along the roads guarded by the Turk. We must find a new source or discover a way through the frozen sea. A man who lives on an island musts learn how to swim.'

'Is that a trade you wish to venture into? The wealth from the East?' Gruffydd rubbed his beard, pink with strawberry juice.

'I may dabble here and there and make a few lucrative connections.' Ambrose replied. 'I have no mind to risk life and soul in pursuit of that particular fruit. But I would encourage any brave enough to try.'

'Indeed,' agreed Gruffydd. 'Considered as such, it is a long way from a modest trip to Italy. Even that holds no attraction for me. A man could be content with his own sweet soil, his own songs sung in his melodic tongue. I'll not stray again from Wales, no matter how sweet and tempting the fruit.'

'But you would send your grandson, who you have told me, you wish to make a bard of?'

Gruffydd smiled 'You know how it is with the young today,' he answered. 'If I do not allow him the freedom to discover what he will, he will never be willing to become what I wish. Another strawberry?'

Emlyn did write his poem to Blodeuedd Hewitt, but he never gave it to her; Gruffydd never allowed him the opportunity, but kept him busy with the new sheep and tasks away from the house. Ambrose left three days later. With him went the wool loaded on to six mules, and seven of Gruffydd's men, jovial to be going on a wild adventure out of Wales that they had never left before. Gruffydd had agreed to join the venture financially and would collect wool from the outlying farms to send with Emlyn and an assistant to the English merchant the following spring.

Leaving the farm in the capable hands of his manager Trefor Hewitt, Gruffydd wasted no time. He set out across his beloved soil with Emlyn in attendance. The long days of early summer were warm and benign. Gruffydd and Emlyn visited castles and grand houses, farms and hamlets and wherever they went they were made welcome in the Welsh tradition. On the rare occasions he was asked, Gruffydd practised the art of the bard with his harper playing to embellish his tales. They arranged to buy wool as they went. Gruffydd attended the many meetings held by the gentlemen of Wales; those selected to judge and license the numerous wandering minstrels and poets. On these occasions many were turned away disappointed and forced to seek other means of earning a living. They did not reach the high standards of perfection required to be named Bard, Harper or Crowther. Those who did, were invited to partake in the Eisteddfod later in the year.

As the weeks progressed, Emlyn became aware of his grandfather's intentions. Gruffydd was re-introducing his grandson to Wales; showing him a deep love for the country and its people. Gruffydd soothed Emlyn's anger and fear by instilling into him the importance of his mother's Welsh origins and the importance of strengthening his own tie with Wales. Most of the time they walked, carrying just what they needed and often spending nights out in the open. This simplistic life was one that Gruffydd had known often and he settled into the rhythm with carefree joy.

At night they sat under the stars warmed by a small fire while Gruffydd's voice rumbled softly through the ancient legends and the colourful history of Wales. Emlyn came to understand the nature of the bardic traditions and the need that drove Gruffydd to preserve them. After many such nights, and after Emlyn's gentle urgings, Gruffydd spoke of his own life and eventually of his daughter Anne. The sorrow that he had held in his heart for so long over spilled, tears sparkled in his eyes and ran into his snowy beard. Gruffydd could weave words like a magician's spellbinding and the picture he drew of his daughter was one that Emlyn grasped and held forever in his memory. There had been nothing ordinary about Anne Morgan. She was as one born of the lofty mountains, the bubbling brooks and the deep forested slopes. It was as if, Gruffydd explained, she had held in her laughter and in her deep, knowing eyes, the very quintessence of Cymru.

Emlyn who saw much of the same in his grandfather, forgot his concerns and opened his heart to all that was revealed to him. When he stood alone on the craggy heights of Eryri Mynydd and saw the mists caressing the deep hollows, he knew that he looked on the breath of the mythical dragon of Wales. The dragon seemed to breath into him and thump through the ground beneath his feet. He was filled with awe and felt forever joined with the spirit of the land. Emlyn faced the mountains and spoke as if making his vow taken before the altar of God. 'I will go and I will do all in my power to seek the mother who had cast me so ill prepared into the world.'

Seeing him after this, Gruffydd had silently embraced him and left him to his own thoughts for the rest of that day.

Emlyn's steps kept rhythm with rhyme and song as they wove over mountains, vales and farm land. When they called at houses and halls, the elders would often engage him in conversation. They asked him about

France and the weak king; about the Netherlands and the bloodied scythe of the Duke of Alva which waged war on the innocent people there. Emlyn often talked long into the night, until too much ale or exhaustion drove him to curl up with the hounds by the hearth, to snatch what sleep he could before Gruffydd woke him for the next day's journey.

In the course of events Gruffydd heard many harpers. Against these, he judged Emlyn's skill. The skill is there he admitted to himself, but what is lacking? The fingers are fluent and dexterous but there is no heart in his playing. He may have suffered in France from the cruel words of his fellow students, but he has never known true hardship, as have so many of these wandering song makers. It seems that the more ragged and desperate they are, the truer their song becomes, as if through suffering only can the beauty and depth be brought to sound. What are worldly possessions when held against the melancholy, heart wrenching voice of their music? Does a man have to suffer to perfect his art?

With this in mind, Gruffydd did not suggest to Emlyn that he compete at the Eisteddfod. He would have liked nothing better than to see one of his blood carry off the silver harp. Emlyn's youth and inexperience were against him. He played without understanding what his achieved skill was capable of producing. Like a popinjay, thought Gruffydd, who imitates with no knowledge of the words it utters. Still, the experience of Italy, of travel and adventure will bring their own reward. The chance to learn the art of commerce will give Emlyn a firm beginning and perhaps will provide the foundation stone on which he can build his future without depending on any but himself.

When Emlyn had turned eighteen and they had been travelling for over nine weeks, he and Gruffydd began the journey home. Emlyn was affected by the deep, ageless magic of the land which Gruffydd had shown him and he felt better able to cope with whatever lay ahead. He was no longer afraid of visiting his uncle and his cousin Owain and even looked forward to it. When he thought about Goronwy and the printing, his pace quickened; for he felt that he had neglected his friend and that Goronwy would not fully understand his reasons. They had heard now and again through the summer that the printing press had been set up successfully. He had seen a few of the pamphlets while travelling with Gruffydd. Some of them were acrimonious about the Queen. The publication of such words amounted to treason and treason resulted in inglorious death. However, thought Emlyn, if the printers had something better to work on, such as the first book of the bible printed in Welsh, it would provide a cover up for the illegal pamphlets.

As they neared home and waited for a ferry to take them across the river Conwy, Gruffydd sighed wearily. 'It seemed to me as if fewer want to hear the tales of old any more,' he said miserably, tossing stones into the river. 'They look to the future with false hearts and want no lessons in what their ancestors did.' He sank back down to the stone where he had been sitting. He ruffled his beard furiously and left it sticking out at all angles, like a hayrick with a large nest in it.

'It won't be lost Tad-cu, but it will have to bend with the winds of change.' Emlyn idly twisted yellow grasses together into a plait. 'If you are afraid that these poems of old will die with you and your generation, then they will have to be kept in the written word.'

'Do you think I haven't though of that?' Gruffydd answered, 'and who is going to write them down? The tales of Pwyll Prince of Dyfed, Math son of Mathonwy, Culhwch and Olwen, the Battle of Rhuddlan Plain, Llewelyn Fawr, all will be lost.'

'There is time enough to write it all down Tad-cu,' said Emlyn earnestly. 'It may be possible even now to begin work on the old tales. After all, we have a printing press of sorts. Once written, they are held forever for generation after generation.'

'Aye, god give me life to see it.'

Emlyn could see the ferry approaching. He said, Goronwy must feel well and truly deserted by now. If I don't go back he shall probably come looking. I haven't even told him about not going back to the Jesuits. That will be the most difficult thing to do.'

'More difficult than walking off and leaving your old grandfather?'

Emlyn looked at him with a worried expression. 'Tad-cu, have you changed your mind about sending me to Italy?'

'I have no intention of stopping you. But, I tell you Emlyn bach, the chances of your finding what you are seeking are minimal. Do not mistake me, I do hope that you find answers; for it will solve many problems but some stones are best left unturned.'

Emlyn recognised the tolerant look his grandfather gave him. But the opportunity offered by Ambrose Chillingworth to travel to Italy was a God send. Emlyn could not wait for the year to turn, so that he could leave. There were a few doubts in his mind though. Gruffydd was obviously hoping that he would return from his adventure with a mind to settle, to spend his life in Moelfre Isaf, raising sheep and aiming to win the Golden Harp at the Eisteddfod. Emlyn was not sure how he felt about that.

Chapter 14 Venice

Where once it had flowed like sand through an hour glass, the gold on the Street of Spice now trickled. The rows of shop fronts and olive-tree lined piazzas that had hummed with the scent of the East, had taken on the pall of decay. Birds nested above the long shut doors. It was not as it had been. But, on this particular day, the street was filled with people with their chatter, bustle and noise. The market awoke and filled with colour and activity, as if twenty years of decline had never occurred.

Uglino now owed everything to the Patron. It had never been the boy's intention to see Andrea killed. Although the death had been explained away as an unfortunate drowning, Uglino was left in no doubt who's hand lay behind the deed, Carlos Grimani. Uglino was terrified. through fear that anything else. Now having discovered all he could on the Street of Spices, he returned somewhat mystified as to what he had learned.

Paolo Grimani waited at the palace for his spy to return. He was having his toe nails clipped by the servant Giuseppe. He was dressed in yellow silk and algae-green velvet, a tall, handsome young man, who in Uglino's eyes resembled a god rather than a mere mortal. Diamonds glinted from the pleats of Paolo's doublet. His light brown eyes shone like those of a wild cat contemplating its prey. 'Well?' he said as soon as he saw his spy.

'There is a cargo of spice,' said Uglino.

'I know that fool. Who is responsible for it?' Paolo asked in a high temper. 'Come on wretch, what else have you discovered?'

'It is a new company. Many companies have sent their agents there already; there is much demand for the goods.'

Paolo swatted the servant away and stood up abruptly, scattering toe nails. 'Where is the Patron? There is some treachery here he should hear of.' He ran for the door with Uglino following.

'Why did I not learn of this?' Carlos Grimani demanded when he heard the details. 'I pay to be told these things before any one else learns of them. How is it that a ship comes loaded with spice and I am the last to learn of it?'

Uglino came forward carrying a tray of Murano glasses and a smoke-green bottle. It was Grimani's own wine from Cyprus, from the rich land and hillsides of vines near Famagusta. His stocks were running low since he had lost this year's cargo to pirates. He accepted a glass, looking thoughtful as he held it up to the window; the deep ruby hue captured the light. 'I should have been informed,' he said quietly. 'News of this spice cargo must be known to everyone else!'

'I have made inquiries Patron,' said Uglino, 'it was thought that the ship carried raw silk. Nothing is known of the owner. The ship is the *Cornucopia*, the one that brought the widow of Alessandro Balsamo to Venice. May I make a suggestion patron?' Uglino failed to keep the tremor from his hands as he refilled the glasses. 'There is another who came on the same ship. It is said that he is a cousin of Bartolomeo Varini. I was unable to discover his name, but he has presented a gift to the Doge, two splendid Arab mares.'

'Two splendid mares?' Grimani echoed. 'Varini wished to sell the salt. Now I know why. Who needs salt when you have spice? When is he due here to discuss the sale?'

'Tomorrow,' Uglino replied timidly.

Grimani turned to his grandson. 'Paolo get over there now and buy all the spice they have.'

'Are you not going to make inquiries first?'

'Idiot! Are inquiries going to fill the hold of a ship? Buy the spice first and then I will ask questions. Hurry now there is no time to waste. Take my manager Zorzo Vecelli with you.'

The merchants of Venice failed to make way for Paolo Grimani when he arrived. They could be forgiven for not recognising his magnificence in their excitement and eagerness.

Standing in the doorway of the little shop which, hither to, had sold only salt, he screamed, 'Out of my way!'

They moved reluctantly and made a passage for him and the secretary to push in front of them, murmuring their disapproval. 'Messer Varini,' he said with a feigned smile. 'I am overjoyed to see that you have recovered from whatever ailed you on our first meeting, remember on the canal?'

Seated at a scrubbed table, Bartolomeo greeted him politely, but he did not stand up nor did he cease in his scribbling. Two buyers from the Loredan family stood beside him. 'How may I assist you Messer Paolo?' Bartolomeo inquired, around a spare quill clenched between his teeth.

'There will be no need for you to continue with all this,' said Paolo Grimani. He waved his arms about to include the spice sacks and the Venetian buyers in one arm swing. 'Your stock is already spoken for.'

'It is,' confirmed Bartolomeo. 'But how came you to hear of it? I have only just been made aware of the fact myself, from these gentlemen.'

Paolo smiled grimly. Loredan? This family are rivals in trade to Carlos Grimani. How could they know of this sale? Paolo ignored them. He said, 'Then I have journeyed here for no propose. You have received my grandfather's wishes?'

'Your grandfather's wishes Messer? I am afraid not. Does he wish some task? Something to do with the salt? I assure you all has been put in order this very morning. You will give him my regards?'

Paolo sighed with a show of tried patience. 'His wishes concerning your stock held here.' he explained. 'Are you lacking in wit Varini! All that is stored here is to be sold to my grandfather Don Carlos Grimani.'

The two Loredan buyers looked aghast.

Zorzo Vecelli, Grimani's manager, looked distinctly ill at ease.

Bartolomeo stopped writing and looked up shaking his head. 'That is not so,' he said around the quill in his mouth. He dipped his pen anew, applying it to the ledger.

'Do you contradict me?' Paolo's voice rose to a squeal. 'Are you saying that all this is sold in such a short time? That there is nothing left?'

'We have been most fortunate.'

'Why did you say nothing of this?'

'You did not ask Messer Paolo,' said Bartolomeo. 'Beside, this has nothing to do with salt apart from the fact that it can be used to flavour the same dish. I could perhaps provide a small amount of pepper for your kitchen. Are you short in supply? I would hate to think the Patron is forced to eat his fish without pepper.'

Paolo banged his fist down on the table. The ink horn leaped and came down spilling its contents. Bartolomeo jerked away, but got splashed just the same. He watched his pains-taking columns of numbers disappear under the puddle of black ink. He threw down his quill and realised he had bitten the other in two.

'This is most unseemly,' said one of the buyers removing his green hat from the table before it took on a darker hue. 'To the early bird comes the worm young Paolo. If your grandfather...'

'Unseemly!' Paolo screamed. 'Unseemly,' he screamed again. 'You push aside the wishes of the Patron of Venice and expect me to behave otherwise? This is an insult beyond endurance! By the time I have finished with you Bartolomeo Varini, you will not be fit to clean fish!'

'Fish?' Bartolomeo said.

'Messer Paolo,' said the man with the green hat. 'It is but one ship's stock of spice. There are bound to be some disappointed. The amount cannot satisfy all. Your behaviour is unbecoming of the position you hold in this city. I and Giorgio Pesaro here have been witness to your threats. I assure you Messer that if a hair on the head of this good man is harmed you shall be held responsible. I shall inform the Magistrate without delay!'

'That will not be necessary,' said Bartolomeo. He stood up dripping ink. 'It was merely words spoken in anger. I am filled with remorse, but what can be done?'

'You will change it,' said Paolo. 'When I return you would be advised to have a better answer for me!' He swept out of the door, passed the disapproving faces, pushing them aside, his own face livid with anger. Almost as an after thought, Zorzo Vecelli ran after him.

Silence reigned behind him. Bartolomeo cleared his throat and turned to Giorgio Pesaro and his companion. 'Do not be concerned,' he said. 'This can be drawn up again. I shall do it this evening and send it by a reliable servant. Paolo will I am sure, find his spice elsewhere.'

'He is not a man of controlled temper,' said Giorgio Pesaro with a frown of distaste.

'Most unpleasant,' agreed his companion. 'That is no way to conduct business. Have a care Bartolomeo. Watch that you do not end up in the Lagoon. I would not put it past him.'

'No Jerome,' Bartolomeo replied, reminded of the empty eyes of Andrea and the fading petals,'nor would I.'

Before Bartolomeo Varini returned home, he called on the secretary of the Senate, Scipione Barozzi, whom Fiorenza had recommended as an ideal choice for their representative in Stamboul. Tomasso had showed little interest. 'My confidence in you 'Tolomeo,' he had said that morning, 'is such that your judgement of the man will suffice.'

Scipione Barozzi was a junior secretary in the Senate and in this position, he often had to undertake tasks which he would have rather have nothing to do with. Age was greatly revered by the Venetians. With age came wisdom. This was true in many cases, but with age also came irascibility, senility, poor health and a tendency to spend one's waning years in sleep. As a consequence, a bright, intelligent mind, like the one contained in Scipione Barozzi, went unused, undiscovered and fobbed off with menial tasks. It infuriated him and there was nothing he could do about it, for he had only held his present position for six years and that hardly granted him recognition as an individual. On the rare opportunities that he had managed to make his views known, he had received bored expressions, yawns and total indifference. The Ten were not the least bit interested nor would they ever be. They would all be long dead before Scipione Barozzi gained the age, the wealth, the position, or the senility and a tendency towards sleeping away the daylight hours.

Barozzi looked daily for a position in which he could use his mind and talent. His family were unknown, his background humble. It was a hard task he had set himself for there was little he could achieve without influential contacts. But, now, the widow Fiorenza Balsamo had offered him the chance to change his fortunes. To be factor of a new company, the details of which he knew nothing. When he had asked why she should offer such a position to him, the widow had smiled charmingly and told him she liked his writings and had attended his lecture at Padua. His knowledge of the Orient was impressive. Would he welcome the opportunity to travel?

Scipione opened his door on the Lanarca salt manager and fixed him with a beaming smile, hoping behind it, that the business was not Lanarca Salt.

Barozzi was a big man but handled his weight with surprising delicacy. When they were seated and served with wine and oysters, Barozzi said, 'If I could learn some details? I would not commit myself to blind enterprise, Messer Varini.'

'Do you know anything of sea-trade?' Bartolomeo asked.

'A great deal,' Barozzi replied. 'Although of practical experience I have none. Do not be concerned Messer, much can be learned from behind the counters of merchants. And books? What path can you not tread in another's footsteps? The world is made open by the written word.'

'It is not enough.'

Barozzi smiled. 'What I lack in experience, I can more than compensate for in knowledge. There is nothing that enters the Lagoon without my knowing of it, where it originated, who bought it and who for, what was paid for it, by what route it arrives and even in what ships.'

'Then you will have heard,' said Bartolomeo gulping down an oyster, 'of a shipment of spice?'

'Indeed,' answered Barozzi. 'The *Cornucopia* arrived from Stamboul. It called at Candia, at Ragusta and at Trieste. I admit that this particular ship hides her source and her identity to a certain extent. The owner travelled with the ship and also with Madonna Fiorenza Balsamo. I assume therefore, that the man is a partner in the Salt Company. I learnt from Alessandro Balsamo, God rest his soul, when the poor man last visited Venice, that he had a partner in business. But I have heard too that the man with the cargo is your own cousin Messer Varini? There is much speculation on the Rialto. The ship carried cloth and spice and some life-stock. At present she is being prepared for a further voyage to the Levant I believe.'

Bartolomeo sat forward frowning. 'Is this common knowledge?'

'Not all,' said Barozzi. 'Although it is known that the spice is much and the quality unparalleled, this may be Rialto gossip. I assume the day of trading went well? The owner is still a mystery. He will not remain so for long. Would I be correct in saying that he is a certain Tomasso di Vincentini?'

'How could you know this?' Bartolomeo asked. His voice was edged with anxiety.

Scipione Barozzi smiled secretively and sipped his wine before he answered. 'I would be fool indeed,' he said, 'to divulge its source. I will say however, that your employer has visited the Serenissima, though I do not know the reason behind his visit, he was there for some time.' Barozzi meticulously wiped his fingers and folded his napkin neatly. He added, 'I do not yet know what you require of me nor in what capacity you wish to employ me. The Madonna's reference to being a manager in Stamboul is the first inclination I have received of the position you wish me to fill.'

'And?' Bartolomeo encouraged.

'And, I would like nothing better. That city has long filled me with wonder and curiosity. If it is your wish that I manage your spice from that side, I can only assure you, that I am delighted and that you will find no cause for regret.'

'You would be required first to sail to the Levant. Would you be prepared to leave soon?' Bartolomeo grimaced at the repetitive taste of oysters.

'How soon?'

'A week? Two?'

Barozzi's eyes widened in surprise. 'It will not be impossible Messer Varini.'

Bartolomeo said, 'You would be required to deal in grain and leather goods though an agent in Alexandria.'

Barozzi looked at him in thought. 'What would we trade for it?'

'Mostly woollen cloth. But until that line of trade is established to the Netherlands, we will fill our hold with whatever the Turk desires. The cloth will go next spring to Stamboul with you, if you agree, as our agent.'

'Holland cloth?'

'English cloth,' said Bartolomeo. 'It is superior and we have established, through an agent in Antwerp, an English merchant who is willing to bring a sample of wool across the Alps in the spring, thus avoiding the competitive Florentine buyers and the turmoil of war in Antwerp. Once the link is established, we can elbow into the Levant demand for wool.'

Scipione Barozzi smiled and shifted his great bulk. 'All being well,' he said with emphasis, 'I would be honoured to join your company.' He did not press the Venetian manager for further knowledge. He knew that his own background would be thoroughly investigated before he learnt more. He had his own sources too.

It was late evening when the warehouse had a visitor. The sun sank into the Lagoon with a blaze of fire, painting it like a lake of molten lava. Tomasso had busied himself all day moving things and the warehouse had lost the Eastern treasure. To where, even Bartolomeo did not know. But Tomasso was looking happy. Dressed in just shirt and hose, he was streaked with dirt and his disordered hair was white with dust. He looked like one of the refuse collectors, who gathered Venice's unwanted debris on to barges in the early hours of the morning. Work done, spice sold to the last ounce, he sat with Bartolomeo on a wall outside, where the canal water lapped the steps and gondolas clove the lagoon. They watched the sun go down and shared a bottle of Grimani's Malmsey.

'Is anyone there?' The voice spoke from the building behind them.

Bartolomeo froze. 'He's back!'

'Who? Our friend Paolo Grimani?'

'Ah! There you are Messer Varini,' beamed Paolo Grimani coming around the corner. The smile was alarming. He was followed by a recognizable little servant.

Bartolomeo rose to his feet and fussed about brushing the wall clean and offering a seat to their visitor. Tomasso sat drinking nonchalantly. His eyes narrowed.

Paolo sat down, cushioned by his furs. 'I have discovered,' he said with a distasteful glance in Tomasso's direction, 'for a task to be satisfactory completed, it is always advisable to undertake it one's self. Don't you agree Messer Varini? Please sit down. Here we share a common interest.'

'What interest?' Bartolomeo inquired suspiciously.

'Have you forgotten so soon? The buying of spice of course. Is that wine?'

'Ah yes,' said Bartolomeo. 'I recall that you require some for the Patron's kitchen.'

'For the kitchen? Forgive me. Earlier today I was most discourteous, I apologise, the folly of youth.'

Tomasso burst out laughing.

Paolo looked at him and then looked closer. 'You are?'

'Tomasso di Vincentini. I meant no disrespect,' said Tomasso, 'But the folly of youth?'

Paolo fidgeted in discomfort. 'I am pleased to find you here, as it is you to whom I must speak. You have suffered some accident?' He viewed Tomasso's dishevelled appearance with an expression of distaste. 'Don Carlos will give you the best price you could wish for,' he finished.

'The offer is generous,' said Tomasso. He poured wine into a grubby, chipped glass and then added, 'But what is it for pray?'

'Why, your cargo of spice from the East. He will take all you have to offer.'

'But we have none to offer you Messer Paolo,' said Bartolomeo. 'I thought I had explained it all to you this morning.'

'None?'

'None,' said Tomasso. 'It is all sold or promised. However if you should wish, I may be able to bring him some next time. But you know how it is? Already the space on my ship is spoken for. We have been successful, God be praised.'

'All? Could you not break a promise or two, Messer Vincentini?'

'As a fellow merchant, you should know the 'folly' of such an action. A merchant cannot risk his reputation. Alas I am sorry to say, there is nothing for the house of Grimani.' Tomasso offered him the wine cup. 'Wine?'

Paolo sighed. 'I do not think you understand the situation,' he said. 'You have been away from Venice, so I can forgive your lack of knowledge. You cannot refuse a request such as this.'

'Cannot? I am a man of renowned patience,' Tomasso replied with an icy voice. 'Already you have insulted me by proposing that I go back on promised sales. Do you now insult me further? I was led to believe your grandfather is a man of impeccable character. I see that I have been misinformed. You will excuse me? I have much to do.'

Bartolomeo felt the hair on the back of his neck rise.

Paolo stood up, overshadowing the spice merchant as his eyes glittered in menace. 'Unless you deal with the Grimani, you will not survive the pace of the Rialto long Vincentini. I give you pause for thought, I give you time to reconsider. But tread carefully, lest you tread in a muck of your own making!' With that, he stormed off with the dignity of a sultan. Uglino ran after him, tripping in his curly toed slippers.

Bartolomeo sat down on the wall. 'He forgot to drink the wine,' he said to the retreating figure. 'Considering that it was originally his, I find that most upsetting.'

Tomasso looked troubled. He clasped his dirty hands together and looked steadily at Bartolomeo. 'So that is Anna's son Paolo. He looks like his father. But there is something about him that strikes a chord of memory. I am not impressed.'

'What did you expect?' Bartolomeo replied. 'He has been brought up a Grimani. All that, that you have just witnessed, is just for show. Paolo can be quite charming and intelligent when allowed to be. Do you think he knows about the a fire at the Grimani warehouse near the Arsenal this evening?'

Tomasso shook his head. They had heard about the unfortunate fire an hour before. No lives were lost and the fire had been kept under control and eventually put out, without causing harm to the neighbouring buildings. The stores kept there, however, were completely ruined. 'No,' Tomasso replied. 'If Grimani knew, he would not have sent his grandson here discussing spice.' He looked out across the canal in thought. 'I am going away for a few weeks.'

Bartolomeo was still suspicious of this Tomasso di Vincentini, who was nothing like he had been. Now Tomasso was off somewhere. To what end? 'Where are you going?'

'To the mainland first. You will have to arrange for Scipione Barozzi to go to Alexandria. Does he know what I want of him?'

'I expect so. I shall fill him in with all the details,' said Bartolomeo. 'When do you leave?'

'In a day or two, after we have sold the salt company. I will be gone for some weeks. Symeon will be a great help to you if you give him a chance to get to know the business. Can you manage?'

Bartolomeo stood up. He waved his bony hands in the air. 'I see! You go off and enjoy yourself and don't mind me, I'll stay here and fight off the Grimani hounds.'

'I was coming to that,' said Tomasso moving from his place by the wall. 'If you are still interested in working for me. And, no 'Tolomeo I did not start the warehouse fire.'

'I did not say that you did!' Bartolomeo replied with an indignant expression.

'But you were going to?'

'Just for a moment. I could not believe it, and if you had I would have no qualms about telling everyone.' Bartolomeo replied. His thoughts however, were of a different nature. You did set that fire. I would swear to it on the grave of my mother. You may not have held the flame Tomasso di Vincentini, but as God be my witness your hand was laid to the deed!

Ignoring him, Tomasso withdrew a small knife from his belt and began to clean his nails, he said,'I want you to find a larger house, preferably on the Grand Canal. Do you know of any suitable?'

'I am sure it would be no trouble after today.' Bartolomeo could not help smiling. In spite of his doubts, he was thrilled at the prospect of trading on the Rialto, alongside the noble families of Venice.

'I want a house on the mainland too and that is the reason why I am going,' said Tomasso. Without raising his head, he added, 'Do you know what became of my parent's home?'

This came as a surprise to Bartolomeo. 'It is still there as far as I know,' he replied, 'though gone to ruin and the fields are unkempt.'

'I wish to own it. Can you find out about that too?'

Bartolomeo looked at him. 'Were you to buy it now,' he said, 'there is a chance that your history will be revealed.'

'Am I not dead?'

Bartolomeo shivered, but not from cold. 'So it is believed, but if you buy the property, minds my be stirred to remember. Would owning it be an advantage? You can't control your trade from the mainland.'

'That last is true, but I can return here whenever a ship is due, if I need to. Soon memories will be awakened 'Tolomeo. Until then, I like it not here, there is too much water. I suppose I expected it to be the same, but Venice is filled with hostile feuds, bickering and...'

'Memories?' Bartolomeo interrupted. He was sorry after that he had spoken. This was the first time that Tomasso had seemed nearly human.

Before he set off for the meeting with Carlos Grimani, the following morning, Bartolomeo thought of the years of effort he had put into the business in Cyprus: the rows of mud houses among their miserable palms; the work force of slaves and peasants and donkeys; the run down house; the two clumsy sailing cogs, round as barrels and as difficult to handle, and the high quality salt collected for so many years from Lanarca lake. When the summer dried the mirror of water, it's surface turned into a sheet of dazzling brightness, whiter than marble. As the salt was taxed heavily and partially owned by the Senate, Bartolomeo had at times, found difficulty in making a profit, even before Alessandro had fallen into debt. For that reason he had often filled the spare room on the cogs with Cyprus grain or sugar and they had ferried back and forth across the waves on the monotonous journey without mishap or harassment.

The day was dry, still, Bartolomeo managed to get his feet wet in puddles on his descent to the waiting gondola. Jacopo manned the oar. He wore a new tunic of pale blue with a symbol embroidered on the back. Bartolomeo paused to examine it, it looked like a dragon or a gecko. Without comment, he sat down under the canopy, his leather satchel on his bony knee. They were well ahead of time and had over an hour to spare before the meeting with Grimani. Tomasso wanted to see Venice from a gondola.

Tomasso embarked without getting his feet wet. It appeared that his intentions were to impress. He was dressed in black. The knee length doublet and hose were fashioned from the finest velvet; the doublet was edged with silver thread and collared with ermine. Underneath, exposed between the elaborate fastenings and the silver lined sleeve-slashes, was a shirt of creamy white silk, sewn all over with neat pleats and encrusted with seed pearls. On his hat sat a nest of jewels the Turkish Sultan would have been proud to wear. At his ear was the earring, both familiar and chilling in the memories it evoked.

'Do you think it wise to appear thus?' Bartolomeo said, when Tomasso squeezed in to sit beside him.

Tomasso grinned and winked. The stone in his earring was the colour of blood. 'Jacopo tell him what you told me,' he said.

'News is on the streets Messer Varini. After all the spice sold, everyone knows whom it came from,' said Jacopo.

'They know it was your spice?' Bartolomeo asked.

Tomasso nodded. He seemed not the least bit upset by the news.

'Will this affect the sale of the salt business?' Bartolomeo added anxiously.

'No,' said Tomasso. 'Tolomeo, you did not tell me how fair was the price of pepper.'

'Yes, it is literally worth it's weight in gold. You must have been to the counting house. We have done well.' Bartolomeo replied. 'I assumed you would have known.'

'I should have brought more. There's more in Constantinople,' said Tomasso.

'Of course,' Bartolomeo replied cynically. The boat remained still. 'It is not Constantinople but Stamboul. Did you not know the Turks had renamed it? It has been thus for a hundred years, or near enough. Are we waiting for something Jacopo?'

'Madonna Fiorenza Caterina Balsamo,' said Jacopo with a flourish.

'She is to accompany us?'

'You did not know?'

No, he did not know. Tomasso, it seemed confided in servants but left him in the dark.

Tomasso said, 'I met her this morning and told her our position. You did not think we could sell without her say so?'

'No, I merely assumed that it was already arranged. For myself, I am delighted we shall be accompanied by the lady. She is the only woman in Venice who can make Carlos Grimani speechless and render Paolo to a quivering, love-sick boy. He crosses his knees and squirms like an eel when ever he sees her.'

'Is Paolo married?' Tomasso asked.

Bartolomeo shook his head.

'So Paolo has no children?' Tomasso burst out laughing, he laughed until tears sparkled in his eyes.

Bartolomeo smiled in return. Yet, he did not see the humour in imparting the information.

'What of the daughter of Grimani's old age?' Tomasso asked.

Bartolomeo said, 'She has been schooled in a convent in France. I have heard that soon she will return to wed.'

'Really? Who?'

'A wealthy old man, no doubt,' Bartolomeo replied reluctantly. 'But not one too old to father a litter of Grimani.'

.'What age is she?' Tomasso had a wicked glint in his eyes.

'Old enough to wed,' said Bartolomeo. 'Thirteen of fourteen, a young bride. Why?'

'I have wealth beyond avarice,' Tomasso replied. 'I am not too old to father children.'

Bartolomeo stared at him with astonishment. There had been many tales in Venice about Carlos Grimani and the young wife who had given him a daughter to lighten his old age. Grimani had been so disappointed to have only a daughter, that he had sent her away. But, rumour murmured that he had now sent for her. The rumours about the girl too, were endless; she was fat and complacent; she was deformed and vindictive; she was a maiden of astounding beauty, a pure virgin of such charm and grace that nothing less than a prince would be fitting to husband her.

Bartolomeo shrugged. Tomasso joked of course. Bartolomeo was saved from further discussion on the subject by the arrival of Fiorenza. She arrived like a breath of spring, dressed in deep blue, with a little hat and a blue feather. They heard her chattering before she rounded the corner. She clattered over the bridge, trailed by her maid looking flushed and Enrico, looking like a forgotten scarecrow. When greetings had been exchanged and all settled in comfort, Jacopo poled out into the water and took his passengers on a tour of San Marco's while they discussed their business.

Tomasso had not intended to accompany Bartolomeo Varini and Fiorenza Caterina Balsamo to this meeting with Carlos Grimani. Now that he had included himself, he felt a thrill of joyful expectancy. He was not now the foolish youth who Grimani had condemned to the galleys. At present he felt no qualms about meeting the great man. This meeting meant that his plans would have to be advanced somewhat, but this would make no difference to the outcome.

There was nothing unique in a loss of cargo to pirates, it was one of the hazards of sea trade and was happening with increasing rapidity, now that the Turks had the expertise that made the Middle Sea practically their own. For a man like Carlos Grimani, this was a small loss, a mere nibble at the foundation of Grimani's riches. Soon, thought Tomasso, the nibbles would become chunks. He would chip away, as if at the trunk of a tall tree and the tree would fall. Before it fell, Tomasso would wither it's leaves with a killing frost, until it's branches were bare and incapable of bearing fruit.

The gondola slid over the calm water, propelled by the single oar. Jacopo's muscled shoulders bunched and slackened, driving the narrow boat past the gorgeous Venetian palaces which rose from the Canal Grande.

'Have you picked one out yet?' Bartolomeo said, light-heartedly.

'Do I need one of these?' Tomasso replied in genuine surprise. 'I had thought of something more modest.'

'If a man does not show his wealth and success, how can anyone be made aware of it?' Bartolomeo smoothed his black lapels and eyed his employer.

'By reputation,' Tomasso answered. When I have it, he thought. The Rialto rang with talk of the haul of spice and the mysterious merchant who had brought it. There had been too many curious visitors at the house on Canal delle Torreselle. That house was too small and poor in comparison. Bartolomeo was right, Tomasso would have to acquire something impressive.

In due time, they arrived at a grand white house. It was set at a corner, where the river streets divided. The graceful pointed arches of the portico rose from the green depths. Above this were two upper floors, with delicately pierced loggias. Surmounting the façade was a crown of carved stonework, so delicate that it looked more like an edging of Venetian lace. The portal was decorated in blue and gold. Above it stood a marble winged lion, smaller than the one on the Doge's palace but just as majestic. Of all the palaces which Tomasso had seen, on his trip along the canals, this was the one he liked the best.

'I'll have this one,' he said.

Fiorenza assumed an expression of mock approval. Bartolomeo did not smile as he was supposed to. Tomasso sat with his head slightly inclined, watching the manager of the Lanarca Salt company. He knew that Bartolomeo was not entirely happy with selling the company. Tomasso had never known whether he would be agreeable to the new company and the scheme to bring down Grimani. He had been prepared to lose this astute lawyer-trained Venetian. But Bartolomeo had made the salt company his life, he had not wed nor had he committed himself to anything else. The question was, why? Was it out of some old loyalty to the woman who had first employed him? What kept Bartolomeo Varini interested enough to be enmeshed in the twists of Tomasso's scheming? Whatever it was, Tomasso was beginning to be glad of it.

Bartolomeo was a man who knew his trade. He kept up with the pace of the Rialto; knew the exchange rates, the demands, the shortages and the glut of commodities. He sought out any items of news which would effect an enterprise before embarking upon it, such as the frequent unrest caused by the overlord ship of Spain in much of Europe, and how this effected the flow of trade that crossed back and forth over the Alpine barrier. With this knowledge, he was not afraid to venture into new markets when the chance was offered. Not only this, but he had an uncanny awareness of human relationships; who should be favoured with a gift; who should be entertained lavishly; who should be snubbed and who should be avoided. In Bartolomeo Varini, Tomasso recognised an ally of inestimable value.

The man who greeted them on the steps was neatly dressed in the black of a clerk and was long faced and clean shaven. 'You are late,' he said impatiently, his brows lowered in a frown. 'Kindly have the goodness to delay no longer.'

Leaving Jacopo, Enrico and the maid Maria, in the boat, the others followed the clerk under the portico, up a flight of steps and into a sunlit courtyard. There were two fig trees casting shade over an ornamented fountain. Silver water bounced and sparkled off a clutch of fat, marble cherubs and tinkled into a series of marble basins, each slightly larger than the one above. At the base there were three mythical sea horses with entwined fish tails and flaring nostrils. Tomasso stopped walking and stood in front of it.

Carlos Grimani did not live in this grand palace all those years ago. He had been rich then, but had not been considered among the nobility of Venice. This grand house and the respect with which he was now held, was evidence of the success he had been favoured with since.

Tomasso had thought that it was going to be easy, to walk in here and face the man who had been responsible for all his pain and misery. But it was not. He had already seen and spoken to the fine Paolo and had felt nothing but anger. He had made a mistake in showing it. But this was different, here, on the Patron's own ground. The fountain splashed irritably and he could see fish fleeting under the wide leaves of a water-lily. Standing in the sunlight, he felt cold and was suddenly afraid. He did not recognise the sensation at first, fear was not something he was not accustomed to, but this was a new fear. He felt that he would not be able to walk and that he would mar the perfection of the fountain by being sick in it. His stomach churned. He felt weak. His legs began to tremble and he caught at one of the rearing fish-horses for support. He stood there for a minute, but it seemed like forever.

Fiorenza touched his shoulder. 'The sculpture was fashioned by Nanni di Bartolo,' she said. She seemed aware of the internal struggle he fought within himself. Her hand closed around his arm and she smiled up at him. She said, 'Will you keep the ugly thing when you take over this palace?'

It was meant in jest and Tomasso released a stifled sound. 'It's monstrous,' he replied. 'I may donate it to the church of San Francesco della Vigna. They could use it as a baptismal font.' He breathing was deliberate, each breath commanded to be calm and normal. His fear receded and sunk to a hidden place within him.

'Messer, Madonna?' The waiting clerk indicated another flight of steps which rose under a dark arch.

The room they entered was sumptuous. Tapestries and carpets softened the walls. In between them, hung paintings framed with gold, depicting the great family in all it's glory. The candelabra were gilt and similar ornament set the room in a dazzling display of wealth. Rich coffers stood against the walls and plush carpets covered most of the tiled floor. At the end of the room Grimani sat at his table. It was an ornate affair, made from African wood, that depicted in it's handsome carving, the fall of

Constantinople at the hand of that famed Doge Dondolo, 'Lord of a Quarter and a Half-Quarter of the Roman Empire.' This table was itself famed throughout Venice, for, from behind it, Carlos Grimani had carved out his own empire. Bartolomeo had explained to Tomasso that the patron used the name of Don Carlos after the Spanish form of address. He did, Tomasso admitted to himself, look every bit a Spanish Grandee. Behind him stood his grandson Paolo who was as expensively dressed and jewelled.

Standing in the doorway Tomasso scrutinised the two men. The youth was Anna's youngest son. Tomasso felt nothing for the boy. He remembered ruefully that he had made Paolo a toy wooden boat when he was just three years old.

But it was the older man who commanded attention. Carlos Grimani was sixty-three years of age. Now fat with gluttony and indulgence, he sat like a toad on a lily pad. Pale, red nosed and perspiring, his face was perfectly still beneath a velvet hat which flopped over one ear. The gown over his doublet was lined with warm glossy fur. His hand lifted and beckoned the three visitors to come forward.

Bartolomeo swallowed and looked at Tomasso, searching for some sign of nervousness. Whatever he felt, the sea prince had learnt to mask his emotion; his expression was faintly bored.

They bowed and Fiorenza curtseyed. Bartolomeo stood very still and so did Tomasso. Paolo came around in front of the table and walked towards Fiorenza. She kept her eyes downcast and flinched when he touched her. He kissed her hand but did not let go his grip. He turned her palm upwards and placed something within it.. The jewel caught the sunlight that was streaming through a high window.

Paolo said, 'A gift which I hope you will find it in your heart to accept.'

Without looking at him, remaining demure and perfectly humble, Fiorenza replied. 'You have my gratitude, but I cannot accept.'

This is not the reason why we are here, thought Bartolomeo. What is this about anyway?.

Carlos Grimani watched the tableaux. His eyes held no expression.

Paolo lifted his other hand and curled Fiorenza's fingers over the gift. He let go and stood back from her with a charming smile.

Fiorenza's hand dropped and the object fell flashing to the floor. It lay beside the open jaws of a woven lion. She lifted her eyes. 'I am bereaved,' she said. 'I mourn the death of my husband. Therefore, I consider the gift disrespectful.'

For the first time, the elder Grimani moved. His head nodded from his thick neck and his shoulders shook with amusement. He rubbed his hands together. 'Do you think the boy courts you Fiorenza Caterina Balsamo?'

'He is a boy,' Fiorenza replied. 'I am old enough to be his mother.'

'Quite so,' said Grimani. 'And you are the proud mother of a marriageable daughter, are you not?'

'Yes Monseigneur. But my daughter resides in Cyprus where she has been educated and reared by my mother's family.'

'But you have sent for her, to share your good fortune. We will consider a match between her and my fine grandson Paolo here. And you will accept the gift from your would be son-in-law.'

Fiorenza dropped to a curtsey again bowing her covered head. 'I am honoured Monseigneur,' she replied. Her dark eyes lifted with their penetrating gaze. 'My daughter is already betrothed to the son of an eminent Cypriot family. It is an arrangement which cannot be broken.'

'It is of small account,' the big man answered. He waved his hand, dismissing the subject.

Bartolomeo risked a glance at Tomasso. Tomasso was watching Fiorenza with an expression of approval. Wisely she made no further comment. She stepped back, as if to exclude herself.

Paolo stood with his arms folded, tapping the thick chain of gold which hung around his neck. He looked to Fiorenza with a smile of triumph.

Carlos Grimani called for refreshment and waved his guests to stools that a servant had arranged by the table. He looked questioningly at Tomasso di Vincentini.

Refusing the stool, Bartolomeo stepped forward and bowed. So far the meeting was a disaster. He said, 'May I present my cousin, Tomasso de Vincentini. He is financier of the newly formed Eastern Spice Company.'

Grimani regarded Tomasso coldly. He sighed. 'Be seated,' he commanded.

Bartolomeo rubbed his sweating hands down his thighs, in futile effort to dry them. 'We have not done business in the past,' he began, 'but you know our company well, for we have dealt in the same commodity. Your esteemed grandson has approached me, voicing your interest in buying the Lanarca Salt Company and I have received word of your interest. Until now, to my considerable regret, I was unable to accept your offer. The reason for this was the absence of the company's owners. Now that this has been resolved, we are willing to reconsider.'

'Resolved?' Grimani interrupted. 'Resolved because the Madonna's husband has passed away?'

'In a manner of speaking, yes.' Bartolomeo shifted his feet uncomfortably. 'Madonna Fiorenza wishes to retire from the salt business and see to the future of her daughter.'

'A matter which we too have resolved. Grimani replied with an inclination of his head towards Fiorenza. 'I have as you know, Messer Varini, made you offers far above the value of your company on previous occasions. Neither you nor Alessandro, when he was alive, would consider a sale. Until now, you have refused. Considering this, I am led to believe that some further misfortune has fallen upon you to induce you to sell now.'

'Further misfortune?' Fiorenza repeated. She artfully dabbed at her eyes with a corner of lace. 'I suppose you could call the death of my gently loved husband, further misfortune if you a man of poor judgement and cold heart. I would not have thought it of you, in spite of our differences.'

'You mistake me Madonna,' said Grimani. 'It was not my intent to injure. The death of Alessandro will be suffered by us all.' He paused to see if she would offer further interruption, but Fiorenza bowed her head. Grimani continued 'Although we all remember him in our prayers and offer condolences to his beloved wife, that is not our purpose here. The salt company is not well favoured. There was a sum paid out recently that has not been mentioned.'

'That can be easily explained, Magnifico,' said Bartolomeo, smiling to hide his fury. This was not knowledge of which Grimani should be aware, let alone speak of. From the satchel he had brought, Bartolomeo pulled out a receipt. 'The sum was paid in due taxes to the Senate and has been settled in full,' he explained. 'All that there is, lies before you. I have drawn up the papers that you will find precise and correct.' With his pride strained almost beyond endurance, he added, 'However if you have no desire to continue further?'

'We will continue, said Grimani. His eyes remained cold and blank. 'So you have no employment now Varini?'

'Me?' Bartolomeo gulped. He had lost control of the situation; he had never had control. Grimani was manipulative and behind all this was sure to lie the resentment he felt towards them because of the previous day's trading. Bartolomeo said, 'My cousin here, Tomasso di Vincentini has kindly offered me employment in his modest business. I find his concern and his offer generous and feel inclined to accept.'

'Modest business,' said Carlos Grimani. His eyebrows lifted. 'I assume we are speaking of the buying and selling of spice?'

Tomasso rose and bowed. 'It is but a sideline,' he explained easily. 'I dabble here and there, a little of this a little of that. A man cannot be too tied to one enterprise.' His earring shone and red sprites danced about the room. He was in perfect control.

Grimani looked at him intently. He said, 'These are the words of a man wise in the art of trade. You have had good fortune in the selling of your spice and made profit enough I would judge, to finance the founding of a new company. I am not over pleased with what I know of this so far. But we will agree on a price for the salt business and I am willing to overlook the insult to my grandson. Is the sum last named for the sale agreeable?'

'We are content to accept,' answered Bartolomeo pleasantly.

The clerk who had guided them by the fountain, sat by the table and scowled over the ledgers Bartolomeo presented to him. He had a sharpened quill grasped in his hand. The lid of the ink horn made an intrusive sound as he unstopped it.

Tomasso looked up and found that Carlos Grimani was watching him, there was no sign of recognition in the tiny eyes. Tomasso held the gaze until the eyes turned away. The silence stretched while Grimani puckered his brow in thought and the quill scraped in the silence.

Grimani expelled a breath. 'Messer Vincentini have you discovered a new source to obtain this scented gold? There must be great risk involved. You have made an agreement with the Turk?'

'We are confident,' answered Tomasso. 'There are ways of avoiding both the Turk and the Portuguese dominance in this commodity.'

Grimani smiled, his cheeks round and polished. 'How fortunate,' he said, 'that you have established such a sure and profitable trade. In Venice a new company must nurture good relations with its fellow merchants and must build up a good reputation to gather trust; for you cannot thrive on profit alone. You may think you have started well, but there are unspoken rules that you would be wise to abide by. The risk in overseas trade has increased with the growing power of the Turks. What if they put an embargo on your ship? What if your next haul was overrun by pirates? What if the spice tax was doubled? Without influential backing and insurance you would be ruined.'

'Do not be concerned Padrone,' Tomasso replied sincerely. 'I own land and buildings and life-stock. The spice ship was funded from profit already gained from other ventures. Where this to fail, the responsibility would be my own, all expenses incurred would be met. However I am gratified by your interest and made wise by your superior insight. What is done cannot be undone. I can only offer my humblest apologies that you yourself gained nothing from the recent supply. Had I known what your standing was, I should have reserved the whole of my stock for sale to you alone. I will not make such an error again. Should you wish to reserve anything I can supply, you have only to mention your needs to Messer Varini here, and they will be met.'

'It is thoughtful of you to consider my needs. Tell me, have you ever considered partnership? You have spoken of wisdom Messer, in this business a financial partner is a valued addition to a new company. If this source of eastern spice is reliable and abundant, should you require a ship or extra moneys, you would be in a stronger position and could well double your profits.'

Tomasso stood up. the reflections from his earring jumped and danced like drops of blood about the walls. Tall and elegant, he bowed to the Patron of merchants. 'What can I say Magnifico? I am overwhelmed by your generosity. I would be honoured to consider your interest.'

Bartolomeo felt his heart miss a beat. He closed his eyes, whispered a prayer and then opened them again. Where had Tomasso learned to bear himself with such superiority?

Carlos Grimani smiled benignly, but in the small eyes, there was nothing but chill. His reputation as the Father of Venice, had been acquired through such acts as this, generous financial assistance to small struggling companies, that invariably left them in debt to him, body and soul. Once in this sorry position, they were ripe for manipulation and ruin. Did Tomasso know what he was doing? Bartolomeo saw the bright future of the Eastern Spice Company dwindle into darkness.

Grimani said, 'Messer, you are obviously a man who is long used to success. Tell me, who are your family?'

'Do not I pray judge me by my family,' Tomasso laughed. 'My mother died bringing me into this world, I was reared by the church and my father was a German shoe maker, or so I was led to believe.'

'I understood that you were a cousin to Bartolomeo Varini here?'

'He does me honour,' Tomasso said, sparing his manager a glance. 'Our relationship is extremely remote.'

'Forgive me, Messer Vincentini,' said Grimani, 'But you must have had patronage to reach the position you have.'

'No parentage and no patronage. I am as you see me. I have reached success through my own effort. A self-made man and a successful one. For that reason you can hope for nothing but gain should we consider participation in business. May I suggest that we meet in five weeks or so, to discuss this further? I am rather pressed for time.'

An expression of displeasure flickered in Grimani's eyes, he was not accustomed to being dismissed. He recovered his pique quickly and stood.

He gathered the stiff folds of his brocade and fur before he offered his guests a curt bow. He shuddered, as if to shrug some irksome doubt. The air was not cold. Something dark and ominous seemed to stir his very soul.

He stood and beheld them all with superiority. Now he was master of the vast amounts of salt to be scooped from the lake at Lanarca. And soon he would look to the Street of Spices to buy and make further profits. He could load up his newly built ship and send it to a Flanders hungry for seasoning. He had lost his Malmsey and his warehouse had burnt down, but God looked with benevolence on Carlos Grimani. To suffer loss only made the fruit of gain all the sweeter. Tomasso di Vincentini was obviously a man to be nurtured and milked when ripened but, with exceptional care.

Chapter 15 Wales

With a wide yawn, Emlyn hung up the last printed page to dry. He stood back, arms folded, his head bent to one side and then the other. His fingers were black with ink and his forehead was streaked, where he had dragged ink through his hair. Fingerprints smudged a page here and there. Before him, hung the printed pages which Goronwy had told him to finish. The pages hung, fluttering in the cold, dark air of the cave entrance. Words danced across the pamphlet, declaring the Scottish Queen Mary as the rightful Catholic Queen of the Realm. He had also had a chance to print a few pages of his translation of Genesis into Welsh, of these, he was exceptionally proud.

Emlyn sighed, he had done what was asked of him which made him one of the rebel printers. All through the night he had worked. Exhaustion mingled with starvation making him light-headed. Beside him crouched a boy from the village, Bran, dressed in blue and brown bits and pieces. His mouth, with teeth all over the place, gaped in a continuous grin. A bird's chirrups came from somewhere. It was still dark but dawn was coming.

The idea of the cave had been Goronwy's. Before this, the Catholics had used a cottage at Tan-y-Bryn which stood in a copse of trees, hidden from the road and Goronwy had printed his pamphlets and drawn in other devoted Catholics to assist him. They held secret meetings and plotted the demise of the Reformers. Worried about discovery, they had been forced to move the press. The hidden cave was on the Orme, *Pen Gogarth*, Dragon's Head, a long headland reaching out into the Irish Sea. The cave opened to a shelf of grass before the cliff edge which plunged down to the sea. Gentle waves muddled the pebbles below. The press was constructed from a cider press, eight feet high supporting a twisted shaft of wood. It stood still now and silent, smelling of new ink.

Now, the sea was the only sound. The darkness paled. There was a stirring in the air, a whispered promise of warmth and sunshine. A gull cried over the sea and behind it another.

Emlyn had not seen his cousin Owain nor approached his uncle's manor. He began to hope that he could avoid the meeting altogether.

There was no love or respect in Emlyn's heart for the man who had sent him away to a Catholic education, and then himself deserted his own Catholicism and turned Protestant. It made no difference to Emlyn, that the reformed England had forced the choice on his uncle, 'to adapt or lose all'. It was not easy for a Welsh landowner to remain Catholic. Many wore a twin mask, like Janus, remaining true but showing a wooden agreement when it was required of them. Emlyn's uncle, Squire Hugh was not one of these. He had embraced the new way whole-heatedly and saw in it common sense.

The squire would have heard from Father Manare at College de Clermont and would know by now that his plans for ridding himself of an unwanted nephew, had come to naught.

Emlyn watched the dawn unfold above the sea. The cave sat in cold shadow; the rocks glistened with moisture. Dew caressed the grass and soaked into his clothes. There were hours of peace to go before Goronwy arrived with his fervent acolytes.

Emlyn had seen the pamphlets, distributed to reach every corner of North Wales. He had read Goronwy's disturbing words. They reminded him of the evening meetings held at the Jesuit college, the heated words that were directed solely against the Queen of England. Emlyn had snarled them himself and raised his own clenched, white fist.

A seed of doubt had been planted in his mind since then. It was in the wild places, where he had walked with Gruffydd Hiraethog, over two idyllic months treading their own ground and wanting for nothing. Emlyn had fingered his harp in smoky halls and Gruffydd's deep, hypnotic voice had retold the old tales.

It was an art for which the need had gone. The very earth seemed to shake with change. Like the army of Llewelyn Fawr, Wales peered from behind her mountains; where witches could still be found pouring over their entrails; where fear was still felt of the Gwyllion and the Gwragedd Annun as they perched on the hidden pathways among the hollow hills. There were places were the foot of Christianity had never fallen. Locked in lakes and streams and hidden vales, the fairy fiddler could still enchant the unwary and set his feet to dance for a hundred years.

The free life on those warm days of summer, had soothed Emlyn and showed him a Wales of which he had never been aware. He saw that he had been caught in a quest for knowledge, imprisoned in the confines of the written word. As a wandering harper, he had found a new knowledge, that of earth and sky and sea, of wind and forest and mountain.

'What life is better than that of a wandering minstrel?' Emlyn said to the deaf mute beside him. 'Following meandering roads and caressing a harp for the price of a meal.'

Above the headland of Pen Gogarth, the sky had blued the sea, but a wisp of the shadow of night still lingered. Birds chattered and twittered in clumps of elder and thorn and sea birds screamed above white-topped waves. The wind strengthened, coming in from the sea and from the cliff face, came the screech of a merlin. Emlyn watched as the bird soared into the air and then became still, as if pinned motionless, as she scanned for prey.

Bran ran into the cave and soon returned carrying a hardened loaf and a stone jug of ale which was flat and murky but Emlyn enjoyed the bitter taste. Biting into the loaf, he realised he was starving and that the bread had only wet his appetite. Turning to Bran he used his hands to frame a mute question, 'Have we nothing more?'

Bran shook his shaggy head, grinning. He grunted and ran back into the cave, he returned with a bow and a quiver of arrows. Emlyn took them and held his thumb up to his companion.

Bran capered about with his hands to his head; fingers held up on either side in imitation of rabbit ears. There were plenty of rabbits about, burrowing into the hillside, from where he stood, Emlyn could see them, nibbling at the flowery grass, crunching on dew soaked stalks with whiskers bristling and velvet ears cocked for danger. Emlyn swung the quiver over his shoulder and walked over the hill with Bran bouncing after him.

The sun was well up when he heard the calls. Goronwy sounded angry because they had left the cave unwatched; Goronwy who had turned sour and bitter now that he faced the realities of a religious war. Emlyn called to him and waved from the crest of a hill. Bran scampered down the slope and Goronwy shouted at him. Bran's ears were shut forever from sound. His mind was trapped in eternal childhood and his blank eyes looked out upon the world of a child of seven. He could see Goronwy's anger and see the mouth that snapped silently at him. He curled up in a ball and whimpered.

'What the Devil are you doing?' Goronwy called as Emlyn approached with two rabbits hanging from his belt.

'Getting breakfast,' Emlyn answered. 'Have you lit a fire?'

Goronwy's voice lifted above all else. 'You left the cave unguarded!'

Emlyn stopped and leaned on his bow; the long slither of polished ash bent to take his weight. He said, 'And what was I to do if it was discovered? Remain here to be martyred? Did you see the printed pages?'

The tension left Goronwy, his shoulders lost the stiffened look and he bent to ruffle Bran's untidy hair. 'It looks good.'

'What we have here is probably the first printing press in Wales.' Emlyn said. 'It could be put to better use in producing works that will be a benefit to all. Why don't we find a better place, somewhere where we need not be afraid of printing?'

Goronwy shook his head, the mop of brown curls untidy in the wind. 'What would be the point in that? This whole project has been for the purpose of spreading Catholic doctrine.'

Emlyn knew more about the press than anyone else. He had come back from his bardic wanderings to find Goronwy's inexperience had brought the scheme to a standstill. It was a simple problem but Goronwy had never had much time to learn the method with which things worked. Emlyn had fixed it and they had moved it to the cave away from curious eyes.

Emlyn loosened the rabbits from his belt and walked to a flat rock over looking the sea. Here he set about cleaning and skinning them with his dagger, tossing the waste into the sea below. He knew without asking that Goronwy would not light a cooking fire, nor allow any to do so in case the smoke attracted curious eyes. The unlikeness of this happening on this remote headland made no difference.

Goronwy watched him impatiently for a time before he turned towards the cave. Voices came from within, Rhys and Tom arguing as usual. They were young Jesuit novices like himself and were good workers, once they settled their differences.

When the rabbits were ready, Emlyn made his way down a steep pathway to the beach where the smoke from a fire would not be noticed. Bran scuttled along at his heels making joyous sounds in anticipation for breakfast.

After some time, Goronwy came down to the beach with an uneasy expression. Emlyn sat in front of a heap of crackling drift wood with the rabbits skewered above the flames. The tide was in. Wind snatched at the wave crests before they plied in, loaded with sea weed, in the water's wake, sea creatures burrowed in wet sand.

Jumping from the path to the sand, Goronwy said, 'Something has happened that will change matters to our benefit and that of our church.'

'What?' Emlyn answered while he readjusted the roasting spit. Either the Queen is dead or England has been overrun by Spain, he thought. Keeping the amusement out of his voice he continued on a less disastrous thought. 'Has the Queen decided to wed Philip of Spain?'

'How could that happen? He is already wed to another, some French princess. Our harlot Queen lost her chance there.'

Emlyn stopped what he was doing and looked up at his friend. 'Goronwy, however sure footed you feel,' he warned, 'speaking slander against the rightful Queen of England will not save you from a headman's axe.'

'Rightful?' Goronwy said mockingly. 'Her grandfather killed the rightful ruler of England at the battle of Bosworth. And her own father declared her illegitimate. The Queen of Scotland has a better claim to the English throne.'

'You will recall,' answered Emlyn with equal mockery, 'that our present Queen's grandfather was a Welshman.'

'Well there,' Goronwy replied hesitantly, 'at least he was Catholic. Soon I, and others like me, one of which I hoped would be you Emlyn Tomas, will be able to say whatever we like about the Queen of England. We can practice our faith as God wills, not hidden away in secret as though we were at fault.'

Emlyn poked at the fire with a blackened twig. 'As long as the Queen says different, we are at fault Goronwy,' he answered calmly.

'Why do you always insist upon that argument?' Goronwy asked bitterly. 'Have you become reformer? Turned away from the true church?'

'Of course not,' Emlyn replied. He stood up flinging the stick away from him. 'What is the matter with you Goronwy? You jump at me on every word. I have not forgotten the vows we made, I have just had time to think and to realise that the world is so much more.'

'Yes I can see that!' Goronwy replied disdainfully. 'Time to think your way out of all the plans we made together. You have forgotten Emlyn, we vowed try to bring Catholicism back to Wales.'

'I did not promise such,' said Emlyn defensively.

'Whether you did or not, I assumed you would because of all we did in Paris and all we were prepared to do when we became priests. What has turned your heart ?'

Emlyn turned towards the sea. 'I have just had time to think and can see nothing but suffering resulting from this. We have spoken of this Goronwy.'

'Suffering?' Goronwy gasped, his voice rising. 'Are we not taught that to suffer for God's cause, to put all our worldly fears behind us is to gain great merit in heaven?' He took hold of Emlyn's shoulder and swung him around to face him. His fingers ground into Emlyn's shoulders.

Emlyn glared at him. 'I was not speaking of personal martyrdom Goronwy, worthy though it is, rather of the pain brought on those who play no part in this. Would you see more innocents suffer because of what you have caused? Already authority questions where all this printed stuff comes from. It will not be long before it is discovered and what then? Would you see Bran here and others like him led to the hanging cross? We tread a forbidden path Goronwy. Few will answer to the call.'

'Because it is forbidden you dare not continue?' Goronwy shouted, his anger mounting. 'Are you so cowed Emlyn?'

Emlyn pulled away impatiently. 'I have seen how matters lie,' he replied. 'Wales does not want the likes of you and I; few martyrs here died for what they believe in. The ruination of the church and monasteries in the old king's time washed over Wales with hardly a ripple. And do you know why? Because in that King and in our present Queen there flows Welsh blood. A Welsh King was prophesied to rule from the throne of England, and this has come to be. There are too few that remain loyal to the Catholic way. We are ill prepared. It will take better men than us to bring the true church back to Wales.'

Emlyn could smell his breakfast burning. He crouched by the fire to turn it. 'Something will come out of all this,' he said soothingly. 'Whatever it is it will not be a return to the old ways.'

In three steps Goronwy was at the fire. He kicked at it, sending sparks flying, crackling into the air. The roasting rabbits, fell from the spit, bounced and rolled, collecting a skin of sand. Bran leaped up grunting and huffing, waving his arms about like a seagull. Emlyn bounded to his feet and frantically brushed at the sparks igniting his jerkin.

Goronwy had turned from him and was halfway up the beach by the time Emlyn recovered enough to run after him. Goronwy swung around to face him. 'That's it for you isn't it? You faithless bastard! Something will come out of all this, but it isn't a something that Emlyn Tomas will be involved in. Let others deal with it, fools like me and Rhys and Tom Tilbury. What have you done in all the time we have been here? I'll tell you what, you've gone off strumming your harp, strolling through the country as if nothing mattered. As if the very laws we were taught by are scattered to the four winds with none to say 'This faith is precious, this faith is right. For this I will live and suffer and die for!' You have not even found the courage to pay your respects to your uncle. You are so busy feeling sorry for yourself that you cannot see further than your own pitiful interests!'

'You know me Goronwy and you know that it is nothing like that!' Emlyn protested running to keep pace with Goronwy's long, furious steps. 'I admit that I have been a little blinded by ambition, but not for the reasons you say. I do not consider myself a saint, far from it. I admit that I have doubts. Do you never question? Do you never ask why things are the way they are? Why do so many turn away from centuries of belief?'

Goronwy stopped abruptly and sat down on a lichen speckled boulder at the base of the cliff. His eyes glinted with a fanatical light, an aspect that Emlyn had never seen before.

'You should have learnt that the first year with the Jesuits!' Goronwy replied. 'Questions lead the soul astray. You more than most Emlyn, should know the danger of that. You have been well prepared. Even here in Wales, far from the lessons of priests, most of the families adhere to the lessons taught them by generations of Catholics. They do not question and nor should you!'

'But they do Goronwy. I have seen it on the road with my grandfather. They question and they do not want the old ways any more.'

Without listening to him, Goronwy continued, 'Wales may act now as a beaten dog, but all she needs is leadership. The majority of people are still Catholic and sheer numbers would overcome the odds. Any who say different, any who stand in our way will feel the sword of God!'

'What are you saying?' Emlyn persisted. 'That you would kill by flame and blade, bring terror to this place? The sword is not the answer nor has it ever been, yet none learn from its ineffectiveness. I would not draw a weapon for the sake of the Catholic, Welsh or otherwise, Goronwy you and I are not soldiers. Wales is adhered to England irretrievably, Wales is under command of the Queen and I, Goronwy, as you know, am loyal to her wishes.'

'The Queen cares nothing for Wales!' Goronwy shouted. 'Her illegitimate head has never once turned in our direction.'

Emlyn sighed with annoyance. 'What would she look to Wales for? Are you not aware of the hostilities the Queen has to face against Spain and France and the Netherlands and from the Pope? There are other matters here of greater import.'

'I am well aware of her predicament.' Goronwy answered. 'But if she were to return us to the true faith then Europe would embrace her with a loving heart. Her difficulties arise from the fact that she has made herself head of the reformed church.'

'She has never appointed herself as such.' Emlyn answered kicking at seaweed and shingle.

'But Protestant Europe has, and it amounts to the same thing. Were she to revert, England would prosper as never before. Can you not see it?'

'No, I can not see it so! England has known peace for a decade. The country is becoming rich enough to stand on it's own already. Jesu Goronwy! What do you think beggared us in the first place? If any wish to undermine the harmony of Elizabeth's England, then yes, we will fall back to the horror and blood letting of Mary Tudor's reign. You and I know of the war-torn fields of France and the Netherlands. Blood and abject misery is what religious reform has brought to these. England will go the same, rebellion brings disaster on us all, whatever we believe in.'

'And what of the Catholics that remain here, adhering to the laws of the church?' Goronwy said, clenching his fist until it turned white. 'Are they to have nothing but persecution? Can they not owe allegiance to the Pope, appointed by God, without fear of the rack and the hangman's rope?'

'They owe allegiance first to the Queen,' said Emlyn. He sat down stabbing at the sand with a piece of driftwood.

Goronwy said, 'If a man cannot stand up for what he believes in, then he is already damned.'

'We do our duty to God by obeying the Queen,' said Emlyn. 'What other choice do we have?'

'And if t he Queen is wrong?'

'Then the Queen suffers eternal damnation for leading her people astray. The blame lies on her head. Our duty is first to the Queen who is equally appointed by God.'

'Are we sheep?' Goronwy cried. 'To go bleating to our master's call even if he guides us over the brink of a precipice?'

'Come now Goronwy. The Queen is our sovereign, our ruler, most are bound to live with her religious doctrine because of the very fact that she is the Queen who's law must be obeyed.'

'The Queen is a devil! Misguided and weak. I wonder if we are ruled by her at all and not by that William Cecil who sits upon her shoulder like a witch's familiar. It's a council of heretics and devils! It is what men believe in their hearts that counts in the eyes of God. They can pay lip service to the Queen and remain faithful behind their own doors.'

'If we do not obey the Queen's law, how long do you think we would last in our fight for Catholicism? We must obey our sovereign in order to preserve our own land and our lives.'

'No! First we are answerable to God.' Goronwy rose to his feet to emphasize his anger he towered above Emlyn like an avenging angel. 'Each man knows in his heart that he is answerable to God before Queen or country. If we have the leadership of Norfolk and the lords of the North then the Catholics will rise up and put the Catholic, Scottish Queen on the throne of England. Every man would pick up pitch folk and scythe and fight for his right to believe as he should. The people must be brought together, a holy army to fight for the true church. Now that Mary Queen of Scots is on English soil, we have only to free her from her imprisonment. In the Netherlands now, the Duke of Alva calls to him all those that have fled the rule of the English Queen. Men who have forsaken family and home to be allowed the freedom of their chosen faith. If we clear the English throne of the usurper, Alva would come to support the Catholics. His army would see order and peace in England.'

Emlyn stared at him in horror. This was treason and he wanted no part of it. The young man who stood before him with the fire of his conviction burning in his every word, was not the same boy who had left so innocently with Emlyn four years before. Goronwy saw himself as champion to the cause. Goronwy was a Jesuit. 'That would never do Goronwy and well you know it,' he said patiently. 'No sane man would wish the bloodshed of France and the Netherlands repeated here. There are none but fools who welcome the interference of Alva and his Hispanicization. Would you have England under Spanish rule? Again?'

Goronwy dragged his fingers through the thatch of mud-brown curls. The anger seemed to melt out of him, as if he was ashamed that he had been so outspoken. 'I would not,' he admitted, 'but I would do all in my power to bring Queen Elizabeth back to the guidance of the Holy Church. It could be achieved. There are enough of us, God knows. Can I count you among us?'

Head down, Emlyn did not answer. He felt hemmed in by Goronwy's looming presence, a Goronwy speaking with the voice of Father Barzini. Emlyn suppressed a shudder. He no longer knew what he wanted and even wondered if he ever had. His uncle wanted him to be a priest, his grandfather wanted to make a bard of him and Goronwy, by the sound of things, wanted him to be a martyr in a cause that he no longer cared for.

Standing over him, hands on hips, Goronwy said, 'Swear to me on the Blood of Christ who died for our sins that you will stand with us!' The words hissed with surf on shingle.

Emlyn looked up, but Goronwy's face was hidden in shadow. Only the light from his eyes showed the intensity he felt in the question asked.

Speaking softy Emlyn said, 'Why do you ask me to give you such an oath?'

'You have been led astray,' said Goronwy in a voice like a priest in confession. 'It is understandable. You have been distracted by the bardic wishes of your grandfather. Although he has helped us form time to time, he does not understand the problems we face. Emlyn, if you search your soul for sin, repent and meditate on the passion of Christ, you will be cleansed. Soon we will return to France, before the winter. There you will be able to find the peace you seek and build on your convictions. You have been too long away from the influence of our true vocation. Swear to me that our differences have not turned you from our purpose.'

Emlyn tried to summon up the courage to tell Goronwy that he would not go back to College de Clermont with him. Suddenly, his ambitions and desire to tramp around Italy in the wake of the English merchant paled into insignificance beside Goronwy's noble ambition. But Emlyn could only see disaster looming for the courageous printers. Somehow, he had to get Goronwy away from there before this happened. He could not look at his friend as he spoke. 'I swear Goronwy, that I will return to France with you.'

'Come then. Let us see what we can salvage of your breakfast.' Goronwy spoke as if he was addressing Bran, all anger gone from his voice. He pulled Emlyn to his feet and threw a thick arm around his shoulders, guiding him back towards the sea, laughing and kicking at pebbles as if nothing had passed between them.

Emlyn soon learned more about he abdicated Queen of Scotland. Mary Stuart, had escaped from imprisonment in Loch Leven castle in May. She had drawn together her followers and engaged in civil war that had led to ignoble defeat at Langside. The Queen of Scotland had failed to pacify her people. They had no mind to follow a queen who had partaken in the murder of her husband and had run off with her lover and married him. After Langside, she had fled to England, asking the assistance of her cousin the Queen of England. Now after months of thought and planning, the Catholics spoke of Mary Queen of Scots as the future Catholic queen of England.

Catholics came to the cave on Pen Gogarth, they gathered bundles of pamphlets and went off again to distribute them wherever they could. The news of Queen Mary's flight into England had filled them all with new hope; that the Scottish Queen was held imprisoned in England, suspected of helping in the murder of her husband made no difference, nor that she had run off and wed the rake Bothwell, who had divorced his wife but twelve days before his marriage to the Queen. The Scots might find it difficult to forgive this faithless queen, but in Wales they felt no such animosity. Here was a Catholic queen. And in the North of England, where she was now held, they considered the possibilities of advantage. While two queens stood on English soil, like opposite queens on a chess board, the realm stirred with the muttering of rebellion.

The ten relatively peaceful years of Elizabeth's reign were not to be repeated. The uneasy relationship between England and Spain was fast approaching a crisis. Across the Channel, Alva continued his bloody war in the Spanish Netherlands and looked towards England to make the next move in his harsh crushing of heresy. The Pope growled and threatened excommunication on the heretic queen and all who followed her. Nearer to home Elizabeth kept the Scottish Queen captive in fear that her release would bring an unfavourable alliance between Scotland and France. Within her own borders England faced the treat of rebellion, Catholic against Protestant, father against son in the turmoil of civil war. Even within Elizabeth's court, schemes were hatched. Plotting ensued in hidden corners for the downfall of the Queen and her secretary William Cecil.

The watch on English ports was doubled. Roads were guarded and travellers were searched. None felt free to journey on England's roads without license or honest intent. Books and papers were discovered and destroyed. Extensive searches revealed printing presses and Catholic sympathizers. Priests were arrested and thrown into the Tower. All loyal to the Queen and to England's prosperity kept a diligent watch and paid spies to infiltrate known rebellious groups and seek out others.

The Catholics became more secretive. They attended meetings and heard mass in cellars, attics and even out in remote fields or lonely moor lands. In Wales they took the sacrament on the slopes of Snowdon. The grey mountainside was their cathedral; the flat, grey slate laid across two smaller rocks, like some ancient table of pre-Christian sacrifice, was their altar. They looked to the noblemen of the North to bring England back under the influence of Rome. They set their own guards and their own spies to watch, to infiltrate and to negotiate with the enemies of the Queen of England. Goronwy's followers rejoiced at the little knowledge they gleaned and fired with enthusiasm, they continued their noble quest, unaware of the tightening of the noose that already surrounded them.

Chapter 16 Wales

After a week of work in which he had hardly closed his eyes in sleep, Emlyn left the busy cave and made his way towards Rhuddlan to visit his uncle. Goronwy, having won his friend back to his side, had returned to his old self. Emlyn had joked and played the fool as he used to in Paris. Goronwy, had joined in on occasion, their disagreement was forgotten. Most of the time they worked. Emlyn saw in Goronwy that special spirit that compelled men to follow him. When he talked, there was conviction in his words and in his manner. Goronwy seemed driven; as if their freedom would soon be brought to an end by discovery. Whatever instinct warned Goronwy, he should have known that Emlyn Tomas would be the one to bring misfortune.

For nearly five months Emlyn had managed to avoid his uncle. Now he was off to pay his respects to the man who had provided for him, given him an education and sent him off to be a priest. Emlyn did not look forward to the meeting. Squire Hugh would be well aware now of how matters stood between his nephew and the Society of Jesus. There was no avoiding it, so Emlyn straightened his hat and walked down the old Roman road that led from the fishing town of Abergele to the river crossing at Rhuddlan.

Eventually, tired and thirsty he stopped and cupped water in his hands from a tiny spring bubbling over the dark peat by the roadside. Stray corn had seeded and ripened by the flow of water. Emlyn gathered a handful and sat on stone rubbing it between his palms to loosen the seed. The road ran straight across flat water-meadows; where black cattle stood knee deep, snatching at mouthfuls of nettle and reedy grass. Tiny in the distance, Rhuddlan castle stood on a rise of ground overlooking the river Clwyd as it spread out over the marshland before entering the sea. Cooking fires spiralled up, softening the line of roof tops that wound up the hill towards the castle. A late afternoon mist blurred the river banks and the sun was hot filling the air with the mellow harvest glow of October.

In the distance, Emlyn saw the stooped figure of an old woman walking with the aid of a stick. She carried a pile of twiggy kindling across her shoulders. In spite of this, she moved rapidly, her stick poking savagely at the road as the distance between them closed.

Emlyn rose from the stone as she drew level and removed his hat. 'Good day old mother,' he said greeting her.

She stopped and peered at him from under her hood; her eyes like bloomed sloes. Her face was a mask of threadlike wrinkles, her nose like a beak. From her ragged clothing there hung bags of sea shells, holed stones threaded on leather, and bundles of dried herbs. She smelled like fish and carried a pot of river eels in her other hand. Emlyn knew who she was; Mafanwy Fawr. She had a reputation for being a witch. No one would point a finger and call her such, they were afraid of what she might do. They treated her with great respect.

She prodded at Emlyn's chest with her walking stick, it was covered with leaves, as if it was still growing. She wheezed and cackled in the old tongue. 'Be sure to have a sound ship beneath thee *Mab-y-Ddarig*,' she said with a wicked toothless grimace, 'the tide is turning.'

A curlew sang and swept above the water meadow. Emlyn blinked. '*Mab-y-Ddarig*' she had called him, Son of the Dragon. The red dragon of Wales that, according to Gruffydd's ancient tales, had been summoned from the mountain by Emrys Wledig Merddin, King Arthur's magician who had called the red dragon to defeat the white dragon of England. *Mab-y-Ddraig*, was a fabled warrior, a hero of Wales who would come again in time of need to save the land and it's people from invasion. Emlyn said, 'What do you mean old one? Why have you named me *Mab-y-Ddraig*?'

Mafanwy Fawr sniffed and shuffled, muttering to herself. She did not answer Emlyn. She stood looking him up and down as if he were for sale. He felt that she could see into his very heart. Eventually she said 'The church not good enough for thee eh? Going against the wishes of the mother that bore thee?'

Surprised at her words, Emlyn said, 'Do you know who my mother was?'

She turned away. She pursed her lips, making a wet, smacking sound. 'Tell ye if ye pay old Mafanwy,' she answered. She lowered her bundle of kindling to the ground, gathered her rags together and sat on the grass by the stream. Tall reeds rustled in the breeze and bog-myrtle released a heavy scent in the warm air.

'I have no coin,' Emlyn said. Then he remembered the gems sewn into his tunic. He knew enough of the old woman not to ignore her words. Without a moment's hesitation, he drew his eating knife and cut through the stitching. He withdrew the scrap of leather that the gems were wrapped in and sat on the ground beside her. He unrolled the cloth. 'I have these,' he offered. 'Take one and tell me what you know.'

Mafanwy pulled at her shawl. She moaned and mumbled. She reached out a clawed finger and pushed the stones about. Selecting the red stone, the one that Fra Sebastiano had said was the best of them all, she held it up to the light.

Emlyn regretted his impulsive action. But the information he may be able to learn from the old woman was of more value to him than the gems, of which he had little understanding.

Mafanwy Fawr shook her head. The shells woven into her skirts clattered musically. In her palm, the light in the deep red stone seemed to awake. Mafanwy whispered with rasping breath.

Emlyn drew back, alarmed.

The old woman threw dust over the jewel and muttered over it as if she were weaving a spell. She shook her head vigorously, dropped the glittering gem and shuffled back.

'What is it?' Emlyn said in a breathless voice.

'A Dragon's stone,' Mafanwy wheezed in a nasal tone. 'I see one stone but there should be three, one for each son of the Dragon's bride.' She broke off with a cackle of laughter. 'This is not for Mafanwy Fawr,' she spat in disgust. 'A spell lies upon the stones.'

Desperate to learn more, Emlyn said, 'Tell me the meaning of the words wise one. I will pay whatever I can.'

'Whatever Mafanwy asks?'

'If it is mine to give, yes.'

She looked doubtful for a moment and then peered down the road as if disinterested. Time stood still. Clouds of midges rose above the stream and butterflies hovered above clumps of hemp-acrimony.

Emlyn touched her shoulder. 'Please old mother, tell me what I need to know. Does my mother still live? Is she the Dragon's Bride you speak of?'

She nodded. 'Three sons, she repeated. 'But only one son of the Dragon.'

Emlyn was puzzled by her words of dragons and a little afraid. He said, 'Will I find what I seek?'

Her laugh was chilling. Emlyn snatched his hand back as if scorched. She rocked back and forth on her heels. 'Oh yes, find so much will wish thee never looked.'

He looked at her in astonishment.

'Mafanwy will ask thee in time for that thou owes.'

Emlyn suddenly felt cold.

Mafanwy reached into her bag of bits and brought out a little purse tied with a drawstring. She offered it to Emlyn.

He backed away and shook his head.

'Take it *Mab-y-Ddraig.* A talisman to keep thee from death. It is from the old ways before the Christ. From time of Emrys Merddin. Not evil. Take what Mafanwy offers thee an' remember that the dragon comes in many guises.'

Emlyn accepted it with reluctance. He watched her for a long time, until she was again reduced by distance, a tiny bundle poking at the roadside with her stick. He stood in the middle of the road, his brow creased in puzzlement his heart thudding with inexplicable fear. He made the sign of the cross. 'Crazy old witch!'

Who would make a *Mab-y-Ddraig* out of Emlyn Tomas? He was quite certain that whoever his father had been, the chances of his being Welsh were extremely remote. Aside from that, the only weapon that Emlyn had ever held was a long bow. He had never shot anything bigger than a rabbit. Only in dreams had he ever been a warrior. Here was no saviour of Wales, but a young man with no family to boast of and a head full of conflicting emotions. As a novice with a scholarly upbringing, he had his share of fights and brawls, usually in defence of his honour, until he discovered he had no honour to defend. None could rise Emlyn to anger now by naming him bastard. But in those early days of childhood and schooling, Goronwy had always stood by him. Goronwy who had been bigger than most boys his age, who could fight with the best of them and win.

Emlyn tried to make sense of the old woman's words. There is one, he thought, who may be able to see the meaning, and that is Tad-cu. Perhaps it is time I told him about the gems too.

A breeze blew off the sea carrying the scent of seaweed. Rain clouds gathered on the horizon; a fast approaching storm after the months of heat. Emlyn took time to replace the jewels from where he had taken them before he continued on his way. He could see the grey ruins of St. Mary's monastery on the shoulder of a hill to the right of the castle. Many of the statues and carvings from there had found their way to Gruffydd's house with Old John Talbot. The walls stood forlorn and robbed of stone. No sound of melodious psalm issued from the broken arched windows. Since Thomas Cromwell had visited it with his evangelist wreckers, spreading the new faith with violence, no monks had lived there. The castle had come under the same heavy hand. Rhuddlan castle, that had stood guarding the crossing of the river Clwyd for over three hundred years, was not so easily brought to ruin. When the dust had settled and the destroyers had moved off, the town's people had moved back behind the protective walls. They had rebuild their shops and houses safe from thieves and the raw wind that howled over the marshes in winter. On the other side, towards the sea, stood the church of St. Mary's, in a nest of yew trees and gravestones. Gruffydd's wife Olwen was buried there with most of her family.

Emlyn crossed the bridge into Rhuddlan. The town was quiet in the late sun, a sprawl of buildings of stone and wood. Most were of wattle and daub with steep roofs either thatched or tiled with slate. Old men dozed on doorsteps with dogs curled at their feet. A group of children played in the mud at the river's edge. There were few women to be seen, most were indoors preparing the evening meal. Emlyn turned towards the castle where a path ran beside the river toward the farm belonging to Goronwy's family. Emlyn had promised to call there on his way. If the rain came in, he knew he might find welcome there, but he was not sure after what Goronwy had told him before he set out to visit Rhuddlan. 'Do not expect things to be as they have been.' Goronwy had said. When pressed, he would say nothing more but had smiled. Emlyn had not been reassured.

At the house of Squire Hugh Morgan, the kitchens banged with noise and delicious smells wafted through the house as the evening meal was made ready. The squire was out shooting duck with the Bishop of St. Asaph, while his wife Elizabeth, meticulously chopped the dead heads off her roses on the front wall of the impressive house. Her step son Owain, had gone off two days ago, after an argument with his father. They expected him back before night fall, report said that he had stayed in Rhuddlan for two days getting drunk with his friends in the Black Horse.

Upstairs, dressing in her bedchamber, was Ellen the daughter of Elizabeth Morgan by her first husband John Boutflower. She struggled out of the 'best' dress she had been forced to try on. It was sky blue, the bodice and sleeves embroidered with white and silver flowers, the hem weighed down with a length of white rabbit fur. It crumpled into a heap at her feet. She stepped out of it as if it were on fire. She was a determined fourteen year old.

'What bedevilment got you girl?' Connie O'Neill chided. She was a round, Irish, grey-haired housekeeper who had known Ellen since her birth and cherished her like a child of her own. She was an old family servant who had been maid to Ellen's mother before her. There were few in Wales who had not heard of the O'Neills of Tyrone. They were a ruling clan from Ulster and considered as wild as their country. Whatever connection Connie O'Neill had with this notorious tribe of wild Irish, she kept to herself and it was many years since she had visited the Fair Country.

'I am not going to wear that!' Ellen shouted 'Why can't stepfather buy me material for another? I'm fourteen and I want a proper dress.'

'All the Saints! It is a proper dress. There's many a girl who....'

'Then give it to them! If I have to wear it I shall scorch it or spill elderberry juice all over it,' said Ellen spitefully. 'Young ladies wear dark colours now, didn't you know? I want a dress as dark as a glass of malmsey, or one the colour of the forest and with real pearls on it, and lots and lots of under-dresses, all covered in lace, like the stuff Mr. Lloyd brings from Flanders for his daughters. I want one shining with jewels like the Queen.'

'I want, I want, I want,' echoed Connie O'Neill, 'and what would you be knowing about the Queen and what she dresses in?' She held a threatening hairbrush in one hand and had brought out her 'pointing finger' on the other.

'Harriet Crew told Wendy Williams and she told me,' replied Ellen tossing her head. 'Harriet Crew was in London less than a year ago and she was presented to the Queen.'

'Tittle tattle!' Connie chuckled, 'she never did anything of the sort.'

'You're only jealous,' snapped Ellen.

'I am not.'

'Yes you are Connie O'Neill!'

'Jealous is it? And what would I be wanting in a fancy court, full of the English and the foreigners? Sit on the stool now and let me comb that nest before you have the birds finding a home there. By the Saints Ellen Morgan, you get more wayward every day. If it's a young lady you're considering yourself now, you'd best start behaving like one Malmsey dress or no!'

Ellen sank down on the stool as if all the air had gone out of her. She stuck her tongue out at her reflection in the oval mirror from Tuscany, making sure first that Connie was watching.

Connie attacked the tangles with vigour. Ellen's hair was a striking dark ox-blood, long and thick and wavy. Her skin was pale in contrast to her dark determined brows and the furious deep-set eyes beneath were the colour of Welsh peat. She winced and moaned continuously as Connie dragged the brush through knots and tresses until it ran smoothly and the hair fell brushed and shining to Ellen's waist.

As Connie plaited, Ellen bit her lower lip. Thoughtfully she said, 'How do you know that Harriet Crew hasn't seen the Queen?'

'Harriet Crew has never been further than her back gate,' Connie replied. 'I can well see how the girl has been brought to allow her imagination to run wild.'

'I knew she was nasty,' said Ellen pouting.

'Well I dare say matters won't change much when she's wed our Owain,' said Connie philosophically.

'I heard him say,' said Ellen staring intently into the mirror, 'that he is going to lock her up in the nearest tower and only use her for breeding.'

'Ellen!'

'And he's going to blindfold himself to do so. That's what I heard. I'm only repeating it.'

Connie picked up a blue ribbon and began twisting it into the girl's hair with a vigour that showed her disapproval. She stood back, head to one side and admired Ellen as she sat like a little girl in her under-dress. Eventually Connie said, 'She's a plain girl for all that. But Owain is not marrying her for her looks is he. Who does?'

'I shall,' Ellen replied raising her chin and looking down her nose.

'There's not a man born fair enough for you my heartlet,' Connie replied affectionately.

In Ellen's heart there was, she was in love with Owain Morgan, but he was going to marry Harriet Crew.

Emlyn Tomas paused by a farm gate that led to Goronwy's house. A slice of orange sun sat above the black clouds, leaving a shaft of brilliant light and a reflection of burnished gold on the darkening sea. The clouds loomed closer, boiling towards the land, full of rain and thunder; there was going to be a spectacular storm. From amidst a haze of gnats, Emlyn watched the light dim. He could see the long Welsh house, the barns, the outhouses and behind them, the hay ricks lit yellow by the last of the sun. He opened the gate, and walked through the orchard. There were baskets on the ground piled with ripe apples and ladders leaned against the trees giving access to the high branches. It all looked familiar and friendly. Emlyn's steps quickened as he neared the farm that Goronwy's family had run for three generations and where Emlyn had found warmth and welcome on the many occasions that he had stayed.

Still some distance from the house, he saw two of Goronwy's brothers stop their work, put down their tools and walk towards him. Goronwy had five brothers, three older than himself, which was why Goronwy had been sent to be a priest in France. The two now approaching were the older two, Geraint and Gerald. They were so alike that they could have been twins.

They were both bigger than Goronwy, with thick set features, the same mob of unruly hair and strength enough to lift a cow. They had both wed while Emlyn and Goronwy had been in France. Emlyn had learnt through letters, that grandchildren already ran about the farm yard causing havoc.

Emlyn waved and called out in greeting, his face lit with a smile.

They did not wave, neither did they smile. They came toward him like a pair of stalking lions.

Emlyn stopped smiling and stopped walking. He stood beside a fenced-off area enclosing a mud hole, full of geese and noisy ducks.

Geraint, the eldest arrived first. His face was white with anger, his mouth set in a hard line, his brows lowered in animosity. He was not going to stop.

Emlyn backed a few steps. 'What's the matter Geraint?' he asked indignantly. 'Wait! It's me Emlyn!'

Wordless, Geraint stretched out, grasped Emlyn's arms in a malicious grip, lifted him from the ground and shook him like a jellyfish.

Emlyn kicked out and struggled.

Geraint threw him over the fence and leaped in after him. Ducks flapped furiously and filled the air with squawks of wrath. Geese stretched their long necks and charged en-mass at the first intruder, hissing and snapping with spiteful breaks. Before the hostility of Geraint's long, vengeful steps, the birds took to the air; those not quick enough, he tossed and booted in all directions, if they stood between him and the target of his anger.

Dust billowed and feathers flew as Emlyn scrambled to his feet. He walked backwards with hands held in front of him to ward off Geraint. He tripped over a grey goose and landed at the edge of the mud hole.

Geraint grabbed him by a handful of shirt and jerkin and pulled him to his feet.

Helpless, Emlyn closed his eyes, resigned to a mud bath.

Instead, Geraint hit him on the side of the head with a fistful of nails.

At least it felt like a fistful of nails, before Emlyn hit the opposite fence, splintered the wood and piled through on the other side. Next he was near suffocated by ducks and geese as they made a bid for freedom. He sat up spitting out feathers. He held his head which was threatening to fall off. His senses reeled, his hand came away sticky with blood. Rain began to fall and Geraint was still coming.

A voice bawled out from the long house. Above the raucous squawking, snapping and sibilation, Emlyn recognised it as a voice to obey on pain of a sound thrashing.

Geraint paid it no heed. Deaf in his anger, his steps did not falter.

Emlyn stood up dazed and stumbled towards the house. He couldn't make any sense out of the situation, Geraint had always treated him with kindness before. He began to run. As he came around the corner of a stone barn, just a hand's reach from his pursuer, a stick came down and crashed across his back with force enough to fell him. He had time to look around to see the stick come up again to catch Geraint under the chin with equal force. Geraint's feet flew up from under him and he fell like a tree. The ground shook as he landed with all the breath driven from his lungs.

Above them both, dressed in grey with an apron, stood Branwen Glyn Parry, a tiny, compact woman, who had borne seven large children and brought them all up to survive. She had her hands on her hips, still grasping her broom. Her face was a picture of contempt. She tapped her foot. Her bonnet had come askew loosening a silver-grey plait.

Emlyn stood up, his head pounded and his right eye was already swelling shut. He could taste blood in his mouth. She was the only woman he had ever loved. He would have liked to give her a big hug and sweep her feet off the ground, as he had done at thirteen; even then he had been taller than her. Instead, he just bowed to her sorrowfully. Then he turned and walked away. It began to rain harder.

Branwen Glyn Parry stepped over her oldest son, who looked as guilty as he had when he'd stolen her hen's eggs at the age of five. She went after Emlyn Tomas in the rain. She caught up with him and pulled at his sleeve. 'Come on inside Emlyn bach,' she said coaxing him. 'I'll fix you a nice bit of food and see if something can be done about that poor eye.'

Emlyn turned to face her, but he kept walking. 'I'll not come where I'm not wanted.'

'Well now,' said Branwen running to keep pace. 'I thought you'd have more sense Emlyn Tomas, after all that's happened. Though I'm not saying it was right of Geraint to go for you like that.'

Emlyn stopped. He said, 'After all what's happened?'

'You don't know?'

'No I don't know.'

'Goronwy can't have told you then?'

'No,' said Emlyn tiredly. It was like trying to get milk from a billy goat. What had Goronwy said? Do not expect things to be as they have been. Well they certainly were not. Emlyn shivered, he had lost his hat in the duck pond, the rain pelted his head and ran down his neck soaking him to the skin.

'It's your uncle,' said Branwen. 'He's fenced off a piece of our land and called it his own.'

'What?' Emlyn couldn't think straight, his head hurt so much.

'Come on into the house now Emlyn,' she said fastening a hand on his arm and urging him to return. 'I'll be catching my death out here. Come in for my sake, we'll leave Geraint in the rain. He can go and look for all the ducks.'

Emlyn followed her. Geraint had gone but Gerald stood in the shelter of the doorway holding Emlyn's belongings. It was raining so hard that it fell like a curtain between them. Thunder rumbled directly over head.

'Lord save us!' cried Branwen Parry, running for the door.

Emlyn followed reluctantly and banged his head on the lintel. He had grown since he had last walked through this door.

All the fuss that Ellen had made about her dress was to do with Owain's wedding. It was due to take place in three weeks time, after all the rents and dues had been gathered by the landlord. At least that was how his tenants saw it. It would be their hard earned rents that would pay for the wedding of Master Owain. They were not far wrong. Squire Hugh, usually a cautious man with money when it came to any but himself, was giving a wedding feast that he hoped would be remembered for decades.

For Ellen it was to be the grandest happening ever, and for Rhuddlan, the grandest occasion since old Hal's reign. Ellen had grown more and more difficult as the day approached. At the age of nine, she had believed that when she grew up she was going to wed her stepbrother Owain who all the girls wanted to marry. Even though he was always horrid to her, Ellen blessed the ground he walked on and dreamed of nothing else from morning till night. After five years, her love was even stronger. During the years when he had been away studying, it had become almost adoration. How long would she have to wait before his eyes looked upon her as anything other than an irksome little sister?

Now he was to marry Harriet Crew and her hopes were ruined. She was aware that there would be some difficulty about marrying her stepbrother and had a vague suspicion that it would not be allowed at all. But she had never thought for a moment that he would go off and marry someone else.

Before the rain had started Owain had returned. He was sober but the marks of his recent indulgence were clear. He was a sickly colour, more green than white, his beautiful eyes sunken and expressionless.

His stepmother Elizabeth sat by the fire in the hall in front of her embroidery frame. On the walls hung tapestries and painted drapes. They depicted mythical beasts, biblical parables and symbols of the seasons. Hanging above the wide door, between the shields and the panoply arms, a tapestry showed Thaleia, Euphrosyne and Aglaia, the three Graces, flowing with joy and radiance. When Owain walked in the house dogs rose sleepily, wagged their tails feebly and padded to the door to greet the young master. Owain ignored them. He walked to the table as if he was half asleep and sunk down on the bench as if he could go no step further.

'You'll drink yourself to an early grave Owain Morgan,' said his stepmother without raising her eyes.

Owain had heard it all before. He offered no response, instead, he reached for the flagon and splashed wine into a cup. 'Where's father?'

'Out,' she answered tersely.

Owain moved from the bench and sat in his father's chair, it had a high back, carved with acorns. He leaned back and put his long legs on the table, cradling the cup in his hand. The firelight lent colour to his face and set his golden hair shimmering. He was dressed in blue and grey and silver and had the air of a nobleman, reclining after supper.

Soon the servants entered with platters and cups and boards of new baked bread. The dogs wandered about getting in their way, sniffing for tasty titbits that were not yet forthcoming. Candles were lit and placed along the length of the table. Here too were ewers and goblets and plate, a display of the Squire's wealth. In pride of place, there were spice shakers and a salt cellar in the shape of winged griffins, heavy with gold ornament. The sounds of argument came from the kitchen and a further commotion at the door announced the return of the Squire.

Without really believing that her stepson would take any heed of her words, Elisabeth said, 'We have the Bishop of St. Asaph visiting, he has been out with your father. Would it be too much to ask that you show the respect due?'

Surprising her, Owain slowly lowered his legs and stood, voicing a groan. He walked to the fire and bent over his stepmother, planting a kiss on the top of her neat head. 'That's fine work mam,' he said, drawing a finger down the side of her embroidery frame.

Astonished, she looked up at him. 'Do you think so?'

He smiled his angelic smile and sat at her feet, warming his hands by the fire. She could almost love him when he was like this, ashamed of himself for drinking so much and suffering because of it. She knew the cause of it. He didn't want to marry Harriet Crew, he didn't want to marry anyone.

Ellen floated down the stairs in a dress that Connie had magically produced. It had belonged to Elisabeth, but had not been seen for many years and Connie had transformed it with her magic needle, not good enough for a wedding feast, but fine enough on Ellen to turn a head or two. The material of the skirt was russet brown, the sleeves green and embroidered all over with intertwined trefoil and violets. Half way down the stairs, Ellen cleared her throat because no one was watching.

The head of the Bishop turned first. He smiled kindly, acknowledging her presence. He was a big man, round and jovial with lots of chins and pale eyes that disappeared into folds of flesh as he smiled. Ellen's mother looked up, her eyebrows rose and her eyes twinkled. Squire Hugh did not raise his head, but concentrated instead on his plate of mutton. Owain got up from his place at the table and moved to stand at the steps watching his stepsister.

Ellen's heart missed a beat and her foot near missed the step that would have ruined everything.

'Is this my sister?' Owain said. 'Ellen you look quite transformed. Has Connie been exchanging secrets with the fairies for spells?'

She resented his baiting but by the time she had made her decent and Owain had taken her arm smiling warmly, she felt as if her heart had stopped beating.

'My Lord Bishop,' said Owain leading her to the table, 'this is my sister Ellen.'

'Delightful, delightful,' said the Bishop. 'Come sit beside me my dear.'

Ellen resented that too. She wanted to sit next to Owain who was still watching her, the Bishop of course would have to be obeyed.

He moved up to accommodate her, patting a place beside him with an over-ringed hand and then moved back again once she was seated, his fat thigh pressed close to hers.

Ellen ate in silence, her food was cold from waiting. Opposite her, Owain who had hardly touched his meal, watched her all the time. From beneath her lowered lids, Ellen could feel his eyes. She felt her cheeks burn.

'You have a fine girl here Mrs. Morgan' said the Bishop of St. Asaph. 'You'll be looking to another wedding before long.'

The squire growled in discontent.

'My thoughts exactly my Lord Bishop, said Owain. My dear sister can only marry someone exceptional'

The words shattered Ellen's dreams.

'But you did not have that land four years ago,' said Emlyn, surprised to be defending his uncle. 'Is it not common land?'

Gareth, unlike his brother Geraint, thought before he acted. He said, 'What difference should that make? Common land is for the use of the common people. We have grazed our sheep there much longer than that. Father only tilled and planted it with wheat so that he could meet the high rents of the Squire. It's good land for crops but now it has been left to meadow and your uncle has put his dairy herd to graze there.'

Emlyn, pressed a soaked cloth to his bruised eye. 'Have you talked to him?'

'Of course many times, each making matters worse. Short of rebellion, there is nothing we can do. There is no law to protect us.'

'Aye,' growled Geraint from where he s at in the corner of the warm room. He had a nasty bruise under his chin. 'He's not going to be content with one field, he'll take another and another, turning poor folks from their only place of work. He'll make beggars of us all. He'll take the forest next and make it his own private land, hanging any who seek deer or rabbit to feed their families. The poor are grist for his mill as they always have been.'

'But you are not so poor,' said Emlyn, 'to consider yourselves as such demeans the plight of those who are.'

'And what would you know of it Emlyn Tomas, wrapped in the silks of your fortunate birth?' Geraint snarled, his animosity unabated.

'More than you know of my circumstance Geraint Glyn Parry!' Emlyn retorted. 'Your family have done well for themselves here, I've seen the new buildings, this is not a farm suffering for lack of success. For farmers such as you there is no better time than now. Look at the demand for wool? for wheat, feathers, ducks, beans, cabbages, wattle, eggs, meat? A well run farm has nothing to fear from enclosures.'

'Well you would know all about that wouldn't you? You being locked up in a monastery for the last four years,' said Geraint caustically. 'We want no interference from the likes of you.'

Emlyn cradled his aching head in his hands and shook it slowly. 'I have not, as you just pointed out, even been here for four years. How could I know what was going on?' he replied indignantly. 'If there is any complaining to do, then that should be my part surely? After all you attacked me with no provocation. I have not even seen my uncle since I came back from France with your brother. For the sake of your mother and father to whom I owe friendship and respect, I will mention it to my uncle. But I would not hold much hope in reclaiming the land if I were you, I doubt that he will even grant me his time to speak of it.'

Geraint stood up, his huge frame blotting out the lamp light 'When Reginald de Grey seized the lands of Owain Glyndwr,' he said looking down, his thick brows plunging his eyes in shadow, 'the uprising of the whole of Wales was the price he had to pay!'

'To God that it could be so!' Emlyn exclaimed. 'If we had such a man among us again, I would be the first to carry his banner into battle! But we do not, let us push aside romance for reality. You know I have no influence with my uncle, my plea would be lost on him.'

'Which means you will not speak to him at all,' answered Geraint bitterly. 'Squirming out of sticky situations is something which you were ever good at.'

That sounded like something Goronwy would have said. Emlyn sat in silence. Goronwy had not told him about the enclosure of land, Goronwy knew the sort of welcome he would receive here and had left him ignorant. Why? To see his fellow student reduced to a pulp by big brother Geraint?

Emlyn looked around the room that was so familiar to him. The washing, hanging above the fire, the big black cooking pot, the statue of St. David on the narrow window recess and the mottled cat, looking fatter than she had four years ago. All looked the same but it no longer felt the same. Old Glyn Parry had gone to visit his brother in Llanrwst for the evening. His wife Branwen, had fed Emlyn with fish pie followed by cooked blackberries. She had bathed his eye with some miraculous potion that had prevented it from swelling shut. He knew his affection for her would never change, but the brothers were estranged now. They were hostile towards him because of what his uncle had brought about, hostile towards him because of what they believed he stood for, no matter that it was untrue.

Geraint said, 'You'll be at the Knappan for Merioneth?' It was not so much a question as a challenge.

Emlyn knew quite well what sort of treatment he would get from Geraint in the burly rough and tumble of the Knappan, that fiercely fought contest between the men of Merioneth and the men of Flint. He stood carefully and took his short coat from behind the door, it was still wet from the rain. Geraint and Gareth made no move to stop him. In the rain and darkness, it would take him two hours to reach his uncle's manor. It would well after midnight before he arrived and that was not going to help his present standing. He placed his hand on the door.

At the last moment Gareth said, 'Will you stay in the barn? There is no room in the house with the children and all. Mam would see us skinned raw if we didn't at least offer.'

Emlyn opened the door and went out into the night. He stood outside in a puddle. The storm rumbled in the distance. Steady rain still fell, silvered from the lamp light by the door. Soon it began to run down his temples and find a way down the back of his neck. Reluctantly but with his mind made up now, he splashed across the yard, swung open the creaking doors of the barn and went inside to sleep warm with the animals.

He was used to rising early, the Jesuits had them all up long before dawn. Emlyn left the farm before the birds sang.

Squire Hugh Morgan of Plas Newydd was a tall, heavy set man of forty-eight, he looked ten years younger, widening the gap further, between his wife and himself. His hair was the same rich yellow-brown it always had been. His face clean shaven and his dress meticulous. His stood by the window of his solar, looking out on to the meadows that stretched out and down to the river bank. He knew that if he had stuck to the old traditional ways, he would not now be able to stand on his own land and plan for it's expansion. It was something that his father Gruffydd, had never understood. As a flower turns it's head towards the sun in order to survive, so must we turn, adapt and prosper, he thought, resting his ringed hands on the window ledge. Look at Sir Thomas Myddleton of Castle y Waun? Now there was a wealthy man, and what of Morgan Williams who had taken his Welsh beer to England and married the sister of the monastery wrecker Thomas Cromwell? Another Welshman who had done well for himself. Better still, the Cecil's of Allt yr Ynys? William Cecil was near as powerful as the queen herself. The ability to adapt had helped them to better their lives.

Squire Hugh Morgan, did not look to the influence of the English court himself. As a near nobleman, he had executive power enough. Here he had the freedom to rule as he wished with little interference. Here he could, if need arose, call in a small army. He was Lord and master. He was better off here in the quiet of Wales, than ever he could be competing among England's nobles. Once his father, Gruffydd Hiraethog had gone, squire Hugh would double his wealth and standing.

The much needed rain had left the land sparkling and refreshed. The storm had also brought in it's wake Emlyn Tomas. his nephew. The nephew whom he had received a letter about.

The boy stood behind him, unusually still, not fidgeting as he used to. He had stood there for a good twenty minutes waiting. His calm gaze on the carpet, showed nothing of the fear he must surely be feeling at this encounter.

Without turning, Hugh said, 'You have taken your time in coming to see me Emlyn. That is well, for it has given me time for thought. You have known me for a man short on affection, so you can have no illusion as to where you stand with me. It is not through affection that a man may carve himself a place in the world. Youth seeks love and foolish adventure and often falls foul of it, whereas a man devoted to the church can be rid of such distraction. Now you are grown, I would have you know why I chose that way for you. Did you think it was to be rid of you?'

Outside the sky was beginning to clear. A goose girl in a blue dress crossed the field on her way to the water's edge. Behind her eight birds stepped in time, their splayed red feet in and out like boat paddles. A flock of starlings squabbled over something grisly beneath the window. Rocking on his heels, Squire Hugh Morgan watched and waited for a response. None came. It was the same on many previous confrontations, Emlyn would never speak while his uncle had his back turned in this way; a game of wills which had annoyed Hugh in the past. It still did, but it had never ruffled his feathers. His anger, on the rare occasions it showed, was calm and deadly. He never lost his temper.

He turned around to face his nephew for the first time in over four years. The grey eyes came up to met his and held his gaze. Emlyn had grown considerably and stood near as tall as his uncle. He still looked thin and underfed, but his skin now held the glow of outdoor life. No doubt this was the result of his wanderings with his grandfather. Squire Hugh knew all about that. Strangely, the boy still had a black eye as he did when he left home. There was the same lack of care about his appearance. His hair needed trimming and his clothes needed replacing.

Hugh studied him. He said, 'Do you remember how you used to ever talk out of turn? And get my hand across your mouth for doing so?'

Emlyn smiled. 'It was the same in Paris,' he said, 'except they have harder hands there.'

'You will go back of course.'

Emlyn raised an eyebrow.

Squire Hugh sat down in a padded chair and folded his hands neatly across his stomach. He said, 'After much thought, I have written to Father Manare explaining who your parents are.'

'Then he and you know more than I.' Emlyn answered.

'I have named your father as the trader my sister ran off with, Cristoforo Grimani.'

'But he is dead uncle and has been for more than twenty years. I am not yet eighteen,' said Emlyn softly.

'What is a year or two between them and a bag of silver?'

'You have made a generous donation to the Society of Jesus and in turn they overlook the dates?'

'Well surmised dear nephew. A mere meddling of mathematics. I did not send you there to be rid of you. You know me well enough to know that I waste nothing. There is power in the church and to have a member of family so attached would be of great advantage to me, and of course to yourself.'

'Even though you are no longer Catholic?'

Squire Hugh leaned forward, turning the wedding band on his left finger, a thick ring of rare Welsh gold. He had to admit to himself that he had been impressed by the boy's ability, reported in full by Father Manare, at the College de Clermont. *'An extraordinary grasp of worldly matters and an inquisitiveness unparalleled. The boy would learn from pauper or prince and take the best attributes from each. It is such gifts that are needed in our church, for we look not back to the contented monk, but forward to a man of God with an ability to adapt, as at home in court as with the poor and needy. Such a priest we could make of Emile were we free to do so.*"

'I had thought then as a Catholic,' said Squire Hugh cautiously, 'that it would be an advantage to us as a family to have you join the church. The gain needs no mention here. Now I know not what such a position would offer. For yourself the advantage still remains. There is nothing for you here Emlyn. As much as Gruffydd wishes to bequeath his land and property to you, it will never be. Where it to be so, the enmity that lies between you and Owain would no doubt develop into a feud. I want strength and unity. The question of faith is not an easy one. I pay lip service to the Reformed Church. How else is a man of standing to survive?'

'A man might just as easily give lip service to the Pope, were it to his advantage.' Emlyn said. Then, reading his uncles thoughts, he added, 'If the authority of the Vatican returned to England, what landowner would give back to the church the lands that he has grown fat on?'

Hugh Morgan threw back his head and laughed. Here was no simpleton. 'You are right Emlyn, no sane man would do as such. That is why a backward step will never be taken. England has fed the Pope for long enough. Still, there is no denying the power of the church in Europe. How watchful we must be of our coasts, for many hostile eyes are turned in our direction. As sure as rain falls, there will be invasion and our chances of surviving are not worth a wager at present. The combined force of Spain, France and the Vatican states, together with those within our own land such as the Catholic Scots, would overrun England and plant a foreign power on the throne. So what do we do, we who own the land and gather our sustenance from it's soil? Would it be a wise advantage to place a foot in either camp?'

Emlyn cleared his throat, nervous but undaunted. 'You consider that wise uncle? The danger of finding yourself thus in time of war, could well leave you squeezed out between the two and left with nothing. Wisdom would not advise a man to be Catholic and heretic both. To serve two masters with equal loyalty is as pointless as playing chess with yourself. Which side would you favour? For favour one in the end to the detriment of the other you would be forced to do. Either way, it is you that will lose.'

Squire Hugh looked at his nephew. Here was one who, though young, had indeed a good grasp of affairs. Older he would be a man to contend with. The sooner he is capped and cowled priest, he thought, the better for us all. No Jesuit would be made welcome on English shores so long as she held to the Reformed Church.

Emlyn said, 'Is that what you fear Uncle? A return of the Catholic church? If that is so, why did you change your faith in the first place?'

'I am forced to do so,' Squire Hugh replied. 'In these times it is safe to follow where others lead. We Welsh are an adaptable race. We have had to be in order to survive. If the king demands of us to cease our allegiance to the Pope, then so be it. First and foremost is family and the power of family cannot be divided between brothers and nephews and cousins and lesser sons, as it was before. Wales was never supreme while brother fought brother, tearing at the land until it bled beneath them. The Act of Union imposed by Henry Tudor brought it's pain. It also brought unity to Wales, were she sensible enough to realise it. Family feuds may still run back and forth in aimless pursuit of dividing the pie, but those of us who have seen the benefits, follow the flow and do not become shoved aside to allow room for Englishmen to stand where we have stood before them.'

Squire Hugh could see the anger in the boy before him, and rightly so. But Emlyn had no standing nor power to call upon to defend his claim on Gruffydd's lands. Gruffydd himself was too tied up with preserving old custom, old habit and old ways to ever look beyond and see the impossibility of his will. 'Make your life with the Jesuits Emlyn,' Hugh advised. 'They are a powerful and respected order. And, from what Father

Manare tells me, your skills are admired and can be of great advantage to them and yourself. The antics of youth are forgiveable, they will welcome you with open arms and be willing to ordain you into their fold now that the question of illegitimacy has been resolved.'

'Yes Uncle,' Emlyn replied submissively.

'Go and see Elisabeth and Ellen, they have asked after you. You will be coming to your cousin's wedding before you leave for France?'

'Yes Uncle.'

'And do you think your grandfather, my father could be persuaded? I have invited many with whom he would wish to meet and I would mend the rift between us.'

Emlyn shrugged and smiled. 'He would be interested to see how you win or lose a game of chess against yourself,' he replied.

After his nephew had left the room, Squire Hugh felt a chill sense of unease. He cupped his chin and tapped his fingers on the table top. For the first time since he had founded his empire, he felt shaken. He had a good head for business and was at the height of his powers. He travelled to markets and even to court where it brought advantage. He held on to influential connections and the responsibilities granted to him for his enterprise gave the powers of an earl. He had heard said of him that he could squeeze blood from a stone were it to benefit the lining of his purse. He found pleasure in the thought.

He could leave matters run their course and lose nothing from it, but nor would he gain. His father's lands, were suitable for grazing only, but Gruffydd was no fool. Where Gruffydd could not plant a profitable food crop, he had looked to other means. From the cattle he now owned, he provided butter and cheese and meat for the markets of England. He had built a tannery and a mill and was working towards the manufacture of cloth on a scale not seen before in Wales. He was inventive, and was digging for alum and growing woad and dye stuffs where he could. Gruffydd kept an eye and ear turned towards Europe where he still had enviable connections. The land that he had bequeathed to his grandson Emlyn, was a great deal more than that of a wool grower.

What was there to do then with Emlyn Tomas, should he decide not to be priest? How would Owain in his constant drunken stupor stand up to this ramshackle cousin, whose appearance belied the quick clever mind that churned behind it?

Squire Hugh sat in thought. He employed men to spy on his father so he knew all about the plans that Gruffydd had made with the English merchant who had called in the spring. They had made no secret of their intention to carry wool over the Alps to Italy. Hugh had laughed when he first heard, but the more he thought about it, the more sense it made. If Gruffydd was successful, he stood to gain a large profit. Squire Hugh sold his own wool at Blackfriars in London. He rarely made the journey himself, but had employed a good man to do the work for him. The cloth market had certainly been disrupted and profits had dropped considerably.

Hugh brushed his lips with the quill feather, his eyes narrowed as he thought of some way for himself to gain from their scheme. Gruffydd was sending Emlyn with the Englishman and Emlyn, if truth were told, was Hugh's responsibility not Gruffydd's. Therefore, if some ill befell the youth, could not the profits find their way legally into Hugh's coffers? Even illegally, if necessary. The man who Hugh employed to take his wool to Blackfriars was John Moore, a man of English and Welsh parents, who would sell his soul to the devil if the price was high enough. He had also travelled a great deal in Europe and knew the wool trade as well, if not better, than most English wool merchants. John Moore knew how to avoid the taxes imposed by the authorities, he was man of considerable guile and cunning. Hugh smiled slowly as his thoughts gathered and grew.

After some time he stood and left his room and made his way up the stairs to the room where the Bishop was staying. He knew that the Bishop of St. Asaph had been speaking to Emlyn earlier that morning. The Bishop was sitting comfortably in the window seat of his room above the kitchens. It was not cold but a large fire burned in the hearth, the Bishop of St. Asaph expected comfort wherever he visited. Squire Hugh hoped that he would not be staying much longer.

'An admirable boy,' said the Bishop when they broached the subject. 'Did you know he had made attempt on a translation of the Old Testament? It is five years since the bishops of Wales were ordered by the Queen to produce such a book. As you know our William Salesbury and Richard Davis gave us an excellent rendition of the New Testament just last year. Beautiful it is. But I fear your boy will have to work hard if he hopes to produce an Old Testament before William Morgan. No relation I take it?'

With a grim smile Squire Hugh said 'The Morgans of Gwydir? Yes as it happens cousins of one sort or another. We do not keep in touch. Why?'

'You ask why?' said the Bishop. 'Why not send the boy to him? I believe William Morgan is working on an excellent translation. A couple of years and we should see it printed.'

'Did you tell him this?'

'Well no, I didn't want to disappoint the boy. William Salesbury would be glad of him too. That man's Welsh is not as refined as it could be. It wouldn't do for the Bible to come to us with language oddities now would it? From what I saw of young Emlyn's Genesis they'd be glad of him.'

'He would never do it. On the advice of Morris Clynnog, I sent Emlyn to France to get a good Catholic education and he is Catholic still. He is trained by the Jesuits.'

The Bishop's face failed to mask his alarm. 'I see,' he said and then, after a moment, 'Jesuits!'

There was a sharp knock on the door and Owain entered. 'Well, have you persuaded Emlyn to return to the papists?' Owain moved from the threshold and entered the room. 'Good day good Bishop,' he said as he sprawled himself in a chair by the fireplace.

There were some aspects of his son that Hugh detested. Disregarding them he said, 'I am not entirely convinced that Emlyn will go. He has some scheme in mind to take wool over the Alps to Italy.'

'Then I may have obtained information that will benefit us both and put Emlyn either at the end of a hangman's rope or in some dark, deep place where we can all forget his existence.' Owain replied smugly, his handsome eyes glinting with mischief.

'May have obtained what information?' said Hugh carefully. Did he want the Bishop of St. Asaph involved in whatever it was?

'There is no definite proof as of yet, but suspicion has been aroused,' said Owain not giving anything away. 'If I could have your blessing to undertake a few inquiries of my own?'

Squire Hugh glared at him. 'You'll have no blessing from me unless I have full knowledge of your intentions,' he replied sternly.

'Ah,' breathed the Bishop. 'This could be an awkward situation indeed. If you are thinking what I am thinking and if it is the reason why I am sent hither and thither making inquiries. Is it?'

'Our Emlyn,' said Owain with a theatrical pause, 'could well be a pamphleteer.'

'But Emlyn is your nephew, Squire,' said the Bishop, 'how unfortunate.'

Realisation struck the Squire instantly. All summer the caustic pamphlets had circulated causing disquiet. There had been much argument and even riots in the trading town of Wrexham. A frantic search had been launched to discover the origin of this libel against the Queen of England. Hugh had never thought that Emlyn was connected with them, but it made sense.

'How do you come by this knowledge?' Hugh demanded.

The sun had broken through cloud and entered the room, lighting Owain's fair hair, the meticulous clothing and the fine features. 'Chatter, an ear turned to the right inn corner. You can pick up more than the pox in a brothel!' Owain laughed. 'There is rumour that he brought the wood blocks for a press in himself, that day at Conwy when I won the horse from him. Where he got the money for such a scheme is a mystery. Perhaps he sold himself in Paris to all those depraved monks.'

'Your vulgarity offends me Owain,' said Hugh in disapproval. 'Practice it on your ill chosen friends if you must, but bring it to this house again and I shall see you feel the whip!'

Owain unfolded from the chair and bowed in mockery. He failed to hide his smile or felt safe enough to show his contempt.

Hugh clenched his fists and took a deep breath before he loosened them. He wished Owain had had the sense to talk of this before hand, in privacy. If Emlyn was caught with the papists, he would be unable to go to Italy with the wool and Hugh's recent plans were worthless. Still, he thought, I'll go ahead with them and send for John Moore, if nothing comes of it then I will have lost nothing. But, if Emlyn escapes discovery and is free to make the journey, I'll have John Moore ready to accompany him. Moore will come up with some plan to discredit the youth alone the way.

The bishop said, 'Money? There are plenty here wealthy enough to finance a printing press. If all this is true, then we may have our problems solved indeed. Yet we must tread with care or the birds in the nest will flee before the captor can move to take them. If we watch and listen, use caution and obtain proof, we can undermine the whole lot of them.'

Owain said, 'Oh, what fun we shall have.'

Hugh stepped between him and the bishop. He said 'I want no physical harm to befall Emlyn. You will make no move against him and whoever he is with, without word first to me. We may unearth not a nest of birds but a nest of adders. Owain I want your word on this.'

Owain smiled triumphantly. 'Harm dear cousin Emlyn! I would never dream of it. The law will harm him better than I could ever hope to. But first we have the Knappan. Let's see if a few years in Paris with the Jesuits hasn't made him too soft for our country sport.

Chapter 17 Venice

Don Carlos paced up and down his room as he waited for his visitor. He did not know what it was about Tomasso di Vincentini that made him nervous, but he would not let this unease stand in his way. Some men were harder to bend than others. Most could be persuaded by coin or promises, but few required threats and violence to bring them to compliance. Di Vincentini had already shown that wealth was not the lure to tempt him, he had enough of his own. It was also reasonable to suppose, after their last meeting, that promises would be received with the same lack of interest. So why had he agreed to this meeting? Forming a partnership with Vincentini could only benefit Grimani's trading ventures, but Vincentini would be better off without such an arrangement. So why?

Don Carlos stopped pacing and stared out of the leaded window. The sky was an overcast, iron-grey. The roof tiles opposite glistened with rain and rivulets ran down the glass and pooled on the ledges. Wet pigeons huddled together in a gutter, cooing softly and ruffling their sodden feathers. Don Carlos liked the pigeons that nested on his roof top. He kept tame ones for carrying messages; they were surprisingly reliable. Over the rain-tattooed canal, a slim gondola approached. There was no show of ornament or bright paint work. It was painted and upholstered in black. Nonetheless, this simplicity spoke of elegance and expense.

Cloaked and hatted in black, Tomasso di Vincentini stood and exchanged a few words with his boatman before he left the boat. Don Carlos noted the gondolier's bright smile; he nodded slowly to himself. He had not been able to find out anything concerning Vincentini: who he was or from what family or patron had he originated or from where his wealth had stemmed. Nothing! Don Carlos made it his business to discover all he could about his associates; he hired men to spy for him on rivals and on friends. All his inquiries had come to naught concerning Vincentini.

The name Vincentini came from a village near Florence. Don Carlos had sent his spy, Frederico there, but the village was no more than a few farms and an inn; no one had heard of Tomasso di Vincentini there.

Therefore, Don Carlos thought, I think the name is an adopted one. This is common practice throughout Italy, a man will often take the name of his patron, benefactor or master, and many are named after their place of birth. So how do I find his real identity? Wherever I have looked I have discovered nothing and his servants are loyal. He arrived here with a ship full of spice and made himself a rich man. His own servants arrived with him and Bartolomeo Varini would rather die than speak a word against his new master. Why Bartolomeo Varini though? Through Fiorenza Balsamo of course! Vincentini had travelled with her, so he had plenty of opportunity to form a partnership while still at sea. As a new comer to Venice, this would serve him admirably. The salt company was in debt, perhaps the widow herself suggested it; she would have been a fool not to! The question is, why, once she had recovered her debts, did she still agree to sell the salt company? Obvious! weight for weight, salt is far less valuable than ginger, nutmeg or pepper. Vincentini probably put her up to it; I would have done the same myself. It proves that both have great faith in this spice supply. Fiorenza Balsamo's daughter had not yet arrived from Cyprus, yet she had ample time to do so. Perhaps, knowing my interest in her as a wife for Paolo, her mother had advised her to remain where she was.

Carlos tapped his fingers on the window ledge. He could not afford to miss the opportunity of a partnership with Tomasso di Vincentini. He had suffered further loss in his mercantile business since the the Spring. Time now was his enemy; he would have to secure loans to keep his trading advantage.

Tomasso felt quite jovial as he passed the grotesque fountain in the Grimani courtyard; nothing of his earlier fears remained. He had dangled the bait and Don Carlos had opened his mouth ready to snap it up. Grimani had had time now, since Tomasso had been away from Venice, to make inquiries and to see that Tomasso's new company was successful. But Don Carlos had not reached the position he held by being beguiled and hoodwinked. Before he swallowed the scheme, he would make sure that no hook lay concealed within. And nor is there, thought Tomasso amused by the notion, not yet!

The wine he was served was excellent, far too strong to be drunk in the early afternoon. Don Carlos paced up and down with his hands behind his back while he spoke, '...therefore you stand to gain much' he was saying.

'What sort of partnership are you suggesting?' Tomasso said. After the initial sip, he had not touched the wine. He sat calmly in a brocade covered chair, his fingers twined loosely together.

Don Carlos stopped in front of the fire. 'You have but one season's success to build your reputation on. You have no share holders, apart from the widow Balsamo, to look to for financial support. This is an admirable state to be in, but it is fragile, so can be broken with the ease of swiping a web.'

'I think you underestimate me,' said Tomasso. He stood up and placed his glass on a small table by the door. 'If you think that by belittling my standing we will reach an agreement to your advantage, then we are wasting each other's time.' He turned after a minimal bow and placed his hand on the door.

'Do not be hasty,' Don Carlos said in an unworried tone, 'and do not, I adjure, assume that I underestimate you or your business. With reputation and secure contacts behind him, a man can raise to great power in this city. Nobility is not come to through royal blood; it is bought in to and agreed to by the Senate. If you aspire to such, then you would do well to listen to my advice. You will not climb to nobility alone.'

'Nobility?' Tomasso cared nothing for position, but matters had taken an unexpected turn. He returned to the chair.

'We will form a partnership,' said Grimani in a lighter tone. 'You will have twenty per cent to begin with. I realise....!'

Tomasso burst out laughing. He struggled to get a hold of himself. He cleared his throat and assumed a serious expression. 'Forgive me Padrone. Before we speak of partnership, there are a few things that must be made clear between us. Venice knows of the loss you suffered in the Spring, your whole consignment of malmsey. They have seen your ships too, limping home in tatters. This has done little to enhance your reputation.'

Grimani lifted his hand and let it drop in a dismissive gesture. 'It is of no account. I agree that I have lost some credit because of this misfortune. It is nothing I cannot recover from with a season's good trading. If you thought my company was injured by this, you have been misled.'

'Then all of Venice is misled,' said Tomasso. 'I have been strongly advised to avoid this meeting. As you point out often, I am a newcomer to the Rialto, but I have connections and my coin can buy information as well as any. Let us suppose that what you say is true, that the loss has cost you little. However when coupled to the burning of a warehouse rumoured to be filled from floor to ceiling?'

'It was empty!' Grimani cried indignantly.

'If you insist Padrone. There is another matter, admittedly known by few, the tale of lightning that fired your vineyards in Cyprus and burned them to the ground.'

'Preposterous! You have been fed lies by one of my rivals, in order to discredit me. If I find out who it was I shall have his tongue severed!'

'The source is trustworthy.'

'How can you believe such fantastical nonsense?'

'I am a careful man,' answered Tomasso narrowing the grey eyes. 'You see, even if I chose not to believe all I hear, and agreed upon a partnership, my own profits could be halved if the percentage I held was as you suggested.'

'You would require fifty per cent then?' Grimani replied, in an incredulous tone. 'I would be ridiculed by my competitors. Were I to share equally in such a venture, my reputation would suffer greatly. My reputation is my strength. Added to influence and experience, I stand with the most successful merchants in Venice. Without these your own company amounts to nothing.'

'Nothing?' Tomasso raised an eyebrow. 'Then why am I here? This season's trading has not been beneficial to you, my own success stands as a shining example beside it. Every sea-faring merchant would wish to get a foot in the spice door I have opened; Venice abounds with handsome offers. Let us not waste each other's time. You are hard pressed to recoup the loss you have suffered whereas I have met with success and hold the promise for future success. It matters not what reputation we hold. Right now, standing here in this room, which of us is the stronger? It would be quite within reason were I to leave here, with no further words between us. What have I to gain from such an ill favoured partnership?'

Don Carlos felt his face redden. How dare this upstart, how dare he! He brought his temper under control. 'Perhaps it is you who underestimates,' he replied. 'I may have suffered a few minor set backs, but my name still counts among the most influential men in this city.'

'I have no doubt as to your ability,' said Tomasso. 'You are a great and respected man. I am sure you bring about my ruin with a mere snap of your fingers, but that would gain us nothing. I need your name and influence and you need my spice to recover your losses. You cannot agree on equal partnership and I will not agree on anything less.'

Grimani sat down on a bench near the fire. He twined his ringed fingers together and looked at Tomasso thoughtfully. He had never guessed that the merchant would know as much as he did, it placed Grimani in a very precarious position. But Tomasso was right in that Don Carlos could silence him forever. He was also right in pointing out the futility of such action. Grimani refilled his wine glass and leaned back, turning the glass stem in his fingers. Eventually he said, 'So what do you suggest?'

'That we do not form a partnership, but agree on something else.'

Don Carlos drained his glass placing it on the shelf above the fire. He said, 'Not a partnership, but a shared venture?'

'Exactly. We both arm and man our own ships, there is safety in numbers. We sail together, buy the produce in Constantinople and return together, each with his own cargo. If you could provide a war galley for further security and pay me a minimal cost for the advantage, say five percent of your profit?'

'That sounds reasonable enough. Too reasonable. Why would you wish to share this source of spice if such little advantage is to be gained?'

'But there is,' said Tomasso. 'You recover your losses, I gain name and reputation. In the future we can deal as partners on an equal footing.'

Don Carlos sighed, this did not ring true. 'How do you propose to gain name and reputation from a single voyage?'

Tomasso said, 'By becoming family. Have you not a daughter of marriageable age?'

'God's blood!' Grimani spat.

Bartolomeo could get nothing out of Tomasso concerning the meeting, apart from the fact that the *Cornucopia* would have company when she next sailed to the Turkish city. He could not believe it at first. Then, when it did sink in, he could think of nothing but doom. 'Why,' he demanded, 'why, in the name of all the saints did you offer him such an advantage? Why bother sending the *Cornucopia* at all? Why not just give Grimani the information he needs and let him make all the profit? For that is what you are doing! I see that neither my advice or Madonna Fiorenza's has made a blind bit of difference. What is the point of forming the Spice Company if we are just to give away all our advantage?'

'Be at peace 'Tolomeo,' laughed Tomasso. They were in a back room of the trading house Tomasso had rented on the Canale Grand. The room overlooked a disused yard where weeds grew and cats lurked in profusion. Weak sunlight slanted through the window. Unconcerned, Tomasso was idly scraping flaked paint off a plaster cherub above the embrasure.

'Well you owe me some sort of explanation,' said Bartolomeo.

'I can't give you one yet,' Tomasso replied. 'Why can't you just believe that all will be well?'

'Because it rarely is,' spluttered Bartolomeo. In spite of this, the company had begun successfully and so far, all had run without a single problem. The *Cornucopia* was due to arrive from Alexandria within days with a cargo that included much needed grain, figs and pomegranates.

Scipeone Barozzi had gone with the ship and had taken to the task with a show of business-like confidence. But the spice was where the profit lay. If they lost their monopoly on this, the business would be doomed. This was why Bartolomeo felt so nervous about having Carlos Grimani share their enterprise.

Tomasso stopped what he was doing and turned into the room. There was an old, warped table near the far wall. On it was placed a small cloth-wrapped bundle that Tomasso had brought with him. The cloth was embroidered with old silver thread and dull sequins. Tomasso undid the ties and pulled the cloth aside revealing strange, milk-white stones the size of a child's fist. They were carved into animal shapes, like miniature deities of forest and sea, exotic and mysterious; there was also an amber necklace and a rosary of white and black pearls.

'I am returning to Florence,' announced Tomasso threading the amber beads through his fingers.

'But you have only just come back from Padua,' Bartolomeo protested. Tomasso had been away from Venice for most of the time, following his own interest in the gem market. Bartolomeo could not take his eyes off the objects on the table. 'What are they?'

Tomasso picked one piece from amid the objects. He held it up to the shaft of sunlight. the soapy stone captured the light and seemed to hold it as if it came from within. It had been carved in the shape of a stylized lion, nothing like the Lion of San Marco, nothing like anything Bartolomeo had ever seen. When Tomasso passed it to him, Bartolomeo held it with reverence, it was a truly beautiful piece of work. He weighed it in his hand. 'Glass?'

Tomasso said, 'It is jade, a stone highly valued in the East. These figures come from China, but the stone does not originally come from there. They pay astounding amounts for this in its raw state. Carved thus, the objects are near priceless. Don't look so concerned, I am not about to disappear to the far reaches of China. I am going to Florence to see Cosimo Medici. He is the only man I can think of who would have the wealth and the insight to buy these. I have also heard rumour about a source of jade in the river Po. I plan to take Symeon with me, he knows what to look for. Even a small amount of this would make a journey to Constantinople worth a great deal more than the profits brought by spice. The Arab traders, who cross the Indian Ocean, would leap at the opportunity.'

'It seems a very slim possibility,' answered Bartolomeo, 'there are too many doubts.'

'Nothing ventured nothing gained,' said Tomasso smiling. 'I have learned that the merchant who troubles himself to attain the unusual and the exotic, stands to benefit well above his competitors. This is how I have made my fortune before I came here, and will continue to do so. If there is no jade in the Po, then I will have lost nothing but time.'

'And the Spice Company?'

'Will continue to flourish as long as it may. If the spice dries up, then we will have plenty of other items with which to trade. A man who places all his eggs'

'I know, I know. Must you keep quoting proverbs? So you are going to Florence to sell this jade and to the river Po to collect some more. What about the *Cornucopia*, she is due back within days?'

'I'm sure you are well able to deal with all that 'Tolomeo. When this building is ready, move the business here. Fiorenza may wish to have some say in what you do. Let her buy the furnishings if she wishes, I trust her judgement.'

'Am I to understand that you will be gone for weeks again?' Bartolomeo tossed the jade lion from one hand to the other.

'Probably for longer. If I have not returned in time, send the *Cornucopia* to Constantinople with Grimani's ship. He will also provide an armed galley. There are lots of pirates about.' Tomasso winked and smiled. He re-packed the glassy objects, forgetting to include the lion. Bartolomeo held it out to him. 'Keep it,' said Tomasso, 'when you sell it, you will be wealthy enough to wed. You do wish to be married don't you 'Tolomeo?'

Bartolomeo shuffled his feet, feeling uncomfortable. Yes, of course he wanted a wife and family. He had even dreamed of asking Fiorenza. He knew what her answer would be, so could only shame himself by voicing his interest. He looked at the carving in his hand. 'Thank you,' he said at last, 'but I shall keep it. If we are to be as successful as you predict, then I shall have women queuing up outside my door, some may even overlook my unhandsome features.'

If the marriage of his daughter Carmelia was the price Tomasso di Vincentini asked, then Don Carlos was, after considerable thought, quite prepared to accept the conditions. Unfortunately, Carmelia had not come to Venice, she was still in France. Don Carlos wrote another letter to Adriana Martinelli, ordering her to send Carmelia at the soonest opportunity.

When the letter arrived, Carmelia was staying with her godmother at the house in Chartres. She loved the country house and spent much time wandering through the gardens and grounds. She had spend a good deal of the summer there and had enjoyed the stay immensely. She met scholars and learned men who gathered under Adriana's roof to discuss topics best kept out of public hearing; these were usually to do with religion and Carmelia had not contributed much. She found greater pleasure in listening to the musicians and poets. One young nobleman had been most attentive to Carmelia. He had written her poems of love and romance. His poems were dull and unimaginative and were a reflection of the man himself. Carmelia had soon tired of his attentions and learned to avoid him, until he realised that she was not the least bit interested. She went hunting and improved her riding skills in preparation for the journey to Italy, but the journey was put off again and again.

Carmelia was not too concerned about this, her joy was complete, apart from one fact that she refused to take any notice of. It was her maid Pellegrina who first brought news of it to Carmelia's ears. Pellegrina was always gossiping and Carmelia had paid little attention at first.

They were both sitting under a cool archway facing an inner courtyard when the news from Don Carlos arrived. Carmelia said, 'I can't understand why we did not begin the journey at the height of summer, when the weather is at its best for crossing the Alps. We could be in Italy by now.'

'Why don't you ask Madame Adriana?' Pellegrina replied.

'I have, often. She tells me each time, that it is not a convenient time to travel.'

'Well I know why,' said Pellegrina. She went on to describe all the details that Carmelia had refused to listen to in the past weeks.

Carmelia placed her hands over her eyes.

'Just because you can't see me, doesn't mean that you can't hear me!' Pellegrina laughed.

'I don't care!' Carmelia replied petulantly. 'It makes me feel better if I can't see you telling me. What should I care if my godmother takes a lover?'

'I don't suppose you should care at all,' Pellegrina said. 'Apart from the fact that you nor I nor anyone else in this household is going to journey to Italy while your godmother enjoys her lover. It's deliciously shocking Carmelia, Madame Adriana is twice his age! I can't blame her though, I'd sell my right arm for a night's pleasure with her Josquin.'

Carmelia remembered Josquin from that day close to Easter when she and her companions had decorated the road with flower mosaics. That was went the young scholar had upset all her work and frightened her. Josquin had sorted out the mess and calmed the novices with his soft voice and startling good looks. He had not continued the journey with the young

Jesuit scholars, but had accompanied the nuns and their charges back to the convent. That was when Madame Adriana pounced on him, Pellegrina had said. And, of course, Carmelia would not listen to her wicked gossip, but now, it seemed that it was all true!

Before Carmelia and her companion had left their convent in Rouen to stay with Adriana Martinelli, Carmelia had received a visitor. The old Franciscan priest Fra Sebastiano, who had come to see her earlier in the year, called to see her before he started on his journey back to Florence. Carmelia had liked him instantly and it was through him that she learned something of the young man who had upset her flower pattern. She was surprised to hear that what he had said was probably true, that he was vaguely related to her. She had also spoken of Lorenzo, who still wrote to her often from Florence. Carmelia had arranged to sent a letter to him with Fra Sebastiano who promised that he would be seeing him. She had been unable to tell Fra Sebastiano much concerning her family and was sorry that her knowledge was so scant. She had resolved to ask her godmother about it. Adriana was not the least bit informative and had dismissed the story of the boy as absolute nonsense. Whenever Carmelia mentioned the subject thereafter, Adriana had reacted with unnecessary scorn and told Carmelia to grow up and stop dreaming.

But who is dreaming now? Carmelia asked herself. She would not dare to mention any of this to Adriana, but if they did not leave France soon, the winter would close the Alpine passes and they would be forced to wait until the following spring.

Don Carlos wrote more and more frequently to Chartres. Adriana pleaded sickness as her excuse not to travel. As the summer turned to autumn, Don Carlos demanded that Adriana hire an escort to see his daughter safely to Venice without her. Adriana had written a reply stating that such an idea was unthinkable. So they remained in France while Adriana enjoyed her young lover and Carmelia watched the leaves turn to gold, brown and eventually fall leaving bare branches behind them.

Chapter 18 Wales

Connie O'Neill put down the basket of sloes she was carrying and bent over double groaning in complaint.

'Don't start all that again' Ellen snapped as she sped past, head in the air, eyes straight forward. 'Really Connie, one would think you were old or something.'

Connie kneaded her back. A breeze rose, brushing her with dust. It was pointless agonising to the girl. Off she went marching down the lane, shadowed by a tunnel of trees on either side with leaves fluttering about her. Connie pushed up the sleeves of her woollen coat and sat down on a roadside boulder. She muttered in Gaelic to herself, then added, 'There's a dear girl you are Ellen Morgan, caring for me an' all. The dear Lord must have His head turned elsewhere today or He'd flatten yer with a plague an' cause yer nose to grow 'till yer fall over it.'

'Why Connie!' Ellen shouted. 'Have you been cursing me from here to there?'

'Aye an' back again, so. I'll not be moved another foot yer heartless hussy.' Her powerful voice carried all the way to Tan y Bryn.

Ellen stopped and turned to face her tormentor, before the whole vale knew their business. The sun on her red hair set it aflame; the wind snatched at the curls and plastered her head with leaves. She walked back, dumped her baskets and slumped down on the grass beside her Irish companion.

Connie said, 'Yer all for walking off an leaving me then? An' me carrying yer sloes for thirty mile or more!'

'It was three miles Connie.'

'Well I can tell yer 'tis the longest three miles I've ever walked. The good Lord only knows why you'd be wanting all them sloes. 'Tis sure me legs will never get me there where you're wanting them.'

'If you don't,' said Ellen tossing her head so the un-brushed tangles fell back and her dark eyes could reinforce her words, 'I shall never speak to you again.'

'That'll be a blessing,' Connie replied. 'I've been wondering if the Lord has been turning a deaf ear on me. It's glad I am to see that He's no longer so distracted.'

'You've got to help me dear Connie,' Ellen said sweetly. 'Otherwise I shan't be able to make what I want to make for Owain's wedding.'

'Make out of them green sloes? They'll all be poisoned for sure. 'Tis a favour I'm doing everybody in not taking them a step further, an' that's me final word on the matter.'

They sat with the flies and bees hovering over the fruit and the sun warming their faces. It was mid-afternoon with the wind growing stronger and more rain clouds piling in over the Irish Sea. Ellen snatched up a daisy and pulled all the petals off, then started on another. Connie closed her eyes.

Ellen jumped up suddenly beside her. 'There! Over there, is that a farmer or something? He can carry the sloes.'

'He's not going our way,' Connie replied stiffly. 'He's not going to be taken up with turning right around and going right back again now is he?'

'Of course he will,' Ellen said. 'I shall ask him sweetly.'

'Aye, there's a devil on yer girl!'

The farmer, or something, came closer. Ellen stood with her hands on her hips, tapping her foot expectantly. When he drew level, he removed his hat trailing goose feathers, inclined his head in greeting and then continued on his way.

'You! Boy!' Ellen commanded. 'I want you to carry some baskets for me.'

'Don't be too sweet dear,' said Connie, 'he might get the wrong idea.'

The boy turned and stood smiling. 'These baskets,' he said, 'all four of them?'

'Yes.' Ellen replied and then added, 'if you would be so kind.'

He bent his head to one side and then the other. He was not examining the baskets. His wide, curious gaze rested insolently on Ellen and Connie.

She picked up a basket with two hands and held it out to him. Her dark brow set in a line that invited no refusal. He took it reluctantly and put it down again.

Ellen said, 'If you do not do as I say, I shall be forced to inform my stepfather how surly and unhelpful his tenants are. I assure you, you will suffer as a consequence. I shall insist upon it.'

'That is assuming that I am a tenant?' He asked.

'Well you are, aren't you?'

'In a manner of speaking,' he replied. 'I would of course be delighted to assist, but I am going the other way, as you can see.'

Ellen swung around to Connie. 'Did you hear that,' she cried. Her cheeks flamed with anger. 'He is not going to help us. He considers it too inconvenient to help his betters!'

Connie shrugged her shoulders. 'You could pay him for the service,' she suggested. 'As like as not he could do with it. It'll buy him a poultice for that eye. What did you do lad?'

'I had an argument with a goose,' he replied. 'As you see she got the better of me.'

'Gooses can be like that,' said Connie with a glimmer in her eye.

Turning back Ellen said, 'I'll give you a copper penny.'

His eyebrow rose. 'A copper penny?' He sat down in the middle of the lane as if ready for a lengthy discussion of the subject. 'A penny a basket,' he suggested.

'Insolent peasant,' snapped Ellen. 'How dare you dicker with me!'

Even that did not wipe the smile from his face, worse still, he laughed. 'If I am to be insolent peasant and the bearer of three baskets of sloes,' he said pleasantly, 'I'll settle for three pennies.'

Ellen said, 'There are four baskets.'

Connie burst into uncontrollable mirth, rolling back and forth on her rock and slapping her rounded thighs. Behind her, a flock of raucous birds rose flapping into the air in distress.

Exasperated, Ellen picked up all four of the baskets and started down the road, staggering under the weight. Sloes spilled and bounced out behind her.

The boy followed, taking his time. When he caught up, he took the load from her after a half-hearted struggle and walked ahead. Connie recovered from her laughter and waddled after them squashing sloes.

Ellen kept the pace brisk, kicking up leaves and leaving a billow of dust in her wake. In her wake too, came Connie O'Neill and the boy with the sloes. He put them down three times, grumbling and massaging his hands before he started off again. Connie took one of the baskets from him. The shadows lengthened, leaves rained from the trees and the sun went behind a grey cloud. The boy joked and laughed and had Connie in stitches all the way. It seemed he knew someone who knew someone who knew someone who knew Connie's second cousin from County Tyrone; Friar Patrick O'Healy, now in France, he explained. After that, he did a remarkable imitation of the Bishop of Cork and changed to the bishop of

Bangor, the bishop of St. Asaph, the Squire himself and, finally the young master Owain.

When they all eventually reached the kitchen, he said, 'What are the sloes for?'

'She wants to poison Harriet Crew,' said Connie.

He found that highly amusing. As he walked away, he sang 'the Wooing of the Tanners Daughter' with different words that made Connie start chortling all over again.

'He's a good lad that one,' said Connie when she had breath enough to do so. 'For the life of me I don't know why you go bestowing your affection on the other.'

'What are you talking about Connie?' Ellen demanded. 'As if I have not had quite enough to contend with today, you have been acting like a jobbernowl with an incurable cackle!'

Connie's grin fell and turned into a scowl. 'I knew him straight off,' she said defensively. 'There's not another like him outside Ireland, where there's lots of them.'

'I see,' said Ellen crossly. 'It's a leprechaun that's been bewitching my sloes all the way from there to here. It seems he's bewitched you while he was about it. It's a pity you couldn't have gotten him to give you his pot of gold while you were at it!'

Before Connie could reply, Ellen stamped off banging the kitchen door behind her.

In the year before Emlyn Tomas had gone off to France, Ellen had been ten, but not too young to see the animosity between the boy and his uncle and cousin. She had followed the advice of her elders and paid him little heed; her eyes were blinded by his shining cousin Owain. Her eyes were still blinded by his cousin Owain. They were puffy from crying. Owain had gone off with the Bishop earlier in the day and was not due to return until morning.

Emlyn returned to the house just before the evening meal and only then, did Ellen realise who he was. Before the meal began, Emlyn and Squire Hugh had an argument about some farmer's land that the Squire had encroached upon. Emlyn had not stayed to share the meal.

The rain had come in with the night, heavy rain. It washed the yard and ran off the tiles, shimmering from the light of the forge like silver arrows. There were workers in the forge, Ellen could hear their laughter from where she stood under the eaves, and could see the flickering shadows with the bright flames behind them. Pulling her shawl over her head, she ran across the yard splashing through the puddles.

Inside there were two men and a boy who was working the bellows. They were making a pot handle from a bar of iron. One end was white hot, glowing and shimmering in the darkness of the smithy. As the blacksmith pounded it into shape, his huge arm rose and fell rhythmically. Orange firelight gleamed in reflection on the beads of sweat standing out from the powerful muscles. His greasy leather apron was singed and blackened from years of use.

Beside him stood Emlyn Tomas, half stripped with his shirt tied around his waist. He was holding the black pot; its handle already fitted to one side. The blacksmith gripped the hot metal with pincers and curled it into a hook so that it fitted neatly on the other side of the pot. Emlyn finished it off saying, something that Ellen could not catch above the heavy breath of the bellows. The boy, the smith's son, stopped his pumping and jumped up at his father's command to fetch ale. The smith moved to a barrel of water and plunged a dipper, lifting it and pouring it over his head and shaking like a wet dog. Refilling it, he handed it to Emlyn who drank from it before dousing himself as the smith had done. They both glistened with perspiration and water, their hair dripping like the rain. The blacksmith went off in pursuit of the boy and the ale.

Emlyn returned to the water barrel. He did not see Ellen standing in the doorway until he cleared water from his eyes.

She said, 'Why didn't you tell me who you were?'

'I would have, had you given me a chance,' he replied. He picked up a rag and began to dry his hands.

'Connie didn't tell me either and she knew.'

'We did not plan it as such, if that was what you thought, it is the first time I have been ordered about by a twelve year old, I suppose I found the situation amusing. Shall we start again?'

'I'm fourteen,' cried Ellen preventing her foot from stamping. 'Why do you always quarrel with your uncle?'

He sat on the rough work trestle and rubbed at his hair with the cloth. 'We only quarrel on Thursdays,' he said 'So today is our day for it.'

Her mother always told her off for being inquisitive. She tried a different line, 'Owain said that you are a Catholic priest, you don't look like one.'

'Nor am I. At present I am a blacksmith, but if you want any more sloes carried I am quite adaptable. Did you make your brew?'

She came into the smithy and watched him pull on his shirt. She said, 'The sloes are for making wine, you need a lot of them because they are not very juicy. You will be here for Owain's wedding won't you? You can taste my brew then, I'll keep you some.'

His smile was startling against his dark skin. He looked like one of the Gypsies who came to Rhuddlan in the Spring. He said, 'What, and poison me along with the bride?'

'You shouldn't listen to Connie,' she replied, 'most of the time she talks nonsense. Why should I wish to poison Harriet Crew?'

'Because you are fourteen and would rather be in her place. Don't worry I won't tell anyone.'

She felt her cheeks burn. For a moment she wanted to deny it, but he was not making fun of her. Perhaps here she could find a friend. He came forward and took her hand in his that was still black from the forging. He was much taller than she remembered.

He said, 'Ellen you are too good for Owain, he would not appreciate you as you deserve. Soon you will find a husband who will love and cherish you and you will forget all this. You are not yet a woman and when you are, you will be so beautiful that you will have princes to choose from. You will wonder what you ever saw in Owain Morgan.'

'You are not much older than I' she replied, 'and you can't know anything about it because you are going to be a priest and they have to be celibate.'

He let go of her hand her. 'Priests have to learn about these things, that they can do without involving themselves in relationships,' he assured her. 'That is why you can always talk to them and they will understand and be able to guide you on the best path to take. I am not a priest yet Ellen, but I can be a brother to you and they are nearly as good. Now be a good girl and go in before you get cold and before the formidable Connie O'Neill comes looking for you.'

She turned on the threshold. 'Will you be here for the Knappan?' she asked.

'I'm going tomorrow,' he answered. 'But I shall be back soon with Owain's grandfather. Do you know him?'

'Gruffydd Hiraethog? Yes, I do, he used to come and visit when my father was alive. I liked him, he always had time for me when I was little. I have not seen him for years. He quarrels with your uncle as well.'

Emlyn smiled at her and then turned away as the blacksmith and the ale arrived.

Ellen ran back across the yard. She was not sure why matters did not look so gloomy any more. That night, before retiring, she kissed her mother and after a moment's pause kissed her stepfather too. In her chamber she pestered Connie with questions about her newly found brother. Connie advised her that the less she knew about Emlyn Tomas the better; that way the boy could be left in peace; Connie had a soft spot for Emlyn Tomas.

The next morning Emlyn left the house and took the long way around to Rhuddlan, thus avoiding any Glyn Parrys or any geese. He had borrowed an old grey horse from his uncle's stable so that he could make better time. He wanted to call on Goronwy at the cave before riding on to Gruffydd and persuading the old man to return with him. Aside from knocking Gruffydd on the head and tying him in a sack, Emlyn could see no other way of bringing him to Plas Newydd.

Riding through a tunnel of golden, sun-speckled leaves, Emlyn laughed at this idea. The wooded path ran alongside a fast flowing stream where autumn leaves spun in the eddies and whirl pools. Emlyn dismounted tying the horse to a tree, and stooped to drink from the stream. He sat down in the warm sunlight and took a little book out of his pack. It was the treasured psalm book that he had brought from his room at Plas Newydd. He had found it where he had left it over four years before, concealed behind a lose wooden panel. It did not contain all the psalms, just a chosen selection, all beautifully illustrated. It had belonged to his mother and Emlyn wished to show it to Gruffydd.

Emlyn prepared to continue his journey. From a clearing in the distance he saw the glint of sun on metal and soon after, heard the jingle of harness and the thud of approaching horsemen. It was too late to hide by the time he realised who the horsemen were. His cousin Owain Morgan and Robert Jenkinson, both overdressed as usual. With them rode four men from the Squire's household.

Seeing Emlyn on the path, they spurred the horses into a gallop and pulled up near him, scattering leaves everywhere as they reigned in their mounts. Then Owain spurred his horse, riding a tight circle around Emlyn. The horse was the Spanish mare won at the Conwy fair. She tossed her head, mane flying and let loose a shrill whinny.

'Just the man we were looking for,' said Robert Jenkinson jovially.

Emlyn stood still, his mouth set in a grim line. Dust settled on his head and shoulders.

Owain pulled savagely at the rein and brought the mare to a trembling stop. He hooked a leg across the saddle, leaning forward and chewing thoughtfully on a finger nail. He looked Emlyn up and down. 'Well, well dear cousin,' he said, 'still dressed in rags? And dear me, where are your sheep?'

'Up the mountain where they should be,' Emlyn replied pleasantly. 'But I see you have a mare between your legs. How does she measure up to Harriet Crew? Certainly she has the girth.'

Owain turned red with anger. He forced the horse forward. Emlyn ducked out of the way but Owain reached down and snatched the satchel from his shoulder, spilling out the contents. The psalm book thumped on to the path. As Emlyn tried to retrieve it, Owain spurred the mare in front of him and swung out of the saddle. 'What have we here I wonder,' he said, picking it up.

Emlyn bounded forward, but Owain tossed it to Jenkinson. Emlyn sighed and stood still, his heart thudding with anger.

Jenkinson couldn't read Latin, but he recognised it as a book of prayers. 'Catholic rubbish,' he said as he gave it back to Owain.

Rhys Llwyd, one of the Squire's men, recognised the book for what it was. 'It's a book of psalms.', he explained, 'I'll not stand by and see you be disrespectful to the word of God, Master Owain, no matter.'

'No matter what Rhys?' Owain asked, letting the book fall. It landed in the stream. 'How unfortunate,' said Owain, 'look what you have made me do.'

Wind gusted through the trees, moor hens clucked in the reeds and the horses stamped and flicked their tails at flies. Emlyn snarled like a dog animal and sprang. He drove with all the power of his shoulders at his cousin.

Owain ducked and hurled himself to one side, staggering on the grass, dragging out the dagger at his belt. Warning came from the others but they did not interfere and turn the master's anger on themselves. Owain stood waiting, his eyes wide in anticipation; his cherubic lips lit with a contemptuous smile. He tightened his grip on the knife but there was no sign of his elusive cousin.

Suddenly, a stick descended and the dagger flew out of his hand. Nursing numbed fingers, he heard the rustle of branches. He could not see Emlyn.

Emlyn said, 'Would you stab me brother? Now we are evenly matched. Care for a stick?'

Owain swung around and saw him standing under an ash tree, his hands empty. Owain jumped. He gripped Emlyn's left arm and shoulder and kicked his body with the full force of his fine leather boots.

Emlyn grunted with the force of it and felt the breath leave him. As he sank down, he moved forward, wrapped his arms around Owain and drove him into the tree opposite.

Owain hit the trunk and roared as Emlyn pinned him down. He kicked out but his foot was caught. He cursed, struggled and rolled dislodging Emlyn. He surged to his feet in a shower of leaves.

Emlyn was up before him. He leaped in. They staggered together grasping for an advantage, tearing at cloth, punching wherever they could. Equally matched neither could break the hold. Owain managed to hook a foot behind Emlyn's leg and they both toppled over, rolling against rocks, branches and tree trunks and buffeted by the solid summer-baked earth.

Owain broke the hold and bound to his feet. His breath was ragged. His lip cut and bleeding. As Emlyn rose beside him, he used his boot again.

Failing to avoid it, Emlyn reeled back from the blow, recovered and came charging back. He threw himself against his cousin with such force that they both crashed over the bank and fell into the stream. They broke apart, both winded and gasping, thigh deep in the stream dripping with water. Owain lunged and felt his fist meet flesh.

Emlyn disappeared under the water, twisted around and came up behind, grasping Owain in a strangle hold.

Owain threw his weight forward throwing his opponent over his head. Emlyn crumbled half in water, half out. Owain crouched waiting for the next attack, taking advantage of the pause to regain control of his ragged breath.

Emlyn came at him like a wild animal. They had fought at first like school boys, now they fought in earnest. The tricks and the dirty fighting they both knew. The hatred manifested itself in blow after blow. The water thrashed, cloth ripped, the dull thud of flesh on flesh resounded through the air. Emlyn felt teeth close on his leg and drew a hissing breath, driving his clenched fist down on Owain's ear until the teeth released him and broke away. The pause gave Emlyn an advantage. He surged forward driving Owain before him with all the power he could summon. The returning blows, kicks, bites and twists fell on him unheeded.

Something grasped him from behind and pulled him backward. He fell and his head went under water. He trashed about fighting to regain his feet. His mouth filled with weed, his limbs refused to obey him. Rough hands held him under until his vigorous writhing ceased. His head came up and he choked and coughed, retching and struggling for breath. Holding Emlyn were Rhys and Jenkinson. They pulled him out of the stream. He collapsed on the bank and dropped his head into his hands, the fight had gone out of him.

On the opposite bank, Owain had been treated in the same way. Now he sat, head on his knees, his fair hair, dark and green with weed. His clothing was in tatters. His body shuddered, gasping for the air that had been denied him. Holding him on either side were two of the Squire's men. Owain too had had enough violence.

When he had recovered his breath, Owain splashed across the stream, limping, bleeding and ragged and swung up into the saddle with a gasp. He sat straight in spite of his hurts. 'This is not finished yet,' he said softly. 'We have yet to play the Knappan.'

Rhys delayed a moment, an apology on his lips but Emlyn waved him off. They left him then, caught up their horses and, without a backward glance, rode off slowly and disappeared around a bend in the road.

After a while, Emlyn walked alongside the stream, until he found the book trapped in the reeds. Emlyn stood on the bank shivering. The beautifully illustrated pages were ruined.

It was some time before Emlyn mounted and continued on his way. He feared that they would have killed each other if they had not been separated. Emlyn was so caught up with the violent events, that he did not notice that he was being followed.

Chapter 19 Wales

Emlyn took a long detour towards the Orme but long before he got there, he met Tom Tilbury who told him that Goronwy had gone to the Holywell paper-mill. He would not be back until the following week. Examining Emlyn, Tom Tilbury's good-natured face glowed in amusement.

'I took a wrong turning and fell off the end of the Orme,' Emlyn said without being asked. He left a message for Goronwy and rode on because the hour was late. It was well after midnight by the time he reached the hill tops and Gruffydd's house. He had ridden over thirty miles, all he could think of was bed. The house was still. The servants had retired but a light came from Gruffydd's work room around the back by the stables. From there too, came the gruff voice, slurred with drunken singing and mumbling to itself.

This was Gruffydd's work room. Behind the mischievous eyes there dwelt the mind of an extraordinary inventor. This skill had been highly valued by Good King Hal. In his youth Gruffydd Hiraethog had been a maker of war engines.

Within the room there were pulleys and wheels and levers and winches, all hanging from the ceiling; extraordinary devices all with a particular purpose. The purpose had previously been explained to Emlyn in detail but he had forgotten most of it.

As he entered he ducked to avoid hanging himself from a dangling loop of rope. In doing so, he knocked a stuffed owl off his perch, narrowly escaping the hooked beak. Stepping back, he trod in something wet and glutinous. His arms spun like a windmill, he grasped the edge of a shelf and upset an open-necked sack. It plummeted to the floor, landed with a dull thud and released a cloud of white powder as malodorous as a pierced puff ball. Emlyn reeled backwards coughing and spluttering. He staggered out of the door, dragging in lungfuls of night air.

Gruffydd's laughter boomed across the yard like a canon. He bent double, his eyes streaming tears. He slapped his thighs as his hilarity reduced to a cackle.

On such a day as this, it was either weep or howl in merriment, with no breath to spare, holding his aching sides, Emlyn's emotions warred with each other. In the end, he spluttered to keep his own pain inducing laughter under control. When he could, he said, 'Did you arrange all that?'

'No no,' Gruffydd replied earnestly, 'merely left a thing here, a thing there. Let events take whatever course they would. I didn't know you were coming and I didn't know it would do that.'

'It?'

'The powder,' Gruffydd replied. His expression had become thoughtful. With a long hand he caressed his beard as if he was scheming. 'It's a little adventurous mixture I brewed up. It's very explosive you know. I suppose if it doesn't work you could always throw it at a Spaniard or two and choke them to death.'

Emlyn groaned. He turned around and re-entered the work room with extreme care.

A stained glass window caught the light of an oil lamp hanging from a bracket outside. The light entered the room on a dust-flecked flood of colour. The window had come from the monastery of St. Mary's outside Rhuddlan. Throughout Gruffydd's house, there were other items rescued from the ruins; stone beasts and angels and rain-spout gargoyles leered from the walls in the most unlikely places.

Inside the work room, Gruffydd pushed an orange hen off a chair fit for a bishop and offered the seat graciously to his grandson. 'It's all right,' he explained above the outrageous clucking. 'Gwynwyn hasn't laid an egg or anything else, so you can sit.'

While Emlyn lowered himself cautiously into the chair, Gruffydd thumped about sending feathers and clouds of dust into the air. Eventually he produced an ancient wine flask and held it up with glee. 'I have kept this since Calais,' he explained. He pulled away the stopper and poured the ruby liquid into two cups. 'I have got hundreds of them, well, enough to last us through your lengthy explanation. Did you bump into Goronwy? Or meet the wrong end of a boar?'

Emlyn released a long, shuddering sigh and closed his eyes. 'Yes,' he whispered, 'and they both bit me.'

'Well, I have good news that will cheer you up.'

'It will have to be something spectacular,' Emlyn replied attempting a smile.

'Yesterday I sent off the wool to Ambrose,' said Gruffydd. 'And I found just the man for the job. He will stay with Ambrose and wait for you to join him, then you can all make the journey together. He knows the wool market inside out, I could not have wished for a better man to employ as our factor. You'll like him Emlyn. His name is John Moore. And, do you know what? I met him in Antwerp five years ago; he's been taking Welsh wool to the English for years. He's even done some work for our Hugh in the past, though I'll not hold that against him. Knowing that I was looking for a reliable man he just appeared and offered his services.'

'Sounds English to me.' Emlyn muttered before he fell asleep.

When he awoke the next day, he was still in the same chair and the hen Gwynwyn, was on his knee. He sneezed and yelped; she clucked and pecked at him. Trapping her fluttering wings, he dumped her on the floor and discovered a warm egg.

He was surprised when he limped outside that the day had already turned to evening. The light filtered through rain clouds with no promise of tomorrow's sun as it sank towards the sea. Mist hung above the forested vale. The hill Emlyn stood on dipped towards Llanrwst where a furious water fall tumbled down from the heights of *Eyre Mynydd*. The peaks of the mountains were hidden by grey, ominous clouds and the harsh rock sides were purple with heather.

'There you are! I thought you were attached to that there chair like a hamadryad,' said Gruffydd coming up beside him. He led a goat on the end of a piece of string. 'There'll be snow on *Eyre Mynydd* before morning, but it won't come here.'

Emlyn sat down on a water barrel, every part of him hurt. After much prompting, he told his grandfather what had happened at Plas Newydd. Last of all he told him about the arrangements Squire Hugh had made concerning the Society of Jesus.

'What!' Gruffydd exclaimed. His white eyebrows met in the middle. 'He wrote to the school claiming that you had a legitimate father?'

'Encouraged with a generous donation,' Emlyn added.

The old man sniggered. 'You know what this means? It means that you now have a father. All you need to do is to get hold of that letter and you can prove to any that you are not the bastard you thought yourself. Instead of ridding himself of an unwanted nephew, the poor fool has provided documented evidence that you are Ann's legitimate son.'

'Why poor fool?' Emlyn muttered. He leaned back against the grey stone wall and closed his eyes.

'Well now, I can see that your wits are addled, not surprising from the look of you,' said Gruffydd. 'Emlyn Tomas you now have, assuming that you can get hold of that letter, a legitimate claim on all that lies before you. Are you lacking in wisdom this day?'

Puzzled, Emlyn looked up at him. Then, slowly the words began to sink in.

'Come into the house,' said Gruffydd. He gently urged Emlyn to his feet. 'We can eat and discuss the matter.'

'Egg?' Emlyn offered, producing one.

It was near dark by the time they entered the house. The rich smell of mutton broth greeted them from a pot bubbling above the kitchen fire. Gruffydd tore a piece of soft bread and dipped it into the gravy. 'Now there's a stew worth waiting for'.

Emlyn sat into a chair near the fire. Gruffydd's white cat came and settled on his knee, digging in her claws. When Emlyn had finished eating, he placed his bowl on the table and leaned back with a contented sigh. He told his grandfather about Goronwy and the argument they had concerning the Scottish queen and the hopes of the Catholics to make her queen of England.

Gruffydd spoke around a mouthful. 'Aye I've talked of such with Talbot, but it is a foolish quest and will come to nothing. You will have to try and talk Goronwy out of such a mad scheme.'

'I have not seen him since,' Emlyn answered. He closed is eyes and smiled to himself. 'Goronwy is so keen to become a Jesuit. He has made a vow to God that he will do all possible to bring England back to the Holy Church.'

'You know what the trouble with vows is,' said Gruffydd wiping gravy from his whiskers.

'I can well imagine,' Emlyn answered; he had made a vow himself a few days earlier. *I swear Goronwy, on the Blood of Christ, that I will return to France with you.*

Gruffydd picked up two beakers and filled them with ale. Handing one to Emlyn, he said, 'Do you still want to go with Ambrose and that John Moore I employed, to take our wool to Italy?'

Emlyn remembered another vow he had made, this one to himself that he had no intention of altering. I will go and I will do all in my power to seek the mother who had cast me so ill prepared into the world. Vows were becoming a hazard. He said, 'I still intend to go, more so now that you have employed a manager to oversee the business.' Emlyn sipped from his ale cup thoughtfully. said, 'Tad-cu, on my way to Rhuddlan I met that old witch Mafanwy Fawr. She said some puzzling things to me about dragons and the wizard Merlin.'

'Agh! She is a strange one aright,' said Gruffydd. He wiped his bowl clean with the remains of his bread. 'Pay her no mind, she's full of tales to frighten children.'

'It was not a tale that she told me, more like a prophesy. She spoke of my mother. She said that she still lived. When I asked her whether I would find her, she said that I would find so much that I would wish I had never looked. And she called me *Mab-y-Ddraig*.'

Gruffydd stopped chewing while he listened to this. 'My Ann? Still alive? How could old Mafanwy know that? It sounds like nonsense to me Emlyn bach. What did you give the old woman? You know, she will say anything for a coin or two.'

'I didn't pay her anything. She would not accept what I offered.'

'And what was that?' Gruffydd asked.

'I offered her gems.' Emlyn said. Gruffydd looked at him with an expression of disbelief Emlyn continued, 'Tad-cu, do you remember the Franciscan friar who brought me to you when I was a child and who I told you came to Paris to visit me?'

'Aye, I remember him well. Old John Talbot kept in touch with him for a while, that must be how he traced you.'

'I agree, but there was a priest in the school, a Father de Sacy, who was also helpful to me and the old friar.'

'I liked the monk. I recall he knew something about siege warfare, an interest we had in common.'

'Remember he mentioned a woman who had come to the ship's chaplain in Cetua and begged him to see that I got to England? I did not tell you that he gave him a handful of gems, to ensure that he did as she asked. Fortunately he was an honest man and saw that I and the gems were delivered to Fra Sebastiano when the ship came to Lisbon. All the chaplain had learnt from the woman, was that I was her mistress' son. The mistress I assume was my mother. As to why she sent me there who knows?'

'It is an extraordinary tale,' said Gruffydd. 'I wonder why did the monk didn't tell me this at the time.'

'The explanation he gave me, was that he thought that I might be in danger of persecution had any learnt my origins. He knew that I had come from a Muslim house. I was baptised in Lisbon, which I think you knew. Fra Sebastiano explained that he knew nothing of the people here. At the time, he felt that the story was best left untold. Before I left Paris, he gave me the very gems that my mother had provided for my safety. These he had withheld for his own reasons. He kept them safe for me and he explained the reason was that he did not know of my family here.'

'Presumptuous fool,' said Gruffydd. 'But he could have been right. I can't imagine Hugh keeping the jewels safe for you. Have you got them still? Emlyn why did you mention nothing of this before?'

Emlyn smiled, 'I would have, but I wanted to be sure in my mind what to do. I do not know their worth, nor what they represent. I thought when I returned, that you wanted me to enter the competition at the Eisteddfod, to try and win the Golden Harp. It just seemed unimportant to mention them then. I have them here.' Emlyn placed the leather pouch on the table.

'The Golden Harp,' echoed Gruffydd. 'Aye I did want that for you and I still do. But obviously not this year, as the Eisteddfod had been and gone, nor next by the look of things. But I can't see lad, why you could not confide in me because of that.'

Emlyn shook his head. 'I am not used to confiding in any one. I feel as if I stand at a crossroads, not a crossroads, rather a road that divides into countless branches. I am at a loss as to which to take.'

'Good God!' Gruffydd cried, 'dear God and the seven mercy's!' He had emptied the gems into the palm of his hand and was gazing at them in wonder. 'These stones are exceptional, look at the settings, they are fit to grace the crowns of kings. Dear God, do you not know what you have here Emlyn Bach?'

Emlyn looked at him with curiosity. 'What do you mean?'

'That they will fetch a great price should you decide to sell them. Dear God, be careful, let no one around here know that you have them. I wish you had mentioned this before, Ambrose would have probably had an idea of their worth. These will make you wealthy lad, if wealth is what you seek.'

'They will certainly be helpful Tad-cu,' Emlyn replied enthusiastically. 'But not yet. Perhaps it would be better to take them to Italy with me, where I will find someone who knows the true value of such things.'

Gruffydd shook his head in disbelief. 'I would advise you not to carry them as such, rather to arrange for them to be kept safe. Are these what you offered Old Mafanwy?'

Emlyn nodded.

'That was a foolish thing to do and no doubt about it,' said Gruffydd caustically. 'Let, us hope the old woman would not know of their worth.'

'But she did.' Emlyn leaned forward and picked up a single gem. 'She said that this one here, was a dragon's eye or something. She did not want any of them because they carry a spell.'

'Perhaps she is wiser than I thought. Witch or not, she would most certainly be accused of theft if such gems were found on her. Still, you were a fool to show her.' Gruffydd admired the red stone, absorbed in its iridescent beauty. 'Dragon's stone eh? Stuff and nonsense if you ask me. You would be better paying no heed to her muttering. You say you paid her nothing?'

'She said that she would have the fee from me in time. I wish now that I had never met up with her.'

'Forget it lad. I'll give her a basket of eggs or something when I see her next. That should keep her happy. Fancy her saying that my Anne was still living though. To see her again would be worth more than any jewel.' Gruffyth wiped a tear from his eye. 'You must keep these gems safe and take care Emlyn. The Italians are two faced like Janus. Be careful who and what you ask. Discretion will serve you better than anything.'

Emlyn grinned, ignoring his split lip. 'Don't worry Tad-cu. I am as discretionary as they come.'

'So I had noticed at Conwy!' Gruffydd laughed. 'And what of Goronwy? I hope you have been careful with this printing business. It could be the ruin of all.'

'Before I can join Chillingworth and the wool, I must return to France with Goronwy, as I have promised him. If I discover the letter written by my uncle, when I return, I will be your legitimate heir. Until then I am irretrievably bound to print pamphlets and probably raise a rebellion.'

Gruffydd released an angry snort. 'I want you to have nothing more to do with the Catholic rebellion. I know it is a lot to ask of you, but consider this, there is a promising future for you here. You could make a good life for yourself. Marry a lass from the mountain and give me some fine great grandchildren to sit on my knee and play with my beard. Here, you can believe as you wish. John Talbot is here and often says mass of a Sunday. If not here, then somewhere remote up the mountain, under the heavens where good Christians can hear the word of God in peace, without fear of being discovered. Would you give me a promise as readily as you gave one to Goronwy?'

'How can I give such a promise? The danger of giving vows is already apparent and I am already involved. We have brought the means with which to spread the word. Leaflets, pamphlets and even books can be printed; there is advantage too in this.'

'Of course I can see the advantages. But not necessarily to your cause, that may well end in disaster. You and I have striven to avert a much greater peril at hand, of which few are aware That peril Emlyn, is the loss of our own language. There I can see great use for this printing press of yours. You have said yourself that if the language is written then it will always remain. If we see Welsh in print this alone will be enough to stimulate an interest and a need for literacy and education.' Gruffydd rose from his chair and took a book from a high shelf above the door. He handed it to Emlyn saying, 'This I have had these past three years it is *Kynniver Llith a Bann,* a Welsh translation of the Epistles and Gospels for the Book of Common Prayer. Did you know that a translation of the New Testament into Welsh was ordered by the Queen? Even now it may be in circulation. This is just one man's work Emlyn.'

'I know well of whom you speak,' said Emlyn, 'William Salesbury, he is no friend of the Catholic church and his Welsh is appalling. The Book of Common Prayer is a Protestant book and we should have nothing to do with it.'

'Rot and nonsense Emlyn! How else am I to read in my own tongue? There is nothing else and until you and the likes of you come to your senses and print books instead of printing incitement to riot, there will be nothing else.'

Emlyn sat in thought for a long time. During his time at the Collage de Clermont he had met Gruffydd Robert and Morris Clynnog, two Welsh Catholics who had fled England on Elizabeth's accession. Their ambition had been much the same, for Wales was still remote enough to hang onto the old beliefs and not to be influenced by the new swathe of thought. They, like Goronwy saw Wales as an island of strength for the Catholic believers. There were not enough learned priests to teach the ways of the new religion to the remote parishes.

Gruffydd gathered up the gems and replaced them in the sacking. He patted Emlyn's shoulder affectionately. 'Return to France, as you must anyway. But do not become further involved here in this mad printing scheme. In spring you are going to Italy remember.'

'Italy,' said Emlyn for the second time that evening. He smiled. 'Is that before or after I have wed a lass from the mountain and provided you with great grandchildren?'

'That's it then,' said Gruffydd, pleased with himself. 'Italy will get you away from your cousin and the priests for a while.'

Gruffydd leaned back in his chair. 'This is my life here Emlyn, breeding sheep, gathering wool and selling the excellent cloth made from it. There were some fine voices at the Eisteddfod though, you should have been there, and there is a new style of harp that sounds like a mournful wind on the mountain. I brought one back with me, I'll show you when you're ready. You should have heard Simwnt Fychan, now there's a man who's learned in the bardic traditions, God bless his Welsh heart.' He closed his eyes and began to talk in earnest. The names flooded through Emlyn's mind, the Druids the musicians, the skill, the acclaim, the disagreements the awards. As always Gruffydd painted a picture fresh, colourful, accurate and amusing. Emlyn could see in his mind, the flags and pennants and the dignity of the Druids and the elation of the awarded. He knew that his grandfather wanted such for him, but he was not yet ready to rise to that particular challenge.

'Ah, you see Emlyn bach, it was like this. First in the world was Gwyddon Ganhebon,' Gruffydd said, 'who made vocal song and Huw the Mighty who made the means of preserving the song and Lydain, the father of the muse, who gave them the rules by which to keep the song. From what these three men began, came the bard and his art as we know it today. The first three bards were Plenydd, Alon and Gwbon and they kept the dignity and the custom of the Englyn Meifwr, the three lines with a common rhyme, the words of ancient poetry handed down through the mists of time. Listen to the way the words sing as if they have a life of their own.

The mountain snow: the stag doth fly,
The wind above the rocks doth sigh,
Love cannot in concealment lie.

The mountain snow: the grove is dark,
The raven black, the hound doth bark,
God keep you from all evil work.

The mountain snow: the crust is sound,
The wind doth twist the reeds around,
Where ignorance is, no grace is found.

Emlyn listened patiently hearing the wind above the bard's rumbling voice and the lonely call of an owl and the crackling of wood burning in the hearth. He listened as he did to all his lessons, fixing the words in his mind so they would never be forgotten.

Chapter 20 Venice/Florence

The Republic of Venice had suffered under the heat of a relentless summer. With no rain, the earth had cracked and the crops had shrivelled before they had come to harvest. Drought brought death and poverty. Those better off had depended on the grain-ships which brought their produce from the islands of the empire. But even these, brought the poor fruits of harvest. With winter came the sea storms, the bitter cold winds and the continuous rain. It was too late now to benefit the earth and those who depended on it's produce.

The newly founded spice company wanted for nothing. A ship came in from Alexandria with a cargo of rice and corn, which Bartolomeo sold for twice the usual value. He had hired clerks and workers and moved to a modest palace on the Canal Grande. For himself, he kept the house on Canal delle Torreselle. Jacopo, Maria and her family stayed with him, as they had lived in the area for most of their lives and the arrangement kept their numerous children away from the intolerant master. Tomasso himself, had not yet returned. He had sent word to his manager and put in Bartolomeo all his trust and confidence. Following his instructions to the letter, Bartolomeo prepared the Cornucopia and Scipione Barozzi to make a winter voyage to Stamboul. With it, much to Bartolomeo's disgust, were going two of Grimani's ships, a caravel and a galley for protection. By then, most of Venice was aware of how much Don Carlos pinned his hopes on the voyage to Stamboul. When the ships returned, laden with spice, it was assumed that all his worries would be over.

Bartolomeo had not been present at the meeting between Tomasso and Don Carlos. He was relieved that they had not formed a partnership. It was more in the nature of a shared enterprise, the outcome of which would dictate future arrangements. Tomasso had not been persuaded into making an agreement which he would later regret. Only Bartolomeo knew of his real intentions and suspected that no joint venture between Tomasso and Don Carlos could be for good intent. Bartolomeo would not forget Tomasso's words. 'In this sweet city which you hold so dear to your heart, resides but one that I would injure, one that I would strip of his wealth, his reputation and all that he holds dear.'

Bartolomeo was burdened by a sense of guilt because of Tomasso's intentions toward Don Carlos Grimani. No physical harm had befallen the great man or any of his household, yet Bartolomeo could not rid himself of the unease.

He walked to San Marco's in the rain, to attend Sunday mass. The members of the trading house accompanied him, all dressed in new attire which showed their success. They were greeted along the way with respect where none had been given before. On the rare occasions in which Bartolomeo could forget the reasons behind Tomasso's success, he thoroughly enjoyed himself. Never had he had such a free hand to practice his talents, never had he had such wealth at his disposal. In the Basilica he even found his eyes straying towards the women. His hopes were rekindled.

Weeks had passed with no sign of the master. Bartolomeo received word that Tomasso had bought a house on the mainland. Bartolomeo was requested to visit it when he could to assess what repairs were needed. The cost had not been drawn from the company funds, but from Tomasso's own considerable wealth. Bartolomeo wondered if Tomasso had had success with his jade and if Cosimo Medici, the Duke of Florence, was dressed in the rich yellow silk that Tomasso had brought when he first came to Venice.

The evening before he planned a journey to the mainland, Bartolomeo had a visit from Fiorenza.

'So tell me all about Tomasso,' she said. She was seated near the hearth in the library. Bartolomeo poured her a glass of wine. She took a sip and set her glass down beside her. 'I know that you know more than the rest of us Bartolomeo,' she continued, 'because of the way he regards you. He did say to Enrico and I that he had known you years ago. He holds Venice perplexed, it is as if he has appeared from nowhere. Now he is gone, is he likely to come back?'

Bartolomeo looked at her seriously. He knew that she was not a chattering woman and that she found greater pleasure mixing with poets and philosophers than the gossip mongers of San Marco's. 'I can tell you a little,' he replied. 'What happened to Vincentini between now and the time I last knew him must remain a mystery. He has told me nothing. I assume he had been trading on the coast of Africa and the Levant.'

'But, you know who he is, Bartolomeo?'

He sighed and squirmed uncomfortably in his chair opposite her. It was not his story to tell. But to be able to share the burden of the knowledge he carried would be a great relief. Could he trust Fiorenza? Or would he be better to steer her away from the subject?

She sat forward, her velvet skirts rustling. The green jewel at her throat caught the light like a glow worm. She looked at him earnestly. 'For example,' she prompted, 'is he married?'

'I don't know,' Bartolomeo answered honestly. He remembered Tomasso joking about the Grimani girl in the gondola before they had sold the salt company. 'He has bought a house on the mainland,' he added to turn her thoughts away. 'It is a ruined crocus farm. Why he wants it, I cannot begin to guess. He has asked me to go and see it. I intend to do tomorrow before the weather gets any colder.'

'Why would he want a run down farm when he has all this?' Fiorenza frowned in puzzlement.

'Perhaps he has tired of the sea,' he offered lamely. 'Saffron is a valuable crop and many merchants have now retired to the land to make their living in better comfort and security.'

'Could it be that he had a wife and family hidden away somewhere whom he wishes to provide a home for?' Fiorenza asked. She seemed determined not to be swayed from her interest.

Bartolomeo admired her hands that were clasped in front of her. They were rounded with tapering fingers. He wished that he could see her hair that she always kept covered. He drew his eyes away. 'Tomasso has said nothing of family,' he replied. 'He has said very little of anything.' He remembered then, the night Andrea had been found in the canal. Fiorenza had not returned to her own residence that night. If she had spent the time with Tomasso, she had been very discrete. 'Are you interested in...er?' Bartolomeo stumbled to a halt, sorry that he had spoken.

'What?'

'Forgive me Madonna, are your inquiries of a romantic nature?' He cleared his throat to cover his embarrassment.

She smiled and blushed. She sank back in the chair and retrieved her glass; twiddling it around in an agitated manner.

Bartolomeo stood to refill his own glass. Fool! he thought to himself. Why ask such a question when you do not want to know the answer? Madonna Fiora is not for the likes of you Bartolomeo Varini!

Fiorenza said, 'I will not deny that I find the prospect of marriage to Tomasso di Vincentini attractive. I doubt if it has ever occurred to him! In fact so unresponsive has he been, that I feel that he may be wed. Be that as it may, there are still questions that need answers. I am being made wealthy by a business of which I know nothing. Enrico and Barozzi know nothing of the master either. He did not even take the trouble to wait to meet Barozzi! You are the only one Bartolomeo, who knows anything about him. Most women might be quite content to be in my position. However I feel unsafe, as if I totter on a precipice. What if he has disappeared?'

'There is no need to feel such insecurity,' said Bartolomeo returning to the fire. 'The spice company is well established and will remain secure whatever happens to Tomasso. He has left all in my hands and left us the freedom to make whatever decisions are necessary for the company's betterment.'

'What of the involvement of Don Carlos Grimani?' Fiorenza pointed out. 'Neither of us had any say in that decision.'

'Grimani has merely sent ships to the same source of spice, there is no partnership. Each merchant takes his own risks. Why Tomasso offered him such a trade advantage, he has not said.'

'Like everything else,' added Fiorenza. 'Many are saying that this new spice merchant is a fool and that some enterprising rival will soon rip the carpet from under his feet and send him tumbling.'

'I doubt it,' said Bartolomeo with a grim smile. He knew that the true reasons for the joint venture had nothing to do with mutual gain either. Carlos Grimani should have looked closer into the fate of his malmsey fleet, before he had taken up with di Vincentini. Bartolomeo felt with a growing certainty, that Grimani would never see his ships return laden with spice next spring.

'You are very loyal Bartolomeo,' said Fiorenza. 'I can see why Tomasso has put his trust in you. But do you trust him?'

'I believe that he would not bring us any misfortune. He wants this company to succeed. He knew your husband Madonna, and would see you content and provided for.'

'Alessandro never said anything about him!' Fiorenza exclaimed petulantly. 'Even that story could be a fabrication!'

Bartolomeo shook his head. 'No, that much, I know is true for it was so when I first met Tomasso.'

Fiorenza stood up impatiently. 'And, are you going to tell me Bartolomeo? Or shall I leave and we will not be friends?'

He turned to face her. Her eyes were alight with challenge, her perfume, heady and exotic. Bartolomeo swallowed nervously. He said, 'Your oath first, that nothing of what I say will pass beyond these doors.'

'You have it,' said Fiorenza without a shade of hesitation. She sat down, arranged her folds of velvet and held out her empty glass.

'To tell the story of Tomasso Vincentini, you have first to follow the tale of another.' Bartolomeo began. 'When first I came to Venice, I found employment with the trading fleet that ran to Flanders and England. The captai'n who employed me was Cristoforo Grimani, a determined young man very like his father Don Carlos. He had a nose for sniffing out advantageous deals and traded at every port we came to. He kept me busy, keeping records of everything he bought or sold. He turned me into the man of the sea trade; making maps, drawing charts, keeping ledgers, reading the weather, the tides, the market, the mood. I knew the price of black pepper in Lisbon, cloves in Algiers, oranges in Cyprus, wool in England and silk in Stamboul.

For four years we traded thus, up and down the Mediterranean, through to the Atlantic, up the coast of Spain to the ports of Northern Europe. It seemed that we were favoured by God, for not only did we meet with success in trading, but we had our fair share of fighting too. There is nothing like a battle at sea to stir the blood! One corsair in particular, we met more often that any other, and always he eluded us. This was Barbarosa, Khair-e-din, that orange haired pirate that plundered the Middle Sea as if it were his own private fish pond. Hate grew like a cancer in the heart of Cristoforo. He vowed to destroy Barbarosa or die in the attempt. You must realise Madonna, that in those days we were young and hot blooded.'

'I have heard of this Barbarosa,' said Fiorenza. 'When I was young, it was the fantasy of many a maiden of my age then, to be captured and carried off by this fabled prince of the sea.'

'Well, before Cristoforo could achieve this ambition,' said Bartolomeo warming to his subject, 'something happened which changed his future and fortunes. He fell in love. It was English cloth that brought Cristoforo and his young wife together. She was Elizabeth Anne Morgan, the daughter of a land owner. Theirs was a thriving business exporting fine English wool to the dyers of Italy. The family was in London at the time, selling the best wool on the market and they were very hospitable people.'

Fiorenza lifted her bent head and interrupted. 'Was it not as rumour says, a marriage of necessity then?'

'No no,' Bartolomeo protested. 'Is that what they still say? Nonsensical gossip! Cristoforo was pierced by Cupids arrow the moment he set eyes on her. Captivated by her beauty and raven hair and the pools of blue she called eyes. In he fell and had no wish to escape. I tried to intervene, I used every scrap of influence I had among the Venetian families in London. They all backed me in my attempts to dissuade Cristoforo from such an unsuitable match. Elizabeth Anne's own family were fiercely opposed to the marriage too.

The lovers were inseparable, tied up in that pure and selfish love that is granted to few. If they could not wed with the blessing of her father, then they would wed without it. She was the light of her father's life was Elizabeth Anne, even a fool could see that he doted on her. I'd say the whole business broke the heart of the man. She was just sixteen and Cristoforo was eleven years older. He was the dream of a romantic young girl, handsome, dazzling and full of excitement and adventure. It is a terrible thing for a man to lose his beloved daughter to a stranger, to have her spirited away to some far, unreachable place. For that is indeed what happened. The lovers defied everyone and she ran off with him, leaving London in the dead of night aboard his galley.

'By the time we returned to Venice, Elizabeth Anne was with child. I always thought that was a grave mistake, but they were blind to the consequences and saw nothing but each other. For the new bride, Venice became an ocean of hostility. Faced with the unwelcome bitterness of Don Carlos and Cristoforo's brother Roberto, she begged Cristoforo to take her home. There were many reasons why he could not do this. He sheltered her as much as possible from the family's disapproval. He took her to a house near Padua. Don Carlos Grimani publicly disowned his son and ordered his family to turn their backs and deny the young couple recognition. They even tried to get me to leave him by offering me money. I don't know why I stayed for to be without the backing of family here in Venice, seemed a fate worse than death. I knew what Don Carlos wanted; he hoped to crush Cristoforo with his rejection and then to bring him back humbled and begging to divorce his English wife. But Cristoforo was made of as stern stuff as his father. He seemed not the least bit upset by the way matters turned out. He was an astute merchant himself and managed in the following years to make a decent living and gain a reputation as a reliable seaman. His wife Anna gave him two sons, Lorenzo and Paolo, whom you know Madonna.'

'This girl was the mother of Lorenzo and Paolo Grimani?' Fiorenza said. 'I did not realise. Perhaps I should tune my ear better to the chattering tongues of Venice.'

'Have you heard enough?' Bartolomeo asked, teasing her.

'If you stop now Bartolomeo Varini, I shall tie a stone to your knees and have you dropped into the Lagoon!'

Bartolomeo looked at her tenderly, she looked like a child eagerly waiting for the completion of the story. She is, he admitted to himself, an extraordinary woman. He smiled at her, knowing that his feelings for her were plainly visible upon his face. 'So,' he began with a deep breath. 'Apart from the animosity of his family, a few years of happiness were granted to Cristoforo, his young wife and the two little sons. Then, while at sea, Cristoforo met again with his old enemy Barbarosa. In the ensuing, ill-advised sea battle Cristoforo risked the Senate's galleys and lost them. He was killed and Barbarosa escaped, a richer man by far that before the encounter.

It was a terrible battle and I myself was wounded, but I will not subject you to the details here. When I returned to Venice, I was cared for by Anna. When I was well enough, she asked me to remain with her, employed in the capacity of manager. She was a brave girl and faced her future with resolve. The debts incurred by Cristoforo from his clash with Barbarosa were formidable. The Senate demanded that the cost of the lost galleys be met from his own estate.'

Fiorenza stirred the embers to life and placed more wood on the tiny flames to drive away the chill of night. From across the Grande Canal came the clamourous ring of the Campanile. Fiorenza's face was bathed in new flame. She looked up and said, 'Please go on Bartolomeo. What happened to her?'

'Anna sold everything she could. She refused the help of Don Carlos and ran the country farm on her own. Her intention was to bring in the grape and olive harvests and use the profit from these to pay some of the debt she owed the Senate. Then she planned to sell the property and use the money to pay back the remainder before she returned to her own country. This was not a promising position for me to be in. But I had been devoted to Cristoforo and came to greatly respect his widow. It was at this time, while she joined the harvesters, that Tomasso and your husband Alessandro, come into the tale. Tomasso's family were crocus farmers at the very house that he has now purchased. He was Tomasso Capaccio then, named after his father. He was not the ideal son his father had wished for; he wanted nothing to do with saffron. He went his own way and even though young, he had already gained a name for himself as a jewel merchant. He was returning home after an absence of three years trading through the seas with Alessandro whom he did much business with. At the time of his return, Anna was gathering olives. Their fateful meeting was eventually to bring disaster, but the outcome of it, was one of loving devotion.'

Bartolomeo stopped speaking. He drained his wine and held his glass out playfully to Fiorenza, as she had done to him. She rose and refilled it; her own wine was hardly touched. Bartolomeo thought that she looked sad.

'Are you too worn to continue?' Fiorenza asked.

'Not in the least,' Bartolomeo replied truthfully. 'I will come to the end of the tale in time.'

'This Anna sounds a woman worthy of admiration. She was so able to love.'

'She was. She had a strength of spirit that nothing could quell. That is, until Don Carlos began to force his influence. So grieved had he been at the death of his son whom he had been estranged from, that he wished to make amends. He wanted Anna and her sons to come into the security of the family. He wanted Lorenzo and Paolo near him, so that he could watch them grow and influence their futures. Anna would have nothing to do with him; enamoured as she was by the colourful gem merchant Tomasso. Don Carlos would not accept her defiance. He tried by persuasion, by temptation, by all in his power to compel her to return to Venice. She resisted it all. Then, by guile, Don Carlos bought the property, the land and buildings which Anna had worked so hard with to repay the Senate. Roberto, Don Carlos' remaining son, took possession of the crocus farm. Anna and her sons were forced to return to Venice.

To understand what happened next, Fiora, you need a better knowledge of Anna. She had about her an unreal beauty, as if she were of the Other-world that is inhabited by sirens and tree spirits; like some fey creature accidentally caught in the realm of men. Once Roberto had encountered her, he was as if under a spell, enchanted by her beauty. He was like someone possessed, he wanted to own her like an article of clothing or a fine hound. She could not escape his attentions, he sent her lavish gifts and seemed to be wherever she looked. Don Carlos only wanted his grandsons, Lorenzo and Paolo He was not captivated by the charms of Anna, and saw the attraction which Roberto had for her as a wicked thing. To hunger after his dead brother's wife was unholy in his sight.

During all this, Tomasso stayed as clear as he could away from the Grimani. But eventually Roberto and he fought. The first time, Roberto was fortunate and escaped with his life. Soon after, Don Carlos sent men to this very house, which belonged to Cristoforo and Anna. I, to my sorrow was not here at the time, nor was Tomasso. Grimani's men took away Anna and her boys. Within a few days, Tomasso challenged Roberto to a duel to the death. They fought with swords and Roberto was seriously wounded. Tomasso was arrested and imprisoned by Don Carlos while Roberto bled his life's blood away under the care of inept physicians. At the soonest opportunity, Anna was sent away, on a ship bound for Cyprus. It was the intention of Don Carlos to place her in a convent as far from her sons as she could be. The ship was never seen again nor was she. For Tomasso he devised a different fate.

Having lost one son and with the other fighting for his life, Don Carlos' hatred was raw. He directed it against Tomasso Capaccio. And not only Tomasso, but his family as well. They were burned to death in their own house, his parents and his little sister Gina. It was said to have been a tragic accident. Tomasso was sold to a Greek galley slaver. Perhaps this inadvertently saved his life, for soon after, Roberto died of his wounds. Had Tomasso been available to the Patron, no doubt he would have met his death too. Indeed it was assumed by all, that he would not last long chained to a galley oar. That was the last I saw of Tomasso Capaccio, until he returned as Tomasso di Vincentini.'

Fiorenza sat in silence. The fire crackled. Eventually she looked up at him. 'Could you do nothing for Anna and her children or for Tomasso?'

'No, try as I might, there was no way I, a mere notary, could break through the influence of Don Carlos Grimani. The whole tale was never told, until now and none knew the truth of it but I and your husband Alessandro. However, Tomasso escaped the miserable death planned for him. He must have founded the Lanarca Salt company a few years later and placed his friend Alessandro at it's helm.'

'I cannot understand why Alessandro never mentioned it,' said Fiorenza.

'He must have been sworn to secrecy. He knew that any mention of Tomasso Capaccio would bring about his own downfall. I believe now, that Tomasso had every intention of involving me in the secret. But Alessandro kept all the correspondence to himself and I remained ignorant all these years.'

'So what do we do now? What could Tomasso's reasons be to come back at all. Unless...' she stopped in mid-sentence. The look she gave Bartolomeo was one of mounting alarm. She whispered, 'Revenge?'

Bartolomeo nodded his head slowly. He said 'Now renew your oath to me, that you will say nothing of this.'

'I would not dare,' Fiorenza replied, 'nor do I dare to dwell on the outcome. Be assured Bartolomeo, nothing of your story will ever leave my lips. I well understand the need for secrecy. Don Carlos did not recognise him did he?'

'No, and why should he? Tomasso is changed beyond recognition and Grimani thinks him long dead. He would never dream that the ghost of his misdeeds had now come back to cut with the scythe of vengeance.'

Fiorenza made the sign of the cross. Her eyes were wide with fear.

'Perhaps it would have been better if you had never inquired after the truth,' said Bartolomeo softly. 'But if you keep it safe, you have nothing to fear. It is late. Jacopo will see that you return to your sister's house safely.'

Early the following morning Bartolomeo had Jacopo ferry him to the quay where ferry boats left for the mainland. It was raining, a thin drizzly rain which soaked into everything. There were only two other passengers waiting for the boat to leave; two women, heavily veiled and cloaked against the weather. Bartolomeo could see them from the gondola as it slid nearer. One was Fiorenza he was sure of it. Few would recognise her in the bundled cloth, but Bartolomeo had watched her the night before, her comely shape and even her slightest movement were ingrained in his mind.

She waved when she saw him and came out from under the shelter of a portico to greet him as he climbed out of the gondola. 'I'm coming with you,' she said. 'Do you mind?'

Bartolomeo didn't mind; he didn't mind the rain any more either. 'Madonna, I would be honoured,' he replied. 'But in this unsuitable weather you will not be comfortable.'

'I do not mind the rain,' she smiled. 'Maria however will grumble all the way. If you can put up with that, I'm sure we shall have a pleasurable journey. Is it far to Tomasso's home? I wonder if he will be there himself?'

'It will be a round journey of three days,' explained Bartolomeo. 'But there are inns in plenty, where you and your maid will find comfortable accommodation. I intended to hire horses in Marghera.' He paused a moment, 'no, Fiorenza, he will not be there,' he added solemnly.

Fiorenza was everything he had hoped. Her conversation was educated and she revealed a greater knowledge of trade that he had given her credit for up to date; he had thought her uninterested. By mid-morning the rain had stopped and they spent the remainder of their journey travelling under a winter sun. They stayed at an inn in Dolo that was nothing like Bartolomeo had described and which gave Maria genuine reason for complaint. Fiorenza did not seem to be upset by the dirt and the grime. She sees beyond such trivia, Bartolomeo mused as he lay awake in his room scratching. They had not mentioned Tomasso once.

The farm that Tomasso had bought, lay in a curve of the river Brenta, about ten miles to the north of Padua. From it's mountainous source, through Lago di Caldonazzo, the Brenta twisted through the Alpine foothills which reached like stretched, forested fingers out across the plain. It wove and curved to the east of Padua, ran and spread adjacent to the Lagoon and spilled out into the Gulf of Venice near Chioggia. Its course ran through fertile lands, watered by the upland snows of winter. Even in the heat of summer there was plenty of water to be had from the streams that ran from the Brenta soaking into the earth. The farm buildings lay between two gentle hills, the land stretching out level away from them. Once, in October, these fields would have been a carpet of crocus flowers.

The house was large and practical. It was built in the popular Roman style, around a central courtyard. Under the broken red-tiled roofs the walls had once been whitewashed, to reflect away the heat of the summer. The surrounding ground was planted with tall cypresses and huge, spreading orange bushes. Vines scrambled over every wall and grew thick were they had fallen to the ground. They were leafless now, the tortuous branches looked as if they were devouring what remained of the buildings. The air was scented with thyme which grew in profusion on the hillsides. It had always been a working farm with no frills of fancy tiles or fountains. It looked as if it had been deserted for many years. The blackened stumps of the wooden outhouses were a sharp reminder of the fire that had taken the lives of Tomasso's family.

Bartolomeo, Fiorenza and Maria rode down from the hill where they had paused. It was crowned with a copse of dark umbra trees from which squabbling birds rose. They could hear the bubbling song of the Brenta that flowed a short distance away. The land was dressed in winter colours; black branches, deep green conifers and glistening earth, still soggy with the fallen rain.

'It is beautiful,' said Fiorenza turning to smile at the spice manager.

'Yes,' agreed Bartolomeo, 'more beautiful than I remember.' There is no need, he thought to question why Tomasso wanted this back. If he survives the ordeal of his revenge, there is no better place to spend the remainder of one's days than here. I understand his vengeance better now that the story is told. I can only hope now that I live up to his expectations, for never was there a fouler man that Don Carlos Grimani. The sins of the past may be allowed a time of rest, but they will bring their own just return. No man should be excused the justice that murder demands. The devil take you Carlos Grimani!

Chapter 21 Wales

Gruffydd watched Emlyn recover from his hurts. He was pleased at how easily the boy absorbed all he was taught about ancient poetry. Something had occurred during Emlyn's absence that had changed him. Gruffydd could not fathom what exactly it was; perhaps it was no single incident, but an overall effect. It had left him in better control of his emotions and with less inclination towards light hearted tomfoolery. But he seldom smiled nowadays and the swaying hips and inviting eyes of Blodeuedd Hewitt, had no effect on him whatsoever.

For two days after he had come back, Emlyn did nothing but sit in the late autumn sunshine, tinkering with the new triple harp or partaking in lengthy discussions with John Talbot. Later he rode to the high hills where the gulls cried and the ewes grew round with the quickened seed of the new rams. Some days he spent on the heather-dressed marsh-lands that lay between the rocky outcrops, where the peat cutters built up their winter stores of fuel. Here the black cattle with long hair weighed down with mud and horns smooth as slate, grazed among red barberries and the purple flowers of autumn thrift.

Other times, he would visit the farm fields, studded with bee hives, where rows of women with baskets or babies at their hips, planted the winter kale while their lips mumbled in prayer to sway the winter storms. The thud and slithers of the withy cutters beat a rhythm to the passing days. When the rain turned the roads to mud, Emlyn went to the barns where new ropes hung, scented still, of hemp, willow and heather and where the grain was laid to dry in preparation for winter. On the steep, rock-strewn Moels, where the north wind howled blowing the trees so that they grew forever bent to its will, Emlyn worked mending the stone walls that wound like serpents up the mountain. Here, rills as white as marble, scribbled down the craggy slopes to plunge into the fern-clothed banks of streams and rivers that led to the sea.

At home, as Emlyn began to appreciate the land that his grandfather owned with such pride, he offered sound ideas where improvements could be made, in irrigation where the soil was thin and in drainage where fields lay water logged for most of the year. Under his grandfather's tuition, he drew designs for cogs and wheels to improve the mill where lowland farmers brought their corn to grind. In the evenings Gruffydd and Emlyn often sat upon the hillside where the magnificence of the Welsh mountain range spread before them as far as the eye could see.

Gruffydd did not need to be knocked over the head and stuffed into a sack to attend the wedding of his other grandson Owain Morgan; he agreed to go quite willing. He felt that his presence would prevent further conflict between Owain and Emlyn. Aside from that, the day following the wedding was the day of the Knappan and no Welshman worth the blood running in his veins would miss that.

On the day of their departure for the wedding., Gruffydd brushed and trimmed his beard and dressed in a respectable gown, lightened with twisted green and gold braid and hemmed with squirrel fur. Emlyn wore a new doublet with a narrow-tabbed skirt fashioned from black brocade with slashed sleeves and padded wings at the shoulders. Gruffydd had chosen black cloth because it was expensive, this seemed a good opportunity to impress upon the family the esteem in which Gruffydd held his grandson.

The two best horses in Gruffydd's stable were brushed until their coats gleamed and the saddles were hung with gilt and tassels. Gruffydd, Emlyn and John Talbot were accompanied by servants and grooms and other men, who made the journey for the Knappan. They were dressed in russet dyed cloth; the first to come from Gruffydd's wool woven by a work force of farmer's wives.

The company rode out before it was fully light. The servants brought the dogs and hawks, in the hope that the pleasure of hunting might avail itself. With them, trying to keep up with the horses, was a motley crowd of neighbours on foot, all eager to take part in the Knappan. They laughed and joked with Emlyn, offering suggestions and carefully worked over plans for success in the game.

They rode down from the mountain and passed through forests lit in the morning light. The countryside was embroidered with golden leaves, and Rowan trees were bright with berries, and Elder festooned with fruit, black and velvet as night. It was over twenty miles to Rhuddlan. Emlyn thought the pace deliberately slow. He said nothing to hurry events. They passed many on the road, crowds travelling to the great event of the year that would begin in Rhuddlan. From there, God only knew where the Knappan would run.

In high spirits Gruffydd sang, his huge voice frightening the birds and the squirrels from the trees.

'You're Welsh blood will be the death of you Gruffydd Morgan,' said John Talbot when the raucous song had quieted.

'Well now.' Gruffydd hummed, 'if a man can't live and die for what he believes in he's no business living and dying at all.'

'There's much good common sense in that,' John Talbot replied.

'There should be more like me,' said Gruffydd dreamily. 'Then Wales would not be governed by the Saeson. We hold only one in eighteen seats in the parliament and if such a man was to speak in his own tongue he'd be thrown out by the seat of his hose. That's what the Act of Union has done for us. Do you remember how it goes Emlyn?'

'All of it?' Emlyn said in dread.

'Just the main bit,' Gruffydd replied. 'To remind our good friend here of the implications.'

Emlyn recited, 'That this said country or Dominion of Wales shall be, stand and continue forever from henceforth incorporated, united and annexed to and with this Realm of England.' He paused and then added, 'One seat in eighteen you say? And how many did Wales hold before that, it can only be less.'

Ignoring him, Gruffydd said, 'Forever,' and spat on the path in disgust. 'Forever the English has become the language of our church and our law, indeed a man is hard pressed to make a niche of his own without it,' he growled. 'Now the way I see it, God had kept us as a people with our own language for a specific purpose and it's our duty as bards to hand on our traditions. Tudur Aled, God rest his soul, told me that and he learnt it from Dafydd Nantmor. I in my turn, have told it to Simwnt Fychan and Emlyn here. I'll not forget it at the whim of some authorizing Englishman just for the ease of it.'

'It's a pity Tad-cu,' said Emlyn, 'that you do not feel the same about the true faith. For with such devotion we may well overthrow the English and Reformer's alike.'

Gruffydd turned to face him, his beard glistened in the sunlight. 'Who says I don't feel the same about the faith?' he answered. 'I helped you with your printing engine didn't I?'

'True,' admitted Emlyn. 'But by befriending William Salesbury, of the abysmal Welsh and Richard Davis, who's Welsh is little better, you have aligned yourself with the Protestants.'

'I'll admit,' said Gruffydd, 'that I am Welsh before I am anything else. And these men have made a positive step for the future of Wales by giving us a New Testament and a book of prayer. I'll befriend any man who devotes himself to the plight of Wales. Now Gruffydd Roberts is a Catholic, he was Bishop of Bangor when the Catholic Queen Mary was on the throne. He's gone from here now for the sake of his health. He serves as confessor to Cardinal Borromeo in Milan. There's Italy for you again Emlyn; you might look him up while you're there. Morys Clynnog went with him and they wrote Yr Athrawiaeth Gristnogol, the book of Christian Doctrine. How they must miss their own beloved land. Both men were well known to me and write still from time to time. You would be well cared for by them Emlyn, should you see fit to visit. I suspect they follow the teachings of the Jesuits like yourself.'

Moving his horse back a pace, John Talbot said, 'At least William Salesbury is not a deceptive man when it comes to the new ideas in religion, no matter that his Welsh is a little eccentric. He believes as I do, that it was the Celtic Church in all its purity that has preserved the Christian faith and kept the Welsh language alive. The Reformation could be seen then, not as a novelty brought from foreign parts, but as a return to the proud past of the Welsh.'

'But you are a priest,' Emlyn replied, 'are you saying then that you do not see the Pope as the head of the Catholic Church?'

'Not at all,' the old man replied. 'The Pope is indeed the head of the Catholic Church as we know it now, but the Celtic Church owed its allegiance to no man far away in Rome. When Rome was overrun by barbarians, the faith all but died out. If it was not for the Irish and Welsh monks and scholars who brought the faith back to Europe, where would the head of the Church be now? Are we to be ruled by the word of God or by the law of the Church? It is understandable that a man can confuse himself sorting the one from the other. The church has grown fat and indolent on its riches. Can a poor man honour the rich who gain by another's loss? Is it Christian to bedeck your gown in gilt and silver? Where in the good book does the Lord ask us to build great hedgehog cathedrals from riches that would better serve the poor?'

'But there is no Celtic Church to speak of,' said Emlyn. 'With respect, what you speak of is idealistic, for no Celtic priest could be consecrated bishop without Rome's authority. If the Church does not show its power by wealth and influence, then no man can respect it. In order to hold his people together, the Pope must wield power. No man can call himself king unless he wears the insignia of God's authority and shows his strength in arms when his authority is questioned.'

'True, true,' agreed John Talbot, 'but the Church has taken advantage of such power. Selling a place in heaven for example, now where's the sense in that? If a man's soul is blackened by sin no amount of coin is going to buy him redemption. I'm not saying that I agree with the Calvinist, but it seems to me that the Church was losing sight of its purpose, straying from the guidance of the Holy Book. The bigger an empire the harder it is to control. That's what happened you see? It split at the seams.'

'Well there's no going back now,' said Gruffydd. 'We'll be invaded for sure. And what is Wales but a back door into England? Spain could well land an army in Ireland, combine forces with the Catholics there and launch themselves on the Welsh coast. No doubt, they could rouse the inhabitants and gather local support. Wales would then be a causeway for invading foreigners.'

'I disagree,' said Emlyn, 'at least a far as Welsh support is concerned. The ruling class that we still have, are more loyal to Elizabeth than they are to ancestral belief. Without our own leaders, what Welshman would follow a completely foreign rule? Better England than Spain no matter how you look at it.'

'I hope you haven't said that to Goronwy,' said Gruffydd Hiraethog.

Emlyn dropped back to leave the elders to their talk. He chatted instead with Twm as they rode along. The man had been Gruffydd's servant for four years. Twm told him of an extraordinary cure for tertian, concerning rats tied to the soles of the feet. Emlyn's spirits rose.

The wedding took place in the afternoon, to allow all who were invited time to attend. St. Mary's was crowded. Ellen thought this was just as well; being small she could bow her head and remain unseen if she should shame herself and cry.

The bride, Harriet Crew was not ugly, nor was she fat. She was pink and blond, admittedly plain, but pleasantly so. She was dressed in a tailored gown the colour of Malmsey with gold piping around all the edges and trailing sleeves, the like of which had never been witnessed outside the court of the Queen of England. Harriet twinkled with jewels. Her hair was the colour of corn and ivory, it hung in ringlets and pleats; twisted round with tiny flowers threaded on to a strand of golden silk. At her temple, it curled as soft as down. Her downcast eyes were cornflower blue framed with amber lashes.

Beside her, Owain stood tall and handsome dressed in contrasting dark-green with a blue waist-length cloak hanging from his shoulders like a tent. They looked stunning together. Admirers named them, amid flushes and laughter, as Titania and Oberon.

Ellen did not cry and even managed to hold her head up. She did not look at the couple who drew every other eye. She smoothed her plain blue dress absently, clenched her gloved hands and looked out the window. There she could see the great crescent shaped bay that ended with the headland of Pen Gogarth, now blue and dim in the distance. Her mother Elisabeth, elbowed her in the ribs. Ellen drew her eyes back to the moment. It seemed as if the whole population of Rhuddlan had arrived to see the young master wed. The church was filled with bared heads and shawled heads; all bent or risen in unison. Squire Hugh's voice could be heard above the rest, mellow and rich it led the congregation in prayer. Ellen fidgeted impatiently. The church was hot.

When she had seen Owain battered and bruised by his nasty cousin Emlyn, she had cried buckets and hated Emlyn Tomas with a venom powerful enough to do murder. It was only later, when she stopped her tears long enough to listen, that she learned what exactly had occurred. Connie told her as she had heard it all from Rhys Llwyd. He was one of the men who was with the two at the time and who had prevented them from killing each other. Connie showed a remarkable interest in Rhys Llwyd. Ellen expected that the affection was returned, so she doubted that Connie had made the story up about the two cousins. Ellen decided then, that she hated both Owain and Emlyn. Her gaze strayed again to the window.

Outside, lit by sunshine, Emlyn Tomas stood on a grave stone that was the same colour as his eyes. It took her a moment to recognise him; he looked so different. He was neatly dressed and graceful. His eyes looked huge and his hair was as dark as forest earth and trimmed neatly. He winked at her and put a long finger to his lips. Beside him stood an old man with furious eyebrows and a mop of wizened grey hair sticking out from his felt hat as if trying to escape. Behind them both, standing with natural dignity was Gruffydd Hiraethog. Under one snowy eyebrow, his exceptional blue eye also closed in a wink. They motioned to her to look away. They were late and were going to pretend that they had been there all along, mingling with the crowd as it left the church.

Ellen turned her attention back to the ceremony, only to discover that it was over. As the echo of the vicar's final blessing faded, they all rose with a rustle of cloth and a whisper. Owain Morgan, who held his stepsister's heart in his palm, was now wed to Harriet Crew. The bride looked disgustingly radiant and most unlikely to be locked up in a tower and visited infrequently for breeding purposes, as Owain had threatened.

When they had all left the church, Harriet kissed her sister-in-law. Ellen froze in the soft embrace and fought to control her tears.

'Ah, there's a lovely bride you are Harriet Crew,' said Connie O'Neill beside her. 'Of course it wouldn't do to be calling you Crew now would it?' She cackled at her own play on words. Poor though it was, it stopped Ellen's tears from falling.

Owain held his new wife's arm in a gesture that was both possessive and tender. His fair curls fluttered in the breeze. His smile was loving. He looked like a guardian angel. He likes his little wife, thought Ellen. She is broad where it matters and so can provide him with a clutch of Morgans as soon as chance avails itself.

Ellen's mother appeared, small and neat in a tailored brown dress. Ellen could tell from her mother's expression, that she was content with her choice of daughter in law. Harriet curtseyed, blushed and smiled sweetly. Elizabeth greeted her with smiling affection.

Then they were amid the other relations, the ones from up the mountain.

Ellen stood back and watched as Emlyn, in one purposeful stride was beside the new bride. His right hand closed on her arm breaking the lover's embrace that had held her to Owain since they had been wed a short time before. Harriet's pinkness heightened. Holding her close, Emlyn kissed her first on one flaming cheek and then on the other. Her eyes closed, her lips trembled. Emlyn drew away looking momentarily startled. And then, surprising them all, he embraced his cousin, whispering something in his ear.

Owain went stiff and turned white, so white that the recent bruising showed clearly on his pale skin. They stood together for a moment. Elegance and beauty mingled, dark and fair, blue eyes on grey. Ellen could almost see the spark of animosity that crackled between them. She held her breath. Owain's colour returned and he offered Emlyn that cruel smile which Ellen didn't like.

'She's a perfect crab apple Owain,' said his cousin without moving his glare. 'Where will you find the time to consume?'

Then someone pushed between the two of them breaking the tension. The person grabbed Ellen as if he was going to carry her off like a pirate. He smothered her in a bear-like hug, whiskers scratching her cheek. She held on and when released, smiled up into the burnished blue eyes of Gruffydd Hiraethog.

'There's no hair like that in all the length and breath of Cymru look you,' he said. He held her at arm's length in genuine admiration. He then introduced her to the other elderly gentleman. The poor man had lost his hat and was having a problem with the wind in his hair.

When the elders had turned to the bride and groom, Emlyn came and stood beside Ellen. He smiled at her. 'Well sister, are you battling the storm?'

Ellen felt a tear run down her cheek; the first she had shed all day. She turned away and hurriedly left his side.

Soon they were all loaded up in a disorganised cavalcade of flower-strewn carts and restless horses, making their way to a feast that promised to surpass all others. Because of the number of guests invited, and uninvited, the Squire had chosen to hold the feast in the castle grounds. He had full support from the people of Rhuddlan; there where many visitors in the town who had come to attend the Knappan so they agreed that the feast could have a double purpose. The October day was still warm as had been prayed for. The evening, when serious feasting would begin, was drawing near.

In a tavern, named after the Castle but called the Bog by any who had frequented its dark, low beamed rooms, orange light pulsed and flickered over walls, tables and faces. Candles burned and melted in dribbles down the side of holders and sconces. The low voices were woven with quiet laughter and resounded under the tarred rafters. It was early yet, but the inn was filled to bursting. Many visitors sat on the banks of the river with ale jugs and drinking noisily.

Shadows elongated the towers of Rhuddlan castle, fingering the fields away from the sea. A torpor descended on the scattered, drifting groups winding their way from St. Mary's to partake in the evening meal. More and more people poured into Rhuddlan. As darkness fell with its gossamer of stars, the little town was ablaze with light. On the paved courtyard within the castle walls, servants had placed long tables spread with white cloths, chairs for the important persons, and benches for everyone else. Lit candles marched down the tables and the cloths were hung with harvest garlands. Pyramids of apples were brought followed by decorative loaves, in the shape of leaping hares and stags and sheaves of corn. Musicians arrived and climbed up to the galley; it smelled of new wood and creaked with every step taken. Nonetheless, they settled down to the groaning, demanding task of deciding upon an agreeable note to begin on, and so continue with the least possible discord.

Braziers were poked awake with new fuel added. From these, an array of silver sparks rose as if to escort the harvest moon appearing huge and laborious over the black mound of Moel Hiraethog.

Below on a bubble of suppressed excitement and with the swish of elegant gowns, the guests began to flow into the lamp-lit courtyard. They stood in small groups talking quietly greeting acquaintances as they arrived. When at last the bridal pair took their seats at the head of the centre table, the rest found allocated places and the noise rose in relaxed chatter. Steaming curls rose from heaped dishes releasing delicious aromas; wine mirrored pin-points of light as it ran and splashed into precious glass; salted brawns and gelatins encircled with bay leaves and pickled barberries, capons and fish, fat pork and goose, pastries and pies all came to the tables carried by squabbling page boys all who wanted to be cup bearers to the fairy-like couple.

The bride and groom were seated in the place of honour. Further down the table sat the Mayor. Beside him, his chancellor and on the other side, Gruffydd Hiraethog and John Talbot. These four elderly men had seen the changes under the Tudors flow through Wales since boyhood, but never once had they missed the yearly gathering at Rhuddlan for the Knappan. Sitting near by were Emlyn Tomas, Ellen Morgan, the stepdaughter with hair like Rowan berries, her mother Elizabeth and Squire Hugh. At the top, sat the beautiful couple, who everybody was talking about, when they weren't talking about the Knappan.

'That wild hog,' said Gruffydd Hiraethog pensively, 'cooked or not, is looking at me.' In front of him, without doubt, sat a wild boar's head set smugly on a bed of rosemary and spinach with roses behind its tufted ears and opaque, pigeon-egg eyes.

'It may be that you dealt it some injustice while it yet lived,' said the Mayor. He was devouring a marrow and raisin stuffed capon. He was round and red with his thin orange hair clinging to his temples and his large jaw chewing contentedly. He was English and because he was the Mayor, they spoke in English.

'Well, if it is not going to turn away,' Gruffydd replied, 'I shall leap upon it and pluck out the eye balls. The creature has no call to stare at me so. I didn't even deal it the death blow. Did you see that! It winked. I can see I shall have to have its garnished tusks as well, before it does me an injury.'

Before him, small hands appeared holding a dish of trout shivering in aspic. This was topped by a yellow tousled head and large child's eyes determined to accomplish the task set to them. The boy bit his lip in concentration. The fish's single, marbled eye shone balefully on Gruffydd. He took up a long eating knife and pocked it. 'Get back you villain,' he shouted. The jellied masterpiece wobbled on a nest of laver bread, a concoction of sea weed and oatmeal, and nearly leapt from the plate as the page boy hurriedly thumped it onto the table and fled.

'I have heard,' said Ellen Morgan, pausing for Emlyn's attention to turn from the fish, 'that in Milan they use a little silver instrument called a fork to hold down their meat while they cut it. An ingenious device is it not?'

'Would it hold back a wild boar though?' Emlyn said, 'or capture a slippery trout?'

The Mayor leaned forward licking greasy fingers, that had served the purpose of that she spoke for as long as he could remember. 'Italians are always inventing useless objects, for equally useless purpose,' he said. 'A nation of cheats cut-throats and poisoners, not worth the trouble of bothering with.'

'Really?' Ellen replied, looking aloof. 'And what of all the painters and builders? The physicians and scholars?'

'And sinners,' added John Talbot.

The Mayor wiped his hands on the table cloth. He said, 'Where you find the highest art and culture, there also you will discover most vile debauchery, the horror of that you would be hard pressed to come by anywhere in the known world.'

'It sounds worth a visit,' said Ellen.

'The highest art and culture,' added Gruffydd in a voice of protest, 'lie right here in Wales. Are you suggesting, my Lord Mayor, that here too lie the vices of which you mentioned?'

'Of course not,' the Mayor replied. Gruffydd Hiraethog was the only man he knew who could say 'my Lord Mayor' as if it was something distasteful he must rid from his mouth in disgust like spittle. The old man's Welshness was tiresome. 'Wales is a shining example of obedience to our gracious Queen,' continued the Mayor. 'There is not a blade of grass nor a knob of rock I would find fault in. The Welsh are an agreeable people in whom I find nothing to criticise.'

'That's what I thought you were thinking,' said Gruffydd smugly.

Glancing up to the place of honour, Ellen was pleased to see that Harriet had a healthy appetite, that Harriet had the manners of a starving savage and that Harriet was exceptionally found of sloe jelly. The sloes had been fermented first and were as strong as wine. Owain's eye's were already heavy from drink. He looked detached, almost forlorn. His eyes were shadowed, he was chewing at a thumb nail.

Dogs licked their lips under tables laden with steaming dishes. Chatter and laughter ran through the courtyard. Music tinkered in the background and more heaped dishes streamed in to be deposited on the over-burdened trestles. Loaves of cheese curds, tarts of honey, pippins and blackberries, wafting cinnamon, mountains of prunes and chestnuts, raisin stuffed apples and spiced honey cakes, all disappeared down glutinous throats.

Clumping through the door of the Bog, Rhys Llwyd squinted through the charcoal smoke to see who was there and who wasn't. The crowd filled every space and the ale flowed copiously. The noise had risen. Talk and laughter, snatches of song, curses, the rattle of dice and a viol player in the corner sawing at his fiddle, all combined in happy confusion. The scents of sweat, horse, unwashed bodies, spilled ale, vomit and food mingled in a stinking miasma that made Rhys' stomach heave. Elbowing and cursing his way through, he found the men he had come to meet. They were sitting, swilling ale and scoffing greasy mutton in a dark alcove that they had occupied since early evening.

'Where is he?' Rhys Llwyd asked, standing above them with his hands on his hips.

'I have no idea,' answered Madog Mathaw. He was a dark Welshman with a huge black beard streaked with grease and a fierce reputation. Most people were inclined to avoid his company. When that wasn't possible, they chose their words very carefully. 'But I would hazard a guess,' he added, 'eating at a finer table than this?'

'Our Aled Jones?' Sinon Ddu piped up. He was a small, thin man seated in the corner. 'You'll not part Aled from Jack willingly, he'll be with his brother for sure.'

'But we have his brother already, yer' daft bugger,' said Madog pounding a hairy fist on the table.

'Did he tell you anything?' Rhys Llwyd asked.

Madog smiled, the wings of his moustache lifting like a raven from a gristle feast. He said, 'Not a thing and how could he, him with not enough nounce to speak a word of sense? He cried though, fancy that, a big lad like him crying like a girl? I'd have never believed it had I not seen it with my own two eyes. No, it's Aled you'll have to get to do the talking.'

Rhys took a place beside them and stretched out his legs on the littered table. He leaned back with his hands cradling his head. 'Well if Aled doesn't turn up tonight,' he said, 'we'll not earn the promised coin and Master Owain will be in a right high temper.'

'Yer'd think him well content tonight with the Crew bitch fer company,' said Madog. He licked his lips and rolled his eyes.

'I hear he is going against his cousin Emlyn Tomas tomorrow,' said Sinon. His thick dark hair fell over his eyes. 'Whole town's talking about it. Pity, I'd like to see that. There better be enough coin to pay for me missing the Knappan.'

'If we miss it at all,' said Madog who hoped the same. 'It's too good a day to send us Willie nilly after a clutch of Catholics. If they had any sense would be here like the rest of Wales not off printing scribble. If we find Aled perhaps we can be done and be back again before the fun starts.'

'It's not us that they want hunting Catholics,' said Rhys tolerantly. 'All we have to do is find out where they are hiding. That is why we need Aled. He's had something to do with the Papists, you mark my word.'

'Well you'll have to get that out of him first,' said Sinon. 'An he'll not give that in a hurry, if I judge him right.'

'Have you looked upstairs?' Madog offered lazily. 'I hear he's attracted to the pleasures of Megan of Marion Mill.'

'You mean you haven't looked?' Rhys sighed fighting down his irritation.

'Well no,' said Sinon, 'I never thought.'

Rhys left them, fought through the drinkers and took the stairs two at a time pushing recumbent bodies aside. He tried every door that led off the upper galley, amid screams of protest. Rhys found Megan of Marion Mills behind the last door. She did not hold Aled in her scented embrace, the man she did hold growled and waved a threatening fist, shouting obscenities.

'Seen Aled?' Rhys asked.

'Be off with you peeping Twm!' Megan screeched. She threw a shoe at him.

'Well have you?' Rhys ducked to avoid the missile. It flew out the door resulting in a howl of indignation in the room below.

'Not since Thursday,' said Megan. She disappeared under folds of blanket and flesh, laughing like a banshee.

The Mayor now felt overfed and immovable as the tables were cleared of the plates and cups. Fresh wine was brought to accompany the music and dancing that was to follow. Ellen had picked at her meat, without the aid of a fork and filled herself to busting with rich cinnamon cakes. She arranged her blue velvet skirts in a comely way and settled down to wait for the spinning acrobats, the Bishop of Bangor's choir boys, the wrestlers and the musicians; none of whom had yet appeared. Speeches had been made and cups downed. Now Gruffydd Hiraethog was called to speak. He was after all, the head of the Morgan clan, no matter that continuous animosity ran between them all.

He sat like a Celt with his mead horn and waited for the chatter to cease. When it did, he stood, smoothed his white beard across his broad chest and hooked his thumbs in his wide belt with its buckle of a golden harp. 'We have heard here,' he began in the deep voice that carried throughout the grounds open to the sky, 'enough talk and well wishes to the couple we honour this night, I shall speak no more of this. I wish them good fortune, wealth and a goodly crowd of Morgans to follow in our footsteps. But of this future, which is theirs and their children's, I would speak.'

The old man stood with pride shinning in his eyes. He spoke of Wales and the soil that was as dear to him as life's blood itself. He made them feel the nobility of Wales and hunger for its freedom. With his deep sonorous voice he reminded them of their glories past; remembered through the songs of the bards and the majesty of words in Cywydd and Englyn. Historical names rose from his heart like birdsong: Pwyll, Branwen, Manawydon and Math; the dream of Macsen Wlegid and Lludd and Llafalys; the bardic verses of Taliesin, Cynddelw, Iolo Goch. He pictured for his audience dreams of past glories as he spoke the famous names into the darkness of night; of Carradoc's brave stand on Morva Rhuddlan's fatal marshes, of Llywelyn's last fight for freedom and of the struggles of Owain Glyndwr.

'I am last among the bards,' he added as he drew his speech to a close. 'And I ask you to arm yourselves, not with cruel swords and the battle cry on your lips, but with the bardic word. Make weapons of the pen and the harp and a weapon of the beloved tongue of Cymru. We are in a similar plight my dear countrymen, to the five men of the epochs of the world, who languished many ages in hell awaiting salvation. From day to day Wales, that was once great, is changing and learning. Our hope is on what is to come.'

By the time Gruffydd had ended, there was not a soul there that was not moved by the compelling gentle voice and the deep sorrow that lay beneath the poignant message. Nor was there a sound, as if the very night had commanded silence and unfolded a listening ear. A gentle wind fluttered through the inner ward, fondling the draperies, fingering the garlands, sighing the breath of night like the turning of a page. A cackle of golden, dancing leaves dispersed the silence. The spell broke, its whisper forged forever behind it.

A hound padded across the floor.

Gruffydd sat down. 'Well now,' he said to John Talbot who was sleeping like a hog on a bed of herbs. 'I'll have my fill of golden beer and we'll hear the song of 'The Poet and the Friar' I've taught Emlyn all the words that are usually left out these days. He'll raise an uproar in a minute or two.'

'What sort of an uproar?' The Mayor opened one eye, remarkably like the marbled eye of the jellied trout.

Gruffydd wiped beer from his moustache. 'Well that depends,' he said, 'on what way you have of viewing things. Are you a liberal minded man, my Lord Mayor?'

'I am, Gruffydd Morgan and a Saxon liberal mind at that!'

'Who would have thought they'd have put an Englishman as Mayor of the Welsh? Pity though,' said the bard lightly, 'for you'll not understand a word of the song. Will he lass?'

Ellen was sitting alone, straight backed and brave. With surprising dexterity, Gruffydd pushed away the chair in which Old John slept so admirably, and hooked Ellen's chair with a hand and a foot, bumping her over the flagstones until she arrived, shaken beside him. He enclosed her in the circle of an affectionate arm. With his free arm, he lifted his cup and took a long swallow. He held up the cup and in a voice that held them all, he hollered, 'I drink to the Knappan!'

So Emlyn Tomas came to play his harp in the ward of Rhuddlan castle, at the wedding of his cousin Owain.

He climbed the creaking steps to the musicians gallery and sat by a brazier with its hot light and sparks escaping like sprites in the wind. At his back was the castle wall, dashed with leaping shadows thrown from the fire sconces. The harp lay under his hands like a sleeping deer. He brought her to life in a tingling cadence that ran around the castle walls whispering in ears both Welsh and English. A boy with a drum started a slow, mournful beat. He stood behind Emlyn and receiving a wink and a foot tap, quickened the beat and maintained it when the harp let loose the power of its enchantment.

Ellen looked at Emlyn Tomas with a new eye. She watched his hands walk like many-legged spiders, spinning silver webs across the trembling strings. But these webs were woven of invisible sound. An imploring invitation to a country dance. Unable to resist, dancers filled the floor. Skirts swirled, faces laughed and feet leapt, trapped in the bewitching sounds of the harper.

Unaware how she had arrived there, Ellen found herself amidst them, on the arm of her adopted grandfather. He preceded to show her that age had done nothing to lessen his exuberant agility. 'An uproar alight,' said Gruffydd Hiraethog. 'But it's not The Poet and the Friar.' If he was disappointed, he had a peculiar way of showing it.

Aled Jones was in a crowd by Rhuddlan bridge. Lights mirrored in the river, its banks and crossing was overburdened with people. Autumn, the season of home fires and soft talk, a time to dance, happy with ale, or tussle a willing maiden. The crowd, drawn to Rhuddlan for the Knappan, were waiting for the fireworks but the fireworks had been left out in the rain the day before. 'Throw them to the fire,' some bright spark suggested, 'that'll dry them up nice.' Aled continued his search for his brother Jack who was a harmless giant of a man, who would never hurt the least creature where he could avoid it.

After they had been dismissed from the short service of Ambrose Chillingworth back in Conwy, Aled and Jack had sought a mixture of employment here and there. They had done some translating for a mercer in Shrewsbury at the wool fair, guided a herd of black cows up the road to Capel Curig and all the way back down again, they had thatched roofs in Llanberis and run errands in between jobs for Goronwy Glyn Parry and his band of pamphleteers.

'Ah there you are my lad,' grated a voice like a moving tombstone. Aled felt a heavy hand on his shoulder.

He stiffened with fear. 'Madog Mathaw,' he whispered. Clearing his throat manfully he said, 'Is this anything to do with Jack?'

'As a matter of fact,' said the villain wrapping a heavy arm around reluctant shoulders and forcing the walking pace, 'that's the very thing.'

By then they were leaving the crowd behind them, coming away from the light of a hundred touches. Aled looked back, seeking a friendly eye, but all he saw were the leaping shapes of merry makers. They were on the opposite side of the bridge now, near the Bog where a crowd with ale pots burst from the doors and littered the space outside. They passed on and Aled was forced along the cobbled alley that ran parallel to the river Clwyd. The lane was hemmed in by the fronts of fishermen's houses and the stone built store-barns that dealt with the small trade plying the river from the sea to the castle. The moon had risen high washing the stone in yellow-grey. They came to the high wall around the church of St. Mary's, where Owain and Harriet were married that afternoon. The large buildings obscured a view of the river.

Madog ducked through the gate in the wall, pushing Aled roughly ahead of him. They cut across the church grounds, passing the grey buttressed walls and on through the graveyard until they reached the wall on the other side. Here the noise of the town was just a murmur in the distance. Their breathing was heavy and loud, intruding on the melodic gurgle of the river as it churned to take the flood of the incoming tide. Madog leaped from the wall to the path below pulling Aled with him. It was a drop of twelve feet of more.

A figure detached itself from a shaft of black shadow. With his nerves already strung to snap, Aled jumped and then cursed under his breath. It was Sinon Ddu, thin as a stick with the angular joins of a grasshopper.

Aled stopped walking, squirming out of Madog's grasp. 'Has something happened?' he asked breathlessly. 'Is Jack alright?'

'Jack's in one of them boat-houses,' said Sinon.

'Well I am not about to follow you and walk into the nasty end of a bludgeon,' snapped Aled 'What is this about?'

'Don't be a fool,' snarled Madog Mathaw. 'The hut is just there, where you can see. You have nothing to fear, some of the sheriff's men are there too so we'll all be nice and cozy. Soft lad isn't he? Your brother Jack'

Mystified and afraid Aled resumed the walk towards the boat-houses that cut dark shadows against the starlit sky. Row boats clunked in the midnight water. They arrived at the door. Aled could hear voices in easy conversation within and see light filtering through the gaps where planking had rotted, a victim to the salt laden winds from the sea.

Sinon Ddu knocked, smiling, shifting foot to foot as if he were about to spring a surprise.

Madog shoved passed him, banging the door open with the heel of his hand. Aled stumbled in behind him. The first sign to meet his eyes was Jack. Jack bent and bound over a grain barrel with the stripes of a whipping stark across his naked shoulders. The big, slow head with a crown of child's curls, turned and stared back, the round face spread into a dimpled smile as innocent as an open bluebell.

Aled didn't look at anything else. 'In the name of Mercy why?' His words were directed at whoever lurked inn the shadows at the side of the shed.

'To obtain quick answers and in order to crush the papists who stir rebellion in this our peaceable countryside.' The man came forward so that Aled could see who spoke. It was Idris Hughes, a sheriff's man who used a whip when he was being lenient.

Aled took a deep breath in attempt to control his growing fear. 'What are you talking about?'

'Jack is not forthcoming,' Idris Hughes replied. He lifted his whip from where it lay on a fish cask, it was stained with blood. He leaned against the wall, the sharp planes of his features lit red in the lamplight. 'The exercise has been a wasted effort,' he said. 'Jack has no more brain than a pebble. You Aled, are a thinking man, I can see that. Therefore you don't need me to tell you what will happen next. I can assure you however that the effort will not be wasted again.'

Aled could find no voice to speak with.

'What I require,' Idris Hughes continued, 'is the printing press and any who print or circulate the slanderous offence against our gracious Queen Elizabeth. To help them in any way is treason and treason is punishable by death. Unfortunately Aled Jones, I count you among such helpers.'

'That's not true!' Aled cried. He wished Jack would stop smiling like that. Jack could have told them nothing as well they knew. Protesting innocence would not deter Idris Hughes from using violence to attain his end. If Hughes did not get what he wanted, Aled and his big brother Jack would not live to see the sun of another day. The river Clwyd that was deep enough to drop a house in and not see the chimney, would make a watery grave. If Hughes did receive the answers he was after then that too promised nothing pleasant for the future of Goronwy Glyn Parry, or Jack Tilbury, Elis Lloyd and Arthur Pennant, who were now at Pen Gogarth, unaware that their secret was out. Their capture would lead to others, including some of the nobility. Aled wished that had those wise heads to confer with, before Idris Hughes threw him and Jack into the river.

The constable uncurled his whip ominously. 'I will tell you what I know,' he said pleasantly, 'so that you have no need to go through a masquerade of denial. A ship came to Conwy in May and left the means for printing upon our shores. With that same ship came Goronwy Glyn Parry and Emlyn Tomas the Bastard. I know of these Aled and I know that you were seen with them the very same day. After that, the hidden press began to disgorge incitement to rebellion. I have since been able to discover that the concentration of activity lies near Pen Gogarth. What I want from you, in exchange for your freedom, is the exact spot and the names of the papists.'

'I don't know,' said Aled fearfully,'believe me, I don't know!'

The door rattled with a freshening of the wind, the lamp flame writhed throwing lurid shapes around the room and the handle of the whip came down on Hughes palm, sharp as a slap on water. His hooded eyes bored into the prisoner with baleful savagery.

At the castle, the minstrel had exhausted them all. Emlyn sat now with his lute, drinking thirstily from a wooden goblet of French wine; wine that had travelled the same route as he had in the spring. He passed it half full still, to the boy who sat on his haunches beside him, the drummer who had kept pace with him and the house musicians all evening. A harp, a pipe, a drum, two creaky viols and a rebec had roused the feasters to dance or to listen when a story was told. All had gone better than anyone had hoped and there was yet another session of feasting on the morrow.

The boy was known as Dai Pysgod, because his farther was a fisherman. He placed his drum between his bent knees and began to tap lightly on the goatskin. Looking up at Emlyn, he said 'Is it true you are running in the Knappan tomorrow against your cousin master Owain?'

'I am running in the Knappan,' said Emlyn. 'Who isn't? As for cousin Owain, no challenge has been issued.' Though no doubt there will be before this night is out, he thought to himself. The drum continued to tap.

Emlyn's fingers woke the lute strings. Slow and quiet at first, no more than the stir of a gulls wing on air, then the pace quickened and the sound increased. Emlyn grinned at the drummer and began to sing in the cywydd rhythm. It was the ancient mode that Gruffydd had asked them all to hold dear to their hearts. Emlyn began the song by Dafydd ap Gwilym, a bard who had lived over two hundred years ago.

> It's a pity the maiden who holds her court
> In the green bush hears no report
> Of my quarrel today on her account
> With the mouse-coloured friar, which I here recount.
> To confess my sins with pious intent,
> As everyone should, to the brother I went.
> I informed him then, as I recall,
> That I was a poet which is known to you all.
> And had doted long on a maiden fair
> Of milk-white skin and raven hair.'

Because his voice was quiet and captive, they came and stood around and listened. Among them, swayed the silver whiskered Gruffydd with his moustache hitched up in a grin and the sloe girl Ellen beside him. She was neither cross nor tearful now. Emlyn wondered what had become of the sloes. She watched Emlyn with a quizzical eye.

> 'And from my confessor no reward
> Encouragement nil, in deed or word.
> Yet I constantly loved her for years and years,
> With aching heart and bitter tears.
> Throughout all Wales I spoke her fame
> Though her chill indifference remained the same.
> So much this maiden had turned my head
> That my heart was set on sharing her bed'

Squire Hugh Morgan apologised profusely to the Bishop of St. Asaph. The Irish woman Connie O'Neill and Elisabeth had taken Harriet away, to sleep off the effects of the strong wine she had consumed in unwise quantities. The drink had caused her to fling her arms around the Bishop and make some rather lewd suggestions to the noble lord of the Church.

'Don't be concerned my dear Hugh,' said the Bishop. He smoothly dabbed at a spill of wine on his fine red gown. 'I am the very soul of discretion. We must thank God that the mishap did no occur here for all to witness. A terrible shame for a bride on her wedding night. Where by the way is the husband?'

'He's in the corner with Jenkinson and Stephen Howell of Tywysog,' said the squire. He did not add that the husband's drinking far outdid that of his new wife. But Owain could hold his drink as long as he was not roused to anger.

'The fact that he has remained,' said the Bishop in hushed tones, 'while his wife has retired, is bound to raise some question. Would it be presumptuous of me to suggest, with the poor girl being taken ill so suddenly, that he join her?'

'He will presently my Lord Bishop,' Hugh answered. He had already spoken to Owain and ordered him to leave or risk ridicule and laughter, which was sure to come sooner or later. Harriet's behaviour had not passed entirely unnoticed. No matter how loyal a servant claimed to be, a little spicy gossip was always welcome.

Laughter erupted from around Emlyn as he drew his song to a close. Owain was gratified to see that Squire Hugh had drawn the Bishop's attention away. Now Owain could make his challenge to Emlyn Tomas for the play to take place tomorrow.

The town players had now taken over. They were setting up their stage, a two storied affair on wheels. The clerk's voice rose blaring out instructions for the order of the play, a moral lesson on the seven deadly sins.

Emlyn crossed the floor and walked straight up to his cousin.

Hugh moved closer to his son so that he could hear what passed between them and prevent either form making further mockery of the wedding feast. Just before the mishap with Harriet and the Bishop, a servant had come to the Squire and told him that Idris Hughes awaited his pleasure. Well he could wait. Hugh hoped that Owain had the sense to keep his mouth shut about the hunt for the Catholic rebels. The whole thing had become a very sticky situation as far as Hugh was concerned.

Stephen Howell left his perch on a convenient barrel and stood beside Owain.

The two cousins stood eyeing each other. 'I offer you my condolences on this your wedding night,' said Emlyn spitefully. 'You hear how quiet it has got? You must be mortified.' He had already heard about Harriet and the Bishop.

Owain leaned gracefully against the wall. His arms were folded and his heavy eyes patient, as if he was dealing with a child. 'It is just as well,' he replied. 'A man needs his rest to play the Knappan. You and I will have sporting opportunity to settle our differences before you go back to serve the monks. You are, I presume treacherously running for Merioneth?'

Stephen Howell shifted uncomfortably. He too would run opposite Owain, owing to where his family lands lay.

'I am,' said Emlyn. 'So are the other four-hundred and twenty-two. It will be interesting. How are we ever going to find each other?'

'I hear the Glyn Parrys are after your blood as well,' said Owain. 'Such terrible accidents are known to happen to culpable conspirators. *Esto castus, en fraudes agnus lupo previo'*

Emlyn looked at him with surprise. He knew that Owain had spent a few years at the university of Cambridge. But Emlyn had got the impression that Owain had left without learning much. To hear him quote Latin now, was the last thing he had expected. He thought about the words and recognised the warning implied. *Beware lamb that you do not come prey to the wolf*

'Well what have you learnt?' Squire Hugh demanded irritably.

Standing in the shadows of the castle wall, away from light and company, Captain Idris Hughes smiled grimly. 'Nothing,' he replied, 'that is, nothing that can prompt us to swift action.'

Hugh swung away with a curse on his lips. 'Then we will take men and overturn every stone and tuft on Pen Gogarth until we do discover something. There can't be that many places to hide a party of papists and their press.'

'They would have it away before we had a chance to act. There are many sir, who would offer to help them, especially now that the Scots Queen stands on English soil. The very air whispers with rebellion.'

'So where does that leave us?' asked the Squire in a commanding tone.

'With no choice but to question your nephew, Emlyn Tomas. He must know what is going on. It is by command of the Justice of Chester and North Wales that we bring these traitors to justice.'

Squire Morgan heard the warning underlying the words. If he wished to keep his name out of the scandal, he must tread with care. 'It is a matter of exceptional delicacy as you know Idris. There would be no advantage in blundering about. Many influential families are still faithful to the old religion and do much for their cause, including financing. It is not our place to bring their battlements down around their shoulders. I don't want my nephew connected with this.'

'So we need to arrest the printers on Pen Gogarth,' said the captain agreeably. 'As we have been able to discover so little. We can only hope to persuade your nephew will lead us there.'

'What of the brothers Aled and Jack? Could you get nothing from them?'

'I hold them still. Aled would have spoken if he could. He nearly foiled us with lies, but he has no idea as to the exact location. Of that I am convinced. We have to find that out from Emlyn Tomas, a Jesuit no less. If your Emlyn wants to remain unconnected and free from imprisonment, he would be well advised to offer all the assistance we require.'

'Then don't approach him about it here,' the Squire replied. 'Owain is wed this day and I will not have Elisabeth upset by the commotion. There are too many here who would rise objection, including my father. If he hears word of this, then he will have Wales up in arms.'

'When then? The Knappan?'

'Yes, that would certainly bring you the privacy you need. Can you take Emlyn on the field and go straight to Pen Gogarth?'

Idris Hughes smiled and unfolded his arms. 'I can,' he answered, 'but will he tell us where to go?'

'I don't want to hear anything about it,' said Hugh distastefully. 'If you link my name with this Idris, you will get nothing but trouble form me.'

Chapter 22 The Knappan

Emlyn stood in a field sticky with mud on the castle side of the river Clwyd. The mist lingered still in hollows, wraith-like as it rose off water-meadows and threaded through the river reeds. The sun rose warmer, blazing the river in a mirror of light so that it was like a silver serpent, coiling the fifteen miles up the valley from Rhuddlan castle to Ruthin castle. From here, the coast was a wetland of salt marshes and sand dunes all the way to Flint castle, situated on the sandy estuary of the Dee. This was the 'field' where the Knappan would be run.

Eight hundred near-naked men stood on Rhuddlan Plain. Drawn from the shires of Merioneth and Flint they were gathered now to capture the Knappan; to run, to kick, to throw, to fight, to cheat and to confuse in all that was foul or fair, to reach their objective. Stripped to tight-fitting hose and armed with nothing but fist and cunning, the men drew up and prepared to do battle. On this plain, eight centuries before, Carradoc King of North Wales had stood to war with Offa King of Mercia. But there was no armour here, no painted Celts with fierce weapons and the cry of slaughter screaming from their wild ranks. Here, with their head cloths of green and red, were fishmongers, bakers and butchers, smiths and gaunters, fletchers, fullers, tanners, mercers, carpenters and potters, clergymen, gentlemen, landlord and farmer. All came in good spirit to chase the Knappan until nightfall when inevitable darkness concluded the game.

The voices that roared in insult were equal to those of their ancestors. Taunts and threats raged across the field; challenges tore from mouth to mouth. All arguments and grudges nurtured through the year since the last Knappan would reach conclusion here. For the duration of the game, the law would sit and look the other way, no matter what happened.

The Knappan was a ball roughly oval in shape and the size of a man's head. It was made of yew wood and soaked in tallow so that the surface was slippery. What little law there was to the game was arranged before hand, so that every man would know, according to his ability, where he was of most value. Out runners kept up with the Knappan's journey as best they could.

Outside the castle walls, benches had been put up for the nobility of North Wales. Above them, their heraldic devices were displayed on flag and pennant; the designs were repeated on the padded cushions on which they sat and in their attire. There were lions, dragons, griffins and eagles and a bewildering selection of other ornaments, depicting the family arms and crests of the nobles. Beneath this rich tapestry were seated the lesser families, the churchmen and the mercers, who were near as richly dressed as their betters. Among the top ranks, Ellen Morgan sat with her mother Elisabeth and her new sister-in-law, Harriet, who looked rather pale. Next to her, was the Squire, dressed in new tawny velvet and behind him stood three pages wearing tabbards depicting the Morgan wyvern on a half shield and the thorn entwined swan of his wife's Boutflower family on the other half. Saddled horses waited in the background for any gentlemen who wished to follow the game. A trumpet blared and a voice like thunder called all to order. An expectant hush settled.

From where he stood, knee deep in bog grass, Emlyn could see Geraint and his brother Gareth. He was certain that the rest of the Glyn Parry's would be there somewhere. Except for one, Emlyn knew that Goronwy wouldn't come. There were stocks of rebellious leaflets stored in the cave and Goronwy had mentioned the advantages offered by the Knappan; with the villages emptied, distribution could cover a wider area without fear of hindrance. He had probably loaded up a mule or two and taken off with the zeal of a crusader. Emlyn smiled to himself, one less Glyn Parry to contend with.

Owain had positioned himself near the centre. His eyes had already found Emlyn's position and marked it. Owain's arms were folded across his naked chest; clothing being a hazard in the game. He was not well built but thin and wiry as a Gypsy dog with long legs capable of running as fast. In the past, Emlyn had been unable to beat him in a race, after four years of near inactivity in Paris, Emlyn guessed that Owain could outrun him still.

Emlyn shifted uneasily. The hand signals came and he acknowledged them. There was a hushed silence everywhere. Then the clerk, fully dressed in a neutral colour, rose to his full height and cried 'Y Ddraig Goch ddyry gychwyn! The Red Dragon shall lead!'

He threw the Knappan.

As law declared, the Knappan flew straight up into the air while beneath, waited the two biggest men from either side. For Merioneth, Dai Patch the blacksmith, who had lost an eye while shoeing a stallion and was all the meaner for it; and for Flint, Twm Teg of Dyserth, a stone mason as wide as a row boat. The twin thick necks swivelled upwards. A sea of faces watched the Knappan soar and spin in the air. It slowed a moment, and then began to fall.

More hand signals, Emlyn just grasped the meaning. He stayed where he was his heart thumping with a mixture of joy and fear.

The Knappan dropped. Thirty men piled on top of it, a mass of heaving bodies, thrashing arms and legs and curses fit to split the heavens. One broke away hunched over, running straight toward the coast. Another followed him and then another fled towards the castle. A further four detached themselves and made for the river. Confusion ensued; deception from the start. Who held the Knappan? In the centre the crowd broke, taking after their various decoys. From amid them a single figure raised, head burnished in the sun. Owain Morgan held the Knappan. He ran like a stag, his long athletic limbs carrying him up the rise toward the village and the sea road. Beside him ran his out-guards, pushing, shoving and bowling over any who sought the capture the ball. In front of him and to all sides ranked the opposition.

Watching with grudging admiration, Emlyn knew that Owain was doomed unless he threw to friendly hands across the river; but before he had the chance, sheer numbers defeated him. The agile runner disappeared under a writhing mass of Merioneth men. The Knappan flew out and was caught and passed from one to another. Whistles pierced the air. Merioneth had the Knappan. It travelled in the capable hands of the tanner from Llanrwst, orange haired Jasper Overbury who had thrown Emlyn into a manure pile when he had kissed Blodeuedd. Hands flayed the air. Emlyn began to run judging where the Knappan would come if Jasper threw it. They were fortunate; Emlyn had the field to himself. The field of Dyffren Clwyd was flat and offered a clear causeway. If he caught the Knappan he could hope for a good run in the right direction.

Jasper was running like a trenchant bull, ploughing through the opposition, casting them aside as if they were nothing but dross. Voices roared. Bare feet trampled the earth. The tanner ducked, swerved and tripped the man who had blocked him. He drew closer, his mouth wide to draw great gasps of air. Emlyn tensed.

Jasper slowed and the crowd behind gained ground. 'Are you right you Welsh bastard!' Jasper shouted.

'Gentle in barding and fearful in war!' Emlyn called running backwards. 'Loyalty and God's speed, just name the meeting place.' The distance between them seemed too far to be reached in one throw. But Jasper threw the Knappan, summoning the best of his strength.

It came at Emlyn with the speed and animosity of a cannon ball. He raced to reach the point of descent. Down it came hurling from the sky like a dead duck. Emlyn got a hand to it but the greasy dead weight of the heavy wooden ball slipped through his fingers. He stumbled, picked it up with numb fingers and ran. It slithered in his grasp as slippery as a fat fish. He wrapped two hands around it and charged away with a thousand feet thundering after him like the hounds of Gronw Bebyr. Borne on wings of exhilaration, feet black with mud, heart thudding with excitement, Emlyn Tomas took flight and sped down the valley road, fighting to turn laughter into much needed breath.

'Well that's that,' said Ellen rising with purpose. 'We're going to the fair aren't we Connie?'

'Are we?' Connie O'Neill offered a grimace of disappointment.

'I'm not going to sit here with an empty field for view,' Ellen insisted.

'Nor are you going off into that hive of sin without an escort my dear,' said Elisabeth sternly. 'You can take Thomas Mostyn with you and be nice to him. Perhaps Harriet would like to go?'

Harriet's white face lit with a smile. She had been quiet for most of the day. Ellen almost regretted the effect of the sloe wine on the new bride, poor thing! Still, further mischief could be better practised with Harriet along for company than without. 'Of course she can come,' said Ellen sweetly.

Most of the men had mounted up and were departing to follow the Knappan. They rode off with their feathered hats bouncing, their satins shimmering and their voices rose in excitement. With a long face, Thomas Mostyn left them and walked back to take up his duty as ward for the young ladies. He was followed by a large hound with soft eyes and a furious tail. Thomas had already suffered under the whipping tongue of his mother that morning, after he had voiced his wish to join the Knappan. It was his duty to look after the young ladies was a further disappointment to him. He was the son of Sir Edward Mostyn, ward of Flint castle and the surrounding estates. As his heir, Master Thomas was considered to be the best match that any mother could wish for her daughter—although there was a rumour that the Mostyn family were active Catholic sympathizers. Thomas was twenty-two, presentable and immaculate in dress. Of dark hair and eyes, he cut a gentlemanly figure and strutted about with the importance of a royal herald. His Latin was faultless, but was mostly lost on those he practised it on.

Straightening his grey hat, so that the red grouse feather fell becomingly; he set off in the direction of the fair, with the three women and the dog in tow. Anyone who was anyone took off after the Knappan with hoots of joy and howls of delight and comments which Thomas chose to ignore.

Elisabeth Morgan was left with a few maids, an old priest who was asleep and the irascible, snowy haired Gruffydd Hiraethog. She eyed him and prepared to do battle. 'The boy runs well,' she said with no pretence of hiding the subject she wished to discuss.

Gruffydd Hiraethog viewed her from one blue eye. 'Owain is a golden youth, swift as the waves, as fleet as the fair swan and as dear as the daffodil. A Philomel with the love of a maid aflower is our Gwri Golden-hair.'

'Do not mince words with me!' Elisabeth snapped. Her hands were clasped on her lap.

Two eyes turned their innocence upon her. 'Mince words…I?'

'You know it is not Owain I speak of, his affairs are settled and his future sorted.'

'Ah,' breathed the bard, 'that life was so simple.'

'Emlyn Tomas,' she said, 'between you and Hugh that boy has been used and misguided. It would have been well that you left him where he was, doing the good Lord's work. I blame you Gruffydd Hiraethog for all the upset between him and his cousin. If you had had the sense to leave your lands to Hugh, as should be, then we could all be back to our ordered lives. As it is, we'll be well blessed this day if they both came from the Knappan intact.'

'Sweet Elisabeth,' said Gruffydd. He crossed his legs running a long hand down a silken leg, smoothing out the wrinkles. 'As much as you would like life to run, as ordered as a violet obeying Spring; the human element denies it all and flowers out of season.'

'What are you talking about?' she snapped.

'That is exactly what I was about to ask you my dear.'

'Then you'll not know that Owain has challenged Emlyn this day? And the Glyn-Parry's are out to get his blood as well, because they can't get the Squire's.'

'What do they want Hugh's blood for?'

'Encroachment on their land, all lies of course.'

'I see,' said Gruffydd pensively. The line of his mouth revealed his distaste for this item of news. 'Well Emlyn's got nothing to do with that, so they have no call to be after him.'

'They have some quarrel they are vowed to settle,' said Elisabeth. 'It started when Emlyn was here last.'

'I thought he fought with Owain that time, in good family custom?'

Elisabeth looked across the field, where the thin clerks and the fat shop keepers were drifting back to the village, their energy spent. She had nursed Owain on that occasion, bathed his bruises and cuts while Owain had sat wincing and cursing his cousin to doom and back. What had he said? I hope the sheriff preserves his life when he catches the Catholics, for Emlyn Tomas is mine to crush! Elisabeth didn't know anything about that and had refused to consider the implications, until now. Was something planned?

Gruffydd tapped his foot to the tune of a creaky viol that floated over from the fair. He said, 'As for Owain, this is nothing new, they can't stand each other. That's common knowledge and where better to sort differences than at the Knappan?'

'Aye, if we have two live boys at the end of it all,' said Elisabeth. 'The future of Emlyn must be decided upon. Hugh wishes him to return to France and to stay there for his own health as well as Owain's.'

'And when he becomes priest,' said Gruffydd, 'he will no longer have need to return. Is that what you would like Elisabeth?'

'That is how it should be, the boy can settle down and be about his business.'

'And this old bard can find his peaceful end and leave his goods and chattels to his good son Hugh, or failing that, to the fair Owain?'

Elisabeth flushed and looked away from the calm gaze.

'That,' said Gruffydd 'would solve all dispute and make the noble squire into a rich man and his son after him. Then your daughter Ellen, will a bride worth her weight in silver. Emlyn can be a good Jesuit and spend his life battling heresy. You are right sweet daughter-in-law, it would serve all well. Soon you will have your prayer answered for Emlyn returns to Paris in the Spring. Did you know Elisabeth, that a bastard is barred from taking holy orders?'

She knew all about that, Hugh had told her and about the return letter he had written to Father Manare to insure that the boy found a place with the priests. Not knowing whether Gruffydd was aware of this, she said, 'So? He can be a monk or something.'

'A monk?' Gruffydd replied thoughtfully. He smiled and then began to laugh.

Elisabeth took a deep breath and fixed him in her shrewd gaze. 'If that is the case, I want you to change your will and be done with all this nonsense,' she said with authority.

'Why?' Gruffydd said. 'No, don't answer, I'll answer for you. Harriet Crew, so recently wed to our Owain, has a brother, at present in Europe. Should this prodigal return, then any claim which Owain has, for the wealth of the Crews will be lost to him and fall to the rightful son. Then Owain would be left with his reputation and purse in tatters. You dear

Elisabeth, knew of that risk when you and Hugh made the match. Owain then being landless, would return to the loving embrace of his father, who was more fortunate in his choice of wife. Or was he I wonder?'

'What are you saying?' Elisabeth demanded, as flushed as a hen comb.

'That the Squire is squire in name only? That your resourceful first husband, John Boutflower insured the future of his only child by placing Plas Newydd in her name. Does it belong in truth, not to you or Hugh but to Ellen and her future husband?'

There was no point in denying it. Elisabeth sniffed and played with the keys at her waist. Beside her the old man laughed like a hooting owl. When she was again in control of herself, Elisabeth said, 'If that were true, would you then change your will and give Hugh his rightful inheritance?'

Gruffydd stopped laughing. 'No,' he replied, 'not for you, not for Hugh and not for the golden boy Owain. I will stick by my law and my will unless Emlyn himself decides different.'

'What of the law of England? Do you refute that too?'

'Never consider it,' said Gruffydd, 'I live in Wales.'

She had to be satisfied with that, for Gruffydd called to his servant and stood up to take his leave. 'Perhaps we could discuss this some other time,' he said with a bow, his eyes twinkling with amusement. 'I am off to the chase. I would welcome you to join me dear daughter-in-law, but there seems to be a shortage of horses. I will look out for the quarrelsome youths, both the bright sun and the dark moon.'

Elisabeth stood up stiffly and eyed him with contempt. Her mouth was set and determined. She hoped the silly old goat would fall off his horse and break his neck. She hoped whatever Owain had planned for the Catholics would happen, so and they could be done with Emlyn Tomas and his overbearing grandfather.

Geraint caught Emlyn Tomas at the top of a rise. Emlyn had seen it coming. He was terrified of Geraint. By then he had run further and faster than ever before. His legs burned in protest, his lungs laboured for air and his feet were cut by bracken and stone. Still holding the Knappan, he had been driven away from the river where the soft black mud had hindered his progress. A group of mean looking Flintshire men had been strung across his path; Geraint was in front crying insults and threats. To avoid them, Emlyn had swung left and toiled upwards. They all followed like hunters after the stag. Through gorse and heather, bramble and shrub, Emlyn had evaded Geraint and the others. He had dodged, raced, changed direction and avoided them with the skill and speed of a hare. They had kept away any members of his own team who tried to reach him. Tempers were high, and fights frequently broke out. Emlyn was near the end of his strength. The ragged chase had taken them up towards a Moel, a headland that overlooked the wetlands like a sentinel.

Now Emlyn could feel the feet pounding behind his. Geraint had closed the distance between them. Straining with every muscle Emlyn fought fatigue to gain the top of the rise. From there he knew that he would see one of his own team, four-hundred men could not just disappear.

Geraint leapt.

Emlyn felt the powerful arms close around his middle. He staggered, recovered and then fell. They both rolled over the rise and down the other side. Emlyn felt the world turn upside-down, the sky reeled. The earth hit with such force that the Knappan slipped out of his grasp and bounded off down the slope. Nettles and brambles twisted, gripped and stung; loose stone and rock battered, bruised and flayed as they both tumbled the steep drop.

At the bottom Emlyn lay very still until he assessed that nothing was broken. He had made a heroic run. Had any of his team been near enough to take the Knappan, it would be well on its way to Ruthin by now. In spite of that, he felt exhilarated. Then he remembered Geraint. He was too late to avoid being hit altogether. He swung away as Geraint's foot hammered into his ribs driving out the little breath he had left.

'Where's the Knappan?' Geraint growled breathlessly.

Bedaubed with thistle fluff and bog mire, Emlyn lay in the grass. His body racked with sobs as he drew in lungfulls of air. His back and arms were crossed with scratches, scrapes and nettle bites as were Geraint's. He turned his head to the sun and shut his eyes. His lips set in a sarcastic smile. 'You're a big lad Geraint,' he said 'for taking on one as incapable as I. If you intend to beat me to a pulp I hope it will be quick for we have a Knappan to run and only four hours of daylight left to do it in. And where are the other Glyn Parry'su?'

Geraint was searching frantically in the bushes. 'Where's the bloody Knappan? Did you have it at all?'

'No,' said Emlyn.

'When they get here they are going to rip you to shreds! God curse you Emlyn Tomas! Where is it?'

Emlyn stood, his breath easing. He said, 'I had it when we crashed down the slope there.'

When Geraint did eventually find the Knappan, Emlyn had wisely disappeared. Geraint climbed the rise. He whistled and cast the Knappan to willing hands. He had not strength to run with it.

The cry of a hawk drew his eyes up towards the Moel. There, his sharp eyes found Emlyn Tomas. He was running again with twelve or more fully dressed men in pursuit. As he no longer carried the Knappan, Geraint thought this strange, unless he thought to deceive. But Geraint had seen the weakened state that the long run had left Emlyn in. Only a madman would take off again after that. Curious, Geraint turned and began to follow at a lumbering run.

Flags fluttered and voices called. Wherever there was a Knappan held, there came the traders, brewers, the bakers and the acrobats. The ladies and their sullen escort stopped Twm the peddler. He was strung with his ribbons and bows, scissors, thread, needles and all manner of baubles. Ellen bought six wooden buttons. Harriet was cajoled into buying the same. There were stalls, booths and pavilions. Outside one, a blackman in a turban boasted that he had a concealed beast that boasted two heads and the tail of a cockerel. There were ballad sellers, jugglers and Gypsies, as bright as meadow flowers; with snapping black eyes and olive skin that reminded Ellen of Emlyn Tomas. There were sliced meats, pastries and pies and apples on sticks, cakes, sausages and sweetmeats with plenty of cordials and beer to wash them down. Connie and Thomas Mostyn were gradually loaded with miscellaneous bits and pieces until they were forced to stop and rearrange it all. Ahead of them Harriet and Ellen chattered amiably without a pause.

They stopped at an enclosed area where they could hear curious growls and scuffling. After a thorough investigation, Ellen squealed in excitement. 'A bear! A dear old bear. We really must stay and watch him fight the dogs. We haven't had a bear baiting since the wool fair in Shrewsbury. The Gypsies must have brought him.'

'That's no place fer a woman of breeding, it's shaming me yer are,' said Connie haughtily.

'I too wish to see the bear,' said Harriet. 'Don't you know that the Queen watches bear baiting. It's her favourite pass time.'

'And you, having been there just lately,' said Connie, 'would be all for knowing what the Queen of England likes and likes not?'

Harriet turned pink.

They all stayed to watch the bear. Thomas Mostyn held on to his hound while it whined and struggled. The bear had no teeth. It looked such a pathetic creature that Thomas felt his mastiff could easily bring it down. The dog seemed of the same opinion. He fought the leash and became frantic, leaping and barking at the strong scent of bear.

People gathered around, talked among themselves, inspected the dogs and placed their bets. A willing audience drifted towards the wicker enclosure as the hounds set up a barking and howling. Hearing them, the bear lifted her head and sniffed the air. The corner of her mouth lifted in a snarl.

Harriet squealed, her eyes aglitter with anticipation. 'I do hope Thomas' dog wins,' she said. 'Shall we place a wager sister?'

Ellen looked at her. 'Has he fought a bear before?' She addressed this to Thomas.

Making a fuss over the well loved hound, Thomas took a moment to answer. 'He will pit his strength against the ungainly beast gladly mistress Ellen, and come to no harm. The bear is old and helpless.'

Ellen folded her arms and watched dog and master and then shifted her gaze to the bear. The great shaggy head swung from side to side. Ellen saw that her eyes were white and sightless. She was tied to a wooden stake, as tall as herself. Her long brown coat was matted and filthy, bald in places and spotted with festering sores. 'She has very convincing claws,' Ellen said, which was about all the poor creature did have to be proud of.

When a suitable crowd had gathered, the dogs were released into the enclosure by the bear owner. He held a whip in his hand. He was a dark hairy man, with a long scar running from eyebrow to chin. Ellen thought he looked strangely like his bear. The scarred face hinted at earlier misfortune with such animals. The creature rose up on her hind legs. She was tied at neck and ankle; her chains ratted a she moaned plaintively. A clawed paw batted at the air in front of blind eyes as if to clear her sight.

At a word from the master, the dogs attacked.

The first blow ripped at the leaping mastiff. It was Thomas Mostyn's. The bear tore open the hound's stomach. The dog dropped, spilling blood and guts as the bear moved in to maul it, sensing its presence by smell alone. The other dogs, seven in number, circled around snapping and barking. The bear's master used his whip to drive the bear off the dog. Thomas' hound lay bleeding into the dirt and panting out his last breath.

Ellen pressed her fist to her mouth in horror. Thomas stood pale with disbelief. Harriet bemoaned her lost bet.

'Faith,' cried Connie O'Neill, 'there now, enough of this slaughter and bloodshed. The lady Elisabeth will be for making chittlins of me own innards if I let you watch another minute. Come away now girls. Master Thomas, 'tis terrible sorry I am to see the poor beastie brought to such ruin, but I'm not for staying and seeing the rest of them go the same way. It's not fitting. Can I offer you a thread of advice?'

Master Thomas turned to face her. His face was bereft of colour and his eyes, wide in anguish. 'Dead,' he uttered.

'As dead as a stone,' said Connie, 'and there's none to blame but yourself. The good lady Elisabeth has put these two girls in your care. I'd not like to be in your becoming hose when she finds out about this shenanigan.'

In a tragic daze, Thomas Mostyn loosed his purse and paid out where his dog had failed him. Tight lipped, he took an elbow of each maiden and marched them off with the Irish woman toddling after them with all the bundles and bits.

In the centre of the village green there was a play being performed by the same actors who had entertained the night before. On this occasion they played out, The Deluge, the story of Noah and the Ark buckets of water were thrown about and the players were dressed up as animals.

Ellen and Harriet clapped their hands. The bear was forgotten. Thomas Mostyn stood glum and sorrowful beside them. Noah's creatures spun and leaped, cocking furry ears, whisking tufted tails, roaring and clucking, mewing and squeaking.

'Do you know Harriet,' said Ellen clasping her new sister's elbow, 'that Noah forgot to take the unicorn on the ark? That of course is why they are not to be found anywhere.'

'All the saints! There's a good deal more than that the good man forgot to take,' said Connie O'Neill. 'And I think he was a wise man to do so. On the isle of Tir na Nog, you'll yet find all manner of foul beings. It was a great aunt of mine that travelled there never to return. I was but a…'

'Mistress Ellen!'

This voice called from across the green. Ellen turned, her dark brow lifted in curiosity. It was Aled Jones, she remembered him for early school days. He was the bully that had called her a changeling. He ran up to the ladies, his face pale, his breath ragged and his hair wet with perspiration. His clothing was torn and dirty as if he had been through the mill wheel. Behind him lumbered a large boy who would be better suited to the Knappan field, where all the rest of his kind were.

'Mistress,' said Aled breathlessly. 'Is the Knappan begun?'

'Are you tup?' Ellen replied.

Aled looked very upset. He said, 'Is master Owain there?'

'Yes,' said Harriet and Ellen in unison, their voices edged with alarm.

Aled breathed a sigh of relief. 'And Emlyn Tomas?…Where?'

Connie answered, 'Running down the river bank last we saw of him with nothing between him and his goal but fifteen miles of bog. Why?'

'I have to find him. Are there any horses left?'

'Well there's one of those Green Men over there on a donkey. Yer could ask him, if yer find his face among all those leaves and twigs and things,' offered Connie O'Neill. 'I dare say he'd be willing enough to lend yer that four legged creature. As for the rest, they'll be half way to nowhere by now, following the Knappan..'

'What has happened?' Ellen asked sensibly.

Aled took a deep breath and wiped his nose with the back of his hand. 'Madog Mathaw is after him with all his men. If they catch him they'll skin him alive.'

'Owain, Jesus mercy!' Ellen cried.

'Owain!' Harriet cried beside her.

'God bless us and save us!' Connie O'Neill exclaimed.

'No, rather Emlyn Tomas,.' said Thomas Mostyn surprising them all. 'Aled I think you had better tell us all that happened.'

Aled looked at him nervously. 'My brother Jack here, was taken last night,' he said licking a cut lip. 'And me soon after, by the sheriff's man, Idris Hughes. We were held in yonder fish barn, but have just now managed to escape. Master Thomas, they are going after them all.'

'Who is going after who?' Ellen demanded.

Thomas ignored her and turned to Connie. 'Can you take them back without me?'

'I'll not move a step until you tell me what's amiss,' Connie said. She placed her bundles on the ground, determined not to budge.

'Nor I,' said Ellen and stamped her foot, 'and nor is Harriet are you sister?' Harriet moved closer to her and wordlessly shook her head.

Thomas Mostyn drew Aled to one side. 'What have you told them about us?' The contempt he felt was evident in the words.

Aled said, 'Nothing. How could I?'

'And they let you live?'

Aled glared at him. 'They may not have, had we not escaped. Are we to stand here yapping about it?'

Thomas Mostyn looked around biting his lip, as if the answer lay waiting for him to grasp. After some thought he said, 'I must find my father and the others with him. They must be warned and given time to cover themselves.'

'And Emlyn?' Aled added caustically

'While they are after him, we are safe and he will not tell them where go. Perhaps we can reach Pen Gogarth first. We would be better doing that Aled. If you and Jack are to escape further capture. No harm will come to Emlyn. He's the Squire's nephew.'

'Who do you think planned all this from the start?' Aled replied in a fierce whisper. 'Squire Hugh, if I know the man. Jack and I can look for Emlyn on the field, I'm willing to risk that, but I doubt that we can reach him in time.'

But there was no time now to think and talk. The Mostyns were catholic and did what they could to preserve their belief as many landowners like them. Thomas had to warn them of the impending danger. He took hold of the girls again, and remained dumb to the constant questions as he marched them up the hill towards the castle. 'You must go home with Connie and the Plas Newydd servants,' he said as they neared their destination. 'Don't do anything or say anything. Is that too much to expect?'

It was too much to expect of Ellen. 'Of course dear Thomas whatever you say,' she replied sweetly.

Madog Mathaw shaded his eyes and peered down the mountain. 'Diawl!' he spat. 'There's the devil, cavorting and gamboling like a March hare. Curse his bones!'

'He'll get away,' said Sinon Ddu lazily. He lay on the grass looking at the clouds scudding like sea foam across the sky. The day was getting cold, and a strong wind swept over the high ground, snatching at hair and clothing. A group of the sheriff's men approached and Siôn rose with reluctance

Emlyn Tomas—the hare— had stretched them all out on a line up the long ridge, forcing them into a dangerous chase among the rocks and ravines of the Moel. They could still see him. Madog grunted and straightened. 'No he bloody well won't.'

After a final, ludicrous leap, that took Emlyn from the peak of a huge rock into the under growth below, he plunged into the thick woodland that cradled the Moel like a laurel wreath and disappeared from sight.

'I'll not take after him any more,' said a voice behind them. Geraint Glyn-Parry had joined them at the bottom of the hill. He was as keen to get his hands on Emlyn as any of them, but for his own personal reasons.

'Nor will we,' said Madog. 'We're going to saunter down this nice bit of hill here and watch him bump into his cousin, nice and friendly like.'

'Is that what this is all about?' Geraint demanded. 'You're to drive him into the net of Owain Morgan?'

Madog was surprised at the anger in his voice'. In a manner of speaking,' said Madog. 'All's fair in love and war and the Knappan.' He produced a leather flask from the folds of his greasy clothing and pulled the cork out with his teeth, spiting over the ridge.

Sinon said, 'He's going to roast him with those other papists on Pen Gogarth, isn't Mr. Mathaw?'

Madog kicked him. But by then it was too late. Geraint was away down the mountain. With a determined, long-legged step, he disappeared in seconds.

'Yer dumb, blundering dung heap! He's got a brother with them!' Madog cried. Swinging around, he let Sinon Ddu feel the full battery of his fist.

The forest closed in cool about him. The wind snatched through the branches and the crackle of leaves and twigs snapped underfoot. Shafts of sun pierced the forest, striping the path where he trod. The heavy smell of rot and toadstool filled the air and seemed to rob him of breath. He was not running, but shuffling, his gait dreamlike, his feet immune to thorn or stone. No steps came behind him; they had given up.

Emlyn had realised they were after him when he had held his hands up and had shown them that the Knappan was gone. They had still kept coming, carrying no colour to identify them. It was obvious, their intent had nothing to do with the game. Once or twice they had come near to catching him. Emlyn had thrown caution to the winds, leaping down a scree slope, bouncing, jumping and slithering, carried on a solid tide of stone tumbling to the bottom. He had lost of three of them there; Hwe Bryn, first time out of an ale jug for a month, the baker from Bodrhuddlan Willie Bara, too fat to run any further and Wyn Pryce who leaped in fright at the chirrup of a grasshopper. Emlyn had even begun to enjoy the chase then, but then the implication began to sink in.

Owain was not among them. Owain would not give the pleasure of catching his cousin to anyone else; theirs was a personal quarrel. Emlyn could not believe that Owain would hire Mad Mathaw and his hounds, they were of a nature alien to Owain, he would not think to speak with the like of them, so these hounds were hired by some one else.

Owain had said, *Beware lamb that you do not come prey to the wolf.*

There had been times as they had grown up together when they had tolerated each other. Owain had offered him a warning that Emlyn had failed to understand. 'Am I then,' whispered Emlyn to the trees, 'the Lamb or the wolf?' If he was the Lamb, that seemed highly likely in his present predicament, then why had Owain warned him? Emlyn was too tired to think beyond the comfort of a tree bole, where he could curl up and disappear like a mole. He stopped running before his legs failed him entirely.

From the woods behind him came the snap of a twig and the soft pad of bare feet rustling the leaves.

Emlyn did want to escape, the need was prominent in his mind; to fight, to run, scuffle, grapple and defy. But further escape was beyond his physical capability. He turned to face his adversary.

There was one set of footsteps approaching, solid and tired. Geraint came around a bend in the path and stumbled to a stop. His breath was torn from over used lungs, his skin flushed with effort and his hair plastered damp across his forehead.

With no hope of succour from the shambling figure, Emlyn turned and willed his floundering legs to walk, to crawl to do anything to free him from the grasp of Geraint Glyn Parry.

'Wait!' Geraint croaked, and then louder, 'Wait Emlyn you are walking into a trap!'

Emlyn sat down where he was. Enmeshed in leaves and fungi, he dropped his head on to his arms and waited.

Geraint walked up to him. 'I was a fool,' he said. 'I'll not harm you. But you are being driven towards your cousin. There are horses at the base of the hill. Once they have you, they are going after the others, the printers with Goronwy.'

'How many?' Emlyn asked, without lifting his head.

'Eight. There are sheriff's men among them,' said Geraint. He dropped on the path beside him.

Clouds blotted out the sun like the cloak of night. Bereft of the glitter of sunlight, shadow swathed the forest in a pall of gloom. Something rustled the under growth, raucous jackdaws beat the air returning to their roost.

Geraint said, 'Rain coming. I know a sheep hut near. We might find something to bind our feet. Have to be quick though. Will you take my hand in friendship, Emlyn Tomas?'

Emlyn looked at him and at the offered hand. Scratched, grass stained and bruised the two hands joined. Emlyn said, 'Why the change of heart?'

'Because I am hot tempered and was looking for someone to blame for what has happened,' said Geraint. He stood and pulled Emlyn to his feet. Then he smiled and ducked his head like a boy. 'Mam said if I touch a hair on your bastard head, I'll have her to answer to and I think she will choose something more damaging than a broom.'

'I like your mam,' said Emlyn with a fleeting grin.

They reached the hut unseen. It was no more than a stone built shelter, thatched once, but roofed now by green moss and stone-crop. There was no more than an hour of full light left. If they could avoid capture until darkness, a chance remained for them to warn Goronwy and the others with him on Pen Gogarth. There was nothing in the hut but old sheep skins. They tore them to strips to bind their bruised feet. The wind had strengthened bringing deeper cold. Emlyn and Geraint peered out from the stone doorway.

'They are in the woods,' whispered Geraint. 'We could make a dash across that field and perhaps reach the trees on the other side, before anyone sees us. I fear we are going to have to do some serious running now, if we are to warn Goronwy in time.'

'We will need horses,' said Emlyn. He had been doing serious running for most of the day and thought little of the prospect. 'How are we going to cross the river Clwyd?'

Ellen felt the horse move restlessly beneath her. She drove her boot heels into its side and the mare lurched forward into a stumbling run. Connie's high pitched protestations rang through the air. 'An' what would I be caring if yer broke yer silly neck, yer great brainless, maudlin goose! Come back here I say! Belial for sure has got yer reason, yer wicked girl! 'Tis sure I am I'll be for the poor house after this...Ellen!'

Ellen drove her stolen horse through the crowds. She used her whip where some were not quick enough to move from her path. The mare tossed her head, stamped her hooves and twisted this way and that as Ellen fought for control. At last, a clear way opened up before her and she urged the animal to better speed, thundering through the fair like a demon. There was one whom she recognised as she drove over the bridge. Gruffydd Hiraethog's servant Twm leaning from his horse to settle some purchase with the peddler.

'Twm!' Ellen called, drawing to an untidy stop before him. 'Where is your master?'

'Down yonder,' said Twm pointing with his chin. Then realising who spoke and caught by the urgency in her voice, he added, 'Mistress Ellen?'

Ellen could see Gruffydd by the water's edge. He was sitting on an upturned boat in deep conversation with Glyn Pysgod. His horse grazed at the tough reeds about the water's edge. The road was filling up now with the players of the Knappan who had dropped out the seek the comforts and warmth of an inn. Ellen pushed her way through them and drew up beside Gruffydd.

'Have you seen Emlyn?' she asked breathlessly.

Gruffydd looked up to her with a smile. The smile faded. 'Ellen lass, what are you up to?'

'I don't know,' she replied desperately. 'But we have to find Emlyn. Aled said they will skin him alive!'

Gruffydd caught up his horse and swung easily into to the saddle. 'Tell me as we go,' he said. He called Twm to follow.

Ellen had ridden since early childhood. She used her skill to good effect now, galloping over the grass beside the river while the wind snatched at her words. Gruffydd's scowl deepened with every word. At the mention of Captain Idris Hughes, he pulled to a stop and began to question the Knappan players.

'Emlyn?' Jasper Overbury said. 'Aye up the long ridge last I saw 'im, running like a madman. Thought it strange at the time, 'im not 'aving the Knappan an' all. Do you know if we won master Hiraethog?'

Gruffydd didn't answer but turned and clattered back over the bridge with Ellen and Twm following. From then it was a hard ride out of Rhuddlan, stretching to a fast gallop across the fields that sloped upwards to the Moel.

A thousand questions crowded Ellen's mind, but she asked none of them. She followed Gruffydd and Twm matching their speed. She tried to hear what she could from the shouted conversation. The clouds released their burden and rain fell in sheets over the water-meadows. There were many stragglers still coming in. Shouting, Gruffydd hurled a barrage of questions at them all. Learning all he could, he left the flat and led the others toward the slopes of the Moel. Thunder rumbled above the sea and mist rose from the trees in pearly silver.

'You are right my girl,' Gruffydd said as they urged the horses to further speed. 'That's Madog Mathaw ahead of us with his pack of hounds. Do you see them?'

Ellen saw a group of men leave the forest just ahead of them and start out across the plain. Gruffydd rode straight up to them. He raised his whip and brought it down on the head of an unfortunate. He drove his horse in among them, his booted feet kicking out viciously. 'What the devil are you playing at Mathaw! I'll have answers or by God Siôn Ddu, there's a thing or two I could tell to your lady wife which will gain you a whipping better than any I could deliver!' The whip came down again, delivered through a chorus of yelping objection.

Twm took the rein of Ellen's horse and held it steady as he watched his master with alarm.

Further up the vale, two men broke from the cover of the trees and ran towards a sloping field. Eight horsemen broke from cover further on still, and pursued them.

'There they are!' Ellen cried. Regardless of the others, she pulled her borrowed mare away from Twm, pushed through Madog's disordered gathering and began to gallop towards the running men. She hadn't really understood what was going on, but Gruffydd's anxiety was enough to impel her to do whatever she could to assist him. They followed her with half formed curses on their lips.

Their horses were fresher and ran all the quicker for it. Ellen felt her hat come loose and tumble off, her hair released from its confines whipped out behind her like a tongue of dark fire. By then they could see Geraint and Emlyn stumbling over thistle and gorse. They were making straight for the river.

Geraint's powerful legs drove him out into the open, Emlyn close behind. The rain came down in torrents, obscuring tree and field and washing the water meadows anew. Before they saw the horsemen, they heard them.

'They have seen us!' Geraint gasped.

Reserving what little strength he had, Emlyn did not answer.

Three horses splashed into view. The great voice of Gruffydd Hiraethog boomed across the field and bounced off the mountain. It reached the runners as they stumbled around. The rain lashed relentlessly. Out from the mist came the thunder of more hooves, wet across the mud sodden grass, rumbling after their prey like devil's huntsmen.

Utterly exhausted, Emlyn saw the ground rear up to meet him. Before he dropped, Geraint grasped a wet arm and hauled him onward. Dazed, numb and beyond thought, Emlyn struggled to keep his feet under him. He saw the approaching horses as if they floated, as if they were not going to stop. One overtook him, swung around and knocked him over. He splashed into a puddle.

'Are you going to sit there all day or are you getting up here behind me?'

Emlyn looked up. It was the sloe-girl Ellen. He rose and crawled up behind her with the agility of a slug. The mare sprung into flight again, the others thundering behind. Emlyn wrapped his arms around the girl, finding nothing else to get a hold on. They did not ride for long, but drew to a stop beside the river. Emlyn spilled to the ground like a sack of grain.

'They will not follow now,' said Gruffydd Hiraethog, bending beside him. 'Good God lad, what the devil have you been up to, did they lash you to a brambly bush?'

'Where did you come from?' gasped Emlyn.

'Twm will give you the gist of it all. I'll take the horses,' said Gruffydd. 'I'll get on to Pen Gogarth as quick as I can. If I can get there before daylight, there should be time enough. Twm give Geraint your shirt and coat.'

Geraint stood shivering, he accepted the clothes gratefully while the bard fished about his in saddle-bag and produced a heavy brown cloak and a spare doublet for Emlyn. In the mist they could hear voices calling.

Ellen dismounted, 'You are not going there on your own?' she cried. 'What will happen if you go?'

'You're a good girl lass,' Gruffydd replied. 'But you go back riding pillion with Twm now. Am I right in thinking that's a mare belonging to master Thomas of Mostyn?'

'He lent it to me,' said Ellen.

Giving Emlyn the clothing, Gruffydd walked toward her and took her hand. He said, 'Aye, and a little objectively I'll grant. If you go back now, none will be the wiser and the mouth on Twm is as closed as a stone saint's. Isn't that right Twm?'

'I'll take her back,' Twm replied, 'but I'm not keen on leaving you to go thrashing off on a night such as this. I'll go in your stead master Gruffydd.'

Gruffydd shook his head in strong determination.

Away from Gruffydd's hearing Geraint said, 'Have you got the reserve for a night ride?'

'I do it all the time,' Emlyn replied in a teeth-chattering whisper. He pulled the doublet on and wrapped himself in the cloak.

Before Twm or Ellen or Gruffydd could do anything to prevent him, Emlyn took the mare's rein and clambered into the saddle.

Gruffydd swung around in fury, an objection on his lips.

'No Tad-cu,' said Emlyn gathering the reins. 'You go home. Where else could I go now that the cat is out of the sack? If I am free to do so, I'll come by there with Goronwy. To remain here will bring nothing but trouble now and not only for me, but for yourself and Geraint and Ellen. You'll need to get away from here before you are discovered.'

'Then take my horse,' said Gruffydd, his whiskers bristling, 'or be labelled horse thief on top of all!'

Emlyn smiled down at him. 'If I get off this one,' he replied, 'I doubt if I'll find the fortitude to clamber on to another. Anyway you'll only ask Geraint to sit on me and then run off yourself. Tell Thomas Mostyn I've had to loan the mare for a while.'

No a keen rider himself, Geraint was struggling to take Twm's horse.

Emlyn moved forward and snatched the rein from his hand, drawing the horse away. He said, 'No Geraint, caring for one Glyn-Parry will be enough to try the patience of a saint. I'll not be delayed with you. You want no further involvement in this. Get home to your mam and your babies, you'll serve us better there.'

'I'll keep up,' said Geraint trying to grasp the rein.

Emlyn rode out of his reach. 'I'll get your brother out of this Geraint and send word as soon as I can. We can travel over Eyre Mynydd and get ship at Aberystwyth for Bristol and from there to France.'

He swept them all with his heavy grey eyes, his lashes starred with rain drops. He urged the mare forward, straight down the bank of the Clwyd. She pawed the air and whinnied in objection. The river flowed fast, brown with mud, swelling in the confinement of the banks and pitted by the rain. The mare tossed her head and backed away. Emlyn fastened his hands in her flying mane, thumped her with his heels and screamed in her ear, it always worked. She leaped for the water and landed releasing a splash that showered the onlookers. Rider and mount went under. The water boiled and two heads arose thrashing for a headway in the spiralling tide. Emlyn slid from the mare's back, holding on to the saddle and swam beside her as she fought the swift current, pushed by its force to angle towards the opposite bank.

'God's speed!' Gruffydd called to the dark head amidst silver splashes. 'God's speed Emlyn bach.'

'God's speed indeed,' said Owain Morgan when he heard the old man's voice echo through the mist. He and twelve others were hidden from view by a screen of twisted willows on the opposite side of the river.

'Matter's could not have worked out better,' said Idris Hughes. He had pulled a leather hood over his head and the rain ran from its brim splashing his gloved hands. 'One of the rare pleasures of life is well organised hunt with the quarry run to the ground at the end of it.'

'This quarry,' said Owain, 'will lead us to his den before the night is out. We will give him time to get ahead before we follow.'

The Spanish mare he had won at Conwy, shivered beneath him and tossed her head freeing a spray of rain. Owain watched his cousin scramble out of the river, the new found clothes soaked and smeared with mud. Emlyn climbed on to the shaken mare and turned her towards the sea road and the cave on Pen Gogarth.

Chapter 23 Wales England

The ride that Emlyn Tomas made that night became dream-like and unreal. He was so highly strung with exhaustion that he was scarcely aware of his surroundings and often lost sight of his purpose. He gritted his teeth and clung on to the powerful horse thundering through the night towards Pen Gogarth to warn the printers that discovery was impending. He was lulled to semi-consciousness by the rhythm and memories of a another ride in darkness swam into his mind unchecked

He was a small boy and his arms were stretched to the limit. He wrapped them around the broad waist of the woman who sat in front of him on the labouring horse. His hands gripped the cloth of the woman's cloak so tightly that they ached. The night was warm and trees clattered their finger-like leaves on a wind that smelled of heat and dryness. The woman turned awkwardly to him on occasion, to shout encouragement and his small voice asked again and again how far there was yet to go. His eyes stung with tears and he felt ashamed; his father said that tears were for girls and little children, not for young warriors who must grow up brave and strong. But he had left something behind that was very precious to him and he was not going back. When he turned to look back there was nothing but the closing darkness and a sky full of twinkling stars.

Sometimes he slept, to be jerked awake when his grip slackened and he half fell. Then his heart would pound with fear and the woman shouted at him to keep him alert. All around them were soft hills which knew that hey were made of sand, though they were painted blue now by the starlight and melted away in the darkness. Eventually he saw lights on the horizon and he could smell the sea. The woman spoke, her voice edged with excitement. She spoke in a tongue that was different to his mother's and different from the soft, guttural words his father used. He could understand them all. The lights drew nearer and the horse strained up a steep rise churning the sand and making grunting sounds. His grip loosened as the woman pulled suddenly on the rein at the top of the hill. He felt himself slip and tried to recover, but the cloth ripped from his small hands and he fell into darkness

Emlyn was sitting in the bracken. He could hear the sea pounding against the cliff face to one side. The air was bitterly cold causing him to shiver. His teeth rattled with cold making his head ache. The mare had not run off, but had strayed to a clump of gorse where it stood with its ears forward, sniffing the wind. Emlyn could not remember falling, but he did not think that much time had passed. He stood up, every muscle hurting. He walked slowly towards the horse, calling softly and holding out his hand. The mare came to him, nuzzling his neck and ears. He griped the mane and swung into the saddle. He knew where he was and that he only had four or five miles to cover before he came to the cave. For a moment he thought he heard pounding hooves, but the sea crashed below him and the wind howled and whined through the rocky heights above. He urged the horse onwards, going a little slower, listening carefully to the sounds of the night.

When he drew near, a voice called out in challenge. He answered with the password Goronwy had told him, and continued down a stony slope. There was a fire in front of the cave and figures milling about a farm cart. Emlyn cursed as he rode into the clearing, nearly all the printers were here, even though it was late at night. He called out questions as he hurriedly dismounted and learned that they had heard some rumour that discovery was imminent and were hastily dismantling the printing press. There were eight men working through the night to clear away all evidence of the work they had been engaged in throughout the summer. Some walked down the steep path leading to the sea, their arms loaded with pamphlets; they had a small rowing boat waiting. The deaf mute, Bran was getting in the way of everyone. Seeing Emlyn, he grunted and jumped up and down, caught up in the excitement.

Goronwy was stacking paper and wood blocks into the cart. Emlyn ran up to him, babbling out an explanation of all that had happened. Goronwy listened in stunned silence then he turned away and shouted orders to the others.

That was all he had time for. Owain, and his men thundered into the well lit clearing with draw swords.

At first, Goronwy could not believe what he was seeing. He turned to Emlyn and gripped a handful of his clothing. 'You fool!' Goronwy cried. 'You have led them right to us!'

Emlyn shook his head adamantly, but they had no time for explanations.

Idris Hughes called out to them to surrender. The Catholic printers ignored him, they chose to fight their way to freedom rather that face the consequences. They scattered, running for their scanty weapons and causing confusion. They were forced to use sticks against swords and knives. Idris Hughes' voice called out and the sheriff's men closed in.

Finding himself in the midst of it all and chilled by guilt, Emlyn stood beside Goronwy, prepared to die beside him if necessary, to show his friend that it had never been his intention to betray them.

Emlyn could see the fool Bran, smiling and leaping about, as if they were engaged in some game. But a sword came down and cleaved his face, slicing through eye and cheek before sinking into his throat. Bran dropped to the ground, his body convulsed in grotesque shudders before death claimed him.

A madness overwhelmed Emlyn then, a hot numbing anger such as he had never experienced before. It flowed through him like liquid fire, took possession of him and turned him into something wild and uncontrollable. He fought like a man possessed, disregarding the blows and the slashing swords, blind and senseless with the spirit of vengeance. He plunged knife up to the hilt, into the heart of the man who had struck down Bran. He felt indestructible and capable then of killing them all, but Owain stopped him.

Owain attacked him from behind. He smashed a rock into the side of Emlyn's head and felled him. Only seconds passed as Emlyn lay on the wet grass, but the blow had knocked the burning anger out of him. When he looked up, Owain towered over him with a sword held at his throat.

'Give up Emlyn,' Owain said. 'We have our differences, but you are of my blood and I would not see that blood spilled on this ground.'

'Better the sword than the hangman,' Emlyn replied, spitting out blood.

'My father has influence enough to save you from that fate. You need not die from this night's work.'

'In truth, I could not be free while my friends here hang!' Emlyn spat his reply.

'You are finished, whether you live or die,' said his cousin. 'After this, you will be named traitor and there is no place in Wales for the likes of you. Better to run now Emlyn, you may yet be able to get free. I will not stand in your way.'

Emlyn stood up, wary of the blade. 'If there is truth in your words cousin,' he replied, 'then give me a weapon and let me fight for that freedom as the others do here.'

Owain stepped back with a curse of anger and lowered his sword. He stood still for a moment and then nodded. He turned, bent to pick up a discarded blade and offered Emlyn the sword to fight with.

Emlyn had rarely held such a weapon. After the trying events of the Knappan and the exhausting ride, he did not have any reserves left. His efforts were pitiful compared to Owain's skill. They fought while the cries and the clash of steel rang about them. Emlyn was blind to the plight of the others. He defended himself as best as he was able. Owain could have killed him during the conflict, but he did not. His quick blade slashed across chest and arms, easily finding a way through the poor defence. He drove Emlyn away from the cave and the light. While he did so, he pleaded with Emlyn to give up.

Emlyn backed away, his breath raw in his throat. He stumbled over bracken and heaved his blade up two-handed to strive off Owain's stinging sword. Owain's movements were fluid and controlled as he drove Emlyn to the cliff edge. The blades locked and Emlyn felt his knees tremble. Straining against the force, he freed one hand and reached for his stabbing knife. He struck out and felt it penetrate the body of his cousin. Owain shuddered against him with quick intake of breath.

The blow did not stop Owain's advance, it lent him strength. Whatever reserve he had fought with at first, was gone. He renewed his attack with fury. Emlyn lost his blade and gripped Owain's sword arm. As they struggled, Emlyn stumbled. He tried to regain a foothold on the loose earth at the cliff edge, but his feet slipped and the strength drained away from him. He felt himself falling into the blackness, as if he had returned to his earlier dream. He felt his body smash into the sea. He felt the cold and the dark but nothing else.

The first sense to return to Emlyn was his sense of hearing. Voices rumbled somewhere in the darkness, deep men's voices with a lighter voice above them. Emlyn could not hear the words. He opened his eyes. At first all was blackness but there was light filtering through the open door that illuminated the room he was lying in. His eyes adjusted. He guessed it to be a store room. There were dim shelves from floor to ceiling on one wall. They were stacked with earthenware pots and sacks of grain. Dried flowers and herbs hung from the roof beams. Emlyn could smell manure and sour milk. He was lying on straw with a rough blanket thrown over him. He could feel the cold seep up through the stone floor. A farm of some sort? he wondered, and how long?

He felt cold and sick, he could not remember how he had come to be here. He supposed that Goronwy had brought him. His last awareness had been one of being heartily sick, with someone supporting him. He remembered the skeletal remains of Valle Crucis towering above him. Before that, was a nightmare of fast riding when he had been tied to a horse or tossed about on the boards of a cart as it thundered through dark nights and rain filled days. There had been a few waking moments after that. His body had rattled with fever and pain. Someone then, must have pulled him out of the sea before he had drown. He opened his eyes and stared up into the rafters. He saw a rat running along a roof beam, pausing to sniff the air, its eyes alight like the eyes of a demon

Then the memory of events preceding this came crowding back into his mind. He closed his eyes and groaned in despair. He turned to the wall with a stifled sob, willing his mind to forget.

'Are you awake?'

Emlyn turned and saw Goronwy framed in the doorway. He held a candle that he placed on the floor as he entered. 'Your eyes are open, you are awake. How do you feel? Its been days. Mary, the farmers wife here, says that you are suffering from the effects of exhaustion and cold rather that from the wounds. They are not deep and will heal soon enough. I have prayed for you.'

Emlyn tried to speak but no sound came. He cleared his throat and tried again. 'Thank you Goronwy,' he managed. 'Did they all escape?'

Goronwy shook his head. He pulled up a three-legged stool and sat beside the straw. 'Rhys and Tom Tilbury are here with us. I saw Morrisy killed and Arthur Ddu. Idris Hughes took the others prisoner. We escaped in the rowing boat we had kept on the shore. That's how I managed to get to you when you fell. We are safe now, at a farm near Hereford with a good Catholic family. We are waiting for others to come, this is a secret meeting place. But we will have to get to the south coast as soon as you are able, and leave for France. Ifan, the farmer here, advised us to avoid Bristol. The port is watched by William Cecil's men. There is a growing fear that Philip of Spain will invade England through her lesser ports. Are you hungry?'

The thought of food made Emlyn feel sick. But he was hungry and the feeling, he guessed was more to do with lack of food than because of it. He said, 'I have killed someone and I stabbed my own cousin.'

Goronwy nodded solemnly. 'It could not be helped. We were all fighting for our lives. We had no choice. If we had been taken like the others, we would be locked up in Beaumaris castle by now awaiting trial for treason. Like you once said to me, our deaths would not stop with a hanging, we'd be drawn and quartered before the ease of death. Morrisy and Arthur are better off dead.'

Emlyn struggled to sit up, fighting the pain and weakness. 'None of this would have happened if I had not been such a fool,' he said. 'They must have known all along that I would come straight to you, once I discovered that Aled and Jack had been questioned by Idris Hughes. Had I stayed away, those men would be alive now and we would be free men. As it is, we are outlawed and cannot go back.'

'I too am to blame,' said Goronwy. 'I who insisted that you stay with us in the first place. I knew the danger and we are not out of trouble yet. Emlyn, none of us thought that this would be easy, we knew that we risked discovery. Although the cost has been high, we have achieved much. We have kept the spirit of Catholic Wales alive and given hope to those who strive for the same ends. When we return, we will be much better prepared.'

Emlyn could feel a sharp pain thumping across his chest. He remembered Owain's blade cutting through leather and cloth and skin. 'When we return,' he said in disbelief. He should have guessed that the experience would do nothing to cool Goronwy's enthusiasm. Emlyn himself had had enough of rebellious printers. He had killed the sheriff's man because of the cruel fate of Bran, who no one would miss and no one would mourn.

Goronwy was still talking of rebellion and revenge. Emlyn could not listen to the words. He felt stained with mortal sin. Would it not be better to give himself up? To face with courage the death he had surely brought upon himself? He thought about Gruffydd Hiraethog and the land that he had seen with newly opened eyes, as if he had been half blinded before. Where now was that promising future? Lines of bardic poetry ran through his mind, the words seemed part of the land. The craggy mountains and rolling hills had awakened in Emlyn the deep love of belonging. He understood his grandfather now, now that none of that promise would be his.

'Do you remember William Allen?' Goronwy was saying.

Emlyn brought his mind back to the present. 'William Allen?' He could remember the man. Allen was the English exile who had influenced the young Jesuits in Paris when he had talked to them, Goronwy had been especially taken by the man. The last Emlyn had heard concerning him, had been from Friar Patrick O'Healy. Allen had gone to Rome to obtain permission from the Holy Father to found his own Jesuit school. From Goronwy's assurance, he guessed that Allen must have been successful.

Goronwy said, 'He is starting a school in Douai, especially for our own countrymen; exiles from Britain like you and I. This will be much better than College de Clermont. We will all be trained to drive heresy out of England, the school is to be for that purpose. All our efforts directed to one cause.'

Emlyn guessed what Gruffydd would have said to this, but he saw no use in pointing the flaws in this idea out to Goronwy. Goronwy paid no attention to what he didn't want to hear. Emlyn said, 'First things first Goronwy. Did you mention food?'

Goronwy stood up and knocked over the stool. 'Yes, of course,' he cried. 'But just think Emlyn how beneficial it will be for us to have our own college? And to train under such a man! We will come back as the priests that this country so badly needs.' He reached the door and turned. 'Have you not said that all we lacked was leadership?'

Emlyn did not reply. Goronwy smiled, his face seemed to shine with an inner light. He ducked under the lintel and left the room.

Emlyn felt dizzy with fatigue. He was not going to Douai with Goronwy. Of that he was certain. I may have lost all, he thought, but I can still go to Italy, even if I have to sing for the cost of getting there. Whatever future life holds for me, I will not be a Jesuit. Nor will I strive to bring England back to the obedience of Rome. That task lies not in my hands, but in the hands of men like William Allen and, God protect him, Goronwy Glyn Parry.

He fell asleep before food arrived.

During the next few days, others came to the isolated farm house that lay on the boarder of Wales and England. They were Catholic and the farm was a prearranged meeting place. They came in the hope of hearing some news, the nature of which Emlyn had not been told. That it was of utmost importance, was evident in the suppressed excitement of the visitors. The farm belonged to Ifan and Mary Stout, it had long been a place for clandestine meetings and messages.

Emlyn purposefully avoided company, he managed to find some task to occupy himself rather than be brought into the lengthy conversations, that consisted of nothing but plotting. He did not want to know what they were all waiting for. He even considered 'borrowing' a horse and making his own way to the coast. He avoided Goronwy whenever he could.

At the end of that week, he failed and Goronwy found him in an outhouse milking the goats. 'William Persons is here,' Goronwy cried on entering. His eyes were aglow with excitement. Goronwy sat in the straw beside him. 'We have been waiting for word from the court. We have managed to persuade one of William Cecil's grooms to inform us of his master's every move. Next time he steps away from the security of London we will be waiting for him.

'Goronwy no!' Emlyn shouted. He rose in one fluid movement and kicked the milk bucket across the floor. 'What do you all plot here? To murder the Secretary of State?'

Goronwy stood. 'Why are you so angry? You know that with his downfall the rest will follow and the Queen, by God's grace, with them!'

'Jesu Goronwy! Do you realise what you are involved in here? This is no printing of pamphlets! This is murder and I will have no part in it!'

'But you already are in it Emlyn,' Goronwy replied. 'It is your fault that we are here in the first place! If you had not led the...'

'I agree that it was my fault. But that does not excuse what you plan here nor does it entitle you to involve me. I cannot condone murder, however just you may believe it to be. Give my thanks to the farmer and his wife. I am leaving!'

'You can't leave,' said Goronwy. 'I sent word to Gruffydd Hiraethog. I told him where we were.'

'How could you drag him further into this?' Emlyn cried. 'Do you expect him to come here?'

Goronwy looked away and bit his lip. 'Of course not,' he answered. 'All I asked of him was money. We need something Emlyn, to pay our passage to France. We cannot live on charity alone nor should we.'

Emlyn waited until his anger was under control before he spoke. 'Charity from Gruffydd is acceptable is it? He will know by now how matters at Pen Gogarth turned out. He will also be watched and will be unable to offer help even if he wished to, which I very much doubt.'

'He will help you though,' said Goronwy. 'I am sure, if nothing else, he will send word. Stay a few days more, you owe it to me Emlyn, after all, I did save you from drowning.'

Emlyn winced. So it has come to this. 'I will stay a few more days,' he agreed reluctantly. 'But do not involve me in anything you do here. Don't even talk to me about it!'

Goronwy smiled triumphantly. Emlyn glared at him until he left.

Twm, Gruffydd's servant arrived at the farm the following day.

Recognising the voice, Emlyn came out of the house to see what all the commotion was about.

'Master Emlyn!' Twm cried desperately. He was held securely between two men who had been watching the road.

'It's all right Twm. They'll not do you any harm,' Emlyn said reassuringly. The men released Twm and returned to their duty.

'I've had a div'l of a job finding this place,' said Twm. 'I was all for turning back, when those two saw me. We thought you were drown' master Emlyn, 'till we got word from Goronwy. Master Gruffydd was in a right high temper.'

'Twm, do you know how my cousin Owain fares?' Emlyn asked anxiously. The thought that he had killed his cousin had been difficult to live with.

'He's well enough considering. You've not done away with him, if that's what you're afeared of. Master Gruffydd thought it best for them all to believe you was dead, for a while at any rate. He sent me with your belongings, much against me will, mind. The whole place is crawling with the sheriff's men. I had a right job getting away. They're looking for them printer's who escaped, you know, Goronwy and all. I'm right pleased to see you master Emlyn and no mistake!'

Emlyn took his arm and led him to the house 'Come on Twm. You'll feel better with an ale jug and a bit of food inside you. You can tell me the rest while you eat.'

Twm knew nothing of what he had carried over the border from Wales. The bundle he had brought looked innocent enough. It contained Emlyn's jerkin with the gems still sewn inside, along with some money and a letter from Gruffydd. With it, there was some extra clothing, a bow and a quiver of arrows. This was tied with the thong that held the bag of 'bits and pieces' that Mafanwy Fawr had given Emlyn on the road to Rhuddlan. He untied it smiling. Its presence showed that even Gruffydd believed something of the old woman's words, despite his objections.

Gruffydd had written the letter in Welsh. As soon as he was able, Emlyn sought privacy in which to read it.

'I had a feeling that drowning would not finish you off, I believe dragons are quite good swimmers. You'll find all you need in the pack I send with Twm. Sending your translation of Genesis seemed foolish so I thought to keep it here for you, sure that you could begin again when the opportunity arise. Do as I suggested with the 'dragon's stones' as soon as you reach France. You know how I feel about all this. What can I say to you? Only come back when you are able. You might find it wise to remain in France until Ambrose Chillingworth comes over with the wool then you can continue on to Italy with him. Try and pick up that item we spoke of in Paris, the letter from your uncle to the priests there. Remember that with such evidence, you will one day be entitled to the land I hold for you. Send me word with Twm and from wherever you find yourself after.

God's speed Mab y Ddraig. Don't forget your music, I have my eye on a certain golden harp.'

Emlyn smiled and cried at the same time. He now had enough funds to make his way to Italy.. But first, he thought, I have to get free of Goronwy, or better still, persuade him to come with me.

He wrote to Gruffydd and sent Twm back to Wales before any thought to prevent him. Twm complained a lot, but had seen the sense of it in the end.

Emlyn stood by the road and watched Twm ride into the distance. Beside him stood Rhys and Tom Tilbury. Both had sent letters to their own families with Twm.

Rhys said, 'I wish to God that I were going home with him.'

'So do I,' Emlyn replied.

'Me and Rhys are thinking we could stay here in England and slip home when all the excitement has died down,' Tom said. He kicked at the stony ground as he spoke. He was ashamed to be backing out now.

Emlyn could understand his reasons. He said, 'You may have a long wait Tom. If you go back to Wales now you will both be arrested. Do you intend to stay here?'

'No,' said Tom. 'Rhys has a brother in Shrewsbury. Don't you Rhys?'

'Aye,' Rhys agreed. 'Me and Tom, well we've no liking for the goings on here Emlyn. Although I admire the men here I can't see this as being the work for God. Why kill in the name of God?'

'Why not?' Emlyn smiled. 'Many have killed and died in the name of God. Who are we to know the rights or wrongs of it? But if your conscience tells you that this is wrong, then go Rhys, and you too Tom. I wish I could come with you.'

'If your heart is not in this either,' said Tom, 'why stay?'

'Because I killed a man on Pen Gogarth,' Emlyn said. 'Besides, they all think I am dead. Perhaps it's best left this way.'

'Dead?' Rhys laughed. 'Died for the cause eh? Well Emlyn Tomas, from what I've heard here, that's better that living for it.'

Rhys and Tom Tilbury were gone the next day leaving no word behind them. Emlyn never forgot those last words, in time, they came to mean more and more to him.

Goronwy felt very angry when he discovered that the two Welshmen had gone without a word. He confronted Emlyn with it as soon as he saw him. 'I suppose you talked them out of becoming Jesuits,' he snapped.

'Not at all,' Emlyn replied. 'Rhys has taken a liking to Megan from Marion Mills. He plans to marry her if he can out of all this. They did tell me they where going and I'll admit that I did nothing to stop them.'

Goronwy shook his head and entered the room where Emlyn was packing his belongings into a sack. He had said nothing about the visit from Twm yet. Goronwy noticed the bow and the sheaf of arrows. He said, 'You'll have heard we are leaving then?'

'I'm leaving,' Emlyn said, 'I didn't know that you were.'

'William Cecil will be coming south himself soon. So why not travel with us, you'll see the sense of it all in the end. Do you remember the vow we made when we first went to College de Clermont? '*I swear to Almighty God that I am ready and shall always be ready to receive holy orders, in His own good time.*' Remember Emlyn? '*I shall return to England for the salvation of souls, whenever it shall seem good to the superior of this college to order me to do so.*' I know that last bit is new. It has been added by William Allen and the founders of the college at Douai. Emlyn we swore to take holy orders!'

Emlyn sat down on an upturned box and looked steadily at Goronwy. Goronwy didn't like that look. Emlyn had not been the same since the miracle of the Virgin's footprints. Emlyn said, 'we were fourteen then. I did not know what I wanted then and nor did you. If you intend to be ordained Goronwy and feel suited to that way of life then, that is admirable. But I have other concern now and...'

'Other concerns! Why? Because Gruffydd Hiraethog has made you his heir? That is now impossible. You know that we are outlawed.'

'...and even if I wanted to, I could not take holy orders. Do you remember Goronwy? They only accept youths from noble families into the priesthood. Being a fatherless bastard, I do not qualify.'

'But they do not know that. And anyway, if your grandfather has named you his heir, that is surely enough to gain you respectability.'

'They do know,' said Emlyn. 'How could they not? Father Barzini went to great trouble to discover my parentage. He knows more than I do. Goronwy, before we left Paris, they made it quite clear to me that I was no longer welcome there.'

'I don't believe you!' Goronwy cried. 'You would have told me before this.'

'Would it have made any difference?'

'No,' Goronwy admitted. 'Look, we need not go to College de Clermont for more than a few days. You and I can go to Douai. Students will come from all over the country. We will be properly trained to wrest England from the grip of heresy. William Allen will not question your origins Emlyn. It is what is in your heart that counts before the eyes of God. You and I will be invaluable to the new school, considering the training that we have already received. Why not come and speak to Robert Persons? He is a man of great foresight and bitterly opposed to the reformation. If you just listen to him, you will know that I speak the truth. God will grant us success. Get your things together Emlyn, we are all leaving within the hour. We cannot stay now that Rhys and Tom have deserted us. If they are captured, they will break under torture and we would no longer be safe.'

Goronwy could not understand why Emlyn looked at him with such an expression of astonishment. At first he thought that perhaps Emlyn had at last understood.

But Emlyn turned away. He clenched his fist and drove it with all his strength into the stone wall, again and again, until his hand bled.

Goronwy did not tell his friends about Emlyn's reluctance. So they spoke to him with confidence as they travelled south. Goronwy noticed how Emlyn always turned the conversation to lesser matters, no one else seemed to notice. Goronwy rode for most of the time in silence with a growing mistrust of the friendship they had shared. He knew that Emlyn felt deeply hurt from being deserted by his mother and unacknowledged by a father. Goronwy knew what it was like to be teased day after day. He had been a fat boy at fourteen, but they had not teased him for long. Like his brothers, he knew how to fend for himself. He was no longer fat but had kept the solid build of the Glyn Parry's. His father said you could tell a Glyn Parry from a mile away. Build was the only thing Goronwy had in common with his brothers now. They seemed dull and withdrawn to their own concerns. They had no time for the troubles that threatened the Catholics who remained true to the rule of Rome. Nor, thought Goronwy sadly, does Emlyn Tomas. But how to bring him back?

In the first days of December, a rider intercepted them outside Oxford. They were staying at the house of a miller. For the price of a meal and a place to sleep, they were sacking the ground flour and were dusted in white.

The news that was brought to them had nothing to do with William Cecil, though it would inevitably lead them to him. A Spanish fleet had been attacked by Huguenot privateers in the Channel. The ships had been forced to seek shelter in the English ports of Plymouth and Southampton. News of this strange visitation had reached the ears of William Cecil. He was by then, on his way to Southampton to visit a certain English merchant by the name of Ambrose Chillingworth.

Robert Persons who led the little troop south, could not contain his enthusiasm. There were seven men in his Catholic army, all on their way to the continent, to the new college at Douai.

'We will let Cecil get there first,' said Robert Persons when they were all gathered around a fire in a barn to hear the news. 'That way, we will discover the reason why a fleet of peaceful ships brings even the Secretary of State from the comforts of court. I have, as some of you know, been in constant touch with the Spanish Ambassador, Guerau de Spes. I have received a letter from him. He states that on no account must the ships be delayed. He has insisted that they are provided with a safe escort to their destination.'

'Does he say where they are bound?' Emlyn asked with growing suspicion.

'The Netherlands. They probably carry troops for Alva. If this is the case, they can hope for little help from the Queen of England. She sees Alva as a dangerous threat to the new religion and well she might. Guerau De Spes is negotiating with Alva, King Philip and the Holy Father. Bring them all together and England will lie at our mercy. De Spes is our powerful ally. With his help and influence, we will raise the Catholics to rebellion and free Mary Tudor. In the meantime, we will do what we can to hinder William Cecil.'

Emlyn felt a chill wash through him. On the other side of the fire, Goronwy was watching him intently. Emlyn said, 'This merchant Chillingworth, what part does he play in all this?'

'I know little of the man,' Persons replied. 'He comes from the same part of the country as Cecil. Rutland or some such place. Perhaps he knows more about the Spanish ships that we do. Still, there is not much this small band can do to free the ships, both ports have soldiers and a town guard. If only we could discover what the meeting between Secretary and merchant is about.'

'But we can,' said Goronwy.

Emlyn dropped his head so that none could see his expression of disgust.

Goronwy continued. 'Emlyn knows Ambrose Chillingworth. He bought wool from your grandfather, didn't he Emlyn?'

Emlyn lifted his eyes and glared at Goronwy. 'He also prevented our discovery and arrest when we smuggled the press into Wales. I would not want any harm to come to him. You and I are in his debt Goronwy.'

'But this is excellent news!' Robert Persons lifted his hands in the air as if about to bestow a blessing. He brought them together sharply. 'You say that this man knows that you smuggled a press into Wales and has not betrayed you?'

'He knew all right,' said Goronwy. 'He stumbled right on to us. He wasn't in much of a position to say anything. He was unarmed and had no one with him. There were half a dozen or more of us. But then, when the bailiff came and started asking questions, Chillingworth guided the man away from us and even saved Emlyn from a session at the village stocks. I would not be surprised if he sympathised with us.'

Emlyn would. He also suspected that Ambrose was more than just an acquaintance of William Cecil. Ambrose Chillingworth was not a stranger to the court of Elizabeth.

'What do you say Emlyn?' Goronwy urged.

'That he is a good man, and we have no right to ask anything from him.' Emlyn tried to remain calm. If there was going to be any violence directed towards Chillingworth or William Cecil, he knew that he would try and prevent it. But how could he warn them and not betray these gallant Catholics?

'I think he could be persuaded to help us,' said Goronwy. 'In fact, he may even welcome the chance.'

'Excellent Goronwy,' said Persons. 'You and Emlyn could go there. Talk to him and find out what his involvement in this ship businesses is.'

'And if he is not interested?' Emlyn voiced the question coldly.

'You will have nothing to fear,' said Persons. 'If he did not betray the printing scheme, he is hardly likely to turn you in to William Cecil now is he?'

Emlyn tried a last time. 'He may well do just that,' he said, 'if he discovers what you intend to do with Cecil.'

'Then say nothing of it,' Persons replied. 'You and Goronwy can go there paying a friendly visit. He will make you welcome I am sure. Once there, it will not be difficult to discover what we need to know. The rest of us will wait on the road for Cecil's return and take him. He only travels with a small guard and in secret. None but us know this. Such an opportunity will not come again. God surely guides our steps.'

'Amen to that,' said Goronwy with finality.

The next morning Emlyn tightened the straps holding his pack to his saddle. He knew now that he must not betray his intentions to his fellow travellers and must work towards gaining Goronwy's confidence.

'You are not with us are you Brother?' The voice spoke behind him.

Brother? Emlyn turned and saw Robert Persons. 'With you sir?'

Persons was a tall man with a full beard streaked with grey and dark intelligent eyes. He was thin and muscular. Emlyn thought he looked more like a soldier than a man of God. There was something threatening about him, though his voice was soft and persuasive. He smiled grimly. 'I can see that you have doubts brother,' he said. 'Prayer and absolute devotion to God; that is where the answer lies. Take example from Goronwy. He is a good young man with strength to live by his convictions, and die for them if need be. You too have that strength brother and could be like him.'

'I think you are mistaken sir,' said Emlyn carefully. 'I admit that I have my doubts. I admit also that I could not be like Goronwy. There are those who lead and those who follow. I follow.'

'You underestimate yourself brother. Goronwy has told me something of your reputation. You are a talented musician I believe?'

'A gift from God,' Emlyn answered humbly. 'Goronwy was kind to have said so.' What else, he wondered, has Goronwy told this astute man? Emlyn felt that he would have to speak now with care.

'Goronwy also mentioned that you have no intention of joining the Society of Jesus. Is this true bother Emlyn?'

'As I have said sir, I do not have the convictions of Goronwy. I feel that I have not been called by God to do his work.'

'You can be dedicated to crushing heresy brother, without the call of God,' said Persons. He placed a fatherly hand on Emlyn's shoulder and guided him away from the horse and the mill, down towards the river. 'First you must learn to recognise your doubts for what they are,' he added softly. 'Do you question your love of God and the true faith? Or are your doubts closer to earthly matters? Such as the justice in ridding this God fearing country of such people as William Cecil, who seek to corrupt it? Come now boy, do not be afraid to answer.'

Emlyn could not think up a reply. If he said 'yes' to either of the questions, Person's suspicions would be further aroused. If his answer was negative, Persons would not believe him. He said, 'The questions are the same. If a man doubted his faith, then so would he doubt the actions of his fellow Catholics. I think the question here is of a different nature.' Emlyn stopped walking. He had no intention of being led further away. He did not want to be alone with Robert Persons. It was not violence he feared, but the man's power of persuasion.

'A thoughtful statement,' Persons said. 'Are you going to re-phrase the question or shall I?'

Emlyn looked away from the penetrating eyes. He stooped, picked up a stone and sent it skimming over the sluggish water. He hoped the action was reassuring enough to put Persons off his guard. Gathering up a handful of pebbles, Emlyn said, 'Should a man choose loyalty to Queen and country or loyalty to the Holy Father? This is what causes me such difficulty. Until I have decided, I cannot take holy orders. But I will not stray from the faith that I have been taught and believe in with certainty.'

Persons placed two hands on Emlyn's shoulders. His hands griped firmly and shook as he spoke. 'Then after this, come to Douai with us brother. You will be shown the true way and we will make a Jesuit of you. Let us leave questions concerning the rights and wrongs of our actions to a time of greater leisure. Tell me brother, what instrument do you play with such renowned skill?'

Relieved that the subject was dropped, Emlyn relaxed. The subject of music was one he could talk about without fear and to whatever lengths Persons wished to push him. He looked forward to the day when he and Persons would part company. He felt that Robert Persons was a man to be avoided in future. Persons and his loyal youths planned to travel to the Netherlands soon after they had waylaid William Cecil.

Chapter 24 England

Ambrose Chillingworth wiggled his toes in front of a roaring fire and sipped his excellent wine. He did have to travel until Spring, so was settled into his Southampton town-house, prepared for the winter, composing letters and managing his substantial financial assets. He thought with pleasure about the quiet winter months ahead of him. He hoped that soon he would hear word from his son Christopher, who was at sea with Jack Hawkins. The fleet had been expected back from the Indies for over a month. Ambrose was not too concerned; the sea and winds were fickle. Hawkins would have difficulty finding suitable currents and winds to return to England if he had left late in the season.

Ambrose had visited the queen's court in September. He had unwritten sanction to act for the Queen in the matter of trade with Venice. She was always thus; ready to reap profit should there be profit to reap and to turn a blind eye if there was not. The Company of Merchant Adventures was interested in restarting trade with the Levant, any enterprising merchant who could make advances in this direction would be well rewarded for his efforts. While in London, Ambrose had held long discussions with them and agreed to a separate arrangement. He would not have to go back to London during the winter. All he had to do now, was get fat and fiddle with clocks and write letters until late March. Leaving Southampton then, he would reach the Alps in time for the passes to be open. Emlyn Tomas was due to arrive before then with more Welsh wool. Ambrose could see nothing but profit on the horizon.

He lifted his cup to the flames capturing flickers of light in the green Murano glass. This, like everything else in the room, reflected his expensive tastes. The room was furnished in shades of red and gold, adding to its warmth. On a long table under the window stood a Nuremberg clock supported by gilded apostles and crowned with heavenly bodies. Ambrose liked the magic workings of clocks, like some sorcerers spell they captured and held to order the elusive nature of time. He owned four clocks. He'd been toying with this one for most of the afternoon. Now he waited for its elaborate telling of the hour with anticipation, sure that it would strike with perfection. There were ten minutes yet to go.

Outside the window, another wet, grey day neared its end. In the narrow streets of the harbour town, rain dripped off the thatched roofs, splashing the cobbles and anyone unfortunate enough to pass underneath, but most people where indoors. Even the town's watchmen, huddled in their shelters, reaching chilled hands to the warmth of hissing braziers. In the harbour, ships creaked as they rose and fell on the swelling tide. Among them were the foreign, Spanish ships; having made the mistake of seeking the protection of England's shore, they now rode to their anchors with empty holds and an English guard; not one of their crew remained aboard.

Ambrose heard the sound of hooves as riders entered the walled courtyard of his residence. He stood and could see them in the fading light from his window. They were hooded and muffled against the weather, with only their eyes visible. Ambrose had no need to see, even the eyes, to recognise one of the riders. He hoped and prayed that he was mistaken. He considered the unlikeness of such a visit from the man he thought of and convinced himself that he was mistaken. Maybe it was just a trick of the light.

There was shouting and a great deal of fuss and then footsteps on the stairs. Matthew, his servant for fifteen years, entered the room with a worried expression. 'Master Chillingworth, 'that is they,' he stammered, 'require a night's lodging.'

Reseated and outwardly calm, Ambrose considered this for a moment. Whoever 'they' or 'he' was, it seemed that an inn was not good enough. 'Who?'

'Your favourite meddler,' said a deep voice behind the servant. 'Good God Ambrose where did you get that infernal clock?'

Ambrose groaned. He had said to himself but a minute ago, please, please dear sweet Lord don't let it be who I think it is. As usual the good Lord had other matters on his mind.

'William,' he said, in as warm a voice as he could conjure up at such short notice. 'The clock was a gift from John Carre of Antwerp, a gift to oil the wheels of enterprise. He wants to start his glass-making in England. He feels I may be able to help the enterprise. I'm dismayed that you don't like the clock William, it's rather handsome I think.'

There were few people in England or beyond, who had the temerity to call this man 'William'. As Secretary of State to the Queen of England, William Cecil actively discouraged it. But Ambrose could. Not only because of their long and lasting friendship, but also for the unstinting service that he had given in obtaining valued items of news and scandal, to add to the palette of espionage for the Secretary of State.

Peeling off layers of dripping clothing the man revealed himself and looked about with expectancy for a cup of wine. Matthew scooped up the shed garments and left closing the door with an ill tempered slam. Nothing was ever the same after a visit from William Cecil.

'Not the best of days for travelling,' Ambrose said handing his guest his own refilled glass for lack of another. 'I expect this might have something to do with our unexpected visitors out there bobbing bows among the fishing fleet?'

William Cecil put down his glass and rubbed his cold hands together, posterior to the fire. 'I'm glad to see that you still have your housekeeper Martha. She's warming up a pie for me.' He looked at Ambrose, an eyebrow raised.'You know the ships are Spanish,' he said with a grimace. 'They were driven here by sea beggars and are not, as some believe, newly arrived from the America's loaded with Aztec gold. Her crew and her nobles, God curse them, have been marched off and her cargo is now safely under lock and key.'

'This could be taken as an affront to his gracious majesty Philip of Spain,' said Ambrose. 'Would I be right in assuming that the ships were bound for the Netherlands?'

Cecil half nodded. He had forgotten how the extraordinary mind of the merchant was usually one step ahead of everyone else. 'Part of a fleet bound for the Netherlands yes,' he replied. 'The rest lie in Plymouth.'

'And you are not letting them go?'

Cecil smoothed his neat black doublet, fingering the silver edging. A letter crackled, hidden in its folds. He knew there was no need to mention the secrecy, either about his visit or the reason for it. He knew Ambrose Chillingworth to be as silent as a stone and as trustworthy. Because of this rare quality, Ambrose had a finger in every pie in Europe.

'You surprise me William,' said the merchant. 'Can we afford to antagonise the Spanish further?'

'It is a somewhat complicated story,' Cecil replied seating himself beside the fire. 'I received a letter from Jack Hawkins. As you know he has made his third voyage to the New World and we hoped it would be the most profitable yet.'

Ambrose looked at him with a worried frown. 'Seven well armed ships, I recall,' he said. 'You invited me to take shares in the venture, I sent my son Christopher. Is anything amiss?'

'They refused to buy his wares at Rio de la Hacha and our brave and foolish Hawkins turned his cannon on the Treasury, letting none leave the port until they had bought his slaves.'

'Turned his cannon!'

Cecil nodded solemnly.

'Fired on the Treasury?'

'Yes, and that was not all. He entered the town and fought with the Spanish, burning most of the town. His own letter unfortunately forgot to mention most of this; I learnt it from other sources. I'm afraid our Spanish ambassador Don Gueru de Spes has heard the news too. I've had quite a task avoiding him. Still, it is best not to believe this until we have further news. Rumours magnify as they travel. Benedict Spinola from the Genoese finical house in London has spread one such rumour, that all Hawkins' ships are lost and he and his men killed. Do not worry Ambrose, I know this is not true. The truth however, is of a more serious nature.'

'More serious?' Ambrose turned pale. His eyebrows lifted his furrowed brow. 'What could be more serious than an act of war against Spain? Or is this to be explained away like the rest, as an act of uncontrollable piracy?'

'King Philip is no fool,' Cecil replied. 'I can't believe that he will start a formal war between Spain and England.'

'God save us William! They have been circling us like hungry wolfs, waiting for an excuse to move in for the kill. Now this fool Hawkins has offered it to them on a silver plate! Are we to believe that the Spaniards will brush it away as a mere misfortune at sea?'

'There have been repercussions.'

Ambrose felt his heart miss a beat. 'What repercussions?'

Cecil took a deep ragged breath. 'To repair his ships Hawkins pulled into San Juan de Ulloa. A few days later, before he had a chance to flee, the Spanish fleet arrived with Don Martin Enriquez, the viceroy of Mexico. Trapped, Hawkins tried to negotiate and bluff his way out but the Spanish villain opened fire. Before he finally got away from San Juan, Hawkins lost a hundred and twenty men and three ships including the flagship...I'm sorry Ambrose, but I know nothing of the fate of your son Christopher. I am sure if anything had happened Hawkins would have mentioned it.'

Ambrose turned away. His mind was in a turmoil. 'He was on the *Judith* with Francis Drake.'

'The *Judith* is safe Ambrose. We can only hope that Christopher is safe also.'

The merchant sank into the chair opposite and dropped his head into his hands, frustrated by the lack of information and overcome by what the news could imply. After some time of silence he said, 'When do they return?'

'It won't be more than eight weeks. They must be well on their way by now and could reach here this month or early January,' Cecil replied, trying to put hope into his voice.

Ambrose knew the futility of worrying while he remained unaware of all the facts. Voyages always carried risk. He remembered his son's smiling face and the sun in his hair as he had bid farewell full of the hope of expanding their interests. He cast worry to the back of his mind. To reassure the Queen's secretary and himself he said, 'There is nothing to be done. Christopher will send word if he is able. Is this then why the galleon is being held here? In retaliation? If you wish to avoid war William, your actions are questionable.'

'No,' said William Cecil sipping at his wine and licking his tidy moustache. 'Retaliation is not the real reason, 'though it may well be believed so. The Spanish ships are kept here and at Plymouth because, although they carry no treasure from the Aztecs they carry wealth of a similar nature. They are bullion ships carrying eight-hundred thousand ducats owed to Alva's troops in the Netherlands.'

Chillingworth looked up in horror. It was an astonishing sum. 'The Queen it seems, tempts the very devil. What can be gained from such rash action?'

'Eight hundred thousand ducats,' Cecil repeated with a grim smile. 'We knew of the planned voyage as early as April from our agents in France. The fleet has been delayed. The money is a loan to Philip from Italian bankers.

'Genoese?'

'Yes. I have discovered from Benedict Spinola, that the gold does not legally belong to Spain until it reaches the Netherlands.'

'You can't just take it the theft would upset Genoa. Hasn't England enemies enough, and what of your Spanish ambassador de Spes? If he is aware of this, he is bound to demand its return.'

'He has also been informed, in all sincerity, that the Queen cannot allow it through the English Channel for fear of piracy.' Cecil paused for a moment fixing the merchant with his pale eyes as if assessing the effect of words before they were spoken. 'The Queen would like to borrow it herself,' he finished.

Ambrose sat back in his chair and thought about that for a while. He knew more than most what the collapse of the Antwerp money-market had meant to the London mercers and therefore to the kingdom. For the past year, the Castilian grandee, the Duke of Alva had crushed the people of the Netherlands in a reign of terror. Through his Court of Tumults, soon known as the Court of Blood, he had condemned and slaughtered hundreds of the lowland's nobility and at every provincial capital, a Spanish garrison had been installed. Their sole purpose was detecting and eradicating heresy through the tortuous horrors of the Inquisition.

After giving him time for thought, Cecil said, 'Someone must convey the queen's wishes to the Florentine and Genoese bankers of the Holy See and arrange to transfer the loan. Negotiations with Benedict Spinola have already been gone into with great detail. He assures us that there will be little trouble, but feels, and rightly so, that the matter should be dealt with in the right quarter and with utmost secrecy. If you agree to undertake the task, it must be now.'

'Me?' Ambrose stood up. 'In December?'

Cecil rose too, and stood face to face, looking directly into his host's eyes. He said, 'Speed is essential, but not to the detriment of the purpose. Have you got some wool or rags you can take along to conceal your true intent? That is if you decide to go.'

Ambrose flinched at the word 'rags'. He thought with some pleasure that William Cecil looked acutely uncomfortable. Let him. There was a limit to what a man could be expected to do for Queen and country. 'Can't you find another?' Ambrose said lamely.

'There aren't any. You're the only man I can trust to get the job done at such short notice.'

'So, I'm to travel all the way across the Alps, at the most unsuitable time of year, sneaking all the way, under the guise of a travelling cloth merchant, peddling rags as you put it?'

'That's it in a nut shell.'

'Is there a personal gain to be gleaned from this madness? Europe is not the healthiest of places for an Englishman to travel at present.'

'Gain?' William Cecil smoothed his neat beard. 'Have I ever shown meanness before?'

'I'll need a week,' Ambrose said, nose to nose with the Queen's secretary.

'You haven't got a week. Weren't you going to go next year anyway?'

'Five days then, or I'm not going.'

'Two.'

Ambrose turned and emptied what was left of the wine into the single glass. He sipped half of it, offering the Queen's secretary the remainder.

Cecil drained it and looked over the rim. 'Am I to take it that you agree?'

Ambrose considered him for a moment. 'Let us say that, if I have four days and if that is all there is to it, I agree, but reserve the right to change my mind.'

'Ambrose!' Cecil exclaimed in exasperation.

'Let's try Martha's pie,' said Ambrose, 'and consider expenses.' As they left the room, he noticed with annoyance, that his clock had not struck the hour.

It was not the end of the night's activity and the arrangement was not, by any means, finalised, whatever else the Queen's secretary might believe.

Hours later the clock from Nuremberg incorrectly clanged out eleven. Ambrose was dressed in a striped nightgown of Egyptian cotton and a bedcap with a tassel on the end. Room had been provided to put up Percy, Cecil's suspicious looking notary, his servant, groom and men at arms. William Cecil was asleep in the warmed room opposite.

Sitting glumly in candle light, Ambrose was plagued with worries. He left his room and made his way down the cold passage towards the room he had been in earlier. Outside the sky was starless. The heavy clouds still poured their deluge over the inhabitants of Southampton. Ambrose failed to hear the arrival of a new wave of visitors as they clattered into the courtyard and woke the servants.

Ambrose poked the fire to life and added more fuel, casting a warm glow over the table where he worked. The clock lay partially in bits around him. He was replacing the skeleton of death armed with a sickle, onto its pivot. When a knock came at the door he jumped, dropped the gilded bones and upset the threesome of cherubs already replaced above.

Matthew entered looking dishevelled with a full lit candelabra in his hand. 'More visitors 'ave just arrived,' he said grumpily. 'You'll never guess who?'

Ambrose fixed the cherubs to their filigree cloud and turned a little key to set them rotating musically around the crown. 'The Queen of England?'.

'As you were already up, I thought you might wish to see them,' added Matthew.

This was too much to expect. 'Whatever are you about?' Ambrose threatened his servant with a tiny hammer. 'Whoever they are, tell them to go find an inn with the charity to open to them at this ungodly hour. They can call back in the morning.'

'They said to tell you it is of the utmost importance and, by the look of them, 'ave ridden far an' mistress Martha says to put them in the store, but the other ones are in there. So she's all for throwing them out the gate.'

Mistress Martha was the merchant's housekeeper who had made a pie for William Cecil. Ambrose reflected that she seemed to have more sense then he had given her credit for. He looked up from his work. 'Then be off with you and do as she says,' he said. 'I'm going to bed.'

Matthew stood hesitantly in the doorway. 'One of them is that lad from the manure pile. Remember, 'e's the grandson of...well 'e did tell me the name but I couldn't grasp it even after three tries, it's the Welshman you buy cloth from, you know the one with the 'arp? I think they're...'

'Gruffydd Hiraethog?' Ambrose rose from the bench where he had been working. 'Is Emlyn here then?'

'That's 'im.'

'Well show the man in! Can you fetch John Moore. What are you standing there for?'

Matthew left, shaking his head and muttering to himself.

Gruffydd's agent, John Moore had arrived over a month ago with the wool that Gruffydd had collected during the summer. Ambrose had stored the wool in his warehouse near the harbour and John Moore had stayed with him to make the arrangements for travelling. Ambrose found him to be a capable man, well used to the problems of travelling in Europe. The man himself was plain spoken and his appearance as ordinary as a starling; the sort of face and personality that left very little impression. Yet Ambrose knew, that this was a deception and that he would be glad of Moore's company on the planned journey.

That had been his intention, until today and the request of William Cecil. Ambrose had not expected Emlyn for months. A chill ran through him when he remembered that Emlyn had been educated by the Jesuits. This will make William Cecil happy, Ambrose thought, to be under the same roof as a Jesuit! Ambrose felt even colder when he also recalled the fiasco of the French ship arriving in Conwy with its suspicious cargo. He still felt uneasy about that day. He had said nothing to anyone about the pamphlets and the printing press. Ambrose prayed that his other guest, the Secretary of State, was a heavy sleeper.

Matthew returned with a visitor. He was a tall serious young man, soaked from head to foot. His brown hair dripped in front of his deep brown eyes. He walked into the room past the servant. With no introduction or apology, he said, 'I would like to speak to you in private

Mr. Chillingworth.' His voice was deep and his words accented with the Welsh of his origin.

'Go Matthew,' said Ambrose dragging a hand across his beard and rubbing his eyes. He recognised this one; he had been the other Jesuit scholar on the ship. 'Matthew bring wine, heat water and food and find some dry clothes.'

Matthew left the candles on the table and left, closing the door quietly behind him. He would have liked to slam it, but he too feared what the night had brought in.

Ambrose Chillingworth leaned back in his chair and folded his hands neatly across his round belly. Although he had seen this young man before, the meeting had been brief and Ambrose could not remember who he was. He said, 'And you are?'

'Goronwy Glyn Parry,' said the Welshman. In the stronger light, his exhaustion was evident. His skin was pale and his eyes were sunk into hollows of sleeplessness. He was visibly shivering with cold.

Ambrose said, 'Get near the fire and warm yourself, I'm cold just looking at you. You are a long way from home.'

'Yes,' Goronwy replied. He sat down on the stone hearth drawing up his knees and sinking his head on folded arms.

Ambrose looked down at him. 'Where is Emlyn Tomas?'

'He is here, seeing to the horses.' answered Goronwy. 'There's been a problem or two. We were betrayed and fled from Wales. We tried to escape through Bristol but word had arrived before us. Running further we were caught outside Glastonbury, but we managed to get away. Don't worry master Chillingworth, no one has followed us here,' he broke off with a boyish smile and then said, 'Emlyn didn't think you would make us welcome.'

'He's right, you are not welcome. You do not know what you have walked into' Ambrose grasped his arm and pulled him to his feet, feeling the icy cold of his skin under the cloth. 'Come,' he said, 'it can wait, you can tell me the tale while you both eat and dry yourselves.'

When they arrived in the kitchen, Ambrose busied himself warming wine while Goronwy stripped and rubbed himself vigorously with a towel; he was a big lad. While Martha was out of the room, Goronwy dressed in borrowed clothes that stretched at the seams across his broad back and muscular shoulders.

With a look of concern Ambrose said, 'Is Emlyn well?'

'Aye' Goronwy replied. 'but we are both exhausted it has been a terrible time and we have hardly stopped to sleep or eat.'

The room with its banked up fire, was glowing and warm. Goronwy accepted the wine offered and drained the cup before seating himself on a bench at the table.

Matthew placed a platter of bread, ham and cheese in front of him and refilled the flagon. He then stirred up the fire and placed new logs on it to dispel the cold.

With a grim smile Ambrose sat opposite Goronwy. He thought of William Cecil upstairs. With a feeling of doom he filled his wine cup, praying that he did not harbour rebellious Catholics under his roof. He said, 'I remember you from the incident in Conwy. You had returned from France with Emlyn. You had better tell me something of what this is about. Has your ambitious printing scheme failed?'

'The printing was brought to an abrupt end,' Goronwy replied. 'At first Emlyn would not have much to do with us. Do you remember the Conwy fair? When Emlyn had to show off and hit that damned bird? After that, his grandfather wished him to become a bard in the old tradition, to finish his learning. His uncle would give him no recognition or place within his home, he told him to return to France and make his life in the priesthood. We had planned the printing together, Emlyn and I while we were at the school. Once I got him away from the influence of his grandfather, I urged him to join us printing the pamphlets. He is too talented to be any man's servant and what use would being a bard be to anyone?' Goronwy paused and stretched his long legs under the table. 'It was his cousin Owain who discovered what we were doing and it was Emlyn himself who inadvertently led the dogs to where we were we worked in hiding. Now we have no choice but to return to Paris. He and I intend to become priests.'

Ambrose controlled is rising anger. He said, 'To turn England back into the arms of the Holy Church? Is that what you intend?'

.'Aye. the Stuart queen had fled Scotland and was being held prisoner in England. She was the centre for which we had all longed and prayed. It was time to raise the standard and time for us to gain her release. There are thousands of good Catholics out there who wait only for the call to arms. To rid this land of its heretical queen.'

Ambrose groaned. 'You will gain nothing by insulting her gracious majesty who, I am bound, out of loyalty to defend,' Ambrose was astonished. It was obvious that Goronwy thought him a Catholic sympathiser. Was it because he had said nothing about the press he had seen in that dark warehouse? This was possibly the worse situation he had ever found himself involved in. He voiced what William Cecil and the Privy Council all feared. 'You would place the Scottish queen on the throne of England?'

'Aye that we would,' said Goronwy, helping himself to bread and cheese, 'and bring England under the protection of the Holy Church. Failing that, the present Queen must be made to settle the succession in Mary's favour.'

Ambrose leaned forward elbows on the table. 'The Scottish Queen is discredited as you know Goronwy. Can you not see the strife this will bring? Did you plot for this at the Jesuit college with Emlyn Tomas?'

'Well yes, for four years. It was our intent all along to do this. Of course we could not know then that we would have Queen Mary to champion our cause.'

'So the Jesuits make you a traitor to your Queen and the interests of her domain. Can't you see, they poisoned you in order to gain your support, to swell their ranks?'

Goronwy controlled himself with a shudder. 'I'll not hear you speak against them. They are a courageous order, an army of loyal Catholics who defend the church against the Huguenots and the Lutherans and the fanatic-like John Knoxes. Why are we forbidden to believe as our ancestors did? Where are the priests? The monks? The faithful Roman Catholics?'

Ambrose raised his hand to calm his visitor. 'Goronwy...'

'They are here,' Goronwy continued, 'they are all here. Wales is full of them, England is full of them. If there were but one man among them to lead. Then we would overthrow the present regime and restore all to God. Now we have that leader. William Allen, a member of our order has returned from Rome with Pope's blessing to start our own school at Douai for English exiles.'

This was news to Ambrose and would be interesting to William Cecil. It portended nothing but trouble as far as Ambrose could see.

Goronwy continued, unaware of his predicament. 'Here in England we have the support of the Duke of Norfolk. He will lift his banner in the name of Christ and the Holy Church and the Northern lords will follow him.'

Ambrose stood up slowly. 'Thomas Howard Duke of Norfolk?'

'Yes,' said Goronwy. He whispered the affirmation as if suddenly in fear of being overhead.

'This is treason Goronwy,' cautioned Ambrose.

'This is no mere treason,' Goronwy answered. He leaned forward with his hands clasped as if to lend power to his own beliefs. 'What if Norfolk was to wed the Scottish Queen?'

Ambrose took a deep breath. He said 'I realise what you would like it to mean, because the North cries out for Catholic rebellion, it does not mean that it is right to throw away the peace and plenty of Elizabeth's reign. There are not two causes to be squabbled over here Goronwy but many. There are those such as yourself, who cling to the old ways before the King Henry changed it all, then those who would like to see a new Catholicism, with no allegiance to Rome and there are Protestants who have brought a completely new light on matters and who follow many different paths themselves. You can not turn back what is done.' Ambrose paused and placed his hands on the table, towering over the Welshman. He said, 'It would have been wise Goronwy, to have enquired about me before you crossed my threshold.'

Goronwy stood up suddenly. A look of horror spread across his face. 'You're a Calvinist!'

Ambrose made his way upstairs, sighing deeply with a tired sadness. There was a rim of light under William Cecil's door. It creaked open. Cecil's notary Percy emerged, like a silent shadow. Ambrose had always disliked the man instinctively. His sharp features and sour expression boded ill for anyone who crossed him. Now he paused at the top of the stair. The look he gave Ambrose seemed to be loaded with gloating spite. Obviously, he had overheard something which had aroused his suspicions.

Ambrose turned and followed for a few steps. He then turned again and walked on. He stopped and sat down half way up his own carved, oak staircase. There were times, he had learnt, when it was best to just wait.

He was certain that Percy must have been listening to Goronwy's ranting from behind the closed door. The man was a born informer. He was probably on his way now to rouse the men at arms, to arrest Goronwy and Emlyn Tomas; the misguided fools who had, like the Spanish ships, come seeking shelter only to be captured again in their haven of safety.

Cecil came out fully dressed, voicing an inquiry.

Ambrose Chillingworth rose to meet him.

Cecil caught his arm. 'Whatever have you dredged in from the cold Ambrose?' His grip tightened as they went down the stair together. 'Percy tells me you have some Catholic printers in for a visit. Could it be that you stand with a foot on each shore?'

'Don't be ridiculous William! What will you say next? That I have Spaniards in my cellar!'

After attending to the horses, Emlyn stayed in the stables in the harness room while he exchanged his wet clothes in to the ones which had been brought for him by the housekeeper, Martha. They were of better quality than anything he was used to. He was cold and so tired he could have curled up then and there and slept with the house dogs. Voices muttered in the background. He heard the deep rumble of Goronwy and the clearer voice of the merchant, Ambrose Chillingworth. He could not hear the words. He could not think clearly, for sleep tugged at all his senses. He looked around the small room. A wax candle burned steadily on a table beside him. Martha appeared at the door, in her hand was a heavy pewter jug. She signalled for him to remain silent. He heard the sound of shouting and Welsh cursing. Goronwy violently protesting. He was betraying himself with every word. The hot headed fool was inviting himself to a stretch on the rack and a hangman's rope. Emlyn moved to the door. Goronwy had probably told the merchant everything. Even so, it was hard to believe, from what he knew of the merchant, that Ambrose had betrayed them.

'They may not know you are here yet.' Martha said with a whisper.

'Who?'

'It's William Cecil. You must be touched in the head to come here with him as snug as a flea in the master's best room.'

'Cecil's here already?' Emlyn pushed her restraining hand away. 'I knew he was in Southampton, but not in this very house! What do you suppose Goronwy has talked us into now?' It was a question to himself. He took a deep ragged breath and walked through the door towards the house

The kitchen door was open and Queen's adviser stood at the table. Beside him, nearest to Emlyn, stood a thin man in the attire of a secretary. On the other side stood a short, bed-robed figure in a nightcap, the merchant Ambrose Chillingworth. On the other side of the room stood Goronwy. He was securely held by two men at arms. There were a further two holding drawn swords behind him.

Emlyn thought frantically, unless he acted now, this would all end in disaster. He summoned up his strength and nerve and raised his voice above the noise in the room. 'I would ask a favour of the honourable Secretary of State.'

When he had every one's attention, he continued, 'In exchange for that favour, I have a piece of most secret information.'

Cecil's face sharpened with interest. The words 'secret' and 'information' were like meat and drink to him. He pursed his lips shrewdly. 'Come sir, whoever you may be. You know that I must hear this secret information from you first. Then we shall see if its importance warrants bargain or favour for traitors.'

Emlyn held his gaze, for the Secretary tried to stare him down. He replied calmly, despite the rising panic he felt inside. 'That I cannot do sir. As to traitor, I acknowledge that for the difference of our loyalties, you could order our arrest and in due time watch us hang. But I doubt you would be alive to see it.'

'How dare you threaten me!' Cecil thundered His pale cheeks reddened and his brow furrowed in anger.

Emlyn shook his head. 'You misunderstand my words. I do not threaten. But I do know of a most serious threat to your life. Why else do you think we came south to seek you out?'

Cecil stared long and hard at the dark young man before him, then relaxed his tone. 'You cannot have known that I would be here, no one but my loyal servants knew of this journey. Come tell me more of this.'

As he spoke he nodded to the men who held Goronwy. They relaxed their hold on him but continued to watch him closely. Emlyn took a few paces further into the room, hoping that his faltering steps would not betray his fear. He said, 'Today we have ridden almost non-stop with Walsingham's men hard behind us. We were making for the coast hoping to take ship.'

At the mention of the name Walsingham, Cecil's interests quickened.

Emlyn continued, sensing that he had made an impression at last. 'There were seven in our party. We parted from the others, Goronwy and I came to seek you here at Southampton.'

Cecil's eyes flared in anger. 'As I said, few know that I am here today. Those who do, I trust. There is no way that you could have known.'

Emlyn lowered his voice but kept his eyes steady. 'With respect, that is perhaps your mistake and one that may prove fatal. Three of our friends were captured in Wales. They are held at Beaumaris awaiting trail. For these men and the life of Goronwy Parry and myself, I offer you a chance to preserve your own life.' Emlyn was aware of the sharp intake of breath from his companion across the room. He could almost feel Goronwy's animosity in the air between them.

'You ask for five lives in exchange for one?' Cecil laughed bitterly.

Ignoring Goronwy, Emlyn answered, 'Your own life sir, as many would agree, is worth a great deal more than that. You can afford it.'

'And if I do not agree, would you let me be murdered, in the name of God?'

'I would not see murder done in the name of God or otherwise if I can prevent it. I hold no personal war with you or the Queen, indeed, it would be foolish to do so if the welfare of England was to be considered. I think you a man of honour it would cost you little to free a handful of over enthusiastic students.'

'But what would it cost when they become an army of fanatics armed with the sword of the Holy Church and the support of the Inquisition?' Receiving no answer, Cecil continued, 'Give me the names of those who wish me harm.'

'I cannot do that until you give your word for our safety. This I will tell you, you are to be assassinated on your way back to London,' said Emlyn. 'Your betrayer is one of your own grooms. I think it unlikely that you will discover his whereabouts. By now he will be well beyond your reach. His name is Jack Blackhill.'

'Good Lord!' Cecil exclaimed. 'The man has been with me for over ten years. I have never been anything but just with him. I would never believe it of him. Are you sure it is he?'

Emlyn shivered and looked from secretary to merchant and heard the soft curses of Goronwy. He said, 'I am sure but he is not so important. There is another who wishes you dead and will be the instigator in...'

Then Goronwy launched himself across the room and hit him.

It was like blowing over a feather. He fell backwards into the arms of Martha. He slid to the floor, closed his eyes and lay still

He could have got up, but he remained where he was. His heart thumped and the blood surged through his veins as clear and fast as the rills down Erie Mynydd. Cecil would have to agree to his terms, wouldn't he?

Chapter 25 England

The day dawned grey, with a harsh wind blowing the rain clouds in from the sea. The ghostly Spanish vessels creaked at their anchorage as the fishing fleet, free as seagulls, sped past, the crew shouting derision and jeering.

Ambrose had been unable to get much sleep for the remainder of that night. His mind was in turmoil. Foremost in his thoughts was the news of his son; he knew well what happened to English seamen in the hands of Spain. If an act of war had been done against Philip of Spain, Ambrose feared that Christopher would be in an exceedingly difficult position, along with the rest of them. Now, William Cecil had asked Ambrose to go to Italy to finalise an arrangements between Queen Elizabeth and the Italian bankers concerning the considerable amount of eight-hundred thousand ducats which had been diverted from its journey to pay Alva's troops in the Netherlands. Ambrose would like to remain in England and wait until he heard word of Hawkins' fleet. In a single night, all his plans for a quiet winter, looking forward to his son's return, had fallen to ruin.

The other matter that plagued him, was the fate of the two Welsh youths. It had not been his intention to lead Goronwy into the talk that had revealed so much of the thought behind the present unrest in England. However, Queen and country came foremost. This line of thought did little to comfort Ambrose. The shared venture he had arranged with Gruffydd was now in question; if Ambrose stood by while William Cecil led Gruffydd's grandson to face charges of treason, his friendship with the Welsh bard would be over and the wool scheme, ruined before it had started. Unfortunately, William Cecil was not a man to be easily swayed from his purpose. Emlyn had come up with a good enough argument to gain freedom for himself and Goronwy, but he had given too much away before securing Cecil's word of honour.

At first light of day, Ambrose had his horse saddled and left the house before any of his guests had stirred. He owed much of his success to thoughtful organisation and planning. His mind, unlike his clock, worked with clear precision and order; no part was ever unaware of what the other was doing and why. If he was to go to Europe as Cecil had asked, there was much to be done.

His warehouse was near the water's edge, joined to a row of others. At this time of year, most were empty. The fame and fortune of the harbour town had dwindled and ship building had declined in recent years. Many of the houses lay deserted, their inhabitants drawn away by the promise of greater fortune elsewhere. Ambrose had remained. He was not fond of the busy, demanding life in London, he liked to stay on the fringe of matters, where an easy escape could be made if necessary. Southampton, he felt, would recover. Its position and harbour were to be taken advantage of.

Ignoring the sleeping watchman, Ambrose opened the double doors of the warehouse. He lit the lamps and carried one to the back to inspect his store of cloth. The room was filled with dark, looming objects, strange shapes and foreign scents. Ambrose lifted the lamp above the stack of Welsh friezes, finely woven cloth and raw wool; dry and well cared for by Gruffydd's agent. There was enough here for a modest cart load or the packs of eight mules. The value would quadruple by the time it reached Italy. Ambrose had already been contacted by an agent in Antwerp, the man represented a Venetian company who had asked him if he would be prepared to do just that. He had not thought that he would be making the journey in winter, it held very little appeal and lessened his chances of success.

Therefore, rather than risk all, other quick profits could be made. Weapons never failed and Ambrose just happened to have six boxes of French guns. He wished he had more time but he was prepared to take the risk, no Englishman would object to him providing arms for the hounded Huguenots; at least no Protestant Englishman. He had done so before. He wondered if there was enough time to arrange a rendezvous at sea with a Huguenot privateer. As it was these privateers who had driven the Spanish fleet to seek shelter here, they were probably still near to the English coast. Ambrose sent a fishing boat out immediately to make inquiries.

Before he turned for home, he called at houses he knew, waking their members with an unwelcome cheerfulness. Wherever he thought it would be profitable, he told of his intention to make a winter journey to Geneva. He collected some letters, arranged to collect others and even saw a rider sent hastily away to bring word from further afield. At all times, Ambrose visited only those who would gain from their silence. A courier, with a reputation such as his, would be highly valued at this unpopular time of year, when the flow of news was slow and the political intrigues of the courts of Europe flourished.

Next, with an itching suspicion, he rode back to the water's edge where the Spanish ships lay awaiting their fate. It had begun to rain with the lightening sky. He noticed a smaller ship loading at the harbour. It was the *Lauris Nobilis*, a small trading ship that made frequent trips across the Channel in all weather; she was obviously getting under way. To Ambrose, the coincidence clearly bore the mark of William Cecil. It seemed that he was sure Ambrose would agree and had already made preparations for the departure. Annoyed, Ambrose nevertheless contacted the sailing master and arranged for his stock to be brought and loaded aboard. He had been expected and it seemed that he had priority, the sailing master was most solicitous. While arranging matters, Ambrose pulled at his ear to hide his amusement, then he went off to talk to the few fishermen who were still on the harbour.

On returning to his town house, he found Martha up. She was in the kitchen busying herself with the morning tasks. 'And how are all our merry antagonists this morning?' Ambrose asked on entering.

She turned round, armed with a runcible spoon. 'Master Cecil is still resting, that's good all things considered. Matthew has gone to arouse the Welshman and the guards. The other Welshman is in Matthews' room. I dare say he'll be as right as rain with a good nights sleep behind him. Leastwise, fit enough for Master Cecil to have them hanged.'

Ambrose shook his head and peered into the pot she was stewing. 'What are you going to feed them on girl?' He backed away in mock horror.

Martha, who was not a girl, but liked being called such, blushed to the lace of her bonnet. 'It's naught but a bit of porridge.'

'Well that should keep our Welsh friends happy, but you'll have to come up with something better for the Secretary of State,' said Ambrose, 'Whatever will he think of us Martha? There's some fish in the basket.'

It was with some reluctance that Ambrose sought the door to his servant's room. With a nod to the armed man outside the door, he entered softly and stood looking down at the sleeping figure tangled with bedclothes. Emlyn's dark hair lay on the pillow like displaced feathers, his thick lashes lay still in sleep. To Ambrose, he looked like a child.

He remembered the talks he'd had with Emlyn before he left Wales, when they had sat around the hearth drinking Gruffydd's wine form Calais. Ambrose had been surprised at the mind Emlyn had revealed during those talks, surprised, because he had first thought the boy shallow and foolish.

Gruffydd thought a great deal of his grandson and would not readily forgive Ambrose if he deserted Emlyn now. What if this was my own son? Ambrose asked himself; indeed, it was quite probable that Christopher faced a similar fate. Hadn't Emlyn shown an unexpected loyalty to Queen and country, when he had been so outspoken the night before? Ambrose smiled grimly to himself, knowing that he would attempt to free Emlyn and the vociferous Goronwy from William Cecil. Perhaps Goronwy had been speaking the truth when he said that they were both going to become priests. Ambrose was surprised at the depth of his disappointment that this thought aroused, but he had not spoken directly to Emlyn yet, and Goronwy's enthusiasm concerning his friend may not be entirely correct.

There was a stirring from the corner of the room. Ambrose turned and to his surprise, found William Cecil sitting on Matthews' chair with an open book on his knee. Saying nothing, Ambrose stood and watched him.

Cecil returned his gaze with a look of amusement. 'What's wrong my friend? Are you wondering whether I sit here out of compassion or malice?'

'Oh. Out of compassion assuredly. In which case,' said Ambrose in speculation, 'You will have no objection to me taking him with me when I leave for Europe. Otherwise I may find it inconvenient to travel.' He held the door open. 'Shall we talk about this outside?'

Cecil rose and walked past him reflecting just how determined this man could be. Outside the room, he turned with a wary sigh and removed a sealed letter from the folds of his doublet. He said, 'We are all players in a royal game here. I am instructed to deliver this into your hands.'

Ambrose knew the seal. His lifted his eyes to meet the pale gaze of William Cecil and fixed him with a glare of contempt. It was a game, this move gave Cecil the advantage where the merchant had held it but a moment before. He turned his back and led the way up the stairs. After a moment's hesitation, Cecil followed.

In the merchant's room above, where celestial bodies chimed the hour, at present without skipping a beat, Ambrose held the letter tempting the newly lit fire to consume it.

'Do you intend to burn it?' Cecil entered behind him.

'I don't need to open it. I can well guess its contents. It's a request from the Queen. You should have given it to me last night.'

'I thought to persuade you,' answered Cecil. He sat in the same chair where he thought he had concluded this very subject the night before. 'I wanted your choice to be a free one. We have known each other a long time. Ambrose, I need you to do this.'

'So not liking my bargain, you now try to compel me by royal signature!' With a deliberate gesture Ambrose tossed the letter into the flames. He said, 'William, I am a merchant. I know it is true that I have dabble here and there in my own interest, but I have helped you on many occasions in the past, I have been your informant and your agent. What I do is my patriotic duty for the interests of Queen and country.'

Cecil released a scoff of laughter. 'Is this task not of the same nature? For Queen and country? Where now is the difference?'

'Not at the cost of the lives of the two young men you have under guard. They are too unimportant to be a source of real threat to you, seek it in another quarter. Let me send Emlyn and Goronwy safely out of the country; then I will do as you and our respected Queen request. Was the letter an order?'

'That we will never know will we? As you seem to have allowed the fire to reduce it to ashes,' said Cecil patiently. 'Why be so stubborn on this?'

'I will tell you truthfully. The boy's grandfather is a trusted friend, you have heard me speak of him often enough. I buy Welsh wool from him. In fact William, you have dealt with the man this very year, over the matter of gaining recognition for the Welsh festival of bards and poets.'

Cecil looked up with surprise. 'Is this the same boy? The grandson of Gruffydd Hiraethog? I have met this boy before then. It was on the occasion of Queen Mary's wedding to the Spanish Prince, God rot him body and soul! The boy was a child then, accompanied from Europe by a Franciscan monk.'

Ambrose sat down opposite smiling. 'I thought that you were in the tower yourself at that time?'

Cecil returned the smile. 'Well I did spend too much time there for comfort, but not on that occasion. I remember the incident though, I knew the friar fairly well then though I did not meet the boy. I recall hearing that he played the spinet for the Queen's ladies,' he paused remembering. 'So Gruffydd Hiraethog is your interest in the affair. I wonder did the old bard win a golden chair or whatever it is they award their poets.'

'No,' Ambrose replied. 'He'd already won his chair in the days when the Eisteddfod was held in secret. It's made of oak anyway, not gold.'

'Meaning that the pagan ceremony continued to be held in spite of the Queen's ban?' Cecil laughed, obviously in better spirits. 'I received word of the boy on odd occasions. He was sent to France for his Catholic education if I remember.'

'To the College de Clermont,' said Ambrose. He waited for the Secretary's reaction.

Cecil's joviality left him, he frowned. 'That college is run by Jesuits! All France is one big melting pot of plotting and intrigues at the moment; Catherine de Medici rules instead of her imbecile son; de Guise schemes with the Scots; the Huguenots beg for England's assistance and the Jesuits worm their way into every nook and cranny of every ruling court in Europe and beyond.'

'It was a mess and still is,' agreed Ambrose sadly. He loved France nearly as much as England. 'The wars of religion have turned the countryside into wasteland. Like the religious wars in the Netherlands, bloodshed and suffering everywhere. Are we to repeat it here?'

But Cecil was still thinking about Jesuits. 'Paris had no welcome for the Society of Jesus,' he said 'The Theological Faculty firmly suggested that they would be better sent to the furthest corners of the earth as Papal vassals to evangelize the unbelieving pagans. Though what those poor lost souls have done to deserve the Jesuits, I can't imagine!' Cecil's expression became serious as he continued. 'There is no place for them here either! This is what I must guard against Ambrose. You are right, we will not have the bloodshed of France and the Netherlands here in England. Many, I know, have fled England. I am sorry Ambrose, I cannot let these boys go to join them. Who knows what this Emlyn Tomas and his like will bring back when they return?'

'In all innocence William, the boy is no political trouble maker. He showed you that well enough last night.'

'Is that how you see it my friend? Jesuits do not live quiet lives. The boy who spoke so boldly last night is not the stuff of which quiet monks are made.'

'A rash judgement, surely? He thought only of the safety of his companions. He is but a scholar. There is no malice here William, just some misplaced loyalty.'

'Do not mistake me Ambrose, I am no tyrant.. However there is much we could learn from these people. For example, how could he have known that I was here yesterday? For a youth of his age the denial of freedom alone would be enough to open his secrets. We would have no need to harm him.'

Ambrose stared down at his hands. He believed Cecil wished no physical harm to the boys. But even he could not guarantee that others would not wish otherwise. Hatred for the Jesuits was growing daily. Walsingham had no scruples when it came to gaining information. Cecil had always favoured the man; he had trained him as his successor. Ambrose decided to try another approach to persuade Cecil. Ambrose smiled. He said, 'Why not let Emlyn accompany me on this mission?'

'No. He is a Jesuit, scholar or not, it would be nothing but foolish to take one such as he on your present task.'

'Hear me out. Assuming the plot to kill you is true, God knows you have enemies enough; it would not be the first time. Emlyn Tomas could well have saved your life. As a merchant, I say you owe him the price demanded.'

'He knows more Ambrose. It's not only my life that is at stake here. If the Catholics rebelled and Spain invaded from the Netherlands and from Ireland, England would be squeezed between them and crushed. Curse the day the Scottish Queen sought refuge in England! She sits in her tower like a temptress, appealing prettily to the foreign Catholic princes for her relief. Any plot we can uncover, places England one step ahead of her enemies.'

'What about confiscating the bullion ships William? That could be seen as retaliation for the attack on Hawkins ships. The attack on Hawkins ships was in retaliation for Rio del la Hacha. It could all accelerate until it becomes outright war. It is as clear as day.'

'Perhaps, but not before we have put our own house in order. If there is to be war it will be when we are ready for it. We must retain control of the situation. I distrust the Duke of Norfolk and the Northern earls. They are solidly Catholic and would take the field for Spain. If they succeeded, they would try to persuade the Queen to return to the authority of the Pope. Failing that, they would put the Scottish Queen on the throne of England and throw all we have achieved to the dogs. I have to know the schemers Ambrose. I would not wish it, but the welfare of a boy cannot be considered against this.'

'It's a dangerous situation surely,' Ambrose said thoughtfully. 'If the Northern earls rebel there is also the danger of French interference, for the Scottish Queen has the support of Guise. Scotland has always favoured France rather than England and they could allow an army to land on their shores.'

'Not that dangerous yet my friend,' Cecil replied with a grim smile. 'France has greater fear of Spain than of England. Consider this, if Philip has to borrow eight hundred thousand ducats from the Italians to pay his troops in the Netherlands, he is no position to finance another war here in England. If we withhold that pay, unrest amongst Alva's troops is sure to follow. Any trouble caused for Alva is an advantage for us.'

'You are right of course,' said Ambrose, puzzled that he had not thought of it. He stretched and yawned, aware that Cecil was deliberately slipping from the subject. But Ambrose was not yet willing to let the matter drop. He said, 'The boy knows nothing of me other than that I am the merchant trader who buys his grandfather's wool. If he is as loyal to the Queen as he showed, would he not make the perfect agent? If not, he need only accompany me as far as Paris. Then I shall leave him at the college. He has helped you already, you never know, he may yet be of greater value to you in Catholic France than as your prisoner here.'

'I will not take the risk.' Cecil was adamant.

Ambrose played his last card. 'Well, it is not a good time for me to cross the Alps anyway. I shall most probably spend the winter there. I advise you to find someone else for your mission.'

William Cecil stood and walked to the window in obvious agitation. Time was never his own. He would have to leave within the hour. Already he had made preparations to return. He had sent one of his own men to gather more men at arms from the walls of Southampton. They were to return the way he had come, in hope of springing the trap that was being set for him. If they succeeded, he would not be lacking sources of information, perhaps more valuable than anything Emlyn Tomas had to offer. It was not really this however that made him to change his mind. He knew that he could drive Ambrose no further. This would surely mark the turning point for the end of their friendship and that was bad enough. But it would also be the end of a mutually profitable relationship. Ambrose knew all the right merchant-bankers and the men of commercial power in Europe. It was the bankers who first heard of the intrigues among the rulers of Europe; it was merchants like Ambrose who heard second.

Without turning he said, 'Do you know the kind of people who now seek the safety of England's shore as they flee from Alva and the Spanish inquisition?'

'Dutch artisans,' said Ambrose, 'craftsmen, millers, weavers, dyers, clothiers and bankers, these are not artisans of course but their craft is valuable to England just the same.'

'Then do you see what keeping that money away from Spain would mean?'

Ambrose answered simply, 'Further hardship in the Netherlands causes further disruption of trade. If the trade moves here, England may grow and prosper. London could become the banking centre for Northern Europe.'

Cecil nodded. 'Then, for this and our friendship's sake, take your young harper Ambrose, and the other with him. They will not be welcome to return to England. I will see what I can do for the others the youth spoke of in Wales, if no mortal deed has been done, I will work towards their release.'

'Then there is much to do, if I am to leave for Geneva within three days.' Ambrose answered. They both smiled and then broke into laughter as if their long friendship had not been on the brink of disaster.

Cecil said, 'Ambrose you have not got three days. You will find...'

'That there is a ship already waiting? The *Lauris Nobilis* is loaded with my cloth since this morning. We shall sail with tomorrow's noon tide. I suppose I had better take Matthew along to look after the Welshmen and I have a good overseer in John Moore.'

Cecil shook his head in admiration. He came forward and grasped his arm. 'You have made me a happy man and the Queen will show her gratitude.'

'God preserve her from her enemies, Catholic, French, Spanish or otherwise,' said Ambrose deliberately.

'Chess is not a game of kings at all,' said William Cecil pensively. 'We would all do well to remember that the queen has more power on the board than any other piece.'

It was not long before William Cecil Secretary of State, was mounted and surrounded by a company of archers. A few of Ambrose Chillingworth's most trusted men accompanied him.. The day was still young and the rain had lessened to a slow drizzle hazing the landscape with damp greys and the murky browns of mud and mouldy leaves. Trees poked the sky with skeletal branches and curls of grey smoke rose from sodden thatch and glistening tile.

Before he set off on an indirect route to London, Cecil bade farewell to the merchant in the courtyard. Ambrose returned the embrace, they would remain friends, but Ambrose had no doubt now how thin he had stretched the bonds of friendship. He felt a strain between them which had not existed before.

Reading his thoughts, Cecil said, 'In my place, I can afford few friends. The one's I have I value highly. Let us hope that in this I have not been wrong.'

'Anything I learn will reach you,' answered Ambrose. 'Keep an eye at your back William and send me word of my son on the *Judith* as soon as you may.'

Cecil nodded and handed him a worn satchel. 'All you need to know is here,' he said. 'Conceal it well for if the Spaniards get hold of it, your chances of survival are not worth a wager. Be careful Ambrose they are already looking for their lost ships.'

'Who else knows of this?' asked Ambrose anxiously.

'Her majesty, myself and two others. They are trusted, you have no fear of leakage. But, a warning, Don Gueru de Spes may well guess our intent. I know that he has written to Alva concerning the ships and urged him to act; in what way, I have yet to learn. I hope that Alva will do nothing without word from Philip. So a little caution will not go amiss. Behind you I will send a courier or two.' Cecil swung into the saddle with a groan of protest. Looking down he said, 'Your greatest danger lies with your own choice of travelling companions.'

As if summoned, the dark, fragile youth walked from the house, his pace measured and slow. He paused at Cecil's nervous horse, grasping the rein. 'Master Cecil,' he said in his musical voice, 'we had reached an agreement. I parted with some of the goods before a price was settled. We are not held, but I would still have your word before I give you the rest.'

Cecil studied him for a moment. 'You have your freedom and that of your companion. The case of the others, I give you my word, shall be looked into the moment I return. The men who wait to ambush me will be apprehended.' Cecil paused and smoothed his beard. 'You however, and Goronwy Parry,' he said firmly, 'must leave England forever. If you return, your lives will be forfeit.'

Emlyn dropped his hand and stood in thought. Banishment! Well, he had already burnt his boats behind him when he had left Wales. Still, this exile was not to his liking. Resigned, he said, 'Those who would change the fate of England have power and influence. Until they find a strong man to lead them, I think you need have no fear.'

'And what of the Scottish Queen?'

'She is no leader, just a prize for the winner surely? With her comes power over England.' Emlyn drew a scrap of paper from his sleeve and handed it to the Queen's adviser. 'This,' he said, 'is for the lives you have saved and for the lives of others you will try to save. It is also for mine, I am grateful. God's speed on your journey.' He stepped back and then added, 'You might look under his floor boards and find what you need to stop his plotting.'

Cecil nodded curtly, gathered his reins and rode out of the courtyard. It was not until Southampton lay far behind him, that he unfolded the scrap of paper and read the name written there. He smiled grimly. His position was stronger returning to London that it had been when he left court. 'A profitable journey,' he muttered to himself. 'God will, that Ambrose has one also.'

Emlyn walked across the courtyard and entered the gloomy interior of the stable. The smell of damp straw and horse manure assailed him. The first thing he saw, was the broad back of Goronwy. The guards had gone with William Cecil, gone too, were the chains that had imprisoned Goronwy through the night. He was prisoner no longer, but he sat where he had spent the night, as if he was still tied and guarded.

'We are free to go to France,' Emlyn said from the doorway.

Goronwy did not turn around. He said, 'At what cost have you bought us our freedom? Who else's life have you so willingly squandered?'

'Don Gueru de Spes,' Emlyn replied.

Goronwy did not answer. Emlyn could see the tightness across his shoulders, and the shuddering breath that ran through him as he fought to control his anger.

'He is an Ambassador so will suffer nothing worse than house arrest,' said Emlyn. He walked into the stable and stood where Goronwy could see him. 'Cecil will have him watched and his correspondence opened, that's all.'

'That's all!' Goronwy raised his head. 'You fool Emlyn! Do you realise what you have done?'

'Of course I do,' Emlyn said righteously. 'William Cecil will not lie murdered on the road. I cannot bring myself to believe that you would agree to such a sly killing Goronwy.'

'You have severed our connection with Alva and the King of Spain!'

'De Spes came to England to answer the accusations concerning the treatment of our English Ambassador in Spain, who had spoken unwisely against the Pope. De Spes came here to preserve the peace between England and Spain. So why does he want Cecil dead? No answer? I'll tell you then. Because he wants England back for King Philip. He wants us under Spanish rule. And that Goronwy is not the return to Catholicism that you envisage.'

'That is not true!' Goronwy thumped his balled fist down on the bench where he sat. 'He intends to overthrow the Queen's government and place Mary Stuart on the throne. Getting rid of Cecil is the first move to bring England under the influence of Rome not Spain. What have you done Emlyn?'

'Mary Stuart will not be allowed to go free,' said Emlyn folding his arms stubbornly across his chest. 'Have you ever wondered why she came to England at all? Why did she not flee to France? The King of France is her brother-in-law. Her uncles are the duke of Guise and the Cardinal of Lorraine. If she really wanted to make herself queen of England that is where she would have gone to raise an army.'

'She is a symbol in this country Emlyn, a head of the Catholic Church.'

'We have argued this before,' said Emlyn, 'and I do not intend to do so now. We have our freedom Goronwy, freedom to return to France.'

Goronwy leapt to his feet trembling with rage. His eyes smouldered, red-rimmed from lack of sleep. 'You are an irresolute coward Emlyn Tomas!' The words came out as a snarl. 'Your loyalties fluctuate at the slightest whim!'

'I do not consider the rack or the hangman's rope a slight whim,' Emlyn retorted. 'If I had not given Cecil the names of his would-be-murders, we would not be here now, free to escape to France and...'

Goronwy did not allow him to finish. 'We would have been freed on the road when our friends, whom you have so cheaply sold, would have attacked Cecil.'

'It is unlikely that they would have met with success,' said a different voice from the doorway. Ambrose Chillingworth walked up to them. 'William Cecil is a cautious man. He is well aware of the dangers that threaten him. Incidentally, how did you get his groom to tell you of his whereabouts?'

'I do not know,' Emlyn answered.

'Then how did you find out? I thought you were fleeing from Walsingham's men,' said the merchant.

'We had help along the way,' Emlyn explained with some reluctance.

Goronwy stepped towards him threateningly. 'If you speak another word of this,' he said, his voice grating savagely, 'I swear to God I will grind you in to this floor until you are unrecognisable! Faithless bastard!'

'Come now,' said Ambrose, alarmed by the intensity of the situation. 'Goronwy you betrayed yourself to me last night by your own big mouth. You are fortunate that I said nothing to the Secretary of State concerning our conversation. But much of it was heard by his notary. If we are to be travelling companions I trust that an amicable relationship be found between the two of you.'

'Travelling companions?' Emlyn looked at him with the hint of a smile..

Ambrose looked at him intently. 'What are you running from?'

It was Goronwy who answered, his voice still bitter. 'I told you last night, Emlyn here led the sheriff's men right to where we had hidden the printing press.'

Emlyn sat down on the bench with an exasperated sigh. He cradled his head in his hands as if it was aching. 'I did not do so intentionally.' he explained. 'My cousin Owain found out about the Catholic printing. When I rode to warn Goronwy and the others, Owain followed with the sheriff's men. I like a fool led them right to the printing press. Unfortunately there were more people there than I guessed. Resisting capture a fight ensued. Some of our own people were killed. In the confusion Goronwy and I and a few others managed to escape. Those who remained were captured. The killing was unjust for we were unarmed. I hold myself to blame for it.'

'As well you should!' Goronwy did not add to the tale.

Emlyn dropped his hands and looked up at him. Since that terrifying incident, they had hardly spoken to each other without argument. Goronwy burned with resentment and accusation. They had never been able to rest long. They had been followed, chased and hunted until the journey became like a nightmare.

'Did Gruffydd send you to me?' Ambrose asked.

Emlyn released a heartfelt sigh and shook his head. 'We had no intention at first of coming here. Then we found help with a Catholic family and discovered through them that William Cecil was travelling here in secret. Goronwy got caught up in the plot for his demise.' Emlyn stood up and faced the man he had fled from Wales with. He said, 'Goronwy I am sorry but it was always my intention to bring warning to Cecil, not to see him killed.'

This was too much for Goronwy. 'You black-hearted traitor!' He swung his fist at Emlyn, as he had the night before.

This time, Emlyn was expecting it. He dodged back out of Goronwy's reach. Goronwy did not follow up his attack. Instead, he stormed out of the stable, his face flushed with anger and his fists clenched at his sides.

'What will he do now?' Ambrose asked gently.

Emlyn did not say anything. For a long time he stood still. Then, turning slowly, he walked across the floor and came to rest by the door. Then he said quietly, 'He will come to France. He is no fool and knows that the fight here is over for now.'

'And you Emlyn? Do you intend to return to the Jesuits?'

Emlyn took a quick breath and held it for a moment. His eyes followed Goronwy's retreating back. He said, 'Goronwy seems to have switched his fiery zeal to the saving of my soul. Goronwy believes that they will guide me back to the straight and narrow and show me the error of my ways. After all this I don't know what will happen, though I have said I will return with him.'

Ambrose shook his head sadly. 'Well I am taking the wool. I have John Moore to manage your part in the scheme, but I would rather that you came too.'

Emlyn turned, his expression a mixture of disbelief and joy. 'You're taking the wool now?'

Ambrose nodded. 'I am never a man to miss an opportunity.'

'In winter?'

Ambrose shrugged. 'So it is winter. I have journeyed in worst weather than anything England can produce, and all for the sake of trade. What is a little cold discomfort in the face of profit?'

BOOK TWO

The Ice Maiden

Chapter 26 English Channel

The sea was a tapestry of dancing, froth-crested waves. The rain clouds had gone leaving an ice-clear sky. The wind snapped the sails, rattling the rigging and snatching at anything that was left loose. The English coast was still close, although they had been at sea for two hours; it was as if the *Lauris Nobilis* was reluctant to reach her destination. Ambrose had made this crossing on countless occasions and he feared that the rendezvous that had been arranged would be missed if the ship continued in this sluggish way. His cloth was stored in the hold. Gruffydd's manager, John Moore stayed with the cargo; he had taken on the responsibility willingly and Ambrose was glad that he had come on the voyage.

Ambrose was huddled in a buff coat, padded with quilting and collared in fur. He sat at a tiny desk in his cabin, attempting to scribble letters. His gloved hand fumbled with quill and ink in an attempt to match the rhythm of the sea. He looked across the cabin to where the six unmarked boxes stood, one on top of the other, boxes packed with wheel-lock muskets. The guns were new and were ironically, French. They had been placed in the cabin so that he could keep an eye on them. On the voyage, he expected to deliver guns to Jacques de Sores, a captain of the Huguenot privateers. Under the command of the Prince of Conde. The Huguenots had made the port of La Rochelle their own and from here the Protestant privateers were free to ply their trade on Catholic shipping. They were practically in control of the Narrow Seas, and had driven the Spanish wages fleet to seek the deceptive safety of England's shore.

Before the *Lauris Nobilis* reached France, she was to meet with a Dutch galleon, *La Huguenotte*, captained by Jacques de Sores. Ambrose would send the boxes across by rowing boat and they would disappear into the hold, leaving no trace of the purchase. There were risks involved but these were not as great as they would be if Ambrose took the arms to a hostile port. What was unfortunate now, was that if the *Lauris Nobilis* continued to sail like a barrel, she would never make the rendezvous.

Abandoning his efforts to write, Ambrose stood up and pulled on a velvet cap with ear flaps, tying the strings under his chin. Grasping his cloak tightly about him, he left his cabin and fought the wind all the way up to the poop deck. Teeth to the wind, he located the sailing master and pinned him to the rail with a long accusing finger. 'Get this foul-bottomed tub on her way and earn the coin you are paid with or by God, by the time I have finished with you, you'll be fortunate to get command of an apple in a bath tub!'

Flinching as the finger jabbed painfully beneath his Adam's apple, the sailing master rose to his full height, a head taller than his antagonist. 'Master Chillingbone I think I should know how to...'

'Well it is quite obvious that you don't!' Ambrose screamed. 'Put out more sail and run before the wind or I'll stuff you in a barrel and have you dragged behind all the way to le Havre. And, if you call me Chillingbone again I'll dispense with the barrel and drag you by your miserable entrails!'

Risking life and limb the sailing master replied, 'I am not bound for le Havre. You did not know?'

'Oh?' Ambrose lowered his finger. 'Are we out for a day's sailing then? To take the air as benefits our health?'

'It is more than my life's worth,' pleaded the seaman. 'The crew, master Chill...Chill, they will not go near there as they fear the Death.'

'The plague? That was over four years ago dizzard!'

'Nonetheless,' insisted the man, hands open in supplication, 'the crew will not go anywhere near le Havre. We have no choice, the harbour at le Havre is closed to English ships. The *Lauris Nobilis* is bound for Dieppe.'

'Was this known before we left Southampton?' Ambrose kept the worry out of his voice. What if they missed the Dutch ship because they were following a different sea route? He would be left with six boxes of guns when he arrived in Dieppe. If he managed to avoid discovery there, he would still have to contact Sir Nicholas Throckmorton, the English Ambassador in Paris, in order to find a way of disposing of the weapons.

'Master Chillingworth?' This inquiry came from the seaman who had loaded Ambrose's wool the day before. His name was William Moon of Gravesend. He was a thick-set man with wide, sloping shoulders and a thatch of coal black hair falling in front of his eyes. He knew about the guns and the arrangement for the disposal of them, Ambrose had worked with Moon before. 'The master's right,' the man added. 'It is unwise for an English ship to be seen near le Havre.'

'Even a scow like this?' Ambrose's worries mounted.

'We've been using to Dieppe or Calais these past months,' Will Moon replied reassuringly. He offered Ambrose a conspiratorial wink.

'So be it,' said Ambrose. He understood well enough the terrors that every one felt about that unforgiving scythe of death that had killed most of the English troops that had landed at le Havre to support the Huguenots. The plague had travelled back with those who survived to reap anew on England's shore. He had also been aware of the possibility of disruption to English shipping. 'Be it Dieppe, Calais or le Havre,' he said, 'we still have to reach there. I suggest Ship-master, that you sail closer to the wind.'

The sailing master raised his voice above the wind and shouted orders in a mixture of guttural French and dockside English.

Ambrose nodded with satisfaction. He grasped cloak and cap and fought the wind back to his cabin and shelter. Above him the sails broadened as the ship heeled up lighter to the stiff breeze of the Channel. The forked lion pennant of England writhed and curled at the change of direction.

On entering the cabin he discovered that his servant Matthew had found food and had cleared a space on the table. Goronwy Glyn Parry had been silent and sullen since the start of the voyage. He sat under the dim light with a chicken bone in one fist and a wine cup in the other. Ambrose studied the Welshman for a moment. Goronwy had offered no thanks for his rescue from the clutches of William Cecil. On being informed that he and Emlyn would be sailing for France with Ambrose, he had merely said 'Good. Then I shall have ample opportunity to rid our cause of a traitor.'

From the way he sat now, in a shroud of determined gloom, Ambrose believed that was just what he intended to do. Emlyn Thomas was nowhere to be seen. 'This voyage,' said Ambrose, 'has made a bad start. I don't like the look of the sky either.' Turning to Matthew he added, 'Where is our other fine seaman, Emlyn Tomas?'

Matthew helped him struggle out of his cloak and handed him a plate of food. 'Emlyn? Sick as a dog an' gone to throw up over the side. There is a storm brewed in 'ell just about to descend on us an' all this tacking about is getting t' nowhere.'

'The captain of this scow is an incompetent buffoon!' Ambrose replied, 'still, we are moving now and may well miss the storm.'

Matthew said, 'I knew that meddlesome Cecil would send us willy nilly, off on some godforsaken journey.'

Ambrose looked at him patiently. 'Keep your views to yourself Matthew Wheatland or I'll have you dropped in le Havre, where I hear the Death reigns still and there's Spaniards all over the place.'

'Aye an' there's Spaniards runnin' up and down the Narrow Seas an' all,' said Matthew. 'Seems they's lost somthin' You wouldna know what all that's about?'

'If you're that keen to be elsewhere Matthew Wheatland, I'd be obliged if you threw yourself overboard.' Ambrose finished eating in silence while Matthew mumbled about everything he could think of.

Behind the ship, the coast of England diminished and disappeared behind a curtain of rain. On a new course, sailing closer to the wind, the *Lauris Nobilis* began to show her paces. She breasted the troughs with white foam streaming astern, as if pulled by dolphins. Emlyn sat on the creaking boards under the rigging. He was huddled, sea-splashed and preoccupied, among the barrels and fish baskets.

Finding him there, Ambrose sat on a barrel out of the wind and regarded him curiously. 'I'd say from he look of you,' he said, 'that you are not a man used to crossing the waves.'

Emlyn's face was green, his grey-blue eyes returned the look from the hollows into which they had retreated. He offered a sickly grin. 'I do it all the time.'

Ambrose gazed out across the wind tossed waves. The ship was away like a gull now, fleeing the soft pinks and murky greys of the coming storm. The sea was rough and winter grey. Ambrose wondered about the earlier delay and whether the sailing master was not quite the buffoon he had thought him. What if the sailing master knew about the prearranged rendezvous and sought to avoid it?

Emlyn took a deep breath to settle his heaving stomach. 'I hope we can reach France before I feel compelled to throw myself overboard.'

Ambrose smiled. 'Knowing the sailing master, I find that unlikely. The man's as wicked as they come, he'd sell his grandmother to a Turk for the price of a jug of ale.'

Emlyn wasn't listening. Heaving himself to the rail and hanging over the side, he was convulsed with retching until he collapsed gagging on a muffled curse.

Ambrose felt obliged to hold an ankle to prevent the poor innocent from spilling overboard. He hauled him in like a fish and settled him to sleep on the damp comfort of rope and canvas. It was hard to equate this sickly figure to the one that had performed those acrobatics to prevent the discovery of the printing press at Conwy harbour. Emlyn seemed a youth of extraordinary talent, yet he didn't seem aware of his potential. He was intelligent enough to see beyond the boundaries set for him by the Jesuits and by his friend Goronwy. But was he astute enough to make a good spy?

The answer to that would depend on whether Emlyn intended to rejoin the Jesuits with Goronwy. Ambrose was half tempted to take Emlyn under his wing and teach him the art of espionage.

In the late afternoon the wind still tore at the rigging and shrouds. The coast of France lay like a smudge of grey on the horizon. A black ship loomed out of the sea from the south and made her way stealthily towards the *Lauris Nobilis.* In his cabin, Ambrose heard the voice of the watch calling out the hour. Matthew dozed near the door, his brows even in sleep were knit in a frown. Above them, came the sound of pounding feet, running across the deck. There was a note of alarm in the babble of voices.

Ambrose awoke his servant and went up on deck. The first thing they saw was the dark shape of the approaching vessel. On light topsails only, the ship bore up to them with ports open with the black eyes of her cannon gleaming in the sunlight. There was a thunderous boom from her guns. A cannon ball plopped into the sea ahead of the *Lauris Nobilis* sending up a plume of water like the spouting of a sea monster. There followed shouts and clunking sounds. Soon the *Lauris Nobilis* lay hove-to, head to the wind.

'Lord save us!' Matthew exclaimed. 'Will you look at the size of 'er. She's closing in. If she's pirate then we're as good as dead. We'll greet the morning at the bottom of the sea if we greet it at all. We gotta 'ave a blind watchman 'ere. I've a mind to throttle the swine, 'ere 'ave this.' With a gap-toothed grin, he handed the merchant an arquebus. 'I'm not going to meet me maker without a black soul or two to bargain me way to 'eaven.'

All the crew who could be spared, were taking up positions for defence. This was a futile action considering the size of the galleon. The *Lauris Nobilis* was of little value and not expecting trouble. They carried no cannon and there were only four archers aboard. No more guns boomed across the water. It seemed for a moment that the galleon would sail by, on her way to whatever illicit cove she had business in. But as she drew abreast of them, she backed sheets and lay head to the wind. John Moore came up on the deck and stood silently beside Ambrose; taking in the situation without voicing questions. He held a drawn sword in his hand. They waited, silent and frozen from poop to mermaid prow.

Ambrose heard the rattle of anchor chain clear across the water and muffled voices calling. 'Well she can board us or sink us as she pleases,' said John Moore. He pushed back his thinning hair and narrowed his eyes.

Fortunately, Ambrose knew the ship's purpose: this was *La Huguenotte*, captained by Jacques de Sores; to whom he had sent word with a fishing boat before he had left Southampton. Ambrose had been alarmed at first, on seeing the size of the galleon. He reasoned that the fisherman must have got his message through and every effort had been made to meet the English ship. Six boxes of new firearms were worth the trouble and on these seas, the Dutch privateers held domination. Much of the cargo they took from Catholic ships was delivered to Plymouth. Jacques de Sores had often sailed with John Hawkins and between them and the machinations of William Cecil, they commanded a navy of considerable strength.

Signals passed between the ships. Ambrose turned to Matthew. 'The boxes in the cabin, go down and get them and bring them up.'

'What?' Matthew's expression was one of suspicion.

'I would be glad to help,' said Moore.

Ambrose turned to him, wondering if he could trust the man. After a moments thought, he said, 'I would rather you stayed with the cloth, Mr. Moore. We do not know whether we face trouble, but it would be best to be prepared.'

'Of course,' Moore replied. He sauntered off. Ambrose had noticed how fond the man was a whistling.

Ambrose waited until he was out of sight before he turned his attention back to his servant. 'The boxes contain guns. They are the reason why the ship is here firing across our bows,' Ambrose explained simply. 'Don't argue with me Matthew there is no time.'

'I might 'ave guessed,' said Matthew with a heartfelt sigh. 'Am I to carry 'em up on my own?' By then they had been joined by Will Moon, who had winked at the merchant earlier. He offered to assist but warned them both to be watchful. 'I have a feeling,' he said, 'that the ship master may know something of your plans Mr. Chillingworth.'

'There's not a great deal he can do about it if he does,' said Ambrose. 'These are Protestant waters.'

In the cabin, Emlyn had recovered from the worse of the sea sickness. It was always this way for the first few hours of a voyage, sea travel was not something he would ever get used to. He had seen the galleon that seemed so huge compared with the hitherto emptiness of the horizon. He guessed her to be Dutch, but knew nothing of her purpose. As a Jesuit scholar, he felt that it would be better to remain out of sight. He was worried about Goronwy, whose loud mouth and opinionated ideals could cause them trouble. Emlyn was alone in the cabin, sitting on some boxes that took up most of the free space. As the sea was rough, this was not easy, more like a fair ride with the ship raising and sinking, slithering him along the smooth wood and back again. The lid of the box he was working at had come loose. He was just about to have a look inside when the English servant, Matthew came into the cabin. His face was a mask of alarm.

'What is it?' Emlyn stood up. 'Are they pirates?'

Matthew recovered his composure. 'I'll be wanting them boxes,' he said briskly. As soon as Emlyn moved out of the way, Matthew grasped the rope handle of the top one and waited for the man with him to take the other side.

'Wait the lid is loose!' Emlyn leapt forward as he spoke.

Matthew swung around to prevent him. Will Moon tripped and lost his balance, dropping his end of the box. There was nothing they could do to prevent the contents from spilling.

'Guns!' Emlyn gasped as he stumbled over them. They looked like a jumble of sticks, then they clattering across the cabin like stiff snakes. Ambrose Chillingworth was selling guns!

'Hold him!' Matthew cried.

Emlyn could not rise in time to avoid him. The seaman had a knife at his throat before he could move. Matthew hurried out to fetch the merchant.

'You are selling guns to the Huguenots!' Emlyn said as soon as Ambrose arrived.

'I am sorry that you discovered them,' said Ambrose, he looked quite morose. 'The men on this ship will prevent your interference. There is nothing you can do now. Are you to be tied like a wild hog or can I rely on your silence?'

'Has the Queen agreed the supply the Huguenots with arms then?' Emlyn asked. He did not move, the point of the knife indented his skin.

'Not as simply as that,' said Ambrose. 'This is purely for my own interests. Do I have your silence? There is a little complication.'

The pressure on the knife lessened slightly. Will Moon said, 'What complications?'

Ambrose looked them in turn. 'We are to play host to two passengers and their servants from this Dutch ship. They wish to go to France.' He turned to his servant. 'Matthew get some men and bring the pinnacle to the other side of the ship. We can have it loaded and away before our guests arrive. With luck, they will not see it nor question if they do.'

Matthew grinned and left the cabin. Ambrose turned his gaze on Emlyn. 'Where, I wonder is Goronwy?'

'If he finds out,' Emlyn replied, 'there will be no stopping him.'

'He will not find out if you are assisting in the loading. Will he?'

Emlyn squirmed.

'If you move I'll cut you from ear to ear,' said the seaman. 'I've slit papist throats before this.'

Emlyn believed him. He felt the warm thread of blood from where the point had pierced his skin. He remained as still as possible, his heart thudding in fear. If Ambrose was intent on selling the guns he would be considerably worried about the appearance of unwanted visitors. Emlyn had no intention of betraying the Englishman, he would lose too much by doing so, but Goronwy would not feel the same, he would act before he thought. To get rid of the guns was the only solution. 'All right' Emlyn said. 'Let us get it done quickly.' They allowed him to stand.

'Now put all these guns back,' snarled Will Moon, pushing him towards the boxes. Emlyn bent, gathered guns in his arms and stood.

Goronwy entered the cabin.

Ambrose closed the door behind him. Goronwy spun around and glanced quickly from one to the other. The seaman still held his knife; he was smiling.

Emlyn could see the thoughts etched on Goronwy's face. He dropped the guns into the box and sprang forward. 'Goronwy wait!'

They collided and crashed to the floor. Goronwy heaved himself over and up. He rushed across the space between Emlyn and the boxes and swept up the wooden lid, it was fashioned of three sturdy planks. Before any could reach him, he swung the lid at the seaman and sent him reeling back. The knife dropped and Will Moon clutched his head. Ambrose had not moved. Goronwy discarded the wood and picked the knife. He held it out in front of him, between himself and Emlyn.

Emlyn said, 'Do you intend to kill us all?'

'For selling guns to the Huguenots?' Goronwy replied. The blade in his hand shook with his anger. 'Deceiving, spurious bastard!'

Goronwy had assumed the worse. Emlyn said, 'Why do you turn on me? You think that I am involved in this? Goronwy put the knife down, there is nothing you can do. This is a heretic ship, they will throw us both in the sea.'

'Not before all this is overboard and you with it. Traitorous pillicock!' He changed to Welsh that was not so good for swearing in but was very colourful nonetheless.

'Emlyn speaks the truth,' said Ambrose, stopping the guttural flow. He was leaning on the door with his arms folded and his expression calm. Will Moon stood beside him, his expression murderous. He made no move to interfere.

Emlyn feared that they would attack Goronwy if he did not solve the problem soon. Would Goronwy use the blade on him if he tried to disarm him? Such thoughts brought further delay. Emlyn stopped thinking and sprang. He parried the knife and drove into Goronwy's chest with a force that knocked the breath from them both. The fell and rolled across the floor, kicking and grasping, struggling over the planks, until the gun boxes stopped them.

'Jesu Goronwy. Get off me!' Emlyn rasped. He knew there was only one solution to this encounter. With one hand he reached for Goronwy's head grasping a handful of brown curls, with the other he held the hand with the knife. Goronwy wrenched his head away and caught Emlyn's wrist in a grip that made the bones creak.

Emlyn grunted. Goronwy's strength and anger out matched his own. He kicked Goronwy and heard the sharp intake of breath. They rose, entwined like lovers, struggling for the knife between them. Emlyn pulled free. With both hands he put all his strength into the hand that held the blade. He forced it down and away and smashed Goronwy's hand against the wall. The fingers opened and dropped the knife.

Emlyn had lost the advantage of position. Goronwy roared like a bear, locked his thick arms around Emlyn's chest and squeezed. Instantly Emlyn felt the blood rush to his head. His feet left the floor, he kicked and struggled without breath. Any more, and he felt his back would snap. The room seemed spotted. His sight blurred then darkened.

There was a crashing sound and a splash. He was released. He fell with Goronwy in a tangle of limbs. Goronwy was still, his head was soaked with wine. Emlyn sucked in great lungfulls of air. The wine ran like blood and puddled about him.

'You took your time,' he gasped. Ambrose stood over them with the remains of a clay jug in his hand.

'What are you sitting around for?' Ambrose said. 'There is work to be done.'

They tied Goronwy to a chair and gagged him. Ambrose secured the opened box. He walked behind Emlyn as it was carried to the deck. Emlyn worked in furious silence. Matters between him and Goronwy had become worse and worse and Emlyn knew how difficult it would be now to mend the rift between them. After a few minutes the six boxes were off-loaded into the pinnace. Emlyn stood back hoping for the chance to speak with Goronwy, but the burly seaman came up to him and kept a tight grip on his arm. There was a long, bloody tear along the man's cheek, his eyes were like daggers.

From the Dutch galleon, a rowing-boat approached. The oars worked as even as fish bones, closing the distance between them. As the longboat drew nearer, Emlyn recognised the fluttering pennant on the jack staff. 'She's *La Huguenotte*,' he said. He had not really believed what was happening until now, he had heard of this ship and knew of the acts of violence the Huguenots subjected their Catholic captives to. He looked nervously at the pinnace loaded with gun boxes, it was still under the lee of the *Lauris Nobilis*, ready to pull away when the rowing boat reached the other side with its passengers. As the row boat neared the *Lauris Nobilis*, they could hear words spoken. It was not one of the many dialects of the Netherlands; this voice had the authority of command. The words were in Spanish. They could see the oarsmen and four passengers, darkly clothed and hooded. One of the men stood, there was a glint of metal from the jewelled broach that pinned his cloak. Emlyn thought that he was probably the galleon's captain.

Ambrose came to stand beside Emlyn. 'The Spaniards will have swords, but no other weapons,' he said, almost to himself.

'Even if your guns were discovered,' Emlyn replied, 'what could these few men do against you?'

'You are probably right, there is nothing they can do but meet their deaths,' said Ambrose. 'Accidents often happen at sea.'

Will Moon spat on the deck. 'These Spanish bastards will be on their way to join Alva's troops. What the devil are they doing aboard a hostile Dutch ship?'

The boat drew alongside. Ambrose, Moon and Emlyn edged forward. A ladder clattered down. Grasping it, the man who had stood in the boat clambered up with the agility of a long practised seaman. Greeting the ship's master at the top, he spoke in Flemish. 'We must have put the fear of God into you captain. We have some Spanish gentlemen for you.'

The sailing master looked pointedly towards Ambrose before he took the offered hand and pulled the Dutchman aboard. He knows now what is going on, reasoned Emlyn, but if he is Catholic he would be wise to remain silent. The sailing master stood in grim silence for a time. Then, turning to Ambrose, he said, 'Am I to understand Mr. Chillingbutt, that your boxes are off loaded?'

'Yes,' replied Ambrose worriedly. 'Don't concern yourself.' The sailing master nodded slowly that turned away to see to the new passengers. Ambrose addressed the Dutch captain. 'Are the passengers really Spaniards?' he asked him.

'The very same,' agreed the captain of the galleon. He was tall and thin with a mass of sun-whitened hair and a contrasting beard split with a smile. 'We were met by the fishing boat you sent as we turned to the English Channel. The Spaniards joined us soon after.' He spat on the deck, showing his disgust. 'They'll be hatching nothing but ill between them I'll warrant. They know nothing of our present business, so let's be about it and away.'

'I could not be more agreeable,' said Ambrose with a heart-felt sigh. 'and the sooner the better. But why in the name of heaven Jacques de Sores, are you carrying Spaniards?'

'The Spanish want passage to France,' said Jacques de Sores. He smiled generously and winked. 'I am a reasonable man when offered a fat purse and it seems they have lost something.'

'Really?' Ambrose felt the colour leave his face. He knew what the Spaniards were looking for...their wages fleet! Jacques de Sores too knew what they were looking for.

Dressed in scarlet and black and adorned with ivory, the first Spaniard climbed aboard. He was of middle height, armed with a sword in a splendid scabbard. He was drenched with sea water. His face was notably handsome and bearded. A red feathered cap crowned his dark hair and gold shone from his ears. Laughing, he embraced the surprised ship master and kissed him on each cheek with a roll of Catalan Spanish. The second Spaniard climbed aboard behind him. In contrast, he was plainly dressed, Emlyn thought he had the baring of a soldier. The sailing master welcomed them in the same tongue, his rendering of the language grated on Emlyn's' ears.

They moved away from the Spaniards. Ambrose was as pale as wax. Matthew examined him with concern. 'Are you feelin' the sea sickness? Is it the Spanish? They are good Catholics by the size of the crosses on them.'

Ambrose glared at him. He said, 'I have no intention of meeting the overdressed gentlemen.'

'The Dutchman says they have no French nor English nor Flemish. Would you guess it?' laughed Matthew.

'Perhaps they would like to borrow Emlyn,' answered Ambrose. There was a warning in his eyes. 'After all he's a good Catholic, aren't you Emlyn? And can get your tongue around those Latinised words; most of the Jesuits are Spanish. I'm going to sleep. Emlyn, I expect you to pay me the debt owed for rescuing you from the Duke of Exeter's daughter.'

The sailor still had a grip on Emlyn. He said, 'Are you going to let this one go?'

'You could toss him to the sea, but what harm can he do? The merchandise is gone. Keep a close watch on the other one until we reach

Dieppe. Emlyn, if any harm befalls me on the rest of this voyage, your friend Goronwy will go overboard first.' His words had a ring of certainty to them. He shuffled off while the waves rose and the downpour increased.

Emlyn knew what the 'Duke of Exeter's daughter' was, it was the rack used for torture in the Tower of London. He also knew that the Queen of England had not turned a blind eye to the plight of the Huguenots. She had sent them guns and cannon to fight their enemies and hers. Like her sea beggars, who harried the Spanish shipping, there would be no evidence that these weapons came from the crown of England. Emlyn stood in the rain and thought about Ambrose Chillingworth.

Ambrose would be paid for the delivery to the Dutch ship in Dieppe. Jacques de Sores sought him out before leaving and handed him a letter and an address. Ambrose smiled, it was one he knew, a draper in Dieppe. Before long the *Lauris Nobilis* was under way again, sloughing through the towering waves.

Ambrose sat down in his cabin and rubbed his tired eyes. The cabin was still a mess. Goronwy had been taken somewhere more secure, to be guarded by Will Moon with the split cheek. Ambrose lit a lamp, though the daylight still filtered weakly through a tiny window. He thought of the Spaniards and of how often the threads of intrigue crossed and tangled without one ever being aware of the other. Then his mind conjured up the formula that drove away all conflicting thoughts. He thought of his childhood home in Rutland; of butterflies and bees, the soft caress of summer sun, the heady scents of lavender, lupin and rose. His eyes grew heavy.

A rapid knock came on the door and the dreams dissolved before him. 'Come,' he invited in irritation.

John Moore entered with a covered basket. He smiled and said, 'A gift from the passengers who have just joined us sir.' He held out his bundle, sweeping the cloth away. It was a basket of Seville oranges. They were halved and scooped out with the flesh mixed with sugar and cinnamon, stuffed back into the skins with a fluff of lace and, tied up with a ribbon. With it was an invitation to dine with the Spanish passengers.

Although he was impressed with the gift, Ambrose was immediately suspicious; he knew what the Spaniards were looking for. He had to accept the gift, but not the invitation. He sent Moore back to the Spaniards his apologies. 'Tell them that I suffer from sea sickness,' he said. 'And John, don't tell them any thing else.'

John Moore spat on the planking, showing his contempt for Spain. He whistled as he swung the door open.

Ambrose finally drifted off to sleep away the rest of the journey to France.

Through the rank smell of salt and the splash of brine, the English ship rode a fair wind and nodded her way towards France. Dieppe was already in sight, the houses were tiny specs of white on a shore of winter browns and blackened greens. The basket remained untouched until Matthew discovered it and took it away. He knew well of his master's distaste for citrus fruit.

Emlyn was standing by the ship's wooden rail watching the gulls circle overheard. He understood the need for Ambrose's caution. He thought a great deal about the Huguenots and their fight against the Duke of Alva. Emlyn could not see that Alva's reign of terror against the Protestants would solve the problem; the more they were oppressed, the better justified they felt to continue fighting and killing. Because of his mixed feelings he wondered if he was the traitor Goronwy had named him.

A neatly dressed man approached him and inquired if he would see the Spanish gentlemen on board. As Emlyn could think up no excuse to avoid them, he followed the man from the deck.

Don Diego de Luzon was seated in his small cabin. There were papers spread out on the table in front of him. He was a handsome man in his mid thirties and a man used to authority. His mother had married a Portuguese landowner, but Luzon's heart was purely Spanish and he devoted much of his life to serving King Phillip and the interests of Spain. He had made this journey often, carrying messages back and forth from Alva to the King. But this was a mission of much greater importance and one which Diego Luzon was determined to succeed in.

He bundled up the papers and handed them to a man who stood behind him. This was the younger man who had accompanied him on board. His eyes were soft and his hands long and delicate. He was introduced to Emlyn as Miguel de Cervantes Saavedra.

The smile with which Don Diego de Luzon greeted Emlyn seemed genuinely warm and friendly. 'Welcome, welcome, my young friend,' he called out in Spanish. 'I am an agent of Don Fernando Alvarez de Toledo, the Duke of Alva, and am here on his behalf.' He turned again to the man behind. 'Miguel, have we got wine to offer our guest?'

Emlyn introduced himself and sat on the stool offered, sipping from the glass of heavy red wine. He had to look up to his host.

Don Diego de Luzon lifted his own glass. 'To your gracious Queen!' He dabbed at his mouth with a piece of lacy cloth and settled back into his chair. He placed his hands together, making a tent of his fingertips, and looked curiously at Emlyn before he spoke. 'You have come from Southampton?'

'Yes Señor,' said Emlyn.

'And what cargo do you carry?'

'I am not a merchant Señor. I am returning to my schooling in Paris.'

Don Diego de Luzon sighed. His eyes travelled down from Emlyn's face to his thighs. 'An admirable youth,' said Don Diego. 'Do you agree Miguel?'

Emlyn shivered, suddenly alert.

Don Diego continued, 'I must assume that if you seek an education in Paris, there is not one fitting for you in England.'

'I am Catholic, if that is your meaning Señor.'

'Alas!' Don Diego exclaimed with a sorrowful expression. 'How unfortunate it is that such a becoming youth cannot feel safe within his own land. It is your England that has brought me from the comforts of my own home. We are both stray souls you and I. But I am rewarded, for you have come from the very place I am sent to make inquiries after. I am seeking after some small matter, one that you in your position may be able to assist me with. I expect help from you and offer friendship. You and I should support each other in these hostile parts where we are beleaguered by enemies.'

Emlyn felt his skin burn. Why did he feel so uncomfortable in this man's presence? He cleared his throat and said, 'I am more that willing to help in whatever way I can, Don Diego.'

'You see?' Don Diego de Luzon exclaimed, turning to his partner, 'the boy is clever. The English have such a clear beauty about them. Tell me young scholar, did you see the Spanish ships in Southampton before you left.'

'No,' said Emlyn. He did not know why he lied, suddenly he felt threatened. He added, 'I saw only the fishing fleet.'

Don Diego's hands rubbed together and his smile lessened. 'I see,' he said. He stood up, cracking his knuckles and came around the table to stand in front of his guest.

Emlyn tensed and lowered his head, nervously fingering the wine glass.

'What about the Merchant you are travelling with?' Don Diego asked.

'Señor? If you wish to find out, why not ask him. He keeps a house there, so will probably know more than I can tell you.'

Don Diego nodded slowly. He stretched out a hand and ran it from the top of Emlyn's boot to the inside of his thigh. He pinched a handful of skin and squeezed.

Emlyn drew in his breath and attempted to pull away. The grip tightened.

Don Diego bent his head to one side as if considering. With his free hand, he caught up a handful of Emlyn's hair. 'No ships,' he said. 'Are you so sure of this?'

Emlyn twisted his head away, hearing strands of hair come loose as the Spaniard released him. The grip on his leg also slackened, but Don Diego's warm hand remained and began to caress.

Emlyn dropped his wine glass and leaped to his feet. He backed out of the room and fled. Behind him, Don Diego and his companion burst into derisive laughter.

Emlyn ran blindly and then stopped abruptly. He looked around the deck and began to move about, busying himself with an assortment of items. By the time the ship was close to the harbour, Emlyn sat with a tangle of string around his hands, there were other objects littered around him. Had Goronwy been there he would have been suspicious. Emlyn looked along the length of rope. It might work, he mused with a private smile. Inaccuracy was the problem, but time was short and one must make do with inferior equipment. The Spanish grandee would look a fool if all went according to plan.

Matthew appeared beside him and held out a basket. Having completed his task; Emlyn accepted a decorative Spanish orange. He held it out over the sea. The sun dipped beneath the rain clouds and washed the sea with colour; the fruit and his hand were stained with red light. Emlyn plucked out a sugared segment, as dark as blood. He could smell the cinnamon. He shivered, for it reminded him of Don Diego. Suddenly, a gull dropped and snatched it from his fingers. The bird swallowed before its head had straightened.

'Good God!' Matthew exclaimed. His mouth stayed open.

Emlyn stood back and watched the thieving gull battle the air currents. Orange forgotten, it wheeled and dived down to the sea for fish, like a bird struck by the hawk. It gave good imitation of being dead as it splashed into the water. Emlyn peered over the side to watch it glide up again. It really was dead! The wings were outspread and the sea-foam of the ship's wake turned the body over.

Matthew was just about to bite into the sweet juices of his orange. Emlyn hit him on the back of the head with such force that the orange dropped and rolled overboard. Matthew bit his tongue and tasted blood.

Emlyn swept up the basket and hurled it over the side.

Matthew swore. 'Y' great blunderin', sheep-shaggin', Welsh goat! The devil take y'! What hare-brained prank is this, 'ave y' taken leave of y' senses?'

Emlyn looked at him in surprise, equally taken aback by his own actions. 'I saw the bird drop dead from the sky,' he explained.

'Fool!' Matthew spluttered. 'What do y' think with? Welsh oats! That bird choked to death on a fish bone. Y' porridge brained loon!'

Emlyn swung around, tripped over his cloak and staggered off down the planking.

'Poisoned!' Ambrose choked on his malmsey. 'A ridiculous idea,' he spluttered. 'You can't poison an orange.'

Emlyn's expression was one of extreme anger. He looked more frightening than Goronwy. The Celts are very temperamental, thought Ambrose. He himself was Norman through and through and proud of it. Emlyn stood at the cabin door with his hands on the casing to steady his balance against the swell of the sea. The wind was behind him, punishing the back of his head so that his hair flung out like sun rays on a map. His back was to the light, Ambrose could only see pools of his eyes, twin lamp-flames floated eerily within like weir lights in a bog puddle.

Emlyn's eyes changed, losing their violence. He entered the room, sitting on the narrow bed with his head in his hands. He said, 'Poisoned oranges make no sense. They were looking for their lost ships, your death would bring them no answers.'

Ambrose stopped dabbing at the wine on his collar lace and froze. 'You knew about the Spanish ships?'

Emlyn's hands dropped; the look he gave Ambrose belonged to an older man. 'Not until they asked me,' he replied.

'And you told them what?'

'They think that their ships are in Southampton and know that we came from there. That is why they transferred to the Dutch ship from their own and why they are on this ship. They invited you to dine with them so that questions could be asked.' He leaned back on the bed, his head against the boards.

Ambrose sat forward and began to sort out the disorder on the table, speaking while he did so. 'Are you saying that failing to attract my interest, they then questioned you? Emlyn what have you told them?'

'Nothing. What could I tell them? Why were the ships there in the first place? Why are they prevented from sailing?'

Ambrose felt the tightness leave his shoulders. No mention of eight hundred thousand ducats then. He said, 'I have no idea, but I suspect that they were driven there by pirates. I heard in a little harbour gossip that the Dutch Sea Beggars were lined up off-shore waiting for them.'

'Are they treasure ships from the Indies?'

'I think not, they were too small and sailed unprotected.'

'Before I came to you in Southampton,' said Emlyn, 'I heard about the ships and knew that William Cecil's visit to you concerned them. I also heard that the English wool fleet, that sailed to Hamburg was so successful, that another was sent in August. You are a wool merchant. It is winter, the season for trade is long gone. Why have you left England?'

'The season for trade is never over,' Ambrose said. He wiped the tips of his quills and rolled them in a scrap of soft leather before packing them away. He was alarmed by Emlyn's knowledge, but would let nothing of his feelings show. 'You have seen the wool and are well aware that I intend to start for Italy early,' he said. 'This venture is for the benefit of myself and your grandfather. There is much to be gained from being an early bird. If the Alps are impassable, I will remain in Lyons or Geneva, but I will still catch the worm.'

Watching him seriously, Emlyn said nothing.

Ambrose had learned already not to underestimate him. At first, Ambrose had thought him quite typical of a French-trained student; the swagger, the manners, the tendency to quote in Latin or better another's quote with Greek, it was all there plus that superior air they practised, proud even if they had not eaten for a week. Ambrose said, 'I'll admit that I hoped to persuade you to come with me. I understand well enough if you don't, after the incident with the firearms. Do you want to go to Paris with Goronwy? Are you of an age to make a priest?'

'I'm eighteen,' Emlyn said, 'or thereabouts.'

Ambrose studied him in silence. Then he said, 'Your grandfather had hopes for you. Was there difficulty over the ownership of the land he wished you to inherit?'

'I am outlawed,' Emlyn replied easily and then, with difficulty, 'I killed one of the sheriff's men during the fight in Wales. It was because the man killed a boy who was with us, the boy was simple and did not deserve such a cruel end. Yet if I could take back what I did I would'

Ambrose nodded slowly. He said, 'Because of this, you will turn to the Jesuits?'

Emlyn smiled bitterly. 'The answer is not so simple,' he replied. 'One born of a father unknown, is considered unsuitable for the church. His mother is considered a whore, her sins are passed on to her son. It is he who must carry the blame and shame for her mistake.'

Ambrose looked with sympathy at the boy. When Emlyn had spoken of the death of the simpleton, his raw suffering had been plain to see. Ambrose felt a strange stirring of affection and curiosity. He thought of his own son Christopher. Did he languish in some harsh Spanish prison with the other English seamen? As Protestant, they would be toys in the cruel hands of the Inquisition. Or did he sail free, bound for England, wiser than when he had left it? Here was one, a little younger perhaps, and still a child in the ways of the world. Emlyn seemed lost, with no place to turn. Again Ambrose was struck by the comparison he made with Christopher, it was as if, were he to help Emlyn achieve his aims, someone along the way would give his own son the help he needed.

Now the grey eyes regarded him across the room, expressed with a mixture of humility and discomfort. Ambrose said, 'If you have ruined your chances of some sort of life at home in Wales and are told that you cannot now be ordained, will you come to Italy with me? My Italian is hopeless.'

Emlyn said, 'Mine is not much better.' He relaxed, as if whatever had burdened him had suddenly flown. 'God's truth! I don't know what I want.'

Ambrose thought for a moment. Emlyn looked much like a Spaniard, but looks alone were not enough to make an agent of the crown. He would wait and watch and judge. Casting the thought aside, he said, 'I could find you a position, for I have many connections, a little disrupted in the present state of war, but still a man of your ability with the pen or lute could find easy employment. A musician can find fame and even fortune. If you are as talented as your grandfather tells me, I may be able to help you obtain a position in Mantua. I am known to Duke Guglielmo and he is a man of the arts; his court attracts many learned men and musicians from all over Europe.'

'Thank you,' Emlyn replied. 'Already you have done more than enough and I remain in your debt. I feel like a ship with no sails, tossed on an aimless ocean. I could feel some hope towards my future if only I were not banned from England!'

Ambrose smiled. 'Your grandfather has started a good business, to which you may be able to return in time, once the heat of the incident has died down, men will forget and you could return; as long as it is not in the guise of a priest. The wool trade is thriving.'

'My uncle has written to the Jesuit school, stating that my father was an Italian by the name of Grimani,' said Emlyn. 'It's possible that it is true, for that is the name of the sea captain who my mother wed, but I have good reason to doubt it. Still the letter itself would act as proof that I am not of illegitimate birth. If I could get my hands on it, my uncle could not contest my grandfather's wish that I be his successor. If as you say, I could redeem myself and return home.'

'So you need to get to the Jesuit college in order to pick up this letter? Will that be a simple task?'

Emlyn smiled ruefully. 'Not in the least,' he replied, 'even less so now that Goronwy has seen the guns that you sold to the Huguenots. He will think that I had something to do with them.'

Ambrose nodded thoughtfully. 'You do not hold that against me do you Emlyn?'

Emlyn smiled.

'I shall talk with your friend Goronwy. I'm sure he will see then that you had no choice in the matter. I am concerned though, will he keep quiet about it once we reach France? I am safe enough here but when we stand on French soil matters will be different.'

'I would have said definitely not before this summer,' Emlyn said. 'Now Goronwy has become very devoted to the eradication of heresy. I don't know what he will do. You may be able to convince him that I had nothing to do with the guns, but I have already betrayed the plot to take William Cecil. Goronwy already has a just reason to condemn me.'

Ambrose rubbed his beard thoughtfully. 'We will keep a close eye on him,' he answered. 'As long as he does not talk to our Spanish friends, I think we will be safe enough.'

Emlyn looked puzzled for a moment then he said, 'If I can get hold of the letter written by my uncle, then we could go to Italy as we had intended, in spite of the fact that you have changed your plans and mine have been changed for me. Are in a hurry to get wherever you are going?'

Ambrose shifted uncomfortably. How much could he tell the boy? Nothing would be best. 'I need to travel as swiftly as I can with the wool. The snow on the Alps will be worse the longer I delay.'

Emlyn sat forward twining his long fingers together. 'I will go back with Goronwy and try to get the letter. I would not have you delayed because of me. John Moore seems a reliable man he can organise the journey. Then I could catch up with you; for the wool mules will slow you down.'

'We will leave it at that then,' Ambrose said relieved. 'And I am sure you have made a wise decision.'

Emlyn stood up and grinned. 'I nearly forgot about Don Diego,' he said. He was out of the room before Ambrose could question his meaning.

The tide was in. The river, filled with weeks of mountain rain, swelled to the grey banks of the estuary and allowed ships to move to the dockside to off-load their wares. The *Lauris Nobilis* came to the end of her journey. Her seamen threw dripping ropes to the shore and her passengers, some ruled by Philip of Spain and some ruled by Elizabeth of England, prepared to disembark for the turbulent shores of France that was ruled by neither.

The ship neared her mooring and Ambrose's cloth was stacked ready to off-load, supervised by Moore. The Spaniards stood with the ship's master, taking their leave. Behind them, were stacked their belongings, beside the half-barrel in which rain water collected. The day had darkened to twilight with a cold wind coming off the sea. This did nothing to disguise the smells of charcoal and rotting herring that hung over Dieppe like a cloud of invisible smoke.

Ambrose came out of the cabin fastening the ties of his fur-lined cap. Laden with their personal bundles, Matthew came out behind him, muttering in complaint. Then Goronwy and Emlyn emerged with their few possessions. Goronwy looked as glum as ever, he had acquired a black eye while in the care of Will Moon. With the printing failure in Wales, Emlyn's betrayal in Southampton and the incident with the Dutch ship behind him, Ambrose thought he had good cause. Ambrose watched him with a troubled mind and felt something of William Cecil's fears.

Emlyn blinked owlishly as he came from the shadows. He looked relieved to have the sea crossing behind him, but to anyone who really knew him, there was a gleam of mischief in his eye. Many of his companions at the College de Clermont had seen that gleam, before he got up to some prank or trickery.

Ambrose saw Emlyn's hand reach up and grasp the ringing cord of the ship's bell. His eyebrows rose in puzzled inquiry. This was not the usual time for bell ringing, there was no change of watch, no signal, no alarm. What was the boy doing? Soon all thought of the bell was driven from Ambrose's mind.

Emlyn vigorously pulled on the rope. The bell set the whole quay side ringing. Heads turned in their direction. The people of Dieppe, who were still at work on the harbour and were ruled by the voice of bells, all looked towards the sound of urgent summons. Voices cried out. Had a fire occurred? Fire was the worse enemy of ships and those who made their wealth by them.

Emlyn's expression was one of impish delight. The bell pull set off a series of inexplicable happenings. Above, on the roof of the tiny cabin from which they had emerged, lay two lengths of guttering, used for loading the hold with ballast or grain. One of these took on a life of its own, it shifted forward and up and then tipped dislodging something stored there. It was a cannon ball; its presence unaccountable. It rolled gathering speed and plopped off the end of the chute. It bounced, hit a plank and shattered a jar of oil. A shower of corn-yellow liquid washed the boards. A rope that was fastened to the plank, suddenly lifted, hissing stiff from where it was knotted to the ship's rail; as it ran behind a Spanish gentleman's knees, the end was inevitable.

It swept the feet from under Miguel de Cervantes and flipped him over backwards. His arms spiralled for balance. His eyes widened as round as wine cups and his mouth parted in a wail of incredulous dismay. Before anyone could move to help him, he sank butt first in to the water barrel behind him. The icy, rank water washed out over the sides of the barrel. Miguel de Cervantes whined as the breath was driven out of him by the freezing brine. His arms and legs thrashed frantically as he struggled like a crab left behind at low tide, on its back and helpless.

Emlyn watched the scene, his face a mixture of astounded innocence and suppressed delight. 'Damn the Diawl!' He guffawed to himself in Welsh. 'I've landed the wrong bloody fish in the barrel.'

He was the first to move to assist the unfortunate man. His face showed the effort he was having to contain his laughter. The sailing master and Don Diego had problems of their own; the deck was slick with oil, and they slipped and slithered, struggling for balance, their dignity in ruins. As soon as he moved forward, Emlyn was confronted with the same difficulty. Failing to keep to his feet, he fell headlong. Hands outstretched he crashed straight into the barrel with the Spaniard in it. The greased surface did the rest. As slow as oil, but unstoppable, the barrel glided and gently parted the ropes, to lurch over the side. There was just enough room between the *Lauris Nobilis* and harbour wall for it to splash into the freezing sea. Miguel de Cervantes howled in dismay as he disappeared overboard.

Chapter 27 Florence

Fra Pietro Sebastiano da Firenze returned to Florence before winter set in; as Emlyn had told him, he did not meet his death in France. He knew that his health would never be what it was and that the aches and pains would be with him till the end. The good Lord was a hard master, but Fra Sebastiano had come home as he had wished. He was staying at the Church of Santa Croce in Florence. It was situated in the district he had been brought up in, near the bank of the river Arno where the dyers lived. These were the true Florentine; it was on their backs that Florence had come to fame through her cloth industry. On these streets Fra Sebastiano had run and played as a boy. It is fitting, he thought, to come home now for the remainder of my days.

The members of the Franciscan order made him welcome and were content if he just spent his remaining days in peace and prayer, but Fra Sebastiano liked to visit his old haunts and do what he could for the people who lived by the river, he was always welcome to sit and talk in the sun or share their meals. On this day, they had given him a gift of two large fish that he was finding heavy to carry home. He rested on a stone block at the side of the street waiting for the younger priest he had noticed walking behind him.

'Good day to you Father,' said the young man as he drew level.

'Good day son, will you carry these fish for me?' said Fra Sebastiano, 'my prayers shall be answered.'

'If all men kept their prayer so simple Brother we would be in a better world than we are.' He reached down and lifted the fish. He held them up and whistled in appreciation.

Fra Sebastiano stood and fell into step, grateful for the willing help. He knew who the young priest was though they had not spoken together. Eventually he said, 'Lorenzo isn't it? You have been recently ordained?'

'That is so, just this summer gone.' He turned back and smiled, swinging the fish like a young boy.

'Will you remain in Florence?'

'No,' laughed Lorenzo. 'I am due to leave for Carrara in a few days. I am engaged to teach Latin, Greek and Mathematics.'

'In Carrara? I did not know it for a scholarly place,' commented Fra Sebastiano. 'Is that not where the marble is quarried?'

'It is Father. But eventually a man might aspire to better himself through education.'

'True, true,' mumbled the old priest. They were near the refectory kitchen. 'Can you gut fish?'

'Gladly. I can cook it and eat it too.' Lorenzo took charge of the situation. He sat the old man by the fire and placed a cup of wine to warm at the hearth. Then he sharpened a gutting knife and set to work. There were few others about; it was late afternoon when all were at work or taking an afternoon rest. Apart from a cook dozing by the bread oven, they were the only ones there. Shafts of light from the high windows slanted into the spacious room, illuminating the ever present dust and sending it sluggishly sparkling to the low ceiling. The day had been cold and the kitchen was warm and comfortable. Lorenzo worked steadily at the fish.

Lorenzo was the eldest son of Cristoforo Grimani and his foreign bride Anna. He was a tall young man with dark hair and penetrating dark eyes above an over-large nose. He did not share the good looks of his brother Paolo, but Lorenzo was of a steadier character with a determination that his brother lacked. Lorenzo had never gotten on well with his grandfather Don Carlos Grimani; they had argued continuously. The topic that had usually caused these disagreements, had been to do with Lorenzo's ambition to join the church. Don Carlos had objected strongly, and eventually Lorenzo had left of his own accord and joined the Franciscans in Florence. Now that he was ordained, he felt at last safe from his grandfather's interference.

Birdsong entered the arched openings. The sound lulled Fra Sebastiano into melancholy, dreamlike thought, in which time stood still. There was something about the young priest Lorenzo that reminded Fra Sebastiano of Emlyn Tomas; the boy whose early history he had felt it his duty to reveal. Fra Sebastiano had further promised that he would find out what he could, should God permit him to return to Florence. Well, he was home now, but he had not been able to discover anything yet. Even the child Carmelia, whom he had visited in France had been unable to tell him anything concerning Emlyn's mother. But she had spoken with great love about Lorenzo, who wrote to her regularly.

His thoughts were interrupted by the tapping footsteps of a young novice as he hurried down the stone floor unaware of the peace he had disturbed. 'Lorenzo!' His voice boomed before he was half way there.

'There is a letter for you. I saw you come in here with the fish. Is it cooked yet?'

'Who is the letter from?' Lorenzo asked, without looking up from his work. 'And get your mind off this fish, it is already spoken for.'

'The messenger was dressed in your grandfather's livery, a sort of unpleasant, olive-green colour,' said the young novice, 'so I imagine it is from Venice.' He drew the letter out of the folds of his habit, glancing around the room for something to eat. The personal seal of Don Carlos Grimani proclaimed the letter's origin.

Lorenzo unhurriedly wiped his hands before he accepted the paper. The novice watched him with eager curiosity. 'You can go now,' said Lorenzo dismissing him. He broke the seal and briefly scanned the contents. A frown deepened on his brow.

'Not bad news?' Fra Sebastiano asked.

'No. My grandfather wishes me to go and visit him again. I know what it will be about, but this time he is too late.'

'Too late for what?'

'To try and make me change my mind about the life I have chosen. I am ordained now and nothing can pull me back to that life I so detested.'

'Come now,' soothed Fra Sebastiano. This seemed a good opportunity to discover more concerning the Grimani family. Pretending he knew nothing of Lorenzo's family, he said, 'I can well understand a parent's reluctance.'

'My father is dead,' Lorenzo explained. 'My brother Paolo and I were brought up by our grandfather, Don Carlos Grimani. I entered this order against his will.'

'Grimani? You are a Grimani?'

'Yes, are you surprised?'

'I am, but not for the reasons you think. Tell me about yourself. I think I may know a distant relation of yours.'

So Fra Sebastiano heard the story of the two young boys who had come to live with their grandfather when their mother had retired to a convent in Cyprus and had tragically died on her journey there. Her story fitted the tale Fra Sebastiano had heard from Emlyn Tomas.

When the story was ended, he said, 'Are you so sure that your mother died?'

'There was some doubt early on,' said Lorenzo, 'some rumour started by an old woman from the area my mother lived. The old woman's' name was Zia Carlina and she claimed to have received word from my mother some months later. But nothing came of it, Zia Carlina failed to produce the letter when it was demanded of her by my grandfather. Why do you ask?'

Now Fra Sebastiano knew that he was on dangerous ground. Should he tell what he knew? Was it his duty to reveal the rest of the tale? Or would he be overturning a bowl of worms and in so doing, bring sorrow and unrest? Lorenzo was looking at him expectantly. Fra Sebastiano struggled inwardly. There was some mystery here that had a flavour of unpleasantness to it, but it was a mystery of the past; to unravel it would certainly answer the questions of Emlyn Tomas and grant him some ease with his own origins. Would it harm Lorenzo, who had chosen his life with the Franciscans and had cut himself from the great family of Grimani?

'Fra Sebastiano?' Lorenzo prompted.

Fra Sebastiano made his decision. I shall do what I can to discover the origins of this story, that was what he had promised Emlyn in Paris. And who knew how much time he had left to do so? 'Leave that fish now and come to sit here with me,' he answered. 'For I too have a tale to tell and it concerns your mother's family.'

That day, Tomasso di Vincentini was also in Florence. He was crossing the piazza on his way to the bridge where the gold smiths lived and worked. Tomasso's financial luck had not left him; he had sold most of his jade to Cosimo I de' Medici, the Duke of Florence. His predecessors had collected works of art and antiques of inestimable value. Tomasso had a good look around the Medici palace and had been impressed. Cosimo I de' Medici himself, collected ancient manuscripts. In the guise of a gem merchant, Tomasso had made some future arrangements with the Duke of Florence. Now he was making his way towards the goldsmith's area, in hope of engaging a master goldsmith.

'Salve! Capaccio!'

Tomasso did not turn when he heard his old name called. He had thought that he might be recognised sooner or later, he would have preferred later. He carried on walking, his shoulders tightening.

'Capaccio! Toma!'

Ignoring the man wasn't working; rather than allow the whole of Florence to hear, Tomasso stopped and turned slowly.

Coming towards him was a heavy-set, black-bearded man in huge Spanish boots, with gold earrings and gold braid all over him. Tomasso recognised him instantly in spite of the gaudy clothes and the overgrown beard it was Gaspare Maria del Monte. Twenty years had fattened him, but not much else appeared all that different. Laughing like a baboon with his arms outspread, Gaspare charged across the piazza. Tomasso grinned and swept off his feathered hat, in preparation for the impact.

'By all the saints!' Gaspare Maria del Monte released his captive. Tears streamed down his round cheeks and soaked into his beard. 'I thought you were dead. I scoured the seas for two years looking for you!'

Tomasso took his arm and led him off to the nearest taverna.

They had met at a harbour inn in Genoa, where Gaspare was from. They had both been very drunk when Genoese eyes met Venetian eyes across the room. They proceeded to fight until neither could stand. There was no love between Genoa and Venice; they had fought for domination of the trade routes for generations. Tomasso and Gaspare had done a lot together since then; in those carefree days when life was a whirl of revelry and adventure. They had bought and sold just about everything that could be bought, sold or stolen when necessity arose. They had travelled, as far as their purses would take them, lingering often to taste the fruits of enterprise in exotic ports and cities. They had traded with hostile Turks, crafty Arabs, cunning Jews, thrifty Egyptians and all manner of Europeans from one end of the Mediterranean Sea to the other. It had seemed then, as if there had been no tomorrow, that each day had to be lived to the full; every dish tasted, every challenge tried, every woman bedded and every enemy fought with honour. Tomasso had not thought much about that time over the years. He hadn't realised until now, how much he had missed Gaspare and all he represented.

Gaspare boasted that he was now the proud captain of a Genoese ship. Then he talked for over an hour about himself and his achievements over the years. Tomasso got pleasantly drunk and discovered to his surprise that he was enjoying himself. Would that life could be so simple!

It was not until they were well into their second bottle of wine that Tomasso remembered Gaspare's words on greeting. 'What do you mean you scoured the seas for two years looking for me?' He interrupted Gaspare's flow.

Gaspare's expression became serious. They had both avoided talking about those last events of their past, to which Gaspare had been witness. Gaspare said, 'What difference will it make now? The years have changed all that was. The reasons for my search need no explanation now.'

Tomasso laughed. 'You wanted to rescue me? That is if you could find me, among the thousands of slaves and prisoners that cleave the sea for their masters.'

Gaspare did not return the smile. He wrapped his hands almost defensively around his cup, his eyes downcast. He said, 'I came to find you yes, but rescue was of secondary importance.' He paused for a moment, biting his lip. 'I followed your wife, Anna, you know when they sent her to Cyprus. I felt that if I could do nothing for you, imprisoned and accused as you were, then I vowed to do all I could for her.'

Tomasso felt a fool for laughing. He had forgotten how Gaspare had felt about Anna. And Anna had loved him too, in her own way, she had treated him like a big brother while Gaspare would have kissed the ground she trod on. Tomasso reached across the table and refilled the cups. He said, 'You are right, the years have altered all. Perhaps it would be wise to allow the ghosts to lie at peace.'

But Gaspare shook his head and continued without lifting his eyes. 'Because she did not die at sea, as everyone seemed to believe, I felt it my duty to do all I could to secure her release from the slavers who held her. I personally delivered thier ransom letter to Don Carlos Grimani. I watched and did nothing when he fed it to the fire.'

'What did you say?' Tomasso felt cold all over.

'Nor did I do anything after. I knew what he would do you see?'

'Wait,' commanded Tomasso in a hoarse whisper. 'Did not die at sea?'

'I was afraid,' said Gaspare. 'Can you believe that? I was afraid of what he would do to me. I turned my back on her and didn't tell a soul. That's why I searched for you, and I have lived with the cowardice and shame ever since.'

Tomasso stood up. He could see nothing of his surroundings. Only in his mind a voice screamed. Anna!

Gaspare rose beside him. 'Toma? Are you all right? You have turned white as a spirit. What is it? You mean you did not know?' Gaspare sat, pulling Tomasso down also.

'What difference will it make now?' Gaspare whispered urgently. 'She probably did not survive long in captivity.'

Tomasso dropped his head into his hands. 'Tell me all,' he said, without removing his hands. His voice sounded tired and far away. He felt as if all his insides had been sucked out, leaving an empty shell.

Gaspare spoke softly, telling all that had happened after Tomasso's arrest and of his own efforts to secure a release for Anna after she and her companion had been taken when pirates had overrun their ship. He had not been able to see her but had haggled for hours with the Arab slave trader, eventually convincing the man that she came from a powerful family who would pay well for her safety and release. Grimani had not been aware of the part Gaspare had played in bringing the letter demanding ransom. He had read it briefly and burned it, as if casting Anna herself on the ashes.

When he had finished speaking Gaspare drained his cup. He had never felt so somber after two bottles of wine. He snapped his fingers in the air and ordered another.

Tomasso remained silent, sunk in the deep sorrow of memory and regret. Anna was not dead. No, that was impossible reasoning. She would be by now, Grimani could have prevented her fate, but he had what he wanted, her sons Lorenzo and Paolo. He had turned his back on her plight.

Gaspare said, 'Will you try to discover what happened to her?'

'Yes,' Tomasso replied. 'I will find out what happened. First I have some business to settle in Venice.'

Gaspare flinched from the pain he saw in Tomasso's eyes.

Tomasso was scarcely aware of him. Fed by new anger, he would follow the path of his vengeance to the bitter end. And if there was anything left? He locked away in the recess of his mind the thoughts that caused such pain. He smiled at Gaspare and spent another hour in his company talking of ships and pirating. Gaspare owned his vessel and had done well on the open the seas, attacking Turks or Venetians, when he could get away with it.

'Do you ever come to Venice?' Tomasso asked, as they left the taverna.

Gaspare winked. 'I could make a visit. Why?'

'I may have some business to put in your direction,' said Tomasso. He could not allow regrets to cloud his thoughts now. He had sworn that he would bring Don Carlos Grimani to his knees and wipe out his bloodline forever. Soon Don Carlos' ships would sail to Constantinople with the *Cornucopia.* Let him hope then that the voyage would be profitable, let him borrow against the promise of success and sink further into debt. Tomasso's true purpose behind this visit to Florence had little to do with gems and the Duke of Florence; Tomasso had come to strike the first murderous blow against Grimani's heirs. Had Anna been alive still, he knew that she would never forgive him. Tomasso had come to Florence to kill her son the priest, Lorenzo Grimani.

Jerome was a mercenary whom Tomasso di Vincentini had hired with enough gold to buy his soul to keep his silence. Jerome made the winter journey to Carrara with thoughts of the rich reward he would receive for kidnapping a priest. He did not question the reasons, the reward was great enough; he would not have to seek work again this winter. He travelled with Vincentinis' servant, Symeon. Carrara was on the western coast of Italy, over a hundred and twenty miles from Florence. It was a quiet sea town, surrounded by horse-shoe shaped walls. The heights of the Apuan Alps rose steeply from the coast. In the village, the piazzas were cobbled in marble and most of the houses boasted marble columns, delicate window frames or some other decorative feature carved from the stone they all made their living from. Jerome was watched with open suspicion when he came to the place, the Carrarini were hostile and unfriendly, it was costly getting information out of them. Eventually the men he had asked, shook their heads and directed him out of the town towards the steep mountain path, pointing upwards. 'Canale di Fantiscritti,' they chimed in unison, naming the quarry where the tiny Franciscan chapel stood.

The chapel was a long way up the milky ravines of marble. A lonely place that few visited while the frosts of winter closed in. The soldier and his quiet companion found a ruined farm house at the base of a craggy hill; from here Jerome went on alone. He was quite glad to leave his companion behind; the man was of a quiet, dignified nature and found little to laugh at in Jerome's brusque humour.

Jerome met no one on the road. He tethered his horse out of sight of the little church, and walked the rest of the way.

He entered the darkness of a little chapel where fat, yellow-grey stone pillars rose to the arched ceiling, darkening as they ascended. Although the chapel was small, Jerome found it awesome and strangely cold; he was not a frequent visitor of sacred places. He made the sign of the cross and stepped in quietly, his heart thumping. A sweeping whisper caught his attention. An ancient monk was moving rhythmically back and forth with a grass broom. Dead leaves that had entered on the wind, swirled and rustled before him.

Holding his sword quiet at his side, Jerome walked on tip toe and crept forward. He pulled his shoulders back and tried to appear normal. 'Where can I find Father Lorenzo?' He whispered. He got no response whatever from the sweeper. Tapping the ancient on the shoulder and raising his voice a pitch or two Jerome said, 'Where's Lorenzo?'

The elderly man looked at him as if he was not there, then slowly his eyes focused; they were watery blue, heavily lidded and seemed filled with the grace of God. He croaked in a kindly voice, 'Can I help you my son?'

Jerome felt guilt seeping through him. He felt reluctant to involve this blameless, old man in the events that were to follow. He pushed the doubt aside and repeated his question, more politely phrased.

After four further attempts, understanding spread over the monks face like sunshine and he smiled up from his bent position. He took Jerome's sleeve and, with the broom dragging behind, lead him to the door, pointing a bony finger in the direction of a tall building. 'Calligraphy, I should imagine,' he said. He returned to his sweeping.

'Thank you,' said Jerome loudly. He hurried out, glad to leave the gloomy confinement. He reached the tower in long strides. A freezing wind whipped at his hair and snatched his breath away in smoke.

The tower too, was cold the whole place was cold and empty. Jerome climbed the winding stair swiftly and opened the door at the top. Inside there was a young man. He was perched on a tall stool, bent over a glittering parchment spread on a high lectern in front of him. An arched window let the same wind enter and curve its chilly fingers around the room. Even the priest, who Jerome thought should be used to such conditions, looked half frozen with his frayed sleeves pulled over his hands and his sandaled feet blue with cold.

'Lorenzo?' Jerome offered a bright smile.

The priest looked up and smiled in welcome. 'I did not expect any visitors up here, but I would be glad of any excuse to leave it. Is there something I can do?'

'I am seeking one previously known as Lorenzo Grimani. I have come from Florence, a journey, I might add, that I enjoyed not in the least,' said Jerome.

'I am he.'

'Then you, my little saint, must come with me.'

'Has my grandfather sent you? Has anything happened?'

'No, nothing of any consequence, just a problem you may be able to help me with.'

'Then certainly I shall come,' Lorenzo replied. Slipping from his perch, he came forward eagerly and opened the door for his guest.

Jerome felt almost sorry for the deception. 'Thank you kindly,' he said with an inclination of his head. This was going to be easier than he thought.

They walked down the narrow stair. At the bottom, the young Franciscan stood in the stark light and offered the same open smile as turned deep-brown eyes on his visitor. He was at least a head shorter than the soldier. Jerome looked down on the circle of shaved hair. Lorenzo had such a trusting manner that Jerome merely said, 'Could you follow me, it's not far, twenty minutes should do it.'

A shadow of suspicion clouded the youth's face. 'Where is it you wish to take me?' Lorenzo asked uncertainly.

Well, he isn't that much of a fool, thought Jerome. He assumed a sorrowful expression and wrung his hands together. 'They told me you were good with animals. My horse has gone lame, I have left him just down the track. If you could assist me in bringing him up here perhaps we can do something for the poor beast. He and I have been many years together.' That seemed to do the trick, the young man, trustful once more, was in total agreement. Without a word, Jerome led him down the path. They had attracted no attention; apart from the leaf-sweeping monk, Jerome had seen no one.

'You are a soldier?' Lorenzo said, behind him. 'For what army do you fight?'

Jerome thought it was a strange question coming from a priest who spent his life in the middle of nowhere. 'For whatever army pays me the most,' he replied.

'I do not condone your profession. The Lord teaches us that it is wrong to take the life of others,' said the priest seriously.

The last thing he wanted was a lecture! Jerome was grateful to round the corner where his horse, uninjured, stood waiting. It greeted him with a snort and a whisk of its tail. Jerome turned and took the Franciscan's arm in a tight grip. He said, 'It would be greatly to your benefit to get on the horse and, as a special favour to me, keep your preaching to yourself.' He pushed his captive against the animal's side.

Lorenzo turned, squirmed away and started to run.

Jerome grabbed at his habit and pulled him off his feet.

At this, the pious Franciscan turned into a wild beast. Kicking, thumping, biting and writhing like a wet fish, he screamed at the top of his voice.

Jerome cursed and fought away the fists and feet that flew at him. He tried to trap the youth's arms and get a good grip on him, but he fought back so desperately that Jerome saw only one way out. Fending off the blows, he lifted the handle of his knife and brought it down on the shaved head with force. The dark eyes stared at him a moment then closed. The priest crumbled. All the frantic energy fled, and he lay still.

Shaking his head in disbelief, Jerome lifted him and laid him like a sack across the saddle. He led the animal down the steep mountain path. The horse stepped gingerly over the shale and Jerome felt relieved. But his troubles had only just begun.

The sun sank out of sight leaving deep, mist-strewn valleys behind it. Half way down the hillside, Lorenzo suddenly slid off. He reached the ground and began to run. Jerome snatched at him and once more, grasped a handful of hood, roughly pulling him back. The worn material tore and left him holding a shred. Jerome did not like to walk, the trek up to the church and back was all he thought he would have to endure; running was even less popular and reserved only for charging an enemy. He cursed and followed the shadowy figure that clambered like a goat up the rock side.

Eventually the youth stopped and concealed himself in the shadow of a boulder. He thought he was hidden, but the sun, coming from under the clouds for a final blaze of light before it sank behind the marble-snowed crags, illuminated his hiding place. Jerome spotted him and ran forward.

But the priest still had some fight in him. He charged out of his hiding place like a cornered fox. Jerome ducked under a flying fist. The young priest, carried by his own momentum, sprawled on the ground at Jerome's feet. He was up and fighting in seconds. Jerome hit the monk, this time, with enough force to knock him senseless and keep him that way for hours.

It was past midnight by the time Jerome reached the outskirts of Carrara. He headed for a ruined farm were he had left the master's servant and the other two horses. The man's name was Symeon and he had been a quiet, brooding companion on the ride from Florence. He was obviously of African extraction, probably a black Arab, Jerome guessed. Symeon had shown little interest in revealing his history. He had been equally secretive about his master. Jerome had seen enough of life to know the wisdom of this silence; he had stopped his questions.

The dark man was waiting at the doorway. Jerome had led the horse for most of the way down, he refused to ride any further until he had a few hours sleep. He unloaded the unconscious priest and dumped him on a pile of dirty hay. 'Meet the good Father Lorenzo,' he said.

'What happened?' Symeon asked.

'He's wild. He attacked me such furiously I had to knock him senseless, twice. I should have taken a sack with me,' said Jerome. Seeing Symeon glare in disapproval, he added, 'He'll recover enough, and I hope he has a roaring headache when he does.'

Symeon bent and examined the youth. 'He is but a boy.'

Jerome ignored him and rolled up in a blanket in the corner. He had near completed his task. Gold would rattle in his purse as soon as they had delivered the priest to Bagni di Lucca, where Tomasso Vincentini waited. Jerome was asleep in seconds.

A few hours later while they prepared to leave, Symeon said, 'We will reach the valley before sunrise, then we will have to ride hard. Our prisoner is awake but refuses to speak to me. You can tie him to the horse if he makes any trouble.'

'Trouble is something you can be sure of,' Jerome replied.

They tied the unyielding form of Lorenzo securely to the saddle. His mouth was set in a line of defiance, his dark eyes bored into Jerome with hatred.

Jerome winked at him. 'Don't worry lad, they are not going to hurt you.' He did not know then, of the fate that awaited Lorenzo Grimani.

As soon as they reached easier footing, they pushed the horses to their limit and thundered over the stony ground. They rode through the soft rolling hills of the Apuan Alps, with the sea to their left, spread out to the horizon in a blanket of glittering glass-blue in the sun rise. Jerome grinned, the Franciscan was no horseman. He sat his horse bouncing awkwardly. If he had not been tied on, he would have left the saddle on countless occasions. By mid morning they reached Querceta where they dismounted on the outskirts to rest the animals.

Symeon took a good look at the young captive. Still mounted, Lorenzo sat pale and miserable. Symeon had tried talking to him, but the young man had spat at him and called him a devil worshipper. Symeon felt inclined to allow him time to burn off his anger. He offered the boy a drink from his leather flask. Tied as he was, Fra Lorenzo still managed to kick at it and sent it flying. Symeon glared at him. 'You may as well accept the situation and make the best of it,' he said.

'Are you going to kill me?'

'Yes!' Jerome stormed up to him. 'If you don't mend your ways, it would be better for us all!'

They left him on the horse. He refused to speak nor would he accept any food or drink from them during the long, fast journey. To escape notice, they kept off the well-used roads and found their way along little-used mountain tracks. Three hours after darkness they stopped near a stream and ate cold food. Jerome tied Lorenzo to a tree. Symeon began to worry. The boy looked pale and sickly but the defiance still burnt in his eyes. Symeon tore a piece off a hard loaf and offered it to him.

The youth shook his head. He licked his lips and said, 'If you were going to kill me, you would have done so by now, so you need to keep me alive for something. I'm not going to eat your stinking bread or help you at all.'

'Then you will die,' Symeon replied with a wry smile. 'Even a Franciscan vowed to poverty, has to eat. You are the only one who is suffering here. Have you ever ridden before?'

Lorenzo looked down and Symeon thought he was as near to tears as he would allow himself to be. A lump the size of an egg had risen on his forehead and from the way he sat, Symeon knew he would be feeling uncomfortable from the hard ride. 'If you take the bread I will untie you,' he said.

Lorenzo nodded agreement and Symeon, feeling pity, struggled with the tight knots and released him. He sat quietly and ate like a starved animal. Symeon dropped his guard. Lorenzo leapt up and began to run. He headed straight up the hillside until he was swallowed up by darkness.

Jerome cursed Symeon soundly. He took off after their captive with surprising speed.

Lorenzo did not get far. He was unable, the exhausting hours had robbed him of energy and the headache that had pounded all day, had become unbearable. He turned to face the whiskered giant who came pounding after him. A full moon had risen, bathing the hillside in pale light and giving them enough light to see. They stood facing each other over a grey boulder.

'I don't want to lay you flat again, but if you give me no choice' Jerome was breathing heavily, tired after the chase.

Lorenzo didn't much care for being laid flat again either. He stood still and out of reach. 'Where are you taking me? Is this some scheme of my grandfather's to get me to come back? Has he paid you to do this?'

Jerome rubbed his beard. He didn't even know of who the young man spoke. 'It's something like that,' he answered as this seemed the easiest course to take.

But it was the wrong answer. Lorenzo ran. This time he gained more distance, but darkness of a different kind made his head swim with dizziness. He dropped to the ground, bruising the thyme. The smell rose around him, strong and dominating. Jerome picked him up and carried him down the slope over his shoulder.

They were on the road before light, cantering at the same terrible bone shaking pace through the rolling hills of Tuscany.

Lorenzo never dreamed that Don Carlos would go to such lengths to bring him back to Venice. Because he believed this was all Grimani's doing, he was not too worried. As long as he did not try to escape, the big Jerome would not harm him. The other one, Symeon, was a mystery. He seemed gentle and solicitous to Lorenzo's needs. His face was bland and expressionless and he spoke rarely. As they drew near to Lucca, Lorenzo began to eat more and to speak more freely. If he was to escape, he would do so nearer to the town, where help would not be difficult to find.

An hour outside Lucca the party drew to a halt and dismounted near a fast flowing stream. They led the horses to drink and Symeon produced a wine flask. He offered it first to Lorenzo, while Jerome watched with a sour expression. Lorenzo lifted the flask to his lips and drank deeply. He thought the wine unusually bitter, but the taste did not deter him from taking a long drink, more to annoy Jerome that out of need. Shortly afterwards, Lorenzo felt abysmally tired. He sat down with his back to a tree and watched the sunlight on the water. It seemed too bright and too dazzling. He closed his eyes, wondering if he was suffering from some fever, and fell asleep.

When he awoke he was not sitting by the river, but was in a room darkened by night. His mouth was dry and his head pounded. A candle burned by the door, its flame fragmented, writhing as if it lived. Lorenzo looked away. He felt that he had been drugged. He knew with certainty that Don Carlos was not responsible; his grandfather would not poison him. Afraid now, he came more fully awake and saw that he was tied to the cot he lay in. He cried out, putting as much anger into his voice as he was capable of.

The door opened flooding the room with warm light. Lorenzo recognised the dark head of Symeon. He entered carrying a plate of food and a cup. 'Where am I?' Lorenzo asked anxiously.

'We are in Lucca,' Symeon explained. 'At a house in the silk weaver's quarter. Can you drink?'

'Drink? More poison? You will have to force it down my throat this time. I will not be a fool twice!'

Symeon placed the cup and plate on a small table by the wall. He stood with his arms folded over his white gown. All Fra Lorenzo could see of his face were his eyes. He thought that the expression they held was one of pity. Symeon said, 'I would strongly advise you to take the drink. It is true that it contains a drug. You will not be able to bear the pain without it.'

'Pain?' Lorenzo whispered. 'Why am I here? I have never seen you before Carrara, what possible harm could I have done you?'

'You have never harmed me,' answered Symeon. 'For this reason I am sorry for what will happen to you. Take the drink and when you awaken all will be over.'

Lorenzo strained against the rope that imprisoned him. He tried to control the mounting terror. After a moment he said, 'What is going to happen?'

'You are a priest,' said Symeon, 'sworn to obedience and chastity. Will you devote your life to this?'

'Yes, so I had vowed,' Lorenzo replied. His voice echoed his fear.

'Then trust me and take the drink. You will be held down and forced otherwise.'

'For what reason?' Lorenzo cried. 'What is going to happen to me?'

But Symeon did not answer. He picked up the cup and approached the bed.

Stiff with fear and defiance, Lorenzo glared at him and kept his mouth set in a straight determined line. He was quite prepared to die rather than accept the fate they, whoever they were, had devised for him. He began to pray silently.

Symeon nodded his head slowly. He returned the cup to the table and quietly left the room. The draft from the closing door extinguished the candle. Lorenzo was left in darkness.

They came back him before long. Symeon returned, and with him a huge man, taller and broader that Jerome. Neither spoke, they didn't even bring light. In the darkness Lorenzo struggled for all he was worth. But the bounds held and the large man caught hold of his head, wrapping a thick arm around his forehead in a painful grip. With the other hand, the man squeezed Lorenzo's nose, so that he could not breath through it.

Dark terror embraced him, his struggles were pitiful. He felt the cup at his lip, but would not open his mouth. He held his breath for as long as he could, sure that God would grant him peace in death before his body betrayed him. As soon as his lips parted to snatch at the air, the cup was crammed into his mouth and the liquid burned down his throat. He swallowed automatically, unable to stop himself, knowing that he could not breathe until he had swallowed. The liquid spilled down his chin but most poured straight down his throat, the same bitterness. He coughed and spluttered and choked trying to make himself vomit. They held him securely until the drug took effect.

Symeon had done this before, under his previous master's direction, but for boys a great deal younger. Then he had been the slave of a physician in Aleppo before his master had died and Symeon had been given as a gift to Ismael the Syrian. But he had not met his new master, he had been passed on to the Venetian merchant Tomasso di Vincentini. Symeon had not thought that he would have need to call on the knowledge he had picked up while with the physician; he had assisted that master often in the castration of boys. Symeon judged Lorenzo to be in his early twenties, a handsome man with a strong, athletic body. Would the wound kill him? Symeon had known Lorenzo for only a few days, but he had seen the courage in the young man. He did not want Lorenzo to die. If he lived, he would never father children.

That of course was what Tomasso di Vincentini intended. Because this youth belonged to Grimani, his seed must not ripen. Lorenzo would feel the vengeful hand without ever knowing the reason. Would he be content with that? Symeon had advised his master to have the youth killed. But Tomasso would not agree to that; for some reason, he would not have the boy's death on his hands. Symeon could not help thinking that death might be preferable.

Symeon turned away and picked up the small sickle knife beside him.

Even heavily drugged, Lorenzo's body jerked with pain and a scream escaped his lips.

Chapter 28 Dieppe

The *Lauris Nobilis* would remain in Dieppe until the out-going tide came to return her to Southampton loaded with smoked fish; then she would dry dock for the winter. Ambrose Chillingworth intended to hire mules to carry his cloth to Rouen. He was concerned though, he had already heard of the dangers of travelling unprotected through the French countryside.

The previous evening, when Ambrose and the others had left the *Lauris Nobilis*, Ambrose had been near crippled with laughter. He had been surprised and shocked at his own behaviour, but watching Miguel de Cervantes Saavedra's unfortunate mishap with the rain barrel had unhinged Ambrose and he had laughed like a baffoon. The Spaniard had been fished out of the sea with nothing hurt but his pride. Ambrose and his company had tumbled into a new inn off the market square. Once settled, he had ordered the best meal they had to offer. They had chuckled over the events that had delighted Ambrose beyond measure. Ambrose had questioned Emlyn about the cause of the incident, but after the sickening sea crossing, Emlyn had pushed dishes aside and cradled his dark, uncombed head in arms. He had fallen asleep where he sat.

This morning, following their arrival in France, Ambrose and Emlyn crossed the market place at the Puits Sale and joined the crowds flowing about their business in the Grand' Rue. Dieppe was a typical harbour town. In its people, it resembled Chillingworth's beloved Calais. Fishermen, tanners, carriers, shipwrights and carpenters thronged the quayside. Maids with buckets and pretty, blushing cheeks, flashed among them with flouncing skirts. The Corps de Garde in their bright livery, kept a serious eye on everyone. Fish packers, net makers, boys with baskets of oysters and women with bundled laundry bustled through the streets. Whatever the season, the babble of the countless tongues of Europe could be heard everywhere.

Ambrose found, to his annoyance after three attempts, that hiring pack mules in December was not as easy as during the height of the trading season. Abandoning hope, he led the way to the house of a draper of long acquaintance. It was the address on the slip of paper he had been handed on the ship. Ambrose had known the man and his wife well when they had lived in Calais. He wondered how Emlyn would react when he saw the payment for the firearms. Ambrose hesitated on the doorstep, thinking up some errant he could send Emlyn on. The door opened and he lost the chance.

The draper's wife greeted them. She had her arms laden with stockings and breech-hose. She was Isabelle Benoit, her silken sleeves embroidered with lilies and festooned with pearls and her rich brown hair, piled on top and woven with ribbons. She dumped her bundle on a passing servant and grasped Ambrose in an embrace of jasmine water and soft, feminine curves. Ambrose made no effort to struggle free and even suffered her numerous wet kisses. She grasped a handful of Emlyn's cloak and pulled him inside like a fly into a spider's web.

'Why Monsieur Chillingworth!' Her voice was high pitched. 'Eugine! Eugine! Look 'oo is 'ere!' She led Ambrose and Emlyn through the shop. They passed the counter and the shelves stacked to the ceiling with cottons, lengths of velvet, coarse woven wool, Florentine damasks, Saxe cloth, tissues and satins. Ambrose looked at it all appreciatively as he sped by.

'There is not a cloth on God's earth Monsieur that cannot be found on Eugine Benoit's shelves,' boasted Isabelle noticing the merchants interest. 'But mon cher, 'oo do not come to buy?'

Then the draper appeared and he knocked his eyeglasses askew as he embraced Ambrose with vigorously. Eugine Benoit was as round as a barrel, pink and bald as an egg. He made up for the lack of hair by displaying extraordinary hats. At present he wore one that resembled an odd, striped sock with a gold bead and a pair of blue tassels on the end.

When he'd recovered from the embraces, Ambrose introduced Emlyn. They were led to a back room with a glass of wine each and the promise of a meal. The meal, Ambrose guessed from past experience, would be excellent. When it arrived Madame Benoit sat close beside him and beamed under his compliments, proud of her kitchen..

Always polite, Eugine Benoit, waited until the meal was completed and cleared away. He refilled the wine glasses before he placed a purse on the table. He gave Ambrose a knowing smile. 'For service rendered,' he said.

Ambrose stretched his legs in the comfort of the room. Isabelle had gone about her tasks. Head to one side Ambrose had admired her behind as she bustled out the door. He and Isabelle shared fond memories. The purse disappeared into the folds of Ambrose's doublet. Without looking at Emlyn, he said, 'Thank you Eugene. I trust they will be of use to you and your friends.'

Eugine said, 'If you have cloth mon ami, I will buy it as I know you are a man of taste. But here in December? I feel this is not the purpose of your visit.'

A wood fire crackled in the hearth. Emlyn remained quiet and attentive. Eugine's question was one he too would like to know the answer to.

Ambrose said, 'I do have cloth, which, apart from friendship, brings me under your generous roof. But the cloth is for Italy and I intend to go with it. I need mules and so far I have been unable to secure any.'

'Mules? All that I have are yours,' offered Eugene. 'They are stabled outside the town and will be sent for immediately. But you my friend, are on a fool's errant?'

'No, I have urgent business there that has nothing to do with wool. I cannot await upon the mood of the weather nor the season. The cloth I carry, is indeed of good quality. I would be a fool indeed to make the journey unprofitable.'

'The Italians have agents in Antwerp. Why not allow me to contact them to take the cloth from you? I could hold it until spring and get a good profit for you. The roads are not safe. It is unbecoming, for you to act like a travelling pedlar my friend. Men can be hired to do this, or is this boy?'

Ambrose sipped his wine appreciatively and shook his head. 'If the cloth were to delay me, I would of course be forced to sell it elsewhere. This is not to my liking as I should lose by such an action. Mad though it may appear, I would like it to travel with me.' He paused and looked at Emlyn. 'I hope that Emlyn here will come on the journey, as he has a share in the enterprise.'

Emlyn smiled but did not reply.

Having eaten twice as much as the merchant, Eugene loosened the ties of his doublet and sighed with content. Isabelle's currant pudding at midday, left him lethargic, agreeable and disinclined to move. He sent a servant to fetch the mules and to lead them to the warehouse where Ambrose had left his merchandise. He persuaded the merchant to spend a few hours talking about old times, when they had both been free of family and care raking money in at Antwerp.

Eugene said, 'You will not go this day. It will take an hour or more to fetch the animals and Isabelle would be most put out if you did not spend a night here at least, she is very fond of you. The boy is welcome too, we have plenty of room here.'

Ambrose remembered how fond Isabelle once had been of him. He hoped Eugine saw his high colour as an effect of the wine. 'Thank you,' he said. 'I would like to accept, but there are a few matters that I must attend to before I am rendered helpless by your hospitality.'

Engine's face shone in the heat of the room as he filled the glasses again, ignoring the merchant's negative words. 'Drink to your content, do not worry, my man will deliver the mules.'

Ambrose sank further into his chair. He said, 'There is another young man with me. He and Emlyn here, are out of sorts at present.'

'Then a man will be sent there to inform your servant and friends of your whereabouts. Will you agree to this?'

Ambrose stroked his beard and assumed a thoughtful expression; he was tempted to stay. The day had been good and the wine too strong. 'You are a good man Eugene Benoit,' he chuckled 'It seems we are stretching your reserves.'

'Not at all, mules are for carrying, wine is for drinking and servants are to serve. Besides I know the whereabouts of a man who is known to us both; a man who will provide protection for you and your cloth from Rouen all the way to Italy.'

'Who?' Ambrose laughed. He was pleased to discover this, as he had intended to hire mercenaries for the journey.

But Eugine was not going to allow his guests to escape so easily. He belched and smiled. 'Let us take some of your precious time and do our best to consume it.'

After three hours they managed to escape the kindness of Eugene Benoit. They walked through the busy streets. Emlyn read signs above shops and sometimes paused and peered down narrow passages that were overshadowed by upper stories. The air was ice cold, cold enough to sober the most determined of revellers. Emlyn had drunk little. He wanted to stay alert. Although he managed to hide it, he was very angry with Ambrose Chillingworth. Emlyn knew that he was being coerced into something that would be detrimental to him. He stopped walking and waited until Ambrose had turned around before he spoke. He said, 'If the Spanish ships were driven onto England's shores by the Dutch pirates, why are they prevented from now continuing on their way?'

'Because the pirates are still out there, waiting like sharks to fall upon them,' said Ambrose.

'They travelled up the Narrow Sea without escort or protection; surely that means they were carrying nothing of great value.' Emlyn paused, 'or do they in fact carry a rich cargo and sailed thus for a ruse?'

Ambrose shrugged. 'Who knows? No doubt the Queen will provide them with an escort when it is safe to do so and send them on their way.'

Emlyn said, 'Are they the wages fleet that Philip has sent to pay the troops under the Duke of Alva?'

Ambrose pulled at his ear lobe nervously. 'I would say that you sail in dangerous waters Emlyn. Such speculation is not for the likes of you and I.'

'Why would the Secretary of State come to visit a cloth merchant in Southampton?'

'He is an old and dear friend.'

Emlyn huffed with impatience. 'Before I left France in the spring,' he continued, 'I discovered quite by chance that Alva's troops did not receive the pay owed to them. That the pay was expected was too widely known; it was too much of a temptation for the brigands who treat the mountain passes as their own empires. Philip could not send the wages over land. One must assume then, that he attempted to send them by sea. If he had sent war ships into English and Dutch waters, he would have been attacked, so he sent smaller vessels hoping that they would escape attention. The Dutch privateers are as aware of the story as France is. They merely had to sit back and wait; anything Spanish coming into these waters would be suspected of carrying a handsome cargo.' Emlyn paused and licked his lips. The day had colder; his breath misted the air.

Ambrose said, 'Is that it?'

Emlyn shook his head. He folded his arms across his chest to keep his hands warm. 'When attacked, the ships turned for England expecting help; we are not at war with Spain yet. William Cecil was as knowledgeable as the rest of them concerning the matter, he has informers throughout Europe. He is also aware that further delay in paying the troops in the Netherlands can lead to nothing but desertion and violence. England keeps the ships and in doing so helps the Protestants in the Netherlands.'

Ambrose bent his head and rubbed his hands together. 'Your reasoning is plausible. However there is one rather large point that you have neglected. Queen Elizabeth has no intention of detaining the ships, to do so would antagonise Philip? No, we are not at war with Spain and nor do we intend to war with Spain. Yet the Queen is not so merciless as to send this stray fleet back into dangerous waters; they must be patient and they must wait until our gracious Queen deems it safe for them to continue. It adds up to a sticky situation for everyone concerned. Now, are we to stand here until we freeze over?'

Emlyn was not yet satisfied with the matter about the ships, but he dropped the subject and fell into step beside the Englishman. When

Ambrose had threatened him on board the *Lauris Nobilis*, Emlyn had been left in no doubt that the threats would be carried out if he did not comply. Ambrose might appear to be mild natured and mild mannered, but Emlyn suspected that there was a much greater strength and determination in the man. Emlyn returned to his earlier scrutiny of the shop signs. He said, 'I was looking for a pawn broker's, somewhere I can leave some valuables for safe keeping.'

'Valuables?' Ambrose said. 'Perhaps I can be of some help. I know Dieppe well. Is it some address you seek?'

Emlyn looked at him and began to shake his head then changed his mind. He said, 'I need to find some banker's agent. Genoese of Florentine? I know not which.'

'The Medici by all means,' said Ambrose. 'That is, if it concerns money.'

Emlyn felt uncomfortable. He shuffled his feet, undecided how to answer. Yet, he did trust Ambrose Chillingworth, the merchant had not sent him away when he had reached the draper's house. Emlyn had been witness to the payment for the muskets, so Ambrose had shown his own willingness to trust him.

'I will point out the right building to you,' Ambrose said. 'You do not need to divulge anything to me Emlyn. Your business is not mine to inquire after.'

'I would value your advice,' said Emlyn. 'It concerns some jewels that my mother left me. Gruffydd said that you might know something of the worth.'

'You wish to secure them?'

'I think that might be wise. He advised me not to travel with them.' Emlyn could see that Ambrose was surprised to hear this; he'd probably thought that Emlyn hadn't as much as two pennies to rub together.

Ambrose said, 'I intend to hire mercenaries in Rouen, so we will be well guarded from there. I would say that Rouen or Paris. Here in Dieppe, you may not find a trustworthy agent. In Rouen there is a Medici house run by the banker Benetto Rovigo. I will write it down for you.'

'I will do as you say, perhaps in Rouen.' Emlyn replied. 'The jewels are worth nothing to me as they are. I would turn them to coin in order to reach Italy.'

Ambrose stopped walking and eyed him with circumspection.

Emlyn stopped and looked back at him innocently.

Ambrose said, 'You will have guessed that this journey has little to do with wool?'

'But more to do with Queen and country?'

'Precisely.'

John Moore had seen to everything. He had even inspected the mules and found stabling for them until the following morning. With him was Goronwy Glyn Parry. Perhaps the man suffers from a melancholy nature, thought Ambrose, for I have yet to see him smile. With that thought in mind, Ambrose found some task for Emlyn. Then he took the other Welshman to the back of the stables were the straw was warm and they could eat the fish he had brought, in relative peace and quiet. They found an empty stall free of manure, even though the smell prevailed.

Goronwy finished the fish and sat with a pile of bones between his feet.

Ambrose said, 'Goronwy, in Southampton, Emlyn may well have saved your life and the others of whom you spoke.'

Goronwy looked up, anger flaring in his dark eyes. 'Am I to abandon all because he was too afraid to sacrifice his life for what we believed in? Do you think for a minute that it was all for my sake? Emlyn preserves himself. He is no fool, even though he acts like one all the while.'

'I had not noticed,' said Ambrose, 'indeed he seemed just the opposite.'

'No?' Goronwy looked at him as if he was a questioning child. 'How do you think the Spanish gentleman suffered as he did? An act of God? Emlyn tumbles through life in chaos. The Society of Jesus never had a moment of peace while Emlyn Tomas pranced under their roof.'

Ambrose stared at the floor to hide his smile. He had thought the incident in the harbour a little close to be a coincidence at all. But Miguel de Cervantes Saavedra had shown no hostility towards Emlyn, he must have assumed that his mishap was an accident. 'If it is as you say, that he caused Miguel de Cervantes to fall overboard,' he pointed out, 'why would he contrive such a thing?'

Goronwy released a bitter snort of laughter. 'Why? Does there have to be a reason? Emlyn probably did it just to see what would happen. Some poor unfortunate will be blamed for carelessness and punished for the curiosity of Emlyn Tomas. I doubt if it has even occurred to him. He never accepted guidance and would always go his own way, but I never believed that he would stoop to betrayal!'

'Goronwy it is not easy to lay down your life for a cause, whatever that cause may be. Sometimes it is braver to live for what you believe in. I think he made the right choice in preserving the life of William Cecil. Where would England be without the wisdom and guidance of Cecil? It was not the man Emlyn chose to safeguard, but what he stands for. Goronwy this is not a time for England's men to leave her. Emlyn was being loyal to what he saw as right, loyal to the Queen of England. I would advise you to do the same. Go, if you must and take your holy orders, I think you will make a fine priest, but do not visit your grievance on England Goronwy. It will end in nothing but a stake of burning fire. Is that a fate you would wish on yourself or even on Emlyn?'

Goronwy stretched his legs out, rustling the straw. He folded his arms across his wide chest as if they were armour. 'I have been a fool Master Chillingworth,.' he said, 'for you are a Protestant and I am sworn to the old ways. We will never agree. But for Emlyn it is different, he is Catholic. Tomorrow we return to Paris and soon after that will enter the service of the church. In time Emlyn will settle and know that it is right.'

Ambrose said, 'Has he agreed to this? You and he may in time gain favour and be able to return to Wales. There are other choices aside from a life serving God.'

'We always planned to become priests together. We thought of the New World and all its promise,' Goronwy explained. The tension seemed to lessen in him. He dropped his defensive arms and picked up a fish bone twirling it in his fingers. His eyes softened in memory. He said, 'Now Emlyn has nothing to return to in Wales, nor do I. His uncle, Squire Hugh has never taken a liking to him and has never treated him as kin. That's why he sent him to be a priest. Emlyn is the son of the Lady Anne, the Squire's sister, or so I've been led to believe. It was before my time but my father told me that she wed an Italian merchant. Emlyn was born too long after he died, to be his son, or so the story goes. She was never heard of again and he believes himself illegitimate.'

Ambrose sat thoughtful for a moment. So the boy was indeed illegitimate, father unknown. His mother was probably dead and in disgrace at that. 'How did he arrive? A basket on the doorstep? Left in the crib on Christmas morning?'

Goronwy raised his eyes. 'He came when he was about six years old. Brought from somewhere in Europe by a priest,' he explained with a faint smile. 'A right little princeling he was. He talked in gibberish and said his father was a Barbary Prince. After that he never spoke of it again, not for love or money.'

'Why not?'

'The squire beat him black. Told him he was the low born son of a devil worshipper, if he was anyone's son at all, and that if he spoke of it, he would be burned to death. It was a terrible beating, we thought for a time that Emlyn would not recover. My mother cared for him, it was two weeks before he could even stand. Emlyn never said anything again, his past belongs to him alone. Squire Hugh had no time for him and believed from the start that Emlyn was some part of a plan to undermine master Owain's inheritance. Emlyn had no protection from his grandfather then, he was away, here in fact fighting for Calais.'

Ambrose nodded slowly. He said, 'Was there any proof of Emlyn's identity?'

'He arrived with some letters but I know nothing of them, 'cept his mother wanted him to enter the church. This suited his uncle, he was Catholic then. He knew that a life in the church could only be made outside the shores of the realm, some place where the lack of legitimate parents would be concealed. In Wales, Emlyn had the name Bastard placed upon him. It has remained so ever since. He had no defence against it.'

'Would knowledge of this not bar him from joining the Society of Jesus?' Ambrose was sure that Goronwy must be aware of this.

'The Jesuits would not throw away a good pot because the pattern on the rim was faulty,' said Goronwy.

Emlyn awoke when it was fully dark. He had fallen asleep in a warm, comfortable bed at the inn. He had decided that he would show the gems to the Englishman before he sought a secure place to leave them; he and the Englishman half trusted each other. But Emlyn was a little reluctant to part with the jewels that Fra Sebastiano had kept for him. If they provided some clue as to what had become of Anne Morgan, Emlyn would need them with him when he reached Venice. He knew very little about bankers and trusted them less; his lack of knowledge making him cautious.

His room was along the corridor behind the common room, a small, neat rectangle with a comfortable bed and an adequate fire. The noise of bawling and the discordant sounds of mandolin and pipe were magnified as he opened the door. He avoided the main room and sought the kitchen. There he charmed a slice of beef and a new loaf out of the kitchen maids.

The inn had filled as darkness fell. Emlyn recognised some of the crew of the *Lauris Nobilis*, they were recounting the tale of the sailing master amongst much laughter; it came out embellished and exaggerated. They greeted Emlyn when they saw him. Although he waved he did not move to join them. The strumming mandolin dragged a bawdy song out of the drinkers. The room was hot and crowded.

He found Goronwy alone at a corner table. He looked sunk in misery and jars of ale littered the table. Emlyn sat opposite and filled a spare cup. Goronwy acknowledged his presence with a hostile glare and then turned away and contemplated the wall without a word. Emlyn ordered more ale and placed his back against the wall and his feet up on the long bench. Goronwy continued to ignore him. If he did glance in his direction, it was with the utmost distaste, as if something unmentionable sat beside him like a succubus come to swallow his soul.

Emlyn waited while they got drunk in silence together. He thought that Goronwy felt no pain at being banished from the place of his birth and held no regrets at the ruin left behind them. He would return with his cross and bring Wales, at least, back to the Holy Church. That was his dream and no state of exile would prevent him from achieving it. Emlyn wanted to try and talk Goronwy into coming to Italy with him. He was afraid of what Goronwy might do if he went to Dounai.

An hour had passed. Emlyn said, 'You can beat me to a pulp if you like, but it is not going to change the situation. Goronwy I have thought long on the circumstances we have created for ourselves. To become a priest is no small matter and it requires a great deal of sensible thought and a devotion that I do not believe I have. I have fulfilled the oath I made to you and returned to France with you. It is not my intention to become a priest. I have tried to tell you...'

Goronwy's fist pounded the table. He lifted his head and glared. The flickering candle shadows made dark wells of his eyes. Within them burnt the glittering light of his fury. He blindly snatched at the ale jug and filled his cup without dropping his thunderous glare; the ale splashed over the rim. He stood up violently, overturning the bench, it slamming against the tiled floor. After a moment's hesitation, he threw the contents of his cup into Emlyn's face.

Emlyn held his gaze without moving a muscle. The beer dripped off his hair, his lashes and the end of his nose. The noise in the inn subsided. The mandolin played on alone. Faces turned to watch and coins jangled hoping for the entertainment of a fight.

Goronwy sneered in disgust and threw his cup. It shattered against the wall, showering Emlyn with pottery shards.

Still Emlyn didn't move. He knew that one blow from Goronwy's meaty hand would probably floor him. He almost groaned aloud at the thought.

To Goronwy, Emlyn's words concerning abandoning the priesthood and all that they had planned together, was the ultimate treachery. He spoke the words he would never have spoken before. 'I was fool to ever expect more from a wretch born of a mother exposing her nether parts at every tavern door! You, like your word, are nothing, with not even a father's name to attach to your own!'

Emlyn dropped his head, dripping ale. How often Goronwy had defended him against such taunts; taunts that had always aroused Emlyn's anger? Now the words left him cold.

'Beat you to a pulp?' Goronwy snarled. 'I would not stoop to soil my hands with you.' Like a maddened bear, he brought his fist down on to the table. The wood splintered and creaked in protest, the jar bounced, splashed and overturned and the candle flew out of its holder, spluttering out in spilled ale.

This time Emlyn flinched. Goronwy turned his back and stormed out of the room. The held breath went out of the watchers with a shudder. Wary eyes followed in his wake. Emlyn sat in the darkness with his head bowed. He thought of William Cecil and the guns for the Huguenots with a gut-wrenching flood of shame. Had he been right? What was right? Church or country? Should a man be forced to choose?

He and Goronwy had sworn to uphold the true faith They had come to France to continue their education. The Catholics who remained behind had attended services at the parish church, to avoid attention, while still practician their own religion in private. They had appealed to the Holy Father for help. The Pope's answer to their problems had been to forbid any Catholic from attending the heretic services, not even on pain of suffering.

To Emlyn the folly of such a judgement was plain to see. Influential families, landowners and learned men, doctors, lawyers, students, and priests, had been forced to take the oath of Supremacy, declaring Queen Elizabeth the head of the church in England; they had declared themselves Protestant to escape prosecution. Men of lesser means had soon followed their example. Others still practised their faith in secret, hearing mass in private houses and giving protection to scholars and priests who strove to preach and hold the dwindling Catholic community together.

Such had been the hopes of Goronwy and Emlyn and many like them. The written word, had already displayed its value in spreading the teachings of Catholicism. Leaflets had been smuggled into England in all manner of ways. The beleaguered Catholics, who bore the brunt of the storm, were not forgotten.

'And what of you Emlyn Tomas?' Emlyn asked himself, in a savage whisper. 'Do I lack courage or do I lack conviction?'

The next day, everything seemed clothed in ice. The sky cleared from darkness, brittle blue and winter sunlight washed the frost with chill glitter. Before they left, Ambrose bid farewell to Eugine Benoit and his cuddlesome wife.

'The flavour of Paris is ill mixed,' warned Eugine, shivering in his nightshirt. 'Peace has been agreed at Longjumeau to end the present religious strife, but it is a peace on lips alone. In reality, a man must watch the company he keeps and keep a sharp eye at his back. Deal only with Huguenots, our own kind, my friend. I'm sending two of my own men with you as far as Rouen, they can return when they are ready. It is unwise to travel unprotected, even the road to Paris is watched by thieves.'

Ambrose smiled. 'I will hire the mercenaries that you told me of Eugine, if they are still in Rouen. They are always at a loss in winter when the fighting is over.'

'I wish you God's blessing Ambrose, for whatever path you take.'

Thanking him and paying him well for the mules, Ambrose left the draper's house with foreboding. He picked up his mules, his cloth and servants and, with some misgiving, his Welshmen. They were both nursing sore heads from drinking too much ale. Ambrose had no intention of travelling to Paris, he hoped to avoid the town and continue on to Lyons and from there to the Alpine road.

After his talk with Goronwy the day before, Ambrose was constantly worried about his choice of travelling companion. He believed Goronwy to be a man of honour and convinced himself that, whatever the Welshman thought of heretical merchants, Ambrose Chillingworth would not be among the condemned. It was over a hundred miles to Paris, he hoped that with forbearance, they could remain in each other's company on the journey they shared.

The cavalcade trailed out of Dieppe through the long frozen shadows laced with ice. Breath misted in the frigid air and the mules grumbled under their burdens. There were few travellers on the road. A shepherd with six sheep and a ram fell in with them, as their pace was slow. He was taking his animals to Paris to be slaughtered for the coming festivities of Christmas and was grateful for the protective company.

By mid-morning when the sun was high but had done little to warm the air, the sound of galloping hooves turned Ambrose's head. He gazed back along the road they had travelled. A group of horsemen bore down on them. As soon as they were in sight, Emlyn turned his horse and rode back to Ambrose's side. 'Do you recognise them?'

'Our friendly Spaniards, who could not keep to their feet on a docked ship?' Ambrose replied with a trace of humour.

It was indeed the overdressed Spaniards with their attendants. When they drew level, they shouted and cursed, driving their spurs to their mounts and creating havoc among the sheep. For a moment Ambrose saw the fierce eyes of Don Diego de Luzon, meet those of Emlyn with a flare of recognition. The Spaniard's pulled their horses to a walk.

Philip of Spain was at odds with France, never sure whether France would support him or turn against him, threatened as it was by Spain's overlord-ship of the neighbouring Netherlands. Philip had attempted to avoid conflict my marrying Elizabeth of Valois, the eldest daughter of Henry II, but that French king was now dead, God rest his soul, and France struggled between the extreme Catholic Dukes of Guise and the determined Huguenots. The Queen Mother, Catherine de' Medici, favoured the Huguenots when it was to her advantage and persecuted them when not. Ambrose felt comforted by the thought that the Spaniards would find little comfort in the court of Charles IX and his dominant mother.

'That is Don Diego de Luzon,' said Emlyn. The riders had drawn level and attached themselves to the company, churning up a shower of frozen mud. 'He is an agent of Don Fernando Alvarez de Toledo, the Duke of Alva.'

'Really?' Ambrose felt the colour drain from his face. 'How do you know?'

'I spoke to him on the *Lauris Nobilis*, remember? He has no French.'

Ambrose remembered, the Spaniards had no French, Matthew had mentioned it and Ambrose, like a fool, had suggested they borrow Emlyn. Ambrose said, 'Do you think that they follow us?'

Emlyn looked at him a moment without offering a reply. Then he smiled and said, 'They have misplaced something as you know. They seem to think that you or I or Goronwy may know something of its disappearance.'

Ambrose swallowed with a gulp and tried to read the expression in Emlyn's eyes. 'And?'

'Fortunately, Master Chillingworth, Goronwy has no talent for foreign tongues.'

In extreme discomfort, Ambrose squirmed in the saddle. He cleared his throat. He looked at Emlyn thoughtfully. There was something he couldn't figure out here and he had a gut feeling that it was something to do with Emlyn's behaviour on the *Lauris Nobilis*. If Emlyn had caused the accident, as Goronwy believed, what were his reasons? 'Emlyn,' he said as sternly as he was able, 'did you have anything to do with the mishap aboard ship?'

Emlyn raised an eyebrow. 'Is that what you think?'

'Well it has been suggested to me that your part was not entirely innocent.'

Emlyn gave a short burst of laughter. 'Goronwy, I expect. He thinks I have a hand in any misfortune that occurs within twenty miles of my presence.'

'Well did you?'

Emlyn gathered his reins to leave, as if he was not going to answer. Then he changed his mind and offered Ambrose a dazzling smile. 'Whatever you may think,' he said 'I had no axe to grind with Miguel de Cervantes Saavedra.'

Which answered the merchants question not at all. Or did it? Ambrose was quite infuriated with the youth. Emlyn suspected that Ambrose had something to do with the stray Spanish fleet; he had come close to the truth. If they were to travel together, there were some matters that must be cleared between them. It seemed as if Emlyn was not ready to trust anyone.

Ambrose pondered his precarious position. Had Emlyn's intended to humiliate Miguel de Cervantes Saavedra? If so why? Had the mishap been designed for another and had not gone quite according to his plan? Ambrose shook his reins and thumped heels into the horse's side, urging it forward. Now he had Spaniards to contend with too. Ambrose had experienced siege at Calais, he was beginning to feel the same closing in of forces.

Queen Elizabeth now held the Spanish gold under the pretence of protecting it. Word would have travelled fast and Don Diego de Luzon may have boarded the *Lauris Nobilis* for the sole purpose of stopping negotiations to transfer the loan in England's favour. He probably knew that the *Lauris Nobilis* had set sail from the very same port as the one holding some of the Spanish wages fleet. Perhaps William Cecil's mistake had been in underestimating the quality of the Spanish intelligence network in England. Ambrose himself was impressed. It meant Spain had at least one agent close to the more secretive happenings at Queen Elizabeth's court. And, although they could know nothing of Ambrose's part in the scheme, it would take no more than an infant mentality to guess it.

Which meant only one undeniable truth, the Spaniards had questioned Emlyn already and probably discovered where his and Goronwy's affiliation lay. That left Ambrose Chillingworth isolated with the suspicion of Don Diego de Luzon pointed solely in his direction. Then he remembered the oranges. Was it possible to poison an orange? And if it was and had failed was there to be another attempt on his life? Emlyn may have guessed a great deal and Ambrose already knew how readily the boy gave up information to escape a difficult situation. 'Emlyn preserves himself,' Goronwy had said. What if Goronwy was right? 'Your greatest danger lies with your own choice of travelling companions,' William Cecil had warned.

Don Diego de Luzon seemed to pay no attention to the English merchant. He pulled his horse in close to Emlyn and spoke to him in soft whispers. Ambrose watched Emlyn stiffen and wondered what passed between them. Then Don Diego reached out a hand, gloved in soft leather and loaded with costly rings. The hand caressed Emlyn's thigh. Even from behind, Ambrose could sense the danger signals, if Emlyn hit Don Diego, he would be arrested and probably lose his life. But the danger passed as Emlyn pulled at his horse, turned and rode back to the merchant's side; his face was as dark as thunder. Ambrose smiled grimly. Was it Don Diego de Luzon who was targeted to end up in the sea at Dieppe harbour?

Don Diego de Luzon watched Emlyn retreat and his eyes met those of Ambrose. He slowed his mount. 'Is he your catamite Englishman?' He laughed and his companions obediently joined in. 'Let me know when you tire of him, he would make good sport!' There was no humour in the heavy lidded eyes, only glittering interest and mocking invitation.

He spoke in Spanish but Ambrose knew enough of the language to understand. Ambrose smiled pleasantly. In English he said, 'May your member wither in your hand. Godless sodomite!'

Don Diego's face darkened, sensing an insult.

With a bland and innocent expression, Emlyn translated Ambrose's words.

Miguel de Cervantes Saavedra who rode beside Don Diego, touched his arm and whispered urgently. The grandee drew himself to his splendid height and glared contemptuously down his nose at Ambrose. The Spaniards drew away and sent their mounts galloping down the frozen road, leaving the slower travellers far in their wake.

The sunlight dimmed as a wraith-like, freezing mist furled around tree trunks. It swirled about the ice-frosted grassy tussocks and lichen spotted farmhouse walls; washing the winter landscape with a brush of indecipherable grey. Gaunt trees lifted threadlike branches, cob-webbed with a filament of mist. The sun hung like a sorcerer's orb dipped in sallow, winter-orange.

It was a hungry winter for France, this of itself was nothing new, but the year's harvest had been poor. What little the country people had gleaned had left them bitter. They were in no mood to watch six sheep, a ram and eight loaded mules go by as if it were the height of summer; there was enough here to provide a Christmas worth remembering for generations. They waited, the thieves with eyes glittering in the frost and cudgels grasped in their skeletal hands.

The possibility of attack had also occurred to Ambrose, not only the possibility, he realised with resignation, but the probability. The two men from Eugine Benoit, were stout farm lads, muleteers who carried thick staffs and wore short blades at their belts. They looked as if they were quite able to use either, but they represented poor defence. Matthew, Ambrose knew, would be armed to the teeth, John Moore too, looked capable of defending himself. Goronwy was thick-set and looked able to plough through a stone wall without blinking an eyelid. And Emlyn Tomas?

Ambrose cursed himself for his foolishness. Don Diego and his party were now far ahead and Spanish coin could wink brightly for eyes sunken in deprivation. Was it possible that they could be hired to attack the English party? Ambrose shook his head, he was allowing his thought to get the better of him. He just wanted to be on his way across the plain of Grandmont and see the walls of Rouen rise up above it.

Matthew, having reached the same inevitable conclusion, turned his horse and rode back between the sheep to join him. 'We should turn back,' he suggested glumly.

Ambrose ignored him. He called to the shepherd who had joined them on the road. 'Henri! Is there a farmhouse near that could accommodate us all?'

Henri rubbed his red, dripping nose with his sleeve and shook his head like a dog coming out of water. His smile was a childlike grin, as if he had achieved something worthy of award.

The two muleteers seemed to catch something of Ambrose's concern. One came up to him with an expression of anxiety. he said, 'Do you fear attack Monsieur?'

'Yes Jacque, I do.' Ambrose rubbed his hands together. Thickly gloved, they were still numbed with cold. The sun dimmed.

'Then we must leave Henri and his sheep Monsieur. Speed is our only hope of escaping if we are attacked.'

'Excellent idea,' Ambrose replied enthusiastically. He had no intention of turning back, there were enough of them to defend themselves against an odd band of rouges. Henri the shepherd would have to make his own way.

'I know the road here,' Jacque assured him, 'and there is one place only on this road where a thief may wait in security. It lies a good half mile from here. If we each take two mules we can start to run and build enough speed up so that we may bowl them over, should they be there of course. Louis thinks he has seen men moving in the mist.'

Ambrose stared at him incredulously. But what other choice did they have if time was as short as that? The very air seemed to press around them and reach with icy fingers deep within their clothing. What sensible thief would want to go aboard on a day like this? A thief paid by Spanish gold?

Emlyn had been listening attentively. He turned to Henri and drew him to one side, no doubt to inform the poor wretch that they could not risk taking him with them. Ambrose watched as Emlyn indicated with his hands a way to cut inland and possibly avoid being seen, easy enough for a man with sheep and a dog, but impossible for mounted men with loaded mules. Henri the shepherd was grinning, as if the idea of armed thieves lying in wait to murder, was an invitation to the winter fair.

Goronwy raised a quarrelsome voice to object in Welsh. Emlyn spoke quietly and whatever his reply, Goronwy simmered back to his brooding silence. He had picked up a stout cudgel somewhere along the way and was swinging it menacingly.

They rode slowly now on the verge of grass at the roadside, holding harness and horse as quiet as possible. The hooves left bruises of crushed frost and moved with soft thuds, hardly audible in the still air. At the front, Jacque was astride a mule with a heavy staff length-wise across his knee. Behind him rode Louis and John Moore, both equally determined. Ambrose pulled at the two mules in his charge. He caught a glint of amusement in Mathews eye. His servant carried a short handled hatchet, capable of cleaving a man's skull with one vicious swipe. In the rear came Goronwy with the rest of the pack animals. Emlyn had disappeared with Henri. Ambrose wondered whether the boy was concerned about the safety of the shepherd or merely concerned about himself. They all watched Jacque for the arranged signal.

His hand went up without a sound, and dropped. He spurred his mount, the mule responded instantly. The others followed and Goronwy let loose the most blood-curdling war cry, Ambrose had ever heard. They rode like madmen, giving voice to their fear and anger.

Dim shapes armed with sticks came at them from the side of the road. A dog barked. From somewhere, sheep joined with terrified bleating. Someone 'Hallooed' out of the mist like a banshee.

Ambrose clung on and guided the horse sure beneath him. A hand reached up and grasped his leg, digging in iron fingers as sharp as bone. Ambrose stabbed at it with his meat-trimming knife, while his heart trembled with revulsion. The hand clung on like a severed claw and endured three stabs before it let go with a moan of bitter defeat.

Hollow eyes glared out of starved, fearful faces. Hands armed with clubs reached out, thrashing desperately. Thieves ran and leapt alongside, shouting to each other in the confusion. There were howls of pain and the sickening thud of wood on flesh. True to his ideals, Jacque clouted his way through the thieves and overrode any that lay in his path. Horses snorted, hooves thundering on the frozen ground. The mules rolled their eyes in terror and plunged into the affray, panic stricken. Matthew howled with joy when his hatchet brought a wail of pain from his victim.

The fog swirled around black-branched shrubs. From the invisible greyness came moans of fear, mumbled snatches of prayer, and a soul wrenching wail of utter loneliness. This was followed by a cackle of wretched laughter and more idiotic 'Halloo's'. Fearful of what lurked to either side, shrieking in the mist, the thieves faltered.

None were slain, but they would not be so careless with their next prey. Nursing wounds, they fled, foul-mouthed with curses.

The horses were still running in fear and it took some time to bring them under control. When they drew to a standstill the mules puffed snorts of steam and stamped their feet nervously.

Out of the mist behind them, came a blot of sheep, they were running as if they were one creature. Mist trailed in their wake and Henri's dog darted around them holding them together. Emlyn appeared next, leading his horse, he had captured a bow, a quiver of arrows and a hat shaped like a toadstool. With ceremony he swept off the hat and bowed, presenting the weapons to a wall of swirling grey. Then the large form of Henri loomed out of the fog. His booming 'Halloo!' shattered the frozen day and made merry with the fear they were all fighting to control.

Emlyn straightened, panting with mirth. Henri swung him off his feet in a brotherly hug.

Ambrose felt his own tension dissolve and joined in the merriment. Goronwy offered a prayer of thanksgiving and all echoed his words with gratitude. He was smiling; it was tight lipped, but it was a smile. Between them they had created utter confusion. The gloomy day had provided a stage for the 'ghosts' that had added to their defence. Somehow the danger and excitement that they had shared drew them together with a sense of camaraderie.

Chapter 29 Rouen

Warping their way upstream against the sluggish flow of the great River Seine, the tall merchant ships came to Rouen. At anchor these majestic ships rode high above the fishing boats, their masts cut the winter sky like insect legs webbed with rigging. Despite the suspicions fear of the English mariners, they were no longer plagued with the Black Death. Rouen was plagued with jealousies; a hunger to possess the water gate to the centre of France. Civil war threatened but trade ferried up and down the Seine making the best of the uneasy peace. France quivered but did not rebel.

With the mist lying deep, the day had darkened early. Ghosted lamps lit the Rue Grand Pont inadequately. The light bloomed dully on the defensive walls and the Archers pacing the ramparts. Some hours ahead of Ambrose and his party Don Diego and his group of Spanish supporters entered the town. They clattered across the cobbles, scattering the people as careless as unruly princes.

When Ambrose's party arrived they were all high spirited and smug with the joy of escape. They parted from the jovial shepherd before they reached the walls; they heard his loud voice calling blessings on them even after he had disappeared into the gloom. With a concentrated frown, Ambrose watched him go. How had Emlyn managed to converse with the idiot? Then Ambrose remembered the simpleton who Emlyn had killed for.

Emlyn's horse was jogging along beside him. Emlyn was grinning. He said, 'Henri is not an idiot, he is deaf. He finds it an advantage to act as if he has no brains though.'

'Yes', said Ambrose, 'I can imagine. I believe the Emperor Claudius managed to live to a ripe old age by using the very same method.'

Once they had entered the town, Ambrose led them all across the market square to an inn he knew. Le Cheval Rouge was clean and superbly run. At the stables in the courtyard, Ambrose left all in the care of grooms and hurried into the warmth of the main room hoping that there would be a meal ready; he became ill tempered if he went too long without food.

Emlyn and Goronwy followed him meekly, too tired to fall on their pride and refuse his generosity.

Tired though he was himself, Ambrose denied himself the comfort of an early night. He sent Matthew to find John Moore, but Moore was not at inn. Ambrose stepped out onto the damp street alone. He pulled his cloak around him and sunk his chin into the warmth of its fur collar. There was a task to be done before he could seek sleep. His friend Eugine Benoit had informed him where the mercenaries stayed in Rouen; drinking away the winter until employment could be found. They were a rough lot and were not welcome at Le Cheval Rouge. Although their coin flowed freely enough, they frequently fought and ruined the furniture. To find them Ambrose would have to wind his way through the narrow, steep streets to the riverside. There the grimy inns piled one atop the other. The streets were dark and dangerous and tinged with the blood of murder. Rats chewed at the entrails of fallen victims and thieves awaited the misfortune of others.

After trying four disreputable inns and parting with two coins of silver, a black-toothed whore, smelling like a barrel of fish skins, pointed out a party of ill kept soldiers of mixed shapes and sizes. They were led, she explained as she fumbled at his clothing for a hidden purse, by an Italian captain, known simply as Angelo.

Ambrose disentangled himself and thanked her, failing to conceal his disgust. But he was relieved; this was the man he sought.

The inn he entered was filled with thick smoke from the cooking fires and stank of stale wine, unwashed bodies and vomit. Ambrose wrinkled his nose and peered in. Two men arm-wrestled in a corner, sweating and cursing each other while others shouted encouragement. A bawdy song emerged from a heap of rags perched on a stool. Wide hipped women fought their way through the heaving, grasping mass, sloshing ale from fat jugs. With a grim smile Ambrose elbowed his way forward. There was a space, a table were one man drank alone. He looked uncivil. His face was lean and scarred from eyebrow to cheek by the stroke of a sword; it was a face moulded by a life of brutality. His eyes were so dark a brown that they looked black and held a surprising hint of drunken compassion. He wore lots of jewellery over ragged clothing. Ambrose smiled. He had not seen Angelo for over ten years.

Reaching him Ambrose said, 'I am looking for Angelo, a mercenary of some renown. Do you know him?'

The man lifted his hard, black eyes, curled his lip, lifted his wine and took a long, slow swallow. He looked the merchant up and down as if judging a side of beef. There were four empty jugs on the table. The single cup was clenched in a heavy, scarred hand with two fingers missing.

Ambrose glared back and wished he had brought Moore with him or even Goronwy. There was no recognition in those dark eyes. He thought the man was not going to answer. With such little space, in the room, why was the table unoccupied but for this one man? He was sure it was the one he sought. But what changes had occurred in the time since they had last met? Was Angelo now some cut-throat, who would kill for the price of an ale jug?

At length the man placed his cup on the table and wiped his black beard with the back of his hand. He indicated the opposite bench with a leering invitation to sit. 'I am he,' he explained belching loudly. 'What do you want?'

'A man sober enough to be employable,' Ambrose answered ignoring the invitation. 'It seems I have been misinformed, the man I seek would not stoop to wallow at the bottom of a wine jug.'

No anger showed but the mercenary became dangerously still. The general conversation, that had babbled around them, ceased. Ambrose looked down at the greying head. Angelo Corberio had aged and gained more scars, but he was still the same fierce Sicilian behind the blood-shot eyes and the unhealthy pallor.

Risking all. Ambrose continued, 'That man, who was once known to me, cleaved his way through the armies of Charles V at the battle of Pavia. He made a necklace of their ears. I see that you are no longer he and I am forced to seek elsewhere.' With a sneer of contempt, he turned his back and faced the door.

If his intention had been to leave, he would have never walked another step. The men who had stopped their chatter, closed around in an inescapable circle. Their eyes shone and the rings from their ears flashed dully in the candle light. These would be Angelo's men, violent, hard-bitten and glittering with the thought of plunder. They smiled in anticipation. Some cracked their knuckles. A blond giant, drew a knife as long as his forearm.

Ambrose felt prickly with fear. He prayed that Angelo's wine-fogged brain would remember before the blood of an English merchant washed the floor of the filthy inn. Angelo had worn his trophy of shrivelled ears when he had fought alongside the English and Lord Grey of Wilton in defence of Calais. Ambrose had won the ears in a drunken wager, much to his distaste. He stood still turning colder by the minute and prayed his shivers went unnoticed. The blade gleamed wickedly. The men began to close in.

Behind him something stirred. Something hiccuped and a great boom of laughter shattered the tension.

In one smooth move, Angelo climbed over the table and thumped Ambrose with a huge meaty hand. His drunken laugh filled the room and bounced about like an apple on a drum skin.

Ambrose turned and grinned, weak with relief. 'If you had let these animals kill me Angelo Corberio, I would never have forgiven you!'

Angelo, still helpless with laughter, charged at his men with a roar, pushing them out of the way as if they were a flimsy wooden fence. They retreated with unsure smiles. The mercenary turned and thumped Ambrose again with such vigour that he sat down abruptly.

'Bring wine!' Angelo commanded, 'and none of your rubbish this time, we have a man of taste in our midst. It is good to see you, you old English heretic. You come strolling in here as if you own the place! You always were a fool with your health Ambrose.'

Ambrose sighed, glad that he was sitting down; his knees had turned to water. 'There was a good chance I would find you here. Unless you had terrorised some village into sheltering you for the duration of winter, or sold yourself to Alva. Was his coin not good enough?'

'What would I know of his coin?' Angelo replied with a puff of exasperation. 'I never saw it nor did anyone else! The fool will loose all his hired mercenaries unless he pays them soon.' Angelo's eyes narrowed. 'I'll not forget that he owes me.'

Ambrose choked on his wine and burst out laughing. He laughed until tears flowed down his cheeks and he was gasping for the chance to breathe. He didn't know whether his humorous outburst was to do with his relief or that he knew why Angelo and his men had not been paid by Alva. Again he was surprised at himself; he had never used to laugh at all. He spluttered, 'Do you care for a trip over the Alps? I hear the view in winter is unsurpassed. You could even gain a little winter gold.'

Angelo looked at him sullenly. Then one corner of his mouth rose and then the other. He nodded his head slowly, his smile spreading. 'Devil Englishman!' Angelo laughed. 'Italy! You have saved my soul. Tell me where we are going, while I can still see the top of the wine jug.'

At the inn of Le Cheval Rouge, Emlyn approached Goronwy. He said, 'I am going to the abbey of St. Ouen for vespers. Would you like to come?'

He knew Goronwy would be unable to refuse, the last time they had been to a Catholic service was over four weeks ago.

Goronwy looked up at him. He said, 'Is there nowhere closer?'

Emlyn folded his arms and leaned against the wall. 'Probably, but it would take just as long to discover where at this time of night. Chillingworth will leave in the morning, he has gone to hire a guard to see him safe over the Alps.'

'And you are going with him,' answered Goronwy.

Emlyn smiled then dropped his head. He was certain now that he would go with Ambrose. He didn't answer, it was not a safe subject. They gathered their cloaks and went out into the cold night dragging tired feet up the crooked hill. Cold water and street sludge crept in through the holes in Emlyn's boots and the inn fleas feasted on the blood of his ankles. Until this eventful year, he had been sure that his path was to be one in the service of God, dedicated to drive the heretics out of England. Now the words of Barzini echoed in his mind. 'I have heard that his father, if he had a father at all, was a heathen Moor and he did not receive baptism until he reached the age of six or seven. Is this a soul destined for the church?'

It would be best for all concerned, including himself, if he found employment elsewhere. A large part of Emlyn wanted to go and sink his miseries in a tavern, to drink as he had never drunk before and to do all the things the Good Lord advised against. If Goronwy had not been there, walking like a solid guardian angel beside him, he may have done just that. He continued towards the church of St. Ouen.

They were late for vespers, their arrival did not escape notice from the choir in the Chapel. Pale faces turned, haughty with disapproval and resumed their prayer. So elaborate was the décor inside of the church, that Emlyn found it difficult to concentrate on prayer. His eyes wandered over stone saints who retained their heads and sumptuous windows that remained unshattered by Reformer's stones.

When the prayers were completed, Emlyn lingered by the sacristy until he caught the attention of a tired choir boy. 'Is Father Mandard here?' Emlyn asked, catching the boy by the elbow.

The boy was a gentleman's son, obvious from the offence he took at being handled. He was polite enough to give a curt nod of his head and point to the darkened side aisle where Emlyn could just make out the outline of an old priest kneeling in prayer near two ancient tombs. The flickering candle light cast eerie shadows over the stone carved features of some more ancient patrons of the abbey.

'What are you about?' Goronwy demanded in a fierce whisper.

'Can you wait for me?' Emlyn answered, 'there is someone I must see.'

'It is not wise to be walking the streets at this hour, any later and it would be suicide!'

'Monsieur, late visitors are allowed to stay overnight with us at the abbey. We have a new visitor's dormitory at the new Hotel de Bourgheroulde. It is finished.'

Emlyn smiled. 'There you are Goronwy it is finished.'

Goronwy looked at him with annoyance. He said, 'We could try the comfort of the Abbey's guest house later, but for now I shall stay with you.'

Emlyn didn't smile although he felt like it. He sought out Father Mandard with determination. If Goronwy accepted that Emlyn really had no further interest in a life with the Jesuits, Emlyn feared that he would only think of the deception and the betrayal as malice. Should he stop now and try to explain the circumstances as he should have done from the start? He feared that Goronwy would turn a blind ear to him if he tried again.

The light in the church was dim. Candles cast leaping shadows and lamps, shielded in red glass, illuminated the pious stone faces of saint and apostle. The church was an encrusted lace-work of carved stone and in every niche and corner, creatures lurked, leering from the dimness. Emlyn looked about curiously. He failed to see the clutch of nuns who were muttering prayers and fingering their rosaries as they moved towards him.

The first nun had her head down and so hit him in the chest and trod on his foot. She leapt back startled, bumping into the one behind and bringing the rest to a staggering halt. Emlyn bowed and apologised and awkwardly stepped out of the way, leaving them room to pass.

The last in line, hurried her steps to catch up with the others. Her rosary swung out behind her and looped around the wooden head of St. Luke on the end of a lectern. The rosary pulled taunt, stretched and burst asunder showering the tiled floor with glistening pearls. She cried out in dismay and bent to gather them up before they all rolled out of sight. Without a thought, Emlyn knelt beside her, his head an inch from hers. She was giggling. He lifted his eyes.

She wore a wimple that came to a point in the centre of her forehead, framing her face in a heart shape. Her large eyes were a warm, mossy-brown sparkling with mischief. Her nose, slightly upturned, gave her an elfin aspect and her smile washed over him like a shaft of sunlight.

'Good evening Signor. Please help me.' Her softly spoken words were in Italian. Her low pitched voice and charming accent added a delicious element of mystery and a hint of excitement to her words.

Emlyn realised that he had forgotten to breathe. Behind him, Goronwy efficiently gathered up spilled pearls as if the world had not come to a standstill. Emlyn let his held breath out in a shudder and couldn't find a voice to answer her with.

She laughed mockingly at him and cast a quick look over her shoulder, towards her companions who walked on, as yet, unaware of her mishap.

Goronwy was too good at collecting pearls, soon he had picked them all up. Beaming like a ripe apple, he placed them in her open hands. 'You will have to count them all mademoiselle,' he explained, 'to see that none are missing.'

Still dazed, Emlyn held forward his fist. His hand opened to reveal the three pearls gathered in his palm.

She put out her tiny hand to take them. Instead she closed her fingers over his and curled his hand over the beads, indicating that he could keep them. 'Can you meet me later?'

Emlyn rose slowly, unable to believe her words. Had he understood her right? He bent to assist her. With a rustle of velvet skirts, she stood, hardly reaching his shoulder and something stirred in his memory. Where had he seen her before? Surely he would have remembered. She turned beside him in time to meet the clutch of nuns returning, with anger and impatience on their faces.

Emlyn revived his tongue and his Italian, 'When?'

She blushed and dropped her eyes modestly. She offered no reply, it was too late. Her companions closed around her, scowling at the Welshmen as if they were devils. They whisked her away, disappearing into the soft shadows.

Emlyn watched until she had gone. He felt cold and empty, as if those precious minutes had robbed him of an essence he hardly knew existed, but suffered all the more for the poignancy of its obliteration. In his hand were the three treasured pearls to remind him that he had looked upon the face of an angel.

Goronwy was standing with his arms folded across his wide chest, he was watching him. 'I assume that she was not the person you sought,' he said, enjoying Emlyn's confusion.

The words seemed to come from a great distance. 'No,' Emlyn replied dreamily. 'I mean yes, but I thought she was a child.'

'You know her?' Goronwy asked.

Emlyn said, 'Do you remember when we were last in Rouen and we stayed in the barn outside the town?'

Goronwy smiled and nodded his head. 'And you spoke of Fra Pietro Sebastiano da Firenze who had found a child in a convent with the name Grimani. You thought she was a distant cousin.' Goronwy's smile widened. 'The petal mosaics and the horse and cart. She was one of the novices wasn't she?'

'I exchanged a few words with her, that's all. How could this be the same girl?' She had said she hoped to meet him later, but had not had the chance to say when. Had it been for amusement? Puzzled and vaguely irritated, Emlyn turned to make his way to the knighted tombs, near which Father Mandard still knelt in prayer.

Out in the cloisters which stank of boiled cabbage and gave the promise of a tasteless supper, Father Mandard turned to face his visitors. He looked older than many mistook him for, his love for the vine and all that came from it had left its mark. 'I hope this will not take long,' he grumbled. 'I am too old to stand out here in the teeth of winter. What can I do to assist you?'

Emlyn bowed respectfully. 'I am sorry Father to disturb you, I learned that a good friend of yours left a message here for me.'

'Being who?'

'A Florentine priest, a Franciscan by the name of Fra Sebastiano. In the past, he has done me great service.'

'I know the man, I know him well. But, what do you mean child? That he did service to you without knowledge of you?'

'I am Emlyn Tomas Father and he brought me as a child to my family and I saw him again in Paris in spring.'

Father Mandard beamed with some inner knowledge 'Merde! You are that boy now grown into a man? The tale is known to me also. You are the child handed to him in Portugal and taken to England in the train of his most Catholic Majesty the King of Spain. We did not believe Fra Sebastiano at first and I always harboured doubts; it became a joke between us. But I too saw him earlier in the year and he told me about you.'

Emlyn felt a sudden fear wash through him. He wished that he had not asked Goronwy to come.

Father Mandard rocked on his heels with his callused hands clasped firmly in front of his round stomach. 'You are educated in College de Clermont and the Jesuits will not have you, they do not want a bastard among their number. So you planned with Fra Sebastiano to go to Italy and seek your parents or what became of them. What is the matter? Did I get the story wrong?"

Burning with shame, Emlyn dropped his head.

Goronwy grasped his shoulder and spun him around to face him. He spoke Welsh. 'This is it eh? You planned all this before we had even left the college! Because the Jesuits won't have you, you turned against them and against me and turned your back on all we stood for! You betrayed us

Emlyn Tomas and were I not a God fearing man, I would strike you down where you stand. Your presence fouls this holy place!'

'It is not so Goronwy! As God is my witness it is not so. You must know that, after all these years do you not know me well enough as least to believe me?'

Goronwy spat. 'How so?' he growled. 'I heard the words from your own mouth when you betrayed Cecil's groom. Who were you going to betray next? Had I not stopped you, I and countless others would now have their heads rotting on London bridge. You wear the badge of bastard around your neck like a mill stone. Because you suffer its hurts, you would pull down others to suffer with you. The Jesuits are not responsible for the wickedness of your mother Emlyn! Nor are those who have befriended you and those you were so ready to sell to the Queen's inquisition!'

Father Mandard came between them shaking his untidy head. 'Gentlemen, if I may call you such, do not raise your voices so. Your anger is misplaced here, take your argument to a tavern or inn yard where you can better vent it.'

'I am sorry Father,' snapped Goronwy. 'But there is no need for further words between him and me now, nor will there ever be.' With that, he turned and stormed out of the cloister. Emlyn heard his rich voice rise high above the roof tops. Goronwy sung of the selling of Llewelyn, the last Prince of Wales, to the English. He sang in Welsh, so that there would be only one to understand his words.

Father Mandard placed a well worn hand on Emlyn's shoulder and patted him like a fretful child. 'I know nothing of this,' he said 'and would rather it remain so, but I feel that I was the cause, although I did not understand your words. If so, I apologise.'

Emlyn felt a sense of terrible loss. He stood staring into the darkness where Goronwy had disappeared. Goronwy's voice was fading, but the sound was so true and powerful that it hung in the air as if captured within the walls of the abbey.

Unaware of his pain, Father Mandard said, 'You will find that Fra Sebastiano has left France. He returned to Italy with a delegation from Milan. After seeking support from the French king, they continued on to the Holy Father in Rome. They wish to rid Milan of Spanish rule.'

Emlyn smiled bitterly and brought his emotions under control. 'There are many who would wish the same Father.'

Father Mandard nodded agreeably. 'I think even the pope has reason to fear the power of Philip of Spain. Do you know that he wishes to be overlord of Ireland once the English queen is excommunicated?'

'I had heard some rumour,' said Emlyn. He remembered Friar Patrick O'Healy who he seen last time he was in Rouen and who had told him about the problem concerning the overdue wages for the mercenaries under Alva's command. And he remembered talking of the future of Ireland with Goronwy; he had talked of many things with Goronwy.

He thanked the old man and made his way back to the inn alone. He knew that Ambrose was not going through Paris. Nor would he be prepared to wait for Emlyn if he was delayed. That won't matter, Emlyn thought, I can always catch up with him on a fast horse. He felt that there was still the matter of the gems to be sorted; if Ambrose was still awake at the inn, he would have a chance to show them to him and get his advice. And his uncle's letter? Somehow he had to make an attempt to secure that too. When he reached the inn he knew that Goronwy would not be there. In the room they shared, Emlyn saw only his own belongings stacked in the corner.

Seeing a light under Ambrose's door, Emlyn lifted his hand to knock. He heard voices within and turned away without disturbing the Englishman.

Ambrose Chillingworth had been escorted back to the Le Cheval Rouge by a troop of loud mercenaries. They were highly amused to see their new master accept charge of a pack of wool-carrying mules. You could laugh a little at Angelo and not get your head bitten off for your affront when he was well drunk. In winter a mercenary must take what coin he could or terrorize someone into providing shelter and comfort; which often ended with a knife between the shoulder blades. Being Italians, most of Angelo's company were secretly pleased. Geneva meant just one cold step into the warm arms of Italy, which would enclose them like a mother's embrace and not scold them for sins they would rather forget.

But Ambrose didn't want them all. Thirty men to escort eight mules and their Englishmen was absurd; beside the cost of feeding them all and dishing out to their constant complaints. 'I want twelve,' Ambrose had said when they had left the inn by the docks. No amount of arguing or cajoling was going to change his mind. It left a dilemma.

Angelo was a good captain to serve under. Although he never showed the slightest affection for any man who served with him. His concern was evident in the harsh way he trained them and then led them to victory and its spoils, or escape if defeat resulted. Anyone who could not endure their initiation, was left to find another master. If Angelo could not provide for them all, he would not abandon them with no employment, while he went shepherding over the Alps.

When Ambrose eventually reached his own room, Angelo appeared in the doorway with a flask and two wooden cups.

Ignoring him, Ambrose sat on the bed and heaved at his damp boots.

Angelo came in, poured the wine and sat on the opposite bed wrinkling his nose. 'Do you really keep feet in those?' he asked, offering the merchant a cup.

Ambrose frowned at him. 'Angelo why are you here? You know my mind and if you are unable to abide by my wishes, tell me now, so I may seek elsewhere.'

'Why not take them all anyway? They are willing enough.'

'And what will they eat?'

'Well there are ways of providing a meal.'

'You are not going to thieve your way to Italy, at least, you are not going to do so in my company. I told you, twelve men and yourself if you wish, but that is all. What do you think I am? Duke? Prince? Why I should travel with an army at my back?'

Angelo emptied his cup with a grimace. 'All right,' he announced, 'it will be as you wish. The others can go back to the Netherlands and fight against Alva, they may find the pay better.'

Ambrose yawned and began to undress. He pulled on a woolly nightshirt before he spoke again. 'I want one of your men to remain here or in Paris and watch someone for me. No more than a few days and then they could both follow us.'

'Watch someone? Play nursemaid or spy?'

'Not quite. As you know Angelo, we Englishmen have an aversion when it comes to Spaniards. For some obscure reason I have been followed by such from Dieppe. There were two of my countrymen travelling with me. One will remain here but the other has some business to attend to before he can join me. I must be sure that neither are approached by these Spaniards and questioned.'

'For some obscure reason?'

'Quite. But if I knew the reason, it would still be obscure as far as you are concerned. It may be that the Spaniard will follow me, in which case there will be no need. I fear that when they see me so well protected, they will question the others.'

'And if they do?'

'The two young men are scholars Angelo. The one returning to the Jesuit College in Paris will be safe enough, as his affiliation will be evident. It is the other that I am concerned about.'

'Jesuits?' Angelo spat. 'So you are asking me to protect him or them if they are approached by these Spaniards?'

'Protect? I doubt that will be necessary,' Ambrose replied, 'one is practically a Jesuit himself. But if either of them talk at length with the Spanish, I need to know.'

'They can have Josquin to look after them,' said Angelo draining his cup. 'He is reluctant to leave his mistress at present. I don't suppose you would consider a few women joining us?'

'What a preposterous idea!' Ambrose scoffed. 'Most definitely not!'

Carmelia lay awake in her bed. To either side of her, other beds stood, each with a muffled novice asleep. All were young girls, training for a life devoted to God. Carmelia had returned to the convent in Rouen when it was evident that she was not going to start the journey home that year. Constant letters from Don Carlos had done nothing to persuade Adriana Martinelli to travel. Carmelia had been disappointed, but she had not voiced her objections; there was next year to come.

Lying awake now, she thought about the boy who had helped her pick up the rosary beads, not the big one, the other who had only gathered up three. She didn't know why she had let him keep them. She guessed that it was something to do with the way he had looked at her. No one had ever looked at her with such intense interest before. It made her feel peculiar, yet it was a warm and comfortable feeling. Her godmother Adriana was constantly telling her how thin she was and how small and how plain.

Camellia had known who the young man was as soon as she saw him; he was the boy who had driven a cart over her flower pattern depicting the Sacred Heart. She had hoped that he would have waited outside the church to talk to her, but she had seen no sign of him. Thinking about him kept her awake. If only she were as free as her maid Pellegrina, who could put on a hooded cloak and leave the convent whenever she pleased.

Carmelia's thoughts were interrupted by a sound at the door. She could see a light. A candle flame seemed to float down the room in her direction. It stopped at the bottom of her bed. Carmelia froze, lying as still as death. A hand reached out and shook her foot. 'Carmel! Are you awake?'

Carmelia sighed. It was the voice of Sister Helen. The hand began to shake her foot vigorously. 'Come child!' Sister Helen demanded.

'What is it?' Carmelia pulled her foot away.

'Put a gown on,' said the nun in a fierce whisper.

Carmelia dressed hurriedly and followed her out of the room. She could not imagine why she was being summoned at this late hour. The two figures hurried through the dark corridors toward the mother Superior's room. Although she asked, Carmelia could discover nothing. Sister Helen remained silent, she was obviously angry but was not prepared to divulge the cause.

The room they entered was filled with light. Carmelia's godmother Adriana and one of the novices, sat by a small table. 'What is it?' Carmelia spoke as soon as she entered, alarm tingeing her voice. 'Is there something wrong?'

Her godmother smiled. She said, 'There is nothing to be alarmed about. We have the opportunity to travel home as soon as you are ready.'

'We? What?' Carmelia stammered. 'Now, in the middle of the night? Its winter.'

Adriana Martinelli seemed to glow with anticipation. 'Indeed my girl,' she said. 'There is a foreign merchant who has hired mercenaries to guard his journey over the Alps. We shall join the party and travel with them. Unfortunately they will be leaving in the morning. So we must be ready ourselves by then. We would be fools to miss the opportunity.'

Sister Helen clasped her hands in front. 'Such terrible dangers!' she cried. 'I do not question your judgement Madame, but in such weather you will most surly suffer!'

'Then you had better be on your knees praying my girl,' said Adriana Martinelli happily. 'It may be the middle of winter, but now that I have my health back, I am going home and Carmelia with me. Where is Pellegrina? She must be awoken and told to get all in readiness. You are still packed aren't you Carmelia?'

'Yes, of course,' Carmelia lied. It would not take her long to gather her few belongings. She could not believe what was happening. Surely it was the most foolish notion her godmother had yet come up with. And the mention of getting her health back was complete nonsense; Adriana had stayed in France for another reason entirely! Carmelia said, 'Madonna how could all this be arranged at such short notice?'

'There are a few matters that still require some attention,' Adriana Martinelli replied. 'But I can see no reason for the merchant to object.'

'You mean you have yet to ask?' Carmelia was shocked further. Was all this fuss in the depth of night, done on a whim?

'Don't question dear,' said Adriana. 'Just go quietly and get your things together. Leave the arrangements to me. Are you not pleased?'

'I am pleased,' said Carmelia meekly. 'I just haven't had time to think. Madonna, could you tell me how you know of this?'

Adriana Martinelli spoke in a voice of tried patience. 'I am acquainted with a certain soldier of fortune who has carried letters for me now and then. His name is Josquin. He knows the captain of the mercenaries who are to guard the merchant and his goods and will be coming with us.'

Carmelia blushed, she knew who Josquin was, Adriana's lover! She curtseyed to her godmother and left the room with Sister Helen in tow. Carmelia had heard all about Josquin, Pellegrina had told her. Pellegrina liked to gossip, her wicked tongue wove yarns all the time; Carmelia had not wanted to believe one of them until now. She was too scandalised to do anything but obey Adriana's request.

The next morning, Ambrose gave up the idea of making an early start. It was not until mid morning, wrapped up in his woollen cloak and layers of clothing, that he was ready to leave. He had heard from the kitchen boy, that before light Goronwy had caught a lift to Paris with a man delivering two butts of Malmsey to the table of Eustace de Bellay, the Gallican Bishop of Paris. Ambrose silently wished the young man well of whatever this future held. Still, he thought, Goronwy might have muttered a word of thanks, it would not have killed him. Emlyn, it seemed, had not gone with him. Nor was he at the inn. Ambrose had received a note from him explaining that he had gone about his business concerning the gems and would continue on to Paris to pick up a certain letter which they had spoken of. Ambrose was a little disappointed, but he knew that they were all pressed for time. He hoped that Emlyn would not take too much time and would be able to catch up with him as soon as possible.

Now Ambrose waited only for Angelo who had horses to collect and men and provisions to organise. Ambrose's own men had been ready for hours and he was impatient to be on his way.

The proprietor of the inn found him in the stables checking the mules with his ill tempered servant Matthew at his side and the more pleasant overseer, John Moore. 'Monsieur Chillingworth?' the inn keeper said politely on entering.

Ambrose turned to face him with an expression of annoyance. 'What?' he demanded.

'Monsieur there is a lady within who wishes words with you.'

'A woman?' Matthew commented with a wink. John Moore grinned.

Ambrose said, 'What does she want?'

'I do not know Monsieur. She begs your pardon if you are put to any trouble. I would judge her to be a lady of some means.'

She was standing in his empty room, alone and dressed all in black, with a concealing veil covering all her hair. No ornament offered relief to the eye, but the cloth was excellent and the lady's bearing was proud and confident.

'Madame,' said Ambrose from the door. 'How may I be of assistance?'

She turned and looked him up and down. Obviously not displeased, she said, 'I am Adriana Martinelli, Signor and I would ask you for a favour.'

She was an attractive woman in her mid-thirties, so Ambrose judged. She had about her something untouchable, a sheen of ice, which allowed a man to look but nothing more. Ambrose could be disagreeable too. 'Madonna, I am honoured but feel unable as I am just about to depart. Perhaps I could send for another?' he replied not moving from the doorway.

'No, that will, not be necessary,' she said. She snapped a Spanish fan open and fanned herself as if the day were warm. 'I am informed that you are bound for Geneva and have a guard of thirty men. I and those with me, beg your company and protection as we travel the same road.'

'I am sorry Madonna, you have been misinformed. It is not possible.' Ambrose wondered how she knew so much about his business. Should he get a leper's clapper and rattle it announcing his businesses, in case any in Rouen had missed hearing it?

'I am sorry that you feel this way,' said Signora Adriana Martinelli. Her fan came to an abrupt halt. 'Let us not be hasty,' she added.

Ambrose entered the room making a point of wriggling his fingers into his gloves. 'It is winter Madame. We have to make good speed for the weather can be unpredictable The pace of my travel would leave you far behind and in danger and discomfort. As a gentleman, I could not even think of it. Therefore I would advise you find better suited companions for your journey. Now, if you will excuse me?'

She didn't excuse him at all. She held him with her cold eyes, her fine arched brows knit in a pretty frown. 'Will you allow me to explain my circumstances?' She sat in the window seat as if he had already agreed.

'But of course,' he answered exasperated, she left him little choice.

'I am here with my charge, Carmelia Grimani. We were to return to Italy long before this. But lengthy illness has prevented us from doing so. The child longs to return home to her family. I cast this unfortunate girl's plight at your feet, Signor and beg you, out of Christian charity to offer her your help. You are not a heretic are you?'

'No Madonna, I am not an unbeliever,' countered Ambrose. 'You have my deepest sympathy and prayers, but I cannot allow such ladies to accompany me. As I said the pace...'

'But you are taking laden mules with you. Surely your speed will be dictated by them? We can travel faster than mules and will give you no trouble. We ask nothing of you, but the protection of your men. You would not abandon us to travel alone? At the mercy of every thief and cut throat? I can see you are a good man, although you are English. You have thirty mercenaries, more than enough for a merchant and his wares. Signor do not turn your heart against us.'

Ambrose squirmed like a worm on a hook. She was really quite becoming in her desperation. 'I have employed but twelve men to accompany me Madame, not, as you have been led to believe thirty, this would be beyond my purse.'

'Then I shall take it upon myself to employ the others,' she replied. 'You will not find me without means. In which case we will all travel well protected.'

'Employ them by all means Madonna,' said Ambrose peevishly. 'You will find them willing to see you through to Geneva and beyond. But I am leaving within the hour if not sooner. I am delayed enough already and cannot wait. I am sorry Madame.'

She stood up, straightening her skirts and snapped her fan with a cool smile. 'But there will be no need for you to wait. I knew you for a gentleman who would not turn his back on our sorry state. We are ready to leave.'

Ambrose sighed and looked up towards heaven, wondering whatever he had done to be visited with such penance. 'What can I say Madonna?'

She smiled genuinely and the cold left her eyes for a moment. 'We are all guided by God Signor. He has placed you on our path to be our champion and saviour. All that remains, is to depart and offer a prayer of thanksgiving for the generosity of your heart.'

Ambrose could not take the women with him. He rose to his full height and matched her cold stare with his. 'I am sorry Madame,' he said. 'I must refuse and will not be persuaded.'

She didn't drop her gaze. 'As we are all ready to travel ourselves,' she answered, 'would you be kind enough to escort us as far as Paris? It is but a short distance. Perhaps there we may find the help to continue our journey.'

'I am not going to Paris,' he replied with finality. 'I apologise Madame, but I must refuse.'

She swept out of the room as white as snow and as cold as ice.

Ambrose shivered, but it was an arrangement that he was heartily glad of. He was a simple merchant and could not be saddled with a harem.

Outside, he found the captain of the mercenaries. Angelo was smiling. He was armed to the teeth and flashing his earrings. He had combed his beard and found a decent set of clothing. 'You see!' he cried, sweeping his arms to include a party of travellers Ambrose had not expected 'We are all going to Italy.'

Ambrose shook his head. 'No! No women.'

There was a twisted grin on the old campaigner's face as he chuckled into his beard. 'The men like you master Chillingworth, you have provided them with a path home, they all want to see their mothers. Still, it is a pity about the women.'

'Well, who am I to stand in the way of such touching reunions?' said Ambrose drily. He walked towards his horse. 'I am not going to Italy saddled with women,' he said aloud to nobody in particular.

Chapter 30 Rouen

Emlyn arrived at the Medici financial agent's house late in the morning and banged on the heavy door. He had spent most of the morning at St. Ouen abbey gardens, but the novice had not come. He smiled to himself now, feeling a fool. The door in front of him creaked open and a neatly dressed man with a pointed beard, looked Emlyn up and down with a sneer of distaste.

Before the door could close, Emlyn pushed passed and shouldered his way in. 'Messer Benetto Rovigo?' he said pleasantly.

'I am his nephew, Ferdinando: he is not here,' the man answered coldly. His face was a mask of contempt.

Emlyn drew a pouch from a fold in his sleeve. He weighed it thoughtfully. 'Are the Medici without a representative in Rouen today then?' he said. 'Perhaps I should approach the Genoese about the deposit of my wealth. Would you be good enough to tell me where I might find the Genoese financier?'

Ferdinando's face melted like a candle. He smiled. He rubbed his hands together. 'I am here acting for my esteemed uncle's interest,' he whined. 'He has gone south for the winter. His health has not been so good this past year. Whatever you required of him, you may also require of me. You wish to deposit some wealth Monsieur? Please come in, come in. Let us discuss this in better comfort. A glass of wine?' He clapped his hands loudly.

'Do you know the business of a jeweller?' asked Emlyn.

'You ask that of a Florentine?' said Ferdinando indignantly.

Emlyn followed him into a small comfortable room. He felt an instant dislike for Ferdinando. He wished that he had not forced his way in. But, he was here now and a greedy man was easy to manipulate. Emlyn refused the wine and got down to business.

When Ferdinando saw the gems, his face lit up. He picked one up and held it to the light. 'Exquisite,' he whispered. He looked at Emlyn suspiciously.

To save himself from been accused of thievery, Emlyn said, 'From my mother, they have just recently come into my possession. My mother has passed away.'

'God rest her soul,' Ferdinando replied without a trace of sincerity.

'Can you value the stones? I would appreciate a second opinion.'

'You have had them valued already?' asked the Florentine.

Emlyn nodded his head thoughtfully. 'A rough estimate only,' he said

'Then I can tell you Monsieur?'

'Tomas.'

'Monsieur Tomas, that these are no ordinary stones. They represent a collection. I would say that these, set as they once were in a necklace would be of considerable value.' He began to arrange the gems in a curve, placing the red stone at the centre. The colours fell into a pattern which Emlyn had not realised before.

Ferdinando fingered his beard. He bent and straightened, keeping his eyes on the necklace. He made a humming noise. 'Very old,' he said. 'See how worn the gold clasp is here? I would say that it is not complete. There are some stones missing. I would judge from the rich quality and pattern of these stones, that the missing ones would be a match for this one. That red stone was probably not the original centre stone. I would hazard a guess and say there may have been one of greater size there in the middle. See there, that is where the missing stones would have gone.'

'At the start of each band of colour?' Emlyn said.

Ferdinando nodded solemnly, as if in awe. 'Rubies,' he said breathlessly. 'There are probably four of these blood-stones missing. If they are anything like this one here, you would want for nothing for the rest of your days, may they be long and prosperous.' He shook his head making tutting sounds. 'Such a pity, such a pity.' He turned to Emlyn. 'I don't suppose you have the rest?'

Emlyn dismissed the question with a wave of his hand. Before this, he had seen the stones as a means to an end. Now, I know I cannot sell them, he thought, they are obviously not from my mother's family. His grandfather Gruffydd, had not known them. Could they be from my father? If so, they could provide a clue. Why would anyone break up a necklace of such great worth? He looked up.

Ferdinando was watching him with glittering eyes. He said 'Do you wish to leave them here in safety?'

Emlyn sat down on a stool beside the table. What I should do, he told himself, is gather them up and sew them back into my jerkin and take my chances with the thieves. Ferdinando does not prompt a feeling of trust. I should have confided in Ambrose Chillingworth; I should have brought him with me. He needed time to think. 'Messer Ferdinando,' he said. 'I will have the wine now, if it is no trouble.'

'Not at all!' cried the jeweller gleefully. 'Take your time, take your time.' He whisked out of the room, his feet dancing.

Emlyn realised that he could borrow money against the value of the gems. He could dress in silks and furs and ride to Italy on a fine horse. The vision was tempting and the jewels glittered on a square of velvet. Emlyn smiled at his dreams, dismissing them; he knew that was not the answer. However, he could borrow enough to buy an ordinary horse, winter clothing and a lute. Gruffydd had shown him how to make a living from music whilst travelling. Such a life had appealed to him them, in the warmth of summer; he had thought it romantic and idealistic. He didn't think like that any more, life would be hard, but it would be honest. If he had been able to leave Wales as he had wished, he would have been better organised financially for the journey to Italy; as it was, he had no intention of living off the charity of Ambrose Chillingworth. Emlyn swept the gems into his hand. He would not borrow so much that he could not earn it back by the time he reached Italy.

He guessed that Ambrose would be well on his way by now, so he needed to find someone else whom he could trust to witness the business. The first name he thought of was Wendelin Tieffenbrucker; the German lute maker who had provided Goronwy with the letter blocks in the spring. The financier, Ferdinando was most helpful when Emlyn asked him to send a boy to the house of Tieffenbrucker with the request.

Soon after, when Tieffenbrucker arrived he was delighted to see Emlyn again. He paid little attention to the gems, but he knew pawn brokers and saw that the business of pledging and borrowing was conducted correctly and legally. Ferdinando was exceptionally helpful and assured Emlyn that the gems would be securely held and left untouched until he returned for them. When they were finished, Tieffenbrucker ignored Emlyn's protests and took him home with him. 'You want to buy a lute you say?'

Emlyn grinned at him and strutted down the road in imitation of Don Diego de Luzon.

As they left the house of the Medici agent, a cloaked and hooded figure emerged from the shadows of the alley behind the house. Like some dark, shadowy wraith it followed the two men through the narrow twisted streets.

In the afternoon when the merchant's cavalcade had left, the Dutchman, Josquin stood by the wall outside the church of St. Ouen. He stamped his feet to keep them warm. He had complained to Angelo about being left to watch a couple of students while everyone else tramped off to Geneva with two cart-loads of ladies. Four days, Josquin had promised and no more. Four days and then he could catch up with the others. Angelo told him that the ladies were inaccessible and if he or any as much as touched one, then Angelo would cut their hands off. Josquin smiled, could get a lot further with Adriana Martinelli. He had no idea then, that she had been refused by Ambrose Chillingworth.

Josquin, although born of a French father, of whom he knew nothing and cared less, considered himself Dutch. He had grown up in Antwerp under the roof of a house of ill repute. It was a childhood in which he had been loved and pampered by many mothers, which he blamed, forgivingly, for his insatiable appetite for women. It was a house that all men were made equal by their desire.

In looks Josquin had few rivals. He was tall, thin and fair as a Viking, with twinkling eyes as blue as the river Schelde. Door's to bed chambers opened willing, but never promised wealth. In Italy, Angelo had promised that he could become a professional Giovanni and make himself a wealthy man doing what he did best. This was an impression Angelo had formed of Josquin when he had joined the mercenaries in the summer, Josquin had done nothing to change it. But Josquin had many talents and was devoted to what he believed in. It was not by chance that he had agreed to make the winter journey to Geneva, he had been hired and well paid by an English agent to watch and follow Ambrose Chillingworth. What annoyed him now, was that the merchant had gone off, while Josquin remained behind employed on some pointless task.

After waiting all morning with no sight of the English scholars, Josquin entered the church. He found an old priest lighting wax candles under a statue of St. Denis. Josquin tried to keep his spurs silent and self-consciously held his sword still. Tapping the old man on the shoulder, he bowed and whispered, 'I am seeking two English scholars Father, they were here last night.'

'Ah yes,' beamed Father Mandard. 'I know of whom you speak. What is your interest?' He snuffed the taper with his fingers. 'They seem in much demand today.'

'I was to see them safely to Paris,' Josquin replied quietly.

Father Mandard placed spare candles in a satchel at his waist. He looked thoughtful, chewing his beard. Eventually he said, 'I myself spoke to one only this morning, the big one. You will find he has already gone before it was light, he left alone. I told the same to the other man who asked. The other scholar was here all morning. Now he has returned to the inn, Le Cheval Rouge. Do you know it?.'

'Thank you father. You say he was here this morning?'

Father Mandard nodded. 'He asked after a lady who was at the church last night. It seems she dropped her rosary.'

'A lady who was leaving this morning too?' said Josquin.

'A Mademoiselle Carmel.' said Father Mandard. He turned back to his candles.

'Father, you have been more than kind. Thank you.' Josquin crept out of the church. At the door he turned around and went in again. 'Father? You mentioned another man asking after the scholars?'

'A Spanish gentleman. He was very polite and he left a generous donation for the church repairs,' said Father Mandard pointedly.

Josquin pulled a few coins from his belt pouch and reluctantly dropped them into the iron-bound trunk beside the door. Father Mandard nodded his head sagely and smiled benignly. He said, 'The man was Don Diego de Luzon.'

Josquin thanked him and left. One of the young men was already on his way to Paris, so there was no need to search for him. At Le Cheval Rouge he discovered that the other one had returned late at night, had risen early and left, but his few belongings were still there. 'Do you know where he went?' Josquin asked the inn keeper.

The man pursed his lips thoughtfully and shook his head. Even Josquin's offer of a bribe failed to get him any more information. But, before he left, a kitchen boy told him the names of the two who had accompanied Chillingworth from England.

Josquin walked the streets in deep thought. He recognised the names, they were the same two young men he had met earlier in the year when he had been on the trail of Friar O'Healy. He smiled recalling the mishap they had suffered on the bridge across the Seine. They had upset the nuns and Josquin had been able to steal an important letter from the Irish friar that he had sent to his employer. If it had not been for that incident, Josquin would have never met Adriana Martinelli. He knew that they were Catholic and that they came from the Jesuit school in Paris, so why were they in the company of Ambrose Chillingworth? There could be a simple explanation; it could be a coincidence that they had been travelling the same road. But Angelo had told Josquin to bring one of the young men with him when he rode after the merchant and his company. So, he thought, what are the Jesuits up to now?

He climbed the clock tower and peered over the old town on the banks of the river, nestling under its defensive hills. In the streets, he asked in inns and bake houses, stables and work yards, churches and poor houses, at every door he discovered nothing. Eventually, he called at the Spanish Residence. A spy hole in the gate opened when he knocked. 'Que?' demanded a harsh voice.

'I am seeking a Don Diego de Luzon,' said Josquin pleasantly.

'He's not here,' the voice answered. 'Went to Paris this morning.' The spy hole closed with finality. Josquin resumed his search.

In his work shop, Tieffenbrucker moved further into the sunlight and grasped the corner of a mound of velvet brocade on the table. He paused to ensure that he had Emlyn's undivided attention. He twitched his yellow moustache and then flicked the red cloth away as if performing a conjuring trick. There bathed in light, lay the lute of Emlyn's dreams. Released from the folds of cloth, the instrument caught the late sun and mellowed under its touch. The top was made of pine and light as a leaf and dense with exquisite marquetry. A gossamer of ivory sat coquettishly shadowed in the rose at the centre. The pear-shaped back was built up in a series of sycamore ribs, lovingly curved, shaped and glued together edge to edge; these too were of incredible thinness. The instrument seemed to tremble as if, where there none to pluck its sensuous strings, it would play of its own accord.

'Come now,' invited Tieffenbrucker. His big hands were open in invitation.

Emlyn picked it up with tenderness. He bowed his head, his long fingered hands poised and prepared, his eyes humble.

Time froze. Not a sound disturbed the workshop.

Emlyn shrugged off the twinge of self-consciousness. He brushed his fingers down the strings. Harmony burst out of the resonant wood, vibrating, echoing from walls to ceiling. The lute was perfectly tuned. He played a fast galliard, that became more complex with each measure. The strings quivered as melody filled and whirled around the room. The apprentices tapped their feet to the race of notes plucked by clever fingers confident and true. The pace slowed then quickened. The lute laughed, danced, wept and moaned, giving voice to every feeling in between. It brought forth the sound and the lutanist made each note his own and played the phrases with a unique, breathtaking style. The master and his apprentices were entrapped by the virtuosity of the artist and the perfection of the perfect lute.

When the haunting magic came to an end it was as if a pall of darkness had descended. Where the unearthly song had dwelt in every fibre of every being, a deprived emptiness was left, with each heart yearning for its return. Tears were running down Tieffenbrucker's cheeks and soaking into his moustache.

Emlyn flashed him a bright grin. All the years of training seemed to have brought him to this moment. He stood awaiting judgement, proud of what he had achieved, unashamed of the demonstration of his skill.

Tieffenbrucker brought his big hands together in applause. 'I have never heard such an exquisite sound. There is no praise I could give that is high enough and no words to describe the pride and happiness you have brought me. You have made me a happy man.'

'I have equal praise for the artistry of your lute, Monsieur Tieffenbrucker,' said Emlyn. He felt prickly with embarrassment.

'You have a wonderful touch and style. Did you learn it from the harp?' Wendelin stroked his chin, his expression thoughtful.

'It is slightly similar to the way I play the harp,' answered Emlyn. 'The strings must be allowed to sing and not be cut off. It was hard to master, but far superior to the use of a plectrum. There is a new type of harp in Wales, my grandfather showed me. You rest your little finger thus,' He demonstrated with his finger resting near the bridge and brought a shiver of response from the treble strings. 'you see?, you have an anchor to work from.' He held the instrument at arms length and admired it. 'All instruments will pall in comparison to this,' he added. 'I shall never play another like it I'm sure, even if I searched through all of Europe.'

Tieffenbrucker nodded his fair head. After a moment, he said, 'Why should you need to look Emlyn? This lute is for you.'

Emlyn looked at him aghast. 'I could not except Monsieur Tieffenbrucker, Yes I could, but I cannot believe you.' He caressed the instrument with loving hands. 'I do not know what to say.'

'Then say nothing. I know of your gratitude, your music speaks clearly of it.'

Emlyn could hardly contain himself. He held the lute close and planted a kiss on its bulbous belly. The apprentices clapped and jeered, 'The little priest has found his true love!'

'Betrothed to a lute! Now no woman will come between him and his hearts desire!'

'Will you keep a place for her on your pillow Emlyn?'

They made rude gestures.

Emlyn smiled at them all, nothing would dull this precious moment. He danced in circles with the lute as his partner and called out sweet endearments to her. Tieffenbrucker's booming laugh resounded off the other, less loved instruments hanging from the wall.

Tieffenbrucker touched the songbird he had created. 'She is for a Philomel, an artist and she would never be happy with another. Take her with my blessing. May she bring you luck.'

With his free hand, Emlyn grasped the German's hand and kissed it. 'You have made me the most contented man to walk on God's earth.'

'Do you know that I am leaving France? I am taking the family.' Tieffenbrucker rubbed his moustache thoughtfully.

'To Germany?' asked Emlyn in surprise.

'To Venice my minstrel, where they appreciate a good instrument maker. I have a brother there who has begged me join him. Tieffenbruckers have made lutes in Venice and Padua for generations, they are the finest musical instruments available in all of Europe. When you decide not to become a priest, that is where you will come to see me next and show the Venetians how a true Orpheus can strike the lyre.'

Emlyn almost told him about his plans for going to Italy himself, but he held back. Tieffenbrucker would surely wait until the spring before he travelled. They talked for almost an hour. Wendelin's wife Eva, brought them a plate full of pastries and a jug of beer. Eventually, Emlyn held up his wooden cup and drank in solemn celebration of what he considered the pinnacle of his life. He bid farewell to the three apprentice lute-makers and Wendelin gave him a leather case for the lute with a strap attached for carrying. Emlyn embraced the big German and left the workshop.

It was late afternoon by the time he stepped out on to the street. The sky was silver and it had begun to snow. It was a light fall, soft puffy crystals with the caress of a feather. There were few people about as most town's people liked to rest at that time of day and resume their work in the hours of evening. If it had been fitting to act so in the streets of Rouen, Emlyn would have cart-wheeled and somersaulted in his elation. He quickened his pace, his heart beating in rhythm with his footsteps. He could not believe his good fortune. He had never imagined for a moment that he, unproven and untested, would own a treasure the King of France would surely envy. And it was a gift! Tieffenbrukler had refused payment with an expression of hurt pride. Emlyn poured out his gratitude in prayer and snatches of song.

In front of him at the corner of the street, stood five men. They stood with arms folded across their chests menacingly. They were watching his approach. Emlyn's steps faltered in doubt. He slowed to a walk.

In Paris between the students, street fights had been frequent. But Emlyn had never been a willing participant. While his fellow students were practising, clashing staffs and swords, Emlyn had been buried in the adventures of Marco Polo or the discoveries of Christopho Colombo or the life of Francis Xavier. He practised with a bow frequently with Goronwy but he knew nothing of sword play.

These men had the same threatening look about them as those students. Emlyn recognised none of them and thought that perhaps he was allowing his imagination to get the better of him. He kept his head down and prayed that they would leave him in peace.

They let him pass then fell in behind him. They chanted imitating his stance, exaggerating his steps. To be called English was something Emlyn found hard to bear, he gritted his teeth and endured it. Two of the men walked beside him, linking their arms in his in a seemingly friendly manner. Emlyn clutched his lute. Another walked ahead of him pacing backwards; his soft voice never ceased taunting. Emlyn kept his head lowered. He knew where he was; if he lifted his eyes from the ground, he would see the spire of the church of St. Joan. He did not think the men would start trouble here in the town's streets. All the same, Emlyn wished he had Goronwy with him, Goronwy who was as big as a tree and would have no trouble tying up all five in a tangled knot before tossing them in the Seine.

Reaching the end of the street, Emlyn could bear it no longer. He wrenched his arms free and broke into a run making straight for the gate of the church. The men grabbed at him. He spun out of their grasp. They tried to trip him, but he leaped clear and raced ahead of them crashing into the gate. He pulled it open, fell through and kicked it shut behind him. It closed off his pursuers but not their mocking laughter. Emlyn shuddered with relief.

He turned. The church was cool and dark. The air was scented with frankincense. Pulling a lectern to the stained glass window, Emlyn peered out, he could see through a break in the glass. His pursuers had gathered into a knot, with bowed heads. They laughed then broke into a line and proceeded to the nearest inn. Emlyn ran to the back of the church, looking for a side door. Running up and down, he eventually found one in a small chapel behind a baldaquin. He lifted the bar and inched it open. Snow was still falling, the streets were silent and empty. Emlyn mentally plotted a course to Le Cheval Rouge before he left the safety of the church. He took another look outside to be sure that no one waited for him.

He could think of no reason why anyone would wish him harm so he stepped out into the snow with confidence. It was soft and slippery under foot. Close to the wall, he walked down a narrow lane; his breath smoked in the frozen air. He stopped, listened and breathed more easily. Leaving the wall's protection, he walked to the end of an alley.

They were waiting for him.

Three men stepped into his path. They jeered and laughed. Emlyn did not wait to find out what they wanted. He spun around and raced back the way he had come. His feet slithered in the slush. He fell to his knees. He sprung up again and pounded back.

The missing two stepped out in front of him cutting off his escape. Skidding to a stop. Emlyn looked behind. The others were closing in.

His eyes flew upwards. A shop sign hung above a closed set of heavy doors. Emlyn slung the lute over his shoulder and tightened the strap. He ran a few steps and leapt. His fingers closed over the snow-laden rod showering him with icicles. The sign creaked and swung against him. He scrambled up. The voices beneath cursed him and shouted for him to come down. A hand reached up and grasped his ankle. Emlyn lowered himself slightly and kicked out at the face below. The man howled in pain and let go his grip. Emlyn found purchase and pulled himself up further. Reaching for the upper coping, he caught the wooden rail and threw himself over a balustrade.

He didn't stop to look back. He was dimly aware of the sound of receding footsteps. He heard the shop sign creak again; at least one had followed him up. He hurried through an empty room to a door opposite that opened on a balcony. The passage ran around three walls, a walk-way giving access to the bedrooms. To one side wooden stairs reached the ground floor. Emlyn ran for them and leapt down three at a time. There was a crashing sound behind him. He glanced back. One of the men from the street snarled at him and rushed forward. Emlyn sped out the front, leaping over a woman on the step. He saw the others at the same time they saw him.

Emlyn turned and sped off towards the river. He jumped over a garden fence and crashed into a pyramid of old pea sticks. They fell clattering about him. He stood dazed and undecided. The snow began to fall harder. The men chasing him loomed closer. After a quick glance around him, Emlyn moved. Skidding in the snow, he jumped over a gate into a lane between two houses.

It was a cul de sac with a narrow passageway at the far end. There were few doors here and not a sign of activity anywhere. Emlyn ran. He heard the shouts and the clamour as the men cleared the gate behind him.

He jumped up banging on shutters, windows, doors and shouting for all he was worth. The pursuers circled him and drove him away from the passage. Emlyn backed further towards a crumbling wall piled with refuse. His heart thumped wildly, the odds were terrifying. He reached the ivy-clad wall and lifted the lute strap from his shoulder. He placed it carefully behind him and turned to face his aggressors. Three of them had black beards, the others clean shaven and younger. Emlyn's heart turned to stone with fear. Could they be from the Spanish party on the Rouen road? One had a split lip from the kick Emlyn had dealt him. They all eyed him with hooded contempt, making chicken sounds and clicking their teeth.

'One at a time!' Emlyn cried, half in plea, half in challenge.

They laughed and advanced. They pushed him around from one to the other.

'English offal!' Snow hit him in the face. The lacing ripped from his doublet.

'Heretic!' A handful of his favourite shirt tore from its sleeve.

He allowed himself to be pushed around without complaint. He felt that it would be pointless to fight. Unable to regain his balance, he went down. His knees jarred on the wet, hard packed ground. Heavy boots thudded into his ribs. One caught the side of his head, ripping across his ear. Emlyn rolled away from the pain and the punishing boots.

Pausing in their play, the men drew away for Emlyn to regain his feet. One approached the lute.

Emlyn struggled up breathing hard, his mind screaming in protest. He dabbed at the blood on his lip and stood unsteadily.

'What have we here cheep cheep?'

'Monsieur, it is but a delivery I am making,' explained Emlyn desperately. Would he leave it? Please God make him leave it.

He didn't leave it. He opened the case spilling the contents and caught the lute before it reached the ground.

Emlyn's heart stopped. 'Monsieur it is for Monseigneur the Cardinal of Lorraine!' He moved a step closer, his hands tightened into fists. He could hear dogs barking, small dogs yapping.

The lute was swinging by its ribbons. The pot-bellied shape swung up and down, back and forth, nearer and nearer to the wall.

A cruel sneer twisted on the man's red mouth.

Emlyn recognised the swing that would reduce the nightingale to splinters.

Time howled around him. Anger flowed through him like a torrent of ice. He could see his clawed hands reaching out in front of him, feel the rush of blood as his legs rose strongly beneath him. His own terrorised cry of agony rent the air. Desperately he tried to defeat the space, to rip through its cloggy slowness and cheat time of its inevitable conclusion.

He collided at the same time the lute hit the wall. The lute didn't break.

Emlyn was unaware of this. Blinded by madness, he hit the man and brought him to the ground. He felt the power of his fists as they beat at the face beneath. He felt the skin of his knuckles split, heard the crack of broken nose bones and the sickening crunch that followed it.

Whatever chances had remained of saving the lute were now gone. Still cocooned in a miasma of fury, Emlyn felt the hands wrench him away. The savage, relentless blows came through a haze of grey smoke, thunder bolts that seemed to hit him and carry on through, punching great holes until there was none of him left un-hit.

They kicked him among the refuse.

Before the sycamore lute splintered, he heard the strings moan as if in anguish. The lute was dashed to death across his shoulders.

Carmelia had never seen her godmother so angry. If the Englishman had been within her reach, Adriana Martinelli was capable of melting him on the spot with her scorn alone. They had not returned to the convent, but had come to Adriana's town house near the river. Carmelia had visited the house on but few occasions. This was where, according to Pellegrina, Adriana met her lover Josquin. Carmelia sat meekly at the window, casting her eyes from side to side as if she would see the man leap out of the furniture.

Adriana refused to unpack. 'I shall leave France with that cursed merchant,' she cried, 'even if I am forced to beg. The insufferable wretch!'

Carmelia looked out at the snow. 'It is snowing harder,' she said. 'Perhaps it would be better to wait until the spring.'

'Most definitely not!' Adriana turned to face her charge. 'I will not be refused by a mere wool trader. Who does he think he is. How dare he refuse our company. Miserable worm!'

'Even he can't get to Italy in this snow,' Carmelia pointed out. 'If it is snowing here think how terrible it will be in the mountains. We might never reach Italy but be frozen to death along the way. It has happened.'

'Snow?' cried Adriana. 'Who cares about snow. It melts doesn't it? There must be some way the man can be persuaded.' She began to pace up and down the room. The household keys at her waist clanged whenever she turned. 'He is English so he's probably a heretic, even though he denied it.' She said came to a stop in the centre of a worn carpet.

'If you do him any injustice, he will most definitely not take us,' said Carmelia. 'Anyway, Pellegrina said that he has already left Rouen. So I don't see what we can do about it.'

'The snow will have delayed him. While it does, we shall have to think of some persuasion to entice him to let us join his party.'

Mademoiselle Pilou had taken syrupy cinnamon cakes to her son-in-law's bakery. Of course he had been forced to agree that they were far superior to his own, he had begged her for the recipe. He was a nice boy when he had a bit of sense hammered into his empty head and listened to his mother-in-law. He had given her a loaf and a length of linen. It was not the best she had seen but, with some embroidery, it would do well enough for undergarments for Tieffenbrucker's daughter Isabella.

She had been housekeeper for the German lute-maker and his family since they had come to Rouen, seven years ago. She remembered the year well it was when the dear King died. It had happened during a joust. The King had died from a splinter in the eye. King Francis, such a chivalrous man! Such a tragic death! All of France had wept. Nothing had been the same since. Strife torn, famine torn, France was ruled in name by his son, in reality by the queen mother, Catherine de'Medici.

Mademoiselle Pilou went out of her way to avoid the end of the street, to avoid the heap of rags that sat there, sun or snow, banging clappers at her. The beggar never failed to extract coins from poor Mademoiselle Pilou as she went past, she with so few to give! They should have the man removed, he was a menace to honest citizens.

Bundles clasped tightly, she made her way through a narrow opening between an apothecary shop and the house of Madame Diane de Ventadour with the birds and the three irritating little dogs. Mademoiselle Pilou disliked being forced to use the dim passage, but it was preferable to the beggar. The day darkened as she brushed against the damp buildings, her hurried steps crunched over the snow sounding like an army of Mademoiselle Pilous instead of one. She stepped in a snowy puddle that soaked right through to her stocking. She heard a rush of footsteps but saw only something small and squeaky scurrying ahead. 'Holy Virgin preserve us!' She ran the rest of the way. At the other end, she paused to catch her breath, her heart pounding.

This was a filthy street, rubbish, peelings, leftovers and dead cats were piled in a disused doorway; even the snow did little to disguise it. At her feet lay something that was not refuse. She bent to pick it up. It looked like a circle of delicate ivory like Monsieur Tieffenbrucker used in his fine instruments, the pretty bit he put in the middle. It was one! What else could it be? Mademoiselle Pilou's eyes picked out the splinters of wood that led like footsteps to the doorway. She saw the soft, worn boots and then the body wearing them and then the blood.

She caught her breath in terror.

She could drop everything and scream or she could walk around and pretend she had seen nothing. She walked around, eyes averted. She had not gone far before she stopped. 'Call yourself a good Christian woman Claudine Pilou?' she said to herself. 'A good Samaritan?' She went back. With a reluctant foot, she pushed aside a flutter of stained cloth and set eyes on Emlyn.

Mademoiselle Pilou dropped everything and screamed. She gathered up her skirts and fled from the courtyard as fast as her damp feet could carry her.

Behind her, from where they were concealed in the shadows, the men returned to the clearing and shook the prone figure. Getting no response they argued among themselves for a moment, then dragged the youth from the corner where he had fallen, and carried him away.

Chapter 31 Rouen

When Emlyn awoke it was dark, he was lying on something cold and he hurt all over. He could hear voices risen in argument. They were speaking Spanish; Emlyn cringed at the memory of Don Diego de Luzon. He lay still, mortally afraid. He heard a door open, saw feet scuffle and then rough hands hauled him to his feet. He had time to see the front of a large town house before he was pushed inside the door. His mind was a turmoil of fear. He recognised the men who escorted him, they were the ones who had chased him through the streets and smashed the lute! Something of Emlyn's fear lessened, replaced by cold anger. He lifted his head and looked about him, his right eye was swollen and blurred his vision. One of the men smiled maliciously at him. They came to a stop outside a closed room. The guard banged heavily on the door and a gruff voice invited them inside.

The room was a small bedchamber, warm and richly furnished. Miguel de Cervantes Saavedra was standing by the hearth, his hands held out towards the flame. Seeing him, Emlyn swallowed. He remembered this man's desperate cry as he had slipped into the sea in a rain butt at Dieppe harbour. If that incident was what this one was all about, Emlyn felt that he had little to be afraid of; they might think that he had caused the accident, but they would never prove that he did; the whole thing was too obscure to contemplate. Emlyn straightened his shoulders, feeling a little braver. The Spaniard turned around and looked Emlyn up and down with an expression of concern. Emlyn returned the gaze, remembering the dark eyes and the poet's face and the derisive laughter that had followed him when he had fled from the attentions of Don Diego de Luzon.

Miguel de Cervantes Saavedra rubbed his long hands together, seeming ill at ease. 'Se–or de Luzon is not here,' he said, 'he has gone to Paris, but it is he who wishes to speak with you.'

'Did Don Diego order you to bring me here in such a violent manner?' Emlyn asked. He kept his voice level.

Miguel de Cervantes turned away. 'I am not a violent man, unless I have rightful cause,' he said. 'I did not order this, but I thought that if you and I had a little talk before Don Diego returns you might save yourself some trouble. It's really quite extraordinary how Don Diego takes pleasure from violence.'

Emlyn shuddered and licked his cut lip. He looked around furtively; the door was closed firmly and two of his assailants stood inside with their arms folded across their chests. 'Talk about what?' Emlyn asked.

Cervantes sat on the arm of a chair, his long legs stretched out in front of him. He said, 'Don Diego is concerned about the fate of a fleet of ships which his most Catholic Majesty King Philip, sent on a minor mission to the Netherlands. As you know, these ships never reached their destination, but where delayed in England. Just tell me what you know of the vessels and save yourself a great deal of trouble.'

'We spoke of this on board the boat,' said Emlyn. 'I told you then that I knew of nothing concerning the vessels. How can I have learned anything more?'

'Perhaps you are as innocent as you seem,' said Cervantes. He sighed as if he found the whole business tedious to the extreme. He began to clean his nails with a small peeling knife. 'However, Don Diego has learned of more concerning the matter. He has learned that the house you stayed at in Southampton was visited by no other that William Cecil.'

Emlyn was shocked. How could they have leaned so much in so short a time. He said, 'I am no friend of William Cecil's and have had no dealings with him, nor have any of the company I travelled with.'

Cervantes shook his head. 'I am sorry for you. I have not the power to grant your freedom, but I will speak to Don Diego when he returns. I do not know what he intends, but he has ordered that you be kept in the cellar here until he can have words with you. Do not despair, if you are innocent you have nothing to fear, beyond a ducking in the Seine in a barrel of brine.'

When Emlyn looked up, Miguel Cervantes was smiling. When he was led away from the room, Emlyn felt that Cervantes' words were genuine and that he was not the enemy that Ambrose had envisioned. Emlyn's fear lessened; but not for long.

The men led him though dim rooms and down flights of dark steps. They were not gentle in their handling. From their conversation which they thought he did not understand, Emlyn heard that they had little respect for Cervantes and that their true master was Don Diego. Their orders too, conflicted with what Cervantes had said. Emlyn tensed and watched for a chance to escape.

They entered a darker passageway and the grip on his arm slackened. Emlyn twisted and charged with his head down, back up the steps. The men cursed and one fell back holding his chin. The other grasped Emlyn ankle and pulled. Emlyn fell down the rest of the steps, the cloth of his hose ripped and the skin of his thigh tore on rough stone leaving a wide gash of raw flesh. After a stunned moment, Emlyn rose slowly to his feet, shaking from head to foot. He stared fearfully at his captors. As they approached him, he flung himself against them, they backed away from the wild attack, but did not retreat. They punched and kicked and threw Emlyn, still fighting, to the ground where he lay half dazed, the breath coming in gasps from his lungs. He saw them move in and was powerless to stop them. He felt the savage kicks that turned him over and over until darkness closed in.

The next day, Josquin called at the inn and discovered that Emlyn had not returned, but his belonging were still with the landlord. Josquin cursed and made his way towards the abbey. It had snowed for most of the night. The night had been cold and the snow lay thickly, concealing the sadness of winter beneath its pristine beauty. Now the snow was already melting and had been churned up by cart wheels and feet throughout the busy morning.

Josquin felt that the elderly priest he had spoken to the day before, knew more than he had told about the situation, and he was the only man who Josquin could think of asking. Father Mandard was in the church snuffing candles again. Josquin realised that it was the same time of day and that the old man probably took on this task as a personal responsibility. He didn't seen capable of anything more strenuous. When he saw Josquin he said, 'Good Morning! You are becoming a regular visitor. Want can I do for you today?'

Josquin was cold from his long walk. He scowled at the priest, but the old man instantly melted his hostility with his benign attitude. Josquin said, 'I am a soldier, Father. It was my intention to follow my captain and accompany an English wool merchant over the Alps. The ladies we spoke of yesterday also hoped to travel under our protection. Unfortunately, the merchant would not accept them in his train, he thought the risks too great.'

'I see,' said Father Mandard raising his eyebrows. 'I am glad that someone shows wisdom in all this. And what has this to do with the boy Emlyn?'

'The Englishman is a friend of the family I believe,' explained Josquin from his limited knowledge. 'They crossed the Channel together with the other scholar. I have been hired for the purpose of taking this Emlyn Tomas to join the Englishman. If he is here, then all is well for I have needs to be elsewhere.' He looked intently at the priest. 'Is he here?'

Father Mandard turned away from him and walked to the arched window. He stood silent, gazing out upon the snow filled courtyard. Josquin shivered and prayed to Saint Thomas for patience, then smiled at the irony in his choice of saint.

'As you know, he came to me a few nights ago,' said Father Mandard without turning. 'He came with Goronwy. Emlyn sought me out to discover some news of a friend of his, a Franciscan by the name of Fra Sebastiano. He and the other argued while they were here; right in front of me. I paid little attention to what they said, they spoke their own tongue. The big youth walked away in a temper. I told Emlyn all I knew and he too left. Then the Spaniard came.'

'And you told him this?'

'Yes. Was I wrong?'

'No father. Thank you.'

After that there was nothing to do but search again. Josquin did not go to the house where he had stayed with Adriana. He knew that she was there, in a high temper; he didn't care much for her when she was like that. Josquin had lived in Rouen for seven years, on and off. He knew enough street urchins to rake the town from wall to wall. Still, he did not learn anything for two days.

Emlyn awoke to the sounds of choking, and realised he had his face in a puddle, or was it a puddle? Lifting his head, his other senses returned. He was shuddering because it was freezing and the cruel cold was worse than anything else. Then came the headache, like an inquisition cap screwed on and squeezing his brains out. Equal torment, smothered his chest so that he couldn't easily get a breath out. His torn shirt did nothing to protect him from the bitter cold. He had a vague thought that he had been here for some time, but even time had ceased to exist.

With a groan and a shallow, stolen breath, he sat up. He felt his eyes. One still felt swollen and crusted with blood. He was not without sight; his fingers waved grey upon grey as his eyes adjusted. So there was light, of a sort, it was dark but it was not night. Above him there was a square of a barred window. Through the grey light he could see the four corners and dribbling walls of the tiny cellar. His hands shook uncontrollably. His teeth chattered, making his headache worse.

He stood up, leaning against the wall and then slid down again. There was no point groping around for a hidden opening, it made him dizzy and there wouldn't be one; that much he remembered from his half conscious efforts. The shivering ran from his head to his toes and encompassed everything from inside out. He curled up, slept and woke. He wished he was dead. A voice spoke inside his head,

'Cariad, you are grown now and will go from the house of women. You must not forget that I am here and come to see me when you can.'

He reached up his arms and wrapped them around his mother's neck. She was weeping and the tears shone with light like the coloured jewels at her throat. He felt his own resolve weaken and choked on unmanly tears. She grasped his shoulders firmly and held him from her. Her eyes spoke of her deep feeling for which there where no words to express. He straightened his shoulders and when her hands dropped, he bowed to her as she had taught him. He turned and walked away without looking back.

Across a marbled courtyard his father waited, with his older son at his side. They were smiling and the small boy returned the smile when he joined them. He was four years old. An age to leave the house of woman and an age to join his brother in learning the art of the warrior.

There was water on the floor rimmed with ice. The cellar was possibly near the river. It had risen enough to soak him and stayed in an icy puddle four inches deep; if he moved he'd fall in. He had drunk the water out of necessity. There was filthy straw and rats that never drown, and crawling things with lots of legs. He was glad he couldn't see them.

An emotional pain inside him hurt as much as the others. Emlyn released a mournful sound when he remembered the lute he had treasured for so short a time before the lovingly fashioned wood had made the last rending sound it would ever make. Emlyn grasped his clothing, attempting to pull the rags together enough to warm him. They had taken everything from him but the ragged clothing and the string around his neck containing a medal of St. Christopher, the pearls he had gathered from the church floor and Mafanwy's charms. He tried to sort his thoughts out through the pain and cold. They were keeping him for Don Diego and if they continued treating him like this, he would probably tell them everything they wanted to know. What did they want to know? It was obvious that he had guessed right in thinking that the Spanish ships had carried wages for Alva's troops. But what did William Cecil intend to do? And in what way was Ambrose Chillingworth involved, for involved he most surely was. Emlyn knew that Ambrose would be well away from Rouen by now. It possible that the Englishman had left enough clues for the Spaniards to turn their attentions on the two scholars who had accompanied him, so that they would not pursue him. Emlyn shook his head, he didn't think that Ambrose would have done such a low deed. But didn't that depend on what his mission for Cecil was? Emlyn cautioned himself not to forget that Ambrose was Protestant and an enemy to all he had been brought up to believe in.

A loud thumping hammered into his mind. He had slept again. Awakening fully, he realised the noise was outside his head, not part of the relentless pain inside. He sat up and listened. Faintly he could hear noise from the streets outside. There was the rumble of a heavy cart from somewhere above him and the sound of feet stamping in unison like a troop of soldiers. A bell rang, a dog began to bark. The sounds gave him no clue as to where he was being kept.

By the late afternoon of that day, Josquin had discovered that Emlyn had called at the Italian banking house and done some business, with a German gentleman to witness it. They seemed to be good friends, the Italian agent had said. Afterwards, Emlyn had gone to the home of the German lute maker.

Josquin was not unduly worried then, he knew of the lute maker and where he lived. As Emlyn Tomas was with him, Josquin would call in the early evening. They could not leave Rouen now because of the threatening snowy skies and the late hour, there was no need to hurry. Besides, Josquin had received a message of a different natured Adriana demanded that Josquin call on her at the soonest opportunity. Josquin smiled. Adriana was a fiery woman to cross; she would be furious that the merchant had refused to take her on the journey. Josquin was impressed with the sound of Ambrose Chillingworth; there were not many who would have the courage to turn down Adriana Martinelli. He made his way to her house, glad that he had allowed her a few days to cool her temper.

'Where have you been!' She shouted at him as soon as he entered the house. 'Do you know that miserable, stubborn...' she went on and on,'if he thinks for one moment that he can say no to me!'

Josquin let her voice her anger and tried not to smile. The girl Carmelia was in the room, standing behind her godmother. She made faces at Josquin, indicating that she had heard all this a dozen times over. Josquin winked at her; she was a timid child as a rule.

'You will have to take us with you,' finished Adriana firmly.

'What?' Josquin looked at her in surprise.

'We will travel quickly and be able to catch up, then he will have no choice but to accept our company,' Adriana said. 'We are all ready, so we can leave in the morning.'

Josquin shook his head. 'I can't do that sweetness,' he replied. 'I have to pick up another of the party before I leave. If you have made your mind up I cannot stop you, but I will not take on the responsibility myself. Angelo would have me skinned.'

'Miserable coward!'

Josquin held her shoulders. She pulled away. He said, 'Adriana, why not wait until the spring? The merchant left Rouen three days ago. Can you not see that it is too late?'

'I should have discovered all I could about the man,' said Adriana. 'He must be a heretic. I should have found a stick to beat him with.'

'What?' Josquin never understood the way her mind worked.

'Not a real stick,' she said scornfully, 'an item of scandal something which I could use to threaten him with if he did not do as I wished.'

'That would be difficult,' said Josquin smiling. 'The man comes from England not France. I doubt if you could unearth any scandal about him here.'

Adriana's expression changed. She turned soft eyes on him and tried a different approach. 'You said that you are joining one of the party who is still here. Perhaps I should talk to him. Where is he?'

'I hope to find out, after you have fed me and pampered me with love,' Josquin replied teasing her. 'Carmelia has met the youth I believe.'

'Don't talk nonsense,' said Adriana. 'How could she ever meet anyone? She's been at the convent until now.' She turned to her charge, 'Carmelia?'

Carmelia was blushing. Eyes downcast she said, 'I haven't met anyone.' She looked up. 'Unless you mean the one in the church a few days ago. My rosary broke and two youths helped me pick up the beads. They were not French.'

'That will be them,' said Josquin. He held the girl's eyes for a moment, wondering why she did not mention her brief meeting with Emlyn in the spring. Carmelia turned away.

Adriana had a familiar look in her eye. Josquin sighed. She was going to be nice to him; she was going to try to persuade him. He was going to resist her. And how much he would enjoy her exquisite efforts to make him change his mind.

Emlyn awoke in the night. There was a rattle of keys in the darkness. The door creaked and orange light spilled in through the opening. The flickering light from a fire brand, clawed the walls and mingled with the shadows behind.

Hands grasped Emlyn roughly and pulled him to his feet. He tried desperately to get his numb legs under him, willing them to move. He was dragged, splashing towards the door. The light hurt his eyes. He saw little but the harsh, bearded faces with ugly smiles; one had a broken nose. They bullied him through a dim passage until they reached a larger room, lit bright from a brazier in the centre.

Emlyn's knees refused to hold him up. He sank to the floor in a well of fear and misery.

There was silence, precious in it's brevity. Then came the sound of clanking metal and the muttering of the guards as they moved about, and further off, the sound of water splashing in a wooden bucket. A spitting brazier splashed the walls with madder flame, there was a sickening scent of scorched meat mingled with charcoal. Two men drew near, one carrying water. He emptied the bucket over Emlyn's head. Emlyn gasped in surprise, the water was warm and scented. He shuddered and winced at the soldier's touch as they pulled off the shreds of his shirt and clothing and began to roughly scrub the cellar dirt from his cuts and bruises. All around, bouncing off the cellar walls, the guard's ridicule and laughter cawed like the call of crows on a battlefield.

To his immense relief, they gave him clothes, of a sort. A coarse shirt, woollen hose, that was worn and patched, an un-quilted tunic that did little to keep out the bone-chilling cold and wooden clogs that he pushed his blue feet into. He stumbled around in them until he fell, sprawling over an out thrust leg. In his pain filled head, came the realisation that they would not wash and dress him for the purpose of torture. Whatever had occurred, it had been a mistake and they would let him go as soon as this was made plain. He tried to ask, but a gloved fist crushed his lips before his sentence was half formed.

They bound him with rope, securing his wrists behind him so tightly that his hands became instantly numb. They kicked and slapped at him with the flats of their swords, until he struggled to his feet. The next shove sent him stumbling up a short flight of steps and out of the door.

He tried to gather his thoughts as he was marched through the building and out into the black night. The cold hit him like a physical blow, driving all thoughts away but a smouldering, relentless loathing. For the first time, he really looked at the faces of his guards and fixed them in his mind for the sole purpose of revenge. There were five of them, their way was lit by flambeaux held in their mailed fists. Their booted feet crunched on newly fallen snow. They had smashed his lute.

Emlyn lost a clog and tried to limp back to retrieve it, but a soldier kicked it spinning into the street until it disappeared into the darkness. He laughed heartily and thumped Emlyn between the shoulders as if he shared the humour of the situation.

Emlyn spat at him.

The soldier cursed and shoved him hard, while retaining the rope end fastened to his hands. Emlyn fell face down, hard in the snow. He lost his other clog. He tore at a mouthful of snow desperately trying to feed his thirst. His shoulders were wrenched back in tearing agony as the rope compelled him to stand. They walked on then, Emlyn's feet soon lost all feeling. He tried to work out where he was, but the snow gave a new look to the narrow streets and the night clothed the buildings in freezing mist.

They came to a large, well built house, surrounded with high walls. Above the gates, limp and snow laden, hung the cross of Spain, lit by twin flambeaux, the Spanish Ambassador's Residence. The soldiers stopped and pounded on the wood, shouting for admission.

Kindly washed, dried, fed and pampered, Josquin reached the German's house in the evening. Gentle, soft mounds of snow had collected in corners and on roof tops It was slowly filling all that had been scraped clear during the day with pure, glistening crystals. Josquin's hat and furred cloak were adorned with scattered snowflakes and they clung to his hair like remnants of silver webs.

'I came to inquire after a certain Emlyn Tomas,' he said when the door opened.

Wendelin Tieffenbrucker recognised the kindred blood immediately. Waiting for no further explanation, he ushered Josquin in to a warm, well lit kitchen. His family and servants were gathered around a table sharing the evening meal. The table was laden with fresh bread and cheese and beer and apples and a ham, still steaming from its cooking and spiky with cloves.

Frau Eva Tieffenbrucker rose, wiping her reddened hands on her apron, and pushed the line of four children along the bench to make room for their visitor. 'Sit down,' she ordered, 'and eat.'

'Thank you,' Josquin replied. He removed his cloak and handed it to the ready hands of a servant. 'You are too kind Madame, unfortunately, I have already eaten.'

'Then take a small amount,' she said. She piled a plate with enough to feed a family.

The Tieffenbrucker's had a guest staying with them. He sat in a corner sniffing and covering his face with his hands. Josquin realised that the man was crying. As the others were politely ignoring him, Josquin did likewise. He smiled, he winked at the eldest daughter, then he sat and ate, finding room for it all.

When the meal was finished, the children obediently cleared all away and scampered off to bed, owlish with curiosity. Josquin had shown them a trick with an egg and won their hearts.

'You say you are from Antwerp Josquin,' said Tieffenbrucker refilling their beer cups and pouring one for his unhappy guest. 'I know Antwerp well, who are your family? It is possible that I know them too.'

Josquin laughed. 'I doubt it, my mother was known by many, but I would not think you a man to have made her acquaintance.'

'You think not?'

Looking at the lute maker's wife, Josquin frankly described his upbringing. Eva turned red as an apple and busied herself wrapping the ham in muslin. Tieffenbrucker stared at his visitor a moment and Josquin feared he had misjudged the man, but the German released his held breath and let out a howling laugh, beating his big fist on the table. He glanced quickly to the corner where his other visitor sat and his laughter died, replaced by a look of deep concern.

Josquin felt uncomfortable, perhaps the man had brought ill tidings that Josquin had rudely interrupted. 'You have been gracious to a stranger,' he said to his German host. 'For that I thank you humbly. It is rare to come across such kindness in these troubled times. Do you know anything of this Emlyn Tomas? Is he here with you?'

Tieffenbrucker made circles in the spilled ale on the table. Looking up with a serious expression he said, 'May I ask you a question that concerns us here? Will you give me an honest answer? You have nothing to fear.'

Josquin looked from one man to the other in alarm. Had he walked into something he would soon regret? 'As well as I may,' he answered.

'Are you Catholic?'

'No,' answered Josquin holding the blue eyes with his own.

Tieffenbrucker seemed to deflate with relief. 'This is my friend Adalbert,' he explained indicating the man in the corner. 'Tell this good Dutchman, Adalbert what has become of your own family.'

'My family!' Adalbert gasped, emerging from a handkerchief. 'What family have I now? My wife is dead, used and murdered by Alva's mercenaries and that dog Don Diego de Luzon the Butcher. The sky was so black, as back as blood. What I had of land lies burnt, my animals butchered, my home in ruin and my brother Friedrich gone! He took a long time to die.'

'God have mercy on his soul!' Eva Tieffenbrucker exclaimed with a hand to her mouth.

'They cut off his ears, And his daughter? No one has seen her since. They show no mercy to the helpless, the infirm, the old, babes in arms even have died on the swords of Alva's men. I cannot tell you my friend how much we have suffered. And the sky was black! The stench, the cries, the blood, it is as if it were a field of battle.'

'That it is Adalbert,' said Wendelin. His eyes were soft with comfort and his shaggy head nodded in sympathetic agreement. 'Against the armies of the Duke of Alva the Huguenots have little hope. He has the power of Spain behind him and, no doubt is sanctioned by the Pope to carry out such dreadful slaughter. Now that the Spanish have such a hold in the Netherlands, I see small chance for England's survival. We hoped once to go there ourselves, you know Josquin.'

'Ja, many of us have fled there already. All it will take is the agreement of Philip of Spain to invade and they too are doomed.' Adalbert broke into sobs, unable to continue.

Eva placed an arm around his shoulder, her eyes bright with tears. 'I beg you to come away with us when we leave,' she said, 'and if you cannot come to Italy, then return to Wurttemberg, return to the home of your parents.'

'I cannot. How could I leave the others to fight alone?'

Wendelin Tieffenbrucker frowned. 'You too will die Adalbert, this war is not for the likes of us. Leave it to those who know the blade, like Josquin here. God will see that justice is done.'

'God! How could God stand by and allow such things to happen?'

'It is man who allows it to happen, not the hand of God.'

'Such carnage is enough to make a man lose his faith forever. If you had seen the pain and the suffering and the ways they have to gain confessions, a man would swear he followed the very devil to escape such torment. Where for them is God?'

'Do not speak so Adalbert! We have not striven this far to lose now. When has death and persecution allowed us to be overcome? All know when they tread this path, that it is not an easy one. These deaths are not the first nor, I fear will they be the last, but God cannot be held to blame for the destructive path of the Papist armies. Go home Adalbert, mourn your dead, regain your strength. To return to the fight now with such bitter hatred in your heart, will bring only death. Where is sweet revenge in that? Go now with Eva, a room has been made ready, and think no more of vengeance. Sleep Adalbert and may God grant you peace.'

Eva helped the poor man to his feet and led him from the room; her voice murmuring words of sympathy, where words could never mend.

Josquin was not a Catholic. Whatever he believed in, he kept to himself. But Angelo was Catholic and so were most of his men who came from Naples and Milan; at present under Spanish rule. They had fought for Alva against the Reformers and could even have played some part in the death of Adalbert's family, had it not happened so recently. This was knowledge Josquin wisely kept to himself, he had not fought alongside them then. He never attached morals to those who paid him, wherever the gain was greatest, there his sword was employed. He was handsomely paid for the information he gathered and for spying as he should be doing now, on Ambrose Chillingworth.

Under the bushy brows, the keen eyes of Wendelin Tieffenbrucker were watching him across the room. 'There is purpose in your hearing this Josquin,' he said. 'You asked me about Emlyn Tomas and I had to know where your interests lay before I could help you.'

'Do you know where he is then?'

'Not exactly and there is some puzzle here, for Emlyn is Catholic, so I can not be sure what has occurred. Adalbert here, mentioned a Don Diego de Luzon who is in Rouen,' said Tieffenbrucker. From a fold in his doublet he produced an object that he placed on the table in front of Josquin. 'This,' he explained, 'is the rose from the lute I made with my own hands and gave to Emlyn when I last saw him. It was found by one of my servants, and so was Emlyn.'

'So what happened?'

'The servant, Madame Pilou, appeared here in an agitated state. When I had calmed her down, she explained that she had found a body, that of Emlyn, beaten and left for dead. We hurried to the place, not far from here, and discovered him gone. I found the shards of the lute, there was evidence of a fight, but it was snowing and the signs were fast disappearing. We searched and inquired where we could. We found out nothing.'

'So how do you make the connection with Don Diego?'

'Through these.' Wendelin spilled three coins onto the table. 'Which we found at the same site. They show the head of Philip of Spain and must have been lost there. Emlyn had already told me of an undesirable meeting with the Don, it seems he took a disliking to the Spaniard. It is a puzzle Josquin and this, that I have offered, is but a guess.'

Josquin sipped his beer thoughtfully. 'I have reason to believe what you say. Have you informed anyone else?'

Tieffenbrucker rubbed his whiskers and shaped the ends of his moustache meticulously. 'I told none of this discovery, it seemed unwise. I have some affection for the boy, he plays the lute like an angel, I have known him for some years.'

'I learned that Don Diego has gone to Paris. I wondered if he followed Emlyn's friend, Goronwy?'

Wendelin picked up the empty jug and crossed the room to refill it from a barrel in the corner. 'I think you are right, for he returned today with a member of the Jesuit college. The Jesuits work closely with Spain, indeed most of the teaching priests there are Spanish themselves. Don Diego's reasons must be urgent for him to have travelled at such speed in this weather.'

Josquin placed a hand over the top of his cup when Tieffenbrucker attempted to refill it. 'No more I beg you,' he said. 'I am going to visit a Spaniard and want my wits about me. If the boy is there and I can get him away, we shall leave Rouen tonight.'

'The town gates are already shut,' said Wendelin.

'There are other means of leaving the town,' said Josquin with a knowing grin. Such an escape would mean involving Adriana. Josquin winced at the thought.

Don Diego de Luzon was seated on a chair of red and gold brocade belonging to the Spanish Ambassador. In that gentleman's absence, Don Diego had made the room his own and favoured the chair to conduct his business from. He was thus seated when Emlyn was brought in. The room spoke of the warmth and the golds and reds of Spain. Servants stood by the walls that were hung with tapestries, flags and Moorish carpets from Granada that were lined with silk. On the table stood Venetian glass goblets cradled in silver and studded with gems and an ewer of intricately engraved gold. One of the servants held a monkey that chewed pomegranates and spat out the peel. In one corner, a tasselled, gilded cage hung with two silent canaries. Next to it, stood a priest with his head down and his hands clasped in front of him.

Don Diego looked quite at home, neat and lissome, with doublet and hose of Lucca silk, a shirt fluffed with Flanders lace and a peacock feather adorning his hat. His eyes were warm and dark above high, aristocratic cheek bones. He wore a beard, neatly combed and as black as tar. Shimmering against the black of his doublet, was a chain holding a gold salamander set with rubies. Behind his chair stood the equally handsome gentleman, Miguel de Cervantes Saavedra. He was again paring his nails with the bronze handled knife. His long fingered hands were delicate enough to belong to a woman.

'You have marred him Jaume,' said Don Diego with annoyance. His voice was surprisingly high and he sulked like a spoiled child.

Jaume, the guard who had been among Emlyn's attackers, offered a gap-toothed smile and pulled on the rope that Emlyn was attached to. 'He is rude and insolent Excellency, but not unduly harmed. We have had small pleasure from him yet, although he is a little cold. He found the shoes we offered him beneath his dignity.'

'Untie him and give him a chair; mind you cover it first, I find blood and filth ruins good cloth.'

Emlyn was quite relieved to sit. He found that his feet had not died but were coming back to life with agony. He sat, head bowed and miserable, rubbing at his numb wrists where the rope had rubbed into his skin.

'We have found,' said Don Diego standing up and peering at Emlyn in distaste, 'that you betrayed your companions in their heroic attempts to bring the true word of God to their forsaken countrymen.'

Emlyn looked at him in horror. 'It is not so Excellency!'

'Did I give you leave to speak scum? No? Then I shall continue. After that you took payment from that carrion that sits behind England's throne, William Cecil, for making further betrayal of your companions. Now you are set upon some errand concerning His most Catholic Majesty's ships that are at present held at the port you yourself sailed from. What has become of the cargo of these ships?'

Emlyn knew it was not the cold that made him shiver. Don Diego's words had frozen him with fear. What had happened? He could not believe Goronwy had done this, but who else could have told him so much? Ambrose knew, but he had gone from Rouen. The merchant had shown him nothing but kindness, but had that kindness been a deception? Had it all been a front?

The guard hit him with such force that he left the chair and sprawled across the carpet. He was wrenched up and placed back in the chair before his head had ceased to spin. They were waiting for him to answer. It was hard not to fight back when his future looked so bleak. Emlyn said, 'It is all nonsense, none of it is true. I know nothing of ships.'

Don Diego turned around and took the small knife from Cervantes. He walked forward with the knife balanced in his hand. He stood in front of Emlyn and placed the blade under his chin, forcing his head up. Emlyn glared at him. The Spaniard smiled contemptuously. 'He is lying,' he said. He laid the blade lightly on Emlyn's cheek.

Emlyn felt the tiny blade pierce his skin. A bead of warm, sticky blood ran down his chin and throat. The blade withdrew.

Don Diego laughed in a high pitched cackle.

Desperately Emlyn said, 'As God be my witness, I know nothing of which you speak.'

The guard, Jaume, hooked a toe around one of the chair legs and gave it a jerk unseating the prisoner again. This time Emlyn remained on the floor. Jaume found it amusing. 'Senior Luzon,' he said, 'I can make him speak, I would enjoy the task.'

'Will that be necessary?' Miguel de Cervantes walked forward, his face a mask of distaste.

Don Diego stood over the prisoner. He said, 'Come now, save yourself disfigurement, I do not ruin beauty needlessly. I will help you *Tomacino.* Tell me what I wish to know and you will be favoured. Continue in this obstinate way and you will wish that God had never granted you life.'

Emlyn rose stiffly to his feet, only to be pushed down again. He had seldom felt the depth of anger that built up inside him and threatened to overspill. With a ragged breath, he held in it check and stood stubbornly, willing himself to silence.

Don Diego made a sound of impatience. He said, 'Such refusal is fruitless! I will not have my time wasted.'

Jaume hit Emlyn. He dropped to the floor.

'This is unacceptable Senior,' said a new voice behind him.

Emlyn looked around. He shuddered with relief when he saw who the priest, it was Father Alonso d'Aguila, the man who had encouraged his music and tried to keep him at the college. Emlyn struggled first to knees, with a nervous look at Jaume, then painfully to his feet.

Facing the Jesuit, he said, 'Father Alonso, thank God. You at least must know that none of this is true. Tell them, I beg you Father, that I know nothing of this.'

Father Alonso d'Aguila looked at him with sympathy. 'Emile my child, I too I find it hard to accept that you have turned against the Holy Church.'

'I have not Father. Why would I? I am as true now as I was before. If Goronwy has told of these things, it is because of an argument or two that passed between us; perhaps he thought to spite me. But not this, I will never believe he wished me this. Can you not ask him? He will tell you the truth.'

'Goronwy came home to us a few days ago. He has told me and Father Manare all that has happened since you both left us, and he wept as he did so. I would call him to testify the truth but he is no longer with us.'

'Then where is he? Send for him before I am committed to torture for this ridiculous accusation. In the name of God I beg you Father!'

'It is too late Emile, he has gone to Douai to the school of William Allen, who trains priests to return to England. If you had not fallen thus, you could have gone with him. The school is founded with the Pope's blessing and will be the salvation of your countrymen.'

'I have not fallen nor erred from the path! This is all a lie.'

Father Alonso shook his head. 'Tell them what you know Emile. Repent and all will be well.'

'Repent what!' Emlyn heard his voice fail. What could Goronwy have told them? Everything concerning the Catholics and William Cecil, surmised Emlyn bitterly. Yet he could not believe it. No matter how he looked at this present situation, there seemed no way that he could talk himself out of it. What could Goronwy have known about the Spanish ships? No one had talked to him during the Channel crossing nor after. Even if asked by Don Diego, Goronwy would have known nothing nor could Emlyn believe that his friend had sold him to the Spanish. Why was Father Alonso d'Aguila here? Goronwy had never been keen on learning music and had had little to do with the Spanish priest. They were all watching him expectantly, if he did not speak he would end up on the floor again. Emlyn's tongue felt too thick, he moistened his swollen lips and croaked, 'Tell what?'

The Spanish priest walked up to him and placed a comforting arm on his shoulder. 'You betrayed a confidence in the house of the English merchant, that much we know is true.'

'Dear God! That was only to preserve our lives and it was a minor matter. We could not have escaped otherwise. That is all there is to it. As for Spanish ships, I was unaware of their existence. I am no seaman, I do not know one ship from another nor does Goronwy.'

'A small matter?' Don Diego's voice was chilling. 'You call preserving the life of a heretic who holds the Queen of England in the palm of his hand, a small matter?'

'She needs none to hold her in his hand! I would say woe to any who tried.' Emlyn instantly regretted his words.

Don Diego banged his fist on the table rattling the gold ewer and the goblets. 'He is lying! See how he loves the strumpet Queen? How could he not know of the ships? Not see the ships that lay in their splendour before him? His ship sailed right past them. Loosen his tongue Jaume!'

Emlyn allowed his head to drop as if in abject despair. Then suddenly, without giving the slightest hint of his intentions, he spun around sharply and made a break for the door.

He violently shoved the priest out of his way. He moved so fast that he reached the door and pushed past the liveried guards. He sped on through the great hall before pursuit began. The main gate was open, letting in a feathery cloak of snow. Feet tramped behind him, outraged voices raised the alarm. He charged and ducked under the crossed halberds of the gate guards, surprising them with his speed. Emlyn stumbled down the steps out into the snow. Snow slowed his steps and he felt that ice had replaced the blood in his feet. He struggled on, desperate to reach the safety of the darkness beyond the gate. Blind with terror, he crashed into a passer-by.

The man stopped him and held him up in a firm unrelenting grip. 'Emlyn Tomas?'

Astonished to see him, Emlyn nodded. 'Josquin!'

The delay cost him dear, for the Spanish soldiers were already racing down the steps towards him. He tried to wrench free but Josquin held him firmly and his struggles came to naught.

Just before the guards arrived, Josquin spoke in a fierce whisper, 'Be ready when I come!' Then he turned to the soldiers with a dashing smile. 'Is this the man you seek? What is he? A thief?'

They smiled in gratitude. They tore Emlyn from his grasp. Josquin smiled and willingly offered to assist.

Emlyn was beyond reason. He cursed and spat at him, and had the small satisfaction of seeing the spittle run down Josquin's face.

Josquin hurried back to the German's house and burst through the gates. Tieffenbrucker was waiting for him. 'I have found him,' Josquin cried. 'He literally fell into my arms, but I had to let him go again. Time is short, they may not keep him there. If we are to rescue him it must be now. Have you got two horses?'

'Yes,' answered the Tieffenbrucker looking confused. Eva came rushing to his side clutching her shawl against the cold.

Josquin grasped her shoulders. 'Madame have you spare clothing and some boots? I noticed he had none. And some food for a journey?'

'You can not travel in this!' She waved at the snow.

'There is no choice,' said Josquin grimly.

'What do you intend to do?' Wendelin asked. 'Did you go to the Spanish Ambassador's Residence?'

'Yes, yes,' said Josquin impatiently. 'He was trying to escape, the guards recaptured him. They will not keep him there. When they have questioned him they will move him to some place more secure. I will make an attempt then, as they will not expect it.'

'How can you do this Josquin?' said Eva, her face lined with anxiety.

Josquin smiled at her. 'I shall have the angels on my side disguised as snow flakes. Would you like to run away with me Eva?'

She thumped him in the chest good heartedly and blushed and smiled. 'You are a devil Josquin.' She took charge, pushing Wendelin towards the stables before she waddled off to the kitchen, shouting instructions.

Josquin shovelled snow away from the stable doors and swung them open. Grasping harness and saddle, he said, 'My own horse is at the inn of the Hat do you know it? I've taken Emlyn's stuff there too.'

Tieffenbrucker chose two horses, with a shade of regret. 'Shall I keep the horse for you? Where will you go?'

'We will try to reach Captain Angelo. I will give you a letter for the landlady. Take my horse in place of these. I know it is an unfair exchange, for these are both fine animals. Let us hope it will not be for long. I will leave these at a farm I know between here and Lyon, and send a message to you. What are they, Dutch war horses?'

'Bred to carry a man in full armour, they will not out pace your pursuers I'm afraid, but for endurance in this weather, you could not hope for better.' Tieffenbrucker had bought the horses at some expense, to take him, his family and all his belongings to Italy in the following spring. They knew no battlefield for they had never gone to war. Now he was parting with them for the sake of a youth who could play his lutes better than any he had ever heard. For the German, who stood now with tears in his eyes and a prayer on his lips, it was a worthwhile sacrifice.

Josquin struggled with the huge horses, trying to work too fast. They were placid, soft eyed and gentle. Wendelin took over the task speaking to them in German. Soon Eva appeared with food and bundles of warm clothing that she handed to Wendelin. She stuffed the food into sacks that could be slung over the saddles. 'You have all you need here,' she said.

Wendelin held out a folded paper. 'This is a letter of introduction to my brother in Venice. Should Emlyn ever find himself there, it will give him a place to stay. My brother will know of him as I have written to him before concerning Emlyn's extraordinary talent.'

'Poor homeless boy,' added Eva. 'Have they harmed him?'

'Not much,' Josquin replied. He did not mention the bruised eyes, the cut lips and the blood nor the beating Emlyn had received when Josquin had handed him back to the soldiers. He had suffered such himself from time to time, a beating could be got over. He saw no reason to worry the compassionate woman, who seemed to think of Emlyn Tomas as one of her own. He swung into the saddle of a grey giant and accepted the bundles of food. 'I will send word to you as soon as I am able, God willing that I succeed,' he said. He tied the lead rein of the other horse to his own.

'God's speed Josquin,' said Eva reaching up and patting his knee. 'My prayers will go with you and with Emlyn.'

Josquin bent and kissed her and then grasped Wendelin's hand. 'This is how I earn my bread,' he said with a tight smile 'Have faith, I am, as your lovely wife says, the very devil with a sword in my hand, but your prayers will not go amiss.'

Seething with anger and the injustice, Emlyn struggled, bit, scratched, punched, wriggled and refused to walk. His mind blindly battled with the looming promise of death and the horrendous suffering he must endure before its mercy was granted.

But, before that bitter-sweet caress reduced him to beg for it, he fought. With fists, feet, knees, elbows, teeth, shoulders and aching head he fought all the way to the snow-softened, blood-brindled steps. Then he struggled all the way up them, shouting and screaming like a demented soul.

His teeth found a guard's ear and crunched down vengefully. His elbow punched in an eye. Frozen feet thumped against noses and a clawed hand squeezed a handful of soft flesh, the other came free grasping a handful of hair. Grunts and snorts mingled with howls of outrage, pain and fury. They all tried to hit him at once, and hit each other while he cavorted like a windmill. All came together in a breath-thieving crush. The blot of heads and limbs staggered, tottered and collapsed, spilling back out the door, and bumping down the steps, sprawling the snow in a medley of disorder.

It was only because they wanted something he did not have to give, that he reached the room alive. Momentarily subdued by violence, he went in quietly between his two bruised guards, into the gold-lit room with its fire and its gold and its jewels, with its Spaniards.

Don Diego watched him with a sneer that wrinkled his nose. Jaume's ear was bleeding.

The fate that awaited Emlyn had not changed, death still beckoned with a bony finger. Dizzy, sick and hurting all over, Emlyn was held together only by anger. His eyes could still see, just. He turned them on Father Alonso d'Aguila.

The Jesuit held his gaze for a moment only then dropped his eyes. His face was cast in a genuine expression of sorrow and deep disappointment. Emlyn couldn't believe that the priest was convinced that what Don Diego had said was true. But the priest's eyes in that fleeting glance, told all; he would look after his own interests first and not risk his position at the Jesuit college for the sake of a failed student. Father Alonso was going to abandon Emlyn to his fate. The Jesuit turned away, hands clasped in front. He walked from the room, his robes whispering across the tiles. At the door he turned and faced Emlyn and blessed him. His ringed hands, flashed off candle light. 'I and our brethren will pray for you Emile Tomas,' he said with a tone of melancholy.

Emlyn drew a ragged breath. He offered no thanks, he no longer owed it. Where there had been a slim hope, he now stood friendless.

The soldier's grip on his arms had slackened. Emlyn tensed, even now, he was ready to spring and wreak havoc if the opportunity arose.

'Take him, rack him, whip him, do whatever it takes to give me answers,' said Don Diego. 'I tire of this.'

Emlyn sprung, straight for him. The gold clattered. The Venetian glass fell, rolled off the table and smashed into smoke-blue smithereens.

Before he could reach the grandee, Emlyn was dragged back.

Don Diego's eyes were wide with alarm. He snarled orders, the Spanish so fast that Emlyn was unable to grasp it. Emlyn struggled. Hands and arms held him now as firm as a serpent's embrace.

Jaume seized one of his hands in an iron-like grip. He slammed it down on the table, forcing Emlyn's fist to open and pressed down on it so hard that it became immovable. Emlyn gasped in pain.

In a lightning arch of silver, Jaume's knife plunged down mercilessly. Through skin, sinew, even shattering bones, it nailed Emlyn's hand to the table.

Pain shot up his arm, snarled across his chest and plunged to his stomach with the force of a blow. He crouched up over it, feeling it fill, screaming in to every corner of his being.

Forbidding himself the release of a scream, fighting nausea, he tried to release his fire-anchored hand. His body shuddered in agony and refused to obey. A babble of Spanish buzzed about him.

'What is this?' said Jaume. 'Do you wish to run Englishman? Oh, I see, you are somewhat hampered. Let none say I would leave a man in need. I will help you.' He withdrew the blade with a vicious twist.

The hand dropped, dragging a flow of blood in its wake. Emlyn curled up like a dead leaf, cradling his hand. He released a moan of anger and pain.

No wind stirred the frozen air, the night was black, silent and empty. This late, none walked the street but the city guards and even these, had abandoned the night to the snow, no man of sense would venture out in this deadly cold. No lamps lit the darkness, buildings loomed unrecognisable, light less and burdened with snow..

Staggering footprints scared the snow like a wound. A huddle of dark shapes emerged through the eerie grey darkness of the night. Curses and complaints were muffled and distorted by the blanket of snow. The group of men hurried to their task envying every shuttered window, where all within slept in warmth and comfort. So bent were they, that they heard nothing outside their own grumblings.

Among them, Emlyn lifted his head and stared into the tunnel of softening darkness which swallowed the street they were crossing. He had felt rather than heard the disturbance in the still air ahead.

In the world of white pain in which he dwelt, all the fight had gone out of him. His only hope of release now, was the gate of death. He tried to tell himself that he would be brave to the very end, but the pain he now suffered caused him to doubt it.. He would be spineless, he would scream like a slaughtered piglet. He would tell them everything and it would not be enough. And none would know of his suffering, no friend would light candles and remember him in their prayers, no mass would be sung to see his soul guided true. Would they let him see a priest?

It began with a muffled rumble.

A slight stirring of the air; a whispered breeze.

A drumbeat so soft none paid it any mind.

Emlyn's heart missed a beat.

He dropped to the ground, pulling the neck rope taunt, choking.

The pounding turned to distant thunder.

A voice rent the air with violence like an axe cleaving through ice.

'Can you run Englishman!'

The Spaniards spun about, snarling their alarm, fighting through layers of cloth to reach their swords.

Still, there was no sign of anything. The ground shook.

Emlyn stood up again slowly, shedding snow. In his head were the words of the man who had handed him, with a dashing smile to the soldiers. Josquin whom he had spat at. 'Be ready when I come!

Emlyn pulled at the strangling rope one handed.

But Jaume was no fool, his own grip tightened.

Emlyn fought for breath, enfeebled by the relentless bite of burning rope and the increasing sense of unreality. He went down, again, clawing at the rope. He found in dizzy surprise, that his spirit was not defeated.

Suddenly, out of the black, trembling night, came an enormous two-headed beast. The great hooves slashed the air, crushed the snow and brought it relentlessly nearer. Upon its back, a rider howled and held aloft a blade of wicked silver.

The soldiers blind with terror, fled calling for God's protection. Jaume hauled Emlyn to his feet. He was not afraid. The knife still gleaming red, came out from its hidden folds.

The beast was upon them, teeth bared, eyes rolling, hooves cutting, breath billowing with hell-like steam.

Jaume berated his men harshly. They turned and shed their dire superstitions when they saw the beast was two horses, one ridden and one not. The size and speed of the horses and the massed confusion had prevented them from action.

The rider still howled. He bent as he drew level with Jaume, and brought down his blade. It sheared through the rope instantly. Jaume stabbed at him roaring with fury, but his blade was ineffective.

Emlyn sat down abruptly when the tension in the rope slackened. Through a fog of unreality he heard his rescuer shout and he struggled to his feet. He began to run after the horses. His feet had long since lost all feeling and pounded the snow by will power alone.

Having collected their wits, the Spaniards leapt to orders and scrambled after him. The drawn swords whitened in the snow's light. With good boots and the terror of Jaume to urge them on, they were soon at Emlyn's heels.

In front of him, the horses had slowed. Josquin shouted encouragement in a voice tinged with panic and anger. To Emlyn the words came as if through a howling tunnel of wind. His pursuers screamed for him to stop, his head spun in white madness. But he kept running. Inch by inch, he drew to the right of the horses. He caught a stirrup with his uninjured hand, nearly fell and failed to pull himself up, the height was too much and his strength had dwindled away like sand in an hour glass. Spanish hands grasped at him, ripping cloth. He lurched on with a wretched sob.

A hand came down reaching for his own. Fear drove him on and fear drove him to reach up the mangled remains of his right hand towards his rescuer. Josquin grasped it and pulled.

Blinding pain lanced through all, threatening to overwhelm him. Some hidden reserve, brought Emlyn scrambling on to the horse's back, clutching Josquin like a drowning man. The following curses dwindled as they were lost in darkness. The powerful horses churned the snow and flew on as if with the wings of Pegasus.

Chapter 32 Voyage to Stamboul

Fra Sebastiano had regretted his decision to make the ten day journey to Venice as soon as he had started. But he had persevered through the cold days and difficult mountainous roads. Who else could have come but he? He was the only one, apart from Father Zenobius the herbalist, who knew exactly what had befallen Don Carlos Grimani's grandson. He was greeted warmly by Don Carlos' wife Juliana. She offered him dry clothing, food that he could not finish and a jug of warm wine which he found no difficulty in consuming. She sat with him and spoke of the great respect she had for her step grandson, Lorenzo. Fra Sebastiano was surprised that her feelings were opposite to those of the husband, but he had heard that she was an exceptionally pious woman who spent a great deal of time on her knees praying for a son. She had suffered from continuous miscarriages over the years that had left her in ill health and with a sharp bitterness which marked her once youthful face and edged her voice.

When she was satisfied that he was well cared for, she led Fra Sebastiano to her husband. She did not enter the room and Fra Sebastiano was glad of this, what he had to say to Don Carlos would cause her pain. The two elderly men sized each other up across the room. Grimani had been reading by the light of the window. He was dressed in a loose robe of red velvet trimmed with white fur like a cardinal. The room too spoke of great wealth; tapestries and eastern carpets covered the walls and cloth of gold edged the soft furnishings.

Grimani offered Fra Sebastiano a seat before he spoke. 'I was expecting my grandson Lorenzo,' he said. 'They tell me that you are from Santa Croce in Florence?'

'That is so,' answered Fra Sebastiano. 'I have come on behalf of your son, Signor Grimani. Lorenzo was unable to make the journey himself on account of sickness.'

Don Carlos sank down on to a chair opposite, his face a mask of concern. 'What has happened?' he asked.

'He had gone to Carrara,' explained the Franciscan, 'to take up his teaching duties at the small community there.'

'I ordered him to come here!' Grimani snapped.

'He has devoted his life to God. I assure you, he thought long and hard before he made his decision. I was with him myself, it was not easy for him to go against your wishes, but he is ordained now and is bound to obey his superior before any other.' Fra Sebastiano paused and whispered a prayer begging forgiveness for his manipulation of the truth. 'We thought him well settled and content enough. No more than a few weeks had passed when he returned. He was left at our gate, sick and unconscious. We could not guess what had happened and presumed that he had been attacked by brigands on the road from Carrara. I thought at first that he would loose his life. But it was most extraordinary how well he had been cared for before he had been brought to us. I am sorry Don Carlos to be the bringer of bad news.'

'Are you saying that he will not live?'

'No, he will live. He is over the worse now, but he will never be the same again.' Fra Sebastiano paused, then could find no other way to break the news to Don Carlos; he made a direct statement. 'I'm afraid to say that your grandson has been castrated.'

'God's blood!' Grimani leaped up from the chair. 'God's blood! Castrated? Who has done this brutal deed? They shall feel the strength of my anger and the harshness of my punishing hand! Who?'

'I do not know,' admitted Fra Sebastiano. 'Lorenzo remembers being captured by two men and brought towards Lucca. He was drugged, and although he fought his captors, they got the better of him and performed this horrendous act. He has described the men to us and we are doing all we can to find them. One of them, he told us was a Nubian. Don Carlos, your Grandson's condition is known only to myself, the physician who tended him and the abbot of our order in Santa Croce. For his sake and yours, we thought it better kept this way. I judged that the cruelty was done with purpose, for the wound was well dressed and he had been cared for afterwards, as if who ever did it intended for him to live. I know that he has entered our order now, but would it be presumptuous to suppose that he had some dealings with a woman?'

'Do you mean that this is revenge for some woman he has wronged? Did he say as such?'

'No he denied it. But young men are not always careful with their affections. Priests too, have their moments of weakness. I felt that his denial was genuine, but what other possible explanation could there be?'

'A eunuch!' Grimani cried. 'A eunuch! I cannot believe what I am hearing. Jesus Christ!' He began to pace the room.

'I am sorry for the pain this has caused you Signore. There is some consolation however.'

'Oh no. There is no such thing. I knew when he chose a life with the church that I had probably lost him. But I hoped to talk him around to my way of thinking. You see Father, the future of this family is at risk. The only male line is through Lorenzo and Paolo. On them I have pinned all my hopes that our blood line will not die. Now Paolo is my only hope.'

'Then we must thank God that you have this other grandson through whom your name will prosper. As for poor Lorenzo, he is a good man of God, I believe with prayer and patience that he will get over this.'

Grimani swung around, his face a mask of bitterness. 'Lorenzo never did what I wanted, he always went against me. He refused to learn how to ride, to fight, to play music, everything I suggested in fact. He even entered the church without my permission. Do you know, Father, he never liked me, even from the very beginning!'

'Perhaps he was devoted to his mother,' suggested Fra Sebastiano. 'He spoke of her in his fever, at first I thought I might find her here, but they tell me she passed away some time ago. She was lost at sea.'

'She was mad.' said Grimani with some malice. 'A sadly disturbed woman. I did all I could for her. In the end I was advised by the very best physicians to send her away, somewhere quiet far from the worries and pressures of life. I sent her to Cyprus, as I have some people there who could watch out for her. The climate, I was told was health-giving. We all hoped that she would recover. But she never reached there, the ship was lost and she was never seen again. Perhaps it was better for her in the end. Her sons became my sons and on them I have placed all my hopes.' Grimani resumed his pacing. 'Forgive me Father, I need to be alone. My servants will see to all your needs. Will you remain here so that we can speak further on this?'

Fra Sebastiano rose, feeling suddenly tired. 'I can remain a few hours,' he replied 'I shall visit your chapel here. Then I will be at the Church of the Frari for a few days, send for me if you should have need. I shall pray for you and your family. May you find peace.'

When Don Carlos turned to him, there were tears in his eyes and a frightening, unquenchable anger. Fra Sebastiano bowed himself out, his mind a whirl of confusion.

The fate of Anna Grimani was a puzzle. Either she had died as Grimani said, or someone was determined to keep the details of her fate a secret.

Perhaps Emlyn Tomas sought the wrong woman. Before Lorenzo had left for Carrara, he had mentioned some doubt voiced by an old woman form Torcello, a Zia Carlina. Fra Sebastiano knew the island well, a peaceful place of mud flats and water birds. Could that woman still be living, after twenty years? Perhaps a visit to the old cathedral of S. Maria Assunta on Torcello would be worth while before he returned to Florence. Fra Sebastiano had not been there for some years and the mosaic of the Virgin was always worth the trouble it took to get there.

Finding the old woman took a great deal of unpleasant foot work and cold boat rides, but the trip to Torcello proved rewarding. Once Fra Sebastiano found the correct place, he was relieved by the news that the old woman still lived and everyone seemed to know her. Willing hands pointed out the house.

He was admitted by a dark beautiful girl, as dusky as a Gypsy. The walls of the house were crowded with brass plaques that depicted obscure saints and their brave deeds. Between them, were paintings and tapestries all faded and dusty. Most of the floor space was taken up with heavy furniture leaving little space to turn around. Layer upon layer of thick carpet muffled the stone tiles. In the lamplight, it looked like a mysterious cave filled with twinkling oriental treasure. Fra Sebastiano was received in the most cluttered room of all. Zia Carlina, in her bright fringed shawl, fitted the room perfectly. She was ancient, her brown skin a mass of wrinkles, her eyes a lively brown still showing her humour.

'You are welcome Fra Sebastiano,' she croaked. 'I was expecting you.'

'You were?' asked Fra Sebastiano incredulously. 'Do you know why I am here then?'

The old woman shook her head. She pushed a cat off a chair and indicated for her visitor to sit on the fur mottled seat.

'My visit concerns a story of long ago good mother,' said Fra Sebastiano settling into the chair. 'The story of a certain Anna Grimani. Did you know of her?'

Zia Carlina cackled with laughter. 'So the dark wings are spread are they? I told him they would come.'

'Dark wings?'

'The wings of the Avenging Angel. I told him they would come, old Carlos Grimani. He would not believe me, told me I was a silly old fool talking nonsense. Now the Devil returns and the doubting man will know no peace until the Devil has slacked his thirst.'

Fra Sebastiano crossed himself. 'I don't know what you mean. I learned that the woman died at sea.'

'That's what he wanted them all to believe, even her boys. You are a priest, so what I tell you will be safe from other ears. I have lived with the secret for many years. I knew I would live to see the end of it.'

'Forgive me Madonna Carlina, but see what? What did happen then?'

'He put the tale about that she was mad,' explained Zia Carlina. 'He took her boys from her and sent her away. Not to a convent you understand, he sold her and her maid to a slaver, just like he sold her lover to the galleys. He could never stand to have blood on his own hands. It would have been better for him had he killed her, that's what I told him. She cursed him and she had the power to make her curse come true.'

'That is preposterous!' Fra Sebastiano had never realised that his search would lead to such dark truths. 'So she lived,' he said. 'I wonder if she may even live still. You mentioned a lover?'

'It was all hushed up after it happened,' said the old woman wheezing. 'Venice is a city of sinners. In those days, I kept a house near to where she lived. She did not frown on my girls and spit as they passed. I befriended her in her grief when her Grimani husband died. But youth recovers and in time she found another. His name was Capaccio and he was a gem merchant.' Zia Carlina sighed and closed her eyes, as if to picture the past. 'Carefree and young he was, and handsome as a god. All my girls fell in love with him and watched for him when he came to visit her. She had sold her husband's property on the main land and had come to live in the house on the Canal delle Torreselle, where that spice manager now lives, he knew her too, he had worked for her husband Cristoforo Grimani. Anna was not mad, she was a good, charitable girl, determined you understand. Never could accept the way things were, never saw that, as a woman, she had no power over her life. Carlos Grimani urged her to be a part of his family. He wanted her sons you see, not the woman herself. She defied him all the way. His urges grew to threats and she tried to run off with Capaccio. All Venice knows what happened then, Grimani took the boys by force and Anna followed them. None of us saw her after that. Then Cristoforo's brother, Roberto challenged Capaccio to a duel and got himself killed. You can imagine how enraged Carlos became now that both of his children were dead. The gem merchant, Capaccio was arrested and accused of murder. He was sent to spend his remaining days at a galley oar. A sad end to the lives of those two lovers. Anna cursed old Grimani. She cursed him and his blood line and I have seen the curse come true. Grimani has a puny daughter who he sent away in bitter disappointment. I knew that it was not finished.'

Fra Sebastiano felt a shiver run down his spine. He did not believe in the superstitious nonsense the woman said about dark wings. Curses were the work of the devil and should not be believed in. 'Was there anything else?' he asked.

'What else could you want,' laughed the old woman.

'Did Anna write a letter to you?'

Zia Carlina rocked back and forth, her old head bobbing on the skinny neck. She cooed to herself softly. Eventually she said, 'Anna wrote a letter to me. I cannot read, you understand, one of my girls read the words. Yes, Anna wrote to me, it was the life of her sons that she cared about. I had some influence then with the nobility of Venice.' Zia Carlina winked and nodded. 'Anna said that a demand for ransom was sent to Don Carlos and she hoped for her freedom. Obviously he did nothing about it. Why would he when he had contrived the thing from the first?' She shook her head tutting. Her watery eyes lifted and regarded Fra Sebastiano. 'What she hoped to gain I cannot guess, nor what became of her.'

'Was she with child?' Fra Sebastiano asked delicately.

The bony shoulders rose and fell, the ancient eyes twinkled with some inner knowledge which Zia Carlina would not impart.

Soon after, Fra Sebastiano took his leave of old Zia Carlina. He tried to forget about her words of avenging angels, but at the back of his mind a tiny voice asked, What of Lorenzo Grimani? Was what happened to him the act of some woman wronged or was it a hand reaching from the past, unwittingly turned upon itself to bring about the curse of Anna Grimani?

There were none now to avenge the fate of Anna and her lover, so the story had best be buried and left undisturbed. If Emlyn came to Venice, Fra Sebastiano felt that he had a right to know who his parents probably were, but the details of their sad lives were best left to God. Would I accept that? Fra Sebastiano asked himself, he knew that he would not and that nor would Emlyn Tomas.

Scipione Barozzi had found his sea legs on the voyage to Alexandria during the summer. He had taken to the sea like a fish, his stomach untroubled. He had earned Bartolomeo Varini's respect, for he had done all that was expected of him as a representative of the spice company and more, he had found a secure market for the future sale of English wool.

It was this subject that brought him now to Bartolomeo's house on canal delle Torreselle. The *Cornucopia* still lay at her mooring at the Arsenal. Waiting with her was the *Maria*, Grimani's cargo ship and a fully provisioned war galley commanded by the redoubtable Cesare Zatta, a veteran of many battles at sea. Scipione Barozzi had so far, endured the harassment from Grimani's agents, concerning the lateness of the season. The question on their lips was, When are we going to sail?

'English wool.' Scipione said as soon as he was shown into the library at the new trading house near the Rialto.

Bartolomeo sat hunched over a pile of documents squinting behind his eye glasses. He looked up, 'It's not here.'

"Madonna Fiorenza,' added Scipione, noticing the woman at the far end of the room. She smiled and came forward. She stood behind Bartolomeo peering over his shoulder.

'The question is,' said Scipione, 'can we afford to wait? It will still be some time before the wool reaches here. If we don't leave soon, Grimani will leave without us.'

'Well that won't do him any good,' laughed Bartolomeo. 'Without the *Cornucopia*, he gets no spice. But I understand the worry and am as concerned myself.'

'The *Cornucopia* is all loaded and ready to go, apart from the space reserved for wool.' Scipione pushed a stack of paper aside and sat down on the table. He produced a notebook and began to flick through the pages, pausing at a column of figures. 'I've already worked out something we could carry instead, glass. The *Maria* carries glass, so it may be over doing it a bit, but they need not know. We can load up without their knowledge. After that, we will be free to sail. I know you wanted to secure a wool market, but we stand to loose much by remaining here selling nothing. The wool markets of Northern Europe are disrupted, even Antwerp has been overrun by mercenaries in the employ of the Duke of Alva. Embargoes have been placed on English shipping so I doubt if we will see much wool next season. Therefore, when this Englishman you are expecting eventually gets here, the cloth will sell well enough here in Venice; he could well be carrying golden fleeces, for it may be the last good quality wool we see here for some time.'

Bartolomeo nodded his head and remained in silent thought for some time. His lips began to move in calculation. Eventually he made a positive sound and added, 'That will leave you and the *Cornucopia* free to sail within a day or two. I am sending Enrico de Martoni with you.'

'Enrico de Martoni?' Barozzi repeated.

'He is Fiorenza's secretary, he's been to Stamboul before.'

'Yes I remember,' said Barozzi. 'I thought he was against the idea.'

Fiorenza laughed, 'Enrico will bend when the reward is great enough. He speaks reasonable Arabic and better Turkish,' she said. 'You have neither.'

Barozzi assumed a miserable expression, in close imitation of Enrico de Martoni.

'I know he is not the most cheerful of companions,' added Fiorenza. 'But he does know his ground, and there are none better than he for keeping correct accounts. Are there Bartolomeo?"

Bartolomeo nodded. He crackled his bony knuckles and leaned back placing his hands behind his head. 'Shall we go over what you need to do once you have reached Stamboul?'

'There is no need,' assured Barozzi 'I am to take up residence in the Venetian quarter in Galata, with the cheerful Enrico. Then I get in touch with a certain Ismael of Syria and, from there, fill the holds of the ships and sent them back to you laden. I stay in Galata for twelve months, strengthening connections and making new ones. When you send a man to replace me, I come back. It couldn't be simpler. Why? Have you received word from our elusive employer, Vincentini?'

'I have, but nothing is changed except for one puzzling instruction,' said Bartolomeo, 'but that is for the return voyage of the *Cornucopia* and need be of no concern to you.'

'But you are going to tell me just the same?'

'On the return journey, the *Cornucopia* is to find some excuse to delay the departure from Candia. Don't ask me why, perhaps Tomasso intends to join with the ship there. I had hoped we would see him before then though.'

'Where is he?'

'Looking for a certain green rock at the source of the river Po,' said Fiorenza. 'Can you believe that?'

'I am willing to believe anything concerning the man, Madonna. Is the river Po running with emeralds? The rumours abound!'

Bartolomeo smiled in agreement. Whatever Tomasso was up to, it could not effect matters concerning the trading voyage now. He put thought of the master out of his mind. 'You will miss your wife and daughter, as it will be over a year until we see you here again.'

'Charlotta?' Barozzi smiled and clasped his hands over his round stomach. 'Good heavens no! And my girl, Lucretia is showing signs of developing her mother's sharpness of tongue.' He winked at Fiorenza and added, 'I shall be glad to get away. Maybe they will learn to appreciate me better! When can I leave?'

'Is it too late in the day to go to Murano?' said Bartolomeo.

Barozzi stood quickly, his smile broadened into a joyful grin, Murano was where the Venetian glass was manufactured. 'If need be, I shall go in the dark,' he suggested. 'Grimani's men won't be able to see me or the glass then.'

Bartolomeo's expression changed to a knowing wink as he added archly, 'Guess who the gentleman-of-the-poop on Grimani's galley is?'

'Surprise me.'

'Paolo Grimani.'

Cesare Zatta, captain of the war galley, cringed as the young man ordered him to increase the speed of the oars; the sea was rough and the weather unsuitable. It was common practice for a merchant's son or a young nobleman to accompany the galleys, as apprentice to the sea. The experience and training was necessary for their futures. Usually though, thought Cesare bitterly, they were under the strict orders of the ship's captain. But Cesare had been informed that this particular young man was to have authority above all others! As captain of the galley, this was a gross insult to Cesare. It had been obvious from the start that the young man had no idea how to run a galley. Paolo Grimani boasted that he had sailed on many voyages, but, if he had, he had learned nothing.

Cesare walked down the gangway towards the oar master. On either side of him the great oars rose and fell in strict rhythm. The war galley was a hundred and fifty feet long and twenty feet wide with three masts. Twenty-six pairs of oars spread out from the ship like the legs of a centipede, each oar pulled by three slaves. These were mostly Turkish and Moorish captives with hate burning in their eyes. If the hate was kept well stoked they rowed well.

'Quicken the beat Luigi' Cesare said. He would not shout the order and subject himself to further embarrassment.

Luigi was a thick set man with a dark weathered complexion, well muscled and as strong as an ox. Beside him, stood a great drum on which he beat out the oar strokes in times of war. His eyes narrowed as he glanced toward the horizon, billowing rain clouds rolled toward them. The galley rose and fell with a sickening rhythm, sinking into the troughs and sluggishly heaving out of them, each time, as if it would be the last. 'I would not advise this captain. There's the mother of all storms on the way.'

'Nor would I,' agreed Cesare, 'but if that foppish youth asks it, who am I to go against his wishes?'

'You are the captain,' said Luigi, 'He is but a gentleman-of-the-poop, the crew will follow your orders before they as much as look at Paolo Grimani. Why risk the safety of the ship and the crew to satisfy the whim of a boy?'

'Because, against my better judgment, I am ordered to do so,' complained Cesare. 'Do not worry. Do you think I would let him sail us to the mouth of hell?'

'Why not ask Quirini to speak with him?' Luigi suggested. 'He can frighten the boy into obedience and no blame will fall on you for going against the Patron's wishes.'

'Frighten him?'

'He'll put the fear of God into him. You know Quirini, his tales are enough to curdle the blood of a corpse. Remember when we had Zeno Sammichelle as gentleman-of-the-poop?'

'Aye,' Cesare nodded, 'he too tried to put his oar where it was not welcome.'

'Until Quirini told him about the sea wraiths that came to feed on men's souls while they slept. We didn't see hide nor hair of young Zeno for the rest of the voyage. He kept to his cabin and wouldn't come out.'

Cesare looked at Luigi appreciatively. They and Quirini had sailed together for many years. 'All right,' he agreed. 'Take the beat up half a measure, just to fool the lad into thinking he has us at his command. I'll send Quirini to him, but I fear Paolo Grimani is made of sterner stuff than our young Zeno Sammichelle. If we cannot stop this madness, we'll chain him to an oar.'

Paolo had never felt as proud and as free as he did now, at sea with command of his own ship. But Cesare had soured his joy. He was standing at the prow, the epsilon below him cut through the waves like a shark. The wind was strengthening by the minute, they were making little headway against it. He knew that Cesare was correct in cautioning such oar speed in these waters, but earlier in the day when the wind was in their favour the two caravels that they were supposed to be protecting had made good speed and where now out of sight. Paolo knew that this too, was his fault, the mist had been too thick to see. Now he knew, that if they did not sight the trading ships soon, he would have a lot of explaining to do to his grandfather. He had been instructed with the utmost secrecy, he was to do all he could on the return voyage, without incriminating himself, to delay the *Cornucopia*, so that the *Maria* could reach the markets of Venice first. But this was the out-bound voyage, on which he had been told to be helpful and friendly, so that no suspicions would arise.

Cesare said that the caravels were ahead of them, and the wind would now be against them too. He had assured Paolo that the sailing ships would have to tack the wind and wait for them. But now the weather had worsened and they would turn to the protection of the coastline rather that fight the winds. Paolo loved the wind and the rain and the tangy smell of brine. 'Would that I could always be thus,' he said aloud to himself, addressing the sea.

'And so you will be, if you do not throw caution to the winds and all of us with it.'

Paolo turned to see who had spoken. It was the red-faced boson, Quirini.

'Do you know, I remember when I was but a lad like yourself,' Quirini continued, 'we were off the coast of Naples when a howling storm, such as this devil's breath approaching, hit us with all the vengeance the sea can spit. We were joined then to the Beirut fleet and had become separated out of folly, a wager I recall, by our young captain, to see who could race the better, sails or oars. Well, out of this storm came the wailing of the Sirens. You've never heard the likes of it, turned a man's blood to ice it did. Then we saw it....'

Within minutes, Paolo was running down the gangway, shouting orders. Quirini had awoken a chilling fear in his heart and made him realise that most disasters at sea were caused by incompetence. Vowing to watch and listen in future, Paolo handed the control of the galley to the commander, Cesare Zatta. But Cesare suggested that they run it together, discussing their moves before they undertook them. The rowing pace eased as they turned toward the dark smudge of coastline.

Within two hours, the galley lay at her anchors under protective cliffs that rose from the sea. Within hailing distance, the two caravels waited out the storm that was growing in intensity. Shamefaced, Paolo stood on the wind lashed deck, knowing that had he driven them further eastward, it was unlikely that any of them would be alive by now.

'You've done well lad,' said Cesare who stood beside him.

Paolo turned toward him with a smile of self-mockery. 'Done well? I could have killed us all.'

'Aye, but you swallowed your pride and we have come to no harm, thanks be to God. You have learnt, and there is no cause for you to feel ashamed. You have acted right and the crew will respect you now.'

'They laugh at me!'

'They are behind you though,' said Cesare. 'It takes more courage to admit you are wrong than to battle on regardless. We will be in Stamboul in a few days and if there is grog to be found in that Muslim infested flea pit, you and I will get drunk together to celebrate your initiation.'

Paolo smiled and bowed extravagantly. The wind whipped at his hair and clothing. 'I shall be honoured captain,' he replied. He did not feel so ashamed now, but he would not forget. These seamen were not like the young men he kept company with in Venice. There was no time for foolish antics on the sea.

Don Carlos had talked long and tiresomely before the *Maria* had put out to sea. Within the first three minutes Paolo had yawned and made a show of impatience. Don Carlos had shown then what a man he was to be feared. Age had not blunted his ability to wound. By the time he had ended the tirade, Paolo had been reduced to pulp and made to feel of less worth that the least scrap of rubbish in the Lagoon. At first his anger had blinded him, he had been consumed with burning hatred. He had turned to the nearest tavern, but no amount of wine had dispelled the miasma of fury and self loathing.

Don Carlos had sent men to find him and had even come himself, to the disreputable inn at the harbour, when Paolo's whereabouts had been discovered. His glittering presence had shamed the inn keeper. But Don Carlos had ignored the foppish attendance. He had eased his great bulk onto the narrow bench and poured two cups of the rough wine.

'Do you hate me Paolo?' Grimani had asked.

Paolo had turned to the wall, away from the commanding, appealing gaze. Was that not obvious?

'Your brother hates me too,' Don Carlos added. 'He could never see beyond that hatred. And great it must be too, for him to leave all this and choose to live like a hermit up some mountain. So, Lorenzo has his way now, perhaps more than he would have wished, but there it lies and I shall not ask of him again.' Don Carlos had reached across the table and grasped Paolo's hand in his.

Paolo tried to pull away and glared at him across the table. He felt the power of his grandfather burn into him. The old man's hand tightened and remained so, until Paolo's struggles ceased and his eyes had dropped in shame.

'In life there occasionally comes a time for change.' Don Carlos' words were softly spoken. 'For you such a time has come. I have placed all my trust in you and given you overall command of the galley.'

Paolo had been stunned. He was to sail! He was to leave Venice in search of glory and, God willing, battle with the infidel!

'You will be gentleman-of-the-poop, this is for appearance sake only. I have informed Cesare Zatta that he will follow your orders. He is a difficult man Paolo, and this decision has done little to place you in his favour. I would advise you to listen to him, seek his opinion in all you do. Matteo Sarzana is to command the *Maria*, I trust his skill and judgment and so should you. Vincentini is sending Scipione Barozzi to represent the company in Stamboul. Do not, whatever happens, get on the wrong side of him. We need him. He will not be returning with the fleet, so we need not worry about what happens out of his sight. Don't mistake me, I mean no harm to befall the *Cornucopia*. I merely wish the *Maria* to get home first. Do you understand me?'

Paolo had understood everything. They had remained in that damp, grimly lit inn for the rest of the night. Grimani had shown a rare side of his character, speaking affectionately of family and loyalty and of his hopes for the future. He looked forward to the wedding of his daughter Carmelia and Tomasso di Vincentini, which would take place perhaps before Paolo returned. His ideas were filled with hope and the promise of prosperity. Paolo had understood and was quite willing to make the changes expected of him, if he was able. He knew he could never make himself into the merchant that Don Carlos wanted him to be, but he could adapt and he could always pay someone to do the tedious paperwork and bartering. The trouble was, old habits died hard, and all he really hungered after, was the glory of war.

After one of the roughest nights Scipione Barozzi had yet spent at sea, he was still jovial and hungry the following morning. He had been very relieved to see the galley limping in towards darkness. Until now, the journey had been without mishap, which in December was an unexpected blessing. Scipione had enjoyed the short stay in Candia, he was an old acquaintance of Sebastiano Venier, the governor. He was surprised to learn that Sebastiano Venier had met Tomasso di Vincentini. That, Scipione assumed, would have been on the first journey Tomasso had made to Venice with his hold bulging with spice and luxury cargo. Sebastiano Venier had also pointed out, that he had found Vincentini unpleasant, and that Scipione was fortunate that he himself had not yet met with the man.

It was one matter in which he was sorry about; Scipione had hoped that Tomasso would have returned to Venice before the *Cornucopia* had sailed, but there had been no sign of the master. What had Bartolomeo said? He's up the Po, looking for green rocks! Well, rich men could afford to pamper to their pleasures or vices. Green rocks though?

Scipione had brought few personal items with him; Bartolomeo had warned him about loading himself down with anything of value. It invariably gets left behind, he had warned, or lost, or stolen, he had added with a note of caution. Scipione Barozzi had no fears concerning his destination and his home for the next twelve months. There were over a hundred Venetians in Galata, working for either the Senate of private enterprise. For many years they had vied for dominance with the Genoese. At present, Genoa was out of favour and the Venetians had control of the market. France was making a few inroads, they had long been allies of the Turkish Sultan. You have to watch the French, thought Scipione as he left his cabin, they have a habit of sneaking in when you are least aware of them. Look how they had branched out down the coast of west Africa, and across the Atlantic where Spain had difficulty watching a coastline that seemed to go on for ever? Scipione knew much about the comings and goings to the major ports of the Mediterranean. He knew better than most of the weakening position and dwindling empire of Venice. No strong foothold would serve them for long, horizons had broadened and ships built like castles, could cross the great deserts of water that separated west form east. Venice with her slim galleys, was outdated, exhausted and forever being nibbled at by the very Turks who so willingly filled her holds in Galata.

Barozzi came on deck just as the *Cornucopia* nosed out of the shallow bay. Ahead he could see the galley and the *Maria*, sailing with a good breeze. Gulls filled the air with noise and the sky with fluttering out-stretched wings. The sea was blue and golden in the morning light, sparkling with froth-topped waves. It seemed as if a hundred dolphins followed them, rising with a flash of beautifully curved backs and glistening grey skin before they disappeared. As the coast faded into the haze astern, islands dotted the horizon, like places of myth, they looked like jewels upon the sea. Most where bare rock, but some where covered by low growing thyme or ancient trees, stunted by the unforgiving winds. Scipione filled his lungs with sea air and expelled it with pleasure.

On a hill, high above the sea, a young man shaded his eyes against the glare. He could see the tiny ships as the sails bellied out in the wind. He dropped his hand and inclined his head in affirmation. This was what he had been waiting for, for the last four days. As the ships left the shelter of the shallow bay, he turned away and trotted down the hill to where his horse was tethered to a olive tree. He scrambled lightly into the saddle and thumped his heels to the horses' side. Koçi was happy that his master had returned from Damascus. Ismael had been gone for many months.

He rode for two hours, for he had ridden far along the cliff tops the day before. Crossing a stretch of grassland, he came in sight of a copse of trees and a circle of felt tents. Above them horses-tails and pennants flew form spears placed in the ground. They were the tents of his master, Ismael the Syrian. Around them sat a dozen men, dressed in rough sheep skin and furs. Across their backs hung their compound bows and leather shields, and at their waists hung the short, curved swords of the Turkomen. The waiting horses were the small Steppe ponies that could carry the riders tirelessly day after day, Ismael had insisted upon their use. The saddle and harness were hung with woollen tassels and plaited braids of yellow, green and red. Across the mares' foreheads were bands of dyed leather, sewn with bright sequins that glinted in the sunlight.

Ismael was standing outside the entrance of the largest tent. Beneath the long fur of his hat brim, a single eyebrow was raised in question.

'I have seen them as you said Lord!' Koçi called out as he dismounted.

The day was cold and clear, frost still sparkled from shaded places. Ismael was dressed in his coat of leopard skin and had his hat pulled down over his ears. He smiled at his slave and looked relieved to hear the news he had waited for in the week that they had camped there.

'Will we go now Lord to the city of cities?' asked Koçi.

Ismael nodded. He clapped his hands once and the men under his command leaped up. They would ride across the peninsular of land and meet the African galley that awaited them.

Chapter 33 France

Jaume and the Spanish guards did not give up their prisoner willingly. They followed through the heavy snow. Josquin looked over his shoulder. The horses had churned the snow in their wake. He could not see the Spaniards but he could see a line of flambeaux bobbing through the darkness.

He stopped the horses, his breath smoking in the cold air. Emlyn's grip at his back slackened. He was holding on with one hand, the other hung at his side, dripping blood into the snow. Through his clothing, Josquin could feel the violent shivering.

Josquin turned awkwardly. 'Can you climb across to the other horse? We will have to ride as fast as we can once we leave the town.'

Emlyn did not attempt such a feat. Instead he slid to the ground and stumbled to the other horse. He stood at its side and reached up with his good hand. After three tries, he failed to pull himself into the saddle. He sat down with a groan of frustration.

Cursing, Josquin dismounted. Casting a quick glance at the approaching fire brands, he hurried to Emlyn's side and pulled him to his feet. Josquin shoved him up into the saddle. 'Can you stay on?' he snapped.

Emlyn nodded silently. They rode faster then, and soon the lights were out of sight. Their tracks were fast disappearing under a covering of glistening snow.

Josquin always thought ahead of his actions. He liked to know what lay behind every choice and every move. He knew that this was why Angelo valued him in the company of fighting men. For not many soldiers of fortune considered the consequence of their actions. It was not always possible however, to plan with any detail. Josquin could not have guessed how he and Emlyn were to escape this situation. Had the weather been any different, he was sure that the guards would have foiled any attempt to rescue Emlyn, and it was no good fooling himself that the boy was capable of the hard ride ahead of them; Emlyn was scarcely conscious.

Josquin kept hold of the reins while he led the mounts through the quiet streets towards the river. The snow was falling so thickly that he could hardly see what lay in front. Adriana's house had an orchard at the back with the trees growing up to the town wall. In the wall was an old door by which Josquin hoped to leave the town; beyond that, he could not plan. The snow would make it difficult, if not impossible to travel. But leave they must, no place in Rouen would be safe enough to hide once it was daylight.

'It would be fine,' Josquin said to himself, 'if Adriana had gone off with the merchant, we could have made our escape undiscovered. As it is, we will be lucky if we escape at all. Unless?' He turned to see if Emlyn was listening. He didn't look as if he was.

'Unless,' Josquin continued, 'She could use you as a beating stick, Scaramouch, to have her way with that stubborn English merchant, Chillingworth.'

'Don't call me Scaramouch!' Emlyn's words were whispered, Josquin only heard them because everything else was silent. Before they reached their destination, Emlyn fell from the saddle and landed with a muffled thud.

'I should have guessed,' said Josquin, 'that they would not teach you how to sit a horse in that Jesuit school.' He leaped down from the big horse.

Emlyn didn't bother wasting breath to reply. Heaved once more into the saddle, he leaned forward and wrapped his arm around the horse's neck. He was so cold that he could not think beyond this simple task. If he fell off again, nothing would induce him to rise.

Josquin led the horses on foot from there. When they reached the house, he clambered over the wall to unbar the gate. The house in darkness and Josquin's hopes rose. Perhaps the mistress wouldn't notice if they were very quiet. But Josquin knew he could not go on without giving Emlyn warmer clothing, and the benefit of a warm fire nor could he continue without some simple care for his injuries. Adriana was renowned for her art of healing, if she could be persuaded in her present state of mind.

Carmelia peered over her Adriana's shoulder and clutched Pellegrina's arm on the other side. They were all dressed in nightcaps and thick gowns with shawls across their shoulders. They huddled behind the kitchen door. Adriana's hair was free from its usual confines. It rippled down her back to her waist, a swath of black tresses. She held a lamp in her hand. She lifted it higher and stood listening to the distant thumps. 'It's coming from the stable,' she whispered.

Carmelia said, 'Can we not rouse one of the menservants?'

Adriana turned to look at her. 'Why? Are you afraid my dear?'

'By the Blessed Virgin, yes!' Carmelia replied in a hoarse whisper.

'It can't be thieves,' said Adriana, 'they are too noisy.'

'Madame, it could be murderers,' gasped Pellegrina. 'What would they care about noise? Who would come out in this snow to our aid?'

Adriana opened the door and marched through the room to the other side. After a moment's hesitation, Carmelia and Pellegrina followed, clutching each other. They followed the mistress out into the snow and ran across the yard to the stable. There was no light inside but they could hear the distinctive sound of horses and a muffled curse that made Carmelia gasp in astonishment.

Adriana turned to them both. 'There is nothing to fear,' she reassured them. 'Unforgivable though the wretch is for uttering such a profanity, I know who he is.'

She pushed the door and lifted her lamp. 'Josquin!' Adriana cried sternly. 'What are you doing here?'

Josquin jumped with fright and dropped the unlit oil lamp he was holding. It hit him on the shin. He grasped his leg and hopped up and down, glaring at her. The stable filled with light as Adriana came forward and hung the lamp on a hook. She tightened the shawl about her shoulders and stood with her arms folded across it.

'Whatever you are going to say,' said Josquin, 'never mind. It is your help we need now Adriana not your scorn.'

She tapped her foot impatiently.

'We need warmth and food,' said Josquin. 'Then we need to escape the town through your postern in the orchard.'

Adriana dropped her hands to her hips. 'What have you done?' she demanded.

Josquin looked heavenward. He knew the language of those hands, soon they would begin to wave about expressively and he would be arguing for an hour or more. In the darkness of the stable, Emlyn was motionless across the neck of the war-horse. Josquin scowled up at him. If he was seriously hurt, escape would be impossible. Emlyn was unconscious by the time Josquin lowered him to the ground.

The hardest of hearts could be brought to sympathy for the ragged creature who lay on the kitchen floor in front of Adriana, but Adriana wanted something first. She covered the boy with blankets, making a tally of his hurts as she did so. She settled back on her heels and fixed Josquin with a look he should be well acquainted with. 'Did you say the boy was some relation of the wool carrier?' she said pointedly.

Josquin was leaning on the wall with his arms folded and his eyes drooping. He was wet and his body shuddered with cold. He dropped his gaze and straightened, kicking at the hearth to express his anger. He said, 'Obviously the man would be overwhelmed with gratitude were you to assist the youth.'

With a smug expression, Adriana turned her attention to the boy's injured hand. He mumbled but did not awaken. She said, 'He cannot travel like this, he will die. Dead he is of no use to me.'

'I cannot believe what I am hearing,' said Josquin 'For the love of God Adriana, just do what you need to make him comfortable, we shall worry about the consequences later. You have my oath that you will go wherever you wish even if I have to hold my sword to the Englishman's throat all the way.'

'It is agreed then,' said Adriana.

Josquin came close to the fire, holding his hands out to its warmth. His yellow hair dripped and his woollen cloak steamed in the heat. He said, 'There is however, one problem that only the hand of God can sway. Snow may be friend as well as enemy. While we are held in its chilly embrace, sweet natured Adriana, use your skill and heal the boy. You would not think it now, but he is worth the effort. You will like him, he's like a whirlwind when conscious.'

'I will need daylight,' said Adriana, 'before I can see to his hand. There may be other hurts too that I will see in better light. If he can be wakened, I will give him a sleeping draught that will ease the pain.'

'Would it not be better to work now, while he is unconscious?' asked Josquin hopefully.

Adriana did not reply, she just looked at him as if he were a child, with a child's simple solutions.

Emlyn was totally unaware of his surroundings. He existed in a different world; away from pain and hurt and cold. He dreamed.

The man who was teaching him was a Mufti, an official in his father's house who taught him the teachings of Mohammed. The Mufti's voice was sharp and authoritative. 'Sit still Saiah ibn Khalil.' he ordered. 'And listen. We believe in Allah and what he sent down to Abraham and Ishmael and Isaac and Jacob and what was given to Jesus and all the Prophets of the Lord. We make no distinction between them. Remember that Mohammed is Rsaool, Messenger and not nabi Prophet. Mohammed is the Messenger of God.'

Saiah's attention wandered. From where he sat he could see his brother through an arched opening. His brother was three years older and had no need to learn the

Koran; he could recite form memory all that he had learned. He was riding the sand coloured horse that their father had presented to him. Saiah watched him with envy, wishing that he too could escape the hooded eyes of the Mufti.

He jumped when the teacher clapped his hands sharply and snapped an order. Saiah dropped his eyes in shame. 'Yes Sidi Ahmed,' he mumbled. He had heard the Mufti's request, he lifted his head and responded to the question. 'The six daily prayers are like a fresh river which runs by the entrance of home. He who washes six times daily will keep himself pure and clean.'

'Five!' The Mufti's voice filled the room. 'Five daily prayers! Five times a day! Fix it in your mind Saiah ibn Khalil. If you cannot remember this simple thing, how can you hope to be the man your father wishes you to become?'

Emlyn opened his eyes. He could remember little after he had held his wounded hand up to Josquin and had been hauled into the saddle in white agony. He didn't try to work out why Josquin, who Friar O'Healy had called a thief, was his rescuer. He seemed to exist between the darkness of dreams and pain-filled consciousness. Fever haunted his mind and racked his body with shudders. His hand was still the centre of burning pain. It lay on his chest with a damp cloth covering it. Emlyn could see little in the dim light. He did not want to look anyway, he was afraid of what he might see and reasoned that it was better to remain ignorant of the damage that caused such pain.

It was more beneficial to think of the reason why he had been treated so harshly. Goronwy may have talked to Father Alonso d'Aguila and Don Diego about what had happened in Southampton, but Goronwy would have known nothing of the Spanish ships. As the fate of the ships had been the main concern of Don Diego, there must have been another responsible for directing the arrest and torment which Emlyn had suffered. If it had been Goronwy, then why had he not mentioned the firearms that had been sold to the Huguenots as well? Emlyn would not believe that his friend had falsely accused him. Emlyn tried to think of some other whom he could blame and vow to avenge himself. He could only come up with the name of Ambrose Chillingworth. if Ambrose had sold him to Don Diego, then why rescue him and Goronwy from the fate William Cecil had threatened? It made no sense.

Emlyn gasped as a wave of pain washed through him. When it receded, he lifted his head. There was a fire lit in the hearth, the red flames were reduced to a molten glow. Beside it there was a chair and he could see the folds of a woman's skirt and her veiled head bowed in slumber. He tried to call to her to discover where he was. His tongue was swollen and his mouth felt as if it were filled with sand, he could not make himself heard. He sank back to the pillow. Pain and thirst had interrupted the flow of his thoughts. He forced his mind back to the conclusion he had reached with reluctance.

Ambrose could have brought him and Goronwy to France in his company with the full agreement of Cecil. The merchant was on some mission of greater significance and must have been aware of the risks he was taking concerning the ships. Emlyn groaned with frustration. The thought that Ambrose had sold him to Don Diego in order to escape discovery himself, seemed as near the truth as he could guess.

'Madame?' he whispered to the dim figure across the room. She didn't stir. Emlyn reached his good hand up to a shelf above him. He could see the dim outline of jam pots. He gripped the edge and pulled himself up, hoping to stand with its support. As his weight increased, the shelf tipped and the pots slid off. They hit him and the straw bed in rapid succession and filled the room with sound as loud as thunder. Emlyn gasped as they thudded onto his chest. He struggled to sit up and his hand dipped into something sticky.

'Mon Dieu!' His companion was started awake. She turned up the wick on a lamp near by and hurried to his side, holding the light above the wreckage.

'Carmelia,' croaked Emlyn in surprise.

She placed the lamp on the floor and turned away. 'Are you a thief too Monsieur that you would try to steal the mistress' honey?' She poured some liquid into a cup for him.

There were pots all around him, some spilling their contents on the heavy blanket. With little success, Emlyn tried to clear the mess, every movement and every breath caused agony.

'Whenever I see you,' said Carmelia returning, 'you are breaking something. Is it always as such with you?'

Emlyn drank the water she held for him. It was cold and tasted like snow; he had never tasted anything better. His fingers were sticky around the cup.

Carmelia efficiently put the pots back on the shelf and mopped up the honey. As she worked she told him where he was and how he had arrived there, just two hours ago with Josquin.

Emlyn felt as if mist filled his mind and snatches of song floated disjointed and meaningless as sleep beckoned. He fought against it and mumbled the words that swam before him. *'As everyone should, to the brother I went. I informed him then, as I recall, That I was a poet, which is known to you all.'* He was acutely aware of Carmelia, as she washed the honey from the fingers of his left hand. He could sense a tender magic in her touch that was unlike anything he had felt before. *'And had doted long on a maiden fair,'* A spasm jerked his injured hand as if it was frozen on a chord to produce the heart-rending cadences of a lute. *'Of milk-white skin and raven hair.'*

Josquin crept out of the bed as not to disturb Adriana who slept like an angel beside him. They had left Emlyn in the kitchen with Carmelia to watch over him. Josquin had commented to his mistress, that the girl was on her knees in prayer for an uncommonly long time for the sake of a stranger.

'The girl is starved,' Adriana had replied. 'She's been shut up behind those walls for so long, is it any wonder she is besotted by the first young man to cross her path? Were she not of so timid a nature, I would worry for the boy's purity. It is a wonder what she sees in him though, with his face such a mess.'

Before he left the room, Josquin looked with gentle affection on the woman he would not give his heart to; would not, because she would never do the same. To Adriana, Josquin was just a passing ship, a lovable rogue to keep her bed warm and her passion satisfied. He owed her nothing, not even loyalty. He was not her only lover.

Once in the kitchen, Josquin approached the corner where Emlyn lay. Carmelia was fast asleep in a chair across the room. Loath to disturb her and call attention, Josquin gently pulled away Emlyn's blanket. Josquin had partaken in enough battles to judge the severity of wounds and had learnt how to treat them. He ran his hands gently over the boys limbs and chest. The rib cage was discoloured and swollen. Probably cracked or broken, thought Josquin, but not so seriously as to cause internal injury. The worse problem was the hand, the cut's and bruises on his face would heal soon enough. but he was in no state to travel. Josquin lifted the cloth from the boy's hand and winced. It was a mess of black bruising and dried blood. Adriana had eventually agreed to sew up the ragged wound but she had done little else. Emlyn moaned and moved restlessly. His eyes opened and he looked at Josquin as if he did not see him.

In a low voice Josquin said, 'We are in the house of an acquaintance of mine, but in Rouen still. The snow has stopped. Do you think you could ride? We are not free yet.'

The eyes closed. Emlyn swallowed and moistened his lips. Josquin found a jug of water on the floor near by. He poured some into a cup and would have helped Emlyn rise to drink, but Emlyn pushed his hand away and sat up with care. He took the cup and drained it with one gulp. He grinned and then changed his mind, his lip was beaded with new blood.

'I can,' he said hoarsely. 'If I can eat first. We are sneaking away?'

Josquin nodded, relieved. The boy showed signs of spirit and courage; all he needed now was endurance. The ride would not be easy for him.

With a great deal of fuss, Emlyn rose and dressed in layers of the clothing that Tieffenbrucker;s wife had provided. He sat at the table to eat the cold meat and bread that Josquin placed before him. Josquin bathed his injured hand. Emlyn felt dizzy. His appetite fled. He endured the pain without a sound, keeping his eyes on Carmelia were she sat curled in the chair asleep. One frightened glance at his hand had confirmed his suspicions it was not the hand of a minstrel.

Josquin whispered quietly as he worked, explaining what had happened and what part he and Wendelin Tieffenbrucker had played in the escape. 'So we will join your merchant and captain Angelo and we will all go to Italy,' he finished.

'Do we have to catch up with them?' Emlyn asked. He didn't touch the food. 'Ambrose Chillingworth knew what would happen to me, that's why he left so quickly. He knew that Don Diego would seek his answers from me.'

'Then why would he charge me to see you safely away from here? I don't think he realised how serious the situation had become. I cannot judge, for I do not know the gentleman. Do you want to avoid his company?'

Emlyn shook his head. 'No. I just want to be well enough when I see him to reduce him to soup,' he replied bitterly. Now he had neither lute nor a hand able to awaken its sweet voice!

Josquin tied off the binding neatly and viewed it with a grimace as the blood began to seep through. 'You can stay here with these gentle ladies if you wish,' he said keeping the concern from his voice. 'They will smoother you with kindness until Don Diego discovers your whereabouts. The comfort of a woman's embrace is too great a temptation for a soldier of fortune, I must flee this scented nest before I grow used to it. There is rumour that there will be war in Spain with the turn of the year, war between Spain and the Moors. A man of the sword could earn good coin hiring himself to one or the other.'

'You would hire your sword to an unbeliever and kill Christians?' Emlyn whispered. 'God forgive you Josquin.'

'Fear not,' said Josquin winking at him. 'One day you may learn that killing one man is much the same as killing another, all in the art of war. So you don't want to come to Spain to kill Muslims or to fight alongside them?'

'Are you serious Josquin?'

'Is that no?' asked Josquin. 'Then we shall go to Italy and the Alps shall open before us like the Red Sea. I am after all, employed by your Englishman. Like it or not, I shall bring you to him. We'll take a meat grinder with us. Are you ready?'

Emlyn followed him from the room. He was the colour of sheeting and his hair was damp on his forehead. 'I have run from my home in Wales, have been banished from the shores of England' he said, 'and now I flee France, all in the space of a winter's month. I doubt either, that Spain would offer me welcome.'

The horses were still saddled in the stable and they seemed content enough. Josquin felt quite affectionate towards them. He lead them out into the snow to where Emlyn waited. There was no light yet of dawn in the sky.

Josquin said, 'Do you really ride as badly as you have so far shown? If I have to stop every few yards to pick you up and haul you into the saddle, we may as well surrender to the Spanish now and be done with it.'

'I can ride well enough,' said Emlyn. 'I want to see what the Italians think of me. They might let me stay.'

Carmelia received the scolding of her short life the following morning. Josquin and Emlyn had gone. Adriana screamed and cursed and tore the house down, throwing things in a fit of temper.

This was a different Adriana to the one who had spoken with such caring, gentle words when Carmelia had been told of her future plans. Adriana was a remarkable woman. At present she was not Madame Adriana Martinelli, that renowned Italian lady of high esteemed reputation. At last her furious eyes came to rest on her godchild. Adriana marched up to her and slapped her with such force that Carmelia sat down abruptly. 'Stupid, senseless girl!' shouted Adriana shrilly. 'All you seem capable of doing is sleeping or crying. The sooner we get you wed and bedded the better. Dispirited novice!'

'It was not my fault,' wailed Carmelia holding her burning cheek. 'You insisted that I drink some wine and it sent me to sleep.'

'Hold your tongue!'

'Madonna, if ever there was a sign from God that this journey was not meant to be, surely this is such?'

'If you think for one moment that I am swayed from my purpose you are mistaken. We leave within the hour. If I as much as catch sight of that miserable beggarly soldier, I shall curse him to eternal damnation! He gave me his oath! It will serve him right if the youth drops dead!' Adriana swung away, brushing Carmelia with her skirts. 'Come on, get up child,' she snapped. 'My steward will accompany us and we shall ride the palfreys to make better time. You shall have to learn as we go along. Where is your idle maid? Pellegrina! Pellegrina!'

Carmelia sat too dumb struck to move. After years of inactivity and regulation, the past night had been one of horror. Carmelia wanted to go back to the convent. She didn't care about husbands and princes any more. If this is what 'outside' was really like she wanted none of it.

They rode out of the town gate soon after it had opened. With Carmelia and Adriana, rode two maids, including Pellegrina, two grooms and four men at arms to see them safely to the protection of Angelo Corberio's mercenaries. The grooms pulled mules behind them, packed with bales of dresses and warm clothing. Adriana assured Carmelia that she could produce anything they might need from those simple bundles. The snow lay heavily, bowing tree branches, overburdening roofs and swathing the land in fat billows of crystal white. The sun shone watery yellow as it rose from the horizon. In spite of the early hour and the weather, there were many people on the road with their produce. The roads were being cleaned. It was nearing the season of Christmas and there was money to be made; geese, swine and cattle were driven into the town market to fill the plates of feasting churchmen.

Carmelia sat her horse wordlessly. Adriana would not allow the women to ride side saddle, she insisted they ride like men. So disgraced did Carmelia feel, that she could not lift her eyes from her gloved hands on the rein. Adriana kept the pace brisk; she and her own maid Marietta, were confident riders. The two girls bounced along beside them. Carmelia was miserable and frozen.

Carmelia's thoughts returned to the previous night. It was true that the wine had made her sleepy, but she had been awakened by the tipping of the shelf. She hadn't mentioned that incident to her godmother. Josquin had not said what had happened, nor who had caused the cruel wound and beating to the boy, so she could not understand why Emlyn had run off with him. She hated Josquin because of what he represented, Adriana's lover. She had seen Emlyn on three occasions. He had ruined her flower mosaic, broken her rosary and upset her godmother's honey pots. Emlyn was no heroic knight from romantic tales, but he was beginning to have the same effect on her.

If Adriana thought that the redoubtable Englishman was held up by the snow, she was mistaken. Ambrose Chillingworth considered snow an oft unpleasant aspect of winter; he respected the limitations that it brought but he was not daunted by it in the least. It did not prevent him from travelling, unless it fell so heavily that he could not see his road. Ambrose, Matthew, John Moore, a few hired servants and thirty mercenaries escorted the wool laden mules across the white landscape, twenty miles ahead of Adriana Martinelli. Most of them were huddled in their cloaks with blue noses and silent in their misery, but Ambrose himself was quite happy. It was less than two weeks since William Cecil had voiced his distaste for the Nuremberg clock in Ambrose's Southampton house. He had nobly saved the lives of two youths, he had made a good profit from the sale of muskets to the Huguenots and he had succeeded in hiring thirty mercenaries, only twelve of whom were in his pay. Good fortune rode with Ambrose Chillingworth. Soon he would see the Alps and soon after, Geneva, the city of Calvin, of who's works Ambrose was a keen reader.

One concern nagged at his content, and that was the whereabouts of Emlyn Tomas. He often glanced back down the road they had travelled, hoping to see the boy, but the road was empty and Ambrose became increasingly concerned that something had happened to Emlyn to prevent his coming. When he voiced his concern, Matthew surprisingly agreed with him, but John Moore laughed at his words and suggested that Emlyn may well have decided to stay with the Jesuits after all and when Angelo's man, Josquin caught up, they would discover the facts. 'Nothing you can do about it now anyhow,' Moore added. 'It's needless to worry Mr. Chillingworth, from what I've seen of the lad, Emlyn can look after himself. I'll swear he's gone to the Jesuits, he talked about it to me often.'

Ambrose still felt uneasy, he was not so sure of this. Emlyn was just eighteen and his upbringing had been sheltered; he was naive about the ways of the world beyond the slow and unchanging peace of Wales. Ambrose pulled his mount to the side of the cavalcade and reined in, indicating to Matthew to do likewise.

'Don't say it,' said Matthew.

Ambrose scowled at him. 'I am worried and...'

'You want me to drag m'self all the way back 'nd look for your fledglin' Jesuit?'

'Would you Matthew?'

Matthew nodded solemnly. 'All right. Say where I'm t' meet with y' an' I'll give 'im five days afore I'm commin' back. I knew this would bring trouble. I said t' myself only...'

'You are wasting time,' said Ambrose, cutting off his complaints. 'This means a lot to me and I know that you are the only one capable of finding him. Do it with a good heart or not at all!'

Soon after, Matthew rode into the snow and disappeared. Ambrose watched him and remained still for some time after, until Moore touched him on the shoulder and urged him to continue, for the days were short and evening was already dimming the sky.

Another solitary figure made his way across the frozen fields of France, travelling north. Goronwy Glyn Parry was on foot with his pack slung over his shoulder and a stout walking staff in his hand. He looked up to the grey sky blending into the flat land all about him. There was not a mountain, a hill or a tussock in sight. Could a Welshman bear to live in such a dull bleak landscape? For the sake of God I can, thought Goronwy, and it will not be forever.

He missed Emlyn's company. Emlyn would be laughing and cavorting through the snow all the way to Douai. But that would not have done, Goronwy knew better than Emlyn that the time for frivolity was over. Goronwy smiled sadly. He knew now that he should have listened to Emlyn and not parted company so sourly. Whatever had caused Emlyn to abandon the Jesuits was of obvious importance to him. His wild spirit would never be tamed for the church unless he had this freedom now. Goronwy didn't envy him his discontent. I have believed, he thought, that because I know what is right, that it would be right for Emlyn too. How desolate he must feel, cast adrift without the firmness of belief to give him comfort. Why dear Lord, could he not share the vision?

He had not stayed any longer in Paris than he had to. As soon as he arrived at the college, Father Manare had summoned him. Goronwy had poured out his bitter tale, concerning Emlyn and the betrayal in England. Goronwy was sorry now that he had said so much, his words had made Emlyn appear a lot worse that he actually was. But Goronwy had felt better afterwards. At least Father Alonso d'Aguila had listened to him with a sympathetic ear. No harm could come to Emlyn. He was probably in some roadside inn with the Englishman on his way to Italy. Whatever the future held for him, Emlyn would have Goronwy's prayers and hopes to strengthen his way. Goronwy felt sure that they would meet again, perhaps as older and wiser men.

He stopped walking and looked back down the road. Mist shrouded the distance and seemed to hold him as if trapped in an alchemist's bowl. He stared up at the winter sky and turned so that it spun above him. How marvellous was the creation of God!

'You get to Rome before me Emlyn Tomas,' he laughed. 'You Bastard!"

He turned and planted his staff firmly in the snow. He lifted his head up and sang, his rich voice breaking the cold silence all around him. He continued towards Douai and the school founded by the Society of Jesus for training the English exiles in the eradication of heresy.

A few days later, Ambrose Chillingworth rubbed his hands together above the flames of the inn fire. In spite of the weather, they had made good progress and the snow had held off for the last day. They had only run into trouble once but the presence of Angelo and his mercenaries had been enough to deter attack. The band of thieves had let them pass in peace. Starvation had driven these desperate men into forming larger groups. Ambrose was glad that he had hired the mercenaries, otherwise he knew, he would not have travelled far without encountering attack.

Ambrose turned away from the fire. He had eaten well and looked forward to a good night's sleep. There was a commotion at the door and it opened letting in an icy gust of wind. As he was expecting Matthew and, hopefully, Emlyn, Ambrose turned to see who had entered. Three women stood on the threshold. 'I want a warm, clean room,' demanded one of them pointing a finger at the proprietor.

Ambrose managed to reach the landing before the same voice stopped him in his tracks. 'Monsieur Chillingworth! How fortunate that we should meet again!'

He turned. The lady was standing at the bottom of the stairs, looking up at him with a bright smile. She pulled her gloves off with sharp sudden movements.

'Madame?' said Ambrose. He recognised her but thought it wise to show ignorance.

'You have not forgotten already?' She spoke loud enough for the whole inn to hear.

Caught with no means of escape, Ambrose descended with heavy steps. 'Madonna Martinelli,' he said, 'how delightful.'

'We travel the same road Monsieur,' she said in her loud tone. 'There are so many dangers these days for women travelling unaccompanied. Surely you will not refuse us the protection of your company?'

Ambrose looked around the room. Angelo caught his eye and offered a malicious grin. The others held expressions of exaggerated pity. Ambrose said, 'If it were possible to accommodate you Madame, I should be only to pleased to offer assistance. As it is, we are a company forced to travel at a pace unsuitable to you. If I might suggest a better...'

'We are all able to ride as fast as the best of you. So please do not be ungracious Monsieur,' said Adriana. She placed her arm on his and guided him back into the room with an air of conquest. 'Besides,' she added, 'Who will care for the poor unfortunate boy?'

'What poor unfortunate boy?' asked Ambrose. What excuse was she going to use now?

'I tended him myself,' said Adriana. 'I would have helped him further if he and Josquin had remained. Have they not joined you then?'

'No,' said Ambrose slowly. He felt suddenly cold. Adriana sat down near the fire and the other women flocked in behind her like obedient ducks.

'I have saved the boy's life mousier,' said Adriana. 'He is some relation of yours, a nephew?'

'Madame, forgive me my ignorance,' explained Ambrose. 'I have no idea to whom or what you refer.'

Adriana knew little of what had actually happened to Emlyn and Josquin. She explained that Emlyn had been badly treated, that he had been beaten, but she did not who by or the circumstances behind it. For her own reasons, she minimised the extent of his hurts, leaving the Englishman to reach his own conclusions.

Ambrose was reluctant to believe everything he heard. He knew that Adriana was determined to leave France; such determination could mean that the whole tale was fabricated to work towards her goal. But the fact remained that Emlyn had still to make an appearance and until he did, the truth could not be discovered. Putting his concern aside, Ambrose crossed the room and explained the situation to Angelo.

'If Josquin is with him, no doubt he will be able to do something, he's a good man to have beside you in times of trouble. Are we to wait here in the meantime?' Angelo responded.

Ambrose said, 'We must continue, at least as far as the place outside Lyons where I have arranged to wait for my own man. Do you think it would be possible to leave here before morning?'

'So to avoid the ladies company?' said Angelo with a wink.

'Precisely.'

'A pity,' said Angelo. 'I like the little maid with the big eyes best. No doubt, the other could be good company, if her claws were cut. I told you the women come from rich families, you might be wise to take them.'

'So you did Angelo,' agreed Ambrose, 'but you are in my employ and not theirs.'

'There are advantages here for us both,' Angelo continued. 'They may even buy your wool from you, as they are merchants.'

'My wool?' said Ambrose in surprise. 'Did I not tell you that it is already spoken for?'

'No, I cannot recall you mentioning such. A merchant must keep his options open though. You will get nothing but praise for escorting them. It is not such a disadvantage to have the nobles of Venice indebted to you. In times of difficulty, you can call in the debt.'

Ambrose rubbed his eyes wearily. Now Angelo was thinking like an Italian, as well he should. What he advised made sense and the cavalcade would be forced to travel slowly as soon as they began to climb towards the Alps. If Adriana's story about Emlyn was true, then Ambrose owed a favour. Ambrose re-crossed the room again to where Adriana was seated with her maids and the child. He was struck by how tired they all looked and realised that Adriana must have set a trying pace in order to catch up with his party.

'Under the circumstances,' he said, 'I would be honoured Madame, if you and your company would travel with me. You have brought carts? Servants?Minstrels? Hawks?'

'No Monsieur,' answered Adriana forlornly. 'We are but as you see us, bereft of every comfort and at your mercy.'

'Quite so,' said Ambrose. 'Then if you do not object to the pace I am forced to set. We will be off before first light. May I ask Madonna why you are in such haste to reach Italy at this unreasonable time of year?'

Ignoring the question, Adriana said, 'What of your nephew Monsieur? Are we not to wait from him to join us?'

'I have sent a man to discover his whereabouts,' Ambrose replied, biting down his impatience. 'No doubt he will join us when he can. It has been a long day,' Ambrose finished. He bowed respectfully. 'Madame?'

Adriana stood. Her hand dropped to his arm and remained there. 'Thank you Monsieur,' she said quietly. 'You will not regret your generous decision.'

'No Madame. I do not believe I will,' Ambrose replied. He was no nearer convincing himself that he had done the right thing when he retired. There was also a nagging worry in his mind about Emlyn's fate. Ambrose lay awake for hours.

The following morning the travellers were up before dawn and soon ready to leave. True to her word, Adriana was also prepared for the journey and gave Ambrose no cause for complaint. There was no sign of Matthew.

Chapter 34 Alps

Now cease my lute this is the last
Labour that thou and I shall waste
And ended is what we begun.
Now is this song both sung and past,
My lute be still, for I have done. Thomas Wyatt

Carmelia hid behind a loaded cart when she heard the sound of horses. She saw two distant riders approaching the inn. The travellers were delayed here, just twelve miles short of Geneva, for three days while the snow piled higher and higher. Since joining Ambrose Chillingworth, they had travelled for ten days and the Englishman had kept the pace as arduous as he had threatened. Carmelia had prayed continuously that some minor mishap would befall them, so that they could rest. Her prayers had eventually been answered when the snow had come again, by then, Carmelia had doubted if she could have gone on for another mile, let alone another day, every inch of her body had ached mercilessly. The long snow bound journey had been cold, uncomfortable and tedious. The inn that they were staying at now, was small, dirty and packed with travellers, mostly from their own company. Carmelia, Adriana and their maids had avoided the company of the soldiers whenever possible. At meal times they joined the English merchant, Ambrose Chillingworth and the captain of the mercenaries. Adriana Martinelli said the mercenary was a devil and that Carmelia must not even dare to look at him. She did, and he always winked at her and joked about her freckles and long plaits as if she was a little girl.

Today the weather had improved and all hoped that soon they would be free to continue their journey. Christmas had come and gone and it had been the smallest Christmas Carmelia had ever known. They had heard Mass in a little chapel ten miles from Lyons. It was the day before they had started the steep climb towards the mountains. Mass had been said by the mercenary's priest, a small nondescript man with a balding head and a tendency to sniff after every sentence. Carmelia disliked him and the thought of him knowing all her sins from confession made her hair stand on end.

Now, it was too near to evening for them to load up the pack animals and continue. Stifled boredom with the endless hours of embroidery drove Carmelia to leave the stuffiness of the inn. She had dressed in warm woollens and crept out into the fading daylight, hoping that the others wouldn't notice her absence.

The jagged mountains stood all around, sharp as icicles with the steep sides shadowed in snowy grey. Towards the inn and the road, the land flattened out a little and the white squares and rectangles showed the boundaries of fields. Bare trees stood here and there and a line of pollarded willows marched down the hillside. Houses squatted around the inn, the thatched roofs covered in white mounds and the ridged shapes softened by drifted snow. Pine trees provided a patch of green, where birds twittered and squabbled over scant scraps from the inn kitchen. A large fire roared outside the barn where the animals were kept, and where most of the mercenaries slept in the warmth of straw. Around the fire, men sat drinking ale, laughing among themselves and rattling dice. The two youngest mercenaries sat together on a log. They were as pretty as girls. Carmelia had heard the servants commenting and giggling about them and Pellegrina had been scolded by Adriana for paying them too much attention.

The two horsemen rode in from the direction of Lyons. They paused at the gate and exchanged words with the guard, before they were admitted to the inn yard. Snow lay across their shoulders and speckled them with white.

Carmelia peered from behind a tree. The rider nearest to her was thin, his face aquiline and familiar. He was bundled up in a huge cloak with a woollen hat pulled down over his ears. He sat slumped in the saddle. As he dismounted, he got his foot tangled up and piled off his horse into the snow with the dignity of a plucked hen. Carmelia shivered with laughter.

His eyes were in shadow. She remembered that they were grey or blue and his hair, invisible beneath his hat brim, was as dark as night. Recovering himself, he saw her and walked forward leading his horse and brushing the snow from the heavy cloak that made him look like a bear. When he removed his hat the dying sun oranged his hair like a halo. The light played tricks and his eyes glowed with a touch of something fey and unreal. He bowed, his cloak coming loose and dragging in the snow.

His voice was deep and musical. He said, 'Did I startle you? Forgive me lady, we met in Rouen at the church. I didn't think that I would see you again.'

She smiled and looked up. She felt she had known him all her life, like some hero out of a well-read romantic tale. His Italian was strange and barely understandable. He smelled of horse and damp wool. If she moved a little she could touch him.

His eyes smiled at her. On his cheek there was a half healed cut. He said, 'When you told me that you hoped we would meet again, did you cast a spell so that we would? For I can think of no other reason why you would be in this frozen place and not safe in your convent.' He paused and then added, 'Carmelia.'

Hearing her name spoken with soft, precise pronunciation, she felt inexplicably sick. 'What did you say?' she stammered.

'I like you better like this, with your hair all starred with snow,' he replied. 'I thought you were a nun.'

She felt lost, her heart hammering like the thundering hooves of a wild horse. She remembered breaking her rosary and he had gathered her beads. She had told him to meet her outside the church, but he had not come.

His left hand disappeared within the folds of his cloak and came out again in a closed fist. He held it up in front of her, his eyes glinting mischief, willing her to guess what he held concealed.

She looked at the hand and then up at him, shaking her head. His gloved fingers opened like a leaf uncurling. In his palm, the three tiny pearls she had given him lay shimmering dully. Carmelia stared at them. They were from her rosary. He had only picked up those three and he had made her laugh. She thought that he did not remember when he had been brought by Josquin to Adriana's house. She had been afraid of him then, because of the way he had looked and she had thought that he was near to death. The marks of his beating had faded but his skin was pallid and his eyes still dark with bruising. He favoured his injured hand which was tucked inside his cloak.

She reached out with a childlike gesture and closed his fingers over the pearls as she had done before. Through the leather, she could feel the cold of his skin. He shuddered under her touch. His dark hair, was wet with snow and hung down from his forehead, cork-screwed in dripping ringlets. She remembered his strange name Emlyn Tomas. 'Go to the fire and warm yourself,' she said, suddenly concerned for him.

It would be improper for Carmelia to sit by the fire in the company of mercenaries, so she lingered in the shadows where none seemed to notice. Their attention was turned on the two newcomers who had ridden through the snow storm. They spoke French that she had spoken more often than her native tongue. Emlyn did not contribute much to the talk but sat still and listened.

Carmelia watched him. He was unshaven, but his beard was not a man's beard, merely a soft shading across his cheeks. He had pulled the glove off his left hand; the other he treated with care. It was wrapped with a thick, dirty piece of red cloth. He had a scar above his eyebrow, a thin white line of some long forgotten hurt. He was seated near the fire, leaning back against a snow covered boulder. His eyes were shut, the long lashes sweeping his cheeks like the lashes of a calf. He held a cup of warm wine, but it was tilted, nearly forgotten.

Both of these men who had ridden in, looked drawn to exhaustion. Josquin too, was fair to look at, blond like a German. Carmelia wondered if he knew that Adriana was here and quite prepared to give him the tongue lashing of his life.

'Well who is he?' asked a voice in Italian. It was the captain, Angelo; the one Adriana Martinelli said was a black devil.

'The youth you asked me to care for,' answered Josquin.

'What is this?' Angelo snapped. 'You were only to watch him to the gates of his monastery, not to bring him with you!'

Josquin looked angry. He said, 'We had some trouble and there was no choice. Angelo I am frozen to the bone and cannot remember the last hot meal we ate. Is there any chance of seeing some hot food before we go into explanations? Is the Englishman here?'

'He has been sent for,' said Rafaelo Gandolfi, the oldest member of the group. He handed Josquin a plate of steaming food.

Josquin accepted it gratefully and sank down before the fire to eat. They all sat around a long, rough table; empty cups, plates and wine bottles cluttered its surface. The air was filled with the scent of hot mutton stew and burning wood. Emlyn rose slowly. He refused the plate of food, but had accepted a refill to his wine cup.

'This is Emlyn Tomas,' said Josquin with his mouth stuffed.

The others grunted in acknowledgement and shuffled along the wooden bench to give him room to sit.

Carmelia shrank back into the shadows of the pines. She tried his name in Italian, 'Emilio Tomasso,' she whispered. She wished then that she was a simple country girl and not the daughter of a wealthy Venetian, whose life was ordered and arranged with no consideration for her own thoughts and desires. She saw Emlyn as a symbol of the freedom she would be denied. Soon I shall be wed to an old man, she thought; soon I will be required out of wifely duty to spread my legs and do whatever it is that they do to you to take your maidenhood. Pellegrina says that it is a pleasure and she does it often enough, and with young men of her own choosing. She may be a servant but she has more freedom than I shall ever know. I am sixteen and will wed an old man and from then on my life will be over, shut away in a rich house, shut away as I always have been. If only I could snatch some freedom before that happens and if only I could realise the promise of love.

She looked at Emlyn and a warm, exhilarating glow stretched to every fibre of her being, encompassing her, running through her as fast, clear water, crackling like ice crystals and awakening her with a thrill of unbearable excitement. She felt as if she stood upon a great precipice and, were she to step off, she would spout wings and fly. Her eyes flooded with tears.

A burst of laughter diverted her attention. It was fully dark now and the English merchant came out of the inn holding a lamp aloft. He wore a magnificent coat of long fur, near as white as the snow and hanging down to his boots. He had been to Russia, she had heard him tell them over dinner the day before and of the wonderful legendary beast the fur had come from.

'Emlyn!' He called out as he drew near.

Emlyn stood up; he upset a plate and knocked over a wine bottle. He did not reply. He just stared. His brows were lowered over eyes that were blazing with anger.

The merchant didn't notice, he smiled and came forward; his hands held out in greeting.

Emlyn swung away, turning his back, and stormed off towards the barn.

Chillingworth dropped his hands and stood with an expression of speechless surprise.

Josquin rose, wiping his mouth with the back of his sleeve. He folded his arms across his chest and eyed the Englishman with hostility. 'I snatched him out of the grasp of the Spaniards,' he explained. 'They took him and threw him in prison. He knew nothing of their reasons, it was something to do with Spanish ships. He is sick and injured and we have fought through snow and storm to reach here. I do not know you Englishman, but I know a little of Emlyn. If you have been the cause behind all this, then you will answer to me as well as him. Young though he is, there is much to admire in him. He has sworn to kill you. He says you threw him to the dogs.'

Ambrose Chillingworth heard this with an expression of astonishment. 'Perhaps you should explain further,' he replied quietly. He gathered the white fur about him and settled down on the bench.

Carmelia heard the shrill voice of Madame Adriana calling for her. She melted away from the group of soldiers. She appeared from a grove of bare branched trees. 'I am here,' she called sweetly. Quieter, she added to herself, 'Sweet Virgin protect me from protectors!' She returned to the inn where a meal was waiting, this time without the company of the Englishman. Carmelia ate little, too tied up with confused thoughts. Adriana always eyed her with suspicion, never letting Carmelia out of her sight for a moment.

Carmelia was particularly pleasant. Inside her still, the wild emotions pounded through her blood and beat a tingling feeling to her very finger tips. She felt as if she was especially alive, like flowers in spring in the glow of the first warm sun. She could hardly contain her joy; she felt enchanted and could not fully understand why. She made no mention to Adriana that Josquin had arrived.

Emlyn found a place to sleep in the straw. He pulled his cloak about him to keep out the cold. The air smelled of damp straw and manure and horse sweat, the barn was gloomy and uncomfortable. Emlyn was exhausted. His burning anger kept away the ease of sleep. The mercenaries who shared the barn had ignored him. He had seen John Moore when he'd entered; Moore's face had been a mask of surprise. Emlyn had smiled ruefully; he supposed that he did not look his best at present.

He and Josquin had ridden near non-stop since the heroic rescue in Rouen. The great horses had been left at a farm that Josquin knew; from there they would be retrieved by Tieffenbrucker when the Spring came. They had hired horses, then to take them on each stage of the journey. For Emlyn, it had been a time of nightmare and pain during which he had scarcely been aware of his circumstance and surroundings. He had lost a tooth from the beating and had two ribs broken. The bruises had faded as the winter days fled by with a thrash of hooves and constant motion. Josquin had bound his ribs, but every breath still caused him pain. His hand had been like a ball of fire, often even preventing him from sleeping. After the third day, he had wanted nothing but to slip from his mount and curl asleep in the snow forever. He remembered waking in an old mill to the smell of roast duck prevailing the air. The next day and the days after, Josquin had given him aqua vitae until he was drunk and had tied him to the horse.

Gradually he regained a sense of reality. He had lost all he owned. The only thing he wore that was his own was a thong of plaited silk around his neck, with the medal of St. Christopher that Gruffydd had given him before he left Wales. On to this too he had threaded the little linen sack of bits which Mafanwy Fawr had given him to keep him from harm. Emlyn smiled; it was not turning out to be a very good charm so far, but he kept it and could not think of a reason why. Josquin had told him that Wendelin had promised to collect the travelling pack that Emlyn had left at the inn in Rouen, so he hoped and prayed that his Welsh manuscript would be safe. He felt that he had failed by leaving that behind and he had failed Gruffydd too, in not going to Paris to attempt to get his uncle's letter that would name him legitimate.

He had never felt so alone in all his life. It was a bitter loneliness. Ambrose Chillingworth would feel his anger. He would have already had a taste of it if Emlyn had not been so cold and weakened with fever. He would have only made a fool of himself.

Under the light of a lamp that hung from the rafters, he unwrapped the damp bandage from his hand. If he moved it, waves of dizzying pain threatened to overwhelm him. The hand was stiff, swollen and useless. Broken bones had forced his fingers to curl around the wound, it still looked angry and raw. Not only the pain upset him, he was terrified of being maimed; which meant loosing the one pleasure he had retained out of the confusion of his life, his talent for the making of music; that magic that flowed from his heart capable of enchanting even the hardest of men and reducing them to tears. He had even been afraid of it at times, afraid to give it full voice, afraid to allow it to flow from him. But he would never deny the pleasure and joy that the creating of music granted him. It was a gift from God, and he was learning how to return it with the utmost confidence and gratitude.

Emlyn's eyelids drooped. He jerked his head back and looked out across the barn. 'I had been learning,' he whispered to himself, 'had been learning.'

He bound up his hand again and sat staring at nothing.

An hour passed before he saw the distinctive shape of Ambrose Chillingworth approach. Emlyn stood up defiantly, feeling sick with hatred. The Englishman carried a flagon of wine and two wooden cups that he set down on the straw between them. The light from the oil lamp illuminated his beard and the fur of his heavy coat. He stood for a while in silence, his serious brown eyes filled with concern.

Emlyn remained standing and held his gaze, silently willing his hatred against the English merchant.

'Whatever you may believe,' said Ambrose sorrowfully, 'I never dreamed for a moment that you would be drawn into this. The Dutchman has explained to me what happened and I understand your hatred. I know that I well deserve it, had I been more trusting of you, none of this would have happened. Will you hear an explanation?'

Emlyn shuddered. The anger that had kept him going mile after frozen mile, was draining away, just when he needed it most. He felt dizzy with fever. He sat down. 'An explanation' he laughed. 'You used me and Goronwy as a cover for whatever you were about.' He paused and drew a ragged breath. 'Are you an envoy for the Queen?'

'Yes,' Ambrose replied with no hesitation. 'It can do little harm if you know now, unless you wish to cut my throat for it.'

'You could have told me,' Emlyn replied with malevolence. 'I am no enemy of the Queen of England. It was that loyalty which came between Goronwy and me. He wanted her captured and marched off in chains to face the Holy Father and I always defended her as the rightful Queen of England. What does the Queen ask of you, that you were willing to sacrifice our lives?'

'Where is Goronwy?' Ambrose asked shifting his weight uneasily, as if he expected the big Welshman to leap out of the shadows.

'In Douai, with a new Jesuit school founded for the salvation of England.' Emlyn replied. He sat and leaned back in the straw; he could hardly keep his eyes open. It was useless to attempt a confrontation, he felt drained and empty. But this man had done him an injustice, however innocent he appeared. Looking up Emlyn said, 'The Spaniards thought that I had turned Protestant for monetary gain. Can you believe that? But you were the one they wanted, you are the one who knows all about the Spanish ships.'

The merchant sighed heavily. He settled in the straw awkwardly and filled the wine cups.

Emlyn took the wine willingly and drank deeply. He said, 'The Privy Council provided you with arms for the Huguenots that you passed to them under the very noses of the Spaniards. Even then, they were after knowledge of their ships, and you knew what had befallen them. They suspected you then. The oranges were poisoned weren't they? Later on the road to Rouen, you saw my reluctance to speak with Diego, you knew I had a grievance against the man. Did you hope then that they would follow Goronwy and I, thinking us Protestants?'

Ambrose shook his head in denial. He looked genuinely upset.

Emlyn continued, his voice hoarse with tiredness and frustration. 'After a visit to the school in Paris, Don Diego returned with the conviction that I had betrayed Goronwy and the whole scheme to print Catholic literature. I see now what an advantage it was for you to have us travel with you!'

'Good God. Emlyn!' Ambrose exclaimed. 'It was nothing of the kind!'

'Say what you will, I am no fool! Your ends are the same as Cecil's. If there are any stray Catholics along the way on whom you can pin the blame, then all the better. The reason why Cecil let me and Goronwy go, was so that any suspicions aroused would fall upon our heads and not your own. I was a fool, but I shall not be so again.'

'Please Emlyn, hear me out.'

'I do not want to hear!' shouted Emlyn resentfully. At the outburst, heads turned in his direction, he lowered his voice, holding his temper in control. His next words were tinged with malice. 'I have thought of nothing but my pleasure in killing you Englishman! I should have listened to Goronwy. He would not condone murder, but I can learn. There are plenty here who will teach me, if I become like them.'

Ambrose sat back, his white brows knit in a frown. 'You intend to join these mercenaries?' he said 'Then, when you are trained to kill, you intend to come after me?'

Emlyn dropped his head. He now owned nothing, maimed and with no employment. Killing Ambrose Chillingworth, he knew, would not be so easy; it went against all he had been taught to abide by.

'Come now Emlyn, you have no knowledge of weaponry or of the coin with which theses men ply their trade. They are rough and brutal. They work for any man who has the most gold to pay them and who does not question their methods. They burn, rape and thieve whenever the opportunity arises. Their cruelty in battle is legendary, through such terror they maintain their reputation. They change sides without batting an eyelid. These are but a handful, their captain Angelo can call up a thousand like these. Would you number yourself among them? You a Jesuit trained scholar?'

'Would you have me thieve and beg my way through life?'

'Have you no pride?' Ambrose answered. 'What of all your grandfather Gruffydd taught you? You are a musician, you can read and write, your knowledge of languages is extensive. These are not the skills for a soldier of fortune. What is a mercenary, other than a beggar and a thief?'

'A musician,' Emlyn said quietly. He swallowed back the well of emotion that roared at him with the voice of thundering water. He closed his eyes. 'A musician,' he repeated. He held out his injured hand. 'I was, but shall never be again.'

Ambrose drew his breath in alarm. He stood up quickly. 'You have not had the opportunity for proper care lad. There is someone with experience of these things here Emlyn; a woman of considerable reputation for her knowledge. I will go and get her. Let her be the judge.'

'I will seek my own help,' Emlyn replied. 'I want nothing from you. You will not play the kindly gentleman with me again. Such deception is godless and degrading.' He took a deep breath and stood carefully. He gathered up his cloak and walked towards a dark corner in the barn, away from the light, away from the traitorous Englishman.

Within the hour Ambrose returned and he brought Matthew and Adriana Martinelli with him. Matthew had returned from his fruitless search four days earlier; the experience had done nothing to sweeten his dour demeanour. Ambrose led them both to where Emlyn lay, at last abandon to sleep. He was nearly buried in straw and did not awake, even when Adriana lifted the cloth from his hand.

She pursed her lips and hummed. 'This is your nephew, the one that I cared for, Monsieur. He did not remain long enough in my company for me to set the broken bones.' She shook her head with a grimace of distaste. 'I'm going to have to re-break it, if he ever wants to get any use from it again. But not here, bring him into the inn.'

'Madame?' Ambrose voiced anxiously.

'It is impossible to say whether or not the hand will mend,' Madame Adriana said with uncharacteristic gentleness. 'He is young and well, we will see.'

Matthew elbowed his way forward. 'A Spanish bastard nailed 'im to a table with 'is dagger, Josquin told me, 'twas to stop him escapin'. Do you want me to knock him on the head with a mallet first? It's the only way you'll get 'im to come with yer.'

Adriana fixed him with a penetrating glare. 'You did say Josquin?' she said coldly.

Matthew ignored her, he had an admirable ability for ignoring women. He moved to Emlyn's side and began to clear away the straw.

Adriana's nostrils flared. 'Josquin,' she said again, the name came out like the sibilant hiss of a venomous serpent. She smiled to herself and tapped her long fingernails together. Her expression softened as she turned to the problem of the boy that Josquin had burdened himself with.

Adriana's room was small and warmed by a fire in the tiny hearth. Her shawl and head scarf hung from the back of a chair steaming dry before the fire. She pushed them aside and hung an iron pot above the flames.

She filled it with water from a jug by the door and rummaged about in her bundle of possessions. From small hessian sacks, she sprinkled herbs and ground spice into the water. The room was filled with a pungent scent, making Ambrose's eyes water.

Although he wore a worried expression, Emlyn did as he was bid and drank a brew of poppy. Within half an hour, his pupils grew huge, as dark as arquebus barrels. Drugged and exhausted, he fell into a drugged stupor.

Ambrose had halted by the door, he felt squeamish. He walked out into the night. It was never truly dark when snow lay on the ground, its whiteness lit up the sky with a diffused misty light. It was warmer than it had been for over a week, the snow was softer as if it melted from the inside out. The fire had died down to a glowing heap of ashes and white-hot twigs, but the heat was still fierce. Ambrose rubbed his hands together, watching the patterns in the smouldering fire.

In a few days he would be in Geneva talking to Italian bankers, drinking expensive wine and tasting the comforts of the life he had left behind. Are you the Queen's envoy? Emlyn had asked. It was the first time Ambrose had thought of himself as such. And the more he thought about it, the more uneasy he became. Was he too a scapegoat for William Cecil? Royal envoys carried news from monarch to monarch, they wore the badge of their trade and rode fast horses, changing them at each stop until they reached their destination. Letters were written more often than not, in cipher. So that if they fell into the wrong hands, the contents could not be understood. To counter that, ciphers were broken, where they could be, and the secrets revealed. In turn, new codes were made, an ever changing method of communication, a web of secret writing stretching from sea to sea.

Ambrose had looked at the sealed letters in the satchel William Cecil had entrusted him with. He had removed the seals and then replaced them, no one would guess that they had been tampered with. The Queen's secretary would have anticipated something like this, so the letters had been coded. Even this, after a life in the mercantile world, Ambrose had worked out and understood. The letters contained nothing that could cause a Spanish finger to be pointed at the Queen of England accusing her of detaining Alva's long awaited gold. Even if I had been taken by the Spaniards, Ambrose surmised, they would have learned nothing, unless they beat it out of me of course.

But they had not. They had taken Emlyn Tomas instead. They had taken him, but not from any clue the merchant had left in his wake. If Goronwy had talked about what had occurred in Southampton, then they would have known that Emlyn had sought to preserve the life of William Cecil. It was only natural to assume then, that Emlyn would be willing to assist the Queen of England. But Goronwy could not have known about the ships, could not have seen what a mesh he had woven around his once, fellow Jesuit. Had Emlyn reached the same conclusion?

'Master Chillingworth?' Matthew's voice came floating from the inn.

Ambrose did not turn from the fire. He felt his shoulders clench.

Matthew came up beside him, he was carrying a pail of snow, he placed it on the embers to melt.

Ambrose spun around to face him. 'What?' he demanded 'Do you place the blame for this on my head too? It would be the first time you ever showed concern for the lad.'

Matthew looked at his feet, shuffling the snow about.

'Matthew did you talk to those Spaniard on board the ship?'

Matthew spat into the fire showing his contempt.

'Remember the oranges that Emlyn threw over board because he thought they were poisoned?'

'Aye, 'e nearly did for me, nearly 'ad me overboard in the process!'

Ambrose pulled at his earlobe thoughtfully. 'Moore brought them to me and you took them from my cabin because you knew I had no taste for them,' he said. 'Did Moore know that I did not like oranges?'

'Well I mentioned to 'im,' said Matthew, 'as 'e was goin' past me, that 'e was wastin' 'is time. But 'e brought them anyway. Didn't have much choice far as I could see, been as them fine gentlemen asked it of 'im.' Matthew stamped his feet and shivered. 'Right cold out 'ere. Are you coming'?'

Ambrose sighed impatiently. He did not know why he felt so angry.

Matthew shrugged, turned on his heel and trudged back to the inn.

Ambrose walked up and down cursing, his breath turned to smoke in the icy air. He took a few steps after his servant and then walked back again. 'God preserve us!' He kicked snow into the fire, waving his arms about uselessly.

Ambrose said, 'I did not hand you to the Spaniard. Inadvertently, it was Goronwy, though I am sure he meant you no harm. Through him, they must have learnt of your dealings with William Cecil. From there they looked no further. In me, Goronwy saw only what I represented, a wool merchant taking his wares to market. He could not have known that I acted for the Queen.'Ambrose spoke to the dark window in front of him.

He had his back to the room and he could see his own reflection in the warped glass. Adriana had left the room and gone off to prepare some medicinal mixture. She would send one of her women to watch the boy through the night and promised to return herself, after an hour of two. It was some time in the still hours of the morning when nothing stirred but the fire in the hearth and the flame of a single candle. Outside, the glass looked shattered with ice crystals.

'I thought the same,' said Emlyn, 'until I saw the guns aboard the ship.'

'Why did you say nothing then?'

'Because Gruffydd trusted you and you had helped us escape from Cecil. Goronwy didn't say anything about the firearms either, if he had I would have known about it. I'm sure Goronwy did not betray me.' He reached up with his free hand and released a moth from a spider web. On the bed cover, the moth fluttered, wings shredded, and toppled over, legs stiff and antennae still in death. It was as white as snow. Emlyn nudged it with his finger.

The candle flame was flickering in its last splutter of wax. Light and shadow vied for dominance. Ambrose lit another and the light strengthened. Now, gazing into the candle flame, Ambrose said, 'I have a son, if God be merciful, I have a son.'

Emlyn stirred and pulled himself up. 'If God be merciful?'

'He was with John Hawkins on his voyage to the New World this summer past. They too ran into trouble with Spain. Most of the fleet were lost. I know not whether he was lost with them, or captured to delight the inquisition. The last news I had was on the night that you came to my house in Southampton. I learned nothing since. You see Emlyn, we all suffer in the name of God. Protestant and Catholic alike. We cannot all be right.'

'I'm sorry,' Emlyn replied, the words soft and heartfelt.

Silence stretched between them. Before long, Emlyn's eyes closed and his breath became ragged with fever. A deep well of sadness brought unaccustomed tears to the merchant's eyes. In the privacy of darkness, he let them overspill and run over his cheeks to soak into his beard.

Adriana Martinelli came back before morning. She shook the Englishman awake and sent him off to sleep in better comfort. She turned to Emlyn. He had cast off the bed covers and lay naked in uneasy slumber, his skin was glistening with perspiration. His arms were well muscled for one so young and Adriana idly traced a long finger nail across his skin, parting the glistening moisture and leaving a thin white scratch from shoulder to elbow. Carefully her pointed nails travelled lightly over the bandaging across his chest and then lower. The skin seem to shudder under her fingers. An amused smile lit her face as her artistic fingers explored. He was unresponsive, sweet and innocent under her hands. She began to caress him more intimately. Nothing!

Emlyn was too far sunk into himself to respond. Adriana withdrew her hand and pulled up the bed covers. Her smile soured. She had not taken a lover for over two weeks.

She left the room and awoke Carmelia, instructing her to sit with the patient. 'You will not need to stay alone here long,' said Adriana. 'Pellegrina will be here to keep you company shortly. Come and fetch me if you need to.'

'Will he die?' Carmelia asked, speaking in a whisper.

'No,' Adriana replied, 'but a prayer or two will do him no harm. You could do that until I return.'

Emlyn is a lutanist, the merchant had said. Adriana knew he would not have made this comment if the boy was an ordinary player, for most educated boys of this age could strum out a tune or two to impress where necessity demanded. It was too soon to say whether this one would ever regain the dexterity required to be a minstrel. Adriana looked long at him before she left.

Left alone with the sick boy, Carmelia felt a thrill of fear. He slept restlessly, turning from one side to the other. Under his good hand there was a dead moth, silvered with spider web. Carmelia brushed it to the floor. The action caused him to stir uneasily, tossing his head as if in adamant denial of something in his dreams. She could not understand the language he spoke. Tentative, she reached out and brushed the damp hair from his forehead. He seemed to go quiet then. His skin was very hot and glistened with perspiration and his chest rose up and down with the uneven rhythm of his breathing.

Carmelia's mouth felt dry with unreasonable fear. She swallowed and took a deep breath, stopping the prayer on her lips before it was formed. Leaning forward, she touched his lips with her own. His whole body jerked from her touch. She jumped and drew back. His grey-blue eyes were open and were blazing brightly as if he was angry.

Carmelia wondered at her foolishness. She dropped her eyes and felt her cheeks burn with shame. She did not know why she had acted so thoughtlessly. When she summoned the bravado to look back, his eyes had shut again and he was asleep.

Had Emlyn been awake, he would have been baffled by the intimate attentions of two women in the space of an hour. But he was far from that place where his body lay so oblivious to reality.

Saiah was riding bare back upon a running horse and beside him rode his brother, adorned with jewels and a dazzling white smile. He was as haughty and as proud as a falcon. The dust was red, tinged with the sinking sun. He could see his father, sitting on a grey stallion far ahead, blurred in the dust. And beside him, stood Saiah's mother; her clothes bright and shining, her hair spangled with silver. She called out to them, 'Dewch i mi fy anwyl plant. Brysia!!' Her voice was tinkling with laughter 'Come to me my beloved children. Hurry!'

Saiah responded eagerly to his mother's laughing challenge to race his brother. He beat his heels on the horse's flanks, urging it to run faster and faster. The earth flew beneath him, a blur of stones and sun scorched grass. His brother laughed at his efforts, his own mount streaming ahead. Saiah sat his horse grimly, crouched over, small, light and determined. The space closed between them. The thunder of hooves filled the sky. His brother brought a whip down slicing through the air, hissing on the horse's flank. Saiah screamed in his horse's ear. It shuddered beneath him, lengthened its stride, pulled level, Saiah clung on like a leech.

There was no smile on his brother's face now. It was distorted with anger. Saiah feared the whip, but it did not come down to score his cheek. The horses were drawing apart, Saiah's surging ahead as if it flew across the earth. Light glanced off golden tassels and mirrored the turquoise sequins. The air held the tang of salt and dry, unforgiving soil. Saiah's horse pulled ahead and he crouched lower, his blood pounding with joy. He would win! He would win!

'I have brought you a book to read.'

The voice shattered his victory. Emlyn awoke and saw olive skin and the large eyes before they turned away. He closed his eyes and tried to grasp the threads of the disappearing dream. His hand hurt but this was a different hurt, it no longer felt like a bag of loose, jagged bones held together by ripped skin. Someone had sorted it all out and stuck them all into a comfortable hurt, if pain was ever comfortable. Dreams still beckoned. He could smell bread, freshly baked bread that made his mouth water. He opened his eyes and saw a loaf swimming in front of him on a pewter plate. Like ghosts, the tendrils of sleep melted away and left a deep pain of longing behind.

'Do you read Italian?' said the girl beside him. 'It is by Baldassar Castiglione il libro del cortegiano'

Emlyn took the bread and held it savouring its aroma, it was warm in his hand. He looked at the girl seated on the mattress beside him with downcast eyes. 'The little nun,' he said around a mouthful.

'Carmelia, by the door, is my maid Pellegrina.'

Emlyn glanced across the room and saw another girl of near the same age. Her heart-shaped face was pale under the dark hood, her cheeks were flushed from the cold, her lips were full and pouted and her black, shapely brows arched in charming disdain. She was stunning to look upon. Emlyn blinked and swallowed a lump of bread whole. Both girls were dressed in sober black; expensive cloth beautifully seamed and unadorned.

Emlyn moistened dry lips. Carmelia offered him a wooden cup filled to the brim with milk. 'Fresh from the goat this morning' she said.

Emlyn took the milk and swallowed it all in one thirsty gulp.

'What happened to your hand?' she said.

Emlyn cleared his throat and mumbled through a mouthful of bread. He felt a prickle of heat warm his cheeks and knew that it had nothing to do with fever. He looked down to see if he was dressed and sighed in gratification, the shirt he was wearing was one he had seen Ambrose wear.

'I thought you might be bored and brought you the book,' Carmelia said. Her cheeks were red and she gazed intently at her hands, but Emlyn could see that she was smiling.

'Why are you here, crossing the Alps in winter?' he asked her.

'I'm going home to Venice,' she said. 'My godmother thought it wise to join your companions as you are going there too. I have lived in France for many years and now I am going home to be married.'

Emlyn smiled. She was so childlike that he could not imagine her being wed. It was not only her age, but her simplistic way of viewing matters. He could not think of anything to say to her and then he remembered the book she had brought. He said, 'Baldassar Castiglione teaches, that where heroic action is forced upon a gentleman, he must be sure to undertake it in full view of his lords and masters, so that his courage can be displayed and thus not go unrewarded. I know this book, the Book of the Courtier, a guide on how to behave in gentle society, how to be a true gentleman.'

'Do you consider the tilting yard and warfare to be gentlemanly pastimes?' she asked, without looking at him.

'I am not a soldier or a knight or a gentleman, Mademoiselle. But I should think it beneficial to be gentlemanly in all matters, including those of war.'

She lifted her head and smiled nervously. 'I think there is nothing more noble than a life spent in fighting for what one considers just and right.

To fight for God and one's country must be the greatest honour.' Her eyes were alight with abstract admiration.

'Quickly! Your godmother is here,' cried Pellegrina from the doorway. She gestured frantically.

Carmelia stood up and looked down at Emlyn. She said, 'Such a man would be rewarded in heaven and could make quite a fortune for himself in doing so.'

Emlyn leaned back on the pillows and closed his eyes with a weary smile. He had seen her in the church at Rouen and his heart had missed a beat. He had stared at her and had been unable to gather up her rosary beads.

'You know we might after all be related,' said Carmelia. 'A Brown Friar came to see me shortly after you ruined my flower mosaic.'

'Fra Sebastiano?' Emlyn asked in sudden interest.

Carmelia nodded and her smile broadened. 'He told me that you were related to Anna Grimani who was married to my half brother Cristoforo, he died before I was born'

'Carmelia!' Madame Adriana Martinelli stood n the doorway. She wore a high headdress with a string of pearls wound about it and looping at the side of her face; it was a face of frozen beauty, frowning in disapproval.

Emlyn sat up stiffly. Speaking Italian, he said, 'Madonna, the child was concerned that I would be suffering from boredom. It was a kindness only.'

'And who are you, that a lady of rank should be concerned about?' Adriana's dark eyes were alight with glittering contempt.

'Emlyn Tomas, Madonna,' his reply was mumbled. He remembered her from the previous night and felt confused. 'I owe you thanks for the care you have given me Madonna Martinelli. I'm afraid I did not know the child's standing.'

Carmelia swung around to face Emlyn. He was surprised to see that she was angry. She said, 'I am not a child!'

He looked at her in astonishment.

She turned and marched out the door with her nose in the air.

'Madonna?' said Emlyn, before the older lady could follow. 'I beg you place no blame upon her head. It was my fault entirely.'

'Then you should known better,' said Adriana. She came into the room and stood close beside him. Her expression softened. She lifted a gloved hand and lightly touched his temple, drawing her hand down his cheek with feathery tenderness.

Emlyn held her penetrating gaze and swallowed nervously.

She smiled and stepped back. 'We are to continue on our way. We have been delayed here for days and the weather rules travellers when they cross the Alps. We are forced to take advantage of this spell of fine weather. Are you well enough to travel?'

Emlyn caught a trace of exotic perfume. 'I am well Madonna,' he replied brightly. 'May I thank you again for your kindness'

She gave him a lop-sided smile and examined the wrappings around his hand. Emlyn watched her with curiosity. Her eyes lifted and scolded him.

There was a piece of flat wood tied to his fingers and bound over and over with cloth.

'This is to straighten your fingers,' Adriana explained. 'How do they feel?'

Emlyn looked at her with wonder. Was it possible that the fingers would heal? He dare not voice the question. 'They are very comfortable,' he stammered.

'Good,' she said looking at him with appraisal. Then she straightened and assumed that hooded contemptuous look. She said, 'If I find you as much as looking at the girl again, I shall have you beaten within an inch of your life!' She turned away. Her beads rattled as she left the room.

Emlyn got up slowly up feeling bemused. He thought he might fall madly in love with Adriana Martinelli very soon.

'Do you plan to spend the winter here?' Josquin poked his head around the door.

'What? No, of course not.'

'Come on then, we're off. You look a great deal better Emlyn.'

Emlyn pulled on his cloak that was hanging on the chair and followed Josquin out of the inn. He wished he could have gone back to bed and slept for a week. He said, 'Why did Ambrose allow the women to travel with us Josquin? Have you inquired?'

'You are greatly improved!' Josquin exclaimed. He thumped him on the shoulder. 'They are Italian ladies under the capable care of Madame Adriana Martinelli, who I have just had the misfortune to bump into. I never expected her to totally ignore me though. They joined the caravan for the protection Angelo and the mercenaries provide. You may as well give up your hopes now Welshman, you'll never get a peek in there. They are way above anything you can ever hope to bed!'

'Jesu! Must you view everything along your own sordid habits!'

'Sordid Emlyn?' Josquin looked offended. 'At least I have the sense not to rise above my betters. I would advise you to follow the same code or....'

'I will get beaten within an inch of my life, I know, I've already been given that lesson once today and it's not full daylight yet.'

Chapter 35 Geneva

A jumble of carts and wagons, mules, oxen, horses and the various owners, rumbled through Geneva Gate. The day was icicle clear, the sky a piercing blue into which thrust the dazzling Alpine spires. Cut into the sparkling ice and snow, valley glaciers scarred the rock with deep, blue shadow. Mountains fell into the sickle lake in perfect mirrored image. At its end, the Rhone flowed away to France. The city of Geneva was a curious assortment of stone and wood buildings. It was a predatory city where the prosperous merchants had filled their cellars from the pickings to be made along the lucrative road between France and Italy.

Ambrose drew his horse to one side, over-seeing the cavalcade. Beside him, on his right, was Giles de Saint Remy, a Frenchman who knew everything about soldiering except for actually fighting. He was employed to organize food and accommodation and to meet the needs of those of Angelo's men who were not in Ambrose's employ. On the merchant's other side were Emlyn and Angelo. The road was furrowed with snow, mud, dung and salt. This had melted to a mush in the warmer air, by nightfall it would be a frozen path of glass-like shards. Even now, in the cold of winter, beggars cluttered about the town gate. They were a shapeless ragged motley with hardly enough flesh on them to see them through the winter.

'The first time I came to Geneva,' said Ambrose, leaning forward to ease his weight in the saddle, 'I was nineteen. And there was not a better place on God's earth for a boy of nineteen to be.'

Angelo burst out laughing, his breath steamed the air, his red-rimmed eyes leaked tears.

Emlyn looked nervously at him.

'You are eighteen are you not Emlyn?' Ambrose continued. He flicked his whip idly in Emlyn's direction. 'I give you Geneva. It is nothing like it used to be, but I am sure we will find that the essential essence still flows in hidden channels.'

Angelo's laughter increased. His shoulders shook and his voice boomed loud enough to cause an avalanche. He said, 'When you hear the song of the Siren little monk, you will be swallowed up whole, flesh, blood, bone and purse!'

Emlyn looked at them both. Angelo had taken to calling him Little Monk. The older men grinned back at him, sharing some hidden knowledge to do with essences and Sirens. It sounded pagan.

'They are not too fond of Jesuits here either,' said Angelo. 'Mind you, they do for an afternoon's entertainment at the whipping post or burning pyre. Do you think our little monk would burn well Englishman?'

'That remains to be seen,' answered Ambrose sharing the joke. 'Fortunately for me, Protestants are welcomed here with open arms.'

Emlyn spat in the snow. He did not know what essential essences were nor the fate of courting the Siren, but he did know to whom this lofty city answered, Calvin: the enemy of the Roman Church, who had died but four years earlier. This was the centre of the Calvin Church; a hive for Reformers. Calvin's teachings directed his followers to a Spartan life with few pleasures. Emlyn was surprised at the intensity of his hatred for this city; the Jesuits had taught him well. He sat silent, damp and sullen.

Giles de Saint Remy conversed in slow Italian with Angelo, organizing the billeting of the men. He argued with difficulty, as his Italian was poor. Eventually he changed to French and added, 'Once a pot is empty it is empty and you will get nothing more from it.'

Ambrose smiled smugly. He understood enough to know that Angelo was a little short of funds for all the men who had accompanied him. Ambrose couldn't think how to say, 'I told you so,' in Italian. He caught Angelo's eye and widened his smile. Angelo turned on the Frenchman and sent him off with his ears burning.

Emlyn's attention was on the road. A fringed Wagon creaked by, dangling oil lamps and behind it rode the Italian ladies. Carmelia rode by, her heart-shaped face peered out from a dark hood; she was grinning.

Emlyn winked back and felt his dark thoughts shimmer away. He smiled crookedly and remembered that if he went near her he would be thrashed by her guardian. Adriana rode straight-backed with her head held high. She looked composed and in control of all she surveyed. She had cared for Emlyn well, always solicitous and gentle, contrary to her normal behaviour. He dreamed about her a lot; even though she was near twice his age, he found her the most adorable of women. His hand lay stiff in folds of cloth bound to the wood, to straighten his fingers. He thought that he could actually feel it healing daily under such tender care.

Angelo's men were happier to be in the company of ladies, though they were forbidden to converse with them and the young girls were not often to be seen at each day's end. On one occasion, on an orange evening, Emlyn had seen Carmelia dancing to a carter's pipe, her maid Pellegrina with her. The two young girls were rosy with cold, giggling and smiling with a swirl of layered underskirts. They had thrown snow and sang soldier's songs until the harsh voice of Adriana had put a stop to it all and sent them scurrying for cover.

Crystal white snow covered the roof tops of Geneva and softly rounded the lines of trees that marched up the slopes. The houses looked welcoming as smoke rose from chimneys and cooking fires. The town roads had been cleared of snow and scattered with salt. Geneva sat smug and warm; its inns tamed by reformers and its ladies of the night concealed from objecting eyes. Geneva that had once been wild, licentious, irreligious and tempting, now it lay clean and good and calm under the eye of the Calvinists. They watched, they preached, they guided and they punished. But still travellers came. For those who knew where to look, Geneva could equal even the Italian cities with its offering of joyful vices.

Apart from its religious aspect, it was a city of bankers and merchants; a city of money. With its chequered past, it did not tempt these wealthy dignitaries to make a permanent home upon its snowy slopes, only to tarry and dip into its flowing riches. Here could be found agents of the Medici, the Arnofini, the Turretini, the Balbani who all kept large houses overlooking the Madeleine. Here, Ambrose hoped to reach a final agreement with the Genoese bankers who had lent money to Philip of Spain to pay his troops in the Netherlands; money that had instead found its way to England's shores. Here too, Ambrose hoped to secure a buyer for the wool he and Gruffydd had invested in.

Once inside the walls of the town Emlyn stood for a while, watching the Italian ladies disappear behind the great wooden gates of a merchant's house across the square.

Coming around a corner, Josquin bundled into him. Righting himself, he said, 'We are all staying at the Pilgrims Rest or the Lady's Cup, depending on how you view the inn. It's not far, are you coming?'

'No he is not!' Ambrose Chillingworth came up behind him.

'Aren't I?' Emlyn said, suddenly annoyed.

'It is no place for a young man,' Ambrose replied.

'Where better for a young man?' Josquin asked. 'Don't worry, I'll look after him.'

Fixing Ambrose with a quarrelsome glare, Emlyn said, 'You told me, but a half hour ago, that there was no better place on God's earth....'

'I know, I know,' answered Ambrose. 'But I was a different sort of young man then I'm afraid to say, and it was but said in jest. We are staying at the house of a Meester Oertel.'

'Oertel?' Josquin recognised a fellow country-man's name. 'Do you speak of Abraham Oertel, the historian?'

'Yes. Do you know him?'

'Not personally,' said Josquin. He was going to mention that Abraham Oertel had been a frequent visitor to his mother's house, but he thought better of it. 'I have heard of him though,' he added. 'He's from Antwerp. A patron of the arts. Why is he here?'

'How should I know?' Ambrose answered irritably; Josquin was always asking questions.. 'Come on Emlyn, you'll like him. Oertel speaks Latin and Greek, if I'm not mistaken.'

Josquin winked. Emlyn released a patient breath and followed the Englishman.

In spite of the merchant's protestation, nightfall found Emlyn Tomas in the Pilgrims Rest. The room was hazy with wood smoke. Eyes glinted and voices rose in raucous laughter. Emlyn was surrounded by mercenaries and had already drunk more wine than he had ever drunk before. He had told them that he wanted to join their ranks. To be a soldier of fortune, they told him, you have first to learn how to drink like one and then to whore like one. Learning to drink like one seemed easy enough more wine spilled down his throat. The soldiers sang bawdy songs; the meaning was lost on Emlyn, he joined in the choruses when he could get his mouth around the words.

In time, they pulled him to his feet and pushed him towards a back room. His head reeled, his stomach churned and saliva flooded his mouth. He felt sick and helpless to prevent whatever jape his comrades had in store for him. Panic enclosed him as he was led through an opening door into a stifling darkness, but he would rather die than show his fear.

Now female voices soothed him and hands surrounded him. He was aware of the ribald comments and that he was the likely butt. Hands clapped, feet stamped, voices chanted, the tempo rising in time with his spinning head.

Before him, on a table, laughing like a demon, sat a large lay. Her laughter filled his head and the sight of her gums with her a few rotting stumps, made Emlyn's stomach heave. His intended fate was becoming shockingly apparent and though his mind screamed to escape, his limbs refused to answer the demand.

Amidst the noise and the stench of sweat, unseen hands held him still. Other hands loosened the ties on his codpiece, pulling at his hose and fondling his genitals. Emlyn struggled and fought, hampered by his injured hand, sick with revulsion. The tempo of the chanting increased; the laughter became demonic to his ears. He howled in protest.

The crone beamed with delight at the thought of this young, soft, tasty morsel. It was not often that she sampled such rare meat these days. She drooled in anticipation and lifting her skirts lay back on the table.

Emlyn was unable to respond with the gallant reflex. The wine and the revulsion that he felt, caused his member to shrivel. Though more than one hand sought to stimulate his failing manhood, the only affect was to further injure his bruised testicles. He fell to his knees and his face landed in the spongy, yielding softness of her groin. He felt coarse hair against his cheek, briefly his eyes focused on flesh marred by pustules and tiny crawling creatures. The growing torrent of saliva met with the up-welling contents of his stomach and poured from his mouth and nostrils.

Ambrose pushed his chair back from the chessboard where he had just suffered an ignoble defeat. His opponent, sat looking smug, his hands folded neatly across his stomach. Abraham Oertel was, as Josquin had said, from Antwerp and was the famed mapmaker and geographer. He was also a follower of the teachings of Erasmus and a keen collector of clocks. Ambrose had not seen him for many years but they had kept in touch, At forty-one, Abraham Oertel was a man of widening girth with a round jovial face and thinning hair, dampened down upon his forehead to cover what was missing. He had a large, round head with pale flaxen hair, a thin nose with a knob on the end and wide, kindly eyes that bestowed a tender glance on the least thing he came across. His education was extensive, but he only brought out his inexhaustible knowledge upon heads which would not be cowed by it.

Yawning and stretching he said, 'You have not improved Englishman I win. Did I not win last time we played?'

'Yes, indeed you did,' admitted Ambrose with reluctance, 'and the time before that. But I am more skilled with clocks than you are, otherwise your German time piece would still be still, if you gather my meaning. What if I had not come along?'

'It would still be dumb and time would suffer nothing from not being counted. Nonetheless, mine is the victory, you are attempting to lessen it.'

Ambrose was annoyed that he had lost the game, but his expression was calm and his irritation remained hidden.

Within an hour of his arrival at Oertel's house, he had been approached by an agent from Venice by the name of Theodoric Molino, who had been waiting for him and the wool to arrive in Geneva. Theodoric Molino had informed Ambrose that if the cloth was of superior quality, the Englishman stood to gain much profit in arranging to sell it to Tomasso di Vincentini, the Venetian merchant Molino represented. 'What a stroke of unexpected good fortune,' the agent had continued 'that has brought your wool to Geneva at this unprofitable time of year. Let no others approach you for its sale my good friend, for you will get no better price than that offered by me. And, if you could see your way into delivering it to Venice yourself before the spring, all expenses will be paid in advance for its delivery. You'll make an even greater profit on the commodity, for the price of wool at present in Venice is soaring! The gain will far outweigh the small inconvenience of travelling a few extra hundred miles in winter.'

Ambrose had been suspicious. He knew how many hundred miles it was to Venice, but the offer was exceptional. Where was the catch?

'Catch?' had said Theodoric indignantly. 'There is no catch. However there is an urgency, for the Venetian company has ships to fill. Tomasso di Vincentini likes to stay a step ahead of his competitors. As a merchant yourself Messer Chillingworth, you will be aware of the advantages in that. Your reluctance is understandable. So, to put your mind at ease, we can settle this now, this very day. Subject only to an inspection of the wool, monies shall be brought to you directly.'

It had all been too quick for Ambrose. He had agreed to consider the offer for a day or two. He had to nearly force the exuberant Theodoric out of the door and had only rid himself of the man by promising to see him the following day.

Abraham Oertel, who had been witness to it all, was in full agreement with the scheme. 'You know how things are Ambrose,' he had encouraged, 'Antwerp is in turmoil, the wool market there is ruined. No doubt it will recover again, but what are the buyers to do in the meantime? They still have obligations to meet. What he says is true, you could not be better placed, you can triple your profits. I am half sorry to have you as guest here, we shall be inundated before long by cloth buyers.' The last had been said in jest, Oertel enjoyed all the activity that, as he had foretold, invaded his door before the day was out. He had turned them all away, his visitor was tired and would arrange to see them in his own good time.

'Master Chillingworth!'

Ambrose was startled out of his thoughts.

Without any show of politeness, Matthew entered the room. His boots, crusted with snow and mud soiled the colourful Syrian rug by the fireplace.

'Well what is it?' Ambrose demanded, half rising from his chair. He recognised Matthew's expression as one of agitation.

'The boy,' said Matthew. 'Emlyn, e's in the Pilgrims Rest with that lot.'

'So? Am I to be his guardian?' Ambrose snapped. 'I dutifully warned him, beside, the loss of his virginity is probably the best thing that could happen to him at present.'

'At the Pilgrims Rest?' Abraham Oertel asked. 'That is the last place for the boy to gain what he is seeking. He will most surly loose his virginity there, of that there is not doubt, but it will surely be the death of him. The place is ridden with the *Morbus Gallicus*.'

'You what?' Matthew said with a vacant look.

'The pox,' said Ambrose enlightening him.

Josquin entered the tavern. After a brief look around the room, he walked towards the curtain, from where all the noise was coming. He paused on the threshold. The room was brightly lit by tallow candles on every table and fire brands bracketed on the walls. A brazier spat and crackled in a near corner. Old Rafaelo Gandolfi had drunk himself unconscious and was sprawled across a table, his beard reddened by spilled wine. The two youngest members of the troop, the Sicilians, as similar as twins, sat arms entwined on a bench in a corner. All the rest, including Angelo, stood in a circle stamping their feet, with girls entwined around their necks in various states of undress. In the centre a fat whore sat astride a table. She was wailing and cursing, flailing her arms about and thrashing her fat legs.

Josquin had been about to take supper with a girl of quite a different nature, she had caught his eye with promise, earlier that evening. But, he had be summoned by the Englishman's servant; summoned to go and pull their young prodigy from the tavern of vices. The sight that met his eyes made the Dutchman chuckle and then the chuckle became a roaring laugh.

Incapable, drunk as a bishop, Emlyn struggled to free himself from fat thighs and a pool of vomit. He was so drunk that his feet refused to obey him and each time he managed to get them under him, they betrayed him and failed like straw stalks. His ankles were tangled in hose.

Josquin had seen all this before. Whenever the mercenaries finished a campaign, their master, Angelo let them loose in the nearest house of ill repute, free to spend their gains. They were always unruly, drunk and disgusting, Josquin had been so himself. If there was a new comer among them, then he would provide this type of sordid entertainment; a sensitive youth would have cut his wrists and bled to death in shame. Josquin walked across the room with long strides. He grasped a fistful of the boy's shirt.

'Leave the lad be,' slurred Angelo with a belch. 'He wants to be a soldier of fortune!' This was followed by a chorus of agreement and struck the audience as hilariously funny.

Josquin ignored them. He pulled Emlyn away from the whore and attempted to get him to his feet. Emlyn staggered and spun like a broken windmill, the bandaging coming loose from his hand. The whore let loose a wail of protest. Hands reached out to prevent the rescue. Josquin lost his grip and Emlyn went down under a forest of legs.

The woman descended and reclaimed her victim. She loomed above him and sat astride him like a succubus. Josquin took hold of the woman by the ample waist and pulled. She clung on to her prey and let out a squeal of protest. Emlyn opened his eyes. They crossed, straightened and re-crossed. He stared up, past the mound of flesh, at Josquin. His dark brows met together in a puzzled frown.

Josquin spanked the woman's behind, hard enough to force her to release the boy beneath. He grasped a handful of her skirts and pulled her to her feet. 'Get away!' He shoved her towards Angelo. 'Go and ply your trade somewhere else, pox-ridden whore!'

Angelo staggered back as the large woman arrived in his arms. She cackled and planted a resounding kiss on the end of his nose. They both tottered backwards into a table, upsetting ale cups and wine bottles, tilting the bench with the Sicilian lovers and splintering a chair as they landed in a confusion of cloth and limbs.

The whole room rang with drunken revelry. The soldiers romped about crowing and sniggering, banging the tables and throwing anything that came to hand. They would all be beaten, burnt or thrown out of Geneva if the Calvinists found them.

Josquin grasped a firm hold on the mess of Emlyn Tomas and dragged him towards the door. He could have carried him, but he was unwilling to ruin the clean set of clothes he had taken such care with to impress the rope-maker's daughter.

'Have I missed something?' Rafaelo Gandolfi raised his head from his stupor to question them as they passed.

Once outside, Josquin dumped his charge in the snow. Emlyn lay as still as a sack of grain groaning with remorse.

With the handle of his knife, and after a few strenuous attempts, Josquin broke the ice on the surface of a water butt by the inn wall. He lifted the youth by handfuls of cloth and dumped him, head first into the freezing water.

Emlyn went stiff then reeled up out of the butt as if he was on fire. He gasped, wheezed and made a peculiar noise in his throat as he fought for breath. He coughed, spluttered and sneezed and slid down the barrel, blue eyes wide open and mouth agape, face as grey as dirty snow. He began to shiver uncontrollably, head lolling and stared up at his rescuer looking perturbed.

Hands on hips, Josquin glared down at him with an expression of contempt. 'Pulling you out of sticky situations is becoming a habit,' he said. He hauled him to his feet and they set off across the snow covered square towards Abraham Oertel's house. There was a group of women wrapped in hooded cloaks crossing the square. Josquin frowned.

Emlyn shuffled along grasping his muddle of clothing together. Occasionally he lost his footing and tumbled over in a disorder of limbs. By the time they reached the middle of the square his body was convulsed in shudders and his feet could no longer hold him up.

'Josquin!' shrieked Adriana Martinelli. 'By the Blessed Madonna, what have you done!'

Josquin smiled charmingly and bowed. 'I, Madonna? Not a thing.'

Adriana dropped down beside Emlyn, her expression anxious. Carmelia Grimani and Pellegrina glared at Josquin.

'Get him inside quickly,' said Adriana calling to the servants who accompanied them.

'He is merely drunk, Adriana,' said Josquin. 'I'll take him with me. He'll sleep it off.'

But Adriana ignored him, as she had done since he had joined the Englishman's party. He had not been surprised to find her there. She was an exceptional woman. He watched with a mixture of admiration and unease as she led her troop across the snow, Emlyn staggering between them. Had she got her claws in the young Welshman?

This time when Emlyn Tomas lay under the care of Adriana, his skin was dry and cool. She had mixed him a drink from her powders and spices and he had revived from his drunken stupor. She thought him a fool for acting as he had so soon after his fever. But he had surprisingly suffered no further harm, loose limbed and drunk as he was. Adriana ran her nails over his chest and arms. She whispered into his unheeding ears. He is so young and untouched, she mused, almost like a maiden. This time, his skin quivered delightfully. His eyes opened, as huge and deep as bottomless wells. He responded to her kisses; at first like a child and then bolder, learning quickly and then unafraid, giving back all that he was given and more. And drunk as he was, she was rewarded with the right response when her hands explored further. She kept him with her for half the night, pleased that he was drunk and scarcely aware of where he was or what he was doing. But he would remember, she made sure that he would remember.

When Emlyn awoke it was still dark and snow fell, clinging to the window in glistening snowdrops. He thought an axe had split his skull and hoped that he would soon be dead. He knew with certainty that if he moved his head would fall off and roll across the floor. Slowly, in fragments, he remembered. A wash of horror ran through him. He struggled to rise and quickly changed his mind. His stomach churned, bile rose in his throat, he let out a shuddering groan. Without moving his head he looked about. There was a lamp alight, a feeble flame, placed on a table near the window. The room was small and neat. He smelled of soap and was wearing a clean shirt with frills around the neck. His injured hand had been freshly bandaged. An ewer and a bowl decorated with silver poppies stood on a stool beside the bed. Emlyn looked at the bowl and willed his stomach to be still.

It was no good. With an almighty effort he heaved himself up and swung his legs to the floor. The room reeled and spun. He reached for the stool, it was too far away. He stood and lurched towards it. He upset the stool and sent the ewer toppling to the floor. It hit the floor boards with a resounding crash.

The door opened a crack. The head of Ambrose Chillingworth, topped by a ridiculous night cap, poked through the opening, like a decapitated demon.

Emlyn stared up at him from his felled position on the floor. He felt his stomach heave and darkness clouded his vision.

Ambrose held a cup to his lips. 'Come now drink,' he ordered.

Emlyn took a timid swallow, it was water and it washed into his tortured stomach like a flood of ice. He felt better. He opened his eyes, choking back tears of shame. 'Did what I remember really happen?' he asked in a whisper.

'That and more I imagine,' Ambrose replied. 'I have not heard the details. So now you have heard the song of the Siren. Two of Adriana Martinelli's servants brought you back a few hours ago. Josquin left you with her last night. I gather that he had little choice in the matter as she was upset at the way you were behaving after begin so recently ill.'

Emlyn bowed his head and shook it slowly from side to side. He wanted to forget, he wanted to wipe out the night as if it had never happened, in his shame, he just wanted to lie down and die. Had he really done what he thought he'd done with Adriana Martinelli?

Ambrose sat on the side of the bed 'Finish the cup of water,' he advised. 'It will do you some good.'

'I can't live with this,' said Emlyn dramatically.

'Of course you can.' Ambrose replied with a stiff smile. 'Whatever happened, it will fade by morning. You are not the first to get outrageously drunk and make a fool of yourself. The others were probably in the same state and will all be nursing equally bad heads by morning. Sleep now, put it out of your mind.'

'I can't!' gasped Emlyn with a shudder of revulsion. The memories of the tavern were bad enough, what had happened afterwards was beyond bearing. Emlyn was too ashamed to speak of it and he hoped that it was just a dream.

Ambrose rose and took the lamp from its place by the window. Turning by the door he said, 'I too have been where you are now. It passes and even in excess, there is a lesson to be learned. Do you still want to be a mercenary?'

Emlyn looked up at him and felt his resolve weaken. In his present state of mind, he hoped he would never see any of the mercenaries again. And how could he ever look upon Adriana Martinelli again?

Ambrose winked and closed the door softly behind him.

Three days later, Emlyn followed Ambrose Chillingworth to the house of Pompeo Diodati, a merchant banker whom Ambrose had travelled so far to see on behalf of the Queen of England. Ambrose had asked Emlyn to accompany him earlier that morning. Emlyn realised that the merchant had taken him into his confidence and that this meeting was one that the Spaniards had hoped to prevent. The mystery of the Spanish galleons was about to be made clear.

New snow had fallen during the night and the sky was pinkish grey, filled with the threat of more. Emlyn had not been out of the house, he had remained in his room for most of the time and still shuddered with shame whenever his mind forced him to remember. He had seen little of Ambrose whom, he learned, was being offered outrageous prices for the Welsh wool. Emlyn dragged his feet through the snow, leaving furrows behind him.

They arrived at the gate, stated their business and were invited inside, Pompeo Diodati was expecting them. Emlyn straightened his shoulders and followed Ambrose. He was surprised that the English merchant had invited him along to witness whatever it was that this eventful journey was all about. For the first time in his life, he wished he was better dressed.

Pompeo Diodati greeted them at the top of the stairs. He was rounded and jovial, he smiled as he rubbed his fat hands together, they twinkled with rings. He was dressed in pale blue silk that covered his fat gut in loose folds. His eyes were an insipid brown. His nose was not the least bit Roman and his was mouth small and pink. 'Welcome! Welcome!' He ushered them into a warm room. 'I have long awaited you Messer Chilli...Ch'

'Chillingworth,' finished Ambrose bowing courteously. 'And this is my notary Emlyn Tomas.'

'Of course, of course!' Pompeo Diodati beamed, his smile spreading to his chins. 'Delighted. You will have wine? My wife Karenina will be overjoyed to serve you.'

Wondering how he had become a notary, Emlyn remained standing and stared about.

A woman entered, she was young, half the her husbands age. Her raven black hair was piled up and adorned with pearls and ribbons. She bore a silver tray loaded with crystal glass and a plate of sweetmeats. She swept into the room, placed the tray on a low table and turned her bright gaze on Emlyn Tomas. She smiled sweetly, walked over to him and took his free hand, looking with sympathy at the other. She led him to a couch and sat close beside him, leaning forward to pour the wine. Emlyn felt his cheeks burn. She smelled nice.

Pompeo Diodati smiled soothingly, offering a chair to his older guest before he seated himself opposite. 'Messer, you have come well escorted. A whole troop of mercenaries!'

Ambrose shifted uncomfortably in the hard chair and cleared his throat. 'It is wise to travel protected in these disturbing times.'

'Indeed indeed,' The merchant banker replied. 'You have come with Madame Adriana Martinelli and the Grimani girl. We had heard of course that her father, the redoubtable Don Carlos, wishes her to return to Venice. No doubt the girl will find a suitable husband in her own country.'

Emlyn went stiff and felt the colour drain away from his face. He stood up dropping his wine. 'That cannot be true!'

They all turned and looked at him with astonishment.

'Yes,' said Pompeo Diodati. 'Is something amiss?'

'No,' stammered Emlyn. He resumed his seat and retrieved his glass. He looked apologetically at the young woman and turned to his host. 'I'm sorry Messer Diodati, please forgive me.'

Ambrose glared at him.

'Quite,' replied Pompeo Diodati. To cover up the embarrassing incident, he turned to Ambrose. 'I trust your journey was satisfactory?'

'Thank you,' said Ambrose stroking his beard, 'Though I do dislike travelling in the depth of winter. It's an uncomfortable experience, don't you agree?'

'True, but we must thank God for your safe arrival in this splendid city,' said Diodati.

'A sweetmeat?' Karenina said, offering him the plate.

Ambrose took something unfamiliar off the plate and smiled with an inclination of his head. They ate and drank and exchanged further pleasantries until Karenina excused herself and they were free to get down to business.

'The Genoese bankers have had dealings in the past with your most gracious Queen,' said Pompeo Diodati introducing the subject for which they had come together. 'We are devoted to such a courageous woman,' he continued, 'and are always only too pleased to do business with your esteemed country.'

'Thank you,' said Ambrose. 'You will be aware therefore as to the nature of our business?'

Pompeo Diodati picked up his glass and assumed a serious expression. 'I have received word by courier only two days ago. I understand that the monies lent to Spain have been misplaced. It is a matter that causes some concern. A great deal of money is involved here and it will cause some upset to the royal house concerned. His gracious majesty the King of Spain would not be pleased to discover our dealings with your Queen.'

'But his gracious majesty the King of Spain,' said Ambrose, 'is in no position to intervene. Am I correct Messer Diodati? Forgive me if I err.'

'There is nothing to forgive my dear Mr Chill...?'

'Ambrose will do if you cannot manage the other. You have a church dedicated to St. Ambrose here? Or was that Milan?'

'Milan,' corrected Diodati. 'The money loaned to the King would not have really been his until it reached the Netherlands. As it never did reach its destination, I assume that it is held in safe keeping by your gracious Queen?'

Ambrose smiled inwardly. Poor Pompeo Diodati was indeed in an awkward position. As manager and spokesman for the Genoese bankers, he carried a heavy burden upon his shoulders. It must be, thought Ambrose, as embarrassing a matter for the Genoese as it was for the King of Spain. Eighty thousand ducats was a great deal of money to mislay. The eighty thousand ducats which at present lay in England, and out of reach of Spain or in fact the Genoese bankers themselves.

'I assure you,' said Ambrose pleasantly, 'that you need have no fear for the safety of your loan to the King of Spain. As you have already pointed out, it is not the King's until it reaches the destination it was intended for. The eighty thousand ducats is held in safekeeping. Her Royal Majesty Queen Elizabeth, wishes to transfer the loan to herself.'

'What!' The Genoese banker wrung his fat hands.

'It is fortuitous that matters are so Signor Diodati,' said Ambrose. 'The seas around Britain are crawling with pirates. As it is, the Spanish fleet was forced to seek shelter in our shores because of them. Had Her Royal Majesty allowed this fleet to continue on its way, the gold could well have be in the hands of sea beggars by now. Where would be the advantage in that?'

'There would be no advantage at all,' admitted Pompeo Diodati glumly. He rubbed his hands together looking flustered. He refused to meet the English merchant's eye. Examining the carpet he said, 'I see that your Queen is a wise and thoughtful ruler. It is gracious of her to take care of the money for us, but transfer the loan? How could she have considered such a thing?'

'Simple,' said Ambrose handing Diodati a refilled glass of wine himself. 'The loan is on English soil already. All that remains is the agreement of your bank Signor Diodati. The Queen, I believe has an impeccable reputation for repaying her loans.'

'Indeed she has,' agreed the banker miserably. 'She is a shrewd business woman. Already she has convinced us to halve her interest on previous loans and has never been lax in her repayments.'

'Well there you are, her reputation speaks for itself.'

'What of the King of Spain?'

'Philip?' Ambrose maintained a mild expression. 'Spain has gold pouring from her domains in the New World. He will find monies soon enough to pay his soldiers in the Netherlands.'

'The next shipment of gold my dear Englishman,' said Diodati, 'will never be seen by the King of Spain.'

'How unfortunate,' exclaimed Ambrose. 'Has he mislaid that too?'

'No,' Diodati replied, his voice tinged with annoyance. 'It will come straight to the Genoese bankers to whom it is owed from a previous loan.

Where now will he get the eighty thousand ducats for the Netherlands troops?'

'He must pray to God for guidance,' Ambrose replied. 'But we are not concerned, for Genoa can afford to be generous to the Queen of England. After all, Genoa stands to gain much from the Spanish gold. May God protect it on its perilous journey.'

At last Diodati raised his watery eyes to meet those of the English merchant. He knew he had talked himself into a corner. He was in truth so upset that he would have wept had he not had company to witness his weakness. He offered a nervous smile, showing his dimples. 'Will you allow me a few days?'

'Certainly,' said Ambrose standing. 'Shall we say in three days then?'

'I shall probably need more,' Diodati replied wiping his brow with a silk sleeve.

'As soon as may be then,' said Ambrose. He snapped his fingers and Emlyn jumped up from the couch and followed him.

'No need to trouble yourself,' said Ambrose as they left. 'We'll see ourselves to the door.' He turned on the threshold and bowed respectably. 'Thank you for your hospitality Messer Diodati, and for the charming company of your wife. You will pass her my regards?'

'Certainly Messer, er....quite. Good day!'

'It is isn't it,' said Ambrose. He left the sad Italian and thumped down the stairs humming an English drinking song.

'So that is what this is all about,' said Emlyn when they had returned to Oertel's house. 'Queen Elizabeth wants to borrow the bullion that was to pay Alva's soldier's in the Netherlands.'

'Quite, if I may quote our friend Diodati,' Ambrose replied. He was standing by the hearth eyeing a clock on the shelf above the fire, the one he had repaired. His hands were clasped behind his back and he rocked back and forth, letting loose an occasional musical hum.

Emlyn sat with his head nestled on a plush cushion on the back of the chair. He had his eyes closed. He could hear the clock ticking and the merchant humming to himself and, from outside, the jovial squeals of children throwing snowballs. It had started to snow again. He said, 'What will you do now?'

'Wait,' said Ambrose. 'From the look of the weather we will be here for some weeks. I am sure a path can be found back to France though, to send a courier with the news as soon as it is settled. I have always felt that the Italian bankers will be delighted to transfer the loan to England. There will be no objections. I will remain here until the snow has lessened. After that, it looks as if I may be going to Venice with the wool. I have accepted part payment already and have agreed to deliver it to a certain Tomasso di Vincentini. Milan and the road to Italy however, will be impassable until the spring.' Ambrose paused and nudged the finger of the clock. Without turning he said, 'Want to come along as we arranged with your grandfather?'

Emlyn said, 'I was going to go to Venice anyway.'

Ambrose turned around. 'I knew that you wanted to go there to discover what had happened to your mother and why you were brought originally from North Africa. I admit I am puzzled about it myself. Forgive me Emlyn, but I think you need a little fatherly advice, would you accept that from me without taking offence?'

'Advice?' Emlyn said. 'It seems to me that I have listened to advice for too long. Wherever I tread I seem to invite suggestions as to what I should do with myself. I'm beginning to think that my future will never be directed by me. Goronwy would make a rebellious Catholic of me, Gruffydd wants me to become a traditional harper and my uncle wants me to become a priest.'

'We are all carried by life's river Emlyn Tomas,' said Ambrose. 'On that river without guidance we have no choice but to flow where life's currents take us. If you do not build a strong ship under you, then you are battered to and fro and are not in control of your destiny.'

Emlyn remembered the toothless grimace of the Mafanwy Fawr on the road to Rhuddlan. '*Be sure to have a sound ship beneath thee Mab-y-Ddarig, the tide is turning.*' Is this what she had meant?

'If you do not seek to guide yourself Emlyn,' said Ambrose, 'others will guide you. You have skills and talents that they can make use of. Goronwy sees in you a saviour for Wales, Gruffydd sees in you a harper who will gain reputation and reward for his skill. Wherever you turn, you seem to attract interest, and not always to your benefit.'

'And you, Mr. Chillingworth,' said Emlyn coldly, 'what would you have me be?'

Ambrose moved away from the fire. 'You told me yourself that you felt like a ship with no sails, tossed on an aimless ocean. It is up to you to take command of your situation. I ask nothing of you. Gruffydd thought that you might benefit from the experience of travel and learn something of the mercantile world. Half the wool we brought here is your grandfather's. He appointed John Moore to see that it arrived safely at its destination and that man has proved his ability, so you need not concern yourself with the scheme. There have been matters that have soured our relationship and I hope you not be influenced by these, as they were not of my making. If you wish to continue to Venice on your own, you have my understanding. However, I would like you to take the responsibility from John Moore; to become involved in what your grandfather and I planned. I will not force this decision on you and I will not have you accompany me one step further unless I have your full agreement.' Ambrose waited for a response. When none came he added, 'Whatever you decide, we will be here in Geneva for some time and I suggest that you make use of it, suggest mind you, not compel.'

'In what way?'

'Ask Angelo to teach you about whores and drinking, but most of all, how to look after yourself in difficult situations.'

'You mean how to fight to with one hand?'

Ambrose ignored his rancour. 'Failing that,' he said pulling at his earlobe, 'you know that our host, Abraham could recommend you to the Medici interests here. They too are merchant bankers like the one we have recently visited, but more powerful. It seems that they have lost their secretary, the man died three weeks ago, and they have been unable to engage another. Why do you not consider this position instead?'

Emlyn stood up quickly. 'I cannot tell you,' he replied. 'Not because I do not want to, but because I do not know myself. It seems as if I have spent all my life scribbling with a quill, one translation after another. I want to learn how to fight and be a soldier.'

Ambrose sat down in the chair opposite, folding his gown about him tidily. He said 'Any man can be a soldier Emlyn. It is not given to many to be able to make music of excellent quality and to be able to do those things that you have been trained in. Do you propose to ignore your learning to satisfy some whim?'

'How would that be possible?' Emlyn said. 'What I am, is what the Jesuits have made me, I cannot change that. It was not of my own choice.' He walked to the door and turned. 'When you are ready to leave for Venice, I would be honoured to accept the responsibility you suggest.'

Ambrose smiled. Before Emlyn disappeared Ambrose said, 'One question.'

'What?'

'In the meeting this morning, why did you splutter your wine at the mention of our Italian ladies?'

Emlyn stared down at the carpet, unsure how to answer. 'It was nothing,' he shrugged, 'a mistake.'

'Come, come. I know you better than that.'

Emlyn looked up, his eyes dark and unfathomable. 'It was the name,' he said softly. 'Signorina Carmelia's father is Don Carlos Grimani. He was also father to the man my mother wed. There could not be two with the same name.'

'Why not?'

'He has adopted the Spanish form of address, few Italians would be willing to do that, especially now that Italy is being overrun by Spain. It must be the same Don Carlos.

Ambrose knew something of Emlyn's past, Gruffydd had told him. He had not thought himself that there would be a connection between the young Venetian girl and that marriage of long ago. He said 'Your mother wed a Grimani?'

'Yes. A merchant like yourself. He was killed in a battle at sea.'

Ambrose looked at him thoughtfully. 'So you think that you may be related to this girl, Carmelia?'

Emlyn offered no answer. Ambrose realised that there was no one to whom Emlyn could turn to for advice or comfort nor, it seemed, had there ever been. He had learned to keep his thoughts to himself. Ambrose said 'Have you spoken to Madame Adriana Martinelli concerning this matter?'

'How could I? I would not know where to begin.' Emlyn replied, his eyes lit with amusement.

It is very difficult to help the boy, thought Ambrose. He said, 'I have talked often to the ladies and Madame Adriana Martinelli cared for you. Would you like me to arrange a meeting with her?'

'No!' Emlyn responded quickly. 'I would rather that you mentioned nothing to her.'

'Oh? And how do you propose to discover the facts?'

'Mr. Chillingworth, I do not want them to know of me yet. I know that it all sounds foolish, but I will not be called bastard by them. It would be better if I could speak with Carmelia alone. She could tell me about her father, but Madame Adriana would not approve of the girl speaking with me though.'

'I understand,' Ambrose replied. And they will learn nothing from me, nor will I interfere more than I have to, he thought. For Emlyn it was important to gain respect. He could not see that his own talent would lead him to the same result. Here, locked by winter to the Alps, there was little to fear for him. As Angelo's employer, Ambrose would ask the mercenary to teach Emlyn the skill of arms, once his hand was healed.

Before Emlyn left, Ambrose said, 'I may be able to assist you in meeting with the girl.'

Emlyn smiled. 'That would be helpful to me, thank you.'

Ambrose stood and straightened his doublet. 'Good, then you will not object to accompanying Adriana Martinelli on a hawking excursion. She left word for me to join her tomorrow at first light and especially asked that you accompany me.'

Emlyn didn't look as happy as Ambrose expected.

Chapter 36 Geneva

In the long weeks that followed, the soldiers of fortune were let loose on Geneva. Boredom turned them to drink and revelry. They did this on the understanding that if they caused upset or broke the rule of the town, they were on their own. Ambrose had clearly stated that he would not stand by them or defend them, nor would they be able to return to his service, once their punishment was over. In full agreement, Angelo enforced this law with no mercy. He found it to be exceptionally effective. There was a whipping post at the Madeleine square, the Calvinists lived by strict rule and were a force to be reckoned with.

The Catholic community were watched carefully by the Calvinists and on one occasion Emlyn was questioned by the authorities. This incident puzzled him, for they had asked him what his intentions were in Geneva and how long he intended to stay; they had also mentioned his educational background with the Jesuits in Paris. How they could have discovered this was beyond Emlyn's understanding. When he mentioned the incident to Ambrose, the Englishman had been concerned and wondered if the Spaniards had traced Emlyn to Geneva.

While Emlyn waited for his hand to heal, he could only watch the mercenaries practising at the butts and the skilful sword play. He tried skating on the frozen edge of the lake and discovered that ice was unforgivably hard. He played chess with Abraham Oertel and won two games out of twenty-seven. He learnt how to play a particular Rutland form of skittles from Ambrose, and won a pair of Spanish boots when he tried it on Angelo. He saw the back of Carmelia's head every Sunday at mass and heard her sing. The service was held in the chapel of the Medici banking house. Although mass was not said in secret, the ceremony did have an element of secrecy about it.

The weather was unpredictable, it was bitterly cold and snow fell on most days, preventing the travellers from continuing their journey. As Ambrose had promised, Emlyn had been able to see Carmelia on the day they went out hawking with Adriana Martinelli. Ambrose kept

Adriana trapped in conversation while Emlyn dropped back to ride beside Carmelia. 'Of course he's my father.' Carmelia had said when Emlyn asked her about Don Carlos Grimani. 'I haven't seen him since I was seven,' she'd added. 'He didn't like me because I was not a boy. He wanted a son more that anything in the world so I was a great disappointment to him. That's why he sent me to be educated so far away.'

'Does he have sons now?'

'No, and serves him right!' Carmelia said childishly. 'He'll have to be content with his grandsons Paolo and Lorenzo. I am so looking forward to seeing them, Lorenzo is a priest.'

Lorenzo and Paolo, Emlyn had whispered to himself, half brothers! He was quite looking forward to meeting them himself. Carmelia could tell him nothing about Cristoforo Grimani and his wife Anna; as she had said in Paris, the subject was not one that her family discussed. She suggested that Emlyn talk with Adriana about the subject. Emlyn would not speak with Adriana. What had happened between them had left him with a mixture of loathing and desire. He never looked at her on the rare occasions that he was in the company of the Italian ladies and he did all in his power to avoid such meetings. Josquin somehow knew what had happened; he told Emlyn, after swearing him to utmost secrecy, that he had been Adriana's lover himself and that she was a woman of insatiable appetite.

During the following weeks, on three separate occasions, Emlyn escaped harm from inexplicable accidents. The first time had been while he was out walking on the forested slopes, an arrow had whipped through his hair and buried itself in a tree trunk an inch from his head. When he'd looked around he'd been unable to find where the arrow had come from and guessed that it was a bizarre happening, a stray arrow shot from some hunter's bow. A week later he was in the dyer's quarter with Giles Saint Remy when a stack of logs collapsed while he was walking past. A worker had shouted in warning and Emlyn had been just able to leap out of the path of the falling logs. The logs had remained neatly stacked there since the Autumn, the workman had explained, he could not understand why they had fallen.

The last accident had been the most frightening and had occurred while Emlyn was skating with John Moore on the frozen boarders of the lake. The ice had splintered and cracked and he'd tried to scramble out of the way as he felt the surface tilt beneath him. He had fallen and begun to slip; he'd cried out in panic, but Moore was too far off to hear him. The icy water had closed around his legs and he had sunk deeper as he scraped the smooth surface for a hold with frozen fingers. He had sunk in to the shoulders before anyone noticed his plight. A group of local skaters had come to his rescue. Knowing the nuances of the frozen lake, they had negotiated the thin ice with skill and had pulled Emlyn to safety, cautioning him to heed the warning flags. Moore had come running up to then, his face a mask of concern, his voice stammering with apologies and remorse. It was not his fault, Emlyn explained, there had been no warning flag where they'd skated. Emlyn could not think of any malicious reason behind these mishaps, yet some inner sense told him that they had not been accidental, even the fall on the ice. He mentioned nothing of the accidents to Ambrose, feeling foolish at the thought of explaining that he felt someone wished him harm.

There were a few incidents when his path met with Carmelia's and even some when they were able to exchange a word or two, Carmelia always laughing and blushing. There was a message in her eyes, a warm, welcoming, glowing message that he always turned away from without acknowledgement. His future plans, he told himself, every time his eyes followed her movements or his ears were alerted to her sweet voice, allowed no room for romantic attachments. In spite of this, he found himself thinking about her for much of each day.

Most of the time Emlyn was with the soldiers, trying to get them to accept him. He put up with a lot, but they were never as cruel as they had been that first night with the whore; Emlyn had not been near that place since. He understood that he was expected to endure this customary baiting or he would not be considered to join the company. He was not always in control of his emotions. At these times, when insult was unforgivable and he was forced into fighting for his diminishing honour, he never lasted long enough to get in one blow. The bouts he had fought with his fellow students in Paris, faded into nothing in comparison. Clearly, there was much to be learnt in the art of warfare. Apart from his skill with the bow, that his injured hand prevented him from displaying, Emlyn Tomas was about as useful to the band of mercenaries as a bent arquebus.

He trailed after them when he was tolerated. At first he tried to form some sort of friendship with the two Sicilians, Alessandro and Celio. They were nearer to his age and seemed to harass him less than the others. He thought too, that they were mild natured, gentle and polite, bred in better society than most of the soldiers of fortune. Alessandro and Celio were cousins and it was rumoured that they were lovers. They were, agreeably, beautiful to look upon. Their faces were like those of angels, their eyes deep and liquid warm and framed with women's lashes. They were thin and graceful and moved like the wild deer that roamed the lower forests. It was not until Emlyn approached the courtyard, where the two were practising their skills, that he was made aware of the reason's for their being in Angelo's employ.

Armed with swords, they were equally matched in skill and elegance. Every movement was a pleasure to watch. They were the best swordsmen in the company; they could demonstrate to perfection every style, old or newly contrived. The first time Emlyn watched, they were aware of his presence and, no matter how small and unimportant the audience, they performed as if to a prince. Emlyn saw then, that this was not just for show. He had been told that none had ever bested them, that every opponent had been skewered through the heart or brought to their knees begging for mercy. Celio and Alessandro were not men to cross nor were they immune to scorn. Nobody teased them., Emlyn had applauded them and admired their skill. During the evenings the company devised often ludicrous methods of entertainment. These usually involved some form of competition. Emlyn joined them with good nature when he could and usually lost.

Emlyn's injuries healed slowly and he began to hope that his hand would mend and be the same as it once was. He went hunting on the forested slopes, trudging through the snow sometimes until darkness. Often he went off alone and forced his trembling fingers to pull a yew bow until the hand grew stronger. Eventually, over seven weeks since he had been injured, he shot a wild boar and brought it in triumph on a sled into the town. Angelo took him off after that and taught him how to handle a sword. In this, Emlyn found his skill left much to be desired. He persevered and grew strong enough to win more of the bouts of friendly fighting than he had at first, but wielding a sword was beyond his capability.

The weather began to improve and the company began to look forward to continuing their journey. On a Thursday after two days of clear sky, Emlyn watched fifteen of the soldiers leaving the town gate carrying shields. Some of the town's people went with them and skipping children trailed after. Josquin was not among them. He sat outside the inn, plaiting leather thongs with which he intended to mend his saddle before the next stage of the journey. They were all leaving Geneva the following morning.

'Where are they going?' Emlyn asked him.

'To play in the snow like children,' Josquin replied cynically. 'They have been drinking all afternoon and have a mind to release their high spirits.'

'Play, doing what?'

'Why not go with them and find out?'

'Are you not going?' Emlyn addressed Josquin's bent head.

Josquin didn't answer. Of course it would be beneath his dignity to play children's games. He had spent most of his time with the rope-maker's daughter or with the Englishman, talking about rulers and the ruled, matters in which Emlyn found little of interest. But children's games, he could understand. The worse he could suffer, he thought, would be a shower of snowballs and there were real children among them with sledges instead of shields.

'You can't come without one!' Giles de Saint Remy's voice rose with objection.

'I could borrow yours,' Emlyn replied.

'Do you think me touched?' spat the Frenchman. 'I am not prepared to walk all the way up that hill twice!' They were standing at the side of the road where the cleared snow was piled up into frozen mounds. Gills de Saint Remy glanced nervously up the narrow path where the others were fast disappearing.

Emlyn said, 'What hill?' He kept hold of the Frenchman's sleeve.

Giles rolled his eyes. 'That hill!' He pointed to the highest slope that was covered with pristine snow from top to bottom.

Emlyn let go. 'Oh, that hill,' he said. He would not be able to find his way up without a guide. 'Will you wait for me while I get a shield of my own?'

'No!' Giles answered sullenly. He stepped away, slipping his shield across his shoulders and ran off to catch up with the others.

Emlyn ran back in the opposite direction. Ambrose had a shield that Matthew had lugged all the way from England.

'No!' Matthew said.

'Why not? 'Ambrose queried. 'If it can't hold Emlyn while he descends the mountain, what good will it be in battle?'

'That there shield 'as saved your skin on many occasions master Chillingworth an' you've no call to treat as if it 'adn't.'

'Oh give the boy the shield Matthew and be done with it. I'll have no cause to use it again.'

''Ow do you know that?' Matthew said indignantly 'We're goin' to Italy aren't we? Don't they always fight each other in Italy?'

'They may well do just that Matthew, but I shall not be a soldier again.'

'Were you a solder then?' Emlyn's curiosity was aroused.

'I have been,' Ambrose replied. 'But as I have told you often enough, there are better ways of making a living. Take the shield Emlyn, may it serve you as it has served me. I never used it to slip down a mountain though.'

There was so much hostility and resentment in Matthew's glare that Emlyn could not accept the gift and thought that if any should have it, then it should be the English servant, who obviously held it in great value. There followed a lengthy argument. It was too late to join the others by the time Emlyn got outside with the disputed shield. He went to watch the men come down though. The shield was./heavy and cumbersome. It was red, painted with a leopard and a lily and chevrons in white and yellow. It stood from the ground to his elbow. Emlyn leaned on it and watched the tiny figures slide down the mountain slope. If he climbed up now, it would be too dark to make a safe descent.

The next morning the party of travellers; Ambrose Chillingworth, his wool and pack mules, the Italian ladies, and a few more merchants who saw advantage in the protection of mercenaries, prepared to leave Geneva. They had also acquired a physician who was on his way to Padua, a painter bound for Rome and an astrologer who held them spell bound with tales of planets and magic. It was a risky business travelling over to Italy this early in the spring. The winter had held them bound to Geneva long enough. Traders and pilgrims were forced, through lack of resource, to continue their journey. Tales reached them of the bands of outlaws who roamed the mountain passes. These men, it seemed had no difficulty in finding a way through the snow-bound roads, so it was assumed that a way would be found, God willing! Emlyn suspected that a desire to reach the Italian markets early had a great deal to do with it. He was glad to be leaving Geneva and he hoped that there would be other slopes to try out the shield as the journey progressed. The opportunity came sooner that Emlyn ever imagined.

Angelo watched Josquin and Emlyn climb up a snow drift. They were tiny in the distance. Angelo had sent them ahead in order to gain a superior view from the top of the high ridge which overlooked the road to Milan.

The party had doubled in number since they had left Rouen. Now there were eight merchants and their servants and three students returning to their studies, among them a Dutch artist with no money who was going to Italy to learn the Venetian method of applying colour to the best effect. There was also the astrologer and the thin physician who had been granted a position in Padua. They all rode unhurried through a deep vale that cut between the mountains. They were surrounded by some of Angelo's men. The rest were riding spread out, expecting danger.

From where he sat his horse above them, Angelo could pick out the merchants by the richness of their fur robes. Did they never learn? More wisely attired in sober colours, the Englishman rode among them. They had skirted Lake Geneva and had been travelling slowly for five days. The weather had induced them to start their journey in early March. It had been fine and bright for the first few days, with no sleet or snow, but with a keen wind, sharp with ice. Then it had became dark with storm clouds and sleet. The monasteries and inns along the way had been exceptionally poorly provisioned. Nevertheless, the travellers wished to continue, they thought that the dire weather would offer them protection from the band of brigands who had raided the last group of travellers who had passed this way. They learned with growing unease that only five had survived.

Angelo had been aware of the presence of the outlaws for the past few days. He knew that the party were watched and that the brigands were many and could choose their own time and place to attack. Angelo looked again towards the ridge. Josquin and the boy were above the tree line, angling towards the right, where the snow cut the sky; where the rock fell away to unknown depth on the other side. The blaring red triangle of Emlyn's shield stood out bright against the dazzle of snow.

Angelo turned to the man beside him, surprised that this man had offered to come up here with him. John Moore was in the service of Ambrose Chillingworth and had been with them since the beginning, though Angelo knew little about him. He did know that Ambrose depended on him for most of the organization of his party. Angelo said, more to himself than anyone else, 'This had been a poor winter for employment.'

Moore smiled. He changed the language to Spanish which they both understood. 'Perhaps you should have stayed with the Duke of Alva.'

Angelo spat in the snow. 'Or gone south into Spain,' he said, 'where the Moors have risen in rebellion against their overlords. The Muslims mercenaries come over the sea from North Africa to fight alongside their brothers in faith. The Moors are paying their hired soldiers more than Spain is.'

Moore looked shocked. 'But most of your band are Italian. Wouldn't they refuse to fight for the Moors?'

'What does it matter?' Angelo thumped his heels into his horse's flanks. 'We are stuck here in the Alps and can do nothing to better ourselves until we reach Italy. That task grows more and more difficult as the days progress.'

'You think that we will be waylaid by outlaws?'

Angelo grunted. 'It is quite probable. That's why I've sent those two up there; if they can see ahead, we'll have a better chance of avoiding trouble.'

Moore shaded his eyes and gazed upwards. 'You have accepted the youth as a mercenary?'

Angelo nodded slowly. He had to admit, that he had seen few who could pull a bow like the little monk, even with two of his fingers tied together. From that first night with the fat whore, Angelo's soldiers had made it difficult for the lad to join them, but he had persevered. Angelo admired perseverance and the boy had more of that than the lot of them. They made things difficult still, and still he came back for more. He wore a foolish grin which Angelo knew was a deception, but it had the others beguiled. Most began to think of him as simple-minded and then had accepted him readily enough. Josquin was unaccountably around whenever the rest chose to go too far with the boy.

Angelo had seen boys like him before. They came to him, unskilled hopefuls, running from an unloved past, casting themselves wholeheartedly into a life that only existed in their imaginations. Reality drove most back to where they had come from. Angelo smiled. He had been a mercenary for most of his life, but it was not a path he would have chosen if he could choose again. He said, 'The boy has his uses. He keeps my men amused and that is not an easy task when we are as delayed as this.'

'He is supposed to be taking wool to Italy for his grandfather.'

Angelo chuckled. 'But you are taking the wool to Italy for him instead. Perhaps he finds the task dull.'

The weather which had started grim, had brightened into blinding sunlight. Icy wind still howled through the rocky gap, snatching at flurries of snow, swirling it and grasping it like an invisible hand, to mould the snow into fantastic shapes shadowed with hollows. The wind hummed as it carved, an incessant, mournful dirge, that even Angelo felt crawl under his skin like a spell.

The shadows were deep, soft blue and hard edged as they cut into the blank glaring snow. On either side of the pass, mountains lifted stiff and sheer. To the right, above all the craggy peaks and undiminished by distance, rose the great dome of granite, the White Mountain, the highest in Europe. Around this massif the towering, glacier-carved heights stabbed into the sky.

Angelo could not see well with the glare from the snow. He pulled down the brim of his hat and shaded his eyes further with his hand as he peered up the steep slope. Emlyn stood, facing downwards from a ridge, he was waving his arms. The language of sign was essential in their profession. Angelo read the signal. He said, 'Between thirty and forty men wait in ambush in a hollow around the next bend of the road, half a mile away.'

'You know that from these signals alone?' Moore asked, his voice tinged with admiration. 'Why not call them to come down?'

Angelo grunted negatively. 'It is not considered wise to call out anything at these heights. The slightest noise can bring the whole mountain down on our heads.' He swung his horse around and ploughed through the snow, back down towards the road were the merchants plodded unaware. Moore followed him slowly. Angelo and his men could hold their own against thirty men, but not when lumbered with the women and the rest, who were not fighting men. The snow had drifted into a hidden trench and Angelo could see that the distance was far to the road. He cursed and urged his horse forward. and waved frantically to the riders below. He saw Gandolfi looking up towards him and, with relief, saw him send a soldier to the front to turn the cavalcade about.

Angelo slowed his pace and looked back to see that the English wool carrier was coming. John Moore had come to a standstill. Puzzled, Angelo pulled up his horse. To his horror, Moore lifted his head and cupped his hands around his mouth. He shouted at the top of his voice.

There was a moment of frozen time. The shouted warning echoed incessantly, as if it were an invisible ball bouncing from cliff face to cliff face, thrown back through the cavernous sounding-board of the ravine. The faces of the men below where all turned upwards and were all fixed with an expression of dread. Angelo felt the sluggish passing of time it seemed to take forever before his eyes picked out the two struggling figures high up the mountain. A deafening roar began to resound through the air, increasing at every second as it echoed form the sheer rock and glacier slopes around the valley.

There had been no need for Josquin and Emlyn to climb as high as they did, to see the men amassed beneath them. They had peered from the edge, where the mountain fell away steeply to the small valley below. Black against the snow, a small army, awaited the coming of the travellers. Sunlight glinted off helms and swords. They looked as tiny as insects, so high did the mountains tower above them. Josquin made a rough estimate of their number, and groaned inwardly. These were men as willing to kill and as hard trained as the mercenaries. Hampered with and mules and women, Angelo would have to turn the group and retreat along the route. Josquin pulled Emlyn down from the skyline and told him to signal to

Angelo and the others. He did not know then what was going to happen, but it did not take him long to guess, nor was Emlyn unaware of the danger they now faced. As Moor's shout shattered the silence. They began to run as soon as the signal was acknowledged.

For them time did not slow. High above them, was a fat bulge of winter snow, overhanging precariously. Josquin too knew just how little it would take to start an avalanche. The snow on the slope was knee deep making it impossible to run. They heard the shout and the thunderous echoing answer of the mountain itself. Neither of them looked back. They flew down in leaps and bounds, the powdered snow clinging to them, icy fingers dragging them to lurch, and stagger and fall.

'We are not going to make it!' Josquin cried, his voice high with panic.

The ground began to tremble. A muted rumble filled the air.

Emlyn pulled the shield from his back as he ran. Then he dropped it and sat on it. He yelled to Josquin, 'Get on behind me!'

Josquin hesitated only a moment before he ran forward. He placed his hands on Emlyn's shoulders and shoved hard, scrambling on to the shield before it ran away from him. They pushed with their gloved hands for further speed. The improvised sled, burnished with bees-wax, slipped over the snow like a Flemish ice-skate.

The rumble became a roar, a terrifying, swelling fortissimo. It was as if they were trapped in the thunder of storm clouds, crunching together, boiling with the wrath of tempest. The sky darkened. The air trembled and the sky appeared to split asunder with the jagged, rumbling thunder of the avalanche.

'Christ Jesus!' Josquin cried. He felt as if his head had burst with the sounds of stabbing and snapping in the air around him. The sled bounced and jostled over the mounds and the ripples laid down by the wind like a frozen sea. They both clung on with aching fingers and snatched breath. The impacts drove the air from them in harsh grunts. The sled dipped and slithered and reached the tree line.

Raw, icy wind clawed at their faces as they crashed through the laden trees They steered where the could, dodging branches and trunks, kicking from the ground or off the trees that they sped past in a shower of dropping snow. Still, they were not fast enough.

Josquin gasped as the jagged end of a sharp branch, dig into his left high and broke, leaving a thick splinter of wood embedded in his flesh. He shouted out and reeled backwards. His back hit the ground hard, dragging through the snow. Grasping a handful of Emlyn's clothing he managed to pull himself back up.

A thinner branch whipped across Emlyn's face, lashing his cheeks and the bridge of his nose. He pulled away suddenly, nearly unseating them both. The upset had slowed them. A mass of snow flew past, crushing the young trees in its path. More followed as the avalanche pursued them rapidly closing the distance. On their present path they would be crushed to death.

'Can we change direction?' Josquin shouted. The words were snatched from his mouth. But something of his meaning must have reached Emlyn. He braced himself, Josquin felt his shoulders tense beneath his hands.

Viciously, Emlyn kicked out at a tree to their left as they thundered passed. The shield lurched, spun and shot off at a right angle. It narrowly missed the fall of a huge slap of ice careering down the mountain with a shower of icy debris. The slope was steeper here, with nothing between the racing shield-sled and the ridge edge.

Josquin had no idea how far the erratic decent had brought them. But he had seen what lay on the other side of that drop. And what didn't. It seemed so ridiculous that he released a bitter snort of laughter. They could not jump clear, for to do so would leave them in the path of the solid torrent behind them. They would be smashed at the bottom of the ravine or crushed by the merciless avalanche. The edge was mere seconds away.

Angelo had stayed where he was. The fall of snow offered no threat to him or the fool who had caused it. Snow would pile up in the roadway and not reach this height. Nor were the others in great danger. They had turned with old Gandolfi urging them forward and up the side of the road were the ground rose steeply.

Carmelia had need no urging. The noise terrified her horse and the same fear ran through her impelling her into flight. The horse carried her to safety ahead of the others, plunging through deep snow drifts with Carmelia clinging like a limpet. Pellegrina came close behind her, her voice raised in cries of panic. Carmelia glanced back and saw that she need not have worried about her godmother, Adriana Martinelli was as capable on horseback as a soldier. Angelo's men galloped around the group of merchants while the mountain exploded with snow and noise. Carmelia drew her mount in abruptly, it quivered beneath her. She looked anxiously up at the falling snow across the valley.

'There!' cried Celio, one of the young Sicilians.

Carmelia followed his pointing finger. At first all she could see was the wrath of the cascading ice. Then, in front of it all, the strange slithering blot on which she could make out the two dotted heads. The shape flew over the ground like a wingless bird, straight towards the edge. Then it was over, hanging for a second before it plunged out of sight. The avalanche blotted out everything, filling the sky with snow and thunder. She could see nothing, it looked as if the whole top of the mountain had fallen, tumbling, crashing and roaring into the ravine below.

It was over as quickly as it began, like a mass of snow falling off a roof top in the thaw. But its repercussions could be heard cracking the air, throwing the snow off other, distant disturbed heights. Carmelia stared into the thinning mist and saw the mercenary captain as he approached. The men looked relieved, they saw how narrow had been their escape from death.

'Why did the fool shout in the first place?'

'Did he not know that he had just killed two men through his foolishness?

Killed! Carmelia's breath caught.

Angelo rode up to them and offered no answer to their questions. He was alone. Carmelia had never seen him look so angry. He called three of his men to accompany him and find the remains of Josquin and the little monk, were there any to be found. Carmelia urged her horse after them. In the confusion, no one called her back.

When they went over the ledge and left the security of solid ground, Emlyn thought only of prayer. He had even felt a thrill of excitement as the shield carried them hurdling out into the sky.

They were flying!

They were not flying, they were falling.

The shield fell like a stone. It landed on a ledge some distance below, then gathered momentum and slid over the edge. Then they were falling again. They hit three more outcrops with sickening speed before they plunged on, still clinging to the shield as if it would sprout wings. The ledges had slowed them and the snow they had dislodged and fallen before them. They both screamed as they made the final drop; voices that were cut off short as they hit the ground. The shield and its burden thumped and sank into three feet of soft snow, undamaged. Josquin and Emlyn sat where they had landed; their eyes and mouths open in disbelief.

Apart from the crackle of distant avalanches, silence reigned. After a long while, Josquin stood up. He bent over like an old man and massaged his back groaning. He made creaking noises as each limb straightened and was found to be unbroken. His thigh was soaked in blood.

Emlyn remained were he was, pinned shrike-wise to the shield; stunned by the incredulity of being alive. He felt wrapped in magic. Nothing could harm you ever, if you had fallen off a mountain and survived.

Noticing that he was, after all injured, Josquin sat down and drew out a knife from his belt. He cut the cloth of his woollen hose and exposed the embedded splinter.

Emlyn jumped to his feet, fell over in the deep snow and then stood again. He examined Josquin's wound with ghoulish curiosity and shook his head, tutting to himself.

'Well?' Josquin. demanded. 'Can you get it out?'

'How?' Emlyn turned pale.

'The end is below my skin, so you will have to cut it out. Slide the knife down a bit where the wood entered. When you have revealed enough to grip, just grab it and pull.'

Emlyn said, 'Do I have to? Can't it wait for one better used to this sort of thing?'

'Why? Are you afraid?'

Emlyn sat back on his haunches and shook his head. He grinned and said, 'Not for myself.'

'Then for Christ's sake do it!' Josquin ordered. He dropped back to lean on his elbows and added, 'It's about time you did something for me.'

'I thought I just had,' said Emlyn. He looked up towards the towering mountain they had just fallen off. He took the knife and although his hands shook, he cut into the flesh and drew out the wood splinter. It was as long as his hand and as thick as two fingers. Josquin shuddered in pain. He held his hand to the open cut when the blood flowed and startlingly marred the snow. The wound was not deep, but looked blue and painful. Emlyn tore a strip of cloth from his shirt and bound the wound tightly.

Emlyn dug the life-saving shield out and sat on it. Josquin seemed to melt like wax, subsiding to the snow with his hands behind his head and a stretched grin, bubbling into laughter. Emlyn laughed with him. They had escaped death and it was wonderful to be alive. Absolute stillness descended, a pall of Godlike silence. Tiny particles of snow, still falling in the aftermath, powdered the air and settled like a loving caress on the two prone figures and the old shield. In time the mist thinned. Dying sunlight poured onto the Alpine slopes and crags, trapping the ice crystals in scintillating gold dust. The burdened trees came alight like warm glowing candles and cast long, motionless shadows fingering across the snow.

Emlyn said, 'Do you think the others are safe?' He stood, brushing the snow from his tattered clothing.

With a plaintive groan, Josquin rose beside him like a half finished snowman. He said, 'Do you think any of them are alive?'

Emlyn looked at him in stunned horror. His mind had not yet considered that possibility, the possible death of the others. 'They would have escaped the fall if they rode quickly,' he replied, more to reassure himself than the Dutchman. They trudged off in what they both agreed, must be the right direction.

After some time, Emlyn realised that Josquin was not with him. He stopped and looked back. Josquin was walking very slowly, moaning and complaining dramatically. Emlyn's body was aching all over; he guessed that Josquin must feel the same, worse with the wound in his thigh. Emlyn trampled back. 'It was only a splinter,' he said accusingly. 'And it is down hill all the way.'

'Only a splinter!' Josquin cried indignantly. 'Is this how you repay me for saving you from death and from saving your from a fate even worse than death?'

Emlyn looked at him with one raised, snow-speckled eyebrow, as if in serious thought. 'If I help you, I shall have to leave the shield behind, to which, you may just recall, we both owe our lives.'

Josquin sat down suddenly and fixed his eyes on the setting sun and the spread of astounding beauty. The mountains looked as if they were made out of pure gold. 'I see,' he said, 'my worth is reduced to that of a scrap of tin. You meant to do that all the time didn't you? That's why you brought the cursed thing!'

Emlyn remained standing and watched the sun with him. After a minute or two he said, 'Shall we do it again? It is a very gentle slope.'

Josquin stood slowly, turning as he did so. He shook his head like a tired beast. 'No!' His lips shaped the word theatrically.

'It was just an idea,' Emlyn replied in a small voice.

They had both seen by then, the group of riders emerge from a blue shadow into the peach-flushed snow below. Angelo's feathered helmet announced their identity. It would take them nearly an hour to toil up to the top of the mound. They would make their way back, to wherever they were camped for the night, in the dark.

'It is a gentle slope,' said Josquin agreeably. He winked at Emlyn. They both scrambled onto the battered shield and pushed off slowly. This was a pleasant ride. If they gathered too much momentum, Emlyn slowed their decent with his feet, dragging them through the snow.

'Besides,' added Josquin when they were halfway down, 'I shall need some daylight to see Angelo's face while I pull out his tongue for shouting.'

The earth didn't tremble, the sky didn't reel, the air didn't boom. The snow stayed where it was supposed to stay, and the golden hill lowered them down its side with a whisper of tenderness.

After the day of catastrophe, Carmelia lay awake on the cold straw pallet. Beside her, Pellegrina lay in peaceful repose. Carmelia had not realised until that day how loud Pellegrina could scream; she was almost as loud as the avalanche. On the other side of the tent, behind a thin curtain of linen, Carmelia's godmother slept. Adriana Martinelli did not like the cold and this had taken her mind off everything else, except for the boy, who's hand she had cured so expertly. Although she would never admit to it, Carmelia knew that Adriana Martinelli had come to care for him, especially since she had discovered from the Englishman that Emlyn had no parents and was all alone in the world. Carmelia wondered if Adriana still felt anything towards Josquin, after all, she had taken him as her lover in Rouen and he had been forgiven. Carmelia had seen him with Adriana more frequently of late and Adriana's joy on learning that both the young men were safe, had not been artifice. A miracle saved them, Adriana had said over supper; a miracle had brought them back safely from the jaws of death. They had even brought food with them. A doe, having escaped death from the falling snow and met it instead at the point of a arrow. Carmelia had seen the kill. Emlyn Tomas had shot it on the trek back.

The Englishman had been upset when they had all returned; his steward John Moore was missing and Chillingworth had taken a party in search of him. Although they had searched until darkness, no sign of the man had been found. The merchant had tried to send Angelo into the darkness to look again, but Angelo had spat in the snow and said that it served the fool right; shouting as he had done.

Carmelia sat up and listened, waiting. All of the women were sound asleep. She groped about in the darkness, found one boot and then the other and swiftly pulled them on to frozen feet. She felt crowded and imprisoned by guardians. During the long weeks in Geneva and on this slow, cold journey, she had not had a moment to herself. She almost wished that she was back in the convent, where it was easy to slip away into the walled gardens and find a place to be alone. Her favourite place, for all the years that she had spent there, had been a little grove where a statue of the virgin stood framed with flowering shrubs and old rose bushes. It was surrounded by tall yew hedges, a tiny, secret place, forgotten and private. Since Carmelia had left the confines of the convent, her days had been filled with changing scenes and brilliant winter colour and faces, most of which belonged to men. Men were a rare sight inside the convent walls. Obviously, that was the reason for all this protection. Did Adriana Martinelli think that should her charge escape her vigilance, she would throw herself at the feet of the nearest man and beg him to seduce her? Pellegrina might. Carmelia hoped that she would have her own choice of man to do whatever women did when they caught one. But she would not, she was going to Venice to be wed to someone of someone else's choice.

She pulled a warm woollen robe over her head and pulled Pellegrina's shawl from where it lay draped across a travelling trunk. Stepping over the four serving women on the floor, she reached the tent flap without disturbing any. She unlaced the fastening with shaking fingers and stepped out into the night.

The tents had been set up in the snow, protected from the worse of the wind by a screen of trees. Outside the tent all were still, asleep under a dome of twinkling stars and a fat moon newly risen. She could see the dark outlines of the sentries on the periphery of the camp. Three more sat by the fire dozing. The mercenary leader was not taking any chances. The light was surprisingly good, she could see the mountains, blue-white against the starlit sky. Carmelia had crossed the Alps just once before, at the age of seven. That memory had faded as had the memory of her mother and father. She had, among her personal belongings, a miniature painting of her mother Juliana. The pretty, heart-shaped face was of a girl hardly older than herself. Her mother had written to her once or twice a year since Carmelia had left as a child. The letters were full of sensible advice and lengthy sermons about God. Carmelia could not guess how time would have changed the face in the picture. Would she know her own mother? All she recalled of her father was that he was large and he had frightened her.

During the journey from Geneva, Carmelia had been captivated by the austere, forbidding beauty of the craggy peaks. At first she had thought them bereft of colour; grey scars whose bare rock rose above snow laden contours, deeply cut by blue shadow. The only show of colour had been in the deep green of the pine trees and these were mostly covered by the cold snow. But the wide spread of snow became like an artist's canvas when the gold of sunlight fell upon it. The rarely seen sunsets had been awesome in beauty; the bloodied sky had spread on every patch of white and washed it with hot madder.

Carmelia tiptoed from one tent to another, avoiding the light from the central fire. If she made for the line of trees off to the side, she would be hidden from the camp. She could obey the call of nature in privacy and get her bottom cold and she could be on her own for a short, precious time. Any longer out in this frozen air, she felt would be unwise. She could see, directly in her line of flight, one of the guards, Flavio, dozing. She gave him a wide berth. He was not asleep.

'Where are you going?' He called out as she tried to sneak past. Although he was young looking, his hair was white.

'Where do you think,' she replied. She stopped and placed her hands on her hips.

'If you are going into the trees, I will follow you, to watch out for you.' His breath smoked through the air. His face was as round as the moon.

'Don't be ridiculous! It is only just there, what harm could possibly come to me?'

He smiled tolerantly at her. 'You could be eaten by wolves or carried off by those thieves we made such a fuss avoiding.'

'There are no wolves here and no thieves either. They are all on the other side of the avalanche. Why should they come all the way back, when we are going in their direction anyway? All they have to do is wait for us to come.'

He took hold of her arm to prevent her from going further.

Carmelia pulled away from him. 'Let me go, before I have an embarrassing accident,' she pleaded. He shook his head. 'If you don't,' Carmelia added threateningly, 'you shall hear from my guardian!'

'I need an ages,' she replied. 'Please Flavio!'

'Promise not to go too far,' he said, his round face beamed with a forgiving smile.

He stepped back. 'Go then.' he said.

She gave him a sweet smile in return and crunched across the snow, leaving the security of the camp behind her. The night was bitterly cold. Once free, she ran to keep warm, she sang and skipped through the night shadows, dodging the snowy branches. She ran until she was out of breath and could run no further. She sat in the snow. There was no one anywhere near her. She was alone with the tall pines and their snowy mantles and a wide area of pure white, printed only with her swirling footprints. A night bird cried and was answered by another far off down the valley. Owl wings spread against the moon.

Carmelia dropped her head into her hands and wept. Long held tears flowed down her cheeks, frozen before they hit the snow. Her shoulders shook with sobs of utter misery. She did not know who would be her husband, but she was convinced that he would be old, Venetian men were renowned for their custom of marriage when they were as old as thirty.

That was bad enough, but what if she was sold off to one older still? Forty? Sixty?

She thought about Emlyn Tomas who was a little older than her. She had seen him near naked and he was like a young boy, like the school boys who swam in the stream near the convent in the summer. She thought of the stories, that had held her spellbound, cherishing her candle to read by, alone in her tiny room. Tales of knights and heroes, of princes and noblemen, all handsome, all brave, all young and all with sweet words of love on their lips.

What if her chosen husband was as old as the man Pellegrina had been with in the stable at her godmother's house in the summer. She had thought that the man was a priest but then realised that this could not be, for priests did not do what he was doing. They had not seen her. Pellegrina had laughed. The man had been fat and Carmelia had seen the sweat running down his face and dripping off his chin as he pushed his body curiously back and forth. Pellegrina had cried and Carmelia had nearly run to her aid. Then Pellegrina had made a different noise, a deep guttural sound that was not pain or fear. Carmelia had run away. She had never mentioned any of this to her maid. Pellegrina had appeared in a new dress shortly afterwards and she had not been harmed at all. Her belly had stayed flat and not grown with a baby in it.

Memory brought a fresh flood of tears. Carmelia was very cold and knew she had better start back before the guard came out to look for her.

'Mademoiselle?' The voice called softly from the trees.

Carmelia jumped up with a gasp of surprise and whimpered in fear.

A figure emerged from the shadows and walked out into the moonlight. 'It's only me,' he called reassuringly in his improving Italian. 'You should not be out here with none to protect you.'

'Against what?' Carmelia said breathlessly.

'Flavio thinks that you have be eaten by wolves,' said Emlyn. 'I see that you are still whole.'

'And are you going to eat me?' Carmelia was suddenly filled with that inexplicable excitement. 'You will have to catch me first!' She gathered her skirts in frozen hands and ran. He had hardly noticed her on the ride back in the dark after he had come down the slope on a sled. Surely this was an invitation that he could not refuse?

He came after her, before she disappeared into the darkness of the forest. He was slow and she had to wait at one stage for him to catch sight of her again. She was breathless with laughter. A tree showered her with snow. It wasn't a tree, it was a snow ball. She looked over her shoulder and still running, gathered snow and pressed it into a hard ball. Her hands ached with cold. When he was near enough, she threw the snowball and caught him between the eyes. He cried out and dropped as if felled by a log.

She waited. He didn't move. She took a few steps towards him. 'are you all right?' she called, creeping closer.

With a wolf howl, he leaped up and grasped her, preventing her escape.

She writhed and struggled and laughed. Then she stood still and looked up at him. His face was lit with moonlight. She could see sickle slithers of light in his eyes, twin replicas of the moon. When he smiled, another white crescent appeared. Her lips parted and her breast rose and fell from the exertion.

Emlyn bent and kissed her.

He held her close to him. She did not pull away. She could feel his taut, cold flesh under the thin shirt he was wearing. He was trembling with cold. Her response, after a moment, was as eager as his. His lips were cold on hers. A frozen kiss. A burning kiss. A kiss which fanned the new flame in Carmelia's heart. She shuddered from head to foot.

He released her, stepped away and stood wide eyed with the shock of what he had done. 'I'm s..sorry,' he stammered. His teeth chattered. 'Will you forgive me? I don't know what...'

'Forgive you?' she said with feigned scorn. 'Never!'

She could see that he did not know what to say. Here, in the privacy of snow-laden Alps, they stood silent, bathed in moonlight. Her lips burned with the memory of their stolen kiss. She could not remove her eyes from him. He looked like some frosty, winter sprite, risen from the icy wastes to claim her soul.

'Not ever?' he asked eventually. His lips curled with the hint of a smile.

She gave him a sidelong glance, her head tilted considering. 'I might if you were to do that again,' she whispered.

They sat together until they were too cold to remain any longer. He gave her his gloves. He said, 'We must go back or your godmother will take a stick to me.'

'To me too,' she replied.

He pulled her to her feet, brushing away the snow. They began to walk, tightly holding each other. Emlyn said, 'You told me that you were returning to Venice to be married?'

It was a hurtful question, considering. She nodded her head and shivered against him. 'I do not know who to yet.'

He said, 'Your father is a great merchant banker in Venice. Your mother is his second wife and he has no other children. You are a treasured girl and there will be suitors clamouring at your door and wailing under your window.'

She could see the light from the camp as they drew near. She moved away from him slightly, her joy marred. He stopped under an arch of branches, sparkling with snow. He turned her to face him. She could see nothing of his face, the moon was behind him. She could hear his teeth chatter. She wanted to cry. She had come out alone to the night wanting nothing but privacy. Now she wanted this bitter-sweet moment in his company to last forever. 'Why?' she asked.

Emlyn shook his head. 'I don't know. Because you gave me the pearls? Because you said we would meet again? If I came to your door in Venice with songs of love, may I hope for a chance to see you?'

'You are laughing at me!' she accused him.

'Is it a hopeless cause then?'

'My family is very wealthy and you have nothing at all. They would throw you in the Lagoon.'

He put his arm around her shoulders and they continued walking. Before they reached the tents, he said, 'You are right, but I might get rich if you wait for me, *Morwyn yr Eira.*'

The strange words snatched at her heart and held it fast. She stopped walking and he stood close beside her. 'What do you mean?' she gasped. 'Is that English?'

'No. It means Maiden of the Snow,' he said looking down at her. He gathered her into his arms and nuzzled her hair. His words were soft and musical and seemed to come from deep inside him. 'When I speak of the deepest thoughts in my heart, I use the language of my heart and my love. You are my snow girl. I name you in Welsh, *Morwyn yr Eira.*'

Chapter 37 Barozzi and the Camel Race

The *Cornucopia*, the *Maria* and the Galley paid tribute at Hellespont, sailed between the two castles, along the Thracian coast, passed Rodeso and Peririthe, into the gulf of Selimbrie and eventually lowered the sails below the seven towers of Stamboul. Rowing, they turned at Seraglio point and entered the Golden Horn, or the Scarlet Apple, if you were Turkish. After two days of negotiations and delay, the voyagers were free to enter Galata. In spite of the lengthy procedures, Scipione Barozzi felt as if he was living out a dream.

It took them over a week to settle in the Venetian residence and ten days had passed before Barozzi was contacted by the agent of Tomasso di Vincentini. While waiting, Barozzi had plenty to keep him busy. Matteo Sarzana, the captain of the *Maria* had proved to be a difficult, unpleasant man who argued with just about everything. When the ships had called at various ports on the journey, he had done his utmost to upset and cross examine every plan. Barozzi, who considered himself mild natured and seldom riled, had difficulty in keeping his temper at times. Now that they had arrived, matters had improved somewhat, Matteo Sarzana was forced to be pleasant for the sake of the contacts Barozzi held with the Syrian spice trader. As soon as was feasible, the ships would be loaded, turned about and sent back, to arrive in Venice before the end of June. Tomasso had assured them all that this would be possible although his notary, Enrico de Martoni voiced his doubts continuously. He was of a very melancholy nature and seemed to be sneezing all the time as if the air of Constantinople was unsuitable to him. Barozzi was glad that he had come, for Enrico's Turkish was surprisingly good.

Early one morning, when the sun began to touch the land with light and the call to prayer wavered over the roof tops, Barozzi was awakened by the house steward. Despite the hour, he had a visitor. Intrigued, Scipione dressed and washed quickly and hurried outside. A young man greeted him and babbled at him, as soon as he appeared. Barozzi sent for Enrico.

'What is the man saying?' he asked as soon as Enrico arrived looking dishevelled and irritable. They stood in the mosaic courtyard of the

Venetian residence. The air was stringently cold. The Arab boy, had brought three well-bred horses saddled in rich trappings.

'He wishes you to accompany him,' snapped Enrico. 'His master has sent him. I should send him away with a beating for his impertinence.'

'Ask him who his master is?' Barozzi interrupted.

The youth smiled, his teeth were beautifully white and even. His eyes were liquid brown with long lashes, shining with the light of pleasure. His skin was smooth and the colour of honey and his dark hair was curled like a young child's. He bowed his head to Barozzi, speaking directly to him as if Enrico didn't exist. 'My master is Ismael the Syrian, effendi,' he announced with pride.

After hearing Enrico, Scipione smiled back. 'Ah good!' he exclaimed. 'Tell him I'll come at once. Enrico, do I need a Janissary as escort?'

'I should think it impossible to go anywhere without one,' Enrico replied. 'I advise you again Messer Barozzi, send the boy away. These people are not to be trusted. Look at those bells at his wrist! You never know what hive of sin he will lead you to.'

'Enrico.'

'He may leave you somewhere and demand payment to bring you back. They are devils these people. You will be robbed and stabbed to death.'

'Enough for the love of God!'

Red faced, Enrico glared at his superior. 'They all think they know it all as soon as they get here,' he said with his nose in the air.

'You may go Enrico, the boy and I will manage with hand signals. His master is the man who will supply us with the spice. I assure you, I have nothing to fear. I shall take my servant Marco with me. Unless you would like to come?'

Enrico turned about and hurried inside mumbling about catamites.

Before they mounted, the boy gave Scipione and his servant a camel hair burnous each, to conceal their European attire. With a thrill of private delight, Scipione pulled the hood up, hiding his round face in shadow. Was this to fool the Janissary guard, who up till then had followed him everywhere?

The Janissary was not fooled for a moment. He and Barozzi had got on quite well together, considering the lack of common language. His name was Ahmet and he was fat and idle. They laughed and smiled a lot at each other. At the gate Ahmet and the Arab boy conversed for some time in Turkish. Barozzi gathered from their expressions that the topic was himself, and was cause for great amusement. At last, the boy mounted and made his way out of the compound with Scipione and Marco following. Behind them Ahmet stood and waved happily allowing them to go without him.

Scipione drank in the sights around him with open curiosity. He could see the tower of Christ, built by Anastasius which overlooked Galata, its dark windows looked like blank eyes, watching the passing of time. This was the first time since Barozzi had arrived that he had left the residency without an entourage of servants and officials. He had eaten Italian, spoken Italian and breathed Italian, while the sounds, scents and essences of Constantinople had beckoned and tempted him from every corner. Disguised in their hooded cloaks, he and Marco blended with the multitude of traders, even if they had not been dressed as such, few would glance their way, for Galata contained a myriad of nations. All tongues and all guises drifted through the markets, some thronging streets with ultimate patience, others waving their arms and raising their voices in loud dispute. Some called out to the young man leading them and he returned their greeting with his bright smile and a wave of his musical wrist.

There were hundreds of ships moored in the harbour. In winter up to a thousand would lie in the half mile of the Golden Horn. Being Venetian, Barozzi gave them a cursory glance before his eyes sought more interesting sights. The riders pulled aside often to make room for rumbling carts, trains of mules or asses carrying veiled women to the public baths or blocking the narrow streets with the burden of alfalfa or kindling strapped upon their backs. At the street sides, steps provided platforms for the selling of goods, burnished brass, tooled leather, beads and baubles and all manner of food stuffs. In Galata inns could be seen, where the foreigners could buy wine. Barozzi wondered if they were all foreigners on this shore, for the Turks had made this their dominion for only a hundred years and before that, it had been the meeting place of nations under Byzantine rule. This gateway to the East contained Turks, Arabs, Persians, Jews, Franks, Venetians, Florentine s, Greeks, Armenians; a multitude of nations and various religions, tolerating each other for the sake of trade.

They soon left the crowded, wooden houses with the places of worship nestled between them like beacons. The road took them upwards, through the luscious greenery of orchards powdered with blossom. They past the walled houses of the wealthy merchants, these were surrounded with flowering gardens filled birdsong.

After an hour, they came to a building that looked as if it had stood since the age of Constantine. Above the ancient gate, a vine clutched the wall with woody fingers, its gnarled branches as thick as forearms. It was twined about by flowering jasmine, the waxy flowers exuding exotic perfume. In the inner courtyard, there were six mounted men in Arab and Turkish dress and a seventh who's hat was trimmed with long fur and who's clothing resembled the style of the White Sheep tribe of Turkoman. He had an air of dignity about him. He was a tall bearded man with a curved blade stuck into a thick silk band around his waist. Although he looked more like a war lord than a trader, Barozzi guessed that this must be the merchant, Ismael. Seeing the new arrivals, he rode forward and greeted Barozzi in Arabic. 'Salaam Aleikum, Peace be with you.'

'Aleikum Salaam, And also with you,' replied Scipione correctly. These were the only words of Arabic he had picked up and remembered whilst in Alexandria. Yet this man was no Arab. Scipione could not place his origin, his eyes were grey and his manner was that of a men used to riches and instant obedience.

When he drew level, Ismael leaned forward in the saddle and smiled. He, 'We are going to a race. I thought you might like to come.'

'God be praised!' cried Scipione. 'You speak Greek!'

'It is the language of Constantinople, we would be lost here without it,' he answered. 'Do you like to place a wager Signor Barozzi?'

'I do, but you have me at a disadvantage, I have little with me,' said Barozzi. He was un-embarrassed by his lack of foresight. A small part of him believed in Enrico's warnings, so he only carried a few coins.

'Then we shall have to ensure that you invest it well,' said Ismael. He winked at Marco and then pulled his stallion around, shouting to his men. They answered in unison, raising their hands, all smiling in anticipation of the days events. Scipione watched with admiration. Their horses were elegant and graceful. 'What a turn of good fortune this is Marco,' he said turning to his young servant.

Marco looked about him anxiously. 'Where are they taking us?' he asked, his voice cracking.

Scipione saw that he was afraid, that he did not see this as an adventure but as a fearful ordeal. He was a small, dark youth of eighteen and had been Barozzi's servant for three years. Barozzi had not taken him when he had travelled to Egypt and had regretted the decision. Marco had leapt at the chance to come to Stamboul. Now he looked as if he was not so sure.

'We are going to a horse race,' Scipione explained. 'That man with the fur hat, is the merchant who will fill our holds with spice. You have nothing to fear Marco. You haven't got any money have you by any chance?'

Marco shook his head and made a visible effort to relax, offering a wan smile.

They left the exotic gardens and the impressive merchant's houses and climbed further upwards. They rode through fields of olive, pomegranate and citrus trees. The earth was littered with rocks and red stone and the grass was a brittle green, a starling contrast of colour. As the orchards receded the land became steep and jumbles of bare rock lay at the base of steep cliffs. Here, stunted pines grew and struggled against the sea winds. After a ride of two hours the party approached an open space where a great crowd were gathered. Craggy rocks rose up behind it, laced with worn paths. Ismael pointed out entrances to dwellings that had been hewn out of the stone, where people still lived. At the base of the rock was a scattering of red roofed houses and walls constructed from small stones. Cypress trees and straggly shrubs provided a little shade. Although the sky was bright, a cold wind blew from the north, snatching at hair and clothing.

Soon Scipione and Marco found themselves left alone. They stood on the outskirts of the crowd, enraptured by the colour and noisy babble of activity. Barozzi identified Ismael by his height and the distinctive hat. He was talking with a stout Arab, waving his hands for emphasis like an Italian. At his side stood a small boy of about six or seven. There were hundreds of camels with bright tassels hanging from their mouths. Barozzi had already given Ismael the little money he carried. He guessed that the Syrian was placing wagers for himself and his guest.

'I fear you have lost your coin,' said Marco. 'They can take advantage of us, for we know nothing of their customs.'

'I shall not miss it,' answered Scipione. 'What interests me more is the reason we have been brought here.'

'Where are the racing horses?' said Marco. 'I see only saddle mounts. Perhaps they mean to race those.'

Scipione looked over the crowd. Some of the camels were ridden by boys, like the one Ismael had near him. 'Camels,' he said. 'We are here to watch a camel race.'

Ismael approached with the child trotting at his side. The boy wore a little embroidered cap made out of felt and a short waistcoat glittering with braid and sequins.

'The first thirty camels will run soon,' Ismael explained. 'The one on the far end with the white trimmings is Shaitan. She is mine. With Bachir Safar here, on her back, she will win.'

'This small child is to ride the camel?' asked Scipione in disbelief.

'We use boys because they are light and can stay with the camel until she reaches the finish. Bachir is famed for his skill and courage.' Ismael placed an affectionate hand on the child's head. Bachir grinned up, his eyes shining with pride. Ismael released him, giving him a little shove. 'Go and find Koçi, brave warrior and make your master proud.'

Bachir ran off, disappearing within seconds. The line of camels waited, bawling and grumbling. Barozzi squinted through the dust. 'How far will they run?'

'Six miles. We will ride ahead to see them. There is nothing quite like a camel race my friend. Wherever they go, the Arabs race their camels. It is traditional and brings the people together. Some will return rich and others loose all they own, it is fate.'

'But they are not all Arabs here,' said Barozzi, even he knew a Turk from an Arab.

'It is so,' agreed Ismael. 'There are Turks here, Serbs, Egyptians, Greeks, Syrians. It is one thing all men have in common, the desire to gamble.'

The crowd, some mounted others running alongside, surged forward. Signals passed from one to another. A single musket shot rang through the air, a muffled thud distinctive above the noise. The camels began to lope forward, the air filled with their guttural complaints. On either side, cheers and shouts urged them on. Riding with the Syrian, Scipione and Marco galloped ahead. Scipione smiled at his servant. Marco's doubts and fears had dissolved. This was an adventure for the young man and his joy was undisguised. They were joined by the youth Koçi, who had collected them that morning Koçi encouraged Marco to leave the company of older men, to race ahead and watch the lead camels. Barozzi was glad to let him go.

'Yala ! Yala!!' the crowd shouted. The camels disappeared in a cloud of dust. The crowd surged alongside calling and waving their arms. Barozzi and Ismael urged their mounts to greater speed. 'I have faith in my Shaitan,'' cried Ismael. 'She will run them all to the ground.'

'Can a horse outrun a camel?' called Scipione above the noise.

'Without doubt,' answered Ismael, 'but not as far. They do not have the brave heart of the camel, their energy is expended in speed not endurance.' He turned with a wide smile 'You will see, for you will be showered with sequins before this day's end, by Allah's will.'

Yes, and by God's! thought Barozzi joyfully.

The shouting increased as the camels passed the half-way mark. The boy Bachir, was hardly discernible among the thirty brown, eager faces, driving their mounts to the finish. The camel he rode was a lighter shade, almost the yellow of butter with a ruff of longer hair around its neck. Shaitan was a few paces behind the two in the lead. They did not use saddles, but a series of straps that held the child riders securely behind the rounded hump. Barozzi could hear the camel's name ring through the air. 'Shaitan! Shaitan!'

'What is the meaning of the beasts name?' he called across to his host.

'Devil,' Ismael laughed. 'They say it is a name of ill luck, but she has proved them wrong again and again. This is but the beginning. I have twelve camels who will run before the day is done.'

Barozzi looked at him with new respect.

An anguished howl rose. Scipione looked up in time to see a camel stumble and fall, its rider going down in a swirl of dust. It looked as if the boy had been injured, but the crowd were not diverted. They were reaching the finish, Shaitan running neck to neck with the leader. Barozzi saw Bachir's face now, a mask of howling encouragement. The camel's stride lengthened and the watchers went wild as she pulled ahead, running free to the finish.

The noise was deafening, a mixture of anguish and elation. Ismael pushed through the throng and made his way to Bachir's side. He lifted the boy down from Shaitan's back and embraced him. Then he turned to his camel and wrapped his arms around her neck, his face as animated as Bachir's. Keeping clear of the mass of bodies, Scipione watched with pleasure. This Ismael was an unusual man, not at all like Barozzi had expected.

This was but the first race and many followed, running up and down the course throughout the day. All watched with the same wild enthusiasm. At midday when the sun had risen warm and bright, Koçi, brought Scipione a plate of figs and pomegranates and a drink that looked like mud and tasted like mud with honey in it. The coins he had surrendered doubled, tripled and continued to grow. Ismael's camels were bred for racing, they all proved their worth. Ismael bet on others too, when his own were not running, he had a good eye for spotting potential winners. He came to share the meal with the Venetian, squatting comfortably under a tree in a posture Barozzi didn't attempt to emulate.

'Do they know or care that I am Venetian?' asked Barozzi.

'They know that you are the man I was expecting and care not. Christian and Muslim can get on when purpose serves. Even the Sultan has made peace with Hungry.'

'He has?' said Barozzi, surprised at this valuable news. He and the Venetian Ambassador had talked of the Turkish war with Hungry only two days before. Now, Ismael was giving him a priceless piece of information. If Turkey had made peace with Hungry, where now would the Sultan turn to make war? This question would cause the Christian powers to draw in their breath with dreaded expectation. Barozzi looked at the trader. Ismael held his gaze for a moment, as if to stress the point he had just made, then he turned away and chose a ripe fig from the plate in front of him.

Like all Venetians away from home, Barozzi knew the value of gathering information. He had been approached by Sebastiano Erizzo, a member of the Senate, before he left Venice. Erizzo had asked him to keep an eye open here, an ear cocked there, to be of whatever service he could to the Republic of Venice. Barozzi had expected this and was secretly pleased. He had known Erizzo for many years and had often assisted him. Barozzi and Ismael talked no more on the subject, but Barozzi was in no doubt that he had been told this for the specific purpose of informing Venice.

As the day drew to an end and the sun began to slant towards evening, Ismael approached the cypress tree where Barozzi stood with the horses. He carried a steaming pot and two enamel cups. Barozzi watched with distaste as more mud-black liquid poured from the spout. Ismael handed him a cup. 'It is the custom now,' he explained, 'for the camel owners or trainers to take part in a final race. It is for pleasure alone and no wagers are accepted. Would you like to try?'

'Fortunately for me,' Barozzi answered, 'I do not own a camel.'

'Then you must take one of mine,' urged Ismael smiling. 'Try Sirocco. He is of a mild temperament and the most lightly to treat a Frank with sympathy.'

'I am a fat man and I have never ridden a camel,' protested Barozzi.

'That is no problem,' said Ismael seriously. 'You will be secured by the straps. It is as simple as riding an elephant.'

'Then I shall have no trouble, as I ride elephants all the time,' added Scipione cynically.

Ismael took his arm and urged him to his feet. Barozzi followed the man with a sinking feeling. He said, 'What happened to the boy who fell in the first race?'

'He did not suffer, by Allah's mercy,' said Ismael. 'We have only lost that one today. Are you afraid? I am sorry, I should not have presumed.'

'Afraid?' cried Barozzi indignantly. 'Me afraid of a camel? Heaven Forbid!'

By the time the camels were assembled, there were more than fifty. Good humoured, bantering laughter accompanied Barozzi as he scrambled onto the camel's back. Next to him rode the stout Arab whom Ismael had talked with earlier. The two large men eyed each other. The Arab smiled, he had pearls woven into his thick beard. Barozzi smiled tentatively, and shifted his weight. With hand signals the Arab showed him how to sit with better comfort and demonstrated how to urge the camel to greater speed when the need arose. The animal began to move, it turned around and around like a dog chasing its tail, heehawing with the voice of a donkey. Barozzi felt quite dizzy by the time the camel was under control.

A Christian among Muslims, Barozzi felt that he must make a good effort in spite of his fear. Someone pulled at his boot. He looked down, it seemed a long way to the ground. Marco stood grinning up at him, his face mirroring the pride he felt. 'Good luck Messer Barozzi,' he laughed. 'Just stay on and try and reach the end in one piece.'

'I have no intention to do otherwise!' announced Barozzi bravely.

Ismael rode towards him to take his place in the line up. He was mounted on Shaitan and looked more like a desert pasha than a spice dealer, more like he was riding to do battle than taking part in a camel race.

There was a period of silence before the musket shot rang through the air. The race began.

Barozzi was alarmed by the motion of the camel. He gripped with his knees and tried to stay on by will power alone. It was not enough. Before long, he began to slide. A rider came up behind him and gave him a good natured shove as he passed by. Barozzi lurched over the opposite side, the ground reeling below him, then righted himself with a wriggle. He clung on wrapping his arms around the swaying hump, his dignity gone to the winds.

What followed was a nightmare. At one stage, Barozzi felt his rump slide backwards, he was in danger of falling and being trampled by the oncoming riders. He tried to pull himself up and slid back further. The air was filled with dust and the clamour of thundering cloven feet. A hand grasped the back of Barozzi's clothing and yanked him forward. The impetus was enough to regain his seat. With a prayer, Barozzi pulled himself up further and schooled himself to endure the unnatural motion. The camel complained and swung her serpentine neck in frustration.

Barozzi saw that his rescuer still rode beside him. Ismael shouted encouragement to him. From what he had seen of the man, Barozzi was surprised that he was not racing to the finish.

'Thank you!' cried Barozzi. 'I'm fine now, you go on.'

Ismael nodded but he did not ride ahead. He spoke to the camels in Arabic and snatched at Barozzi's rein. The camel began to run faster, keeping pace with Shaitan. Barozzi closed his eyes, his lips voicing prayer. He was vaguely aware of the other riders thundering past. 'Holy Virgin protect me!' he gasped through clenched teeth. 'Lord and all the saints of heaven, let me stay on this devilish monster. San Marco get me through this and I shall not place another wager for a year!'

He and Ismael did not win, but they were among the first camels to finish the race. Cheers greeted them as Ismael drew the mounts to a stop. Barozzi could not get off quick enough. He landed on his buttocks with a thud and a puff of dust.

With contrasting agility, Ismael dismounted beside him. 'I should have not forced this upon you,' he laughed.

'On the contrary,' said Barozzi, 'I would not have missed it for all the gold in the Basilica. But nor would I do it again for the same wealth. The good Lord has protected me thus far, to expect more would be testing His patience. Look how they laugh at me!'

'You are a brave man for a Frank,' said Ismael, helping the Venetian to his feet. 'They have laughed at you now, but they admire your courage, you have the stamina of a camel.'

'Thank you, I am sure that was a compliment, but I would appreciate a warning if such a feat is required of me again.'

Ismael smiled. 'Come, we will return before darkness.' He clapped his hands and miraculously from amid the crowds, his men appeared with Marco in tow. 'Well done Signore!' he cried. 'I thought you would fall, praise God that you are safe!'

'So did I,' admitted Barozzi rubbing his backside. 'I am ill suited to racing camels.'

That evening Ismael sent a messenger to the Venetian residence, informing them that Scipione Barozzi would be returning in the morning. Scipione knew that this would not meet the approval of the Venetian ambassador, but he was willing to risk this in order to partake of the feast promised by the Syrian.

The inside of Ismael's house was resplendent with colour. The walls and ceilings were painted with murals of ancient origin, these had been retouched with gold leaf and bright colour. In places the walls were hung with tapestries and appliqué work, it resembled the interior of a nomad's tent. There was little furniture. Richly pattern Persian rugs were strewn in layers across the floor. A collection of rare Canopic urns stood along one wall, the lids depicting Egyptian animals and gods.

Before partaking in the sumptuous meal, Scipione bathed and he had to admit that he felt a great deal better afterwards, he didn't even smell of camel. Marco, he was glad to see, had done the same to comply with the customs of the house. Their clothes too, were taken to be cleaned and they were given a number of Turkish robes. These were worn one on top of the other and fitted Barozzi's ample form with surprising comfort. Marco did not join Barozzi during the meal, he disappeared somewhere with Koçi, Barozzi was not concerned, the youth had managed well enough so far.

The food was plentiful and varied. The conversation light and entertaining. Barozzi tried the new dishes with humorous trepidation. Many were not to his taste but he waded through with an appetite expected of his size. He sat next to Ismael, who translated his comments to the other guests. They were seated on cushions around a low table. The guests were mostly different faces than the ones Barozzi had spent the day with.

Eventually, when the tables were cleared away and more black, hot mud was served in delicate, gem-studded cups, the conversation became more sober.

Barozzi relaxed and sipped the hot liquid with distaste. Servants seemed to appear from nowhere and disappeared again, just as mysteriously. There were nine guests not including himself. They are an odd mixture, thought Barozzi, but then this surely is an odd house. The oldest member of the party looked like an Imam in his dark gown. To his right, sat three men with flowing beards and tall conical hats. Barozzi judged them to be Turks. There was a tall, dignified scholar with a neat pointed beard, Barozzi had learnt that he was Persian. The three men to the right of the Venetian were certainly Arabs. The familiar stout figure of the camel racer who had assisted him sat in the middle. He had been introduced as Abu Abdullah of Ulcinj. The last guest, Barozzi could not begin to guess the origin of. He was small and round with a grey wispy beard and a thin moustache. His skin was of a yellowed hue and he spoke seldom. He listened more to the Greek than the multi-tongued flow of conversation, he was introduced with the peculiar name of Chung K'uei. Ismael himself, played the perfect host, taking little part in the talk but participating through his skill as interpreter.

Now, turning to Barozzi he said, 'Mahmud Reshid asks if the Venetians are ostracised by Rome for their allegiance with the Sublime Port?'

Barozzi looked across the room at the Imam, who had made this inquiry. This was a question he had not expected. Until now, they had managed to avoid the topic of religion, as this most surely was. He answered carefully. 'There are some who have shown objection and others who are encouraged by the progress we have made through trade.'

'Is this objection,' said Reshid, through the Syrian, 'on the grounds of belief? I have heard that your Holy Man in Rome is revered for his piety.'

'I am but a merchant,' answered Barozzi. 'Matters of the church I leave to those most fit to deal with. I am Christian and worship as I have been taught by my elders.'

'In spite of this,' smiled Reshid, 'we have found you a worthy man. Our differences however will always stand between our two people.'

'In my country, religion is not that of the Muslim or the Christian,' said the little, round man, Chung K'uei, giving his views for the first time that evening. 'We are taught that, as God fashioned different plants and trees for different parts of the earth, so are there different ways of praising Him.'

'Do you not then, have wars of religion in your land?' asked Barozzi interested.

'We have our differences,' he replied, 'and there are warriors among our priests as there are with yours, but we have a great respect for life. Some among us will even spare the life of a flea, or sweep the ground as they walk, lest they tread upon some tiny living creature.'

'It is difficult to see how they can survive with such a gentle beliefs,' said Barozzi. 'If they spare the fly, what do they do when a great hostile force comes before them?'

'They do not wish to see the violence of men. They close their eye or turn away their heads. If they live and die well, according to their teaching, they believe that they return to a better life the next time. They spare the flea in case it is a man on the wheel of life, living out one life in hope of a better.'

'Are they not awarded in Paradise if they live honourably?' asked Reshid.

'The idea of Paradise does not enter into it, for the ultimate goal is to reach Nirvana, a state of non-being. In this, is sought freedom from the struggle of life.'

'Do you mean no immortal soul?' asked Barozzi in disbelief, it was a concept he could not imagine. 'No reward in heaven?'

'We do not believe as such. Life is suffering, death is freedom from suffering,' announced Chung K'uei. The talk continued in this vein until Ismael's voice became croaky and worn from use.

It was late by the time Mahmud Reshid rose with fluidity to his feet. He bowed to his host 'Masalaem, peace be with you.'

As if this was a signal, the others rose also and took their leave. When all but the Chung K'uei had left, Barozzi stretched until his bones creaked. 'I cannot remember when I last spent a day of such pleasure,' he said to Ismael. 'I am in your debt. May I ask why you have shown such kindness to a Christian and a stranger?'

'I wanted you to have such a day, so that you would know the people who you will be dealing with,' Ismael answered. 'There may not be such an opportunity again for we must turn to business. When do your ships plan to sail?'

'As soon as they may,' answered Barozzi.

'They will be fully provisioned in a week.'

'Then I stand doubly in your debt,' said Barozzi. 'It will be a great advantage to leave so soon. I thank you for this day that I shall never forget.'

Ismael yawned and smiled tiredly. 'I admit that it was for my own sake as well as yours. I hope that we will have some trust between us.'

'Trust?' laughed Barozzi, 'I think I can trust a man who takes a thin purse from me and gives it back well fattened. But a man who forces me to ride a camel?'

Chapter 38 Milan

Ambrose refused to listen to any argument concerning his decision to halt the journey. And because the mercenaries were in his employ, the other travellers were forced to wait. Most of them joined in the search for John Moore which the Englishman directed. Ambrose could not bring himself to abandon the man, even though Moore's horse had returned during the night and there was no more than a slim chance of finding the man alive.

Ambrose had expected Angelo to attempt to talk him out of the delay; there were outlaws close at hand and the fall of snow would not put them off for long. Ambrose had ordered them to leave the tents erect and to leave the women with half the men to protect them. The merchants complained, the women nagged and Angelo made matters more and more difficult. Ambrose had eventually lost his temper. It was very rare for him to display such anger and he had regretted it. To add further injury to his ill temper, Emlyn was not interested in joining the search and seemed not the least bit concerned. He wanted to stay with the women.

'I can't believe what I am hearing!' Ambrose exploded. 'Your grandfather employed the man, I can't believe that you care nothing for his fate.'

'I'm sorry,' said Emlyn, 'it's not that I am heedless of his fate. I hope the man survived the night; I hope he survived so that I can question him. Angelo too, will have some words to say to him. Moore caused the avalanche and I believe that he did so intentionally.'

'Stuff and nonsense! What are you saying?'

'My grandfather told me that Moore had also been employed by my uncle from time to time.' Emlyn explained. 'I think that Moore is still employed by my uncle. Squire Hugh is my guardian and if any misfortune were to happen to me on the way to Italy, who would get the profits from the wool?'

'Gruffydd Hiraethog, who else?'

'No,' Emlyn shook his head. 'Tad-cu drew up everything in my name. If I die on the journey, the wool profit goes to Squire Hugh. There is some enmity between us, it has been thus for many years.'

'So how have you arrived at this conclusion about Moore?'

Emlyn looked at him, a serious expression in his eyes. He said, 'Do you want the long story or the short; being as you are in a hurry?'

'You can tell me as we go.' Ambrose said. He took Emlyn's arm and led him to where the men were assembled. Emlyn had the sense, he was glad to see, not to resist further.

The men spread out in a long line, toiling up the rise that Angelo and Moore had climbed the day before. They walked slowly, hampered by the deep snow. Nobody shouted the man's name.

Matthew and Emlyn walked with Ambrose across the narrow valley. The sun had dimmed and a mist was thickening on the heights. 'If we 'aven't found him by now, 'e's as good as done,' commented Matthew. 'We wasted a whole day for nought.'

'Well, that won't worry you, will it Emlyn?' Ambrose's voice was laced with sarcasm. 'Emlyn thinks that Moore tried to kill him by calling down the mountain.'

'Could 'a done for us all,' said Matthew.

Emlyn said, 'It all began with the oranges on board the *Lauris Nobilis*. Moore poisoned them hoping that I would eat them. I know it sounds ludicrous, but he knew that you didn't like them and Goronwy was unlikely to eat them, as he was being held somewhere else on the ship. As we three were sharing the cabin, it was reasonable to suspect that I might be tempted by the fruit.'

'Lordy!' Matthew spluttered.

Ignoring him, Emlyn continued. 'Moore saw the Spaniards and spoke with them, he had ample time to point a finger in my direction and accuse me of heresy or some deed that would alert Luzon to me. Moore was with you for some time in Southampton remember, he could have found out about the foreign ships from harbour gossip. He was also present when William Cecil arrived. Moore is an inconsequential type of man, no one notices him around the place. He could have discovered much if he set his mind to it.'

They had come to a stop near the mountain of snow that had fallen in the avalanche. The air had turned bitterly cold and Ambrose indicated that they should begin the walk back. 'But, Moore had no Spanish,' he said. 'How could he have spoken with Luzon?'

'That is what he wanted you to believe,' Emlyn added. 'He has travelled through Europe quite often, it is likely that he had picked up enough of the language to get his meaning across. Luzon needed to discover what had happened to the wage fleet, he was probably prepared to believe anything.

It shows a mark of genius on Moore's part. Who would suspect that he had any dealings in such a scheme?'

'Preposterous!' Ambrose exclaimed.

'Not quite as incredible as all that,' said Emlyn. 'I knew that Goronwy could not have played into Luzon's hands with any idea of what he was doing. It was this faith in him that led me to look elsewhere. I could not believe this of Moore either at first. Then there were other happenings.'

'It is merely speculation,' said Ambrose, 'and not enough to accuse the man of betrayal, let alone murder.' Ambrose rubbed his hands together to keep them warm. He had so much trust in Moore that he found Emlyn's story hard to believe; yet, he could not believe either that Emlyn was making the whole thing up. Ambrose remembered that on the journey from Rouen when he had sent Matthew to look for Emlyn, Moore had said, I'll swear he's gone to the Jesuits, he talked about it to me often. Ambrose had felt something was amiss with that statement; Emlyn had hardly spoken to Moore about anything. Ambrose listened with keen interest as Emlyn went on to explain the 'accidents' when he had escaped injury or death.

'I don't suppose we'll ever know the truth of it,' said Ambrose when Emlyn finished speaking. 'Though I can see why you think Moore caused the avalanche.'

Just then a shout when up and was cut off sharply. Ambrose could see a group of men in the near distance. They were standing around a prone figure that was face down and half buried in snow.

Emlyn reached the scene first and dropped to his knees. He turned the body over. John Moore's empty eyes stared up into the sky. He had been dead for hours and his body was stiff. There was no sign of blows or wounds. Ambrose pulled at his ear lope and frowned. 'Poor John Moore,' he said quietly. 'It would appear that his horse bolted from fright during the chaos and he was unable to find his way. He froze to death, God rest his soul.'

They took the body back to the tents with them. The mercenary's priest gave a little service before they committed John Moore to a cold grave. Afterwards, Matthew brought to Ambrose, the purse, a bundle of letters and few personal belongings that Moore had carried. Ambrose intended to send them to Moore's family when he returned to England. Because of the story Emlyn had told him that afternoon, Ambrose opened the letters and found one that he could not read, but he read the name at the bottom, Hugh Morgan. The letter was written in Welsh and Ambrose wrapped it with the others. He would mentioned nothing of it to Emlyn;

whatever Moore had done, it was over now and Emlyn had no need to fear for his safety. To give him the letter now would only lead to further trouble for the boy. Ambrose decided that the whole matter was best left to rest.

The cavalcade set off at first light the next day. They hoped to reach the St Bernard Hospice before the day was done. Angelo sent the guide ahead to ensure that the fall of snow was passable. They would have to climb over the top. It was a journey of twenty-two miles. The sun came out fully by mid morning. The women left their hoods down and the general mood was one of jovial expectancy.

Instead of his usual antics, which had kept them entertained or irritated throughout the journey, Emlyn was quiet. No one fell off a horse. Examining his clothing, Gandolfi discovered that the laces of his hose were not cut. Checking before he mounted, the mercenary leader found nothing unpleasant under his saddle. There were no spiders, or chickens, or rats in any body's anything. They could ride in peace and admire the scenery. There were tumbling mountain streams; shadowed valleys between soft pristine slopes; grey towers of rock patched with snow blots; swathes of deep forest; goats with clanging bells and long dragging, tangled coats and hawks, high above, wings spread in a sky of startling blue. There were jonquils under the trees, poking up through the snow. Emlyn gathered three and presented them, with everyone watching, to Adriana Martinelli. Ambrose noticed that she had the courtesy to blush and that her charge Carmelia watched the young man with glowing eyes. This was not surprising, they were the two youngest members of the party. Emlyn had about him a vividness that Ambrose had not noticed before. Emlyn was so thin he seemed to consist of nothing but skin and bones, though there was no trace of weariness about him, only energy, pride and agility in his gait and in his every movement. He had changed a great deal since he had arrived with Josquin.

Apart from the show of jonquils, Emlyn rode unusually complacent. He had chosen Gandolfi to ride with, Gandolfi only spoke when he had something to say, which was rare. In warfare there was seldom found a voice to match him. Ambrose was riding beside Angelo. He had always liked him, even from days of old when they had fought the French. Angelo was unchanged. His open brusque manner was easy to deal with.

Ambrose had watched Emlyn over the weeks and still knew him no better. One thing he did understand though, was the boy's need to be a soldier. The need was the same as any adventurous youth. Like a boy out of school, Emlyn embraced his freedom with open arms. Warring between youth and maturity, his moods were as up and down as a bucket in a well.

His life up to now, Ambrose supposed, had been one of restriction and servitude. An unwanted bastard who was shunned by family and denied the hope of ever achieving the position he was born to. There was reason enough for anger there. The one person who had offered him affection, his grandfather Gruffydd Hiraethog, had gone off to Calais, just when the child would have needed him most. The boy had been left in the care of his uncle, who gave Emlyn the position of servant and companion to his son Owain. Ambrose had heard of the disasters of that relationship and even witnessed the cousin's animosity that day in Conwy. Then had come the Jesuit college where Emlyn had been sent at the age of thirteen or fourteen.

Now Emlyn was free of authority for the fist time in his life. He was called little monk the archer by the mercenaries, a title which he obviously appreciated. The journey would be a matter of days only and they all looked forward to Italy. Emlyn rode in silence, his head slightly bowed listening. Gandolfi spoke quietly, his hands talking too as they rode. They travelled downward across the Lombard plain away from the heights, winding down to the welcome change of Spring. They had been together for nearly three months, soon their ways would part. Ambrose had received little news from England. The harsh winter and brought most of Northern Europe to a standstill. Letters were more likely to come to Milan now that it was March and hardy ships could come across the sea to Genoa. Ambrose felt a desperate need for news.

They caught up with Josquin, who was riding alone. He looked pale and uncomfortable. 'Not far now,' said Ambrose in encouragement. He had seen the wound left by the splinter in Josquin's leg. Josquin turned and grinned, he looked like a beardless Viking. It was strange, thought Ambrose, how they were drawn to each other's company. Apart from both being men of the north, they shared nothing in common, unless it was an interest in Emlyn Tomas who they both watched now. Ambrose had a suspicion that Josquin was more than he seemed, but what that implied, he had been unable to uncover. However the Dutchman did show an unexpected knowledge concerning the Queen of England and her beleaguered kingdom.

Ambrose said, 'the avalanche must have been terrifying.'

Josquin eased his weight in the saddle. 'Emlyn and the shield,' he replied, 'if he had not taken it we would not have survived.'

'Why did he take it?' Ambrose asked.

Josquin looked at him and smiled. 'He wanted to ride it back down the slope, we would not have got off that mountain without it.'

Ambrose replied. 'Life could be much easier for him if he bent a little. Why does he want to be a soldier? Have you ever seen one less suited?'

Josquin pulled off his fur hat and dragged his fingers through his hair before he replaced it. He said, 'There is nothing preventing Emlyn from fitting into this life as well as any other. At present he sees it as a means to an end.'

'But how can that be better than what I have offered him?' asked Ambrose perplexed.

'I do not know what position you have offered him,' Josquin replied. 'But you have helped him before, he feels that he is in your debt, perhaps that rules his judgement.'

'I was hoping that you might be able to talk him out of it,' said Ambrose. He did not look at Josquin, he did not want to look away from the sunlit snow, against the deep blue sky, the snow was as yellow as dunes.

Josquin's eyes too, remained fixed ahead. 'Emlyn makes his own decisions,' he answered. 'It is strange how often there is purpose in his actions, even when he plays the fool.'

Ambrose remembered Goronwy's words when he had asked about the unfortunate accident on the *Lauris Nobilis. Does there have to be a reason? Emlyn probably did it just to see what would happen. Some poor unfortunate will be blamed for carelessness and punished for the curiosity of Emlyn Tomas. I doubt if it has even occurred to him.* And the words of Gruffydd Hiraethog, *Emlyn dances to his own drum.* Aye, agreed Ambrose, nor cares that none dance to the same beat. But Ambrose would not let go that easily. He felt that if he guarded this boy's life, then God would watch over the life of Christopher. At times, reason told him that this was futile nonsense, but he did not want reason, reason was cold and merciless. If one lived, then so would the other, this was what Ambrose wanted to believe and what gave him small comfort in the growing fear concerning his son.

The monastery, when they reached it, was a large sprawl of old buildings merging with the rock. There was a narrow bridge across a furious stream. The snow was melting, the rills were flowing and the rivers were pouring into Italy. Half of the company were across the stream. A shrill whistle pierced the air. The Astrologer's hired horse, on the bridge, started walking backwards rapidly.

Ambrose, Josquin and the mercenary captain were at the back so were not effected. The ladies were driven to turn their own mounts. Apart from the Astrologer's acrobatic beast, the other horses were not willing to walk backwards. They could smell fodder and comfort, they were not to be denied it now. Confusion ensued, accompanied with feminine shrieks.

Ambrose said, 'Emlyn.'

'They are going to love him in Venice,' said Angelo. 'Are you sure you don't want me to make a mercenary out of him?'

Swerving to avoid an escaping mule and its pursuer, Ambrose brought his horse under control. 'Why?' he said. 'You yourself have pointed out his unsuitability. You said he handles a sword like a plank.'

'That's true,' the mercenary replied pensively. 'He keeps the men happy though. They like him, he makes them laugh and he can shoot that bow of his. I could use him. But none of this has anything to do with why I asked. As I said, they are going to love him in Venice. They like monkeys and parrots and little dogs, they put them in cages or train them to respond on demand. Little monk will have silk strings tied at ankle and wrist and be required to dance.'

'Will he?' said Ambrose 'I think not.'

The confusion was beginning to settle. The Astrologer was on his feet, having given up on coaxing his horse. He left the horse with his servant and tramped through the gate in a high temper.

Following slowly, Josquin said, 'I wondered how he was going to get his own back on Girolamo Favorino of Pavia.'

'For what?' said Ambrose.

'Girolamo Favorino of Pavia corrected his Greek. Emlyn and he had a disagreement about it when we were passing Lago Maggiore. Favorino won the argument. To contradict the older man would have been unforgivable, so Emlyn has made his horse walk backwards instead.'

'A feat almost as commendable as speaking good Greek.' Ambrose. 'How do you get a horse to walk backwards by just whistling at it?'

That night, because they were in a house of God and because the worse of the journey was behind them, Adriana Martinelli was lenient. She allowed her girls to sing. Carmelia and Pellegrina unpacked a rebec, a guitar, a viol, a flute and a tambour. Adriana Martinelli was presented with the guitar and was a skilful player. Her flock of angelic charges were competent enough to accompany her. The songs were beautifully constructed. The voices, trained in the praise of the Lord, trilled in harmonic melody and succeeded in silencing the mercenaries.

Ambrose sat back and enjoyed all. The food was plain but plentiful, the wine was excellent. Emlyn, he noticed didn't play anything. He sang with Adriana Martinelli and the little Venetian girl and produced a counterpoint to a madrigal in the style of the canzonette. It brought a beaming smile from their host, Fra Bernardo of Castione.

Ambrose saw this gathering, as an end to their journey. Soon they would all part and go their separate ways. What of you Ambrose Chillingworth? he asked himself. He had done his task for William Cecil and the Queen and could still reach Venice to deliver the wool. But most of all, he knew he would soon get word of what had happened to Christopher.

Within a few days Milan came into sight. Emlyn pulled his horse to a halt. He turned in the saddle, one hand holding the reins the other shading his eyes against the glare of bright sun. He would not forget the terror of those far peaks, nor how he had cheated them from taking his life. They gnarled the horizon like brandished broken blades and dared him to return. Emlyn wondered what returning home to Wales by sea would throw in his path, for return he would. He had beaten the mountain, therefore he could walk across the sea. He had crossed the Alps! Hundreds made the same journey every year, but how many in Rhuddlan could boast to that? He turned away, put the dragon's teeth behind him and looked upon Italy. 'Italy, It has begun,' he whispered to the blossom-scented wind.

It was a beginning. For his flight from France had been done in blind terror and he did not want to remember that as a beginning. Emerging from the ice claws of the severe Alps was like a new birth. Ever since he had been tossed upon the world as a child, away from loving arms, scented hair, soft and gentle words, his mind had protected him from metal anguish. He could conjure up the rare memories and embroider upon them to shield himself in fantasy.

His dreams of the past had increased. He recognized that they were not of the gentle greens of Wales, but of the harsher soil of North Africa. More that ever now, he was driven to discover what had become of his mother. Now he would begin to unravel the mysteries. He had known real fear and had survived it. But this was no fantasy, this was the realization of dreams and the time for fantasy was over. Apart from the promise held in a frozen kiss, what lay ahead was clouded in mystery. Emlyn urged his horse forward and did not look back again. He watched Carmelia and sometimes, feeling his gaze upon her, she turned and the smile that she gave him made his heart miss a beat.

Ambrose was expected and made welcome at the home of Philibert Sforza who was an acquaintance of Diodati, the man who Ambrose had finalised the arrangements for Queen Elizabeth with. Philibert Sforza was the grandson of Francesco, the duke of Milan. Philibert was not a man with which general conversation came easy. Ambrose wished he was staying somewhere else. He had come to Milan for news of his son. Without news, he refused to think further. He was wet and tired; tired of snow, tired of cold and tired to death of horses. He requested a bath as soon as politeness allowed. He was informed, to his delight, that water had already been set to warm. Ambrose sighed with pleasure and welcomed the comforts of civilized living. All was soft and welcoming. Ambrose wearily climbed the wooden stair to the room appointed him.

'There's a man already waiting' to see you,' said Matthew bluntly from the door, which Ambrose had yet to enter. 'English, by name of Thomas Becheart.' Matthew added. If the visitor had been anything else, he would not have been allowed to remain there. Matthew was watching his master carefully.

'Bring wine,' said Ambrose. He shouldered past into the room. It was hot and stuffy inside. The windows were shuttered and a large roaring fire burned at the hearth. There was a bed that beckoned, and two chairs and a table large enough to eat off. The walls were wood panelled and hung with relatively new tapestries.

Thomas Becheart wore the livery of a courier. Over it, there was a sleeveless riding jacket made of thick leather and lined with sheepskin; clothing suited to the rigours of the road and the dreadful weather up and down the paths of Europe. Under a fringe of dull brown hair, Thomas Becheart's face was lined like a peasant. He was thin and small with square, callused hands and a tendency to fidget. He handed Ambrose a satchel of letters that the merchant rifled through briefly, before placing it reluctantly on a table at his side.

'From William Cecil,' Becheart said. 'He asked me to let you know how matters lie now with England and the rest of the world.' The courier's voice held a tinge of exasperation.

'Tomorrow would be quite convenient,' Ambrose replied. He took off his travelling cloak and shook out the moisture before hanging it on a hook behind the door. He felt that he could have slept right there on the floor if he allowed his legs to bend.

'I have already waited three days for you sir,' said Becheart. 'I cannot wait another. My horse is saddled and waiting. This very night I am to leave for Padua.'

Ambrose hung up his hat and watched the point dip to the floor before he turned. 'Then we will talk while I eat. Have you eaten?'

The courier smiled warmly, he looked like a different person. 'I have' he answered 'But I would eat again if invited.'

'That's settled then,' said Ambrose, suddenly liking him. The letters could wait. He could wait for an hour or two more. He told Matthew that he would eat in his room and sent for Emlyn Tomas. It was wise, he thought, to let the boy know of the real difficulties faced by England. He knew from the delivery of the arquebuses to the Huguenots, that Emlyn would keep anything he heard to himself. At least, he hoped that he knew. Emlyn Tomas would be invaluable to William Cecil and England if he could be persuaded to work for them. When Emlyn appeared soon after, Ambrose introduced him to the courier as his interpreter. He knew that William Cecil would eventually find out that he had brought the boy with him.

As he had expected, Becheart was more than just a courier. William Cecil had, possibly, the best network of informants in Europe. Settled with wine, Becheart said, 'In retaliation for the Spanish ships and contents that are still held in English ports, the ports of the Low-Countries are closed to England. Alva has laid an embargo on all English property. This was all done before Christmas, soon after you must have left. Her gracious majesty Queen Elizabeth, laid the same restrictions on all Spanish property and trade in England. The chaos this had caused is indescribable, and none of this has been done with the agreement of King Philip of Spain.'

'Was it instigated by the Spanish ambassador, Guerau de Spes?' said Emlyn.

Ambrose looked at him curiously. He was sitting on the bed. There were holes in the toes of his hose. He had left his mud covered boots by the door.

Becheart nodded his head. 'Very much so. Cecil watches him closely and has had the man under house arrest for acting thoughtlessly and risking the frail relationship between England and Spain. De Spes had corresponded with Mary Stuart, who remains imprisoned in England, and he is resourceful enough to be corresponding with her still. Master Cecil feels that the man is the spark that will be set to the fuse.'

'Meaning what?' asked Ambrose. 'The dissatisfaction of the Catholic Lords in the North of England?'

Becheart leaned back in the chair. He looked as if he didn't have the reserve for a night's ride in him. 'That is what Cecil believes. Without proof he cannot act. Meanwhile, to further his ends, de Spes has convinced Alva to keep the ports closed and to disrupt trade with England. The French King Charles, has voiced objection to the piracy that robs the

French merchants and has ordered all English goods to be confiscated in Rouen.'

'If the French king is influenced by the Duke of Alva too,' said Ambrose 'the consequences could be disastrous.'

'It is not King Charles you have to fear in France,' added Emlyn, 'it is his mother, Catherine d' Medici. Charles is influenced greatly by her, not perhaps as much as he used to be. They say that the mettle of his grandfather Francis I, comes out in him sometimes. He wishes to shun the Hapsburgs and Spain. If it were not for the influence of Catherine de'Medici, he would support the Protestant for the sake of peace and prosperity. He has seen how France has suffered. He wishes to make an end to religious disaffection; to give recognition and forbearance to the Huguenots.'

'His brother, Henry Anjou has been suggested as husband for Queen Elizabeth,' added Becheart. 'He is heir to the throne of France.'

'This would be a powerful marriage for England were it not for Catherine de'Medici,' said Ambrose. 'Indeed, we must not forget that she is niece to Clement VII, the pope who excommunicated King Henry and brought forth the schism between England and Rome. Catherine de Medici is Catholic and would not see Anjou wed to Elizabeth, unless she too adopted the true faith. And there lies the rub. Who will wed the Queen of England? She is the only ruling Protestant. Whoever she weds will strive to overcome her faith and with that, England. But without husband, there is no future English king. She will be forced into naming Mary Stuart as her successor or face the domination of Spain.'

Emlyn shook his head. 'She would never condone an allegiance with Spain. It could well be the other way, France would be afraid that England's interest in the Netherlands might overcome her disagreement with the Duke of Alva. We are not yet at war with Spain and such an agreement could be reached. With England and the Netherlands united, France would stand alone against Spain.'

Ambrose looked at him to see if he was being serious. He was. Emlyn never ceased to surprise him. 'Cecil hates Spain,' Ambrose added. 'Such an agreement would never come from him.'

'France is concerned with civil dispute,' said Becheart. 'War with the Huguenots has began again. In England the people sympathize with the Protestants. Weapons and volunteers are already flooding to Coligny.'

'Commanded by whom?' said Ambrose.

'Sir Henry Champernoun and some gentlemen from the west-country,' answered the courier. 'The Queen has voiced her neutrality.

Her sea beggars are making matters difficult for both France and Spain in the Channel. No matter what the threats imply, Master Cecil is afraid a declaration of war from Charles will be the result.'

'War with Spain and with France?' said Ambrose in disbelief.

Emlyn rose and refilled their glasses. He did not refill his own, he had been careful with wine since the night of the whore. Resuming his seat he said, 'From what I learned before we left England, de Spes had been in touch with Norfolk and Arundel and had plotted for the downfall of William Cecil. One plot for his demise was thwarted, but there will be others. Joined in interest with Norfolk, are the Lords Morley the Scottish regent, Montague, Lumley and Darce and most of the powerful Northern earls who are still Catholic, even Leicester was rumoured to be with them. Without Cecil and with the consequent overthrow of England's government, these leaders believe the Queen would be displaced or at least convinced to settle the succession in Mary's favour. Something has to be resolved concerning the Scottish Queen, she can't remain prisoner for ever.'

'Why didn't you mention any of this before?' asked Ambrose, forgetting the presence of Thomas Becheart.

'You didn't ask me,' Emlyn replied, 'nor would there have been any point. I am sure Mr. Becheart here, could tell you as much. I knew of the flavour of discontent and learned much from the Jesuit leader Robert Persons, who I was with before I came to Southampton.'

Becheart looked from one to the other. 'The names of these dissatisfied northern Lords are known to Master Cecil. He can not bring himself to believe in the actuality of rebellion. The Spanish ambassador believes that thousands of discontent Catholics will rise in war when called to the banner of Rome.'

'And the Queen?' asked Ambrose.

'The Queen thinks de Spes is a dreamer and that her secretary William Cecil is not.'

'That I can certainly agree with,' Ambrose said. 'Cecil is not a man to dwell on impossibilities. But what if he is wrong?'

'What could happen,' Emlyn said, 'is that the Northern Lords rebel, gather an army from their own lands, free the Scottish Queen and march on London. Simultaneously, the Duke of Alva lands an army of thousands, probably in Scotland, to march down to their assistance. And Spain harasses English shipping in the Channel to prevent trade. Philip could also land troops in Ireland and invade through Wales. The result would be an England crippled financially, Anglo-Spanish relations rectified and a return to the law of Rome. I haven't even begun to imagine how the French would feature in this. But I think France more likely, from passed allegiance, to side with the Scottish Queen, she was married to the last French King remember, however briefly. She also has Henry Duke of Guise to turn to.'

'Do you agree with all that?' said Ambrose accusingly.

'That is a question which does not matter here,' Emlyn said, looking directly at him. 'What I believe makes no difference to the eventual outcome. Let us hope and pray that William Cecil keeps his place of favour and that the Queen can beguile her enemies. She has proved quite good at that so far. But even the stoutest fortress will fall if enough power is turned against it.'

'There is one power that you have left out,' said Becheart, 'that of Pius V.' He left his chair with a show of reluctance and gathered his hat and riding gloves from the table where he had left them.

'The Pope, one would think, has enough problems with the Spanish rule in Italy,' said Ambrose. 'The worse he can do is excommunicate the Queen. I am surprised he has not already done so. Perhaps neither the Pope or Spain have realised that the strength of England lies in her people. The Queen will need more than prayer to defend her from the sharks that surround her and wait for her to show weakness. Never was there an island as encompassed with so many enemies. There is no abettor to whom the Queen of England can turn and call ally. Her greatest power lies with William Cecil and his web of informers. Knowledge is the key.'

'Aye,' agreed Becheart, 'to be one step ahead of your enemies certainly gives an advantage. But I fear even that will not be enough. I must take my leave.'

Ambrose nodded, hardly paying any attention. He eyes wandered often to the satchel of letters. He knew his impatience would soon get the better of him.

When the door had closed behind Becheart, Emlyn turned to Ambrose with a look of expectation. 'I gather from your expression that you have not had news of the *Judith and your son*' he said.

'I have, but have not yet had a chance to see,' Ambrose replied.

'I will leave then,' Emlyn said with his hand on the door.

'No stay. In fact you could read it to me. I am tired beyond endurance and would rather have company, be the news good or bad.' Ambrose took out of the satchel the letter with the familiar handwriting and the undisguised seal of William Cecil. He must have been sure that the letter would reach its destination. Ambrose sat down near to the fire and closed his eyes.

'*Ambrose*,' read Emlyn with no preamble. '*First I must tell you my friend, what I know is foremost on your mind. The Judith returned in January, much depleted of her crew, including your son Christopher. I can I think, assure you that he was alive and well when he was last seen. There are over thirty prisoners held by the Spanish, they may be sent to Spain before the end of the year. If not, ships will sail from here again soon, if there is word to be found I will do all I can to procure it.*'

He did not hear the rest, thoughts of Christopher as a prisoner could not be driven away. Ambrose rubbed his eyes and groaned. His knees ached, his head ached, he felt lethargic and sleepy.

'Master Chillingworth?'

He looked up. Emlyn stood above him looking concerned. He said, 'Nothing can be gained from worry.'

'I know that,' Ambrose replied crossly. 'But nor is there anything to drive away that worry. What will they do to him? You hear such terrible tales.'

'If he and the others are brought to Spain, they will be taken to Seville and imprisoned to await trial. Foreigners are welcome there and many English merchants have settled there. You too could go when you know for certain. Until then there is nothing to be done. Why not sleep for a while?'

'I will in time,' said Ambrose. 'And you Emlyn? What will you do now that we are in Italy?'

'I would like to go to Padua with Thomas Becheart, if I have your permission.'

'What? You want to travel right now?' answered Ambrose in surprise. 'No indeed I would not give you my permission. But there is no agreement between us, so you do not need to ask for it do you?'

'If you do not agree, then I shall wait here until you are ready to make the journey yourself. I would not go against your wishes.'

'That is well Emlyn,' said Ambrose tiredly. 'Can we speak of this tomorrow?'

The next day Ambrose stayed in bed with a raging fever. His mind was filled with nightmares and darkness. Emlyn sat with him for hours, making no sense of his mumbling. But in the evening Ambrose was more settled and his eyes, when they opened were clear. Emlyn smiled at him and supported his head while he drank. Emlyn said, 'You have had me on my knees all day praying for your soul.'

'That bad eh?' Ambrose smiled weakly.

'No,' soothed Emlyn. 'But Matthew has been skulking about like a hen who's lost her chicks.'

'He worries too much,' Ambrose said. 'It is just a touch of fever.' He paused and regarded Emlyn seriously. 'Emlyn would you ever consider working for her Royal Majesty Queen Elizabeth?'

Emlyn looked at him in astonishment.

Ambrose closed his eyes to rest them, he desperately wanted to sleep.

Emlyn said, 'Do you mean like Thomas Becheart? As a courier?'

'In a manner of speaking. How does the idea conflict with your teachings?'

Emlyn sat, quiet in thought. He had always torn between loyalty to queen and country and to the church. Goronwy had never been able to understand it. Now, Emlyn did not understand it himself. Not yet a year had passed since he had painted his feet with gypsum and carried the miraculous footsteps to the door of Father Barzini. In that time he had lost friends, home and family. He had killed a man, fought, been imprisoned and brutally accused; he had fled from one place to the next in black despair. But he had ridden down a mountain on a sea of ice, seen those mountains reach as far as the heavens; shot a wild boar in the snow-bound forest. And he had kissed *Morwyn yr Eira* a Snow Maiden under the moonlight.

'I want you to take the wool to Venice,' said Ambrose. 'I have no time for the enterprise and no longer care. God has reminded me this winter that I am an old man.'

'What are you saying,' gasped Emlyn. 'You will be well in a few days. You need rest and warmth.'

Ambrose shook his head. His voice was rough and tired. 'No, I do not seek that end yet Emlyn Tomas. But if I have lost my son, there is no point in building up a strong business, for I have all I need and enough to keep me in comfort. Age has come upon me so unexpected, I know that sounds unbelievable, but that is how it is, suddenly you are old. Now I must use all my time and my efforts to learn what has happened to Christopher. Against this, of what importance is wool?'

'Then I shall come with you,' said Emlyn without a moment's hesitation.

Ambrose managed a faint smile. 'I don't want you to come with me,' he replied. 'I want you to do the job I came here to do.'

'the wool?'

'The wool, of course and everything to do with it was my own idea. However it helped to conceal the true reason I visited Geneva, of which you also know. But there is another. Before I speak of it to you Emlyn, I must know where your loyalty lies. You did mention, I recall, that you wished to ride off with Becheart in such a hurry the other day?'

Emlyn hung his head, feeling his blood cool with shame. 'I am truly sorry for that and you are right to think ill of me. I was blinded, I don't know why I acted so irresponsibly.'

'Would it be anything to do with young Carmelia Grimani?' said Ambrose with a tired wink.

Emlyn blushed and felt prickly all over. Desperately he wrung his hands, feeling like a child caught stealing cakes. It was true that he had intended to run after the Italian ladies, believing that they had continued on to Padua. He had since discovered that Carmelia and her entourage were still in Milan, awaiting an escort. Would I have gone? he asked himself, would I have run off after all this man has done for me?

'Emlyn I have grown very fond of you in the months we have spent together,' said Ambrose. 'Your reasons for going to Venice are important to you. I believe any man should know his origins and your quest is noble. But sometimes when we turn over old stones, we are not rewarded by what we find lurking there. Don Carlos Grimani may not take well to a stirring up of the past. As you say that you could not be the fruit of the marriage between your mother and his son, it seems to me that you tread on very fragile ground. You cannot go there, throw yourself on his mercy and expect him to welcome you like a prodigal son.'

Emlyn had no intention of doing anything of the kind, but because Ambrose looked so ill and only meant well, he did not object to the lesson. He swallowed his protests and sat humbly.

'You would be better served,' continued Ambrose, 'if you were discrete in your inquiries. And I very strongly advise you, to put all thought of Carmelia Grimani out of your mind. You will learn that these Italian families are very tightly woven; in that lies their strength. They adhere to each other and are dependent on each other. Some hold such power and influence that even the law and the State cannot function without their favour. Their families are their fortresses; their children a means to strengthen their walls. A foreign stranger, sprouting love poems, would not be made welcome. To try and break through those walls Emlyn, is to sign your own death warrant. It is rare that a youth listens to the wisdom of his elders. Can I hope that you will listen to me?'

'My mother was a foreign stranger,' answered Emlyn, 'and she married into a family such as you describe.'

'Yes she was that. And the man she wed was well aware of the difficulties that could arise. That is why he wed her away from home, knowing that the sacred act of marriage would hold him above his family's objections. Now don't go thinking that you can run off with the young lady in question. Don Carlos may have had qualms about harming a woman who captured the heart of his son, but he will have no such feeling towards a vagabond youth who attempts to take his daughter. He will hound you down and kill you and would be forgiven for doing so. Go as you are Emlyn, and you will be treated like a beggar at the door of a miser. You have no wealth, no degree, no standing whatsoever in that world of sea princes.'

Emlyn knew that the words were true. But what of love? That hand that clenched his heart with such sweet pain would never loosen its grip unless he acknowledged it and bent to its will. Was every corner he turned just to lead him to a blank wall?

'You have to be somebody in Italy,' said Ambrose tiredly, 'if ever you hope to rise to such heights.'

'There is no time to be somebody!' cried Emlyn. 'She will be wed long before I can climb to wealth. Unless I discover a chest of treasure this instant, I cannot hope to compete with her suitors!'

'That is why I suggest that you forget her. No matter how hard and painful you think this, it would be sheer suicide to do anything else. Besides, what can you offer her, to give her security in life?'

But she loves me, thought Emlyn, I know she does. It is as if God placed us on this earth for the sole purpose of being together. Who can go against the will of God? He let his breath escape in a tired sigh and folded his arms protectively about him. 'You are right,' he said at last. 'I will try to do as you advise. But from were I sit, I will say in all honesty that I will not find it easy and may fail dismally.'

'Work,' said Ambrose, 'work cures many ills Emlyn and a wounded heart especially. Now, can you answer my original question concerning the Queen of England?'

Emlyn tried to look cheerful. 'So long as I did not have to work against the church,' he answered, 'I would serve the Queen with my very life. What do you want me to do?'

Ambrose had no strength left to launch into further discussion. He tried to keep his eyes open but before he could answer, he was asleep.

Emlyn left him then and closed the door quietly as he left. He had made no promises and he owed it to himself as well as Carmelia, or so he believed, to see her one more time. Just once before his heart was broken and made forever incapable of love.

The first time Carmelia saw movement on the roof tops, she thought it was a trick of the light. She reached up her arm and drew the thin curtain across the window; she would be better able to sleep in semi-darkness, if sleep she must. The whole house it seemed to have retired for the afternoon. She paused. A shadow moved and disappeared behind the bell tower. It was too large to be a bird or a cat.

Carmelia found Milan gloomy and the house where she and her godmother were staying. The roof tiles of Villa Portormo were dark pink, washed with watery sunlit. Where they could be seen, the walls were white, but most were covered by vines and wall shrubs. Outside her window, tender green shoots had burst into life along the vine branches that clambered up the walls and scrambled over the roof top. Outside, nothing moved. She heard something clatter near by and a moment later, shatter on the tiles of the courtyard. Would a thief dare to rob the house in broad daylight?

Opening the casement, Carmelia leaned out as far as she could and peered down. There was no one in the courtyard and even the dogs were stretched asleep in the sun. The air was cold so Carmelia drew in her head. As she did so, the branches under her hand trembled. Startled, she stepped away from the window with a little cry of fear. The branch continued to move of its own accord. Carmelia watched, transfixed. Then a hand appeared.

Hand to mouth, Carmelia backed further into the room. She stepped behind her travelling chest. Would any hear her if she screamed? Another hand appeared. Carmelia opened her mouth, then she saw that two fingers on the hand were bound together with a scrap of red cloth.

The head of Emlyn Tomas appeared, his eyes as blue as the sky. 'Have you ever heard the tale of Gruffydd ap Llewelyn?' he said clambering over the window ledge.

'Is that what you came here for?' laughed Carmelia. 'To tell me a story?'

'No, I have come for a different reason entirely. But the story concerns a climb such as I have had, except that it was down instead of up and had a less rewarding ending. Can you climb *Cariad*? It's not very far to the balcony, then there's a little jump and a scramble up and down for a bit. The last wall might be a problem. Gruffydd ap Llewelyn used tapestries but they weren't very reliable.'

Carmelia bit her lip, excitement running through her. He talked such a lot of nonsense! She recognized the feeling, it was the same as she felt when she had escaped through the convent wall, but more so. Emlyn sat on the window ledge grinning like a well fed cat. She knew that he would not take no for an answer. She said, 'This is a new dress.'

'Yes,' agreed Emlyn, 'and how beautiful you make it become. Can't you tie it up or something?'

Escaping out the window with Emlyn Tomas was a shocking idea. Carmelia tucked up her skirts and reached her hands out. As they made their precarious decent, Emlyn talked incessantly. Carmelia had to fight down her laughter all the way. In suppressed fits of giggles, death-defying leaps and climbs, they reached the outer wall and negotiated the gnarled fig trees all the way to the top.

Emlyn jumped the fifteen foot to the road. He stood then and held his arms out for Carmelia to do the same.

She was sitting in full view of all, were they awake enough to take note. The distance looked horrifying. His arms had held her like no other arms had held her and his lips had kissed hers where no kiss had fallen before. Carmelia crossed herself and jumped.

Emlyn caught her and staggered about as if she were four times her weight. She held on tightly, laughing and giggling as they proceeded down the road. Her joy at being held thus was unsuppressed. Their merriment ceased simultaneously. Emlyn lowered her feet to the ground. He took her hand and pulled her under the shade of an old plane tree. He held her close and bent his head over hers, covering her hair with soft kisses. He made a groaning noise like an animal in pain.

Carmelia's heart raced, her breath caught short, she trembled from head to foot. Emlyn's kisses reached her forehead, touched her eyelids, as soft as a whisper, and came to rest a fraction away from her lips. She met his eyes, they were dark and deep as wells and spoke of a thousand conflicting emotions. It was she who closed the gap that kept their lips apart. In that kiss, Carmelia surrendered to the emotions that had torn her apart ever since he had upset her flower mosaic of the Sacred Heart. She knew then, that she loved this wild, mysterious youth more than life itself.

She drew away with a suddenness that surprised her almost as much as the kiss had. 'There is a way,' she whispered.

Emlyn looked as if he had awakened from a dream. 'A way for what,' he mumbled leaning towards her with kisses.

'A way to escape the dreaded future that awaits me,' cried Carmelia warming to the idea.

Emlyn's kisses ended abruptly. He looked at her with a mixture of adoration and compassion. His eyes dropped and he shook his head with slow purpose. When his head lifted again, his eyes were the colour of rain. 'You and I *Cariad*, are far removed from each other as islands in the sea. You know that I would be killed before your father allowed me to take you away. And I could not give you the wealthy life you have been brought up to'

'Why should that matter? You insult me by suggesting it!' She cut him off in distress. 'Please tell me there is some hope my love.'

'Carmelia not all men are bad or old. You may be betrothed to a considerate and gentle man. Do not assume, dear love that you will be unhappy.'

Without you? I want you. I do not want anybody else!

Emlyn took her hands in his. She felt his callused fingers run over her sensitive skin. They were like the hands of a peasant. She had seen him rage in fever, near naked before her eyes. She remembered his smile when he had upset the flowers outside Rouen. It was the strangeness of Emlyn which had first attracted her. It was also the sameness, for he too knew what it was like to grow up devoted to Christ, to be channelled and ruled in how to think, how to worship. When she was wed, she would be caught again in a web of no escaping. She wanted to love wholly this glistening spirit who had come to her across the snow bathed in moonlight. Would he understand the need that drove her to ask?

He didn't look as if he would. His expression was one of compassion and understanding, like an older man.

'Do you know what I am asking?' she said. Tears stung her eyes; she had always been prone to tears.

He turned away, his eyes dropped to their loosely clasped hands. He understood and wanted it as much as she did. He looked at her, his eyes stung her with pain. She stood there under the shade of the great tree. Tears scalded her eyes with silver and beaded her lashes like dew.

Seeing them, Emlyn said, 'Your eyes are like the sea into which the stars of heaven have fallen. I know who you are my little flower-leaf,' he paused. 'Why have you chosen me to offer this gift to?'

She nodded her head. 'My love, my own, I am not afraid. You are my heart and my very life from this time hence.'

'*Cariad*,' said Emlyn in the softest whisper. 'This night I'll come to your window and spirit you away onto the deep vale of beauty and everlasting love.'

Chapter 39 Milan

'I do forgive thy robbery, gentle thief.'

No amount of warning would have prevented Emlyn from following his chosen course. He did not think beyond his actions, it was as if this meeting was all his life had been lived for. Blind with love and self determination, he sought to find a way into the house where Carmelia Grimani waited. If he had known then, what the outcome would be, he would have run from there and never looked back.

It had been simple enough, that afternoon to scale the high walls while the household slept; he knew with growing anxiety that he would not be able to repeat this action. Later he stood and watched as a group of riders arrived, dressed in green livery. These were Grimani's men, sent to escort his daughter to Venice in style. Most were men-at-arms, therefore sneaking in was out of the question. Emlyn searched his mind for an answer. He had called at the house of Philibert Sforza but Matthew had not let him in to see Ambrose. 'Be off with yer!' he had cried, 'leave the man sleep while 'e may.'

Emlyn was sitting by a well in a tree lined square outside the Villa Portormo. From here he could see the gate that had remained shut after the escort had arrived. By late afternoon a kitchen maid appeared, swinging her hips to the guard as he complemented her. She brought her bucket to the well and cast sidelong glances at the young man sitting there. She smiled and bowed over her bucket. Emlyn could see the cleavage of her breasts, he made a conscious effort to drag his eyes away. All women had suddenly become a delight to him. If he offered to carry her bucket, could he get inside the walls?

'You have a long way to carry water,' he said. 'Does the house not have a well of its own?'

'It has cracked and run dry,' she answered. Her eyes were dark and long lashed.

Emlyn took the bucket and lowered it for her. He abandon his idea of carrying the water, the guard would see him go in and expect him to reappear. 'You have important guests at the house,' he said as he pulled on the rope.

'Important?' she replied with a short burst of laughter. 'All I know is they make more work. Madonna Portormo has arranged a feast and entertainment, that means I shall be up until morning clearing up after the lot of them!'

'Entertainment?' said Emlyn. 'What kind?'

'Singers, musicians, jugglers, how should I know?' She lifted the water with two hands, making a show of how heavy it was.

Emlyn took it from her. 'The reason I asked,' he said, an idea growing in his mind, 'is that I too am to play there this evening, but I have been unable to discover who else has been employed to entertain. I am requested to come with them.'

She smiled and began to walk towards the gate. Emlyn followed with the water, slopping it over the sides of the bucket. 'That's easy,' she said. 'One of the players is my cousin Sandrino Agazzari. He is putting on some sort of play. You will find him at Santa Maria delle Grazie with the singing master.'

Emlyn handed her the water at the gate and thanked her. He forced himself to walk nonchalantly away, although he wanted to run and leap to express his excitement. He had not picked a lute up since he had held Tieffenbrucker's lute and lost it. He massaged his hand and wondered if he could play. His little finger had set stiff in spite of his efforts to bend it and the hand could not yet close in a fist, nor could it grip with any strength. He had discovered that this was no impediment in his use with the bow, for his fingers were strong, but he had been unable to grip a sword with enough strength to wield it. Until now, he had purposefully pushed the thought of making music from his mind. He knew once he reached Venice that he would have to do something about it, if he hoped to earn a living as a musician. He concentrated on the task ahead of him. The Sicilians, Alessandro and Celio had described to him in detail about the *commedia dell'arte.* This was a new form of street entertainment that was growing more and more popular in Italy. Emlyn had listened with undivided attention to everything he could learn concerning the Italian city states.

His steps slowed as he neared Santa Maria delle Grazie. He had no plans on how to introduce himself. Would he need the name of some famed master to boast of? He knew of none. No musical ensemble or group of players would accept a foreign stranger into their company without references and even then, his presence would be begrudged. The only way he could envisage, was if the musicians lost one of their members suddenly and were unable to replace him at short notice. The only way to do that, thought Emlyn, without causing injury was to get one of them too drunk to perform. It was all highly speculative, but Emlyn could make things happen if he wanted to, he had done so in the past.

Santa Maria delle Grazie belonged to the Dominicans and had gained fame throughout Europe because of a painting of the Last Supper on the wall in the refectory by Leonardo da Vinci. The Dominicans were used to having scholars wander in from all parts, to see the work. Emlyn had no trouble gaining entrance, none questioned him and the few he met greeted him with smiles. In the refectory there were a few novices clearing away the tables and an old man sitting on a bench to one side to oversee the work. As soon as he saw the painting, Emlyn gazed in wonder. It was so real that he felt that he could take a place at the table beside Christ's apostles. He felt moved to prayer.

Surely God's hand had worked this miracle? Emlyn's own devotion to God had suffered neglect since he had started on his travels. There were many Sundays that he had not kept holy. In Geneva attending mass had been near impossible and even before that, when he had been in Wales Emlyn had found little opportunity. If he allowed the inner turmoil caused by this to take a hold, he knew he would be driven to throw himself at the feet of the nearest priest, begging forgiveness. But he never allowed himself to think about it too long.

Ambrose had told him all about the teachings of Calvin when they had been in Geneva, though he had admitted that he himself was not a Calvinist, as Goronwy had believed him to be. When Emlyn had asked him about his own faith, Ambrose had replied, 'That is between God and myself, as should be so with all men, for no one man can tell another in what he must believe and in what manner he must worship. If this were so, there would indeed be peace on earth.' Emlyn's faith had not been shaken. He found no reason to doubt all that he had been taught. Without leadership, men floundered, therefore the Pope too, as head of the Holy Church, could not be deposed. He was God's shepherd, there to guide his flock, to teach, protect and show the path to salvation. Calvin's law was too austere, frowning upon things of beauty and luxury, as if they too did not have their place in God's workings. For every argument, Emlyn found a ready and reasonable answer. He had been taught well by the Society of Jesus.

As he considered the painting before him, he saw it as the ultimate example of the gift of beauty given to man by God. Here the artist had used all that skill in an act of adoration, every brush stroke was a prayer.

Leonardo had given the gift of his talent back to his Creator, he had also given it to man, so that he too, would be filled with the wonder and glory of God and so be humbled.

'Will you stay there? Soon we will be closing the gate.'

Emlyn jumped. The old monk who had spoken was exceptionally small. Emlyn smiled down at him.

'The King of France tried to take that,' the monk informed him.

'That painting?' said Emlyn pointing. 'How could he without spiriting away the whole building?'

'God looks after His own. He inspired Leonardo to do this beautiful work for Santa Maria delle Grazie and here is where it will stay.' He smiled, nodding his white head. 'Still, we cannot stay here. Go to the kitchen and see if you can talk Father Gabriele into feeding you.'

Emlyn never had any trouble charming food out of kitchens. He was fed a bowl of broth and sent off with a hunk of fresh bread. The building was much larger than he had guessed. Soon he thought, I will have to give up this search for this Sandrino Agazzari and to abandon all the plans for the evening, it will be too late. As he left the church, Emlyn saw a boy sitting on the broad steps outside. He too, clutched a loaf and he was dressed in rags. Emlyn sat beside him. Children, he had discovered, could often solve problems that left adults bewildered. Emlyn spun a coin. It was a Venetian ducat. The head of Christ and the kneeling Doge vied with each other as the coin rose spinning in the air. Before it returned, the child snatched at it and it disappeared in his grubby hand.

'You'll get another when the task is completed,' Emlyn said, promising away his worldly wealth. 'Do you know Sandrino?'

The boy nodded, his mouth filled with bread. His eyes shone with eagerness.

After a few pointed questions, Emlyn explained what he wanted to accomplish. He made no mention of Carmelia, but led the boy to believe that he needed the chance in order to draw the attention of the Duke of Urbino to his music, in hope of patronage. 'Do you understand me?' he finished.

The boy shook his head and swallowed. 'Not Sandrino,' he replied. 'Robusti would be better.'

'How so?'

'He can't hold his wine.'

Emlyn grinned. Two ducats were a great temptation for the boy, but he was going to have to work for it and work fast. They put their heads together and began to plot.

Carmelia turned around as she was commanded by Madonna Teresa Portormo. The wide dress swirled about her, shimmering silk the colour of golden sand. Carmelia fingered the loops of pearls that hung from a golden clasp at her waist. The under dress was of cream satin, that showed through at the bodice and beneath the hem of the darker silk. The sleeves were separate, highly embroidered with bullion thread and pearls and tied at the shoulders with tassels. Carmelia had never worn anything like it. Her respect for the father she hardly knew heightened. Not only had he sent the liveried escort, but also a trunk of beautiful clothes and a small casket of jewels. Even thoughts of Emlyn fled at the sight of such luxury.

Carmelia's hair had been plaited while wet, it was piled on top of her head under a damp cloth which did little to match the beauty of the dress.

'A plain girl and small,' pronounced Teresa Portormo.

'Clothes can do wonders for a body, don't you think?' said Adriana Martinelli.

Carmelia's elation dimmed. She was glad her back was turned to her godmother. Adriana had adopted graces and airs since she had arrived; she was exceptionally adaptable. She and their host, a distant relation to Carlos Grimani himself, were of a similar age. They sat in their ruffles of lace and rustles of silk like two birds contemplating a worm. Carmelia jumped when Teresa Portormo clapped her hands sharply.

'Benjamino!' she called to a servant. 'Go and fetch Rosalina and Bettina.' She turned to Adriana. 'They are my nieces, such suitable company for your Carmelia.'

The first thing Carmelia noticed about the girls was that they smelled nice. They were very similar, under thick brows their eyes were dark, Italian brown and clear as a mountain stream. Their black hair was twisted and plaited and curled into red ribbons with fringes. They were dressed in white. Carmelia smiled and returned their kisses wondering how she could tell one from the other. Twittering and giggling they linked arms with her, and marched her out of the room with promises of caged birds and a monkey. Five little be-ribboned dogs, yapped and leaped after them, scurrying under Carmelia's feet.

'It is so exciting sweet cousin!' Bettina squealed.

'Oh yes, Do tell us about it all dear Carmelia,' added Rosalina.

'About what?' Carmelia answered, bemused.

'About your wedding, what else,' cried Bettina.

'I can't,' protested Carmelia. 'I know nothing about it myself.'

'But our aunt Teresa does,' they trilled in unison.

Carmelia stopped walking. She felt a dog collide with the back of her legs. How could they expect her to go and look at birds and monkeys when her very life hung in the balance? Would they tell her? or would they keep her in suspense until the altar? She turned around.

Before she could make a move to go back, the girls grasped her sleeves. They explained in their high pitched voices, that they were to view the animals and garden for an hour and then to rest for a further hour before the evening's celebrations. On no account were they to disturb the older women. They were bubbling with excitement. Resigned, Carmelia followed them. She found it hard to believe that they would rest again before evening. Did they do nothing but sleep here?

I have to escape, she thought desperately. Will Emlyn come? She had visions of being carried away into the moonlit night on a silver horse, with Emlyn, dressed like a prince, clasping her close in front of him. She knew the impossibility of the vision. Emlyn was coming, not to take her away but to take something from her, her virginity and her virtue. One evening on their journey, her godmother had said, 'Virtue and virginity are the greatest burdens a woman has to bear.' This has strengthened Carmelia's decision to shed both to a man of her own choice, before choice was taken from her. She was afraid now, not of what she and Emlyn would share but of the danger she had placed him in. What would happen if they were discovered? Would they kill him? Worse still, what if he did not come at all?

When the girls had left the room, Teresa Portormo turned to Adriana. 'You will not have been told of course, to whom she has been promised?'

Adriana wondered whether she was being asked or was about to be informed. 'Of course, we have heard nothing,' she replied in the same emotionless tone.

'Well I have!' Teresa announced. She reached forward and patted Adriana's hand sympathetically. Her superior demeanour evaporated.

'Who?' Adriana asked fearfully.

'A scoundrel!' Teresa said. She leaned back in her chair to give force to her words. 'Get within a mile of Venice and you will hear talk of the man. Rumour has it my dear, that his wealth is greater that of Midas himself, all gained through piracy and the most despicable acts!'

'A monster!' Adriana gasped. She could not wait to hear more.

'And black,' added Teresa. 'Dark as a Barbary prince. He is vulgar with jewels. He gave the Doge two white unicorns! He has bought the biggest palace on the Canal Grande and has a flotilla of ships spanning the Mediterranean. Some say his riches come from turning base metal into gold, that he is a Necromancer! Not only that, but every woman has opened her door to him! Can you imagine my dear?'

'I can see that somebody can imagine a great deal,' said Adriana sensibly. 'Who is this man?'

'He is a merchant recently arrived in Venice.' Teresa said smiling. 'No one really knows anything about him. That, I suspect is why gossip abounds. And the good Lord alone knows what influence he has over old Carlos. When you think of all the sensible families with suitable sons whom Carmelia could wed. It seems the move of a madman.'

'Not if his wealth is but half as great as you say,' Adriana replied. 'Who?'

Knowing she could keep her secret no longer, Teresa rubbed her hands together and smiled smugly. 'He is Tomasso di Vincentini.'

Adriana felt a shiver run down her spine but she had never heard of the man.

The boy Emlyn had found on the steps of Santa Maria delle Grazie, was about twelve years old and his name was Marino. He was exceptionally quick and clever and he knew everybody. This, he had explained, was because he always talked to the women and paid them complements. They loved him and fed him; sitting at various tables, beneath their chattering heads, Marino learned all the gossip. He promised to help Emlyn only at great cost, because he was a foreigner.

'Robusti never touches the wine,' said Marino.

'Then why are we here?' Emlyn replied, failing to conceal his anger.

'He never touches the stuff because it makes him sick almost immediately,' Marino explained. 'It would only take one cup and he will be senseless for the rest of the night.'

'He sounds just what I'm looking for. How are we going to get him to drink a whole cup? As he knows his failing, he is sure to resist.' Emlyn thought for a moment. What would cause a man to drink without looking at the contents? Something totally inedible, something disgusting and hot. Bad food would betray itself by the smell, pepper was out of the question, so what? 'Horse radish? Mustard?' said Emlyn, voicing his thoughts. But these were not hot enough. 'Arum lilly!'

'What?' questioned Marino looked perplexed.

'I've seen some!' exclaimed Emlyn, 'right outside the walls of Milan, at the edge of the woods, *Arum maculatum*. It's a plant which tastes hot like mustard or pepper, only much hotter. Anyone who ate it would need a drink very soon after. But, how can I feed it to him?'

'By giving him one of Ruggero's special pies,' said Marino grinning. 'I don't know how you were going to do this without me. Perhaps I should demand another of your shining coins.'

'Don't be silly,' scoffed Emlyn. 'Besides, I don't have any. What's so special about Ruggero's pies?'

'Robusti can't resist them, not ever. All we need to do is fill one with this mustard-pepper plant and when he is coughing and spluttering he will drink the wine.'

Emlyn grinned. He had found a kindred spirit in the streets of Milan. They were sitting at the corner of a crumbling warehouse, looking across Piazza Pio to the open gate of Robusti's house. The air was cold as a crypt, the streets looked dull and colourless. From somewhere there came the aroma of garlic and frying onions. Emlyn's mouth watered. They had seen two men arrive at the house. One, Marino had pointed out, was Sandrino Agazzari the other was a tall delicate youth with dark ringlets. Since their arrival, Emlyn had heard snatches of music and raised voices. How much time did he have? He sent Marino off to buy a meat pie and went off himself in search of the lily.

Having dutifully viewed the caged birds and the monkeys, Carmelia left the two Portormo girls and the irritating little dogs and made her way to her room. There, she found Adriana was waiting for her. Adriana patted a place on the bed beside her. 'Come and sit down my very dear Little Dove,' she said softly.

It was the first time she had addressed Carmelia as such since she had come to the convent to inform her of her coming marriage. With a feeling of dread, Carmelia dutifully sat down.

'We will be leaving for Venice tomorrow. You are to wed a Tomasso di Vincentini,' said Adriana. 'I am afraid I can tell you nothing about the man that I know is true. Apparently he has attracted much gossip that you must not listen to. He is an ideal age and has enough wealth to keep you in great comfort. Now do you remember the talk we had in Rouen when we first learnt of this?'

Carmelia bowed her head as the words swam into her mind 'Your chosen husband must receive your respect and duty. Never fall victim to adultery, for that opens the gates of no closing. Your reputation is of paramount importance. Never do anything which will bring disgrace upon you' 'Yes,' she answered timidly. 'You said that you would find me a prince.'

'A sea prince, I recall,' said Adriana smiling, 'and that he certainly is. Are you afraid Carmelia?'

Carmelia looked up and nodded her head. 'What is an ideal age?' she asked.

'He is in his forties, so you will....' Adriana paused. 'What is it Little Dove? Tears!'

Carmelia dropped her head into her hands and wept bitterly. 'Forty!' she cried. 'He is so old! I am doomed to misery!'

'Come, come child. An older man is far better than a young, empty headed fool. He will respect you and hold you in his heart above an older woman. You may well have hoped for a young man little one, but there are few who would be deserving. This is a great time for you and I could not have hoped for a better husband for you. Just think of all that wealth!'

Carmelia sobbed anew. How close to her heart's desire were her godmother's words! But Adriana could not know of what had passed between her and Emlyn, of the meeting Carmelia had hoped and planned for. She realised that the naming of her fear, Tomasso di something-or-other, did nothing to lessen her resolve. Now, more than ever, she felt the need to know love in all its guises, one sweet night of love, before an old, balding man sealed her future and her youth forever.

Adriana said, 'Only I and Madonna Portormo know of this as of yet. It is my hope that matters remain that way, but I cannot be sure that it is not a matter for local gossip. I hope you will not be subjected to questions Little Dove. Do not look so afraid. It is best not to think about it until you have something to think about. If you can make sense of that, we are half way to making you smile.'

Carmelia could not find a smile to answer with. She said, 'Do I have to attend this evening? Can't I plead sickness or something?'

'Most definitely not. Madonna Portormo has invited guests to come and have a look at you. We are to see a Greek tragedy. And what about these dresses! How can you resist showing them off?'

'You said that to display vanity is unbecoming,' Carmelia protested.

'Then you may ignore my advice,' smiled Adriana, 'just this once. Carmelia, Venice is full of evenings such as this and better. This is just the start. You will be swept off your feet in a whirl of music, dance, colour and excitement. Your father has gained much since I last saw him, gained much in wealth and reputation. He is greatly respected and even the Doge listens to his advice. You will be the centre of attention.'

Carmelia cringed. She was afraid of meeting such a life and felt that she would be a sad disappointment to them all.

'I shall send Pellegrina to you,' said Adriana as she stood. 'She will help you to prepare for this evening. Try to keep smiling Little Dove, you look so much more attractive with a smile on your face. Remember that a wedding is a time for celebration and joy.'

Carmelia hid her thoughts, she did not show the anger that seared through her every time she was called 'Little Dove'. She smiled her godmother to the door and even managed to kiss her cheek. Then Pellegrina arrived. Carmelia could not see the point in changing from one luxurious dress in to another. Pellegrina ignored her protests and insisted that she try the green. This dress was the colour of forest in summer. It was made from satin that reflected the light where exposed, and plunged to darkness in the deep pleats of the skirt. The bodice and front panel were embroidered with gold thread in patterns of swirling oak leaves. When Carmelia saw her reflection, she was astonished. Pellegrina had undone the plaits in her hair and it fell rippling about her like weed flowing under water. A touch of gold braid here and there among the dark tresses finished the dressing off perfectly.

Arum *maculatum* was a wild lily with a tuberous root. Emlyn had to dig down deeply in the winter hardened earth before he reached what he needed. Finding Marino waiting with a hot pie, Emlyn cut slithers off the root and pushed them under the pastry crust. Then he sent Marino and the meat pie to Robusti's house. Emlyn followed behind, carrying a bottle of the strongest wine he could find.

'What did you say?' asked Marino before he went through the gate.

'I was praying,' Emlyn replied.

Robusti came out of the house when he heard the boy call. He turned out to be a stout young man with a round glowing face. He was a few years older than Emlyn. Emlyn held his breath as he watched. In a high pitched voice, Marino announced that Ruggero had sent the pie for him to taste, as it was a new recipe. Robusti showed no hesitation. He clasped the pie in two hands and his large mouth opened as he lifted it to his lips making sounds of anticipation.

At that point, Emlyn's courage failed. He ran forward crying out a warning. It came out in French, but he was too late.

Robusti crunched down on the pie and began to chew with gusto.

Emlyn stared at him in stupefied horror.

Suddenly Robusti's mouth stopped, a puzzled look came to his eyes and his face turned vivid red. He choked, spluttered and coughed.

Emlyn was horrified at what he had done and all thought of his deception fled. He anxiously ran to Robusti and patted his back. Marino took the wine bottle off him and handed it to the unfortunate fellow. Robusti straightened and took it without thinking. He tilted his head back and swallowed half the contents without a pause. When he finished, he sat down abruptly on the wall and dropped his head in his hands, groaning pitifully.

Emlyn was devastated 'Are you all right?' he gasped. 'I didn't mean....'

Marino kicked him in the shin. 'Don't go and ruin it all!' he whispered fiercely. And then in a normal voice, 'Here Robusti, take another drink, swill it around and spit it out. I guess Ruggero didn't get the recipe right this time eh?'

The strong drink had gone straight to Robusti's head as Marino had predicted. Robusti's eyes crossed and he stared at nothing while his face worked through a series of comical expressions and his voice emerged in a strangled whining sound.

By then, Robusti's two guests had come out to see what all the commotion was about. They stared in horror at their friend. Robusti stopped coughing and tried to focus his crossed eyes. Vaguely looking at Emlyn he said, 'Wash thash shupposhed to be?'

Emlyn had never seen anyone so quickly effected by drink before, he was quite astonished and could offer no reply.

Sandrino's expression changed from concern to anger. 'You and your greed!' he snarled 'Robusti, you have ruined everything! What in the name of God made you drink?'

'A pie?' offered Emlyn lamely.

'We are doomed!' Sandrino announced theatrically. He waved his arms in the air. 'Woe! All is lost! The only chance we have had all winter. The hours, no days, months of practice all gone to ruin! How am I to buy the red hose I set my heart upon? What a monstrous stroke of ill luck! How are we going to perform now? We are already late, where can we find a replacement? All is woe! All is lost!' He collapsed on the ground sobbing uncontrollably.

Emlyn bit his lip. Marino dug him painfully in the ribs. 'Go on, now!'

The other young man approached and placed an affectionate arm around his friend's shoulders. 'There, there Sandrino. God will provide.'

'What wash ish?' Robusti mumbled.

Sandrino's tear-streaked face lifted to the heavens. His eye's were dark with misery, his noble features, a mask of tragedy. 'God, Ottavio,' he wailed. 'Where is God that a miracle can happen?'

Emlyn took a step forward. 'Perhaps I can help?'

'Who are you? You can sing?' cried Sandrino and Ottavio in unison.

'Sing?' said Emlyn. 'I thought Robusti played but yes, I can sing. My name's er Zacco. Sing what?'

'Zacco?' Sandrino pronounced.

'No, I mean yes,' Emlyn stammered.

'We are to perform a musical drama, the tale of Orpheus and Eurydice,' said Ottavio. 'Robusti has not only learned his part by heart but sings it in the most graceful and moving fashion. How could you hope to match him?'

Ottavio linked his arm in Emlyn's and drew him away to one side. 'We will have little over two hours in which to instruct you,' he explained. 'The piece has a short prologue and four acts. We begin with the songs of shepherds and nymphs who joyously sing at the wedding of Orpheus and Eurydice. When Orpheus returns home his joy is crushed. The messenger of doom announces,' Ottavio burst into song, 'Eurydice is smitten! The serpent has taken away the light of her sweet life!'

'*Tu sei morta*!' added Sandrino coming up on the other side. 'Orpheus wails! He falls upon the earth in bitter grief. He raises up, all power and defiance and vows to snatch his love from the very depths of the Underworld.'

Emlyn groaned. What had he done? 'The deeds of the wicked are repaid ten fold by the Lord thy God!' The words of Father Barzini, echoed through his mind making sense at last! What did they expect, a miracle? Why couldn't Robusti just be a lutanist or a piper or even a shepherd!

'*Ahi! caso acerbo*!' screeched Robusti. '*Ahi fat' empio e crudele! Ahi, stelle ingiuriose, Ahi Ciel avaro!*'

Carmelia sat very straight and very still while everyone had a good look at her. After that, she picked at the various dishes set before her and drank sparingly. Chatter flowed up and down the long table. There was no Duke of Urbino present but a collection of nobles, scholars, a physician, a cardinal, two merchants and a composer. All had brought wives or female companions. Carmelia warmed to their company and thought them good companions who were obviously well used to each other and therefore displayed no pretence. They all teased Carmelia but none mentioned the name of her future husband. She felt they all knew, but were too polite to mention it. This added to Carmelia's fears. What sort of monster could he be if none dared to mention his name? What was his name?

During the meal they were entertained by jugglers and acrobats dressed up as animals; a stag, a rabbit, a griffin and a goat. A musician strummed resolutely on a psaltery, a drummer offered half-hearted accompaniment. Carmelia's worries began to retreat as the wine took affect and the entertainers drew her attention. Further relaxed, she began to take part in the humorous conversation around her, and to laugh quite genuinely at the composer's cutting remarks concerning the animal-headed tumblers. On either side of her, sat her 'cousins' Rosalina and Bettina. Each was a perfect hostess, they laughed when everyone laughed and listened with attentiveness to every snatch of conversation.

Considering the time of year, the dishes presented were delicious. Many were entirely new to Carmelia, she tasted them all without comment. The room was filled with sparkling candlelight, that danced off silver platters, burnished pewter goblets and delicate Venetian glass. A log fire crackled in a hearth that took up half a wall and iron baskets supported clay pots of burning, scented oils. The ladies' dresses were swathes of shimmering silk and satin or heavy drapes of velvet flowing like liquid. Darker in contrast, the men's doublets were trimmed with gold and silver braids, hems and wrist-lets of fur, some with slashed sleeves showing vivid satin lining. Ruffles of lace tumbled down fronts, cushioning neatly trimmed beards. Stiff, pleated collars framed dark, intelligent faces and jewels glinted from neck, ear and expressive gloved hand.

When all had eaten to their heart's content, the tables were pulled aside and seats were rearranged to view the company of players who had been engaged for the evening. The composer placed himself on Carmelia's right. He winked at her, patting her knee with affection. He is very young, thought Carmelia, to have acquired a shining reputation. He had been introduced as Marc Antonio Ingegneri of Cremona. Carmelia moved her knee away. On her other side, Rosalina and Bettina perched together on a chair like twin turtle doves. Next to them sat Adriana and Madonna Teresa Portromo with the little servant Benjamino sitting at their feet.

A group of musicians sat at one end of the room, which had been cleared for the performance. A solemn drum beat brought a shuffle of feet, a clearing of throats and eventual silence. Then a young man entered. He was dressed in a loin cloth, thronged sandals and carried a harp. Carmelia could see his goose pimples. Rosalina and Bettina twittered in whispers. 'That's Sandrino Agazzari!' hissed Bettina.

Rosalina sighed. 'Wouldn't you just die if he as much as looked at you!' she replied with equal excitement.

Carmelia looked at Sandrino Agazzari. He had a noble square-shaped head and the nose of a Caesar. He was capped by a flaxen wig, curled and banded with leaves. He announced the players in a commanding voice and briefly told the tale of Orpheus daring to cross the river of Hades to bring his loved one from death. As he bowed and moved aside, two nymphs floated into the room, their dresses were layers of flowing green linen cut in the shape of leaves. They carried baskets tied with coloured ribbons. Behind them followed three shepherds wearing felt hats and carrying crooks with more ribbons on them. The drumbeat quickened, two treble viols joined in and the nymphs began to sing. The shepherds joined and sung in harmony as Orpheus and Eurydice walked upon the scene. The nymphs threw handfuls of leaves and petals as all swirled around in merriment.

Carmelia clapped her hands with joy. She had never seen anything like it. The tree nymph Eurydice, had a voice as clear as a mountain stream and Orpheus- Sandrino Agazzari, was worth all the admiration Rosalina and Bettina bestowed upon him. Orpheus' love song was filled with such joy and beauty that the whole room, including the hitherto chattering figures of Adriana and Teresa, were struck with dumb admiration.

The musicians blew a fanfare and the actors bowed away from the room, leaving Orpheus to stand alone and announce the first act. The music, the songs and the costumes so captivated the feel of ancient Greece that Carmelia felt she had been spirited away from reality, as if in a dream. The merriment of the players continued until the end of the first act. The second act opened with the whine of crumhorns, two altos, two tenors and a bass. The tone was immediately plunged to a feeling of awesome fear. To Orpheus came the Messenger of Doom, Silvia, wailing that death had claimed poor Eurydice. Tears ran down Carmelia's face as Orpheus wept and grieved in utter desolation. And hope soared in her heart as he vowed to enter the dark reaches of the Underworld and bring his love back to life.

Up until then, the performance had been faultless, actors, actresses and musicians had been in perfect accord. They were so well rehearsed that if a mistake had happened, none of the audience had been aware. In the third act, Orpheus started on his way to Hades singing a lament of such sweet bitterness, that most of the ladies and few of the men wept unashamedly.

Then there was a loud banging from outside the room. The door flew open and Hermes arrived. He was dressed in a a long strip of cloth that he was having some trouble with. Sorting himself out, he sang a line, harmonizing beautifully with Orpheus. He walked three steps, tripped over his winged sandals, lost his winged helmet and his winged stick, entwined with serpents, flew out of his hand and smacked Orpheus across the bridge of his handsome nose.

Orpheus howled in pain and outrage, the phagotum player faltered and the audience burst into uncontrolled laughter. Turning pink, Orpheus resumed his lament. As pale as snow, Hermes gathered up his caduceus, cleared his throat and resumed his song with mock dignity. They recovered exceptionally well, but it was too late, the charm had been dispelled. Tittering laughter and humour-filled conversation flowed around them. As Hermes led Orpheus to the Underworld, to recover his beloved Eurydice, he lost his helmet twice, lost his place in the song more often than he found it, and greeted all with a ridiculous grin that turned tragedy to comedy. Fortunately, all but the players were delighted.

Carmelia stared in stupefied wonder. Hermes was Emlyn Tomas! She had thought that his coming to her would be secretive and silent, but here he was, as bright and loud as a summer day, ruining someone's performance. He had realised early on that he had lost the mood of the sad play, only the songs remained the same as they had been rehearsed. While Orpheus became dark purple with fury, Hermes became funnier and funnier. He hopped, skipped and juggled and pulled the poor Eurydice out of the depths of Hades. The figure of Persephone thundered through a song, warning Orpheus not to look back as he led Eurydice away. The players noted the jovial mood of Hermes, but they would not be swayed out of their serious part. This merely added to the joy of the watchers. Carmelia looked over to where Adriana sat, her godmother too, had recognised Emlyn Tomas. Carmelia turned back to the play.

Still fuming, Orpheus looked back at Eurydice against the advice of Persephone. Eurydice released a plaintive wail as she was thus let down by her lover. She wailed louder as she was led back into the depths of the Underworld.

Orpheus managed to regain some of his dignity as he sang the final lament. His voice was truly beautiful. He held a dagger out and sang to it of death being preferred to grievous life without his beloved Eurydice.

If he had intended to symbolically end his life there, none of the audience discovered, Hermes appeared, mimicking Orpheus. Eurydice followed with her nymphs, then came the shepherds, Silvia and Persephone; all singing the merry tune from the beginning of the play. Most of the audience stood up to applaud them. Carmelia stood with them and so had a clear view of the demise of Hermes. Orpheus- Sandrino Agazzari, strode over to the musicians, snatched up a bass recorder and attacked Hermes with it.

When order had been restored, wine glasses had been refilled and the psaltery player had been placed back in his corner singing Ave Maria, Carmelia approached Emlyn. He was still dressed, or half dressed, as Hermes, sitting by a window with Persephone dabbing at a cut above his eye. 'I'm sorry Ottavio,' Emlyn was saying, 'but once it had started, I could see no other way to continue. Was there nothing I did right?'

'Your singing wasn't too bad,' Ottavio replied, 'not a touch on poor Robusti, but if you had kept to the instructions I gave you, none of this would have happened. Sandrino will kill you painfully.'

'I should not be too concerned,' added Carmelia. 'If your Sandrino's intention had been to impress Marc Antonio Ingegneri of Cremona, I think he succeeded, look.' They looked to where she pointed. Sandrino and the young composer were engaged in deep conversation, Sandrino looked quite smug.

'Heaven be praised!' Ottavio said.

'Heaven be praised, for the sake of your Sandrino or for the sake of you?' asked Adriana Martinelli, who had come up beside them. 'What are you doing here?'

Emlyn stood up and bowed to her, remembering to remove his helmet. Ottavio rose next with a more polished bow.

Adriana ignored him. 'Well?' she demanded. 'Did you tire of the soldier's trade? The wool trade? The vocation of priesthood? Where is your Englishman?'

Carmelia saw a shade of anger flash in Emlyn's grey eyes, but it was gone with equal swiftness. He avoided answering Adriana politely enough, then launched into the rendition of Orpheus and Eurydice with such vigour that Adriana, for once, was speechless. Ottavio too, was swept up in the animated discourse. Emlyn managed to steer them into the room, attach them to Rosalina and Bettina and return to Carmelia alone. She only just managed to stop herself from kissing him.

His eyes shone with mischievous promise. 'What now sweet nymph?'

What next, turned out to be relatively easy, once Emlyn learned where Carmelia's room was. She remained in the hall, looking flushed and pretty, while Emlyn gathered up his clothes and left the room. He avoided the players and the few servants that were about, and ran up the stairs to the upper floor. After trying three doors, he found the right one and slipped inside. The room was in darkness, but he recognised the vine at the window that he had climbed earlier in the day; that seemed days away now. Emlyn found the soft bed and sank down with a tired sigh. He was exhausted but thoughts of his tryst with Carmelia kept sleep away. He had made a mess of Sandrino's play, but he had warned them that what they asked was impossible, a drunken Robusti could not have done any worse.

Emlyn knew that he would suffer with remorse later, but now? Nothing could shadow his joyous anticipation. Ever since he had kissed Blodeuedd Hewitt, Emlyn had wanted more. He had tried prayer, as Goronwy had advised, but that had brought little relief, work had merely taken his mind off girls for as long as the work lasted. But Carmelia was not Blodeuedd Hewitt, nor any girl that he had ever dreamed about. Carmelia's little round face and curious eyes were made to be loved. He had never seen her look so beautiful and could not wait to hold her close to him so that their hearts could beat with one pulse.

When Carmelia arrived an hour later, all such thoughts were driven from his mind. He heard her bid goodnight to Pellegrina at the door, then she entered holding a single candle. Her face was lit by the flame. She looked into the room, her expression like something wild, peering from the undergrowth; a fey creature on the threshold of a dream.

They undressed each other, giggling and blushing. Carmelia's breasts were small, and round, and uplifting, Emlyn bent and kissed them. He tried to be tender, soft and gentle, the way he had once overheard Josquin explain to Gilles de Saint Remy. Once she had shed her own nervousness, Carmelia was like a little animal, playful and highly amused. They laughed and fought, kissed and nibbled until Emlyn eventually caught her and smothered her with kisses. If she had changed her mind then, there was not a thing Emlyn would have been able to do to stop himself. But she held him close and moved against him, her body awakening with every motion. It was as if they were moulded for each other, their desire matched and heightened. Deeply trapped, Emlyn loved her and joined with her again and again.

At dawn when the sky was grey and damp, Carmelia heard the lute strum in the street near by. She heard the voice of Hermes rise up and break the silence of receding night. The love song of Orpheus' brought in the day, silencing the very birds. He had only been gone an hour and he almost got all the words right. Carmelia hugged herself, a thrill of pure delight ran through her from head to foot. 'Dear Lord, is this is love? 'I do forgive thy robbery, gentle thief.'

Chapter 40 Milan/Venice

Emlyn bumped into Angelo as he entered Ambrose's room the next morning. Angelo was dressed for travelling and carried a leather pouch that jingled as he righted himself. 'Well Little Monk?' he said. 'I see that I have lost one of my men. You have changed your mind about fighting and whoring for a living?'

'Where do you go?'

'To sort out a family feud, not my own you understand, but one that promises good reward. That done, I shall come to Venice. I have a married sister there and three grown nephews who all, want to be soldiers. I will visit them all, then I am coming back to your Englishman.'

'To go to Spain?' asked Emlyn, guessing. 'Josquin tells me the Moors pay better than the Christians for hired mercenaries.'

Angelo looked humble. He placed a hand over his heart. 'I am a sinful man, it is true. And you can pray for me. Don't worry, Spain has enough gold for Angelo Corberio. I shall collect infidel ears for a necklace. 'Angelo roared with laughter, thumping Emlyn's shoulder with vigorous good humour. 'So, go and create mayhem in Venice and mind they don't eat you alive! Look up my sister when you are there. She will feed you and pamper you if you tell her that I sent you. Mind what you say though concerning myself, she is a pious woman. Her name is Asarta Chiarini, her husband is Giuseppe. Should you wish to join me again, leave word with her. You will be made welcome.' He clumped down the stairs, his voice yelling up from the ground floor. 'Arrivederci Little Monk!'

'Arrivederci! Mille Grazie.'

Matthew's voice rumbled in grumbles as he showed Emlyn into the room. Ambrose was sitting by the window. He was wrapped in his rich furs and looked like a Russian king, but tired and parchment pale. Josquin sat near the fire with his long legs stretched out to the warmth, the injury he had suffered during their decent of the mountain, was slow to heal and was causing him some trouble. He was dressed in just shirt and hose and didn't look as if he was going anywhere. Emlyn smiled cheerfully at them.

After a night of love and delicious fulfilment, absolutely nothing could dampen his spirits.

They spent most of the morning discussing wool. There was a bale open in front of Emlyn and for a moment, he thought he caught the faintest scent of heather and myrtle as he pushed his fingers into the thick wool.

'I almost forgot,' said Ambrose about mid morning. He smiled and winked. 'There is a letter for you. It arrived with the letters that Becheart brought.'

It was from Gruffydd Hiraethog; Emlyn recognised the handwriting on the worn cover. It had been written before the Spring.

Emlyn,

Matters have died down some since you left, the Catholics have gone into the woodwork, that's how John Talbot describes their disappearance. We both spent some time enjoying the comforts of Beaumaris castle, being questioned by the sheriff. John Talbot told them to start worrying about the Spanish and to leave poor, God fearing folk alone. I only managed to reach the tale of Branwen Daughter of Llyr before they insisted we go home.

Emlyn broke off his reading to laugh, he missed Gruffydd.

Those who were captured have been given their freedom, much to our surprise. I received a letter from William Cecil's secretary, so know the part you played in this. I've made sure the others know it too. Don't worry about being exiled from home, you will find some way to return. You have become something of a hero since you fled. I would not advise you to return yet however, there are still some hot tempers about.

Your cousin Ellen came to visit me with that mad Irish woman. They tell me that Owain and his new wife are not on the best of terms and the house rings with their quarrels. Ellen is to wed a Mostyn, or so Hugh believes, but I doubt they will get her to the altar without tying her up and putting a gag over her sharp tongue. She tells me that she will wed no man until she has been refused by Emlyn Tomas! What wickedness did you get up to when I wasn't looking? The match is impossible, so I suggest you write and tell her so.

I learned too, that you and Goronwy left England with the merchant Chillingworth. I am glad Emlyn, I liked the man and believe that a sound future could be made for you in the world of merchandise. I write this unaware as to what has happened to you since you left England, so write back to your old grandfather! God's speed.

Ti wyddost beth dywyd fy nghalon. You know what my heart says.

Emlyn lifted his eyes and stared out the window. Outside the sun broke through the clouds, lighting the white houses, the vine-covered slopes and the snowy mountains. It seemed a day to be reminded of home and all that had happened there. Emlyn had not thought about Ellen once since the day of the Knappan when she had come with Gruffydd to warn him of the danger. Only five months had passed since then, to Emlyn it seemed more like five years. Well, he assured himself, she would soon change her mind about him and realise it was just a childhood fancy. He had never had a female admirer before. Ellen had been infatuated by Owain that day Emlyn had carried the sloes. With Owain wed, she had just switched her affections. He tried to picture her, surprised how clearly he recalled her rowan hair, her skin as pure as sea shell and her laughing eyes under fine ached brows. In a few years, she would be a beautiful woman. When she married Thomas Mostyn, she would want for nothing. Emlyn loved another.

The voices of Ambrose and Josquin rumbled in the background. Through the window the Alps were painted in sunlight. They were much grander than *Eira Mynydd*, yet there was not the same deep stirring mystery here; through Emlyn had been awed by them more and more as the journey had progressed, he did not feel the same. When he had stood alone on the heights of *Eryri Mynydd* and seen the mists-enfolded hollows, he had looked upon the breath of the dragon of Wales and he had been forever joined with the spirit of the mountain. Emlyn closed his eyes and spoke softy in Welsh.

'The mountain snow: the stag doth fly,
the wind above the rocks doth sigh,
love cannot in concealment lie.

The mountain snow: the grove is dark,
the raven black, the hound doth bark,
God keep you from all evil work.

The mountain snow: the crust is sound,
the wind doth twist the reeds around.
Where ignorance is, no grace is found.'

When Emlyn looked up, Ambrose was watching him with a thoughtful expression. 'All well?' he asked pulling his fur up under his chin.

Emlyn smiled, the thoughts of Wales dissipated like warm smoke. He read the letter to Ambrose.

'Don't tell me they have thrown our Scaramouch out of his own country as well!' laughed Josquin, overhearing.

'Josquin?' said Ambrose pointedly, 'go and make yourself useful and fetch some food from the kitchen.'

Josquin rose and pulled on the soft boots that had been steaming by the fire.

Emlyn said, 'Are you not going with Angelo?'

Josquin shook his head. He took his padded doublet from the back of the chair and pulled it on with slow deliberation. 'I might go to Florence. They tell me the ladies there are thin, whereas in Venice they are fat. I am spoiled for choice, as I like them all, whatever shape they come in. I might go to Spain though....do you think Don Diego de Luzon will be there?'

Emlyn laughed, as he had not believed he could have done at the mention of Don Diego de Luzon. His night with Carmelia seemed to have cured his fears.

Josquin looked at him critically, much the same way as Ambrose had a moment before. Could they know about Orpheus and Eurydice? Emlyn had been careful not to tell the players his real name. He had introduced himself as Zacco which they had not questioned in spite of. Emlyn was keen to be away from Milan as soon as he could, he could understand how Sandrino, Ottavio and especially Robusti, might wish to discover his whereabouts.

Whatever Josquin thought, he kept to himself. He left them then, limping to the door, promising to return with food, wine and a clutch of Milanese ladies of the night.

'Good,' said Ambrose as soon as the door closed. 'There are some matters that we left undecided last time we talked. I'd rather not have Josquin's straining ears in the room, I think he's a spy for someone, but haven't worked out quite who yet. Have you thought about what I have said?'

'About being a spy for William Cecil?' Emlyn laughed. 'What exactly do you want me to do?'

'It is not strictly for William Cecil. In fact he knows little of this, yet I am confident we will have his full support once the facts are known.' Ambrose paused and adjusted his position, as if settling down to a long story. 'As you know,' he continued, 'Portugal has taken over the Eastern trade with Northern Europe since they rounded the Horn of Africa and established bases in India and the Spice islands. The merchants of the Netherlands and Antwerp look to them as suppliers of eastern merchandise. In England we only had to cross the water for our pepper and silk. However, Portugal is threatened by Spain, as are we all, the trade has ceased temporarily and will be much disrupted by the Netherlands wars that have no respect for trade.

Once England had trade with the Levant, but even that has ceased. It is the desire of the Queen to develop new places of trade and profit in any part of the world, known and unknown. Venice has always traded in the Levant and the French have establish good relations there; it was through them that we first gained a foothold, until war and religious dispute ended it all. Europe fears the growing power of Spain which appears to sweep country after country into its zealous embrace. An alliance with the Turkish Sultan would cause the Spanish king some upset and it would certainly hazard them in the Mediterranean.'

'An alliance with the Turk!' Emlyn gasped in disbelief.

'Speculation only,' Ambrose replied reassuringly. 'Don't worry I am not going to send you as envoy to the Sublime Port, they'll probably sell you to the Sultan. What we are more interested in, we as in the Company of Merchant Adventurers, of which I am a member, is a re-establishment of our trade with the Levant, to send there an ambassador and consuls to guide and protect the merchants who eventually settle there. I was requested by two of our prominent members, Edward Osborne and Richard Staper, to discover all I could in view of this. They thought it wise to make inquiries of merchants who already trade there. And where better than Venice could you find those? These inquiries are to be discrete and confidential, that alone will bring its own difficulties, Venice will not take kindly to England nosing in on what they consider their own private trading grounds. But you Emlyn, are better suited to this than I, for I am English through and through and my Italian is appalling. On the other hand, you look like one of them and speak the tongue with better confidence and knowledge.'

Emlyn said, 'I think your confidence in me is over estimated. Angelo tells me that my Italian is peculiar. No true Venetian would believe that I was one of them.'

'No indeed, that is understandable. But you could be one of them Emlyn and maybe you are. If your accent is questioned, well there is an easy enough excuse for that, tell them you were brought up with French or something and learnt Italian as a second language. Your history is unknown so none can question it. We could take precautions and invent a good story. These merchants sail to Constantinople, Egypt and the African coast throughout the year, their galleys and ships can brave the worse of storms, there is nowhere better to establish contacts. Before England approaches the court of the Sultan with an ambassador, we need to discover what our chances of success are likely to be. For example, will our ships be attacked by opposing forces once they reach the Mediterranean? The answer to this can only be told us by Venice itself. What gifts will the Sultan expect? Do we make a separate agreement with the Sultan of Morocco? What will be the price of English wool? Metals? Cloth? Do you see what I am getting at?'

Emlyn tried to settle the fluttering in his stomach. What Ambrose suggested was both frightening and challenging. One thing he was sure of, was that he could not lie his way into Venetian favour, still, some way could be found. He nodded in affirmation.

Ambrose said, 'If we could establish a centre from which to trade here in Italy, the markets for English cloth would double and the profits be much greater. I know this is a is a weighty responsibility for young shoulders to carry. But I have never seen one more suited to the task than you. Apart from what I have already pointed out, you have the ability to remain secretive and that is a rare gift indeed. There is a complex and curious mind behind all that buffoonery and I think you have already learned to use it to gain your ends. There is also one fact here that will be of benefit, make yourself a useful and valuable aid to William Cecil and the Queen and you will be welcomed back to England, or should I say, to Wales as I am aware England holds no appeal for you. So what do you think?'

Emlyn sat in thought. He had learned much concerning Ambrose from Matthew, in a round about sort of manner. It had been a difficult task befriending Matthew at first, but once he had let Matthew beat him in a race in which they had walked on their hands, Matthew had warmed toward him and they had talked more freely. Most of the talk had concerned Ambrose's adventurous journeys to the court of Tsar Ivan the Terrible, when he had traded for the Muscovy Merchant Company. The task that Ambrose now asked of Emlyn seemed simple in comparison to that. So why did Ambrose not undertake it himself? Yet, he was offering Emlyn a chance to redeem himself in the eyes of William Cecil and Emlyn wanted to return home after all this and how much better it would be to return with no fear of persecution. Emlyn smiled, perhaps he hadn't burnt his boats behind him after all. He said, 'I agree, for no cost can be too great, if it gets me home again.'

Ambrose nodded slowly, a satisfied smile lightening his pale face. He leaned forward and grasped Emlyn's shoulder in a fatherly embrace. Releasing him, he said, 'I am going from here to Genoa, where news will be more accessible. It is of the utmost importance to me to discover what has happened to my son Christopher. Without him, I feel little inclined towards the interests of the Merchant Adventurers, the Queen of England or William Cecil. Within a month or two I'll come to Venice and see what you have discovered. Do you know, I never doubted that you would accept.'

'Accept what?' Josquin entered carrying a tray of hot, steaming chestnuts, sliced meats, cold beans, cheese and a loaf. Balanced on top of all, was a wine bottle nested in a woven basket. As there was only one plate, they shared it, as was quite customary in Milan. Emlyn felt a glow of warmth and excitement. But he would be sorry to part company with Ambrose Chillingworth. They had come far together and Emlyn felt a deep friendship for the man.

Ambrose explained that when he felt well again he planned go from Genoa to Seville, to discover all he could concerning the sailors who had been captured by the Spanish after San Juan de Ulloa. He had an acquaintance there, an Englishman by the name of Hugh Tipton, whom he hoped to stay with and whom he seemed to have great faith in.

The three men talked until Matthew chased Emlyn and Josquin out of the room with threats of a flaying if they returned before the evening. Ambrose had retained three of Angelo's men to accompany Emlyn to Venice. Emlyn agreed to leave at first light the next day and with him would go the mules and the bales of Welsh wool that had come as far as Emlyn had.

As Emlyn made his way to the room he shared with Matthew, exhaustion seemed to drop on him like a rain cloud. He had not slept while with Carmelia nor had he wanted to. Now, he could think of nothing else. The box beds were pushed against the wall of the small room, a single chair between them. On Emlyn's bed was a stack of neatly folded clothes of grey velvet and a hat with a brown-red feather. Leaning against the chair back, was an Italian four-course cittern, a lute-like instrument that was very popular in England as well as Italy; though it was considered ignoble when compared with the lute. It was a common instrument, often seen in barber's shops and cobblers, provided to amuse customers while they waited. There was a note threaded through the strings bearing the message, The best I could do at short notice, Ambrose.'

Emlyn smiled and picked up the instrument. He ran his thumb over the strings. The quill for plucking had been tied to a piece of thread and hung from the wooden pegs. The cittern was played with this plectrum, so made less demand on the player. Emlyn sat on the bed and began to tune the strings. He knew he could play now, he had borrowed the house lute early that morning, his fingers had snatched at the strings with the expertise he had known before Rouen. They had been awkward but all he lacked was practice. His stiff, little finger had worked to his advantage, acting as an anchor, allowing the other fingers a greater freedom. He had felt maddened with delight.

When Matthew looked in an hour later, Emlyn was asleep, the cittern cradled in his arms.

Early that morning Carmelia had ridden away from the pink walls of Milan and got a ache in her neck from looking backwards. But no single rider had come galloping to catch the cavalcade. Nor had she expected Emlyn to come, but still she allowed herself to dream. She was dressed in muted pink velvet and carried a little long-haired dog. Beside her rode Pellegrina and Adriana's maid, Maria. Adriana rode in front with a new servant she had acquired. He was the boy of nine years by the name of Benjamino, whom she had persuaded Teresa Portormo to part with. He chattered non-stop about the festivities that were held in Venice for Easter and the Feast of Flowers, that they would all soon witness for themselves. With them, rode the escort dressed in the green livery of Don Carlos Grimani. There were more servants and baggage mules bringing up the rear. This was a different cavalcade from the one Carmelia had accompanied over the Alps. There were no laughing soldiers here, no English merchant and no beloved Emlyn to keep them all in high spirits. This is almost like a wedding party, thought Carmelia with dismay.

She had bid farewell to her 'cousins' Bettina and Rosalina. They wept and promised to see her when the date for her happy union was settled. They had presented her with the little white dog. 'Do tell us who your husband is to be?' Bettina had pleaded. But Carmelia could not remember the full name of her promised husband, just the first name, Tomasso that was nearly the same as Emlyn's. Carmelia refused to think further on it.

There was never a touch of guilt, when she thought of the night before. It had taken three attempts before she had experienced the same pleasure as Emlyn, and then three more, so that she could savour the pleasure more. No matter what happened now, she knew that her heart belonged to him forever. That one night would be hers to treasure through all the years of her life. He had promised to find her as soon as he could. She shook her head, knowing that would not be true. Emlyn had awoken, not only the woman in her, but had brought forth the deep undying love she felt for him. How could she hope to live without him? What if she wed him in secret? Would her father be able to interfere? 'You and I, *Cariad*, are as far removed from each other as islands in the sea. You know that I would be killed before your father allowed me to take you away.'

Emlyn had said that he would be only a few days behind her, already the ache of parting lay over her like a heavy, dark mantle. How long would it be before she would see him again? Once in Venice, would that even be possible? Whatever happened, Carmelia would find a way. Once she was with him again, she would persuade him to run away with her, as she had tried to do while she lay in his arms in the darkness. Perhaps they could go back to France or even England. Surely once there, her father would not be able to pursue them. Convincing Emlyn would be difficult, he seemed to think that he had to have money and riches to support her, while she was quite prepared to live like a beggar so long as they could be together. What of Emlyn's family? Adriana said he was a bastard, well, that did not mean that he had no family, reasoned Carmelia and it was no fault that he could be blamed for. She realised that she knew very little about him.

This journey was much easier than travelling through the mountains. On most nights they stayed in rich houses where they were always made welcome and feasted lavishly; the power of Don Carlos Grimani was far reaching. They passed through Bresca, Verona, Vicenza and Padua, eventually reaching the last stretch to Venice. Carmelia became quieter and quieter, even Benjamino's cheerful company could do nothing to dispel her melancholy. On the other hand, Adriana was filled with anticipation. She appeared to grow younger and more energetic the nearer they came to Venice.

At Marghera a large gondola was waiting for them. It was highly decorative, upholstered in red velvet and canopied in striped silk with tassels and fringes adorning every border and corner. At the prow was a fish-tailed unicorn painted gold, and at the stern, a dolphin with a curly, fluted tail. Carved cherubs and dolphins, holding a garland of vines and lilies embellished the forcola that gave support to the oars. Carmelia had never been in such a boat, her memories of Venice had faded. She could see the changes her father's growing wealth had brought about. The sea was turquoise and the Venetians were jovial and handsome. Servants appeared with wine and food, they welcomed Carmelia like a long lost relative. She climbed into the boat with a sense of excitement. It moved off with hardly a ripple and her melancholy lifted. A young boy, dressed in green and peacock blue, bowed to her like a courtier and introduced himself as Uglino, a personal servant of Don Grimani. Carmelia was glad to find someone to hand the dog to.

'I have two dogs,' said the boy, 'big enough to pull a carriage.'

'Then you can give them that one for breakfast,' offered Carmelia. 'It does nothing but yap and wet itself.'

'Surely not Donna Carmelia,' laughed Uglino, holding the dog to one side. 'He is a creature of some virtue, all creatures are.'

'Do you believe, Uglino, that God placed all creatures on this earth for man's use?' said Carmelia straightening the heavy skirts around her on the seat.

'Most definitely, Donna Carmelia.'

'And women?' added Carmelia, teasing him.

Uglino turned crimson. He deliberately changed the subject. 'We have all been waiting for your arrival with longing. Your respected father will be overjoyed to see you and your beloved godmother. We shall be there in less than an hour.'

Less than an hour! Would he be there? She wanted to ask, but dared not do so, afraid of the answer she might receive.

Don Carlos was waiting for them in the courtyard of his palatial home. A fountain sparkled and burbled, filling the air with a quiet melodious rhythm. An army of servants and slaves stood in attendance, all grinning. At first sight, Carmelia thought Don Carlos very fat, old and stern, but seeing her, his face lit with a smile and the embrace he gave her was welcoming. He kissed her cheeks and stood back with a look of admiration. It was only then that Carmelia noticed the woman standing behind him, she knew this must be her mother, Juliana and she was horrified that she had not instantly known her. There was little resemblance between this Juliana and the picture Carmelia had carried dear to her heart throughout her childhood. Carmelia dutifully moved forward to receive her mother's embrace. There were tears in the older woman's eyes, but her embrace was stiff and formal. 'My prayers are answered,' she whispered in Carmelia's ear.

Carmelia looked nervously about her. Was her future husband here? She thought not, for most were dressed in the Grimani green or wearing gowns of a scholarly nature, and the lappets of lawyers or notaries. Carmelia was introduced to them all, she responded politely, forgetting the names as soon as she heard them, there were so many. She looked for her 'brothers' Lorenzo and Paolo, but they too were absent.

'Paolo has gone to sea, to Stamboul,' said Juliana taking her daughter's arm and guiding her towards the house. 'And Lorenzo is in Florence. He is ordained now. We are very proud of him.'

So Lorenzo had got his way after all, Carmelia was glad, but sorry that he was not here to greet her; he had always been her favourite. Paolo had been spiteful and had pulled her hair whenever he saw the opportunity. It was difficult to think of them as grown men, one a priest, the other sailing across the sea in a galley bound for the mythical East.

After his first greeting, Don Carlos Grimani showed little interest in his only child, he was not a man used to displaying his emotion. As she would not be long under his roof, he made no attempt to develop the relationship.

Emlyn sold the mules on the mainland. The animals had served them well since leaving the house of Eugene Benoit in Le Havre. The mercenaries told him that he would have little need for them on the waterways of Venice. Emlyn paid the men as Ambrose had instructed him and they immediately sought an inn, inviting Emlyn to join them. He declined the offer. For them this was a homecoming, for Emlyn it was much, much more. He sat on the bales of wool, staring out to the sea. He could see little of Venice, as a thick mist obscured the islands and sandbanks. It didn't matter, he knew that it was there, at last he had reached his destination.

This was where Carmelia came from, a floating city out of a fairy tale. This was also where his mother had come as a new bride, far away from her own people and home because of the strength of love she had for a Venetian sea captain. The city beckoned like a temptress. Emlyn shivered. Here he would find the answers he sought. He thought back over the years and the series of events that had guided his steps. He had planned this for a long time. He had drawn a map of the world, with all the animals upside-down on the other side of the equator, a map he had hidden in a wall crack, lest it be taken from him. But he had lost it in the end, left it in an inn in Rouen. Lost too was the psalm book his mother had given him, which he thought had contained secrets. To unlock them, he had paid attention in the Latin classes. But the book had been a disappointment to him, he had not been able to discover its secrets, if ever it had any. Then had come the knowledge imparted by Fra Sebastiano and the little Moorish box with the gems nestled within. Emlyn didn't think he would ever see them again, the letter of mark, showing his ownership had also been taken by the Spanish. He had nothing now with him that could help him begin his search.

What had old Mafanwy said? 'Be sure to have a sound ship beneath thee Mab-y-Ddarig, the tide is turning. Three sons, she had repeated. 'But only one son of the Dragon.' But thou, the only son of the Dragon. Find so much Mab-y-Ddraig, thou will wish thee never looked The dragon comes in many guises.'

He had dismissed the words, old witches gibberish! But now they came back, floating through the reeds on a strand of lost mist, glistening like dew-spun cobwebs. He heard the rattle of sea shells and a breath of wizened laughter. Emlyn shook his head and the vision dissipated like a splash. But the memory stayed. He had paid little attention to the talk he had had with Mafanwy. Because of his religious training, he knew her words could not be true. Who could know the future but God? Now, the words had come back to him as if summoned.

In Italian, he said, 'Who is the Dragon?'

'Dragon?' said a voice beside him. 'Not who, but what. The only dragon I know of is the *Sea Dragon.* A great ship built recently at the Arsenal. You are not the Englishman I have been waiting four days for, but you have the wool. I am Jacopo, from the trading house of Tomasso di Vincentini.'

'You have waited for four days?' Emlyn turned away from the sea and looked directly at the man who had come to meet him, or rather the wool. Jacopo's eyebrows were lowered in a frown. He looked irritable and bad tempered. He indicated with his hand for Emlyn to precede him to the waterside where a boat waited, bobbing on the sea. The short cloak Jacopo was wearing was swept back, Emlyn saw a yellow salamander embroidered on the red lining.

It was mid-afternoon by the time the boat reached the Grand Canal. There were few people about, and those that were, dozed on sunlit benches outside their places of work or sat working lazily on fishing nets or delicate crochet. Cats stretched out on sun-warmed stone, tawny and ginger draping the steps like lush carpeting. Even the pigeons were quiet for the hours of siesta. Emlyn heard only the gurgle and occasional splash from the wake of the boat. He yawned feeling the lassitude in the air. How sensible it seemed to sleep after a meal and a good cup of wine. What a sinful waste of God's time! Father Barzini would have said, even though Father Barzini was a Florentine!

'Jacopo?' said Emlyn in a hushed voice, 'Do you know of a family by the name of Grimani?'

Jacopo smiled. 'Why do you ask?'

Because I am in love with Carmelia Grimani. Emlyn said, 'My master asked me to deliver a letter there. I thought you might know which house.'

Jacopo's black curls rocked up and down with his laughter. Since they had left the mainland, he seemed a very jovial man, Emlyn decided he liked him after all.

Jacopo said, 'Grimani do not live in a house my friend, they live in a palace. I will show you after we have unloaded the wool and been to the trading house.' He paused to manoeuvre around a bend crowded with moored gondolas. They moved into a dark, overshadowed canal. 'We are going now to a warehouse at the Arsenal,' he added. 'You know that the wool is too late for the ship, it sailed a month ago.'

'What ship?' said Emlyn curiously.

'*The Cornucopia*.' Jacopo replied with flourish. 'That is the company's caravel sailing to Constantinople.' He finished his sentence with a wave of his hand, bringing the magical name out of the air like a magician.

Emlyn stared at him spellbound. Constantinople! He said, 'Do you mean that this wool was to go to Constantinople?'

Jacopo launched into an artistic description of the fabled city that he had never seen. Emlyn's eyes grew round with wonder. He listened in rapt silence while the boat sped through the water under the capable hands of Jacopo. They slid in and out of sunlight and shadow, under bridges festooned with algae, past a thousand churches, piazzas and tall decorative houses. Emlyn's ears and eyes were bombarded with wonder. Only when they drew near to the Arsenal and the tall ships was Emlyn's attention drawn away. He had never guessed that so many ships could exist in one place. The masts rose to the sky as thick as fencing. He recognised flags of San Marco, Spain, France, the red cross of the Knights of St. John, many he failed to identify. Here was displayed the true beauty and nobility of Venice. The Arsenal was fabled to be the greatest ship building centre of the world.

'That is the church of San Francesco della Virginal,' explained Jacopo pointing to a building that looked more like a pagan temple that a church. The façade was in the process of being built. Already Emlyn had seen more churches that he could count, all were equally fascinating. The gondola drew nearer and began to nose between the ships. The air was rich with brine and tar, fish and shellac. The huge prows rose like cliffs above the tiny boat. Mermaids, Neptune, dolphins, queens and kings, large-breasted maidens, sea horses and sea dragons thrust out of the sea; giant, terrifying and magnificent. Anchor cables, chains and ropes creaked and swayed entangled in mermaid-green hair. The ships rose and fell in the gentle waves. Occasionally Emlyn saw the crustacean crown, glistening white above the water-line before sinking into the impossible blue. The great vessels were like a dream out of boyhood. To what fantastical shores had these prows pointed? What adventure had they seen and what treasure had they spirited away over the hidden pathways?

The boat thumped to a stop next to a line of warehouses. Above the door of one, there was a crudely painted salamander, like the one on Jacopo's clothes. Jacopo called to the men inside. After some time, a head appeared at a tiny window and looked down on them. Jacopo shouted instructions, his Italian too fast for Emlyn to follow. Soon a crane hook appeared and sank down to the boat. Jacopo fastened it securely and called up. Emlyn heard the voices and the winch as the wool bundles swung wide and began to rise. He thought of Welsh mountains and Gruffydd's sheep with their thick coats, so far away they seemed to come from another world. Who's backs would the Welsh wool eventually keep warm? Emlyn sighed. How wonderful it would be, he thought, to be winched aboard a ship with the wool and follow it to its destination. Venice suddenly seemed a city of adventure and opportunity, a place where any man, had he the courage, could become a prince of the sea and all its wealth.

More men appeared and soon the wool had all disappeared inside the warehouse. Emlyn suddenly realised that he had seen the last of it and that he had not received any form of receipt. He looked at Jacopo with a worried expression. Would the Italians take advantage of his youth and inexperience?

'Do not look so worried,' said Jacopo. 'This is usual, I know. It will be weighted and inspected, now I will take you to the trading house and we will settle the price. You have come a long way and it would be worth your while to speak with our manager, Bartolomeo Varini. If the wool is of excellent quality, there may well be a promising future for you. Did you say your name was Tomas?'

Emlyn nodded. He leaned back on the padded bench, while Jacopo took the oar and talked all the way. Emlyn felt a delicious flow of well being. So far Venice was all he had dreamed and more and somewhere here, Carmelia lived and watched the same sky as he.

The trading house was impressive. The façade was as yellow as buttermilk, carved with beasts and heavenly bodies. There was a freshly painted emblem above the portico; a gold salamander with symbolic flames beneath it. Emlyn craned his neck gazing up at it. Venice gave him neck ache, there was not one corner, he had yet seen that did not invite curious investigation.

Before he left the boat, a tall thin man hurried down the steps to greet him. 'Messer Chillingworth!' he called.

Emlyn stepped out on to the marble steps and nearly got bowled over as the man embraced him. 'We have looked for you for so long,' he exclaimed. 'I had almost given up seeing you! You are young indeed to undertake such a journey. How is your delightful Queen Elizabetta?'

Emlyn tripped on the wet step, righted himself and stammered, 'I'm not....that is, I'm not Ambrose Chillingworth.'

'Excellent!' said Bartolomeo taking his elbow. 'Come in, come in. Explanations can wait. You must be tired. Some wine? I cannot wait to hear of your journey. And in the snow! They tell me it was the worse ever seen.'

Emlyn followed obediently, speech was impossible with this exuberant Venetian. Once inside he was ushered up a flight of stairs, along a corridor and into a large room bright with sunlight. Trying to see everything at once, he was pushed into a soft chair and had an exquisite glass forced into his hand, over-brimming with wine. There were as many books here as there were in Father Manare's room and the walls were lined with curious objects. All the time Bartolomeo Varini chattered non stop. When he did eventually cease, the silence was startling. He was watching Emlyn with an expression of expectancy.

Flustered Emlyn said, 'I'm sorry, what did you ask?'

'Your Messer Chillingworth,' said Bartolomeo, 'I pray that he has not met with misfortune?'

'No, but he was over tired by the journey and had some pressing business that prevented him from continuing. As I was his travelling companion, coming to Venice myself, he asked me to come on there and to see the wool safely delivered. The wool is from my grandfather a business partner of Mr I Chillingworth. I had not expected to be met. Your man, Jacopo, the boatman was very efficient.'

'Yes, he is a man of many talents. You have not been to Venice before?'

Emlyn shook his head. 'I have been to the Arsenal,' he replied enthusiastically. 'I have seen war galleys and great wonders.'

Bartolomeo smiled and settled into the chair opposite, delighted by the youth's childish excitement. Emlyn gave a brief explanation of himself and talked more about the long journey from England. Then he launched into a barrage of questions to do with Venice, and trade, and ships, and pirates, all of which Bartolomeo thoroughly enjoyed. Steering him back eventually to the present, Bartolomeo said, 'Do you have a name?'

'Emlyn Tomas,' Emlyn answered. He had decided to abandon any attempts at changing his name, feeling that honesty would serve him better.

'Do you have a place to stay here in Venice?' Bartolomeo asked. 'There is plenty of room here should you have need.'

'Thank you Signor Varini,' Emlyn replied politely. 'I am grateful for your generosity, however, I hope to look up the brother of a friend in Paris, and am assured that I will be made welcome there. I am at a loss here though, as I do not know where to look.'

'Perhaps I know the family?' said Bartolomeo helpfully.

'They are German lute makers Signore, the name is Tieffenbrucker.'

'I do not know them personally,' Bartolomeo said, 'but they are famed throughout Venice and the Veneto. When our business is complete, Jacopo will take you to the very doorstep. Now, Messer Chillingworth was paid partially for the wool in Geneva, I shall give you the amount owing or you may leave it here with me if you have nowhere secure to leave it. And there is the matter of future supplies to be discussed. Do you have some form of agreement?'

Emlyn concentrated on the matter at hand. Ambrose had given him enough coin to last him for a few weeks if he was frugal. He had no intention of using the wool money unless it was unavoidable. Ambrose had talked at great length to him before they had parted company, informing Emlyn of all he could concerning the cloth trade and Venice and where to keep the money in safety. Emlyn had told him that he wanted to find work for himself in Venice before he attempted to discover anything concerning Don Carlos Grimani. He hoped to find some band of musicians to join, or some ordinary work that would enable him to observe, while blending into the background.

He sipped his wine feeling utterly alone.

Chapter 41 Venice, April

Emlyn stood outside a three storied house near the Arsenal, where Jacopo had left him. He had declined the offer of a ride to the palace of Carlos Grimani, he was not ready yet to visit there, but Jacopo had pointed it out to him. It was not a place that Emlyn would forget; he could find his way there again. The house he now stood outside had a courtyard in the middle and the doors were open. Crowning the high wall to either side were two stone griffins, their heads turned towards the sea; they were splashed with bird droppings. Through the gates, Emlyn could see blocks of wooden planks stacked neatly under faded awnings. Next to these was a work room from which came the rhythmic sound of a saw and a deep voice singing in German.

Emlyn smiled, it was most definitely the voice of a Tieffenbrucker, even the tune was familiar. It was the song about the two cobblers of Baden, one echoing the other to the rhythm of a tapping hammer. Emlyn remembered Baldassar Castiglione's Il Libro del Cortegiano, which Camellia had brought for him to read, and the lessons in taking advantage of a given situation. He took a deep breath and began to sing the second part, as he had once done with Jan Coecke over a pot of ale.

The huge voice, hidden yet from view, faltered for a moment and then began to laugh a deep rumbling chuckle. 'Who is that, turning good German into gibberish?'

Emlyn stopped singing. 'I am a friend of Wendelin Tieffenbrucker,' he called.

'So,' came the thunderous reply, 'there are Wendelin Tieffenbruckers all over the place!'

'That many?' Emlyn yelled.'If you are Herr Theo, this one is your brother from Rouen.'

A copy of Wendelin Tieffenbrucker came out of the shop, brushing sawdust from his leather apron. He was thinner that Wendelin and as he drew closer, Emlyn saw that he looked the ten years older. He was a florid man in his early sixties, his hair showing more white that the wheaten yellow of his brother. He drew abreast and looked Emlyn up and down critically. 'Did Wendelin teach you your German?' he demanded in the same loud voice.

'No,' said Emlyn laughing. 'It usually sorts itself out after a few days. My name is Emlyn Tomas, I have brought you a letter.'

Then Theo howled with joy and grasped Emlyn in an embrace that drove the breath from his lungs. The large, white-haired forearms tightened, pinning Emlyn's arms as his feet left the ground. Theo growled happily. Emlyn wheezed and got dropped then heaved upright. His hand was crushed in a meaty, bear-sized paw and pumped up and down like a treadle. Then Theo propelled him off across the courtyard towards the house. Emlyn's ears popped as Theo's voice erupted like a flattened sackbut. 'Mariebella! Mariebella! Look what the sea has washed up.'

Emlyn came to an abrupt halt, the collar of his new shirt ripping as he was dragged back in mid-flight.

The German's face came close to his, his eyebrow lifted like a caterpillar. 'You are the philomel my brother mentioned aren't you?' Theo asked sensibly.

Emlyn gasped in a miasma of beer and garlic sausage. He gulped and nodded.

'I thought as much,' growled Theo. He shoved his visitor onward with a hearty thud between the shoulders.

The blow drove Emlyn straight through the door. He tripped over the door step and collided with somebody soft, coming the other way.

'Don't take any notice of him,' said a pleasant feminine voice. 'Theo! Stay outside until you are sober!'

'I will not,' answered Theo. The light dimmed as he entered the narrow passage. Emlyn untangled himself from the German's wife. He wished that he had never come.

Theo said, 'If I turn my back, just for a moment, you'll have this boy eating me out of house and home.'

'This what?' said Emlyn, 'did you know I was coming?'

'Know?' spluttered Theo. 'I'm surprised that there are not a band of heralds announcing your arrival and a royal carpet rolled out so that you don't get your precious feet damp and dirtied!'

'Give the boy a chance Theo!' snapped Mariebella. She was very pretty in a Teutonic sort of way, with golden hair as fine as cobwebs. She took Emlyn's arm and guided him down the passage into a dining room, where she sat him in a chair; all the while muttering in German.

'That's right,' howled Theo following, 'sit him down in my chair, feed him off my plate.'

Emlyn jumped up. He said, 'I don't understand Menheer. What is the matter?'

'Wendelin wrote him a letter,' explained Mariebella. 'So we knew you were coming, and he himself is due to arrive here in May. I can't wait to see his wife and children. Eva and I were friends when we were young. Theo is impossible when he is drunk.'

'Drunk!' bellowed Theo indignantly. 'I have only just begun.'

'I can't imagine what sort of letter it could be,' said Emlyn, 'to warrant all this. Have I done something of which I am unaware?'

Mariebella tutted and patted him on the head. 'There, don't be alarmed. Theo will be more agreeable once he had stuck his head in the canal to cool it off.'

Theo was walking up and down making noises like a hungry large animal. 'Give him a place at my table,' he bellowed. 'Give him a roof over his head and worse still....' Theo paused in front of Emlyn, his red face dripping perspiration, 'don't forget that I am to give him the best lute in my shop and be sure to introduce him to anybody and every body that matters!'

Emlyn ducked to avoid the fumes and spittle. He was beginning to realise what had happened. Wendelin must have written to his brother Theo, instructing him to do all these things when Emlyn made an appearance. Wendelin had been very enthusiastic

'*When you decide not to become a priest, that is where you will come to see me to show the Venetians how a true Orpheus can strike the lyre.*' those had been his words when he had given Emlyn the exquisite lute that had ended its short life soon after. Emlyn had played a lute only once since then, that had been in the street in Milan, acting the fool for Carmelia. Orpheus?

It looked as if Wendelin certainly hadn't done him a favour in preparing the way. The last thing he wanted was to live on Theo's charity. He could find a group of musicians to join without Theo's help, especially as Venice was in preparation for the Feast of Flowers, Easter and numerous other festivals that took place at this time of year. Musicians were in great demand.

'Why not give him my bed as well' continued Theo, 'would you like that Mariebella, a nice young man to keep you warm? Never mind me, I'll find a space in the wood pile.'

'I can't play the lute at present,' said Emlyn, in a small voice. He could play now, all he needed was practice, but he had thought of a way out of the awkward situation.

'Theo,' said Mariebella, equally as quietly, her voice held a ring of warning.

'Perhaps I could go and beg at the door of the Frari. Angilbert owes me a handful of sausages, so I can live on those for a while. Then there's....'

'Theo!' screamed Mariebella. 'Stop complaining!'

'Give him the shirt off my back did you say?'

'If you don't shut that oversized mouth, I shall take pleasure in stuffing a lute down it, belly first! Out! Out, out, out!' Mariebella bullied her husband through the door. 'Don't you come back here until you have a civil tongue in your head!' She yelled after him, her hands at her hips to enforce the point. With her husband packed off with a tirade of threats in his ear, Mariebella came back into the house. Three children trooped into the room, all girls, all dressed in green cotton with white aprons over the top. They stared at Emlyn out of identical Lagoon-blue eyes. Their hair hung on either side of solemn faces, six unique, blonde plaits woven out of spun silk; the blonde varied from white to old gold. Emlyn guessed the oldest to be around twelve, with no more than four years between her and the youngest. They stood in a row by the door, reluctant to approach any closer. Emlyn made a face at them. The smallest smiled, covering her pink lips with a shy hand. They shuffled in and scrambled on to the bench opposite.

Soon Emlyn was sitting in front of a plate of food the like of which he had only dreamed of. He couldn't let it go to waste in spite of Theo's words, nor, in the end, could he do it justice. Emlyn's embarrassment faded. He would talk to Theo later and sort something out.

'Carmelia tell them to bring the material into the light so that I can get a good look at it,' said Adriana Martinelli.

Carmelia helped the woman lift the bolt of heavy velvet and carried it outside to a table where the other examples of cloth were displayed; all brought outside at Adriana's command. There were already three shades of grey, two of green, a blue and three of different shades of red. Carmelia added the brown to the rest and cautioned herself to be patient.

The piazza was filled with noise and colour. Voices rose and fell in a constant clamour: thick-set women shouted from balconies; fruit sellers haggled with voice and gesture from behind the pyramids of watermelons.

'Not only is this food,' one called to Pellegrina, who had wandered off, 'but a drink too and water to wash with afterwards.'

Carmelia had never eaten a water melon, she watched with mouth-watering anticipation. She had been with Adriana and Pellegrina at the cloth sellers for over two hours. It was preferable to the endless visits she had been subjected to since they had come to Venice, but it looked as if Adriana would need another hour to decide on the hue.

Against an old wall sat a group of elderly men, talking quietly in the Spring sunshine and watching life unfold before them. Carmelia envied them their content. Younger men with bright handsome smiles tried to catch her interest, she looked away blushing, aware of the old women peering from behind green wooden shutters above.

'I do like the blue best,' said Adriana, 'but it is so hard to decide.'

'The blue suits you,' Carmelia replied without looking. Why should she care what her godmother dressed in for the most talked about wedding of the year?

Adriana flung the blue velvet away from her. 'I think Annina Gattinoni is wearing blue, and if I'm not mistaken this is the very same shade, so that will not do.'

Carmelia sighed loud enough for Adriana to hear. Adriana gave her a cold, calculating look. Carmelia turned away. She had cried every night since she had arrived, seeing the black pool of her future yawing to swallow her up. She thought about Emlyn all the time, as if, by concentrating, she could bring him to her. She had stood by her window in the Grimani palace and willed him to appear. But there were no vines for him to climb and he had not come. She didn't know if he was even in Venice and could think of no way of finding out. She had told only Pellegrina of her utter despair. Pellegrina was the same as the others, she wished that she herself was to marry the rich merchant and could not understand why Carmelia's heart should turn to another. Tomasso di Vincentini had yet to make an appearance. Carmelia didn't care, she didn't want to see him, the longer he stayed away, the longer she would have her freedom. She hoped he had dropped dead somewhere. If not, there was enough time still, to make an escape when Emlyn came. And she was sure he would come, by whatever means.

Eventually Adriana chose a colour of crushed blackberries. She added it to the pile of purchases that had mounted throughout the long afternoon.

'Shall we return to the boat?' Carmelia suggested, 'there is so much to carry.'

'I shall have it delivered. Until then, Pellegrina can wait here,' said Adriana. 'Come child, let us take some food. All this spending has made me faint with hunger.'

The piazza was lined with tables were the Venetians could sit to eat or sit in idleness. Adriana chose a table where nothing could escape her notice. The proprietor arrived, bowing with eagerness. there were few who had not noticed the ladies and their spending skill. Adriana ordered wine, a small wheel of hard cheese, a dish of olives and mushrooms, a pie stuffed with larks and zucchini and a plate of honeyed cakes. Carmelia's request for water melon went unnoticed.

Adriana fixed Carmelia with a look that Carmelia had come to know well, they were going to talk about marriage. Carmelia dropped her gaze and picked a flower out of the jar on the table. She began to pull it apart methodically.

'Are you going to starve yourself to death?' Adriana asked, popping an oily mushroom into her mouth. 'I hoped to put some colour in your cheeks on this outing. I see that you are determined to be melancholy. Carmelia all is arranged and you cannot go against the wishes of your father.'

'Why did we not wait until the Spring to cross the Alps?' asked Carmelia. 'The night we left Rouen was the worse night anyone could have chosen to go anywhere.'

'I needed the Englishman's escort,' Adriana replied dropping her eyes. 'Who knows how long we should have had to wait for another? You will recall that we had intended to leave much sooner.'

'But why the hurry? Why can't I wait to marry. The man might detest me. I am sure I shall not be impressed by him.'

'Well, if you are going to make up your mind before you have even met with him.'

'The man is a scoundrel, everyone says so. They think I can't see their pitying looks and hear their whispered chatter!'

'The unknown my dear, is always frightening. But you mustn't listen to them, they gossip and fill in details that they know nothing about. The man is rich. What else do you need to know?'

'Everything!' cried Carmelia, 'and nothing. I don't want to know anything about him.'

'Then why concern yourself? Listen to me my child, I have not been unaware of the trouble you are going through, who could be? You hardly ever touch your food, your face is the most miserable in the house, you grow thin and pale and cry yourself to sleep. Is the wedding that detestable to you Little Dove?'

Carmelia felt the tears sting her eyes, overflow and pour over her cheeks. She sniffed and tried to regain control of herself. 'You said that you would not see me wed to a monster!' she sobbed.

'Yes I remember, I promised you a prince, and he is that my child, have no doubts about it. I cannot think of any better suited for my favourite little girl. You shall be hung with rubies and all things precious.'

Carmelia dropped her head to her hands and wept bitterly, not caring about the curious stares and Adriana's discomfort. All they ever thought about was riches, and all she ever thought about was a ragged student who had made her laugh and showed her love. She would part with everything to be with him, she would rather live with him in poverty and starvation, than a whole lifetime with the fabled sea prince and his riches.

It was nearly dark when Emlyn found Theo in the work shop with a single candle for company. The room smelled of sawdust and wood sap and the dark shadows of unfinished lutes wavered along the walls. 'Herr Tieffenbrucker?' Emlyn called softly.

Theo did not look up nor make any movement to acknowledge Emlyn's presence.

'I did not come to take a place under your roof,' Emlyn said, 'and I am no longer able to play as I did because of an injury I suffered on the way here. I came only to bring you your brother greetings.'

Still Theo remained silent.

Emlyn stood awkwardly, not knowing how to appease the man. 'I will leave the letter here and shall bid thee goodnight then,' he said lamely. Even this brought no reaction. Emlyn turned to leave. He had to leave if he was to find somewhere to stay before it became too dark to see.

He got as far as the door before Theo followed and placed a hand on his shoulder to stop him. But Emlyn pulled away, offended by the treatment he had received.

'Come on back in. You can stay here, at least for tonight.' Theo invited. 'I am sorry I spoke as I did, it was not your fault but Wendelin's. I admit that I may have got the wrong impression and probably frightened the wits out of you with all that shouting. Have you eaten?'

Emlyn stared at his feet. 'Your wife was kind enough to provide me with an excellent meal,' he replied cynically.

Theo chuckled and pulled at Emlyn's sleeve, enticing him to return to the work room. 'I don't blame you for being bitter,' he said. 'But let us start again. I can give you work if you are without any, and food and you can sleep in the room with my apprentices. Do you know much about working with wood?'

'Not the slightest thing,' Emlyn said, 'and please, do not trouble yourself on my account.'

'Good,' said Theo. 'I don't need any more awkward hands to train. But I need a lad to run errands for me and make deliveries, my old legs are not as good as they used to be. It will serve you well until we find something more suitable. Stay here. Mariebella would never forgive me or speak to me if I allowed you to go. I could live without her speaking to me with no trouble, but her scorn would be unbearable.'

Given such a choice, Emlyn agreed. Even the work suited his purpose. He could get to know his way around and discover who was who in time. Once he was settled and known, he could begin to make enquiries for himself and for Ambrose. Bartolomeo Varini would know much concerning trade with the Levant and therefore may be useful at a later date. He had arranged to return there in a few days, in order to discuss the future supply of wool, a matter in which he was reluctant to become involved, until he had found what he had come to Venice to find. But Ambrose had been kind and Emlyn could not find it in his heart to refuse such a seemingly simple request.

That night he curled up in a heap of old blankets on a pallet in the apprentice's room. There where three of them and none of them were in. For Emlyn the day had been long and tiring. He closed his eyes and pictured the Grimani palace where Carmelia dwelt. He was soon asleep.

The days that followed were a whir of activity. Emlyn got lost on countless occasions, but he began to learn his way around. He thought that Venice must surely be the most dazzling city in Europe. Dominated by the white cupolas of St. Mark's Basilica, the city was a sea of red roof tops, crowned with chimney pots shaped like turbans. The red in startling contrast to the deep, impossible blue of the Mediterranean. He discovered that the life of an errand boy was not an easy one. If he delivered a message or an instrument to one house, they would make use of him, sending him off on some errand of their own. Well dressed and smiling always, Emlyn was soon known and made welcome. All he waited for, was a feasible excuse to visit the house of Carlos Grimani.

He sent Carmelia an anonymous poem, so that she would know that he was close. His Italian improved daily and he improved his German by talking with the Tieffenbrucker daughters, promising to marry them all when they were old enough. Mariebella kept him fed with pastries and cakes filled with honey and spices. He often had the three daughters for company when he had spare time, they demanded tricks and juggles or stories, squatting in the yard where he worked. While running about Venice, Emlyn made a habit of visiting every church he passed to say a Hail Mary, enough prayers would surely turn the Virgin's ear to his humble plea. An opportunity was all he asked and there were a lot of churches.

He did his best to make everything work: he listened to his elders with devoted attention; mingled with the apprentices with a mixture of meekness and good humour, often finding himself the butt of their constant pranks; he did everything that Theo expected of him. One of the men who worked for Theo, Umbaldo who was not much older than Emlyn, attempted to show him how to manage a gondola, with hilarious results.

Occasionally, Emlyn found employment of a musical nature, he played the drum for a shawm player, and the shawm for a ballad seller. The day he played the shawm, he had dropped to his pallet and was asleep before darkness, exhausted from the effort. All the wonderful, enticing instruments that hung from the walls in the work room and were to be found all through Theo's house, Emlyn ignored with increasing difficulty. When he was alone he played music on the cittern Ambrose had given him. This strumpet of stringed instruments, was all he turned his fingers to; with four strings, it had its limitations, but Emlyn looked for every trick and intricacy the instrument offered, developing his skill and strengthening his hand until he could play as well as before.

Crossing the yard one evening, Theo paused and listened. His scorn for the cittern lessened somewhat. He stood for a very long time. His thoughts on Emlyn Tomas brought a furrow to his brow. Was it possible that Wendelin had been right?

Whenever he could, Emlyn watched the Grimani house and came to know the faces that came and went. Sooner or later, he knew he would recognise one for whom he had run messages or delivered one of Theo's instruments to. He was more fortunate in the end, ten days after his arrival in Venice, Pellegrina appeared, on her way to the flower market with a group of chattering house-servants. Emlyn followed the gondola, not by water, but by the narrow streets, passages and bridges that wove through the city. When he reached the flower market, he charmed a single, early rose from a flower girl and approached Pellegrina with cunning. She had offered to share his bed on more than one occasion during the cold winter nights in Geneva.

'Sweet life where have you been?' Emlyn cried as soon as Pellegrina saw him.

'Ah, its you' She yelped in delight, looking around to be sure her companions could see her. 'You are alone?'

Emlyn knelt before her, his face set in earnest, his voice soft and musical as he mentally translated the Latin he had chosen. *'Take thou this rose, O Rose, since Love's own flower it is. And by that rose thy lover captive is.'*

She clapped her hands together.

Hating himself, Emlyn continued, *'Smell thou this rose, O Rose, and know thyself as sweet, as dawn is sweet. Look on this rose, O Rose, and looking, laugh at me. And in thy laughter's ring the nightingale shall sing.'*

Pellegrina blushed to match the flower's hue. She reached out a hand and accepted it, while the whole flower market looked on appreciatively.

'Kiss thou this rose, O Rose, that it may know the scarlet of thy mouth.'

'Ahh,' they all sighed.

'O Rose, this painted rose is not the whole. Who paints the flower paints not it's fragrant soul.'

'I never knew!' Pellegrina gasped. 'I thought that you and....'

'Can I see you alone?' Emlyn leaped to his feet. 'Just for a moment or two?'

Hearing this, Pellegrina's friends giggled and urged her to go to the empty booth that Emlyn indicated. They would see her from where they stood, so nothing unethical could occur.

'Pellegrina I'm sorry, but it was the only way I could think of.'

'Sorry?' said Pellegrina, her eyes full of promise.

'It was not meant as it seemed. The words were a deception.'

'What!' Pellegrina's beautiful eyebrows curved in scorn. She took a deep breath and opened her mouth. Emlyn placed a hand over it before any sound could escape. Pellegrina turned rose pink; her chastising words smothered.

'Wait, before you condemn me,' whispered Emlyn furiously. 'Pellegrina you are not disappointed, you never wanted me anyway. I have no money nor shall I ever. I need an excuse to visit the Grimani house. I must see Carmelia. Will you help me, and your mistress who I know is dear to you?'

Released Pellegrina spluttered, 'I have never come across nonsense.'

'I know, but what could I do?'

Pellegrina's breast lifted and fell becomingly. She deliberately crushed the rose in her hand, letting the petals fall to the ground. 'You want to pretend that you are coming to see me, when in reality you will visit my mistress?'

'That was my intention, sly and wicked though it be.'

'She cries all the time,' said Pellegrina, still angry. 'I believe she will die before she will take the marriage vows expected of her. I will do what I can. Perhaps she will listen to you for she will not listen to anyone else.' Pellegrina's eyes dropped, sparkling with tears.

Emlyn felt a cold shiver run through him. He could not bear to think of his new found and precious love pining away for need of him.

At the house on Canal delle Torreselle, Bartolomeo Varini put down his quill and powdered his writing meticulously. He stood with a yawn and stretched until his stiff joints creaked. It was raining, as if Venice was not wet enough already. The downpour, thick as curtain, tattooed the canal below the leaded window and produced a continuous pitter-patter and gurgle of watery sounds as it spilled in rivers from the cinnabar roof tops. The day was dim and drab, casting its uninspiring gloom into every corner. Bartolomeo turned away and sought the comfort of the fire. The flames were low, struggling against the damp chill. He rubbed his hands together and stared into the hypnotic flames. Across the room Symeon sat at a high table, his quill tipped in gold, its scratching the only sound in the room. He had returned without Tomasso, shortly after the *Cornucopia* had sailed and was busy embellishing a book that Tomasso had ordered from Paolo Aldus. Bartolomeo recognised it as Capurnicus Mathematica. Symeon had told him that Tomasso had ordered ten copies at great expense and wanted them decorated with gold, to give as gifts to customers. Bartolomeo thought the gesture rude in its generosity, what customer deserved such a fabulous book? He couldn't think of any.

No, there was one who had received an embellished book who Bartolomeo thought deserving, that was Fiorenza. Tomasso had provided her with a house near Fontego della Farina, where she awaited the coming of her daughter Florinda. The girl it seemed, was reluctant to leave Cyprus, she was betrothed to a Cypriot youth by the name of Antonio and had used her love as an excuse in reply to her mother's urgent letters. Then had come news of a sadder nature; Antonio had suffered an unfortunate accident and had drown. Florinda's letter had been filled with sorrow and she stated that she could not now leave as soon as she had planned. Fiorenza, had been obviously disappointed. She called to see Bartolomeo two or three time a week during the following weeks. For a while he had hoped that she came to see him, but her interest was obviously with Tomasso whom she always asked after, as it turned out, in vain.

They knew now that when Tomasso returned, he intended to wed Carmelia Grimani. Bartolomeo had been furious when he found out. He had stormed up and down the spacious trading house, cursing Tomasso beyond the reach of God. Tomasso with his usual habit of absence was not there to explain himself. Bartolomeo had been determined to spill the whole tale to Don Grimani, he had even put on his cloak and hat and stormed out of the house. It was Symeon who had prevented his going, had coaxed him back inside and cautioned him not to act too rashly. The girl was not wed yet, there was time enough for Tomasso to explain himself when he returned.

Hearing raised voices, Bartolomeo moved to the window. Outside in the downpour, a loud argument was taking place between two gondoliers. The canal was narrow here, so the right of way was often disputed. Under the window Bartolomeo could see that two vessels were tangled. The tall prows, notched with six metal teeth, were locked together in battle like two angry geese. The curses and shouts that brought in the particular heavenly saints who protected every gondola in Venice, fulminated the air as did the oars and animated hands of the gondoliers. Bartolomeo watched as an old man approached with a dripping hat and a decorative walking stick. He bowed and offered his arm in assistance to the passenger. The youth took the arm offered and leapt to the steps, passing a coin into the man's hand. The gondolier shouted after the boy for money. He turned, walking backwards, and showed them empty hands. He shrugged and backed straight into Jacopo who was coming out to see what all the fuss was about.

Smiling, Bartolomeo opened the window and heard the voices.

'He said that he had no coin before I brought him here!' shouted one, from the gondola the youth had left. 'El *ganzer* is paid for holding his elbow out, while I remain poorer from rowing him all the way!'

'Does he think that we do this for nothing!' rejoined the other gondolier, forgetting the first cause of the argument.

'Where have you brought him from?' asked Jacopo.

'From San Marco,' said the youth. 'I have paid him. He is trying to swindle me!'

'San Giovanni Battista!' cried the boatmen.

'Madonna!' cried the other.

'The boy made a mistake Alvise,' said Jacopo, signalling the visitor to silence. 'Here,' he added holding out his hand and rattling the coins within, 'this will cover the cost of the journey and your trouble.'

He ushered the soaking youth through the door before further objections could arise. Bartolomeo entered the kitchen and waited by the door. He recognised the youth now, he was the one who had delivered the wool to the trading house. Emile? The visitor made straight for the warmth of the fire, his eyes alight with humour. He shed his soaked cloak and ruined hat, dropping them to the floor. Jacopo brought him a towel and gathered up the wet clothes. The boy dried his hair with vigour, it fell in dripping cork-screws to his shoulders. 'Thank you,' he said. 'I have been more wet than dry since I got here.'

'You are fortunate that the gondoliers did not dump you in the canal,' said Jacopo.

'It is true what I told you,' mumbled the boy from under the cloth. 'I would not pay the man twice, even if I could.'

'There are a few, unfortunately who are not to be trusted. Alvise being one of them,' said Jacopo, 'but it is not wise to point this out, when there is no one to witness your story. The barcaiolo are loyal to each other and, for the most part, are loyal to their trade. You were unlucky to pick Alvise.'

'He picked me. As I am a stranger here and it was raining I had little choice. I have never seen such a wet place as this, even home is a desert in comparison.'

Bartolomeo came fully into the room.'I have heard that accent speaking in Italian before,' he said. 'Where exactly did you say you were from?'

Emlyn stood up and offered a dripping bow. He said, 'From Wales, I mean from England.'

'Well which is it?' said Bartolomeo. 'I have learned that there is a difference between the two.'

Emlyn looked at him seriously, his wet hair hung over his eyes. 'You have?' he said, obviously surprised.

Bartolomeo nodded and felt the hair at the back of his neck rise. There was something very startling about this Emlyn Tomas. 'How may I help you?'

'You asked me to return, to discuss wool.' Emlyn answered.

'Ah yes I did, didn't I?' laughed Bartolomeo. 'I had not expected you so soon. Do you plan to return to England then?'

'Not for some time,' Emlyn replied, 'but I shall be writing to Ambrose Chillingworth and thought I might inform him of any future plans. He plans to come here within a few weeks. Crossing the Alps in winter is not a journey he would like to repeat. So if we could arrange what you require, the wool could reach you before then.'

'You are a step ahead of me,' laughed Bartolomeo. 'And you are right, for one so young. Is your family in the wool business?'

'In a manner of speaking,' Emlyn replied, in his non-committal way.

When he was dry, Bartolomeo led him to the library to talk about wool. All Bartolomeo had to guide him, was a letter from Tomasso that Symeon had brought. It contained a tall order, considering the state of the wool market, he was to acquire enough to fill the hold of the *Cornucopia* for next year. Emlyn Tomas seemed to know a great deal about Antwerp and the market, it did not sound very promising. But England would be searching for new markets and if Tomasso's company could take advantage of the situation, they would both benefit. Scipeone Barozzi was in Constantinople so they would have to employ another agent to travel to England, and this youth seemed the ideal choice. He knew the markets and the state of England and the Netherlands; he already had good contacts in the trade. But when Bartolomeo mentioned it, Emlyn Tomas turned him down. 'It could all be arranged if Ambrose Chillingworth was here,' he replied. 'I cannot commit myself to such a scheme at present, but will do all I can to assist you, in return for a small favour.'

'Being what?'

'The company of Merchant Adventurers in London wish to re-establish trade with the Levant.'

Bartolomeo looked at him in surprise. 'This company wishes to sell English wool in the Levant?' he cried. 'I could not possibly assist you. Venice still has interest in the Levant and would not welcome competition. It was Venice that took English wool to the Levant in the past, not England. You will find hostilities wherever you inquire. I understand the desire, but believe your masters have sent you here on a fool's errand.'

'I see the reasons for such an objection,' Emlyn replied.

For a moment Bartolomeo saw the anger in his eyes and wondered where he had seen those eyes before. The youth was a fool to expect such favour from Venice, discretion would have served him better.

Emlyn's anger cooled. 'Venice needs wool and England can provide it,' he continued. 'Her own trade in the Netherlands has been disrupted. Can there not be some agreement made between Queen Elizabeth and the Senate?'

'Even if they agreed upon re-opening the trade, how would the wool reach here? Can England bring the wool by sea?'

Emlyn rubbed at a scar on his right hand. He said, 'It would not be feasible. A fleet would not be allowed too pass Gibraltar; Spain and Portugal have their own markets here.'

Bartolomeo laughed bitterly. 'Spain and Portugal are slowly bleeding Venice dry, along with the rest of us. We are not the power that once we were, the trade we monopolised from the East comes to us now from Lisbon at three, four times the price. If we do not pour new blood into this city we are doomed to decline.'

'The Portuguese domination of the spice trade has benefited England. It has been much cheaper for us to buy from the Netherlands than from Venice. Now, Spain and the Duke of Alva are doing all in their power to prevent England from reaching her usual ports of trade and are stemming the flow of goods coming to England. We both suffer from the same hand. Is this not a good enough reason why we should reach an agreement which will benefit us both?'

Bartolomeo shook his head slowly. 'It is not a question for the likes of you and I, young Emlyn. Spain would not look on a Venetian fleet with any more favour than she looks upon England. Gone are the days of the rich Flanders galleys. The world has widened and we are living in the afterglow of our power and strength. I doubt that Venice could provide ships herself for such a feat. Even wood for building ships comes from the Crimea through the Black Sea; we have none of our own. Bringing the wool over the Alps too, would be near impossible now that Spain has become such an aggressive power. Such a train would have to have an army to protect it, therefore the cost would outweigh the profit, the enterprise would be worthless. If England wishes to renew her trade with the Levant she will meet nothing but opposition from the Senate. As did France when she tried to elbow in, in the same manner.'

'Then let us think small,' said Emlyn. 'Instead of Doge and Queen, one company could make a partnership with another. Such as the one you manage and the one I represent.'

'Unthinkable' said Bartolomeo with finality.

Emlyn rose and nodded solemnly. He took his leave of the spice manager, Bartolomeo sent him back with Jacopo in their own boat. Bartolomeo watched until the they disappeared. He was sorry that he had dismissed the youth so finally. There was some sense in what he suggested, but the gulf of space and time divided the scheme, and history taught that it could not be halted, captured and repeated. He was sure that an attempt a return to the old ways of success, was not the path to new beginnings. But he did not dismiss the subject entirely. When Tomasso returned, they could discuss whether it was feasible or not; even Spain could be persuaded if advantage was to be gained.

On the day that Carmelia arranged to meet Emlyn, she received a gift from Tomasso di Vincentini.

That morning she had tried to sit still and sew, in her excitement, this had been impossible. Instead, she paced the portico, up and down the marble squares, with the little dog yapping at her heels. Her steps were even and purposeful. When she reached the wall, she spun round, belling scarlet skirts, and paced down the length of the passage again. She carried a book of poetry, idly held open in her hand. It was a book of sonnets by Gaspara Stampa, relating the poetess' tragic love for a nobleman whom she was too lowly to marry. It seemed to Carmelia very like her own position, with the roles reversed, love turned to torment, joy to pain, fulfilment with utter loneliness. Does love arouse such passion and bring about such suffering? she asked herself.

Now, floating in a miasma of joy, she would not think on that other aspect of love. It was four days since Pellegrina had returned from the flower market, four impossibly long days.

Adriana emerged from the shadowed archway leading to the main part of the house. 'There you are my dear,' she called.

The dog began its ear piercing yapping. Carmelia gathered him in her arms and the yaps reduced to growls. She was getting used to him now, and thought she might even like him eventually.

Adriana joined her and linked her arm through Carmelia's free one. 'I've been looking everywhere for you child. Come and see what your husband has sent you.'

'He's not my husband,' snapped Carmelia sharply.

'Yes dear, I know that,' Adriana replied patting her godchild's hand. 'Don't judge him too harshly, at least wait and see what he has sent you.'

'I care nothing for his gifts,' said Carmelia scornfully.

Adriana sighed wearily.

By the fountain at the bottom of the white marble steps, stood the most beautiful creature Carmelia had ever seen; a mare as white as Alpine snow. Her mane had been plaited with silk. The Spanish saddle was small, better suited to a lady, it was tooled with swirling patterns and leaping hares with emeralds for eyes. The harness was fashioned from woven dyed leather and hung with tiny bells. The mare's skin was so light that Carmelia could see the blueness of her veins at flank and delicate arched neck.

Carmelia stood on the steps overlooking all the excitement; the grooms and servants had all come out to have a look. Carmelia stood stiff and haughty, her face cold and indifferent.

In contrast, Adriana was circling the horse smiling and chattering gaily. She ran her fingers over the jewels and gasped in wonder. She looked up to Carmelia and the smile dropped. Leaving the mare, she climbed up to where Carmelia stood. 'Are you not pleased Little Dove? The animal is a dream, you are the most fortunate girl in Venice.'

'If you like her so, you may have her,' announced Carmelia. 'What is the point of a horse in Venice anyway?'

'Your father has a summer house in the Alpine foothills and Vincentini has a grand house and rich farm lands on the Brenta. Where better to own such a beautiful animal?'

'I do not care for it,' said Carmelia. She swung around and marched up the steps.

Behind her, Adriana's expression became one of angry concern. She could not understand the girl. From the carefree, laughing travelling companion she had been, Carmelia had become a miserable wretch near starving herself, then, miraculously changed to the joyful girl again, full of youth and laughter. Adriana thought that she had come to terms with her future. This display proved Adriana wrong. She went in search of Pellegrina.

She found her in Carmelia's bedchamber, chattering with the maids who should have been at their tasks. Adriana sent them off with acerbic words ringing in their ears. 'What has happened to your mistress?' she demanded as soon as she and Pellegrina were alone.

'I can't think what you mean Madonna.'

The girl is a terrible liar, thought Adriana, look at the way she ducks her head and blushes! 'Pellegrina you must tell me the truth, you have nothing to fear. Whatever you say will reach no other ears. Carmelia is as dear to me as a child of my own.'

'There is nothing to tell,' said Pellegrina, her dark eyes darting to Adriana and away again.

'Very well,' stated Adriana 'Bear in mind though, that if you are being dishonest with me, I shall make your life an utter misery.'

Pellegrina curtsied.'Mademoiselle,' she mumbled. She had shared Carmelia's life since they had both been children, to be parted from her, especially now that she was to marry the rich merchant, would be unbearable.

The Basilica of St Mark's with its Gothic crown of marble crockets and pinnacles, dominated the brick-paved Piazza San Marco. It was the largest open space in Venice, overlooking the Lagoon. Running the length of the

Piazzetta, the Ducal Palace stood in glowing pink splendour, its canopied balcony piercing the sky like spear heads lined up for battle. Emlyn had gone that morning to the Basilica with Theo Tieffenbrucker: it was the first opportunity Emlyn had had to see the famous building from the inside. Theo had matters to discuss with the choirmaster. San Marco's Basilica swallowed them all without a ripple. Plastered in gold and precious plunder, the Basilica was the high altar of Venice: a symbol of the power and glory of the Republic. It housed such an abundance of gold that the very air was suffused with glistening, opalescent dust. High above, majestic domes and soaring arches were plated with icons and mosaics of shimmering gold; exotic, awesome, opulent and filled with the spirit of God.

Emlyn and Theo walked through the Moorish portal of Saint 'Alipio, they were tiny against the bejewelled backdrop. As they approached voices rose on a mournful chord; the singers were at practice for the celebration of Easter. Seeing that Emlyn's attention could not be commanded until he had seen everything, Theo left him to wander, while he sought the choirmaster.

Emlyn paced the the marble flooring. Above him in blue and gamboge yellow, was depicted the wailing and weeping of the multitude, the drunkenness and death of Noah and the tower of Babel; from which all fell speaking gibberish. Emlyn knelt at the back of the great church feeling as insignificant as an insect. He bowed his head and laid his doubts before God. He knew what Carmelia would ask of him, that they flee from Venice and seek a life of their own, come what may. Emlyn knew by then who she was to wed and when. If they were to do as she asked, it would have to be soon.

If Emlyn left Venice, he would never find the answers he had come so far to find; he would be as troubled as he had always been. Would his love for Carmelia overcome that fear? Emlyn had no doubts that they could make a reasonable life for themselves, wherever they were, he was confident that he had enough skill and learning to find work.

But, but, but! He dragged his fingers through his hair in frustration. Coming here had not been easy, he had left a trail of chaos in most of the places he had passed through, to leave now unfulfilled, went against all he had believed important and essential to his future well-being. He was aware that all this had lessened in the face of love, but felt that he at least had to try and see Don Carlos. Emlyn remembered the day he had stood on the mountain to make his vow. 'I will go and I will do all in my power to seek the mother who had cast me so ill prepared into the world.'

Could he have forgotten such a promise? No, for not once had he turned from his purpose. So what to say to Carmelia? He could not do as she asked, but if he did not, he knew that he would loose her, that she would pine away trapped in an unwanted relationship. If she found out who he was, might not the same thing happen? 'God what do I do?' he said aloud to the gold and glitter of the Basilica.

When Theo was ready to return, Emlyn was not to be seen anywhere. Theo was surprised, it was the first time Emlyn had been unreliable. When he reached the workshop again, Theo asked Umbaldo.

'He came, he went, he came, he went,' said Umbaldo with a wave of his hand. 'Now he's back again,' he added by the time Theo got to the door, on his way out. 'Didn't you hear him?'

'Why? Is he singing in his terrible German?'

Umbaldo shook his head and returned to his task. Theo had grasped that Umbaldo and some of his other workers were disappointed about something, probably to do with Emlyn, he surmised.

Emlyn was sitting on a low stool in the room he shared with the apprentices. He was writing, his untidy head bent over a page of music. Seeing Theo, he straightened and offered his usual smile, slightly absent minded. He said, 'Don Carlos Grimani is said to be a man with a great love for music, and a man who will only hear the best there is to be found.'

'Why did you come to Venice?' asked Theo.

'Because Venice is where the best lutes come from.'

Theo bent reached forward and took the page from his knee. He gazed at it, his frown deepening. As much as he loved the sound of the lute, Theo had never mastered the instrument. He knew enough to recognise the intricate piece of music before him. When he looked up, Emlyn was watching him. Theo said, 'Can you play this?'

'I composed it,' Emlyn answered.

'For what? To sell? Are you forced into finding other employment?'

Emlyn laughed. 'Ambrosio Bragadin needs a piece to impress a certain lady. He did offer to pay me for it.'

'And how did he know to come to you?'

'I wrote another for Girolamo Mei, a Greek scholar I met at the printer's house, remember the chitarrone you mended for Paolo Aldus, charging him twice the price so that he doesn't break it again? Girolamo Mei and I got to talking about printing music.'

Theo waved his hand impatiently. 'Can you play the piece?'

Emlyn nodded, his smile disappearing. When he saw that Theo was still watching him, he grasped the cittern from where it leaned on the wall.

'The music is written for a lute,' said Theo holding a hand out to stop him. 'I shall bring you one.' He only walked as far as the door, opened his mouth and roared across the yard. 'Umbaldo!'

Umbaldo appeared at the window and Theo shouted his instructions. 'Bring me my lute!' 'My lute' always meant the very best lute, that Theo kept in the house. Umbaldo walked over, moving with the slowness of a grazing cow. By the time the lute arrived Theo was aware that Emlyn was to have an audience.

Emlyn blushed when he accepted the instrument. He tuned it with surprising speed. Then a light came into his eyes that he bestowed on each member of the little gathering of errand boys, apprentices and master craftsmen. Emlyn struck the first soul wrenching chord.

On the pretence of visiting Carmelia's great aunt, who lived on the Riva del Ferro near the Rialto Bridge, Carmelia and Pellegrina set out with one manservant for company. This was Uglino, one of the servant's whom Carmelia knew as Don Carlos' spy. They would leave him waiting in the gondola and he would be none the wiser.

When they arrived, a servant informed them that the lady was out. Knowing this before hand, Carmelia insisted that they remain as the journey had been tiresome. She and Carmelia were shown into a tiny walled garden at the back of the house. There they sat sipping sweetened wine, waiting. Pellegrina had told Emlyn about the house and the two visits that Carmelia had made previously, and had arranged for them to meet there.

He was over an hour late. Carmelia was close to tears and Pellegrina had thrown a shawl about her shoulders and insisted that they leave. 'No,' snapped Carmelia. 'We will stay until dark if necessary.'

'It is nearly that now. I cannot see why you persist with this fascination for that boy, he is a vagabond.'

'Fascination?' gasped Carmelia. 'Vagabond! I love him Pellegrina, I shall never love another. I know that as sure as day be-gets night!'

'And what will you do when your husband leads you to the altar?'

'I shall not be there,' announced Carmelia with finality. 'And don't think you can lecture me because I won't listen! Go and turn your charms on Uglino or something, I don't want you here.'

Pellegrina marched off, so beautiful in her anger that Carmelia felt like a brown sparrow in comparison.

Soon after, the vines trembled and Emlyn came spilling over the wall in a shower of leaves. He looked drunk and was wet from the thigh down.

Carmelia flung herself into his arms and clung to him weeping like a child. Emlyn kissed the top of her head and whispered to her in his own tongue.

'Let us go from here beloved, right now,' begged Carmelia breaking away. 'I can climb that wall like I did in Milan. We can get into your boat and be away. None can search for us until daylight, by then who knows how far we could have travelled?'

Emlyn laughed, his eyes filled with affection. 'I haven't got a boat,' he said, indicating his soaked hose. 'Besides it will not work. There are things I must do before I attempt such an escape.'

'I don't care about the things you have to do,' cried Carmelia. 'I thought you cared about nothing but our being together.'

'I don't little flower leaf. But I can not shrug off my responsibilities so easily. We will not have long to wait.'

'How long then?'

'Until the Easter festivities,' Emlyn said, 'when Venice is masked and besotted with wine. Do you not see *Cariad*? Masked, we will be anonymous and be able to go where we will. It will not take me long to do what I need to do here. Then we shall return to Wales together.' He cradled her face in his hands, kissed her brow, her eyelids and kissed her mouth.

Carmelia eagerly returned his kisses and felt the tenseness of his passion as he crushed her lips. She moaned under his touch. She could feel his warm, wine-scented breath and shivered as his fingers traced a line down her back. His hands moved to her hips, stroking, caressing. He pulled her close to him, letting her feel his desire. The magician's hands cupped her breasts sending thrills of answering need running through her. Emlyn pressed her with hungry kisses, he held her so close that she could feel the thundering of his heart. He ran a hand down the length of her skirt, gathering up the material until he touched her flesh.

Carmelia giggled and pulled away snatching at the cloth of her skirts. 'Not like this!' she squealed. 'Not here like field peasants!'

Emlyn grinned like a wolf and chased her around the small enclosure, they were both near helpless with laughter. When he caught her, she felt the laughter disappear and instead was inflamed by the same need. She returned his kisses, burying her face in his hair. This was not the innocent passion they had first shared, it was something new, something wild and forbidden.

Chapter 42 Venice

On a day bright with the promise of summer, Fra Pietro Sebastiano da Firenze returned to Venice. With him, travelled Fra Lorenzo Grimani. They came on a fishing boat from Ravenna, winding through the intermittent sandy islands and grass spiked mud banks. Before they saw Venice, they saw the snow-capped mountains that rose sunlit and sparkling to the north. The sea was rich with fish, eels, crabs and shell fish and the sky was busy and raucous with sea birds. A flock of long-necked water birds flew over the boat, the susurration of their wings filling the air and their honking cries echoing across the Lagoon. The two Franciscans stood at the prow, with the faded sail bellying out behind them, casting them in shadow.

'This is the best way to come to Venice,' said Fra Sebastiano. 'Suddenly it is there, appearing out of the sea where nothing stood before.'

Fra Lorenzo's smile was wide and generous. 'I have not done this for years,' he replied. 'I am ashamed to say that I was never one for the sea. As a child I wanted to travel to the furthest reaches of the earth and see all the wonderful things that lay therein. But never once did I consider realising this dream by means of water.'

'You may yet achieve your wish,' said Fra Sebastiano. 'Our superiors are keen not to allow the Jesuits to carve the world between them. We must go where they go and beyond. They are too influenced by Spain and Portugal to spread the word of Christianity to these heathen people. Believe me, I know the folly of forcing one belief in place of another, the more pushed, the more they resist.'

Fra Lorenzo leaned his arms on the boat rail and watched the Lagoon approach. 'I have heard much that is admirable about the Society of Jesus, though I admit that such a name rankles me. These are troubled times for the Holy Church. A strong order is needed with new ideas to battle against the Reformers.'

Fra Sebastiano made an exasperated sound. 'There must be some among them that deserve credit,' he admitted. 'Unfortunately, I have yet to meet any. Do you remember that day when you carried the fish for me? In the kitchen when I told you of your half brother Emlyn Tomas and his quest to discover his parents?'

Lorenzo turned to look at him. 'The supposed half-brother?'

'Not so supposed. He has arrived in Venice, perhaps you should find him.'

'There have been many like him,' the young priest broke in, 'many who claim to be illegitimate sons of Don Carlos Grimani, or sons of my father Cristoforo or my uncle Roberto.'

'But none from England, I mean Wales?'

Lorenzo laughed. 'No, only the one you told me of, so there may be some truth in it. It is a fantastic tale and if it were not for the part you yourself played in it, I would be hard pressed to believe. If the young man is here in Venice, no doubt we shall meet, but I will not seek him out. Can I persuade you to stay with us at the Grimani house Fra Sebastiano?'

'That I cannot do, as much as I would like to. There are duties at our church to which I must attend. But I will not miss the coming wedding. I have heard that it is to be a quiet ceremony.'

'That is what this Vincentini has requested. For once, I think Don Carlos will be glad not to have to make a show of wealth. Until Paolo and the *Maria* return, he will be hard pressed to find the funds.'

'The rumours are true then, that his empire is crumbling?' said Fra Sebastiano, remembering the chilling words of old Zia Carlina.

'My brother Paolo tells me everything,' Lorenzo laughed. 'He does not even use a code in his letters, so the news is anybody's. I am sorry that he will not be here for Carmelia's wedding, and he will miss the Easter festivities. Poor Paolo, this is his favourite time of year.'

Fra Sebastiano wanted to ask his companion, whether he had told Paolo of the dreadful maiming he had suffered when taken from Carrara. Lorenzo had recovered remarkably well. He was much admired by the few who knew what had happened, including Fra Sebastiano. The young Venetian had pushed the incident from his mind, neither did he hunger for revenge or even knowledge of who and why. Fra Sebastiano understood this reaction. Lorenzo was closer to God than most men; he put his trust and destiny in the hands of God whole-heartedly. Whatever befell or awarded him in life, he believed firmly that God's will was at work. As a servant of God, he bowed to His judgement and questioned not. He cared nothing for wealth and influence, and ever placed his duty to family second to his duty to God. He had come to Venice now, only for the sake of Carmelia, the little girl he remembered with love and had not seen for nine years.

It seemed unlikely on reflection, that he would speak to Paolo about his suffering; Paolo was not blessed with the same peace of mind and spirit, he would overturn every stone until he discovered who had done the deed.

Fra Sebastiano had come now, because Emlyn had written to him from Milan, saying that he would be in Venice. Fra Sebastiano had few duties to attend to, being elderly and greatly respected by the community at Santa Croce, he was able to come and go as he pleased. But he always informed the abbot of his intentions and never failed to ask permission. The correct approach, he had discovered in his varied life, was invariably the most rewarding.

Bartolomeo Varini adjusted his eye glasses and skimmed through the ledgers before him. Occasionally his quill scraped against the paper, came away, dipped in ink and resumed its scratching. The year's business had run from success to success, the misery of Lanarca Salt was a thing of the past. Bartolomeo did not feel comfortable in the palace on the Grand Canal, although it was over thirty years old, it had an unfinished feel to it, as if it was about to be left empty again. Tomasso had had it painted yellow, which Bartolomeo found intolerable. In spite of this, it was busy, filled with clerks, and a miscellaneous collection of people who busied themselves running back and forth or scribing endlessly. Enrico de Martoni, had organised most of that, Bartolomeo would be happy when he came back, miserable though he was. Bartolomeo had received word that the *Cornucopia* and company had left Stamboul in the first week of March. He estimated that the ships would reach Venice in the next seven to ten days. I can hold the bastion until then, he chuckled to himself.

'Messer Varini?' said Jacopo from the door, in that manner of his that never seemed quite right since Tomasso had influenced him.

'Well?' snapped Bartolomeo. 'Am I to squeeze it out of you?'

'There is no need,' laughed Fiorenza, sweeping into the room. 'Did you swallow something horrible Bartolomeo? Or did you get your hose get wet crossing the piazza this morning?'

'No, I...'

'Well something has rubbed you the wrong way. Aren't you pleased to see me?'

'Of course,' beamed Bartolomeo, feeling his control flow away, forgiving her chattering. It had been weeks since she had last called. In fact, thought Bartolomeo, since the startling news about Tomasso's intended marriage to Carmelia Grimani. Although Bartolomeo was furious about the arrangement, he found some joy in Fiorenza's position, when the peacock folds his tail, the more interesting birds can be seen behind.

'I intend to leave Venice,' said Fiorenza. She unfastened her cloak and tossed it towards Jacopo who still lingered by the door.

'Go away Jacopo,' said Bartolomeo. He was devastated by Fiorenza's words.

'You are angry,' cried Fiorenza.

'Why go? Is it because of Tomasso and the Grimani child?' ventured Bartolomeo bravely.

'Of course not,' snapped Fiorenza, her cheeks burning with colour. 'I'm sorry Bartolomeo, that was foolish of me; I have behaved like a young girl caught in romantic fantasy. Is this wedding some form of repayment for the wrong done to Tomasso by Grimani so long ago?'

'Most certainly,' agreed Bartolomeo with a sigh.

'What will happen to the girl?'

'I don't know. But I would not think him capable of doing her harm.'

'Do you know where he is?'

The catch in her voice made Bartolomeo look up. Tears sparkled in her eyes. He said, 'I received a letter a few days ago, it was from Padua. Near though he is, he obviously cares nothing for the girl's anxiety. He is due here shortly before the wedding. Don Carlos himself, stopped me outside the Ducal Palace and asked me the very same, *'There is plenty of time,'* Tomasso wrote, '*to get to know her after we are wed.*' I am sorry Fiora, he is not a man who can see beyond his own designs.'

'Meaning what?' broke in Fiorenza. 'I do not understand how this marriage can grant him satisfaction.'

'Nor I. I cannot begin to guess. Fiora, he would not have made you happy, he is but a shell of a man, burnt out with bitterness.'

'You are most probably right,' agreed Fiorenza. 'It may surprise you to know that this is not the reason why I am leaving Venice. If my daughter, Florinda can not or will not come here, then I shall go to Cyprus. I have missed my family terribly.'

'What of your partnership here?'

'I need little enough. Send me only what I ask and use the rest to better my daughter's future, you are no stranger to wise investment.'

'Thank you, you will not regret your decision. But could there not be another way? I mean, why not re-consider?'

'No Bartolomeo, I have thought long on this and my mind is made up.'

Ask her! Ask her you fool! Bartolomeo's alter-self screamed in his mind. Fiorenza was already at the door. 'When are you going?' he gasped weakly.

'I will remain for the Festival,' she replied, 'a last masked, magical night that can only happen in Venice. I shall leave a week after.'

Bartolomeo swallowed audibly. 'No doubt I shall see you again then, before you leave?'

Fiorenza re-crossed the room and took his hands in hers. He thought they looked so small and shapely compared to his long, bony fingers, messed together like haphazard spider's legs. The joined hands were ill matched, as if to illustrate their incompatibility. Before she left, Fiorenza stood on tip toe and kissed him on the forehead. Bartolomeo cursed himself for his cowardice. The touch of her lips burned long after.

Emlyn sat in the workshop watching Umbaldo's deft hands as he set the marquetry on a lute face. A shaft of sunlight shot through the window, stabbing the intricate work and washing it like burnished copper. In spite of his size, Umbaldo's work was unequalled. Serving an apprenticeship was a waste of time for Umbaldo, his talent and imagination far exceeded that of the master craftsmen in Theo's employ. But Theo had seen the boy's potential early and had bound him with a contract before he could be spirited away by the promise of rich patrons. Umbaldo had turned his craft into an art. Emlyn sighed, this was something he had never attempted, but his fingers itched to have a try. He said nothing, Umbaldo would only laugh at his awkward attempts.

This was one of the few times when Emlyn was not rushed off his feet, he felt at odds having time to spare, it meant he would have to think. Whenever he thought, Carmelia came into his head and drove all others thoughts aside. He knew with certainty that what they had done was wrong, and with equal certainty that it was right.

Umbaldo and the other apprentices had been talking all morning about the Festival of Flowers and Easter and the regatta, there was no place better to be in than Venice in the Spring, they told Emlyn. You can be whatever or whoever you like at the carnival, so long as you are masked and unidentifiable. This worked to Emlyn's advantage, he had told none of them of his plans. Only Pellegrina provided the link between him and Carmelia, through her Emlyn sent verses of love and adoration; he also sent her the details of his scheme to get her away from Venice. Through Pellegrina, Emlyn learned all he could concerning Palazzo Grimani and she had told him that Carmelia would send him a token if she thought the plan feasible. He would ware a red mask for the festival, so that she would know him by it. It was less than a week to the feast day.

The attitude of the apprentices and craftsmen had changed since Emlyn had played for them, and he knew that Theo was doing what he could to introduce Emlyn to Don Carlos Grimani. There were others of much greater fame with whom Emlyn could find a position as lutanist, in the old tradition, but 'Grimani' was the name on all Venetian lips. Once Emlyn had planted the idea in Theo's mind, Theo had agreed that Don Carlos was a good choice of patron, for if all eyes were focused on the Grimani and the coming wedding, so should they focus on Emlyn Tomas.

If he had not been smitten by love for Carmelia, Emlyn could find a bright and profitable future in Venice. He was aware of this, and even wondered at times if he was nothing but a fool to be steered from his purpose by love. Love was an emotion that brought selfishness, irrational decisions, and an abandonment of sanity. As it did to my mother, thought Emlyn; she who left home and family, who deserted all for her own ends and broke her father's heart for the sake of love. Is it her impulsive nature that now visits me? Will I suffer the same tragic end as she?

But Emlyn had not abandon this cause. He believed that once he had Carmelia safely away from Venice, he could return and fulfil his oath. Once installed as house musician, he would have time enough to discover the truth concerning his mother and her fate. The only danger he could envisage, was discovery in the act of elopement. If he was found with Carmelia during their escape, he did not expect to survive. Don Carlos would have every right to order him killed outright. And Carmelia? What would happen to her if she were to wed the man intended? Pellegrina had told Emlyn that her mistress would die before allowing herself to become another man's wife. It was that desperation that Emlyn could not understand nor believe. Surely not even love could drive any to commit a mortal sin, and so be condemned to burn in hells' fire for eternity.

Theo entered the workshop, ducking under the lintel. In his hand, he carried a red mask, covered in sequins. When he reached Emlyn's side, he held it up with a finger, so it dangled from its strings. 'For you,' said Theo. 'A servant brought it. Do you have an admirer?'

'I hope I am not expected to wear it,' Emlyn said while the others laughed around him. He smiled in return, but inside, his mind was in turmoil. Why so outwardly! Had Carmelia's mind deserted her? He calmed his fears, none could know from who the token had come. They tried, with ribald humour to discover his secrets. Emlyn invented a different tale for each apprentice who badgered him for answers.

Theo ordered them all back to work. Then turning to Emlyn, he said, 'There is a group of madrigal singers come to Venice for the festival. They have agreed to let you join them and you will have plenty of opportunity to show off. They sing outside the basilica in the piazza San Marco. There too, will be everyone that matters, including Don Carlos. His musician will introduce you only if you impress the man.'

'Impress him?' said Umbaldo, 'Emlyn will leave him stunned, especially if he has a decent instrument.'

'I was coming to that,' snapped Theo. 'Umbaldo, like the bull you are named after, you have a habit of putting your horns in where they are not required.'

Chastised, Umbaldo turned red. Theo drew Emlyn to the end of the room and presented him with a perfect lute. 'It's not a gift,' he said, 'you can pay me when you are able.'

'Then give me a lesser one,' Emlyn said, 'the last perfect lute I held came to a sad end.'

'I have received word that my dearest brother Wendelin is due here this evening. Don't think I am afraid of him, I'm not. But if he sees that I have ignored his advice concerning you, he will be hard to pacify. The instrument is a good one as you will discover and will keep both you and Wendelin happy.'

Emlyn smiled. 'I shall be very glad to see him,' he said, and meant it.

Theo turned to leave and then turned back again. 'One more thing.' He pulled a fold of paper from his belt. 'You are very popular today, this came for you, a Franciscan novice brought it.'

When alone, Emlyn opened the letter. There were a few words written in a beautiful hand across the centre of the page. 'I am here, at the church of the Santa Maria Gloriosa dei Frari. Come when you can for there is much we can discuss. Guess who's here too?' It was signed Fra Pietro Sebastiano da Firenze.

Eager to go and visit the Franciscan at once, Emlyn stepped across the yard with the lute wrapped securely and held under his arm. He stuffed the red mask into his doublet where no one could see it. He had reached the griffin mounted gates, and just had time to see something charge straight at him, before it hit.

The blow caught him on the side of the head. His feet left the ground for a dizzying moment then he landed, crushing the lute beneath him. He hadn't even opened his eyes, before the thing hit him again, this time, across the bridge of his nose. Pain exploded inside his head. He fought blindly, hitting out and crab-walking backwards, fighting to regain his feet and see what was happening.

Through a film of tears, he recognised who it was immediately, Robusti, whom he had nearly poisoned in Milan. He was bigger than Emlyn remembered. Behind him, approaching with equal intent, came Sandrino and Ottavio. Emlyn lurched to his feet and abruptly sat down again, his head still reeling.

Theo's bellow, put an end to it all, before they could close in and do murder, which was what Emlyn feared. Theo's long stride carried him to the gates that he closed with flourish, trapping the assailants in the yard. He stood, feet slightly apart, big hands on hips and snowy head thrust forward. All work had ceased, the workshop emptied. Umbaldo came to Emlyn's side and helped him to his feet. 'What has happened?' he asked anxiously. 'These are the players who are to assist you in your ambitions, surely you have not fallen out with them already?'

'These?' gasped Emlyn. 'Hell couldn't have chosen more unwisely. We have met before, they have a grievance against me.'

Robusti considered himself, first and foremost, an actor. He commanded the centre of the courtyard and held them all spell-bound as he recounted the near tragic tale of his poisoning by the wicked foreigner. The same, who they, poor misguided souls, had taken in and were prepared to defend!

Emlyn stayed where he was, dabbing at his bleeding nose with his sleeve, his dreams and schemes falling into fragments before him. He stood straight and assumed an innocent expression. There was nothing he could say or do without jeopardizing his and Carmelia's future. His mind was numb, he could think of no way to answer them. He could not tell them about Carmelia, that the whole thing had been for the sake of love.

On cue, Sandrino took up the tale of the ruinous night in Milan when the same knave had wheedled his way into their confidence and proceeded to make a mockery of their refined performance. By the time he had finished, all eyes were turned on Emlyn and none of them were friendly, including Umbaldo's.

Emlyn was ready to answer, for the sake of Love. He said, 'I was driven to do the deed. I beg your forgiveness, poison me in return, if you must. But bear with me meantime, so you will know that I am not the villain you name me.'

The crowd relaxed a fraction and Emlyn saw some expressions soften. He had known Gruffydd Hiraethog command a hall of hundreds with just his voice alone. But Emlyn did not intend a story here, he would tell them the truth and let them judge him accordingly. Well, he amended, the truth as far is fitting, with a little adaptation here and there.

He said, 'I made a vow to a chaste and beautiful maiden. A sweet nymph so far above my standing, that I risked all that I could but glance upon her, to attempt to draw her sweet eyes toward me. Harder is he than iron whom such beauty could not stir, colder is he that ice that such fire could not scorch. I challenge any one of you if you were to look upon her you would be as smitten as I. She, sweet and gentle virgin, has looked upon me with favour, and God be eternally praised, her love is returned. Are we to deny Love? Are we to be ever ruled by our standing? I promised her that we should escape together. I followed her to Venice for the purpose of finding her and wedding her before any can move to interfere. Is she not as free a spirit as the birds that soar above the sea? Can not we be granted the happiness and fulfilment we deserve?'

'I don't believe you!' cried Sandrino. 'Who is this mythical maiden? Point her out to us and show us that she shares your devotion.'

'I cannot,' said Emlyn shaking his head in mock desolation. 'If we were discovered, her family would have me killed and worse still, cause great grief to her and injure her pure innocence.'

'Sweetly put chevalier, but not convincing enough!' laughed Sandrino. 'Produce the maid and we will stay the beating you so justly deserve.'

'The red mask!' cried Gian, the youngest apprentice. 'The favour of a lady?'

Emlyn stared at Sandrino, imploringly. 'I tell you truth. I would rather die than betray her. If Love cannot stay your hand, do what you will.'

'Gladly,' grated Sandrino, not the least swayed.

'Wait!' cried Ottavio. He came to stand between them, facing Emlyn. 'Show me then,' he suggested quietly. 'For I am the least angered by this. Show me, then Sandrino and Robusti will hold by my word.'

'Not so!' snapped Sandrino.

Ottavio turned to him. 'We did not do so badly that night. You especially Sandrino, for you were granted an appointment from Marc Antonio Ingegneri of Cremona. Which was what you desired.'

'That does not excuse the rogue. It would not be difficult to uncover his lies, for what women left Milan the following day to come to Venice? Not Rosalina and Bettina, nor their respected mother, it was the Grimani party. He is besotted with Carmelia Grimani and is urgent to wed her before the next man does!'

'You are correct but for one small detail Sandrino,' said Emlyn. His words were grating but his heart pounded in fear. 'The wrong lady,' he added coldly.

Sandrino howled with laughter. 'Then it must be the young and lively Madonna Adriana Martinelli! Such wonder that a youth can find desire in a woman three times his age! Pure and chaste did you say?'

Umbaldo elbowed his way between them. 'Didn't you say that you travelled from France with them Emlyn?' he said innocently.

Emlyn, had he the freedom, would have gladly throttled him. The situation had gone from bad to worse. 'Neither the lady nor the godmother,' he replied.

'Do we not consider ourselves as gentlemen?' said Ottavio. 'The insulting of respected ladies is beneath our dignity. The real injury was done to Robusti, it is for him to decide.'

They all fell into arguing. Emlyn sat down where he was. He recognised the stinging sensation of his eye swelling shut. It did not seem as bad as some he had suffered, Goronwy's brother had hit him harder. He reached out his hand and gingerly touched the lute wrapping, it felt like broken egg shell.

'What was it you told me about the last perfect lute you owned?' asked a voice above him.

'Much the same as has happened to this one,' said Emlyn sorrowfully. He gathered up the cloth, hearing the jangle of shards inside and held it upon his knee, devastated at what had happened. Was there ever such a day as this?

'Well I should have listened then, as I should have listened to Wendelin,' said Theo.

'Orpheus and Eurydice, did you really cause such ruin to these fine players?'

Emlyn merely nodded. What was the point in denying anything now?

'Orpheus was a musician,' said Theo. 'From his lyre came sound of such sweet melody and refinement that the birds and wild creatures gathered to listen to him. Music is in your soul Emlyn Tomas; not even Love will entice you from it.'

When Emlyn looked up, Theo had gone.

Emlyn reached Santa Maria Gloriosa dei Frari by evening. The sky was the colour of lemon rind, lighting the tall houses with a brilliant wash of gold. Announcing his intentions, Emlyn was shown to a small garden by an elderly man dressed in a brown Franciscan robe. The monastery was very different than College de Clermont, but there was something familiar about the cloisters and the dully clad friars who offered Emlyn smiles and greetings as he passed.

Fra Sebastiano was sitting on a bench, with a book open on his knee, he was fast asleep. When the elderly monk moved to awaken him, Emlyn gently pulled him back and shook his head. 'Leave him to his sleep,' he whispered. 'I can come back later. In the meantime I should like to visit your church?'

The friar nodded and smiled. He guided Emlyn through the building speaking softly as they walked. 'We came here when our founder St. Francis of Assisi, was still living,' he explained as if he himself had witnessed the happening over three hundred years before. 'Begging then from door to door, sleeping in peace in the porticoes of the churches. Who would think that from such humble beginnings we would have one of the finest churches in Venice?'

The church and monastery was a large complex of buildings. The cloisters and school surrounded two wide courtyards that they crossed before coming to the Gothic church. Once there, Emlyn was left alone. The golden evening light poured through the large rose windows, the great church was unexpectedly bright, Emlyn felt small and insignificant. He found to one side, a small chapel where he was better able to kneel in quiet prayer. He spent over an hour with his head bent over clasped hands and would have stayed longer, if a hand had not touched his shoulder and brought him from his solitude.

At first he saw only feet, but even these betrayed their owner. They wore sandals and were large and freckled. Unbelieving, Emlyn looked up and gasped in surprise.

'Saints alive! It's yourself, Emlyn Tomas of the White Virgin,' said Friar Patrick O'Healy. 'Tis sure the good father told me you'd be here, but I'd not thought him to be telling me the truth.'

Emlyn stood, his stiff knees creaking. 'What are you doing here?' he asked as they made their way out of the church.

'Visiting the man himself, though he's not seen fit to find the time for me yet.'

'Fra Sebastiano or Pope Pius?'

'That's the very man. I took meself to the Vatican to talk to him about Ireland. T'was while I was there I bumbled into yon old padre, an' him all for persuading me to come here. There must be a great deal of sinning going on, for there's a great many churches. Have you seen them yourself?'

Emlyn laughed, suddenly his worries diminished. 'I could hardly miss them now, could I?'

'She can call herself Queen of Ireland for all the good it'll do, she'll not get the O'Nieills bowing and scraping nor the rest of us.'

Emlyn assumed he was speaking of Queen Elizabeth and that he had come for much the same purpose as the last time he had visited Rome. Pope Pius had not had time to see him then either. As Ireland adhered to the Holy Church and was a suitable place to launch an attack on Protestant England, Emlyn could not understand the delay caused to Friar O'Healy, nor could he feel anything but relief that it was so. England had enough to cope with.

They found Fra Sebastiano in the same secluded spot. He embraced Emlyn as if he were a lost son and questioned him about his black eye. Emlyn bit back the tears that stung his eyes. They were unable to speak freely for the first hour or so, as Friar O'Healy accompanied them to the refectory and sat through the evening meal talking about Ireland.

When they were alone, Emlyn and Fra Sebastiano walked away from the church and found a quiet seat, overlooking the Rio della Frescada. The night was warm with a dry, spicy scent in the air. Fra Sebastiano explained that this was the smell of the North African desert brought in on the wind. 'Your dear mother would have known the same scent,' he said. He described his previous visit to Venice and something of his visit to old Zia Carlina. Before he revealed what he had discovered, he said, 'I am going to ask something of you Emlyn, but I do not ask you for promises, if you believe what I ask impossible.'

Emlyn had listened in silence up until then. He looked expectantly at the priest.

Fra Sebastiano released a weary sigh. He said, 'When you have heard all I tell you, can I hope that you will forget all this and return to your home? You are a young and talented man, your whole life waits for you, whatever happened in the past can have no bearing on your future.'

'I know what you are trying to tell me,' answered Emlyn. 'Ambrose Chillingworth, the Englishman I travelled with, informed me of much the same, overturn long settled stones and you uncover only worms.'

'The man spoke true. Italy is not like England, if you put a step wrong here and offend the wrong people, you will pay dearly. No wrong goes un-avenged in Italy, no matter what the cause. I am afraid that you will become involved in a tangle of no escaping. What you need to know happened twenty years ago and is forgotten. They may be some who wish it to remain so.'

'But not I,' said Emlyn. 'I have not come here to turn about and go back again. You say that in Italy no wrongs go un-avenged, if injustice was done to my mother, who can avenge her? We may not be as passionate in England, but nor do we turn away from injustice and are just as capable of extracting the cost from the offender. I can give no promises until I hear what you have found out.'

'Then I must be content with that and pray that God will guide your choice,' said Fra Sebastiano. 'There are two versions of what happened, you must decide which is nearer to the truth. The first I have been told, is that your mother suffered from an ailment that effected her sanity. Don Carlos took the boys from her and sent her to a convent on Cyprus to recover. But her ship was attacked by pirates or met a storm at sea and she never reached there. But we have you Emlyn, so we know with certainty that Anna Grimani did not perish at sea. We must assume that she was taken by a slaver. The old woman Zia Carlina had a different tale to tell. She claimed that Don Carlos arranged it all, that he was fully aware of her captivity and ignored the demand for ransom when it came, her disappearance was a solution to his problems at the time. There is no proof of this Emlyn, no one knows the truth but he.

'Your mother took a lover, a young jewel merchant by the name of Tomasso Capaccio, which, incidentally, may explain the jewels your mother left to you. Unfortunately during those last days in Venice, he became involved in whatever conflict existed between Anna Grimani and Don Carlos. The outcome being, he fought with a man and killed him. Capaccio then paid the penalty for the deed. He was accused, imprisoned and spent his remaining life as a galley slave. When you came to us as a small child, you told me that your mother often called you Toma. It is quite likely your father was this jewel merchant. Unfortunately, there is no way to discover anything further.'

'Could we not discover who it was he fought with? It may have some bearing on what happened to my mother. It is not enough for me to know only this, there are too many questions left unanswered. If she was so in love with this merchant then why did she go to Cyprus in the first place?'

'It was the will of Don Carlos,' said Fra Sebastiano. 'Perhaps at the time his was the best solution. The man your probable father killed was Roberto Grimani, Don Carlos' only living son.'

'No man kills without purpose,' said Emlyn bitterly. 'If it was a fight in which this Roberto was killed, how can the deed be so punishable? One man against another? I must still face Don Carlos and ask him for the truth.'

'That may not be a wise thing to do. He and your mother did not get on very harmoniously. The 'truth' you hear from him may not be the one you wish to hear. Awakening old conflicts, may turn him against you completely and you will discover nothing.'

Emlyn said, 'I had intended to be discreet in my inquiries, if I ever got as far as the door. Up until now, I have found no justifiable reason to present myself. I had hoped to introduce myself to his music master, and gain an appointment through him. If I had a chance to play for Don Carlos, I feel sure that he would employ me.'

'That's where I come in,' laughed Fra Sebastiano smugly. 'One of our brethren in Florence, is a Grimani. In fact, from all account, he is your half-brother Lorenzo. I travelled in his company on the journey here.'

Emlyn felt a surge of excitement. He said, 'I had learnt that Paolo had gone to Constantinople with Grimani's trading ships and that Lorenzo was in Florence. What is he like?'

'You'll like him. He is gentle and considerate, never has a harsh word to say of anybody. I have rarely met one better suited to the service of God, which he has devoted himself to. He was ordained last summer, much to Don Carlos' annoyance. I have told him of you Emlyn.'

Emlyn looked at him in surprise. 'And?'

'At first he dismissed the possibility. But he will talk to you and is probably as curious as yourself. I have met your Don Carlos too, and have been made welcome there. We shall go together and if you are as good as you say you are, then we will find opportunity to employ your talent. You may also discover in Lorenzo some of the answers you seek. Although he was but a child when all this occurred, he has fond memories of his mother. It will be interesting to discover if his memories of her are alike to yours.'

They talked long after that, until the night grew cool and Fra Sebastiano showed signs of tiring. Emlyn stayed at the monastery. He fond no chance for sleep, while in the company of Friar Patrick O'Healy. But Emlyn was happy, the Irishman was like a breath of fresh Celtic air.

When Emlyn returned to his room at Tieffenbrucker's house the following morning there was a familiar looking travelling pack on his bed. He stood for a moment in the doorway, just staring at it. The last time he had seen it was at the inn in Rouen. Wendelin had arrived in Italy and had brought Emlyn's possessions as Josquin had said he would do. Emlyn sat down and pulled carefully at the draw strings. Just inside, wrapped in oiled paper was Emlyn's translation of Genesis. He opened it and saw the words swim before his eyes, Welsh words that aroused so much emotion, so much that was dear to his heart.

Before he greeted Wendelin, Emlyn hurried out of the gates with the manuscript. He had already sought out Paolo Mannutio, but had been unable to talk with the printer about the possibilities of printing in Welsh. The printing house founded by Theobaldo Mannutio, known as Messer Aldus, was on the corner of the Campo di San Agostino, near the Scuola di S Giovanni Evangelista. Until he had come to Venice, it had been a quiet and peaceful corner, but the printing house and the new methods employed there, had attracted much interest and many learned men had come to gather in discussion, to rub shoulders with famed scholars or to assist Aldus with their critical experience and knowledge. There were hundreds who wished to see their own work in print, but Aldus had had little time or patience for those who asked the impossible. When he had died, Aldus had left the business to his son Paolo and although the fame of the printing house had lessened with the increase of others, it still maintained an air of scholarly seriousness and still remained a place for intelligent men to meet and exchange ideas.

When Emlyn arrived he paused by the door and read the inscription that old Aldus had placed over the entrance. *'Whoever you are, Aldo requests you, if you want anything, ask it in few words and depart, unless, like Hercules, you come to lend the aid of your shoulders to the weary Atlas. Here will always be found in that case, something for you to do, whoever you may be.*

Emlyn heard the clank and clatter of printing presses in the near distance, but he could not see them. Instead he saw a long room sectioned off periodically with screens behind which scholars worked in strict silence, pouring over their writings, editing work to be published. There was a smell of old books, leather and ink. Paolo Mannutio sat at a table at the end of the room, bent over his work. He was in his fifties, with a thatch of untidy white hair and thick white eyebrows knit in concentration. Emlyn approached as quietly as he was able and remained standing unacknowledged. He cleared his throat.

'Be about it and be off,' said Paolo Mannutio without lifting his head.

Emlyn smiled thinking the man very like his father who had written the words above the door. 'Messer Mannutio, I have heard that you print works in Greek and Latin.'

'Yes, yes,' he said impatiently. 'I have no time to waste. What do you want?'

Getting straight to the point, Emlyn said, 'I came to inquire whether or not you might consider printing in a Celtic tongue. The Holy Bible translated into Welsh.'

This time the brown eyes lifted from what they were doing and eyed Emlyn with a spark of interest. 'Welsh?'

'It is not a tongue known outside the confines of Wales. But I have been most careful in the translation.'

'Not known?' smiled Mannutio. 'Well there you are mistaken. I have printed in your tongue before, not more that a year ago. I remember it well for we worked closely with the man who commissioned it. He is confessor to Cardinal Borromeo in Milan.'

Then suddenly Emlyn recalled the conversation he had had with his grandfather and John Talbot on their way to Owain's wedding, the mention of a certain Gruffydd Roberts who had fled Wales and come to Italy when the catholic queen Mary had died. And another who had gone with him, Morys Clynnog. '*Gruffydd Roberts is working on a book of grammar in the rhythmical style of Cicero. You would be well cared for by them Emlyn should you see fit to visit. I suspect they follow the teachings of the Jesuits like yourself.*' Emlyn had not thought of them since. He regretted the opportunity he had missed while he had been in Milan, what a pleasure it would have been to see and speak with another Welshman so far from home. He said, 'Yr Athrawiaeth Gristnogol, the book of Christian Doctrine. Was that the work you printed?'

'No, it was a book of Welsh Grammar. I liked the man. Roberts or something like that. What you ask will cost you and you do not look like a man with the coin to pay. The Bible is an exceptionally large manuscript.'

'I know something of the cost,' Emlyn replied, 'and you are right to judge me incapable of producing it at present. That is why I have only brought the book of Genesis. It is printed already, but I should like to see it done in the proper manner, we were a little limited when I and my companions undertook the task.'

Mannutio nodded, his hair falling forward. He un-wrapped the manuscript Emlyn had brought and gasped in surprise. 'This is unacceptable!' he pronounced. 'Look, there are even finger marks on the first page!'

Emlyn hung his head. 'I am aware that it is far beneath your standards, but we have no printing presses in Wales and this was produced under the most trying circumstances. In the words the value lies and these you will find are as correct as they can be.'

Paolo Mannutio looked at him seriously. 'I am not a man to put down the efforts of others,' he said. 'But in all honesty, there is no point in producing just the Book of Genesis. It would not be worth the time and effort here. Now, if you have the whole of the Old Testament translated, even if hand written, then you can ask me again. Your fellow countryman in Milan may be able to assist you if you have not the funds yourself.'

Emlyn gathered up the pages and tied them up again. He bowed respectfully and thanked the printer before he left. He felt bitterly disappointed, but was not the least bit put off by what Mannutio had told him. He agreed that the printer was right. When he and Carmelia were away from Venice, Emlyn would look up Gruffydd Roberts, and perhaps between them, they could produce a work that would benefit Wales and the Welsh tongue. Old Mafanwy had called him Mab-y-Ddarig, a saviour for Wales, well there were other ways of saving Wales than running amok with sword and spear.

Emlyn was surprised how happy he felt to see Wendelin and Eva. Theo's yard had been transformed into a play area for children, fair heads bobbed up and down. The air rang shrill with laughter while all clamoured for attention. Theo's Italians gave up any hope of getting work done, their natural love for children brought them all out to watch or play.

Emlyn e was smothered by Wendelin first and then Eva, he emerged from the Theo-type bear hugs gasping for breath. Wendelin held his shoulders and examined him with scrutiny. 'You are no longer a boy,' he pronounced as if the wonder had just that moment happened. 'All broadened out in to a handsome young man to woo the Italian ladies. From what we learned from Josquin, Eva and I were concerned for our little fledging. I see our worries were unfounded. We saw Josquin in Milan and the English gentleman with whom you travelled. So now we are all in Venice, where life begins and music is on every breath of wind. You have seen the children, they have talked about you all the way over the mountains.'

Emlyn grinned. 'They have all grown too,' he said. 'Now Messer Theo will be forced to employ teachers instead of lute makers.'

'You have seen your things that we brought?'

'Yes, and am in your debt for that and the help you gave me on leaving Rouen. I prayed that no trouble would come of it.'

'Ah, trouble!' said Wendelin woefully. He winked and turned to his wife, gathering her and pulling her towards him in an affectionate embrace. 'We had a visit from your Don Diego. Eva showed him the door,

Didn't you my little savage. You should have heard her Emlyn. There's a woman for you, who need weapons when you have a tongue like that whipping to your defence. The man never even got a single word out.'

Eva thumped her husband's chest. 'Men!' she exclaimed. 'What would men be without women to defend them?' She stood on tip toe and planted a kiss on his red nose. Then she turned to Emlyn with a look of motherly concern. 'You are recovered from your ordeal Emlyn?'

'Perfectly,' Emlyn smiled. 'And your horses, did you get them back?'

'We received a message from Josquin and picked them up a few weeks later when the snow had cleared,' Eva explained. 'They are in Padua now with a cousin, no point bringing them here, they would have to swim, but they have served us well.'

'I have brought you something else,' said Wendelin. He broke away from Eva's embrace and dug into his tunic. He produced a pouch that he handed to Emlyn with a wink.

Emlyn recognised it immediately. He pulled at the draw string and poured the contents into his palm. Light winked off the gems sending a dazzle of dancing colour about the room. 'How can this be?' He was suddenly overjoyed.

'The agreement we made with the banker Ferdinando Rovigo, entitled us both to collect them. I bullied them out of him myself. Now you can be a rich man for a short while.'

'How can I ever repay you,' asked Emlyn. He was acutely uncomfortable with the favours this German family had done for him. 'And your brother Theo,' he added.

'He was helpful to you?' said Wendelin. 'I told him to be.'

'He has showered me with generosity.'

'Kind of you young Emlyn, but over generous,' said Theo entering the room. 'But we have done well enough. And you were right in your judgement of his skill Wendelin, he has left us speechless.'

'I had my doubts,' said Wendelin. 'I thought to have heard of Emlyn's fame as far off as Geneva. By now such talent should have made you your own master.'

Theo turned red but before he could speak, Emlyn said, 'I suffered a minor injury that set me back a month or two. It was at Rouen, but I am recovered now and ready to take Venice by storm.'

Eva grasped his hands and turned them over in her own, examining them and tutting over the ragged scar. Emlyn endured it, growing more and more uncomfortable. He was saved from further embarrassment by the arrival of Theo's wife Mariebella, announcing that the meal was ready to be served and it promised to be a treat. Eva had brought bundles of edible gifts over the Alps with her, they all filed out of the room with promises of sausages, spiced cabbage, cakes and a feast fit for the Doge's table.

When the talk had lessened, Emlyn managed to talk privately to Theo. He said, 'I am sorry for the lute. I will pay you as soon as I am able. And for the disruption to your workshop and yard.'

'Forget it,' said Theo with a wave of his hand.

'I insist,' said Emlyn. 'How could I do otherwise and remain at peace with myself?'

'If it makes you feel better, then by all means do as your conscience demands.'

Emlyn rubbed at his eye. It was quite black today, he was surprised that Eva had said nothing about it. He said, 'What happened with the players? I didn't wait to find out.'

'They do not care for you to join them and so have refused. They are willing to forget what you did but not to forgive. What that means is anyone's guess, perhaps they look for a way to repay you in kind. It might be wise to avoid them. Why Grimani anyway? I can find you a better patron, a true lover of the art of music, Count Marco Verit^ or Alessandro Franganesco, both of Cremona, Viadanna, Maestro di Cappella at the cathedral of San Pietro in Mantua, Martinengo Maestro di Cappella of San Marco, here in the Serene Republic of Venice. I will speak to the Procurators.'

Emlyn listened with abstract attention. He would need such influential men when he escaped Venice. He refused to consider the possibility of 'if'. Ambrose had once said to him 'Never if, it, whatever it may be, either is or isn't, 'if' doesn't enter the question.'

BOOK THREE

The Salamander

Chapter 43 Sea Battle

The Venetian caravels sped over the Aegean Sea with the grace and ease of birds on the wing. Behind them, the war galley beat the sea, cleaving through the waves as the oars rose and fell in unison. The sailing ships carried their own master's cargoes and a certain enmity had grown between them. As captain of the *Cornucopia*, Marco Erizzo refused to speak to Cesare Faliero, captain of the galley or Matteo Sarzana on the *Maria*, until they showed respect for his position as overall commander.

On the *Maria*, Matteo Sarzana glared across the sea space and hoped the *Cornucopia* would sink, taking Marco Erizzo with it. He had been instructed by Don Carlos Grimani to find some ploy to delay the *Cornucopia* and so reach Venice ahead, Don Carlos liked to have the upper hand.

Aboard the galley, Cesare Faliero knew nothing of this, but had been instructed to follow the orders of Sarzana above the orders of Erizzo. He found little to admire in either of them. So far, he had found no cause to disobey one in order to appease the other, he was insulted, in truth, that it had been asked of him. The most experienced of the three sea captains, Cesare knew the folly of disunity at sea. Soon they would arrive in Crete where they could hopefully heal their differences. Both Caravels rode low in the water, the holds filled with eastern luxuries. They had each tried to be secretive with each other. Cesare had seen the barrels of spice and grain that made up most of the cargo. He had seen the carpets, brass, leather, lacquer-ware and iron bound boxes These last, judging by the way they were guarded, probably held gems and gold. Cesare shook his head, he was not impressed by it all. The only item of cargo that had aroused his interest was a box of compound bows, like the ones the Turks used when shooting from horseback. They were aboard the *Cornucopia*, along with Turkish saddles and harness as were many personal items that Scipeone Barozzi had been instructed to acquire for Tomasso di Vincentini.

Apart from buying slaves to replace the four oarsmen they had lost on the out-bound voyage, Cesare and his crew had little to occupy them in the Turkish city. He had kept a close eye on Paolo Grimani and had come to like the young man in spite of his misgivings. At times, Paolo was wild and uncontrollable; if he decided upon a course of action, nothing would deter him from it. He had got into some sticky situations in the pursuit of adventure, but his charm and wit and ready purse allowed him to escape unscathed. Cesare and he had learned to respect each other in the matter of drinking; for a youth of twenty two years, Paolo had a remarkable capacity. He had also shown an assertiveness with Matteo Saranza, bullying him into sacrificing a barrel of mace to make room for a terra-cotta vase of immense proportions that was reputed to have come from the court of the Empress Theodora. Cesare had been with Paolo in the dark narrow street where they had been led by an enthusiastic boy of ten. The Greek dealer had been very convincing. Cesare had commented that the jar was remarkably well preserved for its years. He did not add that, there were another three dozen very similar jars just around the corner with the very same legend attached.

Hearing Paolo approach, Cesare turned away from the salt-laden wind. Paolo's movements were self assured now; he sauntered up the walk-way between the rowing benches as if he were a lord out for an afternoon's hawking. The confidence was justified, Paolo had achieved all his grandfather had asked of him. All that remained was to deliver the laden caravel to Venice. There had been rumour that Don Carlos had suffered further financial set back. If that were so, thought Cesare, the old man would be more that compensated when the cargo came in aboard the *Maria*

'Remarkable,' said Paolo as he drew level. 'The wind has risen in our favour. It will be a relief to be free from the clatter of oars for an hour or two. The slaves we bought to replace the ones we lost are having an easy time of it. Quirini has put the three of them at the same oar, they have no sense of rhythm. Their oar is up while the others are down and down when the rest are up. Still, it is a small set back, considering the luck we have had so far. I can't wait to get home. How long do you think it will take?'

'Just over two weeks, if we do not delay too long in Crete.'

'Then why go there at all?'

Cesare only offered the tolerating frown that Paolo recognised as meaning, in the hands of God. This was a term they had become used of hearing while in Stamboul, where everything was in the hands of God, or rather Allah.

Paolo smiled. 'Forget I asked'

'I find no fault in your enthusiasm,' said Cesare. 'Don Carlos will be proud that you have done all in so short a time. God has granted us favour. In all my years running these seas I have never known a trading voyage to go so smoothly. Some credit must go to Scipione Barozzi and that Syrian who arranged it all.'

'Well the Syrian is not here,' said Paolo with a mischievous grin, 'so we can take all the credit for ourselves.'

Cesare shrugged uneasily. 'It all ran so smoothly that I was suspicious until we actually got away; afraid that some custom official or mishap would delay us. I would not have been surprised if we had been stopped by the Turkish officials and forced to pay exorbitant fees before we were allowed to leave, the Turks have that sort of humour.'

'Put worry from your mind Cesare,' said Paolo confidently. 'We are safe now and sail further from threat with every wave. We are strong enough to deter the most daring pirate.'

'Aye,' said Cesare nodding his grey head thoughtfully. 'Yet I cannot feel the same surety while there is such enmity between us and Vincentini's caravel.'

'While we are at sea we are safe enough,' said Paolo looking over the waves to where the *Cornucopia* followed. 'Another reason why stopping at Crete is unwise,' he added. 'Even I, who never shies from a good quarrel cannot understand why Marco Enrico remains so stubborn and argumentative. I shall advise Vincentini to be rid of the man. Perhaps I could recommend you Cesare, to captain his tub?'

Cesare laughed. 'I am a galley man young Paolo. Let me feel the pounding of a warship under my feet not the sloppy wallowing of a wind dependent ship. If you want to place a spy aboard Vincentini's ship, you will have to find someone else.'

A swift North African galley pulled into a bay of the once Venetian island of Negroponte. Shortly afterwards, a pinnacle pulled away rowing towards the rocky shore. It carried Ismael the Syrian and his retainers. As the boat drew nearer, Ismael could see a group of horsemen waiting on a hill above the beach. He nodded his head when he made out the pennants fluttering above them and saw the pre-arranged signal he had been expecting. The boat ground on sand and pebbles. Three oarsmen leaped into the shallows and drew the boat in, so that the master would not get his feet wet. The red leather boots trod on dry land, the ornamental tassels swinging. Ismael turned and smiled at the large Arab sea captain who stood beside him. 'Salaam Aleikum. Peace be upon you my friend!'

'May Allah guide you swiftly,' said the captain, patting Ismael's shoulder affectionately.

'How long can you wait?' asked Ismael.

'Until the moon is once again full in the heavens. To expect me to survive on miserable Greek lamb any longer would be punishment indeed.'

'The feast we will celebrate when I return, will more that make up for your suffering. Abu Abdullah.'

'You could leave me your servant Koçi,' suggested Abu. 'I would pine away, should any misfortune befall the gracious creature.'

Ismael laughed lightly. 'You have Saiah on board your ship Abu, let him be your companion.'

Soon after, Ismael, his servants including Koçi, and five armed men climbed up the embankment from the beach and joined the waiting horsemen. There were mounts waiting for them; fast mountain horses, well suited for the rugged terrain of central Greece. There would be no comfort and little rest until the land was crossed and they came in sight of the sea on the other side.

As he rode away from the coast, Ismael prayed that the three war galleys would be waiting for him when they reached the Ionian sea, he did wish to waste any time. He was not concerned that they would miss the *Cornucopia* and the *Maria*; these would most certainly call at Crete for supplies and be delayed. There, Ismael knew, they would discover an order from the Senate for a cargo of grain for the Venetian Republic. The last summer's harvest had been poor and Venice depended on her Islands for extra grain. Ismael was not interested in the grain. He had filled these ships with treasure. Now he would take it back again.

Ismael had gone to a great deal of trouble to pamper to the Turkish Sultan's love for wine. He had stolen Cyprus wine from Venetian ships the year before; it was Sultan Selim's favourite. Sultan Selim was a generous lord if served well. Bestowed with such favour, nothing would stand in Ismael's path. Soon he would be counted among the wealthiest merchant princes in Constantinople, that was, if he should desire it.

He thudded his heels into the horse's flanks and heard the harness ring. His heart was filled with joy. Above the riders, rose the harsh rocky mountain slopes, bare of soil and vegetation, sharp against the clear sky. On the gentle wind came the stringent scents of thyme and pine. Behind him, Koçi, began to sing an amusing love song. The men laughed at him and one snatched at a wild olive branch and placed it between his lips whilst waving his arms in the air like the dusky Gypsy dancers of Balatmahalle.

'It is not so very long since I saw that very ship in my harbour,' said Sebastiano Venier, the governor of Crete. 'I remember the owner well.

Tomasso di Vincentini. He was travelling with Fiorenza Caterina Balsamo and Enrico de Martoni.' He smiled tenderly, remembering the lady. 'I'm sorry to see that Scipione Barozzi is not with you.'

'Barozzi has remained as Vincentini's agent in Stamboul. Vincentini, like my own master, has no need to suffer the ardours of the sea excellency,' commented Matteo Sarzana, the commander of the *Maria*. He and Cesare stood at the governor's window overlooking the harbour. Paolo sat sprawled in a chair, ill tempered because he had been unable to persuade Cesare and the others from coming to Crete.

'I remember Vincentini's jewels,' said Venier.

'He has done well for himself since then, lavish to the extreme,' said Matteo Sarzana with an air of contempt. 'Funny how wealth make more wealth. When the *Cornucopia* returns he will be richer still. Don Carlos too, stands to recover his losses.'

'He is fortunate in his choice of galley captain,' smiled Venier. He and Cesare Zatta had fought together against Genoa in numerous sea battles. 'Is it Marco Erizzo who captains the *Cornucopia*?'

'He is a good seaman,' said Cesare. 'However, the ship is commanded by Enrico de Martoni who is nothing more that a notary. Let us hope he leaves matters of the sea to those better suited. There have been troubles enough.'

'How so?' asked Venier.

'We serve under two masters,' said Sarzana. 'Vincentini and Don Carlos. Enrico Martoni will continue to be difficult because of that alone.'

'Then let him sail alone with Vincentini's ship,' laughed Venier.

Cesare laughed with him. 'Martoni is not a fool. He will not sail without the galley.'

Paolo unfolded from the chair and joined them. 'My grandfather tried to persuade Vincentini to treat this as a joint venture,' he explained. 'Vincentini refused to entertain the idea, insisting that we each take our own risks. Even protection from the war galley would not induce him to change his mind. Enrico de Martoni is probably being awkward because he was told to be. We both race for the Venetian markets. Vincentini is the only man I have ever known to go against the wishes of my grandfather. But Don Carlos has his measure.'

'Which is?' asked Cesare.

'Greed, the same as most men,' said Paolo. 'His wealth will soon be shared by Don Carlos anyway so I can't see why there has to all this secretiveness.'

'Shared?' said Venier, curious.

'Did you not know?' laughed Paolo, 'everyone else does. Vincentini is to become one of the family, son-in-law, to be precise. He is to wed the only child of Don Carlos, my dear cousin Carmelia. So why the competition?'

'Whatever the reason,' said Cesare, 'we need to keep the ships together until we reach friendly seas.'

When they had left the governor, Sarzana drew Cesare and Paolo into the privacy of his own room. 'Much as I dislike what I am about to reveal to you,' he said in a secretive whisper, 'I am under Don Carlos' orders and it would be more that my life's worth to go against him. It is essential that we reach Venice before the *Cornucopia*. I have been instructed to do all I can to achieve this. I will not stoop to sabotage, but we have a faster ship and if we can devise some way of delaying Enrico de Martoni and Vincentini's caravel, only if for a half day, we should have no problem reaching our objective.'

'I have sailed these seas since I was a child,' said Cesare crossly. 'Never have I deserted a fellow ship and I do not intend to do so now.'

'It sounds like common sense to me,' said Paolo. 'Don Carlos wishes to score a point against Vincentini, perhaps to teach him a lesson as well as to make the better profit. The *Cornucopia* has sailed alone before. If I have to, I shall sail with it and even throw myself overboard to reach our objective.'

'Then whatever you do will be without my support,' snapped Cesare. 'I'll have no part of it. We are agreed to remain together.'

'You have no choice in the matter,' said Sarzana. 'You are Grimani's man and under his command. Verbally, a man can agree to anything. When we lose the other caravel, it will seem like an accident; who knows the rule of the wind? Enrico de Martoni will never suspect our intentions. We will wait until we are within six or seven days of Venice before we act, by then I should have come up with some idea to achieve the separation.'

Paolo grinned disarmingly. He is a true Grimani, thought Cesare. It is strange that Don Carlos has not seen his potential. But Paolo has not the cruelty and guile of his grandfather, perhaps that may come with experience and avarice. I am but a pawn in the game of great men, now I question my own loyalty, a matter which I have never had cause to question before.

Ismael pulled his horse to a halt on top of a rise overlooking the sea. The wind fluttered the fur around his hat and snatched at the ties on his padded jacket; on the tie ends, golden acorns hung and winked in the bright sun. His mare stamped and ached her neck; Ismael mumbled to her in Greek until she stood quietly. He had pushed the men and the horses hard allowing them little rest. Now, he knew he would reach the desired coast line before nightfall.

Stretching out before him lay the Gulf of Patras and the land mass of Morea opposite. The Ionian sea was a starling blue seeded with gem-like islands. Some of these were still Venetian, but Greece and Morea were under Ottoman rule. So too was the finger of sea that ran from Lepanto to Corinth; an ideal harbour for Turkish shipping. This sea would have run into the Aegean if not for the isthmus of land that joined the mainland to Morea.

The Gulf of Patras provided Ismael with an ideal position from which to launch his attack. These islands provided provisions for the Venetian ships. He was not afraid of re-enforcement's coming to the ship's aid for there were no galleys at the Ionian islands. Ismael spurred his mount and rode down to join his men.

Before the end of the day they reached the hidden bay where the three black galleys lay on the water and the smoke from cooking fires spiralled up from the beach. The riders drew their mounts in and gathered on a ridge above the sea. They smiled and joked, the master had pushed them hard but they had got here and all was as he had told them.

The sun washed the sea in brilliant splendour. With great reverence and relief, Ismael spread his mat on the ground and bent in prayer towards Mecca.

When the Venetian ships reached the Ionian island of Zante, Matteo Sarzana left the *Maria* and went ashore to greet his family who had moved there from Tuscany. The Caravels lay in the harbour, loading water and grain and the galley lay close to them. No other large vessels lay at anchor, only a few Greek fishing boats, their nets stretched drying out in the sun. The Venetians had made good time sailing from Crete and had heard mass together before Matteo Sarzana had left his caravel. He could now see the ships from the flat roof of his sister's house, where the family had gathered to share a meal.

'Can I come with you uncle?' This question came from Sarzana's eight year old nephew, an undersized boy who never stopped chattering pointlessly.

Sarzana cuffed him across the ear. 'Don't be stupid boy!'

His sister looked up from her plate as the boy cried out. 'Luigi! Don't bother your uncle,' she scolded 'He is an important man with no time for children.' Then seeing Luigi's tears, she added, 'Perhaps he will take you to sea when you are older.'

A Greek servant reached the top of the open steps huffing and puffing. He approached Sarzana and bowed lower than he was already bent by age. 'Messer Sarzana, there is a messenger from your ship who wishes to speak with you urgently.'

Sarzana nodded and made his way down the sunlit steps to the pebbled courtyard below. There, he stopped in astonishment, the messenger was Enrico de Martoni, the miserable looking notary from the *Cornucopia*. He was pacing up and down with his hands clasped behind his back and his pointed face knit in a frown.

'Messer de Martoni?' said Sarzana with a minimal nod.

Enrico marched up to him. 'I acknowledge that we have our differences,' he said, 'but something has come up which must push them aside at present.'

Sarzana felt the colour drain from his face. Had Cesare betrayed his designs? Calming himself, he said, 'What has happened?'

'We have lost our anchor. The chain snapped,' explained Enrico reddening with shame. 'The earliest another can be brought to replace it, is twelve hours.'

'Chain snapped?' Sarzana stared at him in astonishment. He had judged the *Cornucopia* unfit for the voyage from the beginning. During an argument with Enrico de Martoni in Stamboul, he had said that the ship was a disgrace and should not carry the pennant of San Marco bringing shame upon the Serene Republic of Venice. But the caravel had proved her worth up until now. The grubby sails, unvarnished wood and unkempt crew had made no difference to her performance at sea. He saw that Enrico had resumed his pacing and was fidgeting, too flustered to speak.

Sarzana said, 'I have never heard of such a thing, not ever. Any seaman worthy of the name of Venetian should know enough to see the worn links of his anchor chain rusting through. But I forget, you are no seaman are you Enrico?'

'I will admit to the truth of that,' said Enrico with surprising humility. 'It was an oversight. The chain was not immediately visible, being below the water line. I cannot forgive myself for the mishap and the delay it will cause us all.'

By the blood of Christ, a miracle! thought Sarzana. He felt a warm smugness wash through him. 'I am sorry Enrico,' he said sorrowfully, 'but we cannot possibly wait for the *Cornucopia*.'

'What!' spluttered Enrico, his face darkening with anger 'That is totally unacceptable! We have an agreement and I hold overall command of the flotilla, however small it may be. Until we reach Venice you must do as I say or I shall inform the Serenissima!'

'I am sure the Signori would understand,' said Sarzana. 'After all, who would remain under the command of a man who has dropped his anchor into the sea unattached to his ship!'

Enrico pointed a finger at Sarzana and waved it threateningly. 'If you desert me, you can be sure all Venice will hear of it!'

'They will first hear of your incompetence,' Sarzana replied. 'And we do not desert you. Here at Zante you can wait for the fleet. You can join them in two months and return in safety. Don Carlos would no look kindly on me if I delayed needlessly. Even you Enrico would not escape his wrath, were you to be the cause of it.' He paused. 'Six hours. If you have not sorted your troubles by then, we shall be forced to leave without you. You cannot say then, that I have been unfair. Now, if you will excuse me? I do not see my sister often.'

'God curse you Matteo Sarzana! I should have expected such shoddy treatment from a Tuscan.'

Matteo was not angered by this. Turning up the steps he paused and looked over his shoulder. 'If you would be so kind,' he said, 'could you ask Paolo Grimani and Cesare Zatta to meet with me here? My dear sister has invited them to dine. I would not dream of disappointing her.'

'Do your own running about you pox-ridden, cowardly bastard!' screamed Enrico. He leaped up and down on the spot, waving his clenched fists and spluttering curses.

Unable to believe his good fortune, Matteo Sarzana whistled as he ascended the steps and even ruffled Luigi's dark curls affectionately.

The three pirate galleys sped out across the Ionian sea. On the leading one, Ismael stood at the bow; his red cloak caught the wind and billowed out behind him. Beneath a protection of hardened, moulded leather, his chain-mail flashed in the bright sunlight. A scimitar hung at his jewelled belt along with a short sword and curved dagger. His malicious smile was bright against the darkness of his skin and beard, his fierce eyes echoed the colour of the sea. At his ear, a single jewel winked malevolence from a claw of gold. He folded his arms across his chest and watched the distant sails of a single caravel and a Venetian war galley.

Behind him, stood his servant Koçi. The armour he wore seemed to devour his small frame. His eyes were wide with fear. He had seen his master fight battles before, but Koçi was not a warrior and had stood far out of harms way. As far as he knew, Ismael had never fought at sea. Because there was nowhere to hide this time, Koçi would fight beside him. He had never killed nor drawn a sword before. He was numb with fear and felt with certainty that he would not have the courage to do what was expected of him. The armour was uncomfortable and made him feel bulky and awkward.

Moistening his lips, he said, 'Lord, there are only two Christian ships.'

Ismael did not seem bothered by this. He did turn around then merely inclined his head and continued to look out to sea.

The corsair galleys were rowed by slaves. As the wind would be against them until they attacked, the galleys moved by oar alone, their low profile in the deep troughs made them almost invisible to the approaching Venetian ships. Palisades lined the sides of the galleys. Behind these, some thirty men on each side, crouched with short, horned Turkish bows. Each of these two-hundred bowmen had a full packed quiver of arrows at his back. The weapons they carried did not have the distance of the arquebus or muskets that the Christians would surely use, but at close quarters their accuracy more than made up for the loss.

The pirates looked wild and savage. They had already come to respect their master; one of their number had been left ashore, nursing a stump where his right hand had been severed at Ismael's command, this, for the theft of a horse from a nearby village. Judging from the Syrian's display of anger, the man had been lucky to escape with his life. They had not fought under Ismael before, but they held no doubts to his ability as he stood now like a hawk eyeing a tasty morsel.

The gap between the ships shortened. Ismael realised that by now the alarm would have been raised on the Venetian ships. His galley waited like a hornet poised to attack. The other two pirate galleys had swept far out on either side. Along with one of these galleys, Ismael intended to drive between the caravel and the Venetian galley and then turn on the galley, leaving the caravel to the corsair approaching now from the direction of the Greek mainland. The Venetian galley presented the greatest threat; Ismael knew the power of these Venetian war ships. The caravel would be armed with a few cannon but these would be poor defence unless they could be brought to bear on the manoeuvrable African galleys that lay low in the water. The corsairs were experienced enough to avoid this danger and would be protected from arquebus fire behind the stout palisades. The only true defence the caravel could hope for lay with the wind. But this too, was not now in their favour, it blew them straight into the arms of attack.

The Venetian war galley approached under full sail, which meant the slaves would be rested and better prepared to manoeuvre in battle. These, Ismael guessed would be Turks and Moors mostly and if Ismael's careful arrangements bore fruit, the slaves would all be aware of the promise of freedom if they hampered their Christian overlords.

Paolo could see the powerful ramming beak of the epsilon, just under the surface of the sea. He straightened from his bent position and looked towards a lone black galley ahead of them. The wind was brisk, stirring the heightening waves to froth.

'She carries no identifying pennant and her sails are secured,' said Cesare who stood with him eyeing the vessel with a grimace of distaste.

'Then she is prepared to do battle,' said Paolo excitedly. 'How can she hope to win against us? She is but half our size.'

'Don't be misled by size. A galley such as this is the type favoured by corsairs for her manoeuvrability. If I am not mistaken, there will be others nearby.'

'Other galleys!' cried Paolo. For the first time since they had sighted the galley his expression turned from joy to alarm. The distance was closing fast.

'We should have waited for the *Cornucopia* instead of listening to men who are ruled by greed instead of common sense, or by men who are not even here to see the consequence of such greed.' Cesare spoke, angrily. Then realising who he was with, he added, 'I mean no disrespect to your grandfather Paolo, but too often are battles fought and lost from a distance.'

'Surely you do not believe that we will fail against such a pitiful vessel?'

'One against one no,' said Cesare. 'But what about that one?' He pointed to the left. The masts of another galley were just visible above the swell of the waves.

Paolo looked and scanned the horizon. 'For me this promises much glory Cesare,' he said softly.

'God is with us my friend, although the *Maria* is too far astern to be of much use yet.' He grinned at Paolo and added, 'Let us prepare to do battle.' Turning away he lifted his voice above the wind and called his men to arms. Then he called to the ship's priest and told him to be swift with his prayers.

Like most Venetians, Paolo believed that the Adriatic belonged to Venice alone. On Ascension day, when the Doge went out in his bucintoro to wed the sea, the Adriatic too was considered Venice's bride. Flowing between the Italian coast line and the harsh rim of the Balkans and churned into fury by fearful storms, the Adriatic ran for five hundred miles. All ships in these waters were required to dip their colours to Venice and to call at her docks and warehouses and pay their dues. The power of Venice was still something to be reckoned with but, with the loss of the island of Mordon, 'The Eye of the Republic', the power was in the balance. The Turk now ruled much of the Middle Sea and even dared to harass the home waters of Venice and threaten her shipping.

Paolo bristled from the insult. He knew their confidence had been misplaced. If the *Maria* were attacked, there was nothing the galley could now do for her defence. Paolo prayed that the *Maria* would flee with the power of the wind behind her, and carry Don Carlos' goods to safety. But we, he whispered to himself, shall bring glory in our wake.

With the sails trimmed for speed, Cesare chose to attack the nearest galley. Using wind and oars, he hoped he would have enough speed to outmanoeuvre the corsair galley and attack it from astern; ramming the smaller vessel at its most vulnerable point amidships. If they could strike with the power of the epsilon, half the battle would be won. The weight of the immense Venetian galley could cleave the lesser one in two. Only then could he take on the other enemy vessel.

The drumbeat quickened, the oars cut through the water driving the galley forward. The slaves bent to their task with the sweat running down their naked backs and hatred burning in their eyes. Behind the palisades, the bowmen braced themselves for the shattering impact. The cannon were primed and the musketeers readied their weapons. They were rowing with the wind in their favour, the sea-spray danced and slapped the boards. The Lion of San Marco snapped and writhed above the strident green chevrons of Don Carlos Grimani.

Hand on the rigging, Cesare yelled over the heads of his men, ordering the vessel to begin the turn which would bring them into position for attack. Paolo braced himself against the swell. He held his sword ready drawn. Ten minutes, he estimated. The galley was sluggish in the turn, Paolo could hear Quirini's powerful voice roaring out instructions and the angry hiss of the slave master's whip as it snapped across the backs of the oarsmen. They were free from their shackles but even this would give them small chance of survival if the galley was overpowered and sank, few could swim. Paolo frowned at the unevenness of the strokes, the oars were loosing rhythm.

The lighter corsair galley had a shallower draught and was closing in swiftly, with deadly intent. Turbaned heads lined the ship's sides; sun glinted off arrow, spear, shield and helm.

Cesare shouted to Quirini, urging him to regain control of the galleys pace. The oars faltered and then regained rhythm, bringing the galley around to face her enemy. But the delay had lost her the advantage. Cesare cursed the missed opportunity. The oars swung from their grommets, spooning through the sea.

Sprayed in mist, the galleys sped, hissing, spiting and thrashing the sea like multi-legged sea monsters. Nearer and nearer they closed. The sky darkened, filled with a hail of deadly, glittering arrows. They hung in the sky a moment like a tangled net before they fell; whining, whistling and thudding into both ships. Then came the screams of men, some in pain, but most from the sheer joy of battle. Cannon boomed and the lighter roar of the muskets spewed fire and smoke.

Paolo did not know what made him turn when the galleys where within seconds of collision. Closing in, another black galley thrust through the waves, epsilon cutting the water like a shark fin. 'Cesare the other's behind us. Black hearted bastards!' shouted Paolo. He was not afraid. Let them come and feel the bite of his Venetian blade!

Cesare did not hear him and, if he had, there was nothing he could have done; for the distance had closed and the vessels crunched together. They did not hit head on, they slithered together, the corsair nudging aside at the last moment. Her oars rose with fluidity out of the sea, towering like a forest of saplings above the galley.

For the Venetian galley, it was too late for such a manoeuvre. Her oars cracked and snapped, trapped between the two vessels. Above the roar of noise, rose the screams of agony from the dying slaves, impaled, stabbed, shredded, by splintering shards. Ignoring this, the Venetians had already thrown the grappling hooks locking them to their enemy's side. Armed with sword and shield, Paolo leaped the bloodied water between the ships, the cry on his lips an echo of galley battles for centuries.

'For God and San Marco!'

And from the corsairs, an answering cry rent the air. 'Allah w' akbar! Allah w' akbar! Allah w' akbar!'

Aboard the Venetian caravel, Matteo Sarzana had tried to go about on a wide tack as soon as he received the signal from Cesare. Pirates! The *Maria* was running briskly before a stiff south easterly breeze when the signal had come. Her wide mainsail was bellied out taut, straining at the rigging with full thrust. Changing course so dramatically was a dangerous strategy but Sarzana attempted it anyway. Panic gave a high nervous edge to his voice as he gave the commands. By the time the ship had answered to the helm in as light a turn as the helmsman dared, the wind took the sails aback in a wild fluttering of cloth and loose rigging. Blocks clattered with a deafening roar as the *Maria* lurched, wallowed and crabbed up, loosing way and almost to a stop. Sarzana realised the enormity of his mistake. If he had continued, he could have easily outrun an oar powered galley. Now nothing could save him, for the *Maria* lay in the path of an on coming galley, its oars pounding the water with incredible speed.

'Lord God,' cried the ship's chaplain who stood beside Sarzana. 'They will cut us to ribbons. We must surrender to the dogs!'

The bow chaser on the corsair galley fired, releasing puffs of smoke before the noise boomed across the water. The grape-shot shredded through the rigging and cut the sails to shreds, a master stroke, rendering the wind dependent ship powerless and crippled. The *Maria* was not a war ship and was ill equipped for battle. She carried twelve bowmen, the rest of the men were sailors, but they armed themselves well enough. A servant brought Matteo his sword and shield, and hastily helped him strap on his armour.

The chaplain screamed at him to surrender. Sarzana pushed him aside. 'They are after our cargo you fool,' he snapped. 'We shall not be sunk, so we shall fight.'

'God have mercy on us all,' wept the chaplain. 'There are hundreds of them.'

'Get control of yourself. Fight beside us or get on your knees and pray!' ordered Matteo Sarzana, his face a mask of contempt. 'If necessary, throw yourself overboard to put an end to your snivelling panic. Courage is what we need now, not fear.'

'Fear?' gasped the chaplain incredulously. This was the last word he ever uttered. An arrow thudded into his neck and drove him to the deck, his face fixed with an expression of disbelief.

Sarzana ducked behind his shield. The crew milled about in panic, only the bowmen fought to defend the *Maria*, they fired and reloaded with efficient rapidity. Most of the arrows clattering uselessly against the galley's palisades. The few that found their mark were not enough to lessen the odds. The galley kept up its alarming speed until the last moment. Her oars lifted and the grappling hooks snaked through the air, clawing at the railings and ripping into the boards like dragon's claws.

Sarzana fought to control his own fear. He rallied his men and charged to the side as the corsairs swarmed up the ropes and scrambled aboard. They screamed their savage war cries, swords, eyes, and smiles glinting with macabre pleasure.

Sarzana's sword rose and fell as he fought for his life in blind fury. The bowmen and crew fought with equal ferocity. All around, the noise of battle reigned, the cries of triumph mingled with the screams of death, the sickening wet thud of blade on flesh, hammering feet and the constant clash of steel. The planks were soon slippery with spilled blood, littered with the dead and the dying. Limbs and bodies splashed into the sea until it reddened with gore. Above it all came the cry of gulls, waiting to feast like carrion crows.

In the thick of the fighting, Sarzana cried out as a mace glanced off his helm, the blow sent him sprawling. He scrambled to his feet as the same aggressor swung the mace in a killing stroke. Barely avoiding it, Sarzana brought his own weapon up, two handed and plunged it into the corsair's unprotected chest. Warm blood spilled over Sarzana's hands as the man keeled over, blood frothing from his lips. Sarzana could not withdraw the blade. He snatched up the mace and whirled it about him in a silver glittering arc of death.

Even though every Venetian fought for his life, they could do little to staunch the attack. These pirates were wicked men who lived by no moral code and who terrified their enemies with their merciless slashing and blood-curdling war-cries. Vastly outnumbered, the Venetians fought with desperate courage and fell like scythed corn. The survivors stood together, back to back, causing many of their enemies to fall in screaming agony. Below, the sea rolled over, dark with blood and littered with bodies.

They were driven further and further, until the remainder fought finally at the bow of the ship; hacking and stabbing at the impossible flow of fierce-eyed demons. Sarzana stood in front of the men, his mace held out and his free hand, open palmed towards the enemy. 'For the love of God enough!' he cried.

For a moment afterwards the fighting continued, then suddenly, at a strident command, the pirates drew back. A tall, bearded man pushed his way forward and nodded curtly to Sarzana. Dressed in splendid robes, he was un-scratched and, having taken no part in the fighting. Speaking Greek, he said softy, 'Throw down your weapons and no further harm with befall you.'

Sarzana dropped his sword. He turned to see that his men obeyed the order. His eyes widened in alarm when saw only eight still standing. There were as many again, who lay or sat in exhaustion, nursing their wounds. Without delay, the corsair captain ordered the prisoners bound and had them marched or dragged on to the waiting galley.

Black despair swamped Matteo Sarzana. Bloodied from the battle, shocked by the intensity of the brief attack, he watched as the crew of the *Maria* were replaced by the fierce men of mixed origin. They killed those who were too injured to move. The caravel was rigged with some spare canvas and the rigging restored to temporary working order. The *Maria* able to limb behind the galley. She turned her bow and dead bodies plopped into the sea in her wake.

When the two galleys crunched together, Ismael made no attempt to board the Venetian vessel nor did any of his men; they stood with drawn weapons and waited for the onrush of Venetians. As Ismael had planned, the Christians had been unaware until too late of the second pirate galley. This had come up on the opposite side, to take their ship while her crew fought with the other.

The Venetians were veterans of sea warfare. Even with the odds piled against them, they were not prepared to give in without a fight. They knew their fate if they lost. Many preferred to die in battle than live out their days in slavery, far from Christian fellow men. They swarmed aboard the African galley with the ferocity of cornered wolves. A forest of blades clashed through the air, glinting wicked silver in the harsh sunlight. They rose and fell, crashing against shields, slicing through flesh, and rose again, as bloodied steel.

Koçi scuttled out of the way and hid under the benches, where the slaves sat slumped at the oars, exhausted from the demanding pace. Even these Koçi feared, he stayed far enough away so that only the hatred in their eyes could reach him. He turned to watch the battle. The three ships had come together, the decks of the Venetian galley flocked with dark-clad pirates, the remaining Venetians fought for their lives.

Ismael was well able to care for himself, there were few swordsmen who could match his speed and skill. He had cast off his cloak lest it hinder him. Distinctive for his height, he scythed through his enemies like a god, undaunted, untouchable. In the space of five minutes, Koçi saw the flashing blade drink the blood of three infidel.

Dead bodies and writhing wounded began to clutter the boards, hindering the fighting. The cries, the thuds, the crashing and the sickening screams seemed to go on and on like a vision of hell. The air was thick with agony and violence. Blood and viscera spilled on to the rowing benches and ran between the planking. Amputated limbs spun into the sea, fountains of pumping blood spewed from severed arteries.

Tears ran from Koçi's eyes, he bit his lip until it bled. Racked with sobs, he drew himself into a ball and buried his head in his arms, hiding from the ghastly sights. If he could block off the sounds as well, his fear convinced him that all would disappear.

The fight continued longer than seemed humanly possible. Ismael's sword arm was numb, he felt heavy exhaustion slow his reactions and began to feel the blows he had taken. The Venetians were finished, but like the youth with whom Ismael now fought, they seemed incapable of accepting defeat. Ismael had to fight hard to keep his opponent at bay. The young man fought with a skill learned since childhood and produced a surprising amount of tricks and feints to gain advantage. Ismael did not want to kill him.

Some of the Venetians tried to return to their ship before it was overwhelmed. Men scrambled up the sides, swinging their swords to slash at all in their path. In the water some still fought, hampered by heavy armour and the dragging of the sea, most who fell perished and their cried rang through the air unheeded. The Venetian captain was still alive; he was holding on to the mast, his right arm red with blood. His voice however, was not impaired as he called to those who yet lived. He face was masked with horror as he called them to surrender.

As soon as he heard this, Ismael ordered an end to the slaughter, even as he still fought himself. 'You heard your captain,' he cried. 'Yield!'

'Never!' snarled the youth. He pressed his attack with greater vigour.

Ismael fought defensively while the young man exhausted himself trying to get a thrust passed the scimitar. Ismael watched for an opening. Soon as opportunity presented itself, he moved in. His blade caught his opponent's weapon under the hilt and sent it spinning across the boards.

Disarmed, the youth stood glaring; breathing heavily, his eyes wild and angry.

Ismael braced himself against a physical attack.

It did not come. Apart from the groans of the wounded, all else was still.

'It is done Paolo,' said the Venetian captain walking to the young man's side. He gripped his shoulder and regarded Ismael with insolence before he bowed. 'Cesare Antonio Leone Faliero,' he announced. 'We have fought honourably and courageously for what is ours. I ask you to show mercy to my men and spare their lives.'

'I do not take slaves,' said Ismael coldly. 'You are the property of these men who have bettered you. Go with them now and you will suffer no further harm.'

Koçi lifted his head, he knew from the sounds that the fighting had ceased. It seemed to have lasted for hours, yet the sun had hardly moved in the sky. The wind had strengthened and the swell of the sea was greater. Koçi could hear the heart-broken sobs of the slaves as they wept and mumbled their Christian prayers, still shackled to their benches. Koçi looked at them with compassion, how they must have prayed and hoped for Christian victory and freedom.

He could see the other slaves, those that had rowed the Venetian galley, Muslims who had been freed. They were ragged, half-naked men with shamefully shaved heads; this did nothing to mar their joy as they boarded Ismael's galley. As they came on board, they passed Ismael and each freed slave dropped to his knees before him, touching the hem of his gown with grateful lips. Koçi smiled with pride. He had taken no part in the battle, but this did not lessen the pride he felt in the rough men he had sailed with, but most of all, for the master he served.

The prisoners were ordered aboard their own galley to man the oars, a point that amused the men who's positions they refilled. Ismael gave the captured galley to the corsairs to reward their day's work. They would gain much from its sale and the sale of the slaves. The prisoners walked with defeat and misery on their faces. It was a sorry end thought Koçi, for men who had fought so bravely. He looked at the last one in the line. He wore no helm but could be singled out by his bright silken hair, a fair youth, as bright as Apollo. As Koçi was watching, the man stumbled and fell to his knees. He got to his feet again slowly, as if injured. Ismael had turned away with his back to the prisoners. Before any could move to stop the young Venetian, he leapt towards Ismael, with a knife flashing in his hand.

Koçi cried out, 'Master! Behind you!'

Ismael turned swiftly. There was nothing he could do to avoid the descending blade. Koçi heard the grunt as the knife stabbed into his master. Koçi snatched up a weapon and leapt towards the Venetian, bringing his own blade down on Ismael's attacker. The knife lifted stained with blood, he stabbed down again, weeping and howling in distress.

'Stop!' Ismael caught the back of his slave's tunic and pulled him away.

As Koçi straightened, Ismael hit him. There was no mercy in the blow. All Ismael's anger and pain came behind it. It caught him on the side of the head and sent him sprawling across the blood brindled benches.

After a moment of blackness, Koçi sat up and shook his head. His vision blurred, his head rang with pain. But greater than this, was the deeper injury, that Ismael had found cause to strike him. When his sight cleared, he saw Ismael crouched beside the youth, tearing away at the ineffectual armour, pushing aside the clothing. The man was unconscious, a pool of blood widening beneath him.

Koçi staggered to his feet and came to stand behind his master. Ismael pressed a bundle of cloth against the youth's side, within seconds it was soaked in crimson. 'Why master,' Koçi sobbed, 'Why, when so many here dead are dearer to you than he?'

Ismael shuddered, his hands against the wounds slackened. He stood unsteadily. His Greek physician hovered behind him. Ismael ordered him to examine the youth's hurts and stood, waiting anxiously while he did so. When the Greek looked up, he shook his head. 'The chances of him surviving this are not good Lord,' he pronounced.

'Use all your skill Kyriakos,' Ismael replied. His voice was raw with emotion.

Koçi shrank away from the burning in his master's eyes. Ismael was deathly pale, his eyes black with a pain no physical wound could bring. Koçi threw himself on the boards in front of him. 'Lord, if I have offended thee, kill me now and end my misery!'

Ismael said, 'If the boy dies, you will die. Preserve his life as if it were your own.'

'My life is worth nothing master.'

Ismael turned away. He faltered and then sank to the ground. Koçi was just in time to prevent his master's head from hitting the palisade.

As soon as Paolo had fallen, Cesare turned and hurried back. Even in his anxiety, he was surprised to see the tall corsair strike the servant. The boy looked as if he would snap from the blow. Cesare sat on the planks beside the prone figure of Paolo. The heir to the Grimani trading empire, lay as still as death. The fair hair was curled with perspiration and plastered to his forehead. Over the sunken eyes, the lids were blue and his skin was as pale as sea-foam. A trickle of bright blood spilled from the corner of his mouth.

Cesare looked up at the man who was tending him, he too looked pale and drawn with exhaustion, but his grey eyes were stark with concern. Cesare had seen enough wounds to judge Paolo's as probably fatal. Yet, the corsair desperately tried to stem the flow of blood.

His eyes bored into Cesare. 'Hold this firmly,' he rasped. He took Cesare's hand, smearing it with blood and pressed it against the wound.

Only when the man had risen and a Greek physician had taken his place, did Cesare realise the corsair's words had been in Italian.

Cesare had his own share of hurts from the fighting. It is only now, he thought, that the blows, stabs and cuts are felt by the body; in battle we are immune, armoured by God.

'Will the lad live?' asked a voice behind him

Cesare was gratified to see that Quiniri had survived the day. 'We can only pray,' he replied sadly. 'Only by God's hand does he live yet. I see that He has seen fit to preserve your life Quiniri.'

'You too my friend,' answered the boatswain. 'Are you fit to pull an oar?'

Cesare rose unsteadily to his feet and laughed bitterly. He saw the eyes of his conquerors watch him with expressions of disbelief and respect. There was no laughter in Cesare's eyes, He knew what his future held, he would face it as bravely as he could, there where none to pay the ransom to free him from slavery. He scanned the wreckage with tired eyes and bid his own farewell to faces he recognised among the dead. Some still thrashed weakly in the water; they were ignored and would be left to die. What, he wondered, would have happened had he returned with news of Paolo's death? Poor brave Paolo who had only ever wanted the glory of battle.

Chapter 44 Venice

Fra Sebastiano took Emlyn to the Grimani house on the Thursday before Easter. Venice was already festooned with garlands and pennants. Rich, savoury aromas filled the warm air and mingled with the heavy scent of flowers. Donenico Alfani, the Franciscans' boatman chattered merrily as he steered the gondola through the busy canals. Many of the vessels were plied high with flower baskets on their way to adorn the numerous churches. The gondoliers had stuck flowers in their hats or tucked them behind their ears. They ferried their boats with a sense of urgency, calling excitedly to one another as they sped on their way. Emlyn felt the atmosphere like the calm before a storm, as if some catastrophic event was about to burst with a clap of thunder above the maze of canals and the jumble of ancient buildings.

In contrast, the courtyard of the palace was quiet and serene, the laconic splashing of the fountain lulling even the flowers to nod their heads as if to sleep. Emlyn and Fra Sebastiano entered through a line of potted Madonna lilies, their scent heavy in the air.

Fra Lorenzo was reading in his room that overlooked the fountain. '*Go rather to the lost sheep of the house of Israel. Do not possess gold nor silver nor copper in your belts: nor scrip for your journey, nor two coats, nor sandals nor a staff; for the labourer is worthy of his hire.*' He looked up, his thoughts were too intrusive to concentrate on the words of the gospel. His grandfather's attitude towards him had changed since they had last met the previous Spring. They spoke little now, but Lorenzo read the painful accusation in Don Carlos' eyes, as if he had been bitterly betrayed and suffered greatly when his grandson had taken holy orders. Lorenzo was sorry that there as so little understanding between them. Like the scripture he had just read, Lorenzo had made his decisions and would not turn them aside to appease of his grandfather.

Carmelia was the only person he had come to see. The little girl he remembered had grown into a determined young lady, with still, that mischievous look about her that he loved so well. She and Lorenzo and taken to each other immediately, as if the years apart had never been. It did not take Lorenzo long to discover how fearful she was about her coming wedding. He did what he could to reassure her and ease her fear. He had not met Tomasso di Vincentini and ignored the gossip that flowed like wine. As Carmelia had not met him either, Lorenzo found it difficult to understand the basis of her fear. Perhaps marriage did not appealed to her; perhaps she would have preferred to devote her life to the service of God as Lorenzo had. The decision unfortunately did not lie in her hands. Don Carlos needed the reassurance of grandchildren, a continuation of the family. Lorenzo had turned his back on that responsibility. He realised grimly that now could not have it even if he wished.

He saw the familiar figure of Fra Sebastiano walk into the courtyard beneath his window. Beside him walked a young man who Lorenzo had not seen before. With a stir of unease, Lorenzo hurried down to meet them.

Fra Sebastiano introduced him as Emlyn Tomas, a friend of long standing. Lorenzo caught the knowing wink from the older man. He guessed that he stood in front of his half-brother. He was certain of it. The captivating smile was the same as Paolo's. The eyes were different, a darker, less intense blue and his hair was as dark as Lorenzo's own, but put this youth and Paolo together and there would be no mistaking the shared blood. Lorenzo guessed Emlyn to be five or six years younger than Paolo, a youth just grown to manhood. He seemed ill at ease, even overawed by his surroundings, glancing up at the portico as if afraid of what he might find there. Lorenzo smiled in welcome. 'Come out of the sun,' he invited. 'I'll scare some wine from the kitchen.'

'You couldn't scare a snail from its shell,' laughed Fra Sebastiano. 'We have no need of wine, the day is too warm and I shall spend it in sleep if I drink.'

'Perhaps your companion has a stouter heart?' said Lorenzo looking at Emlyn.

'No, I am afraid I am much the same,' he replied quietly. His eyes were cast to the ground.

Lorenzo thought it best to broach the subject they shared, rather that subject the boy to further embarrassment. He said, 'Fra Sebastiano tells me that you and I may be related, even brothers?'

Emlyn looked up then, his eyes dark with emotion. He said, 'My mother was Anne Morgan. She came to Venice as wife of your father, Cristoforo Grimani.'

'Forgive me, I mean no disrespect to you or what you tell me, but that is impossible. You are obviously too young to have been any child of hers.'

'So I have been told, ever since I first asked. But I know it to be so. I have come here to discover how. I know the story of our mother's supposed fate. I stand here as proof that it is not the truth.'

Lorenzo stared at him in astonishment, the man and the words suddenly understood. He did not want to believe what he was hearing. The last time he and Paolo had seen their mother, they had been small boys, screaming in terror as they were led away; their mother filled with tears and deep sobs as she implored Don Carlos to let her stay with her sons. Neither of them had ever seen her again, but they had heard her cries ring through the house long afterwards. Lorenzo still felt the wrenching pain when he thought of her. Paolo had been too young for the memory to effect him much, but Lorenzo had remembered. They had heard soon after that she had drowned at sea. Lorenzo had never forgiven his grandfather. It was the one wrong he would never find it in his heart to forgive. Now, he was surprised to realise that what he was hearing was quite likely to be true.

Emlyn placed a gentle hand on his arm. 'She could not have died Lozo,' he said.

Lorenzo thought it strange that this man automatically used the name which Paolo called his older brother. When he looked at Emlyn, he saw and recognised his own pain mirrored in the blue-grey eyes. He did not know why he saw it there. He returned the embrace and felt the tension between them dissipate like wind-blown floss. The three of them sat under the shade of a fig tree, in a quiet corner of the courtyard where their presence went unnoticed. They exchanged stories, the brothers eager to learn from each other. Fra Sebastiano contributed little, content to see some of his own puzzling story solved. Once relaxed, Emlyn had a winning way about him, the old priest could see Lorenzo's liking for him and he was glad that at least one bridge had been crossed without a scathing.

After an hour Emlyn stood up, his eyes lowered in concentration as he looked at Lorenzo. 'We must confront your grandfather with this,' he said. 'Only he knows the real truth.'

'He may be no wiser than you,' said Fra Sebastiano, feeling uneasy. 'I feel that the utmost care should be taken, as I have warned Emlyn before.'

'But with the three of us together,' said Emlyn, 'how can he avoid giving us the answers we require?'

'You are both right,' agreed Lorenzo. 'But there will be four of us. My brother Paolo will be back within a few days, no longer than a week.

I feel that it is only right that we should wait for him. It will give us more time to think on how we are to approach Don Carlos. In the meantime, we will have to devise some means of keeping you here Emlyn, or at least for you to visit. There is so much we have to tell to each other.'

'We have already solved that problem,' said Fra Sebastiano with a smile. 'Emlyn is an accomplished musician, so he tells me, come to Italy to better his chances in life. He thought to approach your grandfather in hope of patronage.'

Lorenzo looked thoughtful for a moment. 'That may not be as easy as it once was. My grandfather has lost interest over the years. But we will try, in a roundabout sort of way. It may be just what he needs to take his mind off his worries.'

'Is that before or after we place more upon his shoulders?' said Fra Sebastiano with wry humour.

'Before,' laughed Lorenzo. 'The servants tell me that there has been much music and laughter here since Adriana Martinelli arrived. It would be best to approach Don Carlos through her.'

'The lady and I are already acquainted,' said Emlyn. 'She and her charge joined our company while crossing the Alps.'

Lorenzo smiled. 'That is news indeed and can only help our cause. Would now be a suitable time to approach her?'

Emlyn swallowed and grinned. 'Admirable,' he said with a bow. He had waited long enough. Whatever fears he now felt, he would not allow them to stand in his way. He and Fra Sebastiano followed Lorenzo through a maze of corridors. They heard the music before they emerged into the sunlit garden at the back of the merchant palace. It was surrounded on three sides by the house and on the forth by a high stone wall, green with vines and hung with bird cages. Chairs and a low table were set in the centre. There were about nine people there, apart from the green liveried servants. Some carried or played instruments, others read or joined in the singing. This was the sort of gathering Emlyn had hoped for when he had first come to Venice. At the centre of the group were four women and amid them, Carmelia Grimani standing with a lira da braccio held to her shoulder.

Emlyn froze, his breath halted, his heart hammered. Carmelia stood before him, as pure as Aphrodite herself, risen from the foamy waves. There was a deep sadness in Emlyn, this haunting, delicate loveliness was to wed some gross brute, twice, three times her age! Dewi sant no! By the Virgin, by all the saints, no! He turned away, feeling the hot sting of tears in his eyes, afraid that all there could see their naked suffering.

But Carmelia was better than him in this. She had faltered in her playing but recovered quickly enough, looking at the newcomers with innocent expectancy.

'Well, well. Little monk,' said Adriana Martinelli in that voice she had used with him during the journey to Italy. 'You do turn up in the strangest of places. Did the role of Hermes tire you?'

Emlyn bowed and kissed her hand like a gentleman.

'Little monk,' whispered Lorenzo beside him. 'Are you a monk too, Emlyn?'

Adriana took Emlyn's hand in hers. She turned it over much as Eva had done, and examined the puckered scar. She said, 'Does it work as well as you hoped?'

'Better,' said Emlyn, 'as I hope to demonstrate to you.'

She drew him aside and questioned him at length about Ambrose and even wished to know what had become of Josquin. Emlyn told her all he knew, feeling uncomfortable in her presence. He remembered what she looked like under the stiff, costly clothing. He felt his skin burn and his eyes drifted to where Carmelia stood with Fra Sebastiano.

'You could not have come to a better place for music,' said Adriana linking her arm through his. She introduced him to each person there.

The names meant nothing to Emlyn, famed though many were. There was but one among them to whom all Emlyn's thoughts were directed. Eventually he greeted Carmelia. He grinned at her while his inner emotions were in a turmoil.

She played her part well, in greater control than he, but her heart spoke through her eyes. 'My love, my own!' she whispered when they were unobserved.

What followed, was the best time Emlyn had yet spent in Italy. The afternoon was warm and pleasant with a fresh breeze coming off the sea. Music, conversation and song flowed through the gathering. They played games, challenging each other to feats of skill on each instrument, passing them around from one to the other. Emlyn took up each challenge and played well enough, not to impress but to show his competence. Adriana, Carmelia and he played French tunes and sang lively Breton songs, encouraging the others to join in the chorus. Fra Sebastiano relaxed and added his voice to most of the songs, it was no compliment, for he was not gifted with a voice for music, but he enjoyed himself immensely. Lorenzo slipped away for a short period, explaining that he would search out his grandfather and beg him to join them.

Adriana embarrassed Emlyn by telling the story of how she had come to assist him when he had come to them sick and wounded and of how he had defied the mountain on a shield. When pressed, Emlyn explained away his injury as a mishap in a tavern. Adriana, he was gratified to see, did not contradict him.

Servants brought food and wine as the afternoon lengthened. When they were all fed and relaxed, Emlyn took up a lute and played for them. He chose a Welsh love song, the words meaningless to them all. But the words needed no explanation, combined skilfully with the intricate fingering of the lute, they wove the melancholy of deep sadness into an emotion each man and woman there could not help but feel to the depths of their hearts. For Carmelia alone was the song meant and Emlyn knew from her expression, and from the tears that dewed her eyes like stars, that she understood implicitly.

Having plunged them all into sweet misery, Emlyn then strove to lighten their hearts. He played a fast country dance. Within minutes, one took up the tabor, another braved the shawm and soon they were restored to their high spirits joining in with voice, instrument or just tapping feet. Though there were none there, who could quite shake off the haunting beauty of the lutanist's foreign love song.

On his way through an upper corridor, Don Carlos paused and walked to an open window that overlooked the garden. Behind him, standing with his usual patience was Giuseppe the old steward. Don Carlos stood quietly, listening to the sweet incomprehensible song. 'You and I are old men Giuseppe,' he murmured, 'in all our years, have you ever heard anything like that before?'

Understanding his master's tone, Giuseppe joined him at the window. 'Not ever my Lord,' he agreed. 'Who would think man and lute capable of such a pure and blessed music?'

Don Carlos rubbed his chin thoughtfully and looked at his life-time servant, Giuseppe rarely spoke his mind. Don Carlos said, 'It speaks to the heart so directly; a sweet suffering like love. It is many years since my ears were so wooed. No wonder Lorenzo bid me listen. Is the player aware of the control such talent brings?'

'Most surely my lord. See how he holds them spell bound, even though he is not an Italian.'

'Find out who he is Giuseppe and bring him to me in an hour. I would hear more of this that has the power to drive away my concerns.' When Giuseppe had gone, Don Carlos did not move away from the window.

Music had once played a great part in his life. He had not known until he heard these soft and gentle notes, how much he had missed the art. Not Italian, Giuseppe had said. From here, the boy looked much the same as the others, though Don Carlos knew Giuseppe would be correct in his guessing, he invariably was. Don Carlos could only see the top of the boy's head and the long able fingers spinning out their special magic along the lute strings. It was a sound new to the merchant's ears and that, he guessed was the attraction. An impressive player and an ornament to a nobleman's household.

When the young man was brought to him an hour later, Don Carlos had retired to his bedchamber. He had not been well over the past few weeks and found the heavy clothing a discomfort. Uglino had helped him change into a comfortable robe of red damask and had left a flagon of malmsey, ready poured for his master. Giuseppe entered the room with the lutanist and introduced him as Emlyn Tomas.

He stepped forward, bowing as gracefully as a courtier. He had brought Adriana's lute from the garden. When he lifted his head, Don Carlos gasped in surprise. The boy's exceptional looks were stamped forever in Don Carlos' mind, but not from the youth who now stood before him. He had never thought to look upon this elfin, bewitching face again, he had thought it forever gone from him, except in dreams buried in the past where it belonged. The youth stood, eyes downcast, waiting with still patience while Don Carlos struggled with the memories he had evoked unawares. Don Carlos sighed. It is just a coincidence, he told himself, what my conscience will not allow to rest has come back now to haunt me. 'Are you English?' he said sharply.

'Yes my Lord.'

That explains it, thought Don Carlos reassuring himself. All Englishmen look the same as we all look the same to them. The similarity is slight and caught me off guard. 'I would like you to play for me. My grandson Lorenzo tells me that you are in Venice to better yourself. If you meet the standard I require, I will offer you employment.'

'I am overwhelmed my Lord. I pray the music will be pleasing to your ear.'

Emlyn entertained Don Grimani until darkness. He left with no word of reassurance, but he was not concerned. Emlyn had practised for uncountable hours on the pieces he had chosen to play, knowing them to be popular in Venice. Don Carlos' enjoyment had been clear to behold and they had talked to some length about the harp. He told Emlyn to come back after

Easter, to discuss his future. Emlyn left feeling as if he walked on air. Thoughts of Gruffydd came to his mind and memories of the exhausting hours of teaching the bardic law and the skill of the harper.

He was so filled with pride that at first, he did not hear the hiss that issued from an alcove he passed. A little hand reached out and grasped his sleeve. Carmelia pulled him into the shadows. There were no words spoken between them, Carmelia clung to him. She felt so right there, so close to him, standing in the curve of his arms, moulded to fit exactly. He kissed her eyes, her head and her lips.

'I have wept all day and all night since I last saw you,' she whispered. 'Do not despair sweet love, for they were tears of the most pure joy.'

'And I am enslaved to worship thee,' said Emlyn speaking with kisses into her soft, scented hair.

'Only God can take you from my heart though death,' she sobbed. 'I will not live a single day if you will not have me and take me from here. Whether I live or die, I place that trust in your hands.'

'No *Cariad*, do not place such a burden upon me,' pleaded Emlyn. He held her as tight as he could without crushing the breath from her. How could she utter such words? What if he failed to find a means of escape before Tomasso di Vincentini took her as wife? If any death came of this, it would not be hers, but that of the old man who chose such a young and innocent bride to satisfy his unhealthy appetite.

They talked little in that short time they had together. As always in each other's company, their passion awoke and made demands of them. 'Sweet impossible love will you have me?' whispered Carmelia, her voice thick with tears.

'How can that be?' said Emlyn smiling down. Fighting his desire he pulled away from her, holding her at arm's length, seeing the answering passion burn in her eyes.

It was Adriana's call that broke the spell and caused them to realise where they were and the dangers that they braved.

'Carmelia!' Came the call again.

'She has seen us!' gasped Carmelia.

When Emlyn looked he could see no one. He left Carmelia then, promising to wear the mask she had sent to him, so that she would know him in the crowded square of San Marco. She clung to him in desperation and his heart was wrenched as he pulled her small hands away and left her standing alone.

Emlyn found Fra Sebastiano and Lorenzo in the kitchen; they were admiring some delicate Blancmanges. Emlyn smiled at them, showing in that smile the triumph he had felt.

'Well Maestro?' said Fra Sebastiano. 'I have always mourned the lack of musical voice, the good Lord saw fit to bestow upon me, but never more so than now. Fra Lorenzo here has offered to return to the monastery with me if you are detained by your admirers.'

Emlyn shook his head. 'I can't wait to get away,' he said. 'Wait until Theo and Wendelin hear what has happened.' He chattered happily as they left.

Adriana found Carmelia outside the private chapel in the west wing of the house. Glancing around to ensure that they were alone, Adriana said, 'I know who you were with my girl. What can you be thinking of? Do you know what people will say if they see you in the company of a young man, any man, just days before you are to be wed?'

'Their words cannot hurt me,' snapped Carmelia. She felt that nothing could hurt her now that Emlyn had found a way to come to her.

'Words?' said Adriana. 'Words will be the least of your worries when I have finished with you!'

'Whatever do you mean?' Carmelia's confidence faded rapidly. She was sure that Adriana must have seen her and Emlyn together, but how?

Her godmother folded her arms and shook her head in a slow meaningful manner. 'I have often told you that lies breed lies Carmelia Grimani. You had better stick to the truth and nothing but.'

'What truth?' cried Carmelia evasively.

'It's no good playing the innocent with me. Do you think me blind? Do you imagine for one moment that I did not see the way you looked out for that boy every step of the journey?'

'I didn't!'

'I have not survived three marriages without learning what passes between man and woman. I thought it was just an infatuation, that it would pass, but I see that I was much mistaken. When you set eyes on him in the garden this afternoon, it was fortunate that I was the only witness to what silent messages passed between you. I watched, at first unable to believe. I followed and I waited. My reward, distasteful though it be, was to see you in his arms like a common whore. Why do you think I shouted to you?'

Carmelia's hands flew to her mouth, 'God protect me!' she gasped.

'I know what it was just! Do not mistake me for a fool. Now we know what all the long faces were about and the starvation and the constant weeping. Stupid girl!'

'Should I not follow my heart?' sobbed Carmelia desperately. Could she appeal to this, the one person who knew her better than any here? 'I love him! As God be my witness, I cannot and will not live without him!'

'Love is for the hedgerow and has no place in your life.' Adriana breathed deeply and fought down her anger. She loved Carmelia dearly. She knew by what she now saw and had seen in the eyes of Emlyn Tomas, that Carmelia spoke the truth. The two youngest members of that travelling party had fallen in love somewhere between Geneva and Milan. Adriana had not realised the depth of feeling they held for each other and had been unable to prevent the fated couple from making this mistake. She put her arm around Carmelia's shoulders. 'Come Little Dove, dry your tears.'

Carmelia pulled away. 'I don't want to marry that man! Why should I? You promised that I would not have one such as he!' Her words trembled with crying. 'You promised me a prince!'

'And you have found a pauper!'

'You promised I should find happiness!'

'That is not mine or any ones to give,' Adriana said gently. 'And I have not broken any promise I made you. We know nothing about this boy. It is evident to me that he has no wealth to keep you as you deserve. He is parent less and has yet to make a path for himself in life. Marriage will not only ruin your chances, but also his. Don Carlos will kill him before he allows such an ill suited match. Believe me Little Dove. I speak the truth.'

Glazed with tears, Carmelia's eye's implored her to grant the impossible.

'As you love him child, let him go and do your duty to your father.'

'I cannot! Nor would he accept that we should be parted.'

'If he is the boy I cared for and spoke with often, I think he would.'

'Then I am dead.'

'How dare you speak so!'

'If it is possible to live in death, that is what you condemn me to.'

'You are being totally unreasonable,' Adriana's voice rose. 'What do you think Don Carlos will think when he hears of this?'

'Do not tell him,' begged Carmelia.

'I have no intention of telling him. He will not find out through me, but he will find out. Of that you can be sure, as nothing escapes him. Do you want to hear that your little monk has been found floating dead in the Lagoon?'

'Don't I beg you, do not speak as such!'

'It is for you to decide child. Do as your duty demands or I will be forced to act.'

'Am I to be doomed to a life of utter misery? Never knowing the touch of a lover's lips, the caress of a lover's hand?'

'Now you are being foolish,' snapped Adriana. 'Will you sacrifice your chastity as well as your sanity?'

Carmelia's tears stopped, her eyes flamed with anger. 'You yourself told me that the heaviest burdens a woman has to bare is her virtue and her virginity. I no longer bear either!'

Shocked to her soul, Adriana hit Carmelia hard across one cheek and then the other. 'Liar!'

'It's the truth,' cried Carmelia backing away. 'It's the truth, even though repellent to you. I gave him my chastity. I did it with every part of me willing and ready, begging him to satisfy my need.'

'Stop this instant!'

'I did it to bind him to me in every way I could. Once they discover that I am not the prize they thought me, the wedding will be called off.'

Adriana turned away. The girl must be lying! She would not dare, this was just another lever to persuade all around her to her will. What had happened to the timid, fearful, obedient convent girl? Adriana could not bring herself to believe Carmelia. Clearly some answer must be found for the problem. Carmelia did not have much time left and time was what they needed. Adriana looked fully at the stricken girl. 'I will do what I can for you my dear,' she said softly. 'You must tell me no more of your lies. I shall speak to your father and ask him to reconsider the marriage to Tomasso di Vincentini. If I cannot persuade him to change his mind, then we must pray that I can convince him to postpone it. If a later date is agreed upon, who knows what we might achieve?'

Carmelia fell into her godmother's arms. 'I did not want you to know,' she wept. 'I would not have subjected you to this, after all you have done and been to me.'

'I will not deny that I am bitterly disappointed in you my girl. Your happiness has always been of paramount importance to me. If I am to help you, then I want something in return. You are to promise by the love you hold for the youth, that you will not, whatever happens, attempt to meet with him again.'

Carmelia hung her head. 'That will be difficult if he is to be here at Don Carlos' request. I will do all I can to abide by your word. Only for how long?'

'For as long as is necessary. Now dry your eyes and for the sake of all, try to look cheerful about your future.'

'That will be more difficult still,' said Carmelia. 'I hate to even think about this Vincentini. I hate everything about him. He is certainly no prince.'

Exasperated Adriana said, 'Then you are a greater fool that I took you for. Who but a prince could court you thus? With dresses and jewels and everything a grateful woman could wish for.'

'My father has provided all this,' Carmelia insisted indication the rich dresses she wore.

'Think again Little Dove.'

Carmelia looked aghast. She pulled at the material as if to rid herself of it. 'How can that be so? The coffers of clothes and caskets of jewels are given by my father.'

Adriana shrugged. 'Perhaps your father thought it not worth a mention; all this was sent by Vincentini. What difference does it make? Be content with that and, for the love of heaven, behave as is expected of you.'

Flushed with shame or anger, Carmelia turned away and marched off towards her room, already pulling at the laces of her bodice.

Adriana stood still until she had disappeared, sure now in the face of such determination that everything Carmelia had said was true, all of it. Adriana sniffed and wiped a rare tear from the corner of her eye. She went in search of Don Carlos. She would talk to him and do what she could. She would also talk with the fool boy. If Carmelia could not be persuaded to abandon him, then Adriana felt sure that with pressure applied she would persuade him to leave Venice and never reappear. Privately Adriana was insulted that Emlyn Tomas had ignored her since that night in Geneva. And, because of what had happened between them, brief though it had been, Emlyn Tomas could not ever have Carmelia. Adriana had enough coin to bribe the rouge with and enough influence to deter him, if he thought to improve his standing by marrying his betters!

Adriana had known Don Carlos for many years. Their families had strengthened each others wealth through marriage in previous generations; Don Carlos' first wife had been Adriana's cousin. Adriana had come to live with her as a child and had been a companion to her sons Cristoforo and Roberto.

Adriana found Don Carlos in his favourite room. It ran the length of the portico with unadorned pillars on either side supporting the vaulted ceiling; this was painted night-time blue with stars picked out in gold. The walls were painted with scenes from Roman mythology, unlike most

Venetians, Don Carlos favoured the revival of ancient Roman to that of ancient Greece, Rome was closer to his heart. He was sitting under a mural depicting the Muses, seven young maids dancing with Apollo on a background of red marble, each carrying the symbol of their art. The room was used for relaxing and reading, numerous windows overlooked the piazza at the back of the palace.

Adriana's skirts rustled as she made her way down the length. She had taken the trouble to change before she had come. Her dresses, one laid over the other, were of satin, in warm orange and deep blue. How refreshing she found the fashions of Italy after the numerous, heavy layers she had become used to in France. She wore all her pearls, twisted about her neck and woven into her hair plaits and a Spanish silver broach that she had received from a fond lover and had always cherished.

Don Carlos was partially concealed behind a red curtain trimmed with tassels, it was loosely hung and could be drawn across the opening for privacy; or eavesdropping, recalled Adriana remembering easier times. She drew level and found his eyes upon her. There was no love shared between them nor had there ever been when Adriana had lived here as companion to his first wife. They held each other in guarded respect. He had changed greatly since Adriana had gone to France with his young daughter. He was no longer the powerfully built, barrel-chested man who had commanded attention as soon as he entered a room. Adriana though he looked old and harmless, pale with the sicknesses of old age. She was not deceived, he still wielded the same power and commanded the same awesome respect.

She had not intended to bother with any meaningless conversation, but it was he who spoke first. 'Giuseppe tells me that you and my daughter travelled in the company of that young man who was so entertaining this afternoon. You should have made a gift of him to me. I would have seen that he received the patronage that his talent deserves, such light should not be hid under a bushel.'

Adriana felt the colour leave her face. Clasping her hands in front of her, she said, 'We did not hear him play on the journey, Carlos.'

Don Carlos rose stiffly and brushed passed Adriana as he walked to a window. His limp was pronounced, he had kept to his bed for a week, the whole house aware of the pain his gout caused. 'I have decided to employ the youth to entertain the guests at Carmelia's wedding feast. I may well find other work for him, quite charming for a foreigner. Something will have to be done about his appearance though, he looks like a wandering minstrel. Black is always effective against the vividness of youth, don't you agree?'

As this was the last thing Adriana wanted to happen. She said, 'There was rumour that he was an untrustworthy youth, with tendencies to thieve. He kept company with the mercenaries. I hope you will keep this in mind.'

Don Carlos gazed out of the window and made a dismissive sound. Adriana moved forward to where he could see her, determined to accomplish the task she had set herself. 'Carlos I want you to reconsider the arrangements you have made for Carmelia. She is very young and needs time to get used to the idea of marriage before she is plunged head first into a disagreeable union.'

Without turning, without the slightest change of expression, Don Carlos said, 'No. I will not go back on my word for any man, or woman, even a daughter. She will do as I demand. There is no question of like or dislike, merely dutiful obedience.'

'She is your only child! If she was content there would be no cause for concern. I do not want her to be unhappy. A delay may well be all she needs, even a month would be enough. It is all so rushed and she has not even met the man yet.'

'Had you come when you were meant to, there would have been time enough. The fact that time is short lies on your shoulders, not mine. I will talk no further on it, the arrangements are made.'

Adriana wrung her hands together nervously; he was one of the few people who could unnerve her. 'Where is Tomasso di Vincentini?'

'In Padua. He will be here shortly after Easter. We shall have a celebration and you may judge him for yourself. Am I asking her to wed a hunchback? A lunatic? A leper or an incompetent ancient? No. I find her one of the wealthiest men in Venice. He is respectable, presentable, rich and influential. I find the best for my only child, and she needs time to get used to the idea. Preposterous!'

'Could we not persuade him to wait then?'

'He is a busy man, he will not wait nor shall you mention this again. Adriana you, more than most, know my will.'

Adriana's anger lent her the strength to continue with her plea. She was no stranger to finding weaknesses and applying pressure when nothing else worked. 'If you refuse to listen to reason,' she said coldly, 'I might be forced to betray a confidence or two.'

Don Carlos gave up his scrutiny of the garden and turned. Adriana was surprised at his expression, it was neither harsh nor angry. 'You will do no such thing,' he snapped. 'Now go away from me before I have you physically removed, as I do most unpleasant persons who cross my purpose.'

Adriana rose to her full height, gratified to see that age had dwarfed the great man. With hooded lids she looked down on him. 'I am not unaware of how you endeavour to remove any who dare to stand up to your despotic will! I however, refuse to be counted among them. I don't know how you can dare to tempt me so. A whisper in the right ear Don Carlos Grimani, and your popularity, reliability and respectability will be worth less than a butt of fish heads!'

He waved his hand dismissing her words. 'What do you think you hold over me, foolish woman? Time has passed Adriana, no one cares any more and those that did are all dead and gone.'

'Oh?' exclaimed Adriana in mock surprise. 'Your grandsons might be interested to know that their mother still lives and in what circumstances.'

For the first time, Don Carlos' brow furrowed. He released a snort of laughter. 'You can't possibly hope to revive that one. And what good would it do you? You have no proof to support your accusations. You can not harm me by malicious gossip.'

'Can't I? There may be but a few who would believe my words and two who most certainly would. Threats do not frighten me Carlos. If I were to suffer one of your 'accidents' you can be sure some ugly truths will follow. I have not come here to do battle with you and left my back unguarded.'

Don Carlos' large frame shuddered as if an icy wind had entered the hall. His fat fingers closed around Adriana's arm, but the grip was not vice like or even intimidating. It was gentle yet urged her firmly to walk back to the tapestry seat.

'I can see,' he said, 'that there is need here for some swift education. I am not a man in the habit of revealing my concerns to women, but I see no other course left to me.'

Adriana sank into the seat opposite and endured his intimacy as he took her two hands in his, clasped across the space between them.

He sighed and again the shudder ran through his body. 'Everything you see here, eat, stand on, sit or lie upon, even breath, is held in surety against the formidable loans that have been forced on me.'

'I don't believe you!' snapped Adriana. 'If you think this is some sort of threat?'

'No.' He shook his head. 'If you must, you may examine my books, my ledgers, speak with Zorzo Vecelli, my manager. You will find that the great trading empire of Don Carlos Grimani has been eaten away by disaster and misfortune. Ever since I lost the Malmsey fleet last spring, my fortunes have gone from bad to worse. If I do not regain the balance through this marriage I have secured for Carmelia, I am doomed to end my days in a debtor's cell. When I fall, so will everything and everyone else, including you Adriana. In Carmelia's future lies our salvation. She is my daughter and in spite of that unfortunate turn of fate, I love her and have done all in my power to ensure that she has a firm future in front of her. Foolish child! What more could any girl wish for?'

As this sank in, Adriana felt the same shivering chill run through her. It was so awesome that she could not even begin to consider the implications. 'What about the *Maria*?' she asked on whispered breath.

Don Carlos gave a short, bitter laugh. 'A dip in the ocean, a mere sip to moisten the lips of the bankers who hold me so securely. I have kept up pretences, there are very few who know the truth; you will keep it that way if you wish to come through unscathed. If Tomasso di Vincentini knew he was betrothed to a pauper's daughter, do you think he would wed her? No of course not, what sensible man would? Go forth with your slanderous gossiping Adriana, and see what you do to us all.' Don Carlos released her hands and stood up.

He pulled the bell cord above the seat and an answering chime rang in the ante chamber. Within minutes Uglino appeared, his dogs at his heels. 'Ah there you are!' called the patron. 'Give an old man the support of your shoulder.'

Uglino immediately came to assist him. 'I am going to Monte Paganella for the summer,' said Don Carlos pleasantly. 'You have never been there have you Uglino, never left Venice? You will like it there, mountains and a lake and plenty of room.'

They shuffled off, down the long room, slim and fat, old and young, Don Carlos' voice rising and falling. The hounds padded behind, their claws clicking on the marble.

Chapter 45 Easter

To celebrate Easter, the Grimani household turned out with its usual splendour. Dressed in their finery, aglitter with gems, they trooped into San Marco's Basilica to attend the long mass. San Marco piazza was flooded from the aqua alta, the high tides of spring. Another inch and it would have spilled into the basilica, as it was, it was quite convenient for everyone, they were rowed right up to the central portal and hardly had to walk at all.

With Don Carlos were his wife Juliana, her two sisters and their husbands with a group of angelic daughters, Adriana Martinelli and Carmelia. Behind them stood a crowd of various cousins, two or three times removed. There were priests and nuns and the rest of the Grimani household; the notaries, accountants, artists, musicians, house servants and gondoliers, maids, pageboys, including Uglino and a fool and a dwarf. Don Grimani liked to have a good turn out. It was a show of power and wealth that left no man in any doubt of his standing. The fact that it was an illusion was known to few. In his finery, Don Carlos looked magnificent and he was greeted with great respect.

Incense filled the air, tickling noses. The smoke curled up the marble pillars, the vaulted ceilings and cupolas as it had done for hundreds of years. Voices joined, moaned and sung out the mass to celebrate Easter. The basilica tolerated their presence and soaked up their sacred music. Eventually with the final blessing the congregation rose with a rustle and a creak, a cough, a sniff and a whisper. The crowds thinned and left the House of God. Outside, the water level had dropped and they were able to take part in the Doge's procession across the square, taking their exalted places and looking as opulent as was expected of them. The air was hot and humid. When the solemn duties were over, the atmosphere of carnival broke over Venice like a tidal wave.

Uglino stayed at his master's side all through that hectic morning. He knew his master well now and was no longer afraid, Don Carlos had become like a father to him. Before they returned to the house, Don Carlos drew him aside, out of hearing of the others. He bent to Uglino's ear. 'I want you watch with the eye of a hawk,' he whispered. 'This time, it is my daughter who you are to watch. Remember when you told me she went to meet some gallant while pretending to visit her great aunt?'

'Yes my Lord, but I could not be sure, I did not see much.'

'You can be sure my faithful Uglino. Now you must find out who it was.'

Uglino fumbled with his tunic ties. 'The Madonna Carmelia does not like me, she will know if she sees me.'

'Then you must use the cunning I have taught you, watch, but do not be seen. Is her maid faithful?'

'Mistress Pellegrina doesn't like me either. But I have delivered some messages for her from time to time. A few days ago there was a matter which I thought to draw your attention to, but I have not had the chance.'

'Well you have it now. Speak.'

'I believe that mistress Pellegrina has a lover my Lord. I delivered a token of hers to an address which she swore me to secrecy; I did not think that included you my Lord, so I will not be forsworn. I did not think anything of it at first, it is not my place to question.'

'You are right Uglino, it is your place to obey the master who loves you. Tell me more.'

'It was a mask my Lord, a red mask that I had seen the lady Carmelia sew with her own hand. I thought, surely she would not go to such trouble for her maid's lover? Perhaps mistress Pellegrina borrowed it, or perhaps it was intended for another?'

Don Carlos smiled and rubbed his hands together. 'And the address to which you delivered this token?'

'To the German's house my Lord, the one who makes the musical instruments. There are many working there. I did not discover for whom it was intended.'

Don Carlos straightened and looked thoughtful. 'A red mask,' he said, as if to himself. 'A mask to be identified among many, a token by which the giver will know the receiver. Perhaps we are closer to our quarry than we guessed, for all go masked at carnival time. Watch, my hawk. Even you can tread wherever you will. You shall have a disguise in which none will know you. Before this day's end, you and I will know who the wearer of the red mask is. But caution little hawk, none must know of your surveillance. Return to me with anything you learn.'

Carlos Grimani already had his suspicions, it was obvious considering what he already knew. He was sorry, for the young man's music had been unique and had given him great pleasure.

Alone, Emlyn watched the water ripple behind the gondola as he poled it through the Rio della Frescada. The Venetian stroke, used to manoeuvre the slender boats, was not easily mastered and he had endured many hilarious soakings to remind him of his lack of skill. Umbaldo had given up teaching him. Away from prying eyes, he had tried out some complicated manoeuvres, causing the boat to weave from side to side, but, when he was least expecting it, the boat seemed to ditch him as if it had a mind of its own. On this occasion, he was determined to master it. The gondola had eyes painted on the sides and the name San Francesco written in curved lettering across the stern; a statue of the saint stood at the prow beneath a gilded sea horse. Emlyn had discovered that the gondola was more than a mere boat in Venice, it represented the spirit of the water city and its people. Those who built the vessels and those who steered them over the canals were a special breed who guarded their secrets jealously. Emlyn had been warned that as a foreigner, he stood little chance of remaining dry on whatever journey he undertook for, he was not a gondolier and no amount of skill could ever make him one.

He was in the centre of the canal when the pole slipped out of his hand and stuck in the mud as he and the boat sped on. It slowed and came to a stop with a soft thud against the wall. Tall houses rose straight out of the water on either side, seeming to frown down in scorn. Long tendrils of moss-green algae spread out across the surface of the water, and clothed the precipitous walls in the green velvet. He stared into the shadowy depths, concerned about his predicament. There were no other oars on the boat, so he splashed with his hands but the heavy gondola made little response. There were two choices left to him. He could ruin his best clothes by paddling to the pole in what looked like exceptional unsavoury conditions and was probably too deep, or he could remain sitting like an idiot until someone came along and laughed at him, making him feel the complete, miserable fool he was.

He heard the muffled sounds of Venice, but the only sound near him was the continuous plopping of water, unnerving in the dark, cool canal. After ten minutes of waiting, he stood up and taking a deep breath, began to sing. His voice bounced off the walls and echoed down the damp passage. He sang of forsaken by love, a song that Umbaldo had taught him and that brought a touch of humour to the humiliating situation. It was not long before he was rewarded for his efforts. An answering voice, picked up his lament and carried it through the next verse. Soon a slender gondola came into sight. Emlyn murmured a prayer of gratitude, it was Donenico Alfani who regularly brought flowers for the Franciscan church further down the canal and ferried the Franciscans on their various duties about Venice.

Donenico was smiling, a smile repeated in the three chins beneath it. He was a round, jovial, bear-like man, well used to threading his way through the Rio della Frescada. He poled through the water with balance and enviable poise, catching up the stranded pole with deft precision. 'Ah, Emlyn, I should have guessed, caught up the creek without an oar again? How can a foreigner hope to be a Venetian? Your San Francesco was no man of the sea Emlyn, perhaps you should name your boat after another or carry with you an image of the Virgin of the Fishes.' He drew up beside the stranded gondola.

'Thank you Donenico,' Emlyn laughed. 'Saint Francis has guided me well enough up 'till now, it would be no justice for me to desert him for an occasional mishap.'

'Such faith will be well rewarded. Do you go to the masquerade, to lay your heart at the feet of some unsuspecting maiden?'

'I have no lady in mind,' replied Emlyn evasively. 'But, I would not miss the festival for all the treasure in the Basilica.'

Donenico laughed. 'Such a night of gaiety, for grand balls and youthful love, and you look so fine. I will not toss you into the water. Instead, we will finish our song and between here and the Canale Grande, I will show you how to steer that tub of yours.' He tipped his weight forward, leaning on his pole, hardly disturbing the surface of the water. Emlyn started up the song again and they progressed on their melodious journey. Donenico's strong voice broke off occasionally with a word of advice or encouragement.

For Easter, all of Venice turned out to take part in the festivities. The singing Gondoli poled through the gleaming water towards the Grand Canal. Boats of all shapes and sizes ferried up and down. From the windows, far up above, women reached out with smiling faces, shouting and gesturing frantically to each other across the water space. Their lustrous hair, caught up in swathes of cobweb lace, fell in raven coils intertwined with flowers. 'Maria! Maria!' shouted Donenico Alfani.

Flowers rained down and a powerful voice boomed. 'Is that you fat Donenico?'

'It is I, sweet Aphrodite. And look what I have brought for you, the Golden Apples of Hesperedese.' Donenico held up a basket of fruit as bright as the fiery sunset. His eyes crossed as they soaked up the vision of milky half moons framed in provocative lace that hung temptingly over the window ledge.

'Keep the fruit for your wife Donenico,' shouted sweet Aphrodite. 'Give me instead the pretty boy with you.'

This time, with the flowers, cat calls and hoots of suggestive laughter rained down. Emlyn blushed from the soles of his feet. With all his strength, he leant heavily on the pole and pulled the vessel away, the jeers and invitations increased as the sounds faded.

They joined the thick flow of highly decorative gondolas piled with flowers and filled with oarsmen, costumed in colours to match their vessels and the noble houses they represented. Emlyn thought their own boats looked dull and dwarfed as they sped past a sky-blue bissone, elegantly furbished and looped in white garlands with life-size silver dolphins at the prow. Donenico called out greetings and received light hearted insults in return. Emlyn concentrated on steering, loath to have a mishap in view of all.

The colours of the sun deepened, painting the fragile rooftops in gentle, soft oranges and golds. Emlyn bid farewell to his rescuer. Separating from Donenico, his gondola swirled into the Bacino di San Marco. The brilliant evening spread out before him as far as the flat sea horizon, dotted with marshy islands and the long, mist shrouded, Lido. Other boatmen were silhouetted by the orange sky; their voices raised in song and laughter. It was a magical time of day, when the lamps winked on the crowded narrow boats. Moored to striped poles, they swayed rhythmically on the waves like a flock of sea birds. On the quay, doors in the tall buildings stood open, glowing with welcoming light. A wave of jovial conversation floated across the water, Emlyn could feel the undercurrent, a bubble of excitement and expectation. He began to nudge around the tied boats, until he found a space into which he could squeeze his own vessel unnoticed.

Over his shoulder-length ringlets he wore a peculiar hat folds of ash-grey velvet gathered into a headband that flopped over one ear like an un-stuffed cushion and sprouted a red feather. Grey too were his short doublet and soft hose. The doublet was lined with fine, red linen, that showed through the wide, slashed sleeves gathered at the elbow into a long cuff. On to each arm, four silver bells had been sewn by Tieffenbrucker's daughters. A small Venetian knife hung at his belt in an unadorned scabbard of leather, a long, thin blade fabled for its stealth. These were the clothes Ambrose had given him. Such fashion was only suitable for the English court or in Venice, where all vied to outdo each other in dress and splendour. Emlyn had only worn them twice, on his two visits to the company house, the time when he had that had brought the wool and when Bartolomeo Varini had refused to consider his proposition concerning the Levant Merchant

Company. Ambrose had said that clothes can make a man and Emlyn had to admit that he felt good thus attired.

He pulled on his mask, it was the red one covered with sequins. Although the mysterious provider was a puzzle to Theo and Umbaldo, they had guessed it was a lady's choice and had teased him non-stop about it. Since then, Emlyn had seen Pellegrina and finalised the details of his and Carmelia's escape. The mask, she had told him was the way that she would be able to identify him in the crowds. When Emlyn had returned from Don Grimani's house, he discovered that Theo and Wendelin had arranged for him to join a group of musicians who were engaged to entertain the bishop of San Marco and his guests outside the basilica. Because they had gone to such trouble, Emlyn had not told them about his success with Don Carlos and the promise of more, none of which would happen anyway if he ran off with the patron's daughter.

He felt as if he walked on a narrow ledge, one foot put wrong and he would fall. He knew he was ambitious in his scheming and had left little margin for error. If he failed to snatch Carmelia from the palace or was discovered, there was little time to make another attempt. The plan was simple and this simplicity worried him. But what other way was there with time running against them? He had even thought to delay the groom, but he did not know the man or his whereabouts.

Snatches of song and shrill women's laughter cut through the air. Ready for the masquerade, Emlyn gathered up the newly borrowed lute in its soft cloth wrappings and stepped onto dry land, feeling the thrill of carnival thumping through the ground beneath him. The bells jingled musically.

Carmelia was hemmed in by great aunts, cousins, her exceptionally quiet mother, Adriana Martinelli and a collection of maids and servants. With them too, sat Don Carlos and Lorenzo, who was now a priest, and Fra Sebastiano whom he had brought to the house with Emlyn. There too, were numerous people to whom she had been introduced briefly, but she could not remember who was who. Madonna Teresa Portormo and her daughters Rosalina and Bettina had arrived from Milan the morning before, in order to attend Carmelia's wedding and to celebrate Easter in Venice. They were all seated under fringed, silken canopies, in front of one of the many wine shops that lined the water front. As was customary, they had been invited to join the bishop of San Marco in a feast of celebration under the stars.

Actors, with faces painted stark white and dressed in domino costumes, began their conjuring tricks, receiving awesome cries and a shower of coins for their efforts. They bounded up and down, as agile as monkeys, spinning shimmering swords that they danced around with complicated, daring steps and energetic acrobatics.

The various guilds had collected in groups about the piazza, Carmelia tried to guess what they all were by their attire. Some were darkly cloaked with anonymous face coverings, but the tanners and curriers were obvious in their leather aprons, decorated with burnt in designs, as were the artists with their gold-trimmed hats, and the guild of weavers and silk dyers, and the gifted glass-blowers from Murano. The people ambled in swirls of colour, light and music from one show to another. The wine flowed more rapidly and the severe vigilance of Carmelia's guardians, over her and each other, began to slacken as they watched the flood of festive entertainment unfold before them. Bettina and Rosalina, after permission was granted, got up to dance with mysterious masked companions. Carmelia thought it unfair. Adriana had told her that the her meeting with Don Carlos had been unsuccessful. Heartbroken, Carmelia now pinned all her hopes on Emlyn. She was careful to follow Adriana's advice in keeping up appearances, but that was getting more and more difficult.

She sat, delicate and pale with her hair all hidden in a close fitting veil. A fringe of black threaded beads hung at her forehead, dancing when she moved. Her eyes peered under the tassels. She desperately wished for an escape from her cushioned confinement, but no opportunity had arisen; when one did, she was determined to break away. She knew Emlyn would be here before long and that she could not as much as look at him for fear of discovery. But masked? It was hard for her to keep her excitement in check.

Late that night, or in the early hours of the morning when all were retired, Emlyn would come to her window and in the darkness they would make their escape. The palatial house was well guarded both night and day, for it contained much of the material wealth Don Carlos had accumulated. No stranger could enter unseen. Leaving the building was a great deal simpler. A long passage that ran the length of the house on the upper level, gave access to a back entrance and a set of steep steps that led to the canal. Four strong doors were placed at intervals through the passage, they could not be opened from the outside as they were all barred. The only way to pass them was from the inside, where the bars could be lifted. Once he had entered the house, Emlyn would have little difficulty leaving, if he was careful not to be seen. And Carmelia would leave with him, and never look back.

'Dearest, delay not,' Carmelia whispered. 'Light of my eyes, I live not without thee.'

The square was filled with noise and music. Masked, she hoped to slip amongst them and disappear into their familiarity. Jugglers, fire-eaters and acrobats flowed across her vision. Traders appeared, daubed with gaudy face-paint. They sold sweets, cakes, confetti, fruit and cooked mushrooms as white and round as moonstones. None wore a mask of red sequins. Carmelia clapped her hands, enthralled by their performances. She felt warm and excited, wanting to leap and dance and sing, blending with them all. She would let nothing pass by her unseen, but her eyes were not big enough to take it all in, she felt she would burst if she could not express something of her emotion.

'Do not stare so Carmelia!' chided her mother scornfully.

Carmelia pulled her gaze away from a group of young musicians, who had cleared a space in front of the bishop. They whirled around, grasping skirted companions in dance to a rapid drum beat. Carmelia, as much as she wished to join in, remained, small and childlike, hidden in the cage of her relations. Her spirits began to flag. A lute joined in, weaving a fast galliard above the noise, so expertly played, that all other sound seemed to dim in comparison. Carmelia's heart missed a beat.

'Ah there he is,' said Don Carlos to the bishop. 'The youth is talented beyond most.'

Horror struck, Carmelia watched as Emlyn, red masked, emerged from the crowd, his lute hanging from his hand. She thought he looked splendid, he had found a decent set of clothing and was obviously out to impress. He did not glance at her, but bowed before Don Carlos, speaking so softly that she could not hear the words.

Carmelia was grateful for her mask, which she pulled down, for her expression was clear to read, should any see it. She had no idea what Emlyn was up to, and prayed that he would not jeopardize their plans for escape. What if he was asking Don Carlos for her hand? Heaven forbid! She would never see him alive again. No, she reasoned, his purpose must be some other.

After nearly an hour of unbearable suspension, Carmelia edged further away from the table. A group of madrigal singers entertained the gathering and got through five sessions before she managed to summon up enough bravado to escape. Emlyn from his place with the entertainers, had still made no glance in her direction. How could he not look at her, just a brief meeting of eyes would be enough!

The attention of her guardians was taken up in buying pasta filled with sweet raisins and shaped like stars and cartwheels, and pastries wafted a rich spicy scent of cinnamon and cloves. Hidden in the shadows, Carmelia stood up, moved discreetly behind her chair and slipped away. No one had noticed, no voice demanded her return. She felt that luck surrounded her on this wild night, giving her freedom. A freedom that she had rarely felt. She checked that her mask was secure and, slipped through the crowd. Her steps hopped and skipped, instead of behaving in the strict, lady-like manner in which she had been taught from infancy. She hugged herself gleefully. Here I am, nobody and everybody all at once, she thought. The world is at my feet and I am dancing on it.

The music had stopped and an argument was taking place. Carmelia moved closer. Seeing her, Emlyn winked. He said, 'I don't want to play that one all over again Renato, find another to play it, this place is probably crawling with musicians. Why can't we play something better suited to the festival?'

'Al l right,' replied the one called Renato. He was an elderly, bent musician who was obviously at pains to keep his players from wandering off. For emphasis he held out his hands, palms up. 'I'll find another. Just play until I do. And drink some more wine, I don't like you when you're so disagreeable.'

Carmelia pushed to the front of the group. She bounced up and down like a child and said 'Yes, do play another.'

'What will I receive in return?' asked Emlyn. His face lit up in the flare of a yellow firework. He winked again at her.

Carmelia stared up into the sequin-framed blue eyes. 'I dare you to a dance,' she whispered. She cast her gaze to the ground and stared at her blue slippered feet, suddenly afraid. Emlyn's eyes had warned her to be cautious. But she could feel the magic in the air and persisted. 'If your music pleases me, your reward shall be a dance.'

The older man Renato, laughed. 'Listen to the child Emlyn, how can you refuse such promise?'

'I am not a child,' yelled Carmelia stamping her foot, then, realising that she was behaving just like one and that her quick temper could ruin an interesting evening, she smiled beseechingly. She remembered Emlyn calling her a child when they were in Geneva, then she had displayed the same anger, the price to pay for a small stature.

'He'll play,' said Renato, looking at her with a raised eyebrow.

Emlyn walked over to the drummer for a few words before he stepped back and swiftly checked his lute strings, they hummed as he concentrated on tuning them up. With a nod to the drummer the music began and immediately captured the crowd. Trapped in an invisible net of irresistible motion, they moved and turned to the steady rhythm. The half concealed faces were bright with smiles and sparkling eyes. Carmelia stood where the lamps were dim, afraid of being recognised, and watched her lutanist with adoration.

Renato returned with a bird-masked man carrying a shawm, another with a rebec and a piper, dressed in a moth-eaten lion skin. They immediately added their music to the lute and drum.

With a jerk, Carmelia was swept into torrent of swirling figures by a stranger. A loud thump on the drum announced a quickening to the pace. Faster and faster the stomping, country dance sent them all in a compelling whirlwind of motion. They flew around, skirts belling out and shrieking with high pitched laughter. More and more of the crowd joined the dancing throng. The melody tempted even the elderly to cast aside their reservations and join in the animated jubilation. Confetti and egg shells filled with rose water, began to fly, bursting on heads and shoulders, pervading the air with heady perfume. Carmelia flew as free as a bird into the grasp of a bear and on to a magnificent cockerel, a dark magician, a fool, a feathered serpent; on and on, arms linking through as they passed. Venice knew better than any other city how to enjoy a carnival.

When the music stopped silence descended like a blanket, time stood still for seconds. Then the dancers and the onlookers erupted into a roar of applause, for the musicians, for each other and out of pure joy.

A melody rose again, it was quiet and flowed calm and soothing over the variety of hats, tiaras, horns and headdresses. Carmelia stood breathless and exhilarated. A voice behind her said, 'I believe this dance is mine?'

She turned and smiled. 'Your music was beautiful.' Taking off her cloak with precision she handed it to Renato who stood breathless beside her. Lights sparkled off the jewels sewn onto her organdie overdress, a translucent midnight blue. 'I hope you are a prince. I will dance with nothing less,' she said to her sequin-masked companion.

'Tonight, I put my heart at your feet, my arm at your service and my destiny in your keeping. I am whatever you would have me be. The king of the Magic Mountain, the Emperor of Cathay, Prince of the Golden Sun God or the Man on the Silvery Moon.'

'Which will it be?'

'It is for you to choose little princess.'

'The man of the Silvery Moon?'

'An excellent choice.' He grasped her hand and pulled her in to the confusing medley. The marching thump of drum, the whistle of pipe and the jangle of a gypsy tambourine sent Carmelia's slippered feet in motion. Her heavy skirts swayed and shimmered as she danced. In these arms and with the promise of a future together, her joy was complete, nothing could have made her happier.

A burst of fireworks filled the sky with new born stars. They twinkled, trailing glowing cinders which poured through the night. Before dying, others took their place, pinks, yellows, oranges, golds, greens and blues soared, bursting and sparkling upward like a thousand sequins. Booms, crackles and bangs cut through the air, fire wheels spun dizzying and squibs hissed quietly before they rent the air with a thunderous devil's tattoo, followed by the rapid explosions of fire-crackers and the accompanying squeals of their unfortunate victims.

Throwing caution to the winds, Carmelia and Emlyn toured the stalls and watched everything they could. They were joined by masked young men with decorous women on their arms, a gaggle of noisy children and the magnificent cockerel. They saw a puppet show, were spun around on a bright carousel, stuffed themselves with sticky cannelloni, took a ride on a donkey dyed blue, were garlanded with chains of sweet smelling jasmine and were dragged up and down mysterious staircases, to play pranks and empty pails of canal water over unsuspecting ladies in their glittering gowns. They were showered with cheap baubles and beads and flower petals. All were captivated in a turbulence of thrilling, delirious madness.

After two hours, Emlyn escorted Carmelia back towards her family, filling her ears with promises on the way. 'But a few hours more, sweet mermaid.'

'That's more than I can bear,' she answered, looking up at him with tears threatening to fall. 'You hold my life in the palm of your hand.'

Emlyn kissed her, first on one damp eyelid and then the other. 'No it is I, that Love has wounded unto death,' he whispered.

Carmelia returned home exhausted and in deep trouble with her mother and Adriana. Their anger failed to penetrate her euphoria; she floated on a silver cloud. She went to her room and lit a lamp in the window as she had agreed with Emlyn. He had tried to urge her to go to the door at the end of the passage alone, assuring her he would be there waiting, all night if necessary. But she was afraid to escape alone. Uncaring of the hour, Venice still glowed and sang with celebration. Carmelia did not intend to fall asleep, but as soon as she sat down on the soft bed, her will betrayed her and she was asleep in seconds.

Emlyn had told Umbaldo that he had fallen in love with a lady's maid. This had not been hard for Umbaldo to accept after the visit from the Milan players to the Theo's yard and the trouble that had followed. Emlyn had further explained, that when all were asleep or drunk after the festival, this girl had promised to be his, but only if he could get to her room. 'It's a matter of a window,' he'd explained. 'I need you in the boat while I scale the wall.'

'Am I to wait,' said Umbaldo, 'while you have your evil way with a maiden?'

'Of course not,' said Emlyn laughing. They had both drunk too much wine. Earlier in the day, Emlyn had taken a boat to the sleepy canal that Pellegrina had told him about. He had lit a fire brand and climbed the slime covered steps to a bolted door at the top. It was ancient. The hinges were rusted with mould furring the damp wood. He had tried it but it held solid to its casement. He had left the fire brand knowing that they would need it to find their way on the gloomy steps. He had Carmelia would make their escape in a small rowing boat that he would row to the mainland in the darkness. Emlyn believed that the night belonged to him and Carmelia and nothing would or could stand in the way of their ambition. He had never been more wrong.

It had begun to rain gently by the time Umbaldo and he approached the back of the Grimani house in the depth of night. They saw the lamp sparkle in the high window. Behind which, thought Emlyn lovingly, Carmelia waits with bated breath and sweet, soft kisses. He had no knowledge that he had been watched and followed and was watched still from a dark passage where a boy in the guise of a cockerel had concealed himself. There was a tree growing on the canal bank, its branches conveniently leaning over, a mere leap away from the small balcony where a single candle burned in its glass casing. Emlyn scrambled out of the boat and up the tree trunk with the agility of a lizard.

Umbaldo stood rocking the narrow boat and shouted up. He had no idea where he was; his mind befuddled with wine, had kept no sense of direction.

Emlyn signalled for silence. He was hanging off a branch. The branch was creaking piteously informing him of its reluctance to hold his weight any longer. If he did nothing, he would end up wet. Below him in the darkness was the narrow, slimy, little-used canal and opposite him, three floors up, a solid brick wall. Just out of reach was Carmelia's balcony. It had seemed like a good idea from the ground, now Emlyn realised he had misjudged the distance. The branch creaked as he inched along a bit further. Then his legs slipped, the wood bent and Emlyn dangled over the canal like fish bait. He began to swing himself and with an almighty effort and an imploring prayer, left his precarious security and flew through the air, long limbs flapping.

He hit the balcony with a thud, threw his hands out and grasped a smooth stone pillar. His fingers began to slip. The pillars were plain and unadorned affording little grip. He hung desperately trying to swing his legs up without loosing his tentative hold. His heart beat wildly with the thought of the fate awaiting him below. He swung his legs up again and again until he managed to wrap one around a pillar. He hung there for a moment, then spilled over the stone railing in a sprawling, untidy heap. He stood up and dusted himself off, his doublet marred with dust. Without looking back, he walked regally to the open window and stepped inside.

The room Emlyn entered was lit by a single candle, its light barely reached the canopied bed where promised delight lay waiting for her lover. Emlyn moved with care through the dark room. Was she not ready? But, in the dim light, Venus waited, pulling aside the bed covers.

Emlyn did not need inviting twice, there was enough time, or so he convinced himself. He hurriedly undressed. Her face was in shadow but her dark hair, long and rippling down her back caught the light in soft waves. She giggled in the darkness. She was wearing a loose robe of dark orange over a pale chemise and sat with her back to the light, knowing that she presented an attractive temptation. Emlyn stared at her in open admiration. She came close up to him, dragged her delicate fingers through his damp, tangled hair and planted a light kiss on his willing lips. Emlyn reached out and held her as if she were made of Venetian glass and kissed her gentle mouth. There was no need for words between them.

Totally under her spell, Emlyn was smitten by tender passion. It was a night for love with the distant sounds of the festival floating through the open window. This is what heaven must be like or perhaps hell, he thought with a pang of guilt, guilt that was soon forgotten as she held him close.

He undressed her, his movements and hers now urgent. The danger of their situation heightening their desire. She was so sensitive, so passionate, a feathered touch made her cry with ecstasy and implore him for more. He cupped her breasts and sucked at her nipples until they stood proud. His kisses explored her neck, her ears and found her lips. His hands wandered down, stroking silken skin, tangling with the springy hair between her thighs. Carmelia bit back a scream. She kissed him with increasing hunger, caressing him so that he groaned in anticipation, his need near unbearable. She wrapped her legs around him, and he could wait no longer. He pushed into her, the touch sending shudders through them both. He pushed in further, began to move until she writhed like a serpent beneath him. Blind in her need she matched his rhythm.

She was as yet, unaware that his seed already had found its destination, when they had first made love in Milan. Carmelia was now two months pregnant.

As soon as Uglino saw where the red-masked man was going, he left his hiding place and hurried to the front of the house. The other man in the boat had crawled under the canopy to sleep. Knowing how urgent the situation had become, Uglino ran all the way to Don Carlos' room and bounded through the door.

Don Carlos was not asleep, he was sitting under a spray of lit candles, a cat sat purring on his knee, oblivious to Uglino's hounds that slept at the master's feet. He had already observed his daughter's behaviour and identified the man she had spent over two hours with. He could not at first believe that her behaviour had gone unnoticed, but the others had all enjoyed themselves too much to be aware. Uglino had watched the lovers and had reported back to his master every move they had made.

Uglino skidded in now, wet and mud splattered, his feathers in tatters. 'He is in her room!' he spluttered. 'Got in through the window from outside!'

Don Carlos smiled, a warm satisfied smile. How well he had judged the situation. He yawned and continued to stroke the cat.

'Aren't you going to do anything?' said Uglino, his voice squeaking.

'In a while,' said Don Carlos quietly. 'Sit down Uglino, dry yourself by the fire, there is time enough, it will soon be dawn. When you are dry, go back and watch the door.'

And what to do with such a lover? he mused. It explained Carmelia's behaviour. Of course she did not want to marry Tomasso di Vincentini when she had a young, virile man to give her childish heart to. And what enterprising young man would refuse such a tender and promising fruit? Don Carlos was amused by the situation. What if I do nothing? Would they run off? Wed in secret? No, that could not be allowed to happen, Vincentini must have his bride. What an amusing twist of fate it would be to present him with used goods. Is the girl too pious? She seems timid enough to keep her legs crossed, but, appearances can be deceptive and if she has any of my spirit, her appetite will be demanding. Why else invite the lutanist to her room in the darkness of night?

If I tread with care, then I will have a lever with which to do injury to Vincentini. Care though! He must not be scared away from the promised partnership. I do not like him, he has that chilling air of confidence and superiority that I detest in any but myself. In all honesty, he makes me feel small! No one has ever achieved that before, I take it as a personal insult. I have been unable still, to discover anything about the man, Vincentini hides his tracks well. That, I will admit to myself alone, is admirable and I am not in the habit of admiring anyone. So a lever is needed, anything to get under that cool exterior. If I can pluck nothing from his past to use as a bludgeon, then I shall create one from this unwise choice Carmelia has made. She will still fulfil her purpose and wed him. Only afterwards, shall he learn that she is not as pure as she appears. But what if she is? There is always a slim possibility that the youth is a well behaved gentleman and has not taken advantage of the situation. To be sure I shall question the maid, ladies always share their loves and hates with their maids. Pellegrina is a pretty girl and vain like most women. Extravagance and pampering, that's what wins them all in the end.

Uglino returned, slipping into the room quietly. It was less dark, a pale light announced the coming of dawn. Don Carlos stood up, dumping the cat on the floor. He rubbed his eyes, scratched his chin and yawned while requesting a warm cloak. Smiling, Uglino wrapped the garment around his shoulders and they left the room. The house was silent and dark. When they reached Carmelia's door, Don Carlos turned the handle, it opened with no resistance. The room was empty, the bed rumpled, still warm and the candle spluttering in a pool of wax. He swung around alarmed. 'Where?'

'They were here when I came for you my lord. Not much time has passed. They must have gone through the upper passage. They could escape the house that way.'

'On no account can that be allowed to happen!'

'My lord, if we hurry through the concealed passage and cut through the chapel we will meet them on the other side, before they reach the outer door.'

Don Carlos hadn't run for many years, he found the experience unpleasant. The house was riddled with hidden passages, many long forgotten. Rosa the whore, had used this one to come and go on his demand; it was quite free of cobwebs but pitch black. They ran through, Don Carlos huffing and puffing, Uglino leading him along by the arm. They nearly collided with the fleeing lovers who just managed to dodge out of the way before they were seen. Carmelia and Emlyn had reached the large door at the end of the hall, that would open to their freedom. Uglino was just about to leap out of concealment when Don Carlos stopped him and whispered fiercely. 'Say nothing and do not be surprised by what I do and say. There is method in my actions.'

He strode out into the passage, singing a refrain and rubbing his hands against the cold. Out of the corner of his eye, he saw Emlyn push Carmelia behind a threadbare curtain, where she was concealed from view, but there was nowhere he could hide himself.

'Ah!' Don Carlos cried, assuming an expression of pleasant surprise. 'Emlyn Tomas wasn't it? You are here so early. I did say this morning didn't I? I did not expect such punctuality, you are an early bird!'

Emlyn stared at him, his mouth closed and opened, his face as red as an apple, his guilt written all over him. He moved away from the curtain.

'Never mind,' said Don Carlos cheerfully. 'As it happens I am up and about. Old men do not sleep so well you know. Music, music that is the answer. It is yet hours until daylight, you can come and sing for me. Whatever are you doing up here anyway? Were you lost?'

Chapter 46 Tomasso

Fiorenza had spent Easter and the three days preceding it at her sister Giovanna's house, Ca' de Paradiasia. The days had sped by in a whirl of activity and enjoyment, she felt physically and mentally exhausted. That was the main reason she had returned to this house to spend her final night in Venice. She was due to sail for Cyprus the next day on a ship owned by Francesco Cornaro, who was a friend of her Cypriot family. Fiorenza had been in Venice for nearly a year, most of that time she had spent in this quiet house which Tomasso had found for her. Bartolomeo Varini had visited her often, informing her on how the business was running and proving a valuable and thoughtful friend. She was aware of the depth of his feeling towards her and had been quite flattered by his awkward attentions. She had not shown him any encouragement. She did not feel any love towards him and would not allow herself to become trapped again in an unhappy relationship. She had had enough of that with her deceased husband. Besides, Bartolomeo deserved better; she had given her heart to another, foolish though it was.

Even though Tomasso had been away from Venice for most of the time, he was never out of her thoughts for long. In the privacy of her room, she had wept long and deeply when she had heard that he was to make Carmelia Grimani his wife. Fiorenza could not feel hatred towards him, she knew that the arrangement was not born out of love. Whatever devil drove him, she had no power to intervene. If it weren't for his determined vengeance, she knew that she could have made him happy; could have made him forget and bury the past.

The spring had been warm and idyllic. Fiorenza had spent many afternoons sitting in this tiny courtyard. It was a sunlit area, protected from the sea winds by high walls. On one wall there was a an ornate shell shaped bowl beneath a lion's head from which water spouted. The walls were criss-crossed with overgrown roses, now just coming into flower. It was a peaceful place to sit and chatter with Giovanna and the many friends she had made since coming here. Often she was content to sit alone, working at the lace making which a Murano neighbour had taught her how to master. In many ways, Fiorenza would be sorry to leave. All her belongings were packed into barrels and a sea trunk, ready to be loaded onto the ship when she boarded.

She had let her servants go to enjoy the festivities that still continued in Venice. Her maid Maria had gone to spend the last day and night with her relations. Fiorenza had just kept the house steward Cassio, an elderly man, slow and stupid but pleasant with it. The atmosphere of carnival had hardly touched this piazza, it seemed as always, sleepy in the late afternoon sun, the sounds were distant and muffled. Fiorenza examined the lace she was working on and marvelled at the feeling of deep peace. When the hand bell rang at the gate she was startled, the sound was so intrusive. She guessed that it must be Bartolomeo since he had already sent a message to inform her that he would call before she left. She threaded a sewing needle carefully through the lace and set it on the table beside her. She heard the slip-slap of the steward's sandals as he made his way from house to gate. Behind her, in a reed cage, the tiny bird Giovanna had given her began to chirrup softly. It had been very noisy at first but had gradually become quieter and quieter. She thought she would open the cage and let it go before she left the house, it was obviously pining away in captivity.

Because she was expecting Bartolomeo, she did not look up when Cassio returned. "You can go Cassio," she called knowing that he was going to buy a few last items she needed. "Don't forget the lilies for Madonna Bianchi!"

He was gone by the time she looked up and saw her visitor. He was standing in the shadow of an archway. It was not Bartolomeo. He was tall and darkly dressed, in one hand, he held a wide-brimmed hat with an ostrich feather. Fiorenza's heart beat quickened. She stood up slowly, the thread bobbins rolling to the floor unnoticed. 'Tomasso?'

He walked into the sunlight smiling and stopped beside the fountain on the wall. He folded his arms and tilted his head to one side, looking at her with interest. There were no servants with him, which was unusual. She thought he looked thinner and a little care worn. She returned his gaze with equal scrutiny. He looked different. His skin was darkened by the sun, but for all that, she thought he looked pale and his eyes looked dark, tired and vulnerable. Fiorenza smiled, she had never thought to see him so unguarded with his expression. Her heart went out to him. She wished that he loved her, it would have been so natural to fall into those arms. She ached with longing.

She said, 'If you stand there long enough, I could use yours instead of the lion's head. It is not working well at present. Your head would make an interesting replacement. I may start a fashion.'

'Unfortunately my head is firmly attached,' he answered, his eyes smiling. He rubbed his eyes and walked forward slowly and carefully as if he was creeping though a room of sleeping children.

Fiorenza frowned. 'What has happened?' she said, suddenly alarmed.

He looked decidedly uncomfortable, reluctant to speak, unwilling to unburden himself but desperately needing to. He sat in the chair she had vacated and threw his head back, staring at the sky.

Fiorenza said, 'We are alone here. I shall fetch some wine.'

She noticed on her way to the house, the heavy dark cloak Tomasso had dropped by the gate. It was too warm for such a garment. He had come concealing his identity with the hooded cloak. Fiorenza assumed he had his reasons for secrecy and he knew she would not betray it. Was he uneasy about the wedding arrangements that he had made months ago with Don Carlos? The girl, Carmelia was young enough to be Tomasso's daughter. Was that what caused him such discomfort? Fiorenza took her time collecting the wine, instinctively knowing that her guest needed time to collect himself. She could see him though the window, sitting as still as she had left him, the only movement was the fluttering of butterflies on the roses behind him.

When she returned, she poured the wine, topping up the glasses with clear water before she spoke. 'You look tired Tomasso. Would you like to sleep? You will not be disturbed.'

He smiled at her, his eyes crinkling at the corners, bright as a child's. 'Tired, yes,' he replied, his voice was rough. 'They come and find, the tired travellers, green herbs and ample bread and golden youth that once could course the stag, is stooped above his stick, a tired old man,'

Puzzled by his nonsense, Fiorenza said, 'There are many at the Grimani house who doubted if you would come at all.' The topic had to be broached, but there was no way she could hide the bitterness in her voice.

He looked up at her, pain for a moment fleeting through his eyes. 'I am sorry Fiora that we cannot have what we should nor be as we call to each other to be. You are the loveliest creature in Italy and I am without heart or soul.'

A shuddering sob ran though Fiorenza. She swept up a glass and drank half in one swallow. She turned her back to him, folding her arms across her breast to stop the anger that boiled there. There was so much she wanted to scream at him, so much of her pain and anger which he deserved to hear, and her scorn at the choices he had made and the suffering he had caused her. She bit her lip, it was near impossible not to fly at him, to lash him with her tongue. From what she had learned of Tomasso, she knew he would storm off, snatch up his cloak and bang the gate behind him as he left; most men seemed to do that when a woman got the better of them. She held her peace, but it was some time before she turned.

He was asleep! His head was cradled in his arms on the table, sprawled across her lace and bobbins! How could he? How dare he!

Something made her stop halfway across the courtyard and turn back. She touched his head gently. He didn't stir. She ran her fingers through his hair to brush it from his face. It was damp and tangled, the skin underneath burnt like fire. 'Tomasso?' she called out, kneeling beside him.

He didn't move. She shook his shoulders. The motion caused him to fall. As if boneless, he crumbled to the ground, unconscious to the world about him.

Don Carlos kept Emlyn beside him for most of that day, demanding him to perform for this or that person, for this or that occasion. For Emlyn the day was a nightmare. Cruel fate often brought Carmelia into the room where he was or caused her pass him as he traipsed from one place to another. He could see that she had been crying. She was pale and hollow eyed and made no effort to hide her emotions from him and from any who saw. He read anger in her eyes and accusation, as if he was responsible for their failure to escape. And he was and felt it. If he had not been persuaded to stay and share love with her they would both now be free of Venice. He had no chance to talk with her and even Adriana, who was always with her, seemed hostile. At first, when he had recovered from his fright, Emlyn had felt only relief that they had not been discovered, impossible though it seemed. He thought that perhaps the old man's eyesight was failing, for he must have been near blind not to have seen his daughter making her bid for freedom. Then Emlyn felt the bitter disappointment clawing at him constantly. It had been difficult to get through the day without madness seizing his senses. He left when it was dark, having promised Don Carlos that he would return in three days to entertain at the feast held before Carmelia's wedding, and stay to entertain for the one after.

Three days! Three days in which to come up with a solution. On his way back, Emlyn did not go straight to Theo's house, he went to the first church he came to. It was ornate and Gothic like most in Venice, but Emlyn paid little attention to ornament. He knelt beneath a statue of the Virgin, and stayed there until his knees had gone numb and his hands ached, so tightly did they grasp the lectern before him. No answer came; no miracle to whisk him and Carmelia to freedom.

On his way through the dark streets and over the narrow bridges, he struggled to think of some delay he could cause to Tomasso di Vincentini. He knew the man was reported to be in Padua and guessed that he must be no his way to Venice by now. Could the man be waylaid on the road? Then, for what purpose? Murder? He pushed the thought from his mind knowing that he was incapable of such a wicked act. What else could stop the marriage from taking place?

There was one solution that he had thought of before and which Carmelia had been in full agreement with. He could wed her himself in secret. As his wife she could not become another's. But who would perform such a sacrament? What priest could be convinced of their love and see justice in their union? There were none he knew who would ask no questions. Bribery would make a dark beginning to their life together. Yet Emlyn was not beyond considering it. He had the jewels that Wendelin had brought, his only connection with the mother he had come here to find out about. That promise, which had ruled his life until now faded into insignificance compared to his need for Carmelia. Surely he could find some dishonest priest who would take the gems to perform the ceremony; provided he could find a way to get Carmelia away from the place for long enough.

Emlyn no longer felt the pull form the past that had first driven him to come to Venice. Fra Sebastiano had solved some of the riddle. After his talk with Lorenzo, Emlyn was fairly certain that their mother had been taken into slavery and that he had been born in a Muslim household. It was possible that he was just the son of a galley slave. Emlyn could not come to terms with that solution. It did not match the faded memories and the frequent, haunting dreams in which he had a father; a man on a fine horse, dressed in rich colours, with rings on his fingers and a jewelled scabbard hanging at his side. Emlyn wondered if they were just thoughts, conjured up to satisfy his loneliness in childhood. He dismissed the idea, a man could not control his dreams. Suddenly his mind cleared. Fra Sebastiano!

He had run across a plank bridge and turned into the street that would take him in the direction of the Friary, before his steps faltered and came to a stop. He sat down on the step of a dark house and dropped his head into his hands. Carmelia was right to blame him, he had been a thoughtless fool, carried on a wave of confidence, too inexperienced and young to really think out and plan what had to be done. Was he now prepared to drag the old priest into this mess?

Emlyn was exhausted, he had not slept the night before nor eaten since the festival. The strain of events had drained him of any residue of energy. He knew that he could not ask Fra Sebastiano to help him. The Franciscan would have to refuse and that would cause them both embarrassment and regret.

It began to rain. Emlyn stood and walked on, dragging his feet through the puddles, desperately forlorn, utterly miserable. Goronwy had been right all the time, he thought, I should have gone with him and become a Jesuit. And Mafanwy reading my future with her bones and bits, and Ambrose, with his warning about overturning stones. I have created nothing but chaos all around me and brought disappointment and sorrow to all I touch.

He stood by the water's edge, looked into the depths and wondered if drowning hurt. He had been close to it once before, when he had fought with his cousin in Wales. Then Goronwy had pulled him out of the sea. There was no one now to whom he could expect help from. The Lagoon was no answer. He realised that he was no more capable of taking his own life than he was of taking the life of Tomasso di Vincentini. He saw no one when he returned and the room he shared with the apprentices was empty. Emlyn curled up under his blanket, his heart heavy with sorrow. He was asleep within seconds.

The next morning he was awoken by Umbaldo shaking his shoulder. "Come on slug-a-bed, you have a mysterious visitor waiting by the water steps."

Emlyn groaned and opened one eye. Umbaldo stood over him with a half eaten sausage in one hand and a loaf in the other. "I assume the night's adventuring was a success by the look of you," he said. "You're not even undressed."

Emlyn swung his legs to the floor and shook his head to clear the horrors that lurked there. They did not go away. "Who?" he asked, dragging his fingers through his tangle of hair.

"Well it would not be a mystery if I knew who," said Umbaldo. "Here," he pushed the sausage and bread at Emlyn. "You look as if you need this more that I do."

Emlyn hesitated, then took the food, a conscious decision to live on and try again.

Umbaldo took him to the canal where a gondola waited by the steps. It was black with no show of decoration or identifying symbols. Whoever wished to see him was concealed beneath the hooded canopy. Emlyn climbed aboard and ducked through the opening. It was dark inside, its occupant a single woman, hooded and veiled. He could just make out the shadow of eyes and mouth behind the thin cloth, but he knew who it was by her perfume, Adriana Martinelli.

'I assume you know why I am here,' she said.

Emlyn sat opposite her, to stand was impossible. 'I have no idea.'

'For the sake of my charge Carmelia, who had the misfortune to fall in love with you and is now broken hearted and sick with weeping.'

Emlyn closed his eyes, the words stabbing like a physical pain, emotion running through him like a fever. So she knew. She waited for him to answer. He opened his eyes and tried to read her expression; the veil was too thick and the light too gloomy. He said, 'The simplest answer for her happiness and mine would be to let us become man and wife. I hold her just as precious to my heart, and love her with every fibre of my being. If it is for her sake that you have come, you must know her heart and mine.'

'I care not for your heart. She is not for you,' snapped Adriana.

She threw a purse at Emlyn. He caught it, hearing the dull jangle of coins inside. It gave a sour taste to his mouth. He burst into laughter, a acrid, bitter sound, insulting in its tone. 'What is this?' he asked tossing the purse in his hand.

'Spanish Reals. You will find them acceptable wherever you go and there are enough there to see you back to your own home in comfort.'

'I will not be bought.' Emlyn stood up, bowed over by the limited space. He dropped the purse on Adriana's knee and climbed out.

She called after him, 'You would be wise to reconsider. If you will not be persuaded by this means there is another, less gratifying.'

'Nor will I be threatened!' he shouted back to her.

'I shall tell her,' shouted Adriana. 'I shall tell her how you lay with me. Does she know of the brand you carry on your shoulder?'

He no longer cared if any heard. Heads appeared at the workroom window. Her threats came after him and followed him until he was too far to hear them.

Tomasso awoke in darkness and heard the whisper of waves. There was a soft glow of light from a yellow candle under a shuttered window. He did not know where he was. If he was on the galley, then it lay in calm waters. When he spoke, his voice was hardly a whisper. 'Koçi?'

The candle seemed to waver, the light revealed a bed curtain of gold damask, caught with gold thread. His eyelids were heavy, he let them close. Perhaps in darkness, he could find reason and remember where he was.

No answer had come to his call. If Koçi was there with his hurt, adoring eyes, he would have come. Where then was Mahmud and Abu Abdullah?

Was he with Kyriakos? Yes, that must be the answer, Kyriakos would have left him to sleep if he was tired and would not allow any to arouse him. What was it Kyriakos had said? 'They give you the name Chameleon, Lord, as you change colour in different places.'

No, his name was not Chameleon, it was Capaccio. His father was a crocus farmer, a kind, gentle man who lived each day as if it were his last. Gina his sister running with her skirts loaded with lemons, they bounced behind her rolling into the sunlight. It was the day the goats escaped. His mother, pushing back her hair as it escaped from her bonnet, her hands, white with flour. She had nursed him when he had broken his arm falling out of a tree. No, it was not he who had fallen, someone else had fallen out of an olive tree and broken his arm in the process, a tree spirit who he had fallen in love with. Anna.

Snatches of thought and dream mingled. Then he accepted the dark reality and knew that his father was dead, his mother and sister burned to death in their own house. So he was not at home. There was something, something his mind had tried to tell him, but he thrust it away like a child's nightmare, for it echoed with violence and was red with blood. His mind cleared enough so that he felt the deep hurts and remembered Fiorenza. Why had he come to her? Too many questions, too much pain. Darkness closed in.

The next time he awoke, there was no confusion in his mind, but he would not think of the immediate past. It was still dark outside. He could see Fiora by the candle light. She was reading in a chair beside him, lit with golden light. Her face was as still as marble, her lips slightly parted, a crease above her brow.

Tomasso lifted a hand and felt the bandaging around his ribs and waist. When he looked up, she was watching him with soft eyes. He whispered to her, 'How long?'

She shook her head slightly, a sad smile. 'Do not speak.'

He closed his eyes and heard the splash of pouring liquid. Then, she was lifting his head, holding wine to his lips. He swallowed a little and sank back on to the pillows. She sat on the bed. She looked different. Then he saw that her hair was free from any covering. He had never seen it before. It was beautiful, not grey as he had suspected, it was dark and long, playing tricks with the light. She swung it over her shoulder. He reached out and captured a handful. It ran through his fingers like spun cocoons. A drop of moisture splashed on his hand. Fiora was crying.

This hurt him more than the pain in his side, but he did not know why. He had come here because he was wounded and Fiora would not tell anyone of his presence. He had known enough women to guess that she would do as he wanted because she had fallen in love with him. Her tears betrayed her. 'How long?' he asked again, dreading her answer.

'This is the second night,' she replied. 'You should have stayed wherever you were when you took these wounds. You have done yourself nothing but ill in travelling here. I was afraid you would die.'

'Who else knows?'

'I send word to your servant Symeon. It is he who has cared for you. My own steward knows too, he had to carry you here and there is one other, but he does not know the extent of your wounds. I told him you were tired and suffering a slight fever. It was Bartolomeo.'

'I have much to thank you for. Did I, did I speak, rave in fever?"

'You called out often, foreign names, words I could not understand. Who is Koçi? A woman?'

'No, a young man I know, of a different place.'

Fiorenza stood, her skirts rustling in the darkness. The light wavered as she crossed the room. She stooped to the candle, a hand shading it, lips pursed to blow the flame. It that frozen moment, Tomasso saw her with the eyes of love. They stung with tears, tears he had not shed for near twenty years. Too late!

Then the room was dark. There was nothing he could do now to stop the flow of memory. He thought of all the planning that had brought him this far. It was not a matter of days, weeks or even months, for years he had lived with the flame of vengeance as his guide. He had been a young man when he had made the oath to destroy Carlos Grimani. Nothing had quenched that flame of hatred, he had nurtured it and been directed by its light. Carlos had not only taken Anna from him but had methodically destroyed all that Tomasso Capaccio had loved and cherished. Tomasso had been condemned to the slow, humiliating death of a galley slave, but every pull of the oar had fed his hatred, every lash of the whip had given him strength. All that he had been, had drained away and into the empty shell had come the dark avenging spirit armed with the Reaper's scythe. With this he would slash through everything that ever was Don Carlos Grimani, his wealth, his empire, his loves, all that he had made and become.

It was not ended yet. Although Grimani was not yet aware, his empire had tumbled, one grandson was castrated, the other most probably dead. The strength that Tomasso needed to achieve his ends had been weakened; doubts had crept in, draining his resolve. He remembered the violence of the battle at sea. The odds had been against the Venetian galley all along. There was no honour in Tomasso's victory, he had abandoned honour to reach his aim. He had not considered the lives lost at sea neither Christian nor Muslim. The corsairs had been content with the capture of the galley and the slaves. As Ismael, he had paid them well. The *Maria* he had kept for himself and sent it on to Cyprus. Cyprus was where he had established the foundation of his own empire. There too, was the wealth he had procured from Grimani. Tomasso had chosen Cyprus as the final battle ground, but he knew now that the end would come before that.

His own determination had now been shaken by the blade of Anna's son, Paolo. Had she not asked for his promise, to watch her sons grow? He had been unable to fulfil that promise. It had never been his intention to harm them personally, though harm they would inevitably suffer through the downfall of Don Carlos their provider. Tomasso had intended to entice them away. But Lorenzo had already chosen his path in life. Tomasso had seen him at Santa Croce in Florence, a young Franciscan with the glow of conviction in his eyes, one who had turned his back on the Grimani riches to live his life in simplicity and devotion. Lorenzo was lost to Don Carlos already, with no help from Tomasso. But that had not been enough for the angel of darkness. Anna had cursed Carlos and his seed and Tomasso had made the curse a reality, in spite of the cost.

Paolo was the only one who had known his enemy and faced him with a sword. Tomasso had left him in the care of Koçi and Kyriakos, the Greek physician. If the boy lived, he would go to Cyprus as a prisoner. But Paolo would be fortunate to survive the wounds he had received. Tomasso had never intended that Paolo should die.

He struggled to rid himself of it all, it seemed too heavy to carry. He felt as if he was drowning. The pain of his wounds burned through him. His skin was on fire, his breath ragged and laboured. It would be so easy to die now. Something held him, trapping him in reality. Fiora's voice came from far, far away. 'Don't. Whatever it is that torments you!'

He was aware of her presence. She lay on the bed beside him, her arm laid across his bandaged chest, as if to hold his spirit down. Her head was at his shoulder, her hair touching his skin. He awoke more fully and placed an arm around her, holding her close, feeling her tears scald across his skin. Then he felt the stirring of her desire and his. He laughed weakly at the irony of it.

Bartolomeo called the following morning. He had done as Fiorenza requested and had said nothing of Tomasso's return to Venice, but matters could not be ignored for much longer, by the end of the week, Tomasso should be married. Tomasso was seated in a chair under a window, a book was open on his knee. Fiorenza was in the square, cutting the roses with Symeon holding her basket. The chopping sound ceased when Bartolomeo called from the gate. Tomasso could not see them, but he could hear the talk clearly.

Bartolomeo said, 'Is it Tomasso, arriving sick, which has prevented you from leaving? Francesco Cornaro's Cyprus-bound ship has left without you.'

'It is of no account. I shall take the next, which is due to leave the day after Tomasso's wedding,' answered Fiora.

'If he still had the strength to go through with it!'

'Don't be misled. He has risen from his sick bed and is quite prepared to wreak havoc on any who try to prevent him from going his way. Insufferable as ever. Against my advice and Symeon's, he is up and dressed. He has been reading all morning, but will be glad to see you.'

Tomasso closed his eyes for a moment, feeling the lightness of his lashes brushing his cheeks like the flutter of a moth's wing. The wound fever had not left him, but it didn't matter, he only needed a few more days.

Bartolomeo ducked under the low lintel and entered the room. He stood just inside looking argumentative.

With a sudden smooth movement, that hurt more than he had expected, Tomasso stood up. 'Ready for a feast, 'Tolomeo?'

'You are going then. I hoped you had changed your mind.'

'Well I must meet the girl before I bed her.'

'She is a child,' said Bartolomeo scornfully.

'Sixteen? I have bedded younger. In fact the youngest was ...'

'Don't tell me,' snapped Bartolomeo. 'The details of your sordid life are best left unspoken.'

Tomasso smiled. 'Then let us by all means speak of ordinary things. What needs doing?'

They spent the rest of the morning talking business. Bartolomeo felt his enthusiasm ebbing as they progressed. There was something missing in Tomasso, as if he was, in truth not the slightest bit interested in business. Eventually Bartolomeo gave up trying. Instead he said, 'What do you intend to do afterwards?'

'After I am married? I have thought no further.'

'What of Don Carlos? Is he then to discover who his new son-in-law really is?'

'I thought we had agreed not to speak of this,' said Tomasso, his voice weary.

Bartolomeo sighed visibly. 'You have appointed me your manager, I have to know something of your future plans.'

'You know them well enough.'

Tomasso looked out the window, they could hear Fiorenza's shears and Symeon's easy laughter. It was quiet and peaceful, the streaming sunlight was warm and kind. After some time, Tomasso looked away and shifted his weight uncomfortably. He closed his eyes. It would be so easy to sleep. He guessed that Bartolomeo thought he was asleep. The manager stood up to leave. Tomasso said, 'Tolomeo, did you bring the papers I asked Symeon to find?'

Bartolomeo returned to his chair. He drew he papers out of the satchel he had brought. They were deeds of ownership, concerning the Spice Company.

Tomasso took them from him, and began to read through, eyes darting from side to side, until his head ached. When he had finished he handed them back to Bartolomeo. 'The company is yours if you want it.'

Bartolomeo looked at him in surprise. 'What do you mean, mine?'

'Tolomeo I cannot stay here, once Venice learns who I am. I want you to have the company, you and Fiorenza.'

'But that's preposterous! We are well established now, the spice alone' will make us rich, it already has.'

'I know all that. It is yours, you made it into what it has become. The connections will still be there, the *Cornucopia* is yours when she returns.'

'What of the partnership with Don Carlos?'

'There never was one. I never intended there to be one. There is no written or verbal agreement between us. No doubt his hopes are high, for he believes differently. I shall have pleasure in seeing his sorrow.'

'Tomasso, I have to ask again if you intend to go through with this arrangement. The girl Carmelia is innocent of the hurts you've suffered. You have gone too far. Must you marry her?'

'It will be as I have decided. The risk is mine not hers. I will not harm her 'Tolomeo. She can have my parent's old house on the Brenta. That is why it has been restored. It is for her.'

'And where will you be, while we are all enjoying the fruits of your endeavours?'

Tomasso shook his head, trying to rid it of the storm of pain. He closed his eyes to blessed darkness. Sometimes nightmares became reality and he did not know one from the other. He had thought nothing could stop him, but now his own body hindered him with weakness. He could hear 'Bartolomeo's voice, weaving in and out of focus. He felt a hand on his shoulder, shaking him gently. Concentrating hard, Tomasso drove away the devils that plagued him.

Bartolomeo was close to him, kneeling by his chair. Seeing Tomasso's eyes open, he moved away, his expression concerned. 'You won't be doing anything will you?' he asked accusingly. 'For the simple reason that you do not expect to survive.'

'I don't know,' said Tomasso. He tried to put strength into his voice, he didn't want interference now. The less the notary knew the better. He found a smile from somewhere. 'Let us dress in our silks and velvets, adorn ourselves with our finery. Can you send word to Don Carlos that we shall be there to attend the feast?'

'You are in no state for a feast.'

'I will manage. Symeon is a good witch doctor when he puts his mind to it. He used to castrate boys. He will find some brew to keep me charming.'

Bartolomeo turned pale. Tomasso laughed at him, his senses confused. Symeon would have to find something to keep him alive until he was through. And Symeon must leave Venice before Lorenzo Grimani recognised him and brought Tomasso's plans to ruin.

Chapter 47 Feast

The guests gathered throughout the day at the Grimani's house. From the number of people who arrived, the feast promised to be an extravagant success. Already the long hall was nearly filled. Most were respected merchants; gold traders who knew the African deserts like the spice and silk merchants knew the Middle Sea. Some were notable members of the Senate, with a train of notaries and relations hovering about them; others were the Venetian noblemen who made an appearance whenever occasion invited. It was an excuse for the young men to show their finery; short doublets tight buttocks and slender, muscular legs clad in tight fitting hose. Doublets were puffed, padded and pleated, hung with rich cloth, caught up with tessellated brooches. Hair was strung with pearls, aglitter with gems or tucked under shimmering raw silk wigs. Under the soft glow of wax light, Venice lived up to her scandalized reputation; a time of festivity and carnival, a time for masque and romance. The great ladies gathered and swooped together, a host of butterflies above a pond of chatter and babble. And, like butterflies, they showed no reserve in their splendour. Swathed in silk and velvet, taffeta and brocade, bedecked in gold, pearls and a bright spangle of jewels, they circled on belled skirts, smiles suggestive, eyes a sparkle.

There were a few frowns to be seen here and there, these were the bankers usually attired in black. They stood with heads bowed together and saw only the needless cost to be met; their last favour to Don Carlos Grimani before the axe would fall. But it wouldn't fall, they assured themselves. Vincentini had sent word that he would be delighted to attend, God curse his black soul! And Grimani's boat would come in, sooner or later if not delayed by storm or piracy. They hoped the ship's holds were filled to bursting.

Much to everyone's delight, Tomasso di Vincentini arrived with Fiorenza Caterina Balsamo. The relationship between he and the widow had been food for much speculative gossip. Now the guests looked on, eyes glittering with interest. Some argued that they could hardly have arrived otherwise, he and she being part-owners in business, and they did have the long-limbed Bartolomeo Varini trotting along behind. Whatever the relationship between them, it would soon end. The widow had missed one ship to Cyprus, it would be foolhardy to miss the next. And the gentleman? The sooner he settled down with his new young wife the less the tongues would prattle, that was a pity, considering what entertainment the ladies of Venice had gleaned from the mystery. Surrounding him, eyes from sixteen years to sixty, peered from behind fans and fanciful masks or watched with open curiosity, some wondering if he was Italian in his tastes.

One look at Vincentini and even the most frugal of bankers could put his mind at rest. Vincentini had not adopted the flash and colour of the younger men, as all had expected. He was dressed in black, a quilted silk doublet of knee length worn over hose and soft boots. His wide belt was fashioned in a series of golden coiled snakes, each with a jewel for an eye. The red jewel, winking balefully at his ear was worth a loaded galleon. He showed no shyness in displaying the wealth which had Venice drooling with gossip all winter, they were gratified to see that at least that part had been true.

There was much chatter concerning Carmelia, who had yet to make an appearance. What a fortunate girl she was, some said with good wishes, and others said with jealously. Had they heard of the house he had built for her? A villa in the Roman style, a rose garden, a mosaic courtyard, orange trees and such horses, a wonder to behold. And the gifts he had showered upon her since she arrived in Venice; the gems, the cloth, the snow-white palfrey, the furs, carpets, tapestries, the list was endless. And today, a falcon with golden jesses and a diamond in her hood the size of a pea!

Tomasso wove among them all with impeccable courtesy. He astonished most of them with a short display of the knowledge he had concerning their affairs, sometimes it was possible only to move a pace or two down the floor. Finally he left Fiorenza and Bartolomeo to deal with them and reached the end of the room. There Don Carlos waited with his wife Juliana. Between them stood a small girl, hands clasped in front of her, eyes downcast. She was dressed in a plain grey dress, overlaid with Venetian lace. She was not wearing any of the gifts Tomasso had sent to her.

She was very like the way he had thought of her, on the rare occasions she had entered his mind. A quiet girl with the stamp of the nunnery in her meekness. He was surprised at how young she looked, like a pretty child half the age she actually was. She stood without moving, her head still bowed as Tomasso bowed and nodded his way through the greetings and introductions. He said something to Juliana that made her smile and blush and caused Don Carlos to interrupt what he was saying and open the door behind him, indicating that Tomasso and his daughter enter.

There was a maid inside who closed the door behind them and sat on a low stool beside it. The room was small, panelled with wood and hung with red Damask. Carmelia's head was still bowed; she had not looked at him once. Tomasso reached out and placed a gentle finger under her chin, inducing her to raise her head. Her eyes were deep brown with a green light to them like a mossy pool, they were filled with hatred.

Tomasso stood back and folded his arms. So, she was not as he had expected. 'Are you so afraid of me Carmelia?' he asked softly.

She did not reply. Her head dropped again, the blazing eyes downcast.

Tomasso thoughtfully stroked his beard. 'Did you think me a monster? I admit I add many years to your own and may seem monstrous in your youthful eyes, but look upon me. Am I so detestable?'

She looked up, the hatred had lessened, replaced by something unfathomable. Her mouth was set in a straight line, a nervous hand partially covering it.

Tomasso crossed the room to the window seat, gathering her hand in his as he did so. He pushed a small white dog off the padded seat and sat down. He drew her towards him, retaining one hand, which trembled under his touch. He brought out a ring and placed it on her finger, it was too big and slid on easily, the heavy stone forcing it to turn inwards. Tomasso righted it and brought her hand to his lips, kissing lightly. 'You have nothing to fear Carmelia,' he said. 'What can I do to still your trembling heart?'

She pulled her hand from his grasp. That she hated him was obvious, but Tomasso could not understand why. He knew of the defamatory talk that had circulated in his absence. Perhaps the girl had been terrified by this, believing she was promised in wedlock to the very devil. In this short time he had alone with her, there was nothing he could do or say to prove such talk was nonsense. He would never harm her nor make any demands of her physically or spiritually. He did not greatly care, but it would be better to have some friendship between them. It was only necessary that she become his wife, and therefore wife to no other.

'My lord?' she said, her voice surprisingly strong and controlled, 'I beg you to reconsider.' She rung her hands together and failed to hold back the tears. 'My lord, my heart is given to another. Where you the godliest man on earth, I could never love you.'

Tomasso smiled grimly. So that was the answer, she had given her heart to some gallant Venetian nobleman. He had heard that many frequented the house, with sonnets and poems, in futile hope. He stood up, taking both her hands in his. 'Love? Love is but a passing fancy. You will get over it little Carmelia and be better blessed because of it.'

'No my lord, I speak the truth. Were you to deny me my heart's desire, I should pine away like a caged bird. My love could never be yours. If you take me to wife I shall hate you forever!'

'Hate me if you must,' said Tomasso, running out of patience. 'I think you will find that to your loss, not mine. Is this how you envisage your future with me?'

She nodded, biting her lip, tears running down her cheeks.

Tomasso was surprised to feel pity for her, such consideration for anyone hadn't entered his scheming before. He desperately wanted to sit down. It is because I am ill, he reasoned, aware of the stiffness and aching limbs, the burning pain in his side. And because, thus weakened, Fiora has broken down the invisible wall I built from which to engineer my revenge. It can soon be rebuilt, it is already.

He let go of Carmelia's hands. 'It is unfortunate that you are so disinclined. Love or hate make no difference. The die is cast and we are ruled by its falling.' Tomasso walked to the door and winked at the maid with the promise in her eyes.

Carmelia ran after him. 'Please my lord, I beg you to heed me!'

Hand on the doorknob, Tomasso turned.

She looked woe-begotten and forlorn, her eyes and face pleading for his understanding. She caught his arm and dropped to her knees beside him, eyes imploring, voice beseeching.

Annoyed, Tomasso pulled her to her feet and pushed her gently but firmly away from him. 'You will excuse me. We have a feast to endure before we can be free of each other's company.'

He left her then, his head pounding, his senses reeling. Her voice screeched, shrill and tearful behind him, the thickness of the oak door doing little to muffle her depth of feeling.

Behind the closed door, Pellegrina leapt to her feet. 'What can you be thinking of! How could you dare to speak to him like that?'

'Do you condemn me too!' screamed Carmelia. 'You of all here you should know my heart Pellegrina. You alone have given me comfort and known of my suffering.'

'And I wish to God we had never come here. It is for you, for your own sake that I must speak. You are blinded by foolishness. He is a fine looking man, you could not hope for better, considering his age.'

'His eyes are cold.'

'Is it any wonder, after the way you have treated him? You are fortunate that he did no worse than glare at you. That is enough to show that his character is good. Why not give him a chance, before you fall on him with your wicked tongue.'

'Because I have already given myself to another. Mind, body and soul!'

Pellegrina took hold of her shoulders and embraced her, not wanting to hear any more. 'It is as I thought,' she said soothingly. 'All this worry has put you out of your senses for a while.'

Carmelia pulled away, hitting out as she did so, slapping her maid soundly across the cheek. She backed towards the window. 'Why don't you believe me?' she cried accusingly. 'I have given myself to Emlyn Tomas. In God's eyes I am already his wife!'

'In God's eyes? You are not married to him Carmelia, how could you!'

Carmelia turned away, glaring out of the rain splashed window. The day had grown dark and overcast. When she spoke Pellegrina hardly heard her, but Carmelia did not repeat herself.

Pellegrina stood, one hand to her stinging cheek, and took a step towards her. She was horrified at what she thought she had heard. 'What did you say?' she asked with dread.

Carmelia swung round, her eyes blazing. 'I said, I am with child. How else would you have me put it?'

'Jesus, Mary and Joseph!'

'So I cannot belong to any man can I, other than he that has planted his seed upon me. I am carrying Emlyn's child. He is the one I have chosen as husband. I care not for any other and, if I am to suffer disgrace to meet my ends, then so be it.'

'Holy Mother in heaven,' gasped Pellegrina. 'Do you know what you are saying? Do you have any idea what they will do to him? They will take him out from here, strip him and have him flogged to death, or even worse.'

'Stop it Pellegrina!'

'Do you think you will suffer for this? I can assure you that it will be nothing compared with what Don Carlos will do to him. Your little monk will have he skin flayed off his back and while he is still alive …'

Carmelia screamed, her hands over her ears.

'His agony will be made to last. Can you stand by and witness that?'

'Enough! You are just trying to frighten me. We shall get away from here, he and I, far, far away.'

'Frighten you? It is I who has been frightened by what you have revealed to me. How long have you been thus? Does Emlyn know?'

'Since Milan,' said Carmelia. She tossed her head as if she were arguing about the price of fish in the market. 'No one knows but you.'

Pellegrina counted rapidly on her fingers. 'Two months! Why could you not wait?' she cried. She sat down on the floor.

'How can you say that? You are hardly a maiden of pure virtue yourself.'

'No. I lost my virginity at the age of twelve, to a sailor. I have never looked back since. But I am a lady's maid and you are the lady. There is a great deal which lies between us. You are forced to maintain a good reputation Carmelia, the disgrace could well break you. If Vincentini takes you from here soon after the wedding, he could delay the news of the child when it comes, and still claim it for his own, may even believe so.'

'I will not be his wife!'

'Then you condemn your lover.'

'Only if you tell,' sobbed Carmelia. 'Which you will not, which you cannot.'

Pellegrina bowed her head. Don Carlos had given her a brooch of Spanish silver and a bracelet of mother-of-pearl. He had been kind and attentive, he was a surprisingly good lover for his age. She had given him her solemn oath to inform him of all Carmelia's secret meetings. Don Carlos suspected his daughter's affections had already turned to some one other than her intended. Pellegrina was used to giving oaths and breaking them. She had said nothing about Emlyn. She felt that she could not betray Carmelia, they had been together too long. But this was madness. Perhaps there was a way. She said, 'If I were to tell your father, it would only be for your own good. There is only one thing that will prevent me from doing so.'

'How dare you bargain with me! Do you think your word will be believed against mine? I shall deny everything!'

'Deny as you wish,' Pellegrina shouted. 'Your own body will soon betray you. How long do you think you can hide your condition?'

Carmelia's eyes flooded with tears, but her voice was still determined, even in the face of the impossible. 'I shall tell Emlyn, and we shall leave here and never look back.'

'In the two days that are left to you? Don't be a fool Carmelia. Give me your promise and I shall say nothing.'

Carmelia broke down into uncontrolled weeping. After some time her tears lessened and she looked up. 'I know what you will ask of me,' she said in a frightened whisper.

'Then give me your word. Promise me that you will never see Emlyn again, that you will go through with the ceremony and be dutiful to your husband. When this time has passed you will know I speak with wisdom.'

Carmelia sank to the floor, convulsed with sobbing, her face caged in trembling fingers. 'You can have my oath!' she cried, 'But I shall hate you forever.'

'Like you will hate Tomasso di Vincentini? You promise yourself a miserable future. You always were a selfish girl Carmelia Grimani and will continue to be so until you drown in the muck of your own making!'

Carmelia wailed in misery.

Pellegrina dropped to her knees beside her, despairing on how to comfort the girl and make her presentable for the guests who waited in the adjoining room.

Tomasso had taken his place near the centre of the feasting table, next to his future father-in-law. Next to Don Carlos sat his wife Juliana, the plainest dressed woman in the room. Next to her, an empty chair. The absence of the bride send tongues wagging anew.

Bartolomeo was unconcerned, he was seated between two ladies, Adriana Martinelli one side and on the other, Fiorenza. He was delighted.

Adriana said, 'If I did not know better, I would swear that I know your employer.'

Bartolomeo felt suddenly cold. He took a hasty gulp of wine, spluttered and burst into a fit of coughing.

Fiorenza smiled at him. 'You should not eat and drink at the same time Bartolomeo. Are you in a hurry? I am sure there is no need, look at all this food.'

Adriana turned her astute gaze on her. She said, 'Of course you would know, being his partner.'

'Know what?' said Bartolomeo. His Adam's apple bobbed up and down.

'All about this Tomasso di Vincentini,' she added. 'It is Vincentini isn't it?'

Bartolomeo stuffed a piece of capon into his mouth and began to chew fastidiously.

Fiorenza leaned forward to see around him. 'Messer Tomasso is incredibly secretive,' she said. 'He had made his fortune trading in the Levant and Morocco. Was it Morocco Bartolomeo? Something to do with gold and salt from Africa where they worship idols. It is all very romantic, you should get him to relate his stories to you one day.'

Adriana nodded. 'I shall endeavour to do so.' She held Fiorenza's gaze for a long minute before she looked away.

Bartolomeo sighed with relief. He guessed that he had not heard the end of it, but if he could avoid the topic for the next few days, there would be little Adriana or anyone else could do if they learned the truth. Bartolomeo had become increasingly suspicious about Tomasso and wondered if he really cared what was going to happen afterwards. They are all the same, he mused, one as bad as the other, once the thirst for revenge gets a hold on them. He remembered that rainy night, before Tomasso had come, when he had sat in the warehouse, with the prospect of a debtor's cell yawning in front of him as a result from the debts owed by the Lanarca Salt Company. It would have been a sad end, but somehow it looked clean and honest compared to what had happened since. Bartolomeo could leave his present employment now with greater confidence. His reputation had grown with the spice company's success. He had to admit that the only thing holding him loyal still, was the affection he felt for Fiorenza. He could not bear the thought of her being tarnished by Tomasso's deceit. Once she had gone from Venice, Bartolomeo could leave, he would not accept the gift of ownership that Tomasso had offered him.

As Fiorenza had pointed out, the food was plentiful, in fact it was still arriving from the kitchen, heaped platters and flagons of wine carried in and served by pageboys. Bartolomeo looked around the tables. There were many faces he knew here. Don Carlos' grandson, Lorenzo had chosen to sit in the least honoured place, with an elderly Franciscan. An insult to Don Carlos perhaps? The young man was as strong willed as Don Carlos himself, no amount of influence had drawn him away from his vocation. With them sat a young man who looked vaguely familiar, but he was masked as many were, so Bartolomeo could not be sure. There was a notable collection of persons of means gathered here. The masks, the power, the plucked brows, the gauze, the silks and tinsel all sugared in diamonds, all gathered to dine sumptuously.

His scrutiny was interrupted by the arrival of Carmelia Grimani. Her eyes were red and puffy, but she offered and brave smile to the many onlookers and took her place without glancing at her future husband. She sat meekly, eyes downcast, picking at her food. The babble of conversation grew louder, frequently accompanied by laughter. In the gallery above the hall, the musicians made no attempt to compete with the noise, they plucked and played in the background, keeping their best for later entertainment. The guests had been promised a play by the Milanese actors later in the evening.

Bartolomeo, suffering from hiccups, ordered his glass refilled, determined to make the most of the evening. If he drank enough, who knows? He might even find the courage to tell Fiorenza his true feelings. He looked up at her and his courage failed. Her eyes were so often on Tomasso, with a little frown showing her concern for his health.

A burst of laughter dragged his eyes away. The young man who had been seated with the Franciscans was standing on the table, tossing fruit into the air. Bartolomeo saw that he was dressed in the manner of a fool, with glass baubles glinting off his costume as bright as real jewels. He leaped down, without breaking his rhythm and began to walk forward. The guests threw items to join those flying from hand to hand. He caught some but let most fall unheeded, to include them all would have been impossible.

'Good God!' exclaimed Bartolomeo, his hiccups gone. 'It's the young man who brought us the wool.'

Fiorenza said, 'That youth juggling?'

'The very same. Perhaps he has tried to entice Don Carlos in his ambitious scheming.'

'What scheming?' asked Fiorenza. 'I have heard that he is Don Carlos' new lutanist, superbly talented in more ways than one. Bianca told me.'

'I can imagine,' agreed Bartolomeo. 'He would like Venice to move aside from their trade with the Levant and give England a bite at it. I refused to consider the proposition he put to me. It seems he has found success elsewhere.'

'Whatever next?' said Adriana. 'He travelled with us from France. I have seen him change from monk to merchant, from merchant to mercenary and from mercenary to musician, all in the space of three months.'

'Well now he is juggler,' laughed Fiorenza. 'Or should it be magician? Perhaps he is working through all vocations beginning with 'M''

'Talented yes,' said Adriana, her eyes cold, 'and scheming. He has wheedled his way into Don Carlos' favour. He made a shambles of the players we watched in Milan, they were the same group we shall see tonight. Perhaps he intends to ruin their performance again. I have never known one to wreak such havoc as he, let us hope he tumbles his way out of favour with equal rapidity.'

Bartolomeo pushed aside his plate, feeling sick from the amount of march-pane he had consumed. 'I wonder if Don Carlos is thinking of buying English wool instead of Spanish.'

'I have no idea,' said Adriana. 'However, if you know of anything that will discredit the young man, I will be more that grateful to hear of it.'

Bartolomeo smiled at her, wondering exactly what more than grateful meant. He had not forgotten what the youth had suggested and had half hoped that he would have returned to discuss matters further, once Bartolomeo had spoken with Tomasso. But business was far from Tomasso's mind and the opportunity had not arisen. He turned to Adriana, noting her expectant expression. He said, 'No, nothing. I quite liked the boy, Thomas Em-something.'

'Emlyn Tomas,' corrected Adriana with displeasure.

The juggler was half way up the room by then, his antics watched by most of the guests. He made lots of mistakes, all of them ending with someone getting soaked or sprinkled with sugar or almonds, or something sticky and ruinous to their fine cloth. Knives, plates and a single orange flew through his hands. He had broken two of Don Carlos' costly glasses and had now added another to his spinning hoard. Often the breakables returned to the table with the same deftness with which they had been swept up. Some of the mistakes were contrived to awe the guests and keep them laughing. He stopped in front of Don Carlos and the honoured guest, the items slapping through his hands and spinning with impossible speed.

When the accident happened, it looked innocent enough to those who were watching casually. To Bartolomeo, it looked inexplicably deliberate. Emlyn had let fall a carving knife. It landed in front of Tomasso, point embedded in the table a hair's breath from his hand. The juggler then scooped up a wine glass, making no attempt to prevent the contents from spilling over Tomasso's embroidered sleeve, before it flew to join the other objects. Then a cup fell, out of the centre. In his attempt to catch it, Emlyn stumbled and lost control for a moment. He tipped over a bowl of chopped octopus in greasy sauce, before his baubles fell out of the air. They all, including the octopus, landed on and around Tomasso di Vincentini. There could be little doubt now that it was all deliberate.

The insult drew a gasp from the watching guests. Bartolomeo was surprised when he saw Emlyn's face. His smile was contemptuous, his eyes, framed by the red sequins of his mask, were bright with challenge. Tomasso's reaction was even more astonishing. He stood up so fast that the chair fell behind him. He was ashen, his expression a mask of disbelieving horror. He appeared to fall, but recovered quickly enough, offering a weak smile and stood while servants attempted to clean the mess from his clothing.

The failed juggler remained standing, offering no assistance and no apology. His eyes remained on Tomasso, ignoring Don Carlos who spoke to him sharply. Bartolomeo strained to hear better.

'What was it you said about him?' asked Fiorenza. She had stood as soon as the first knife had fallen, watching Tomasso.

Bartolomeo shook his head in puzzlement. 'It looks as if the young man has a grievance against our honoured master. I was not aware that the two had met. Perhaps Tomasso could not be tempted by English wool either.'

'It is nothing of the sort,' said Adriana calmly. 'Emlyn Tomas is challenging your renowned master to a duel.'

'Whatever for?' cried Bartolomeo and Fiorenza in unison.

Adriana looked exceptionally angry. She too had risen from her place. She said, 'You may as well know, as all here will soon, if they have not guessed already. The challenge is for the hand of Carmelia.'

'Good God!' exclaimed Bartolomeo.

'Sweet Virgin, no!' cried Fiorenza.

'The youth is a fool,' Bartolomeo added. 'Tomasso is probably the best swordsman in Venice. Don't worry Fiora, he will never accept.'

The room had become silent and still. The only movement was from the older Franciscan who walked the length of the hall and placed a hand on Emlyn's shoulder.

Tomasso had resumed his seat. He leaned back with a refilled glass in his hand. He had recovered a little and looked slightly amused. Don Carlos too, looked as though he was enjoying himself, he had said nothing since his first reprimand. The juggler stood in front of them, ignoring the priest at his side, waiting for an answer to his challenge.

Tomasso sipped his wine thoughtfully. He slowly shook his head. 'Duels are forbidden within the confines of Venice. The answer is no. Whatever your grievance, do not I pray, visit it on my head.'

Emlyn didn't move, nor drop his gaze. 'Then I shall fight you outside Venice, anywhere you choose. Refuse my challenge and be named craven coward. My grievance is against you and no other. Meet my sword and I shall see you beg for mercy!'

'Emlyn!' cried the Franciscan. 'What madness is this?'

'Do not be concerned father,' said Tomasso. 'The boy has drunk too much. I take his words lightly. He is a foreigner I believe, not used to the civilities of his Italian betters.'

The group around them burst into laughter that spread quickly through the room.

Emlyn's voice cut above them all. Few understood the implicit meaning behind the words, but Bartolomeo did.

> *'Look you, even as once Judas was a traitor to his Lord,*
> *So, O king, thy princes gave thee in betrayal to the sword.*
> *O beware, beware the treason! Lamb, the wolf is in the fold.'*

And so did Tomasso. Apart from the first shock, he showed no emotion. He turned to the elderly priest, addressing him by name. 'Fra Sebastiano, if you remove the boy from my sight I shall forgive him. It he crosses my path again, I will not feel such generosity toward him. Perhaps when he is sober, you will explain to him the folly of challenging his betters.'

Bartolomeo let his breath out. How could the youth have said such a thing? How could he possibly know anything concerning Tomasso and the truth behind his actions? 'O beware, beware the treason! Lamb, the wolf is in the fold!

Carmelia unaccountably burst into tears. To everyone's astonishment, Emlyn Tomas spun away from the table. He flipped down the room, hands to feet, hands to feet in spinning acrobatics. He reached the end and without pause, wind-milled back again in cart-wheels and arrived a little breathless, back where he had started. His face was fixed with a wide grin. From his ragged clothing he produced a stick with a jester's head on the end, hung with bells. He waved it in front of Don Carlos and his guest and then bowed extravagantly, spinning on his heel to include them all.

'Good God, he was jesting!' gasped Bartolomeo in relief. He realised that Fiorenza had been squeezing his arm. She was pale, she released him with a shudder which echoed his own feelings.

Don Carlos clapped his hands and abruptly the servants and pageboys began to clear the mess away and talk resumed.

Bartolomeo heard the patron address his fool. 'You are fortunate that I do not have you beaten and thrown to the fishes Emilio. Was this out of some malice? Or meaningless drunken chatter?'

'Think what you will,' laughed the fool. 'No wine has touched my lips. I think you well know my mind.'

'Concerning Carmelia here?' laughed Don Carlos. 'Silly boy. You are a worthless troubadour. Now leave me before I do as I have threatened. You were employed to entertain!'

'I thought I had,' came the cold reply. 'And I have only just begun.' Emlyn stormed away. There was nothing jovial now in his bearing.

'How romantic,' said Fiorenza. 'A troubadour and a nobleman's daughter. How very, very sad.' She dabbed at her eyes with a scrap of lace.

'There is no truth in it,' snapped Bartolomeo. He was annoyed, knowing the real reason for such display. But then, Fiorenza had never been shy to make her feeling's known. Had I been that youth, would I have challenged the treacherous rogue for his cruel indifference to sweet Fiora? Does age and inability excuse me from doing so now?

Emlyn had not re-entered the hall, he stood facing the wall in an adjoining room, the lute hanging from his hand. The wall was a hand's breath from his face. He stared at the wood panelling without seeing it. Before he had met Carmelia, this would have been the highlight of his musical dreams, all the years of devoted fingering, preparing him to display his craft in front of such influential men as these. But none of it mattered now. He knew they expected him to work miracles, Don Carlos had seen that word was passed around concerning his new lutanist. Emlyn had understood most of the sly remarks made in his wake and the others he had guessed at, they thought his position as lutanist was of a secondary nature. Most of the Venetians here were aware of Don Carlos' taste in lovers.

Don Carlos had kept Emlyn with him for most of the last two days, since Adriana had offered him a purse of Spanish reals to leave Venice. He had not ignored her threats, but reasoned that there was little she could achieve of a forceful nature while he stayed thus in the patron's favour. That had meant tolerating the fat fingers stroking through his hair, tracing a line down his neck to his lace collar or fondling his thigh while he played. Emlyn had treated all the suggestive talk with the innocence of a monk, thanking the patron for the compliments and deliberately misunderstanding the rest. He had seen Don Carlos become quite annoyed at times.

But Emlyn did not want the man's special favour, he no longer sought to better himself through his talent or anything else. He had come to the house again only in hope of seeing Carmelia. That had happened just once, when he had seen her walking thorough the portico with her white dog bouncing at her skirt hem. Her eyes had not been filled with scorn, only love and the light of hope. Seeing him there, she hoped that he would again attempt to spirit her away.

No answer had come to Emlyn's prayers. He had become desperate tonight and made a fool of himself. He had tried to entice Vincentini to agree to meet him with drawn swords. Vincentini's reaction had only served to bring ridicule on Emlyn's head. He had tried to belittle the man with Latin, that snatch from an old poem that had come into his head. He remembered his cousin Owain quoting the same words to him in warning. Apart from insult, Emlyn had not meant anything by them, he had been surprised at the reaction of Vincentini though, the man had near swooned. Perhaps he was indeed guilty of some treason along the way, who could know? But Emlyn felt that the shock had been greater than that. He smiled sadly, he had certainly given the man a fright and had him fooled for a while.

'Emlyn?'

The voice pulled at the strings of his heart and he turned. Carmelia stood by the door, dry eyed and composed. She had a look about her which he had never seen before, a calm serenity like a statue of the Madonna. Emlyn knew then that he had lost her.

'I have come to say good-bye,' she said.

Emlyn's heart thudded in his breast, threatening to burst. She came up to him, stood on tip toes and kissed his lips lightly. 'I still love thee and will do so until I die,' she whispered.

'Then why?' he croaked.

'I have decided to do my duty. That is all there is to it.'

Emlyn swung away from her, blinded by shameful tears. 'Because you have seen him, and find him not so detestable after all? Because you have seen the jewels glittering from every part of him? Because you see a life of ease ahead of you?'

'You know that nothing you say is true. My heart is as it will ever be, held in your hands. We were doomed from the start, but were too young and blind in each other's light to see it. Whatever you say or do Emlyn, you know that I am always yours and, in truth I tell you this, I will never belong to another.'

Emlyn desperately gathered her in his arms and pulled her close, burying his face in her hair. 'Do not speak so Eira Morwyn.'

'The truth must belong to us now,' her words whispered in his ear. 'There was always something held from me by you. I know you have loved me as well as you could Emlyn, your heart will not be broken, you can live on and find love again.'

Emlyn lifted his head and frowned down at her. 'What are you saying Cariad? You have plucked the heart from my breast and can still speak so?'

Carmelia shook her head, her hair shimmered dully. She reached a hand up and placed it over his eyes closing them. He felt her lips on his and returned her kiss. All that they had ever been to each other went into that single kiss and that bitter sweet embrace.

Then she broke away from him and he felt as if something vital had gone from him. She said, 'Promise me that you will leave Venice before I wed.'

He held her as she pulled away. 'Wait Cariad!'

Her eyes pleaded with him. He unfastened one of the jewels he had sewn onto his fool's doublet. The gem was as clear as water. He opened her palm and placed the tiny gem in her hand. She stared down at it and tears fell onto her hand. 'Keep this, my precious love,' said Emlyn. 'Hold it to your heart when you think of me. I shall always be with you in spirit.'

Carmelia sobbed and closed her fingers. 'It is like a drop of rain! I shall wear it unto death.' She gave him one desperate look and was gone, a swirl of skirts disappearing through the door.

Pain lanced through Emlyn like a spear. He dropped to his knees, shuddering with loss, stricken with a terrible sense of doom. No matter what she said, he could not understand her reasons. He had lost sight of everything in his fight for her, nothing mattered but her; all was faded and meaningless. Could she cast him aside now, when there was nothing left of him but his love for her?

It was some time before he saw through the madness that had seized him. His mind cleared. She was so much braver than he, her heart was greater, her Christian soul stronger. She had made the decision with admirable courage. Now he should be strong for her, bear the short time he had to remain here then go from her life so that he did not cause her further pain.

Emlyn took Tieffenbrucker's lute from the wall and walked to the hall, filled with sad courage and a depth of emotion that he had never experienced. He took the chair they had provided in the centre of the room, like a minstrel at royal court. He had prepared nothing for this night. Had he come with the Milanese players as Theo had arranged, his performance would have been of a different nature, strengthened by the support of others. He had been vaguely aware of Sandrino, Robusti and Ottavio working through their Orpheus and Eurydice in the background, and the applause of the guests as he had held his love in that final embrace.

A stillness descended, all were content, over fed and in need of gentle repose. He had been sitting for some time, the guests coughing and shuffling around him. Across the room Carmelia was watching him. She smiled sweetly, willing him to be as brave as she. He brought his mind to concentrate on the task at hand. He would give them what they craved, he had the power to make them weep, wrenched by music and word. He held their heart strings in his hand, when they had been brought to their knees by sweet sadness, he would makc them dance. Dance as they had never danced before, he would not free them from the spell until his hands bled.

A series of melancholy chords trilled from his fingers. He looked directly at Carmelia, not caring that all would see and know to whom his love belonged, to who his song was meant.

As Emlyn began to play and sing, his own heart told him that up to this moment he had never really understood the music which was in his soul. Each note and musical phrase, each word and idea of the heart-rending melody, seemed to come from somewhere deep inside, a whole dimension of his being which he never knew existed. He could feel the music draining him, but it was a deep satisfying feeling that at once was agony and joy, blended into a deep mysterious experience. He was completely unaware of his audience. If he was still expressing his love for Carmelia, it was on a level which was beyond his understanding.

The last notes of his music hung as if to be eternal in the hushed air of the banqueting hall. The audience were stunned. No other sound stirred in the falling silence. They all seemed lost, as if some essential essence had been drained from them. Nearest to him, Fra Sebastiano and his half-brother Lorenzo sat like two dull birds on a fence, their faces wet with tears. This was mirrored throughout the hall. Don Carlos was actually holding his wife's hand and patting it affectionately. Beside him the groom looked as though his emotions had been stripped raw, seeming to show the terrible hunger and loss which Emlyn himself suffered.

He could not leave them thus. He stood and began to play. He played as he had at the carnival and had them all up on their feet in seconds, without the help of drum, viola, sackbut or flute. He had expected the musicians in the minstrels' gallery to ruin his performance at any moment, it would be his just reward, after the trouble he had caused them in Milan. He smiled, not caring, and laughed with the guests who danced to his demand.

Ottavio joined him first, crossing the room through the dancers, a drum at his waist, the drum sticks already beating out the rhythm. Behind him came Sandrino, a forgiving smile lighting his face. He stood beside Emlyn, placing his Viola in the new favoured position at his shoulder and added its voice, enriching the dance. Lastly came the piercing brilliance of Robusti's shawm, swirling through the room an octave higher than the lute. There were few there who had ever experienced such a night, most would remember it until the end of their days.

Tomasso had risen and signalled to his company before he took leave of his host. Bartolomeo stood and offered his arm to Fiorenza. She was a little breathless from the dance the manager had swept her up in, unable to resist the lure of lute in the hands of such a talented player. Bartolomeo looked exhilarated. They joined Tomasso by the door where he stood with Don Carlos and Juliana, going over the final arrangements for the ceremony. He was very brief and he was aware that his farewell was not as courteous as it should have been.

Outside the air was cool, the night clear and full of stars. The reason for Tomasso's hurried farewell could no longer be ignored. He leaned on the nearest wall and was heartily sick. Bartolomeo knelt at his side, lending him the support he needed. He wiped the blood from Tomasso's mouth without comment.

Jacopo arrived, holding up a lantern. He directed them down the steps to the waiting boat. Tomasso stumbled, scarcely able to put one foot in front of the other. He was afraid of the blackness that crowded him, not afraid of what it represented, but that it would make him forget something important that must be spoken of. As soon as he was seated and the dizziness eased, he said 'Who was the troubadour?'

'An Englishman, the one who brought the wool,' said Bartolomeo, rubbing his tired eyes. 'Did you note the way Don Carlos enjoyed your discomfort, it must have been arranged.'

'Yes, but how?'

'He will have gone to some trouble finding out all he could concerning you.'

'He would have found nothing,' said Tomasso. 'I have covered my tracks well, it is as if I do not exist. I gambled with him, knowing that he would be in greater need of the gain I could bring him than in discovering exactly who I was. Even if I were named Capaccio, I should deny it.'

'He is a master chess player this Grimani. He plans carefully before each move. He must have learnt something. Otherwise, why would the youth quote such lines to you? It was as if he knew your very soul.'

Tomasso sighed tiredly. 'That, I cannot guess, much as it puzzles me. There is however, another possibility. In the brief time I spent with my betrothed, I discovered that she is foolishly besotted with some young man. And that was probably the troubadour. The challenge itself was serious, the rest was thrown in jest.' Tomasso leaned back on the cushions. The sickness welling up in his stomach. It was pitch black under the canopy but from somewhere, the jewelled earring found light and winked blood red in the darkness.

Bartolomeo knew there was more troubling Tomasso, he could but try, though he did not expect answers. 'How can you be sure?' he asked.

'There are other things which puzzle me, said Tomasso wearily. 'The jewels on his doublet …' His mind seemed to be wandering. 'Anna. There are other matters.'

'You should rest,' said Fiorenza speaking for the first time since they had left. 'My house is the most private, where you will not lightly be disturbed and Symeon is there.'

To their surprise, Tomasso agreed. Then he said 'Symeon must get away from here.' But soon he was asleep and they did not discover what he meant by this. They continued in silence, afraid to voice their fears. Jacopo's oar plopped into the water, sending the long boat surging forward.

When they arrived at Fiorenza's house there was a messenger waiting for them. The *Cornucopia* had arrived late that evening and with it, had come the news of the sea battle and the loss of Don Carlos' trading ship and galley. There was a survivor, a seaman who had been with Cesare Faliero on the galley and who had urgent news for them. The messenger explained that the seaman was waiting with Fiorenza's notary, Enrico de Martoni and with the captain of the *Cornucopia*, Marco Erizzo.

Bartolomeo left immediately with Jacopo to make his way towards the Arsenal. The news of the disaster was terrible, but Bartolomeo realised with dread that he had expected something like this to happen; he knew that Tomasso had no intention of doing Grimani any favours without extracting some cost. It had never occurred to Bartolomeo that the cost would be so great.

Tomasso was asleep, Fiorenza beckoned to Symeon to leave the room. She led him to the kitchen where the lamps burned brightly and a breeze blew through the open shutters.

Symeon did not wait for her to voice the question that was on her mind, he had sensed her unease. He said, 'Madonna he will not survive if he does not go from here and seek help.'

'I had guessed as much Symeon,' she replied quietly. 'Tell me of his hurts, how did he get them?'

'I know not Madonna. From what I have come to know over the years, I would say they were wounds received in combat.' Symeon dropped his head, unwilling to tell her more.

Fiorenza slid on to the bench across from him and leaned her arms on the table. 'Tell me about yourself Symeon. Where did you first meet Tomasso di Vincentini?'

'When my old master died, an Arab trader sold me to a Syrian and this Syrian sold me to the owner of the *Cornucopia*, Tomasso di Vincentini. It was a few days before we left to come here, on the same ship as yourself.'

'And how did he get you to agree to come?'

Symeon's smile widened. 'He bought me Madonna. It was for him to decide how best to employ me.'

Fiorenza gave a gasp of surprise. 'Bought you? You are a slave and I did not realise.'

'I am not any longer Madonna. Though my family were so and theirs before them. I am the only one among my brothers and sisters who is not a slave. They would be happy with such news.'

'You must be grateful to the man who freed you.'

'Messer Vincentini is a good man,' said Symeon. 'Madonna, a devil rides him and torments his soul.'

'I know of that devil Symeon and from where it has come. I only wish that I, or you, or anyone could rid him of it before it destroys him.'

They talked long into the night. Strange companions, tossed together by their love and concern of the roaming spice merchant, who had come into their lives and enriched them. By the end of it, Fiorenza was certain that Tomasso had somehow been involved in the recent sea battle. But the reasons why and how he had come to Venice at such speed, remained a mystery.

When the news reached Don Carlos Grimani, he was bidding his last guests goodnight. He made the messenger wait, seeing that the man's news was not going to be good, from the expression on his face. Whatever ill tidings he brought, Carlos wanted to hear them in privacy. He cheerfully waved off the last barges and boats and returned inside, the messenger following at his heels.

'Out with it,' ordered Carlos as soon as the door closed.

The messenger dropped to his knees. 'The *Maria* is lost Lord!'

'What!'

'Your ships were attacked by corsairs at the Gulf of Patras. They overran the caravel and then turned on the galley. Lord all is lost!'

Carlos stared at him in disbelief. 'Paolo? Where is my grandson Paolo?'

The messenger dropped his head and a great sob ran through him. 'The *Maria* was captured and the galley. I heard that your grandson fought admirably, but fell to the enemy before the galley was overwhelmed.'

'Who has said these things? Did you see what happened?'

'There was a survivor Lord, The *Cornucopia* picked him up a few hours later. He is with Vincentini's manager, Bartolomeo Varini.'

Carlos breathed deeply to calm himself. 'Are you telling me that the *Cornucopia* was not with my ships when this attack happened?'

'She had been delayed at the island of Zante. Your ships were forced to continue without her. Don Grimani, it was by your own order that your ships make all speed to Venice.'

Carlos suddenly felt cold, a deep creeping cold that seemed to come from within him. 'Is my grandson dead?'

'It is believed so, God have mercy on his soul.'

'Bring this survivor to me.'

'He is with Bartolomeo Varini,' the messenger stammered.

'I will see and speak with him. Who else knows of this terrible disaster?'

'All of Venice will know by morning Messer Grimani. It is not possible to keep such news private. The crew of the *Cornucopia* have left the ship, they will spread the word like wild fire.'

Don Carlos nodded solemnly to himself. He would not allow himself to show emotion. Thoughts rushed through him like a howling wind and foremost in his mind was the terrible certainty that the attack had been intended all along. He said, 'Find me this survivor. I cannot act until I have heard from his lips exactly what happened.'

He turned away, his steps were heavy and his shoulders bowed with sorrow. A stifled sob escaped his lips as he made his way towards the house chapel. Where was there to turn, but to God?

Chapter 48 Venice

Tomasso awoke in the late afternoon. He was alone in the room with which he had become familiar. He lay still and stared at the ceiling. It was painted with fish and an enormous whale with the legs of Jonah disappearing into its gaping mouth. The work was childish, but the colours were bright and it had a certain charm to it. It was better to think thus, of nothing. He felt greatly improved from the long sleep. He could judge from the slant of the sun what time of day it was. By this time tomorrow, he would be married, he reflected.

So now the end had come. The thirst of his vengeful blade would soon be satiated. The wake of destruction did not concern him. Should he care that Fiorenza had offered him love? She would not feel so inclined if she truly knew him. Bartolomeo was better acquainted with the truth, but he had remained loyal, in spite of his misgivings. So had Symeon and Koçi and all the rest who had assisted him one way or another in his revenge. He had paid them well, let them be content with that.

Grimani's feast had been a trial. He had gone through it without trouble, just. The youth had nearly caused his undoing, the mad juggler with Anna's jewels sewn on his clothing and Anna's eyes behind the glittering mask. How could that be? Had he drunk more wine than he had thought? Had his mind conjured up an illusion? The accidents, the spillage's, the challenge, these could be explained away as the actions of a jealous youth. But then, there was the poem; the accusing words that were so near to the truth. Only Bartolomeo could have betrayed the truth to Carlos Grimani, but that could not be the explanation either, because Bartolomeo had not known about the jewels.

These jewels came from a necklace that Tomasso had given to Anna many years before. He had made his fortune as a gem merchant. He knew his precious stones, and those he had known particularly well, one hung from his ear. Tomasso reached up and felt it tangled in his hair. He unfastened it and held it to the light. It was a large ruby clasped in a gold, a fanciful dragon's claw, a meaningless symbol fashioned to intrigue. There had been nine of them altogether, of different colours, different fittings, all strung on a necklace of gold links. It was an ancient necklace and like many ancient treasures, bore its own legend, if separated, the stones would eventually come back together, no matter how far they were from each other. Tomasso spun the earring and watched as it caught the light, alluring, magical and awesome. He had believed the legend himself once, and then dismissed it as his mind grew cold with time. It was ridiculous now to think that there had been any truth in it.

He smiled remembering. Anna had held up her dark, heavy hair and kept her eyes squeezed shut as he had fastened the priceless necklace about her slender neck. But when she had seen it in the mirror he held, she had turned pale and refused to wear it. She had never given him an adequate explanation for her dislike of the gift. She had said that it was not for her, that it made her shiver. When he had next seen her, she had pulled it apart and given him back the large centre stone, the dragon clawed ruby that he had kept ever since. Had she believed in the legend? Had the gesture been to remind him to hold on to that belief?

He had not thought much on what had happened to the other stones, for soon afterwards, events had taken a wicked turn and all that was, was no more. He had supposed that her jewels had gone to enrich Grimani's coffers. Since his return, he had seen one, a sapphire in a setting resembling the petals of a flower. It had been part of the brooch that had fastened Paolo's cloak, on the day that the spice had been sold, the same day Grimani's warehouse had burned down. A gem sparkling as clear as sky, bleak in the memories it had evoked. Tomasso had forgotten the incident, until he had seen the juggler. Would Grimani be fool enough to give such precious stones to a vagabond minstrel, because he admired the good looks and the shapely legs in the stripped hose? It made no sense, Grimani was a merchant, such an action would not suit him nor could he afford it. Grimani would have need of every bauble under his roof to starve off bankruptcy. Yet there was no denying that those same jewels had been in the Grimani house. The boy had them sewn onto his bright doublet and worn them with little care as if they had been glass. Indeed that must have been what he thought for such vulgar display spoke of shocking bad taste.

Tomasso dropped the earring onto the table beside him. Unexpected tears stung his eyes, the painted whale blurred.

Anna, how hast thou come hither like a celestial being to awaken all my love? I do not acknowledge God's superiority as a ruler of men. If, sweet love, thou wilt scorn me and deny me my right of vengeance, I will take mine own life and thus end my sorrow.

His stomach felt like an empty sack inside him. He would not eat, not yet, the memory of last night's agony was too fresh in his mind. But he needed to drink.

As if he had heard the silent summons, Symeon appeared at the door with a ewer in his hand, a cloth over his arm and a bright smile stretching from ear to ear. In his other hand, he carried a steaming bowl. Tomasso's stomach churned as the smell of stewed mutton reached him. 'Take the food away Symeon. I do not care for it.'

'Then you will die master.'

'I am not your master. You are as free as the sunlight.'

Symeon walked into the room, placing the items on the table. 'You have given me freedom and self respect. Out of gratitude and for the love I bear you, you are my master still.'

Tomasso dropped his head on to the pillow. There was no reasoning with a man such as Symeon.

'May I speak freely master?' said Symeon.

'When have you done otherwise?'

'There is much that concerns me master.'

'Is not concern, the lot of any God fearing man?'

Symeon's smile disappeared. 'This is so master, some more than others, especially those who have a devil in their souls. The woman here master, she is a good woman. I knew as soon as I first saw her, that she would be suitable to keep your bed warm and take away your troubles. She is old, I see that, but age brings wisdom and that she has in abundance.'

'Did you also learn that I am not a man to be pampered and irritated by slaves? I do not intend to take you with me when I leave, had I meant to I would have kept you slave and had your wagging tongue removed.'

Symeon's black face seemed vacant without his usual smile. 'Then keep me as a servant master,' he replied miserably. 'I have seen that the Venetian gentleman here, have servants to care for their needs. Take me as such.'

Tomasso sat up carefully and poured his own water. He was getting soft, if he stayed here any longer he would most probably fund a house for the poor or take holy orders. He said, 'You have served a renowned physician before, would you like to do so again? I can find some worthy man who would be glad of your experience. Padua is full of them.'

'What do the Italians know of doctoring?' Symeon said cuttingly. 'They take blood from wounded men and drill holes in heads to relieve headaches.'

'Do not dismiss their skill too readily Symeon, they could probably find something to teach you yet. You will have to leave Venice, to remain here is foolish. Are you not aware that Lorenzo Grimani is here? If he should see you, you will not be free for long.'

'Master, I am satisfied where I am, so long as I may serve you,' said Symeon with finality. He took the cup from Tomasso and refilled it, as if to prove a point.

Exasperated, Tomasso made one last attempt. 'I have brought you here from the slave markets of Galata Symeon. If you come back with me, I shall return you there.'

'Why master? Is it because I am knowledgeable about your double identity? Because in your heart you are a Muslim?'

'That is not the reason Symeon nor is what you say the whole truth. If I agree to take you with me, will you leave now?'

'Where would you have me go?'

'I have arranged for a ship to meet me tomorrow after the wedding. It is owned and captained by Gaspare Maria del Monte. He is an old friend whom I met in Padua. The ship is at *Chioggia.* Go there, my faithful Symeon, and wait for me. If you are discovered here in Venice, it will cause me a great deal of trouble.'

Symeon scratched his ear thoughtfully. 'Master, you force me to speak plain. I know you care little for your life, but if you wish to finish this vendetta against your enemies, you will have to remain living to do so. And, to remain living you must heed my humble advice, you must rest and heal or death will claim you.'

'Death?' said Tomasso with a whispered laugh.

'Do not tempt it, lest it hear you. And there is the matter concerning Donna Fiorenza.'

'What matter concerning Donna Fiorenza?' said Fiorenza walking into the room with her arms laden with folded clothes.

Symeon turned in surprise. He stammered the start of an explanation.

Tomasso said, 'He thinks I have chosen the wrong lady for wife.'

'So do I,' said Fiorenza with no hint of embarrassment, 'but I am not going to waste my time in telling you so. However, I will attempt to point out, that you should wait until you are well, we don't want you swooning in the marriage bed. Whatever will the child think?'

Tomasso closed his eyes. As Ismael, no woman or slave would dare to speak to him thus. He cautioned himself, forbearance. It would not be for much longer.

Umbaldo saw Emlyn return to the workshop late that morning. The apprentices were bent over their work, the room had become hot and stifling. The only sounds came from the clatter of tool, the clank of wood and the sighs from Theo as he mopped his brow.

Head down, shoulders slumped, Emlyn crossed the courtyard. He reached the water butt at the corner of the wood store and grasped the rim with two hands. By the time his feet left the ground as he ducked into it, most of the apprentices were watching. They began to laugh; the water butt had grown two legs that were kicking up into the sky.

Frowning, Theo tapped a block of wood on his table. The laughter lessened, then began anew. Umbaldo stood up and walked to the window. The braver apprentices abandoned their work and followed him. Theo thumped his block of wood again and demanded to know what was happening.

Luigi offered an explanation. 'Master, the water butt is about to walk off, that is, if it doesn't drown first.'

With an expression of hard suppressed patience, Theo crossed the room to join them. The legs were kicking above the barrel, they sank further in, splashing water out.

'It's Emlyn,' said Umbaldo.

'Perhaps he can't get out,' offered Luigi.

'Perhaps he doesn't want to,' suggested Marino.

'Well, if he intends to drown, why not use the Lagoon? It's much easier,' commented Orio, the Master Craftsman.

'It is obvious that he has dropped a scudo into the barrel,' said Sangallo. 'It must have been his last one.'

Umbaldo opened the door and walked out into the sunlight. The splashing had creased.

'He has met with failure and ridicule,' said Theo sadly. 'What a terrible waste of talent.'

'They probably threw him out,' said Marino, 'he must have tried to ravish Don Carlos' daughter.'

'his love has refused him,' offered Luigi, 'now he drowns himself and his sorrow.'

Umbaldo reached the barrel and peered inside. He could see murky shapes and bubbles, but not much else, the butt was standing in deep shadow. The boots were still visible, sticking out the top. Umbaldo scratched his chin, to pull on them would result in a soaking and his clothes would shrink. He continued scratching thoughtfully.

It was Theo who solved the problem. Pushing Umbaldo aside, he put his shoulder to the barrel and pushed. It rocked its blocks. Umbaldo added his weight and the second attempt brought success. The water butt tipped on it's side, drenched them with water and then began to roll.

Curses, coughs and splutters boomed from inside it as it gained momentum. The apprentices poured out of the workshop. Theo and Umbaldo started to run behind.

Over the cobbles it bounced, boots spinning, water slopping out.

Peals of laughter erupted from the younger men. They bounded after, tossing their caps in the air as if it was a holiday. They hoped the butt would roll through the gate and plop into the canal, but a loose stone set it askew. It veered and bounced towards the wall, emitting a howl of anguished protest. It hit with a resounding crash and burst asunder. Emlyn crawled out as wet as a seal. The stone griffin, which had rested on it's foundations for a hundred years, tottered, slewed to one side and toppled, without the use of it's stone wings.

Emlyn was sitting amid the wreckage, legs splayed, eyes empty, mouth agape. The griffin landed in the space between his legs and exploded into a thousand marble shards. Unperturbed, Emlyn rose from the ruins of his adventure like a wet phoenix. He took a step forward and then tripped over the metal loop that had once held a rain butt together.

Theo, Umbaldo, masters and pupils erupted into uncontrollable laughter. Umbaldo pulled Emlyn to his feet and shook him, to see if he was still in one piece. Emlyn's eyes crossed, he gulped a breath and groaned. Umbaldo said, 'Were you trying to do away with yourself? Surely there must be a simpler method?'

Emlyn placed a hand on his chest and pushed him aside. 'Whatever can you be thinking of?' he croaked. 'I'm just clearing my head.' Dripping puddles, he squelched back across the yard, ignoring everybody and disappeared into his room. His head re-emerged. The rest of him followed. He gave a sweeping, dripping bow to his audience, stepped back and slammed the door shut.

Theo gave them a minute to recover and then clapped his hands sharply. They all returned to work apart from Umbaldo. Theo looked at him for a moment and then nodded.

Emlyn sat on the edge of his sleeping pallet. He was soaking the straw and the bed covers. His arms were folded across his knees, his head sunk upon them. There was a growing puddle at his feet. He was shivering, Umbaldo could hear his teeth clattering like crustaceans. Umbaldo swept up a towel and threw it at him. He squatted on the floor and waited.

Apart from the shudders, Emlyn didn't move.

Umbaldo said, 'Are you no longer Don Carlos' favourite Giovanni?'

Emlyn moaned.

'What did you do, ruin the Milan Player's rendition of Tristram and Isolde? Steal the family jewels? Rape the daughter? The mother?'

Still no reaction.

'take advantage of Fra Lorenzo? Don Carlos himself? I've heard the rumours about Don Carlos.'

Without lifting his head, Emlyn said, 'All those and more. I also drank everything, right down to Don Carlos' last jug of malmsey. I was merely nursing my sore head.'

'Then it must be a great burden to you,' Umbaldo answered, 'as you nearly drown it and the rest of you with it. Theo is very cross about the griffin.'

Emlyn looked up. His skin was white, his eyes were red rimmed and bloodshot. They held a look that caused Umbaldo to flinch, something burning intensely which spoke of excruciating pain. In a soft voice, Umbaldo said, 'Was it such an utter and complete failure?'

Emlyn stood up and began to strip off his sodden clothing. They were torn and caked with marble dust. In places, spots of blood showed were stone had cut skin.. Eventually Emlyn said, 'It was not like that. I haven't brought disgrace to Theo's door. I was inundated by admirers. They took me off to a tavern and we all got outrageously pickled. I can't remember, but we didn't rape anyone, at least, I think I would have remembered.'

'Then what is the matter?'

'Nothing,' said Emlyn drying himself with care. 'I have had a taste of the promised dish and find that my appetite has fled.'

'Meaning what?'

Emlyn's head disappeared under the towel. He stood naked, his skin raised in goose bumps. His body was surprisingly muscled, Umbaldo had thought him just skin and bone, Emlyn looked more like a soldier or a labouring peasant. He dropped the towel across the bed and looked at his friend seriously. 'I am leaving Venice.'

'Why? Now you have got where you wanted to be, why run away?'

'I told you, I have tasted of it. I spit it out in disgust. Venice is everything vile that it boasts to be.'

'It is not Venice that you spurn,' said Umbaldo, his voice raised. 'It is your failure to entice away a girl who has more sense than her love-stricken minstrel. She weds another and you stick your head in a rain butt with no intention of coming out.'

'I could not drown today and leave Venice tomorrow could I? You are right though. To remain here and see her with another might induce me to murder. Do you know of a boat? What about the one you row home in the evening?'

Umbaldo stood. 'Take the common ferry,' he said crossly. 'They leave twice a day from Santa Chiara, or hire a man to take you across. Why ask me? I care not in what manner you run from those who have helped you.' Umbaldo crossed the room and pulled open the door. A flood of sunlight spread across the floor.

'Wait Umbaldo!' Emlyn called.

Umbaldo turned, but remained by the door.

Emlyn finished tying the points on his hose and hurriedly pulled a jerkin over his shirt. 'Come back in,' he said gently. 'The light hurts my headache.'

Umbaldo hesitated a moment then shook his head. He walked out and slammed the door behind him. He did not go far, but stood in the hot sunlight, his arms folded across his chest. After ten minutes, he returned and looked in at the window. Emlyn was asleep, limbs thrown wide across the pallet, pale face nestled in a crown of tangled damp hair, burning eyes closed in exhausted sleep.

Emlyn awoke to darkness, he had slept all day. His head ached less and his stomach growled with hunger. His mind was clouded with the shreds of screaming dreams. Heads had bobbed up and down in his nightmares, decapitated and shouting at him in accusation.

'*You will rue what you discover!*' shrieked Mafanwy Fawr's wrinkled head.

'*Are you going to leave your old Grandfather*?' Gruffydd asked mournfully.

'*You know that I am right!*' said Goronwy's mouth scornfully.

'*They will hunt you down and kill you,*' warned the head of Ambrose, it had appeared upside-down.

Then Camellia, floating as if in water, '*I am thine, and so long as my life endures I will be thine only.*'

Emlyn had screamed himself awake. He sat in the darkness. It was still early, he could hear the clamour from the kitchen, Eva's chastising voice, a child's howl. The aroma of frying onions and garlic caused Emlyn's stomach to heave.

'*Thine for eternity.*'

Emlyn shook his head.

'*Without thee, I am as nothing, for I do not live. Death is all I can embrace without thee.*'

Emlyn stood up and splashed his face from a water-filled basin beside the bed. He took his travelling pack from a hook behind the door and stuffed his still damp clothing into it. Need it be so? Was destiny written by the hand of God?

When he had pulled the strings of the satchel tight, he glanced around the dim room. There were yet four items of his that he could not tuck away like clothing; the bow he had fashioned from yew, the shield on which he and Josquin had escaped the avalanche, the cittern Ambrose had given to him in Milan and lastly, the worn, tattered Book of Genesis, written in Welsh for the first time ever. Emlyn stood with his arms folded and glared at them. They were symbols of all that he had been; the Holy Book for the Jesuits; the cittern for the bardic harper; he bow and quiver for the mercenary. And the shield? What did the battered shield represent? The fool?

He had spent the last year in conflict with all he had encountered. Had he been more thoughtful, he could have lessened the antagonism between himself and his cousin Owain, he could have been more humble and obedient to his uncle. But he had upset them both with his arrogance and self determination. Even Gruffydd, who had wanted him to follow the traditions of the bard, he had turned away from. Ignoring the call to his heart and soul, he had pushed it all aside. With the Jesuits, most of whom had been kind to him, he had taken only what he wanted, spurning their advice, ignoring their concern. Worse still, he had betrayed Goronwy who had been like a brother to him; with whom he had planned great things. How much better it would have been to have gone with Goronwy to Douai, to give Goronwy the friendship and support he had needed. They should have talked further and not parted company in anger and discord.

The self indulgence had not ended there; during the journey to Italy, he had ignored the guidance and resented the support of both Ambrose and Josquin. Even Angelo's offer, out of a rough kindness, for him to join the mercenaries, Emlyn had refused. He had not wanted their intrusion, but they had given it regardless, he had been too caught up with himself to acknowledge them. The names ran through his head like a clattering water mill; Ambrose, Josquin, Angelo, Fra Sebastiano, Father de Sacy, Wendelin, Theo, Eva, and even Adriana Martinelli who had shown him what physical love was. But the worse folly had been practised on Carmelia. He had bullied his way into that house in Milan, again using others to get his way. He had taken from Carmelia that purity which he should have treasured, made sacrosanct. Upon her had his greatest harm befallen.

'My heart is in your hands and no others, nor ever will be.'

Emlyn rubbed his eyes, trying to rid himself of the haunting whisper. He picked up the manuscript. It smelled of sea. He closed his eyes. It was not this sea, this gentle Middle Sea of impossible blue. It was another sea, far to the north; a sea of ominous grey, towering walls of brine topped with furious foam; a sea that clawed at the base of the Dragon's Head, frothed and boiled in savage storm. He could almost hear the gulls cry. And see the purple slabs of rock, the blunted grass with it's tapestry of wild rose, cushioned thyme and tiny fairy harebells; see the great clouds ride the storm sky like rearing horses, like soldiers to war booming across the sea, like monks to prayer riding against a sky of pellucid blue. The shapes and colours, the mystery of images, ethereal yet existing from the dawn of time to eternity.

Emlyn opened the door and walked out into the night. He passed the gate, crunching shards of stone griffin, and stepped to the edge of the canal. With no further thought, he dropped the Book of Genesis into the water and watched it spiral into darkness. He felt no remorse, let some other, wiser man complete the task; he was done with it. 'You were right Tad-cu,' he spoke aloud. 'I am no saviour of Wales. It is not my hand that will forever forge the word of God in our beloved tongue.' Sinking with the manuscript were any hopes he had harboured concerning Goronwy and his noble cause to bring Catholicism back to Wales and England.

With the same determination, he returned to his room, swept up the cittern, and left again. He ignored Umbaldo calling to him and left Theo's enclosure. Within half an hour he had reached his destination, a pawn broker's shop. Light streamed through the windows, shadows of activity within. The premises were open. The Medici symbol hung above the door, casting moon-round shadows on the wall. He pushed the door open.

After a short time, he stepped out without the cittern Ambrose had bought for him. Instead, he carried the item he had exchanged for it, a sword. The blade was old and had seen some use judging from the nicks and marring along the blade. It had been fitted with a rapier handle and was surprisingly well balanced, considering its oddness. It was the best he had managed to get, the pawn broker complaining that the cittern was of little value. Emlyn knew he had been cheated, but he was not concerned, it would do until he managed to get one better, if he managed to get one better. As he walked, he thought of the cittern, it had been hung on the wall alongside two lutes, a viol and a mandolin. He would not return for it. Music was dead in his heart, he had purposefully cast it from him, but not without pain.

When he returned he found a plate of cheese, bread and a sausage, Umbaldo, caring for his welfare! Ravenous, Emlyn ate it all.

What he had kept were the tools of war, bow, quiver, shield and the long dagger that Wendelin had brought from Rouen. Angelo had told him that he would be made welcome if he chose to return. Emlyn had made his decision. He felt that he had destroyed the symbols of what his choices had been, all but for one. Although the shield was fitting for the vocation he had decided upon, it was awkward, heavy and old fashioned. Did he need to lug it across Europe in his search for escape? It was not even pleasant to look at, scarred and dented, from it's use as a sled. It reminded Emlyn of sun and snow and a snow-white maid with hair as black as night and eyes filled with stars. 'Morwyn yr Eira,' he whispered, 'Maiden of the Snow.'

'As God be my witness, I shall not live without thee!'

There was a delicate tap on the door. Emlyn rose and opened it. He looked down. Three heads as fair as moonlight, gazed up at him with Lagoon-blue eyes, Theo's daughters. Their expressions were solemn. Emlyn dropped to their eye-level, his own expression softening. They wrapped their arms about his neck and shoulders.

'Bado says you are leaving,' said Ršsi, the eldest.

'You can't if you are going to marry us,' chimed the middle one, Erminia.

Little Agnes burst into tears.

'He can't marry us all anyway,' said Ršsi thoughtfully. 'He could if he was a Muslim man, I suppose.'

Emlyn included them all in his embrace and in his soft laughter. He said, 'If I have to, then that is what I shall be.'

'Won't God be cross?' asked Erminia.

Emlyn sighed. How was he to extract himself from this? Releasing them, he stood and brought a pouch from a fold in his jerkin. He pulled at the draw strings and poured the contents into his hand. He had four gems left. He chose his favourite, a diamond as clear as a tear, and replaced it in the pouch. The other three he held in his open palm and crouched down once more to the little girls. Their eyes widened in wonder. 'These are promises,' Emlyn said. 'They are trapped in pretty glass for you to keep.'

'Do they promise that you will marry us?'

'Do they promise that you will come back?'

'I want the blue one!'

Emlyn presented the sapphire to little Agnes, it was the same colour as her eyes. 'They promise that we will always be friends,' he explained. 'I cannot marry you because I will be an old man when you are young and beautiful maidens.'

They mewed and questioned and demanded a story before he managed to get them back out the door. He felt as if he had bound them to him somehow, that the gems would come back together as if by magic to from the original necklace.

'It is like a drop of rain! I shall wear it unto death.'

Emlyn caught his breath as the words swam into his mind. He pounded his fists against the wall. Why? Why did she keep calling to him? Must she plague his every waking thought as if, as if something in her words … He shook his head, it began to pound intolerably.

'Promise me that you will leave Venice before I wed.'

She who had given him everything, would not now leave his mind. Was she prepared to take her own life rather than belong to any other man? She had given him herself, body and soul. Would she now give him her life too? Sweet beloved, is this what your persistent whispering means?

Emlyn's headache grew. He didn't want to think any more. The best remedy for his present state of mind, he reasoned, was to collect Umbaldo and fall into a tavern.

Don Carlos Grimani spent that night on his knees in the chapel adjoined to the palace. The weight of his sins crushed heavily upon him, but greater was his sorrow. The news of Paolo's death had shocked him and left him weeping inconsolably. His dreams and hopes, all that he had worked for and become, were shattered like broken crystal. No amount of weeping, no amount of prayer, no amount of bitter regret could change the crushing events that had followed each other like a line of felled trees. Everything was gone, blown by one fell wind after another. Sweet Jesus Why?

The sailor who had survived and seen the attack on Grimani's ships had been questioned at great length. He had seen Paolo fall, had seen the blood upon his breast. 'He was dead my lord, or as good as.' From the conviction of these words, Don Carlos had at last accepted the bitter truth. The last of his male bloodline was dead. How cruel was God! How cruel was fate! All that was left was one woebegone daughter.

Don Carlos had learned from the faithful Uglino that the meddling vagabond had stolen her purity, had planted his seed in her womb. Don Carlos had sworn Uglino to silence and even tolerated the presence of the lutanist, with no outward show of the knowledge he had learned. After the wedding, the boy Emilio would be stabbed in some dark street and tossed into the Lagoon, as he so justly deserved. Such caution now was necessary to keep the news from Vincentini. Would he take Carmelia as wife if he knew the truth? No, what decent, self respecting man would. So all must be kept concealed, at least until after the wedding. However, the seaman who had survived the sea battle had sworn that he had seen Vincentini with the corsairs! Commanding the corsairs! The man's mind was added by his ordeal, such a thing was impossible. Still, Carlos had kept the man here, offering comfort and as much food as he could consume. Carlos need time now to consider what had happened and time to weep.

Tomasso di Vincentini. The name stuck like an apple core in Grimani's throat. But in this one man, lay his hope of salvation. Vincentini and his wealth would enable Don Carlos to rise from the flames of ruin like the phoenix. Carlos was old, he deserved better, he would live the remainder of his life in the splendour he had become accustomed to and be held in high esteem by the nobility of the Senate. As son-in-law, Vincentini would be bound to honour his wishes and provide for him. And Carlos believed that he might see a grandchild or two before the end came. All seemed lost, but a glimmer of hope remained.

'Vile beggar!'

Don Carlos lifted his head in surprise.

'Deceitful, malignant fool!'

Without looking around, he recognised the voice.

'Darksome meddler! Foul villain!'

He could not believe that he was hearing such words from one who had always been so pious, obedient and intimidated.

'How dare you kneel in this house of God. Slayer of innocents!'

It was Juliana! Don Carlos stood, his knees stiff from hours of kneeling. He turned to face his wife. She was clothed in black, her face as white as candle wax, her eyes burning scorn, words grating, trembling finger pointed in accusation. Don Carlos took a step towards her. 'Juliana.'

'Come not near me. Devil's spawn! Your house is cursed. Your seed is barren!'

'You are ill my dear, distraught. Let me summon Adriana.'

'Well you may. Sodomite! Raper of children!'

'Stop this at once!' Don Carlos hurried towards her.

She backed away, nimble footed, knowing that he could not catch her. 'Summon her!' she screamed. 'She who has been your lover, she who bore the child you thought to come from your loins. Adriana takes many lovers, she always has. And did you believe Carmelia was your own daughter. Fool! You are cursed. I will not carry the dark secrets of this house a moment more. Let all know that Don Carlos the lover has nothing in his member but spittle! How you have scathed me all these years. I have carried the blame for your inability. I was called barren and treated like an abomination. Had I but taken a real man to my bed, then God would have blessed me with the child I craved.'

Don Carlos ceased in his attempts to seize her or try to understand her caustic words. He was out of breath, his heart pounded viciously. He had to stop her vile mouth before the whole house was roused. 'I command you to stop!' he shouted 'How dare you speak such intolerable lies. I have fathered two fine sons!'

Juliana laughed. The sound was maniacal, a wretched, cracking howl of ridicule. 'Fool!' she screamed. 'All these years you have been deceived. Your first wife Eugenia knew your incompetence. After six years of unfruitful marriage, six years of continuous verbal battering, she took the only course left to her. She took a lover and from that union brought Cristoforo into the world. She took another lover and …'

'Shut you foul mouth!'

'… brought Roberto into the world. Where do you think your Adriana thought up such a scheme to fool you? Adriana was already pregnant when she came to your bed. Laughable dotard! She and I went away so that she could have the babe in secret and so that I could call the child my own. Carmelia is the child of her lover, Roberto and Cristoforo were sons of Eugenia's lovers. Thrice deceived! No child has ever sprouted from your seed!'

'Liar! Filthy, foul mouthed witch!' His anger gave him the strength and speed to reach her. He trapped her against the wall. His hands closed about her throat.

Still she managed to speak, her words stifled and gurgling. 'Kill me Carlos and all Venice will know. Did you think I have not guarded against that?'

Don Carlos released her neck and transferred his grip to the front of her gown, ripping the cloth. 'Then I shall have you locked away, like the mad woman you are. Send you from here somewhere dark and imprisoning where none can hear your unforgivable lies.'

Juliana pulled away. Her veil had come loose, her greying hair fell about her like a mantle. She shook her head, the long tresses flying. She backed out of his reach and spat at him. Her laughter grated on his ears. 'You tried that once didn't you,' she grated. 'You tried the same trick with Cristoforo's wife, Anna. I know now why she never reached the destination you threatened her with, you killed her before she got there didn't you. Vile murder! You will not do the same to me. You are ruined. You have no power over me or anyone else. Everything is lost, even those you thought your own blood. Rot in hell's fire!'.

'Nothing is lost,' said Don Carlos coldly. 'All will be as I intend it to be. Vincentini will wed my daughter Carmelia and all will be resolved.'

'Vincentini?' she spat. 'Vincentini! He has your measure. This is all for his sake not yours. his is the ultimate revenge.'

'What lies do you conjure up now, wicked harlot?'

'Ask Adriana,' she screamed. 'I will do nothing to prevent the sword from falling.'

Don Carlos reached out to grasp her, but she sped away, her laughter echoing through the chapel. He did not try to pursue her. She could do nothing to harm him locked up in her room, as she soon would be.

She ran to the door and swung it open. An icy draft put out the candles, plunging the chapel in darkness. She turned then, ghostly in the grey light. 'I leave you with this Carlos,' she grated, 'but only to cause you pain. Adriana suspected him, as soon as she saw him, she knows who Vincentini really is. He is the hand behind your downfall, you stupid old man. Your hopes are all in vain.'

When she had gone, he wrung his hands, cried out in a wild, wretched voice and broke into bitter sobs.

Chapter 49 The Duel

Carmelia and Adriana arrived early at the Church of I Carmini. This church had always been favoured by her father; he had been married here himself, twice. The façade was greyed by time and pigeons. This was where the marriage ceremony was to take place. Carmelia followed her godmother down the aisle, passed the choir and into a side chapel where they were greeted by Father Antonio. The unfinished frescos showed scenes from the history of the Carmelite Order. The interior was cool and serene, conveying an air of grace and luminosity.

Earlier that morning, Carmelia had endured two hours of dressing and hair pulling and fuss. Gifts from her future husband had flooded through the door into the bridal chamber; silks and furs, costly enamels and a casket of jewels fit for an emperor. She had never seen her godmother display such nervous agitation as she did then, pacing up and down, talking incessantly.

Carmelia herself had never felt calmer. She had made her peace with God and was not afraid. This was but a single day to get through, she had no intention of seeing another. She had prepared the poison herself, pouring it into the ewer of wine that stood on a silver tray with two clear, long stemmed glasses, awaiting her happy return on the arm of her husband. She would never lie with Tomasso di Vincentini and give to him what another already owned.

When the dressing and painting and hair arranging had been completed, she had stood in front of her mirror and had not recognised the young woman who gazed back at her with an air of peace and serenity. The dress was of ivory silk and cloth of gold. It was worked heavily with glittering embroidery and seed pearls. Strings of pearls looped to her waist and were threaded through the ringlets of her hair. More were sewn onto the slashed sleeves where the cloth of gold was puckered and pulled through the silk. There were four under-dresses, each a darker shade of ivory. These were embroidered with silk lilies and each was revealed where the overdress was gathered up in loops, a few inches from the hem. Her slippers were gold and aglitter with sequins. At her neck hung a single precious stone as cold as a raindrop. The reflection had seemed unreal, like a princess out of romantic fantasy; a highly decorative shell with nothing solid within, as if her soul had already departed.

Carmelia knelt below a statue of Our Lady of Mount Carmel, her own namesake. Her prayers were whispered, begging forgiveness for the mortal sin she had sworn to carry through. Should she tell a priest what she intended to do? Could she be granted God's forgiveness before the deed was done? Would such a priest be sworn to secrecy? It seemed unlikely, she would not confess; let this remain between her and God. And if God were merciful, she would not be condemned to hell's fire for eternity. Tears welled up in her throat, she choked them back, tears were for the past, now she must stay strong to fool them all.

Carmelia's mother Juliana, had not come. The news of Paolo's death had caused her to shut herself in her room in a state of misery, so Carmelia had been told. Beside her now, Adriana's skirts rustled as she rose from kneeling. She said, 'It is stifling in here. Shall we go outside my dear? There are some rose bushes in the cloister.'

Carmelia would rather have stayed where she was, protected from questioning by the peaceful presence of Our Lady. But she dutifully rose and followed her godmother from the chapel. At the far entrance, people had already begun to arrive. Carmelia could not endure the empty words they would offer.

The chapel had been cool, outside it was like stepping into a boiling cauldron. Although early yet, the day was fiercely hot and still. Madonna lilies filled the small garden with heavy perfume. In her layers of cloth and glitter, Carmelia was at once uncomfortable with the heat.

Adriana linked her arm as they walked under an arbour of budding roses. At the far end, she stopped and turned to face her charge, taking both her hands and holding them together. 'I praise God that you are no longer distraught, little dove,' she said softly.

Carmelia did not drop her gaze. 'Through prayer I have found the strength to do my duty, Madonna.'

Adriana gave her hands a jerk in irritation. 'Don't call me Madonna. We know each other better than that. I cannot bear your coldness. Is it the price I am to pay for forcing you to marry against your will?'

'No godmother. I am just tired, I slept little and my manner is subdued.'

'Are you afraid?'

'A little. Yet he seemed a goodly man.'

Adriana let her hands drop. 'You know what will be expected of you?'

Carmelia nodded. She had tasted of the joys of love and was glad that she had done so.

'Do not worry Little Dove, within an hour or two it will all be over and you will begin a new life. Soon your parents and family will arrive. Before then, you will have time to compose yourself and to find peace in your heart.'

Carmelia continued walking. 'I already have,' she said wistfully.

Tomasso too, was dressed in wedding finery. The clothes were black, the velvet doublet, striped in bands of dark red. It was quilted and pleated and cleverly sewn with curling leaves. Solid gold acorns hung from the silk ties. About his shoulders, hung a chain of gold and precious stones and his short cloak was clasped with a brooch of gold filigree and clustered black pearls. Smiling, Symeon held out a wide brimmed hat, adorned with a graceful ostrich feather. Tomasso placed it on the bench beside him, while Symeon buckled on his sword. The scabbard was decorated with shimmering mother-of-pearl. On his right side hung a matching dagger. The weapons were highly ornamental and did not look as if they had ever been wielded in action.

They had come to the butter-yellow palace, early the previous evening. Tomasso had been blunt with Fiorenza, it had marred the gratitude he felt towards her. He had told her not to come to the Church of I Carmini. She had replied that she had nothing better to do while she waited for the departure of the ship to Cyprus; it was not due to sail until late afternoon. Tomasso would have to endure her presence, like it or not. But she had not followed him here and he did not think she would come to witness the wedding.

Unfortunately Symeon had disregarded his advice about leaving Venice and Tomasso had been forced to an anger he rarely allowed himself to express. Symeon was leaving within the hour.

Bartolomeo stood in the doorway, with his thin arms folded and his expressive face frowning with all its lines. They were in the room where they had once discussed the value of jade. The knees of Bartolomeo's hose had no bulges or creases, his clothes were new, he looked surprisingly tidy. He said, 'Do you think yourself well enough? No one else does.'

'Line up the virgins 'Tolomeo. I am as fit as a bull and have an appetite to match.'

'Is it is too late now for you to listen to reason?'

'No, 'Tolomeo. Give me one word of advice and I shall have you trussed up like a hen to market. Then you'll miss all the fun.'

'Heaven Forbid,' said Bartolomeo sarcastically. 'I wouldn't miss it for all your jewels. After all, this has been twenty years in the making. Will you confront Grimani?'

'None of your concern.'

'Do you intend to stay in Venice?'

'Neither is that.'

'What about the Eastern Spice Company? Would I be right in assuming that you intend to marry the girl, confront Grimani and die in the process?'

Tomasso sat down beside his hat. 'Assume what you will,' he snapped. 'I have told you not to care for me.'

Bartolomeo said, 'In spite of your path of destruction, I find that I do care for you. So does Fiorenza.'

Tomasso looked at him gravely. 'Thank you 'Tolomeo. And don't look so mournful, we may yet live to see another day. Let us be joyful. I am to wed a maid more delightful to the soul than frankincense and myrrh is to heaven. Twixt now and then, I am the happy groom. Could you not mould your oversized features into a smile?'

'A r ictus perhaps. I can promise no better.'

They left the palace followed by a retinue of liveried servants, with Tomasso's salamander depicted on their cloaks. On the Grand Canal, a gondola waited, it was festooned with garlands and bows of silk. Jacopo waited with his pole in his hand, he was standing with an air of importance.

'Master?' Symeon was standing alone on the steps.

Tomasso turned back to him. 'Go with God, my friend.'

Symeon bowed, his hand over his heart. 'And may He give you peace, Master.'

When Don Carlos left the chapel, he had been unable to discover the whereabouts of his wife Juliana. He hoped that she had the sense left to keep silent and dutifully attend Carmelia's wedding. Don Carlos should be at the church himself, but Juliana's words had forced him to seek solitude, to find time to think. The servants, attendants and a scattering of Juliana's relations waited at the front entrance, all dressed sumptuously, all with expressions of impatience, all overdressed in the heat. Don Carlos ignored them all and strode up the wide staircase to the long hall where the feast had been held a few days before. The room was unoccupied. He closed the double doors behind him and leaned back against them. He felt old and tired and closed his eyes attempting to calm himself. He felt encouraged by the riches that had flowed into the house earlier, Vincentini's gifts for the bride. The bridal room was filled with rich cloth and Carlos himself had seen the jewels. He had locked the room now and the key was in his pocket. He felt that there might be some chance of picking over it before the nights entertainments.

What lies Juliana had invented concerning Vincentini! Had he done her some injury in the past that she should feel such venom? Did it follow, that she knew more concerning the man than Don Carlos had been able to discover for all his money and effort? Vincentini is the hand behind your downfall! Your future is but ashes!

Don Carlos groaned. Could there be any truth in that? It was true that Vincentini had arrived in Venice about the same time as the disasters had begun. He certainly had the wealth to bring the Grimani trading empire to its knees. And I have never liked him, thought Don Carlos, I've always felt uncomfortable in his presence. Why?

Should he send Uglino to fetch Adriana? What could she know of the man, she had been out of Venice for years. Something from the past then, but what? The eyes? the infernal earring? Think!

Don Carlos felt again the deep pain in his chest. Then the name came to him as if lightening had struck.

'Capaccio!' he gasped. 'Tomasso Capaccio!'

Capaccio, the man who should have met the ignoble death of a galley slave. But he had not. He had lived!

He had lived!

He had waited!

He had harboured his vengeance like a miser and grown rich in order to battle on an equal footing. The malmsey ships! The burned warehouse, the burning of the vineyards in Cyprus, one foul deed followed after another. Weak with realisation, Don Carlos sank to a padded seat against the wall and stared sightless at nothing. 'God's wounds!' he exclaimed 'The maiming of Lorenzo! Paolo? Did he meet his death by the same foul hand? Yes: it all made sense.

Don Carlos stood with cold deliberation. There was no time to lose. Capaccio had to be stopped, to be killed, before he took the life of Carmelia and ended Grimani forever. Don Carlos paused at the door. Would it not be more fitting to secure the rogue's wealth first? Wait until the ceremony was over before he was confronted with his crimes? But Capaccio must be silenced. What good would come of regurgitating the past? The curse of that wicked foreign woman has come to pass! God's blood, how I regret not strangling her there and then. She has haunted me ever since. Fiendish witch!

Don Carlos swung open the door and yelled for his steward. Giuseppe came instantly to the summons. Filled with the strength of hatred, Don

Carlos hurried down the steps. 'Get the men armed,' he snarled. 'Get me the city guard, at least a dozen!'

Pale with fright, Giuseppe ran off to do his master's bidding.

Carmelia stood under a blossom laden cherry tree. It was the only scrap of shade she could find in the enclosed garden. The heat was relentless, even the blossom was wilted and browning, the scent sickly. On three sides of the square were the church and adjacent buildings, the forth was a high stone wall that rose from a canal on the other side. The base of the wall was damp and green with algae.

From where she stood, Carmelia could see the priest, Father Antonio, under the archway. He was waiting for her to go and pray with him and endure his counsel. She should not have come early, the waiting grated on her frayed nerves. Beside the priest stood a larger man with whom he was conversing. Carmelia recognised him as the kindly Franciscan who had come to the house with Emlyn, Fra Sebastiano. She had liked him and was glad that he was here. She hoped that he could give some comfort to Lorenzo who was distraught about his brother's death. Carmelia could not feel the same depth of sadness; she had hardly known Paolo. She could not feel anything. It seemed as if she had been drained of emotion, that with her parting words to Emlyn had gone her heart and her depth of feeling.

Petals rained down upon her like falling snowflakes, they settled on her bodice, lodged in the clutter of pearls and gold braiding. She felt insufferably hot, but she would not return inside. Not yet was she brave enough to face the onslaught of good wishes and the curious stares. Adriana had left her and gone in search of some watered wine to ease her fears and discomfort.

Carmelia bit her lip and felt the tears well up again. Whenever she thought that she had her emotions under control, her thoughts would stray to Emlyn and the tears would begin. What a sorry bride she would make. How long now? Fifteen minutes? Ten?

'Did I ever tell you the tale of Culhwch and Olwen, the daughter of Ysbaddaden?'

Carmelia's breath caught, that soft, beloved voice with its foreign cadence. She knew it so well. Had he come now in spirit to invade her thoughts? To haunt her to the very end?

More petals fell out of the tree, the branches swayed.

She knew the voice spoke from her mind but she answered anyway, softly in a whisper as she had done in Milan. 'Is that why you came here? To tell me stories?' Her voice was tight, controlling her emotions.

There was no wind, so why did the petals fall? She turned and peered up into the branches.

Emlyn was perched on a forked branch. He smiled down at her. 'Do you think you could climb a tree?'

She gasped, wanting to scream with joy. 'I have a new dress on,' she replied, her words barely controlled.

'Bring it with you,' said Emlyn. 'We can live off it for a year or more. For eternity, if your heart desires. Can't you hitch it up or something?'

Letting the tears flow, Carmelia looked quickly behind. Both priests had turned away to greet Adriana. Was there enough time?

'Come quick, my little flower leaf,' said Emlyn. He reached down, his hand open to help her climb.

'They will see me!' Carmelia cried.

'This is the only chance we have Cariad. Climb!'

Carmelia ran to the trunk of the tree, tucking up an armful of shimmering skirts. She could not reach Emlyn's hand. If he came down, he would surely be seen. She reached up and grasped a lower branch.

'Carmelia!' shrieked Adriana. 'What are you doing? The dress child, you will ruin the dress!' She hurried across the rose garden. She snatched up at Carmelia, preventing her escape.

Carmelia turned to her. 'Please let me go godmother.'

'Go where? Have you gone out of your mind?'

Emlyn dropped down beside her causing Adriana to jump with fright. 'You!' she gasped.

He said, 'As you love her Madonna, let her come with me.' He was still hidden from the others, shaded by the blossom tree.

Adriana's cold eyes softened. She looked intently at Carmelia and seemed to see to her very soul. 'You haven't got a hope of escaping,' Adriana said softly. 'But I will not stand in your way.' She grasped Carmelia's hands and her face was filled with love. 'Fly then my Little Dove. My heart and prayers will be with you.' She pulled Carmelia into a close embrace. When she released her, there were tears in her eyes. 'Go children. I will distract the priests and hold at bay any who come looking. There are things I would say to you, sweet daughter, but no time to speak them. Hurry away now, Vincentini will be here in a few minutes and your father must be here already.'

Emlyn reached out and took Adriana's hand. He raised it to his lips. 'God grant you happiness Donna Adriana.'

'And you Emlyn Tomas,' she replied with a sorrowful smile.

He kissed her hand and released it. It that split second, he read the pain in her eyes.

Adriana turned away and did not look back. They saw her draw the priests inside the building, before they made their escape. The tree topped the high wall. Hampered as she was by the rich cloth, Carmelia managed with Emlyn's hand always ready to guide her. He had tied a rope to get them down the other side to a narrow ledge onto which they could step. A rowing boat was tied to a hoop, waiting. Carmelia was stunned with joy.

It was pure chance that the bridegroom should come by the same waterway towards the Church of I Carmini and see the lover's make their escape. Tomasso ordered the boat to stop and pull towards the embankment. "'Tolomeo go to the church and keep them all happy until I return.'

'What are you going to do?' said Bartolomeo alarmed.

'Bring my bride to the altar,' said Tomasso. 'Don't worry, they will see their folly when I catch them. Hurry now, there is no time for one of your lectures.'

'You won't kill the boy?' said Bartolomeo, reluctantly climbing out with the servants.

'No. But Don Carlos will if he finds out. I'll catch up and talk sense into them. Don't worry, I'll give the boy my pearls and he can disappear. I will not be denied my wife. And for God's sake don't tell anyone, or we'll have an army of wedding guests on our tail. Can you imagine the sight?'

Bartolomeo watched helplessly until the gondola was out of sight. He felt that he would have to see this through to its conclusion. Tomasso had never listened to him, nor would he now. Bartolomeo made his way to the church with dragging steps and a foreboding sense of doom weighing him down. He could see from the activity as he approached, that something was known. The first person he met with was the elderly priest he had seen with Emlyn on the night of the feast. 'Fra Sebastiano? What is amiss?' he asked.

'Chaos,' smiled the old Franciscan. 'Don Carlos has not yet arrived nor your employer, Vincentini. Now the bride has disappeared. The usual setbacks on such an occasion.'

Bartolomeo liked him instantly. The friar seemed calm and unperturbed. He was seated on a low wall outside the church. His hands, clasped on his knee, were threaded with a rosary. Bartolomeo sat down beside him and removed his new hat to fan himself. Ignoring Tomasso's advice, he said, 'I fear all is not so simple. The bride has run off with a lover. I saw them. Vincentini has gone after them to talk some sense into them. I think it best if we mention nothing to the others yet. All may yet be resolved. Fra Sebastiano?What is it? Are you in pain?'

'No, no.' said the friar, recovering from whatever had caused him to grow pale. 'Who is the lover?'

'Why the lutanist. The one you were with.'

'Blessed Saints, no!'

Bartolomeo stood up, alarmed by the man's reaction.

'Where are they?' cried Fra Sebastiano rising beside him.

'I don't know. They could be anywhere. Don't be concerned, Toma will catch up with them. Believe me, he will not let the girl escape.'

'Toma? Do you mean Vincentini?'

'Yes. He is not a man to give up what he himself wants. You don't know him, never was there a man so determined.'

Fra Sebastiano shook his head. 'You do not know Emlyn Tomas. If he has decided to run off with the young lady, there is little short of death that he will allow to stop, him.' He paused, a shudder running through his large frame. 'How strange life is, to repeat itself so.'

Bartolomeo looked at him in puzzlement. 'You know this young wool trader well?'

'I have known him since he was a child, on and off over the years. He came to Venice for the purpose of discovering his mother's fate. Now he repeats history by making the same mistake as she.' He shook his head sadly. 'Poor, foolish boy. His mother ran off with a Grimani you know. Now he does the same. As tragedy ended one, I fear it will end this too.'

Bartolomeo shivered, in spite of the heat. Run off with a Grimani? What did the man mean?

Fra Sebastiano grasped his arm. 'Where did you say you saw them?' He began to move away, pulling Bartolomeo in his wake.

'At the back of the church,' said Bartolomeo hurrying to keep up. 'What Grimani? Which Grimani did his mother run off with?'

'It was a long time ago,' the friar explained. 'When Don Carlos had two sons. I believe they both died tragically. This one was the oldest.'

'Cristoforo?' cried Bartolomeo. He paused in mid-step and caught at the Franciscan's sleeve. 'That's impossible. Fra Sebastiano I knew these people. I worked for Anna and Cristoforo Grimani as notary. She had two sons, Lorenzo, who belongs to your order and Paolo, so recently lost at sea. She could not have had any more children. Cristoforo died and she ...'

'Was thought to have died too. I know.' said Fra Sebastiano. 'She did not. She lived to give birth to another son. Had I known that you had been with them, I could had saved myself a great deal of trouble.'

Bartolomeo paced up and down like a caged animal. His mouth opened to speak each time he changed direction and then snapped shut again.

'I'm sorry that the news upsets you so,' said Fra Sebastiano seeing his concern.

Bartolomeo released a howl of anguish. Suddenly he sat on the ground, his head cradled, shaking in denial.

Fra Sebastiano bent and touched his shoulder. 'We must help these misguided young people,' he said. 'If we can find them.'

Bartolomeo dropped his hands and looked up. 'It is not only the young who are misguided. You cannot know what this means and I cannot begin to explain it to you. Tomasso Vincentini is not who he seems.'

'Nor is Emlyn,' said Fra Sebastiano with a smile. 'I don't think he has yet confronted Don Carlos with the truth of his birth. I know he had every intention of doing so, at least, I thought I knew, until now. Only Lorenzo knows that they are half brothers. I advised them both to treat the subject with the utmost delicacy. Don Carlos will not take kindly to being reminded of his past misdeeds.'

Another idea suddenly struck Bartolomeo. He leaped to his feet. Taking the friar's arm, he hurried to the waterside, frantically looking for a boat. 'How old is this Emlyn?' he snapped.

'He is not certain, about eighteen, perhaps a little older mow. He was born in captivity. As a small child he was delivered to me from a Portuguese ship out of Cetua. He had hoped to discover the truth by coming here to Venice.

'He could be,' Bartolomeo swore under his breath. 'God in heaven! He must be the son of Capaccio!'

'I would say that was quite possible,' said Fra Sebastiano. 'You do mean I think, the gem merchant who was condemned to the galleys? He was said to be the woman's lover.'

'Don't you see what this means?' gasped Bartolomeo.

'You are upset. And understandably so.'

'No Fra Sebastiano. Tomasso di Vincentini is Tomasso Capaccio. They are one and the same! He was her lover yes, but he was also her husband. They married in secret, hoping to escape Don Carlos. Tomasso survived the fate Don Carlos had devised. He came here for the purpose of vengeance. He has been breaking down the wealth and power of Don Carlos ever since he got here a year ago.'

'What are you saying! You knew this and did nothing to stop it?'

'To my shame, no.'

'Then you can't be aware of the full range of this man's hatred. What of Grimani's ships?'

Bartolomeo froze. 'Surely you can't mean he had a hand in that? In the death of Paolo Grimani?'

Fra Sebastiano grew paler. 'I was not thinking of that, no. Yet it makes sense, in view of what I do know concerning Lorenzo. Could this Tomasso have arranged the attack on Grimani at sea?'

'He could have. He has spent many years trading with the East. He returned to Venice last week in a poor state of health. It was only after the night of the feast that I learned that his fever was caused by serious wounding. If he had travelled here quickly, overland, he could very easily have taken part in that battle. He has offered no explanation as to how he came by the hurts.'

'This must be what old Zia Carlina tried to tell me about dark angels,' cried Fra Sebastiano. 'Who else knows of this?'

There was a commotion outside the church. Bartolomeo looked across and saw Don Carlos arrive in a barge. He was dressed in a red cloak trimmed with ermine. Around him, were not festive guests, but armed men showing the emblem of the Arsenal guard. 'Grimani must have reached the same conclusions as we,' said Bartolomeo breathlessly. 'If he finds Tomasso, he will kill him and ask questions later.'

Fra Sebastiano pulled him towards the building, out of sight of the others. He said, 'The armed men have probably come to arrest Emlyn. If they take this Tomasso too, then he will answer for his crimes!'

Bartolomeo shook his head. 'Don Carlos will kill him to prevent the whole of Venice learning the truth. Grimani will salvage what he can of his diminished influence and probably be compensated by Tomasso's wealth for the misery he has suffered. You have not heard all Fra Sebastiano, but Tomasso may well find sympathy. Many in the Senate owe him favour and many will understand and even admire his actions. He is Venetian and we Venetians avenge the wrongs done against us. But what if father fights with son!'

'Then it is our duty to find them before further wrongs can be done. And to save the sacrificial innocents who have been dragged so insensitively through this insanity. Lord, I beseech thee, provider of the needy, grant to us a boat.'

A gondola slid into view, sweeping into the canal at a furious pace. Bartolomeo recognised the sky blue tunic of Jacopo. He cried out and waved. He said, 'Fra Sebastiano, truly thou art a holy man. You must have the ear of God.'

'Amen,' intoned the Franciscan. 'But I am a proud and ungracious man, for I prayed that the boat would carry your galley slave too. That is a wish God has denied me for my arrogance.'

Emlyn soon realised the drawbacks of his limited knowledge of the waterways. They all looked the same to him, nor had he expected pursuit so soon. If they were able to reach Riva degli Schiavoni without notice, they could lose themselves in the crowds and reach the place where Umbaldo waited with a rowing boat to take them out of Venice. It had all been arranged over emptied wine bottles the night before. Emlyn had drunk too much to keep his secrets to himself, but he did not regret his loose tongue and was grateful to Umbaldo for the help he promised. It was still possible on foot, if they could get away from the water unnoticed. Carmelia assured him that she knew the way over the bridges and through the passages. Emlyn's awkward handling of the boat was causing more and more delay, the gondola following, was catching up fast.

He managed to turn the vessel and punted it towards the embankment, while Carmelia squealed encouragement. Her eyes sparkled with mischief and her laughter clawed at his heart. He knew then that he had been right in returning for her. He could not bear to think of her married to Vincentini. Keeping one hand on an oar, he snatched at her hand as she leaned across and pulled her to her feet. They staggered across the boat and jumped the remaining distance to the steps of the canal. Emlyn pushed the boat out into the water with the oar, hoping that it would cause delay to the approaching gondola. Carmelia tugged at him, urging him to hurry. 'We are wasting time! We need to go that way,' she cried pointing. 'They will reach there before us because they will know the piazza.'

He still found time to hold her close and kiss her. Then he took her hand and they began to run. Buildings rose on three sides of the market square, closely packed together. A small archway and a cobbled street offered the only means of escape.

Already the gondola had pulled swiftly over, ahead of them. The boatman was skilled and sent the craft slipping over the water with the ease of a Lagoon duck. Four men jumped to the shore. Emlyn saw that he and Carmelia could not hope to escape, no matter how fast they ran.

They stopped. Emlyn knew that he would need all his skill now to escape by some other means. He pulled Carmelia behind him. She clung to him with a cry of fear.

Vincentini stepped off the gondola and stood regarding them with one eyebrow raised and his hands open in front of him; it was as if he offered them sympathy, for they had lost the game.

Facing him, Emlyn did not believe the same. He did feel cold with fear. He and Umbaldo had been drunk when they had hatched this scheme. Then, it had seemed simplicity itself, now it looked utterly foolish and had brought Emlyn to face this glittering dangerous man.

Emlyn had not thought for a moment that he'd be forced to fight for the freedom he and Carmelia desired. Behind him, Carmelia was silent. Would she expect him to fight? He remembered the book she had brought to him when he had lain sick in Geneva, Baldassar Castiglione, the perfect knight, chivalry, righteousness and justice. It is one thing, to pretend to live by such a code when not called to practice it, but quite another when faced with reality. I am not a courtier, nor am I even a gentleman. I am a nameless bastard. I have allowed my folly to cloud my reasoning and spurned help when offered. All of them, I have used like tools to gain my own ends. Now, only when love has claimed my heart, can I see the selfishness and the foolishness of my ambitions. I will not desert her to the fate arranged for her, she whom I have hurt more bitterly than the cruellest of slave masters. God forgive me. What little honour I have, I must now find to fight and die with.

Vincentini removed his hat and combed his fingers through his thick greying hair, then he replaced it; his eyes shaded by the wide brim. He walked towards them, his eyes on Carmelia. He held out his hand to her. 'Come my lady, we have a wedding to attend. We must not keep the guests of Grimani waiting, they may think that we have changed our minds.'

Emlyn stepped forward. He said, 'You did not give me a satisfactory answer to my challenge. I repeat that challenge now.'

'Challenge? But you know that I am to be wed. Where this not so still, I would not deem it fitting to cross swords with anything less than a gentleman, and he, not a beardless youth.'

'You will not take her from me,' said Emlyn calmly. 'Not unless you draw my life's blood first.'

Carmelia 's grip tightened on his arm. 'Emlyn, do not speak so!'

Emlyn pulled away. 'I am no puffed up gentleman, but you will cross swords with me! By all that I believe in, I swear you will not take her from me. She is all that I have, all that I hold dear to my heart. You shall not wed her, until I lie dead on this ground. By my honour I swear this.'

Emlyn caught at Carmelia, ignoring her weeping protest. He pushed her towards where Tomasso's men stood, watching with evident amusement. Emlyn stepped back and drew his sword.

Vincentini folded his arms across his chest. He looked down at his feet and sighed wearily. 'I had rather hoped to keep my clothing unsoiled,' he said contemptuously. 'Could we not postpone this, until a more suitable time?'

'Curse your black soul! Fight me you craven, gutless bastard! Coward I called you and coward I call you now. If you think her unworthy of the mettle of your sword, then make your peace and leave us.'

Vincentini's men held Carmelia securely. She cried out and sobbed, begging them both to cease in their antagonism.

Vincentini turned to her. 'Do not be distressed Donna Carmelia. I will not kill your troubadour, merely teach him a lesson. Now, be a good girl and cease your wailing, it distracts me.'

Emlyn stood in the piazza armed with his weapons, sword in his right hand, twelve inch dagger in the left. His mouth was dry with fear, his eyes wide, his limbs taunt as bow strings. He watched his opponent advance. Similarly armed, a contemptuous smile on his lips, Vincentini snapped the air with his blade and attacked.

There was no hesitation, a flicker of movement. A sharp click and slither as blades met. Emlyn sidestepped to avoid the silver flash of oncoming dagger. They broke apart and Vincentini gasped as if Emlyn's blade had caught him, but he quickly recovered and his laughter broke the silence between them. 'Are we to play? Are we to dance, you with lute and I with ire?' He came again, blade slashing.

Emlyn parried, stepping back and back again. The sword jarred in his hand, weakening his grip. His left hand came up with the dagger, desperately batting aside the longer blade as it drove towards his chest. He opponent disengaged, as yet, just playing, testing Emlyn's skill and strength. Emlyn's rapid footwork had kept him at bay. He was no swordsman, but he knew about fighting. Sheer strength and determination might give him a chance. His eyes darted quickly around the piazza. There were houses behind him, closed doors. There were enough objects scattered about to use if opportunity arose. Emlyn could not afford the honourable rules of swordplay. The dagger was more familiar to his hand. Even left handed, he got close enough to snag at shirt and doublet. Whenever he could, he used his knees, elbows and feet, but he could not catch Vincentini. He too, it seemed, was aware of the dirtier type of fighting, but already the strain was telling on him and Emlyn felt a surge of hope.

It was too late now to regret his lack of skill. If he was to die here on this foreign shore, then so be it. He had not heeded the warnings shadowing his future. Why not take Little Monk on? Had laughed Angelo, one night when the Sicilians had sparred in a tavern. They had all laughed and he with them. Why not take Emlyn on, he handles a sword like a plank, the finest plank wielder in Italy!

So far, Emlyn had fought in defence only, stunned by the speed of Vincentini's blade and the constant use of dagger. Vincentini's smile widened. He had judged his opponent to be lacking, and had need only to close in for the kill.

Emlyn braced himself and the fighting began in earnest. The long blades clattered together, slithered, clashed and chimed. Emlyn ducked, swerved from the dagger and backed frantically away from the stinging arch of fury. Sparks flew as his misjudged blade clashed against tile and stone, each time jarring his hand, further weakening his grip. Vincentini's attack was vicious, a whir of glittering silver. Only Emlyn's skittering footwork saved him from the point of sword and stabbing dagger. He could not attack.

Vincentini was a master swordsman. His mind controlled, his limbs obeyed, his eyes never drifted from their purpose. His elegant wrists, arms and shoulders were in perfect accord. Had it not been for his wounds and weakness, he would have defeated Emlyn within minutes. His blades were menacing and powerful. Once, twice, they broke through the erratic, unlearned defence, parting leather, linen and skin, coming away reddened. The daggers sparkled in the harsh light, up and over, darting like solid flame, swords flickering like serpent tongues.

Within the first few minutes, they had crossed the piazza, Emlyn forever backing, circling, using his sword as if it were a baton, warding off the raining blows, miraculously avoiding the brutal attack. Their breath was ragged. Their movements were repeated in the dancing shadows, back and forth across the square. Emlyn used every ruse and trick he could think of. His right arm was numb, locked about the hilt in a death-like grip. His dagger, better managed, was unable to break through. Each feint was instantly dealt with. After his first vicious speed, Vincentini had visibly slowed, but nothing escaped him, he allowed no opening. Emlyn recoiled incessantly, his palms slick, his shirt and jerkin soaked with sweat and trickles of blood.

Tomasso had soon realised the weakness of the blade that tried to better him. The youth was incapable of riposte or counter thrust. Tomasso had not broken effectively through the wild defence nor managed to send the mismanaged blade spinning away, Emlyn managed it like a broadsword more often than not. Could he not see that fail he must against superior skill?

Tomasso moved in. He was already tired, his limbs beginning to drag. He chose a different approach, which his inexperienced opponent could not be aware of. With both blades Tomasso attacked to the left. His sword slashed at shoulder and upper arm. His dagger sliced across the knuckles of the dagger hand. The knife fell. Tomasso leapt back, to avoid the sword descending from the right like an axe. He was not quick enough and felt the sting as the point scratched his cheek. He moved in again, hoping to find his antagonist shaken. Tomasso put as much strength as he could into the downward blow. Emlyn's sword flew from his hand and clattered on the cobbles.

Tomasso cursed himself for not following it through to the finish. He was slowing now, feeling the giddiness return. He had forgotten the agility of this youth, shown on the night of Grimani's feast. Emlyn ducked, somersaulted backwards and scrambled to where his sword lay. He swept it up and gripped it with two hands, crouching, ready for the next assault.

Tomasso lowered his point to the ground. If this was to continue, he could not put in the same vigorous effort; let the boy do all the running about and exhaust himself. His blade would never strike true. It was only his foolish stubbornness that had prevented him from realising it. Breathless, Tomasso said, 'Yield. Preserve your life and walk from this a better man.'

Emlyn spat at him, too exhausted to do anything else.

Tomasso stood quiet, a respite to get his breathing under control, to fight off the waves of dizzying pain from the unhealed wound dealt by that other youth. There was something about the two that was similar, it was not his skill with a sword. Tomasso had hoped that he could easily break through this awkward defence, to teach the boy a lesson and send him off. But he could see in the burning eyes, the courage and determination. It could only end in blood. Tomasso stood back and allowed Emlyn to retrieve his dagger. Then he moved in.

It was as if the sun stood still, fixed in the heavens, harsh and bright upon the scintillating blades burning the figures, one richly clad in dazzling braid and gems, the other dull in leather and torn cloth, blood soaking through at shoulder and chest. The girl who watched was motionless, frozen in the grip of her captors.

Emlyn had better control this time. The blades touched, engaged and broke off, as swift as light. He attacked thrice, each time Tomasso caught and turned the stroke aside. Emlyn retreated to defence against the strong, pliant blade and the dagger wielded in the exquisite dance of death. There was nothing Tomasso did not know of the classic sword play. Even in this, there was something of grim, glittering beauty, of reluctant admiration. Emlyn persisted, met every brilliant attack, clashing, beating and delaying the ultimate conclusion.

In his pride Tomasso fought expertly, intensely fast, ignoring the increasing pain. Constantly he hit Emlyn's blade away, moving out of the dagger's reach, freeing his sword for the lunge. Each time, Emlyn skittered away and came back again. The blades met, fused by light, the flats slapped and scarped. Emlyn's blade slithered down and hit Tomasso's counter guard and locked.

Using all the strength he could summon, Tomasso wrenched his sword free and stepped back, ducking under the glittering dagger that followed. Had he his normal energy and speed, he would have won against this fearless wretch long since. As it was, his weakness made him slow and his swordplay was becoming careless. He realised that he was stretched to the limit, his breathing rough, his concentration blurred by extreme pain.

Then he saw his advantage and took it. Emlyn's arm was rigid, his blade level. Tomasso forced it down with the flat of his own and circled it. Emlyn did not recognise the disarming move. He struggled to free his blade.

Tomasso moved in to end the game. He relaxed his right hand and brought up the left, using the dagger hilt to hit Emlyn's weapon from his hand. Emlyn's dagger spun away. He wrenched his sword back, twisting out of range, his hair whipping across his face. He came back with starling speed. His bunched fist pounded into Tomasso's side.

White hot pain drove Tomasso staggering backwards. He dropped his own dagger, clutching at his side. Blood welled between his fingers.

Emlyn stepped back breathing heavily, sweat running down face and neck. His eyes were wild, but registered the surprise he felt from the effect of his blow.

Tomasso recovered quickly, his own sheer will dominating the agony. Now it must finish. His next advance was merciless. He drove Emlyn the length of the piazza, drove him to stagger and stumble, frantically warding off the ferocity of the relentless sword. Tomasso's blade whirred in a blur of glittering death, a scythe chopping the air where his fleet-footed opponent had stood a moment before. He beat Emlyn further towards the edge of the square where the water flowed black and sullen.

As the sword rushed towards him, Emlyn suddenly dropped to his haunches, bleeding hand to the ground, weakened sword uplifted to skewer Tomasso as he came.

Tomasso's blade clashed through the air where Emlyn's head had been a split second earlier. Tomasso stumbled. Experience saved him from the intended piercing. He twisted away and fell heavily, his sword yet upraised to fend off the renewed attack. He was shaking, his breath came in short gasps, his side burned with fire. To save himself, he kicked out as Emlyn came. Emlyn stumbled back from the force of the blow. It gave Tomasso enough time to rise and catch his breath.

Emlyn was slower to rise and recover. He was too tired, his arms aching from shoulders to wrists. He fought like mad man, immune to the slashes and nicks he failed to avoid. He was aware of the nearness of the canal. Tomasso would not make the same mistake twice, he drove him once more towards it. Emlyn ducked under the sword and ran to one side, hitting down as he did so. He gained nothing, the water was once more behind him.

Tomasso relied on that stretch of murky water. He looked to it as a saviour and fought steadily to gain the advantage he needed. Black spots appeared before his eyes, he shook his head to clear away the dizziness. He used his sword like a whip, allowing no chance for the lesser blade to win through. He relentlessly drove Emlyn back, knowing that this was the last he could expect of his draining strength.

Emlyn went down, caught by a discarded lobster pot. His blade was still for the fraction of a second which Tomasso needed. With his only remaining power, Tomasso drove the deadly length of steel to cleave the unprotected neck. A flicker of regret behind it.

Tomasso's sword fell on the barrel of a arquebus.

'Enough!' Cried the strident voice of Bartolomeo Varini.

The shock was enough to lose his grip on the sword. Tomasso fell to his knees, utterly exhausted and blind with pain, vaguely aware of outside interference.

In that glittering moment, when Emlyn had seen death descend, he had thrown himself backwards and splashed into the canal. The water closed over his head. He didn't struggle, he was scarcely conscious of thought.

Fra Sebastiano rolled up his sleeve and plunged his arm into the dark water. He could see the top of Emlyn's head, hair waving like seaweed as it spread out from the still form. Fra Sebastiano reached down, grasped a handful of hair and pulled.

Once his head had cleared the surface, Emlyn began to struggle and thrash about. Fra Sebastiano did not have the strength to assist further. It was Jacopo who pulled Emlyn to the side and heaved him half out on the step. Emlyn lay retching and coughing, streaming with blood and canal water. Jacopo produced a flask of aqua vitae and forced some between Emlyn's lips. He hit Jacopo's hand away and came reeling to his feet, clawing at the wet hair that marred his sight. Jacopo stood back.

Carmelia struggled out of the loosened grasp of Tomasso's men and ran to Emlyn's side. Tomasso too, was standing. Emlyn glared at him over Carmelia's head.

Bartolomeo and Fra Sebastiano exchanged glances. They could all hear the sound of running feet and the unmistakeable clatter of weapons. Fra Sebastiano grasped Emlyn's shoulder. 'You have to get away from here Emlyn. Grimani is coming with armed men to arrest you both.'

Tomasso backed a few steps to lean against a warehouse wall. He had retrieved his weapon and stood it between his feet, resting his hands on the hilt. He closed his eyes.

Bartolomeo moved towards him. 'Tomasso?' he said. He thought his employer looked terrible.

The eyes opened and regarded him vacantly. With a jerk he let go the sword and shook his head. Then he bent to pick it up once more, his expression better controlled.

Helping him, Bartolomeo said, 'Get into the gondola, Jacopo can have you away from here in no time. Tomasso? This young man here, whom you have nearly killed is, he is Anna's son.'

Tomasso threw his head back with a burst of bitter laughter. 'Another one?'

'You are not listening to me!' snapped Bartolomeo. The sound of the approaching guard came nearer. If they did not leave now, they would all be trapped.

Tomasso dragged shaking fingers through his dishevelled hair and assumed a more serious expression. 'Go on,' he invited.

'Don't you see? Anna did not die at sea as we believed.'

'I know.'

'You know? Then why? Why this path of destructive vengeance?'

Tomasso straightened, one hand on his side where blood soaked through his clothing. He looked worn to death, but his voice was stronger when he spoke, strong enough to command the attention of them all. He said, 'The wrong done to my wife was but one. Have you forgotten 'Tolomeo the sickening stench of burning flesh? Have you stopped your ears against the agonized screams of women consumed by flame?'

'Tomasso I was not there,' said Bartolomeo softly.

'By all in heaven, what are you saying?' gasped Fra Sebastiano.

Tomasso continued. 'Do you not hear the wailing of the murdered, those stabbed to death in dark places where none could bear witness? Bury the past, is that what you would have me do? I have lived there in that time. There where revenge has been my succour.'

'Not like this!' cried Fra Sebastiano. 'What you have done is devil's work.'

Tomasso ignored him. Instead, his eyes rested on Emlyn. They had fought with vicious intent and near succeeded in killing each other. Emlyn returned the scrutinizing gaze, his brow furrowed in puzzlement.

Tomasso said, 'Anna's son? But not a Grimani.'

Emlyn's eyes lowered. He said, 'If you were known to my mother, I hope you were kinder to her than others were.'

'Your mother was my own dear wife,' Tomasso answered softly. 'Could it be that you are a child we made between us? Or are you the spawn of some vile slave dealer with which Grimani exchanged her for gold?'

Emlyn took a step towards him, anger again alight in his eyes. Fra Sebastiano restrained him.

Bartolomeo stepped between them. 'If we are to discover the truth, this is not the place to do so. Tomasso, there is no time!'

Tomasso walked past him and stood before Emlyn. He said, 'I am happy that my sword did not end your life. Son or not, your courage is seldom found. If you find a teacher you will make a formidable opponent.' He paused and took Carmelia's hand, smiling at her. He put her hand in Emlyn's and pushed them gently to the water edge, where the gondola bobbed up and down. 'Jacopo, take them both as fast and as far as you are able.'

'Messer Tomasso,' Jacopo said, a plea in his voice,

'No: I will remain. I can delay Grimani for a short time. There are matters we have yet to broach. Do as I bid. Now.'

Emlyn helped Carmelia climb into the boat, then he turned back and said, 'I will not leave you to face him alone.'

Tomasso smiled. 'You are the cause of his ire. Will you have him ruin another woman's life? If you are not here, no harm will befall the rest of us. Act the gentleman Emlyn Tomas, for surely you have proved that you have it in you. Take your princess and rescue her from the wrath of the dragon.'

Emlyn knelt and bowed his head. 'There is much left unsaid between us. Be you father or not, will you grant us your blessing and forgive me for wounding you?'

'You have both,' said Tomasso.

His eyes were filled with pain as he watched the gondola slip speedily away. 'You did not wound me,' he said to himself, 'I was wounded a long time ago by the same love you now have for your princess.'

Through the archway came the first of the Arsenotti. They were shouting.

Heavy with sadness, Bartolomeo said, 'You should have gone with them. Now Grimani will kill you.'

'And you 'Toloemo, will stay and pick up the pieces.'

'I did once say as much, didn't I? You said that there would be pieces to pick up, should any want them, but they would not be yours.'

Tomasso dropped his sword and straightened his shoulders. 'Then you must ensure that this is dealt with in fairness. I am unarmed, and, if truth be told, I could not endure another duel with swords. But, give me strength and the opportunity, and I will win just as well with words.'

Then they were surrounded. Tomasso's men put hands to weapons, but did not draw them when Tomasso commanded them to be still. Don Carlos Grimani was the last to arrive. An elderly man, whose intelligence lived, shrewd as a fox, behind the pursed eyes, the many-chinned face, the giant bulk swathed in ermine-trimmed velvet. His tiny eyes glittered coldly. 'Where is my daughter Capaccio?' he demanded.

Fra Sebastiano answered, 'The young birds have flown, Don Carlos. We were unable to prevent their escape. It was some time ago.'

Don Carlos shouted to his men and some ran off to pursue the gondola. Then the Don turned his gaze on the man who had brought about his ruin. 'Tomasso Capaccio, in the name of God, I arrest you. In the name of my grandsons Lorenzo and Paolo, I condemn you to Hell's eternal damnation. May the skin on your bones be split and burned and your eyes be plucked out and fed to you. May your genitals ...'

'Don Carlos, this is unseemly,' interrupted Fra Sebastiano.

'... be roasted in the fire pit in front of your own severed head. May your heart be torn from you and ...'

'Is that before or after I have eaten my eyes?' asked Tomasso.

'In the name of justice!' cried Bartolomeo, the lawyer. 'I beseech you, let us not be overwrought. We are sensible men here.'

'Justice?' said Tomasso, with a trace of amusement. 'Justice, that jewel of inestimable value. Yes: let us all seek justice. Do what you will Grimani, I am ready.'

Don Carlos snarled, 'I would murder you where you stand, but such an easy end would display a mercy I cannot find it in my heart to allow, it lacks profound suffering.'

'Then lead me to the Senate, let me answer your accusations,' Tomasso said. 'Then we will see who is forced to swallow his eyes!'

'You are a traitor to the Republic of Venice,' continued Grimani, a glint of knowledge in his shrewd eyes. 'You dabble with the infidel. Are you even a Christian, I wonder? I am secure in my position, I have nothing to fear from your untruths.'

'Untruths? Who here has mentioned untruths?' said Tomasso.

Bartolomeo looked at him sharply. Tomasso's voice had weakened. He swayed on his feet. He stepped back to the support of the wall, folding his arms across the cloak Bartolomeo had lent him to conceal the tell tale signs of the duel he had fought.

'The day is insufferably hot,' put in Fra Sebastiano mildly. 'I suggest that we retire to more comfortable surroundings.'

'By all means,' said Don Carlos. 'But Capaccio remains my prisoner.'

'Then we shall accompany him,' offered Bartolomeo, ignoring Tomasso's glare. 'Lest any be tempted to do violence,' he added.

Grimani's men moved towards Tomasso and led him to the waiting boat. They did not touch him, he seemed to hold them at bay by the scorn of his eyes alone. Before he boarded he turned to face Bartolomeo and said 'Go to the Ducal Palace and find Ser Sebastiano Erizzo, he is uncle to Marco Erizzo, who captains the *Cornucopia*. Tell him what has happened here and be guided by him.'

'Erizzo the Senator?' Bartolomeo replied in surprise. 'I think you would be better served if I stayed with you.'

Hearing their exchange, Fra Sebastiano turned from the boat and came to stand beside them. 'I will stay with Messer Tomasso,' he said 'There are a few things I wish to speak with him about.'

Tomasso smiled tiredly. 'Considering the boy I nearly killed? Do not mistake me Brother, I am indebted to you and value your company. Left alone with Grimani, I don't think I will survive for very long.'

This was what Bartolomeo feared and he too was grateful to the old Franciscan. But why must he go now to the Ducal Palace?'

Seeing his doubt, Tomasso said, 'I think this matter would be better placed in the hands of the Senate. Seek out Ser Erizzo and tell him this ...'

Don Carlos noticed the delay and his voice rang out, ordering his men to bring the prisoner aboard the boat where he waited.

Tomasso held up a hand as if to quiet him. The men moved closer put did not touch Tomasso. Bartolomeo marvelled at his command. Tomasso's long fingered hands trembled and the rings flashed in the fierce light.

He looked directly at his manager and spoke softly. 'Speak these lines to Erizzo, Tolomeo and recite them exactly.

'On stranded isle the sea doth moan and casts her frothy, milk-white foam,

Upon this shore of sea-born land, love's first step has trod the sand.'

The time is nigh, the youthful moon walks forth to rule where lovers swoon.

Crowned with a single, silver star, she casts her ruby light afar.'

Bartolomeo stared at him incomprehensibly, sure that his employer was raving in fever.

'Repeat them to me,' said Tomasso.

Bartolomeo responded without fault. Then Don Carlos roared and broke the tense stillness. Tomasso allowed himself to be led away. Fra Sebastiano followed, his white head bent and his old fingers gathering up the rosary at his waist. Bartolomeo turned away reluctantly. He broke into a run as he crossed the square to make his way towards the Ducal Palace. The words of Tomasso's rhyme ran repetitively through his mind.

Chapter 50 Venice Escape

The air was still and hot. Not a sail nor a pennant stirred on mast, not a scrap of washing fluttered. The insufferable heat had driven most people indoors. The waterways of Venice and the narrow streets were still and silent.

Uncomfortable in the heat, Carmelia had taken off three of the stiff underdresses, though she could not bring herself to abandon the costly wedding dress. The horror of the duel in the piazza was behind them, at last her thoughts were free to reason. Beside her, immune to the heat, Emlyn was shivering, his teeth chattering like leper clappers. He had not spoken, his eyes stared straight ahead, his mind had closed in after the appalling events. Carmelia wished that she could feel the same. She had known the madness which had crept upon her during the past weeks; her bursts of temper and her fits of uncontrollable tears were growing demonstrations of her inability to cope with life outside the protection of convent walls. Emlyn had been her strength during the journey over the Alps. He had not known how much she had depended on the mere sight of him or how long she had lain awake thinking of nothing else. She had never questioned who he was, she had not wanted to know. He became what she had wanted him to be, a knight for the court of Urbino, a prince who lived by the code of Castione, of course he had been none of these things, but that had not mattered, so enamoured with the lustre of fantasy had he been in her eyes. Then it had ended, Venice had snatched her dream away. Of Emlyn, it had taken away the illusion and cast him in the mould of an ordinary man. He had been thrust out of her sight and out of her reach. When the cruel demands of her new and frightening life had swamped her, he had not been there to still her fears.

So who was this Emlyn Tomas, if he was not that man she had thought him? She had assumed because he travelled with the Englishman that they were connected through the wool business, but they had parted and Emlyn and come alone to Venice. She could not fully understand what had passed between Emlyn and Tomasso, yet she was certain that she had altered the plans of both. She had been willing to kill herself for one and because of the other. She need not do so now, nor could she; that madness was behind her. Somehow, witnessing the two men fight, she had been made aware of her own stupidity and of the inexperience that had led her to make all the wrong decisions.

The boatman, Jacopo broke the silence with the clank of his pole as he put it down. He pulled off his blue tunic and offered it to Emlyn.

Emlyn shook his head, he was already steaming dry in the fierce sun. Then he changed his mind, recognising the kindness of the gesture. He pulled the garment on. Carmelia was grateful, it covered the mess underneath, though he did not seem seriously hurt.

'Do we bob up and down until we reach Constantinople?' Jacopo asked. 'Do you remember how you wished to go there?'

Emlyn nodded, without returning Jacopo's smile.

Carmelia burst out, 'Can you take us to the mainland?'

Emlyn touched her arm. 'Cariad, we can't go yet. If we could reach Riva degli Schiavoni, I have a boat hidden near there, with provisions for our journey and a friend who will help us. Unfortunately I do not know where we now are. Jacopo?'

'It is not far, easier to go on foot. I myself could take you to a place of safety and go for the boat myself. There are boats following us, though they have not seen us yet. I could put you ashore and continue as if you are still with me. They will not catch Jacopo.'

'There is no place of safety in all Venice,' moaned Carmelia.

After a pause, Emlyn said, 'She is right, We should go now Jacopo, I feel that we will not have another chance.'

Jacopo never knew what it was that killed him. One moment he was straightening from the pole thrust, the next, he was clawing at his throat, dying as he hit the water.

Carmelia screamed.

Emlyn leaped up and tried to catch Jacopo, but he was not quick enough. The pole splashed into the canal. Another arrow thudded into the wood beside him. He pulled back and began to paddle with his hand away from where the shafts had been fired. After a moment, Carmelia bent and added her efforts. Jacopo's falling body had nudged the gondola towards the shore and the distance was short. As soon as they bumped to the embankment, they scrambled ashore and ran towards the buildings to escape the sight of their pursuers.

The harsh light had softened. A faint haze of mist radiated from the sun, the harbinger of storm clouds that lay on the horizon. The bruised greys and mustard yellows blazed intermittently with stabs of blue light.

The canals and Lagoon shimmered with silver, as still as mirrors. For all that, the heat had not lessened, it grew stronger and with it, the rising stink of rotting fish and refuse, of excrement and stagnant water. The streets, the houses, the churches and the squares remained shrouded in eerie silence.

Emlyn moved furtively, he warned Carmelia to remain quiet. The silence was so profound that he felt that if a needle were dropped it who send strident echoes around the piazza. They ran down the Via delle Rossini, that ran parallel to the Grande Canal and led to the Rialto bridge.

Clutching her skirt, Carmelia hurried behind, her slippers making no sound on the cobbled paving. The shock of what had happened had left her limbs numb. She wished they had been able to stay on the water. Emlyn had given her a dagger that she carried with distaste. She watched Emlyn with new eyes. Outwardly, he looked a ragged mess, incapable of the task that faced them. But she knew the lines of developed muscle under the torn clothing, the inner strength which gave him the grace of movement displayed in love making and in playful acrobatics. She had seen too, the courage and determination with which he had faced Tomasso, a courage that she could not hope to emulate. He was not the prince she would have him be, but she loved him all the more for that. Yet, now he frightened her. She did not know the man she was running off with. He had assumed an air of authority that she could not question. She did everything he bid her.

He came suddenly to a stop and she collided into him. 'Be still!' he warned.

They had come to a crossing where the Rio delle Giovan intersected the Rio da Cersa. They could see the Grand Canal through a gap in the tall houses. They hid in a doorway and peered around the corner. Carmelia heard a splash and the lazy coo of a pigeon. A dog barked, a child began to cry. A bell chimed and then another.

'Wait here,' whispered Emlyn. He stepped out of hiding, crouched down and scuttled along a line of empty fish barrels on the wharf. Carmelia lost sight of him and immediately felt afraid. Clutching the knife, she followed, using the same caution.

Emlyn had not gone far, he had rounded the corner and stopped. Carmelia paused and crouched down, so that he would not see her. Why so cautious? If she had been left to herself, she would have hitched up her skirts and run all the way to wherever they were going. She was nervous of Emlyn's silence and of the anger that burned in his eyes. He had called her the name her liked to give her, so surely the anger was not directed towards herself. Morwyn yr Eira. Snow Maiden.

But he was withdrawn, silent and reserved. Had he guessed that she had meant to take her own life? She had wanted him to know, she had desperately wanted him to come for her and he had. She felt a wave of shame burn her face and tighten her stomach. She could see the back of his head. His hair was dry, fluffed up like a floss flower. He was very still, listening. He had guessed that she was there. Without looking, his hand waved her back. Carmelia returned to the doorway, Emlyn close behind her.

'What is it ?' she whispered fiercely.

He lifted his hand and brushed a damp strand of hair from her forehead. His eyes were soft and his hand gentle; it was filthy and stained with blood. 'Are you tired?' he asked.

'Why? Are we going to swim?' Carmelia found a brave smile for him.

Emlyn brushed her cheek. 'You will have to swim for both of us if we do,' he replied, keeping his voice to a whisper. 'There are three men by the bridge. They saw us escape the boat and are expecting us to cross.'

Carmelia leaned around him and stared out into the sunlight while trying to stay concealed. She could see nothing at first; then the two men appeared and walked in their direction. She snapped her head back. 'They are from my father's household. Emlyn, let us go from here!'

Emlyn said, 'There are also four behind us. We are better off staying here.'

As he spoke, a bank of heavy grey cloud obscured the sun. A feather-light breeze caressed their faces. A soft, faraway rumble announced the coming of the storm. Emlyn smiled at her. 'No one will find us Cariad. Do as I say and Venice will talk of this for years.'

'I think we have already achieved that,' Carmelia smiled. 'Lead the way Orpheus. I thy Eurydice, will follow. But not I hope, to the underworld.'

'Trust me,' he answered, 'I've done this before.' He pulled her close into the deep shadow, his arms about her.

She could feel the heat of his skin against her back. Her heart thumped so wildly that she thought it would betray them with its drumming. The footsteps came closer, followed by the clang of scabbard against stone. The sound seemed to thunder through the narrow passage. Carmelia stiffened and held her breath. Emlyn silently kissed the top of her head. She got the impression that he was enjoying himself.

The guards came, paused and then continued on past the dark opening. The steps receded, until they met up with the others coming from the opposite direction. The words they exchanged were just a mumble. Then there was silence, descending like a blanket over Carmelia and Emlyn as they clung together in the doorway.

After some time, Carmelia whispered, 'Let's run. Please Emlyn, let's run. I cannot stand this creeping about. What are we waiting for?'

'They will not give up the search so easily. If we go now they will see us. We will wait for the rain.'

'That could be hours!'

Emlyn's arms tightened about her. 'I can think of no better place to be,' he said. 'You can tell me why your father has arrested Vincentini, I mean Capaccio.'

'Because he is a murderer and he was supposed to be dead. My father sent him to the galleys years ago, before I was born.'

'So he was the gem merchant who fought with your half brother Roberto over my mother.' said Emlyn. 'Fra Sebastiano told me about that. It would explain the piece of jewellery she left to me. The gem around your neck comes from the same necklace. So does the earring that he wears. It must be the connection, it must be what my mother wanted me to know.'

'But you do not believe it?' asked Carmelia.

Emlyn shrugged. 'If Capaccio is brought before the Senate he will denounce your father's crimes against my mother, Anna. Did you know that Grimani sold her into slavery?'

Carmelia shook her head. 'Then there is nothing this Tomasso can do without proof and she is the only one who could provide it. It would be his word against my father's and my father will have some story concerning the incident. The authorities will believe him because he is still highly thought of in Venice. It would be better for us to get as far from here as possible now and forget the lot of them.'

'Believe me Cariad, if I were free, I would do just that. I came here to discover who I am. Should I run off now that all is made clear? To leave this unknown father to face imprisonment and death?'

'Emlyn you nearly killed him yourself. Just because you find that you are his son, you cannot free him from the crimes he has committed against my family.' Carmelia was growing impatient.

'No,' said Emlyn quietly. 'But I can stand by him and I am living proof that cannot be gainsaid. Capaccio's crimes were in retaliation, an eye for an eye.'

'Revenge!' scoffed Carmelia. 'Capaccio was punished for the murder of Roberto. Roberto was killed because of something he did. How long must it go on? Why must you and I become involved? It is all in the past. What about our future?'

Emlyn adjusted his position, they were cramped in the small space. He said, 'I agree that two wrongs do not make a right. Nonetheless, I have to do what I can. I am bound by duty as his son.'

'But what about us!' Carmelia repeated desperately. 'What would be the point of this day's events?' She struggled to free herself and turned to face him. 'Why did you come for me Emlyn?'

'It is not only duty, it is also blood,' he replied calmly, ignoring her last question. 'I could never hold my head up again if I run now.'

'My father will have you killed like that boatman, as soon as you make an appearance. Emlyn why did you come for me?'

He kissed her and she pulled away. He dropped his eyes. 'You will be safe Cariad.'

'I will not go back!'

'There is no danger now. You will not be facing a forced marriage, now that Tomasso's true intent has been revealed.' Emlyn pulled her to her feet beside him.

Carmelia stamped her foot. 'He is an evil man!' she cried. 'He has caused ruin and hardship for my father. He has killed innocent people to satisfy his vengeance. How can you now say that he is more important than I am?'

'I don't,' said Emlyn turning away. 'But, for once, I am not considering my own desires. I must try to free him. I may have a chance. Carmelia please believe in me.'

'I won't go back!'

'Then let me take you some place where you will be safe until this is over. Then I will come for you and we will leave this place and never look back.'

Carmelia bit back her tears. 'We can leave now Emlyn,' she pleaded. 'Going back is foolish and dangerous. If you are killed,' she stopped, biting her words back. She could not tell him of the child that grew within her. To do so would force him to agree to follow her wish. As much as she wanted him to, she could not use the child as a lever.

He held her at arms length, his gentle eyes upon her. 'I came for you Cariad because I love you,' he said. 'I will not be killed. I promise.'

She looked up at him, suddenly believing in him and accepting his decision. 'Where will you take me?'

'To a family I know and trust. They will care for you until I return.

Carmelia pulled him towards her, burying her head on his shoulder and soaking the blue cloth with tears. Some emotion inside her seemed to erupt like the breaking of a dam.

He caressed her hair and whispered in his own tongue. When she was composed, he tilted her head and kissed her softly, smiling when he drew away. He took care to look around before they left their concealment. The first heavy drops of rain hit the ground and rattled off the roof tiles.

Bartolomeo Varini's first impulse had been to stay with Tomasso, but then reason had cautioned that he could best serve his employer and friend from outside. They were faced now with a legal conflict. Bartolomeo had set off at once.

Grimani's men did not take Tomasso to the prison near the Ducal Palace. Instead they took him to Don Carlos' house and had him locked up in a lower room. Fra Sebastiano offered to stay with the captive and no persuasion from Don Carlos would sway him from his resolve.

For many years Fra Sebastiano had been concerned one way or another, with the life of Emlyn Tomas. Now that the mysteries were about to unfold, he would see the story to its end. He also had a great deal to say to Tomasso Capaccio. Tomasso remained silent on the way to the palace; even Don Carols' berating tongue would not bring a response. Fra Sebastiano guessed that the captive was harbouring his reserves for the forthcoming conflict.

Once they reached the grand house, Grimani had them both shown to a small room with sparse furnishings. He sent them wine and food and his own physician to see to Tomasso's needs. Seated in the only chair in the room, Tomasso waved the medical man away, but accepted the draft of poppy syrup, swallowing it in one action. Then he ordered the physician from the room. The man objected strongly and put up a querulous protest. Fra Sebastiano banged on the door. When it opened, he grasped handfuls of the physician's clothing and shoved him out, banging the door behind him. Fra Sebastiano knew enough about sword wounds and did not have much faith in what he knew of Grimani's man.

When he turned back into the room, Tomasso was violently sick. Afterwards Fra Sebastiano helped him to the narrow pallet and unfastened the gold lacing of the soaked doublet. Tomasso was scarcely conscious, the vomiting had weakened him considerably.

Fra Sebastiano whispered a prayer of thanksgiving when he saw that Emlyn had not attempted to take the life of his newly found father, these hurts were not recently taken. The chest wound was serious. Although there were signs that it had been well cared for, Tomasso had undone that care by not resting until it was healed. The wound had become inflamed and had sent Tomasso into a rising fever. Fra Sebastiano worked in silence, his deft hands repairing the damage with as little discomfort as possible. When he had finished, Tomasso's fever-bright eyes opened and studied him.

Retiring to the chair, Fra Sebastiano did not speak the chastising words that he felt should be voiced. Instead, he spoke of what he knew concerning Emlyn's childhood and upbringing, of his schooling with the Jesuits, the influence of his grandfather and of the sheer determination that had brought him to Venice to seek answers to the mysteries of his past. The old priest's voice rose and fell his own emotion unhidden. When he was done, the silence stretched between them interrupted only by the faint, muffled sound of church bells.

Tomasso stirred in discomfort. His eyes were underscored with shadows, his skin the colour of sheeting. He had endured both the physical pain and the mental anguish in silence. He closed his eyes and said, 'It is too late now.'

'You may be right,' said Fra Sebastiano unfeelingly. 'I can't see you escaping Grimani's accusations. But I think you knew that before you began. Was it all worthwhile?'

'It matters not, good brother. I will answer to God soon enough, maybe long before the executioners shadow falls upon me.'

Fra Sebastiano rose and walked to where the flagon of wine stood, left by Grimani's servant. He filled a cup, adding a pinch of a nostrum which he'd found in the physician's medical bag. While he worked, he said, 'With rest and care you will live to stand trial. There is always hope that you will escape the fate Grimani has devised for you. You do have some influence with the Senate.'

'Its too late for me to get to know the boy,' Tomasso responded. 'I am unable to be a father to him but I can provide for him. Do you think he would accept responsibility for the Spice Company?'

Fra Sebastiano looked up in surprise and returned to the bedside. 'He would need help, for he is young and inexperienced in the world of merchants.'

'He would have all the help he needs. Bartolomeo would stay with him as manager and most of the staff would be willing.'

'You would do this for him without even being sure that he is really your son?'

'He is Anna's son,' said Tomasso. 'He could marry his Carmelia if he held such a position in Venice.'

'Doing this, I fear that Don Carlos Grimani would get his hands on your wealth in spite of all.'

Tomasso seemed to sink further into the pillow. 'I would ask Emlyn and Carmelia to wait a few years before they were married. Emlyn would have a chance then to learn the business and to convince the Senate that he is a worthy suitor for the girl.'

Fra Sebastiano nodded slowly. 'This would certainly solve their problem. It is an exceptional offer. But what about you?'

The corners of Tomasso's mouth lifted in a faint smile. 'The physician's cup was poisoned,' he said.

Fra Sebastiano looked at him with an expression of disbelief.

'Believe me, I would not have made myself vomit at present, unless there had been dire need.'

In stunned silence Fra Sebastiano found the cup that had contained the poppy syrup. He sniffed it and wiped the inside with a finger, tasting tentatively. He frowned; there was a bitterness there that shouldn't have been. Could it be true? 'Why would Grimani attempt such a deed?' he asked.

'It does not make sense,' Tomasso answered softly. 'He has great need to recover his reputation and restore his wealth. I assumed that he hoped to do so by accusing me. If he won his argument, the Senate would see that he was compensated for his loses and this would come from my own purse. He stands to gain nothing by my death now.' He paused then added, 'I think my death was intended by another.'

'Perhaps Grimani has no wish to dig up the past. 'Fra Sebastiano chewed his lip in thought. 'Having you dead would ensure that no one would ever hear of it. As it is, the misfortune that has befallen him by your own doing, places him in a strong position when he cries to the Senate for justice. Tomasso?

Fra Sebastiano was not surprised to see the merchant asleep. Tomasso's ringed hands lay across the new bandaging and his face was as peaceful as a child's. Left alone, he would be as vulnerable as a child, powerless to defend himself against an assassin. Fra Sebastiano felt forced to remain, to guard against such a possibility. He considered the problem Tomasso had put forth.

Who else had a grievance against Capaccio?

All his vengeance was directed against Grimani. In other quarters, Tomasso was spoken of with great respect.

While he waited, Fra Sebastiano send for paper ink and quills, for Tomasso to write his will when he was able. The old Friar sat on a low stool and folded his hands on his knee, his rosary running through his fingers. He was nearly asleep when the door opened suddenly.

His fellow Franciscan, Lorenzo burst into the room holding a dagger at his side. He crossed the floor and stood for some time. His hands were clenched, white fists; one gripped the hilt of a Venetian dagger. He stared down at Vincentini.

Fra Sebastiano watched in silence. Tomasso was unconscious, seemingly innocent, unaware of the blade that hovered above him. It was obvious to the old Franciscan that Lorenzo had reached the same conclusion as he had, Tomasso was responsible not only for the death of Paolo, but also for his own cruel maiming.

When he spoke, Lorenzo's voice was surprisingly calm. 'I'm going to kill him. God help me!'

'It is simple. And can be done without the assistance of the Almighty,' Fra Sebastiano replied quietly. 'It fact, this is the best opportunity you could wish for. He lies there unconscious of your presence and unaware of your intent. Plunge the knife into his heart while you can. He cannot defend himself nor make his peace with God before death claims his soul. Lorenzo, it is as easy as gutting the fish that you cleaned for me in Milan, remember? It was that day when we first spoke of your half-brother Emlyn. You look now upon the father that Emlyn came so far to find, a man who dearly loved your mother. Your heart is too great for this vile deed Lorenzo. If this is your grandfather's wish, then let him do the deed.'

'You do not know,' Lorenzo responded. 'My grandfather is a ruined man. He walks about muttering obscenities. And I know that Paolo's soul will not find peace until his murder is avenged. The strength of blood cries in my veins!'

Fra Sebastiano shook his head. 'No, my young friend, that is not the truth. You are called to serve God. You are sworn to poverty, chastity and obedience. Murder is no less called murder when done with the hand of vengeance.'

'I cannot forgive the wrongs he has done against us!' Lorenzo's voice rose. He twirled the blade nervously in his hand.

'Your duty is first to God. You know this better than any. And have always known that God chose you to serve Him. You have defied your grandfather for this choice. Can you stain your hands now with the blood of this man? Lorenzo, he loved your mother so absolutely that he has been driven his whole life by the need to avenge her.'

Lorenzo's eyes turned at last towards him, they were bright with anger. 'His devotion was not great enough to stop him from the maiming and murder of her sons! Am I to be regarded in less esteem if I avenge the wrongs done to me!'

Fra Sebastiano stood and took a step towards him. He was alarmed by the rise in Lorenzo's voice and the terrible pain in his eyes. Clear in his mind must be the agony of his own suffering at this man's command. Fra Sebastiano reached out his hand. Lorenzo flinched under his touch and backed away, holding the blade in front of him.

Fra Sebastiano looked at him with deep pity. 'Do you threaten me Lozo? I am as defenceless as Tomasso Capaccio, who has not yet been found guilty of the crimes you accuse him.'

Lorenzo released a cry, as desperate as a child's. He dropped the knife and sank to floor shuddering in anguish. He covered his face with his hands and wept.

There was some commotion at Theo Tieffenbrucker's house and workshop that afternoon. First had come the Englishman, dressed in a fine, black serge doublet trimmed with fox fur and a puffed up velvet hat with four square gems on the brim. With him, had come a younger, fair haired man named Josquin, who was Dutch. Wendelin had greeted him as if he were a long lost brother. They had explained that they had gone first to the house of Tomasso di Vincentini and had found only a lone woman and a miserable notary who complained all the while. The woman had explained that the whole household had gone to a wedding. She had directed the English merchant to Theo's house, where he had hoped to find his fellow countryman, Emlyn Tomas.

Emlyn had gone; all his belongings with him. None knew where, but hoped to find out as soon as Umbaldo turned up. They had been seen together the night before, after Emlyn had up-ended the rain barrel and knocked the griffin off the gate. Then Theo's daughters had all chimed together like musical bluebells and shown the visitor the glass beads that Emlyn had given them.

The Englishman, who answered to the fine Alpine name of Ambrose, was surprised at the sight of the baubles. He had drawn Theo to one side and explained to him that they were not fashioned from glass but were gems of great value. Why Emlyn had parted with them, neither could guess. Theo had a task extracting them from his three little girls. Once surrendered, he had locked them away with promises attached. The visitors had stayed at Eva's invitation. The day was too hot to go tramping about Venice and the smells from the kitchen too tempting to resist.

It had begun to rain when Umbaldo came back. With him, to everyone's surprise, was a small woman. She was concealed by a heavy cloak. Once inside the gates, she pulled down her hood.

'It's Carmelia Grimani!' said Ambrose Chillingworth in astonishment.

'Umbaldo!' shouted Eva.

'Umbaldo?' questioned Theo threateningly.

Umbaldo's cheeks burned. 'She is Emlyn's, Messer Theo. I can't explain now. Emlyn is in some trouble and I have to get back.' He was already at the gate when the Dutchman caught up and stopped him abruptly. Umbaldo was uncharacteristically sharp with him. 'There is no time!' he insisted.

'What kind of trouble?' asked Josquin.

Umbaldo shook his head. 'It would take too long to explain.'

'Then you can explain as we go,' said Josquin.

They both left, leaving the girl standing alone behind them. She unfastened the cloak and let it drop, as if it was too heavy for her to hold. She was dishevelled and her hair had fallen from the ribbons and loops of pearls. Eva and the girls squealed in delight, the others gasped in astonishment. The dress Carmelia Grimani was wearing was fit for the Queen of England. The girl was distraught and tearful. Eva rushed forward, arms outstretched in hen-like protection. 'Poor, poor child,' She cooed, gathering Carmelia into a bosomy embrace. Eva led her into the house, shooing the others aside. She would allow no questions until the foundling was comforted and fed.

They all knew by then that Carmelia Grimani should have been attending her own wedding. Theo was surprised to see Ambrose Chillingworth smiling affectionately.

Tomasso had tried to absorb all the words that Fra Sebastiano had told him concerning Emlyn Tomas. He knew without question that the story was true; he had felt sick with shock when he had first seen Anna's eyes staring at him in contempt the night of Grimani's banquet. The eyes had blazed with the same light that had set the gems ablaze on the youth's bright tunic. Tomasso had thought it some hideous mockery. When he heard the young man speak words of betrayal in Latin, he had nearly lost hold on his sanity.

At Fra Sebastiano's incessant urging, he opened his eyes. There was another in the room with him, Lorenzo, the young priest Tomasso had ordered maimed rather than killed. Tomasso held the young man's gaze, undaunted by its fierceness. Lorenzo was holding a knife and Tomasso was vaguely aware that he had tried to use it but had been dissuaded by the older man.

'Did you kill my brother Paolo?' asked the younger Franciscan.

'No, I did not,' Tomasso answered. 'I do know however, that your brother still lives. He is in the care of an excellent Greek physician. He is strong, I believe he will survive.'

'How do you come by this knowledge?' Fra Sebastiano demanded.

'I too have spies father, a merchant is lost without them.'

'Why did you not say so? It would have brought such solace to those who suffer, like Lorenzo here and his step mother, Donna Juliana. Where is your Christian duty?'

Tomasso smiled. 'I found out only this morning and would have been more that willing to put grieving hearts at rest, but I have been somewhat detained, as you know.'

Fra Sebastiano released an exaggerated burst of laughter. 'Are we to believe that you played no part in that sea battle?'

'Would you not like to keep all this questioning for the trial?' said Tomasso, hoping that the old man would have the sense to drop the subject. 'That is if I get that far,' he added.

Fra Sebastiano huffed in annoyance. He was not going to drop the subject, his voice rose with the next accusing question. 'Did you deliberately wound this innocent priest?'

Tomasso found it difficult to keep his gaze steady on the young Franciscan. He said, 'It was done by my order. I will pay any compensation he asks.'

'Even your life?' Lorenzo's voice was as cold as his eyes.

'If it is what will satisfy the crime I did against him. As I seem to have required a son, I should …' He could not continue. He had not had a chance to consider matters yet. The two Franciscans watched him coldly. Tomasso closed his eyes feeling that he had suddenly lost the game and must now pay the loser's forfeit.

Lorenzo said. 'I do not want your life. If you die because of all this, that would be God's will, not mine.'

'Holy Virgin protect us!' Fra Sebastiano gasped.

'As horrendous as what he did to me,' Lorenzo replied coldly. 'He deserves no better. Let him feel the bite of the gelding knife!'

'Lorenzo,' Fra Sebastiano's voice was filled with pain.

Lorenzo stood up leaving the dagger on the bed and glared chillingly at the merchant. 'I leave you an hour to contemplate your fate. I shall return with men as strong as those you set against me and as heartless. If you have the least scrap of honour left, plunge the dagger into your black heart. It is your only alternative.'

He reached the door and turned his head back. Tomasso saw that his eyes were as expressionless as his grandfather's.

Fra Sebastiano stepped towards him and stopped. 'Brother Lorenzo, will you pray with me?'

'No, not yet. But I would ask you to pray for me.'

The door closed, the lock turned and they were once more alone. Tomasso did not touch the dagger. Watching him, Fra Sebastiano said, 'He is not as he seems. I fear he would like you to take the decision from him.'

Tomasso didn't express the amusement he felt. After a moment he said, 'I thought he would ask for something else as recompense. I'm glad he didn't.'

'What could be worse than the castration he threatens!'

Tomasso sat up slowly. 'Father, I can see that you are a God-fearing man and a righteous one. These threats are empty. Grimani has no right to hold me here. You have seen two attempts on my life, will you witness another, perhaps a final one?'

The Franciscan resumed his seat, his expression troubled. 'It seems long ago now,' he said, 'but in truth it was only this morning that I spoke at some length to Bartolomeo Varini. I know the reason behind your ungodly actions.'

Tomasso cursed.

'No, do not be angry with your manager, Varini is too good a man to carry the burden you have placed on his shoulders. You say that you are unjustly confined here. I sat here in prayer while you mumbled in fever. It was strange to hear a man mutter in a tongue foreign to his blood while in such duress. I assumed that this tongue was one more familiar to you than your own. I spent six of my long years in what you call by the old name of Constantinople.'

Tomasso was uncomfortably surprised. Feigning amusement, he said, 'What was it, Greek? Turkish? Arabic? Persian? or did I use some other tongue?'

'It was Arabic,' Fra Sebastiano replied, 'with which I am familiar. You are your own betrayer. From your outcries I know what the sight of your wound already told me. You took part in that sea battle. You have much to answer for and much to be admired for. This plotted revenge is the work of a true craftsman.'

'Yet I have not completed it.'

'Nor will you, thanks be to God.'

While life remains in me so I will, thought Tomasso. It was too late now for priests, for regrets. It was too late even for sons. If he started to think along those lines, all would be in vain. He had come to seek one end, the destruction and death of Carlos Grimani and see it he would, or die in the attempt.

Bartolomeo was kept waiting for over an hour in the grand outer room of the Ducal Palace. The words that Tomasso had told him to remember still ran through his mind as he paced up and down, infuriated by the waste of time. The biggest question in his mind was what had happened to Tomasso? Had he been raving in fever when he had spoken the rhyming lines? They made no sense and Bartolomeo felt that he would be made to look foolish reciting them and would not be able to explain why.

The senator, Sebastiano Erizzo came himself to see Bartolomeo. He walked into the long decorative hall alone. He looked about fifty, with a drooping moustache and a neatly trimmed beard around an easily smiling mouth. His eyes were large and dreamy giving him an endearing appearance. He greeted Bartolomeo in a friendly manned and linked an arm through his, guiding him towards a door at the far end. He had already heard about the troublesome events of that morning. Venice, he explained, was chattering with the details of the story.

Bartolomeo pulled up short before they reached the door. 'Signore, I have come straight from there,' he explained. 'The matter is of some urgency. My employer Tomasso di Vincentini has been made a prisoner of Don Carlos Grimani.'

Erizzo nodded enthusiastically. 'Yes, yes, I to have heard that this is how the incident ended. You must be greatly alarmed.'

'Vincentini insisted that I come here and give you a message. He believes that these matters should be dealt with by the Senate.'

Erizzo frowned. 'He sent you to me? I do not know the man, although he employed my nephew as captain of his trading caravel, the *Cornucopia*.'

'He told me to tell you this,' said Bartolomeo. He recited the four lines of poetry as Tomasso had asked.

Erizzo stood with his head bowed, stroking the ends of his generous moustache. 'I don't understand,' he said when Bartolomeo had finished.

'I am totally baffled myself. Added to this, Vincentini said that you would know what to do on hearing these words. There is a long standing vendetta between himself and Carlos Grimani. While he is this man's prisoner, Vincentini fears for his life. The sooner he is taken from there the better.'

'You want me to use the influence of the Senate to have him brought here?'

'Yes, before further harm befalls those who are involved.'

Erizzo stood in silent thought. Then he nodded solemnly. 'Perhaps we should have them all brought here,' he suggested. He replaced his hand on Bartolomeo's elbow and resumed walking. It was he who drew back sharply next, as a thought came to him. He turned to Bartolomeo and gripped his other arm. 'There is only one possible explanation behind the words of this poem. Speak the lines again'

Bartolomeo did as he was asked.

'Ah!' Erizzo cried, suddenly dropping his hands. 'The success of Vincentini's new company has depended on a source of un-taxable spice. Is this correct? It's all right, you don't have to answer, but you did employ a certain Scipeone Barozzi as your Stamboul agent?'

Bartolomeo nodded, perplexed.

'Barozzi worked here you know, for many years. When Vincentini first came to Venice, he came from Stamboul where he trades with the Turk. His supplier is Ismael the Syrian. Don't be alarmed. Scipeone Barozzi is a Venetian before he is anything else, his letter was full of praise for this Syrian. Your Tomasso Vincentini uses Ismael as his supplier. Ismael the Syrian is also an agent for the Signori of Venice.'

'What!'

'He spies on the Sublime Port. His information comes to us through the Venetian Ambassador in Stamboul and it is always written in verse.' Erizzo smiled hugely and hurried towards the door. 'Come on,' he called, 'there is no time to waste. We must first get these lines written down and decipher them.'

'I'm sorry Signore,' said Bartolomeo following, 'but I still don't understand.'

Once in the corridor, Erizzo snapped his fingers and called to a young clerk who was walking towards them. Erizzo instructed the man to summon eight men-at-arms and wait for him at the south entrance. Bartolomeo was gratified, whatever other plans Erizzo was considering, he was prepared to go to the Grimani house with armed men. The Senate were now interested in the conflict between Vincentini and Grimani and would be better able to deal with it than anyone else.

Erizzo led Bartolomeo to a side room and sat him down at a small table. He placed a piece of paper in front of him and dipped a quill into the ink horn. 'Don't you see?' he asked. 'Write it all down and I will explain as you go.'

As Bartolomeo wrote, the words took on meaning and he thought that he grasped vaguely what they were about. When he had finished, he powdered the lines and blew gently on them before he handed them to the Senator.

Erizzo read quickly and then looked up. 'I will need to show this to one or two people before we visit the house of Grimani.' He smiled smugly. 'Can you wait in the barge?'

'Can you not explain the meaning to me first?' Bartolomeo asked impatiently.

Erizzo spoke softly. 'It is like this. Vincentini has just recently returned to Venice. Somehow, he carries a message from this Stamboul agent, Ismael. It is reasonable to believe that Vincentini knew of Ismael's connections with Venice. By instructing you to recite these lines to me, Vincentini is compelling the Senate to intervene. He has information that Venice needs and hopes to exchange this for the protection.'

'But he was in Florence and then Padua,' said Bartolomeo softly.

'That may be so, but these few lines show me that Vincentini has his own supply of information, it matters not where he received it. The lines explain themselves. They speak of the isle of Aphrodite which is Venetian Cyprus. They suggest that our power there is threatened. No harm must befall Vincentini before we learn more. Unfortunately, he has tangled with a man of great reputation who holds much influence here.'

Once he was outside, the six armed men fell in behind Bartolomeo and followed him to the water edge. They had a barge waiting, a large boat that could accommodate them all. Bartolomeo settled under the canopy and waited in stunned silence. He watched the rain patter on the canal and he remembered.

How did you get through the Turks? he had asked on that night when Tomasso had first come to Venice. 'On a camel,' Tomasso had replied, standing under a sky bright with a sickle moon. Earlier that evening, Bartolomeo had learnt that Tomasso wanted to sell the Cyprus based Lanarca Salt Company to Grimani. He had said, '*Because the Isle of Aphrodite lies in the claw of the sickle moon.*' The Ottoman sultan Selim had turned his eyes on Cyprus.

Now the words of the poem swarmed into Bartolomeo's mind. The time is nigh, the youthful moon walks forth to rule where lovers swoon. With cold, growing dread, Bartolomeo realised that it was all very possibly true.

Chapter 51 Venice

While Bartolomeo Varini sat waiting and worrying in the barge outside the Ducal Palace, Emlyn stealthily made his way through Venice. The sky darkened and a fierce, twisting wind came howling over the Lagoon, carrying the dark cloud like swarf from the glass kilns of Murano. Emlyn kept to the dripping shadows and dark places, always watchful for Grimani's men. He was not afraid, the mountain had taught him that fear was self-made. If you gave in to it, it could paralyse or overwhelm you. However, he was not in that type of danger now, this was of a different nature and he was freely walking towards it. What he had left behind, he did not think about, to do so would have made him turn back. His goal was that rare and precious flower Carmelia, but there was much to be done before he could reach for her.

All the evidence suggested that Tomasso Capaccio was his father. All apart for one crucial point that he had mentioned to no one, his own conviction that they were all wrong. He doubted at times what his mind told him, how much easier matters would be if he accepted the stories as truth. But they were not enough, his dreams told him a different story. These might be conjured from his imagination, but until he had further proof, he could not abandon them. He pushed the memories to the recess of his mind, where they always had dwelt shimmering like star-shine.

Emlyn reached the Spice Company's trading house and stood gazing at it. The wind blew in from the sea, lashing him with rain, yet, a break came in the heavy cloud and the palace was momentarily bathed in sunlight. The gold-painted salamander above the gates, blazed like a beacon. Emlyn narrowed his eyes. The dry-leaf voice of Mafanwy Fawr whispered like the wet palm fronds slapping against the walls, *Remember that the dragon comes in many guises.*

Emlyn smiled, seeing the deceptions of such a warning. Was the salamander in the guise of a dragon? or was the dragon in the guise of the salamander? If he believed what the old witch had told him, he could look upon this as further proof that he had followed the trail to the end. He pulled at the strings around his neck and the bag of charms lay in his hand. He knew what lay inside; there was a scrap of adder skin, a sharp tooth, a dried bunch of herbs that reminded him of far off moors, and a small pebble with a hole in it. Why he had kept them, he could not understand. Like the recurring dreams, the charms belonged to mystery, something which spoke as if through the voices of past lives. It was an inexplicable magic that did not belong to the faith he had been taught to believe.

He walked through the front entrance which was open. There were groups of people gathered in the long counting room. Most were dressed in the dark gowns of clerks, the others in the plainer dress of workmen, some wearing the blue doublets like the one Jacopo had lent to him. As none of these approached him or asked him his business, Emlyn walked through the room. The conversation around him ceased and they all eyed him with suspicion.

He was just about to push the far door when it was opened from the other side. A man came through carrying a sea trunk. He thudded into Emlyn's chest causing him to stagger back. The man dropped the heavy chest with a grunt, just missing Emlyn's feet, then he turned on his heel and returned the way he had come. Emlyn heard a woman's voice on the other side of the door. He looked behind. The men who worked for Tomasso di Vincentini were still glaring at him with hostility. Their boatman, Jacopo had died whilst helping Carmelia and himself escape. These men knew who Emlyn was and made sure that he was aware of this. Emlyn turned away as the door opened once more. A woman stood in the doorway, as still as a painting. Her dress was of red satin, a deep, shadowy red that suited her dark complexion and scornful eyes. Over her head and shoulders she wore a dark shawl, fringed with deep-blue silk. Emlyn knew who she was, Umbaldo had told him about the mistress of Tomasso di Vincentini. He was looking at his father's mistress, Fiorenza Balsamo. Emlyn felt the rain water run from his wet hair down his neck and shoulders he resisted the urge to shiver as they regarded each other in silence.

Emlyn said, 'You know what has happened Madonna?'

'That you ran off with the promised bride of Tomasso di Vincentini? You challenged him to a duel and nearly killed him? or you had him arrested by Grimani and his cut-throats?' She clasped her hands together and clenched them until her knuckles were white. 'I do not know how you can dare to come here!'

Emlyn saw that she was near to tears and trembling with anger. He stood back. 'I am sorry that my presence upsets you Madonna, but I had to come here. I may be able to help Capaccio.'

'Who are you to call him Capaccio?' she demanded. She stepped closer to him, her expression changing to a worried frown. She dropped her voice as she spoke. 'Are you telling me that Grimani has discovered who he is? Tell me how you know or I will let these men have their way with you and believe me, they will not need to be told twice.'

Emlyn shook his head. He hadn't realised until he had entered this house how utterly exhausted he was and how much his body throbbed with pain from the hurts that he had ignored. Conflict was the last thing he wanted. He said, 'May we speak privately Madonna?'

She was perceptive in reading his expression. When she had led him to the privacy of the inner hall, Emlyn turned to her and said, 'Madonna, forgive me, but there is little time. If you know that Vincentini was once named Capaccio then you must know something of his story?'

She nodded once, her eyes downcast. 'I know enough to be aware of the danger he faces left at the mercy of Grimani. Capaccio's men have told me what he has been accused of.'

'What?'

'Murder, piracy, treason, shall I go on?'

'Is any of it true?'

'Of course not, how could it be? If this is brought to trial, he has charges to lay at Grimani's door too. Grimani will have him murdered before any questions are asked and, failing that, will see him face the hangman. You have run headlong into a tangled web here. What is your name?'

'Emlyn Thomas, Madonna,' he added. 'I have indeed, but you will never believe how further entangled it has now become. I have no intention of harming him, but must speak with him. Will you help me?'

Ambrose watched as Carmelia came into the room. She was wearing a plain brown dress that she had borrowed from Eva, it was tucked and gathered to fit her small frame. When she looked up, tears rimmed her reddened eyes. Instinctively, Ambrose held out his hands to her. She stood and ran to him like a little girl and clung to him, burying her head in his shoulder and soaking his fine English cloth with tears.

He responded in the only way he knew; by patting her shoulder and soothing her with soft mumbled words. After a long time, her tiny, shuddering frame eased. Ambrose produced a handkerchief for her. She accepted it, turning away. Ambrose wandered to the latticed window, hands clasped behind him, giving her time. The room was still warm, despite the wash of gloomy grey light. Rain drummed the window, gathered in every leaden diamond and overflowed.

He had come to Venice hoping to find a ship bound for France or, with luck, England. It was the need for negotiation that pulled him back now to his own shore. He had discovered that his son Christopher was being held in Seville, with some of the prisoners from Hawkins tragic voyage. Ambrose needed to get into the thick of things, to gather information and funds and to petition the Queen herself if necessary. He was returning to England with Matthew and Josquin and he intended to take Emlyn Tomas with him. He was not taking Carmelia Grimani. He had to talk to her about that before she left the room.

Without turning, he began to speak. His voice was soft as it had been when he had told her tales of Russia while sitting out an Alpine storm when they had all been drawn together by the dangers of that journey they shared. This time, Ambrose spoke about Gruffydd Hiraethog and of the nature of the land to which Emlyn had given his loyalty and love. He spoke as he had heard Gruffydd speak in the late evening they had spent together. He told Carmelia of Emlyn's future as a wool grower and landowner and of his responsibility to his grandfather. When he had finished speaking, silence reigned, in spite of the musical patter of the rain. He heard the rustle of Carmelia's skirt as she stood and he turned at last to face her.

She crossed the room with dignity. She reached up and touched his shoulder. Tiptoed, she kissed first one cheek and then the other. Ambrose blushed.

Carmelia said, 'Could you send your servant to fetch Madonna Adriana? I will not wait here for Emlyn, nor have I any intention of returning to my father's house, there is nothing for me there.'

'What do you intend to do?'

'To leave Venice. Adriana has a sister living in the country where we can stay.' She smiled weakly. 'I made the decision to leave him before. I can do it again.'

Ambrose looked at her with pity. Her words were brave but they were not the words of her heart. The pain of her decision was plain to see, but he did not attempt to change her mind, she would come to know the wisdom of her decision. She had a new smile on her face when she stood back and her eyes were dry. She was not quite the little girl he had thought her to be, the smile was pure woman. Ambrose saw something there, that made him wonder if her decision had been genuine.

Emlyn waited alone in the room which he'd been shown into. There was an old warped table in the centre, a few stools and a long bench pushed against the wall. He sat on a stool and listened to the rain beat against the shutters. The door was open and he could see the woman through the doorway. She was speaking earnestly with the man who had earlier carried the travelling trunk. Emlyn heard him addressed as Enrico de Martoni.. The voices were raised in argument. Emlyn leaned against the wall and closed his eyes, too distracted to listen to their rapid Italian.

When they came into the room it was the man who spoke first. 'We have all been informed that Vincentini has been detained at the Grimani palace. It is doubtful that he will survive the wounds your blade dealt him.'

Emlyn was not willing to play at this deceptive Venetian game. He was amused and could not prevent the short burst of ironic laughter. 'I did not touch him,' he explained. 'I could not touch him. I am no swordsman. I believe he could have killed me had he wanted to. I see that you do not believe me, nonetheless, it is the truth. Would he not be better served in devising some way to free him?'

'He knew that this would come,' said Enrico. 'I think we can be sure that he planned for this with the same chill practicality that he planned for everything else.' Enrico laughed bitterly. 'He does not want rescuing and would not thank us for our interference.'

'That's absurd Enrico,' cried Fiorenza. 'He could not have known that he would be let down by his own health.'

'Are we to believe that he suffers from some ailment?' Enrico replied scornfully. 'The flux? Swamp fever? Terrarium. You know as well as I Madonna that the fever and sickness he suffers is from wounds received more than a week ago during a sea battle.'

'What are you saying?' Emlyn asked. He stood slowly. 'Did I fight with a man already disabled?'

'You were not to know,' said Fiorenza.

'That does nothing to ease my conscience,' Emlyn snapped.

Enrico turned to him. 'So, you are not responsible for his hurts but he gave you the chance to escape, or so we have heard. Why did you not take it?'

'This matter is a great deal more complex than you imagine,' said Emlyn, sighing with impatience. 'I could not go.'

'Then where is Carmelia Grimani? Did you send her back to her father?'

Emlyn sat down. 'She is safe enough,' he replied. These people could not know what lay between himself and Carmelia. They could not know of the death she had promised herself if she had wed Tomasso Vincentini. She held Emlyn as close to her and as inescapable as a shadow. He had sent her with Umbaldo to Theo's house and told her to wait for him. He did not know what future they would have. But he was learning the past and knew that if he walked from here now, he would never know the peace he sought and never be free to give her the devotion such love demanded.

There was a soft but firm rap on the window shutters outside which caused them all to start with fear. Enrico crossed the room and opened the shutters. The wind and rain blew in as a figure climbed in from outside. 'Symeon!' Fiorenza gasped. 'I thought that you had left us.'

'I did Madonna,' he said smiling. 'I heard at the harbour about what had happened and I came back. Is the master well?'

'He is alive, if that is what you ask,' snapped Enrico.

Symeon's smile disappeared. 'He would be angered if he discovered that I was here, that is why I have used this window and did not come here openly.' He took the woman's hands in his and added 'I could not go until I found out his fate.'

Emlyn recognised the man, he had seen decorating a manuscript when he had called to see Bartolomeo Varini about the wool.

He sat quietly while they explained all that had happened, but he became increasingly impatient, feeling that time was being wasted. He thought of Carmelia and of how anxious she would become at his long delay. Silence fell. He looked up and saw the three pairs of eyes watching with mixed expressions. Enrico de Martoni looked sceptical, Fiorenza Balsamo looked angry and the man they addressed as Symeon looked concerned. Emlyn guessed that they now knew of his own supposed relationship with Tomasso. Throughout the day they must have heard different accounts of the duel and what had happened afterwards.

Emlyn said, 'You may well blame me for what has happened and I agree that much blame falls upon me. But I was not aware of these other matters that my, that Capaccio was involved in. I did not tell Don Carlos who he was. I didn't know myself. I can get into Grimani's house unseen. I have done so before and I can get out again, but I must go now.'

Fiorenza crossed the space between them and sat on a stool beside him. She took his hand which was still covered in blood and grime, the long gash glistening across his knuckles. She said 'You had a chance to escape from Venice with Carmelia, yet you came back to rescue him?'

He pulled his hand away and stood up.

Fiorenza rose beside him saying, 'Sit down. There is much you should know before you risk such a venture. All of us here like and admire your father, in spite of all his efforts to discourage friendship. We would all rather see him safely away rather than face trial and worse.'

Emlyn sat down, sleep dragged at his limbs and slowed his mind. He accepted the glass of wine that Symeon poured from a newly broached bottle. The glass was smoky blue with a twisted stem ringed in gold. He had never drunk from anything so fine before; the contents tasted like the wine he had drank at Ambrose's house in Southampton in what seemed like years ago. Fiorenza folded her arms and leaned back against the table. Her voice was as soft as the wind as she told of what she knew concerning Tomasso di Vincentini.

Don Carlos leaned heavily on Uglino's shoulder as he made his way down the passage that led to the prisoner's room. Half way, he shuffled to a halt and stared out through an open archway where the rain fell over the roof tops. He had not heard anything concerning the whereabouts of his daughter. He knew that she could not escape Venice now without notice, he would deal with her in time. At present Carlos had other matters on his mind. The remaining women in the house, he was sure were plotting against him. He had not seen Juliana since the vile lies had poured from her mouth. He had never liked her, she was a pious, frozen bitch who had always come to his bed with the utmost distaste. It was like embracing cold marble. He hadn't been near her for years, she was always off praying somewhere and he had scarcely been aware of her presence in the building. All her bitter spite, he reasoned, had now taken possession of her. He supposed Juliana had locked herself in her room with Adriana Martinelli. God only knew what the two witches were hatching between them. These too, Don Carlos would deal with in time.

He continued on his way. He knew that he had acted too rapidly dealing with this Vincentini or Capaccio. Had he had time to think and plan, he would have been able to keep the whole matter private. Instead, the whole run of incidents had taken place in public, by now every gossiping tongue in Venice would be rattling with repetition and exaggeration.

So, mused Carlos grimly, you want this out in the open Tomasso Capaccio? Very well, I shall take much pleasure in relating to the Signori how you viciously attacked Venetian ships in the guise of a corsair. The only penalty for such a traitorous act is execution. I have the survivor of that dishonourable battle, a witness who saw everything and whose words will take you to a quick grave!

But wait, I already know what a cunning mind you have. Before the final tale of betrayal against the Republic of Venice, I shall list my other grievances and lay them at their feet. Let the Signori of Venice see what sort of man you really are.

And what can you say in your defence? That you are Tomasso Capaccio who was condemned to the galleys by the Senate twenty years ago? Should any be brought to believe this incredulous tale, what would be the good of it. If the Senate did not help you then Capaccio, why should they listen to you now? They all believed my story then and will do so again. Still, no harm can come of finding out what you hope to gain from this public inquiry, in which you can only succeed in condemning yourself.

They reached the room and Don Carlos nodded to the guard to unbolt the door. 'Uglino?' Carlos said, turning to the boy, 'I want you to get rid of the Franciscan meddler for a while. Take him to comfort my dear wife. They should get on famously.'

This was not as easy as Carlos had hoped and he had to withstand a finger-wagging lecture before the friar even agreed to move away from the door. Carlos rose to his full height. 'I have no intention of harming my prisoner,' he said. 'I am insulted that you should suggest as much. I admit that my words to him when he was arrested were a little colourful, but I was in great distress, you will agree. I have every intention of hearing the scoundrel beg for mercy when he is condemned to death by the Council. All of Venice will want to witness the fate of such a villainous, black-hearted pirate. You have no need of concern Fra Sebastiano. I beg you, go to my wife, she will be comforted by your presence. My son Lorenzo tells us that this man says dear Paolo may yet live. Such a wicked lie when we are all so deeply shocked by the death of our little Paolo. He was such a sweet and cherished youth.'

Fra Sebastiano left eventually, following Uglino, who offered to lead him to the distressed women. Don Carlos momentarily watched the boy. He had become very fond of Uglino.

Tomasso Capaccio did not rise when Carlos entered the room. He remained seated at ease, propped up by pillows on the bed. Although his face was in shadow, Carlos could still see how pale and drawn he looked.

Carlos was privately pleased; he had no doubt as to the man's capability to defend himself in court, the more strain placed upon him now, the less able he would be. But Capaccio did not look concerned; his dark gaze was unwavering, penetrating and cold. It was the coldness of indifference, as if not even his own hatred could warm the hollow depths. Carlos smiled, perhaps fear could arouse some emotion.

With great pleasure, Don Carlos meticulously explained all that he had heard from the seaman who had survived the sea fight.

Throughout, Capaccio remained silent and hardly moved.

'Well?' Carlos ended. 'I wonder what defence, if any, you intend to offer against such serious charges. Your hopes of course are futile, but one can always speculate.'

Capaccio stirred and smiled faintly. 'These accusations are absurd. No one will ever believe them.'

'There are many ways to prove that the seaman's story is true and even you can do nothing to escape from the truth.'

'So why are you here? If you are so sure Grimani, what is it that you fear I will reveal?'

Carlos released a snort of laughter. 'I am not afraid of anything that you can bring against me. You speak no doubt, of matters which occurred many years ago. They are blown like dust to the wind.' He turned away, paced up and down for a few minutes and stroked his chin. 'However, there might be a slim chance of your escaping this with your life.'

Capaccio shifted his position and looked at Carlos with one eyebrow raised.

'Compensate me,' said Carlos, 'compensate me for all that you have taken from me. You know that I can force this from you anyway. Save us both the trouble by arranging now to hand over your wealth and business interests to me. In return, I shall make sure that you reach that ship that you were hoping to join. I see that you are surprised at the scope of my knowledge concerning your plans.'

'I am impressed,' Capaccio replied. 'But, as so often, you are mistaken. You have belittled yourself in begging Grimani. You will get nothing from me.'

'So what do you intend to do? Regurgitate the past? Wring out a tear or two with lies? None will even listen for your piracy is a matter that touches the very heart of Venice.'

'Time does not absolve murder. I have planned long for your downfall. How often I have imagined my sword at your throat, for the final act of vengeance. I see now that I have achieved that end without the need for a blade. You are a ruined man Grimani. You are already dying before my eyes, just as my Anna promised.'

Don Carlos moved forward swiftly and lifted his hand. 'You will change your mind by the time I have finished with you!' He brought his hand down in a vicious blow that caught Capaccio across the side of his head. Carlos swung away and left the room without looking back.

The story of Tomasso Capaccio was new to Emlyn and greatly saddened him in its detail about his mother. He was young enough to see Tomasso's vengeance as heroic and just. Yet his admiration was not complete, he was aware of the chilling brutality behind a man of such determination. Emlyn had to devise some incredulous scheme to free him before Grimani came to know that whole story and had him killed. Emlyn smiled as a familiar thrill ran through him; only Goronwy would have recognised the smile and known what it represented, but he was far from here. Emlyn looked at the others. Could he convince these older, more experienced people to follow a beardless youth? Emlyn stood and bowed slightly, making no comment on what he had heard. 'I have to go,' he said. 'You can come if you like, I would be grateful to have your support.'

Fiorenza reclaimed his hand. 'You will still attempt to free him?'

'Madonna,' said Erizzo, 'we are supposed to be on our way to Cyprus, I caution you not to become involved.'

'The providence of God has kept me here,' she replied. 'Why else would he have sent such a storm?'

Emlyn's admiration for her rose. She did not look like a mistress, though she was pretty in a motherly sort of way. Her smile mirrored something of his own readiness.

Enrico looked miserable. 'I cannot possibly allow this Madonna. There can be only danger awaiting any attempt we make.'

'Messer Tomasso does not want to be rescued,' Symeon added.

'Be quiet Symeon,' snapped Fiorenza, not without warmth.

Emlyn said, 'There will be little danger for any of you. All that will be required, is that you wait with a boat where I tell you. If Messer Enrico is willing, he and I shall bring Capaccio to you and then you can make your escape to the ships at harbour.'

Fiorenza nodded enthusiastically. She fastened her shawl about her head. 'The storm will be over by midnight and by dawn a ship could sail. If we go aboard with an extra passenger and oil a palm or two with silver, no questions will be asked. What ship did Tomasso send you to Symeon?'

'The ship's master is a friend of his,' Symeon explained. 'He is a Genoese by the name of Gaspare. Messer Tomasso met with him in Florence and arranged this voyage. He hoped that he would be leaving with his new wife. Madonna, Messer Tomasso would not be pleased to be freed from the house of his enemy.'

Emlyn took the cloak that Enrico offered to him and pulled it over his shoulders.

'What do you intend to do?' Enrico asked, his fear was not well concealed.

'I don't know,' said Emlyn. 'The good Lord will provide. We have already seen evidence of his interest,' He grinned at Fiorenza. He remembered that he would also have to extract Fra Sebastiano from the dilemma.

It was not until they were all in a the rowing boat moving downstream to Grimani's palace, that Emlyn remembered Symeon's objections. He turned to Symeon who was not looking pleased and said, 'Why would he not be pleased to be rescued?'

Symeon said, 'He would not wish to leave his enemy alive behind him when he flees from here.'

Fiorenza made an expressive noise. 'If we do not free him, Tomasso will leave Venice vertically, wrapped in chains and dropped into the Lagoon under cover of darkness. If Bartolomeo has been able to convince the senate, they will demand an inquiry. Grimani's past history will be revealed and turned against him. Grimani can not afford a public hearing, nor do I think Tomasso could escape the charges against him. They will both lose out.' She paused to include them all in her sweeping gaze. 'What does a merchant do when he becomes as wealthy as Tomasso?'

'Found a bank?' suggested Enrico.

'Exactly,' said Fiorenza. 'But he hasn't. He had no need to. I have seen the accounts. Large sums of money have been transferred without explanation to the coffers of some very prominent noblemen. Tomasso is owed great favour. He has prepared for this as with everything. He may have hounded Grimani and his family to near ruin but he has not touched the man himself. I believe, Tomasso wanted to keep that until last. Unfortunately he could not prepare for his present predicament; the egg has broken before it was fully grown. You are right Symeon, he will not welcome our interference. As it is, we are his only hope for freedom. Would you like to resume rowing?'

As the small boat got under way again, Fiorenza said, 'If only we knew what had happened with Bartolomeo and the Senate.'

'It is probably too late anyway,' Enrico replied. 'Grimani is no fool, he could have already thought of that. I doubt that we will find what we are looking for. If the Franciscan is with him still, he may be alive. Grimani would not have any but trusted men to do murder and witness the deed, Unfortunately it would be easy enough, one would suppose, to be rid of the old priest, to send him off on some pretext.'

'Fra Sebastiano is no fool either,' said Emlyn. 'He knows much concerning the story. If he is aware of a threat, he will stay with him to insure that no harm befalls him.'

'Accidents happen,' said Enrico, 'which even priests cannot prevent, and he is an elderly man.'

'Stop this!' Fiorenza cried, her voice shrill with fear. 'We will keep our minds on what is and not what might be!'

It was fully dark by the time they arrived where Emlyn had directed them, an unlit canal at the back of the tall Grimani palace, the dark unused steps leading up to the single heavy door. It was locked as Emlyn had suspected. He said, 'There is a tree further down, you can't see it from here, it gives access to a balcony and window. From that room, the doors can all be opened from inside, there are four of them at the top of the house, an area little frequented, and they lead to this one. Madonna, if you wait here with Symeon in the boat, we will bring Capaccio to you.'

'We!' Enrico squealed with horror. 'I haven't climbed a tree since, I've never climbed a tree!'

The tamarisk tree was swaying in the wind, it looked thin and frail. Emlyn didn't mention the branch that had cracked under his weight when he had last used this way. He was better prepared this time, he had brought a coil of rope from the boat. Still, one of them would have to climb up to the balcony and then guide the other, It couldn't be Enrico de Martoni, he was too unused to such an endeavour. Ignoring his protests, Emlyn swung up into the branches. It was the second tree he had climbed up in one day, the other had been covered with scented blossom that had fallen and caught in Carmelia's hair like flakes of snow.

Tomasso was fully clothed when Don Carlos Grimani came into the room accompanied by five armed men. Two of them pulled him to his feet and held him securely.

'Where are you taking him?' Fra Sebastiano demanded.

'To the prison,' Grimani snapped, 'where he can await his reckoning in better suited surroundings. I have received word that the Senate are sending a barge to pick him up. Come if you wish, if you think him in need of prayer, which he most certainly is.'

Tomasso struggled needlessly. There was not much he could do apart from split a lip and nose of one of his guards. He stopped struggling and allowed them to bind his hands behind him. He knew the methods of Carlos Grimani and he knew that the man was not telling the truth. He said as much to the Franciscan, speaking in Latin.

He did not know which way they took him, for they pulled a rough grain sack over his head. He used his other senses as best he could. He heard Fra Sebastiano protesting and his slower steps following until they faded from hearing. His captors didn't tell him about steps and doorways until they tired of his constant stumbling. He knew instinctively that Grimani was not with the men who pulled him through blind rooms and ascending steps. he moved his feet, counting the steps, there were sixty, then a corridor. He was stopped four times while locks rattled in doors, then pushed through. The last one opened on to fresh air and Tomasso could smell the rain.

The men didn't speak. Where they to take him somewhere dark and private and slit his throat? Had Bartolomeo got through to Senator Erizzo at all? Once outside, Tomasso felt that he might have a chance of escaping. He did not try it now, they had climbed sixty steps inside the house, so must descend before they came to the water level.

It was some natural instinct in Symeon that stopped Fiorenza from running to the top of the dark steps when they heard the lock turn. The sounds were wrong, too loud. Symeon pulled her back along the narrow ledge out of sight. 'Forgive me, Madonna,' he whispered in her ear. His hand was clamped across her mouth. She did not struggle after the first surprise, she was at once, as cautious as he. She nodded her head and he released her, signalling for her to back further away from the dark tunnel to safer ground. There were no lamps to see by. They crouched behind a row of rotting barrels and strained to hear above the rain. They heard a grunt and a curse and the thud of a man falling.

'The boat!' Fiorenza whispered furiously.

They had forgotten the boat in their hurry to hide. Whoever used the hidden doorway could not fail to see it even in the darkness, they would practically fall into it. Symeon had good eyesight, he made out the shapes of five men with a sixth in their midst, different for the misshapen sack covering his head. Symeon knew that this was Tomasso, the man who had changed his life and given him freedom. Symeon would rather die than leave him to this unjust fate. He was not unaware of his own danger, if Lorenzo Grimani beheld him, Symeon would be identified and only death could result.

Warning Fiorenza to remain where she was, he edged forward and saw the prisoner make a bid for freedom. Tomasso threw himself into he canal. But he could not see and his judgement was wrong. He hit the side of the boat nudging it away and fell half into the water by the embankment. It might have worked if he had been quicker, but one of the men grabbed at him and caught a bunch of clothing. They pulled him back and hit him with something hard so that he dropped and lay motionless. Symeon backed away and bumped into Fiorenza.

'What can we do?' she asked in anguish.

'We must follow them,' Symeon replied.

'How, by swimming? And what about the others? We must find them first. As I cannot climb a tree in this gown you will have to go Symeon. I will follow the boat on foot.'

'That is too dangerous Madonna, you would be alone and unprotected.'

'Then be quick. The sooner Enrico and Emlyn know what has happened the sooner they can follow.'

Symeon put a finger to his lips to caution her to silence. They crouched lower behind the barrels and watched.

Tomasso had been thrown into the boat and four of the men climbed in. The locks creaked, the oars splashed and the boat moved passed their place of concealment, sweeping towards where the canal entered another. The man they had left, returned up the steps and they heard the door lock from the inside. When they were out of hearing, Fiorenza leapt to her feet and pulled her shawl from her head. 'I'll leave a trail,' she suggested pulling at the blue silk fringe.

'Madonna, this is not wise,' warned Symeon.

'We can do nothing on our own Symeon,' she answered. 'Go quickly and find the others. Tell Enrico to find Bartolomeo and you follow me with Emlyn.' She was off before Symeon could do anything to prevent her. Symeon made his way rapidly along the water edge looking for the tree the young foreigner had spoken of. It was not hard to find or to climb. A length of rope had been lefty, tied between the tree and the balcony. Symeon swung over with ease and was soon standing in an unlit bedchamber, the partially opened door was rimmed with faint light. Before moving towards it, Symeon shuddered, not from cold but from a growing fear. He had learned to relay on the accuracy of his instincts. It warned him now to go back the way he had come. But he did not have that choice open to him. He moved forward, his heart hammering, his eyes wide with fear.

Emlyn had reached the lower part of the house. He and Enrico had separated on entering in order to search every room. The lower house was filled with light and activity. Crouched at the top of a flight of wide stairs, Emlyn could see the front door through which Don Carlos had recently left with a group of his men at arms. Emlyn had recognised some of them and he knew what type of men they were. Emlyn wonder if he should follow, but he was reluctant to leave the nervous Enrico de Martoni behind. He remained hidden and listened. He could hear muffled voices behind closed doors. When there was no one in sight, he crept down, crossed the tiled floor and placed his hand on the door. Suddenly there came sounds of approaching footsteps from outside and some one pounded on the door. Emlyn sprang back and ran to one side. He flattened himself against the wall and edged behind a hung tapestry. It was inadequate cover, the bulge of his body would be seen by any who looked closely. A servant came running and opened the door. It swung back providing further cover. Three men entered, two clothed in the livery of the Ducal Palace and the other ...

Emlyn nearly betrayed his presence in his surprise, the other man was Matthew Wheatland, the servant of Ambrose Chillingworth. His presence could only mean that Ambrose had come at last to Venice. Emlyn smiled to himself, he couldn't have chosen a worse time! The Arsenotti had come to collect Tomasso di Vincentini. The house servant they addressed looked perplexed and argued with them for some time. There was more commotion and more men entered the building. Among them was a splendidly dressed gentleman with a drooping moustache and Bartolomeo Varini.

'Don Carlos is not here,' said the steward descending the stairs. Emlyn recognised old Giuseppe, Grimani's personal servant. 'He has left on some urgent business.'

'Is the lady Adriana here?' said Matthew in his rough Italian. He was pushed aside while further questions were put to the man. Giuseppe was extraordinary slow in answering and Emlyn guessed that he was delaying them on purpose. But for what purpose? It seemed to go on forever while Emlyn tried to slow his heartbeat and keep his breathing under control.

Adriana appeared with Carmelia's maid, Pellegrina. They paused at the entrance of the room, both looked strained and tired. 'Matthew?' said Adriana pleasantly.

Matthew bowed awkwardly, 'My lady,' he mumbled.

Adriana walked into the hall. 'Luigi,' she called to a servant, 'fetch lamps, its like a crypt in here.' She turned to Matthew. 'This is a day for happenings. Now what brings you to Venice on such a foul night?'

'I've a word for yer ear mistress,' Matthew replied, indicating that they should speak in private.

'Madonna Martinelli?' Bartolomeo Varini, detained her with a hand on her arm. 'I beg a moment only. Is Tomasso di Vincentini here?'

'I believe so,' Adriana replied, 'though I have not seen the man myself.' She pulled her hand away and guided Matthew to a corner where they could speak in privacy.

'Fools!' A new voice spoke from the top of the stairs. Emlyn peered around the edge of the tapestry. Fra Sebastiano was on the stairs, but it was not he who had spoken. Madonna Juliana Grimani floated down the steps with her hand on his arm. She was dressed in black from head to foot and wore a thin veil over her face. 'You hoped to find Carlo here and he has flown,' she added as she came down. 'What are you after? The furniture? The hangings? Silver and pewter? You will find that there is little to be had.'

'You must not distress yourself Juliana,' said Fra Sebastiano softly.

Senator Erizzo walked towards her and took her ringed fingers. He bowed and kissed her hand. 'Madonna, we are not your husband's enemy, do not be alarmed. You will of course be aware of the distressing events of today. I have come only to take your husband's prisoner to safer custody.'

'But he is not here,' said Giuseppe. 'Don Carlos has already had him taken to the Ducal Palace. Did you not pass them on the way?'

Senator Erizzo, looked impatient. 'Then you must instruct your master to attend a private inquiry on the morrow at the hour of ten. We will have this matter settled before it gets any worse.'

Emlyn's impatience grew as he waited for them all to sort themselves out and leave. Juliana Grimani stayed on the stairs, her face pale and hard behind the veil. Emlyn realised that she had plans of leaving herself, for travelling trunks stood near the front entrance.

He felt a sense of relief, there was nothing he could now do for Capaccio, it could have been feasible to free him from here, but from the Ducal palace would be impossible. Emlyn stood still, feeling the tiredness seeping through him. He would go back now to Carmelia. He would hold her close and caress her scented hair with kisses. He waited another ten minutes but Juliana did not move away. Soon after Adriana reappeared with Matthew in tow. 'We know where she is,' she called to Juliana.

'You have found Carmelia?' Juliana cried, her voice edged with anxiety.

Adriana embraced her. 'We shall all leave together,' she said. 'Get Giuseppe and Matthew to load the boat and we shall leave immediately. You will feel so much better once we are away, we will all be better off without the attendance of men. The four of us shall journey together. How I love the Brenta at this time of year.'

Emlyn stiffened. They were obviously talking of taking Carmelia away, but why? He had to get to her before them to find out. He had a suspicion that Ambrose had some hand in this. How often elders stepped in and interfered, always thinking that they knew what was best for all concerned. Emlyn cursed under his breath. As soon as the women were turned away, he stepped out of hiding and edged stealthily back up the steps. Once at the top, he ran, regardless now of discovery, nothing would prevent him from reaching Carmelia.

What did stop him was physical. He skidded around a dark corner and collided with two people coming the other way. It took him a moment to realise that it was Lorenzo and Enrico. 'Emlyn!' they cried in unison. 'Emlyn, something terrible has happened,' added Enrico.

'I know,' said Emlyn, 'and this time, no one is going to talk me out of doing what my heart tells me. Lorenzo, you are a priest, will you come with me? Will you give the sacrament of marriage to me and Carmelia?'

Lorenzo looked at him as if he had gone crazy. 'What are you saying?,' he said after a moment. 'Emlyn it will have to wait.'

Enrico took hold of his arm. 'Don Carlos has taken Vincentini.'

'To the Ducal Palace, I know. There is nothing I can do for him now. If this comes to trial, I will speak for him if you think it would help, but I have no time now. Lozo, I have to get back to Theo's house. I left Carmelia there.'

'He was not taken to the Ducal Palace,' said Lorenzo. 'My Grandfather had him blindfolded and tied and taken out through a hidden way.'

'You must find him, for his life is in danger,' Enrico insisted

Emlyn groaned. Suddenly torn two ways. 'If Capaccio was taken that way he would be seen. It was the way we used ourselves. Madonna Fiorenza is there waiting, she will follow and let us know where he has been taken.'

'You would leave this to a woman!' Lorenzo said coolly.

'It is so,' said Enrico. 'Symeon came to find me. He told me to find Bartolomeo,'

'Well I know where he is,' said Emlyn, 'he is on his way back to the Ducal Palace expecting to find Capaccio there. Where is Symeon?'

Enrico released an uncharacteristic bitter laugh. 'He was afraid to stay here, he said death awaited him within these walls, can you believe that? He has gone to join Fiorenza. She has followed the boat that left with Tomasso. I came to find you and found this good man instead. If you hurry you will catch up with them.'

Emlyn looked at his half-brother, but he saw no offer of help in Lorenzo's cold gaze. Enrico de Martoni had to find Bartolomeo. So he was on his own. He left them with a heavy heart and made his way rapidly through the house and out on to the balcony. The walkways, where they existed were narrow and washed with sea water, but they were well lit and planks had been placed were the flooding caused inconvenience. Emlyn splashed passed the towering palaces, ran under dripping balustrades and leaped over flooded doorways. He found Symeon waiting for him at the corner of an old fondaco and they continued in silence.

Tomasso knew where he was, he did not need his sight to recognise his surroundings. They had brought him to a warehouse, which brought a little relief, for it meant that they had some other use for him before they dropped him into the Lagoon. The warehouse was his own. He had first greeted Bartolomeo here when there had only been salt cones staked against the walls. Tomasso had filled the room with Eastern treasures and the perfume of spice. He recognized it now by those scents, this came to him in wafts, like the sounds. The men who had brought him were breaking open the casks of cinnamon, ginger, mace and cardamom that the *Cornucopia* had so recently brought back from Constantinople.

Tomasso was amused and grateful to feel the emotion, for it meant that he was not finished yet, in spite of the punishment he had taken and the constant pain. He remained still, feigning senselessness. He was not surprised that Grimani had chosen to bring him here for the final accounting. He should have guessed that Grimani would want the final word before death. Who had sent him the poison then? Lorenzo? Adriana? Carmelia herself? Who did not matter, for he was beyond their animosity now. It was a pity though, that he had been discovered before his end was reached.

He heard a door open and felt the draught. The warehouse had always been guarded by men he had believed were trustworthy, but all men had a price, they could have been bribed to disappear. He hoped that was what had happened and that they had not lost their lives defending his property.

It could have been so different, thought Tomasso with a sigh of regret, had I not held the sickle of vengeance in my righteous hand. What he had Bartolomeo had built in one active year was nothing but admirable. They had a trading house on the Rialto, a good ship and the funds for another that was being built at the Arsenal. The contacts in Constantinople and Alexandria were good for a number of years. Bartolomeo had worked hard and well to build up the business, to employ the clerks, the factors and the workmen needed to keep it all together and running smoothly. There was now enough accumulated stock and wealth to keep it so, to grow and expand to other Italian cities, Florence, Sienna, Pavia, or even further afield to France, Spain, England and the Netherlands, which would be a smack in the face for the Portuguese who dominated the sale of spice and pepper in Northern Europe.

He heard footsteps approach and braced himself as someone snatched the cloth from his head. He was sitting against grain sacks, his hands and feet tightly bound, they had grown numb and useless. The warehouse was filled with light, they had found the box of Russian candles that he had reserved for the Bishop of San Marco, they were all lit. When his eyes had adjusted, Tomasso could see the ruin of costly spice spilled across the floor, ochre, amber and cinnamon. The air was filled with it, causing more than one irritated nose to explode into fits of sneezing.

Don Carlos was seated at the desk. He was eating, his jaws moving rhythmically as he eyed his enemy. Tomasso hadn't eaten for a long time, his stomach burned as if he had swallowed ground glass. His fine clothing was ruined, ironically the gold acorns still swung from loose lacing, but the braiding was torn and the seed pearls had found their way into some quick thinker's doublet. He recalled them being torn when he had tried to throw himself into the water.

Grimani continued to chew; his cold eyes fixed unblinking.

Tomasso didn't hold the gaze, he was too tired and the spice was making his eyes sting. He closed them. He was still alive. Even without his tasbih, he could count the ninety-nine most beautiful names of God.

Senator Erizzo was eager to talk with Tomasso di Vincentini so Bartolomeo knew that he would not have much change of seeing Tomasso himself before morning. Bartolomeo was surprised at what he had been handed by the old Franciscan before he had left. He had read the will that Tomasso had entrusted to him. It was unsealed but had been witnessed by Fra Sebastiano and another, a name that was unfamiliar to Bartolomeo. Tomasso had obviously accepted Emlyn Tomas as his son and was in no doubt that he himself would not escape this situation alive. Bartolomeo sat beside Erizzo and showed him the will. Erizzo laughed. 'Why not go and find the youth, if possible, not only to inform him of his astonishing good fortune, but also to instruct him and Don Carlos' daughter Carmelia, to come to tomorrow's meeting?' He said this with a firmness that turned the suggestion into an order.

The boat pulled in to let Bartolomeo off before it reached the Ducal Palace. With leaden steps, Bartolomeo disembarked and stood watching the barge until it turned and disappeared around a corner. He nodded slowly to himself as he walked. He had mistrusted and feared Tomasso in the year they had spent building up the new company and he had been jealous of Fiorenza's attraction to him. He realised now with great sorrow, that he had come, in the end, to respect Tomasso and even to like him a great deal. Whatever Tomasso had done, he was not the evil avenger that he thought himself to be. Clutching his cloak around him in the wind and rain, Bartolomeo made his way to the house of the German lute maker, hoping to hear of the whereabouts of Emlyn Tomas, who could now be his new employer. Tomasso had included a note for Bartolomeo asking if he would stand by the youth and manage the company as he had done for over a year. Emlyn was not Venetian and it would not be easy for him to gain favour without good council. He would also be at the mercy of the more shrewd traders, who were quite capable of fleecing him of his newly acquired riches.

Bartolomeo had crushed all the hopes he'd had of winning Fiorenza's affection. He guessed that the storm would have delayed the ship she intended to join. She would know by now what had happened that morning and Bartolomeo did not like to think of her in distress. He would call to see her before he returned to his own home on Canal delle Toreselle, he would explain what had happened since and try to put her mind at rest. Knowing her as he did, Bartolomeo felt that she would remain in Venice now until the matter was settled; she would remain until the bitter end.

Theo Tieffenbrucker greeted him warmly and took him inside the house. 'Emlyn is not here,' he explained. 'He sent Carmelia here with one of my apprentices.'

'Really?' Bartolomeo said in surprise. He thought that the lovers would have fled from Venice by now.

'She was in great distress, but the Englishman seems to have sorted the whole thing out. Carmelia has gone with her godmother Adriana Martinelli, just a short while ago.'

'Gone where? Is Emlyn with them?'

Theo shrugged. 'No one seems to know where Emlyn is. Umbaldo came back with the Dutchman after an extensive search. I had assumed that Emlyn and she had planned to meet somewhere. Would you believe that she had a horse brought here? And a falcon!'

'What Englishman?'

'Me I presume,' said a man standing just inside the front door. He bowed and added, 'Ambrose Chillingworth, at your service.'

'Mister Chillingworth! We were to have met much sooner than this. It was my employer who bought your English wool.'

Chillingworth smiled warmly. 'And you speak English! I am delighted to meet you.'

'Bartolomeo Varini.'

'I hope the wool was to your satisfaction,' said Ambrose. 'Perhaps we could discuss further sales while you are here. I have some sound ideas to put to you or to your employer if he has a mind to hear me. Will you come in out of the rain?'

'I have also heard a little of your hopes for expanding England's trade, from Emlyn Tomas,' said Bartolomeo. 'I would be more than happy to assist you under normal circumstances, but much has happened and I am rather pressed for time.'

'Then Emlyn did speak to you concerning English trade with the Levant?'

'He did, and I turned him down. I was prepared to discuss matters further, but he will be free to trade as he pleases now that he has come into such a fortune.'

The Englishman looked at him in puzzlement.

Bartolomeo took the documents from his satchel and handed them to him. 'These are the deeds of ownership for Emlyn, should you discover where he is. He has been made heir to the wealth and trading business of Tomasso Capaccio.'

Ambrose Chillingworth laughed while Bartolomeo stared at him in surprise. When he had recovered himself, Chillingworth wiped the tears of mirth from his eyes. 'I heard from Carmelia that Emlyn had found his father. I cannot tell you how overjoyed I am to hear this confirmed.'

'Well I'm afraid that it is not as simple as it appears, Capaccio will stand trial for the crimes he has been accused of. Emlyn does not know what his father has done for him. Will you send me word if he comes here?'

'Most certainly,' said Chillingworth merrily.

'I have been instructed to inform him of another matter too, which is most urgent,' said Bartolomeo. 'He is to come to the Ducal Palace tomorrow at the hour of ten. This is an order by senator Erizzo and it is one that Emlyn must not ignore. If you will forgive me sir, I have much to see to. Perhaps we will meet again in better circumstances.'

Chillingworth bowed again. 'I would be happy to do so.'

Soon after, Bartolomeo left and hired a boatman to take him to Tomasso's butter-yellow palace. The boatman talked of the disastrous Grimani wedding, which seemed to be the subject on every tongue. Bartolomeo offered little response until the boatman mentioned the death of Jacopo. This was sad news to Bartolomeo and he sat in silence for the rest of the journey. He had known Jacopo and Maria for many years and he felt as if a part of himself had been extinguished with Jacopo's death. It was such a terrible waste of a good man's life, a father who had seen one son die, but who had so many other children to support.

Bartolomeo felt drained mentally and physically. He wished that Tomasso had told him more about the business in Stamboul and what exactly Tomasso had done in the twenty years that he had been away from Venice. There may be something there that could save him from the hangman's noose. If he had been spying on the Sublime Port, there was a chance that the Senate would be lenient. Symeon had probably known more about Tomasso's secrets than any of them, but Symeon had left, Tomasso had sent him away with no explanation.

Chapter 52 Venice

Tomasso stood for a long time waiting. Don Carlos was eating sugared figs and pickled lemons and a dish of scented candied fruits lay open on the desk. Tomasso had paid a fortune for them. Grimani did not look up, his fat fingers probed a clay jar and emerged with a blood red fig. He popped it into his mouth, the syrup running down his padded chin.

He was dressed in loose robes with a napkin tucked at his chin. His sleeves were rolled to the elbow like a manual worker, revealing thick, strong forearms as hairless as a child's. He wore a soft hat, the pleats of velvet falling to one shoulder like an empty sack; it was blue and banded with gold braid with a single jewel above the forehead. Beside him lay his eating knife the ornate hilt winking in the generous light. He wiped his fingers meticulously. His small eyes lifted and glittered like agates. He said, 'Release his hands and strip him of doublet and shirt. He is not going to do anything foolish, are you Capaccio?'

'That depends,' said Tomasso. Someone cut the rope behind him, he felt the sting of a spiteful blade before he brought his hands to the front and rubbed at his wrists. He added, 'after all, you are eating my lemons.'

'Lemons?'

'That is what all this is about,' Tomasso answered, 'lemons and spice, silk and baubles. On my death, with no named heir, my wealth will go to the Signori of Venice.'

'You are cunning, I'll grant.' Grimani dabbed at his jowls with napkin and handed it to the boy, Uglino who stood behind him. 'I will not be rushed. We will come to lemons and heir when I am ready. You have no man servant, allow mine to undress you.'

Tomasso didn't struggle. The same blade that had nicked his wrist, parted the fine quilting of his doublet, sheering through lacing and cloth with the ease of cutting butter. He felt darkness crowding his mind when the bandaging too was cut and pulled away. He reeled and steadied himself.

Grimani had picked up his knife, he was cleaning his nails with it. His eyes shone with malice as he watched and expression of delight spread his rolling chins. 'As we had guessed!' he exclaimed. 'An old would, but not much older than a week a little more. A wound received in battle, in fact a battle at sea in which you bravely led pirates to fall upon Venetian trading ships. And what do we do to our enemy the unbeliever, the enemy of the Holy Church? Pluck out his tongue, scoop out his eyes, slice off his circumcised member and feed it to him? Would such a death gain him the gates of Paradise?'

The words had no more effect on Tomasso than they had the last time he had heard them. 'I have heard it told,' he replied, 'that Allah is merciful.'

'I take that to be an admission that I speak the truth,' Grimani smirked. 'Further proof lies in the ease by which you obtain your eastern goods. Why, I ask myself, go to Stamboul for spice when it can be easier obtained in Alexandria? Because taxes can be avoided and a greater profit made. You told me so yourself. Taxes can only be avoided through the favour of the Sublime Port, indeed, the favour of the Sultan himself. What do you do for such privileges Capaccio? No, do not bother to answer. You have been clever, but I have been more so. Venice is at peace with the Turk. It is known that you have visited the Signori on occasion. What secrets you must have discovered to send to the Turkish Sultan. Not content to war with me alone, you have included Venice herself in your retaliation. Were I a compassionate man, I would understand, for they turned their backs on you in your need.'

'Then hand me to the Signori and let them be my judges. They may make their accusations and ask their questions, to which I will respond as best I am able. You however, will not beat me into confession, interesting though you may find it.'

'I am not a crude man unless necessity demands it.' Grimani's voice rose as he spoke. 'But violence breeds violence and you have some deeds to answer for. Who but an unbelieving Muslim would take from a man all that he values and yet leave him to live with that loss? A bull for the cow, a ram for the ewe, a hog for the sow, a tooth for a tooth and an eye for an eye. My grandson Lorenzo is timid. I am quite prepared to act on his behalf.'

Tomasso remained silent. The cup fills, should we care whether with bitter or with sweet? Drink on! Know that long after us, the sickle moon must keep her long-determined course.

Grimani spun the blade in his hand, it folded dark with light as it turned. 'I see that you are not afraid. That is well, I admire a brave man. Even the finest pot can be crushed with the right pressure applied. I wonder did Lorenzo scream as you will scream? I wonder did Paolo beg for his life as you will beg for death? I'm afraid that there will not be much left of you for the Signori to question.'

He placed the knife on the table and folded his hands together. 'I want all that you have taken from me,' he continued. 'I know that this is impossible. How could you un-drink the malmsey? Un-burn the warehouse and the Cyprus vineyards? Can you rebuild my ships? How do you give back to a man the means of fathering children? And you cannot give back a life once taken. We have learned that you have a son by the witch who is at the start of all this. I heard this from Lorenzo, my dear grandson who heard it from that old Franciscan that was so determined to see matters dealt with fairly. He is a pleasant boy, Emilio; skin as soft as silk, curls as charming as a girl's and his voice, a nightingale. We will keep him close to us, shall we Uglino? We will teach him the higher arts of love. His beauty and slimness will compliment me.'

'You are mistaken,' said Tomasso. 'It is common surely, for the bastards to crawl out of the woodwork when the 'father' becomes rich. He is not one of mine, I never laid eyes on him before he attempted to kill me. Take him to your bed, if that is your desire. You will extract your daughter first, for the sake of some decency?'

He expected to have something thrown at him or a snapped order to bring the blows. None came.

Grimani pursed his lips and leaned back, the chair creaking under his weight. 'Carmelia, you will be glad to know, has been found. Do you still want her as wife. It could still be arranged.'

'A simple solution to your problems and mine,' said Tomasso. 'What a pity the boy interfered before I could bed her. Summon her by all means. Do we have a priest?'

'They are easily obtainable. When you are presentable the bride and priest will be here.'

'Were I to wed Carmelia,' said Tomasso, 'I would not live long afterwards, my wealth will be secured first no doubt. I cannot possibly agree nor see how you thought I would.' Tomasso laughed. 'When first the sky's wild horses won their saddles, when Jupiter first blazed and the Seven Sisters spanned the heavens, my fate was proclaimed from God's judgement seat. How can I err? I act as written. In Sha Allah.'

'You disappoint me.' Grimani stood, his face flushed with anger. 'You are not a brave man after all. You hold your wealth above the life of your son.'

'Let the Signori decide my fate,' said Tomasso. 'Or do revelations of the past worry you? They will be known, whether I die or not.'

'I think I believe you,' said Carlos calmly. 'Having lost all, what further harm can befall me? A drowning man may as well bemoan the rain. Sign to me your business and your property and you will be free to take ship from here and, for the sake of the life you hold so cheap, never return. I might consider sparing Emilio also.'

Tomasso said, 'It is not death I fear, hell is the furnace of my suffering. I would that I could take your soul there too. I must be content that you are knocked from your tower and know absolute defeat. You are too old and detested a man to recover now, your remaining years will be spent in mourning and in memory of the dead who have worked their vengeance through me.'

Grimani nodded his head once. The men behind Tomasso moved forward. He dropped under their blows and sank into a well of darkness.

Fiorenza has left threads of blue silk to indicate which canals the boat had taken. Symeon and Emlyn followed quickly for it seemed as if she had unthreaded the whole of her shawl to be sure that they would know the way. The trail drew them from the Rialto into the intricate back waterways. They eventually reached a wide canal lined with warehouses. It was still raining thinly and the wind had dropped. Without a moon, the night was deep black and the waters a leaden grey. Symeon saw a shift of movement and pointed to where Fiorenza stood concealed partially by a line of fishing nets. She had been looking out for them and signalled for them to approach cautiously.

They crouched down amongst the damp ropes and Emlyn looked across the square. He noticed first, the door of the nearest warehouse, it was painted roughly with a salamander and two lamps burned fitfully on either side. There was a wooden pier running off to one side out into the water, a mere walkway cluttered with barrels and coils of rope. A long rowing boat was tethered alongside. In front of the warehouse four men stood conversing quietly. There were no windows, bit light streamed out from beneath the closed doors.

Symeon spoke in a whisper beside him. 'They have brought him here, to his own warehouse?'

'I don't know why,' Fiorenza answered. 'I have not seen Don Carlos, but he could be inside, there is a door at the front. I am so afraid for him!'

Emlyn knew of whom she spoke. He touched her and smiled at her. That she loved Capaccio had been plain to him from the start. Yet he had obviously turned away from her when he had chosen to marry Carmelia.

Emlyn shook his head, bewildered by the irrational choices that had been made in all this. He explained quickly to her what they had learned, his eyes constantly straying to the guards who wandered about restless in the rain. 'Now you must go back with Symeon,' he added. 'Someone must inform the proper authorities before further harm befalls anyone.'

She gripped his arm and shook him. 'Tomasso will have to stand trial if the Senate become involved!'

Symeon answered her. 'Madonna, they already are involved, that's why they sent a barge to collect Messer Tomasso.'

'There is to be an inquiry held tomorrow, to which all concerned are to attend.'

Fiorenza's voice showed the depth of her love as she pleaded. Emlyn felt drawn towards her; what man could not heed such selfless devotion? She said, 'Symeon, you out of us all know more about Tomasso, tell me truthfully was he the instigator of the attack on Grimani's ships? Did he in fact lead the attack himself?'

'I have not heard this from his lips,' Symeon answered softly. 'Yet, my heart tells me that it is so. He is a man of many guises and I have guessed much of what he was before he came here. To tell what I know would betray a trust that I hold as dear as life. I will not break it.'

'Then the Senate will have no choice but to condemn him to death, for he has struck Venice herself in attacking her merchant ships.'

'He would not face such a death as that with fear Madonna,' Symeon answered with a dreamy quality in his voice. 'It would be preferable to death by the hand of his enemy in whose grasp he now lies.'

Emlyn hissed them to silence. Two of the guard where approaching with their weapons drawn. 'Go quickly!'

'What of you?' Fiorenza objected.

It was too late. Raised voices reached them and the men began to run. Emlyn leaped to his feet. He pushed Symeon and Fiorenza away. 'Take her Symeon. I will distract them and lead them away.'

'You will be taken!' Symeon warned as he moved.

'I intend to be,' laughed Emlyn. 'Once inside I'll have better chance to upset Grimani's plans, while you hurry back.'

Symeon grasped Fiorenza's arms and guided her into the darkness. Emlyn leaped over the fishing nets with such suddenness that the guards were too startled to react before he had passed them. He ran with all the speed he could muster straight towards the warehouse.

The other two men ran forward to cut off his escape. Emlyn ducked and swerved away changing direction. All four men followed in close pursuit. Emlyn could hear the confusion of voices and heard others join the chase. He ran to the wooden pier. There was water all around him, so they would catch him eventually. As was his habit, he used whatever came to hand, cavorting, diving and leaping as he avoided their clumsy attempts to trap him. He grinned, having gained his objective and drawn them away. He laughed and led them on a merry chase that lasted longer than even he had thought possible. They caught him in the end because he couldn't swim.

Soon after he arrived at Tomasso's trading house, Bartolomeo learned that Fiorenza and Enrico had gone off over two hours ago with the young foreigner; one even said that he had seen Symeon with them, who they all thought had left Venice that morning. Bartolomeo guessed that the three or the four of them had gone to Grimani's house and that they would soon learn what had happened and return here. A servant brought him a plate of bread, cheese and olives and a flagon of wine. Bartolomeo forced himself to sit calmly and eat, while his thoughts ran in a turmoil. The servant returned a few moments later with a dripping messenger in tow. He wore the livery of Senator Sebastiano Erizzo.

Bartolomeo looked at him with dread, knowing from his expression that his news was not good. 'Speak, speak!' he said impatiently.

'Signore, the prisoner never arrived at the Palace,' the man explained. 'A man came soon after my master discovered this. He was your notary, Enrico de Martoni, he informed Signore Erizzo that the prisoner had been taken to a place of secrecy and that Madonna Fiorenza Balsamo and a servant had followed, promising to send word as soon as they could. You are required to return with me Signore, for that is where they will come to. Signore Erizzo has summoned men in readiness.'

Bartolomeo stood up slowly, the words sinking in like syrup. He saw then that he had been a fool. He had allowed himself to forget the viciousness of Grimani. He pulled on his damp cloak and motioned to the man to precede him. He made his way through the counting room, questioning the few men that remained there. They could tell him nothing more. He began to run before he reached the door, suddenly afraid for Fiorenza's safety.

He was brought up short outside by a cry that wrenched at his heart.

Fiorenza was running towards him from the water edge. She threw herself sobbing into his arms. Bartolomeo nearly cried out from the intensity of his feeling. He wrapped her in his arms and held her close. 'Fiora, Fiora,' he whispered with all the music of his heart.

She drew back and looked up at him. Her hair hung loose about her and her face was streaked with dirt. Her tear-rimmed eyes were deep wells of emotion. 'They have him!' she cried, 'There is no time! Grimani has him at our warehouse. He will kill him Bartolomeo!'

'Be calm Fiora,' said Bartolomeo, 'You are safe now.'

'We followed the boat that took Tomasso, Symeon and I and the young boy Emlyn,' she said, stumbling over the words in her panic. She grasped his arm and pulled him towards a waiting boat. 'Emlyn was taken by Grimani's men in order that we could escape and inform the Senate, he risked his life. Symeon and I ran for all we were worth. But Emlyn's ruse did not work. We were followed and could not move fast enough. Symeon pushed me into a doorway and he ran out to them armed with nothing better than an oar. I saw them fight and knew that he stood little chance of success. So I came here with all speed. Quickly, I beg you!'

'Wait,' said Bartolomeo. 'We must be better prepared.'

She pulled at him, her face a mask of anguish. Bartolomeo patted her gently, 'A moment only,' he explained. He ran back to the building and ordered the clerks, the workers and boatmen to arm themselves with whatever they could lay their hands on and to pile into the boats. Senator Erizzo's messenger objected persistently, until Bartolomeo paused by the door and gripped his shoulder. 'Go to Erizzo,' he said in a tone that invited no argument. 'Tell him to bring his men to the warehouse of the Spice company, he knows where it is. And hurry!'

Tomasso felt a little of his strength return when he had eaten the meagre plate of food and drank the wine that a charitable man had passed to him. He had been brought to the front of the building and was sitting against a wall. At one end of the long store room, barrels were stacked from floor to ceiling. Tomasso knew what was in them, he could read the Arabic inscriptions on the sides. But he did not look at them for long. He looked instead at the youth who sat on the window seat gazing out of the window.

How had the Franciscan arrived at the conclusion that this was his son? He did closely resemble Anna in the falcon-grey eyes and the dark ringlets and a certain graceful delicacy of his posture. He sat very still, one knee drawn up with his left hand draped over. A fire brand in the wall sconce threw fey shadows dancing about the walls.

Such characteristics could be shared by a people, thought Tomasso, the Welsh. He had only ever met one. He dismissed the idea, people came in all shapes and sizes from whatever parts. Emlyn's other hand lay still beside him, like the rest of him, it was dirty, it was bound with a scrap of

Venetian lace that Tomasso recognised but could not recall from where. Tomasso smiled to himself and shook his head.

The movement, slight though it was, broke Emlyn's trance-like stillness. He looked across the room, his eyes slightly bemused. They cleared and widened with curiosity.

Tomasso drew his knees up and folded his hands across them. He had been given a shirt to replace the one he had lost, it was of inferior quality. Tomasso said, 'Tell me about your mother.'

He answered without hesitation. 'My memories are from childhood sir. She wore sequins in her hair and jewelled slippers. Her voice was like the rain filled streams of Eryri Mynydd murmuring softly through moss and fern. Her touch was a soft and delicate as a new-born leaf,' He paused and closed his eyes. 'Do I remember the same woman that you once loved?'

'I do not know,' said Tomasso. 'I believed that in all that is to come from this that at least you and Carmelia would escape unscathed. Why are you here?'

'I could not go,' Emlyn said. 'I tried, believe me. But I could not walk away form the reason I came here to Venice.'

'I know,' Tomasso interrupted. 'Fra Sebastiano told me a great deal about you. You are a son to be proud of Emlyn Tomas.'

'Do you think that it is true?'

'That you are my son? Do you doubt this yourself?'

'I was about six when I left my mother's home. I remember a different man as father. Until now I have been afraid to name him.'

'The Franciscan tells me that you came from a Muslim house, is this the reason?'

Emlyn nodded and smiled faintly. 'It was the reaction of others that made me fearful. By coming here, I hoped to discover what exactly had happened to my mother and how I had come to be there in the first place. The man I remember is an Arab or a Turk,'

'And are you so ashamed that you do not recall his name?'

'Ashamed? I am not ashamed, nor ever have been. His name was Mohammed Khalil.'

'It is perhaps a Turkish name, but I do not know it.'

'How could you?'

'Names, Emlyn, can be used like clothing, they can be assumed or discarded as expediency dictates.'

'As you nave done so yourself?'

'Capaccio is my true name Emlyn. Vincentini is a name I have adopted for a number of years but I have also had others. Change was forced upon me and had I not adapted where necessary, I would never have survived. I have been both poor and great and have followed many trades, often taking on an identity to suit the situation, for I have travelled far and mixed with many peoples.'

'All in order to came back here and wreak your revenge?'

Tomasso nodded. 'The reasons are mine alone and I am not prepared to discuss them. It is too late now in my life for me to be a father to you, but I have provided for you in giving you the ownership of the company I created here. Do you not see Emlyn? That you will have nothing to fear now in Venice. No one will prevent you from marrying the woman you have chosen. Wealth pushes aside all prejudice and animosity.'

Emlyn sat for a long while in silence. Tomasso guessed at his fears, for they were his also. Grimani would think that he now held of the only possible lever that would make Tomasso change his mind. No matter what he now hoped for, Tomasso was afraid that neither of them would leave here alive.

Eventually Emlyn said, 'And if I am not your son?'

Tomasso dropped his head back and a great sigh ran through him. 'I do not act thus because you are or are not my son. It is so because of your mother Emlyn. I know that you are hers, I do not even need to see the gems she gave you, for she is formed again in you. She lived to give birth to you and to watch you grow.'

'With your knowledge,' Emlyn replied, 'could you not have searched for her? Would the reward not have been greater?'

'There were few people who knew what really happened and I was not among them. I thought for all those years that she had died when her ship had been attacked at sea. I only learned of the truth recently. Her captors send a ransom demand to Grimani. He read it and then he put it to the flames. As far as he was concerned, he was well rid of her. I do not know what happened to her afterwards and when you came to be. It is possible that she was carrying my child when this occurred. We had two weeks of complete togetherness before Grimani axe fell and split us asunder. He always planned well, this was the secret of his success. When he acted, he acted swiftly. Anna was sent away from Venice a few hours after she was taken. I knew none of this then. God had deserted me, for had I known I would have given my life to free her.'

Tomasso shifted his position feeling the tendrils of sleep pull at his every nerve. 'There was that between her and I that was formed in Heaven,' he continued softly. 'It was the love of Tristan and Isolde, of Lancelot and Genevieve, and like so many pure meetings of hearts and souls, it was doomed from the start. Such love is only love, an unblemished completeness like the pearl unto the oyster, the bee unto the flower. Who am I that I should be so blessed?

'I survived the punishment that was set upon me. I survived because the light had gone from my soul. I became the opposite of what I once was. I was not a man but a horned weapon, a blade of unbreakable steel; forged by the searing ambition of Carlo Grimani and strengthened by the slave-master's whip. My hands became as callused as my heart as I gripped the oar and fed upon the black bile of vengeance. She and I, far apart as we were in our origins, were crafted for each other. Where love blesses with such godliness, woe betide the man who seeks to part the two halves. Had I known Emlyn, that she had lived, nothing would have prevented me from finding her.'

Tomasso stopped speaking. He dragged his hand across his forehead and through his hair. He did not know why he had spoken now with a depth of feeling he had kept hidden for years nor why he had said as much to this strange youth who watched him with Anna's eyes. He looked up and said, 'If you have found such love as this Emlyn, as you fought with me, fight now to keep her by your side.'

'And if I should lose her,' Emlyn said, 'will I become as embittered as you have allowed yourself to become?'

Tomasso smiled. 'Every man seeks his own way, though we are not always free to choose the path we follow, they are chosen for us by circumstance. I have walked crooked paths and righteously so, but I would have had it different, had I been allowed to choose my way.'

'I too,' said the boy smiling easily. 'I will tell you what I know and then let us judge whether we share the love of the same woman, one as husband, the other as son. He looked discomforted at first, dropping his head and grasping his hands together, but when he began to speak, his nervousness disappeared. Tomasso recalled the same untidy head bent over a lute and the long fingers spinning out a magic that had entrapped them all.

'I was named Emlyn by my grandfather, he holds a very special place in his heart for my mother. I don't think he ever forgave her for leaving the way she did and I like to think that she sent me to him because of it. Her name was never mentioned in my uncles house, where I was brought up. I usually ended up with a clip around the ear if I mentioned her and sometime much worse. So I forced her out of my mind and only seldom allowed myself the pleasure of her memory.

Tomasso closed he eyes and listened. The voice was soft, the cadence and fall of expression, compelling. Emlyn spoke of fragmented memories from childhood, the colour of a different land, the sound of courtyard fountain and the laughter of women. A young child's pictures of a loved childhood in a house of pampered women. Then of the lessons; the archery, horsemanship, the reading of the Koran and of the wild ride through the night and the long journey that followed, taking Emlyn eventually to the house of his relations.

Silence followed when he had ended. They had both tried to portray the essence of their feeling. Tomasso had felt that this was necessary, whatever happened, they would not have this chance again. He was surprised that Emlyn had sensed this and responded the way he had.

Emlyn looked across to him and smiled. 'My mother called me Toma.'

Tomasso felt a wave of utter weariness wash through him; a weakness, as if something inside him had broken. He opened his eyes when noise intruded and light flooded through the door. Grimani men entered and roughly pulled them both to their feet. When Tomasso drew level with Emlyn, he felt an odd glow of smugness and felt with certainty that he was looking upon his own son. Emlyn met his gaze and offered a brave smile.

Don Carlos showed none of his earlier control, he was agitated and angry. In the bright candlelight, his face flushed and his scant hair, curling damp on his forehead. When his prisoners arrived, he walked straight up to Tomasso and prodded his chest with a walking stick. 'Changed your mind Capaccio?'

Tomasso slowly shook his head,

'I'm glad,' said Don Carlos. 'You see, I have already started the fun a little early. You will find my methods of violence are more poignant than yours. I believe in instant retaliation.'

Carlos stood in front of Emlyn and grasped a handful of the thin flesh on his cheek. Emlyn winced and tried to pull away, but the grip on him tightened. He endured the unpleasant touch with burning hostility in his dark eyes. Don Carlos' fingers relaxed and patted with mock affection. 'Poor boy,' he said, 'He wanted to interrupt our little gathering by informing the Senate. Silly child.'

He stepped back and clapped his hands sharply. Two men standing in the doorway nodded and disappeared. 'I am sorry to disappoint you both,' Don Carlos said in a silken voice, 'Poor Emilio, your scheme came to nothing.'

Tomasso knew nothing of what Emlyn had planned. He waited with a growing sense of fear. When the two men returned, they dragged another between them. They came into the room and dropped the body on the floor.

That it was a dead body was plain to see; no life pulsed through Symeon's veins nor pumped through his generous heart. Carlos kicked the still form over and Symeon's mutilated face revealed his suffering. The sound that escaped Tomasso's lips was like a wounded animal. He was not aware that he had moved, yet he was on the floor beside the body, trying desperately to pull the stained clothing over Symeon's face. His own tears splashed his hands. He shook with despair and knew that what had broken inside him, was the strength and blind resolve that had kept him on this path of vengeance.

'Exquisite, is it not?' said Don Carlos. 'To see so great a man brought to his knees by the death of a mere servant. I am gratified to see such suffering. How much greater my pleasure will be to see you witness the prolonged agony and death of your own flesh and blood.'

Emlyn had remained perfectly still, although he was no longer held physically. He was shocked and horrified; but a short time before, Symeon's dark hands had pulled an oar with him. This was a man who he had come to admire and respect, but who now lay unrecognisable apart from those long, tapered hands. Emlyn recalled Enrico's words, *he was afraid to stay here, he said death awaited him within these walls, can you believe that?'* Still Emlyn could not believe what his eyes told him.

Even in the pain of his grief, Tomasso was startled by what happened next. He knew that the boy was agile, he had witness it while they had fought, but nothing had prepared him for this desperate attempt for escape.

Emlyn suddenly dropped and spun away from the men behind him. He scuttled off and had run half way across the room before anyone realised what was happening. The guards followed, cursing. Emlyn climbed over furniture, scrambled up bales, twisted and turned from every attempt to trap him. He threw objects with deft skill, bringing men to their knees; if any reached out and caught a hold on him, he seemed to explode in a whir of flying limbs. He reached the far side and leaped up the wall like a monkey, reaching for the high window.

Don Carlos watched it all with no show of alarm, if anything, his face showed slight amusement. He knew that Emlyn's attempts were futile. His small, pouched eyes turned to Tomasso with a gleam of unhealthy pleasure. 'Such spirit,' he whispered licking his lips. Then he lifted his voice and shouted to his men, moving a pace or two away.

Tomasso was strengthened by the hatred this man fed to him. He had noted the eating knife discarded on the table and Grimani's men were fully occupied. Still crouched, he moved to the other side of Symeon's body and stood slowly, inching toward the table.

Emlyn had reached the narrow window ledge and was hammering at the wooden shutters. The men below, cursed him soundly as they attempted to reach him. One found a boat hook, a long staff with a metal claw at the end. Emlyn tried to avoid it as it came up to strike him from his perch, but he could not move far without losing his purchase. At the third attempt, the hook slammed into his leg and hooked into his flesh. He cried out as the man pulled and tumbled from the window ledge. He landed among them.

Tomasso took advantage of the confusion. The knife was in his hand in a moment. With no hesitation, he spun it and gripped the blade, lifting it to throw at the broad hated back now turned to him. At the same instant that he made the throw something crashed into him. The impact sent him sprawling and the knife clattered on the tiles.

'Patron!'

Don Carlos spun around with surprising speed. He quickly saw what had happened. His faithful boy, Uglino had saved him from death.

Tomasso struggled to a rise but, Uglino picked up the knife and held it to his throat.

'Shall I kill him Padrone?' Uglino asked, the words hissed through clenched teeth.

Grimani called to his men to attend him.

To Tomasso's surprise, they did not obey the summons, though they were momentarily distracted. Emlyn rose from their midst like a mad dog. With unbelievable strength he wrenched himself from the captive hands, his feet kicking out with vicious intent. They fell away from him, stumbling out of the way. He was off again.

Now Don Carlos was angry, his voice rose, threatening dire consequence to any who failed him. He turned to Tomasso and stood towering above him. He shook his fist, his eyes red with anger, his lips moist with spittle. 'Such a death you will witness now Capaccio that you wish you had never been born,' he growled. 'And after the agony of your son, you have your own end to look forward to. I promise you, you will look forward to both deaths. You will beg for them!'

His men chased Emlyn with drawn swords. He was stumbling now, his movements clumsy and ill judged. Yet his luck held until he reached the main doors. Incredulously, he ran back a few paces straight towards the swords. Then he turned and head down, shoulder forward, he charged straight at closed double doors. He seemed to fly into them and the crash resounded around the room. The doors opened with ease and Emlyn Tomas staggered out into a cluster of men armed with pikes.

Tomasso groaned. He admired the boy's foolish attempts and the fierce courage that drove him to fight to the very end. Perhaps he had forgotten the guards outside the building, perhaps he was beyond caring. Tomasso realised the pressure of the blade at his throat had gone and knew that he now awaited the unfolding of Don Carlos' terrible threats. He closed his eyes and gathered his last strength.

'Thank the Saints!' a familiar voice cried. 'We are in time. Tomasso?

He didn't open his eyes as a thrill of near unbearable relief flooded through him. Some one was bending over him. 'Tomasso?'

He said, 'There is only one thing I want 'Tolomeo.'

'What?' Bartolomeo Varini asked on a bubble of laughter.

Tomasso looked at him, to be sure that he was not dreaming. 'Find me a bed, any bed will do. And leave me there for a few days.'

'Give me your oath that you will not attempt to escape and you can have one at the Ducal Palace.'

Tomasso looked at the other man who had joined them. 'Signore Erizzo. You got the verse then?'

Senator Erizzo nodded solemnly. 'I will do what I can for you, but I can not promise you your freedom or your life. All will be heard and decided at an inquiry in the morning.'

There was a great deal of confusion milling about him at first, Tomasso was scarcely aware of it. Emlyn came and sat beside him while they waited to join the boats. He did not speak. Life was suddenly very precious to Tomasso. He saw a bedraggled figure standing in the doorway, her hair loose about her and her dress torn, Fiorenza, a brave, sad smile playing on her full lips.

The wind had dropped and the light rain fell straight, tattooing the water and making fire-flies of droplets in the twin pools of lamplight outside Theo's gate. Numb with fatigue, Emlyn came and paused. He felt that one more step was beyond his ability. He stayed where he was, his head pelted with rain, his hair hanging straightened from its curls by the weight of water. Every part of him was soaked. The water level had risen, washing over the flagstones and pooling around the shattered stone griffin, though the head had not shattered in the impact. The cruel beak was frozen into the silent cry of a hawk, the hollow eyes were filled with water that overspilled like black tears.

Emlyn shuddered and looked towards the house. He knew that she wasn't there. No Carmelia waited for him behind those warm, square windows that spilled a welcoming light into the yard. He closed his eyes and flung his head back, tasting the rain. How easy it would be to turn from here and to disappear into the labyrinth that was Venice. He had found love and lost love, he had found a man that he could call father, but he had lost him, or soon would. Mafanwy had warned him that he would find regret at the end of his search and that he would wish that he had never come. She had been so right. Would he have been happier if he had never attempted to find out the truth behind his birth? Was the name bastard so hard to bear?

'My soul cleaves to the land that bred me,' he whispered to himself, 'and to the soil that ran once through my fingers. Blood is of no account when compared to that enchanted place, to those deep wooded vales hung with sweet memory. And to that pure harmony of harp and song which races the blood like mountain streams. I should have claimed that beloved land as father, for no man has been greater bred than I. It is to my sorrow, that my eyes were not opened to this truth sooner.'

Emlyn heard a door open behind him and saw lamplight spread to where he was. He turned and saw Ambrose Chillingworth standing in the doorway with the lamp held aloft. He was smiling. He said, 'Emlyn Tomasso Capaccio the younger, I believe.'

Emlyn sighed and trudged forward, at least he would not have to explain that part. He was glad to see Ambrose and shook the hand that was held out to him.

Ambrose said, 'I sent Carmelia off with Adriana Martinelli.'

'Did she go willingly?'

'Oh yes,' Ambrose replied enthusiastically. 'We talked at length, she and I. I did not influence her, she made the decision on her own.'

'What decision?'

'She and Adriana left for the mainland before nightfall with another lady and a few maids and men to see them to their destination. She needs time Emlyn, no one has allowed her any since she arrived here. She told me to give this to you.' He held out a small roll of paper tied up with a ribbon.

Emlyn was still standing in the rain, as he unfurled the paper, the single written line became wet and began to wash away.

'*Be happy sweet love, wherever you go. Love, fare thee well.*'

Emlyn let it fall, the ink ran like dye, the ribbon a bright scar on its surface. He answered her aloud, his voice raw with pain. 'No Cariad, you know where lies my heart.'

'Are you coming in?' Ambrose held the door open. 'You can leave the rain outside. She has made a wise decision Emlyn. I see that it is difficult for you to accept. But it was by her own will. You are both young enough to recover from this doomed relationship.'

Emlyn came out of the rain. Nothing had been Carmelia's own will since she had come here. He did not believe that she had gone away from him without being influenced by either Ambrose or Adriana or some older busybody who thought he was acting in her interests.

It the warmth of the kitchen, he felt dizzy. He was vaguely aware of pulling off the sodden clothing and of being rubbed dry by Matthew. The kitchen fire warmed him and he felt sleep drag at him, pulling him into the comfort of its darkness.

He awoke a short time after. He was seated on a bench by the fire, slumped over the table. Someone was prodding painfully at him.

'Emlyn?'

He opened his eyes and saw Josquin bent over him, a hand on his shoulder. 'Why are you here?' he asked in confusion.

'I've been all over this Godforsaken watery place looking for you. Can you sit up?'

Emlyn had not forgotten the wounds he had suffered in his duel with Tomasso and afterwards. Now he felt as if they had been dealt him anew, as Josquin applied the thick potion that Eva had given him. Emlyn was surprised that she was not there herself. He sat in silence as Josquin bound the long sword cut that ran across his ribs, his hand had been bandaged while he slept. He moved his fingers stiffly, gratified that the hurts were nothing more serious than duelling cuts, delivered to force him to surrender.

Josquin talked quietly; he spoke of Spain and the war with the Morriscos, of the growing fame of Don John, King Philip's bastard brother who led the king;'s army against the Muslims, driving them to the sea. Emlyn half-listened and felt a surge of gratitude towards Josquin, he did not want to speak of the immediate past.

His relief was short lived. He hadn't realised that Ambrose was in the room.

Ambrose said, 'So now you are a rich merchant. Emlyn do you see what this means?'

Emlyn shook his head, he didn't know what Ambrose was talking about.

'He has made you the owner of his Spice company.'

Emlyn slowly pushed Josquin's hand aside and turned around. Ambrose was seated behind him on a comfortable chair by the window. He held a glass of wine in his hand and his feet tapped to a silent beat. He looked as smug as a cat with the cream. In his other hand, he held a rolled document with a broken seal. 'It's all here,' he explained. 'You have seventy per cent of the company, some woman owns the rest. You have a ship called the *Cornucopia* and secure suppliers in Stamboul itself. And in Alexandria,' he paused and his smile widened. 'And, Emlyn you have a chance to redeem yourself in William Cecil's favour. You can supply the base from which England can trade with the Levant, and anywhere we wish to go. This has all turned out wonderfully.'

Emlyn stood up quickly and gripped the table for support. 'Do you have any idea what you are saying?'

Ambrose's smile dropped. 'You are not pleased?'

'Is this why you told her to go? Is this why you got rid of Carmelia? I never took you for a cunning bastard, fool that I am. I should never have trusted you! Never have listened to your vile scheming!'

Ambrose rose, his expression alarmed. 'Wait Emlyn!'

Emlyn left the room and walked out into the yard, seeking the solace of the room he had shared with Theo's apprentices.

Someone splashed after him with a lamp. 'Emlyn, 'ere lad!' Matthew called.

Emlyn turned, Matthew had never called him by name before.

''Ave yer seen what she left 'ere?' Matthew was grinning. 'In yon stable, a lady's palfrey.'

Emlyn crossed to the shed indicated and saw the white horse standing out of the rain. She wore a bridal sewn with silver bells and had been given fresh hay that she munched in content. Emlyn ran his hand over her back and she nuzzled him affectionately. Matthew crossed to her other side and grasped the rein. He shook it so that the bells chimed. Emlyn looked over the horse's back and saw where the rein was held in Matthew's hand. There was a roll of paper tired securely between two bells. Matthew winked. He walked passed Emlyn and went out into the yard leaving the lamp behind.

Emlyn's finger's shook as he untied it. He sank into a pile of straw and held it as if it were some rare and precious gift. The light was dim but he could see Carmelia's neat writing across the page. *Beloved, your Englishman has told me all about your family and the land from which you come. Take me there, I can't wait to see it with you. My horse is fleet of foot, be thou swift in coming love. They are taking me to Vicenza, to the Palazzo Chiericati that overlooks the market square.*

Emlyn felt tears of joy sting his eyes.

Chapter 53 Venice The Trial

Word of the previous day's events had run like water through the canals of Venice. Many curious onlookers had gathered outside the Ducal Palace, as thick as pigeons in the warming sunlight, and as quarrelsome. Voices were raised calling for the blood of the prisoner who had attacked Venice's ships and sent Venetian seamen to their watery graves or to man the oars of heathen galleys. At times the mood was ugly and scuffles broke out; there were some in the crowd who supported Vincentini, having known his generosity.

Inside the palace, in the room chosen for the meeting, men began to arrive and gather in groups. The sun rose and filtered through the high leaded windows, washing the rich furnishings and décor in blots of vivid colour from the stained glass. As this inquiry would cover many topics concerning the city, a prestigious collection of Venice's nobility and churchmen filtered into the room, followed by their secretaries and clerks. There were a few high-ranking officials from the Doge's entourage, evident in their scarlet robes and members of the High Council who were the governors of the Republic. Churchmen by the dozen and the ten feared magistrates who were chosen by the city to keep it free from plots and spies and to judge its criminals.

Senator Sebastiano Erizzo stroked his drooping moustache, his eyes roving over the men on who's judgement the fate of Tomasso Vincentini / Capaccio would be decided: Pietro Barbarigo, a man notable for fairness; Domenico Foscari and Alessandro Contarini, both ruthless in their dealing with piracy; Giacomo Diedo, the chief magistrate; Alvise Da Mosto, named after his grandfather, a renowned seaman; the Bishop of San Marco himself, Pesaro and Balbi, names known to every Venetian. Marco Corner, Giustinian and Dandolo, who Erizzo had asked especially to attend, as their interests like his, were with the network of spies that provided Venice with valuable information.

Don Carlos Grimani came from a very old and respected bloodline. The Grimani had been at the centre of Venice's affairs for generations;

there was even an adjoining room named in their favour which displayed the family coat-of-arms on the ceiling. Don Carlos was quite at home in these hushed, elaborate surroundings, his name synonymous with the greatness of the Republic. He was seated now, smiling, surrounded by his friends and colleges. He owed money to many of them, but they smiled with him, masking their concern in spite of his assurances. At his side, sat the boy Uglino, who, to all appearances, he had adopted as his own son. The only close relative there was Don Carlos' grandson, the young priest of the Franciscan order Lorenzo, who sat to one side, his hands clasped in front of him and his brows knit in a frown.

Just inside the room, sat the foreigner, Emlyn Tomas who had caused so much disruption and who Don Carlos accused of absconding with his daughter Madonna Carmelia. Many here had witnessed the young man's skill with lute and agreed that his talent was rare, but he would find no patronage now, having disgraced himself. He was dressed in black Venetian cloth, plain and unadorned. He sat un-fidgeting, his eyes roaming over the lavish frescos, the clusters of marble cherubs supporting garlands and cornucopias filled with abundant harvest and all manner of bird and beast. The ceiling was aglow with gilt framing, the paintings, visions of heaven. The sheer power of Venice radiated from the walls, creating a hushed, awesome atmosphere, intimidating to a newcomer such as he. He had chosen to sit where few would notice him, as if daunted by his surroundings.

An elderly friar approached him, walking with the aid of a stick. They exchanged a few words before moving further into the room and taking their place beside Bartolomeo Varini and Enrico de Martoni. Voices muttered, hands gesticulated through the room like butterflies. There was a tension in the air like the calm before a storm.

The voice of the court officer attempted to rise above the babble, his words half heard as he read. 'At the insistence of Doge Pietro Loredan. Accusations brought against Tomasso Di Vincentini, otherwise know as Capaccio.' He sped briefly through the preliminaries; all there knew the reasons behind the inquiry.

Senator Erizzo recognised most of the faces, there were a few he did not know, mostly among the witnesses of Don Carlos Grimani. In time, the tiered benches filled and the clerks settled at the lower seats behind tables, their quills sharpened, their papers spread. Voices dropped in expectancy as the usher called for silence. Chairs scraped, throats cleared and eyes swivelled as the two pike men stood stiffly at the open door. Four of the prison guard entered, clad in burnished breastplates, chain mail and plumbed helms. Behind them walked the prisoner and behind him, another two guards.

The guards withdrew. Don Carlos gazed at the prisoner dispassionately as the usher addressed him. Capaccio answered, his voice controlled and audible.

Senator Sebastiano Erizzo, head of the Senate's secrete network of spies, leaned back in his seat and frowned. He was not looking forward to the long proceedings to be gone through before anyone even mentioned Cyprus. The night before, when Capaccio had been brought to the Ducal palace, he had not spoken to anyone. He had been cared for by the Doge's own physician, but he had made no further mention of the four lines of verse he had sent to the palace. Here he would be questioned at length and here he would be judged. If found guilty of the charge of treason, the penalty was a final one. Erizzo suspected that he would hold out to the very end and only then bring forth the matter concerning Cyprus, perhaps to save himself from the fate that many already spoke of as decided.

There had been many men far from the shores of Venice, who had at some time had dealings with the Syrian trader who had come down the road from Samakand and brought camels loaded with eastern luxuries. They had come to know him briefly as a man with an uncanny gift for knowing the markets and with an ability to obtain anything the heart desired, at a price. Yet there were none of those now at the Ducal Palace who would know Tomasso Capaccio as Ismael the Syrian. Had there been, they would have recognised the same unaffected self-assurance and the proud, princely bearing.

He was dressed in simpler attire to that they had come to expect, yet, even stripped of his jewels and finery, he commanded a begrudged respect. He stood before a table in the centre of the long room, his hands clasped, his head slightly bent as if listening.

Bartolomeo Varini, the Spice Company manager, crossed the room. He was darkly attired and wore a cap with ear flaps. He spoke a few words to his employer and Capaccio shook his head. On his way to his seat, Varini's keen, intelligent eyes scanned the room, narrowing at the sight of Grimani's group, gathered on the right hand benches.

Soon after, Don Carlos Grimani stood and cleared his throat. 'I beg your indulgence my Lords,' he said. 'Before we proceed, may we be given some explanation for the unseemly hurry with which this matter is being brought before you?'

The chief magistrate, Giacomo Diedo answered. 'We are here to learn the facts of a matter that stretches back over many years. So that the truth may be more easily accessible, it was decided to hold this meeting as soon as possible; facts, as you know Signor Grimani, have a habit of becoming unclear if left to idle.'

Grimani spluttered with indignation. 'Are you suggesting that I …'

'I suggest nothing Signore. You may be seated.' Diedo's eyes swept around the room, dwelling momentarily on the prisoner who stood calmly in the centre. 'It is known,' Diedo added, 'that the vendetta between Don Carlos Grimani and Messer Tomasso Capaccio is one of many years endurance. It is not the habit of the Signori to interfere over much in quarrels where duty and loyalty to family bring men to conflict. Yet this vendetta has touched upon the interest and safety of Venice herself. Serious charges are here by brought against the person of Tomasso di Vincentini, otherwise known as Capaccio. Oaths will be sworn and all concerned will be heard in due course. Signor Grimani?'

Don Carlos stood again, this time he seemed grown in stature. He looked in perfect control; a proud, dominating man confident of his standing and reputation within these walls of the Ducal Palace. 'The first strike that this man made against me,' he began, 'was done before anyone here had seen or even heard of the spice merchant Tomasso di Vincentini. My ships had left Cyprus with a cargo of Malmsey, sugar and grain. They were attacked before they even reached Rhodes. Vastly outnumbered they were overrun and the fight was short and brutal. The crew were murdered or sold into slavery, God only knows. The two vessels were brought to Rhodes at night and left there, damaged and unmanned.' He paused, straightening a fold in his ermine-trimmed cloak.

'It was a mystery to me why the good vessels were abandon like this. As you can imagine my Lords, this caused great complications with my insurers and is a matter still unsettled. This has been a heavy loss to me and to all those to whom I am patron and employer. I know now, what truth lies behind this puzzle. That man, who sits before you so smug and sure of himself, that vile, black deceiver, attacked my ships in the guise of a pirate prince!'

A mumble, a rustle ran through the room.

'Preposterous isn't it?' Grimani added. 'Nevertheless, it is the truth, but we will return to that. Although I can produce no witness to support this accusation, I learned that Vincentini, on his first voyage from Stamboul to Venice, called at Naxos and took on a cargo of wine. It was mine. Each cask bore the burnt in symbol of my trading house.'

'Signore?' Diedo broke in. 'Without producing any witnesses to strengthen these accusations, is it wise to make them?'

'You find them hard to believe?' Grimani conjectured in an insulted tone. 'I assure you I am aware of the dangers of false accusation. You will see in time, how I arrived at this conclusion. 'We have yet to consider what happened after. So, Vincentini comes to Venice rich beyond avarice. His cargo of spice is sold before it hits the counters. So great is the demand that he elbows respected merchants aside and sells to whom he pleases. Personally, I am annoyed at this and make no pretences about my feelings. He seeks to amend matters between us by urging the widowed Fiorenza Balsamo to agree to sell the Lanarca Salt company, which I had been interested in buying for some time. When her husband was alive, he was so determined to refuse all offers, that I had virtually given up my interest. I discovered only later that Vincentini had been his partner in business. And Vincentini, as we have seen, had no need to hang on to a small, work intensive business. So I bought the Salt Company. What financial trouble this has already caused, the business was in debt and in dire need of investment, makes me realise what malice lay behind the sale. I am certain that he meant nothing good to come of it.

'Throughout the year, one disaster followed another until my business interests tottered on dangerous ground. My warehouse burned down and my remaining cargo with it. As many of you here are aware, I have for some time, held property on the Island of Cyprus; the Malmsey business can be profitable, when free from piracy. But it was not piracy that ruined my vineyards. The slaves I use as workers, men and women as well treated as my own family, were incited to rebellion by this Vincentini, or by his representative. They tore up the vines, brought the distilleries to ruin and set the buildings afire. I have a sworn statement from one of these workers who remained faithful to me which my lawyer is willing to read out to the court.'

He sat down, is expression controlled and nodded to his lawyer and manager Zorzo Vecelli. Throughout the reading of the slave's account, Capaccio remained still and composed. Senator Erizzo watched him, looking for some sign of weakness. Although pale and minimal in his movements, Capaccio had summoned some inner strength and stood as if slightly bored with the proceeding. Erizzo smiled, they had but began and contrary to what he had hoped, the subject of Cyprus was mentioned frequently.

'We are aware Signore,' said Diedo when Vecelli had finished reading, 'That you yourself have not visited your holding in Cyprus.'

Remaining seated, Don Carlos said, 'My Lord, what you say is true. However I have an excellent factor, recommended to me by Signor Corner there.' He nodded across to the Cypriot-born Marco Corner. 'I have no complaints against the man, he still has my utmost trust and it was not in his power to prevent what happened. I knew nothing of Vincentini's deceit then. Knowing of my plight, he came to see me. We spoke at great length and Vincentini offered me a share in his lucrative business. He suggested that my trading ship, my last trading caravel, should join his in the next voyage to Stamboul. As his was the greater expense and I had nothing to back me should the venture fail, we both agreed that Vincentini would wed my only child Carmelia. By doing this, he would gain the respect and influence that takes many years to earn. On the face of it, it appeared to be a sensible arrangement and a promising venture. My grandson Paolo sailed with the fleet on a war galley accompanying them for protection. So I sent my *Maria* to Stamboul with Vincentini's *Cornucopia.* Although I continued to have the worse luck a merchant feared, I was filled with hope for the success of this venture. I sent for my daughter and awaited her coming with eagerness.'

He stood up, his demeanour sorrowful. 'You all know what became of that sad enterprise and what became of my dearly loved grandson Paolo, and of all the men who sailed with him. But we will wait yet to hear that heart-rending tale. Unaware of the fate into which my ships sailed, I was caught up with the wedding preparations for my daughter. I was concerned that Vincentini was not in Venice when she arrived, for she had been delayed on her journey and there was little time left until the ceremony. But Vincentini sent her gifts every day and my fears dissolved. As an influential merchant of this serene republic, I learned all I could concerning the man I had dealings with and I set out to discover what was known about my future son-in-law. Nothing!'

Grimani spread his hands to emphasize his point. 'Nothing,' he repeated. 'He had no family and I even thought that this might have shamed him and this shame had prevented him from revealing it to me, for what man can raise to power in Venice without the strength of his family behind him? I made further inquires, I sent men far and wide to discover what they could.'

He paused and moistened his lips. 'During these weeks, I had taken into my house a young foreign lutanist. The boy's talent was extraordinary and as he was not of this city, I took pity on him and was quite prepared to offer him patronage or else recommend him to the Procurators of San Marco's itself. That same young man sits before you my Lords. His

English name is Emlyn Tomas, in Italian it would be Emilio Tomasso. A coincidence?'

A babble of comment rose and all eyes turned towards the foreigner. He swallowed nervously, but did look away. An expression of puzzlement marked his brow.

'You may think,' Don Carlos continued, 'that I have veered from the point. But hear me now and you will no doubt arrive at the same conclusion. While we awaited the day with mounting expectancy, Vincentini had yet to return to Venice. In his absence the boy Emilio came and went as he pleased, my house was open to him. In spite of this kindness he seduced my dear, precious Carmelia and turned her heart against me. At first I turned a blind eye, thinking the girl moonstruck by the youth, a condition she would soon get over once she was married. Emilio had such charm and such talent, that one was lightly to overlook his behaviour. So, three days before the wedding, Vincentini came back and attended a feast I held in his honour. He spoke with my daughter and she seemed committed to her promising future. Arrangements had gone so far now that when I heard the terrible news concerning my ships and my grandson, I was in no position to cancel the wedding. I was under great pressure for I had to borrow heavily and was now in terrible debt.'

There were murmurs of agreement in this, most of Grimani's debts were to the senate itself. They all knew what pressure he was under and few sympathised. The morning had worn away while Grimani placed every misfortune at the feet of Capaccio.

'On the very morning of the wedding which was just yesterday,' Don Carlos resumed, 'I learned at last who Tomasso di Vincentini really was, Tomasso Capaccio, a man who I had come across many years before and had seen thrown to the galleys for the murder of my son Roberto. The traitorous murderer had survived and now came to get his revenge. I knew that I must stop him before harm befell Carmelia, even then I suspected that Vincentini had been involved with the attack on the ships. I was much pressed for time, for Carmelia had already left for the church. I called my men-at-arms and hurried to intercede. Unknown to me at the time, this vile foreigner Emilio, had taken Carmelia from the church and was in the process of dragging her away from Venice and her beloved family! We have all heard here what happened next. Vincentini fought with the youth. I can only assume that this was under some pretext, for I have leaned since that Emilio Tomasso is the son of Vincentini.'

Senator Erizzo looked up in astonishment. Emlyn Tomas sat with his head bowed. Bartolomeo Varini spoke to him quietly. The old Franciscan leaned forward and interrupted them, indicating the centre of the room. Erizzo switched his gaze. Tomasso Capaccio looked as pale as death. Erizzo called over an usher and arranged for a chair to be given to the prisoner; to have the prisoner pass out at this stage, would undoubtedly annoy them all. Capaccio sat down and after a moment seemed better for it.

'I arrived too late to prevent the foreigner from running of with my daughter,' said Don Carlos. 'And this, against her will. But Vincentini did not escape me. I had him arrested and took him under close guard to my own house. The elderly Franciscan there, will testify that I offered no harm to the prisoner, even though my heart burned with the pain of his betrayal.'

Don Carlos dabbed at his red-rimmed eyes with a scrap of lace. 'There are times in our lives my Lords, when we are forced to act against our natures,' he explained when he had recovered control. 'And so it was with me. When the city had been searched and no sign of my little girl had been found, I became increasingly anxious and my dear wife was distraught. Already we were a house of mourners, for we knew then of the fate of Paolo. I confess that I did receive word from Senator Sebastiano Erizzo that the prisoner was to be brought here, or rather to the prison. I was desperate then and perhaps acted unwisely. I had Vincentini taken to his own warehouse and had him questioned closely concerning the whereabouts of my dear child. He resisted all efforts, and I am sorry to say, I used some violence to gain my ends. The son Emilio, made an attempt to rescue his cursed father. My men took the foolish boy and brought him to me. Now I felt that I had the upper hand; Vincentini would tell of the whereabouts of Carmelia if I threatened the life of his son. I was confident that all would be resolved without further ado. Once I had heard the truth, I had every intention of delivering the prisoner to be judged for his dire crimes by the Signori of Venice. Alas! The chance did not come, for it was at this time that Senator Erizzo himself intervened. My Lords, I stand now before you, having told you nothing but the truth, but I ask that you bear with me a little longer. You have yet to see how Vincentini arranged this cruel and unjust revenge.'

Giacomo Diedo clapped his hands sharply together, perhaps sharper than he intended. 'We have been informed Signore that your daughter is now recovered and in safe hands?"

'That is so my Lord, her whereabouts was made known to us. My dear wife and the lady Adriana made all haste to meet with her and have taken her to safety. I can only thank God for His providence.'

'There is much here that remains unclear,' said Diedo. 'Thank you Signor Grimani, you must be tired and may sit. We will examine the facts in greater detail before we proceed with further charges. Prior to that, there will be an hour's recess.'

The doors were opened and the guards invited to enter. The atmosphere in the room lessened. Men coughed and spoke quietly as they rose. Erizzo stood and made his way to Capaccio's side. He was sitting still, one hand on the arm of the chair the other laid across his waist. Senator Erizzo said, 'You will need some fortitude to defend against all that.'

He merely nodded and stood smoothly.

Erizzo said, 'You might wish to discuss the art of poetry, while you have the opportunity?'

A faint smile played across his mouth. Without a backward glance, Capaccio walked from the room between the guards. The undisguised hostility of the audience was evident in the insults they called after him. Erizzo followed, even though his hopes of learning anything more were minimal.

Emlyn Tomas made no move to stand, he sat in pensive thought, going over all that he had heard in his mind.

'Well!' Bartolomeo exclaimed. 'We will have some trouble sorting through that ridiculous nonsense.'

'Yet, there is some truth there,' said Fra Sebastiano, 'and I fear there is worse to come.'

'Do you believe that he arranged to attack Grimani's ships?' Emlyn asked.

'I know it,' Fra Sebastiano replied, 'and so do you Emlyn and Messer Bartolomeo here. But before we come to that, what of the charges we have heard?'

'I imagine Tomasso will refute most of them,' said Bartolomeo. 'I have prepared enough evidence for him to escape some of it. But what would be the point? If he is guilty of piracy, that alone will be enough to condemn him.'

Fra Sebastiano stood stiffly. 'I will meet you outside, there is a lady waiting to hear how things proceed.' he explained. 'I may be able to pull a string here and there that may help. If he was not the father you have come so far to find Emlyn, I should not care to side with him. It would be just that he answer for his crimes, before man and before God.'

'I know Fra Sebastiano,' said Emlyn, 'and thank you for your efforts.' When the friar had gone, Emlyn turned to Bartolomeo and said, 'It was all lies, the bit about Carmelia.'

Bartolomeo nodded thoughtfully. 'Unfortunately it was not all lies about the theft of Grimani's malmsey, I saw those casks myself even though I will swear otherwise. Emlyn be prepared for the worse, I have a feeling that Tomasso cares not what happens to him after this, I doubt if he will offer much in way of defence, it is as if he is already resigned to his fate. Although it is hard to believe that Grimani has broken the spirit of a man who has schemed for twenty years in order to avenge the wrongs done him. He must at least want the death of Grimani himself.'

'It was the death of Symeon,' Emlyn said softly. 'Perhaps it was one death too many, perhaps we are wrong, and destroying all that Grimani had and to to leave him suffer his remaining days in poverty, gives Tomasso a deeper satisfaction. There must be some other means to free him.'

'There is nothing we can do except fight for his freedom with words,' said Bartolomeo. He told me once that he could just as well fight with words as with swords. Yet, when I spoke to him before the meeting began, he forbade me to interfere. It maybe that he yet has some die to cast of which we are unaware.'

By mid afternoon when the meeting resumed, the day had grown warmer and the air in the room was still. Voices rumbled into silence. Don Grimani's eyes rested maliciously on his opponent. Tomasso Capaccio leaned back in his chair his head bent, much as he had been before. He did not show the anger that gave him the strength to continue.

It was Grimani's lawyer, Zorzo Vecelli addressed the magistrates this time. 'My lords, is it any wonder that Don Grimani acted as he did? We have heard the chilling, calculated path of vengeance Vincentini undertook. Wrecked with grief, worried to the point of sickness by the disappearance of his beloved daughter, Don Grimani had no choice but to arrest and question Vincentini. My lords, some among you may be aware that the prisoner suffers from wounds taken in combat, I believe the Doge's own physician has tended the man. Don Grimani had found out himself how he came by them. You may ask why he chose to take Vincentini to his own warehouse and the reasons are plain enough, when you consider what had happened previously. Don Grimani hoped that he might discover some of his own stolen goods stored there, goods taken from the *Maria*. He also hoped to learn the tragic circumstances of his grandson's death. When he had secured both Vincentini and his base born son, the youth attempted to divert the guard whilst Vincentini made an attempt to kill Don Grimani. It was only the quick action of his servant Uglino that prevented the murder, the boy will tell you himself. I can only thank God that the Arsenotti came when they did. Had they not, I believe that Don Carlos would have given his own life in order to bring this man to justice.'

'Are you telling me,' interrupted Diedo, 'that Don Grimani and over a dozen men were in danger of being murdered by an injured man and a beardless youth? And was it not Bartolomeo Varini who's quick action prevented the murder of Vincentini?'

'Is this what he has led you to believe?' Don Carlos laughed.

'We will hear the youth,' said Diedo. 'Does he speak Italian?'

'I do, my Lord.' Emlyn came forward his manner composed and respectful.

'Can you relate to us how you came to be at the warehouse in question?'

'I learned that there was some concern for Capaccio's safety while he remained in Don Carlos' hands. I spoke of this to Madonna Fiorenza and Enrico de Martoni. We hurried to the trading house and were joined by Capaccio's notary, Symeon. He waited outside while I and Enrico went to discover what we could. Symeon saw Grimani's men taking Capaccio out through a back entrance, he hurried to tell us and we followed.'

'And Madonna Fiorenza Balsamo?' Diedo inquired. 'Was she not further involved?'

'She was my Lord, but I think it unworthy to involve the lady in this needlessly. We had sent Enrico to inform the city guard of what was happening and Madonna Fiorenza came with us. When we discovered where Capaccio was being held, I stayed and diverted the guard while the others ran to get help. Grimani's men brought me inside and imprisoned me with Capaccio. Grimani had caught Symeon and killed him. he had the body cast at our feet when we were brought before him.'

'Scurrilous Lies!' Grimani was on his feet, his face flushed and his knuckles braced on the seat in front.

'You may not have done the deed,' Emlyn shouted at him, suddenly losing control, 'but your hand was upon the blade that killed him!'

'I will not hear this!' Grimani thundered.

'Silence!' Diedo's voice proved louder still. 'Any raised voices and the offender will be taken from this room. You will continue in a quieter manner.'

'I tried to escape.' Emlyn cotinued, 'I tried to get away, for what I saw, brought a madness to me. Symeon had not had an easy death and I was afraid that Grimani had found Madonna Fiorenza too.'

'Did you see Capaccio take a knife to Don Carlos Grimani.'

'No my Lord, I was too busy fighting for my life and his.'

Suppressed laughter floated through the room. The young man certainly had a way with him and he had gained some sympathy. Taking advantage of this, Emlyn added, 'I never ran off with Carmelia against her will.'

The atmosphere relaxed a little more. Don Carlos sat down his anger mounting.

'She and I had know each other for many months,' Emlyn continued. 'We had crossed the Alps together. Madonna Adriana, her godmother, joined our travelling party as we had the protection of a group of mercenaries. I knew nothing of Tomasso Capaccio, I was travelling with an English cloth merchant. I was in love with Carmelia Grimani before we ever reached Venice. We were powerless my Lords, to act in any other way than that which we did. I know how irresponsible this was and I would not have acted so had I known that death would result from my actions. Grimani's men shot the boatman who attempted to get us away from danger. His name was Jacopo.'

Senator Erizzo stood up. 'There is this matter of the deaths of Capaccio's boatman Jacopo and that of his notary Symeon which needs some explanation. This needless slaughter …'

'I beg your pardon Senator,' said Don Carlos rising to his feet. 'Are we to weigh the deaths of two servants against the death and enslavement of Venetian seamen? The theft of Venetian ships and their cargo? The theft of the grain they carried to fill the fondacos of Venice and feed her hungry? The man Symeon was killed when he attacked my men and I have never heard of the boatman. How dare you lay these deaths at my door!'

'Calm yourself Signore,' Senator Erizzo spoke softly.

"I have never been calmer,' Grimani answered. 'I charge Vincentini with the lowest cowardice that a man can stoop to. Had he, as he claims, had an axe to grind with me, then willingly I would have faced him with sword and dagger. I would have given my own life to save the life of my grandson and to save the shame and humiliation he has brought upon my family and honoured name. Are we to side with a villain who is no more than a wandering pirate? Every jewel he wears will have cost in blood. This is not an honourable man, this Vincentini has taken on the guise of a corsair and plagued our shipping and murdered our seamen. There is only one end for such as he. Let him wring your hearts with tales of woe twenty years passed. Are we to believe his wicked fables? Let him better beg for the mercy of God fearing men!'

A hush descended. Don Carlos sank to his seat. He looked sick and old and his voice had lost its earlier vigour. Yet he had not lost his touch. The pain he still suffered from the deeds of the prisoner was evident to all. Across the room, Fra Sebastiano's hair clung damply to his reddening forehead. He sipped from the watered wine they had been provided with. Emlyn returned to sit beside him, pale and dark eyed, shifting uncomfortably. Bartolomeo Varini, perhaps more used to such gatherings, sat with lips compressed his gaze fixed in front of him. At times his expression had shown disgust and disbelief and occasionally he looked his employer. Capaccio was already showing signs of tiredness, his pallor colourless, his eyes underscored with pain.

Bartolomeo Varini moved to stand but Tomasso waved him to remain seated, Bartolomeo's expression was querulous and he whispered in protest. Tomasso smiled briefly and stood to speak.

He bowed gracefully to them all. 'My Lords, gentleman. In order that all here may know from what this vendetta stemmed it is my intention to speak first of these matters. I may well wring your hearts with tales of woe twenty years passed. Are we to forgive murder because of the passing of twenty years? Is a man any less guilty of the act?'

He sat down, silently cursing the weakness and closed his eyes for a moment. 'My father was Zante Gabrielle Antonio Capaccio, and my mother Daniella Francisca Corsi,' Tomasso began, determined to be straightforward and give a brief account. 'She was with child when they wed, but in spite of her protests, he would not believe that the child was his; he said that she had been tempted by some passing mercenary and that it was only his Christian duty to make her his wife. I was born in that same year that they wed and Zante never acknowledged me as his own; a son to follow him and run the farm as he grew older. We made a good living growing the crocus fields around the river Brenta. We all worked together when the flowers spread like carpets to give us saffron. My mother was unlucky with children and all but myself and my sister Gina, died before they reached manhood. It was a sad house because of this. Constant conflict with my father eventually drove me to leave home at the age of fourteen.

'I came to Venice and took to the sea. I learned the ways of the wind and sea and the nature of the galley and the sail ship. For over six years I also learned the craft and cunning of the merchant. I became good at what I did and developed a keen interest in the buying and selling of precious stones. At times I came back and visited my family, this was for my mother and sister's sake, for Zante Capaccio offered me no welcome under his roof. Still, I persisted and it was on one such visit that I met Anne Elisabeth Morgan, and my life was changed forever.'

Tomasso felt as if he was drifting away, as if nothing of his surrounding held solidity. He forced his eyes open and pulled himself into reality with a conscious effort. 'At first our relationship was nothing but stormy. We did not see much of each other, though I had heard about the death of Cristoforo Grimani at the hands of Barbarosa and I knew her for his widow. He had left her in great debt and she was shunned by her husband's family; this was market gossip, anyone could hear for the asking. The farm she ran was five miles down river from our own and there was much admiration for the widow among those who worked for her and in the locality. She was not afraid of working among them, of hitching her skirt like a peasant and hardening her hands to any work that needed doing. She treated them all with warmth and friendship but they knew her anger if they crossed her and respected her for it. When the harvest was done at the end of that season. Don Grimani's remaining son Roberto Grimani came to her home. He informed her that his father had relented and had paid off the debts she was working so hard herself to meet. It turned out that Roberto now owned the farm that had belonged to his dead brother and Anna was invited to return to Venice with her two sons Lorenzo and Paolo. But Anna had plans of her own and could not be induced into living where she had been previously made unwelcome. Nor was it possible for her to remain where she was, for the house, the orchards, olive groves and vineyards and all who worked there, now belonged to Grimani. She came to Venice and lived at the modest house Cristoforo has kept for his use.

'The relationship between Anna and myself had not developed into anything more than a wary acquaintance. I had come myself to Venice a few weeks before; I had some business to conclude before I was due to sail for Genoa. Before I left, Bartolomeo Varini, Cristoforo's secretary who had stayed with his widow, came to see me. He informed me that Anna wished to sell her jewellery and some oddments from the house in order to raise money to return to her father's home in England. When I arrived at the house, the place was in turmoil. Roberto Grimani had called to see the mistress and even from the bottom of the stairs I could hear their quarrelling. As I held the lady in high esteem and I was young, generally acting before I took thought, I became involved. After heated words between Roberto and myself, we fought; I unarmed and he with sword and dagger. Anna brought the conflict to an end by cracking a wine jar over Roberto's head and calling her whole household to see him to the door.

'From then on, Roberto and I were at war it seemed. I did not leave for Genoa; I could not leave Anna alone to deal with the animosity of Roberto and his father, Don Carlos. In the two months that followed I gave my heart to Anne Elizabeth Morgan and asked her to be my wife. During this time, there was a lot of pressure placed on her by her father-in-law. He made it plain that he wanted Cristoforo's sons to come and live with him. She was constantly afraid that she would be parted from her children. We married in secret, feeling foolishly that we would be safe as man and wife and that no man could come between us. But secrets are the very air of Venice and this one became known in a short time. Don Carlos sent his son Roberto to challenge me. God knows, I tried to avoid it, I endured the most base personal insults without being moved. But he would have his way and there is only so much a hot-headed young man can take. We fought the duel and I struck the blow that killed him. I knew then that if we were to have any chance of peace, Anna and I had to leave the city. There were many places I could take her, even to England if she wished, we had discussed it and were prepared to act quickly.'

Tomasso could suddenly see her. She walked into his mind, little Paolo slung on her hip, her face shinning, her eyes laughing. She had a stray feather in her hair, they had been on the Lagoon all day, prodding about the sandbanks. He had shot a wild duck and little Lorenzo cried, seeing the shaft through its breast.

'Signore? Do you wish to retire?' The usher's voice spoke beside him.

Tomasso had not been aware of the man's approach. 'No,' he answered. He waited until the usher had retired before he took up the tale. It is not far now, he told himself.

'When I returned after the duel, Anna and her sons were gone. Soon after, I was arrested by Don Carlos and accused of Roberto's murder. He was grief stricken and enraged, he had lost both of his sons in just over a year, now Lorenzo and Paolo were more important to him than ever before. His revenge on me was brutal and unforgivable. My father, Zante Capaccio was killed outside a tavern in Padua. My mother Daniella and my sister were burned alive in their own house while they slept. This was never mentioned in my trial, which was a shameful mound of lies, one atop the other all the way through; whenever I protested I was physically silenced. I was sent to the galleys to live my remaining years as galley slave. I was told a few months later by a fellow slave that Anna had been sent to Cyprus to take the veil, Her ship never reached there and she died at sea.'

'Lies! Wicked, incredulous, black lies!' Don Carlos' voice roared through the room like muted thunder.

'Please be seated, Signore,' ordered Diedo. 'All will be heard and then decided upon.'

Tomasso stood up, feeling that standing would keep him more alert. He gripped the back of the chair and scanned the room. 'As you see my Lords, I survived the fate intended and escaped the galleys. Everything that I have done since then, was for one single purpose, to visit my vengeance on Carlos Grimani.' He lifted his eyes and fixed them unmoving on his enemy.

'When I visited Florence some moths ago, I spoke with an old friend who told me that Anna's fate was different to that I had believed. Perhaps she went to a crueller slavery than mine, for she was sold by a slaver, a man who although he made an attempt, could not induce Don Carlos Grimani to pay the ransom for her release. She was carrying my child then and he was born in captivity. Somehow she managed to send him away from there to her home in England. That is the connection between myself and Emlyn Tomas and we did not know of each other until yesterday.' Tomasso paused feeling as if a weight had been lifted from him.

'You see me stand accused by Carlos Grimani of crimes we have heard related at some length,' he added. 'Much of what you have heard has a grain of truth to it, much has been woven out of recognition. You are aware now that vengeance lay behind my actions and I do not call upon this truth to act in my defence. Had I sought the justice of a court to settle this vendetta, I would have done so. The justice of the Signoria did not serve me then nor to I seek such now. I came to Venice for the sole purpose of destroying Don Carlos Grimani and all that he had become. I have spoken of this so that you may know that Grimani is not the law upholding citizen he would have you believe. Judge me as you will, but I ask that you judge too, the cruel acts for which this man is held to account.'

A gasp ran through the room. They had all expected him to deny the charges not bolster them. He was offering no answer to the lies and half truths Grimani had thrown at him.

'My Lords,' Senator Erizzo brought the room to silence. 'There are many complexities here. Are you saying Signor Capaccio that you are willing to admit to the charges this gentleman has brought?'

'I do not refute them,' Tomasso answered.

'Because you feel you are being ill judged?' Diedo asked. 'We have heard with what low esteem you consider us. Signor Capaccio, we are here to learn the truth and you are required to answer the charges, regardless of the reasons that lay behind them.'

Tomasso bowed. 'As you wish my Lord,' he replied. 'may I suggest that Messer Varini speak for me, as he is well acquainted with the truth?'

Giacomo Diedo nodded sagely, his composure ruffled.

Bartolomeo Varini came forward and began without delay, for which many there were grateful. Here, it seemed that at least he was in his element. 'Gentleman, I will speak of what I know concerning these incidents and can produce proof for anything I relate. Concerning the first charge, the theft of malmsey. Perhaps Don Carlos will be relieved to hear that most of the crew from those ships have been freed from captivity.'

'How can you know of this?' Diedo asked.

'Messer Capaccio is a much travelled merchant my Lord. He has many sources of information. Word reached us but a few weeks ago and the prisoners were released after some negotiation.'

'Forgive me,' said Diedo, 'but I fail to see why you should concern yourself with the plight of these seamen? Can you produce any of them to ascertain the truth in this?'

'The reason I will admit, was one of self interest. I believed then, that we had a future partnership with Don Carlos and I was but protecting our future interests. Some of those seamen reached Venice yesterday. I believe they await outside so can be summoned without delay, they will no doubt give an account of the theft from Grimani's ships.'

'How is it that I heard nothing of this?' Grimani protested. 'How is it that a man imprisoned for murder can partake in harbour gossip while I, an up righteous citizen of Venice remains ignorant?'

'Signore,' Diedo said. 'We are interested to hear what witnesses you have brought to clear up this matter.'

There was a shuffling and whispered chatter. A plainly dressed man rose from the back bench behind Don Carlos. 'I am a sailor my Lords. I sailed with di Vincentini on the voyage form Stamboul on board the *Cornucopia* when he first came to Venice. We called at the island of Naxos on the way and picked up a cargo. It was malmsey wine, the barrels branded with the Grimani symbol.'

'This man was dismissed from our service for theft,' answered Bartolomeo with a dismissive gesture. 'He is fortunate that he got off so lightly. It is true my Lords, that the *Cornucopia* picked up a cargo of wine at Naxos, the rest is a jumble of convoluted nonsense to discredit my employer. Our own captain, Marco Erizzo will assure you of this. Madonna Fiorenza Balsamo sailed on the same voyage and will tell you the same.'

Senator Erizzo stiffened. He had been afraid that his nephew, Marco would be called to speak. He had spoken to the captain himself, but Marco was loyal and secretive, whatever Capaccio said, Marco would verify; Tomasso Capaccio had some very influential connections. As he had guessed, Marco Erizzo, Captain of the *Cornucopia*, defended Capaccio's story. There was no quarrel the seaman could use against him. The council deliberated for a moment and advised Grimani to drop the charge of the theft of malmsey for lack of evidence.

Don Carlos flushed with anger and many of those watching mumbled in agreement. 'I am undaunted,' Grimani said. 'He may well wriggle out of that particular mess for the space of a breath. My lords, I mentioned that we would come back to this and so we have. We may well end as we began, with the piracy of Venetian ships. He used the same method of attack then that he used later when he brought his godless hoard down upon the *Maria* and her galley. I need say nothing here that cannot be better told by a man who witnessed the vile deed from start to finish. I have here with me one Albagigi, a Ragustan seaman in my employ for many years.'

Albagigi shuffled nervously as he stood. He had the dark skin of Armenia, further darkened by a hard life at sea. He smiled toothlessly and bobbed his head up and down. His account of the sea battle was convincing, for he was not a man blessed with a wide imagination. His telling was straightforward, his obvious distress moved Grimani to tears. He had seen the *Maria* attacked from a distance, the galley where he had served for three years, was overrun by the corsairs and unable to offer any assistance to her fellow ship. After this Albagigi stumbled to a halt, his fearful eyes turned on Tomasso Capaccio.

'And how did you come to survive this terrible ordeal?' Diedo prompted. 'Come now, there is nothing to fear.'

'I was thrown into the sea honourable Lord, whilst I fought,' said Albagigi. 'The galley was forced to surrender, even then I could see the Messer Paolo was not ready to give up. He fought with the leader of the corsairs and it was some time before the man overcame him. Messer Paolo was foolishly brave, he could not accept defeat. When they led him off the enemy galley, he suddenly broke away. He ran back with a blade raised in his hand. I saw him strike the leader, I saw the knife come away reddened. Then there was a blur of movement and one of the corsair's servants ran forward and killed Messer Paolo. I saw him fall, honoured Lords. His breast was red with blood. On my mother's grave I swear, on the Holy Book I swear, that the man who sits at the centre of this room was the same man who led the pirates in attack against the ships of Don Carlos Grimani. On my mother's grave, honoured Lords.'

Giacomo Diedo stretched his legs and waved the man to return to his seat. Many here had been swayed by his simple account and now they eyed the prisoner with renewed hostility. Diedo said, 'We have heard much concerning the conduct of Signor Grimani and I pray, covered now the most serious of the charges against Tomasso Capaccio as well as the lesser.' He turned to the prisoner. 'Signor Capaccio, you have heard the story related by this honest seaman. How do you intend to answer?'

Tomasso waited a moment before replying. Bartolomeo Varini was standing, his face expressing concern. Fra Sebastiano kept his head bowed as if in prayer. Emlyn Tomas never took his eyes off the man that had claimed to be his father. Perhaps amongst all that were gathered there, the face of Don Carlos Grimani was the clearest to read; he was grey with exhaustion but his eyes were calm and his smile smug and self satisfied. Tomasso said, 'My Lord, I have nothing to add.'

'We are all tired here,' said Diedo, 'I understand your reluctance to continue, but this is a court of law and every man concerned with these matters will be heard and judged fairly. Please continue.'

'As I said my Lord, I have nothing to add to the seaman's account of what happened.'

There was a murmur, a rustle of clothing as men shifted and made to rise, their expressions, a mixture of disbelief and growing anger.

The chief magistrate's voice rose above them. 'Signor, you understand that by declining thus, you are in fact admitting to these acts of piracy?'

'I am aware of my predicament,' Tomasso said clearly. 'I offer no defence.'

Voices rose from murmurs of disbelief to shouts. Men began to leave the benches, disordered and noisy. Diedo called them to order with difficulty. 'It is late my Lords, and many if not all here, are in need of nourishment. As we have progressed so far, I suggest that we rejoin in two hours to decide the matters put before us today. May God guide us in justice.'

This was followed by plaintive cries. The mood grew ugly. The doors swung open and the guard entered, their stamping feet causing onlookers to hesitate on their way to the floor. Tomasso Capaccio sat with his head bent, resting on his clasped hands, as if all the energy had drained out of him. A few scuffles broke out, men shouted for his blood. The guard elbowed their way through and grasped a hold of the prisoner as they hurried through the doors.

Emlyn sat through the confusion without moving. Bartolomeo Varini's gaze remained on the door where the prisoner had left. Faces loomed in front of them both, ugly with anger and spiteful laughter. Insults spilled about them like arrows. Bartolomeo answered none of them. He only reacted when Fra Sebastiano took his arm and said, 'It might be wise to leave here, the mood is not going to improve. Come outside, there we can consider what has happened. Emlyn?' They left followed by derision and laughter. Only Enrico Martoni reacted, answering with equal acidity.

'He never intended to defend himself,' said Bartolomeo when they reached privacy.

'Then what has today been about?" Emlyn questioned, his voice raw with emotion.

Bartolomeo shook his head in perplexity.

'I believe that he knew he could not escape,' Fra Sebastiano said. 'Yet he felt a need to place before the Signori the facts behind his vengeance. I think he still hopes that he can bring down Grimani at the same time.'

'I never took him for a fool,' said Bartolomeo. 'Where the hell does he think he is? Can he not see that he has dug his own grave?' He looked around. 'Where's Enrico?'

'Here.' Enrico rejoined them Fiorenza running behind. He added, 'I have told her.'

Bartolomeo felt his heart sink further. 'Fiora, I would have saved you this.'

'Have they condemned him to death?' she demanded anxiously.

'As good as,' offered Fra Sebastiano.

'Then we must get him away from here,' she snapped.

'In the name of heaven, why?' Fra Sebastiano's voice was so sharp that they all looked at him. 'You have all helped him as much as can be expected for a man guilty of such horrendous crimes. Emlyn because he is the father he came so far to find; Madonna Fiorenza because she has given him her heart and you Bartolomeo out of loyalty you were tricked into feeling. Enrico here, for no reason other than his own friendship for you all. What sort of man is this? You all believed him a merchant trader, but it is clear that he is something else entirely. A wicked man with the power to deceive and to command devotion from his followers that even murder cannot lessen.'

'He did not admit that he had done this,' Emlyn protested.

'He did not need to,' Enrico answered. 'He knew that he would be found guilty anyway and perhaps thought to save himself the trouble. And what will happen to us? Are we to be dragged under with him? Is the Spice Company he began to die with him?"

'Do not speak so Enrico,' Fiorenza pleaded.

Bartolomeo rubbed his tired eyed and dragged his long hands over his face. 'He has already rid himself of the company,' he explained. 'It now belongs to his son Emlyn Tomas.'

Emlyn looked away. 'I don't want it,' he answered. 'What do I know of trading ships and spices? I never asked for it. I've hardly had time to think.'

'Is this the young Jesuit scholar I once knew?" Fra Sebastiano asked, 'The young man who could never get enough knowledge to suit his needs? Emlyn, you are not in the habit of running from a challenge, and this will perhaps be the greatest yet.'

'I know you mean well,' Emlyn answered. 'Perhaps we could talk of this some other time, for I am too confused.'

'And me,' said Bartolomeo with forced joviality. 'Lets go and find out what Doges eat for dinner. Food has been provided, and if you are willing to face the lions out there, then so are we. It is not the end of your father yet, I have a feeling that he is indeed much more than we've been led to believe and he might gain his freedom yet.'

'How?' Fiorenza snapped, 'because if he can't come up with some means of …'

Bartolomeo took her arm and began to walk. 'Tell me,' he said, 'do you ever read poetry?"

'What does that have to do with anything?'

'It may have a great deal to do with Tomasso Capaccio.'

Senator Sebastiano Erizzo had hurried after the guards who escorted Tomasso Capaccio from the room. But again, Tomasso would not speak to him of anything concerning the four lines of verse. 'Am I to wait until you are beheaded?" Erizzo had taunted him.

'Until I am judged,' Tomasso answered. 'If the Signoria deal with matters fairly, I will sprout poetry until dooms day. If I consider them unjust, you will learn nothing more.'

Erizzo was furious, the man was a fool, surely he could see that he had tied his own hanging knot. As he hurried through the corridors in search of Giacomo Diedo, Capaccio's words suddenly made sense. He was not speaking of his own judgement, but that of his enemy Don Carlos Grimani.

Erizzo shut himself in a private room with Giacomo Diedo, Giustinian, Dandolo and Marco Corner. He also invited a Signor Marcantonio Bragadin, who was an old and trusted acquaintance of his and who knew much concerning the Venetian owned island of Cyprus.

They came out after an hours discussion and reentered the long room where the day long court had been held. Many faces that had attended earlier were missing. It seemed a foregone conclusion that Capaccio would be found guilty so they had returned to their homes. Don Carlos Grimani was there with his grandson Lorenzo and all his supporters. The members of the Spice Company had returned with the young man, Emlyn among them. Lastly, Tomasso Capaccio entered with the guard. He took his place without reacting to the hissing and derision.

The magistrate, Diedo wasted no time. 'My Lords, this case has been discussed at great length by myself and my colleagues. As the prisoner Tomasso Capaccio as not refuted the charge of piracy against him, the decision of the court will be made known in due course. But we have heard much here today and will concentrate first on our decisions concerning Don Carlos Grimani. Signore, you may stand.'

Don Carlos rose with an air of smug satisfaction. 'My Lords,' he said bowing to the council.

'Signore, as we have heard today, you are in a great deal of debt to the Senate, your bankers and privately. It is the decision of the court that your trading house on the Rialto shall be returned to the Senate, as well as your remaining stock, ships and businesses.'

An awesome sigh followed. Don Carlos' smile disappeared.

'As the Grimani are an old and much honoured family of Venice, it has been decided that you will be provided with a modest house in a quite area of the city and granted a small pension for your immediate needs. We understand Signore that your wife has retired to Vicenza and has expressed a wish to take the veil. She has assured us, by letter, that you need have no worry concerning the care of your daughter Carmelia who she will provide for from her own funds. We admire her decision.'

'This is sheer madness!' Grimani spluttered. 'Are you daring to judge me!"

'Signore, the decision is final. It is true that you are much reduced in status, but we see this as happening through your own folly. Apart from the last charge brought against Tomasso Capaccio, we attach no blame to the prisoner for your misfortune. If you were any younger Signore, the penalties would be much harder on you.'

'I demand to see the Doge!'

'As you are aware Signore, Doge Loredan has little to do with the laws ruling this city. He entrusts that to his loyal council.'

'You can not sentence me to a life of poverty! I demand Capaccio's head!'

'Your demands are heard. You will now be silent.'

'How dare you insult a Grimani. You miserable fool! Do you think that I, Don Carlos Grimani, Patron of Venice can be spoken to with such disrespect. How dare you assume to punish me!'

'You are perhaps a little agitated,' said Diedo, 'and perhaps unaware of your predicament. This council has considered the matters concerning Anne Elizabeth Morgan and were it not for the name, Grimani, you have brought to shame, the penalty for your cruel treatment of this woman would have been much greater. As it is, you are permitted to return to your house to collect a few personal items. In the morning you will be accompanied by a guard who will close and lock the doors after you and to whom you will present the key. Be seated and thank God that you may walk from here with your life.'

It was obvious to them all that Grimani was having great difficulty accepting this. Erizzo thought that his supporters seemed to edge away from him a little. It was some time before his complaints ceased and only then when he was threatened with dismissal.

Giacomo Diedo now turned his attention to the prisoner. 'Signor Capaccio, on examination of the facts put before us, we find you innocent of all but one of the charges, and this, the most serious. The Serene Republic of Venice abhors piracy. There are many here and within the city who have benefited from your own generosity in the past, but even this can not soften the charges against you. Because you have been a respected merchant in this city and have in some way enriched her, your punishment shall be undertaken in the privacy of the prison grounds. Tomasso Capaccio I hereby sentence you to be taken from this court, imprisoned and brought forth at tomorrow's sunrise to face your execution.'

'Execution!' Grimani was on his feet again. 'Send him to the galleys were he belongs. Let him have the slow death I once promised him. If I am to suffer then so should he. Hanging is too good for him! Chain him to the oars of a good Venetian galley so that many may witness the fate of the traitorous scum who has done the same to their fellow citizens!'

The whole room erupted with shouts of agreement. Faces darkened, the hatred for piracy mirrored in each one. Diedo called out, but none would hear him. 'My Lord,' cried Erizzo coming to his side. 'It might be better to do as they say.'

'The decision of the council is final!" Diedo spluttered.

'What difference will it make, the manner in which Capaccio meets his maker? In this it might prove wiser to bend the rules. Die he will, have no doubts of that. This way, it just takes a little longer and goes somewhere toward appeasing Grimani.'

The guard had entered and stood protectively around Capaccio, even using the butts of their maces to keep the crowd at bay. They and Diedo eventually gained enough silence for him to speak. 'We retract out previous decision concerning the manner of Capaccio's fate,' he shouted. 'At tomorrow's sunrise he will be taken to the galleys to spend his remaining life as galley slave. May God have mercy on his soul.'

Bartolomeo thought, even up to the last moment, that Tomasso would find some means of escaping this fate. He pushed his way forward until he found Senator Erizzo. Before he could speak, Erizzo said 'I know what you are thinking, but he would tell me nothing more. I thought last night that he was too sick to talk of it, now I see that we shall never hear. The price he asked in exchange was not within our power to give.'

'What price?"

'I believe he wanted the death of Don Carlos Grimani.'

Bartolomeo shook his head but did not reply. He watched while Tomasso was led away. In spite of his pain and obvious exhaustion, Tomasso walked as tall and as proudly as he always had, with no show of humiliation.

Bartolomeo waited, hoping to get permission to see his employer one last time. Fra Sebastiano and Emlyn waited with him and saw Don Carlos Grimani leave the room. There was a terrible change in the man, he looked as if he had aged ten years since he had entered that morning. His steps were painfully slow, his weigh leaning heavily on the boy who walked beside him. Uglino was dressed in the green livery of the once powerful house of Don Carlos Grimani, the green seemed like a mockery. Grimani looked broken and defeated and few of those who had arrived with him, left with him. His grandson Lorenzo walked at his other side, lending the old man his support.

'In every man there is some goodness,' said Fra Sebastiano.

'Not in that one,' Bartolomeo replied.

But Fra Sebastiano merely nodded his white head. Don Carlos had said nothing of the maiming of Lorenzo, even though this would have brought him such sympathy that his own end might have been kinder. He had said nothing perhaps because of his pride, but Fra Sebastiano though it more lightly that Don Carlos had sought to protect his grandson from humiliation.

Chapter 54 Venice End Game

Don Carlos Grimani stood outside the Ducal Palace while Lorenzo went to summon a boat. San Marco's piazza was empty, rain glistened off the moon-lit tiles and sculptured walls. A solemn bell chimed and faint, harmonious sounds rose from San Marco, it was boys singing a many-voiced canon, the smooth sounds bringing in new voices until the air seemed to fill with them. A figure moved across the lit clearing towards them. Don Carlos sighed heavily, wishing that he could sit down, for his legs felt weak and unable to support him. Apart from Uglino, there were no servants attending him that he could command. He accepted this with deepening sorrow.

'You are a good boy, Uglino,' he said. 'You have stayed with me knowing that I am brought to such shameful ruin by that black hearted pirate and his miserable son.'

'Say the word Patron, and I will kill the youth.'

'You would do that for me?' Don Carlos patted the boy affectionately.

'You are a father to me,' Uglino replied. 'I will serve you until my life's end.'

Don Carlos smiled. 'My end will come before yours Uglino, I am an old man made older by those that turn against me.'

'Where do we go now master?' Uglino asked, desperation tingeing his voice.

'We'll go home,' Grimani answered, 'at least for a short time. Do you know Uglino, they think they have the better of me, but I still have the key to the bridal chamber and no one has taken anything from there.'

'The casket of jewels!' Uglino giggled. 'The casket of jewels that Vincentini had delivered the day of the wedding. And the silks and ornaments. Are they yours for the taking?'

'Of course they are mine,' Don Carlos said triumphantly, 'What use are such baubles to a galley slave? Or to a nun for that matter. I should have left the girl where she was.'

'I thought we were doomed to poverty.' Uglino's smile widened.

'I have one or two things squirrelled away, dear boy.' Don Carlos saw Lorenzo meet with the man approaching and converse with him for a moment before they came on together. The man looked familiar but Carlos could not quite place him. Was it possible that he owed money somewhere that he had forgotten about? That would not be difficult, he mused, and they can't all have a piece of the crumbling cake.

'This gentleman is Girolamo, from the house of Alvise Mocenigo,' Lorenzo explained.

'My granduncle sends his deepest regrets to you Signor Grimani,' the young man said bowing respectfully. 'He has sent his own barge to bring you to our house and welcomes you to stay as long as you need. His house is yours.'

Don Carlos exclaimed and grasped at Uglino for support. Tears rimmed his tired eyes. 'I am overwhelmed Signore!'

'Our families have worked for Venice for many years Don Carlos. Did not your aunt wed a Mocenigo?'

'She did indeed, but it was some time ago. She has passed away, God rest her gentle soul.'

'My granduncle was most upset went he heard what had happened. He considers you part of his own family, and families gather strength from each other.'

'Quite so young man, quite so. I am humbled by his offer of friendship. May we call at my house on the way?'

'By all means,' said Girolamo. 'I have men with me who will assist you in anything you require.'

As they made their way towards the barge, following Girolamo's lamp, Don Carlos bent to Uglino and spoke out of hearing of the others. 'Do you know Uglino, what I have heard whispered in those halls we have just left?"

Uglino bent closer.

'Our exalted Doge Pietro Loredan, is a very old man and his health is failing.'

'God preserve him,' Uglino responded.

'No, rather let God see him to a comfortable death,' Don Carlos continued. 'It is considered highly lightly that Alvise Mocenigo will be our next Doge. A kind man, a man with a heart of gold.'

Tomasso was taken this time, not to the comfortable room in the Ducal Palace but across the narrow canal to a cell in the prison building near by.

The cells were beneath the level of the Lagoon, tiny rooms with moisture glistening on the grimed walls and a single pallet in the center. When the heavy doors closed on darkness, Tomasso sank on the pallet with a sigh of utter exhaustion. There were no physicians to tend him, no rich food and strong wine to slake his hunger and blunt his pain, no blankets nor furnishings of any sort. He had been condemned to death on the galleys and this was where he would spend his last night in Venice. Don Carlos Grimani had walked from here a free, if ruined man.

The guards had handed Tomasso a cloth-wrapped bundle, laughing while they told of the lady who had left it and who had waited through the long hours in hope of seeing him. She had paid them handsomely for the earring, a red bauble they thought of little value.

Tomasso unwrapped it, his fingers identifying the fold of paper, a letter he could not read in the darkness, and the familiar dragon-claw and ruby. The rest was clothing which he was grateful for. He sent his silent thanks to Fiorenza and his silent regrets.

He was very tired and felt again that floating sensation that he had known in the courtroom. He did not intend to sleep, for he was expecting Senator Erizzo to come and plague him with questions, but his eyes grew heavy and he stretched out in the limited space, hearing the scuttle of rats before he sank into nightmares.

It was not Senator Erizzo who broke his uneasy slumber, it was Emlyn. 'Even Grimani couldn't have come up with something as dire as this,' he said. 'My grandfather Gruffydd, told me that he was in prison for a while after I left, he gained his freedom by boring his jailers to death with Welsh legends. I wish that you could have met him.'

Tomasso sat up. 'Are you suggesting that I try the same?' he answered.

'No, but I thought you might like some company. Fra Sebastiano wanted to come too and Bartolomeo. But you are not in favour at present and I was informed that you can see a priest from here if you wish.'

He had brought a candle which he set between them in a pool of melted wax.

'I did not think I would see any of you,' Tomasso replied. 'Where is the redoubtable Erizzo?'

'Outside waiting to speak with you, he let me come first, but I can't stay for long. I wanted to speak of this company that you have handed to me.'

'Don't you want it?'

'No. At least I don't know. I'm not yet ready to decide. There seems so much that I need to do, to see.'

'Then leave it in the hands of 'Tolomeo, I assure you, it could not be better placed. Go off, do whatever you wish, find your maiden and marry her. As head of the house of Capaccio, you can even do it in style, with pageboys and trumpets. Then, if you are still reluctant, give the company to 'Tolomeo. I tried once to do just that; he refused. I would not force this on you Emlyn, against your will. Yet you would be wise to consider very carefully what such a position would do for you.'

I am not Italian,' said Emlyn smiling. 'I am Welsh and that land calls me back. I can't be a merchant trader here as well.'

'Why not?' Tomasso replied. 'You can be whatever you want to be, have I not shown you that?'

'By being Tomasso di Vincentini and Capaccio?' He paused when Tomasso did not answer. 'And,' he added reluctantly, 'a corsair?'

'And much more. My faces have been many. Are you ashamed to call my father, Emlyn?'

'No. Whatever you are and have been, I know what has driven you and can only find admiration in my heart.'

'I hope that you are not wrong in your judgement.'

Emlyn opened his hand and held it to the light. 'I gave the others away,' he explained. 'But I thought this might help you.'

Tomasso took the tiny gem and after a moment, placed the ruby earring beside it in his palm.

'There was no time for me to get anything more,' said Emlyn. 'It might buy you some comfort.'

'Keep it, keep them both,' said Tomasso. 'I thank you for the gesture, but I have no need of these, not now. And be wary of who you give them to, they have a habit of coming back together.'

Emlyn accepted them with some reluctance. 'I shall not give them away, even though they are unlucky.'

'Why do you say that?' Tomasso asked surprised.

Emlyn shrugged. 'I don't know. I showed them to a mad witch once and she felt the same. She said that there was a spell on them, she said they were five stones for the five son's of the Dragon's bride.'

'Dragon's bride?' Tomasso laughed softy. 'Well, the dragon takes on many shapes, the salamander, the chameleon, perhaps she was not as mad as you thought.'

'If you were free would you find her?' Emlyn asked almost in a whisper.

'Anna? If I were free I might find out if she yet lives. But I would not come into her life unless absolutely necessary. I have caused her enough pain both then and now, were she to know it. If your mad witch spoke true, Anna will have other sons to give her happiness and comfort, where're she may be.'

Emlyn stood and paced up and down in the limited space. 'There must be some way you can escape this!'

Tomasso smiled and yawned, his eyes growing heavy.

'Are you not afraid?"

Tomasso shifted his position, his hands resting on his knee. His eyes looked hollow in the weak light. He shook his head and said, 'Go to the door and ask Erizzo to bring Marcantonio Bragadin to speak with me.'

They spoke quietly of unimportant things until the two Venetian gentlemen crowded in to the tiny cell. Erizzo looked unfriendly and mistrusting, Marcantonio Bragadin looked interested after the surprise had left his face. He had met this man before, under much different circumstances. He was about to say this very thing, when he caught Tomasso's eye and was warned to silence. Erizzo asked Emlyn to leave, but he argued and threatened until Tomasso spoke. 'Send him for some wine,' he said, almost mischievously. 'That is if you intend to keep me from my bed.'

Bartolomeo Varini eventually left the Ducal Palace. Enrico and Fra Sebastiano had already escorted Fiorenza home, as the hour was late. There were no boatmen awake and no gondola waited for him, so he walked through the light rain. The streets were dark and the canals gurgled merrily, looking more like tar than water. For the past two days Bartolomeo had fought for the freedom of Tomasso, in one way or another, they all had. And Fra Sebastiano was right in saying that the man didn't deserve such friends and such loyalty. 'But Tomasso is no ordinary man,' Bartolomeo spoke aloud to himself. 'Such great men should not end their days at a galley oar. Some nobler way should have been decided upon. Yet how could that be? Piracy is the worse crime against the Republic of Venice. And why did they believe a poor sailor who must have been bribed to say what he did? Was it a way out?'

When he reached the trading house he paused. A lamp spluttered outside the gate illuminating the salamander above. The building was still only half ready for what they had intended, the rooms still smelled of new paint and wood sap and Tomasso had spent such a short time there that he had lost his way more than once. Once inside Bartolomeo found that Fiorenza and Enrico were still up. Fra Sebastiano had stayed with them and fallen asleep in a chair. They sat around the old table where they had talked with Emlyn. Fiorenza's eyes were red-rimmed and her uncovered hair had come loose. It seemed they were prepared to sit the remaining night away, bolstered by wine. Bartolomeo smiled at her. 'Any wine in that bottle?'

She poured him a glass, her eyes searching.

'I was unable to see him,' Bartolomeo replied. 'Emlyn has stayed and we may speak briefly with Tomasso tomorrow, if we are early enough. Fiora, I would not think it wise for you to come.'

She smiled sadly. 'I would have liked to say a word or two to him. What are we to do Bartolomeo?'

He shook his head. 'Nothing. It is over. Tomasso came here to destroy Grimani and he pushed all else aside for this one aim. At times I thought him inhuman.'

'No, he was as human as the rest of us,' said Fiorenza. 'The ship is still here, the one that Symeon was supposed to be on. The one Tomasso had arranged to take him to Cyprus.'

'Then perhaps you can make use of it,' Bartolomeo suggested gently. 'Go away from here Fiora, there is nothing but regret left for you, were you to remain.'

She pushed her hair behind her ears impatiently. 'He once told me that I could not hope to be in a better position than that of a rich widow. He said, Have you thought of becoming a courtesan?'

Bartolomeo laughed, suddenly feeling better. He felt that he had lived more vibrantly this past year than he had since youth. It is only a year, soon forgotten, he tried to persuade himself.

When they sent Emlyn to fetch the wine that Tomasso had asked for. He took advantage of the opportunity and ran up and down passages, peering in darkened rooms, seeking some way that he could free his newly found father. There were many guards about and although they were relaxed they challenged him, displaying their alertness. The prison was like a fortress, the walls so thick and the doors so heavily guarded that even a mouse would not escape unnoticed. Still, Emlyn tried searching until the men became suspicious of his reasons and sent him back to the lower level.

He stood waiting outside the door for some time after he had knocked. He bunched his fists and pounded on the thick wood. The lock turned and Erizzo let him enter. 'Where is the wine?' he demanded.

Emlyn eyed him suspiciously before he returned to the door and stooped to pick up the bottle and cups. He heard the voice of Marcantonio Bragadin. 'Five hundred!'

'For each bastion,' Tomasso answered. There were papers spread out on the pallet and he held a quill in his hand. 'Without those reinforcements, you would never hold the city. I know that Venice believes herself strong in Nicosia, because the walls are newly strengthened, but without strong leadership, they will still fall to the Turkish army. Advise the Signori to replace the present governor.'

Erizzo folded his arms and pursed his lips. 'That would be Nicolo Dandolo, I thought him an able man.'

'Able?' Tomasso scoffed. 'The Sultan's army are exceedingly powerful, to face them you need to put Cyprus in the hands of a proveditore with the highest military qualifications. You will get nothing from the Cypriots themselves, they are not loyal to their Venetian overlords.'

Erizzo shook his head. 'I still can't believe that the Sultan will not war with Spain, indeed many in Italy hope as much. They have no love for their Spanish overlords either. Without further proof, it will be difficult to convince the Senate.'

'Then Venice will lose Cyprus as she has lost her other islands. There is no further proof. Have you received word from Scipeone Barozzi?'

'You knew that he worked for us?"

Tomasso nodded and accepted the wine that Emlyn handed to him. His hand shook. 'I would not have employed him otherwise.'

'Last we heard,' said Erizzo, 'was that he had been contacted by a certain Ismael, and told that the Sultan had agreed a peace with Hungary.' Erizzo smiled. 'He also mentioned something about a camel race. This Ismael has been a good source of information for Venice. Scipeone assures us that the man has access to the Sultan's court itself, perhaps even has the Sultan ear.'

Tomasso leaned back on the damp wall. Emlyn could see the shudders running through him, more and more often. This was not a good place for a sick man to be, Tomasso would probably die here if he had time. His eyes were shut and his hair clung wet to his forehead.

Erizzo too had noticed. He said, 'We will leave you with what peace remains to you. I am sorry that I can not help you now. The Senate will not believe what you have told me without further proof and so will not grant you your freedom. I am sorry Signore.'

Tomasso responded with a huff of contempt.

'Well I believe him,' said Marcantonio Bragadin, 'in fact, I fail to understand why the Turkish Sultan has not already taken Cyprus.'

'You are a soldier Signore,' said Erizzo. 'Perhaps you see this in a different light. The Serenissima will not act for the simple reason that there is a treaty of peace existing between Sultan Selim and us. The Sultan would be a fool to turn Venice against him, as we are his gateway to the west in matters of trade. This is the argument the Signori will put forth, and it is a sound one.'

They allowed Emlyn to stay, seeing that he would not leave willingly, and filed out with words of regret.

Before the door closed on Senator Erizzo, Tomasso said, 'Scipeone was hopeless on a camel.'

Senator Erizzo halted and turned.

Tomasso opened his eyes. He said, 'Remember this: no Tomasso Capaccio, no Ismael the Syrian.'

The palace of Don Grimani was in darkness. There were no servants even to light his way up the wide staircase. He was worried for the light from Uglino's candle showed that word had gone around already that he was bankrupt; they'd been in the palace, those he was still in debt to and probably others who saw advantage in quick action. The floors were bare, the walls were bare, every ornament and painting had gone. 'I have been so kind to them all,' he moaned. 'Now they leave me. Faithless deserters!'

His heart hammered, his breath came in short, painful gasps. He paused often on the way up and reaching the top, leaned against the wall, sending Uglino ahead with the key to see if the room had been plundered. The light Uglino carried back immediately put his fears at rest. He held aloft a candelabra with seven candles burning brightly through the passage, no thief would have left such a treasure. Uglino smiled. Holding the light up with two hands he beckoned to his master to follow.

The room was untouched. A mantle of moody dark velvet lined with sable lay across the bed. The brocade cover beneath shimmered under the candlelight. On the coffers, swathes of flowing silk seemed to run like water to the carpet. Jewellery and trinkets lay on a table top where the light illuminated the tall Venetian glasses and wine ewer. On the window seat the casket of jewels stood invitingly on a cushion of red velvet. Everywhere there seemed to be light, glancing off carved furniture, gold-threaded tapestries and fold of satin. It was like a cave of treasure compared to the rest of the building.

Carlos lowered his bulk on the bed. 'God has answered my prayers,' he mumbled. 'If those who have offended me were lying dead at my feet, my joy would be complete.'

'Vincentini is as good as dead,' said Uglino, 'and I shall kill the other before another day has ended.'

Don Carlos chuckled. 'Bring me the casket, my precious boy and learn like my enemy did, that time is unforgiving and the sword is as sharp now as it will be twenty years hence.'

The lid was stiff and he struggled for a moment before it opened. Light spilled out, all manner of colour and sparkle greeted his eyes. He plunged his fat fingers through the gems, gathered them up and let them spill; their size alone was enough to tell him their value. He sat for a long time, pouring them from his fingers to the casket, some fell and glittered on the bed-cover and on the carpet at his feet. He felt sick and old but he was comforted to see that his life would still be to the standards he had been accustomed to.

He looked towards the window and stood when he saw the slight greying of the sky. Had he been that long? Something crunched under his foot. He peered down. A powder of coloured sparkles lay underfoot. He bent closer. Glass! Coloured glass!

'Uglino!' he shouted. He looked around and saw that he was alone. Uglino had left him and he knew why. Uglino would never go unless he had good reason, before another day is ended, he had said and had not understood that he had been told to wait. Don Carlos gripped the casket and sent it flying towards the window. The leading buckled under the impact, panes of glass flew out spiralling into the dark canal below. The casket crashed on the floor, its contents sprayed across the carpet. Don Carlos stamped on them, crushing the fake gems underfoot. He screamed in anger and frustration. He staggered about sobbing and tearing at his clothing. He threw objects about and ripped at others, the bed hangings and tapestries, the velvets and silks.

Exhausted, he snatched at the wine and filled a glass to the brim. He sank on to the ruined bed releasing a wail of anger. 'You will know Capaccio!' he screamed. 'You will know that your son was killed by my order! Let that burn your black soul while you live!' He dabbed at his eyes.

He lifted the glass and drank all, in one long, thirsty swallow.

The dawn came chill and damp; it was still dusky grey as a group of guards left the prison, their captive walking in their midst. The younger man walked beside him, both unspeaking. A barge took them to where the galleys waited. The cask makers paused to watch and the orange sellers lowered their baskets to stare in open curiosity, much had been told in the markets and on street corners concerning the prisoner. A Genoese ship lay off shore and the high prows of the Venetian trading vessels rose high above. Emlyn remembered when he had first come here, excited at the sight of these proud ships and Jacopo had told him of the wonders of the sea. There were three galleys to escort the trading fleet on a voyage to the Black Sea. The galley slaves were bent, half asleep still, over their oars.

Senator Erizzo shouted greetings to the captain and did not object when Emlyn followed his father on board the nearest galley. Capaccio was chained hand and foot. He walked between the guards with bent head watching his awkward steps. The slaves eyed him with hostility and the crew called out insults and spat on the deck. They pushed him roughly to a space on the benches beside a thief from Anconda. The man watched without sympathy as the new slave was chained to the bar on the deck.

Tomasso's head lifted and his eyes met Emlyn's. He smiled and said, 'Don't worry I've done this before, it wont take me long to get the hang of it. Go now, my gallant son and reap the earth of its riches.'

Speechless, Emlyn turned before Tomasso could see the tears.

He walked without being aware of where he was going. He felt as if in one hand he held future happiness and in the other, past bitter grief. He waked and walked until he came to a stop in front of an old church wall. His anger and frustration overwhelmed him and he beat at it with his fists. With a shuddering sob he buried his head in his hands and sank down on to the step.

Dawn broke over the roof tops of the Turkish city of Stamboul and lit the minarets and the domes of palaces and mosques. On the eastern outskirts of the city, far from the Topkapi Palace and the Suleymanye, the house of Abu Abdullah of Ulcinj bustled with activity. Abu stepped out into the early light and laughter merrily. He had spent an entertaining night with the gifts that Ismael the Syrian had left to greet him on his return from the Greek coastline. Three nubile black girls, all exactly the same. Abu thought them so beautiful and so charming that he had hardly left their side since his return two days since. His boys were jealous.

'My beloved friend,' said Abu to nobody in particular, 'I was offended when you gave the slave Symeon away to some Venetian. Now I forgive you, for you have made my life rich. I shall make them all my wives, if I can persuade the others to retire. Allah is great.'

As the call to prayer rang over the roof tops, Abu spread his prayer mat and faced Mecca with joy in his heart.

The same lamenting chant wavered across the Golden Horn and floated through an open casement in the Venetian fondaco. Scipeone Barozzi yawned and stretched, his limbs creaking. He had awoken while it was still dark, unable to return to sleep, he had spend over an hour writing a coded letter to the Signori of Venice.

From his window, he could see across the water to the city. He watched as fishing boats pulled away from the shore. The harbour chain was down and larger ships began to move, the sails swollen with the swift breeze from the Marmara Sea.

A dog barked, a woman scolded and somewhere, a camel grunted. Scipeone smiled, remembering other camels and a man of extraordinary character and understanding. The same man that had informed him that Sultan Selim no longer hungered after the conquest of Vienna. Barozzi could see now, the reason's behind the Syrian's priceless information. Sultan Selim was not at war with Hungary, but he was intending to war with someone. Only the day before, Barozzi had seen the cavalry enter the city, led by the Sultan's commander, the proud Mohammed Khalil, with his sons riding equally proud behind him. And in the harbour below, was gathered the massive war fleet of Ali El-Uluji, Pasha of Algiers. The ships were being made ready for war.

Would it be Spain? Barozzi mused, or would it be somewhere of much greater import to the Signori of Venice? Cyprus?

Tall cedar trees swayed in the morning wind, dwarfing the old farm house which lay in their shadow. A young man stood outside the door, carrying a broken sandal. With needle and thread, he squatted beside the rough road that twisted down from the heights past the building and continued down the valley towards Kalopanayiotis. The house was built partially of timber and partially of mud-bricks coated with a thin layer of plaster. It was shabby and uncared for, the sun-baked roof showing wide cracks that had not been repaired after the rains. On the opposite side grew young carob trees and wild olives. Dominating both sky and landscape, the Trošdos mountains rose bleakly from the fertile valley. Capped in snow, they cut the deep-blue sky and descended in tawny browns, heliotrope and amethyst before the deep green of the cedar forests spilled onto the lowlands.

A bell clanged in the distance, a mournful sound like the lowing of a cow. The young man tied off the thread and broke it with his teeth. He stood up and slipped a brown foot through the mended straps. The bell clanged again, this time closer and continued more muted. He walked into the sunlight, pausing to ruffle the forehead of a donkey that grazed on the roadside before he climbed to the top of a rise. He brushed silken, black curls from his forehead and shaded his eyes. Coming towards him, there was a cart drawn by bullocks with bells and coloured wool around their blunted horns. Hay stuck out from the sides of the cart, a small load, hardly worth the trouble. He returned to the house ducking into the cool darkness.

Inside he was greeted by an older man, a Greek physician, with a lined face and kindly eyes. The other man in the sparse room, did not speak. He was of the same age, yet a striking opposite to the youth who had entered. Instead of dark, his hair was as bright as corn. He was pale and hollow eyed, as thin as an athlete; he had a look about him as if he had been long at sea or had suffered a long illness. He listened to the short conversation, his knowledge of Greek to poor to grasp the meaning. He heard the ox bells and guessed their meaning. He stood and walked slowly, an arm held protectively across his abdomen. He sat on a log in the sunlight and watched the cart approach. Beside it walked a shepherd, a long, hooked staff in his hand and a goatskin bag over his shoulder. He was dressed in rough woolen cloth and had a striped rag tied about his head.

The other two came out, the Greek carrying a bundle and the dark youth a purse which he tossed idly from hand to hand. The Greek spoke in stumbling Italian. 'It is perhaps three days journey,' he said, 'perhaps for you, four. There will be ships there and you have enough coin to see you home in great comfort. Remember to take the mixture I have prepared for you, it will make you strong and keep away evil humors.'

The fair man stood and embraced him, thanking him in his halting Greek. The dark youth held out the purse and the two young men regarded each other in silence. No word had passed between them since they had been together. The wounded man did nothing to disguise the hatred he felt. He nodded slowly and accepted the purse, tucking it into his loose peasant clothing. They helped him into the cart and made sure he was comfortable before it lurched and continued onward. They stood in the road watching it grow smaller with distance and disappear into the haze; the bells sang out their mournful complaint until distance silenced them.

The dark youth crossed the road, waded through bright gladiolus and caught up the dragging rein of the donkey. Without a backward glance, he mounted and thumped his heels, making clicking sounds to urge the donkey upwards.

He rode for over an hour until he tuned away from the rugged heights and entered a sheltered valley. A stream gurgled beside him, its banks sprouting greenery and delicate pink flowers. The soil here was rich and deep and soon he was riding through fields of blue linseed bordered by orange trees. He stopped by a rocky outcrop and the donkey immediately began to graze. The valley dipped further from here, a lush expanse of grass grew on the sides of the road, bushed like hair by the wind. At the far end the ruins of some ancient temple blended with the landscape. The builders had found a statue of Apollo when they were clearing the ground, they had fixed its head back on and set it at the center of the courtyard of the new buildings which were rising on either side. The main house was near complete, an elegant sprawl of arches and fluted tile, of white washed walls and wide open rooms designed in the style of the Moors of Granada. It was furnished simply as was the owner's habit, though he had not yet come to live there. The stables running down one side, were half-finished and already horses, mules and camels had been brought to fill the stalls. The air had a spicy scent, carrying the sound of children's laughter and the high joyful shrieks of women behind the walls.

Koçi urged the donkey forward, glad to be free at last to come to the house of his master. This was where Ismael had chosen to settle, here on the isle of Aphrodite that had known many conquerors; and would know more, for Cyprus was rich in grain, sugar, pomegranates, olives, dates, figs and profitable metals. And its rich malmsey wine was much favoured by the Sultan of the Turks. Ismael knew the way the wind would blow, the peasants already said of him, 'For the prosperous person, even the cock lays eggs.'

In Theo Tieffenbrucker's work yard, Umbaldo forked fresh hay into the manger. The previous day, he had saddled the white horse as Emlyn had asked him, but Emlyn had not returned from the Ducal Palace and the palfrey had been unsaddled and returned to her make shift stall. They had found out how matters had progressed, the Englishman had sent his servant Matthew to the Ducal Palace and he had related all that had happened. Umbaldo was saddened for his friend and had asked Theo for some time to go and find him. Theo too was quite moved by all that had happened, he got on famously with the English merchant, they and Wendelin had spent most of the night talking, over numerous jugs of beer.

As Umbaldo stepped out, he caught sight of a boy standing by the gate, but when he looked again there was no one there. Umbaldo frowned and investigated further. He had recognised the green livery and the boy wearing it; he had often laughed and joked with the apprentices about Don Carlos' pet catamite, Uglino.

A voice called him back to the yard and he returned, forgetting the incident. He sat down at the wide kitchen table where breakfast had been laid for Theo's workers. The apprentices chattered about Emlyn's duel with Tomasso di Vincentini, none of them knew the truth behind the story and they had already embroidered it with fantasy. Umbaldo remained quiet, unwilling to contribute.

There were many people who knew Uglino and even if they hadn't the livery he wore told where he belonged. He had come to the workshop of the German Lute maker when it had still been dark. No one had seen him as he had crept through the gates and wandered about the outer buildings. He had been surprised to find a white horse there that he recognised. He had not entered the house, but he peered into the workshop and the room where the apprentices slept; there was no sign of Emlyn Tomas. Uglino had been undecided whether to return to his master or to wait. In the end he had waited, hoping that the young man would return with the coming of daylight. He had seen the man walking across the yard, yawning and scratching his chest, and heard the horse whinny in greeting. He had ducked back when the man had spotted him, and hidden when he came to look further. He returned now to loiter near the gate.

Uglino had never killed anyone. Don Carlos had got rid of the nasty Andrea for him and Uglino had loved the man ever sine, he was a father to him and a protector. Now Uglino would return the favour by killing his enemy. He was bound by loyalty, but Uglino had never killed before and he was afraid. The knife he carried was a slim, long blade, a deadly weapon which had become popular in Venice. Uglino ran his thumb along the edge. He cried out and drew his hand back, sucking at the blood, it was not the first time it had happened. It was an example of the age and experience he lacked. He wondered seriously if he would be wiser to wait, to bide his time and strike when he was better prepared.

An eight year old boy came bounding towards the gate. He stopped abruptly when he saw Uglino. Uglino glared at him, hoping he would go away. He didn't. Instead he leaned forward and whispered in Uglino's ear.

The youngest of the boys came late to the table, he grinned at Umbaldo and the apprentices, obviously bursting to tell them some scrap of gossip he had heard in the fish market. He waited until he had swallowed a mouthful of bread before he told them.

He said, 'Don Carlos Grimani is dead.'

'What!' Umbaldo felt cold with alarm, thinking immediately of Emlyn.

'Dead as a doorpost,' said the boy. His eyes shone with enthusiasm. 'His tongue was sticking out, his eyes were bulging, there was vomit all over the place. They say he died in unbearably agony. His face was purple!'

'Who killed him?' This was the question on Umbaldo's lips, but he did not speak it. The Englishman, Ambrose Chillingworth had spoken from the door.

'The death cup,' the boy replied. 'Took his own life and is it any wonder? The Council of Ten stripped him of all he had. He was ruined and Bianca told me, that his wife had run off. He went to his home and swallowed poison.'

Umbaldo felt a flood of relief. 'Does Emlyn know?' Chillingworth asked.

'Doubt it.' The boy stuffed his mouth. 'Only just been found.'

Umbaldo stood and pushed passed the Englishman, running out into the yard. Chillingworth caught his arm. 'Where are you going? Do you know where Emlyn is?'

'Watching the Black Sea galleys?' Umbaldo suggested caustically, pulling away.

'Wait, I'll come with you.'

'You'll never keep up,' snapped Umbaldo. He felt hostile towards the man; Chillingworth had betrayed Carmelia's presence and had her sent off. Umbaldo knew where she was going, Emlyn had told him and that he had every intention of following, on the horse she had left for him. Emlyn would want Capaccio to know what had happened and the man himself would surely be better able to cope with the fate they had sent him to.

He pushed his way through the markets and walkways, leapt over the humped bridges and dashed through dark passages. Umbaldo knew all the short cuts to the harbour. He skidded around a corner, overturned a basket of lobsters and got tangled in a fishing net. He ran on, the fisherman's curses following him. As soon as he rounded a corner on to the water front, he started yelling Emlyn's name, loud enough to reach the roof tops. He rushed about searching through the crowds, rudely elbowing any that stood in his way.

'What?' said a voice behind him.

Umbaldo spun around, 'Emlyn, thank God!' he gasped. 'He's dead, Grimani is dead!'

Emlyn stared at him dully, his face white as sheeting, his grey eyes widening.

'He took poison. Am I too late?'

Emlyn took off without answering. Where Umbaldo had been rude to the pedestrians, Emlyn was outrageous. He ploughed through them like hurricane sending them tumbling until they opened up before him like the Red Sea. Umbaldo followed, unable to catch up.

Two of the galleys had pulled out to sea, the other had just pulled away from the quay, her great oars moving smoothly through the Lagoon waters. Emlyn never even stopped, he took a flying leap across the widening gap.

Umbaldo staggered to a stop and gasped in disbelief.

Emlyn landed awkwardly across the oars, scrambling for a hold as they lifted. Voices shouted, the oars faltered. Sheer willpower got him up and over the side of the galley. Hands reached out to catch him, the galley slaves cursed. Emlyn flew out of the snatching hands, lurching forward, staggering along the planking. They chased him and crashed into him as he came to an abrupt halt.

Where he had seen his father chained to an oar, there was now an empty space.

'Took him off, the lucky bastard,' said the thief from Anconda.

Emlyn looked at him in puzzlement. Then he lifted his eyes and looked out to sea. The Genoese ship was preparing to sail, waiting only for a small skiff that made its way towards her. Some instinct caused Tomasso Capaccio to look around. He stood up, balancing himself easily. He waved and shouted.

Emlyn could not hear the words, but he saw him smiling and knew then that his father was free.

They took Emlyn back to shore with some trouble and with angry voices threatening to put him in the place the other man had left. Emlyn grinned at the seamen. He grinned at Bartolomeo Varini who greeted him when he reached the quayside and grinned at Senator Sebastiano Erizzo who returned the smile and winked.

'What happened?' Bartolomeo asked anxiously.

Emlyn addressed Erizzo. 'Is he free because Grimani is dead?'

Erizzo made a negative sound. 'Do you recall what he said to me last night, just before I left the cell?'

Emlyn nodded, perplexed.

But Erizzo offered no further explanation. He looked out to sea with a satisfied expression, then he turned away and walked off. 'Tell Bartolomeo,' he called over his shoulder.

'What?' Bartolomeo said, grasping Emlyn's arm.

Emlyn said, 'Capaccio, my father spoke just one line. He said, 'Remember this: No Tomasso Capaccio, no Ismael the Syrian.'

Bartolomeo hit his forehead with his hand. 'Of course! Don't you see? It all makes sense!' He burst into laughter. 'The cunning bastard!'

They stood and watched the wind filled the sails of the Genoese ship as she nosed out to sea. A ship which belonged to Gaspare Maria del Monte, an old friend of Tomasso Capaccio's, who had waited as arranged and come into unfriendly waters when Tomasso had not appeared. The ship was named *Aphrodite* and she was bound for Cyprus.

Emlyn did not know what it was all about nor did he care, there would be time for explanations.

Bartolomeo narrowed his eyes and searched the ship from stern to prow. He could not see the shawled head of Fiorenza. He remembered her soft eyes as she had bid him good-bye and her soft lips as she had kissed his cheek. She had not wanted anything more and he had watched her gondola from a window. He thought now, that she would have retired to her cabin, turning her back on all that Venice had been to her. How ironical that she would win her Tomasso after all.

He turned from the sea and regarded the young man beside him. Another Tomasso?

No. This was a different mind; a strange, complicated mind on the verge of manhood; a talented, idealistic youth, torn by conflicting emotions. He had shown courage and a singular determination that would mark him out against other men. Perhaps he shared the keen intelligent mind of his father, that remained to be seen; certainly, he had the brave spirit of his mother Anna.

Bartolomeo's mind began to turn to accounts and ledgers and all that had been left undone in the chaotic days since Tomasso had come back to Venice. Tomasso, who had known exactly what he was doing, because he lived in two worlds; he changed his colour like the chameleon; like the salamander, he brought both good fortune and bad.

'I'm hungry,' said Emlyn.

'German sausages?' Umbaldo suggested.

THE END

Acknowledgements

I firstly thank my husband Kevin, for his inexhaustible knowledge of so many subjects most especially history, art and superior design. He has an inexplicable ability to find answers to most problems great and small.

Tara and Joseph you know how grateful I am to you for your patience and all you have put up with and have understood.

Bernard Gavin is not only an excellent editor, he is also a great source of inspiration, intelligence and humour and has travelled with me on this ambitious adventure to the end.

I am also grateful to Joycey for never giving up on me, her exceptional and persistent encouragement brought this book eventually to completion.

Renata, thank you for your help and support, especially your friendship.

Rhiannon, thank you for the Dragons.

This story would have never been told had it not been for the genius of Dorothy Dunnett, a great author of historical fiction whose influence encouraged me to become a story teller.

Lightning Source UK Ltd.
Milton Keynes UK
UKHW04f0716111018
330335UK00001B/36/P

9 781546 296492